NIGHT LORDS

THE OMNIBUS

AARON DEMBSKI-BOWDEN

BLACK LIBRARY

A BLACK LIBRARY PUBLICATION

'Shadow Knight' Originally published in the electronic magazine *Hammer and Bolter*
© Games Workshop Ltd 2010-2011.
Soul Hunter © Games Workshop Ltd 2010.
'Throne of Lies' first published as an audio drama © Games Workshop Ltd 2010.
Blood Reaver © Games Workshop Ltd 2011.
'The Core' first published in the *Fear the Alien* anthology © Games Workshop Ltd 2010.
Void Stalker © Games Workshop Ltd 2012.

This omnibus edition published in Great Britain in 2014 by

Black Library,
Games Workshop Ltd.,
Willow Road,
Nottingham,
NG7 2WS, UK
10 9 8 7 6 5 4 3 2 1

A CIP record for this book
is available from the British Library.

UK ISBN 13: 978 1 84970 612 4
US ISBN 13: 978 1 84970 676 6

See Black Library on the internet at

blacklibrary.com

Find out more about Games Workshop
and the world of Warhammer 40,000 at

games-workshop.com

Printed and bound by CPI Group (UK) Ltd, Croydon, CR0 4YY

It is the 41st millennium. For more than a hundred centuries
the Emperor has sat immobile on the Golden Throne of Earth.
He is the master of mankind by the will of the gods, and master
of a million worlds by the might of his inexhaustible armies. He
is a rotting carcass writhing invisibly with power from the Dark
Age of Technology. He is the Carrion Lord of the Imperium for
whom a thousand souls are sacrificed every day, so that he may
never truly die.

Yet even in his deathless state, the Emperor continues his
eternal vigilance. Mighty battlefleets cross the daemon-infested
miasma of the warp, the only route between distant stars, their
way lit by the Astronomican, the psychic manifestation of the
Emperor's will. Vast armies give battle in His name on uncounted
worlds. Greatest amongst his soldiers are the Adeptus Astartes,
the Space Marines, bio-engineered super-warriors. Their comrades
in arms are legion: the Imperial Guard and countless Planetary
Defence Forces, the ever-vigilant Inquisition and the tech-priests of
the Adeptus Mechanicus to name only a few. But for all their
multitudes, they are barely enough to hold off the ever-present
threat from aliens, heretics, mutants and worse.

To be a man in such times is to be one amongst untold
billions. It is to live in the cruellest and most bloody
regime imaginable. These are the tales of those times.
Forget the power of technology and science, for so much has
been forgotten, never to be re-learned. Forget the promise of
progress and understanding, for in the grim dark future
there is only war. There is no peace amongst the stars,
only an eternity of carnage and slaughter, and the
laughter of thirsting gods.

CONTENTS

AUTHOR'S INTRODUCTION

I'VE BEEN WAITING years to write this foreword, and now that the time has come I'm not sure what to say.

This trilogy changed my life. Please excuse how dramatic that sounds, and bear with me.

When I sent the first draft in to my editor (the ever-patient Nick Kyme) during one of my many crises of faith, he called me back with worrying swiftness. I was shaking, literally shaking, when he told me he wanted me on the Horus Heresy team – because of the first half of the first draft of what was only my second novel. My first novel, *Cadian Blood*, hadn't even reached its publication date yet. That was the first change, and it was a terrifying one.

As for the second? The dedication in *Soul Hunter* was: 'Katie, will you marry me?'

She was leafing through the advance copy (the one authors get to read through and cringe at all the things it's too late to change), and I'll never forget the way she looked down at the page with a slow-dawning smile when she saw those words.

The dedication in *Blood Reaver* was in thanks to Vince Rospond of Black Library, who babysat me in New York and Chicago when I was over there for signings and conventions, and who was responsible in ways I never quite understood for the American sales that changed my career yet again. It really should have been a dual thanks, including Rik Cooper (also of Black Library) for the very same reason, but I didn't realise that at the time. The guilt haunts me to this day.

The dedication in *Void Stalker* is notorious in my family. It's dedicated 'To the new Mrs. Dembski-Bowden. Well, both of them.' That was a reference to the fact Katie had said yes to the *Soul Hunter* dedication, and the fact she was pregnant with what our midwives assured us was a girl. The girl promptly turned out to be a boy. So before Alexander Timothy Dembski-Bowden was born, he had a book dedicated to him under the mistaken belief he was going to be female. Graham McNeill mocked me for it in the dedication to his novel *Priests of Mars*. That man knows nothing of mercy.

But you can probably see my point. When this trilogy began, I was working part-time in video game design, part-time in RPG design, and spending the rest of my time writing the stories I actually wanted to write. By the time the trilogy was released, I was a new husband, a new father, and a *New York Times* bestselling novelist.

(I'd also gone from trembling in Dan Abnett's presence to being pals with him, which is still pretty weird for me to think about.)

So these books mean a lot to me.

It should go without saying (and yet, I'll say it anyway) that these novels stand on the shoulders of giants. *Lord of the Night* was one of the early Black Library's best novels, and though the tides of Warhammer 40,000 lore have shifted and changed in the decade since its publication, the book still offered a glimpse of primarchs before anyone else showed primarchs, and Chaos Space Marines doing more than dying to Imperial gunfire on account of being the Bad Guys. It was a trailbreaking book, and I still treasure my copy. For reasons of obvious affection, Talos's philosophies on the VIII Legion mirror those espoused in *Lord of the Night*, and rather than ignore the book in the quest to carve my own niche, I hearkened back to it several times. I had to be careful with the IP changes and dated lore – and no matter how much I wanted Talos and Zso Sahaal to be 'right', the evidence of published background was against them, suggesting that they were both ultimately deluding themselves.

But that's the point. *Doubt. Confusion. Interpretation.* Showing one side as the blatant and obvious truth is the easiest thing in the world. Presenting different, credible perspectives, any of which might be true, is the tough part.

That's what I tried to do with First Claw. From the very beginning, I wanted this to be a story of perception, a tale of how 'your focus determines your reality', to steal a favourite quote on the subject. None of the warriors in First Claw really agreed on anything, as none of them saw the past or the future in the same terms. They were brothers in every sense of the word, but that didn't mean they liked each other. They would fight together and willingly die for one another, despite often not being able to tolerate one another's company off the battlefield.

On a related note, some of the most frequent and warm feedback I've received about the series has been from active and former soldiers, who've written to me or said at signings that they recognised the sentiments of brotherhood and loyalty that show so strongly between the members of First Claw. They often tell me how familiar it felt, how those bonds closely reflected their experiences in the armed forces. I appreciate anyone who takes the time to say they like my work, but those kinds of comments are particularly humbling.

Part of the appeal of these stories is the fact that Septimus, Octavia, and First Claw are always the underdogs. I like underdog stories – I like reading them and I like writing them – and you don't get much lower than Talos's warband. They're also cowards (realists?), at least in comparison to most characters you might expect to see in a 40K story. They run from the Blood Angels in *Soul Hunter*; they hide behind the Red Corsairs in *Blood Reaver*; and they only face the eldar in *Void Stalker* because there's nowhere left to run. Talos and his brothers do vent their wrath on their enemies, but in true Night Lord style, it's rarely ever in a fair fight. When they're backed into a corner and forced to fight back, even when they have home court advantage, victory comes at a heavy price. Nothing is ever easy for them. They lose limbs. They lose brothers. They lose respect, for themselves and for each other.

One of the themes I was keen to show was the erosion of a Chaos Space Marine warband – and its leaders – over time. The Night Lords are undeniably a Chaos Legion (proving that there are an infinity of ways to 'fall' to the Ruinous Powers) no matter how little affection they have for the notion of gods. There's no 'worship' of Chaos here, just as there's nothing so brazen and obvious with many warbands. Chaos isn't a religion; that's just one manifestation of how mortals interact with it. On a more visceral, real level, it's the insidious touch of pride, of self-righteousness, of emotion out of balance. 'Taint', in terms of tentacles and claws, isn't the whole deal at all. It's not just about 'falling', or crossing an invisible line that makes you a Bad Guy.

And these Chaos Space Marines struggle. They run out of ammunition. The *Covenant of Blood* needs repairs. They suffer the mistakes of the past, taking horrendous casualties over the course of the series, as does the crew of their warship, running parallel with the changes within Talos.

Talos was very much the straight man of the series, the foil against which most of the other characters bounced their personalities and ambitions. In a story about perspective and change, it's mostly his perspective we see – and whether it's true or not, I wanted it to be believable. I wanted it to feel credible, I wanted people to see why he was certain it was real, even as they wondered if it ever could be.

By the end of the series, Talos is forced to face many of the things he's ignored as unimportant or denied as irrelevant. He's lower in some ways, and has risen above his roots in others. He changes over the course of three novels, and makes the series' final decisions in facing those changes.

As for Septimus and Octavia, they were unexpected fan favourites – I get as much positive feedback about them as I do about Cyrion. They came into existence because I love getting human perspective on the warriors of the Space Marine Legions, and because I thought it would be interesting to see more 'normal' characters interacting with a Chaos Space Marine warband. They were a joy to write, and I only wish I'd spent more time with them.

Before I sign off ('at last!', I hear you cry), I just wanted to take the time to thank Jon Sullivan for the beautiful and inspiring covers. His artwork sold countless more copies than my name on the cover ever could.

To those who know First Claw well from dog-eared copies of the original books, I hope you enjoy the reunion. To those who are about to meet Talos, Cyrion, Uzas, Xarl, Variel, and Mercutian... I wish you luck with them. You'll need it.

The completed Night Lords Series is dedicated with heaps of gratitude to my in-laws – Christina, Keith, Thomas, and Greer – for all their help, as well as their patience in putting up with some English fop coming over to Ireland and stealing their daughter.

Aaron Dembski-Bowden,
Omagh, February 2013

SHADOW KNIGHT

The sins of the father, they say.

Maybe. Maybe not. But we were always different. My brothers and I, we were never truly kin with the others – the Angels, the Wolves, the Ravens…

Perhaps our difference was our father's sin, and perhaps it was his triumph. I am not empowered by anyone to cast a critical eye over the history of the VIII Legion.

These words stick with me, though. The sins of the father. These words have shaped my life.

The sins of my father echo throughout eternity as heresy. Yet the sins of my father's father are worshipped as the first acts of godhood. I do not ask myself if this is fair. Nothing is fair. The word is a myth. I do not care what is fair, and what is right, and what's unfair and wrong. These concepts do not exist outside the skulls of those who waste their life in contemplation.

I ask myself, night after night, if I deserve vengeance.

I devote each beat of my heart to tearing down everything I once raised. Remember this, remember it always: my blade and bolter helped forge the Imperium. I and those like me – we hold greater rights than any to destroy mankind's sickened empire, for it was our blood, our bones, and our sweat that built it.

Look to your shining champions now. The Adeptus Astartes that scour the dark places of your galaxy. The hordes of fragile mortals enslaved to the Imperial Guard and shackled in service to the Throne of Lies. Not a soul among them was even born when my brothers and I built this empire.

Do I deserve vengeance? Let me tell you something about vengeance, little scion of the Imperium. My brothers and I swore to our dying father that we would atone for the great sins of the past. We would bleed the unworthy empire that we had built, and cleanse the stars of the False Emperor's taint.

This is not mere vengeance. This is redemption. My right to destroy is greater than your right to live.

Remember that, when we come for you.

* * *

He is a child standing over a dying man.

The boy is more surprised than scared. His friend, who has not yet taken a life, pulls him away. He will not move. Not yet. He cannot escape the look in the bleeding man's eyes.

The shopkeeper dies.

The boy runs.

He is a child being cut open by machines.

Although he sleeps, his body twitches, betraying painful dreams and sleepless nerves firing as they register pain from the surgery. Two hearts, fleshy and glistening, beat in his cracked-open chest. A second new organ, smaller than the new heart, will alter the growth of his bones, encouraging his skeleton to absorb unnatural minerals over the course of his lifetime.

Untrembling hands, some human, some augmetic, work over the child's body, slicing and sealing, implanting and flesh-bonding. The boy trembles again, his eyes opening for a moment.

A god with a white mask shakes his head at the boy.

'*Sleep.*'

The boy tries to resist, but slumber grips him with comforting claws. He feels, just for a moment, as though he is sinking into the black seas of his homeworld.

Sleep, the god had said.

He obeys, because the chemicals within his blood force him to obey.

A third organ is placed within his chest, not far from the new heart. As the ossmodula warps his bones to grow on new minerals, the biscopea generates a flood of hormones to feed his muscles.

Surgeons seal the boy's medical wounds.

Already, the child is no longer human. Tonight's work has seen to that. Time will reveal just how different the boy will become.

He is a teenage boy, standing over another dead body.

This corpse is not like the first. This corpse is the same age as the boy, and in its last moments of life it had struggled with all its strength, desperate not to die.

The boy drops his weapon. The serrated knife falls to the ground.

Legion masters come to him. Their eyes are red, their dark armour immense. Skulls hang from their pauldrons and plastrons on chains of blackened bronze.

He draws breath to speak, to tell them it was an accident. They silence him.

'Well done,' they say.

And they call him *brother*.

* * *

He is a teenage boy, and the rifle is heavy in his hands.

He watches for a long, long time. He has trained for this. He knows how to slow his hearts, how to regulate his breathing and the biological beats of his body until his entire form remains as still as a statue.

Predator. Prey. His mind goes cold, his focus absolute. The mantra chanted internally becomes the only way to see the world. *Predator. Prey. Hunter. Hunted.* Nothing else matters.

He squeezes the trigger. One thousand metres away, a man dies.

'Target eliminated,' he says.

He is a young man, sleeping on the same surgery table as before.

In a slumber demanded by the chemicals flowing through his veins, he dreams once again of his first murder. In the waking world, needles and medical probes bore into the flesh of his back, injecting fluids directly into his spinal column.

His slumbering body reacts to the invasion, coughing once. Acidic spit leaves his lips, hissing on the ground where it lands, eating into the tiled floor.

When he wakes, hours later, he feels the sockets running down his spine. The scars, the metallic nodules…

In a universe where no gods exist, he knows this is the closest mortality can come to divinity.

He is a young man, staring into his own eyes.

He stands naked in a dark chamber, in a lined rank with a dozen other souls. Other initiates standing with him, also stripped of clothing, the marks of their surgeries fresh upon their pale skin. He barely notices them. Sexuality is a forgotten concept, alien to his mind, merely one of ten thousand humanities his consciousness has discarded. He no longer recalls the face of his mother and father. He only recalls his own name because his Legion masters never changed it.

He looks into the eyes that are now his. They stare back, slanted and murder-red, set in a helmet with its facial plate painted white. The blood-eyed, bone-pale skull watches him as he watches it.

This is his face now. Through these eyes, he will see the galaxy. Through this skulled helm he will cry his wrath at those who dare defy the Emperor's vision for mankind.

'You are Talos,' a Legion master says, 'of First Claw, Tenth Company.'

He is a young man, utterly inhuman, immortal and undying.

He sees the surface of this world through crimson vision, with data streaming in sharp, clear white runic language across his retinas. He sees the life forces of his brothers in the numbers displayed. He feels the temperature outside his sealed war armour. He sees targeting sights flicker as they follow the movements of his eyes, and feels his hand, the hand clutching his bolter, tense as it tries to follow each target lock. Ammunition counters display how many have died this day.

Around him, aliens die. Ten, a hundred, a thousand. His brothers butcher their way through a city of violet crystal, bolters roaring and chainswords howling. Here and there in the opera of battle-noise, a brother screams his rage through helm-amplifiers.

The sound is always the same. Bolters always roar. Chainblades always howl. Adeptus Astartes always cry their fury. When the VIII Legion wages war, the sound is that of lions and wolves slaying each other while vultures shriek above.

He cries words that he will one day never shout again – words that will soon become ash on his tongue. Already he cries the words without thinking about them, without *feeling* them.

For the Emperor.

He is a young man, awash in the blood of humans.

He shouts words without the heart to feel them, declaring concepts of Imperial justice and deserved vengeance. A man claws at his armour, begging and pleading.

'We are loyal! We have surrendered!'

The young man breaks the human's face with the butt of his bolter. Surrendering so late was a meaningless gesture. Their blood must run as an example, and the rest of the system's worlds would fall into line.

Around him, the riot continues unabated. Soon, his bolter is silenced, voiceless with no shells to fire. Soon after that, his chainsword dies, clogged with meat.

The Night Lords resort to killing the humans with their bare hands, dark gauntlets punching and strangling and crushing.

At a timeless point in the melee, the voice of an ally comes over the vox. It is an Imperial Fist. Their Legion watches from the bored security of their landing site.

'What are you doing?' the Imperial Fist demands. 'Brothers, are you insane?'

Talos does not answer. They do not deserve an answer. If the Fists had brought this world into compliance themselves, the Night Lords would never have needed to come here.

He is a young man, watching his homeworld burn.

He is a young man, mourning a father soon to die.

He is a traitor to everything he once held sacred.

* * *

STABBING LIGHTS LANCED through the gloom.

The salvage team moved slowly, neither patient nor impatient, but with the confident care of men with an arduous job to do and no deadline to meet. The team spread out across the chamber, overturning debris, examining the markings of weapons fire on the walls, their internal vox clicking as they spoke to one another.

With the ship open to the void, each of the salvage team wore atmosphere suits against the airless cold. They communicated as often by sign language as they did by words.

This interested the hunter that watched them, because he too was fluent in Astartes battle sign. Curious, to see his enemies betray themselves so easily.

The hunter watched in silence as the spears of illumination cut this way and that, revealing the wreckage of the battles that had taken place on this deck of the abandoned vessel. The salvage team – who were clearly genhanced, but too small and unarmoured to be full Astartes – were crippled by the atmosphere suits they wore. Such confinement limited their senses, while the hunter's ancient Mark IV war-plate only enhanced his. They could not hear as he heard, nor see as he saw. That reduced their chances of survival from incredibly unlikely to absolutely none.

Smiling at the thought, the hunter whispered to the machine-spirit of his armour, a single word that enticed the war-plate's soul with the knowledge that the hunt was beginning in earnest.

'Preysight.'

His vision blurred to the blue of the deepest oceans, decorated by supernova heat smears of moving, living beings. The hunter watched the team move on, separating into two teams, each of two men.

This was going to be entertaining.

TALOS FOLLOWED THE first team, shadowing them through the corridors, knowing the grating purr of his power armour and the snarling of its servo-joints were unheard by the sense-dimmed salvagers.

Salvagers was perhaps the wrong word, of course. Disrespectful to the foe.

While they were not full Adeptus Astartes, their gene-enhancement was obvious in the bulk of their bodies and the lethal grace of their motions. They, too, were hunters – just weaker examples of the breed.

Initiates.

Their icon, mounted on each shoulder plate, displayed a drop of ruby blood framed by proud angelic wings.

The hunter's pale lips curled into another crooked smile. This was unexpected. The Blood Angels had sent in a team of Scouts…

The Night Lord had little time for notions of coincidence. If the Angels were here, then they were here on the hunt. Perhaps the *Covenant of Blood* had been detected on the long-range sensors of a Blood Angel battlefleet. Such a discovery would certainly have been enough to bring them here.

Hunting for their precious sword, no doubt. And not for the first time.

Perhaps this was their initiation ceremony? A test of prowess? Bring back the blade and earn passage into the Chapter...

Oh, how unfortunate.

The stolen blade hung at the hunter's hip, as it had for years now. Tonight would not be the night it found its way back into the desperate reach of the Angels. But, as always, they were welcome to sell their lives in the attempt at reclamation.

Talos monitored the readout of his retinal displays. The temptation to blink-click certain runes was strong, but he resisted the urge. This hunt would be easy enough without combat narcotics flooding his blood. Purity lay in abstaining from such things until they became necessary.

The location runes of his brothers in First Claw flickered on his visor display. Taking note of their positions elsewhere in the ship, the hunter moved forward to shed the blood of those enslaved to the Throne of Lies.

A TRUE HUNTER did not avoid being seen by his prey. Such stalking was the act of cowards and carrion-eaters, revealing themselves only when the prey was slain. Where was the skill in that? Where was the thrill?

A Night Lord was raised to hunt by other, truer principles.

Talos ghosted through the shadows, judging the strength of the Scouts' suits' audio-receptors. Just how much could they hear...?

He followed them down a corridor, his gauntleted knuckles scraping along the metal walls.

The Blood Angels turned instantly, stabbing his face with their beam lighting.

That almost worked, the hunter had to give it to them. These lesser hunters knew their prey – they knew they hunted Night Lords. For half a heartbeat, sunfire would have blazed across his vision, blinding him.

Talos ignored the beams completely. He tracked by preysight. Their tactics were meaningless.

He was already gone when they opened fire, melting into the shadows of a side corridor.

HE CAUGHT THEM again nine minutes later.

This time, he lay in wait after baiting a beautiful trap. The sword they came for was right in their path.

It was called *Aurum*. Words barely did its craftsmanship justice. Forged when the Emperor's Great Crusade took its first steps into the stars, the blade was forged for one of the Blood Angel Legion's first heroes. It had come into Talos's possession centuries later, when he'd murdered *Aurum*'s heir.

It was almost amusing, how often the sons of Sanguinius tried to reclaim the sword from him. It was much less amusing how often he had to kill his own brothers when they sought to take the blade from his dead hands. Avarice shattered all unity, even among Legion brothers.

The Scouts saw their Chapter relic now, so long denied their grasp. The golden blade was embedded into the dark metal decking, its angel-winged crosspiece turned to ivory under the harsh glare of their stabbing lights.

An invitation to simply advance into the chamber and take it, but it was so obviously a trap. Yet... how could they resist?

They did not resist.

The initiates were alert, bolters high and panning fast, senses keen. The hunter saw their mouths moving as they voxed continuous updates to each other.

Talos let go of the ceiling.

He thudded to the deck behind one of the initiates, gauntlets snapping forward to clutch the Scout.

The other Angel turned and fired. Talos laughed at the zeal in his eyes, at the tightness of his clenched teeth, as the initiate fired three bolts into the body of his brother.

The Night Lord gripped the convulsing human shield against him, seeing the temperature gauge on his retinal display flicker as the dying initiate's blood hit sections of his war-plate. In his grip, the shuddering Angel was little more than a burst sack of freezing meat. The bolt shells had detonated, coming close to killing him and opening the suit to the void.

'Good shooting, Angel,' Talos spoke through his helm's crackling vox-speakers. He threw his bleeding shield aside and leapt for the other initiate, fingers splayed like talons.

The fight was mercilessly brief. The Night Lord's full gene-enhancements, coupled with the heightened strength of his armour's engineered muscle fibre-cables, meant there was only one possible outcome. Talos backhanded the bolter from the Angel's grip and clawed at the initiate.

As the weaker warrior writhed, Talos stroked his gauntleted fingertips across the clear face-visor of the initiate's atmosphere suit.

'This looks fragile,' he said.

The Scout shouted something unheard. Hate burned in his eyes. Talos wasted several seconds just enjoying that expression. That passion.

He crashed his fist against the visor, smashing it to shards.

As one corpse froze and another swelled and ruptured on its way to asphyxiation, the Night Lord retrieved his blade, the sword he claimed by right of conquest, and moved back into the darkest parts of the ship.

* * *

'Talos,' the voice came over the vox in a sibilant hiss.

'Speak, Uzas.'

'They have sent initiates to hunt us, brother. I had to cancel my prey-sight to make sure my eyes were seeing clearly. *Initiates*. Against *us*.'

'Spare me your indignation. What do you want?'

Uzas's reply was a low growl and a crackle of dead vox. Talos put it from his mind. He had long grown bored of Uzas forever lamenting each time they met with insignificant prey.

'Cyrion,' he voxed.

'Aye. Talos?'

'Of course.'

'Forgive me. I thought it would be Uzas with another rant. I hear your decks are crawling with Angels. Epic glories to be earned in slaughtering their infants, eh?'

Talos didn't quite sigh. 'Are you almost done?'

'This hulk is as hollow as Uzas's head, brother. Negative on anything of worth. Not even a servitor to steal. I'm returning to the boarding pod now. Unless you need help shooting the Angels' children?'

Talos killed the vox-link as he stalked through the black corridor. This was fruitless. Time to leave – empty-handed and still desperately short on supplies. This... this *piracy* offended him now, as it always did, and as it always had since they'd been cut off from the Legion decades ago. A plague upon the long-dead Warmaster and his failures which still echoed today. A curse upon the night the VIII Legion was shattered and scattered across the stars.

Diminished. Reduced. Surviving as disparate warbands – broken echoes of the unity within loyalist Astartes Chapters.

Sins of the father.

This curious ambush by the Angels who had tracked them here was nothing more than a minor diversion. Talos was about to vox a general withdrawal after the last initiates were hunted down and slain, when his vox went live again.

'Brother,' said Xarl. 'I've found the Angels.'

'As have Uzas and I. Kill them quickly and let's get back to the *Covenant*.'

'No, Talos.' Xarl's voice was edged with anger. 'Not initiates. The real Angels.'

The Night Lords of First Claw, Tenth Company, came together like wolves in the wild. Stalking through the darkened chambers of the ship, the four Astartes met in the shadows, speaking over their vox-link, crouching with their weapons at the ready.

In Talos's hands, the relic blade *Aurum* caught what little light remained, glinting as he moved.

'Five of them,' Xarl spoke low, his voice edged with his suppressed eagerness. 'We can take five. They stand bright and proud in a control chamber not far from our boarding pod.' He racked his bolter. 'We can take five,' he repeated.

'They're just waiting?' Cyrion said. 'They must be expecting an honest fight.'

Uzas snorted at that.

'This is your fault, you know,' Cyrion said with a chuckle, nodding at Talos. 'You and that damn sword.'

'It keeps things interesting,' Talos replied. 'And I cherish every curse that their Chapter screams at me.'

He stopped speaking, narrowing his eyes for a moment. Cyrion's skulled helm blurred before him. As did Xarl's. The sound of distant bolter fire echoed in his ears, not distorted by the faint crackle of helm-filtered noise. Not a true sound. Not a real memory. Something akin to both.

'I... have a...' Talos blinked to clear his fading vision. Shadows of vast things darkened his sight. '...have a plan...'

'Brother?' Cyrion asked.

Talos shivered once, his servo-joints snarling at the shaking movement. Magnetically clasped to his thigh, his bolter didn't fall to the decking, but the golden blade did. It clattered to the steel floor with a clang.

'Talos?' Xarl asked.

'No,' Uzas growled, 'not *now*.'

Talos's head jerked once, as if his armour had sent an electrical pulse through his spine, and he crashed to the ground in a clash of war-plate on metal.

'The god-machines of Crythe...' he murmured. 'They have killed the sun.'

A moment later, he started screaming.

THE OTHERS HAD to cut Talos out of the squad's internal vox-link. His screams drowned out all other speech.

'We can take five of them,' Xarl said. 'Three of us remain. We can take five Angels.'

'Almost certainly,' Cyrion agreed. 'And if they summon squads of their initiates?'

'Then we slaughter five of them *and* their initiates.'

Uzas cut in. 'We were slaying our way across the stars ten thousand years before they were even born.'

'Yes, while that's a wonderful parable, I don't need rousing rhetoric,' Cyrion said. 'I need a plan.'

'We hunt,' Uzas and Xarl said at once.

'We kill them,' Xarl added.

'We feast on their gene-seed,' Uzas finished.

'If this was an award ceremony for fervency and zeal, once again, you'd both be collapsing under the weight of medals. But you want to launch an assault on their position while we drag Talos with us? I think the scraping of his armour over the floor will rather kill the element of stealth, brothers.'

'Guard him, Cyrion,' Xarl said. 'Uzas and I will take the Angels.'

'Two against five.' Cyrion's red eye lenses didn't quite fix upon his brother's. 'Those are poor odds, Xarl.'

'Then we will finally be rid of each other,' Xarl grunted. 'Besides, we've had worse.'

That was true, at least.

'*Ave Dominus Nox*,' Cyrion said. 'Hunt well and hunt fast.'

'*Ave Dominus Nox*,' the other two replied.

CYRION LISTENED FOR a while to his brother's screams. It was difficult to make any sense from the stream of shouted words.

This came as no surprise. Cyrion had heard Talos suffering in the grip of this affliction many times before. As gene-gifts went, it was barely a blessing.

Sins of the father, he thought, watching Talos's inert armour, listening to the cries of death to come. *How they are reflected within the son.*

ACCORDING TO CYRION'S retinal chrono display, one hour and sixteen minutes had passed when he heard the explosion.

The decking shuddered under his boots.

'Xarl? Uzas?'

Static was the only answer.

Great.

WHEN UZAS'S VOICE finally broke over the vox after two hours, it was weak and coloured by his characteristic bitterness.

'Hnngh. Cyrion. It's done. Drag the prophet.'

'You sound like you got shot,' Cyrion resisted the urge to smile in case they heard it in his words.

'He did,' Xarl said. 'We're on our way back.'

'What was that detonation?'

'Plasma cannon.'

'You're… you're joking.'

'Not even for a second. I have no idea why they brought one of those to a fight in a ship's innards, but the coolant feeds made for a ripe target.'

Cyrion blink-clicked a rune by Xarl's identification symbol. It opened a private channel between the two of them.

'Who hit Uzas?'

'An initiate. From behind, with a sniper rifle.'

Cyrion immediately closed the link so no one would hear him laughing.

* * *

THE *Covenant of Blood* was a blade of cobalt darkness, bronze-edged and scarred by centuries of battle. It drifted through the void, sailing close to its prey like a shark gliding through black waters.

The *Encarmine Soul* was a Gladius-class frigate with a long and proud history of victories in the name of the Blood Angels Chapter – and before it, the IX Legion. It opened fire on the *Covenant of Blood* with an admirable array of weapons batteries.

Briefly, beautifully, the void shields around the Night Lords strike cruiser shimmered in a display reminiscent of oil on water.

The *Covenant of Blood* returned fire. Within a minute, the blade-like ship was sailing through void debris, its lances cooling from their momentary fury. The *Encarmine Soul*, what little chunks were left of it, clanked and sparked off the larger cruiser's void shields as it passed through the expanding cloud of wreckage.

Another ship, this one stricken and dead in space, soon fell under the *Covenant's* shadow. The strike cruiser obscured the sun, pulling in close, ready to receive its boarding pod once again.

First Claw had been away for seven hours investigating the hulk. Their mothership had come hunting for them.

BULKHEAD SEALS HISSED as the reinforced doors opened on loud, grinding hinges.

Xarl and Cyrion carried Talos into the *Covenant's* deployment bay. Uzas walked behind them, a staggering limp marring his gait. His spine was on fire from the sniper's solid slug that still lodged there. Worse, his gen-hanced healing had sealed and clotted the wound. He'd need surgery – or more likely a knife and a mirror – to tear the damn thing out.

One of the Atramentar, elite guard of the Exalted, stood in its hulking Terminator war-plate. His skull-painted, tusked helm stared impassively. Trophy racks adorned his back, each one impaled with several helms from a number of loyalist Astartes Chapters: a history of bloodshed and betrayal, proudly displayed for his brothers to see.

It nodded to Talos's prone form.

'The Soul Hunter is wounded?' the Terminator asked, its voice a deep, rumbling growl.

'No,' Cyrion said. 'Inform the Exalted at once. His prophet is suffering another vision.'

SOUL HUNTER

PART ONE

TRAITORS' UNITY

'My sons, the galaxy is burning.
We all bear witness to a final truth – our way is not the way of the
Imperium.
You have never stood in the Emperor's light.
Never worn the Imperial eagle.

And you never will.

You shall stand in midnight clad,
Your claws forever red with the lifeblood of my father's failed empire,
Warring through the centuries as the talons of a murdered god.

Rise, my sons, and take your wrath across the stars,
In my name. In my memory.
Rise, my Night Lords.'

– The Primarch Konrad Curze,
at the final gathering of the VIII Legion

PROLOGUE
A GOD'S SON

IT WAS A curse, to be a god's son.

To see as a god saw, to know what a god knew. This sight, this knowledge, tore him apart time and again.

His chamber was a cell, devoid of comfort, serving as nothing more than a haven against interference. Within this hateful sanctuary, the god's son screamed out secrets of a future yet to come, his voice a strangled chorus of cries rendered toneless and metallic by the speaker grille of his ancient battle helm.

Sometimes his muscles would lock, slabs of meat and sinew tensing around his iron-hard bones, leaving him shivering and breathing in harsh rasps, unable to control his own body. These seizures could last for hours, each beat of his two hearts firing his nerves with agony as the blood hammered through his cramping muscles. In the times he was free from the accursed paralysis, when his reserve heart would slow and grow still once again, he would ease the pain by pounding his skull against the walls of his cell. This fresh torment was a distraction from the images that burned behind his eyes.

It sometimes worked, but never for long. The returning visions would peel back any lesser torment, bathing his mind once more in fire.

The god's son, still in his battle armour, rammed his helmed head against the wall, driving his skull against the steel again and again. Between the ceramite helmet he wore and the enhanced bone of his skeleton, his efforts did more damage to the wall than to himself.

Lost in the same curse that led to his gene-father's death, the god's son did not see his cell walls around him, nor did he detect the data streaming across his retinas as his helm's combat display tracked and targeted the contours of the wall, the hinges of the barred door, and every other insignificant detail in the unfurnished chamber. At the top left of his visor display, his vital signs were charted in a scrolling readout that flashed with intermittent warnings when his twin hearts pounded too hard for even his inhuman physiology, or his breathing ceased for minutes at a time with his body locked in a seizure.

And this was the price he paid for being like his father. This was existence as the living legacy of a god.

THE SLAVE LISTENED at his master's door, counting the minutes.

Behind the reinforced dark metal portal, the master's cries had finally subsided – at least for now. The slave was human, with the limited senses such a state entailed, but with his ear pressed to the door, he could make out the master's breathing. It was a sawing sound, ragged and harsh, filtered into a metallic growl by the vox-speakers of the master's skull-faced helm.

And still, even as his mind wandered to other thoughts, the slave kept counting the seconds as they became minutes. It was easy; he'd trained to make it instinctive, for no chronometers would work reliably within the warp.

The slave's name was Septimus, because he was the seventh. Six slaves had come before him in service to the master, and those six were no longer among the crew of the glorious vessel, the *Covenant of Blood*.

The corridors of the Astartes strike cruiser stood almost empty, a silent web of black steel and dark iron. These were the veins of the great ship, once thriving with activity: servitors trundling about their simple duties, Astartes moving from chamber to chamber, mortal crew performing the myriad functions that were necessary for the ship's continued running. In the days before the great betrayal, thousands of souls had called the *Covenant* home, including almost three hundred of the immortal Astartes.

Time had changed that. Time, and the wars it brought.

The corridors were unlit, but not powerless. An intentional blackness settled within the strike cruiser, a darkness so deep it was bred into the ship's steel bones. It was utterly natural to the Night Lords, each one born of the same sunless world. To the few crew that dwelled in the *Covenant's* innards, the darkness was – at first – an uncomfortable presence. Acclimatisation would inevitably come to most. They would still carry their torches and optical enhancers, for they were human and had no ability to pierce the artificial night as their masters did. But over time, they grew to take comfort in the darkness.

In time, acclimatisation became familiarity. Those whose minds never found comfort in the blackness were lost to madness, and discarded after they were slain for their failure. The others abided, and grew familiar with their unseen surroundings.

Septimus's thoughts went deeper than most. All machines had souls. This he knew, even from his days of loyalty to the Golden Throne. He would speak with the nothingness sometimes, knowing the blackness was an entity unto itself, an expression of the ship's sentience. To walk through the pitch-blackness that saturated the ship was to live within the vessel's soul, to breathe in the palpable aura of the *Covenant*'s traitorous malevolence.

The darkness never answered, but he took comfort in the vessel's presence around him. As a child, he'd always feared the dark. That fear had never really left him, and knowing the silent, black corridors were not hostile was all that kept his mind together in the infinite night of his existence.

He was also lonely. That was a difficult truth to admit, even to himself. Far easier to sit in the darkness, speaking to the ship, even knowing it would never answer. He had sometimes felt distant from the other slaves and servants aboard the vessel. Most had been in service to the Night Lords much longer than he had. They unnerved him. Many walked around with their eyes closed, navigating the cold hallways of the ship by memory, by touch, and by other senses Septimus had no desire to understand.

Once, in the silent weeks before another battle on another world, Septimus had asked what became of the six slaves before him. The master was in seclusion, away from his brothers, praying to the souls of his weapons and armour. He had looked at Septimus then, staring with eyes as black as the space between the stars.

And he'd smiled. The master rarely did that. The blue veins visible under the master's pale cheeks twisted like faint cracks in pristine marble.

'Primus,' he spoke softly – as he always did without his battle helm – but with a rich, deep resonance nevertheless, 'was killed a long, long time ago. In battle.'

'Did you try to save him, lord?'

'No. I was not aware of his death. I was not on board the *Covenant* when it happened.'

The slave wanted to ask if the master would have even tried to save his predecessor had the chance arisen, but in truth he feared he knew the answer already. 'I see,' Septimus said, licking his dry lips. 'And the others?'

'Tertius… changed. The warp changed him. I destroyed him when he was no longer himself.'

This surprised Septimus. The master had told him before of the importance of servants that could resist the madness of the warp, remaining pure from the corruption of the Ruinous Powers.

'He fell by your hand?' Septimus asked.

'He did. It was a mercy.'

'I see. And the others?'

'They aged. They died. All except for Secondus and Quintus.'

'What of them?'

'Quintus was slain by the Exalted.'

Septimus's blood ran cold at those words. He loathed the Exalted.

'Why? What transgression was he guilty of?'

'He broke no law. The Exalted killed him in a moment of fury. He vented his rage on the closest living being. Unfortunately for Quintus, it was him.'

'And… what of Secondus?'

'I will tell you of the second another time. Why do you ask about my former servants?'

Septimus drew breath to tell the truth, to confess his fears, to admit he was speaking into the ship's darkness to stave off loneliness. But the fate of Tertius stayed trapped within his forethoughts. Death because of madness. Death because of corruption.

'Curiosity,' the slave said to his master, speaking the first and only lie he would ever say in his service.

The sound of booted footfalls drew Septimus back to the present. He moved away from the master's door, taking a breath as he glanced unseeing down the hallway in the direction of the approaching footsteps.

He knew who was coming. They would see him. They would see him even if he stayed hidden nearby, so there was no sense running. They would smell his scent and see the aura of his body heat. So he stood ready, willing his heartbeat to slow from its thunderous refrain. They would hear that, too. They would smile at his fears.

Septimus clicked the deactivation button on his weak lamp pack, killing the dim yellow illumination and bathing the corridor in utter blackness once more. He did this out of respect to the approaching Astartes, and because he had no wish to see their faces. At times, the darkness made dealing with the demigods much easier.

Steeled and prepared, Septimus closed his now-useless eyes, shifting his perceptions to focus entirely on his hearing and sense of smell. The footfalls were heavy but unarmoured – too widely spaced to be human. A swish of a tunic or robe. Most pervasive of all, the scent of blood: tangy, rich and metallic, strong enough to tickle the tongue. It was the smell of the ship itself, but distilled, purified, magnified.

Another demigod.

One of the master's kin was coming to see his brother.

'Septimus,' said the voice from the blackness.

The slave swallowed hard, not trusting his voice but knowing he must speak. 'Yes, lord. It is I.'

A rustle of clothing, the sound of something soft on metal. Was the demigod stroking the master's door?

'Septimus,' the other demigod repeated. His voice was inhumanly low, a rumble of syllables. 'How has my brother been?'

'He has not emerged yet, lord.'

'I know. I hear him breathing. He is calmer than before.' The demigod sounded contemplative. 'I did not ask if he had emerged, Septimus. I asked how he had been.'

'This affliction has lasted longer than most, lord, but my master has been silent for almost an hour now. I have counted the minutes. This is the longest he has been at peace since the affliction first took hold.'

The demigod chuckled. It sounded like thunderheads colliding. Septimus had a momentary trickle of nostalgia; he'd not seen a storm – not even stood under a real sky – in years now.

'Careful with your language, vassal,' the demigod said. 'To name it an affliction implies a curse. My brother, your master, is blessed. He sees as a god sees.'

'Forgive me, great one.' Septimus was already on his knees, head bowed, knowing that the demigod could see his supplication clearly in the pitch darkness. 'I use only the words my master uses.'

There was a long pause.

'Septimus. Stand. You are fearful, and it is affecting your judgement. I will do you no harm. Do you not know me?'

'No, great lord.' This was true. The slave could never tell the difference in the demigods' voices. Each one spoke like a predator cat's low snarls. Only his master sounded different, an edge of softness rounding out the lion-like growls. He knew this recognition was due to familiarity, rather than any true difference in the master's tone, but it never helped in telling the others apart. 'I might guess if told to do so.'

There was the sound of the demigod shifting his stance, and the accompanying whisper of his clothing.

'Indulge me.'

'I believe you are Lord Cyrion.'

Another pause. 'How did you know, vassal?'

'Because you laughed, lord.'

In the silence that followed those words, even in the darkness, Septimus was certain the demigod was smiling.

'Tell me,' the Astartes finally spoke, 'have the others come today?'

The slave swallowed. 'Lord Uzas was here three hours ago, Lord Cyrion.'

'I imagine that was unpleasant.'

'Yes, lord.'

'What did my beloved brother Uzas do when he came?' The edge of sarcasm in Cyrion's voice was unmistakable.

'He listened to the master's words, but said none of his own.' Septimus recalled the chill in the blackness as he stood in the hallway with Uzas, hearing the demigod breathe in harsh grunts, listening to the thrum of his primed battle armour. 'He wore his war-plate, lord. I do not know why.'

'That's no mystery,' Cyrion replied. 'Your master is still in his own war armour. The latest "affliction" took hold while we were embattled, and to remove the armour would risk waking him from the vision.'

'I do not understand, lord.'

'Don't you? Think, Septimus. You can hear my brother's cries now, but they are muffled, filtered through his helm's speakers and further constrained by the metal of his cell. But if one wished to hear him with a degree of clarity... He is screaming his prophecies into the vox-network. Everyone wearing their armour can hear him crying out across the communication frequencies.'

The thought made Septimus's blood run cold. The ship's demigod crew, hearing his master cry out in agony for hours on end. His skin prickled as if stroked by the darkness. This discomfort – was it jealousy? Helplessness? Septimus wasn't sure.

'What is he saying, lord? What does my master dream?'

Cyrion rested his palm against the door again, and his voice was devoid of the humour he'd hinted at before.

'He dreams what our primarch dreamed,' the Astartes said in a low tone. 'Of sacrifice and battle. Of war without end.'

CYRION WAS NOT entirely correct.

He spoke with the assurance of knowledge, for he was all too experienced with his brother's visions. Yet this time, a new facet was threaded through the stricken warrior's prophecies. This came to light some nine hours later when, at last, the door opened.

The demigod staggered into the hallway, fully armoured, leaning against the opposite wall of the corridor. His muscles were like cables of fire around molten bones, but the pain wasn't the worst part. He could manage pain, and had done so countless times before. It was the weakness. The vulnerability. These things unnerved him, made him bare his teeth in a feral snarl at the sheer unfamiliarity of the sensation.

Movement. The god's son sensed movement to his left. Still pain-blind from the wracking headache brought on by his seizures, he turned his head towards the source of the motion. His ability to smell prey, as enhanced as every sense he possessed, registered familiar scents: the smoky touch of cloying incense, the musk of sweat, and the metallic tang of concealed weaponry.

'Septimus,' the god's son spoke. The sound of his own voice was alien; scratchy and whispered even through the helmet's vox speakers.

'I am here, master.' The slave's relief was shattered when he saw how weak his lord was. This was new to them both. 'You were lost to us for exactly ninety-one hours and seventeen minutes,' the slave said, apprising his master in the way he always did after the seizures struck.

'A long time,' the demigod said, drawing himself up to his full height. Septimus watched his master stand tall, and was careful to angle away the dim beam from his lamp pack, casting its weak illumination onto the floor. It still provided enough light to see by, bringing a reassuring gloom to the hallway.

'Yes, lord. A long time. The afflictions are getting longer.'

'They are. Who was the last to come to me?'

'Lord Cyrion, seven hours ago. I thought you were going to die.'

'For a while, so did I.' There was the serpentine hiss of venting air pressure as the demigod removed his helm. In the low light, Septimus could just make out his master's smooth features, and the eyes as black as pools of tar.

'What did you dream?' the slave asked.

'Dark omens and a dead world. Make your way to my arming chambers and make preparations. I must speak with the Exalted.'

'Preparations?' Septimus hesitated. 'Another war?'

'There is always another war. But first, we must meet someone. Someone who will prove vital to our survival. We must go on a journey.'

'To where, lord?'

The demigod gave a rare smile. 'Home.'

I

NOSTRAMO

A LONE ASTEROID spun in the stillness of space. Tens of millions of kilo-metres from the closest planetary body, it was clearly no natural satellite belonging to any of the planets in the sector.

This was good. This was very, very good.

To the keen eyes and knowing smile of Kartan Syne, the hunk of rock twisting endlessly through the dead space of Ultima Segmentum was a thing of beauty. Or rather, what it represented was a thing of beauty, because what it represented was money. A great deal of money.

His vessel, a well-armed bulk trader by the delightfully ostentatious name *Maiden of the Stars*, sat in a loose orbit around the vast asteroid below. The *Maiden* was a big girl, and she threw her weight around when it came to tight manoeuvres, but while Syne hated a little meat on his women, he loved a little bulk to his ship's hull. The sacrifice of speed for greater profit was worth it.

Pirates were no issue. The *Maiden* bristled with weapons batteries, all bought with the profits of his mining runs. Often he'd settle for a finder's fee, but in cases like this – and cases like this were few and far between – he felt the need to fall into orbit and set his servitor teams on the sur-face to start digging. They were down there now, lobotomised lords of their own little mining colony. It had only been a handful of hours since planetfall, but already his automated crews were hard at work.

Lounging in his command throne, Syne watched the occulus screen as it displayed the asteroid spinning below, grey-skinned and silver-veined, a massive shard of untapped profit. He glanced at the data-slate in his hand for the hundredth time that hour, reading the figures from the planetary scan. He smiled again as his dark eyes graced the numbers next to the word 'Adamantium'.

Holy Throne, he was rich. The Adeptus Mechanicus would pay well for a hull full of precious, precious adamantium ore, but better yet, they'd pay a High Lord's ransom for the coordinates of this rock. The trick would be to leave enough ore here for the Mechanicus's exploratory vessels to confirm the intense value, but still have a cargo hold full of collateral when he approached them. Given the amount of the rare metal woven through the vast asteroid below, that wouldn't be a problem, not at all.

He glanced at the figures again, feeling a smile break out across his handsome face. The glance became a gaze, and the smile became a grin. This smirking leer was broken less than three seconds later, when proximity alarms began to ring across the *Maiden*'s untidy bridge.

Servitors and human crew moved about the circular chamber, attending to their stations.

'A report right about now would be just wonderful,' Kartan Syne said to no one in particular. In answer, one of the servitors slaved to the navigation console chattered out a babble of binary from its slack jaws.

Syne sighed. He'd meant to get that servitor replaced.

'Well, I'm none the wiser, but thanks for speaking up,' Syne said. 'How about an answer from someone who isn't broken?'

Blood of the Emperor, this was bad. If another rogue trader had chanced upon this site, then Syne was entering the murky waters of profit-sharing, and that would end in tears for all concerned. Worse yet, it could be the Mechanicus itself. No finder's fee, no hull full of rare ore, and no room to negotiate, either.

Navigation Officer Torc finally looked up from his monochrome screen and the bright runic writing trailing across it. His uniform was about as official as Syne's own, which meant both men would have looked at home in an underhive slum.

'It's an Astartes vessel,' Torc said.

Syne laughed. 'No, it's not.'

Torc's face was pale, and his slow nod halted Syne's laughter. 'It is. Came out of nowhere, Kar. It's an Astartes strike cruiser.'

'How rare,' the trader captain smiled. 'At least they're not here for the mining, then. Bring us about and let's have a look at this. We might never see one again.'

Slowly, the view in the occulus changed from a gentle blur of stars to settle on the warship. Vast, dark and deadly. Jagged, long and lethal. Midnight blue, wreathed in bronze trimmings, blackened in places from centuries of battle damage. It was a barbed spear of violent intent: the fury of the Astartes in spaceborne form.

'She's a beauty,' Syne said with feeling. 'I'm glad they're on our side.'

'Uh… She's on an approach course.'

Kartan Syne turned from the majestic view to frown at Torc. 'She's doing what now?'

'She's on an approach vector. It's bearing down on us.'

'No,' he said again, without laughing this time, 'it's not.'

Torc was still staring at his data display screen. 'Yes, it is.'

'Someone give me its transponder code. And open a channel.'

'I've got the identification code,' Torc said, his fingertips hitting keys as he looked into his screen. 'It reads as the *Covenant of Blood*, no record of allegiance.'

'No allegiance code. Is that normal?'

'How am I supposed to know?' Torc shrugged. 'I've never seen one before.'

'Maybe all Astartes vessels do this,' Syne mused. It made sense. The Astartes were famously independent of traditional Imperial hierarchy and operation.

'Maybe.' Torc didn't sound too sure.

'How's that channel coming along?' Syne asked.

'Channel open,' murmured a servitor, its head attached to the communications console via several black cables.

'Let's get this sorted out, hm?' Syne lounged in his throne again, clicking the vox-caster live. 'This is Captain Kartan Syne of the trading vessel *Maiden of the Stars*. I have claimed this asteroid and the profit potential therein. To my knowledge, I am in no violation of any boundary laws of the local region. I bid you greetings, Astartes vessel.'

Silence answered this. A pregnant silence, that gave Syne the extremely uncomfortable feeling the channel was still live and the Astartes on board the other vessel were listening to his words and choosing not to reply.

He tried again. 'If I have erred and claimed a source of profit already marked by your noble forces, I am open to negotiation.'

'Negotiation?'

'Shut up, Torc.'

Torc didn't shut up. 'Are you insane? If it's theirs, let's just go.'

'Shut *up*, Torc. Do the Astartes even mine for their own materials?'

Again, Torc shrugged.

'We have precedent to stake the claim,' Syne pressed, feeling his confidence ebbing. 'I'm just trying to keep our options open. Need I remind you that there's also the matter of over a hundred servitors and several thousand crowns worth of heavy-duty mining equipment on the surface of the asteroid? Need I remind you that Eurydice is down there with the digging teams? We won't get far without her, will we?'

Torc paled and said nothing for a moment. Needless to say, he'd been adamant in his advice to keep Eurydice on board and curtail yet another of her 'I'm bored, so I'm going' jaunts off the ship.

'The cruiser's still bearing down on us,' Torc said.

'Attack vector?' Syne leaned forward in his throne.

'Maybe. I don't know how these vessels attack. They have one hell of a forward weapons array, though.'

Syne liked to think he was a genial soul. He enjoyed a laugh as much as the next man, but this was getting quite beyond the realm of light entertainment.

'Throne of the God-Emperor,' Torc swore in a soft voice. 'Its lances are primed. Its… *everything* is primed.'

'This,' Syne said, 'has crossed the border into ridiculous.' He clicked the vox live again, failing to keep a note of desperation out of his voice. 'Astartes vessel *Covenant of Blood*. In the name of the God-Emperor, what are your intentions?'

The reply was a whisper, edged with a smile. It hissed across the *Maiden*'s bridge, and Syne felt it on his skin – the chill of the first cold wind that always precedes a storm.

'Weep as you suffer the same fate as your corpse god,' it whispered. 'We have come for you.'

THE BATTLE DID not last long.

Combat in the depths of deep space is a slow-moving ballet of technology, illuminated by the bright flickers of weapons fire and impact explosions. The *Maiden of the Stars* was a fine enough vessel for what it did; long-distance cargo hauling, deep-range scouting and prospecting, and fighting off the grasping attentions of minor pirate princes. Its captain, Kartan Syne, had invested years of solid profit into the ship. Its void shields were well-maintained and crackling with multi-layered thickness. Its weapons batteries were formidable, comparable to an Imperial Navy cruiser of similar size.

It lasted exactly fifty-one seconds, and several of those were gifts; the *Covenant of Blood* toyed with its prey before the killing strike.

The Astartes strike cruiser drew closer, opening up with a barrage of lance fire. These cutting beams of precision energy slashed across space between the two vessels, and for several heartbeats, the void shields around the *Maiden* lit up in flaring brilliance. Where the lances stabbed against the shields, a riot of colours rippled around the trader ship, like oil spreading across the surface of water.

The *Maiden*'s shields endured this beautiful punishment for a handful of seconds, before buckling under the warship's assault. Resembling a popping bubble in almost all respects, the void shields collapsed with a crackle of energy, leaving the *Maiden* defenceless except for its reinforced hull armour.

Kartan Syne had the wherewithal to get his bridge crew together by this point, and the *Maiden* returned fire. The barrage from the trader's conventional weapons batteries was monumentally weaker than the lance strikes of the Astartes ship. The *Covenant of Blood* drifted ever closer, its own shields now displaying the rippling colours of attack pressure, except – much to the unsurprised dismay of Syne – the warship's shields showed no strain at all. The approaching vessel ignored the minor assault. It was already firing its lances a second time.

This time, with the shield bubble popped, the lances ate directly into the *Maiden's* hull. Predatory incisions were made in the steel flesh of the prey vessel, and the lances tracked and turned, beams of cutting laser fire neatly slicing through the lesser vessel's armour. The *Maiden* had barely responded, yet it was already listing, losing stability, and shaking apart from half a dozen detonations across its length. The *Covenant* had picked the paths of its lances with due care, targeting explosive sections of the ship: the engine core, the plasma batteries, the fuel chambers.

The strike cruiser broke off, its engines roaring into the silence of space to put distance between itself and its crippled prey.

On the *Maiden's* bridge, as his ship rattled and shook with myriad explosions, Kartan Syne glared into the occulus screen as the graceful warship speared away. For a sickening moment, he recalled when he'd hunted grey lynxes on Falodar, and the time he had seen one of the great cats kill one of the equine beasts that served as its preferred prey. The lynx had struck in a blur of movement, ripping great wounds in the horse's throat and belly, then retreated to watch the creature bleed out and die. He'd never forgotten that. At the time, he'd suspected the planet was tainted somehow, to breed such behaviour in the fauna.

'You remember Falodar?' he asked Torc.

There was no response. The bridge was a maelstrom of shouts and alarms, as the crew and servitors fought hopelessly to hold the ship together. The noise annoyed Syne. It wasn't like their struggles could actually achieve anything now.

Syne was still watching the occulus when the final lance strike came. He saw it reaching out towards him, a beam of migraine-bright white that hurt his eyes, seeming to stretch an impossible distance across the stars.

It arrived in a flash of burning light that blessedly silenced the panic around him once and for all.

EURYDICE MERVALLION SAW the *Maiden* destroyed in orbit. She stood staring in horrified awe as it exploded under the lance strikes of another vessel, but even peering into space through her magnoculars, the enemy ship was too distant to identify with any clarity. Whatever it was, it outgunned the *Maiden* by a vast degree. That meant she was probably dead, too.

As deaths were concerned, this was hardly how she'd imagined she would go out. Perhaps it was her mutational gift that led her to such assumptions, but she'd always assumed her end would come when Kartan Syne ordered her to find a way through some horrendously difficult warp storm, and the *Maiden* was another 'lost with all hands within the Sea of Souls' footnote in some minor chronicle. She certainly never assumed she'd live to be interred in the undervaults of House Mervallion, but that suited her fine, anyway. House Mervallion, as Navigator Houses went, wasn't worth much in her eyes.

And truthfully, not in anyone's eyes.

Mervallion was one of the lesser-known families within the myriad cluster of minor Houses: small, lacking influence, providing relatively mediocre Navigators, and largely devoid of wealth – all of which added up to why the Navis Nobilite had seen her assigned to a semi-respectable (at best) junker like the *Maiden of the Stars*, under the command of a weasel like Kartan Syne.

Still, despite the weakness of her bloodline and pedigree, she figured she deserved a better death than *this*.

The camp, such as it was, was unfinished. A bulk lander sat in the heart of the base, surrounded by teams of servitors still unloading the mining vehicles and drill columns. In an ungainly, cheap and uncomfortable atmosphere suit topped by a glass sphere for a helmet, Eurydice watched the black sky, ignoring the servitors around her. They shambled around in their modified protective suits, machine parts spinning, tensing, locking and unlocking as they wheeled equipment into position and constructed what should have been a fully-functional mining operation.

She couldn't help feeling annoyed. What a stupid, pointless way to die. Even if the unknown enemy up there didn't land, she was still marooned. Her lander wasn't capable of warp flight, so her ability to find the Astronomican didn't matter a damn, and she had no supplies for any serious travelling even if she did somehow have the capacity to leave this barren rock behind.

What she did have was an indefinite air supply within the lander, about three weeks' worth of food, and about one hundred servitors that were still getting ready to mine adamantium from a mineral-rich asteroid. The mindwiped slaves lacked the intelligence to realise their mother ship was now nothing more than debris in space.

Not for the first time, she regretted taking the job with Syne. Not that she'd had any choice, of course.

Three years earlier, she'd been dressed in the black toga traditionally worn by her family while on Terra, kneeling before the Celestarch of House Mervallion in his throne room.

'Father,' she had said, head cast down.

'Eurydice,' he replied, his voice flat and toneless as it bleated in a metallic drone through the bulky voxsponder unit replacing the lower half of his face. 'The House calls upon you.'

Those words sang through her body like a chill in her blood. Nothing would be the same again. At twenty-five standard years of age, duty had finally called her into service. Still, she couldn't meet his face. Eurydice knew her father was lucky to have survived the destruction of his speeder six months before. The juvenat surgeries to repair his body had been both extensive and costly, but he was far from the man she remembered from her youth. House Mervallion, even as part of the Navis Nobilite, could hardly afford to flush a fortune into the regeneration treatments the Celestarch would need to restore himself to wholeness. She hated to see him so ruined.

But it was his burden to bear. He had chosen to ignite the rivalry with House Jezzarae. He had signed the contract that brought about the death of Jezzarae's heir. As far as she was concerned, Eurydice figured her father deserved his speeder being sabotaged. She had no time for the petty feuds and revenge debts that linked the Navigator Houses more completely than any bonds of blood.

'Who has purchased the talents of our House, father?'

It would be wrong to say she'd dreamed of this day. At least, not with any real excitement. Between House Mervallion's station and the fact she was the eighth of her father's daughters, laughably distant from even scenting an inheritance, she'd known as long as she could remember that she was destined for life on some mass-conveyance scow. No glory, no honour, no excitement. Just a pittance bleeding back to the family coffers.

But she couldn't help it. Now the moment had come, she dared to imagine what lay ahead. The thrill of hope prickled her skin, and she felt herself smiling. Perhaps she would be chosen to guide one of the Imperial war vessels through the Sea of Souls, part of the Imperium's unending crusades. Perhaps even the Adeptus Astartes…

'The rogue trader,' her father said, 'Kartan Syne.'

The words meant nothing to her. Nothing, except to kill her hope like a candle guttered by sudden wind. No rogue trader dynasty of any worth would stoop to purchasing a daughter of House Mervallion.

It had been a satisfactory three years, though. Of course, fending off Syne's smirking advances had been no treat, but she'd seen a wealth of the segmentum in her tenure as the *Maiden*'s Navigator. She came to know the ship as well as she knew the crew. Awake or asleep, she would hear the old girl's voice in the creaks of the hull and the grumbling engines. She was a placid thing, the *Maiden*, and her complaints were gentle. Eurydice had liked her.

But it had been unfulfilling. Of course it had. Especially when one considered the money hadn't even been all that great. True, she'd raked in more than she would have expected, permitted a small allowance to her personal finances as well as the tithe to House Mervallion, but she was hardly living comfortably. Syne was always spending massive sums of Imperial crowns on upgrading his precious fat matron of a ship, and wasn't that just *so very hilarious* in light of recent events. Good job, Captain Syne. All those guns certainly helped when it really counted.

Very calmly, with another glance around the camp and its busy servitors, she spoke a stream of curses that would have made any within her family utter a prayer for her apparent degeneracy. Several of the words in this barrage of invective were made up, but remained obscenely biological.

All of her worries quickly became moot, however. Unarmed, stranded on an asteroid, not as rich as she'd like to be (and doomed to die within the month anyway) Eurydice watched a fireball streaking down from the starry sky.

'Tomasz?' she spoke into her vox-mic, hailing the mining operations chief. She wasn't entirely alone down here, but a dozen technicians and the pack of armsmen with her hardly mattered if the enemy was capable of ending the *Maiden's* journeys in the blink of an eye.

'Yes, my lady?' came the response from the other side of the camp.

'Uh. Problems.'

'I know, my lady. I know, we see them coming, too. You must get to safety.'

'Really? Where's safe?'

He didn't respond. She looked over her shoulder at the four armsmen; they never left her side when she was out of her trance chambers. They were staring as well, over to the horizon, at something inbound.

'Lady Mervallion,' the leader, Renwar, voxed. 'We need to leave the site. Come with us.'

'Sounds fun, but I'll die here, thank you.'

'Lady…'

'You can run if you like. I think with Syne dead, you're excused from needing to guard me with your lives.'

'Lady, the secondary landing site–'

'Is over two weeks' march from here,' she laughed. 'You think we can outrun their landing vessel?'

'Lady, please. We have to go.'

'I don't have to do anything. We don't have time to fire up the lander, and we'd likely be shot down if we tried. And while the four of you look awfully proud with your shotguns, I doubt they will do much against whatever is coming our way.'

The soldiers shared worried glances. 'Lady,' Renwar said, not meeting her eyes, 'can't you… use your powers?'

'My what?'

'Your eye, my lady. With all due respect. Can't you kill them?'

Her forehead itched. Covered with a black bandana, her third eye, the gift of her Navigator heritage, pulsed softly beneath the material. She wanted to scratch, which was impossible in her glass helmet.

What could she say? Her powers were weak? Her eye didn't work that way? She'd never even tried to employ it in such a manner?

'Just go,' she sighed. 'Syne is dead. We have no way off this rock, and I'm not coming with you to the second camp.'

The men moved away in silence, and she felt their relief all too clearly. Guarding her had been a pleasure for none of them. Fear came with the duty. She was too different. She saw into the warp, and no sane soul wanted anything to do with those who stared into the empyrean.

The thought never depressed her. From birth, it had always been this way. The unease of other humans was so ingrained within her perceptions that she barely noticed it happening.

'Tomasz?'

'Yes, my lady?'

'Are you taking the servitors?'

'We planned to leave them as a distraction, my lady.' She chuckled at that. Bloody cowards. Eurydice waited as the technicians and armsmen started their low-gravity loping run to the south.

Soon she was alone but for the continued unpacking and unloading of the hundred servitors all around. The fire in the sky grew, drawing closer. Whoever or whatever had killed Syne and the rest of the crew – she wouldn't exactly call them her friends, but Torc hadn't been so bad – was evidently on its way to kill her.

'Well,' she said, using a word that had featured heavily in her last tirade, 'shit.'

THE LANDING PARTY consisted of four demigods and one mortal. Septimus, in an old atmosphere suit, trailed behind the lords Cyrion, Uzas, Xarl and his own master. Their boots made the gunship's gang ramp shake as they stalked down to the asteroid's silver-grey surface.

The human slave allowed himself a moment of smiling reflection as he glanced skyward. It wasn't much of a sky – just stars, like always, no clouds or sunlight – but it was enough of a change to keep him smiling as he followed the demigods.

Septimus's master led the small group, clad in his battle armour, breathing the chemical-tasting recycled air within his helm. His visor display, tinted crimson through ruby eye lenses, flickered from servitor to servitor as the squad moved through the small camp. In his dark fists was an ancient bolter, loaded and primed, though he doubted he'd have cause to fire it.

'Servitors,' he said, for the benefit of those back aboard the *Covenant*. 'Technical servitors, outfitted for mining. I count a hundred and seven.'

'Perfection,' drawled a voice over the vox. It was a wet, burbling growl, like a wolf with a throat full of tumours. Septimus's own vox-link allowed him to listen to the demigods speaking. He shivered at the voice of the Exalted.

The squad moved in patient precision around the camp, utterly ignored by the labouring servitors. The bionic slaves paid them no heed at all, mono-tasked as they were to perform their current operations.

'Final count is one hundred and seven,' Septimus's master repeated. 'Most of these could be easily refitted for our use.'

'Who cares?' another voice snarled. Septimus watched as Xarl stopped in his patrol ahead. Skulls, some alien and some human, were mounted on Xarl's war-plate. Several dangled on chains from his belt, forming layered faulds that covered his thighs. 'We did not come here for mindless slaves.'

'Yes,' one of the others growled, most likely Uzas. 'We must not delay here. The Warmaster calls us to Crythe.'

'Septimus,' the master said, turning back to his servant. 'Confirm the asteroid is what we seek.'

Septimus nodded, already scanning a gloved handful of dust and small rocks. His handheld auspex display showed a series of green bars in perfect alignment with a previously imprinted pattern.

'Confirmed, master.'

The bulk lander from the *Maiden* towered above them all. Its armament was pathetic, but with the most irritating timing imaginable, the single laser turret mounted upon its hull opened fire on the demigods below. Inside the grounded ship, Eurydice Mervallion sat at the helm console, directing the turret's aim through a distorted pict-link, scowling at the blurry screen and not hitting a damn thing.

Outside, the squad remained unharmed, taking cover behind six-wheeled ore loader trucks and drilling tractors. They watched the lone turret unleashing its minor rage, the red beams pulsing into the dusty ground, nowhere near any of them.

'Under fire,' Cyrion voxed to the *Covenant*. He sounded amused.

'Barely,' Septimus's master amended.

'I've got this one,' Xarl said, rising out of cover, his bolter in his fist. It shuddered once, the echo of its fire transmitting over the vox but not in the airless atmosphere. On the side of the lander, the single weapon detonated under the kiss of the explosive bolt shell.

'Another glorious victory,' Cyrion chuckled in the silence that fell afterwards. Septimus couldn't help but smile as well.

'Do we truly have time for this idiocy?' Xarl grunted.

'Someone is alive in there,' Septimus's master said quietly. The squad looked up at the cargo lander, its blocky sides and the gaping maw of its landing bay, lit from within by dim yellow light. 'We must face them.'

'This is insignificant prey,' Xarl argued.

Uzas grunted an agreement. 'The Warmaster calls. Battle awaits us in Crythe.'

'Yes,' Xarl voxed back, 'let this weakling prey rot.'

Cyrion spoke up, cutting them off. 'This prey is someone capable of managing a hundred servitors. They almost certainly possess technical skill. Such skill will be of use to us.'

'No,' Septimus's master breathed. 'The prey is much more than that.'

Xarl, draped in skulls, and Uzas, his dark armour sporting a cloak of light brownish leather that had once been the skin of a hive world's royal family, both nodded their reluctant assent.

'A prisoner, then,' Xarl said.

'Night Lords,' came the wet growl of the Exalted, 'move in.'

THEY DIVIDED UP once they were inside. The lander was large enough that even separated it would take them up to fifteen minutes to sweep the entire hulk. Uzas took the storage decks and the cargo hold. Xarl made for the bridge and the crew deck. Cyrion remained outside, watching over the servitors. Septimus and his master moved towards the engineering deck.

Septimus drew his own weapons as he followed the reassuring bulk of his master. Two laspistols, Imperial Guard standard issue, were gripped in his fists.

'Put those away,' his master said without turning around. 'If you shoot her, I will kill you.'

Septimus holstered the pistols. The two figures moved down a row of silent generators, each one twice as tall as a man. Their boots clanked on the metal gantry of the floor. Beyond the threat, which was hardly out of character for any of the demigods, something in his master's answer caught his interest.

'Her?' he asked over a direct vox-link to his master.

'Yes.' His master advanced, his weapons undrawn but his gauntleted hands tensed into claws. 'Even had I not seen her in my vision, I can smell her skin, her hair, her blood. Our prey is female.'

Septimus nodded, shielding his eyes again from the glaring illumination of the strip lighting above. It ran the length of the chamber, just as it had in the previous three chambers.

'It's bright in here,' he said.

'No, it's not. The ship is on low power. You are just used to the *Covenant*. Be ready, Septimus. Do not, under any circumstances, look at her face. The sight will kill you.'

'Master–'

The demigod held up a hand. 'Silence. She is moving.'

Septimus couldn't hear anything, except his master's vox-clicks as he changed channels to address the rest of the squad.

'I have her,' he said, and calmly turned to catch a blur of shrieking movement that launched at him.

EURYDICE HAD BEEN watching from her darkened hiding place between two rumbling generators. She had no weapon except for a crowbar that she'd scrounged from her tools, and although she'd been scowling alone and telling herself she would go down fighting, kicking and screaming, that pledge faded a little when she saw the two figures coming down the gantry. One was a human, armed with two pistols. The other was a giant, well over two metres tall, and wearing archaic battle armour.

Adeptus Astartes.

She'd never seen one before. It was not a pleasant sight. Awe met fear, mixing to form a feeling of dread in the pit of her stomach and a sour taste that doggedly coated her tongue no matter how much she tried to swallow it. Why were they attacking? Why had they killed Syne and destroyed the *Maiden*?

She retreated into the shadows, willing her heart to calm, and gripped her crowbar in sweating fists. Maybe if she aimed for the joint where his helmet met his neck? Throne, this was insane. She was dead, and there was nothing she could do about it. With a mirthless grin, she suddenly regretted all the mean things she'd said to… well, to everyone. Except to Syne. He was always an arse.

For all her faults, her spiteful tongue among them, Eurydice Mervallion was no coward. She was the daughter of a Navigator House, even if their name wasn't worth spit, and had looked into the madness of the warp and guided her ship safely each and every time. The sight of a demigod stalking closer to her made her head ache and her guts tighten, but she kept the promise she'd made to herself. She'd go down fighting.

They drew near, walking down the aisled gantry. Eurydice's forehead itched with fierce sensitivity, and with her free hand, she pulled off the bandana of black silk. The recycled air of the lander's internal atmosphere tingled unpleasantly on her third eye, even closed as it was. As naturally as drawing a breath, she opened the eye slowly, feeling the uncomfortable tingle intensify, on the edge of irritation now. The tickling connection of the eye's milky surface meeting the air forced a shiver through her body. It was a sickening sense of vulnerability. The eye saw nothing, yet it felt the warm, scrubbed air brush over its soft surface with every movement she made.

She was ready. Eurydice clutched the crowbar in both hands again.

The giant passed slowly, and as he did, she leapt at him with a cry.

The crowbar banged against his helm with the dull clang of iron on ceramite. It was a strange sound, half a metallic chime, half a muted and echoless clank. She swung with all her strength coupled with a rage born of desperation. The impact would have staved in the head of a human, and had she chosen her target better, Septimus's skull would have collapsed under the blow, killing him instantly. But she chose the Astartes.

That was an error.

The bar had already struck three times before she realised two things. Firstly, her furious strikes against the giant's helm were barely even causing him to move his head. His skull-faced helmet glared at her with ruby eye lenses, juddering only slightly under each of her flailing strikes.

Secondly, she hadn't landed yet. That was what sent her into a writhing panic. He'd caught her as she jumped, and was holding her off the ground with his hand around her throat.

The realisation hit her when he started to squeeze. The pressure on her throat choked her so suddenly, so completely, that she didn't even have time to squawk a cry of pain. The crowbar landed one last time, deflected from his forearm by the dark armour he wore, before it clattered to the ground with a reverberating clang. She couldn't hear it; all she heard was her own heart thundering in her ears. Eurydice kicked out at him as she dangled, but her boots clacking against his chestplate and thigh armour met with even less success than her crowbar had.

He wasn't dying. Her eye... it wasn't killing him. All her life she'd heard tales that allowing any living being to stare into a Navigator's third eye would result in some arcane, mystic, agonising death. Her tutors had insisted this was so – a by-product of the Navigator gene that granted her this obscene and priceless mutation. No one understood the reason behind it. At least, no one in the ranks of House Mervallion, but then Eurydice knew she'd only ever had access to tutors of relatively poor quality.

She stared at the giant with her third eye wide and open, as her human eyes narrowed in breath-starved pain. Yet the Astartes stood unfazed.

She was right. Had the demigod looked into her sightless eye the colour of infected milk, he would have died instantly. But behind the crimson lenses, his own eyes were closed. He knew what she was. He had foreseen this moment, and a true hunter didn't need every sense to bring down prey.

Her vision started to swim. She couldn't tell if she was really being pulled closer to him, but his skull helm filled her sight, bone-white and blood-eyed. The giant's voice was low, inhumanly low, grinding like distant thunder. As her vision misted and finally blackened, the demigod's words followed her down into unconsciousness.

'My name is Talos,' he growled. 'And you are coming with me.'

SEPTIMUS'S MASTER WAS the last to leave the asteroid. He stood on the surface, his boots leaving eternal prints in the silver-grey dust, and he looked up at the stars. Stars he didn't recognise from the last time he'd stood upon this rock and stared up into the heavens. This asteroid had been a world once – a planet far from here.

'Talos,' Cyrion's voice crackled over the vox. 'The servitors are loaded. The prisoner is ready to be taken to the mortals' decks aboard the *Covenant*. Come, my brother. Your vision was true, there was much to discover here. But the Warmaster calls us to Crythe.'

'What of those who fled?'

'Uzas and Xarl have ended them. Come. Time eludes us.'

Talos knelt, seeing how the dust clung to his black-blue armour in an ashen covering. Like sand sifting through his fingers, he watched a fistful of the dust cascade from his open hand.

'Time changes all things,' Talos whispered.

'Not everything, prophet.' That was Xarl, his voice pitched in respect as he waited in the gunship. 'We fight the same war we've always fought.'

Talos rose to stand once more, making his way to the waiting Thunderhawk. Its engines cycled live, blasting dust away in all directions as it readied for the return flight, where the *Covenant of Blood* waited in orbit.

'This rock came a long way,' Cyrion voxed. 'Ten thousand years of drift.'

Uzas chuckled. It wasn't that the emotional significance was lost on him. It was simply that the situation held no emotional weight in his mind at all. He couldn't have cared less.

'It was good to come home again, hmm?' he said, still smirking inside his helm.

Home. The word left a burning afterimage in Talos's mind – a world of eternal night, where spires of dark metal clawed at the black sky. Home. Nostramo. The VIII Legion's home world.

Talos had been there at the end, of course. They all had. Thousands of the Legion standing on the decks of their strike cruisers and battle-barges, watching the shrouded world below as the end rained down upon it, piercing the caul of cloud cover, tearing holes in the dense blanket of darkness in the atmosphere and revealing a venomous illumination: the orange glow of flame and tectonic ruination blazing across the surface. The skin of the world split, as if the gods themselves were breaking it apart out of spite.

And in a sense, they were.

Ten thousand years before, Talos had watched his world burn, shatter, and crumble. He'd watched Nostramo die. It was sacrifice. It was vindication. It was, he told himself, justice.

Talos's boots thudded on the ramp as he boarded the gunship. Once inside the hangar, he cast a single glance at the herd of lobotomised servitors standing impassive in the deployment bay, and thumped his fist against the door lock pressure pad. The ramp withdrew and the blast doors slammed shut in a grinding chorus of hydraulics.

'Do you think we'll ever see another shard that size?' Cyrion asked as the Thunderhawk shuddered into the air. 'That must have been at least half a continent, all the way down to the outer core.'

Talos said nothing, lost for a moment in the memory of raging fire flickering through breaks in dense cloud cover, before an entire world came to pieces before his eyes.

'Back to the *Covenant*,' he finally said. 'And then to Crythe.'

II

VISION

'Surprise is an insubstantial blade, a sword worthless in war.
It breaks when troops rally. It snaps when commanders hold the line.
But fear never fades.
Fear is a blade that sharpens with use.
So let the enemy know we come. Let their fears defeat them as
everything falls dark.
As the world's sun sets...
As the city is wreathed in its final night...
Let ten thousand howls promise ten thousand claws.
The Night Lords are coming.
And no soul that stands against us shall see another dawn.'

– The war-sage Malcharion
Excerpted from his work, *The Tenebrous Path*

TALOS WALKED THE corridors of the *Covenant*, wearing his battle armour
without the confining presence of his helm. While he lacked the vision-
enhancing modes the helmet's sensors offered, there was a comforting
clarity in piercing the ship's darkness with his natural sight.

The mortal crew struggled to see in the blackness, their eyes too weak
to perceive the trace illumination emitted by the ship's powered-down
lighting. They were permitted lamp packs, allowing them to see in the
dark when they must move from one part of the ship to another. To the
Nostramo-born Astartes, the gloom simply didn't exist. Talos moved
through the wide passageways, nearing the war room, which had long
since become the meditation chambers of the Exalted. A natural attuning, coupled with the genetic manipulations performed on his brain
during his ascension into the ranks of the VIII Legion, meant he saw the
Covenant's interior as clearly as dawn on a far brighter world.

Cyrion, clad in his own war-plate, drew alongside. Talos glanced at his
brother, noting the creases of strain around Cyrion's black eyes. It was
strange to see one of his fellow legionaries show signs of age, but Talos

was under no delusions. Cyrion was struggling under the pressure of his own curse – one that weighed upon his brother far more heavily than Talos's own visions wracked him.

'You're not coming in with me,' Talos said, 'so why are you following?'

'I might come in,' Cyrion replied. Both of them knew how unlikely that was. Cyrion avoided the Exalted at all costs.

'Even if you wanted to, the Atramentar will bar your way.' They walked through the labyrinthine halls of the great ship, accustomed to the silence that framed their presence.

'They might,' conceded Cyrion. 'They might not.'

'I'll let you keep that mistaken belief for another few minutes, Cy. Don't ever say I am not a generous soul.' Talos scratched the back of his shaven head as he spoke. One of his implant ports, a socket of chrome in his spine just above his shoulder blades, had started aching these past few days. It was an irritating, dull pulse at the edge of his attention, and he felt the vibrating hum of the symbiotic coupling there that merged him to his armour. The machine-spirit of his war-plate must be appeased soon, and Septimus would need to be set to work preparing the unguents and oils that Talos used to tend to his inflamed junction sockets. The invasive neural connections from his armour into his body were growing aggravated from the amount of time he spent in battle. Even his inhuman healing and physical regeneration could only cope with so much.

In better days, several Legion serfs and tech-adepts would have tended to his bionic augmentations and monitored his gene-enhancements between battles. Now he was reduced to a single slave, and as talented as Septimus was as an artificer, Talos trusted no one to come near his unarmoured form – not even his own vassal, and especially not his brothers.

'Xarl is looking for you.'

'I know.'

'Uzas, as well. They want to know what you saw while afflicted.'

'I told them. I told you all. I saw Nostramo, a shard of our home world, spinning in the void. I saw the female Navigator. I saw the vessel we destroyed.'

'And yet the Exalted summons you now.' Cyrion shook his head. 'We are not fools, brother. Well... most of us are not. I make no claims for Uzas's state of mind. But we know you are going to meet the Exalted, and we can guess why.'

Talos cast him a sidelong glance. 'If you are planning to spy, you know you are doomed to failure. They won't let you in.'

'Then I will wait for you outside,' Cyrion conceded. 'The Atramentar are always such wonderful conversationalists.' He wouldn't be distracted. 'This summons is about your vision. We're right, aren't we?'

'It's always about them,' Talos said simply. They walked the rest of the way in silence.

The war room was at the heart of the ship – a vast circular chamber with four towering sets of doors leading in from the cardinal directions. The Astartes approached the southern door, taking note of the two immense figures flanking the sealed portal.

Two of the Atramentar, chosen warriors of the Exalted, stood in wordless vigil. Each of the elite Astartes wore one of the Legion's precious remaining suits of Terminator armour, their hulking shoulder guards formed of polished silver and black iron forged into the snarling skulls of sabre-toothed Nostraman lions. Talos recognised the two warriors by their armour's insignia, and nodded as he approached.

One of the Terminators, his war-plate etched with screeds of tiny golden Nostraman runes detailing his many victories, growled down at Talos and Cyrion.

'Brothers,' he said, the words a slow intonation.

'Champion Malek.' Talos nodded up at the warrior. He was head and shoulders above most mortal men himself, well over two metres tall. Malek, in the suit of ancient Terminator plate, was closer to three.

'Prophet,' the voice drawled deep and mechanical from the tusked helm. 'The Exalted summoned *you*.' He punctuated his words with the crackling threat of his gauntlet's claws wreathing themselves in coruscating energy.

'You,' the Atramentar repeated, 'and you alone.'

Cyrion leaned against the wall, magnanimously gesturing for his brother to go ahead without him. His theatrical bow brought a smile to Talos's pale features.

'Enter, prophet,' said the other Atramentar warrior. Talos knew the figure from the heavy bronze hammer it carried over its shoulder. Its Terminator helm, instead of sporting the half-metre tusks Malek favoured, was marred by a vicious bone horn spiking from its forehead.

'My thanks, Brother Garadon.' Talos had long since given up demanding that others stop referring to him as a prophet. Once the Atramentar had followed the Exalted's tendency to use the term, it had spread across the *Covenant* and stuck fast.

With a last look back at Cyrion, he entered the war room. The doors closed behind him, sealing with a click and a hiss.

'So,' Cyrion said to the silent, towering Terminators. 'How are you?'

ONLY TWO SOULS were present in the room: Talos and the Exalted. Two souls facing each other across an oval table that had once seated two hundred warriors. Around the edges of the room, banks of cogitators and vox-stations sat idle and silent. Centuries before, they had been manned by live crew: Legion serfs and a small army of servitors. Now the *Covenant*'s remaining crew strength was focused on the bridge and the other vital sections of the ship.

'Talos,' came the draconic growl from the other side of the table. The darkness was ultimate: so deep it took Talos's vision several moments to tune through the blackness and make out the other figure in the chamber. 'My prophet,' the Exalted continued. Its voice was as low as the purr of the warp engines. 'My eyes into the unseen.'

Talos regarded the vaguely humanoid shape as his sight resolved into an approximation of clarity. The Exalted wore the same relic armour so revered by the Atramentar, but… changed.

Warped. Literally. Occasional flickers of warp lighting rippled across the surface of the armour. The witchlight gave off no illumination of its own.

'Captain Vandred,' Talos said. 'I have come as ordered.'

The Exalted breathed out, long and soft, the amused exhalation ghosting through the air like a distant wind. It was the closest the creature could come to laughing.

'My prophet. When will you cease this use of my ancient name? It is no longer entertaining. No longer quaint. Our forgotten titles mean nothing. You know this as well as I.'

'I find meaning in them.' Talos watched as the Exalted dragged itself closer to the table. A mild tremor shook through the chamber as the creature took a single step.

'Share your gift with me, Talos. Not your misguided reprimand. I control this. I am no pawn of the Ruinous Ones, no avatar of their purpose.'

The chamber shuddered again as the Exalted took another step. 'I. Control. This.'

Talos felt his eyes narrowing at the old refrain. 'As you say, brother-captain.' His words caused another breathy exhalation, at once as gentle and threatening as a blade stroked across bared flesh.

'Speak, Talos. Before I lose what little patience remains to me. I indulged your desire to seek a rock in the void. I allowed you to once again walk the surface of our broken home world.'

'My desire? My *desire*?' Talos pounded a fist onto the surface of the war room's central table, hard enough to spread a cobweb of cracks from where his fist landed. 'In a vision, I saw a fragment of our home world in the lightless black, and I led us there. Even if you don't believe that's an omen, it still brought over a hundred new servitors into the ship's crew, and a *Navigator*. My "*desire*" greatly benefited the Legion, Vandred. And you know it.'

The Exalted drew a breath. As the air was sucked into the commander's altered throat, it sounded like a banshee's wail.

'You will address me with respect, brother.' The words were meaningless; it was the softness of the warning that made Talos's blood run cold.

'I stopped respecting you when you changed into… this.'

'Standards of decorum must be maintained. We are the Eighth Legion.

We are not lost to the madness that grips the others who failed alongside us on the surface of Terra.'

There were a hundred answers to that, each more likely to get him killed than the last. With a swallow, Talos finally said simply 'Yes, sir.' This was no time to argue. In truth, it never was. Words changed nothing. The corruption within the Exalted ran too deep.

'Good,' the creature smiled. 'Now speak of the other truths you saw. Speak of the things that matter. Tell me of the wars,' the Exalted finished, 'and the names of those doomed to die.'

So Talos told him, immersing himself in the flames of those memories once more, and...

...at first, there is nothing. Darkness, blackness. It is almost like home.

The darkness dies in a genesis of fire. White-hot and sun-bright, it sweeps across his senses. He stumbles and falls, kneeling on the red rock of another world. He's lost his holy weapons... his bolter and blade... When his vision clears, they are not in his hands.

A sudden strength invades his system. His armour's senses track the waxing and waning of power and life within his body, flooding him with stimulants to keep him in the battle even when his inhuman physiology would require succour. They rush through his blood now, electrifying muscles and deadening nerves.

As they reach his brain, his vision clears. Coincidence or providence, the warrior doesn't care. Rubble everywhere. And there, shattered and cast aside like a puppet with cut strings, another warrior in the colours of the VIII Legion. Talos moves to him, knowing he must reach the fallen brother before anyone else.

He makes it. Targeting sensors flicker and beep as they lock onto other figures moving through the insane dust-smoke all around, yet he's the first to reach the broken corpse. But no sword... no bolter...

His targeting crosshairs zero in on the fallen warrior's blade, outlining it in a threat display reticule and streaming data about the sword's construction. He blink-clicks the details of metal composites and power capacity away, and grips the blade with both hands. A press of his thumb on the activation rune starts the chainsword roaring.

The others are closing in now. He has to be fast.

The chainblade kisses the dark ceramite armour of the dead Astartes, grinding against the war-plate for several fevered seconds before biting through. Talos carves in a quick sweep, hurling the sword aside once it has performed its function.

One of the others is Uzas. He bounds forward like a beast, ignoring Talos, his hands tearing at the dead warrior's helm. By the time he has pulled it free, Talos has retreated from the scavenging, carrying the severed forearm he earned. Once the meat is removed from the armoured arm, the gauntlet could be reworked and...

* * *

…THE EXALTED BREATHED out once more, its laugh-breath exhalation.
'Who was it?' he asked. 'Who will fall, to be plundered in death?'
'It was… They wore…'

…armour of midnight blue, like everyone in the Legion. But the helm's faceplate is painted red, a leering scarlet skull. Talos…

'…DIDN'T SEE CLEARLY,' he said to the Exalted. 'I think it was Faroven.'
Talos closed his right hand into a fist, listening to the quiet growl of the servos in every knuckle joint. The gauntlet was stiff, and Septimus had said several times it would soon need to be replaced. It was old, that was all. The years had worn it down, and although much of his armour had been replaced over time, his gauntlets were both pieces of his original Mark IV war-plate.
It did not trouble him to think of looting his fallen brethren the way it might trouble a mortal to plunder the dead. The Night Lords Legion had lost much since their failure to take the Throne of Terra, and their capacity to forge new Astartes armour was severely limited.
Looting the dead was a forgivable necessity in the endless war.
Talos opened his hand, slowly articulating his fingers. 'Yes,' he said as he watched the hand move, thinking of the night to come when this gauntlet would be replaced by another. 'It was Faroven.'
The Exalted made a sound Talos had heard many times – a grunt of dismissal, callous and curt.
'When he dies, you are welcome to whatever you take. His demise will be no loss to the Legion. Now continue. An explosion. Rubble and smoke. The plundering of Faroven's wargear. And then?'
Talos closed his eyes. 'And then…'

…he sees his sword. There, lying across a spill of rubble, the gleam of the blade already dulled by a thin layer of dust. He scrambles for it, his boots crunching on the gravel underfoot – rock chunks that were the towering wall of a manufactorum until moments ago.
The blade is in his hands, a masterwork of form and function. The hilt and cross-guard is crafted from bronze and polished ivory, forming the outstretched wings of an angel. Between the wings, set into the base of the blade on both sides, rubies the size of a mortal man's eyes have been cut and shaped into crimson teardrops. The blade itself is forged of adamantite stained gold, with High Gothic runes hand-scribed along the weapon's length detailing a long and illustrious lineage of fallen foes.
Talos had killed none of them, for this blade was never forged to be his. He grips it now, feeling the reassuring weight of the stolen weapon, as comfortable in his hands at this moment as it was a decade before when he'd taken it from the dying grasp of an Imperial champion.

Aurum. *The blade was called Aurum – the power sword of noble Captain Dumah of the Blood Angels. Its kiss was death; like all power weapons, a ravaging energy field tore apart solid matter with every strike. But Aurum was forged when the Imperium was young, when the tech-priests of Mars were as much artisans as keepers of secrets.*

Three times, Legion brothers have tried to kill him for this sword. Three times, Talos has slain his kin to defend this prize.

He rises, activating the power cell within the hilt, burning the dust from the golden blade in a hissing rush. Lightning, tight and controlled, dances across the sword's length, bright enough to hurt his Nostraman eyes.

Talos moves across the rubble. The sounds of battle are returning now. The rubble-dust is clearing. He has to find his bolter before the enemy comes to sweep through the sector they've just annihilated with unbelievable firepower.

He… he can't find it. What is that accursed noise? That thunder? The world is falling apart…

Blood of the Ruinous Ones, where is that weapon…

He…

…STAGGERED UNDER THE wave of memory, as real to him in the war room as it was when the vision first struck. The Exalted grunted its displeasure.

'What is wrong? What happened next?'

'The sun,' Talos said. 'The…

…sun has died.

He raises his head to the sky, all thoughts of seeking his bolter forgotten. A moment before it was high noon, now the sky is dark as dusk. An eclipse. It must be an eclipse.

And it is.

In a way, it is.

Targeting reticules lock on the behemoth that swallowed the sun. Information Talos doesn't see slides in jerky lines across his retinas, beamed into his eyes from his helmet's sensor interface.

Alarms chime in time to the warning runes' flickering, and as he looks up, he recalls why the explosion had levelled this part of the city. He looks up at the explosion's cause.

Warlord-class. His sensors flicker the words over and over, the alarm chimes becoming screams in his ears, as if he doesn't know what he is seeing. As if he needs to be warned that it's death itself. Over forty metres of Mechanicus vengeance has come to destroy them all. It's taller than any buildings that remain standing.

Its gargantuan weapons pan and aim, tracking the ant-like forms of the Astartes below. Its arms – cannons the length of trains – split the sky with the sound of a thousand gears grinding – just aiming, not even firing yet. Lower, they aim. Lower.

The city shakes again, even before the Titan fires, purely because the iron god is moving. The vox fires into life, voices bellowing in anger as the Imperial war machine strides closer.

'Heavy weapons!' *he roars into the vox general channel.* 'Land Raiders and Predators, all guns on the Titan!' *He doesn't even know if there are any of the Legion's vehicles left in one piece, but if they don't form a response of some kind, the Titan will end them all.*

With the sound of habitation towers falling, the Titan takes another step.

And with the sound of a world dying, it fires again.

Talos…

…OPENED HIS EYES, only then realising they'd been closed.

The Exalted had come closer while Talos was in the grip of the vision. 'Titans are no surprise,' the creature said. 'A forge world is the Warmaster's priority target within the Crythe Cluster.'

Talos shook his head, his lip curling slightly as he made out the edges of the Exalted's horned visage in the dark.

'We are going to be slaughtered. We will stand in the path of the Mechanicus's god-machines, and our eyes will burn in the light of their fire.'

'And what of the Warmaster's own forces?' the Exalted pressed, his eagerness lending an edge of impatience to his burbling tone. Talos was reminded of a deep cauldron brought to the boil.

'What of them, sir?'

'My prophet,' the Exalted drawled, with an unfamiliar hint of kindness. Talos tilted his head to regard his leader, suppressing a growl. The Exalted was trying to mask his irritation, most likely, to keep his pet seer from losing his own temper at the questioning. 'Talos, my brother, you see so much, yet so little.'

The Exalted smiled – a portrait of too many fangs and acidic drool. Talos glared into his lord's black eyes, and the twisted face of a man he'd once admired.

'That is my question,' the Exalted leered. 'Where *are* they? Do you see them? Do you see the Black Legion?'

'I can't…

…*see them. Anywhere.*

Above, the metallic gods make war. Titan against Titan in the ruins of a shattered city. The air is a solid storm of cannonfire bursts and thunderous grinding as war machines loose their wrath upon one another. The Titans have forgotten that battle playing out around their feet now, and the Night Lords – those that remain – regroup in their towering shadows.

Talos reaches his transport, the Land Raider's sloped, dark hull like a beacon in the maelstrom around. And that's when he sees Cyrion, still half-buried in rubble, almost a thousand metres away.

It's not a clean sight, nor an instant identification. The distance is significant, and at first Talos just sees a struggling figure emerging from stone wreckage, the minute movement catching his eye purely by chance.

He blink-clicks the visor's zoom symbol. A name rune flashes up on his retinal display – Cyrion – as his targeting systems lock onto his brother as an invalid target.

He breaks into a run.

Another target – Uzas, Invalid Target – flashes up in runic code. Uzas reaches Cyrion first, climbing down the rubble behind the staggering, wounded Astartes. Talos runs harder, faster, somehow knowing what's coming.

Uzas raises his axe and…

'…AND WHAT?'

'And nothing,' Talos replied. 'It's as I've said. The Warmaster will send us against the Titan Legion of Crythe, and we will suffer severe casualties.'

The Exalted let the silence extend for several moments, letting his voiceless displeasure speak for him.

'Am I dismissed, lord?' Talos asked.

'I am far from satisfied with this meagre recollection, my brother.'

Talos's smile was crooked and genuine. 'I will endeavour to please my commander next time. As I understand it, prophecy is not an exact science.'

'Talos,' the Exalted drawled. 'You are not as amusing as you think you are.'

'Cyrion says the same, sir.'

'You are dismissed. We draw near to Crythe, so make final preparations. Ensure your squad is in midnight clad within the hour. We strike at the Crythe Cluster's penal world first, then move on to the forge world.'

'It will be done, sir.' Talos was already leaving when the Exalted cleared his throat. It sounded like he was gargling something that was still alive.

'My dear prophet,' the Exalted grinned. 'How is the prisoner?'

III

THE WARMASTER CALLS

'Nostramo has died, and with it, our past.
The Imperium burns, promising a future of ash.
Horus failed, because his plans grew from seeds of corruption – not
wisdom.
And we failed because we followed him.
We do not do well when leashed to the wills of others,
And when bound by the words of leaders that do not share our blood.
We must choose our wars with more care in the centuries to come.'

– The war-sage Malcharion
Excerpted from his work, *The Tenebrous Path*

EURYDICE AWOKE TO a darkness so deep she feared she'd been blinded.
She sat up, her shaking hands feeling the relative softness of a cot bed
beneath her. The smell around her was a strong mix of copper and
machine oil, and the only sound apart from her breathing was a distant
but ever-present background hum.

She knew that sound. It was a ship's drive. Somewhere, on a distant
deck, this vessel's great engines were propelling it through the warp.

The image of a skullish helm leering at her with crimson eyes drifted
through her returning memory. The Astartes had taken her.

Talos.

Eurydice moved her hands to her throat, feeling the tenderness there,
aching to the touch, hurting to breathe. A moment later, she reached for
her forehead. Cold metal met her questing fingers. A small, thin band of
iron or steel… fastened to her forehead. It covered her third eye. She felt
the tiny rivets where the plate was drilled and fixed to her skull, just the
right size to imprison her genetic gift.

There was the sudden clank of a bulkhead door opening, whining
open on old hinges. A blade of light, muted and yellow, stabbed into
the room. Eurydice drew back from the painful brightness, squinting to
make out the source.

A lamp pack. A lamp pack in someone's hand.

'Rise and shine,' the figure said. He entered the room, still nothing more than a silhouette, and seemed to be adjusting the lamp pack in his hands. For a moment, everything went black again.

'May the Powers take this bastard thing,' the man grumbled. Eurydice wasn't sure what to think. She was tempted to fly at him blindly, lashing out to knock him down and flee. She would have, she was sure of it, if her head would just stop spinning. With the return of vision, even for a moment, came the realisation that she was sickly dizzy, right to her stomach. She doubted she could even stand up.

Light was restored when the man switched the lamp pack to a general glare instead of a focused beam. Still very dim, the cone of light projecting from the pack spread across the ceiling and illuminated the cell-like room with a glow almost reminiscent of candlelight.

Her dizziness peaked as her returning vision swam again. Eurydice threw up the remains of her last meal aboard the *Maiden of the Stars*. Torc had cooked. Catching her breath, she spoke in ragged gasps.

'Throne... that tasted bad enough going in.' The sound of her own voice shocked her. It was as muted and weak as the light from the lamp pack. That Astartes, Talos... he'd half-strangled her. Even the memory made her blood run cold. His eyes, drilling into her own, red and soulless and devoid of humanity.

'Don't say that word,' the man's voice was soft.

She looked up at him now, wiping her mouth on her sleeve and blinking exertion tears from her eyes. He looked about thirty, thirty-five. Scruffy hair hung in ash-blond locks to his shoulders, and silvery yellow stubble showed he'd not shaved for several days. Even in the darkness, with his pupils enlarged to see in the gloom, she saw his irises were the green of royal jade. He'd be attractive if he wasn't a kidnapping son of a bitch.

'What word?' she asked, touching her sore neck.

'*That* word. Do not use Imperial curses or oaths on this ship. It will offend the demigods.'

She didn't recognise his accent, but it sounded strange. He also pronounced every word carefully, taking care to form his sentences.

'And why should I care about that?'

She was proud of the defiance she forced into her voice. *Don't let them know you're scared. Show your teeth, girl.*

The man spoke again, his soft voice a contrast to her scathing demands.

'Because they have little patience at the best of times,' he said. 'If you anger them, they will kill you.'

'My head hurts,' she said, gripping the edge of her cot. Her throat tensed and saliva thickened on her mouth. Throne, she was going to be sick again.

She was. He stepped back a little, avoiding the ground zero site of her messy purging.

'My head is on fire,' she said afterwards, and spat to clear her mouth of the last traces.

'Yes, from the surgery. My masters did not want you killing me when you awoke.'

Again she felt the metal plating covering her forehead, blinding her third eye. The panic she thought she was hiding so well pushed that worry aside in favour of another. Through the murk of her thoughts, she voiced the first of a thousand questions she desperately needed answered.

'Why am I here?'

He smiled at that, a warm and honest smile that Eurydice could have gladly punched off his handsome face. 'What the hell is so funny?' she snapped.

'Nothing.' His smile faded, but remained in his eyes. 'Forgive me. I was told that was the first thing everyone asks when they are brought aboard. It was the first thing I asked, as well.'

'So why is that funny?'

'It isn't. I just realised that with you among us, I am no longer the newest in our masters' service.'

'How long was I out?'

'Eight standard hours.' Septimus had counted the exact minutes, but doubted she'd care about that level of detail.

'And you are?'

'Septimus. I am the servant of Lord Talos. His artificer and vassal.'

He was annoying her now. 'You speak strangely. Slow, like an idiot.'

He nodded, his face set in calm agreement. 'Yes. Forgive me, I am used to speaking Nostraman. I have not spoken much Low Gothic in...' he paused to recall, '...eleven years. And it was never my first language, anyway.'

'What's Nostraman?'

'A dead language. The demigods speak it.'

'The... the Astartes?'

'Yes.'

'They brought me here.'

'I helped bring you aboard, but yes, they did.'

'Why?'

Septimus cleared his throat and sat down, his back to the wall. He looked like he was settling to get comfortable. 'Understand something. There is only one way off this vessel, and that is to die. You are here to be offered a choice. It will be simple: life or death.'

'How is that a choice?'

'Live to serve, or die to escape.'

The truth surfaces, she thought with a bitter smile. She could feel the fragility of her grin, like all her fear was trapped behind clenched teeth. It turned her tongue cold.

Aaron Dembski-Bowden

'I'm not a fool, and I know my mythology. These Astartes are traitors. They betrayed the God-Emperor. You think I'll serve them? Throne, no. Never.'

Septimus winced. 'Be careful with that word.'

'To hell with you. And to hell with serving your masters.'

'Life in their service,' Septimus said in a musing tone, 'is not what you might expect.'

'Just tell me what they want from me,' she demanded, a shake in her voice now. She gritted her teeth again to stop it.

'You are gifted.' Septimus tapped his forehead. 'You see into the immaterium.'

'This can't be happening,' she said, and at last her voice was as soft as his. 'This cannot be happening.'

'My master foresaw your presence on that world,' the slave pressed. 'He knew you would be there, and knew you would be of use to the Legion.'

'What world? It was just an asteroid.'

'Not always. Once, it was part of a world. Their home world. But that's not important now. You can navigate the Sea of Souls, and that is why you are here. The Legion is not what it once was. Their flight from the Emperor's light happened many centuries ago. Their... what is the word? Inf... Infra... Damn it. Their resources are running out. Their relics and machines of war are eroding without maintenance. Their mortal attendants are succumbing to age.'

Eurydice didn't resist the urge to smirk. 'Good. They're traitors to the God-Emperor.' She felt a little of her spirit returning, and risked another smirk. 'Like I care if their guns don't fire.'

'It is not that simple. Their inf... infra–'

'Infrastructure.' Throne, what a simpleton.

'Yes. That's the word. The Legion's infrastructure is shattered. Much knowledge has been lost, and many loyal souls; first in the Great Heresy, and then in the wars since.'

She almost, almost said, '*My heart bleeds*', but settled for a silent smile, hoping her discomfort didn't show through it.

Septimus watched her, sharing the silence for several moments.

'Was your life before coming here really so wondrous,' he said, 'that this opportunity has no value to you?'

Eurydice snorted. That question wasn't even worth answering. Being kidnapped and enslaved by mutants and heretics wasn't a step up from anywhere. She was just surprised they weren't torturing her yet.

'You are not thinking clearly,' Septimus smiled, rising to his feet. She realised with an uncomfortable swallow that he was carrying two holstered pistols at his sides, and a hacking machete the length of her forearm strapped to his lower leg.

'You will witness sights no other mortals ever have the chance to see.'

Does he think that's supposed to be tempting?

'I'd rather not damn my eternal soul just to learn a few secrets.' She hesitated, watching him carefully, the smile in his eyes and the way he lounged comfortably against the wall. His easy grace unnerved her. He was hardly a lunacy-driven heretic, like she'd expected to find in a vessel of the Archenemy.

'Why are you here?' she snapped. 'Why did they send you?'

'You are afraid, and it's making you angry. I can understand that, but it would be better for you if you kept your temper. I must report every word of this to my master.'

She hesitated at that, but wouldn't be cowed. 'Why did they send you?'

'Acclimatisation,' he smiled again. 'Easier on you to speak with another human, than one of the Astartes.'

'How did you come to be here?' she asked. 'Were you kidnapped?'

He shrugged a shoulder, and his jacket whispered with a rustle of smooth material. 'It's a long story.'

'I've got time.'

Without warning, the ship shuddered violently, shaking to the sounds of the hull straining. Septimus braced himself by gripping the wheel-lock of the bulkhead door. Eurydice swore as the back of her head smacked against the wall with bruising force. For a few seconds she saw nothing but dancing colours.

'No,' Septimus said, raising his voice over the shaking of the ship. 'Time is the one thing we don't have.'

Eurydice blinked annoying tears of pain from her eyes, listening to the protesting hull as metal squealed and screamed. She knew this sound, too. The vessel was falling out of warp, breaking into real space.

In a hurry.

'Where are we?' she yelled.

Her answer was a shipwide vox message, crackling with distortion, echoing from thousands of speakers across the myriad decks of the *Covenant*.

'Viris colratha dath sethicara tesh dasovallian. Solruthis veh za jass.'

'And that means *what* exactly?' she shouted at Septimus.

'It... doesn't translate well,' he called back, already working the wheel-lock.

'Throne of God,' she muttered, the words swallowed by the shaking all around her. 'At least try!'

Sons of our father, stand in midnight clad. We bring the night.

'It means,' he looked back over his shoulder, '"Brothers, wear your armour. We are going to war". But as I said, it doesn't translate smoothly.'

'War? Where are we?'

Septimus dragged the door open and moved through the oval portal. 'Crythe. The Warmaster, blessings upon his name, has summoned us to Crythe.'

Septimus stood in the doorway. Waiting.

'Crythe was days away…' she said. 'Weeks, even.'

'My masters know many secrets. They know the warp and the pathways through, in the shadows away from the False Emperor's light. These will be the paths you will also learn to walk.' He paused, as if considering her. 'Are you coming?'

Eurydice watched him for several moments. Was that a joke?

He didn't look like he was joking.

She rose on unsteady legs, hesitantly taking his offered hand. The ship juddered again and she knew that, at least, was not the warp drive catching its breath.

Septimus led her from the room, his lamp pack beaming the way. He noticed the look on her face as the ship rattled and shook.

'It is weapons fire,' he said, reassuringly. 'We are under attack.'

She nodded, but had absolutely no idea why he seemed so calm about it.

'Where are we going?' she asked.

'My master told me of the Legion's attack plan.'

'So?'

'So we are going to be ready in case that plan goes wrong. Do you know what a Thunderhawk is?'

RINGING A WORLD called Solace, the vessels of Battlefleet Crythe were stalwart in their defence, punishing the invaders for daring to assault an Imperial planet. It would be recorded as the largest void engagement ever to occur in the sector, with casualties in the millions.

The *Covenant of Blood* had torn back into realspace in the middle of an orbital war.

THE CRYTHE CLUSTER.

Five worlds, spread across five solar systems, allied in profit and a shared defence. Brought into the Imperium of Man during the Great Crusade ten thousand years before, it was an empire within the Imperium – a lesser reflection of fair Ultramar in the galactic east.

Hercas and Nashramar: two hive worlds with productive, stable, sprawling populations forming the core of the star cluster. These were supplied in turn by Palas, an agri world with a climate so ideal and harvest potential so rich it exported enough resources to feed the entire cluster.

The fourth world was Crythe Prime itself, named for the Imperial commander responsible for bringing the region into compliance with the Emperor's will after the decadent years of Old Night. Once, it had been a populous hive-world – the third of the trinity: Crythe Prime, Hercas and Nashramar. Several thousand years ago, its mineral deposits were exhausted by the ceaseless efforts of the Mechanicus and the planetary economy collapsed. Refugee transports left the world in increasing numbers over a number of decades, and rather than leave the barren world alone, a recolonisation was undertaken by the Adeptus Mechanicus itself.

The Crythe Prime of late M41 was an industrious forge world, equipping the sizeable and well-trained Crythe Highborn regiments of the Imperial Guard, and serving as the manufactorum home world of the Titan Legion, the Legio Maledictis.

The fifth and final world was Solace. Here, based around an orbital shipyard fortress, was the heart of Imperial strength.

The planet below the star fort was a third populated world, though unlike Crythe Prime, Solace had always been devoid of mineral worth and natural resources. The world was a barren rock, empty but for the hive-like prison complexes rising from its surface, home to hundreds of thousands of criminals drawn from across neighbouring sectors and the hives of the Crythe Cluster. A penal world, guarded by the might of the Imperium, used as a base for Imperial Navy and Astartes counter-piracy efforts in the star cluster. Only Crythe Prime, in the augmetic grip of the Mechanicus, was a stronger target.

Lord Admiral Valiance Arventaur commanded the unbreakable might of Battlefleet Crythe. Countless escorts, dozens of cruisers, all led by the jewel in the battlefleet's crown: the colossal Avenger-class grand cruiser, *Sword of the God-Emperor,* a city of cathedrals running down the ship's spine, home to thousands of souls.

Had this been the entirety of the Throne's might in the sector, still it would have stood as a defiant and implacable foe, but the lord admiral could also count on the support of a garrison of the noble Astartes Chapter, the Marines Errant, who were permanently on deployment to crush the piracy rife within the sector. Their vessel, the Gladius-class frigate *Severance,* was a lethal blade used against the heretics that dared prey upon the trade routes of the Emperor's loyal subjects.

It was to Solace that the Warmaster first brought his wrath. Break the defences of this fiercely guarded world, tear the strength from the Holy Fleet, annihilate the Astartes presence here… and the Crythe Cluster would surely fall. So went the great Despoiler's plan.

The Exalted's plan fit neatly within this framework. To succeed before the Warmaster's eyes, he would call upon his calculating, tactical genius.

TALOS VIEWED THE interior of the pod through the ruby hue of his helm's eye lenses. His squad didn't even take up half of the twelve thrones within the confines of the pod. They needed to recruit soon. The losses incurred the past few decades had hurt the remnants of the VIII Legion's Tenth Company to the point where – at best – the Exalted could raise no more than fifty Astartes.

The process to engineer new warriors was painstaking and slow, and the Legion's forces aboard the *Covenant of Blood* were severely lacking in fleshsmiths and technicians capable of gene-forging children into Astartes over the course of a decade.

Xarl always commented on the empty thrones. Every time the squad came together in a drop pod, a Thunderhawk, a boarding pod, their Land Raider... anywhere they stood ready in the moments before an engagement, he would bring it up.

'Four of us,' he grunted, right on schedule. 'This is bad comedy.'

'I'm just aggravated it was Uzas that survived on Venrygar,' Cyrion said back over the vox. 'I miss Sar Zell. You hear me, Uzas? It's a shame you made it instead of him.'

'Cyrion, my beloved brother,' Uzas growled in reply, 'watch your mouth.'

For a moment, Talos was back in his vision, seeing Uzas's axe rise as he approached from the rubble behind Cyrion...

'Sixty seconds,' a mechanical voice blared over the pod's speakers. It jolted Talos back to the present with a sickening lurch of perception.

'I'd like to state,' Cyrion said, 'that this is the most foolish use of our forces I can recall.'

'Noted,' Talos said softly. It wasn't his idea to use a pod deployment, but complaining about it now wasn't going to change a thing. 'Stay focused.'

'Furthermore,' Cyrion ignored his brother's reprimanding tone, 'this will see us all dead. I guarantee it.'

'Be silent.' Talos turned in his throne, making his restraint harnesses pull tight over his bulky war-plate as he faced his squadmate. 'Enough, Cyrion. The Exalted gave us our orders. Now sound off.'

'Uzas, aye.'

'Xarl, ready.'

'Cyrion, aye.'

'Acknowledged,' Talos finished. 'In midnight clad, on my mark. Three, two, one. Mark.'

All four back-mounted power generators clicked live, feeding artificial strength through their suits of armour, boosting their physical levels far beyond even the inhuman power already within their gene-engineered bodies. Talos's visor display powered up, filtering his crimson vision with scrolling white status text, ammunition counters and dozens of stylised icon runes scattered at the edges of his sight. He blink-clicked three specifically, frowning as one of them kept flickering in and out of focus.

'Uzas,' he said, 'your identification rune is still unstable. You said you'd get that fixed.'

'My artificer... suddenly died.'

Talos clenched his jaw. Uzas had always been murderous with his slaves, be they Legion serfs or augmented servitors. He treated them like worthless playthings, toying with them to sate his own private amusements, and the only reason his armour was even sustainable was because he plundered his fallen brothers with a diligence few other Night Lords adhered to.

'We do not have the resources for you to entertain your bloodlust with the murder of slaves, brother.'

'Maybe I can borrow Septimus to repair my armour.'

'Yes, maybe,' Talos said. Not a chance, he thought.

'Forty-five seconds,' the launch servitor's voice crackled.

'Stow weapons for transit,' Talos ordered.

He checked his bolter one last time, turning it over in his fists. A beautiful weapon, and one that had served him well since before the Great Betrayal. He'd fired the weapon on Isstvan V, and scythed down countless numbers of the Salamanders Legion as part of that fateful battle. Just holding the boltgun in his gauntlets was enough to give him a thrill of pleasure, as real and tactile as a flooding rush of combat stimulants from his armour's drug infusion ports in his spine and wrists.

It was called *Anathema*. The name, in flowing Nostraman script, was embossed along the side in black iron. Talos held the weapon lengthways against his right thigh, as if holstering a pistol. He blinked at a small icon on the edge of his display, and the thick electromagnetic strip along the firearm's edge went live. With a clank of metal on metal, the bolter clamped to his leg, waiting to be drawn in battle once the release icon was confirmed with another blink.

With his bolter secured, he checked the sheathed blade – too long to be tied to his hip while he was seated – secured to the pod's sloping wall by strips of magnetic coupling. The angel wings of the crosspiece hilt were the white of fine marble. The ruby teardrop between the wings glittered in the red gloom, darker than its surroundings, a drop of blood on blood.

Aurum and *Anathema*, the tools of his trade, his relics of war. His lip curled as his heart started to beat faster.

'Death to the False Emperor,' he breathed the words like a whispered curse.

'What was that?' voxed Xarl.

'Nothing,' Talos replied. 'Confirm weapon check.'

'Weapons stowed.'

'It is done.'

'Weapons, aye.'

'Thirty seconds,' the voice issued forth again. The Dreadclaw-class pod began to shake as its thrusters cycled up to full power. Although it would be fired from its socket, the pod's attitude thrusters still needed to be burning hot to guide them on target.

'Tenth Company, First Claw,' Talos spoke into the general vox-channel. 'Primed for deployment.'

'Acknowledged, First Claw.' The voice that replied was low, too low for even an Astartes. The Exalted was on the bridge, speaking to the squads preparing for battle. Talos listened to the other squads sounding off as the pod started to shake with increasing violence.

'Second Claw, ready.'

'Fifth Claw, ready.'

'Sixth Claw, aye.'

'Seventh Claw, primed.'

'Ninth Claw, prepared.'

'Tenth Claw, ready.'

None of those squads were complete, Talos knew. The centuries had been unkind. All of Third Claw had been slaughtered at the Battle of Demetrian, by the accursed Blood Angels. Fourth and Eighth Claws had both died piece by piece, battle by battle, until the last surviving members were absorbed into other under-strength Claws. Uzas had been Fourth Claw once. Talos hadn't been thrilled by that particular inheritance.

'This is Talos of First Claw. Give me a soul count.'

'Second Claw, seven souls.'

'Fifth Claw, five souls.'

'Sixth Claw, five souls.'

'Seventh Claw, eight souls.'

'Ninth Claw, four souls.

'Tenth Claw, six souls.'

Talos shook his head again. Including his own squad, it racked up to thirty-nine Astartes. A skeleton crew would remain with the Exalted aboard the *Covenant*, but it was still a grim figure. Thirty-nine of the Legion were ready for deployment. Thirty-nine out of over one hundred.

'Soul count confirmed,' he said, knowing every Astartes on the vessel was patched into this vox-channel. He doubted the significance of the figure was lost on any of them.

'Ten seconds,' the servitor intoned. The pod was shuddering in its cradle now alongside the six others, like a row of jagged teeth pushing from a giant's gums.

'Five seconds.'

The vox was filled with a frenzy – dozens of roaring Astartes, calling out for vengeance, for blood, for fear, and the memory of their primarch. Inside First Claw's pod, Xarl howled long and loud, a sound of unrestrained glee. Cyrion whispered something Talos couldn't quite make out, most likely a benediction to the machine-spirits of his weapons. Uzas cried out a string of oaths, promising bloodshed in the name of the Ruinous Powers. He invoked them by name, crying out like a fanatic in ecstatic worship. Talos bit back the urge to rise from his restraint throne and shoot his brother dead.

'Three.'

'Two.'

'One.'

'Launch.'

IV
VOID WAR

'It has been said by tacticians throughout the ages of mankind that no plan survives contact with the enemy. I do not waste my time countering the plans of my foes, brother. I never care what the enemy intends to do, for they will never be allowed to do it. Stir within their hearts the gift of truest terror, and all their plans are ruined in the desperate struggle merely to survive.'

– The Primarch Konrad Curze,
Allegedly speaking to his brother, Sanguinius of the Blood Angels

THE EXALTED SAW void warfare as infinitely more graceful than any surface attack.

He excelled in personal combat and had reaped a bountiful harvest of life with his own claws, but it wasn't the same. Such savagery lacked the clarity and purity of a void hunt.

Even in the years before he became the Exalted, when he had simply been Captain Vandred of the Night Lords Tenth Company, he had taken his greatest battle-pleasures from those moments of orbital and deep space warfare where everything played out to perfection.

And he was no simple observer in those moments. He prided himself on making the perfect battles come to pass, and it was a pleasure he'd taken with him through all his changes. It was a matter of attuning one's perceptions to the realities of scale and dimension involved within a void war. Most minds, mortal and Astartes alike, could not truly fathom the distances between ships, the sheer size of warring vessels, the scars left by each and every type of weapon against hulls of different metals…

This was his gift. The Exalted *knew* void war, seeing its grandeur within his swollen mind the way other men saw the weapons in their hands. His vessel was his body, even without the primitive tech-links engineered by the Mechanicum to merge man and machine. The Exalted bonded with the *Covenant* by familiarity and his modified perceptions. Merely by standing on the bridge, he felt the ship's heartbeat in his bones. Simply gripping a handrail allowed him to hear its screaming voice as it fired its weapons. Others would feel nothing more than vibrations, but others were blind to such nuances.

The *Covenant of Blood* had a fine history of pulling through engagements against long odds and taking part in some of the most savage conflicts to involve the VIII Legion. Its reputation – and, by extension, the reputation of the warband that had once been the Tenth Company – was assured through a record of space battles won, largely thanks to the void warfare skills of the Exalted.

As his precious, prided vessel broke into realspace, the creature that had once been Captain Vandred stared at the eye-shaped occulus screen that dominated the forward wall of the strategium deck. His own eyes were unchanged by the mutations that had twisted his physical form, remaining the pure black of the Nostramo-born, and these obsidian orbs glittered with reflected light from the dozens of crew consoles and the detonations lighting up the occulus before him.

By necessity, the strategium endured a greater level of illumination than the rest of the ship, so the mortal crew could perform their duties with ease. The Exalted spared a sweeping glance around the multi-layered chamber now, ensuring all was in readiness.

It seemed so.

Servitors slaved to their stations jabbered and droned and worked consoles with a mix of bionic and human hands. Mortal crew, including several former Imperial Navy officers in service to the Legion, worked at stations of their own or supervised teams of servitors. Few consoles or strategium positions stood empty. Operations here were far too critical to suffer under a lack of manpower. It was almost the way it should be, the way it had been before the Great Betrayal, before the slow decline of the Legion's strength had begun, and the Exalted revelled in this echo of a greater age.

He took all of this in within the space of a single thump of his heart, before returning his attention to the occulus once more.

And there it was. War in its grandest form. A theatre of destruction where hundreds, even thousands of lives were lost with the passing of each second. He allowed himself several moments to drink in the sight, to relish the sight of the life-ending explosions, no matter which side sustained the casualties.

The feeling threatened to edge into euphoria, and the Exalted clawed his focus back. He had not earned his title by weakness and self-indulgence. Duty came first.

The Exalted likened void war to the feeding frenzy of sharks. Few memories of his pre-Astartes life ever bubbled to the surface of his warped memory, but one in particular returned to him each time he brought his passions to bear in spaceborne battle. As a child, on several coastal journeys with his father, he had witnessed the eyeless barrasal sharks that would group together to hunt the great whales of the open ocean. They would form a pack, yet without any real bonds, for they rarely aligned their movements or worked together – they simply did not kill each other as they hunted the same prey. When each shark would strike at an exposed killing point on the great whale, it was instinct, not cooperation, that drove them. Instinct for the quickest kill.

Void warfare seemed much the same to the Exalted now. Each ship was a shark swimming in the three-dimensional battlefield of space, and only the most talented fleet commanders could harness their instincts and bring their forces together into an efficient hunting pack. The Astartes creature smiled, baring black gums and fanged teeth as he watched the occulus. He was no fleet commander. His own talents had never been in bringing about such a pack unity.

In fact, quite the opposite. He had no desire to inspire tactical union within the fleets he sailed with. All he cared about was the dissolution of order within the enemy's armada.

The easiest way to win a void battle was to ensure no enemy commander achieved tactical unity for his own forces. If their overall cohesion was compromised, each vessel could be isolated from any potential support and torn apart, alone, piece by piece.

It was an approach the Night Haunter had honoured the Exalted for on no small number of occasions. As the primarch himself had said, it was worthless to know an enemy's plans. The foe should be defeated before his plans even come into play.

THE WARMASTER'S CRYTHE invasion fleet had translated into the system several days before – that much was obvious to the Exalted as soon as the Night Lords strike cruiser tore from the warp. Dozens of broken hulks of vessels, their shattered metal skins declaring allegiances to either side in the conflict, hung powerless in the void, destroyed in the opening phases of the war.

The Exalted ordered its helmsmen to guide the ship through this silent graveyard, engines burning to reach the main battle, where the Warmaster's fleet had at last forced the Throne's forces into an orbital defence.

The creature's eyes drank in the sight of ancient names on the flickering hololithic display. Great vessels that had waged war for thousands of years, their names and titles etched into the flooding tides of the Exalted's memory despite the turning of time.

There, the *Ironmonger*, which served the Legion of Primarch Perturabo. There, the *Heart of Terra*, still with the scars it earned when it laid siege to the world it was named for. And ringed by dozens of smaller vessels, in the heart of the storm, the *Vengeful Spirit*.

The Exalted gestured with its claw.

'Make for the Warmaster's flagship as you transmit our identity codes, then break formation and engage ahead of the fleet.'

The *Covenant of Blood* streaked into the maelstrom of the orbital battle, and the Exalted pictured the command decks of Imperial vessels as another mighty ship joined the Archenemy host. Console alarms would sound, orders would be shouted… It was delightful to envisage, even if just for a moment.

But the *Covenant* was vulnerable. It burned its engines white-hot as it powered past the *Vengeful Spirit*, past the Chaos vanguard.

This had to be done fast.

Even a cursory glance at the occulus revealed to the Exalted that the battle result was inevitable. The Imperial fleet was doomed. He watched the icons on the wide holographic display table before his oversized command throne, seeing their slow dance through three dimensions. In a matter of moments, he saw the outcomes of each icon's motion, calculating the many ways every vessel might move in relation to the others. A game of many – but ultimately finite – possibilities, unfolding before his eyes.

Again, he looked to the occulus. The forces of the False Emperor were still numerous enough to inflict severe harm upon the Warmaster's attacking fleet, and that was what counted. Victory at too high a price was no victory at all.

As he grinned, his eyes leaked tears of oily blood. The dark tears ran cold down a face as pale as porcelain, showing every vein beneath in thick, black cables. Muscles in his face strained and his tear ducts tingled. The Exalted was not used to smiling. It had been too long since entertainment of this calibre had been forthcoming, and better yet, the Warmaster was watching.

It was time to make the most of it.

Two Imperial ships stood out from the pack. Two targets that had to be destroyed in order to dissolve the hopes of tactical unity. The Exalted had marked both of them, and relayed his desires to the strategium crew. They worked now to make his intentions a reality.

The *Covenant of Blood* raged through the battle, taking incidental damage on its void shields from the few fighters and light cruisers that had reacted fast enough to its sudden arrival. A speeding shrike of blue-black and bronze, it speared between two ships of similar size to itself, ignoring the barrage from their broadsides.

By the time they had come about to give chase to the diving blade of a ship that had evaded them, they were already engaged by other vessels. These new attackers bore the black and gold of the Black Legion, the Warmaster's own Astartes.

The *Covenant of Blood* didn't even slow down. The Night Lords hunted larger prey.

An Astartes strike cruiser was a powerful ship, excelling in actions of surface bombardment and blockade-running. In void warfare it was a dread enemy, for while it lacked the offensive capability of a battle-barge or heavy cruiser of the Imperial Navy, because of its armaments and dense shielding, it would make short work of most vessels of a similar size. Had the Exalted joined the orbital battle above Solace by lending the fury of the *Covenant*'s lances and weapons batteries, the Night Lords would have made a significant and useful contribution, worthy of praise.

That, however, was not enough.

The greatest threat from an Astartes strike cruiser was its cargo. While the *Covenant* had weapons capable of levelling cities and shields that could take punishment for hours on end without flickering, its deadliest and most feared weapons were already leashed into their deployment pods and awaiting the moment of launch.

The Night Lords cruiser was a huge and weighty ship, yet graceful despite its bulk. It rolled, shark-like, slow and smooth, as it dived towards the much larger Gothic-class ship, the *Resolute*. The Imperial cruiser was a monument as much as a warship: a small city of cathedral-like structures jutted from its central spine, and its aggressive beauty was an inspiration to the small fleet of support ships that streamed around it, orbiting like satellites in its presence.

The occulus aboard the *Covenant* was blinded by the release from the *Resolute*'s lances. The larger ship was still target-locked on the Warmaster's attacking vessels – it had had no time to bring its furious weapons array to bear on the new arrival yet – although the support ships in its shadow began to power up to destroy the racing Night Lords cruiser plunging into their midst.

The Exalted watched as one of the icons situated behind the *Covenant*'s symbol winked out of existence. The *Unblinking Eye* was no more, coming to pieces under the final assault of the *Resolute*. A Black Legion ship: one of the Warmaster's own.

Strange, thought the Exalted, to have endured for millennia, just to die here. The *Unblinking Eye* had been at the Siege of Terra ten thousand years before. Now it was debris and an ignoble memory of failure.

Then it was the *Covenant*'s turn. The strategium shuddered again, and not gently.

But the shields were holding, the Exalted knew. He felt the ship's skin as keenly as he felt his own. Three ships firing abeam, and… something more.

'Shields holding,' a mortal officer called to the command throne. 'Weapons fire from three light cruisers and incidental fire from a fighter wing.'

Fighters, it chuckled. How quaint.

The Exalted instantly assimilated this information into his overall vision of the icon formation ballet unfolding before his eyes. The *Resolute* had been his first target because its shields were already down. He'd known from the moment the battle hololithic display had flickered into life that, from its place in the formation, the Gothic-class cruiser had fallen back from the fighting to restore its void shields. The minor fleet spinning around it like parasites only confirmed his deduction. It was one of the larger ships in the Imperial fleet, swarmed by protectors as it sought to restore its defences. It was clearly key to the defence.

The Exalted snarled harsh manoeuvre orders, and the *Covenant* strained to obey. It began below the *Resolute*, and with engines howling, it climbed hard. Shields still holding, rippling as they reflected incoming fire, the strike cruiser sliced almost vertically up past the *Resolute*'s starboard side. The Night Lords ship presented almost no target to the masses of broadsides, though they fired anyway. It was a curious move by the standards of traditional void warfare. Running abeam of the ship would have allowed for a more standard exchange of heavy broadside batteries as the ships coasted alongside each other, but lancing vertically seemed to achieve nothing at all. Although the *Resolute*'s broadside volley went tearing off into space, completely wasted, the *Covenant*'s weapons batteries would have also done almost nothing – if they had actually fired. The guns of the Night Lords vessel remained silent.

Aboard the *Covenant of Blood*, all of the human strategium crew were still crying out or throwing up in the aftermath of the insane gravitational forces from the manoeuvre. Several had passed out. The Exalted wiped bloody tears of joy from his cheeks.

That had been divine.

'Confirm,' it said simply to the servitor at the pod launch console.

'Seventh, Ninth and Tenth Claws deployed,' the half-machine slave murmured in response.

'Contact?' it demanded.

'Confirmed,' came the toneless reply. 'Boarding pods confirm successful contact.'

A moment later, a familiar voice crackled over the strategium vox-speakers.

'Exalted,' it said in the deep resonance of the Astartes. 'This is Adhemar of Seventh Claw. We are in.'

All this smiling made the creature weep more aching tears. They had just run a gauntlet of Imperial vessels through the heart of the enemy fleet, and by the time the officers of the *Resolute* realised what had happened, three squads of Astartes would be butchering their way to the command decks.

Truly, that had been divine. The *Resolute* and the fleet leadership on board were as good as dead. Once the other Imperial crews heard of the slaughter aboard their key vessels, fear would spread like a merciless cancer.

One down, one to go.

'Helm,' it said as the strategium shivered under another barrage. 'Make for the *Sword*. All power to the engines.'

'Lord,' an officer close to the throne cleared his throat. 'The enemy flagship's shields are still raised.'

Not for long. 'Approach vector: insidious predation.'

'Aye, lord.'

The Exalted licked its lips with a black tongue. 'Fire all forward lances and torpedoes at hull section 63 as we move across her bow. Time the firing of the bombardment cannon to coincide with the exact moment our lances and torpedoes strike.'

That was no easy feat. A dozen servitors and mortal officers hunched over their consoles, working their controls and calculations.

'It will be done, lord,' assured the nearby officer.

The Exalted couldn't recall his name. Either that, or it had never learned the human's name, it wasn't sure. The creature knew the man as its bridge attendant, and that was all it needed to know. 'But–' the man hesitated.

'Speak, human.'

'My lord, Exalted of the Dark Gods… This attack vector will bring us within the *Sword*'s firing solution for fifteen seconds.'

'Thirteen,' the Exalted corrected with a death's head grin. 'And that is why as soon as we fire our prow weapons, the ship will execute a Coronus Dive, full burn on the engines with port thrusters overloaded by seventy per cent. We will roll while holding maximum sustainable negative yaw and pitch for ten seconds.'

The officer went paler, if such was even possible for a man who hadn't felt sunlight on his skin in decades.

'Lord… we're too large a vessel for–'

'Silence. You will coordinate this attack run with main armament weapons fire from the vessels *Ironmonger*, *Vengeful Spirit*, and the *Blade of Flame*. Align with their strategiums and inform them of our intent.'

'As you say, lord.' The officer swallowed. His eyes, the Exalted noted, were a particularly rich brown. They did not flicker here and there in his nervousness, as did most mortals' in the presence of the Exalted, but he was still reluctant to speak his mind in the presence of his liege. The reasons for this were fairly obvious, of course. Arguing with the Astartes always, always ended in blood and pain.

The ship moaned a long, agonised heave as it passed through the forward fire arc of another sizeable cruiser. Again, the Night Lords ship declined to defend itself, letting its shields take the impacts while it stormed to its chosen target.

'Speak, human,' the Exalted repeated. 'Entertain me with your thoughts in these moments before our victory.'

'A Coronus Dive, lord. The g-forces alone are likely to kill us, and the attitude thrusters will be offline for weeks with the burnout. The risks–'

'Are acceptable.' The Exalted nodded to the officer. 'The Warmaster is watching, mortal. And so am I. Bring my wishes into being, or you will be replaced by one more capable of doing so.'

The officer should have known better. When he turned back to his station and whispered under his breath 'This will destroy the damn ship...' he should have known the Exalted would hear.

'Bridge attendant,' the Astartes smirked.

The man didn't turn around. He was too busy working his console, sending binary orders to the minds of the strategium servitors to prepare for the madness to come. 'Yes, lord?'

'If this is not flawlessly done, I will feed you your own eyes, and you will die tonight, skinless and howling for mercy that will never come.'

The bridge fell quiet, and the Exalted grinned wetly.

'I do not care about overhauling the attitude thrusters, nor the slaves that will die in the repairs. A Coronus Dive, as close as this vessel can come to such a manoeuvre, timed with weapons fire from the three named ships.

'*Do it now.*'

IT WAS BEYOND audacious.

The *Ironmonger*, *Vengeful Spirit* and the *Blade of Flame* pulled into position, supporting the Night Lords' manoeuvre by firing their weapons in a coordinated burst, though from a significant distance. The Exalted suspected their own captains aligned with his plan out of amused curiosity rather than the belief it would actually work, but then, their lack of courage was their cross to bear.

Almost every fleet captain on both sides stared – at least for a moment – at the *Covenant of Blood*, the only vessel of the Warmaster's fleet to run the gauntlet of enemy lines, as it sliced past the massive Avenger-class grand cruiser *Sword of the God-Emperor*. Many captains also recognised, to their disbelief, that the ship was in the initial movements of a wrenching, spinning, maddened Coronus Dive.

It began its attack run in the face of incredible firepower. Ghosting through the great ship's fire arc, the *Covenant* suffered the rage of the *Sword*'s forward lances and weapons batteries which were already spitting torrents of fury against the enemy ahead. The Night Lords vessel endured the assault of supreme weapons fire that had been destined to hit other Chaos ships, and its shields first cracked, then shattered, within a matter of moments.

To all observers, it seemed the *Covenant of Blood* was sacrificing itself in a ramming run. And it would succeed, too. That much weight, inertia and explosive capability would burn out the *Sword*'s shields and gut the ship to its core.

But the *Covenant* didn't ram its prey.

It returned fire just as its shields died, unleashing a blistering barrage of lances, solid shells and plasma fire from its prow weapons batteries, as well as a precisely timed single magma bomb warhead, principally designed for surface attack, from its bombardment cannon.

This payload struck the *Sword* just as massed fire from the three other Traitor Astartes vessels coordinated their prow weapons on the same target. It was as close to the shark-like unity of the black sea sharks as the Exalted could have imagined, but that was hardly foremost in the Night Lord commander's mind.

All of this unleashed punishment was enough, barely, to achieve the Exalted's desires. The colossal *Sword of the God-Emperor*, pride of Battlefleet Crythe, flagship of Lord Admiral Valiance Arventaur, no longer shimmered behind an invincible screen of rippling energy.

Its shields were down, overloaded by the sudden savage assault of the Astartes strike cruiser.

The Exalted was not a fool. He knew void war, and he knew the capabilities of his foes, the strength of their weapons, and the power of their vessels. He knew the *Sword of the God-Emperor* was bristling with failsafes and auxiliary generatoriums, and his attack had inflicted no real damage to the enemy flagship beyond temporarily overloading its shields by giving them too much to absorb at once. They would be back online within moments – a minute at the very most – multi-layered and strong once more.

The *Covenant of Blood* veered sharper than a cruiser of its size had any right to do, throwing itself into a potentially terminal rolling dive alongside and past the grand cruiser it had almost rammed. Alarms hammered the senses of all her crew across the ship. The bladed spear of a vessel roared down into its dive, taking secondary fire from the *Sword*'s broadsides as it plunged past. It didn't return fire. A single volley from the mighty Imperial flagship pounded the *Covenant*'s port weapons batteries into nothingness.

Still twisting as it slid past, the *Covenant* trailed a path of shed debris. Halfway through its plunge, the Exalted felt that one perfect moment of connection with the battle.

Here.

Now.

Even as his ship was being torn apart by Imperial guns, he felt the moment with unbroken clarity, and growled a single word.

'Launch.'

'THREE,' THE SERVITOR'S voice had said.

'Two.'

'One.'

'Launch.'

Talos felt his world lurch from under him, every muscle locking tense. It wasn't a feeling of falling, exactly, nor one of dizziness. His altered senses were resistant to matters of unbalance and unreliable perception. Where a human would have been painting the pod's interior with vomit and passing out from the pressure of launch, the Astartes on board merely suffered mild sensations of discomfort in the pits of their stomachs. Such was the blessing of biologically reconfigured perceptions.

'Impact in five seconds,' the pod's automated voice chimed from everywhere and nowhere at once. Talos heard Uzas wheezing into the vox, gleefully counting down the seconds.

Talos counted silently, bracing when a single second remained. The pod's guidance thrusters kicked into life with a jolt almost as bad as the impact that came a moment later. The pod smashed into its target with hull-breaching force, echoing within the pod itself like a dragon's roar.

A rune flickered on his retinal display in twisting Nostraman script, and in the shuddering aftermath of impact, Talos hammered a fist onto his throne's release pad. The restraints unlocked and disengaged, and the four Astartes of First Claw moved from their seats without hesitation, weapons clutched in dark fists.

The pod's hatch opened with a grind of tortured metal and a hiss of escaping air pressure. Talos spoke into the vox, his voice smooth and assured as he looked out into a steel-decked arching corridor: his first view of the interior of the *Sword of the God-Emperor*.

'*Covenant*, this is First Claw. We are in.'

V

SWORD OF THE GOD-EMPEROR

'Poison will breach any armour.
When faced with an invincible foe, simply bless his bloodstream
with venom.
His own racing heart will carry the poison faster throughout his body.
Fear is a venom just as potent.
Remember that. Fear is a poison to break any foe.'

– The war-sage Malcharion
Excerpted from his work, *The Tenebrous Path*

LIEUTENANT CERLIN VITH listened in on the vox-net, from his position on
the bridge.

Orders had come from the highest authority: repel the boarding party
currently rampaging through the operations decks below the bridge.
Cerlin knew there were other boarding parties moving elsewhere across
the ship, but they would be handled by other squads of armsmen. Vith
had his orders, and he intended to see them through. His men guarded
the bridge, and he had a host of reinforcements on the way.

He wasn't worried. The *Sword of the God-Emperor*, his home for the past
twenty years, was as grand a ship as any in His Majesty's Holy Fleet. Over
25,000 crew called the warship home, even though a sizeable chunk of
those were slave labourers and servitor wretches working their lives away
in the sweathouse enginarium decks. You didn't board a vessel this big.

At least, Vith amended, not if you intended to survive.

It was true enough that the *Sword* wasn't in front-line service, anymore.
Equally true, the glorious ship had been sidelined from the major battle-
fleets, but she still stood as the invincible jewel in the crown of Battlefleet
Crythe. It was a sign of the times, that was all. The Avenger-class was a
brawler, a close-range battler, designed to rage into a maelstrom of enemy
ships and give out a beating twice as bad as any it took. It had the firepower to do it, but fell out of favour with admirals over time, when such
blunt tactics were frowned upon by an increasingly defensive Imperium.

This is what Cerlin told himself. This is what he believed, because the officers said it so many times.

Cerlin's beloved *Sword* wasn't out of the running forever. She was just out of fashion. He'd told himself this time and time again, because although he was just a soldier in service to the Golden Throne, he took great pride to be serving where he was. Above all, Lieutenant Cerlin Vith ached for front-line service once more. He burned to gaze out of a port-hole and see the blackish bruise of distorted warp space that made up the Great Eye – the nexus of the Archenemy's influence.

So he wasn't worried now. The *Sword of the God-Emperor* was unbreakable, undefeatable. The shaking of the ship was the endless vibration of its own guns unleashing hell upon the accursed Archenemy. When the shields had fallen a short while ago, they'd been raised again within a single minute. And even if they fell again, the hull wreathing them all in protective, loyal armour was as strong as a righteous man's faith.

Nothing, but nothing, would ever kill the *Sword*.

He repeated these words within his mind, not a trace of desperation in his silent voice. The fact they'd been boarded was… Well, it was madness. What sane enemy would ever attempt such a thing? He literally couldn't conceive of the tactics at play. What fool of a commander wasted the lives of his men by hurling a handful of them into a ship that boasted over twenty thousand souls ready to defend it?

It was time to teach the first boarding party the error of their ways.

Apparently their vessel had pulled some nice stunts to get them here, if the vox-talk from the strategium was anything to go by.

Well, whatever the truth, they'd managed to come aboard a ship that hadn't seen invaders in over a dozen years, so maybe the admiral – blessings upon his name – was right. Maybe this *was* serious.

But Cerlin had a reputation for dealing with serious business. That was why more often than not, he was the one that saw duty defending the command decks.

Vith led the decorated platoon known as Helios Nine, with a record of distinction and superior marksmanship that wouldn't have shamed an Imperial Guard sniper. He handpicked the men and women of Helios Nine, turning down promotion twice in the last ten years because he didn't want to be raised above the station he felt best suited him. Commanding a dozen armsmen squads would mean he had a lot of mediocrity in with his finest soldiers. Commanding Helios Nine meant he commanded nothing but the best of the best.

Helios Nine even dressed like they meant business. On the occasions they were tasked to descend into the depths of the *Sword*'s belly and bring some order to the criminals and scum labouring beneath the civilised decks, their sleek, dark carapace armour with its flaring sun symbol on the chestplate was a sign for every slave and serf to look busy and keep to the rules. Helios Nine – the 'Sunbursts' and the 'Niners' to the con-scripted slave colonies in the ship's bowels – were well-known for their ruthless demeanour. A famous predilection for a merciless eagerness formed the core of their reputation, brought about from many instances of executing slaves that dared hint at disobedience or dereliction of duty.

Helios Nine numbered fifty men and women, spread across the command decks, squad by squad. Forty-nine of Vith's favourite killers standing ready for the enemy, and Vith himself with the lead squad, backing the admiral's throne.

Every member of Helios Nine packed a shotcannon for maximum short-range damage without risking the ship's hull. He didn't need to look around to know his men were ready. They were born ready and had trained to be readier every day since. Nothing would take them down.

Lieutenant Cerlin Vith believed this without a doubt until the first reports came in over the vox.

'...bolters...' one of the crackled cries had said.

He'd swallowed, then. *Bolters.*

That wasn't good.

More reports crackled in his ears, flooding in now from armsmen squads elsewhere on the ship. The transmissions were broken and patchy, distorted by the running battles as well as the war raging outside the ship. But he was hearing more words he didn't like, more words he didn't want to hear.

'...require heavier weapons to...'

'...falling back...'

'...Throne of the Emperor! We're...'

As he stood in the centre of the low-ceilinged chamber of the main bridge, Cerlin tapped the micro-bead vox pearl in his ear, adjusting the needle mic to the edge of his lips.

'This is Vith. Enginarium teams?'

'Affirmative, lieutenant,' the response from the squads defending the ship's plasma drives crackled in his ear. The teams guarding the engi-narium chambers were, if memory served, the Lesser Gods, the Death Jesters, the Lucky Fifty and the Deadeyes. Vith had no idea which officer he was talking to – the vox wasn't clear enough – but they were all solid, dependable squads. Not Helios Nine standards, by any means, but good enough in a scrap. The reception was punctuated by violent shrieks of distortion that prodded at Cerlin's hangover with cruel fingers.

'I'm getting vox chatter about bolters and all kinds of death breaking loose,' he said.

'Affirmative, lieut...' the voice repeated. 'Be advised that boarders are...'

'Are what? That the boarders are what?'

'...st...'

'Command team? Enginarium defence command team, this is Vith, repeat.'

'...th... es...'

Wonderful. Just wonderful.

It was easy to immerse himself in his own world, removed from the larger battle. The bridge was a chaotic hive of activity: naval officers shouting and moving from console to console as they devoted their attention to the war raging outside the ship. Servitors chattered and droned as they obeyed the orders called at them. Almost a hundred crew, human and lobotomised slave alike, working to keep the *Sword* unleashing its full lethal potential against the enemies of the Golden Throne.

With a moment's effort, Vith blanked it all out. His world was restricted to snippets of incoming vox chatter, and the immediate area around Lord Admiral Arventaur's throne. Raised on a platform to look down upon the bridge below, the throne accommodated the admiral's slender, jacketed form with apparent comfort despite the arching backrest made from the curving ribs of some strange xenos creature. Admiral Valiance Arventaur reclined in his bone throne, his temples thick with cables and wiring that bound him to the chair, and in turn, to the ship's systems.

Vith knew the admiral – eyes closed and seemingly lost in meditation – was allowing his consciousness to swim within the ship's machine-spirit. He knew the admiral felt the hull like his own skin, and the racing efforts of the crew within the steel halls like the blood that beat through his own body.

And again, Vith cared little for it. Keeping the old man alive was all that mattered. The admiral had a war to fight, and it looked like Vith did, too.

The thunder of the ship taking hits was still audible, but the hull itself was stable for the moment. Several of the armsmen shared glances.

'Sir,' one of the ones closest to the front of the column said to Cerlin. 'I know that sound. I served on the *Decimus,* and we did several boarding actions with the Astartes. The Marines Errant Chapter, sir.'

Cerlin didn't turn. His gaze remained fixed on the sealed and locked double doors in the starboard side of the chamber. The thunder was coming from there, and he knew the sound, too. It had taken a moment to recognise, because he'd never expected to hear it on board his own ship.

There was no mistaking the distinctive boom of bolt weapons.

They'd been boarded by Astartes. Traitor Astartes.

Finally, confirmation of the enemy was coming from all angles. Naval ratings relayed to each other that the enemy ship diving past them was a confirmed Astartes vessel, excommunicated for heresy, registering as the *Covenant of Blood.*

This was really information that would have been more use to Vith before he'd been comfortable on the command deck with only fifty men.

'Helios Nine,' he voxed to the soldiers scattered across the outer ring of the chamber. 'Enemy nearing the starboard doors. Show no mercy.'

He spared a glance at the lord admiral, seeing the old man sweating, teeth clenched, eyes closed as if in the grip of some strenuous nightmare.

The starboard doors exploding inwards stole his attention right back to where it should have been.

WHEN THEY HAD first come aboard, Talos had disembarked from the twisted wreckage of the hull where the pod had impacted, *Aurum* in one hand, *Anathema* gripped in the other. Despite ten minutes of infrequent fighting since then, he'd barely fired his bolter once. The same with Cyrion or Xarl. The squad was conserving its ammunition for when it really counted – once they reached the bridge.

Their pod had struck the enemy ship in the densely-populated upper gunnery decks, and the resulting slaughter was a time-consuming annoyance that had grated on all their nerves.

Except Uzas. Uzas had loved every moment of ploughing through the terrified crew as they put up what defences they could with tools and personal sidearms. The bark of his bolter was like a hammering in Talos's head, unwelcome and aggravating.

At one point Talos had slammed his brother against the arching wall of one passageway. Under fire from a retreating rabble of gunners ahead, he had thudded Uzas's helm against the metal wall and snarled through his speaker grille.

'You are wasting ammunition. Control yourself.'

Uzas writhed out of his brother's grip. 'Prey.'

'They are *unworthy* prey. Use your blades. Focus.'

'Prey. They are all prey.'

Talos's fist cannoned into the other Night Lord's face, denting his helm's faceplate. It slammed his head back into the wall a second time, louder than gunfire. From the cluster of mortal crew at the end of the passageway, a solid round clanged from Talos's shoulder guard. He ignored it, blinking to clear his visor display of the flashing warning runes.

'Control yourself, or I will end you here and now.'

'Yes,' Uzas had finally said. 'Yes. Control.' He reached for his fallen bolter. Talos could see the reluctance in his brother's movements as Uzas clamped the weapon to his thigh plate and drew a chainsword.

His restraint had not lasted long. As the squad came to another chamber that housed one of the grand cruiser's weapon turrets, he'd opened fire on the servitors that hadn't received orders to flee when the human crew had run moments before.

Talos led on, no longer caring if Uzas fell behind. Let him gorge on his need to instil terror. Let him waste his efforts on mindless servitors, just for the hope of seeing a flicker of fear in their eyes before the end.

They moved with speed, slaughtering the ill-equipped crew that were foolish enough to stand before them. Most lacked the courage to remain, or had the good sense to flee, but not all of the mortals ran.

Sergeant Undine of the armsmen squad Final Warning stood his ground, as did a total of seven of his men, their shotcannons firing a barrage down a narrow corridor at the advancing Astartes.

Talos's slanted eye lenses flickered with dull threat warnings, and his helmet's sensor muted the sound of their ammunition striking his war-plate to the sound of hailstones clattering to the ground. Undine's courageous last stand, and that of the valiant members of Final Warning, ended several seconds later when Talos waded through them, swinging *Aurum* with several annoyed curses. These delays were getting on his nerves, and while shotcannons offered little threat to his armour's integrity, this kind of massed fire might strike a vulnerable joint or socket, and slow him further.

And not all those who failed to flee offered any real resistance. Dozens of mortals stood in paralysed awe, locked in terror, as giants from mankind's nightmares strode past them. They stood open-mouthed, muttering nonsensical benedictions and pointless prayers at the sight of Traitor Astartes in the flesh.

Talos, Cyrion and Xarl ignored these. As they moved on, the sound of a chainblade told them that Uzas was apparently not content to let the fear-struck wretches live.

Finally, Talos thought as he rounded yet another corner.

'The bridge is beyond these doors,' Xarl said, nodding at the sealed portal ahead. At the end of the wide thoroughfare corridor, the double doors stood closed and grim. Uzas pounded a fist against them, just once, resulting in nothing more than a small dent and the clang of ceramite against adamantium – a rock meeting an anvil.

'Prey,' Uzas said. The others heard his voice thick with saliva. He was drooling into his helm. 'Prey.'

'Be silent, freak,' said Xarl. The others ignored Uzas as he started to claw at the locked bulkhead like a caged animal needing release.

'These won't blow,' Cyrion said. 'Much too thick.'

'Chainblades, then.' Xarl was already revving his up.

'Too slow.' Talos shook his head and hefted *Aurum*. 'This has already taken too long,' he said as he advanced with his stolen power sword.

HELIOS NINE WAS ready when the Night Lords hit them.

Under Vith's orders, they'd taken up positions around the bridge chamber. The sheer number of adjacent passages offered a wealth of cover and corners to shoot around. The bridge crew were too rapt in the orbital war. They had their duties to attend to, and although nervous glances were cast at the starboard door, every officer present needed his attention on the void battle, which kept them hunched over consoles and staring up at the wide vista offered by the occulus screen.

No one, least of all Helios Nine, had expected the reinforced doors to give way so easily. Over a metre thick, metal layered upon metal, the doors had stood unbroken since the ship's construction almost two thousand years ago.

Vith cursed as the explosion sounded. The Traitor Astartes had cut their way deep into the doors in order to lay explosives at the point where conventional detonators could actually sunder the command deck bulkheads.

Throne of the Emperor, where were his reinforcements?

'Helios Nine!' he shouted over the vox, without any idea if they could even hear him over the echoing thunder. 'Repel boarders!'

Unseen by Vith and any of the armsmen, the old admiral's eyes opened. Bloodshot, intensely blue, and narrowed in rage.

THE EXPLOSION, AND the clutch of blind grenades that followed, was the signifying event that pulled the mighty *Sword of the God-Emperor* out of the close-pitched void war.

In many of the records that would come to be written on the Crythe War, the Avenger-class grand cruiser remained a powerful force in the Imperium's defence until its eventual destruction. Admittedly, the storming of its bridge was the blow that crippled the ship, leaving it robbed of some of its former effectiveness, but it continued to fight with all honour.

History can be a humorous thing indeed, when written by the losers.

Curiously absent from Imperial records documenting the battle was that the *Sword* spent its final half hour of life in relative indignity, robbed of its glorious fury and its expected honourable last stand. Instead it unleashed its reduced rage, directionless and limping, while it was systematically torn apart by the Warmaster's cruisers – among them, the *Covenant of Blood*, which was not shy about opening fire on a vessel even while its own Astartes were on board. A swift and decisive victory demanded no less, and Astartes engaged in boarding actions were trained to withdraw immediately upon completing their objectives.

The blind grenades thrown by First Claw rattled as they skidded across the mosaic-inlaid floor of the bridge chamber, detonating within a half-second of each other. A thick burst of black smoke spread from each grenade, and while the smoke screens belched out by each device were nowhere near enough to blacken even half of the vast bridge, that was never the intention with which they'd been deployed. The four grenades clanged across the deck towards the forward gunnery station and exploded there, blinding the dozen officers and servitors at the prow weapons consoles.

As the Naval ratings staggered back from the blinding cloud of smoke, the servitors remained where they were – slaved to their stations and emitting monotone warning complaints at the low level electromagnetic radiation in the cloud that stole their sight.

At that moment, the forward guns of the great *Sword* fell silent.

On another vessel, the Exalted grinned, knowing First Claw had reached the enemy bridge.

Several of the *Sword*'s bridge crew cried out blessings to the immortal Master of Mankind. Among them, only the most pious and the most desperate actually believed the God-Emperor would save them.

Helios Nine, blessed with a paradise of cover in the form of angled work stations and railings, raised their weapons as one, drawing beads on the savaged starboard door.

A figure emerged, blacker than the shadows from which it stalked. Vith took in the sight – a towering killer, too large in all ways to be considered human, clad in bulky ceramite plate forged in a forgotten era. He drank in the details within the space of a single heartbeat: in one hand was a blade of gold, as long as Vith was tall, sparking with lethal power and still dripping molten metal from the door it had sliced through. In the other fist, an oversized bolter with a wide muzzle, open like the maw of some great beast.

Its helmed visage was painted with a skull's staring face, bone-white over midnight blue, with glaring red eye lenses lit up from within. A scroll, tattered and burn-marked by small-arms fire, was draped across its left shoulder, the surface of the creamy paper covered in runes alien to Vith's eyes. On the other shoulder a clutch of short chains hung from the ceramite, bronzed skulls hanging from the dark iron links like morbid fruit, rattling as the figure moved.

Vith's tearing eyes took in one detail above all others. The ruined Imperial eagle across the figure's chestpiece, carved from ivory and since marred by blade strikes to scar the symbol in a simple but effective act of desecration.

The armsman leader had no comprehension that the Night Lord had taken the chestpiece from a fallen Astartes of the Ultramarines Chapter a few years before. He had no idea that ten thousand years ago when this warrior had first worn his own war-plate, only the favoured III Legion, the Emperor's Children, had been granted the honour of wearing the aquila upon their armour. He had no idea Talos wore it now, even defiled, with a comfortable sense of irony.

What Vith did know, and all that mattered, was that a Traitor Astartes had come into their midst, and that unless he ran – maybe even if he did run – he was a dead man.

Vith was many things. An average officer, perhaps. A little too fond of his drink, certainly. But he was no coward. He would die with the words so many Imperial soldiers had died with on their lips across the millennia.

'For the Emperor!'

As noble as the sentiment was, his cry was utterly swallowed by what the Night Lord did next.

* * *

TALOS'S RETINAS WERE bombarded with chiming runes flickering across his visor. Target upon target upon target, detailing white flashes where weapons were visible. A single step into the chamber, he didn't raise his weapons, nor did he seek cover. As soon as he emerged from the broken doorway, he threw his head back, blanking his visor of all the threat runes, and he *screamed*.

It was a roar no unaugmented human could ever make: as resonant and primal as a feral world reptilian carnosaur. The roar, already inhumanly loud, was amplified by the vox speakers in Talos's helm to deafening levels. Powered as it was by his three lungs, the cry stretched out for almost fifteen seconds at full strength, echoing through the corridors of the *Sword* in a flood of sound. The crewmen plugged into their consoles felt it physically, sending tremors through the vessel's steel bones. Across the ship, tech-priests and servitors linked to the ship's systems felt the machine-spirit soul of the *Sword* shiver in response to the unearthly roar.

On the bridge, Lord Admiral Valiance Arventaur, at one with the *Sword*'s machine-spirit in a way infinitely more intimate than any other, began to cry blood.

All of this went unnoticed by the armsmen surrounding their commander. They, like every other human in the sweeping circular chamber, were on their knees, hands clutching at their bleeding ears. Several would have killed themselves to escape the sense-shattering sound, had they been able to reach for their guns, which lay discarded where they fell.

Talos lowered his head, seeing the threat runes blink back into existence. The smoke cloud was thinner now, but drifting to cover much of the command deck. Everyone, every single mortal on the bridge, was prone. The *Sword* idled in space, most of its guns fallen silent. Talos imagined the Warmaster's fleet converging on the ship now, the eyes of every captain glinting with murderous intent.

Time was short. The Claws deployed on the *Sword of the God-Emperor* had a handful of minutes to achieve their mission objectives and get back to their pods before they were killed in the coming destruction.

In that moment, something happened that Talos would never forget to his dying day. From fifty metres away, through a break in the smoke and past the staggering forms of deafened crew, he met the admiral's eyes. They bled thick red tears, the same trickles that ran from his nose and ears, but his expression was unmistakable. Never, in the countless years Talos had made war against the servants of the False Emperor, had one of the Imperial wretches glared at him with such hatred.

He treasured the moment for the single, blood-warming instant it lasted, then whispered a single word.

'Preysight.'

At the soft command, his suit's machine-spirit complied, masking the red-tinged view of his eye lenses in a deep, contoured series of blues.

Through the smoke, even through the cover of consoles and work stations, the bridge crew were revealed to him in a maelstrom of blurry
orange, red and yellow smears of heat sources against the cold blueness
around.

Cyrion, Xarl and Uzas stepped up behind him, and he heard their
whispered commands as they activated their own hunting vision.

With thermal sight active, they stalked forward, blades and bolters
coming up to spill the blood of the *Sword*'s best and brightest as the
mortals scrambled to recover their weapons.

THE ADMIRAL WAS the last to die.

By that point, the bridge was a charnel house. Through the dissipating smoke that finally succumbed to the emergency air scrubbers, all
one could see were the ruined bodies of a hundred crew and their slain
defenders, Helios Nine. The four Night Lords moved here and there, taking chainswords to consoles and ripping the nerve centre of the failing
Sword of the God-Emperor to pieces.

The names of the slain were meaningless to Talos, and he had no idea
that the last to fall by the admiral's throne, shotcannon pounding out its
ignorable bark, had been Cerlin Vith.

Vith wheezed out the last of his life through his ruptured lungs, unable to lift his chin from his chest. He had been irrelevant to Talos, an
irritating thermal blur, and the Night Lord had dispatched him with a
simple thrust of his golden blade. As Vith fell, Talos kicked him from the
throne's podium, his attention already elsewhere as Vith's head cracked
on a railing and the mortal descended slowly into death.

Lord Admiral Valiance Arventaur stared up at the creature who would
be his murderer. The blood-coloured eyes of Talos's helm stared down
at the old man merged to his chair. Now, it made sense why the admiral
had not raised himself up in the bridge's defence. The mortal did not
exist – in the flesh – below the waist. His uniformed torso was directly
bound to his command throne by snaking cables sutured against his
pelvis, linking him bodily to the ship as surely as the tendril-wires in
the back of his head tied his consciousness to the *Sword*'s machine-spirit.

Talos wasted perhaps a second wondering when the admiral had sub-
mitted to this invasive, restrictive surgery, and how long he had been
confined here – a living piece of the vessel he commanded – bound to
his throne as a half-human mess of flesh, wire, cables and fluid exchange
tubing.

He wasted that second and then, gripped by curiosity, he wasted
another by asking 'Why would you do this to yourself, mortal?'

He never got an answer. The admiral's unshaven chin trembled as he
tried to speak. 'God-Emperor,' the old man whispered. Talos ignited his
power blade again, shaking his head.

'I saw your Emperor. A handful of times, back in the age before he betrayed us all.'

The sword slid into the admiral's chest with sickening gentleness, inch by slow inch, charring the dusty white Battlefleet Crythe uniform as the powered blade burned the material where it touched. The blade's tip sank into the bone of the command throne behind the mortal's back, forming yet another bond between the admiral and his station.

The effects were immediate. The bridge lighting flickered, and the ship itself groaned and rolled, tormented, like an injured whale in the black seas of Nostramo. The admiral's death flooded the ship's machine-spirit, and Talos withdrew the blade in a harsh pull. Blood hissed on the golden blade, dissolving against the heat.

'And,' the Night Lord said to the dying man, 'he was no god. Perhaps not a man,' the Astartes smiled, 'but never a god.'

The admiral tried to speak once more, his hands trembling as they reached out to Talos. The Night Lord gripped the dying shipmaster's frail hands and left them folded over the blade wound in his chest.

'Never a god,' Talos repeated gently. 'Know that truth, as you die.'

With the admiral's last breath, the lights on the bridge failed forever.

THE CREW OF the *Sword of the God-Emperor* might have regained control of their ship, except for two factors in the Night Lords' attack.

First and foremost, the teams of crew and armsmen that reached the bridge found the helm and every control console in the room ruined beyond use, displaying the jagged wounds left by the chainblades of First Claw. Using low-light visors to see in the darkness, these would-be saviours also found the admiral dead in his throne of bone, his face set in a twisted expression that lay somewhere in the ugliness between pain, hatred and fear.

The command decks might have been savaged beyond fast repair, but the under-officers aboard the *Sword* had only to ensure the grand cruiser could move from the battle, and its armour could easily sustain it until it could thrust clear of the orbital war. Efforts were redoubled in tech crews and officers racing to the enginarium decks, which was where the second factor came into play.

Talos and First Claw had not been alone.

The second impediment to regaining any semblance of control over the ship was that the secondary enginarium sector was in the hands of the enemy. While this section of the ship was nowhere near as vital to overall function as the main engine decks, it was a significant disruption to power flow and drive efficiency. The Night Lords hadn't hit the primary sections and allowed themselves to be drawn into protracted firefights. They'd hit all they needed to hit; enough to take the *Sword* out of the fight with a minimum of delay and effort.

Teams of armsmen stormed the massive engine chambers seeking to oust the invaders, but Second and Sixth Claws had left their pods with their bolters barking, and held their ground until the order to leave. When that order finally came, the defiant Imperials retook the subsidiary enginarium chambers, only to find a farewell gift left by the Night Lords, who had fastened explosives to the same hull section that their pods had breached in the first place. When the detonators counted down to zero, the explosives took out a vast section of the already compromised hull wall, leaving a sizeable portion of the secondary enginarium decks open to the void.

This killed any hope of crew transit to and from the primary enginarium decks alongside the starboard edge of the grand cruiser, and left the secondary engines silent and dead. Directionless, with neither a brain nor a beating heart now that the bridge and enginarium were disabled, the *Sword of the God-Emperor* rolled in space, naked without its shields, taking a million scars from the weapons of the Warmaster's fleet.

In the space of half an hour, a handful of Astartes had killed several hundred Imperial souls, kept the two key areas of the vessel disrupted and only loosely in loyal control, and made their escape after ensuring no significant repairs could be made in time.

Aboard the *Covenant of Blood*, the Exalted – already anticipating the praise he would receive from the Warmaster – ordered the helm to run close to the suffering *Sword* and be ready to receive boarding pods back into the starboard landing bays.

His personal screens mounted in the arms of his command throne spilled digital data in a ceaseless stream of green runes on a black setting.

Second Claw had disengaged and awaited retrieval.

Sixth Claw, the same.

Fifth Claw… no contact. No contact since launch. The Exalted suspected the pod had been destroyed almost as soon as it left the *Covenant*, hammered into nothingness by the pulverising fire from the grand cruiser's broadsides. A shame, certainly. Five souls lost.

But First Claw… Their pod was still attached. The last to be fired from the *Covenant,* their pod hadn't impacted as close to their target objectives as the others.

'Talos,' the Exalted drawled.

'THIS ISN'T HAPPENING.' Cyrion had to smash his chainsword against the wall to free it of the spasming, screaming armsman he'd impaled. 'We're not going to make it in time.'

First Claw was embattled in the myriad corridors between the bridge and the gunnery deck where their boarding pod had struck the hull. Around them, the great ship shuddered violently, already breaking into pieces. The Night Lords had no idea how much of the *Sword* was still intact, but from the screams trailing across the hacked enemy vox, there wasn't going to be anything left worth speaking of within the next few minutes.

They'd met a flood of Imperial crew coming their way, which at first had been a surprise and had quickly become an annoyance. As they'd butchered the mortals running at them in the low-ceilinged corridor, Xarl had joked that it was amusing to see humans running towards them for a change.

'Makes the hunt all the easier,' he smiled.

'You say that,' Cyrion replied, 'but you have to wonder what they're running from if *we're* a more pleasant option.'

Xarl reached for a running female officer, grabbing her by the throat to drag her into a headbutt that caved in the front of her skull and snapped her spine. He hurled the body into the oncoming horde, knocking several people from their feet to be trampled by the advancing Astartes. Her blood was smeared across Xarl's helm, starkly dark against the skull-white of his painted faceplate.

'I see your point, brother,' he said to Cyrion.

As Talos listened to the scraps of enemy vox that reached his ears, *Aurum* rose and fell with mechanical precision, almost without any attention at all. A picture built up in his mind – a picture of the ship ahead and the horrendous damage it was taking as the Warmaster's fleet picked it apart like a flock of vultures worrying a fresh corpse.

'It seems,' he spoke calmly, 'the gunnery decks between here and our pod are taking the brunt of fire from our fleet.' His bolter roared once, but the range was too short. The high-calibre shell pounded right through a running Imperial's chest and out his back, to explode against the wall beyond.

Cyrion chuckled as he saw.

'What do we do?' Uzas, more coherent now, asked as he laid about left and right with his combat blades. 'Can we cross the suffering sections?'

'Gravity is out, and they are ablaze,' Talos replied. 'No, we need to get back to the bridge. Close to it, at least. Even getting to the pod will take too long. The ship is in pieces already, and the crew are swarming like ants in a kicked hive.'

'Then we kill our way there!'

'Be silent, brother,' Talos told Uzas. 'The sheer number of lives we need to end is the main reason this will take too long. The gunnery deck must be in pieces by now. These mortals are coming from there.'

'How do you know?'

'Uniforms, Xarl,' Talos replied.

Xarl, always one to need the proof of his own eyes, grabbed another human attempting to flee past. The man's uniform looked like every other – white and generic. What was Talos talking about? He lifted the struggling man off the ground by his greasy hair, holding the officer's yelling face close to his bloodstained faceplate. Through the vox speakers in his helm's snarling mouth grille, Xarl's voice came out at insane volume.

'*Tell me where you are stationed. Is it the gunnery de–*'

The officer – quite deaf now – hurriedly drew a pistol in shaking hands and fired it point-blank into Xarl's face. The small slug pinged against the ceramite, knocking Xarl's head back a little before ricocheting with a wet crack back into the man's own forehead. Xarl took one look at the deep red groove in the man's skull and dropped the corpse, swearing in Nostraman. He could hear that bastard Cyrion laughing over the vox.

'Fine,' he said, ignoring Cyrion's laughter. 'Why the bridge?'

'Because it has several decks beneath it that won't explode if a lance strike hits them,' Talos said. 'And because I'm going to do something we may regret.'

With those words spoken, he blink-clicked the spiralling rune on his retinal display that represented the *Covenant*.

THE EXALTED LISTENED to its prophet's voice more than the actual words he spoke. Talos sounded calm, but there was a hard edge of irritation in the Astartes's tone. They were cut off from their pod, and it would evidently take too long to fight through the panicked crew.

It nodded its horned head as it relayed the orders to a servitor manning one of the lance gunnery stations.

'You. Servitor.'

'Yes, lord.'

'Lock a single lance on the three decks beneath the main bridge of the enemy flagship. Cut at the angles I am transmitting now.' It tapped a blackened claw on a number pad mounted on the arm rest of its throne. 'Break off fire after exactly one-point-five seconds.'

Yes, that should be enough. Penetrate the hull. Cut deep, excise the metal meat, without doing too much damage. Tear a chunk of hull away, and expose the command decks to the void. It might just work, too.

It would be a shame to lose the prophet if this failed.

'Lord,' spoke one of the mortal officers. The Exalted noted with only faint interest that the man still wore his old Imperial Navy uniform, from over a decade ago.

'Speak.'

'Servitors in Bay Five report a Thunderhawk is readying to launch. It requests clearance.'

The Exalted nodded again. It had been expecting that. 'Let it go.'

'Servitors also report, Exalted one, that the crew is not Astartes.'

'I said to give them clearance,' the Exalted burbled, low and wet, saliva stringing between its fangs.

'A-as you say, lord.'

The Exalted turned to the gunnery servitor it had addressed before.

'Ready, lord,' the servitor murmured.

'Fire.'

THE SHIP SHUDDERED again, more violently than ever before.

'That was close,' said Xarl. His suit's stabilisers kicked in, but he'd almost had to grip the arching wall of the passageway for support. First Claw had withdrawn to the command decks, no longer seeking to carve their way through fleeing human crew elsewhere. Here, in the darkness of the halls webbing beneath the bridge chambers, the Night Lords sheathed their blades and locked their bolters to thigh guards with magnetic seals. The ship's lighting here was dead, a legacy of the lord admiral's murder and the wounding of the *Sword*'s machine-spirit, and four pairs of crimson eye lenses glared out into the blackness, seeing everything in crystal clarity.

Distantly, as the ship's tremor subsided to a background shudder again, Talos's helm auditory sensors picked up a faint sound wave: a series of metallic clangs, faded with distance.

'You hear that?' Xarl asked.

'Bulkheads closing,' Cyrion acknowledged.

'Move faster,' Talos ordered, and the squad broke into a run, their heavy boots thundering on the steel decking. 'Move much faster.'

Dimly, in his right ear, he heard a familiar voice.

'Master?'

The Night Lords sprinted through the blackness, rounding several corners and smashing aside the few crew that lingered, hiding and panicking, in the darkened hallways.

'The squad,' Talos breathed into his vox mic, 'is using frequency Cobalt six-three.'

'Cobalt six-three, acknowledged, master.'

'Confirm our location runes.'

'Locator runes sighted on my augury screens. Lord Uzas's rune is flickering and weak. And... Lord, the ship is breaking apart, with eighty per cent damage to the–'

'Not *now*. Has the *Covenant* fired?'

'Yes, master.'

'I thought so. We seek the closest deck to the voided sections of the command levels.'

The silence stretched for five seconds. Six. Seven. Ten. Talos could imagine his servant scanning the hololithic display of the degrading grand cruiser, watching the locator runes of First Claw as they navigated the tunnels.

Twenty seconds.

Thirty.

Finally... 'Master.'

The shuddering was so violent that both Cyrion and Uzas were thrown from their feet. Talos staggered and left a dent in the hull where his helm crashed into the metal. The ship was coming apart now. No question.

'Master, stop. The left wall. Breach it.'

Talos didn't hesitate. The wall – which looked no different from any other in their headlong flight through the dark passageways of the command decks – exploded under the anger of four bolters.

Beyond the wall, just for a moment, was fire.

Beyond the fire was nothing but the infinite night of space, sucking the four warriors into the void with a greedy breath.

PAIN FLOODED HIM.

Talos looked down... up... at the planet below... above. A dreary rust-red rock decorated by thin wisps of cloud cover. He wondered what the air would taste like.

Stars spun past his field of vision, and he stared without truly seeing.

Then, a slowly-turning cathedral, a palace of stained glass and a hundred spires, on the back of the burning *Sword*. He saw none of this, either.

Blackness took him for a moment, which blessedly dulled the pain. When it passed, he tasted blood in his mouth, and was blinded by the bright warning runes flashing across his vision. He tried to vox Cyrion, Xarl, Septimus... but couldn't recall how to do it.

Pain, like light from a rising sun, bloomed in his skull again. Voices spoke in his ears.

'Armour: void sealed,' one of the runes said. Talos tried to move, but wasn't sure he could. There was no resistance to his movements, no traction to anything he did, to the point he wasn't sure he was moving at all.

His vision turned once more, revealing pinprick stars and shards of metal spinning slowly nearby. It was difficult to see clearly, and that worried him more than anything else. One of his eye lenses was darker than it should be, blurry and black-red with dim, watery runes. Blood, he realised. There was blood in his helm, coating one of his eye lenses.

One of the voices resolved into something approaching clarity. It was Xarl, and Xarl was swearing. Xarl was evidently swearing about blood.

Talos's vision turned, and then he saw Xarl suspended by nothing, drifting in the blackness, his brother's skulls on chains floating around his armour like a dozen moons orbiting him. He felt thunder, a powerful tremor, as Xarl's reaching hand slammed into his chest.

'Got him,' Xarl grunted. 'Hurry up, slave. My leg's smashed to hell and I'm bleeding into my armour.'

Septimus's voice came from the garbled darkness. 'I'm drifting in now.'

'Do you have the others?'

'Yes, lord.'

'Confirm you have Uzas.'

'Yes, lord.'

'Huh,' Xarl's voice lowered. 'Shame.'

Talos, now blinded by the blood smearing both his lenses, gripped Xarl's wrist as his brother held him. He felt his senses refocusing, and although he was sightless, the unearthly silence and weightlessness told him all he needed to know. He was in space, without any propulsion, turning in the darkness without any control at all.

'This,' he said through gritted teeth, 'was the stupidest idea I've ever had.'

'Glad you're still alive,' Xarl laughed, his voice hard and edged. 'You should have seen the way you hit your head on the way out.'

'I can feel it now.'

'Wonderful. You deserve it. Now shut up and pray that accursed little runt you trust doesn't crash our damn Thunderhawk.'

VI
AFTERMATH

'If there is nobility remaining within Konrad's Legion, then it is hidden deeply beneath too many layers of twisted lusts, deviance, and disobedience. Their ways are foolish, ill-considered and a hindrance to the orderly flow of controlled war. The time is coming when the Night Lords must answer for their behaviour and be brought back into the doctrine of Imperial warfare, lest we lose them to their own deviant hungers.'

– The Primarch Rogal Dorn,
Recorded commentary at the Battle of Galvion, M31.

TEN MINUTES AFTER First Claw had destroyed the wall separating them from the vacuum of space, the four of them stood in the strategium of the *Covenant of Blood*, arranged in a half-crescent at the base of the Exalted's raised throne. Two of the Atramentar – Malek and Garadon again, Talos noticed – flanked the former captain, their weapons deactivated but held at the ready.

The Exalted paid little attention to the mundane aspects of the orbital war now. The beauty of its void dancing was done, and it merely awaited the accolades due for its boldness. For now, the Exalted was content to let its under-officers move the ship into the formations of the larger battle and add the strike cruiser's formidable guns to the onslaught.

Battlefleet Crythe was finished. The *Resolute* and the *Sword of the God-Emperor* were well on their way to becoming burned-out wrecks in orbit around Solace, and the lesser ships were being savaged by the over-whelming firepower of the Warmaster's fleet.

The deck shook as the Exalted nodded its acknowledgement down at the four warriors of First Claw.

'Nicely done,' the creature said.

Talos was bareheaded. His helm had been mauled in the final escape from the burning *Sword*, when the pull of the void had crashed his head against the breached wall as he was sucked out into space. Xarl

was limping and favoured his right leg – he'd almost lost it in the
same instant that Talos had narrowly escaped decapitation – and even
his enhanced Astartes physiology was struggling to re-knit bones that
had almost been reduced to gravel. Cyrion and Uzas were physically
unharmed, but Cyrion's internal organs were still tense and working
in frantic heat from the brief time in the void. His war-plate had been
compromised by an unlucky shotcannon spread that had damaged his
chestplate, and he'd needed to hold his breath for several minutes once
his armour had vented all air pressure in space. Uzas, with a lucky streak
the other three had long begun to curse, was grinning, utterly unscathed.

'You are insane, Vandred.' Talos spoke up to the command throne on
its raised dais. His shaven head was a mess of scabbing and dried blood-
trails as his gene-enhanced Larraman cells clotted his blood at the wound
on his crown.

Immediately, the atmosphere soured. Both of the Atramentar brought
their weapons to bear: Malek hunched the shoulders of his brutish Terminator war-plate, and thick claws slid, crackling with force, from the
armour's oversized gloved fists. Garadon's hammer hummed with building energy as it sparked into life.

Talos might have been handsome had he been left as a man. With
his enlarged Astartes features, he'd ascended from the ranks of classi-
cal humanity, but there was still something recognisably imposing and
inspiring in the way he looked. His black eyes, stony with rage, glared
up at the Exalted, and Talos had no idea just how much he resembled a
sculpted marble statue from the heathen ages of Old Earth.

'What did you say, my prophet?' the Exalted asked, purring the way a
contented lion might.

'You,' Talos pointed up at the altered figure with *Aurum*, 'are insane.'

The ship shivered under the attentions of Imperial guns. No one paid
attention, except for the mortal crew at their stations that ringed the
unfolding scene between their masters.

The Exalted licked its fangs. 'And by what leap of the imagination do
you arrive at such a conclusion, Talos?'

'There was no need for such risks. I heard about Fifth Claw.'

'Yes, a shame.'

'A *shame?*' Talos almost went for his bolter. His hesitation was evident
in his body language, for Malek of the Atramentar stepped forward. Both
Cyrion and Xarl raised their bolters and aimed at the elite guards either
side of the throne. Uzas did nothing, though they all heard the chuckling
from his helm speakers.

'Yes,' the Exalted said, utterly unfazed by the standoff. 'A shame.'

'We lost five Astartes in a single operation. For the first time in *millennia*, Tenth Company is below half-strength. We have never been so weak.'

'Tenth Company,' the Exalted smirked, preening and condescending.

'Tenth Company has not existed for millennia. We are the warband of the Exalted. And this night, we have earned much honour in the eyes of the Warmaster.'

The confrontation would change nothing. Talos lowered his blade, letting his anger bleed from him like corruption from a lanced boil. He buried the urge to blood his sword with the life fluids of the Exalted. Sensing the change in him, Cyrion and Xarl lowered their bolters. Champion Malek of the Atramentar stepped back into position, his tusked helm watching impassively.

'Fifth Claw is no more,' Talos said more quietly. 'We are in dire need of recruitment. We cannot function for long with barely forty Astartes.'

He let the unwelcome words hang. Every one of them knew the decades of attention and effort recruitment would require. To sustain a company's fighting strength, it needed a great deal of materiel and expertise to gene-forge new Astartes from prepubescent male infants. The *Covenant of Blood* lacked almost all of what would be required, which was why no recruitment had been done since the Great Betrayal. The remains of Tenth Company had been fighting with the same warriors since the Horus Heresy.

'Change is inevitable,' the Exalted growled. 'The Shaper of Fate is with us, and it knows the truth of this.' At those words, the Atramentar both nodded their heavy helms in respect. Uzas grunted a monosyllabic sound that could have been respect or pleasure. Talos felt his skin crawl, and his dark eyes narrowed.

'Who are we to answer the demands of the Ruinous Ones? We are the Night Lords, the sons of the eighth primarch. We are our own masters.'

'The Shaper of Fate demands nothing,' the Exalted said. 'You do not understand.'

'I have no wish to understand the entities you are enslaved to.'

The Exalted smiled, patently false, and waved a clawed gauntlet. 'I am tired of reminding you, Talos. I control this. Now leave before First Claw joins Fifth in no longer existing.'

Talos shook his head at the threat, disgusted it had even been made, and smiled back before stalking from the strategium.

Once they were outside the bridge, Cyrion voxed to Talos. 'He is worse than before.'

'As if that was possible.'

'No, brother. His fear. I can feel it boiling beneath his skin. He is losing the fight with the daemon that shares his body.'

SEPTIMUS AND EURYDICE were still in the port hangar bay.

The Thunderhawk *Blackened* sat on its landing pad, occasional jets of pressurised steam venting from its ports as the raptor-like gunship cooled. The boosters at the rear of the troop-carrying attack ship matched the gunship's name, the engine exhausts charred from decades of orbital and sub-orbital flight. Septimus was diligent in ensuring *Blackened* remained in as good a condition as could be expected, but he was an artificer first and foremost, not a tech-priest. His skills lay in repairing and maintaining the master's weapons, not keeping an ancient gunship flying.

Eurydice watched the slave as he sat on the deck of the landing bay in the shadow of the Thunderhawk, turning his master's skull-faced helm over in his hands.

'This,' he said to himself, 'is not going to be easy.'

It was a miracle the helm hadn't come to pieces: it was severely dented on the left side where Talos's head had smashed into the edge of the breached wall once the vacuum had pulled First Claw into space. Eurydice said nothing. She was still unnerved by the shaking of the ship, and replayed the last hour over and over within her mind. Powering up the Thunderhawk… Taking it out into the middle of an orbital battle… Throne, this place was insane.

Septimus looked up at her, his jade eyes narrowed. She wondered if his thoughts matched her own. As it happened, they did.

'It's not always that bad,' he said without a smile.

She grunted what might have been an agreement. 'Is it ever worse?'

'Often,' Septimus nodded. 'If you think the Astartes are bad, wait until we go to the crew decks.'

She didn't answer. She didn't want to know.

Septimus held up the oversized helm once more. 'I should get started on this.' But he didn't move. He was lingering, she knew.

Finally, she bit. 'You're not allowed to leave me alone.'

'The only way you may leave my presence is if one of us is dead.'

Her forehead, and her permanently sealed third eye, ached with sudden ferocity. It felt as though her warp-gaze sought to stare through the steel and slay the foolish, cocky slave before her.

'I hate it here,' she said, before she even realised she was going to speak.

'We all hate it here,' he nodded again, speaking slowly, and not just because of his awkward Gothic. He spoke as if stating the obvious to a slow child. 'We all hate it here, more or less. We are worthless to them. They are demigods.'

'There are no gods but the Emperor,' Eurydice sneered.

Septimus laughed at that, and his casual blasphemy grated against her. 'You are a heretic.' She said the words softly, but unpleasantly.

'As are you, now. Do you think the forces of the Throne would welcome you after even a short time on board a Traitor Astartes vessel?' His humour faded. 'Open your eyes, Navigator. You are as ruined as the rest of us, and this ship,' he gestured at the dimness of the launch bay around them, 'is your home now.'

She drew breath to argue, and he held up a hand, cutting her off.

'Enough arguing. Listen to me.'

He let the skullish helm rest on his lap as he scratched the back of his neck. 'This is the Tenth Company of the Eighth Legion. Thousands of years ago, they would have had serfs and servitors and Astartes enough that me taking a relic Thunderhawk out into the black would have been punishable by death. They lack resources, including the souls to serve them.'

'A fitting fate,' Eurydice smiled coldly. 'They're traitors.'

'You think that smirk you wear hides your fear.' He met her eyes and stared for several moments. 'It doesn't. Not from me – and definitely not from them.'

The smile left her face as quickly as it had arrived.

'I don't deny that they are heretics,' Septimus continued, 'but let me put it another way. Have you ever heard of Lok III?'

She reluctantly moved to join him, seated on the Thunderhawk's gang ramp in the gloom of the spacious hangar bay. Across the cavernous area, other Thunderhawks sat idle and silent, untouched in years. Decades, perhaps. Cargo trucks and munitions loaders sat equally lifeless. Fifty metres away, a lone servitor lay slack and unmoving on its back, its grey skin rendered greyer by the touch of dust. It looked like it had lost power and collapsed, left there to decay in the presence of these venerable war machines. Eurydice couldn't take her eyes from the corpse. Its skin was withered and drawn tight against its bones, almost mummified, though actual decomposition was probably delayed because of the machine parts fighting off decay in the organic sections that remained.

She shivered. It was all too easy to see how this ship was a hollow image of itself.

'No,' she said at length, taking grim comfort in his body heat as she sat next to him. The *Covenant* was so cold. 'I've never heard of Lok III.'

'Not much to hear of,' he admitted, then lapsed into silence, thinking.

'I've not seen much of the galaxy,' she said. 'Syne kept most of our prospecting runs within a handful of sectors to save on journey costs. Also, I...'

'You what?'

'My family, House Mervallion, is on the lowest tier of the Navis Nobilite. I think Syne was worried about pushing me too hard. Worried his Navigator was of... poor quality.'

Septimus nodded, with a knowing look in his eyes Eurydice didn't like. When she expected him to comment on her confession, he merely cut back to his previous line of conversation.

'Lok III is far distant, close to the region of space known to Imperial records as Scarus Sector.'

'Half the galaxy away.'

'Yes. I was born there. It wasn't a forge world, but it was close. Manufactories covered the planet, and I worked as a hauler pilot, ferrying cargo to and from the orbital docks down to the manufactorum that employed me.'

'That's... nice.'

'No, it was boring beyond words. My point should be obvious. Yes, I'm considered a heretic because of my allegiance. Yes, I am indentured to traitors who make war upon the Throne of Terra. And yes, there's darkness within this ship that hungers for our blood. But I see things in a realistic light. What I have now is better than death. And once you learn how to walk in the dark places here... it's almost safe. It's almost a real life.

'I lived a life of repetition – another tiny cog in a vast, dull existence. But this? This is different. Every week will bring something new, something incredible, something that takes my breath away. Rarely in a good way, I confess.'

She looked at him. He was *serious*.

'You're serious,' she said, for lack of anything else to say.

'I am. As an artificer and a pilot, I'm given a great deal of freedom on the ship. I am valued.'

'A valuable slave.'

He narrowed his eyes as he looked at her. 'I am trying to keep you alive. If you don't adapt to this existence, your life ends. It's that simple.'

After a long pause, she asked, 'Are you happy?'

'I suspect you think that's a very insightful and cutting remark.' Septimus gestured around the hangar bay again. 'Of course I am not *happy*. I am a slave to heretical demigods, and I live on a vessel touched by indescribable darkness. The mortal crew lives in fear of the things that stalk the ship's lightless decks, and those things are not always the Astartes.'

Septimus chuckled after he said the words, the sound low and devoid of mirth. In his hands, the skull helm grinned up at them both.

'So how did they take you?' Eurydice asked.

Septimus didn't look up from the helm. 'They attacked Lok III. I was originally taken to serve as a pilot, and the hyp... hypno–'

'Hypnotic?'

'Hypnotic. Yes.' Septimus spoke the word a few more times as if tasting it. 'I'm not sure if I forgot that word, or just never knew it. As I said, Gothic was never my first language. But the process was agony. They teach through mental conditioning and hypnotic implantation programs that burn information directly into the mind. That is why I can fly a Thunderhawk – though even after a decade, not with the skill of a true Astartes pilot.'

She scanned the hangar bay again, imagining how it would look as it should have been: a hive of industry and activity, crew running here and there, servitors and munitions loaders rattling and clanking across the rune-marked floor, the howling of turbines as gunships roared in the moments before launch.

It must have been so impressive. It was, she hated to admit it, close to what she'd hoped for herself: guiding the vessels of the Astartes across the stars.

'He has you fixing his armour now,' she said, looking back to Septimus. 'Is that a demotion?'

'Technically, a promotion. Artificers are the most respected serfs in a Legion's armoury.'

She laughed, the sound alien and echoing in the hollow hangar bay.

'What's so funny?' he asked.

'You're not exactly up to your neck in respect.'

'You only say that,' he smiled, 'because you have not seen everything, Octavia.'

'Why do you call me that?'

'Because I am the seventh of my master's servants. And you are the eighth.'

'Not likely.'

'Already your defiance is fading. I hear it in your voice.'

'You're imagining it.'

'That's a shame.' He rose to his feet, the broken helm in his hands. 'Because if I am, you'll be dying very soon.'

As TALOS CONFRONTED the Exalted, and as Septimus spoke with Eurydice, the last vestiges of the orbital battle played out to their inevitable conclusion. Battlefleet Crythe was annihilated, and the few surviving vessels that managed to flee into the warp are of no further relevance to this record, though most distinguished themselves in their own ways when they merged with other sector battlefleets.

Consolidation came next.

The Warmaster's forces had destroyed the Imperial Navy presence in the area, and his fleet hung in the atmospheric reaches above the penal world, Solace. The insignia displayed by the vessels of his gathered fleet were myriad. The slitted Eye of Horus marked a full seven Black Legion vessels – a massive portion of their mighty fleet – while the fanged skull of the Night Lords was evident on both the *Covenant of Blood* and its much larger sister ship already among the fleet, the battle-barge *Hunter's Premonition*. The majority of the fleet was made up of bulk transports carrying legions of the lost and the damned: Imperial Guard and planetary defence forces that had turned traitor and sworn allegiance to the Warmaster's cause across recent campaigns. All in all, the Warmaster came to Crythe with the capacity to unleash over two thousand Traitor Astartes and more than a million human soldiers. Pride of place within the fleet was given to the vast hulks belonging to Legio Frostreaver, once of the Mechanicum of Mars. A full Titan Legion at the Warmaster's beck and call, numbering almost a dozen god-machines of varying classes.

Such a Chaos fleet was rarely seen outside of the Warmaster's holy wars against the Emperor's worlds, and word of this gathering of the

Archenemy spread throughout the nearby Imperial planets, with fearful talk of a new Black Crusade in the Despoiler's name.

With Solace fallen and the Navy crushed, the war for the Crythe Cluster was only just beginning. Long-range scanners told a grim tale, unnerving even for the captains of this lethal battlefleet. The forge world, Crythe Prime, remained ringed by a vast fleet answering to the Adeptus Mechanicus, which had steadfastly refused to answer Battlefleet Crythe's hails for help. Curiously, the Marines Errant vessel *Severance* had withdrawn to Crythe Prime to side with the Mechanicus instead of fighting and dying with the Imperial Navy.

Time was of the essence, and every officer in the Warmaster's fleet knew it. The Imperium of Man would answer this aggression with fury of its own, and alongside Naval reinforcements, Imperial Guard and Astartes armies would be en route from the moment the first astropathic cries for aid had been sent by the beleaguered Battlefleet Crythe.

The *Covenant of Blood* pulled close to its kin-ship, the powerful battle-barge *Hunter's Premonition*. The larger ship had been one of the Legion's flagships before the scattering of the Night Lords over the centuries, and it was an awe-inspiring sight to those who hadn't gazed upon an example of their Legion's strength in many years. Even the Exalted, though he was loath to admit it, felt moved by the sight of the princely vessel, a lance of midnight blue edged in gold and bronze.

He wanted it. He wanted command of that vessel, and all upon the deck saw that need burning in his obsidian eyes.

The destruction of Battlefleet Crythe was not the only reason the Warmaster had ordered Solace taken first. Just as important as the death of the orbital defenders was the preservation of the population below. Had Lord Admiral Valiance Arventaur been more familiar with the Archenemy – instead of spending most of his career fighting eldar raiders – he might have turned the guns of his beloved *Sword of the God-Emperor* on Solace itself, destroying the population centres of the penal world and denying the Warmaster his prize. Ultimately, this would have done much more to save the Crythe Cluster.

But, of course, he had not. He had died with a sword in his heart, whispering incoherent curses at his murderer.

The Chaos fleet hung in space around a world with almost a million prisoners: rapists, murderers, heretics, thieves, mutants and criminals of a thousand other stripes – all held in appalling conditions and discarded by an Imperium that loathed them for their deviance.

Within the hour, while the hulks of Battlefleet Crythe were still flaming wrecks in space, the Warmaster's troop ships began their landing. On the surface, hundreds of thousands of potential new warriors watched the skies burn, staring up through the windows of their cells as deliverance – and freedom – came for them.

VII

THE SURFACE OF SOLACE

'Talos. The prophet of the Night Lords. Bring him to me.'
– Abaddon the Despoiler
Commander of the Black Legion, Warmaster of Chaos

TALOS AND XARL locked blades.

The sparring chamber was, like most of the *Covenant*, a shadow of its former activity. In the centre of the chamber, which was tiered and inclined much like a gladiatorial arena, the two Astartes duelled alone, Talos's deactivated power sword clashing against Xarl's stilled chainblade. With respect to the weapons' machine-spirits, the brothers practised with their own swords instead of practice blades, but kept them unpowered.

Xarl's chainsword was a standard-issue Astartes weapon, incredibly tough and resistant to damage, with vicious serrated teeth honed to monomolecular points. But *Aurum*, the blade taken from a slain captain of the Blood Angels, was a relic of incredible potency. A standard power sword would sunder even an honourable blade like Xarl's *Executioner*, and *Aurum* was closer to an artefact than a weapon. They duelled without the crackling blue fire of the power sword and the roaring whine of the chainblade.

In a way, it was worse. Their movements reeked of training instead of true battle. Talos always felt the relative silence of sparring to be unnerving and unsatisfying, and it was times like this he dwelled most on how he had been gene-forged and bred for the battlefield. He was a weapon more than a man; never was it more obvious than in the moments of his disquiet.

By mortal standards, it would have been considered a duel of the gods. The blades sliced the air faster than the human eye could follow, clash upon clash in a storm of relentless speed and force. Had any Astartes been witnessing the fight, they might have seen with a deeper clarity. Both warriors were plainly distracted, their thoughts elsewhere, obvious in every minute hesitation and flicker of the eyes.

Around them, banks of human-sized passages formed into the arena walls had once housed a small army of combat servitors, engineered for practice and destined for destruction under the blades of the Astartes that came to hone their skills here. Such days were long past. The halls where the servitors had trundled from storage-engineering chambers beneath the arena were silent and lightless, another reminder of a time now gone forever.

Talos felt his anger swell up as he leaned back and deflected a throat cut. Melancholy was not something that sat well with him. It was alien to his thoughts, yet of late it would cling there like it belonged.

That made him angry. It felt like a vulnerability in his defences, a wound that wouldn't heal.

Xarl sensed the frustration in his brother's blows, and as their deactivated swords locked again, Xarl leaned in close. Their faces – already similar due to the genetic enhancements that moulded their bodies – glared into one another with mirrored anger. The bitter gaze from their black eyes met as surely as the blades in their hands.

'You're losing your temper,' he snarled at Talos.

'I'm annoyed that I need to go easy on you because of the leg,' Talos growled, nodding almost imperceptibly down at Xarl's healing limb.

In response, Xarl hurled his brother back with a laugh, disengaging with surprising grace for one who relied so often on fury to win his fights.

'Do your worst,' he said, smiling in the darkness. Like all areas of the *Covenant of Blood* restricted to the Astartes alone, the sparring chambers were utterly lightless. No hindrance at all to the dark eyes of the Nostramo-born, but in former days combat servitors had required night vision visors and aural enhancer sensors to aid with detecting movement.

Talos came on again, his guard high as he executed a flawless series of two-handed cuts from the left designed to force Xarl onto his right leg more and more. He heard his brother's pained grunts as he defended himself.

'Keep it up,' Xarl said, still not even breathing heavily despite the fact they'd been duelling at an inhuman pace for almost an hour. 'Still need to get used to taking weight on this leg again.'

Instead of pressing the attack, Talos stopped.

'Hold,' he said, raising a hand.

'What? Why?' Xarl asked, lowering *Executioner*. He looked around the silent, dark arena, seeing nothing but the empty rows of witness seats, hearing nothing but the dim growl of the ship's orbital drives, smelling nothing but the sweat from their robed bodies and the faint tang of centuries of weapon oil. 'I sense no one nearby.'

'I saw Uzas kill Cyrion,' Talos said, apropos of nothing.

Xarl laughed. 'Right. That's good. Are we going to fight or not?' In a moment of uncharacteristic concern, Xarl tilted his head to regard his brother. 'Has your head not healed? I thought it was fine.'

'I am not joking.'

In the darkness, pierced with ease by the vision of one born on a sunless world, Xarl saw his brother's black eyes regarding him without a trace of humour.

'Are you speaking of your vision?'

'You know I am.'

'You saw wrong, Talos,' Xarl said, spitting onto the decking. 'Cyrion is easy to hate. He is corrupted in the worst of ways. But even a rabid fool like Uzas would never kill him.'

'Cyrion is true to the Night Haunter,' Talos said.

Xarl snorted. 'We've had this argument before. He is an Astartes that knows fear. That is as corrupt as can be imagined.'

'He understands fear.'

'Does he still hear the daemon warring within the Exalted?'

Talos let the silence answer for him.

'Exactly,' Xarl nodded. 'He can sense fear. That is unnatural. He is corrupted.'

'He senses it. He does not feel it himself.'

Xarl looked down at his chainsword, silent in deactivation. 'Semantics. He has been corrupted by the Ruinous Ones, as surely as Uzas has. But they are still brothers, and I trust them – for now.'

'You trust *Uzas*?' Talos tilted his head, curious now.

'We are First Claw,' Xarl answered, if that justified everything. 'At least the corruption within Uzas is visible. Cyrion is the dangerous one, brother.'

'I have spoken to Cyrion about this many times,' Talos warned, 'and I tell you, you're wrong.'

'We'll see. Tell me of this vision.'

Talos pictured again the sight of Uzas, an axe in hand, moving over the rubble of a shattered building, leaping at Cyrion as he lay prone. He explained it to Xarl now, as faithfully as he could, omitting nothing. He spoke of the blaring war horns of the Titans above and the dusty grey stone of the fallen buildings, still magma red in places where the rock had been cooked by the towering god-machines' guns. He described the fall of the axe, the way it hooked into Cyrion's neck joint, and the blood that flowed in the moments after.

'That does sound like Uzas,' Xarl said at length. 'A vicious kill, and perfectly made against helpless prey. I am no longer so sure this was a foolish joke of yours.'

'He despises Cyrion,' Talos pointed out. He moved to the side of the arena, where *Aurum*'s sheath rested against the metal wall. 'But I have been wrong before,' he said over his shoulder.

Xarl shook his head again. He looked more thoughtful than Talos had ever seen him, which was disquieting purely for its unfamiliarity. It occurred to him for the first time that perhaps Xarl was one of those that invested great faith in his prophetic curse. He seemed almost... unnerved.

'When?' Xarl said, 'A handful of times in how many years? No, brother. This has the stench of unwelcome truth to it.'

Talos said nothing. Xarl surprised him by speaking more.

'We all trust you. I don't like you, brother – you know that. It is not easy to like you. You are self-righteous and you take risks as foolish as the Exalted sometimes. You assume you lead First Claw, yet were never promoted above any of us. All you were was an Apothecary, yet you act like our sergeant now. By the False Throne, you act like the Captain of Tenth Company. I have a hundred reasons to dislike you, and they are all valid. But I trust you, Talos.'

'Good to know,' Talos said as he sheathed the blade and stood once more.

'When were you last wrong?' Xarl pressed. 'Humour me. When was the last time one of your auguries went awry?'

'A long time ago,' Talos said. 'Seventy years, perhaps. On Gashik, the world where it never stopped raining. I dreamed we would see battle against the Imperial Fists, but the planet remained defenceless.'

Xarl scratched at his cheek, musing.

'Seventy years. You've not been wrong in almost a century. But if Cyrion does die, and you were right that he isn't corrupt, we could use his progenoid glands to gene-forge another Astartes in his place. No loss.'

Talos considered drawing the blade again. 'The same could be said for the death of any one of us.'

Xarl raised an eyebrow. 'You'd harvest Uzas's gene-seed?'

'Point taken.' And it was. Talos would sooner burn that biological matter into ash before he saw it implanted within another Night Lord.

Xarl nodded, clearly distracted as Talos carried on. 'If this comes to pass, I will kill Uzas.'

Talos wasn't even sure he heard him.

'I will think on this,' Xarl replied, and without another word, he walked from the arena, descending into the deeper darkness of the ship. After the awkwardness of the brotherly candour a moment before, this was much more like the Xarl Talos had grown to tolerate – stalking off in silence, keeping his counsel to himself.

Caught between the desire to follow Xarl and seek out Cyrion, Talos was denied the choice a moment later.

Thudding footsteps drew his attention as another figure emerged at the first tier of witness seats. Lightning-marked armour, too bulky even for Astartes war-plate.

'Prophet,' said Champion Malek of the Atramentar.

'Yes, brother.'

'Your presence is required.'

'I see.' Talos didn't move. 'Inform the Exalted I am currently engaged in my meditations, and will attend him in three hours.'

The sound of a rockslide avalanche rumbled from the hound-like helm of Malek's Terminator armour. Talos assumed it was a chuckle.

'No, prophet, it is not the Exalted that demands your presence.'

'Then whom?' Talos asked, his fingertips stroking the sheathed hilt of *Aurum* at his hip. 'No one demands my attention, Malek. I am no slave.'

'No? No one? And what if the presence of the Night Lord prophet was demanded by Abaddon of the Black Legion?'

Talos swallowed, neither scared nor worried, but instantly on edge. This changed things.

'The Warmaster wishes to speak with me,' he said slowly, as if unsure he heard correctly.

'He does. You are to be ready within the hour, along with First Claw. Two of the Atramentar will accompany you.'

'I need no honour guard. I will go alone.'

'Talos,' Malek growled. Talos still looked up at him. None of the Atramentar had ever used his name before, and he felt a terrible gravity within the use of it now.

'I am listening, Malek.'

'This is not the time to stand alone, brother. Take First Claw. And do not argue when Garadon and I also stand with you. This is a show of strength as surely as the Exalted's tactics in the void war.'

It took several seconds, but Talos finally nodded. 'Where is this meeting taking place?'

Malek held up a massive power fist, his Terminator armour clanking and the servo-driven joints snarling as he moved. Four blades slashed from his knuckles, each one as long as a mortal man's arm. At a command word Talos didn't hear, the lightning claws lived up to their name, becoming wreathed in a crackling power field that brought stark, viciously flickering light to the blackness of the arena.

'Solace,' Malek replied. 'The Warmaster walks the surface of his most recently conquered world, and we are to meet him there.'

'The Black Legion,' Talos said after a few moments, a dark little smirk crossing his features. 'The Sons of Horus, with a heritage of treachery as great as their fallen father.'

'Aye, the Black Legion.' Malek's claws slid back into their housing on the back of his massive armoured fists, locked until reactivation. 'Which is why we are going in midnight clad.'

* * *

THE SURFACE OF Solace was the mixed, dusty red-brown of old scabs and burned flesh. It was an ugly world in all respects, even down to the taste of the air. Because of intense volcanic activity raging across the southern hemisphere for centuries, the myriad mountain ranges breathing fire into the atmosphere left the thin air tasting of ash across the planet.

The spires of the penal colonies were no easier on the eyes than anything else on the surface: towers of red stone, clawed and brutish, jutting like broken blades from natural mountain formations. The Gothic architecture so beloved of many Imperial worlds was in evidence here, but in its crudest and most unskilled execution. Whoever designed the prison spires of Solace – if indeed any real design had taken place at all – knew all too well how the world would be home to souls that barely counted as part of the Imperium. His prejudice against the prisoners that were destined to come to this world and rot under its dull skies was all too obvious in the architecture.

The Night Lord Thunderhawk *Blackened* streaked across the weatherless sky, its pilot adjusting thrust output as the gunship broke from orbital to atmospheric flight.

'On approach,' Septimus said, easing back on one of the several levers that handled the gunship's thrust. In the creaking control chair, which was obviously made for a larger pilot, he clicked a cluster of switches and watched the vivid green hololithic terrain display – updated every few seconds from auspex returns. Altitude dropping gently, speed falling, he spoke without taking his eyes from the console's displays.

'Internment Spire Delta Two, this is the Eighth Legion Thunderhawk *Blackened*. We are on southern approach. Respond.'

Silence greeted his attempts at communication.

'What now?' he asked, over his shoulder.

Talos, armoured and armed, standing behind the pilot's throne, shook his head. 'Don't bother repeating the hail. The Black Legion is hardly noted for excellence in re-establishing infrastructures upon the worlds it conquers.'

Cyrion was making final reverent checks over his bolter. 'And we are?'

Talos didn't turn to his brother. In the spacious cockpit, where all of First Claw stood behind Septimus and Eurydice in the pilot and co-pilot thrones, Talos watched the thin, dusty red mist breaking apart over the front windows as they closed in on their destination.

'We do not conquer worlds,' Talos replied. 'Our mandate is not the same as theirs, nor is our ultimate aim.'

Keeping himself out of their debate, Septimus waited until he was sure they would say no more. 'Five minutes, master. I'll bring us down on the spire-top landing platform.'

'Your flying is improving, slave.' It was Xarl who stepped forward, resting a gauntleted hand on the back of Septimus's chair. There was nothing comforting in the gesture. Septimus could see their reflections in the viewscreen. All without their helms – Talos, handsome and stern; Cyrion, weary with a half-smile; Xarl sneering and bitter; and Uzas, dead-eyed and licking his teeth as he stared at nothing in particular.

And Eurydice. He noticed her reflection last, still unused to her presence. She met his eyes in the reflection on the cockpit window, and offered him an expressionless glance that could have meant anything. Her hair, scruffy and chestnut brown, framed her face in choppy locks. The iron strip still concealed her third eye, and Septimus often found himself wondering just what it would look like.

She wore the ragged, dark blue jacket and trousers of the Legion's serfs, though getting her into the loose uniform had been no easy feat. She'd only relented to Septimus's insistence when he pointed out how bad she smelled still wearing the same clothes they'd captured her in weeks before.

They hadn't branded her, yet. The tattoo beneath his clothes that covered his shoulder blades itched as if in sympathy with his thoughts. A winged skull, in black ink mixed with Astartes blood.

If she gave her allegiance – if she survived – she'd be branded soon enough.

Ahead of them, the thin mist parted to reveal a clawed cluster of peaks, topped by a spire that could only be their destination. Talos and the others reached for their helms, sealing them in place. Septimus was familiar with the differences between them, as familiar to him as their natural faces. Cyrion's helm was older than the other death masks, a Mark II design with narrowed eyes and an almost knightly aesthetic. He wore few trophies, but his armour was decorated in great detail with jagged bolts of blue-white lightning. Twin storm bolts streaked from his ruby eye lenses like forked tears.

In contrast, Xarl's helm was the newest – a Mark VII piece, taken from a recent engagement with the Dark Angels. He'd ordered one of the few remaining artificers to modify it, with a hand-painted daemonic skull covering the faceplate. He displayed trophies with relish and pride: alien and human skulls hanging from chains across his armour, scrolls of past deeds draped across his shoulder pads.

Uzas wore a grim-faced Mark III helm, the paintwork crudely done with little care. Stark against the dark blue was a red palm print with splayed fingers, done with his own hand dipped in blood and pressed against the helm's face.

Talos's helm, a studded Mark V design freshly repaired by his servant's craftsmanship, featured a skulled face of creamy bone, with a Nostraman rune branded black into the forehead. When Septimus had been reshaping the helm on the artificer deck of the *Covenant*, Eurydice had asked what the sigil meant.

'It's like "in midnight clad",' he said, repainting the bone face with both reverence and the ease of familiarity. 'It doesn't translate well into Low Gothic.'

'I'm getting tired of hearing that.'

'Well, it's true. Nostramo was a world of high politics and a compli-cated underworld that infested all layers of society. The tongue has its roots in High Gothic, but much had changed through generations of unique phrasing by faithless, trustless, peaceless people.'

'Trustless and peaceless aren't words.' Despite herself, she smiled, watching him work. She was growing used to his stumbling attempts to speak the universal tongue.

'My point stands,' Septimus said, painting bone white around the left eye lens. 'Nostraman is, by Gothic standards, very grand and overly poetic.'

'Gangsters like to think of themselves as cultured,' she said with a curl to her lip. To her surprise, he nodded.

'From what I gather of Nostraman history, yes, that's the conclusion I draw as well. The language became very... I don't know the word.'

'Flowery.'

He shrugged. 'Close enough.'

'So what does that symbol mean?'

'It's a combination of three letters, which in turn stand for three words. The more complex a symbol, the more likely it is that a number of con-cepts and letters make up the final sigil.'

'Sorry I asked.'

'Fine,' he said, still not looking up from his duties. 'It means, directly translated: "Ender of lives and collector of essences".'

'What is it in Nostraman?'

Septimus spoke three words, which sounded beautiful to her ears. Smooth, delicate, and curiously chilling. Nostraman, she decided, sounded like a murderer by her bedside, whispering in her ear.

'Shorten it for me,' she said, feeling her skin prickle at the sound of his voice speaking the dead language. 'What does it mean, direct translation or not.'

'Equivalently, it would mean "Soul Hunter",' he said, holding the helm up now and examining his work.

'Is that what the other Night Lords call your master?' Eurydice asked.

'No. It is the name bestowed upon him by their martyred prima-rch father. His favoured sons within the Eighth Legion held... titles, or names, like that. To the Legion, he was Apothecary Talos of First Claw, or Tenth Company's "prophet". To the Night Haunter, lord of the Eighth Legion, he was Soul Hunter.'

'Why?' she asked.

And Septimus told her.

THE THUNDERHAWK SETTLED on the landing platform with a gush of vented steam and the clank of its landing claws locking, taking the gunship's weight. Under the cockpit, the gang ramp lowered on groaning, grinding hydraulics. Once it had slammed down onto the deck, the Night Lords disembarked, weapons armed.

Talos led the way, *Aurum* active and *Anathema* drawn. First Claw came behind him, bolters up. Behind them, with servo-joints growling and heavy boots thudding onto the decking, came the Terminator-clad Atramentar warriors Malek and Garadon.

In the moments before *Blackened* had touched down, Septimus had been ordered to stay with the gunship. Although she wasn't included in the order – in fact, the Night Lords were still essentially ignoring her – Eurydice remained with Septimus.

'Septimus,' Talos had said, 'if anyone approaches the Thunderhawk, warn them once, then open fire.'

The serf had nodded. *Blackened* possessed a vicious armament: several heavy bolters mounted on the wings and flanks of the vessel, crewed by limbless servitors slaved directly to the gunnery consoles. The weapons were also fireable from the main cockpit console, which was fortunate considering the depleted state of Tenth Company's servitor complement: only half of the Thunderhawk's heavy bolter turrets were actively crewed. Several of the other gunships aboard the *Covenant of Blood* completely lacked a servitor crew.

The Astartes moved with cautious speed. The decking was clear, open to a starlit sky only thinly veiled by colourless clouds. At the north side of the thruster-burned platform, a small shelter with a double door led into the spire beneath.

'Looks like a lift,' Xarl nodded to the small building.

'Looks like a trap,' Uzas murmured. As if on cue, the double doors opened with a whirr of mechanics, revealing four figures lit by the internal lights of an elevator.

'I was right,' said Xarl.

'I probably was, too,' Uzas persisted.

'Silence,' Talos growled into the vox, and the order was echoed by Malek of the Atramentar. Talos considered objecting to the champion issuing orders to his squad, but then technically, First Claw was no more his to command than it was Malek's. And Malek held overall rank.

The dark figures left the wide elevator, stalking onto the platform with a graceless, lumbering stride that matched the Terminator-gait of the Atramentar.

First Claw raised their bolters in perfect unity, each one drawing a bead on a different figure. Malek and Garadon brought their close combat weapons to bear, flanking the Astartes.

'Justaerin,' warned Malek. They knew the term. The elite Terminator-armoured squad of the Sons of Horus First Company.

'Not any more.' Talos didn't lower his bolter. 'We don't know if they have kept that title. Times change.'

The four black-armoured, red-eyed Terminators approached, their own weapons raised. Brass-mouthed double-barrelled bolters, and an ornate arm-mounted autocannon with twin barrels the length of spears – all aimed at the new arrivals. Where the Night Lord Terminators wore dark cloaks around their bulky forms, spiked trophy racks arced from the Black Legion's hunched backs, displaying a varied selection of Astartes helms from various Imperial Chapters. Talos recognised the colours of the Crimson Fists, the Raven Guard, and a number of Chapters he'd never encountered. Inconstant Imperial dogs. They divided and bred like vermin.

'Which one of you is Talos?' The lead Terminator's voice came through his helm speakers like a detuned vox – all crackles and rasps.

Talos nodded at the Black Legionnaire. 'The one aiming his blade at your heart, and his bolter at your head.'

'Nice sword, Night Lord,' the Terminator rasped, gesturing its storm bolter at *Aurum* pointed at his chestplate. Talos sighted down the golden blade, reading the lettering across the warrior's armour: FALKUS, in faded indentations.

'Please,' Cyrion voxed over the intra-squad channel, 'tell me that rhyme wasn't his attempt at wit.'

'Falkus,' Talos said slowly, 'I am Talos of the Eighth Legion. With me is First Claw, Tenth Company, as well as Champion Malek and Garadon, Hammer of the Exalted, both of the Atramentar.'

'You give yourselves a lot of titles,' said another of the Black Legion Terminators, the one with the long-barrelled autocannon. His voice was lower than the first's, and he sported a horned helm similar to Garadon's.

'We kill a lot of people,' Xarl replied. To punctuate his words, he trailed his bolter across the four Black Legionnaires. It was posturing of the most brazen, unsubtle, even childish kind. It galled Talos that such theatrics were necessary.

'We are all allies here, under the Warmaster's banner,' the cannon-bearer said. 'There is no need for such a display of hostility.'

'Then lower your weapons first,' Xarl offered.

'Like the nice, polite hosts you are,' Cyrion added.

One of the squad, Talos wasn't sure who, had privately voxed back to Septimus on board *Blackened*. He knew this because the heavy bolters mounted on the starboard cheek and wing tips rotated to lock onto the four Black Legion Terminators.

Nice touch, he thought. Probably Xarl's idea.

The Warmaster's warriors lowered their weapons a moment later, evidently neither gracious about the fact, nor with any real unity of movement.

'They move carelessly,' Garadon voxed, his disgust obvious in his tone.

'Come, brothers,' said the first Black Legion Terminator, inclining his brutish helm. 'The Warmaster, blessed scion of the Dark Ones, requests your presence.'

Only when the Black Legionnaires stalked away first did the Night Lords lower their weapons.

'You remember when we used to trust each other?' Cyrion voxed.

'No,' Xarl said.

'Let's get this over quickly,' Talos cut in. No one argued.

THE PRISON LOOKED to be in a riot.

As they descended, the lift's windows revealed floor after floor of expansive red chambers flooded with howling, screaming, fighting, running prisoners. On one floor, the windows showed a yelling man's face, his fists beating on the glass and leaving bloody stains. He fled as soon as he saw what occupied the interior, which was lucky for him, as Uzas had been about to fire his bolter and end the fool's life.

'These will all be rounded up by our slaver ships, ready for the war against the forge world,' the cannon-bearing Legionnaire growled in his guttural cant. 'For now, we are letting them enjoy their first taste of bloodlust since they were incarcerated.'

'We freed them,' the leader, Falkus, said. 'We deactivated their restraining cells and granted them their liberty. They are using their first acts of freedom to butcher the internment guards that still live.' He sounded both proud and amused.

Muted through the lift shaft walls, gunshots could sometimes be made out amongst the howls. Evidently, not all the guards were going down easily.

The lift trembled once as it came to a halt on a floor that looked no different than any other. A horde of prisoners, many bare-chested and armed with cutlery or chunks of furniture as weapons, seemed to be beating each other to death with great enthusiasm.

Until the doors opened.

Of all the founding Legions to turn from the light of the False Emperor, Talos most despised the Black Legion, the Sons of Horus, for how far they had fallen in the years since their primarch father's death. In his eyes, they were an amalgamation of every sin and deviation across the sphere of mortal experience, armed and armoured as Astartes without a shred of the nobility that they once possessed. They consorted with daemons en masse, fighting beside them and listening to their warp-whispers for shards of wisdom. Just as the Exalted, daemon-corrupt and a shadow of the man he once was, revolted Talos – so too did the Black Legion in their wanton embrace of the Ruinous Powers.

But as the lift doors opened, he felt, just for a moment, a glimmer of why they lived as they did.

The floor before them was a long chamber with a central corridor and walls consisting of cells on both sides, looking across at one another. All the cell doors stood open. Smeared here and there were the remains of guards slaughtered by the newly-freed prisoners. And the prisoners themselves – perhaps three hundred gangers, murderers and violent criminals – were all suddenly silent.

Silent and kneeling, their heads bowed towards the lift.

The Black Legion Terminators heaved their spiked bulks from the lift, tromping down the central corridor without paying any attention to their worshipful supplicants. Their power was obvious. They did not live in restraint, suffering through a lack of slaves, taking pains not to reveal themselves to an enraged Imperium. And that, just for a moment, spoke to Talos. He understood them, even though he hated them.

The Night Lords followed, and Talos suspected the others were as eager to reach for their sheathed weapons as he was. Humans brought to obedience through fear; that he was used to. But this… this reeked of something else. The sense of something sulphurous was in the air, not entirely drowned out by his breathing filters. Something sorcerous or daemonic, perhaps, to inspire such terrible reverence in such a short time.

At the end of the corridor, another set of doors led into a square chamber, the lights dimmed almost to nothingness. As soon as the doors closed behind them, Talos heard the melee in the prison block begin once more. Somehow, that sound was more reassuring than the silence.

The chamber they had arrived at had been a mess hall. In the initial riots following their freedom, the prisoners had devastated it utterly, and what remained was a junkyard of broken tables, stools and the corpses of twenty-two guards and inmates in varying states of dismemberment. Several other doors led deeper into the internment complex, but Talos would never see any more of the prison than this.

'What a creature man is…' said a figure in the centre of the wrecked room, '…to spend its first moments of freedom destroying its own lair.'

The Black Legion warriors knelt, their joints emitting low snarls at the unfamiliar movements. Terminator armour was not designed to pay reverence to others. It was designed to kill without end, without mercy, without respite. Talos's jaw clenched at the sight of the Warmaster's elite bowing down. Even the Atramentar, Tenth Company's finest, never knelt before the Exalted.

The figure in the centre of the room turned, and Talos met the eyes of the most powerful, most feared being in the galaxy. The figure smiled warmly.

'Talos,' said Abaddon the Despoiler, Warmaster of Chaos. 'We must speak, you and I.'

VIII

WARMASTER

'When in the heart of the foe, show only your strength.
Never bare your throat, never sheathe your sword.
We are Astartes. Not diplomats. Not ambassadors. We are warriors
all.
If you are within the enemy's fortress, you have already breached
his best defences.
You hold all the advantages.
Use them.'

– The war-sage Malcharion
Excerpted from his work, *The Tenebrous Path*

ABADDON SMILED AS he spoke.

A smile was the last thing Talos had been expecting.

In his own suit of Terminator war-plate, the Warmaster dwarfed his
men and the Atramentar alike, and the consummately crafted black ceramite he wore was bedecked in ornate finery, emblazoned with brass and
bronze edges, and bearing the glaring, slitted, fire-orange Eye of Horus
on the centre of his chestplate. A cloak of grey white fur, the hide of
some huge wolf-beast, was draped across his massive shoulders. As with
his elite warriors, his back sported spear-like trophy racks, each of them
impaling a clutch of Astartes helms. Several of them were at the right
angle to stare lifelessly at Talos, their dead gaze an unsubtle reminder of
the millions of lives lost to the Warmaster's machinations in ten thousand years of rebellion and heresy.

His right hand ended in a vicious power claw of archaic, unique design.
The bladed talons, as long as an Astartes's arm, curved and glinted in
the half-light of the flickering wall lamps. Horus, favoured son of the
Emperor, had worn that gauntlet in the Great Crusade and the Heresy
that followed. He'd used it to slay the angel Sanguinius, and wound the
Emperor unto the edge of death. Now the dread weapon graced the fist
of his gene-son, the leader of his fallen Legion.

That weapon alone almost brought about the urge to kneel, to show respect to the one who carried the blades of ultimate heresy.

But it was the Warmaster's face that drew Talos's attention above all else. Abaddon would never be considered handsome, and the regal lethality emanating from him was nothing a human could project. His face was lined and scarred from centuries of battle, the marks across his pale skin speaking of a thousand battles on a thousand worlds. His head was shaven but for a topknot of his blue-black hair.

In his eyes, Talos saw the death of the galaxy. They burned with inner light, made bright by the dreams of conquest that infested his every waking moment, yet tinged with desperate fury, a longing to inflict vengeance upon the heart of the Imperium.

Like Chaos itself, Abaddon was a clash of contradictions.

And Talos hated his warm, welcoming smile. He could almost smell the corruption beneath the man's skin, a rank scent of charred metal and polluted flesh that teased the edges of Talos's senses.

'You smell that?' he voxed to First Claw.

'Yes,' from Xarl. 'I smell spoiled meat and... something more. They are ripe with corruption, all of them. The Terminators are likely mutated under their armour.'

From there, their replies deteriorated in usefulness.

'The Warmaster smells like he's been boiling human flesh in engine oil,' Cyrion ventured, slightly less helpfully.

All Talos got back from Uzas was an acknowledgement blip – a single burst of quiet static indicating an affirmation.

'I thank you for coming to meet me, brother,' the Warmaster said, his words graceful where his voice was not. It rumbled from his throat, guttural and feral, another contradiction to add to the growing list. Talos wondered how much of this was intentional, designed to throw supplicants off-guard when they came before the great Despoiler.

'I have come, Warmaster,' Talos said, and his targeting reticule locked onto the Black Legion commander, flashing white as it registered the weapons on his person. The Talon of Horus. The storm bolter attached to the great lightning claw. The blade at the Warmaster's hip.

Threat, a Nostraman warning rune flickered across his retinal display. Talos didn't dismiss it from view.

'And you do not kneel,' Abaddon said, his growl not quite letting the words become a question.

'I kneel only before my primarch, Warmaster. Since his death, I kneel before no one. I mean no disrespect.'

'I see.' Talos's attention was drawn to the Talon of Horus for a moment as the Warmaster gestured with the scythe-like claws to the door. 'My brothers, and honoured Night Lord guests... Leave us. The prophet and I have much to discuss.'

Talos's vox-link clicked live. 'We'll be nearby,' Cyrion said.

'We will remain with the Justaerin,' Malek grunted. Talos could hear his eagerness with troubling clarity.

Cyrion had picked up on it, too. 'You sound like you want them to start something.' Neither of the Atramentar replied, though the others could make out muted vox clicks as the two Terminators shared private communication.

Once they were alone in the ruined mess hall, Talos scanned the room, his eyes panning over the wreckage.

'This is not the kind of place I had expected to find you, sir.'

'No?' Abaddon stalked closer, his movements lumbering in the heavy plate, yet somehow more threatening than other Terminators. It was the economy of his movement, Talos realised. The Warmaster's every movement was precise, measured and exact. He wore the armour like a second skin.

'A destroyed mess hall in an internment spire. Hardly the place to find the one who once led us all.'

'I still lead you all, Talos.'

'From a certain point of view,' the Night Lord allowed.

'I wanted to walk the halls of this prison spire myself, and I have neither the time nor the desire to stand upon worthless ceremony. I was here, and I demanded your presence. So it is here that we meet.'

Talos felt his skin crawl at the superiority in the commander's tone. Who was he to speak to one of the sons of Konrad Curze in this way? A captain in a broken Legion, now twisted by the favour of daemons. He deserved respect for his might, but not obeisance. Not fealty or subservience.

'I am here, Warmaster. Now tell me why.'

'So I might meet you, face to face. The Black Legion has its share of sorcerers and prophets, Talos.'

'So I have heard.'

'They are precious to me, and vital to my plans. I take great heed of their words.'

'So I have also heard.'

'Indeed.' The hateful smile came again. 'I wonder to myself, where do you fit in? Are you content with the existence your Legion offers you? Do they respect your gift for what it is?'

And then it was clear: he knew what this was about. How alarmingly unsubtle...

The Night Lord suppressed a growl of anger, eyes narrowed on the flickering *threat* rune that still played across his visor display. His armour's systems tracked his rising heartbeat and, suspecting battle, flooded his veins with potent chemical stimulants. It took several moments for Talos to exhale a shivering breath and speak, ignoring the burn of his energised muscles.

'I am a breed apart from the creatures you call sorcerers, sir.'

Abaddon ceased his vague pacing, looking at his reflection in the silver sheen of his claws. 'You think I do not detect the disapproval in your tone?'

'Evidently not, my lord. It is disgust, not merely disapproval.'

Now Abaddon looked to him, the claws of his relic Talon slicing the air in silent, slow strokes by his side. It almost seemed a habit of his, the way a bored man might crack his knuckles. The Despoiler's claws were always in motion, always cutting, even if it was just air.

'You insult me, Night Lord,' Abaddon mused, still smiling.

'I cannot change the heart of my Legion, Warmaster. I am as you name me: a Night Lord. I am no warp-touched sorcerer, or fallen weaver of spells. I share the gene-seed of the Night Haunter. From my father – not the Ruinous Powers – did I inherit this... gift.'

'Your honesty is refreshing.'

'I am surprised you think so, Warmaster.'

'Talos,' Abaddon said, facing the Night Lord once more. 'Another Black Crusade is in the making.' Here he paused, holding up his claw, and Talos was forcibly reminded of a painting he had once seen of Horus, clutching a burning world in that same gauntlet. He'd assumed, at the time, the world was supposed to be Terra. Ironic then that the painting depicted Horus's ultimate failure – in his grip burned the one world he couldn't conquer.

'This time...' the Warmaster closed his unnatural eyes, and the silver talons trembled, '...this time, the fortress worlds around the Cadian Gate will burn until their surface is nothing but an ashen memory. This time, *Cadia itself* will die.'

Talos watched the Warmaster, saying nothing, until his self-absorbed ecstasy faded and he opened his eyes once more. The Night Lord broke the silence that stretched between them by walking to the corpse of an inmate and kneeling by the body. The man had bled a great deal across the remains of the table he lay upon, but had died from the intense blunt trauma to the side of his head. Talos dipped his first two fingers in the congealing puddle of the mortal's blood, raising them to his speaker grille in order to inhale the coppery scent.

He hungered to taste it, to let the life matter flow through his gene-enhanced form and absorb it into his veins, so he might sense a ghostly echo of the man's dreams, his fears, his desires and terrors.

The wonders of Astartes physiology – to taste the life of those whose blood you have shed. Truly, a hunter's gift.

'You seem unimpressed by my assurance,' the Warmaster said.

'With respect, sir, all of your previous crusades have failed.'

'Is that so? Are you one of my inner circle, to judge whether my plans came to pass and my objectives were met?'

Talos flexed his hand, the gauntlet that would soon be replaced by sections from Faroven's armour. 'You do harm to the Imperium, but never truly advance our cause. Are you asking if the Night Lords will stand with you as you attack Cadia? I cannot speak for my Legion in its entirety. The Exalted will follow you, as he always does. I'm sure many more of our leaders will do the same.'

Abaddon nodded as if this confirmed his point, the veins under his cheeks darkening as he grinned.

'You speak of disunity. Your Legion lacks a figurehead.'

'Many claim to be the Night Haunter's heir. The Talonmaster has vanished, but his claim was no stronger than any other, even with his possession of one of our symbolic relics. Too many other leaders have similar items once carried by our father. Captain Acerbus leads the largest coalition of companies, but again, his insistence reeks of desperation and need. No true claimant has come forth, as you did with your Legion. Our father's throne sits empty.'

'Again, I hear the disquiet in your words.'

'I am not hiding it, Warmaster.'

'Admirable. So tell me: does your heart not cry out to take that throne yourself?'

Talos froze. He hadn't expected this. He'd suspected the Warmaster would seek to use his curse in some way, perhaps even drawing him into the ranks of the Black Legion as a pet advisor. But this...

This was new. And, he suspected, it was a bluff designed to throw his thoughts into disparity.

'No,' he replied.

'You hesitated.'

'You asked a difficult question.'

Abaddon walked closer to Talos, his boots crushing debris beneath each thundering tread. The helms and human skulls impaled upon the trophy racks rattled together, birthing a clacking melody like some barbarous musical instrument.

Threat, the rune flickered, and the Night Lord looked through his red vision at the Warmaster no more than ten metres distant. He couldn't help but compare him to the original bearer of the title. Horus, beloved son of the Emperor, Lord of the Eighteen Legions. Talos had only seen the First Warmaster once, but it was a moment of devastating potency in the storm of his memory.

'I saw the First Warmaster once,' he voiced aloud, without meaning to.

Abaddon chuckled, a series of throaty, predatory grunts. 'Where?'

'Darrowmar. We fought alongside the Luna Wolves in the capital city.'

'The Luna Wolves.' Abaddon openly sneered at the use of his Legion's first name, before they'd become the Sons of Horus in honour of their primarch, and long before they'd become the Black Legion to expunge the shame of their father's failure. 'Days of blindness and war based upon the darkest of lies.'

'True. But they were days of unity,' Talos said, recalling the majesty of Horus at the head of his Legion, his armour of grey-white polished to a finish of ivory and pearl. He was human, but... more. Astartes... but more. Contained within the First Primarch was all that was great and glorious within humanity, distilled to perfection by the fleshsmiths and geneweavers of the Emperor's hidden fortress-laboratories.

To stand within his sight was to bathe in light, to be flooded by inspiration more vital and real than the stinging chemicals pumping through Astartes blood. In his eye-aching brilliance, Horus drew everything to him – merely by taking the field, he ensured he was the fulcrum upon which everything spun. He became the heart of the battle, a maelstrom of slaughter, untouched by the mud and the blood of the battlefield even as he reaped the lives of the foe.

And Talos had barely seen him. He'd formed his opinion of the living god from the other side of a cityscape battleground, seeing little more than the juddering images allowed by his helm's zoomed vision as he sought to assess the Luna Wolves' front lines. It had been like glancing at a moving painting of an ancient hero.

He looked at Abaddon. *How times change.*

'What do you recall of Warmaster Horus?' Abaddon asked.

'My eyes hurt in his presence, even from a distance,' Talos said. 'I am Nostramo-born,' he added, knowing that would explain everything.

'You Night Lords. So literal.' The thought seemed to entertain him, which struck Talos as petty beyond belief. Clarity came upon him in that moment. Abaddon was an avatar for what the Traitor Legions had become. Talos watched him now, knowing neither of them were the equals of their primarch progenitors. None of the Legions could make that claim. They were all mere shadows of their fathers, and their fathers had failed.

The thought was a humbling one, and the weak claws of melancholy reached for his conscious mind again. These encroaching thoughts he dismissed with a scowl, refocusing his attention by acquiring target locks on the weakest points of Abaddon's armour plating. Precious few existed, but he felt his armour's machine-spirit responding, awakening again, teased back into anger. It helped him focus.

'You have still not stated your reasons for summoning me, Warmaster.'

'I will be blunt, then. After all, we have a crusade to forge in the coming days. Tell me, prophet, have you seen anything of the Crythe War in your recent visions?'

'No,' lied Talos immediately.

'No.' The Warmaster narrowed his eyes. 'Just... "No". How very declarative.'

'I have seen nothing that will help you plan, nothing that will bring you new information or aid in any way.'

'But you have seen something.'

'Nothing you have any right to know.'

The claws chimed quietly as they clanged together, Abaddon closing and opening his gauntlet just once. 'I am not famous for my patience,' he said slowly, his voice ripe with threat. 'But it is enough that my suspicions are confirmed. You are a seer, and you have seen what will come.'

'You seem to care a great deal about my visions. I thought you had sorcerers of your own.' A streak of amused pride coloured his words. Abaddon didn't seem to notice, or to care if he did.

'They are having difficulty piercing the warp's veil. You, evidently, have done what they cannot. You have witnessed the future. It should not surprise you that a commander would wish dearly for such information.'

Talos said nothing, knowing what this was building up to.

'Talos, my brother. I have an offer for you.'

'I refuse. I thank you for the honour of whatever this offer might have been, but my answer is no.'

'Why so blatant a refusal?' Abaddon scowled now, the first time he had, and the grimace revealed filthy, blackened teeth behind his bluish lips.

'If you are offering me the chance to lead the Eighth Legion, I refuse because it is an impossible task, and not one within your power to grant. If you are asking me to leave my Legion, I refuse because I have no interest in doing so.'

'You reject my offer without hearing it.'

'Your offer will not be in my interests. There is little of any Legion in what remains to us, Warmaster. I no longer believe we will be the death of the Imperium. I no longer believe we are true to our fathers. Corruption has its claws deep within many of us.'

'Then why do you still fight?' Abaddon's glower remained, his teeth clenched and his eyes raw in their open glare.

'Because I have nothing else. I was born to fight, and forged in the fires of war. I am Astartes. I fight because it is right that we fight. The Emperor abandoned the Great Crusade, and demanded humanity pave the way for His ascension to godhood. I don't expect to topple Him from the Golden Throne, but such hubris, such evil, must always be opposed.'

'And what of Curze?'

Talos stepped closer, his muscles bunched. 'You will not speak his name with such disrespect, Abaddon.'

'You think you intimidate me, worm?'

'I think I address your primarch by his title as the First Warmaster, despite his ultimate failure. You will do the same honour for the lord of my Legion, who was vindicated even in death.'

'Then tell me, what of the Night Haunter? Does his murder mean nothing to you?'

'The Emperor betrayed my gene-father. Even without the Great Heresy's ideals, the need for vengeance alone would be enough for me to live my life only to see the Imperium fall.'

At this, Abaddon nodded again. 'I respect the Night Lords as brothers, but you are right. You are a broken Legion.'

'And you are not?'

The Warmaster turned, his voice dropping to a threatening murmur. '*What* did you say?'

Threat, threat, threat, the rune flickered.

'Do you fight, Warmaster, because you believe you can still win? After centuries of defeat, after failed Black Crusades, after infighting and war has bled your Legion dry and draped you in ignominy among the other Legions? Is it not true your men are slaved to daemons to make up for the great losses you have sustained since the death of your primarch? You leech strength from other sources, because your own Legion's might is almost gone.'

Silence answered this proclamation. Talos broke it again.

'This meeting is a facet of that. You wonder about how my power will benefit your failing armies.'

Abaddon might have laughed. It would have been the act of a great leader to laugh, to humour a lesser warrior, to bring him around to his own way of thinking through persuasion and empathy – even were it all false. But Abaddon was not such a leader. He was shrewd enough, at least, to guess Talos would never be fooled.

The storm bolter barked once. Two shells roared from the muzzles, two bolts thrown by screaming daemon mouths shaped from dirty brass. Talos's chestplate – the defiled aquila of polished ivory resplendent upon it – cracked under the impact, but it wasn't the bolts themselves that brought him low. In a burst of inky mist, black gas streamed around him.

On his knees before he could even blink, his retinal display registered alarms and flashing runic warnings of life signs plummeting. His armour's machine-spirit was enraged, and he felt the rising desire through his connection junctures to slaughter anything living before him. The Astartes instinct. Defending oneself by killing all threats.

The machine-spirit of Talos's armour was a bastardised, hybrid sentience of anger, pride and caution, born from a meshing of the many suits of armour he had cannibalised for use over his years of war. It growled in his blood now, howling through the socket ports in his skull, his spine, his limbs, firing his own rage. He recognised its frustration instantly from the runic display on his visor. It was unable to reconcile depleted life warnings with the insane fact that, somehow, all of the ammunition counters still read at maximum.

He was wounded without returning fire. This was unnatural. It was not how wars were fought. It had never happened before.

'Preysight,' he demanded from his armour's soul. His vision blanketed in thermal vision, a facade of cold blues, but still somehow failed to pierce the choking gas.

And he *was* choking. That in itself was insane. Each breath drew in another wisp of the black gas, filtering in through his cracked chestplate, its scent like that of burning tar and its taste like the burned earth a week after a battle. He felt the muscles in his throat and chest spasm, tightening like cables of iron. Life runes flashed in alarm – runes he'd never seen before.

Poison. He was actually being poisoned.

'Abaddon!' he roared, immediately horrified at the breathy whisper of his voice. 'You die for this…'

It was when he heard the answering laugh that Talos drew *Aurum*. It took him an indeterminate number of heartbeats to realise the blade had fallen from his nerveless grasp to clatter on the wreckage covering the ground. All he tasted was blood and charred soil. All he felt was the cold, cold pain of his lungs going into spasming shock-lock.

'I have an offer for you, prophet,' the Warmaster's voice came from somewhere he couldn't see. He could barely raise his head. He hadn't even managed to look at the split aquila on his chest and assess the damage to his armour. The draining charts and numbers filtered across his vision told him all he needed to know about his condition.

Poisoned. How was that even possible? The gas… daemon-mist…

Kill him before you die.

The thought rose unbidden from the depths of his mind, and – for a moment – the unfamiliar sense of it left him cold. It was closer to a thought than a voice, an urge rather than an order, and in that doubt lay the answer. This close to death, the machine-spirit of his war-plate pushed easily into his fading mind. It was an invasion of unpleasant pressure, so much colder and more focused than the primal emotions and survival instincts usually massaged against his conscious thoughts. Those were easily ignored; tamed with a moment's concentration. This was a lance of ice to the brain, strong enough to twitch his limbs in a dying attempt at obeying the words.

'And,' the Warmaster continued, 'if you will not hear this offer from me, you *will* hear it from my allies.'

'THAT WAS A bolter.'

As soon as he'd said the words, Cyrion raised his own boltgun and levelled it at the bullish helm of Falkus. 'That,' he said again in a lower voice, 'was a bolter. Tell me I'm wrong.' He had the audio readout displays of his helm at the edge of his vision to assure him that he was absolutely correct, but he was caught off-guard and needed to buy time.

The Night Lords and Black Legion squared off in the central aisle, surrounded by a hundred and more kneeling prisoners.

'Abaddon,' they had been chanting. 'Abaddon... Abaddon... Abaddon...' with all the conviction and reverence of a religious rite. But they'd stopped the moment the Night Lords raised their weapons.

'Storm bolter,' corrected Uzas, and they all heard the smile in his voice. 'Not a bolter. Two barrels. Talos is dead. Life rune is unstable.'

It was true. A single bark of a bolt weapon in the distant mess hall, and the life rune had started flickering on the edge of their retinal displays.

As the standoff stretched out, the Black Legion Terminators remained impassive. *Easy for them*, Cyrion thought, *backed up by over a hundred fanatics.*

'Talos,' he voxed. Nothing. He switched channels with a blink at the right rune. 'Septimus.'

Again, nothing. He blinked at a third rune. '*Covenant*, this is First Claw.' Silence.

'We're being jammed,' he voxed to the squad.

'Night Lords,' Falkus of the Black Legion murmured. 'There has been a regrettable incident with your Thunderhawk. Come. We will provide alternate transportation back to your ship.'

'Fight them,' Xarl voxed. 'Kill them all.'

'Blood and skulls and souls,' Uzas sounded like he was drooling again. 'We must fight.'

'Keep your damn heads, you fools.' This from Garadon, Hammer of the Exalted. 'Even we would be overwhelmed in this place.'

'Aye,' Cyrion nodded. 'We find answers first, then take whatever vengeance is deserved.'

'*Fight*,' stressed Xarl. The ignominy of being marched out of here was clearly too much for him. 'We can't leave Talos here.'

'The Legions stand on the precipice of battle with what happens in this moment,' Garadon's gruff voice cut into Xarl's threatened raving. 'And they outnumber us in orbit as well as on the surface. Bide your time, and strike when the prey is weakest.'

'You are a coward, Garadon,' Xarl snarled.

'And you will answer for that slur,' the Hammer of the Exalted replied. 'But lower your bolter. This is not a fight we can win.'

The Night Lords lowered their weapons and allowed themselves to be escorted from the hall. Jeers and laughter followed them as the prisoners rose to their feet. Several hurled bottles or fired stolen shotguns into the air, triggering alert runes across the Night Lords' visors.

'Every single one of these wretches will bleed for this,' Xarl promised. Affirmation blips came back from every member of the squad. A bottle struck Uzas on the side of the helm, and the others heard him laughing.

'What the hell is so funny?' Xarl snapped.

'They played us for fools,' Uzas was grinning. 'Killed Talos. Killed Thunderhawk crew. Captured our gunship. Clever moves. Is it wrong to be impressed that they outplayed us so easily?'

'Shut your mouth,' Xarl said. 'They didn't *kill* Talos. His life rune's still live.'

'Same difference. He's theirs now. Good riddance.'

Cyrion ignored their bickering. Surrounded as they were by kneeling mortals, his secret sense was afire with sensation. Every one of these humans was afraid beneath their masks of worship. Their fears bled into his consciousness in trickling spurts of conflicting voices.

...don't want to die...

...freedom, at last, will they let us go...

...a trick, they'll kill us...

Cyrion closed his eyes, feeling their mass fear threatening to overwhelm his own thoughts in a sickening blur of barely-understood emotion. As a child, he had fallen into the sump-lake in the depths of Joria Hive's underhive foundations. Unable to swim, in the endless seconds before his father had saved him, he'd been sinking slowly into the black, staring up at the fire-lit lightness rippling on the water's surface above. Being around too many humans always reminded him of that one moment, when he'd felt himself fading, swallowed whole and forgotten by some vast extraneous, remorseless force. He'd known he was dying, staring up at the dimming half-light above, feeling everything within his mind slipping from his grasp.

He knew the same now. The feeling was the same, coming with the familiar cold, dull realisation of inevitability. It was just taking much longer to happen.

Cyrion's vision focused as he concentrated on the voices in his vox instead of the whispers within his head. He switched to helm speakers again, letting some of his anger bleed into his tone.

'You. Son of Horus.'

One of the Black Legion Terminators turned, still lumbering forwards. 'Night Lord?'

'What, exactly, has occurred to our Thunderhawk?'

'An event of the most terrible misfortune,' he said, and Cyrion picked up the muted vox clicks as the Black Legionnaires laughed over their internal squad channel. 'As a courtesy, we will return you to orbit with one of our own transports,' Falkus said.

At the end of the hallway, the lift doors rumbled open again. An Astartes in black power armour walked towards them, a smile on his pale features and a glint in his dark eyes.

Cyrion voxed to the others as soon as the newcomer began walking towards them. 'You were right after all, Uzas.'

The Night Lords watched the approaching figure, each one recognising him, each one resisting the urge to aim their weapons and open fire.

Uzas nodded, still amused. 'I told you it was a trap.'

'My brothers, my brothers,' the newcomer said. The oily pools of his eyes drank them in one at a time. 'How it pleases me,' he spoke in fluent Nostraman, 'to see you all again.'

SEPTIMUS AND EURYDICE were still in the cockpit.

Septimus was both annoyed and worried, though he tried to let neither of these emotions show. In fairness, he wasn't doing a tremendous job of it. Eurydice could tell the words he occasionally muttered in Nostraman were curses. She was doing an equally poor job of seeming unafraid, but the Astartes had been gone for long enough to set Septimus's teeth on edge and she found herself infected by his worry.

The vox had died almost an hour before, as soon as the Astartes had descended into the prison spire. With a sudden, sharp crack of feedback, connection had been lost and static was all he'd heard from any of the Astartes since then. That in itself didn't worry him. He doubted there was anything here that could do the demigods any real harm. He was, however, worried about himself and Eurydice.

To no avail, Septimus had been trying the vox once every five minutes since it failed. He could reach neither First Claw in the complex below, nor the *Covenant of Blood* in orbit, and this was starting to smell suspiciously like a trap.

It was time to consider his options.

He'd briefly considered taking off and staying on-station by keeping the gunship in hover a few dozen metres above the platform. That, unfortunately, wasn't viable for two reasons. Firstly, his orders had been to stay where he was. Secondly, even had he broken his orders to take off, *Blackened* didn't have the fuel for sustained hovering on its atmospheric thrusters – at least, not if it wanted to break orbit and return to its waiting strike cruiser. The fuel readouts showed, at his best estimate, that he could burn the engines for perhaps fifteen minutes before he would need to return to the *Covenant*. If his master emerged and needed immediate extraction while he was away, or even while he was burning fuel in an unnecessary hover, they might not make it back into the void.

No. It wasn't even worth considering. So with the doors sealed, the gang ramp closed and the weapon turrets trained on the lift building, Septimus waited, eyes narrowed to slits, watching the ship's sensors and deluding himself into thinking he didn't look as worried as he was.

'Will you relax?' Eurydice asked, shattering his self-deception.

Her boots were up on the control console, and she leaned back into the oversized co-pilot's chair with creaking squeal of leather. Septimus, by comparison, was arched forward over the auspex display, watching the green pulse sweep over the screen every six seconds. It pulsed outwards from an icon of *Blackened* in the centre of the screen.

She made a noncommittal grunt, trying to get his attention.

'What?' he said without looking. Another pulse.

'You're worried.'

'Something like that.'

'When will they get back?' Another pulse, still nothing.

'Do I look like they involve me in their plans?' he laughed, though the sound was forced.

'Just asking. What are you worried about, anyway?'

'The prison below us. Specifically, the inmates.' He nodded to the data-slate resting on the arm of his chair. Its display screen listed a screed of information in tiny green letters. 'This is Internment Spire Delta-Two,' Septimus explained. 'The prisoners kept here are awaiting execution, though they are kept alive to serve a span of years in deep tunnel mining operations as slave labour. These aren't recidivists or minor criminals. They're murderers, rapists and heretics.'

'But the doors are sealed.' An edge of hesitancy crept into her voice now, just a thin suggestion of doubt.

'No door is invulnerable. The flank bulkheads would stop anything I can imagine, but the main gang ramp works through regular hydraulics. It's sealed and locked, but... Look, I'm not worried. Just being prepared.'

'Prepared for what, exactly? Why would anyone rush an Astartes gunship? Talk about a death wish.'

'I don't know. I expect most wouldn't come near us. If they did? Well, maybe some might want to try and flee the planet by stealing the ship. Or maybe, given their incarceration here, they're not all that sane to begin with. Or...' he trailed off.

'Or *what*? Don't just start a sentence like that and leave it hanging.'

He shrugged. 'Maybe if they had learned there was a woman on board...'

She nodded, but he could see she was struggling to maintain her bravado. 'This gunship has, well, guns, right?'

'It... does.'

'I don't like the way you said that.'

'Half of the weapons are inactive, including the main battle cannon. Ammunition is low, and the heavy bolters on the gunship's flanks are no longer slaved to servitors.'

'Why not?'

Another pulse. Another blank screen. 'Because the servitors are dead. They have been for years, and I was the one tasked with dragging the bodies from their ports.'

After several moments of silent staring, another console screen chimed. Septimus turned in his throne, leaning forward to examine the readout.

'Well, well, well...'

'More bad news?' she asked him, not sure she really wanted an answer.

'Not exactly. Another ship just took off – and not one of the bulk landers down there on the plains. This ship was a Thunderhawk-class vessel. Black Legion identification signals.'

'Meaning?'

'The auspex chimed because it registered First Claw on board the ship as it headed into orbit.'

'What? They left us here?'

Septimus was still watching the screen. 'Not all of them. No signal from Talos. He's still in the prison complex.'

He was not a man who enjoyed these kinds of mysteries. Septimus turned from the screen to hit a few console keys. *Doors: Secured*, a flashing icon on the console read. It was the third time he'd checked the doors in the past hour.

As Eurydice drew breath to ask another question, the auspex chimed again. There was nothing foreboding in the sound. It was almost melodic.

'Damn it,' said Septimus, rising from his throne.

Eurydice sat up. The auspex was singing now, tinny chime after tinny chime. 'Are we in trouble?' she asked.

Septimus was staring out of the forward window, at the open elevator doors, and what came spilling out of them.

'Oh, absolutely,' he said, drawing both of his pistols.

'Then give me one of those,' she said as she stood, following his gaze.

'Take them both,' he said, handing them to her before leaning over the control console. 'And don't think about shooting me.'

She gave him a withering look that he never saw. Septimus hit a long sequence of console keys, his fingers a blur.

'What are you doing?' she asked.

'This,' he said, and the gunship's functioning heavy bolter turrets lit up with fire as they unleashed their rage.

JERL MADDOX COULDN'T believe his luck. Freedom.

Freedom.

Freedom after eight years in this damn hellhole. Eight years of eating the cold, bitter grey paste that passed as food, morning, afternoon and night. Eight years of fourteen-hour shifts under the earth of this accursed rock, digging and digging and digging in the vain hope of striking a handful of ore. Eight years of backaches, blurred vision, gums burning from infection, and pissing blood after every beating from the guards.

Yeah, well, payback had come sure enough. He clutched the shotgun to his chest, racking the slide just to enjoy the feeling. Click-chunk. Oh, *hell yes*. This was something else. He'd taken the weapon from Laffian, but that was all good because Laffian had been one of the worst guards in R Sector.

R Sector – 'Omega Level Transgressions Only' – was home no longer for Maddox, and the fact he could still feel Laffian's blood on his face was just that little extra touch of victory.

That was payback, too. Payback for the time Laffian had smacked Jesper around so bad the poor fool's eye had popped out from his broken head. Maddox grinned, the stench of his teeth making his eyes water. Laffian hadn't looked so cocksure with his chest blown open and his leg hacked off at the knee.

He'd screamed about his kids, too. Yeah, like that would make a difference. Maddox's grin became a snigger.

'Shut your mouth, Blackjaw,' someone next to him said. Maddox swallowed, pressing his lips together. In the close confines of the lift car, which was an uncomfortable fit for almost fifty of them, several of the men curled their lips or swore at him in grunting monotone.

'Sorry,' he mumbled, but that just got them complaining again. It wasn't his fault. His gums were infected. His teeth were black and loose in his jaws – the few that remained, anyway. Wasn't like they had access to a doctor in R Sector, was it? And they smelled just as bad, anyway. Fifty of them all sweating and bloody in their white overalls…

'You stink, too,' he muttered. Bodies started to move, to turn in his direction. Maddox lowered his head a little, avoiding all eye contact as the man ahead turned around.

'What's that, Blackjaw?' It was Indriga, a solid two metres of tattooed muscle and knife scars. He'd been stuck on R Sector for killing and eating some poor hab-wife.

'Nothing. Nothing, Indriga.'

'Damn right, nothing. Now shut your mouth before we all throw up.'

He kept his head down, doing his best not to smile. He couldn't help it, though. He kept seeing Laffian howling and thrashing around with no leg… And the trembling smile became a blurted cough of a snigger. A droplet of warm, thick saliva plopped onto the stock of his stolen shotgun. Laffian's gun. He laughed again.

The men around him turned away, swearing. He likely would have died then and there had the lift not ground to a halt and the doors opened. The thin, ash-tasting air floated in to meet them as the prisoners looked out onto the landing platform.

'There it is,' Indriga said, already walking out.

It was a ship – a small vessel by troop ship standards, and that was about the only frame of reference Maddox had; he'd been Imperial Guard before his arrest for… whatever they'd said he'd done. He hadn't done anything, and he knew it. No way. Not him. He was Guard, through and through. Damned if he could even remember what they'd insisted he'd done wrong, now…

Someone shoving him forward jolted his senses back to the present.

'Let's take it,' one of them said.

It was vaguely hawkish, with downswept wings, and it was dark blue, like the colour of the deepest oceans. The thought of that made Maddox's stomach quiver and bunch. He hated the sea. He couldn't put his head below the surface without imagining *something* deep down there, looking back at him.

He was one of the stragglers, while most of his fellow prisoners ran forwards with their stolen clubs and guns held high. Their saviours – the god-warriors in black – had chosen some of the strongest and fittest inmates in R Sector to come up here and perform this sacred duty. There were people in this ship, and they had to die. The gods had spoken.

And, *hell yes*, one of them was supposed to be a woman.

It was good to be free. It was good to be the chosen champion of the gods that had bestowed upon him the freedom he so richly deserved. Even the awful air tasted better than usual.

These were the thoughts swirling around Jerl 'Blackjaw' Maddox's mind as he died. When he went down, he was still too lost in his thoughts of freedom to really comprehend what was happening to him, and he died with his body in pieces, still smiling, and still smelling terrible as he laughed without any sound leaving his lips.

The turret cannons on the gunship blazed away, bolt rounds streaming out to thump home into yielding flesh only to detonate a moment after impact. Inmates were reduced to shattered husks of meat and bone, thrown across the landing platform in ugly smears. From the vox speakers mounted on the Thunderhawk's exterior, a voice spoke calmly in heavily-accented Gothic.

'Welcome, all of you,' Septimus said. 'Please enjoy the last mistake you'll ever make.'

CYRION CHECKED HIS bolter again, then clamped it once more to his thigh armour.

'Stop that,' voxed Malek. 'You look irritated.'

'I can't think why,' Cyrion sneered.

First Claw and their Atramentar escorts sat in the restraint thrones of a Black Legion gunship, their surroundings vibrating as the Thunderhawk juddered through the atmosphere.

'Will they take *Blackened*?' Cyrion asked. 'It would be a foolish error if they tried.'

'They just wanted Talos,' Xarl said. He clicked the blinking rune that confirmed a private channel with Cyrion. 'And the Atramentar knew it would happen. They were here to ensure we did not step out of line, and backed down at the first need to shed blood. The Exalted planned this.'

Cyrion's voice was tired. The weight of the prisoners' fears, although faded now, still rested heavily on his mind. 'I grow weary of this, Xarl.'

'Of what?'

'The treachery. The death of trust. Of my mind aching from the silent weeping terror of mortals.'

Xarl said nothing at first. Sympathy was not in his blood. 'You are tainted, Cyrion,' he said at last.

'Something like that,' Cyrion replied. He took a breath. 'The Exalted has always resented Talos's position in the Legion, as a favoured son of our father, but this was a step too far. To attempt to kill him? Is Vandred insane?'

Xarl's response came after a bitter laugh. 'What makes you so sure he wanted Talos dead? Out of the way, certainly. Perhaps among the ranks of the Black Legion. A gain for both Abaddon and the Exalted.'

'Like Ruven,' Cyrion said.

'Yes, brother,' Xarl said, his voice lower now. 'Like Ruven.'

EURYDICE SWORE WITH feeling as the Thunderhawk shook again.

'Throne, I don't want to die here.'

Septimus didn't turn to look at her. His focus was entirely on the ammunition readouts, which were dropping with heart-wrenching speed. He clicked the vox live.

'This is the Eighth Legion Thunderhawk *Blackened*.'

'It's not working,' Eurydice swallowed her panic at his desperate attempts. 'The *Covenant* can't hear you. Talos can't hear you.'

'Shut up,' he replied. 'This is the Eighth Legion Thunderhawk *Blackened*, hailing the battle-barge *Hunter's Premonition*. Do you read?'

'The… the what?'

'Another one of our ships is in orbit,' he said. 'One of the Night Lords' flagships.'

'Why aren't you shooting?'

He didn't even need to glance at the ammo displays. 'Because every gun that can track a target this close to the hull is out of shells.'

The cockpit shook again, this time hard enough to throw Eurydice back onto her chair.

'Throne!' she shouted. Septimus winced.

'That wasn't good. They're inside.'

'*What?*'

He didn't answer her. 'This is the Eighth Legion Thunderhawk *Blackened*, hailing the battle-barge *Hunter's Premonition*. Please respond.'

Voices could be heard yelling in the deck below. The prisoners that had survived the annihilation offered by the heavy bolters were definitely inside now.

'Damn it.' Septimus abandoned the console and pulled the curved hacking blade that was strapped to his calf. 'Worth a try.'

Eurydice tossed him one of the pistols.

'Looks like I won't be guiding your heretic masters through the Sea of Souls after all.' She smiled a nasty little grin, somewhere between bitterness, terror and triumph.

Septimus raised his pistol at the closed cockpit door. 'We'll see.'

IX

FOUR GODS

'Our brothers run to the edges of the Imperium to cower in the shadows of the Dark Gods that protect them. Only we, the Night Lords, the sons of Konrad Curze, are strong enough to stand alone. We will bring our wrath upon the empire that betrayed us, and though the ages may see us divided and broken by the endless war ahead, we will stand untainted until the stars themselves die.'

– The war-sage Malcharion
Epilogue of his work, *The Tenebrous Path*

TALOS OPENED HIS eyes to nothingness.

To one who saw through pitch darkness as naturally as a mortal man saw in daylight, this was both unwelcome and unfamiliar. He turned, still seeing nothing, unsure if this was because there was nothing to see in the blackness or if he had lost his sight. It occurred to him with no small amusement that he'd inflicted this very fate on so many mortals over the years, forcing them to awaken in the darkness of the *Covenant*'s interior. A cautious smile spread across his lips as he enjoyed the irony.

The air was cold on his flesh.

Flesh? At the first hints of the sensation, he could see himself now – his hands before his face, bone-white and blue-veined, and his tunic of dark weave. He was out of his battleplate. How could this be? Had his wound been so terrible that First Claw had cut him from his armour and...

Wait. His wound.

His pale hands pulled open the front of his robe, baring his chest to the darkness. His torso, a pale, sculpted echo of ancient Romanii marble statues of their warlike gods, was unbroken by any wound. Across his sternum were the junction plugs and connection sockets required to link into the powered systems of his armour, and he could make out the hard shell of the black carapace implanted beneath his skin, forming the sub-dermal armour that sheathed his form in additional protection and allowed him to interface with his battleplate's senses.

But no wound.

'Talos,' a voice spoke from the blackness. He turned to meet it, hands reaching for weapons that didn't exist here, wherever here was.

The speaker was a Night Lord. Talos recognised the armour instantly, for it was his own.

In the nothingness, he faced himself, staring at his armoured image with something approaching fury.

'What madness is this?'

'A test,' his reflection said, removing its helm. The face beneath the helmet was, and was not, his own visage. Eyes of silver stared back at him, and the centre of his forehead was branded with a stylised rune of sickening devotion. The burn mark was still fresh, still trickling blood down his reflection's face.

'You are not me,' Talos said. 'I would never wear the slave mark of the Ruinous Powers.'

'I am what you might be,' his image smiled, revealing teeth as silver as his eyes. 'If you were bold enough to unlock your potential.'

And if you will not hear this offer from me, you will hear it from my allies. The Warmaster's words came back to him now, trickling into his consciousness as the blood trickled into his reflection's alien eyes.

'You are not one of the Ruinous Powers,' he said to the image before him. 'You are not a god.'

'Am I not?' it replied, smiling indulgently.

'No god would be so brazen, so unsubtle. You would turn your eyes upon one soul? Never.'

'I turn my eyes to a trillion souls with each passing moment. It is the nature of a god to exist in such a way.'

An ugly thought clawed its way up from Talos's doubts to reach his lips. 'Am I dead?'

'No,' the god smiled again, 'though you are wounded in the world of flesh.'

'Then this is the warp? You have taken my spirit from my body.'

'Be silent. The others come.'

He was right. Other figures manifested about him – one behind, one to the left, one to the right, taking the cardinal points around where he stood in the darkness. He couldn't focus upon them. Each time he turned, he saw nothing except the others existing at the edges of his vision.

'This,' said the first figure, 'is what I offer you.' He reached out a gauntleted hand to Talos. 'You are keen of mind and great of vision. You know your armies of god-sons will fail without true gods to lead them. Your flesh gods have fallen. Your fathers are slain. You are godless, and in godlessness lies defeat.'

'Touch me and die,' the Astartes warned. 'Mark my words, false god. If you touch me, you will die.'

'I am Slaa Neth. I am the One Who Thirsts. I am a god, more than your gene-father ever was. And this,' the figure repeated, 'is what I offer you.'

Talos…

…opened his eyes to a battlefield.

A battlefield he claimed, heart and soul. The enemy, the Imperial army, was reduced to a graveyard of wrecked tanks and corpses that reached from horizon to horizon.

He stood above his warriors as they kneeled before him, feeling the pleasant sting of some vicious new battle chemical stimulant flooding his veins. He was wounded, for there were cracks in his swollen armour where reddish ichor flowed down his war-plate. These wounds, great rents and rips in his flesh open to the chill air of the battlefield, ached with a pleasure so intense he cried his thanks to the stars above.

Was this what it was to be a primarch? To laugh at wounds that would destroy even an Astartes? To feel war as an amusing diversion, while crushing a million enemies under the might of invincible armies?

Perhaps this was what the Night Haunter had felt. This exaltation. Blood slick claws tore fresh rents in his cheek as he scratched himself, laughing at the delicious pain. Pain itself became a joke to those who could never die.

'Prince Talos,' his troops were shouting up at him. 'Prince Talos.'

No, not shouting. Worshipping. They bowed and cried and prayed for his attention.

This…

'…IS WRONG,' TALOS growled. 'The Night Haunter was never exalted above us as a perfect, immortal being. He was moribund and cursed, stronger for all the trials and agonies he endured.

'This,' he finished, turning from Slaa Neth, 'is not how he lived. It is not how I will live, either.'

'Cyrion,' the figure smiled. Talos hadn't ever smiled like that in his life.

'What of him?' the Astartes narrowed his black eyes, instinctively reaching for weapons that weren't there.

'His soul has felt my caress. Your brother hears the fears of every living thing. My gift to him.'

'He resists.'

'On the surface, he resists. The parts of his mind that shout silently relish the sounds of weeping souls. He feeds on fear. He enjoys what he senses.'

'You are lying,' Talos said, but his broken conviction was evident in the growl. 'Begone.'

The first figure faded with a laugh, unseen by Talos, who now stared at the second. He wasn't surprised to see another image of a Night Lord, his own armour facing him once more. Talos felt a smile creeping across his lips at the sight: it was his armour laid bare, the cannibalism and repairs left unpainted and visible to the naked eye. His chestplate was still the deep blue of the Ultramarines. The armour of his leg was the royal yellow of the Imperial Fists, and the thigh guard attached was the gunmetal grey of the crippled Steel Confessors Chapter. A harlequin's display of colours and allegiances made up the figure's war-plate, and Talos lost himself in the memories of where and when each piece was taken. Most, he'd not even thought about for years. Decades, even.

The shoulder guard ripped from the corpse of a Crimson Fists veteran was a particularly pleasant recollection. They'd fought hand to hand, an uncomplicated brawl of fury against fury, gauntlets pounding cracks in each other's armour until Talos had managed to crush the other warrior's windpipe. Once the loyalist Astartes was strangled into unconsciousness, Talos had broken his spine and smashed his skull open against the hull of First Claw's waiting Land Raider. With the Crimson Fist finally dead, the Night Lord let the body fall to the ground.

Strange, how the centuries were affecting his memory. He'd believed once that his recollection was almost eidetic. Now, he realised he'd forgotten the most ferocious three minutes of fighting in his entire life.

The second figure removed his helm, showing a face that mirrored his own but for the curving symbol tattooed on its pale cheek.

'You know me,' the second figure said, and it was right, Talos did know. He recognised the faintly patronising cadence in the man's speech, and the sickly sweet scent rising from his armour. The same smell emanated from the Exalted.

'You are the Shaper of Fate,' Talos said. 'Vandred is one of your slaves.'

The figure nodded, his black eyes a perfect image of Talos's own. 'He is one of mine. A champion of my cause, a beneficiary of my gifts. Not a slave. His will is his own.'

'I believe differently.'

'Believe what you will. He is of some value to me. You, however, could be so much more.'

'I have no interest in...'

...power.

That was the first sensation that drummed from his twin hearts, as though they pushed strength itself through his body with each dual beat. This was not the laughable power of blithe immortality and pleasure, but something altogether more familiar. He turned his head to regard the others on the command deck.

The Atramentar, all eight of them, knelt before him. Beyond them, the bridge crew worked their stations; each and every one a human with a servitor aide, all working diligently.

He gestured to the Terminators abasing themselves before him.

'Rise.'

They rose, taking their places flanking his throne.

As clear as the sound of his own breathing within his battle helm, as real as his own red-bathed sight, he felt the sudden surety that one of the Atramentar would speak. It would be about the Exalted's punishment.

'Lord,' growled Abraxis, the Atramentar warrior closest to the throne. 'The Exalted awaits your judgement.'

He knew then, before he even spoke, that the Exalted would break under thirty-eight night cycles of physical and psychic torture. The Atramentar could provide the former. Talos himself would provide the latter.

'Mark my words, brothers,' Talos said. 'He will not last forty nights under our care.'

The eight Terminators nodded, knowing he spoke the truth, knowing he had foreseen it in the winds of fate.

'We are one hour from our destination, lord,' said one of the mortal bridge officers. Talos closed his eyes, and smiled at the images he saw imprinted in his mind.

'When we re-enter real space, seek the engine signatures of three freighters using the third moon as shield against auspex returns. Cripple them quickly, and ready First, Second and Third Claws for boarding actions.'

The whispers began. They thought he couldn't hear them – the whispers about his new power, about Tenth Company's resurging strength. Let them praise him in whispers. He needed no obsequiousness to his face.

Talos relaxed into the command throne, letting his thoughts drift into the infinity of what was yet to come, feeling the skeins of fate like a thousand threads under his fingertips. Each strand led to a possible future that played out before his eyes, if he merely concentrated for a single moment. The future...

'...IS UNWRITTEN.' HE took a breath, feeling naked without his armour and swallowing the rising urge to slay these apparitions before him. 'I am a seer, and I know the path of the future is darkened by choices yet unmade.'

His reflection, in its salvaged armour, shook its head. 'I can offer you the secret sight any mortal must have in order to pierce the mists.'

'My second sight is pure.' Talos spat on the chestplate of the patchwork armour, where – much to his discomfort – the Imperial eagle still shone undefiled. 'Yours is the bane of sanity. Leave.'

He turned to the third, aware of a buzzing sound that felt almost tactile, crawling against his skin. Flies covered the armour of the third figure, fat and blood-red, though patches of occasional blue showed through the insect vermin as they swarmed over the armour's surface in a rippling, random tide.

The figure wore no helm. The face was his own, blighted by swollen sores and infected cuts. Through cracked lips which bled a thin orange fluid, the figure shook its head, and spoke with the voice of a grunting, drowning beast.

'I was summoned here,' it said, 'but you will never be one of my champions. I have no use for you, and you have no will to wield the power I offer.'

Talos fixed on the first point of cohesion in all this foolish madness. 'Who summoned you?'

'One of your kind wove his pleas into unspace for a flicker of my attention. A magus, begging into the warp.'

'An Astartes? A Night Lord? A human?'

The figure faded, taking its rank stench into oblivion as it went.

'Who *summoned* you?' Talos cried into the darkness.

When silence was the only reply, he turned to the fourth and final figure, the act of facing it bringing it into being.

The last figure showed the greatest deviation from Talos's own image, and that alone set the Night Lord's lip into a disrespectful sneer. This figure, unlike the others, was in motion as if unable to remain still. It swayed from foot to foot, hunched over akin to a beast ready to leap, breathing rasping from its helmet's vox speakers.

The armour itself was red, the red of a body's darkest blood, edged in bronze so filthy it looked as dull and worthless as copper. It was still his armour, but lacking his familiar trophies and sporting fresh battle damage, as well as the repainted surfaces and bronze modifications, made it an unnerving sight. Seeing his most treasured possession so twisted…

'Make this good,' he said, teeth clenched.

The figure reached up, removing its helm with shaking hands. The face it revealed was a mess of scars, burns and bionics, framing a malevolent grin.

'I am Kharnath,' it grunted through the toothy smile.

'I know that name.'

'Yes. Your brother Uzas cries it as he takes skulls for my throne.'

'He is one of your slaves?' Talos couldn't tear his eyes from seeing his own face so damaged. Half of the head was replaced by oil-smeared bionic plating that fused with raw, inflamed skin at the edges. The flesh that remained was blistered and uneven from burn scarring, or darkened by badly-sealed cuts from what must have been horrendous blows to offset the enhanced healing of Astartes physiology.

Most unnerving of all was the way he swayed, hunched over and ape-like, with the same dead-eyed grin Uzas wore when trying to maintain his attention on a difficult conversation.

'Blood,' it wheezed, 'and souls. Blood for the Blood God. Souls for the Soul Eater.'

'Is Uzas your slave? Answer me.'

'Not yet. Soon. Soon he will stand as a champion among my warriors. But not now. Not yet.'

'Whoever summoned you to win me to your allegiance has wasted their time. This is almost laughable.'

'Time is short,' the figure still grinned. 'And such sights I have to show you.'

Talos had more insults to offer, more rejections to voice, but found he couldn't speak. His lungs locked, feeling like slabs of quivering stone behind his fused ribs. It was a savage echo of the moment he'd been poisoned, and he felt the same sensation as the meat within his body shuddered, stealing his breath. This time, as he fell to his knees, his breathless wheezes weren't curses, but laughter.

The warrior of blood was fading. Talos knew in the world of flesh, his lungs were purging the taint that brought him here.

'Witness my gifts,' Kharnath said, desperate now, ferocious in his eagerness. 'See the strength I offer. Do not abandon this one chance!'

'Go back to hell,' the Night Lord grinned through bloody teeth, and vomited black mist into the nothingness.

Talos opened his eyes again.

Immediately, he felt vulnerable. He was on his back. Prone.

Filtered through the red of his visor display, he recognised the scarred ceiling of the mess hall, and his targeting reticule marked three figures standing above him. He did not know who they were or what their presence indicated – all three were mortals in dark robes marked by blasphemous symbols, backing away as soon as his consciousness returned.

'Preysight,' he said, and their vague identities were further masked, reduced to the rich blur of thermal traces.

The first died as Talos rose to his feet and pounded his fist into the human's face. The Night Lord felt the man's head give with a wrenching snap of skull bone, and the corpse spun away without another sound. He was on the second robed figure before the first had hit the rubble-strewn ground, gauntlets clasped around the mortal's frail neck, eliciting several wet clicks as he squeezed and twisted. The mortal's eyes bulged as the sound of dry twigs snapping echoed into the air. Once the man's head was wrenched backwards, after several seconds of teasing enjoyment, Talos let that body fall in turn.

The third figure was trying to escape, running for a set of double doors that led deeper into the prison complex. Three sprinted strides brought the Night Lord within reach, and he clawed at the fleeing heat-blur. The thermal smear screamed in his hands.

He wasn't even hurting it, yet.

Talos lifted the smudged miasma of reds and yellows off the ground, and voided his preysight. A human face, male, middle-aged and weeping, met his natural vision.

'*Going somewhere?*' the Astartes growled through his vox speakers.

'Please,' the man wept, 'please don't kill me.' Through his helm's olfactory receptors, Talos scented the cloying incense on the mortal's robes, and the sour reek of his breath. He was infected with... something. Something within his body. A cancer, perhaps, eating at his lungs...

Taint. He reeked of taint.

Talos let the man stare into the impassive skulled face of his helm for several more beats of his panicked, mortal heart. *Let the fear build.* The words of his gene-father, the teachings of the VIII Legion: *Show the prey what the predator can do. Show that death is near. The prey will be in your thrall.*

'Do you wish to join your friends in death?' he snapped, knowing his helm's speakers turned the threat into a mechanical bark.

'No, please. Please. *Please.*'

Talos shivered involuntarily. Begging. He had always found begging particularly repulsive, even as a child in the street gangs of Atra Hive on Nostramo. To reveal that level of weakness to another being...

With a feral snarl, he pulled the man's weeping, pleading face against the cold front of his helm. Tears glistened on the ceramite. Talos felt his armour's machine-spirit roil at the new sensation, like a river serpent thrashing in deep silt. It woke again to feed on the mortal's sorrow and fear.

'Tell me,' the Night Lord growled, 'your master's name.'

'R-Ruv–'

Talos snapped the mortal's neck, and stalked from the room.

Ruven.

RUVEN RESISTED THE urge to shrink before the Warmaster's displeasure.

Abaddon's claw scraped less than lovingly over the sorcerer's shoulder guard, tearing the oath scroll that was bound there. Several strips of the hallowed parchment ghosted to the ground, floating patiently on the breath of an invisible wind.

'He has awakened early,' Abaddon repeated Ruven's last words back to him.

'Yes, my Warmaster. And,' – he hated to add this – 'he has slain my acolytes.'

Abaddon gurgled laughter through a fanged maw. 'You were of the Night Lords before you came to my Legion, yet their actions surprise you now.'

Ruven inclined his helm with its lightning bolts painted onto the black ceramite. He was both intrigued and confused by the Warmaster's rhetorical statement.

'Yes, my Warmaster.'

'That makes your carelessness doubly entertaining.'

Abaddon and Ruven stood on the ground floor of the prison complex, overseeing the ragged march of convicts towards the waiting slave ship that rested, slug-shaped and fattened for cargo capacity, on the dusty red plain beneath the prison mountain. Legion serfs, servitors and the hulking form of black-clad Astartes directed the column of convicts, occasionally serving out beatings or – in a few instances – executions, if a convict's jubilation at freedom brought him to attempt an escape.

Robed acolytes, dressed identically to the humans Talos had slaughtered only minutes before, walked alongside the column, proselytising about the glory of the Warmaster, the false rule of the Golden Throne, the abominations done in the Emperor's name by His armies, and the inevitability of the Imperium's demise in the name of justice. Several of these priests shrieked at the thousands of prisoners in gibbering tongues unknown to all but the Dark Gods' favoured servants, seeking any recognition within the convicts' eyes, hoping to stumble across a Chaos-tainted individual and raise such a blessed scion of the Ruinous Powers out of the ragtag cannon fodder regiments of slaves being formed from the prison world's population.

Solace would be stripped bare of life before the sun rose.

The sorcerer, Ruven, still said nothing.

'Your acolytes were worthless anyway,' Abaddon said. 'Listen to these preachers, howling about the unworthiness of the False Emperor. Such theatrics. And for what? Every soul upon this world was betrayed by the Imperium. Discarded, hated and forgotten – purely for the sin of living their lives as they chose. These men need no ideology beyond learning they will be given the chance to earn vengeance through bloodshed.'

'If my Warmaster does not approve of the methods of the acolytes I have trained–'

'Do I sound like I approve?'

'No, my Warmaster.'

'Cease scurrying, Ruven. Where is the Night Lord prophet now?'

Ruven closed his eyes, resting his gauntleted hand against the side of his helm as if trying to make out a sound in the distance.

'Making his way to the landing platform, my Warmaster.'

'Good.' The Astartes helms spiked by the Despoiler's trophy racks clattered together as Abaddon turned to the sorcerer. 'You were foolish to let your acolytes remain as long as they did.'

'I was, my Warmaster. Their chants were necessary to maintain the vision, but the prophet threw off the toxins quicker than I had anticipated.'

'Am I to assume he resisted your attempts at conversion?' Abaddon's voice betrayed just how little faith he'd had in the idea from the beginning.

'He refused the Dark Ones, my Warmaster. To their faces. This was not some minor conjuration – I summoned reflections of the Four Powers. A trickle of power from the winds of the warp, each to offer their gifts.'

The blasphemous symbols branded onto Abaddon's flesh burned and itched with maddening intensity. 'What did he see? What was so easy to refuse?'

'I know not, my Warmaster. But his vision was true. I felt the presence of the Four. A momentary glance of their attention, if you will.'

Abaddon chuckled. The sound lacked even a shadow of humour. 'Grotesque and unsubtle, but deeply amusing.'

'Yes, my Warmaster.'

'Return to orbit, Ruven. Your work here is done.'

The sorcerer hesitated, clutching his staff made from the fused bones of tyrannic-breed xenos. 'Do you not wish to me intercept the Night Lord and make another attempt?'

Abaddon watched the column ahead, where one of his Black Legion Astartes was dragging a screaming prisoner from the line. With a single swipe of a blade, the human's head left his shoulders.

'He has been made to feel vulnerable, and his Legion looks even weaker in his eyes. The cracks already in his resolve will soon split wide. This was never about converting the puritan bastard in one fleeting moment. It was merely the first move in a much longer game of Regicide.'

'Shall I inform the Exalted of our failure?'

Abaddon grinned. '*Our* failure?'

'*My* failure, Warmaster.'

'Better. No, I will speak with the Exalted myself and inform him that his pet seer survived untainted. Vandred was a fool to think it would happen so quickly.'

'Then I shall do as you bid, my Warmaster.'

Abaddon didn't answer. Such an obvious statement needed no affirmation. Instead he turned, irritation touching his feral features for a moment.

'Did you at least kill the slaves?'

The Exalted had won the orbital battle for him in a fraction of the time Abaddon had planned for. The least he could do to repay the Night Lord commander was a little favour like that.

'*Bleed the slaves on board the Thunderhawk,*' the Exalted had asked. '*But allow nothing to be traced to either Legion.*'

'*Whatever you wish, brother,*' Abaddon had replied. '*What reason do you have for making this look like some nonsensical accident?*'

The Exalted had smiled to hear it described like that. '*A petty reason, but a necessary one. Eliminating the allies of a potential rival. My prophet gathers his resources. He will not take my place as commander.*'

Abaddon found that rather quaint. The Exalted's claws had to be clean of this murder. Amusing to see how subtle these Night Lords could be when they chose.

'I sent fifty prisoners, my lord,' said Ruven. 'Their Thunderhawk was overrun, and the other Night Lords returned to orbit in one of our ships.'

'Fifty.' How amusingly excessive. 'Against how many?'

'Two slaves.'

Abaddon nodded, looking back at the columns of freed convicts. Fifty against two, and the crime apparently blameless.

At least something had been done right.

TALOS HAD BEEN unable to reach any of First Claw on the vox, nor had he made contact with *Blackened* or the *Covenant of Blood*. He suspected jamming, though to what purpose, he couldn't begin to guess. Killing them all down here made no sense at all, for there would be no gain for the Black Legion. While Abaddon may have had a thousand faults, with overconfidence first among them, he was not a fool. His grasp of tactical insight had only grown stronger over the centuries.

Then again, nothing the Black Legion did was ever particularly predictable. Once, Talos thought, they were the best of us.

How the mighty are fallen.

As the lifter doors opened, he stared at the bodies spread across the landing platform. It took no time at all to see they had been sectioned by heavy bolter fire. Talos's attention immediately fixed upon the Thunderhawk, silent on its grey clawed landing gear, its forward gang ramp lowered. Black streaks of burned and twisted metal showed on the blue hull where explosives had been employed to wreck the ramp's hydraulics. The convicts had evidently been extremely well-equipped.

Talos was already walking forward, crushing meat and bone underfoot, his blade and bolter at the ready.

'Hnnngh,' one of the nearby corpses wheezed at him. Talos didn't break stride. He glanced at the black-toothed, bleeding ruin of a man, and destroyed its head with a single bolt shell. The gunshot's report echoed off the Thunderhawk's hull.

'Septimus,' he voxed.

The answer he received did not please him.

X

THE HUNTERS HUNTED

THEY HAD TAKEN her.

They had defiled *Blackened* with the foul mortal scent of panicked fear; they had torn Septimus to pieces, and they had taken Eurydice.

Talos sheathed his blade and locked his bolter to his thigh, kneeling by the command throne where Septimus lay unmoving. Dark smears of blood across the floor showed where the slave had dragged himself. He lounged in the pilot's throne, sprawled like a puppet with cut strings, a mess of bloody bruises, broken limbs and shattered bones.

He still breathed. Talos wasn't sure how.

The Night Lord kicked a convict's corpse aside, removing his helm and kneeling by his artificer. The rich scent of flowing blood and the reeking stink of recent death assailed his naked senses. Septimus coughed flecks of fresh blood to his sliced lips, turning to face the Astartes.

'They took her,' he said, his voice surprisingly clear. 'Master, I'm sorry, I can't see. They took her.'

Talos withdrew a syringe and a roll of self-adhesive synskin bandage weave from his thigh-mounted narthecium. The supplies he bore now were a hollow shadow of the old Apothecary tools he'd once carried, but those were lost an age ago, on a nameless world in the years after the Great Heresy split the galaxy.

The first thing he did was inject a cocktail of blood coagulant, pain-killers and Astartes plasma into Septimus's thigh. The second was to bandage what remained of his slave's face.

'They took her,' Septimus said again as the weave was wrapped around his eyes.

'I know.' Talos rose to his feet again, after spraying disinfectant on the open wounds of the mortal's legs, torso and arms. He tied off the worst gashes with tourniquets, and left the bandages within Septimus's reach on the control console.

'You must use the rest yourself. The bandages are by the secondary thrust levers.'

'Yes, master.'

'They used explosives to breach the main ramp doorway.' It was not a question.

'Yes, master.'

'Understood. Rest, Septimus.'

'I can't see,' the slave repeated. His voice was still strong, but his head lolled with the onset of both shock and the effects of the syringe's contents hitting his organs. 'They took my eyes.'

'They took one of them. The other is damaged, but not lost.' Talos was searching the corpses, each one felled by las-rounds or vicious hacks of Septimus's feral world cleaver. The two serfs had fought like tigers before being overwhelmed – the evidence of their defiance was all around, mutilated and silent in death.

'If I can't see,' Septimus rested his head against the rest of his throne, 'I can't fly us back to the *Covenant.*'

'That is not important at the moment. Do you know what happened to First Claw?'

The slave swallowed, the sound thick and wet. 'Back in orbit. A Black Legion Thunderhawk.'

Talos breathed out through clenched teeth. An unsubtle trap that, nevertheless, they had all walked right into.

'Be silent,' he said to Septimus. 'Do not move.'

'Are you going for her?'

'I said to be silent.'

'Hunt well, master.'

'Always.'

Talos, Astartes of First Claw, Tenth Company, VIII Legion, stalked towards the cockpit doors. He gripped his stolen power blade in one hand, and with the other he replaced his helmet, blanketing his sight in the murder-red of his targeting vision. Over his shoulder, the inhuman warrior spoke four words to his wounded slave, the promise emerging from the skull helm as a mechanical snarl.

'*Back in a minute.*'

IT HAD BEEN a long time since the hunter had moved with such purpose.

Too long, he realised. He had lost grip of his own purity, ignored the simple power brought about from being true to one's nature.

He found the instincts flared into life as soon as his twin hearts started beating faster. He ran, the boots of his ceramite second skin pounding on the metal decking. The sound was a welcome warning, a tribal war drum, the threatening heartbeat of an enraged god. The hunter would take no pains to mask his approach. Let the enemy know that death was coming for them.

He moved through the prison complex, corridor by corridor, not trusting the lift to deliver him, placing his faith in the strength of his own renewed vigour. It dawned on him as he sprinted that in the hour since his poisoning and the awakening from his magus-induced vision, a thick sluggishness had settled into his bones. This weakness faded now, purged in the flow of honest adrenaline.

Eurydice. Curse them for taking her, and curse the Black Legion for engineering this petty little trap. She was to be the *Covenant*'s Navigator. Talos would stand for nothing else, not after seeing so clearly in his vision how she would be discovered on the surface of Nostramo's remnants.

Lower and lower into the complex, he ran with unrestrained pleasure at the battle stimulants tingling through his blood. His war-plate's machine-spirit wanted this hunt. Its dim sentience was alive and sharing his joy. They both needed this.

In the corner of his visor, a rune burned its way into his sight. The Nostraman numeral 8. It pulsed with a heartbeat of its own, listing life signs and distance from his position in urgent red lettering. The surgery that blocked Eurydice's warp eye with a small iron plate was not the only modification the Legion's servitors had made to the Navigator. Implanted in her throat was a locator beacon, ticking its position to any Night Lords tuned to its frequency. A standard implantation for the slaves of the VIII Legion.

It took exactly six minutes and thirty-one seconds to reach the basement generatorium chambers. Almost seven minutes of running through stilled, lifeless corridors, past empty cells, and an equal number of hallways still dense with the sweating mortal flesh of convicts waiting to be loaded into slave ships. Some of them had reached out to him, mistaking him for one of their Black Legion saviours. The hunter answered their worship with swings of his blade as he ran, not allowing himself to slow down even to end their irritating blasphemies. Angry, scared cries followed in his wake each time the sword sang. These grunts and bestial shouts of animals herded for the slaughter, panicked by a larger predator, almost brought a grin to his lips. The hunter tried not smile, though their very existences amused him.

So weak. So scared.

Six minutes and thirty-one seconds after he had left the Thunderhawk on the landing platform, Talos reached the basement. Able to survive the drop, he'd fallen the final three floors by tearing open a sealed elevator chute door and leaping into the darkness. He landed with an echoing thud that rang out throughout the prelim chambers of the generatorium floors.

Wasting no time, Talos resumed his sprint, running headlong through the empty control room. Great windows took up one wall, facing out into a vast domed cavern, housing the grinding, clanking generators powering the sprawling prison complex above. Each of the twenty generators stood five storeys tall – edifices of hammering pistons, whirring cogs and thrumming power cell units wedged into their sides like the scales of some caged reptilian beast. Between this miniature city, walkways and gangways were illuminated by the flashing red of emergency lighting.

His vision wavered, rippling lines of distortion dancing across his lens displays. Runes warped and cancelled. Electrical distortion. A great deal of it. It was killing his helm's input receptors.

So much power. Talos scanned the control room, large enough for a staff of thirty or more, though devoid now of all life. *Void shields?* This much power couldn't be purely for lighting the multi-towered spire above. These generators must also power the prison's void shields, preventing orbital bombardment or meteor strike.

Defending a fortress full of criminals from death, though they were slated for execution anyway? *Ah, the wasteful ignorance of the Imperium of Man.*

Anathema boomed out a volley of bolt shells that hammered in a wide spread across the control consoles before him.

His vision cleared. Darkness fell. Silence, at last, followed.

It was not an immediate process. At first the darkness was broken by the crackling death rattles of the destroyed consoles, lighting the blackness like bolts of lightning. When the ruined control consoles spat their last, his vision stabilised just as darkness fell. True, absolute darkness, imaginable only by those who lived life without ever seeing the sun.

Next came the silence. The twenty generator towers took almost a minute to die. Great hulks, strangled of attention and starved of willpower without the guiding signal of the control consoles. Within the observation room, failsafe systems roared into life with flashing red sirens. Talos emptied the rest of his magazine into the failsafe station, turning his head from the resulting explosion.

Once more, there was darkness. The generator towers rattled and clanked and whined down into stillness over the course of another forty-six seconds, and then, blessedly, there was silence over the self-contained generatorium city.

Talos crashed through the control room windows, falling twenty metres, landing smoothly on the ground floor's decking with a tremendous bang of ceramite on iron. He looked into the darkness, listened to the silence, and breathed a single word.

'Preysight.'

Indriga wasn't spooked.

He was, however, losing his temper. The others were getting twitchy with the lights going out and the generator towers dying. The girl wasn't struggling anymore, but that was hardly any reassurance. She'd already bitten and clawed chunks out of Edsan and Mirrick, and Indriga had a feeling lurking at the back of his mind that the dangerous bitch was just waiting for the right moment to lash out again.

Between two powering-down towers, the four men froze in the darkness. The crash of destroyed glass had reached them even over the towers' death whines. Handheld lampsticks speared into life as Indriga and Edsan turned on the shotgun-mounted lights they'd taken from slain prison guards.

The girl moaned, coughing loud enough to make Indriga jump.

'Shut her up,' he whispered. 'And keep your damn light on the ground.'

Edsan obeyed, lowering his stolen gun so the beam was no longer lancing off into the avenues between the towers. 'You just messed your pants, Indri. I saw you jump like you were shot.' It wasn't mockery in Edsan's voice. It was something not far from panic.

'I ain't spooked,' Indriga whispered back. 'Just lower your Throne-damned voice.'

Edsan didn't reply at first. Indriga sure looked spooked, and that meant bad things. Indri was a hive ganger like most of them, but his skin was black with tats listing his kill counts and blasphemous beliefs. You didn't get that big without being vat-grown or significantly cut up and put back together by some augmetic-hungry doc, that's for sure.

When his nerves got the better of him, he said 'Indri. There's four of us, right? That's good, yeah?'

'Yeah.'

Edsan had the distinct feeling Indriga wasn't listening to him at all. That was nothing new – Indriga was big news in R Sector, he'd never had time for small-time players like Edsan – but this time, it wasn't like Indriga was brushing him off out of disrespect. This time, Indri just looked like he could smell fire around the corner and was thinking about making a run for it.

It was weird. Looking at him now, he was like one of the beefy attack dogs Edsan's boss used to use in pit fights. Gene-changed to be hulks of slab-like muscle and wide jaws, and before a dog fight they'd be tense and shivering, staring off at stuff only they could see. They were glanding stimms, sure, but it was still weird to see an animal so... focused. Indriga looked like that now. Shivering but rigid, staring at... Well, that was the problem. Like those ugly dog-things, he was staring at the Emperor only knew what.

'You see something?' Edsan whispered.

'No. Can hear it, though.'

And then, just like that, Edsan heard it, too. Maybe the girl did too, because she moaned again, earning a slap from Mirrick, who was still bleeding, still back there with her. A new noise blended with the fading howl of the generators. Something rhythmic, like the metal *thunk-thunk-thunk* of... of... of something. Edsan didn't even know what it sounded like. He'd never heard it before. His slippery mind fixed on the only comparison it could hold on to in his rising panic. *Like the footsteps of a giant.* When he would learn the truth of the matter less than a minute later, he'd be horrified to see how accurate he'd been.

Indriga raised his shotgun. 'Someone's coming.'

'For her?' Edsan swallowed. Indriga's slow caution was shredding his nerves. This was bad. Maybe they could leave the girl and get out of here. 'Indri... Are they coming for her?'

Eurydice spoke for the first time since she'd been taken. Through swollen lips, she sneered the words, 'No. He's coming for you.'

OF THE EMPEROR'S sons, one had always stood apart from his brothers.

Through a twist of fate that would herald the human race's eventual unmaking, the twenty progeny of the Emperor were stolen from their father. As vat-grown infants – who had been painstakingly flesh-forged as biological masterpieces in the labyrinthine gene-labs beneath the surface of Terra – they were engineered to be all that was idyllic and noble in the human form. Avatars, as it were, of mankind's perfection.

Their exaltations and degenerations are chronicled in numerous tomes of mythology and factual record, variously forgotten by most mortals of the Imperium in the ten thousand year span, sequestered by the Inquisition, or so distorted by the passage of time as to barely resemble the truth.

Though all twenty sons would one day be reunited with their sire as the Emperor reached out to conquer the stars in His Great Crusade, nineteen of these sons were raised, for better or worse, by surrogate mentors. Their incubation pods plunged from the skies of twenty worlds, and twenty planets played home and paid homage to godlike beings that would rise to shape the destiny of each world as they grew to adulthood.

On Chemos, a world of manufactories and pollution so thick it blanketed the sky in a drape of vile orange mist, the primarch Fulgrim rose through the ranks of drone workers and executives to become the lord of the fortress-factories, heralding in a new age of resource and prosperity for his people.

On Caliban, the austere primarch known as the Lion grew to lead a glorious crusade of knightly orders against the tainted beasts of his home world's forests. On Fenris, legends have the Primarch Leman Russ first raised by the vicious wolves of that icy world, then reaching his majority to lead the barbarous warrior clans as their greatest high king.

On a nameless world, its title long-lost to the mists of time, the Primarch Angron reached adulthood as a pit slave, shackled by the lords of his apparently civilised planet, forever twisted by the experiences of his bloodthirsty maturation.

For better or worse, fate had each Imperial son raised by others, shaped by instructors, guides, mentors, friends and enemies. Only one primarch grew up alone, hidden from the eyes of humanity, guided by no hand and taught by no elder.

He would come, in time, to be known by the name his father had chosen for him: Konrad Curze. To the people of Nostramo, the world forever wrapped in nightfall's embrace, he was – at least at first – altogether less human. Never did the primarch bear a human name there.

The child survived by living feral in the shadows of humanity's towers. He scavenged in the alleys and streets of Nostramo Quintus, the planetary capital, a sprawling metropolis that covered a sizeable portion of the northern hemisphere. Crime here, as it was across all Nostramo, was as rife as life itself. With no moral compass beyond the evidence of his own eyes, the young primarch began the work that would shape his existence.

The seed of his endeavour was humble enough at first, at least by the standards of Imperial justice. Street-level criminals; the murderers, the rapists, the thugs, gangers and muggers that populated the dark avenues of Nostramo Quintus soon began to whisper a name that flowed from their lips with fearful tremors.

The Night Haunter.

He would kill them. Barely into his teens, the boy would witness an act of violence or crime, and he would leap from the shadows, feral and enraged, butchering those who preyed upon their fellow humans. This was how the nascent core of his humanity sought to enforce order upon his surroundings.

Fear, primal and true, was something the young god understood all too well. He saw its uses and applications, and he saw how those in the thrall of terror were so much more pliant and obedient. In those black streets, he learned the lesson that would shape his Legion. Humanity did not need kindness, indulgence or trust in order to progress. People did not comply with law and live lives of order out of altruism or shared ideology.

They obeyed society's tenets because they were afraid. To break the law invited justice. Within justice was *punishment*.

He became that punishment. He became the threat of justice. Known criminals were left for all to see come the weak dawn: crucified and disembowelled, chained to the walls of public building and the ornate doors of the wealthiest gang leaders and syndicate bosses. Always, he would leave their faces untouched, twisted with the silent and fixed scream of an agonising death, for he knew the dead gazes of the slain triggered a deeper empathy and realisation within the hearts of those who met their glazed stares.

Years passed, and many more died. Soon enough, the Night Haunter was reaching his pale, grasping hands into the higher tiers of society, beating, strangling and slaughtering the ringleaders, the organisers, the officials at the core of the city's corruption. The fear that so thickly saturated the streets soon choked the halls of the wealthy and powerful.

The rule of law reigned. Victory and compliance through the threat of punishment. *Order through fear.*

It is said in the records of the VIII Legion that when the Emperor came to Nostramo, he spoke these words to his long-lost son:

'Konrad Curze, be at peace, for I have arrived and intend to take you home.'

The primarch's reply is also recorded. *'That is not my name, Father. I am Night Haunter.'*

Perhaps the sons of Konrad Curze, had their sire been raised upon another world and learned different lessons, would have been more typical Astartes, and the VIII Legion a far cry from the driven creatures they were at the edge of the 41st millennium. But the sons of the Night Haunter learned every lesson their gene-father did, carrying the same truths with them down the centuries.

'Soul Hunter,' the primarch had once said to Talos.

'My lord?' he had answered, unable as ever to meet his father's direct gaze. He concentrated on the Night Haunter's midnight war-plate, decorated by lightning bolts painted by the finest tech-artisans of Mars, and bearing the skulls of so many fallen foes on chains like hanging fruit.

'Soon, Soul Hunter.'

The melancholic tone of his lord's voice was not new. The whispered reverence was. Surprise made Talos raise his eyes to his father's face, gaunt and nearly lipless, the pale, dull grey of sunrise on a dead world.

'Lord?'

'Soon. We run from the hounds my father set at our heels, and vindication must be bought with blood.'

'Vindication is always bought with blood, lord.'

'This time, the blood-price will be mine to pay. And willingly, my son. Death is nothing compared to vindication. Die with the truth on your lips, and your life's echo will never fade.'

His father spoke on, but Talos heard none of it. The words were like a blade of cold fire in his gut.

'You will die,' he breathed. 'I knew this would come, my lord.'

'Because you have seen it,' the primarch grinned. As always, the smile was without any mirth. The Night Haunter had never, to Talos's knowledge, displayed any human emotion approaching genuine humour. He was amused by nothing. He enjoyed nothing. Even the bloodiest moments of war set his features in a grim mask of concentration and infrequent disgust. Battle-lust seemed beyond him, or he had transcended its feverish joys.

This was the result of sacrificing one's humanity for the good of the Imperium's people. And he would be repaid for his great sacrifice – repaid by the Emperor's assassins seeking his lifeblood.

'Yes, lord,' Talos replied, his mouth drying, his deep voice like a child's compared to the throaty rumble of his father's. 'I have seen it. How did you know?'

'I hear your dreams,' the primarch replied. 'We share a curse, you and I. The curse of foreknowledge. You are like me, Soul Hunter.'

It didn't feel like an honour. Despite feeling no greater kinship with the primarch than in that moment, there was no honour, just a sense of vulnerability that threatened to eclipse even his awe at standing in the shadow of his godlike gene-sire. They would share words only once more before the Night Haunter greeted his death, and without it being spoken, Talos knew this, too.

What brought these thoughts flooding back to his mind now? The rush of instinct, the thrill of the hunt? Galvanised, Talos broke into a run. Eurydice's life rune pulsed on his retinas like the unstable ticking of a broken engine. She was wounded, that much was clear. Her implantation was crude and functional, revealing little of specifics. He heard Eurydice's muffled breathing, the heightened heartbeats of her captors, and exaggerated his footfalls so they would know he approached.

Then, when he judged the moment right, when he could hear them whispering their fears to one another, the hunter ghosted into the shadows, turning his tread soft, standing in wait.

One of the mortals walked past the Night Lord's hiding place between two man-sized capacitor cylinders, his skin reeking of grime and terror-sweat. Talos resisted the urge to lick his lips.

'Greetings,' he said in a low, smiling voice.

The shotgun bucked and blasted noise into the silence. The convict had fired his weapon in panic even before he turned. He had less than a heartbeat of looking into the blackness, seeing a pair of arched red eyes glaring, before Talos was on him.

His death was regrettably quick, and Talos mourned the chance to make it last. The corpse, its neck snapped, fell to the metal decking with a crumpling thud. The Night Lord was already gone.

'Edsan?' someone called. 'Edsan?'

'He's dead,' said a voice behind him. Mirrick managed a breathless, wordless grunt of surprise before his head left his shoulders. Talos ignored the tumbling body, but caught the head before it fell.

Gripping it by its lank, greasy hair, he moved on through the darkness. In his gauntleted fist, the head still twitched with facial tics for several moments.

The third to die was Sheevern.

Sheevern had remained with the woman, standing over her with a power maul in his hands. Like most of the prisoners, he'd acquired the weapon from an enforcer guard in the riot. Unlike most of the prisoners, he was innocent of the crimes he'd been incarcerated for.

Sheevern was no heretic. He was serving his sentence for ties to a deviant ruling cult from a world that had forsworn the Dictate Imperialis, and broken from Imperial rule. As a politician in the regime, he had been charged with heresy when the Imperium of Man came to take the world back from the grasp of the tainted rulers, despite the fact that he'd argued against secession from the Throne. He found it bitterly ironic to be serving a life sentence for heresy, when he'd spent a good twenty years in office, secretly indulging his true lusts and urges without any of his actions coming to the light. The blood of five women and two young men was on his hands. Sheevern regretted nothing. He didn't believe he had anything to regret.

'Indriga?' he called out. No answer. By his feet, the woman whisper-laughed again. He thudded a boot into her side, feeling something – a rib or two, maybe – snap under his kick. 'Shut the hell up.'

His ears itched. A buzzing, like a swarm of insects, was irritating his senses. 'What the hell is that sound?' he muttered, clutching the maul tighter in his thin-fingered hands.

It was the thrum of live Mark IV Astartes war-plate. Talos emerged from the darkness ahead of him, illuminated only by the dim glow of Sheevern's personal lamp pack.

'Catch,' the Night Lord said. Despite the growl of his helm's vox speakers, he sounded almost amiable.

On instinct, Sheevern caught what was thrown. He cradled it one-handed for a moment before dropping it with a gasp. His hand and arm were warm with blood. Mirrick's head banged on the gantry floor.

'Wait,' Sheevern begged the resolving shape. 'I didn't touch her!' he lied. Eurydice's bare foot hit the back of his knee as she lashed out in a furious kick.

Sheevern stumbled, righting himself just in time to meet the Night Lord's bolter hitting his face. The muzzle of the oversized weapon hammered into his panting mouth, making shards of his teeth, the cold metal forcing its way to the back of his throat. He barely had time to squeal a muffled protest before the bolter bucked and sheared the chubby former politician's head clean off.

Talos backhanded the headless body aside and stared down at Eurydice. She was battered and bruised, her clothing torn, one eye swollen shut. She still looked a lot better than Septimus had, though. Nothing here wouldn't heal, at least in regards to the physical damage she'd sustained.

'We are leaving,' said Talos.

'There's one more,' she said faintly through slug-fat lips. 'The big one.'

'We are still leaving,' he said, reaching down for her.

With the Navigator over his shoulder and his bolter clutched in his free hand, Talos made his way back through the generatorium chamber.

* * *

'THIS IS INDRIGA,' the convict spoke into a hand vox. He crouched in the darkness under the foundation support girders of a silent generator tower, his words emerging as a sneering whisper. He wasn't made to hide. It took all of his willpower not to get out there and brain the armoured monster that was making its escape.

'Speak,' replied a sibilant male voice.

'Lord Ruven,' the prisoner said, 'he came for the witch.'

'This leads me to wonder, however, why you are still alive.'

The words were stuck in Indriga's throat for several seconds. 'I hid, lord.'

'Has he gone?'

'He's leaving now.' A pause. 'He took the witch.'

'What do you mean he *took* her? Why would he take a corpse?'

Indriga swallowed, and the sound travelled down the vox. Ruven growled a sigh.

'We brought her with us,' Indriga said. 'We wanted to–'

'Enough. Your mortal urges are meaningless to me. You failed to comply with the most basic orders, Indriga. And now, you will die for it.'

'Lord…'

'I would start running, if I were you.'

Indriga lowered the hand vox, his lip curling in disgust as he heard the armoured killer's footsteps drawing near again. Evidently, he was coming back to finish the job.

Must've heard me whispering…

Indriga needed to see. He clicked the shotgun's underslung lamp active, and leapt from his hiding place with the beam of light like a lance before him.

The towering armoured form swivelled in the half-dark, no doubt protecting the witch he was carrying. Indriga's shotgun barked once, twice, a third time and a fourth, each impact blasting a hail of shot that cracked and clattered against the ceramite war-plate.

Talos turned in the second Indriga's shotgun clicked dry. Eurydice, over his left shoulder, had been shielded from harm when he'd spun to avoid the gunfire. The massive bolter fired once, aimed low, and the bolt pounded into Indriga's stomach. It detonated a moment later, leaving the convict in pieces across the walkway. The largest piece, consisting of Indriga's chest, arms and howling face, remained alive for twelve agonising seconds. Talos ignored its shrieks, reaching for the hand vox the dying prisoner had dropped.

'Prophet,' said the voice on the other end of the channel.

'Ruven,' Talos said softly, 'my brother. It has been a while, brother. I should have recognised your unsubtle handiwork when your four "gods" babbled without sense for so long.'

'Ruven of the Black Legion now, and Eyes of the Warmaster. I assure you, Talos, you do not know of what you speak.'

'The Exalted says the same. I am weary of the protests of the corrupt and the ruined. The Warmaster has betrayed the other Legions before, but this is crude and brazen, even for him.'

'So you say, brother. You have no proof beyond a cracked breastplate that he was even involved. And who would care? The Exalted? He is Abaddon's creature, and always has been. One squad of the Night Lords walking into an obvious trap is no concern for the coming crusade.'

At Talos's feet, Indriga breathed his last. The silence was unwelcome, for the idiot's howls had been curiously pleasant.

'Your thuggish little cultist is dead,' Talos said as he moved away.

'I will hardly be weeping over that. Tell me, why was it so easy to refuse the Four Powers? Did they offer nothing that tempted you? Even for a moment?'

'The purpose of luring me to the planet's surface escapes me, brother,' Talos said, looking down at the human wreckage. 'You must have known I would never leave the Legion.'

'The Eighth Legion is *weak*. The Exalted seeks to discard you. You have little love for your brothers, and above all – Abaddon himself takes an interest in you. Does that mean nothing to you? How can this be so?'

Talos was already moving, cradling Eurydice as he walked.

'I am going to kill you when next I see you, Ruven.'

The Night Lord had foreseen the Navigator's importance, and almost lost her only days later. This foolish venture had also almost cost him Septimus. Might yet still cost him Septimus, if he didn't survive the restorative surgeries.

Carelessness. Carelessness beyond reckoning.

'Mark my words, Ruven. Whether you are the Despoiler's pet or not, I will cut you down.'

'Why did you refuse the Powers? Answer me, Talos.'

'Because I am my father's son.' Talos cast the hand vox aside and kept walking.

'It was good to speak with you again, my brother. I missed your simple sincerity and literal nature. Talos? Talos?'

Talos felt Eurydice stir as he ascended the stairs to the next level.

'Thank you,' she said softly.

He had no answer to that. The words were too unfamiliar.

PART TWO

THE OLD WAR

'There will come a time when our Legion is shattered across the stars.
When the powers we spurn become allies to which many turn.

The paths of your future are closed to me,
And they are yours to walk alone.
But I know this.
The war that fires our blood now will still rage in ten thousand years.
Bleed the Imperium. Tear it down, tear it apart. Show no mercy.

But watch yourselves. There is no traitors' unity in the Old War.
Trust your Legion brothers.
And trust no one else.'

– The Primarch Konrad Curze.

XI

THREE WEEKS LATER

THE SLAVE LISTENED at the door.

From within, he heard sounds of movement, dully penetrating the metal. With a hand he was still not used to using, he pressed the entrance key, triggering a toneless chime within the room. Footsteps came closer, and the door opened on hissing gears, sliding to the left. In the doorway stood another slave.

'Septimus,' said the room's occupant with a smile.

'Octavia,' he replied. 'It's time.'

'I'm ready.'

The two Legion serfs walked down the darkened halls of the *Covenant of Blood*'s mortal decks, where the illumination strips along the ceilings were forever tuned to twilight. It was enough to see by, even for those unused to a sunless life, but it would hardly pass for twilight on most worlds.

Octavia still found herself glancing at him every few moments when they were together. The surgeries were still fresh, his skin still adapting, and where his augmetics met flesh, the telltale redness of fading inflammation was still in evidence. His left eye, the one he'd lost to the convicts that stormed the Thunderhawk, was now a violet lens set in a bronze mounting that reached out to cover his temple and cheekbone. Octavia, in her life as the daughter of a Navigator House, had seen a great many augmetic enhancements in the courts of Terra, not least of all her own father's. By general standards, Septimus's bionic reconstruction was relatively subtle. It was certainly above the poorest-grade cybernetic 'slice and graft' surgeries available to even many wealthy Imperial citizens.

Still, she could tell none of that was any comfort to him. She watched him hit the door release with his gloved hand – the hand he had lost along with his eye. She had yet to see the augmetic hand and forearm he now bore, but she heard the rough mechanics of its servos buzzing and clicking as he moved. Upon his throat and chest, the outward bruises had mostly vanished, but the memory of the violence done to him was still clear in the way he moved. Although he was healing and the three weeks had shown huge improvement, he was still stiff and obviously sore – walking like an old man in the winter.

They walked together through the lower mortals' decks of the *Covenant*. Octavia doubted she would ever get used to the… the community down here. Unlike the upper decks, which housed valued serfs and officers, the non-essential mortal crew inhabited these darkened decks, occupying civilian quarters much as on any other military vessel, but they were twisted and shaped by their allegiance to the Night Lords. They reminded her of vermin, living down here in the darkness.

In the untraceable distance, down unknown numbers of winding corridors, someone screamed. Octavia flinched at the cry. Septimus did not.

As the two serfs moved down the wide steel corridor, a cloaked figure, hunched over almost onto all fours, scrambled across their path from one adjacent passage to another. Octavia didn't even want to know who or what it was. Cold water dripped in an irregular rhythm from a tear in the metal overhead. A punctured coolant feed somewhere, a hole in the vessel's veins, slowly leaking icy water through a rusty wound. It was hardly an uncommon sight. Maintenance servitors never made it to this part of the ship.

'Why did we have to go this way?' she asked quietly.

'Because I have business here.'

'Why are these people even tolerated? Do the Astartes hunt them for sport?'

'Sometimes,' he admitted.

'Is that a joke?' She knew it wasn't, and wasn't even sure why she voiced the words.

He smiled, and she almost froze in her tracks. It was the first smile she'd seen from him in almost a month. 'They have their uses, you know. Future artificers. Potential servitors. Failed officers that may be useful one night in a position of lesser responsibility.'

She nodded as they approached what looked like a market stall made of scrap metal, raggedly built into the side of the corridor.

'You need power cells?' the sore-ridden old man at the stall asked. 'Cells for lamp packs. Fresh-charged in a fire. Good for another month, at least.' Octavia looked at his withered, gaunt face, at the cataracts milking over his eyes.

'No. No, thank you.'

She assumed they didn't need money in the bowels of the *Covenant*, but she couldn't imagine how anyone acquired anything new for barter, either. She also had no idea why they'd stopped here. She gave Septimus a look. He ignored it, speaking to the elder in the worn serf tunic.

'Jeremiah,' he said in Gothic.

'Septimus?' The elder offered a shallow bow, respect evident in his bearing. 'I'd heard about your misfortune. May I?'

Septimus flinched at the question. 'Yes, if you wish.'

He leaned closer, and the old man's trembling hands rose to meet the serf's face, shivering fingertips lightly stroking across the healed skin, the bruises that remained, and the new augmetics.

'This feels expensive.' The man's smile was missing several teeth. 'Good to see the masters still bless you.' He withdrew his hands.

'Apparently they do. Jeremiah, this is Octavia,' Septimus gestured to her with his ungloved hand.

'My lady.' The elder offered the same bow.

Lacking anything else to say, she instinctively forced a smile and said, 'Hello.'

'May I?'

Octavia tensed just as Septimus had before. She could count on one hand the number of times another person had touched her face.

'You… probably shouldn't,' she said softly.

'I shouldn't? Hmm. You sound like a beauty. Is she, Septimus?'

Septimus didn't answer the question. 'She's a Navigator,' he cut in. Jeremiah's reaching hands snapped back, fingers delicately curled in indecision.

'Oh. Well, that was unexpected. What brings you here?' the old man asked Septimus. 'You don't need to scavenge like we do, so I'm guessing it's not a need for my fine wares, eh?'

'Not exactly. While I was wounded,' said Septimus, 'the void-born must have had her birthday.'

'That she did,' Jeremiah nodded, absently rearranging the fire-blackened power cells, stringed trinkets and handheld machine tools on his scrap metal stall. 'Ten years old now. Who'd have guessed, eh?'

Septimus gently scratched. His gloved fingertips stroked the irritated seam where his bronze augmetic plating met his temple.

'I have a gift for her,' he said. 'Would you give her this, from me?' The artificer reached into his belt pouch and withdrew a silver coin. Octavia couldn't make out the detail stamped upon its face – Septimus's gloved fingers obscured the majority of it – but it looked like a tower of some kind. The old man stood motionless for several moments, feeling the cold, smooth disc in his palm.

'Septimus…' he said, his voice lower than before. He was edging on whispers now. 'Are you sure?'

'I'm sure. Give her my best wishes, along with the seal.'

'I will.' The elder closed his fingers around the coin. Octavia could tell the gesture was reverent and possessive, but there was a sick desperation in there, as well. It reminded her of the way a dying spider's legs curled close to its body. 'I've never held one before,' he said. After a pause, he added 'Don't look at me like that. I won't keep it.'

'I know,' said Septimus.

'May you continue to be blessed, Septimus. And you, Octavia.'

They said their goodbyes to the trader and moved on. Once they were around a few corners and safely out of earshot, Octavia cleared her throat.

'Well?' she asked. Her own fate was forgotten in the wake of the enigmatic gift-giving she'd just witnessed.

'Well, what?'

'Are you going to tell me what that was about?'

'Time flows in an uneven river within the void. You're a Navigator – you know that more than most.'

Of course she knew. Her look told him to get on with it, and she noticed his false eye whirring and focusing as its socket mechanics tried to mimic the raised eyebrow on the undamaged side of his face.

'There is a soul on this ship, more important than most. We call her the void-born.'

'Is she human?'

'Yes. That's why she's important. The Great Heresy was thousands of years ago. This strike cruiser hung in the heavens of Terra, as part of the greatest fleet ever amassed – the horde of the First Warmaster, Horus the Chosen.'

Octavia felt her spine tingle at the words. She was still new to this, new to the *Covenant*, new to her own developing treason against the Golden Throne. She could barely even frame her own evolving place on this ship in words that confessed to her treachery. To hear of this very vessel that harboured her being part of the Horus Heresy's final moments, the assault on Terra... She shivered again. The blasphemy made her skin crawl, but there was a delicious edge to the sensation. She was living in the echo of mythology. She stood with the shadows of a greater age, and even being near the Astartes was invigorating. They felt more than any souls she had ever met – their rage burned hotter, their bitterness was colder, their hatred ran deeper...

It was the same within the metal threaded bones of the *Covenant*. Until Septimus had spoken the words, she'd never been able to form the feeling into something comprehensible. But she *felt* the ship. She felt its wounded pride in the rumble of its engines, like an eternal growl. Now she understood why. The Heresy was not mythology to the VIII Legion, not some sequestered insurrection that was more legend than history. It was a memory, seared into their thoughts, just as their ship bore weapon-fire burns that still scarred the skin of its hull. The vessel itself was marked from the war it lost, and its crew shared the grim recollection, their lives stained with the knowledge of failure.

This vessel had rained its fury upon the surface of Terra. The Astartes on board had walked the soil of Imperial Earth, screaming orders to each other as they slaughtered the loyal defenders of the Throne, their bolters barking in the shadows cast by the towers of the God-Emperor's vast palace.

Neither fable nor ancient parable to these Astartes. Memory, twisted by time's loose grip in the warp.

'You look light-headed,' said Septimus.

She had slowed down without realising, and met his unmatching eyes now with a weak smile.

He continued. 'It's easier to understand when you realise where the *Covenant* makes its haven.'

'The Eye of Terror,' she nodded slowly.

'Exactly. A wound in our reality. The warp reigns there.'

Even as a Navigator, even as one of the rare few with the genetic deviance allowing them to see into the Sea of Souls and know the warp more intimately than any other mortal, it was a struggle for Octavia to cling to this shift in her perceptions. Stories forever abounded of vessels lost in the warp for years or decades, and arriving weeks ahead or behind the intended translation date was an unbreakable, unchangeable part of flight through the immaterium. When ships sailed through the second reality, they surrendered themselves to the realm's unnatural laws.

Even so. This was a span of time she could barely comprehend. The differential made her mind ache.

'I understand,' she said. 'But what has this got to do with your gift?'

'The void-born is unique,' Septimus replied. 'In the time the *Covenant* has been active since the Great Betrayal, she is the only soul to be born on board.' He saw the questioning look in her eyes, and cut her off. 'You have to understand,' he clarified, 'even at full crew complement, this was never a vessel that ran with decks full of conscripted slaves. The crew was always small and elite. It is an Astartes vessel. With the decline over the years... Well. She is the first. That's all that matters.'

'What was the gift?'

'A seal. You'll receive one yourself after your surgery tonight. Do not lose it. Do not give it away. It is the only thing that will keep you safe on these decks.'

She smiled at this habit of his. Every crew member of the *Covenant* said 'tonight', never 'today'.

'If it's so important, why did you give it to her?'

'I gave it to her *because* it's so important. Each seal is inscribed with the name of one of the Astartes on board. The rarest of them show no names, and ensure the bearer is protected by the entire Legion. In ancient nights, it was tradition for a personal serf to attend to each warrior. They carried a seal marked with their master's name, signifying their allegiance and dissuading other Astartes from entertaining themselves by harming such a valued slave. The coins mean little now the old traditions are remembered by so few. But they are still acknowledged by some. My master is among them.'

'You wish her to be protected?'

'Most of the Astartes do not even know she exists, and would not care if they did. Their attention is forever elsewhere. But she is a talisman to we "mere mortals" of the *Covenant*.' He smiled again. 'She's a lucky charm, if you will. With my seal, she is under the guardianship of Talos. Any who meet her will know this. Any who threaten her will die by his hands.'

She considered his generosity, not liking where her thoughts led. 'And what about you? Without that seal…'

'Priorities.'

'What?'

'Priorities, Octavia. Focus on your future, not mine.' He nodded to the doors ahead, dark and sealed at the end of the corridor. 'We're here.'

'Will you be waiting?' she asked him. 'When this is over?'

'No. I am retrieving First Claw from the surface within the hour.' He hesitated. 'I'm sorry. If I could…'

'Fair enough.' She touched the metal band implanted on her forehead. Strange, the things one could get used to. With a smile, she said, 'I'll see you soon.'

Septimus nodded and the Navigator entered the apothecarium. As the doors opened, the servitor surgeons powered up from their sterile silence. Septimus watched them until the doors closed again with a grinding clank. They were a familiar sight for him, having been in their care for weeks himself.

He checked his wrist chron once Octavia was out of sight, and made his patient way back through the ship. The war on the surface of Crythe once again demanded his presence.

OCTAVIA EMERGED TWO hours later. The band of restrictive metal was gone from her forehead. She wore a headband of black silk, given to her by Septimus for this purpose, to use when the time was right. It neatly covered her third eye.

In her pocket was a silver Legion medallion, handed to her by a nameless Astartes who presided over her surgery. He hadn't said a word the whole time.

She turned it over in her hands, seeing the same tower symbol minted into the metal. A hive spire. Somewhere on Nostramo, most likely. On the other side, the impression of a face, lost to time's wear, with the faint inscription '*Ave Dominus Nox*'.

This she could read, for it was High Gothic, not Nostraman. *Hail the Lord of the Night*. The ruined face, smoothed by age, must be their father

– the Night Haunter. She looked at the featureless visage for a long moment, then pocketed the coin.

Staring into the darkness, she suppressed a shiver of fear. This was the first time she'd been out of her quarters without an escort. The seal in her jacket pocket was cold comfort in the bowels of the *Covenant*. What guarantee did she have that anyone down here would care if she carried the coin?

Her hand vox crackled, and she knew who it would be. Only two people ever voxed her, and Septimus was planetside.

'Hello, Etrigius,' she said.

'Are you coming for another lesson tonight?'

She reached up to touch the silk bandana, and a wicked little smile creased her lips.

'Yes, Navigator,' she said.

'I will send servitors at once,' he replied.

She thumbed the coin in her pocket, and stared into the darkened corridor ahead.

'No need,' she said, and started moving, her heart beating in time to her hurried footsteps. Eyes – unseen by Octavia but not unnoticed by her – watched as she walked the blackened halls of the tainted ship.

LONG BEFORE HE had earned the honour of wearing the war-plate of the VIII Astartes Legion, Talos had ghosted through the streets of his birth hive on his home world. It was a life lived in the darkness, a life of avoiding stronger predators and carefully choosing weaker prey.

He knew he'd come late to the Legion, and the fact pained him. Nostramo was already forgetting the lessons learned under the claws of the Night Haunter. Scant years after the great Konrad Curze had ascended into the heavens to wage war with his Imperial father, the world he left behind began its inexorable backslide into familiar degeneracy.

Street gangs carved out territories in the habitation and industrial sectors; little princelings marking their claimed turn by runes painted on walls and – in echo of the Haunter himself – the remains of enemies prominently displayed where their kin and brethren would take heed.

Talos had known Xarl even then. They had grown up together, sons of mothers widowed in the underworld wars that broke out once the shadow of the Haunter was a fear of the past. Before their tenth birthdays, both boys were accomplished thieves, inducted into the same gang claiming their hab sector as its domain.

By the time the boys were thirteen, both were killers. Xarl had killed two kids from a rival gang, peppering their bodies from an ambush with his heavy-calibre autopistol. He'd needed both hands to hold that gun, and the sound it made when it fired… A deafening boom that split the silence.

Talos had been there when Xarl made his first kills, but had shed no blood himself that night. His own first murder had been the year before, when a storekeeper had sought to beat them for stealing food. Talos had reacted before his conscious mind even gripped the situation – a brutal, primal flash of instinct that saw the storekeeper coughing and gasping on the floor, Talos's knife buried to the hilt in his heart.

Even now, while the galaxy had turned ten thousand years since that old man had last drawn breath, he still remembered the strange friction of the blade slamming home.

It stayed with him, that sensation: the scratching twist as the first thrust buckled, defeated by the weak armour of the man's rib bones. Then the way the blade had sped up as it slid between the ribs, sticking fast with a sickening, meaty whisper of a sound.

Blood immediately came from the man's lips. A spluttering spray. Talos felt the flecks of spit-thinned blood on his cheeks, his lips and in his eyes.

They'd run in a panic, Xarl half-laughing and half-crying, Talos in stunned silence. As always, they took to the streets, hiding there, making the dark city into the haven their homes would never be. Places to get lost, ways to stalk prey, a million ways to move unseen.

These were the lessons he took with him to the stars, when his own ascension came. These were the instincts he relied on when he stalked the night-time cities of a hundred and more worlds.

Uzas's voice, voxed from some distance away, was agitated.

'I've found a Black Legion Rhino. It's a wreck. This must be what happened to Ulth Squad.'

'Survivors?' Talos asked.

'Not even any bodies.' They all heard the regret in his voice. Bodies meant armour, and armour meant salvage.

'Mass laser fire damage.'

'Skitarii,' put in Cyrion. The Mechanicus footsoldier elite. It stood to reason – no one else would have laser fire capable of totalling an Astartes transport.

'You hear that?' Uzas said. 'I hear something.'

'How truly specific,' Cyrion chuckled.

'I'm getting it, too,' Xarl cut in. 'Broken vox, scattered chatter from other frequencies. Other squads.'

'The Black Legion?' asked Talos.

'No,' Xarl replied. 'I think it's us.'

Talos moved through the ruined manufactory as he listened to his squadmates. His red-tinted sight took in the stilled machinery, the idle conveyor belts, the tall roof with its shattered stained glass skylights where once the scene of the Emperor-as-Machine-God, coming to ancient Mars, had filtered the brilliance of the night sky.

Stars shone down now, illuminating the gargoyle-decorated building with silver silence. Whatever they had made here would never be made here again. The place was a tomb.

'The vox is unreliable,' Cyrion said. 'What a revelation. Everybody, hold positions, I'm going to contact the Warmaster and let him know.'

'Shut up, fool,' Xarl snapped. 'Talos?'

'Here.'

'Frequency Scarlet sixteen-one-five. You hear that?'

It took a few moments for his helm's vox-link to shift and scan nearby signals. He continued to walk through the silent manufactory, bolter and blade at the ready. Soon enough, voices prickled at the edge of his hearing.

'I hear it,' he voxed back to the others.

'What should we do?' Cyrion asked, dead serious now. He'd heard it, too. 'That's Seventh Claw.' There was a pause as he called up data, most likely on his auspex's data screen. 'The armament manufactorum, to the west.'

Talos idly checked his bolter, whispering praise to the machine-spirit within. The vox on the surface of Crythe was a savage, fickle thing, never reliable, always punctured and scrambled by the Mechanicus's arcane technology. Since the Legions had made planetfall, squads had grown used to the violated vox and being cut off from one another.

The fleet orbiting Crythe was blessedly free of the worst of the forge world's twisted vox-screeching, but the squads on the surface were forced to listen to an unending howl of code mangling their signals. Even vox fed through the ships' systems were still often subject to bizarre ghosting, added voices, and delays of several hours. Many times now, squads had responded to positioning information and orders that were half a day out of date.

'They're trying other frequencies to summon reinforcements,' Talos said.

'That's my guess,' Cyrion agreed.

'The Exalted will not be pleased if we abandon our recall orders.' Uzas sounded pleased, his voice low and scratchy. Talos forced the image of himself so battered and bloody, speaking with the same voice, from his mind. *Blood for the Blood God,* he'd said in the vision… *Souls for the Soul Eater…Skulls for the Skull Throne…*

'To hell with the Exalted,' said Xarl.

'We're going to Seventh Claw,' Talos said, already blink-clicking a Nostraman rune to open another channel. 'Septimus.'

'Here, master.' The signal was choppy, swamping the serf pilot's voice in jagged crackles. 'Scheduled retrieval in fourteen minutes. En route to your position.'

'Change of plans.'

'I don't dare ask why, lord. Just tell me what you need. This isn't

Blackened, there's only so much I can do in a transporter.'

'It's fine. Full burn to my position, combat retrieval protocol, then full burn to coordinates Cyrion is transmitting now.'

'Lord... Combat retrieval? Is the sector not clear?'

'It's clear. But you will be taking First Claw and our Land Raider to an engagement zone west of here.'

'By your command, lord.' Talos heard Septimus take a breath. The mortal knew the Exalted had demanded First Claw's recall. 'Actually, I've changed my mind. I do want to know. May I ask what exactly is going on?'

'Seventh Claw is pinned down. We are going to break them out.'

'Forgive me for asking again, lord. What is pinning them down, that requires First Claw *and* its Land Raider?'

'A Titan,' Talos said. 'Now hurry.'

XII
SEVENTH CLAW

THE STREET SHIVERED under its tread.

Dozens of windows facing the avenue shattered in their frames and dust rained from the walls of broken buildings. The thunder of its splay-clawed feet wasn't even the loudest aspect of its presence. Louder still were the roaring whines of its great joints, great mechanical shrieks that split the air as it walked. And louder yet, the cacophonous bellow of its weaponised arms, burning the air when they sucked in power to fire and illuminating the world around it with the light of blinding dawn as they released their fury.

Adhemar of Seventh Claw crawled through the rubble of what had, moments before, been a habitation block. His vision flickered and hissed, all sense lost with the damage taken to his helm. Even his life readouts were scrambled, displaying nothing of use, nothing he could make out. With a curse, he tore the helm from his head, freeing his natural senses. The air was ash-thick and vibrating with the resonant booms of the Titan's stride. It was still some way down the avenue, bringing its guns to bear once more. Seventeen metres tall, almost as many wide, it hunched in the road, taking up so much of the street that its brutish shoulders made squealing tears in the buildings as it raked them with its bulk.

The Astartes knew those armoured shoulders shielded several crew members at work around the inner reactor, chanting their irritating prayers to the Emperor in His guise as the Machine-God. The fact he could not slay them, the fact he had nothing which he could even deal damage with, galled him almost beyond apoplexy. He glared at the canine head of the Titan, picturing the three pilots inside, leashed to their control thrones by hardwiring and restraint harnesses.

How they must be laughing right now…

Adhemar's throat and lungs tightened, filtering out the dust in the air as though it were a poison. Ignoring this biological reaction, the Night Lord dragged himself to his feet and ran behind the still-standing wall of a nearby building. The street, which had once been the main thoroughfare of a habitation sector, was a tumbledown wasteland in the wake of the Titan's anger. One of its weapons, like a gnarled right fist, was a multi-barrelled monstrosity that hurled hundreds of bolt shells a second at its targets below. Every impacting shell chewed a metre-wide hole in the Warhound's steel and stone surroundings. With thousands of shells fired every minute, Adhemar wasn't surprised at the level of destruction. He was merely surprised he still drew breath.

Most of his squad didn't share that fortune.

An ugly chime rang out, reminiscent of a cracked bell calling the Imperial faithful to morning prayer. Adhemar's muscles locked solid as he remained where he was. It was the echolocation pulse of the Titan's auspex. If he moved, it would know where he was. Hell, if it even sensed the minimal heat of his power armour, it would know... but he was counting on the Titan's systems being aligned to hunt larger prey.

Fifty metres down the road, shadowed from the moonlight by two towers that had escaped its opening wrath, it stood on its backwards-jointed legs, wolfish cockpit-head grinding left and right on servos that whined at agonising volume.

He heard the next attack before he saw it – the grunted cough of a missile launched nearby. From the second level of a ruined building, a streak of howling smoke slashed across the street. Adhemar moved to watch the missile's course, narrowing his eyes as his Astartes cognition instinctively took in the details of the warhead's angle and the certainty of its impact point.

Denied his vox, he whispered to himself.

'Mercutian, what are you doing...'

The missile exploded in a fragmentary starburst against the Titan's faintly-shimmering void shields, and the Warhound was already responding. The great left fist came up on roaring gears with punishing speed.

Inferno gun.

Adhemar was back in cover within a single heartbeat, not because he was in the line of fire, but because to look at the weapon firing would be to invite hours of blindness. Even with his eyes closed and head turned away, the son of Nostramo felt the brightness assault his retinas with jabs of migraine-coloured pain. The massive gun fired with the challenging roar of a feral world predator, blasting searing air in all directions from its heat exchange vanes.

Adhemar exhaled a lungful of the burning air, feeling it scrape his throat. He knew without looking that the chemical wash of vicious liquid fire had flooded the building, dissolving everything within. The expected crash came moments later, as the building's structure withered under the superheated force of the assault.

Was it his imagination, or had he heard a moment's cry from the vox of his helm in his hands? Had he heard one of his brother's death screams?

Mercutian was undeniably dead. Brave, without a doubt, to think to harm the Titan with one of his last rockets, but the gesture was futile even before he took aim. Picking the god-machine apart once its layered shields were down was one thing. Getting those shields down in the first place was quite another.

Adhemar hooked his sundered helm onto the magnetic coupling of his belt, and reached for his auxiliary vox within a thigh pouch. The earpiece felt alien; he was so used to the enclosing sensory magnification of his helm.

He doubted there was anyone still with him, but it was worth the attempt.

'Seventh Claw, status report.'

'Adhemar?'

'*Mercutian?*'

'Aye, brother-sergeant.'

'How in the infinite hells are you still alive?' It was an effort not to raise his voice with incredulity.

'You saw me take that missile shot?'

'And I thought I heard you die.'

'Not yet, sir. I made a tactical withdrawal. At speed.'

Adhemar resisted the urge to laugh. 'So you ran.'

'Ran *and* threw myself from the third storey of that building's south-facing side. My armour's a mess and I lost my launcher. Adhemar, we've got to get to the Rhino. The plasma gun is–'

'Not going to take down a Warhound Titan.'

'You have any better ideas?'

A grinding chorus of immense gears started up down the avenue again. Adhemar risked another glance around the edge of the wall.

'Bad news. Do you have visual?'

'I'm in the adjacent street, sir. I can't see the beast.'

'It's found the Rhino.'

The Titan had indeed. It hunched, every inch the feral predator, glaring down at Seventh Claw's troop transport nestled in a narrow alleyway. The collapse of the last building had revealed its dark armoured hull. Rubble from the fallen hab block was scattered across its roof, leaving bursts of gunmetal grey where the blue paint was scraped away.

'I have an idea,' Adhemar voxed.

'Adhemar, sir, with respect… we need to get out of here. There's no honour in this death.'

'Be silent. If we can get its shields down…'

'That's an impossible "if". If we could fly or piss plasma, we'd have the job done, too. None of those things will happen.'

'Wait. It's moving.'

The howl of great gears intensified. Adhemar watched, whispering a prayer to the machine-spirit of his Rhino, the faithful vehicle that had carried him across countless battlefields. He knew its interior as well as he knew his own armour. He could read the tank's temperament in the grunts of its idling engine, and feel its arrogance in the clank and ding of every gunshot that sparked harmlessly from its hull.

The Rhino's name in High Gothic was *Carpe Noctum*. 'Seize the Night'.

The tank that had carried Seventh Claw since the Legion's founding on pre-Imperial Terra died an ignoble death, expiring with a twisted, protracted groan of tortured metal. The Warhound Titan stood for half a minute, its splayed right foot-claw grinding the tank into the street. The greatest injustice was that the tank had met its end in such an undignified manner purely to spare the Titan's ammunition reserves.

You'll pay for that, Adhemar swore. *You will bleed and scream and die for that.*

The Titan finally raised its foot clear of the wreckage, scraps of bent metal falling from its talon-toes. In its wake, still in the behemoth's shadow, the crushed hull of *Carpe Noctum* looked especially pathetic. It was impossible to reconcile the image of miserable ruin with the great-hearted, indomitable tank that had raced him into battle a thousand times and more.

Seventh Claw was dead. Heart and soul. Even if he and Mercutian somehow survived the next few minutes, they were destined to join one of the other Claws in the ragtag remnants of Tenth Company.

Adhemar watched the lumbering Titan stalk down the avenue, hunkering left and right, coming closer with each pounding tread.

'Mercutian...'

'Aye, brother-sergeant.'

Not brother-sergeant after this. Not a chance. 'We need to find Ruhn and Hazjarn. They had melta bombs.'

The Warhound thundered past.

Adhemar froze, back pinned against the wall. A great shadow fell across him as the Titan blocked out the moon. It stood only thirty metres away, pistons hissing and venting air pressure – a beast breathing, sighing after a long hunt. Its back was to him now, as it stared down the avenue, seeking targets. Another dull clang rang out as its echolocation auspex sought returning signals of movement or heat. The wolf was sniffing for prey.

'Repeat, sir.'

'Ruhn and Hazjarn. They had our melta bombs.'

'They're useless with the Titan's shields up. You know that.'

'They're our only chance. We could mine the road ahead of it. Have you got anything better to be doing, or did you come here in midnight clad just to die with the others?'

'I've got Ruhn on my locator, sir. But not Hazjarn. Can you see him?'

'I can't see anyone's signals – my helm is damaged. I saw him fall when the hab block came down on us. I know where to dig, but we'll need to be fast.'

'I've got no life signs from anyone except you and I,' Mercutian said.

Not at all surprising, Adhemar thought, watching the Titan panning left and right on its torso axis. The sound was like thunder in a valley.

'It's facing away. There's a sixteen second break between its auspex signals. The scanner wave will pass over us within the first second or two. Move only three seconds after the damn thing clangs. Freeze the moment you hear it pulse.'

'Yes, sir.'

They waited for several heartbeats, until the dull ring chimed once more. More windows facing the street shattered under the reverberation.

One. Two. Three.

'Move.'

THE TRANSPORTER HANDLED with weighty sluggishness compared to *Blackened*. Although the Thunderhawk variant was marked by a more skeletal mid-frame, it cradled the bulky shape of the squad's Land Raider in its underside hull claws. The weight counted. Septimus felt it in every bank and turn.

Septimus brought the flyer lower, streaking over the tips of hab blocks, stabiliser thrusters burning hot. Go too low, and he risked entering the Titan's weapon range before they knew for sure where it was. Stay too high, and their auspex wouldn't give an accurate return on where the enemy machine was.

'I'm getting significant thermal flare at the end of a major avenue just north of here.'

The voice of his master came over the vox. First Claw waited within their battle tank. 'Pull in low, release clamps at the other end of the avenue. If you get killed while causing the distraction, I'll lose my temper, Septimus.'

He grinned. 'Duly noted, lord.'

The transporter's stability engines burned hotter and angrier as they took the vessel's weight in full, all forward thrust lost as it coasted lower to the ground, between the stunted remains of Titan-killed hab blocks. Engine wash blackened the street below.

Six hundred metres or more down the avenue, the Titan saw them. The Warhound reared around, back-jointed legs easing it into an awkward reverse turn. Its arms rose in lethal salute.

'Imperial machine is acquiring target lock,' Septimus voxed. 'Twenty… Fifteen… Ten metres above ground.'

'*Ave Dominus Nox*,' Cyrion said over the channel.

'Hunt well, Septimus,' Talos added.

'Claws detached!'

Freed of its burden, the Thunderhawk transporter bucked skyward, overcompensating engines roaring.

Warning runes flashed across his console screens. *Target lock.* The serf wrenched the guidance sticks to pull the flyer into a vicious roll. From the avenue below, streams of massive-calibre bolt shells sliced through his engine wake. He punched out at two levers either side of his control throne, and the protesting boosters cried out with fresh fury. The amount of thrust he was demanding from the transport was usually reserved for breaking back into orbit after a landing. To use it in atmospheric flight, to use in a cityscape...

Septimus knew *Blackened.* He knew the Thunderhawk could've taken this and more. He wasn't so sure about the transport. It juddered and creaked and whined all around him, complaining down to the rivets in its hull.

Spires flashed by in a dizzying blur. Septimus climbed and brought the flyer into a sharp turn. As he lined up the nose with his target below, acquisition runes glimmered across his main data screen.

The transport's missile launchers came alive, pods opening like unfurling flowers.

'I hope this works...'

THE TREADS OF First Claw's Land Raider had been in motion before it even hit the ground. They whirred and spun, chewing air, hungry to grind over the street's surface.

'First Claw!' came a voice over the tank's interior vox.

Talos blink-clicked a tuning rune. 'Adhemar?'

'Talos, by the claws of our father... What are you doing here?'

The Land Raider lurched as it crashed to the street, its cycling treads already tearing up the concrete at full speed. Cyrion, at the tank's driving throne, turned the huge vehicle to the right, moving through a wide alley into a parallel side street. Within the tank's gloomy, red-lit insides, the rest of the squad checked their weapons.

'Take a guess,' Talos replied, and pounded his gauntlet against the door release. Night swept in, temperature gauges on retinal displays falling as the chill wind hit their armour. Talos, Uzas and Xarl leapt from the moving tank, scattering into the ruined hab towers.

'It's not the scenery, is it?' Mercutian's voice crackled. 'We'd have warned you away.'

'We appreciate the effort, brothers,' Adhemar voxed, 'but even a Land Raider is scrap metal against a Warhound. We're honoured you would join Seventh Claw in death.'

'Silence,' Talos barked. 'Where are you in relation to the Titan?'

'I could spit and hit it,' Mercutian replied. 'We're in its shadow, with melta bombs to mine the road.'

'Save them,' the prophet ordered. 'First Claw, move up through adjacent streets to link with Seventh Claw. Cyrion, bring *Storm's Eye* in fast, just as agreed.' There was no sense trying to hide the Land Raider. The Titan's auspex would scent its heat and power source from a kilometre away.

'You plan to take it down with your Land Raider?' Mercutian whistled low. 'A good death.'

'Enough of your negativity,' Adhemar snapped. 'Brother, tell me you've landed with a plan.'

'I landed with a plan,' Talos said. He ran through the rubble-strewn street, sighting the Warhound as it unleashed withering rivers of fire into the sky. 'The Titan is about to become the victim of an unpleasant distraction. When we strike from the sky, follow my orders exactly.'

'Compliance, Soul Hunter,' Adhemar said.

THE THUNDERHAWK TRANSPORTER was lightly armed compared to its troop-carrying gunship counterpart, but not entirely lacking in offensive capability. Wing-mounted heavy bolters made up the anti-troop comple-ment of its weapons array, backed up by the capacity for six under-wing hellstrike missiles.

Septimus had been flying the Thunderhawk *Blackened* for years, and had performed strafing runs on enemy positions many times in the past. This attack run was marked by several uncomfortable differences to his usual participation in a battle. First among these was that the transporter lacked the main cannon armament of the more familiar Thunderhawk. Secondly, it could withstand significantly less damage on its hull mid-sections. Thirdly, as Septimus ran the flight path adjustments through his conscious thoughts, he reached an ugly conclusion: *This bastard turns like it's underwater.*

The tank-carrier dived, and dived hard, like a spear from the night sky cast at the cruellest angle.

The Titan fired up at him. He could imagine its crew in their restraint thrones, unwilling to allow such a prize as an Astartes lander to escape its clutches, commanding their god-machine to send its anger skyward in a relentless hail of bolt shells, thousands at once.

The transporter jerked away from its dive, rolling so hard the pressure slammed Septimus painfully against his throne. The inertia of his attack run would, if he kept this up for much longer, either kill him, tear the ship apart, or both. But the lance of lethal shells slashed past.

Altitude meters chimed in alarm. Velocity readouts did the same. The vessel itself was screaming at him.

Septimus dragged at the control sticks, ramming the thrust levers a moment later. The transporter powered closer, its angle less insane.

Septimus had held out as long as he could, not wanting to broadcast his intent, but the Titan crew had to know now. They would recognise this manoeuvre. Not a strafing run with the cannons. A bombing run.

TALOS CROUCHED WITH Adhemar in the ruined ground floor of the hab block. With the walls almost completely levelled, they had an unopposed view of the street. Both warriors gripped plate-sized melta bombs in their hands, watching the Titan in the middle of the avenue as it fired into the sky.

Adhemar, older than Talos and showing it with his head bare, grinned toothily at the prophet. 'If this works…'

'It'll work.' Talos was almost smiling behind his own helm, glad that Adhemar had survived the Titan's initial assault.

Above, the transporter began its howling descent, racing closer by the second. The Titan locked its legs for support, and opened fire with a fresh volley from its Vulcan mega bolter.

SEPTIMUS CAME IN between the towers of hab blocks. Low now. Even lower.

Low and close enough to graze the Titan's shoulders with heat wash when he passed overhead. When only two hundred metres separated the knifing flyer and the firing Titan, as he heard dangerous clashes on the hull from shredding bolter fire, Septimus pulled back and climbed again.

The Titan tracked its flight, but the ancient, time-honoured joints couldn't keep pace with the speeding flyer as it nosed up into the final stage of its attack run.

Septimus was holding to the thrust and altitude levers too tightly to risk letting go. The flyer was wounded, venting black smoke from several critical points, and he didn't dare take his hands from the controls for a moment. Leaning sideways in his throne, he cursed the fact this ship was made to be piloted by oversized gene-forged Astartes instead of mortals. With a Nostraman invective, he kicked out at the clamp release console the very second his targeting rune flashed green, green, green.

Septimus's boot heel smacked the lever up from *Secure* to *Armed*.

Aimed downward like six separate blades, the missiles spat from their pods and fell, howling, from the sky.

AT THIS RANGE, near-suicidal as it was for the Thunderhawk, the Titan had no chance to intercept the missiles.

The impact was a sight to behold. It burned into Talos's memory as fiercely as it burned into his eyes.

The missiles struck with savage force, hammering into the Titan's void shields with the force of a falling building. They exploded as one, and the flare momentarily blinded the one Night Lord that couldn't resist watching it all play out.

Talos stared, seeing nothing until his eye lenses frantically cycled through filters to compensate for his blindness. Sight returned, blurred by smears of retinal pain, just in time for the Astartes to see the War-hound stagger back a step, its right leg moving back to support its tilting weight, clawed foot grinding into the ground.

Its shields seemed fluid and malleable, swirling like oil on water, dissipating and sparking back to life as the internal generators strained to maintain the power feed to the void shield projector. Talos could almost see the tech-adepts working around the central column of the Titan's juddering fusion reactor, like a spine running through its torso and beneath its dense shoulder armour.

The Titan's shield crackled and flared with a sudden burst of dissipating energy. Deep within its armoured body, a low and rising thrum built up, muted but still audible to the Astartes in hiding. The Warhound's internal systems were bracing, feeding additional power to prevent a complete shield shutdown. Its voids were on the very edge of failure.

'Night Lords,' Talos voxed, smiling his crooked smile. 'Move in for the kill.'

THE MACHINE-SPIRIT HOUSED within the immense bulk of the VIII Legion Land Raider *Storm's Eye* had been honoured time and again for its aggression. Scrolls and pennants marking dozens of glorious victories moved in the wind as they hung from its hull. On treads that had churned the earth of countless worlds, it powered from the side street, acting as much on its own bloodlust and instinct as it was obeying the suggestions from the flesh-master at the controls.

Its prey... Its prey was immense. *Storm's Eye* sensed the boiling heat of the Titan's plasma reactor; felt the fierce pressure of the giant's glare as it drew a target lock. Yet *Storm's Eye*, the soul of the machine, knew nothing of fear, nothing of retreat, nothing of cowing to intimidation. It tore into the avenue, treads crushing and grinding the rockcrete beneath its weight, flanking the towering foe.

Storm's Eye clawed and spat at the larger predator – its spitting venom was a withering hail of high-calibre bolt shells from its hull-mounted turret, its talons raking the enemy's flesh were Kz9.76 Godhammer-pattern lascannons, each side turret unleashing eye-aching beams of merciless laser energy from two barrels slung side by side.

It clawed and clawed and clawed, ripping at the prey's fragile shimmer-skin, tearing at the half-seen protective shield.

Something burst. The shimmer-skin. *Storm's Eye's* talons had peeled the final layer of shimmer-skin away, leaving the foe cold and exposed. The enemy staggered with violent kinetic feedback as something broke within its body.

Storm's Eye heard the flesh-masters shouting to one another. It sensed their blood-excitement and shared their hunt-hunger. The joining of battle-hate pushed the tank's soul even harder. Its claws ached with death-heat. The cooling touch of maintenance would be a blessed relief after this hunt.

The prey was still strong, and it was still fast. The flesh-master guided *Storm's Eye* at hunt-kill speed across the avenue, reversing from the larger foe without ceasing fire. It was a battle to keep the tank's hull-body away from the murder-claws of the colossal predator. Like a shark seeking prey, *Storm's Eye* moved left and right in a weaving motion, engine-heart burning hotter and hotter, claws tensing and hissing with the killing heat.

The foe finally turned fast enough. No longer prey... No longer threatened...

It roared its own reply at *Storm's Eye*, machine-soul to machine-soul, and with the wrath of a predator-god, it clawed back.

TALOS VAULTED ANOTHER broken wall, sprinting across the avenue into the shadow of the firing Titan. With its Vulcan mega bolter chattering a thunderstorm of shells at the Land Raider's retreating form, the enemy war machine had a greater threat to worry about than the Astartes at its feet. Still, it knew they were there. A clanging auspex return from the Titan sent warning runes flashing across Night Lord retinal displays, but even as the towering foe turned and sought to crush its weakling prey, the weakling prey was already acting.

Talos was the first. *Aurum* crackled with energy in his fist before a single slash carved a malicious streak through the armour and engineering of the Titan's ankle. Even one-handed, the blow would have felled a tree or carved a mortal in half. Talos's own gene-enhanced strength, amplified tenfold by the artificial muscle fibre of his war-plate, was the pinnacle of mankind's genetic manipulation coupled with some of the Machine Cult's closest-guarded secrets rediscovered from the Dark Age of Technology.

The golden blade sliced and sank into the armour plating, biting deep into the mechanics beneath. This alone was nothing, a pinprick of a wound caused in a heartbeat's span. Talos snarled with effort, his muscles unused to being so tested as he wrenched the blade deeper, impaling and sawing through the cables and rods and pistons that served the Titan as tendons.

Machine-blood spat from the carved metal, sheeting Talos with discoloured lubricant and oil. Its next auspex pulse sounded like a wail. With a replying cry of exultant anger, Talos slammed his other hand against the jagged wound he'd carved. There was a hollow clunk as the melta bomb adhered fast.

Adhemar and Xarl were next, clamping their own explosives to the wound's edges. Talos was already sprinting to safety as Mercutian slammed his incendiary home. He sighted Uzas.

Uzas, who was not laying his explosives with the rest. Uzas, who stood under the towering, stamping Titan and fired his bolter up at the war machine's chin. Did he think small-arms fire was ever going to puncture a hole in the armour of a Titan? Did he think the crew within that head-cockpit felt his gunfire as anything more than a whispered irritant against the hull-skin of their walking sanctum?

Xarl's voice barked over the vox, caught between anger and disbelief. 'What's that damn fool *doing*?'

Talos didn't answer. He was already running back.

Cyrion's influence made it all the more difficult. Sight-stealing bright-ness flashed in colourful blurs across Talos's eyes as the Land Raider down the avenue maintained heavy fire with its Godhammers. Talos closed his useless eyes, running blind between the Titan's crushing legs, relying on his other senses to guide him.

Beneath the pounding stamp of the enraged Titan's tread...

Beneath the mocking, deafening waspish buzz of constant lascannon fire...

There. The thrum of power armour. The heavy chatter of a bolter like an impish giggle in the wake of the superheavy weapons at play. Most identifiable of all was Uzas's gleeful voice risen in the howling of names Talos had no wish to know. Names which cast him back – just for a moment – to his vision of Abaddon's 'allies'.

He threw himself at the sounds, shoulder-charging Uzas ten metres across the street with the dull crash of ceramite armour plates clashing hard. Still blind, he ran to his brother's rising body, and powered his fist into Uzas's helmed face.

Once, twice, a third time and a fourth.

With a weak growl, Uzas staggered on shaking legs. Talos headbutted him, the Nostraman rune on his forehead shattering one of Uzas's red eye lenses. Feeling his brother go limp, the prophet hooked his fingers in Uzas's armoured collar, and dragged the fool into the relative cover of a half-fallen hab block.

He looked up to see his death. The Titan's arm, the one not releasing a torrent of murder down the avenue at Cyrion and *Storm's Eye*, aimed directly down at him. The arm itself was longer than a battle tank, suck-ing in light and heat through side-vanes as it amassed the power to fire.

An inferno gun. It would liquidate him, Uzas, the stone of the build-ing, the concrete of the street, in a wash of sun-fire.

One thought burned through his mind as Talos stared up at the trem-bling cannon.

This is not how I will die.

The explosives bolted to the Titan's ankle detonated, as if the prophet's silent words shaped fate itself.

* * *

PRINCEPS ARJURAN HOLLISON grunted a weak murmur, because it was the only sound he could make. Something was crushing his chest, blocking all attempts to breathe, and pressing him back against his throne. The pressure that forced him hard against his throne made the hardwiring needles and probes socketed to his spine and skull push far deeper than they should, effectively impaling him. He could feel the dim, pulsing throb of internal bleeding in his head and chest as his vision swam, and...

No. It was the Titan's pain. Still linked to the enraged, crippled form of *Hunter in the Grey*, the princeps was drowning in the god-machine's overwhelming pain.

And its overwhelming indignity.

It had fallen. Not in glorious battle. Not in war against a stronger foe. The Titan, Warhound-class, assembled in the hallowed and sacred forge-factories of Alaris II – noble and knighted Mechanicus world – had *fallen*. Stumbled. Crashed to the ground, now prone to the ant-like bites of lesser prey.

The cooling reactor core of the humbled giant bled helpless rage into Arjuran's mind. Just as the Titan lay prone, so too was he defenceless against its maddening anger. He couldn't move his head to unplug himself. Rage flooded him, terrifying in its intensity and inhumanity, rendered worse by the very fact it could not be escaped. The twisted metal crushing him (the pilot throne of his faithful morderati primus, Ganelon...) was unmovable. His hands beat weakly, worthlessly, against the restraining weight.

He became aware that not only was he crushed, but that he was at an angle. His right arm and leg, as well as the right side of his head, were numb with dull pain from being forced against the metal wall of the cockpit. *Hunter in the Grey* had twisted as it fell, coming down on its side.

Arjuran had a fragmentary burst of short-term memory. The pain in his left fist as the inferno gun streamed killing fire into the sky, a useless release as the Titan toppled.

Then the thunderous crash.

Then blackness.

Then pain.

Now the rage.

ARJURAN WAS SHIVERING and drooling, half-senseless from the fury of his fallen Titan, when the roof of the wolf-headed cockpit was torn away. Not that he was aware of it, but his body was spasming every few seconds with violent jerks, banging his cracked skull and broken leg against the wall. The Titan's mortis-cry, an ululating wave of channelled hatred, was slowly killing the one crew member still alive. But then, *Hunter in the Grey* had always been a wilful and vindictive engine.

Arjuran gasped and wept as a dark figure dragged him from the throne. He gasped in relief, wept in thanks, as the plugs and cables snaked from his skull and spine.

Even now, deprived of the invulnerable shell of his *Hunter*, he could not care that he had traded one death for another. Blessed succour from the dying Titan's poisonous emotion. That was all that mattered.

Held limply in the gauntlets of the enemy, Princeps Arjuran Hollison, born of the dynast-clans ruling the Legio Maledictis of Crythe Primus, once the commander of one of his home world's precious god-machines, stared into the emotionless red eyes of his captor.

'My name is Talos,' the dark warrior growled. 'And you are coming with me.'

XIII
SEEDS OF INSURRECTION

'It is possible to win and lose at once.
Think of the war that rages for so long that a world is left worthless
in its wake.
Think of the swordsman that slays his foe at the cost of his own life.
Think, finally, of the Siege of Terra.
Let those fateful nights burn into your memory.
Never forget the lesson learned when Horus duelled the false god.
Triumph bought with too much blood is no triumph at all.'

– The war-sage Malcharion
Excerpted from his work, *The Tenebrous Path*

TEN THOUSAND YEARS ago, before humanity was riven by the betrayal of
Horus the Chosen, Tenth Company returned home to Nostramo.

Tenth Company, 12th, and 16th – three battle companies returning
from the Great Crusade to be honoured by their home world.

The Night Lords were never like their brother Legions. They came from
a world without warrior traditions stretching back through the centuries.
The fortitude that girded them for the rigours of the Emperor's Great
Crusade was born of a world that knew fear, knew blood, and knew
murder – more than any other globe in the Emperor's grip. The people
of Nostramo knew these aspects as a natural part of life. The acceptance
of such darkness bred a Legion colder than any other; a Legion willing
to discard its humanity in service to the Throne.

And this is exactly what it did.

This was an age when the Night Lords were the emergent Imperium's
most powerful threat. A world resisting the Imperial Truth could be
conquered by the drudging half-mechanical Iron Hands or the massed
precision of the ever-loyal Ultramarines. It could be brought to compliance by the howling hordes of the Luna Wolves – who would one day
become the Black Legion – or the avenging wrath of the Blood Angels.

Or it could suffer the crippling evisceration of society offered by the untender talons of the Night Haunter's chosen sons.

Fear was their weapon. As the end of the Great Crusade neared, even as the Night Haunter's brother primarchs looked askance at their moribund, wayward kinsman, the Night Lords were the Emperor's most potent weapon. Entire worlds would surrender their arms as their scanners revealed that the Astartes vessels that had translated into orbit bore the runic symbols of the VIII Legion. In these waning years, the Night Lords encountered less and less resistance, as deviant societies abandoned their defiance rather than die under the claws of the most feared Imperial Legion.

Their reputation was hard-won through hundreds of campaigns, unleashing their specific brand of terror upon those they conquered. It was never enough to take a world in the Emperor's name. To cement the Master of Mankind's rule, populations must be utterly quelled into obedience. Obedience through fear. A Night Lords strike force would ravage the heart of a world's leadership, crucifying the bodies of its rulers on public address pict-screens, burning the monument-houses to the planet's false gods, and systematically peeling back a society's skin to expose the weaknesses beneath. In their wake, shattered populations lived the lives of loyal, silent Imperial citizens, never even whispering a word of rebellion.

And as the years passed, resistance faded.

The gene-forged warriors of the Night Lords grew discontent with this. Not only discontent, but bored. When the order came from Terra – the insane demand that the Night Lords and their primarch father return to suffer the chastisement of the Emperor – discontent and boredom faded to be replaced by the birth of a new emotion. The Night Lords grew bitter.

They, who had whored their humanity away in the fires of the Emperor's wars.

They, who had allowed themselves to be moulded into the Imperium's truest weapon of terror.

They were to *pay* for these deeds, like sinners kneeling before an angry god?

Indignity. Madness. Blasphemy.

The last Night Lords to set foot upon the surface of Nostramo were the warriors of Tenth, 12th and 16th Companies. A homecoming of special rarity, for few Astartes ever saw their home worlds again, and Nostramo was hardly renowned for doing honour to its sons fighting away in the Emperor's wars.

The parade was modest, but sincere. A gesture from the captain leading the three companies, as the expeditionary battlefleet refuelled and made repairs in the docks above Nostramo. Fifty Astartes from each company would make planetfall and march down the main avenue of Nostramo Quintus, leading from the spaceport.

Talos remembered thinking even at the time it was a strangely emotional gesture. Yet he'd descended to the surface in *Blackened*, along with the other nine Astartes of the full-strength First Claw.

'I do not understand,' he'd said to Brother-Sergeant Vandred, who was still centuries away from becoming the Exalted, and still months away from becoming Tenth Captain.

'What is there to understand, Brother-Apothecary?'

'This descent. The reception on the surface. I do not understand why the Tenth Captain has ordered it.'

'Because he is a sentimental fool,' Vandred replied. Grunts of agreement sounded from the others, including Xarl. Talos said no more, but remained sure there was more to it than something so simple and senseless.

There was, of course. He wouldn't find out what for many months.

During the parade itself – which was almost alarmingly populous – Talos clutched his bolter to his chest and marched bare-headed with his brothers. The experience was dazzling, though almost without sound at first. Little cheering took place, but the clapping soon became thunderous. The ambivalent people of Nostramo, in the actual presence of the Night Haunter's sons, cast aside their apathy and welcomed their champions home.

It was not humbling. Talos was more confused than anything else.

Were these people so ardent in their love for the Imperium that they welcomed the Emperor's chosen born from their own world? He had spent his youth on this world, hiding and running and stealing and killing in the black backstreets of its cities. The Imperium had always been a distant, ignorable thing at best.

Had so much really changed in a mere two decades? Surely not.

So why were they all here? Perhaps curiosity had dragged them from their habs, and the uniqueness of the moment was breeding the excitement now.

Perhaps, he realised with a bolt of guilty unease through his spine, the people thought they had returned permanently. Returned to reinstitute the cleansing laws laid down by the now-distant Night Haunter.

Throne... That was it. That was why they were glad to see them. In the absence of their lost primarch ruler, the populace hoped for the Haunter's sons to return and take up his duties. The primarch's lessons were being unlearned, the imprint of his silent crusade on society was a thing of the past. Talos had lived here himself, barely believing the world had once been a bastion of control and order under a gene-god's rule.

Now it became humbling. To feel the weight of terrible expectation willed from the crowd. To know they were destined for crushing disappointment.

It became worse when the crowd started shouting names. Not insults, *real names.* It wasn't en masse, but individuals in the groups lining the avenue shouted names at the Astartes, for reasons Talos couldn't quite guess. Were they yelling their own names, to receive some kind of blessing? Were they screaming the names of sons taken by the Astartes, hoping those very same warriors now walked this wide street?

Few moments in life had been as difficult for Talos as this. To feel himself so separated from the life he once led, that he couldn't even guess what other humans were thinking.

The thin line of enforcers keeping the crowds back broke in several places. Small-arms fire banged out, putting down the few members of the mobbing crowd that sought to walk with the Astartes. Only a handful made it to the ranks of marching warriors. They weaved this way and that, looking lost, looking drunk, staring up like frightened, fevered animals into the faces of the walking warriors.

A middle-aged man scrabbled at Talos's chestplate with dirty fingernails.

'Sorion?' he asked. Before Talos could answer, the man fled, repeating the same whispered question to one of the Astartes two rows behind.

At no point did the Legion stop marching. Pistol-fire broke out as the enforcers, in expensive business suits, took out one of the mortals in the avenue that strayed far enough from the Astartes to guarantee a kill-shot without hitting one of the armoured giants. None of the enforcers wished to risk his own death by missing and hitting the revered armour of the Night Haunter's sons.

An elderly woman harassed Xarl. She was barely over half of his height.

'Where is he?' she shrieked, wasted hands scratching at the marching warrior's armour. 'Xarl! Where is he? Answer me!'

Talos could read the discomfort in his brother's face as Xarl marched on. The old woman, beneath her mop of wild white hair, saw him paying attention. Talos immediately faced forward again, feeling the old woman clawing at his unmoving arm with her weak grip.

'Look at me!' she pleaded. *'Look at me!'*

Talos didn't. He marched on. Weeping, wailing after him, the old woman fell behind. 'Look at me! *It's you! Talos! Look at me!'*

An enforcer's gunshot ended her demands. Talos hated himself for feeling relief.

FIVE HOURS LATER, back aboard *Blackened*, Xarl had sat next to him on the restraint couches.

Never before – and never again – would Talos see his brother's face marked by such hesitancy.

'That wasn't easy for any of us. But you did well, brother.'

'What did I do so differently?'

Xarl swallowed. Something seemed to dawn behind his eyes. 'That woman. The one from the crowd. You... didn't recognise her?'

Talos tilted his head, watching Xarl carefully. 'I barely saw her.'

'She said your name,' Xarl pressed. 'You truly didn't recognise her?'

'They were reading our names off our armour scrolls,' Talos narrowed his eyes. 'She said your name as well.'

Xarl rose to his feet, making to move away. Talos rose with him, gauntlet clamped on his brother's shoulder guard.

'Speak, Xarl.'

'She wasn't reading our names. She knew us, brother. She recognised us, even after twenty years and the changes wrought by the gene-seed. Throne, Talos... You must have recognised her.'

'I didn't. I swear. I saw only an old woman.'

Xarl shrugged off Talos's grip. He didn't turn around. His words echoed with the same finality as the gunshot that had silenced the old woman's pleas.

'The old woman,' Xarl said slowly. 'She was your mother.'

THESE THOUGHTS ECHOED in Talos's mind now, on the return to orbit from the war-torn surface of Crythe. The memories, which so safely hid within his unconscious at all times, broke through the surface now.

The mood aboard the transport was grim, despite the victory First and Seventh Claws had just achieved. The death of a Titan, even a Warhound-class Titan, a lesser cousin of the city-crushing Warlords and Imperators... This deed would be etched onto their war-plate, and machined onto the armour plating of *Storm's Eye*. Nostraman runes would tell the tale of their triumph until the night when their bodies lay cold and Legion brothers came to scavenge the relic armour.

But the mood remained dark. Victory at such a savage cost was barely a victory at all. Talos recalled similar words written by the war-sage Malcharion, in the years after the Haunter's assassination.

And with that thought, with that connection made, Talos's roiling mind – already lost in the coldest, deepest and most furious pits of memory – turned blacker still.

Assassination. Murder. *Blasphemy.*

The last time he had wept was on that night, that night of wrenching agony, standing with thousands of his brothers and watching the traitorous whore leave the fortress-monastery, her gloved hands clutching their father's head by its lank, black hair.

Hours before, Talos had shared his last words with his gene-sire.

'My life,' the primarch had said, head bowed before a gathering of his captains and chosen, 'has meant nothing.'

The bowed god weathered the shouted denials of his favoured sons, who all fell silent as he spoke again.

'Nothing. Yet, I will amend that with my death.'

'How, lord? What glory will your sacrifice bring to us?' These words from the Talonmaster. *Zso Sahaal*. First Captain.

The same questions were uttered from a dozen lips.

'We cannot prosecute the crusade against the Imperium without you,' declared Vandred, not yet the Exalted, not yet Captain of the Tenth, but already considered so gifted by the Haunter in matters of void war.

The Night Haunter smiled, somehow without animating his face beyond warping the blue veins beneath his cheeks.

'Our crusade of vengeance against the Imperium, against my father's false ascension to godhood, spins upon a fulcrum. Every life we take, every soul that screams in our wake – the rightness of what we do hangs upon a single aspect of balance. Name that aspect. Name it, any of you, you who are my chosen.'

'I will,' said a voice from the loose crowd.

The Haunter nodded. 'Speak, Captain of the Tenth.' At those words, Talos glanced at his own captain. So did Vandred.

Brother-Captain Malcharion stepped forward, leaving the ranks of the company leaders, to stand one step closer to his primarch.

'The rightness of our crusade is justified because the Imperium is founded upon a lie. The Emperor is wrong in all He does, and the Imperial Truth His preachers propagate is flawed and blinding. He will never bring order and law to mankind. He will damn it through ignorance.

'And,' Malcharion nodded his head, mimicking the primarch's earlier bow, 'His hypocrisy must be answered with revenge. We are right because He wronged us. We bleed His flawed empire because we see the truth, the decay beneath the skin. Our vengeance is righteous. It is justice for His scorn of the Eighth Legion.'

Malcharion was taller than many Astartes, his bare head showing seven implanted silver rivets around his right eyebrow, each one a mark of honour meaning nothing to any outside the Legion. A ferocious fighter, an inspiring leader, and already composing works of great tactical and meditative value. It was all too easy to see why the Night Haunter favoured him with captaincy of the Tenth Company.

'All true,' the father said to his sons. 'But what is the Emperor learning by our defiance? What do the High Lords of Terra learn as we slaughter the citizens of their void-kingdom?'

'Nothing,' said a voice. Talos swallowed as he realised it was his own. Every unhelmed face turned to look at him, including the primarch's.

'Nothing,' the Night Haunter said, closing his black eyes. 'Nothing at all. Righteousness is useless, if we alone know we're right.'

He had told them before. Told them his intent. Yet this cold, ironclad confession still undermined the inner preparations each one had made to deal with the death of their gene-sire. All the questions previously quelled broke loose, and the grim acceptances paved over doubts were shattered.

Here was the chance to argue. To defy. To challenge fate. Voices rose in protest.

'It is written,' the Night Haunter murmured. His whispered words were always enough to bring his sons to silence. 'I feel your defiance, my Night Lords. But it is written. And more than that, even were this a destiny to be battled and resisted, it is *right* that I die.'

Talos watched the sire of the VIII Legion, his own black eyes narrowed.

'Soul Hunter,' the Night Haunter said suddenly, gesturing with a hand that resembled a marble claw. 'I see understanding dawn in your eyes.'

'No, lord,' he said. Talos felt several of the captains and chosen eyeing him, hostile as ever at the way their primarch singled him out for the honour of such a deed name.

'Speak, Soul Hunter. The others understand, but I hear your thoughts. You have framed it in words better than any other. Even our honourable and verbose Malcharion.'

Malcharion nodded in respect to Talos, and the gesture gave him impetus to speak.

'This is not entirely about the Legion.'

'Continue.' Again, the marble claw invited more.

'This is a lesson from a son to his father. Just as you instruct us in the principles to continue this crusade, you will show your own father, who watches all from the Golden Throne, that you will die for your beliefs. Your sacrifice will echo in your father's heart forever. You believe your martyrdom will set a fiercer example than your life.'

'Because…?' The Night Haunter smiled again, a fanged smirk that had nothing to do with delight.

Talos drew a breath to speak the words he'd seen in his dreams. The words his gene-sire would speak before the assassin's blade fell.

'Because death is nothing compared to vindication.'

'SIXTY SECONDS TO dock,' Septimus said in muted tones.

Talos would not be jarred from his reverie. Deeper. Deeper. Away from the sight and scent of damaged power armour and bleeding skin, away from the pitted and cracked hull of both the transport and *Storm's Eye* gripped within the carrying claws. Away from the two squads of men with their annihilated numbers, their tainted souls, and their bitter victory.

Deeper.

'NOSTRAMO WAS BLIGHTED,' the primarch said.

It would be the final time Talos spoke to his father. Konrad Curze held his son's helm, turning it over in his hands, white fingertips tracing the Nostraman rune upon its ceramite forehead.

'Soul Hunter,' he whispered the name. 'Soon, in the nights to come, you will earn the name I have already given you.'

Talos did not know what to say, so he said nothing at all. Around them, the black stone chamber of the Haunter's throne room remained silent but for the sounds of their armour reflecting off the walls.

'Our home world,' the primarch said, 'was more than blighted. It was ruined. You know why I killed our world, Talos. You sense the honour-less, murderous nature of the Legion now.'

'Many sense it, lord.' Talos drew in the ice-cold air. His breath steamed out. 'But we are a weapon against the Imperium. And we are righteous in our vengeance.'

'Nostramo had to die.' The primarch continued as if Talos had said nothing. 'I tried to tell my brothers. I told them of Nostramo's backslide into lawlessness and cruelty. The recruitment had to halt. My Legion was poisoning itself from within. The planet *had to die*. It had forgotten the lessons I taught with blood and pain and fear.'

The Night Haunter stared past Talos, at the black wall of his chamber. A thin trickle of saliva made its way down his chin from the corner of his mouth. The sight made Talos's main heart beat faster. It was not fear. That would be impossible, for he was Astartes. It was... unease. Unease at seeing his primarch so unstable.

'Assassins come. One will reach this palace. Her name is...'

'M'Shen,' Talos whispered. He had dreamed the name himself.

'Yes.' The primarch's tongue flicked out to lick at the trailing drool. 'Yes. And she, too, does the work of justice.'

The Night Haunter handed the helm back to Talos, closing his eyes as he lowered his slender, armoured form onto the throne. 'I am no better than the millions I burned on Nostramo. I am the murderous, corrupt villain that the Imperial declarations name me. I will greet this death gladly. I punished those who wronged. Now my own wrongs will be punished in kind. A delicious and balanced justice.

'And in this murder, the Emperor will once again prove me right. I was right to do as I did, just as He is right to do as He does.'

Talos stepped closer to the throne. The question that left his lips was not the one he'd intended to voice.

'Why,' he said, eyes burning with something akin to anger, 'do you call me Soul Hunter?'

The Night Haunter's black eyes gleamed, and the enthroned god smiled again.

'AND WE'RE DOWN,' Septimus said. 'Docked and locked, powering down now.'

Talos rose to his feet, leaving the restraint couch.

'Septimus, see to the Navigator. Ensure her surgery occurred without complications.'

'Yes, lord.'

'First Claw, Seventh Claw,' Talos said. 'With me. We are going to speak with the Exalted.'

'THE WAR ON the surface is costing us dearly.'

'The losses are acceptable.'

Talos eyed the Exalted's visage, twisted and leering in a parody of pale Nostraman flesh.

'Acceptable?' the prophet asked. 'By what standards? We have lost nine Astartes since we made planetfall. The Warmaster is throwing us against the hardest targets on Crythe.'

'And we break them.'

Imbedded within every pure Astartes was the capacity to generate acidic spit. In loyalist Chapters descended from flawed gene-seed, this ability was occasionally hindered, stunted or absent altogether. The Night Lords were not impure. At the Exalted's obdurate display, Talos felt his saliva glands tingling, responding to his annoyance. With a whispered curse, he swallowed the burning venom, where it would dissipate harmlessly in his stomach acids. It stung on the way down his throat.

'Yes, we break them. And we break ourselves upon them. We are fighting the *Mechanicus*. The Warmaster is bleeding us against targets ill-suited to our Legion's warfare. Titans and servitors and tech-guard? We are wasted against an enemy too inhuman to feel fear.'

'It is not the role of a warrior to whine when he is deployed outside his ideal battlefield, Talos.'

'Then by all means,' Adhemar interjected, spreading his arms wide, 'come down to the surface, Excellency. Bloody your claws with the rest of us. Allow your precious Atramentar to fire some bolts in anger. See for yourself!'

The older Astartes grinned, wolf-like and keen, as the Atramentar either side of the Exalted's throne growled through their tusked helms. 'We just crippled a Titan,' Adhemar's dark eyes shone with amusement, 'so don't think you raising those weapons is any deterrent to us telling the truth.'

The Exalted burbled a wet chuckle. 'You are in fine spirits for a sergeant that so recently led his men to their deaths.'

The smile was wiped from Adhemar's face. Talos looked between the two Atramentar – Garadon and Vraal – in their bullish Terminator plate. Tense. Ready.

But they would not act. He was sure of it.

'Enough of this madness,' Talos said. 'We are hurled like fodder against insane resistance, and ordered to scout ahead of the mortal armies. *Scout ahead? Astartes?* This is no way to wage war. Fear is our greatest weapon, and that blade is blunted in this conflict.'

'You will fight because it is the will of the Warmaster,' the Exalted sneered. 'And it is *my* will.'

'Seventh Claw is destroyed.' Talos's fingers ached to draw *Aurum*. He knew, with icy certainty, he could ascend the dais and ram the golden blade home in Vandred's chest before the Atramentar cut him down.

Sorely, sorely tempting.

'Did you harvest their gene-seed? You were my Apothecary once. It would grieve me to think you had forgotten your former duties completely.'

'I cut them from the bodies of the slain myself,' Talos replied. And he had. With his combat knife, he'd cut the progenoid glands from the chest and neck of each killed warrior. Adhemar, with tears in his eyes, had packed the discoloured organs in freezing gel, storing them in a sealed stasis crate aboard *Storm's Eye*.

Six souls lost. Lost to the warp. He imagined his men, brave warriors all, their shades howling as they drifted through the Sea of Souls.

'Adhemar and Mercutian are First Claw now.' Talos was adamant. 'That is not a request.'

The Exalted shrugged, moving weighty armour and bone spikes. Matters of unit size and assignment were beneath him.

'And let us be clear, Brother-Captain Vandred. This war will see us dead. The Warmaster will bleed the Tenth to the bone, because we are expendable to him. The survivors will, by virtue of no other choices remaining to them, join the Black Legion.'

'The Warmaster, a thousand praises upon his name, has granted his forgiveness for your… outburst… on the surface of the prison world.' The Exalted's ruined teeth glistened unpleasantly. 'Do not abuse his generous nature, Talos.'

Talos looked to the Atramentar. Garadon had been there. Had he not explained the truth of the matter?

'The Warmaster sought to create divisions between the landing party. He wanted me because my second sight is not blinded, as his own seers suffer. I cannot believe you still refuse to the see the light of truth. Garadon was with us. Surely he–'

'The Hammer of the Exalted relayed all that occurred. The only flaw the Black Legion was guilty of was allowing our Thunderhawk to be overrun by prisoners.'

'Are you *insane*?' Talos took a step closer. Both of the Atramentar brought their weapons to bear: Garadon hefting his hammer, and Vraal's lightning claws sparking into hostile life. 'They blew the main ramp door open with explosives.'

The Exalted did not answer, but the smile revealed all. It knew. The Exalted knew, had always known, and did not care. The loss of Talos, no matter how precious a commodity his prophetic gift was, would be an acceptable sacrifice in the name of the Warmaster's continued goodwill.

Talos's next words came out as a whispered threat. 'If you think I will allow you to lead the Tenth into the grave because you hunger so fever-ishly for Abaddon's good graces, you are sorely mistaken.'

'You seek to usurp me, Soul Hunter?' The Exalted still smiled.

'No. I seek leadership for the surface conflict. I want to win this war and still have a company to come back to.'

'Promoting yourself? How droll.'

'Not I, Vandred.'

Finally, the Exalted reacted. It rose from its throne on squealing armour hinges, its slanted, birdlike eyes narrowed.

'Do not speak his name. He slumbers too deeply. He will not awaken. *I* am the Exalted. *I* am Captain of the Tenth. You will obey *me*.'

'Enough, Vandred. You will not lead us on Crythe, and we are dying to your desire in order to please the Warmaster. We are fighting an enemy that lacks any human emotion. They do not feel fear, and they will not panic. It is costing us life and resources to destroy such a foe in grinding, traditional warfare. If their morale can yet be broken, it will not be done with bolters and blades. So we will use our own machines. The machines they once made for us.

'I am going to the Hall of Remembrance,' finished Talos. 'First Claw, with me.'

With those words spoken, he stalked from the bridge, guarded by the sacred weapons of the newly-forged First Claw.

OUTSIDE, CYRION STOPPED.

With the doors closed behind them, he leaned against the wall, head down, as if stunned. A tremor overtook his right arm, and he held onto his bolter only because his fist tightened in an uncontrolled clenching of tendons.

In a broken voice that reached only Talos, he said, 'Brother. We… must speak. The Exalted's terrors are flooding him. He is finally drowning in them.'

'I do not care.'

'You should care. When you spoke of the Hall of Remembrance, what remains of Vandred within that tainted shell was weeping in fear.'

THE EXALTED AND its guardians watched the squad leave. As the doors slammed closed in the Astartes' wake, Garadon lowered his ornate ham-mer, resting its haft on his shoulder once more. The black lion's face of his shoulder armour roared silently in the direction of the sealed doors.

'I will never understand why the primarch honoured Talos so highly,' the Atramentar said.

Vraal, on the other side of the Exalted's command throne, voxed his own thoughts. 'He is fortunate. Luck favours him. He dreamed of the Navigator. Now he takes a Titan princeps prisoner. The Warmaster him-self will praise that capture.'

'You sound disgusted, brother.' Garadon's own voice was as cool and toneless as ever. 'Does his fortune offend you?'

Vraal had still not retracted his lightning claws. They hissed and sparked in the gloom of the bridge, sending harsh illumination flashing along the contours of his bulky Terminator armour like sheet lightning.

'It does. He offends me with each breath he draws.'

'Vraal,' the Exalted slurred, its voice thick with bitter mucus.

'Yes, my prince?'

'Follow them. I do not care how it is done, but the ritual of reawakening must be desecrated.'

'Yes, my prince.' Vraal nodded his tusked helm. The servos in his ancient war-plate growled at the movement.

The Exalted licked its fanged teeth, uncaring of the blood it drew.

'Talos must not be allowed to awaken Malcharion.'

XIV

CAPTAIN OF THE TENTH

'I do not want this.
I have served with loyalty and honour…
Throw… my ashes into the void.
Do… not… entomb me…'
– Final words of the war-sage Malcharion

THE SLEEPER DREAMED.

He dreamed of battle and bloodshed, dreams that warped the boundary between memory and nightmare within his sluggish mind.

A world. A battlefield. *The* battlefield. Armies of millions laying waste to each other in a relentless grind. Bolter fire, bolter fire, bolter fire. So loud it bleeds into other senses. So loud it becomes blinding, so loud it tastes of ash. The sound of bolters firing is more familiar to him than the sound of his own voice, so deeply is it ingrained within him.

The spires of a palace that spans a continent. The towers of a fortress like no other – a bastion of gold and stone to rival the imaginations of even the greediest gods.

He would die here. This he knew, for it was memory.

He would die here, but would not be granted peace.

And still, the bolters fired.

THE ORNATE PLATINUM surface of the sarcophagus stared back in silence, still draped in thin, gentle tendrils of wisping steam as the stasis field powered down.

It was ornate and beautiful in the way *Storm's Eye* would never be. The Land Raider, enhanced by vicious spikes and ornate armour restructuring, was artistry of a sort: revelling in the Legion's reputation, fitted with chain racks to display crucified enemies even as the battle tank cut down hundreds more.

Storm's Eye was limitless aggression and the infliction of woe upon the enemy. The machine-spirit within, reflected by the ceramite without.

But this was artistry of a different, nobler breed.

The sarcophagus was rendered in platinum and bronze, depicting one of the greatest days of battle ever to take place in the history of Tenth Company. A warrior in ancient war-plate stood, head raised back to the sky, clutching two Astartes helms. His right boot rested upon a third, driving it into the ground.

The image had never been defiled with exaggeration. No mound of skulls, no cheering crowds. Just a warrior alone with his victory.

The helm in his right hand sported a jagged lightning bolt etched onto its forehead, with a barbaric rune upon its cheek. The helm of Xorumai Khan, swordmaster-captain of the White Scars Ninth Company.

The helm in his left hand was crested and proud, even when torn from the body of its wearer. It was marked only with a clenched fist upon the faceplate, and the High Gothic rune for *Paladin*. Here was the helm of Lethandrus the Templar, a renowned champion of the Imperial Fists Legion.

Lastly, beneath the warrior's boot, the helm of a third Astartes. This helm was winged, marked by a tear-shaped drop of blood – displayed here as a ruby – on the helm's forehead. Raguel the Sufferer, captain of the Blood Angels Seventh Company.

The warrior had slain these three souls in the span of a single day. A single day of hive warfare outside the walls of the Imperial Palace, and the warrior had cut down three champions of the loyalist Astartes Legions.

Clanking cranes lifted the huge sarcophagus from its stasis pit in the marble floor of the Hall of Remembrance. Servitors operated the lifting equipment, their mono-tasked mechanical precision a necessary part of the ritual of reawakening. Talos watched the hulking coffin of platinum, bronze and black ceramite – the size of two Astartes in full Terminator plate – as it was lifted clear of the pit's restraints. Tubes, feeds and cables, each with a sacred use, trailed down from the sarcophagus as it hung aloft. These fibrous snakes dripped coolant, beads of moisture collecting in the funereal air after such a long immersion in the stasis field.

First Claw watched in silent reverence as the sarcophagus was carried across the chamber and lowered with programmed care. Several more servitors waited below the lowering coffin, clustered around the towering form of an armoured carapace three times the height of an Astartes. Their hands, replaced with industrial claws and technical tools, busied over the machine body, making the final preparations for the sarcophagus's mounting upon its front.

Dreadnought.

The word itself sent a pulse of ice through his blood, but it was nothing compared to the reality before his eyes. A Dreadnought: the ultimate blend of man and machine. The form of an Astartes hero, encased within an ornate sarcophagus and forever suspended in amniotic fluids on the very edge of death, controlling the nigh-invulnerable ceramite body of a walking war machine.

The ritual so far had taken almost two hours, and Talos knew several still lay ahead. He watched the servitors at work, machining clamps into place, locking struts, testing interface ports...

'My lord,' said Tech-Priest Deltrian. 'All is ready for the Third Juncture of the Ritual of Reawakening.'

The man, robed in black, had augmented himself to the height of an Astartes with none of the inhuman muscle-bulk. To Talos, he resembled the skeletal harvester of life from pre-Imperial Terran mythology. It was an image shared across the stars by so many colonised worlds, even those that had evolved independently of far, far distant Earth. *A reaper of souls.*

Deltrian's face, visible from under the black cowl, seemed to play to this conceit for reasons Talos had never fathomed. A silver skull grinned at the Astartes. The face was formed from chrome and plasteel shaped to the man's facial bones – perhaps even replacing skin and bone itself.

A voxsponder unit, like a coal-black beetle on his still-human throat, emitted Deltrian's mechanical voice.

The unblinking eyes were glittering emerald lenses, dewy with a faint sheen from the moisture spray that hissed subtly from Deltrian's tear ducts once every fifteen seconds. Talos had no idea why the tech-priest's eye lenses must be kept moist, they were hardly human eyes in need of lids and juices to prevent them drying out.

As with all of Deltrian's inhumanities, it was something Talos respected as personal, despite his curiosity.

'You have the Legion's thanks, honoured tech-priest,' the Astartes said, continuing the traditional phrases expected of him. He glanced around the marble-floored chamber, its walls thick with arcane machinery, pits sloping into the floor holding even more wondrous technology. He looked back to the tech-priest, and added on a whim: 'Our thanks, as always, Deltrian. You are a dutiful and trusted ally to us.'

Deltrian froze, machine-still. The servitors banged and clanged and fused and attached and drilled. The tech-priest's emerald lenses clicked and whirred, as if seeking to adopt some form of facial expression. The skull of his face never stopped grinning.

'You have violated the traditional exchange of vocalised linguistics.'

'I merely meant to show gratitude for the duties you perform. Duties that too often remain thankless.' Talos's black eyes didn't break the sincere stare. 'I apologise if I caused you offence.'

'It was not an error to amend the vocalised linguistical exchange?'

'No. It was intentional.'

'Analysing. Processed. In reply, I would state: thank you for your recognition, Astartes One-Two-Ten.'

Astartes One-Two-Ten? Talos smiled as understanding dawned. First Claw, Second Astartes, Tenth Company. His original squad designation.

'Talos,' the Night Lord said. 'My name is Talos.'

'Talos. Acknowledged. Recorded.' Deltrian turned his death's head grin on the lowering sarcophagus. 'Through the invocation of the Machine-God, through the blessed sacrament of unity between the enlightened Mechanicum and the Legions of Horus, I shall endeavour to revivify the warrior before us if the cause aligns with the First Oath. Make your vow known to me.'

Slipping back into the formal exchange, Talos replied, 'In the name of my primarch, who loved and served Horus as the brother he was, I give you my vow. The Eighth Legion makes war upon the Golden Throne and the Cult of Mars. Return to us our fallen brother, and Imperial blood shall run. Renew his strength with your secrets, and together we will bleed the false Mechanicum of its lore.'

Here Deltrian paused again. Talos wondered if he had spoken the oath incorrectly. He'd studied the texts, but this was the first time he had undertaken the ritual himself.

'Your avowal aligns with the First Oath. My secrets will be employed in our mutual favour.'

'Wake him, Deltrian.' Talos met the tech-priest's gaze, his voice lowered. 'A storm is coming. A reckoning. We need him to stand with us.'

This, too, was a break in the prescribed ritual. Deltrian paused to process it.

'You are cognitive of the probability of failure? This warrior-unit has resisted reawakening on all four previous attempts.'

'I know.' Talos watched the sarcophagus, golden with great deeds, being fastened in place on its war machine body. 'He has never awoken. He did not wish to be entombed.'

Deltrian said nothing. To refuse the honour of becoming so close to the Machine-God made no sense to the Mechanicum priest. With no comprehension of the emotions at play, he simply remained silent until Talos spoke again.

'May I ask a question?'

'Permission is granted, with the acceptance that no lore of the blessed Mechanicum shall leave the minds of its holy servants.'

'I respect that. But I will be leaving an… honour guard here. To watch over the ritual. Is that an unacceptable breach of tradition?'

'It was once considered tradition to maintain an honour guard in the Hall of Remembrance at all times,' Deltrian said. In a moment of almost eerie humanity, the machine man tilted his head to the side while the smile remained on his unchanging face. 'How times change.'

Talos nodded to that, smiling himself.

'Thank you for your patience, Deltrian. Cyrion, Mercutian and Xarl will remain here. They will not interfere with your work and worship, I assure you.'

'Your orders are recorded.'

'I wish you well, honoured tech-priest. Please summon me for the final stage of the rite. I wish to be present.'

'Compliance,' the augmented man said. After several seconds, Deltrian added almost awkwardly, 'Talos?'

The Astartes turned with a growling whirr of armour joints. 'Yes?'

Deltrian gestured with a long-fingered skeletal hand to a wall-mounted life support pod. Within its glass walls, suspended in amniotic fluids and connected to external systems by a tangled weave of cables and wires, the naked form of Princeps Arjuran Hollison floated in chemical-induced slumber.

The tech-priest emitted a blurt of machine code from his throat-vox; the sound equation of a pleased smile. 'This one will have many uses. Much to be learned from him. My thanks for the gift of this most valuable weapon.'

'Return the favour,' said Talos, 'and we'll consider the matter even.'

'WE NEED TO discuss matters of rank.'

Bare-headed, sporting a short black beard salted with flecks of grey, Adhemar walked alongside Talos through the darkened halls of the *Covenant*. They were descending deeper through the ship, heading from the artificer and machinery deck, making their striding way to the mortal crew quarters.

'What is there to discuss?' Talos asked. A rare vitality was flowing through him. *Hope*. Something he'd not felt in a long time. He'd not lied to the tech-priest; a storm was coming. He could feel it in his blood. It threatened to break with every beat of his heart. Tenth Company would be changed forevermore.

The two Astartes' bootsteps echoed from the black steel around them.

'I outrank you.' Adhemar's voice came as if he were grinding rocks with his teeth.

'You do,' Talos agreed. 'Why does that seem to make you uncomfortable?'

'Because rank means nothing with the Tenth ruined. Beneath the Exalted is the Atramentar. Above the Exalted is no one but his hateful gods. All else is unworthy of his notice. Ninth Claw has been leaderless for three months now.'

Talos exhaled, shaking his head. Truly, the Legion had fallen apart.

'I had no idea.'

'I am First Claw now,' Adhemar affirmed. 'But who leads First Claw? The former brother-sergeant of Seventh? Or the former Apothecary of First?'

'Do I look like I care?' Talos rested his hand on the pommel of sheathed

Aurum. 'I'd be satisfied with the company holding together for the duration of this war. You lead. You earned your rank.'

'Has it never occurred to you that perhaps you've earned a higher rank than the Exalted grants you?'

'Never,' Talos lied. 'Not for a moment.'

'I see the lie in your eyes, brother. You are not gifted with deception. You know full well you should lead First Claw. You merely offer me the position from respect.'

'Maybe. But the lie is sincere. You have the rank. Lead and I would follow.'

'Enough games. I have no wish to lead your – our – squad. But hear me well. Your actions for the betterment of the Legion may be altruistic and made without thoughts of personal glory. But they do not look that way to the Exalted.'

They waited at the sealed doors to an elevator, staring at one another in the pitch blackness, seeing each other's features perfectly. Talos breathed slowly before answering. Even the mention of the Exalted was fuel for his suppressed fury.

'These are not your words, Adhemar. This talk of suspicion and deception… It is not your way to learn of such things. Who is this warning from? Upon whose behalf are you speaking?'

From the hallway behind them, a voice said: 'Mine.'

Talos turned slowly, cursing himself for being too lost in his inner conflicts to have heard another close by. Even though the newcomer was unarmoured and wearing only the traditional Legion tunic, the prophet should have heard his approach.

'My behalf. Adhemar speaks on my behalf.'

Adhemar nodded his head in respect, as did Talos, to Champion Malek of the Atramentar.

XARL AND CYRION had never been close. Conversation, such as it was, always remained stilted between them when it occurred at all. Idle chatter was not an Astartes trait, and that tendency was only magnified when the two Astartes in question despised one another.

Bolters held to chests, they walked in opposite directions around the marble-tiled chamber of the Hall of Remembrance, passing each other twice on each circuit. Mercutian, his armour sigils yet displaying his allegiance to Seventh Claw, stood guard at the great double doors, his helm turned to face the form of the Dreadnought.

Deltrian puppeteered his servitors with occasional blaring snarls of machine code. According to his directions, the cyborged minions went about the painstaking process of readying the Dreadnought for a full reawakening. Upon its front, the mounted sarcophagus stared across the room, brazen with its glory in a way Malcharion never was in life.

On the sixth time Cyrion passed Xarl, he opened a vox-channel to his brother.

'Xarl.'

'Make this good.'

'What are the chances of this working?'

'Of the war-sage waking?'

'Yes.'

'I am... sceptical.'

'As am I.' A pause stretched out, and the channel fell dead after several minutes. Cyrion blink-clicked it open again.

'The Exalted will not allow it to happen.'

'That is not news to me, brother.' Xarl sighed over the link. 'Why do you think we are here? Of course the Exalted will attempt to stop this ritual. What still eludes me is why I can scarcely believe things are falling apart so completely.'

'The Exalted fears this. He fears Talos, but he fears the awakening of Malcharion even more. You haven't sensed what I have.'

'I have no desire to. Let us not dwell on talk of your corruption.'

'I *sense* fear. I do not feel it. It's a... perception. Like people whispering on a detuned vox, where only scraps of meaning break through.'

'You are touched by the Ruinous Powers. Enough.'

Cyrion pressed on. 'Xarl. Listen. Just this once. Whatever war is taking place within the Exalted, it is one Vandred lost long ago. He barely exists as the man we followed into battle after the Siege of Terra.'

They passed one another again, neither warrior giving sign of acknowledging the other, despite their argument over the vox. Mercutian still stood in orderly silence.

'*Enough,*' Xarl snapped. 'Do you think I will react favourably to learn you understand the mind and soul of that twisted wretch? Of course you know his secrets. You are as warped as he is. His corruption is on the outside, bared to the eyes and displayed in the ravaging of his flesh. Your decay is within. Hidden, and all the darker for that fact.'

'Xarl,' Cyrion said, his voice softer. 'My brother. In the name of the father we share, listen to me now if never again.'

Xarl didn't reply. Cyrion watched his silent brother approaching as they came around to meeting on another half-circuit of the chamber. As they passed, Xarl gripped the rim of Cyrion's shoulder guard. It was a strange and awkward moment. Even though the red lenses of both their helms, Cyrion felt his brother making eye contact for the first time in several years.

'Speak,' Xarl said. 'Justify yourself, if you can.'

'Imagine,' Cyrion began, 'a secret voice within everyone. A voice that speaks of their fear. When I am with you, with Talos, with Uzas... all is silent. We are Astartes. "Where fear fills the mortal shell, we are hollow and cold".'

Xarl smirked as Cyrion quoted Malcharion's writings. Apt, very apt.

Mercutian's voice crackled over the vox. 'Keeping secrets from your new squadmate?'

'No, brother,' replied Cyrion. 'Forgive us this momentary disagreement.'

'Of course.' Mercutian's link went dead again.

'Continue,' Xarl said.

'It's… different around mortals. I hear their fears, like a chorus of shameful whispers. You kill a mortal and see the light die in his eyes. I hear him silently weeping, hear him whispering of a home world he will never see again, of a wife he was so afraid he would never lay eyes upon one last time. I… rip these thoughts from every mind I am near.'

The taint of the psyker, Xarl thought. In the years of the primarch's glory, such wretches would be purged from the Legion, or shaped according to rigid codes of behaviour and use. A wild psychic talent was an open door to possession and corruption by the soulless beings of the warp.

'Continue,' he said again. The word was much harder to speak this time.

'You cannot imagine what the Exalted sounds like to me, brother.' Cyrion's own voice was broken and hesitant, struggling to give the concepts a form in words. 'He shrieks… lost in the darkness of his own mind. He shouts our names, the names of Legion brothers dead and alive, imploring us to find him, to save him, to kill him.'

He took a breath before continuing. 'That is what I hear when I stand near him. His torment. His terror at the loss of control he suffers throughout his existence. He is no longer Astartes. His possession has allowed him to feel fear, and it has rendered him truly hollow. Terror bores through him like the tunnels of a hundred worms.'

Xarl realised he was still holding Cyrion's shoulder guard. He released it immediately, fighting down the snarl in his voice. 'I could easily have lived without that knowledge, brother.'

'As could I. But my revelations were not spoken to make you uncomfortable. The Exalted is two souls – Vandred, shrieking his slow way into oblivion, and something else… something formed from his hatred and meshed with the mind of another. When Talos threatened to awaken Malcharion, it was the first time I have heard both souls howl. Vandred's remnants and the daemon that claims him – both feared this moment.'

'We are here,' Xarl insisted. 'We stand watch over the rites of resurrection. If the Exalted truly fears this event and sends… dissuasion, it will not matter. Threats and oaths. Who of the Atramentar is truly ignoble enough to make war upon his brothers? Malek? Never. Garadon? He is the Exalted's creature, but he is no match for three of us. Any of the Atramentar would fall, and the Exalted is precious with the lives of his chosen elite.'

'You assume their lives are equally valued. No, brother,' Cyrion said. 'He will send Vraal.'

Both warriors turned as the great doors rumbled open again. Cyrion was already voxing to Talos.

'My brother, it's beginning.'

The reply was terse. 'First Claw. At any sign of aggression, you will engage and slay the target. *Ave Dominus Nox.*'

'Cyrion,' Xarl racked his bolter as one of the Atramentar entered the Hall of Remembrance, 'I hate it when you are right.'

MALEK SHARED THE lift to the lower levels with Talos and Adhemar.

'You cannot afford to be this naïve,' he said, his face as grim and set as white granite.

'I am not being naïve,' Talos said. Despite his respect for Malek, the Atramentar's tone fired his blood. He couldn't keep the edge of defiance from his voice. 'I am acting in Tenth Company's best interests.'

'You are acting like a blind child.' Malek's voice was iron-stern now, and his black eyes glared. 'You talk of Tenth Company's best interests? That is exactly my point. Tenth Company is *dead*, Talos. Sometimes preservation of the past is a step backwards. I do not advocate change for change's sake. We are talking about the reality of our war.'

'The Night Haunter would never–'

'Do not dare speak of our father as if you know him better than I.' Malek's eyes narrowed, and his voice became an animalistic growl. 'Do not dare assume you were the only one he held private counsel with in his final nights. Many of us ranked among his chosen. Not you alone.'

'I know this. I am speaking of the legacy he wished for us.'

'He wished us to survive, and to defy the Imperium. That is all. Do you think he cared about the ranks we marched in and the titles we wore while we did our duty? We are barely over thirty Astartes. Squad unity is destroyed. Leadership is weak. Resources are stretched to the limit. We are not Tenth Company of the Eighth Legion. We haven't been for almost a century of our own time... and ten millennia of the galaxy's span.

'Do you truly remain blind to what you are doing?' Malek finished. He shook his head, as if the mere thought was impossible to fathom.

'I am willing to concede–'

'The question was rhetorical,' Malek grunted. 'Anyone can see it. You chance upon a hundred servitors just as our resources are almost bled dry. You walk the surface of our shattered home world, and anyone with their eyes open saw that as an omen. Then you steal a *Navigator*, of all the things to discover! Now a Titan princeps. You rail against the Exalted and speak of awakening the war-sage...'

Adhemar cut in. 'Talos, my brother. You are rebuilding the company to your vision. The Navigator was the boldest step. If the *Covenant* somehow lost Etrigius, the entire company would depend upon you, upon the

Navigator you control. We couldn't even break into the warp without your… permission.'

'Etrigius is in fine health,' Talos said. But they were words he couldn't back up. Navigators may enjoy inhuman longevity because of their mutations, but Etrigius – who forever kept himself shrouded in his personal observation chambers close to the ship's prow – had barely been seen by anyone except the Exalted in decades. Octavia had access to his section of the ship, but her meagre reports through Septimus had mentioned nothing of Etrigius's mental or physical state. He seemed unchanged.

'I am of the Atramentar,' Malek said, the tones heavy with import. Talos understood immediately. Malek would never break an oath to reveal the secrets of his liege lord, even if he despised the Exalted. But he was free to let Talos know he had obviously accompanied the Exalted into Etrigius's presence.

Perhaps the discovery of Octavia on Nostramo's surface was a more direct threat to the Exalted than Talos had realised.

She would need to be guarded. Guarded vehemently. And Malcharion's reawakening…

'Mercutian, Cyrion and Xarl stand watch in the Hall of Remembrance,' he said to Malek. The robed warrior nodded, his statuesque face resigned.

'That is probably wise. How long has the ritual been taking place?'

'Four hours. The Dreadnought's chassis was being powered up and consecrated when I left. They had not yet begun to wake the sleeper.'

'The odds are not in our favour,' Adhemar said. 'He has never awoken, even once.'

'And he did not go into that sarcophagus willingly,' Malek added.

Talos's vox crackled live, interrupting further discussion.

'My brother,' said Cyrion. 'It is beginning.'

VRAAL STRODE INTO the Hall of Remembrance.

The roaring lion's head of his right shoulder guard, marking him as one of the Atramentar, sported a pattern of random gashes and cuts, the marks of infrequent repairs after countless battles. The rest of his Terminator war-plate followed suit. Scars marred the midnight surface, the lips of these carved chasms gunmetal grey where repainting was in order.

Old blood still flaked his gauntlets. Although any matter on his lightning claws was burned away each time he activated them, gore would streak his gauntlets for weeks after he bloodied himself in battle.

The others misunderstood this as irreverence. As *disrespect*. It was almost laughable.

What greater honour to the machine-spirit of his armour was there than to display the wounds it had won in battle? What nobler reverence could be paid than revealing with pride all the scars that had failed to see him slain?

Thrusting from his armour's hunched back were trophy racks made from bronze spikes, each with Astartes helms and their oversized skulls clattering together with every step he took.

Vraal licked his teeth as his red-tinted displays locked onto every living being in the chamber. There, the servitors tending the silent Dreadnought, like mindless worshippers. There, the tech-adept Deltrian working over a console of arcane lights and switches and levers. There, the new blood of First Claw, dour Mercutian, standing in the shadows of the great doors to Vraal's left. There, Cyrion and Xarl, bolters held to chests.

The Atramentar noticed a warning rune flicker briefly. He was being scanned by an auspex. Deltrian, surely. Vraal gave the watching tech-priest an acknowledging nod as he stalked further into the room. The spindly machine-creature bowed back in respect. Hateful thing. A curse on the Mechanicum, that such filth was necessary to the Legion's operation.

Vraal was under no illusions about his presence here. The Exalted was playing its game with care, for to oppose Talos openly might incite full-blooded rebellion. What remained of the Tenth would be broken, some following the Exalted, others joining the prophet. For Vraal, the choice was no choice at all. The past or the future. Talos represented the former. What was there in the past but failure and shame?

It would be a relief when the prophet was finally killed. Well did Vraal remember his disappointment when the Exalted's plan to whore Talos off to the Ruinous Powers failed so completely. The Despoiler had allowed the prophet to escape with no resistance – Abaddon had even failed to kill the two slaves Talos evidently treasured – and Tenth Company was burdened with the prophet's irritating anachronistic meddling once again.

Maddening. Like an unscratchable itch.

No, Vraal was under no illusions at all. Open conflict was out of the question. It would galvanise Talos's emergent faction. One of the favoured Atramentar could never be used. It would be undeniable proof the Exalted was acting against the prophet. But not wild, unpredictable Vraal. Oh, no. Vraal would be mourned for his 'vicious temper' and 'choleric humours', while the Exalted waxed lyrical about how he deeply regretted Vraal's terrible disruption of the resurrection ritual.

His bitterness left him uncontrollable, the Exalted would say. *Vraal's actions bring shame upon us all. Such disunity…*

Yes, Vraal could almost hear his eulogy spoken now. The Exalted had sent him here to die, spending his life for the good of the warband. So be it.

Of course, this new plan to awaken Malcharion had to be put down with tact.

With nuance.

With *subtlety*.

Vraal's claws slid from the sheaths on his gauntlets. They sparked and crackled, wreathed in killing lightning.

'Brothers!' he called joyously into the vox. 'Everyone in this room is going to die!'

A moment later, he was wading into bolter fire, laughing through the speakers on his tusked helm.

Chunks broke away from his trophy racks, the shattered pieces thrown behind. A tusk from his own helm splintered. His chestplate cracked. His knee guard split, spraying ceramite debris to the ground. A storm of bolter fire hacked and chipped at his Terminator war-plate.

This was almost fun.

The three weaklings from First Claw were falling back, presenting unified fire that was doing nothing to suppress the Atramentar's advance. Vraal heard Deltrian's mechanical voice bleating over his vox.

'Why would you do this! This is blasphemy! This chamber is consecrated to the Machine-God!'

Ugh. Would that Vraal's armour had any ranged weapons... He could silence the wailing tech-priest once and for all. As it was, his lightning claws flared as if in response to his anger.

The three Astartes opposing him were backing away, edging towards the still form of Malcharion and unrelenting in their fire. This was irritatingly tactical. Vraal knew killing them was only a secondary concern, no matter how pleasurable it would be. He needed to end Malcharion's resurrection, once and for all. They stood in the most obvious way of that: simply tearing the Dreadnought's form apart with his claws.

Ah, well.

Vraal broke into what approximated a run for an Astartes encumbered by the near-invulnerable shell of Terminator armour. Not making for the defiant Astartes. No, that would be suicide without doing his duty.

'Tech-priest!' Vraal staggered as the withering hail of bolter fire shattered his lower leg plating and interrupted the workings of the servos. 'Come! We must talk, you and I!'

His stumbling, limping run had a sickening speed all its own. The reaper-like tech-priest did not leave his control console, even as Vraal slammed his right claw through the sacred machinery. Disappointingly, nothing exploded.

A particularly well-aimed bolt threw his head to the side for a moment. Most likely from Xarl. That bastard was known for being a wicked shot.

But the Astartes held back now. Vraal stood among the control consoles, thudding closer step by step to Deltrian. They wouldn't risk exploding bolts damaging the machinery. He raked both claws out to the sides, lacerating more blessed Mechanicum technology.

How curious. The defilement made the tech-priest weep. He was weeping what looked like oil, running down his skullish silver cheeks in dark tracks. Vraal took in this intriguing fact in the span of half a second. He used the rest of the second to ram the four curved knuckle-blades – each a metre in length – straight through Deltrian's torso.

'Hnnkhsssssssshhhh–' the tech-priest wheezed, cutting off in a blurted babble of static.

'Very wise,' Vraal chuckled, pulling the blades back. The resistance within the adept's body had felt unpleasant and inhuman. There was little joy in rending apart false machine-life. Deltrian fell back, his black robe clutched closed even as he fell to the marble floor.

A proximity warning rune flickered a moment too late. One of First Claw was on him.

Spinning, claws up to guard, Vraal faced the other Astartes.

Xarl's bolter kicked at close range, snapping one of Vraal's claws off in a shower of bolt shell debris. His chainsword howled down a heartbeat later.

'Just... *die*...' Xarl breathed over the vox. His grinding chainsword blade skidded across the Atramentar's hulking armour, biting into surface metal without penetrating deeper.

Vraal disengaged with a shrug of his shoulders. His Terminator war-plate boosted his already inhuman strength far beyond standard Astartes armour. And as to the odds of a chainsword piercing it... Well, at least Xarl was keen. It made things all the more amusing.

Vraal raised his right gauntlet – now missing a talon – and caught the chainsword between crackling sword-claws on its second descent. The revving blade immediately started eating its way through the softer joint armour and servo fibres of Vraal's gauntlets. With a grunt of effort, the Atramentar twisted his arm. The claws sparked with a flare of power as they met the trapped chainblade, and severed it with a wrenching snap.

Disarmed, Xarl leapt back, casting his ruined sword hilt aside as it coughed into death, and bringing his bolter to bear again.

He didn't fire. A warning rune told Vraal why, and he spun to meet the threat of Cyrion and Mercutian behind.

They came at him together, leaping with gladius blades drawn and reversed like plunging daggers in the hands of assassins. Cyrion's stab clattered aside from the dense war-plate, and Vraal smashed the Astartes aside with a slash of his claw that tore through Cyrion's armour.

Mercutian's thrust bit, and bit deep. It was a moment of shocking, sickening intimacy – a wrath-inspiring violation – when the two Astartes met one another's gaze through their crimson eye lenses. The gladius was a cold, hateful heaviness in Vraal's stomach, and even as his enhanced physiology coped with the wound by sealing the haemorrhage, he felt it being torn open again with Mercutian yanking the blade upwards.

He'd breached a soft joint in the armour. *And this... this was pain...*

Vraal hadn't quite remembered how much it hurt, it had been so long since he'd felt it.

Impacts struck him from behind in a staccato burst. The rhythm was utterly familiar. A bolter on full auto. *Xarl was… firing… and he needed to…*

Free himself… from the blade…

Vraal lifted his claw. The suit answered slowly, sluggish with the damage it was sustaining. Mercutian kept pulling the blade up, carving through Vraal's innards even though the blade was blocked from moving too far by the Atramentar's dense chestplate.

He spat blood into his helm and backhanded Mercutian away. The other Astartes snapped back like a puppet with its strings tugged too hard, and smashed into the ruined control console.

Mercutian was down. Cyrion was… *Ha!* His blow to Cyrion had severed the wretch's arm at the elbow. He was still picking himself up, shouting his hate through the vox as he looked for his bolter.

Xarl. He had to deal with Xarl. Xarl was always the dangerous one.

Blinking blood and sweat from his eyes, Vraal turned to do exactly that. He launched forward, claws powering towards Xarl like seven short lances.

Xarl cursed even as he moved, throwing himself to the side, muscles aflame, faster than he had ever moved in his gene-extended life.

The tips of Vraal's right claws caught him. Xarl clenched his teeth as the three blades sliced and penetrated his armour. A moment of agony pulsed through his left thigh, and he crashed to the ground on dead legs.

Vraal's estimation of the situation changed. Deltrian, that spindly machine-freak, was crawling away towards another wall-mounted console. He looked injured. Was that right? Did machine-men suffer injury? Damage, perhaps.

Cyrion was advancing again, one-armed and gripping his gladius, the pain of his wound doubtlessly swallowed whole by his armour's injection of stimulants and nerve-killers directly into the bloodstream and brain. Mercutian was back up as well, unarmed. His blade had broken in the fall, and he must have expended all of his bolter ammunition. Xarl, ever defiant, had drawn his bolt pistol and was aiming it from where he lay on the ground, unable to stand with his leg half-severed.

That was the moment Vraal realised he was probably going to win.

'Brothers, brothers,' he laughed. 'Who dies first?'

'Do your worst,' Xarl barked, opening fire again. Flashing runes blinked across Vraal's display as the bolts hammered into his head and chestplate. *Aiming for the neck joint,* Vraal knew. He was still laughing, still advancing, when Xarl's pistol clicked empty.

But… that sound…

…wwrrrrRRRRRRRRRR

Vraal's bloody face contorted as he scowled at the rising noise. *What the hell?*

It was the sound of a Reaper-pattern double-barrelled autocannon powering up. It was followed by the throaty mechanical *clunk-clunk-clunk* of autoloaders cycling into life.

Vraal turned in time to see it open fire. When it did, the Hall of Remembrance shook with the sheer volume of the weapon's discharge. Storms ferocious enough to bring down hive towers had done their destructive work with less volume and rage. Servitors too mindwiped to cover their ears suffered ruptured eardrums. The helms of First Claw filtered the sounds to tolerable levels, but every one of them had teeth clenched against the noise.

Vraal heard it all, with damning clarity, because it was happening to him.

Six mass-reactive explosive shells – each one capable of killing a Rhino transport on its own – smashed into the Atramentar in the space of three seconds. The first destroyed his chestplate and would have seen him dead in moments through the horrendous blood loss from his mangled insides. He was spared this death as the second shell killed him instantly, exploding against his tusked helm and annihilating his head and right shoulder.

The other four shells impacted and tore the remains to pieces. In three seconds, nothing remained of Vraal of the Atramentar beyond shards of broken armour and the wounds carried by First Claw.

The storm passed.

The thunder faded.

On ancient servos, the massive form of a bronze-edged, blue-armoured Dreadnought stepped forward. It was heavy enough to shake the room. The cannonfire had been nothing compared to its howling servo joints and cacophonous tread.

'L-lord?' Mercutian whispered.

'You're awake...' Cyrion breathed. 'How...'

In a guttural, vox-altered boom, the Dreadnought spoke from speakers wrought into its ornate chassis.

'I heard bolter fire.'

XV
REBORN

THE EXALTED RECLINED on its throne, forcing its face into a smile.

'It is a blessing to see you, brother.'

The hulking shape of Malcharion dominated the *Covenant*'s bridge. Light from the console screens flickered across his body's dark ceramite hull.

With the ship idle in orbit, the crew, those human enough to care, were free to cast sidelong glances at the incredible sight in their midst. Malcharion stood alone before the commander's raised central dais. The Dreadnought was tall enough that its sarcophagus was level with the seated figure.

Alongside the walls, every Astartes not engaged in planetary operations had gathered to witness the resurrection – and the first meeting with the Exalted. Talos and Adhemar stood in rapt awe. So did most of the others.

Around the Exalted's throne stood the Atramentar. All of them, except for Vraal. Seven warriors, the Terminator elite, in an orderly half-ring behind the throne. Malek and Garadon stood closest to the Exalted, as always.

For the longest time, the war machine said nothing. The Exalted watched with its slanted black eyes, raptor-like in his attention to detail. It fancied it could almost hear, under the ever-present hum of the Dreadnought's back-mounted power generator, the occasional bubbling swish of the amniotic fluid within the sarcophagus as whatever remained of Malcharion's mortal body twitched.

'You have changed,' the Dreadnought boomed.

The Exalted's smirk did not fade, indeed it became suddenly more genuine. 'As have you, brother.'

The machine made a noise akin to a grunt of acknowledgement. It sounded like a tank shifting gears.

'You are uglier than I remember.' Another gear-change grunt, this one closer to a chuckle. 'I would not have believed it possible.'

'I see your period of inactivity while the rest of us waged our father's war has not dimmed your... humour.'

'Do not bore me back into slumber with your dour nature, Vandred.'

'I am the Exalted now. You would do well to heed that, Malcharion. Time has changed many things.'

'Not everything. Hear me, Vandred. I have awoken. Torn from an enternity of nightmares, each one a memory of our greatest failure. The Soul Hunter tells me that war calls once more. You will tell me of this war. Now.'

The Exalted's lips curled. *The Soul Hunter.* Sickening.

'As you wish.'

THE BATTLEFIELD HAD several names. None of them quite carried the weight of true import. This was to be the decisive conflict, the moment of truth.

Located in the highest reaches of the northern hemisphere's mountain range, it was the bastion of Mechanicus strength above the equator.

To the invaders, grudgingly impressed by the curving rock formations and the fortress-factories built into them, it was the Omnissiah's Claw. A theatrical name, but apt: the mountains resembled steel fingers reaching for the heavens, as if the fortresses could tear the invader vessels from orbit.

To the cold cogitators and tactical logic engines of the Mechanicus defenders, it was simply Site 017-017.

Seventeen-Seventeen, the main foundry of the Legio Maledictis, heart and soul of Crythe Prime's Adeptus Titanicus forces.

And void-shielded so densely that orbital bombardment was utterly beyond hope. Ironically, such a defence was pointless. Abaddon had made it clear to his captains and commanders that Seventeen-Seventeen was to be captured, not destroyed. Such a base would be able to repair, outfit and construct Titans to serve in his coming crusade. At the very least, huge quantities of materiel and resources could be plundered from the fortress-factories here.

Time, however, was growing short. Astropaths across the fleet told of whispers within the warp. The Imperium's response to the invasion would arrive within weeks.

The Blood Angels. The Marines Errant. Countless regiments of the Imperial Guard. Abaddon had ventured far from his haven within the warp anomaly known as the Eye of Terror, where the Imperium could never follow. While he had chosen a fine target in Crythe and hit the world with the decisive power of this hastily-assembled fleet, victory must now come quickly or be abandoned altogether. Already the month of war had been drawn out too long, and ground taken at too high a cost. The Mechanicus and their accursed champions in the Legio Maledictis were defiant, indefatigable foes.

If astropathic premonitions were accurate, the Imperium's battle-fleets en route would present unbreakable might. Here, the forces of the Throne sensed their chance to bring the Despoiler to justice. Navigators and other psychically-sensitive souls among the Chaos fleet told of a great wave of pressure rolling from the warp, like the thunderheads of a coming storm. Every warrior within the Warmaster's armies knew this for what it was. A convergence of warp routes, the way a fleet of ships would drive waves of water before their prows. Invisible currents within the Sea of Souls lashed at the Crythe Cluster as countless Imperial vessels burned their engines hot to defend the forge world and avenge the worlds already fallen.

It all came down to Seventeen-Seventeen.

Crythe Prime had to be taken.

The endgame had begun.

THE NIGHT LORDS of Tenth Company's remnants were tasked with making up part of the spearhead in the initial assaults. Alongside them would be their kin from the *Hunter's Premonition*.

With masses of traitorous Imperial Guard now siding with the War-master, along with the penal legions harvested from Solace, the Night Lords of *Hunter's Premonition* and the *Covenant of Blood* had a handful of foundries and fortress-factories marked as objectives.

The Black Legion, far outnumbering the Night Lords contingent, was assigned to larger numbers of similar factorum objectives. Talos no longer detected any obvious signs of the Warmaster seeking to bleed the VIII Legion ahead of his own troops.

Necessity stole any such favouritism.

FIRST CLAW'S ARMING chamber was a hive of activity.

Serfs and servitors attached armour into place, machining it closed and sealed. Septimus was one of them, checking the joint seals of Talos's armour, ignored by the Astartes as they spoke.

Cyrion held his arm out as a servitor attached his vambrace and gaunt-let. Everyone in the room caught a glimpse of the new augmetic limb, its metal surface a dull, oceanic grey, still uncovered by synth-flesh. Soon enough, the naked steel and titanium arm was armoured in the midnight blue of his battleplate.

Weapons were blessed and honoured. Oaths were sworn. Spinal sock-ets were penetrated by the invasive connection needles of power armour locking into place. Vision was tinted murder-red by helms descending over faces.

'I have not seen Octavia since long before her surgery yesterday,' Cyrion ventured. 'How does our Navigator fare, artificer?'

Septimus did not look over from where he was fastening an oath scroll to Talos's shoulder. The parchment was the white of fresh cream, detailing in Talos's flowing Nostraman handwriting all of the mission objectives, and his blood-sworn promises to succeed in each one. Oaths of Moment like these were no longer common within the Legion. Xarl also wore one, but Mercutian, Uzas, Cyrion and Adhemar abstained from the tradition.

'She is well, Lord Cyrion,' said Septimus. 'I expect she is with Navigator Etrigius again. They spend much time in discussion. They... often argue, apparently.'

'I see. My thanks for the work you did on my bolter.' As he spoke, he held the weapon up, looking over it as he cradled the weapon in his gauntlets. The name *'Banshee'* was written upon its side in swirling Nostraman script.

'A pleasure to serve, Lord Cyrion.'

'How is the void-born? Is she well?'

Septimus froze as he checked the rivets of Talos's shoulder guards. 'The... the what, Lord Cyrion?'

'The void-born. How is she?'

'What's this now?' Uzas asked, suddenly interested.

'She is a mortal, brother. Beneath your concern,' said Cyrion.

'She is... well, thank you, Lord Cyrion.'

'Good to hear. Don't look so surprised, we're not all blind to the goings on of the ship. Take her my regards, will you?'

'Yes, Lord Cyrion.'

'Did she like her gift?' asked Talos.

Septimus forced himself not to freeze again. 'Yes, lord.'

'What gift?' Uzas sounded irritated to be excluded.

'A Legion medallion,' said Talos. 'This mortal is treasured by some of the crew. Apparently, treasured enough to warrant my protection.' Talos turned to Septimus again, and the slave's blood froze. 'Without my permission.'

'Forgive me, master.'

'I heard holes were drilled into the coin, and she wears it as a necklace,' Talos continued. 'Is that desecration, Cyrion? Defiling Legion relics?'

'I think not, brother. But I shall take the matter up with the Exalted. We must be certain of such things.'

Septimus's smile was forced, and he swallowed again. He tried to speak. He failed.

'Forgive us a moment's levity at your expense, Septimus,' Talos said. He flexed his fists, rotating his wrists, testing the ease of motion. His right gauntlet was definitely stiff. A replacement must be found soon.

Faroven. Faroven, the brother that Talos saw die in a dream. From his body, would the new gauntlet come.

His end cannot be far away now.

Cyrion clamped his bolter to his thigh on its magnetic coupling. 'Aye, it's been a long time since we were mortal. Strange how you forget how to joke.'

Septimus nodded again, unsure if even now Cyrion was making fun of him, and still far from comfortable with such 'humour'.

'By the way,' Cyrion added. 'Take this.'

Septimus caught the coin easily, one hand taking it out of the air on its downward arc. It was a twin to Talos's own coin, silver and marked the same, but for Cyrion's name in the written runes.

'If you're going to give mine away and doom me to watching over a ten-year-old girl,' Talos said, 'I need to keep you alive somehow.'

Septimus bowed in deep thanks to both of them, and finished his duties in humbled and confused silence.

It HAD TAKEN Octavia barely five minutes to decide that she didn't like Etrigius at all.

According to the *Covenant*'s Navigator, he had known upon first seeing her that he disliked her. This was the kind of fact he found necessary to share.

Etrigius wasn't even remotely human anymore. That was little concern to Octavia, and nowhere near as shocking to her as many of the more mundane aspects of life aboard the *Covenant*.

She was a Navigator, a scion of the Navis Nobilite, and even if her House name wasn't worth an iota of respect in the great and wide galaxy, she was still a daughter of humanity's most precious bloodlines.

She knew what the Navigator gene did to all of her kind in time. In that regard, sitting with the no-longer-human form of Etrigius was disconcerting, but never truly unnerving.

Much worse was his penchant for glorifying his own existence.

These nightly lessons were now her duty – he'd made that clear the first time he'd demanded her presence weeks before – but they were far from pleasant.

Etrigius's domain was the antithesis of the gloom that pervaded the *Covenant*'s innards the way blood ran through a body's veins. He claimed a modest chamber close to the ship's massively-armoured prow, and bathed the room in oppressive white light from glow-globes mounted on the walls. Octavia found the brightness hard to bear after the ship's dark halls. Her warp eye remained covered, but her human eyes wept stinging tears each time she came to visit the other Navigator in his den. The illumination of false sunlight after a month of night.

'Can you dim these lights?' she asked the first time she'd been granted admittance by Etrigius's robed slaves.

'No,' he said, seeming to muse. 'I dislike the dark.'

'It might be said that you're on the wrong ship.'

Camaraderie had threatened to bloom between them at that moment. They had one thing in common that no other soul shared. Yet instead of a unity forming, they'd quickly descended into bickering and vague tolerance.

Etrigius's attendants – not one of them unaugmented and younger than sixty – admitted her to 'the master's gallery'. The title was appropriate. An entire wall was taken up with pict screens reflecting dozens of views from different points of the ship's outer hull. As it was, the screens showed the rest of the Warmaster's battlefleet, and the world the *Covenant* orbited.

In the warp… the screens would come into their own. Octavia had to admire the wish to see every angle of the ship as one guided it through the sea of souls.

The rest of the chamber was much less admirable. And much less tidy. Clothes were piled here and there, strewn across the floor, as well as jewellery. When she'd first entered, her boot had crunched a golden earring into the ground. Etrigius, thankfully, hadn't noticed.

Octavia suspected Etrigius had been handsome at one point. If not handsome, then at least well-presented. Before his service in the Great Crusade and the century of chronological time since. She formed this opinion from his voice and bearing, both of which remained cultured and polite despite his many other changes from the near-human he'd been at birth.

His skin was grey. Not the wan tone of a sunless existence, nor even the pale grey of the dead or the dying. It was grey the way a deepwater shark's belly was grey: fish-like but unscaled, thick, completely inhuman.

His fingers were almost armoured in gold and ruby, such was the number of rings he wore. Octavia was no expert, but what confused her was that the rings varied in quality from the exquisitely valuable to the almost worthless. What seemed to be the only common factor was that each ring was a shade of red set in a mounting of gold.

The Navigator's many-ringed thumbs and fingers each possessed an extra joint. Octavia would lose track of what she was saying if she got lost in their eerie, hypnotic, curling movements. Fingernails more akin to a feline's claws sickle-curved from the tips of Etrigius's grey fingers. These he used to stroke the tattered leather of his observation couch, forever seeming to engineer new splits in the material.

The rest of Etrigius's body was masked by a robe of the same deep blue favoured by the Legion's warriors. His domed head was smooth enough for Octavia to be sure no hair ever grew there, and his 'human' eyes were always masked in pressurised goggles with thick clear lenses, featuring some strange violet fluid swirling within. She'd asked what the liquid in his lenses was, asked how he even saw through the murk, but he'd deigned not to answer. Etrigius did that a great deal. Evidently, he only answered topics he found worthy of discussion.

'They have freed your warp eye,' he murmured, with something resembling awe.

She touched the bandana tied around her forehead. 'I think they must be coming to trust me. I mean, after I took the name... After Talos saved me...'

'I was not informed of this. Why was I not told you were to be unblinded?'

'Is it any of your business?'

'I am the Navigator for the *Covenant of Blood*. Any issue pertaining to the warp is within my purview.'

'I've been sitting here an hour listening to you. You only just noticed the metal was gone from my forehead?'

'This was the first time I have bothered to face in your direction,' he said, and it was true enough. Etrigius was not enamoured of eye contact.

'I am tired of feeling helpless on this ship,' she said, more to herself than to him.

Etrigius smiled, for once, with apparent sincerity. 'Do not expect that to fade, girl.'

She watched him in silence for several moments, hoping he would continue.

'We are at once slaves and slavemasters,' he said. 'Enslaved, yet valuable beyond measure.' Etrigius gestured to the screens, displaying the Chaos fleet orbiting Crythe. 'Without us, these traitors are crippled. Their endless crusade could never be fought.'

Octavia's gaze never left the grey man's.

'Did you choose this life?'

'No. And neither will you. But we will both live it, all the same.'

'Why would I wish to seal myself away in here?' she countered.

'What Navigator can be satisfied without a vessel to guide?' The words left his lips with a sickeningly condescending sense of kindness.

Octavia shook her head without realising she was even doing so. An unconvincing denial, truly no more than an instinctive need to say no.

Etrigius smiled that same smile. 'You hunger to sail the stars, as we all do. It's in the blood. You can no more hide that desire than you can hide the need to breathe. When the time comes, when the Astartes ask you to guide them... you will say yes.'

Octavia once more felt the potential for a connection between them. She could have used that moment to ask for revelations about navigating the warp without using the guiding light of the Emperor's Astronomican. She could have said any one of a hundred things to bridge the gap between herself and her fellow Navigator.

Instead, she rose to her feet and left.

A cold-blooded sense of inevitability had stolen her tongue.

* * *

WHEN SEPTIMUS FOUND her, she was in Blackmarket.

In the *Covenant*'s mortal decks, a communal chamber linked many of the individual halls and quarters, and as the Great Crusade played out across the galaxy, the Legion's loyal servants and slaves came to use the chamber as a trading post and a place to gather. The black market, as it was back then, derived its name from the perpetual darkness of the chamber, only marginally dispelled by lamp packs and glow-globes. Even with a full crew in better days, the mortal decks had endured the same scarce illumination as they did now.

Fifty or so people crowded the chamber. His status ensured he received respectful nods or greetings from most of them, even from the clusters of rival gang emissaries here to trade for ammunition and power packs. Here, in all its shadowed glory, was a microcosm of fallen Nostramo, born afresh in the blackness.

One old woman pressed her grimy hands to the bronze surface of his augmented temple and eyebrow.

'It's not so bad,' she smiled, exposing rotten teeth in her otherwise kindly, lined face.

'I'm getting used to it.'

'The surgery took you from us for too long. Weeks! We worried!'

'I thank you for your concern, Shaya.'

'Nale's gang was killed close to the enginarium decks.' She dropped her voice. 'None of the others are claiming responsibility. There's talk it's another beast, come from the deepest dark.'

Septimus felt a grim mood settling firmly on his shoulders. He had been part of the hunting party to slay the last warp-creature that spawned in the bowels of the ship.

'I will speak with the masters. I promise.'

'Bless you, Septimus,' she said. 'Bless you.'

'I... heard Octavia was here?'

'Ah, yes. The new girl.' The old woman smiled again, gesturing to a market stall with a small group of people stood around. 'She is with the void-born.'

With the...? Why?

'My thanks,' he said, and moved on.

Octavia was indeed with the void-born. The little girl, her pupils eternally huge in the gloom into which she was born, was showing Octavia a selection of articulated string puppets. Octavia stood at the stall, run by the void-born's ageing mother and father. She smiled and nodded down at the girl's presentation.

Septimus came alongside the Navigator and bowed to the void-born's parents. They greeted him and remarked on how his wounds were healing.

'I had to get away from Etrigius,' Octavia said in Gothic. 'I have the medallion now,' she added almost defensively. 'So I went for a walk.'

'The ship is still dangerous, medallion or not.'

'I know,' she replied, not looking at him.

'Do you understand anything she's said?' Septimus nodded to the little girl.

'Not a word. Her parents have been translating some. I just wanted to meet her. The respect she receives is incredible. People keep coming over, just to speak with her. Someone paid for a tiny lock of her hair.'

'She is revered,' Septimus said. He looked down at the void-born, who was staring up through her ratty and snarled mop of long black hair.

'Athasavis te corunai tol shathen sha'shian?' he asked.

'Kosh, kosh'eth tay,' she smiled back. A beaming smile on her face, she held up the silver Legion medallion, holed through and strung on a leather thong cord. She wore it like a medal of honour. 'Ama sho'shalnath mirsa tota. Ithis jasha. Ithis jasha nereoss.'

Septimus offered her a little bow, smiling despite his black mood.

'What did she say?' Octavia asked, trying to hide her disappointment at the Nostraman conversation.

'She thanked me for the gift, and said she thinks my new eye is a very nice colour.'

'Oh.'

The void-born started babbling, pointing up at Octavia. Septimus smiled again.

'She says you are very pretty, and asks if you are ever going to learn Nostraman, so you can talk to her properly.'

Octavia nodded. 'Jasca,' she said, then in a quieter voice to Septimus, 'That's "yes", isn't it?'

'Jasca,' he replied. 'It is. Come, we need to talk. I'm sorry I've been away since your surgery. It has been an interesting day since we last spoke.'

HE SHOULD NEVER have been awakened.

Had he not served with heart and courage and loyalty? Had he not slain the primarch's enemies? Had he not obeyed the orders of the First Warmaster? What more did life demand of him?

Now he walked once more, striding through the waking world. *And for what?* To witness the degeneration of everything the Legion had once been. To stand defiant against Vandred while Tenth Company crumbled in the final moments of its decay.

This was not life. This was an extension of an existence he had rightfully left behind.

He was two bodies. A mind divided between two physical forms. On one level, through his most immediate perceptions, he felt what was now: the vehicular strength of his tank-like body. The massive arms jointed by grinding servos. The claw capable of mangling adamantium and ceramite. The cannon capable of annihilating entire platoons of men.

An unbreathing, tireless avatar of the Mechanicum's unity between flesh and machine.

All of that could be dissolved within a single moment's lapse in concentration. These immediate sensations were an effort to maintain. In the moments when the ancient warrior let his focus waver, he would feel himself, his mortal husk, encased within the sarcophagus and suspended in cold, cold, cold amniotic fluid.

These truer sensations were sickening to dwell upon, but Malcharion's attention tore back to them time and again. His legless, one-armed husk of a body, gently cradled in icy, gritty fluid. The back of his head and spine was a vertical splash of jagged, awkward pain as machine tendrils and mind impulse unit brain spikes needled his ravaged body, forcing his thoughts into junction with the Dreadnought body.

Sometimes, when he tried to move his left arm – the claw-like power fist – he felt his true limb, the wasted fleshly limb, thumping weakly against the side of the amniotic coffin that housed his corpse. The first time he had tried to speak to Vandred, instead of the piercing tendrils within his mind carrying his thoughts into vox-voice, he had felt his true mouth open. Only then had he realised he *breathed* the freezing fluid now. It was how he stayed alive. Oil-thick and numbingly cold, the amniotics circulated through his respiratory system. The ooze caked his lungs, a dead weight within a helpless, strengthless body.

A long time ago, he had battled alongside his brothers of the Iron Hands Legion. After those wars had ended, he battled against those same brothers. Malcharion knew their beliefs well. It was unconscionable to him that such stoic, resilient warriors found this eternal entombment to be some kind of glorious afterlife.

'I will lead the next surface assault,' he'd boomed at the gathered Night Lords. The warriors of his Legion bowed their heads or thumped fists to breastplates in respect. In pride! Incredible. They saw only what was on the outside. They had no conception of the withered corpse within as its starved face pressed against the front of its coffin.

'We are the Lords of the Night. We are the sons of the Eighth Legion. And we will take Seventeen-Seventeen, so that for a thousand years the Imperium will lament the hour of our coming to Crythe.'

The cheers had been loud and long.

'Prepare a drop pod,' the Dreadnought demanded. 'I stand in midnight clad once more, and my claws thirst for Imperial blood.'

The cheers roared louder.

An eyeless, tongueless, one-armed corpse floated within the god-like machine, knowing it would soon taste war for the first time in ten thousand years.

XVI

SEVENTEEN-SEVENTEEN

'I have noticed an anomaly.

Many Imperial records have come to deal very kindly with the Crythe Cluster Insurrection, but praise is most often levelled at the saviour fleet led by the arriving Astartes of the Blood Angels Chapter, rather than the initial defence of any individual world. Critical eyes were most often cast at the 'dubious resistance' put up by the Adeptus Mechanicus in the defence of its principal bastion in the northern hemisphere, Site 017-017.

Indeed, that site's survival is often entirely attributed to the instability of the Archenemy's forces upon Crythe Prime and the well-noted tendency of the Traitor Legions to fall upon one another at the slightest provocation.

Entire mountains were hollowed out to make room for the blessed Titan foundries of the Legio Maledictis. Had the Despoiler's war been successful, these would have been a resource of overwhelming value: used, plundered and stripped of their worth before the arriving Imperial fleet bestowed its infinite vengeance upon the accursed forces of the Warmaster.

Those rugged mountainsides were thick with elite Mechanicus skitarii, like lice in a beggar's hair. Arranging thousands of individual landings across the entire mountain range would have taken a great deal of time that remained unavailable to the Despoiler.

At this stage, the Warmaster believed only weeks remained before the first Blood Angel battle-barge would soar into the system to bring the God-Emperor's justice. Abaddon, a thousand curses upon his name, knew this from his own astropathic sources. Prisoners captured after the war confirmed this to us.

Such foreknowledge is the only conceivable explanation for a massed surface landing on the plains before Site 017-017's foothills. In essence, Abaddon cast his hordes planetside and hurled them 'at the front gates', as it were.

I have heard it said that our greatest weapon against the Archenemy is the foe's own nature. That may indeed be so. Fate was most certainly on the side of righteousness the day the Night Lords and Black Legion within the Crythe offensive turned against one another.

No Imperial record I have been able to trace details exactly why Abaddon's command over portions of his army broke so completely, nor does it explain what – if anything! – the forces of the Archenemy sought to gain from their untimely division.

If such internal conflict is down to anything more than the maddened behaviour of tainted, once-human beasts, it is unlikely to ever come to light.'

– Interrogator Reshlan Darrow
Annotation in his pivotal work: *Faces of the Despoiler*

FIRST CLAW SHUDDERED as one.

'Breaching atmosphere,' Adhemar said to the others within the confines of the drop pod. 'One minute.'

'Why the rough deployment?' Cyrion asked.

'Anti-air fire,' Mercutian grumbled.

'This high? Not a chance.'

'It's just a rough ride down,' said Adhemar. 'Weather patterns, rising heat, high pressure. Stay focused, brothers.'

'Blood,' Uzas was mumbling. 'Blood and skulls and souls for the Red King.'

'Shut up,' Adhemar growled. 'Shut up or I'll tear your head off, stuff it with frag grenades, and use it as the ugliest explosive ever made.'

'He can't hear you,' said Cyrion. 'Ignore him. He always does this.'

'Blood for the Blood God,' Uzas's voice was thick and wet. He was salivating again, venomous drool coating his chin. 'Skulls for the–'

Talos slammed the palm of his hand on Uzas's helm, crashing the side of the helmet against the headrest of his brother's restraint throne.

'Shut *up*,' he snapped. '*Every* mission. *Every* battle. *Enough.*'

Uzas didn't react at all.

'See?' Cyrion said to Adhemar.

Adhemar just nodded, his thoughts his own. 'Thirty seconds.'

'This is not going to be easy,' Mercutian said. 'Are we going in with the Violators and the Scourges of Quintus?'

'They're to the east,' Talos answered, 'between us and the Black Legion. Just remember your targets. We break in, we kill the unit commanders as ordered, and we break out to our own lines.'

'Twenty seconds,' Adhemar noted.

'This is not about attrition,' Talos said, repeating Malcharion's words at the briefing, 'and we're dead if anyone tries to turn it into a fair fight.'

'Ten seconds.'

'Kill, and break away. Let Abaddon's mortal followers bleed for him.' Talos couldn't resist the grin that coloured his words. 'That's not our job.'

IT WAS A decent plan on the surface, but with obvious risks.

The squads that volunteered for this, across all of the Traitor Legions and renegade Chapters, were given poor odds of survival.

In front of the Exalted and Malcharion, Talos had demanded First Claw be part of the assault.

Like all troops, the Mechanicus's skitarii, despite their training and augmentations, had proved time and again they suffered when severed from their battlefield leadership. The Warmaster's forces, seeking to capitalise on that potential weakness, hurled elite squads of Astartes into the warzones below – each unit tasked with the assassination of several tech-adept commanders.

First Claw's pod crashed to the earth, throwing soil skyward from its landing crater. With timed bursts, the walls slammed down to form ramps, and First Claw charged from their restraint thrones, bolters up and blazing as they ran out onto the plainsland – a vast plateau before the foothills of Seventeen-Seventeen's crag fortresses.

Their pod had come down onto a battlefield, in the middle of an enemy regiment.

An ocean of foes writhed beyond the clearing dust of their downed pod. The distant figures of Titans, a host of classes and patterns, duelled in the distance.

The closest of the god-machines was at least two thousand metres away – a towering, enraged Reaver spraying the ground with immense firepower – and still it was huge beyond reckoning compared to the surrounding enemy. Instinctively, it drew the eyes.

As the Astartes disembarked, weapons opening up, their vox calls to each other immediately took on a tone of amused desperation.

'Try not to die here, brothers,' Mercutian muttered. 'I'm in no spirits to look for another squad.'

Cyrion laid waste to three heavily-augmented tech-guard, bolts detonating in the flesh-parts of their bodies and blowing them apart.

'This looked much easier on the holo-maps!' A brute with four mechanical extra arms rumbled towards him, waving a bizarre array of mining tools formed into weapons of war. Cyrion dodged a drill the size of his leg as it powered past his head, and rammed his gladius into the skitarii's bawling mouth. The blade bit, sank in, and impaled the skitarii's altered brain.

'I've got zero confirmation of the first target,' he said, holding back several more tech-guard with full-auto bolter fire. His aim was off. Shaky and loose. Hard to align his bolter with his targeting reticule.

The new arm. A hasty surgery and a simple augmetic. It would need a great deal more reconstructive work before he was satisfied with its performance. Still, with these odds, it was impossible to miss.

The ground was treacherous underfoot, rendered uneven by the bodies layering the plain. Their drop pod had killed a fair few of the enhanced Mechanicus soldiers when it hammered down into the heart of the regiment's formation. Those around the impact zone were still scattered and fighting to form a decent resistance to the enemy in their midst.

'Landing is never an exact science, eh?' Adhemar ended a brief duel with a skitarii possessing treads instead of legs. He wrenched his combat blade from the creature's eye socket, launching at the next closest. 'Zero sighting of the main target.'

Talos's attention kept flicking to his retinal display, keeping track of the squad's increasing spatial division.

'Xarl?' he voxed. No answer. He spun as he lashed out with *Aurum*. The distance was bad. The blade's tip snicked through the throat of a looming tech-guard behind him, instead of taking the head clean off.

'Xarl, answer me.' Talos kicked the staggering skitarii with the severed jugular away. Cycling through sight modes, he tried to get a clear view of his brothers through the mass melee.

'North,' came Xarl's voice. 'Closer to the front line. I can't confirm. The fighting is densest there.'

'I'm too far away for confirmation,' Adhemar voxed back.

'As am I,' Talos cursed. 'Cyrion? Mercutian?'

'Little... busy...' Mercutian replied.

'Too far,' breathed Cyrion. 'Can't see. Fighting.'

'Souls for the Soul Eater!' Uzas screamed. 'Skulls for the Skull Throne!'

'No one asked you.'

Through a sea of stabbing drills, slashing blades, punching fists and cutting las-fire, Talos carved and gunned his way forward.

Something impacted on the side of his helm. *Anathema* barked in that direction, ending whatever threat had been there. *Aurum* twisted to deflect a skitarii's two lashing machine arms. Talos thudded his ceramite boot into the chest of a tech-guard to the right, caving in the warrior's armour and puncturing his lungs with broken ribs. *Aurum* flashed again in a vicious arc, cleaving through another tech-guard's torso as *Anathema* roared three shells into the heads of three other skitarii.

The downed tech-guard, carved in two, flailed at Talos's legs with its remaining functional arm. The Night Lord stamped on the howling saw blade to smash it into uselessness and crushed the soldier's head a moment later.

'I'm having a wonderful time,' Cyrion voxed to him, breathless and sarcastic.

'You and I both,' Talos said, his teeth clenched. He spared a half-second's glance in the direction of the monstrous Reaver. It was closer now, but only barely, siren horns wailing above the battlefield – a challenge or a warning to those underfoot. It dwarfed the defeated Warhound by no small degree.

'Traitors!' one of the attacking skitarii yelled. 'Kill them!'

Talos gunned him down with a bolt in the face, and waded on.

Uzas made the kill.

The tech-adept was called Rollumos, a name he'd chosen himself, and any name he'd been born with was forgotten long, long ago. He was, by the calculations of his own internal chronometers, one hundred and sixteen years of age. At least, the few remaining flesh parts were. Close, so very close, was his ascension to perfection. Only seventeen per cent of his flawed mortal form remained. A glorious and worshipful eighty-three per cent was iron, steel, bronze and titanium, all consecrated and ritually thrice-blessed daily in the name of the Machine-God.

He hesitated to call himself a Master of Skitarii, not out of modesty but out of private shame. His role was a vital one, certainly, and not without its honour. Yet a grim, too-human ache remained within his cranial cogitators. A master of what? Slave soldiers?

He deserved better. He deserved more.

Solace lay in deception, and shame could be quelled by the same deceit. Outwardly he embraced his role, endlessly modifying his physical form so that he might wage war alongside his augmented warriors. He lied to his peers and fellow adepts. How they believed him! How they processed and chattered confirmation for his apparent scholarly focus within the physicality of front-line tactical/battle immersion.

Like the avatars of the Machine-God that they were, the great engines of Legio Maledictis strode across the plains, towering above Rollumos's own pedestrian, humble, insignificant accomplishments. Oftentimes he would ascend the gantries when only menials were present, and run a mechadendrite across the armour of an inactive Titan, his inner processors generating picts of himself working on a god-machine, striving to bring forth the soul of the engine from its silent bulk.

Tormented by his own position in the Legio's hierarchy, at least he hid his displeasure from the unblinking eyes of his more respected brethren. That was cold comfort, but enough to keep his shame hidden.

It was no matter that this hierarchical deceit placed him within harm's way. His body was significantly enhanced to deal with the kind of threats faced by tech-guard infantry, and he had no worries of sustaining personal harm.

And yet, this deceit was one he came to regret in the final minutes of his life.

They were dropping Astartes into his regiments.

Astartes. Entire squads of them. A night-dark drop pod lashed ground-
ward, pounding into the plain some five hundred and eleven metres
from where he stood, deep within a phalanx of his favoured skitarii.

Rollumos cogitated their allegiance. The winged skull symbol. The
forks of lightning inscribed upon their armour. The... immediate and
total viciousness of their assault, bolters discharging and blades hewing
into precious augmented skitarii flesh.

Night Lords. This was not optimal.

As Rollumos directed a greater number of his soldiers in the direction
of this closest pod and its troublesome burden, the first regrets were
just beginning to sink in. These regrets reached their peak – and ended
abruptly – exactly seven minutes and nine seconds later.

'Kill,' Uzas voxed to First Claw. He wasn't even out of breath. 'Target
slain.'

Uzas raised Rollumos's metal head in one hand, like a primitive tribes-
man bearing the skull of a murdered foe. The tech-guard around him
shrank back as he howled.

'Who's next?' Cyrion asked. The others heard the pounding of weapons
against his armour transmitted over the vox. 'I'm already bored of this.'

'Skitarii Captain Tigrith,' Talos answered. 'Look for banners. Further
north.'

First Claw returned to the *Covenant of Blood* nine hours later.

Septimus and Octavia were waiting for them in the hangar bay, both
mortals dressed in their Legion serf uniforms. The Thunderhawk bringing
them back was *Nightfall*, one of the only other gunships still functional
within Tenth Company. Two other squads disembarked first. First Claw
came last, and Octavia swore softly under her breath.

Almost ten hours of solid fighting at the front line had taken a clear
toll. Cyrion's arm was limp and unmoving, the hastily-attached augmetic
limb having given out hours before under the relentless demands of
battle. Xarl's collection of skulls hanging from his armour was reduced
to no more than scarce fragments of bone dangling on a few remaining
chains. Uzas and Mercutian both bore horrendous damage to their battle
armour: las-burns had carved blackened furrows through the ceramite
or burned it black on deflected impact; huge axes and chainblades had
chopped the images of their edges into the dark plate elsewhere.

Adhemar was bareheaded, his face decorated with bloody cuts, already
scabbed and sealing with his enhanced physiology.

Talos was the last to leave the Thunderhawk. The defiled Imperial eagle
upon his chestpiece sported some intriguing new desecrations. One wing
was now severed by a blade's impact, unjoined to the rest of the image,
and the eagle's ivory-white body was black – charred by a flame weapon
was Septimus's guess. Talos's right hand was locked into a curled claw,

rigid and unmoving. Evidently, the gauntlet had finally failed, and would need a great deal of care in its repair.

Septimus noticed two things immediately, the first of which was how much effort it was going to take to repair Talos's armour. The second made his blood run cold.

'Where's his gun?' Octavia asked. She'd noticed it, too.

'I lost it,' Talos said as First Claw strode past.

'Lord, where are you going?' Septimus said.

'To see the tech-priest, and the Tenth Captain.'

DELTRIAN ATTENDED TO Malcharion personally.

The damage he'd sustained in the desecration of the Hall of Remembrance was almost fully repaired, though several joint-motors within his upper body were still functioning at half-capacity, their systems untested at full power.

Although it wounded him with secret shame to adopt such a human reaction to his injuries, he cursed Vraal each time his diminished physical aptitude caused an adjustment in his motion and movement.

The tech-adept and several of his servitors worked on the Dreadnought's hull, resealing, repairing, amending and reshaping. The Hall of Remembrance echoed with the sounds of maintenance.

Talos had greeted Deltrian formally upon entering, but quickly lapsed into vox conversation with the ancient warrior.

'Forgive me for the rudeness, tech-priest,' the Astartes said, replacing his helm back over his head. 'It is necessary if we are to speak over the noise.' Deltrian had bowed in response. The sounds of holy maintenance were loud by necessity. Through such song was praise offered to the Machine-God.

'Captain...' Talos voxed.

'Captain no longer. Speak, Soul Hunter.'

'The plains are ours.'

'A fine landing site, they shall make. The siege begins with the dawn.'

'It will be close. Even if we take the city within the week...' Talos trailed off. Malcharion knew as well as he did. Time was not their ally. The Blood Angels were less than three weeks away.

'Abaddon's seers are still sure, are they not?'

Talos snorted. 'I heard from his own lips that they are failing him all too often these nights.'

'Then why does he trust them?'

Irritation – and doubt, Talos realised with a jolt of unease – had crept into Malcharion's vox-tone. He was a warrior from an age when almost no psychic tolerance pervaded the Legions. Such abominations were either barred from loyal service or strictly trained and regulated, not relied upon as part of a war's planning.

'He works with what he has. In this case, astropaths across the fleet confirm it.'

'Does Krastian agree?'

'Krastian is dead, sir. Slain sixty years ago. We have not had an astropath on board since.'

'For the best, perhaps. Psykers. They are deviants and not to be trusted.'

'The astropaths aboard *Hunter's Premonition* align their predictions with the Warmaster's own. The relief fleet is still weeks away.'

'Hnnh.'

'How was your first battle, sir?'

Malcharion had already answered this question several times. Upon his own return to the *Covenant*, visitors from several squads came to pay their respects and speak about the surface conflict.

'Glorious, brother. The splash of blood against my armour... The exaltation of ending a legion of lives with cannon and fist... It will be a great triumph when we take this world in our father's name.'

Talos smiled. Barely.

'Now tell me the truth.'

The servitors attending Malcharion paused momentarily as the Dreadnought made a gear-shifting grind of a sound.

'Joyless. Passionless. Lifeless.'

'Are you are angry at me for waking you?'

'Were I angry, brother, you would already be dead. I would erase you from my sight the way I annihilated that Atramentar bastard Vraal. I never liked him.'

'No one did.'

'I do not understand what is needed of me. That is all.'

Talos considered this for a moment. 'Do you realise how you sound to me, sir? To all of us? How your voice hangs in the air like the echo of thunder, and stampedes across the vox?'

'I am not obtuse, boy. I am not blind to this form's inspirational qualities. But I am dead, Talos. That is the truth, and it will tell in the end.'

'Tonight was a fine victory. Not a life lost. We make planetfall again in three hours. Dawn will see the mountain fortress-foundry breached.'

'And I will pretend to care, brother. Have no fear.'

'I heard how you rallied Ninth and Tenth Claws on the field of battle.'

'All I did was kill for hours and bellow at the enemy.' Another grinding sound clunked from the depths of the Dreadnought.

'What was that?'

'My auto-loader cycling,' Malcharion lied. It had been how his behemoth body translated a chuckle. 'Now dispense with the formalities, Soul Hunter.'

'I could live without you calling me that, sir.'

'And you think I am inclined to agree with your desires? I am Malcharion the Reborn, and you are an Apothecary with delusions of command.'

'Point made,' Talos smiled.

'Enough foolishness. Why are you here? What troubles you?'

'I lost my bolter.'

'Hnnh. Have mine.'

'"*Have mine*"?' Talos laughed. 'With such great reverence you treat Legion relics.'

'I certainly don't need it any more.' The war machine raised and lowered its twin-barrelled autocannon. Two servitors working on the barrels emitted error sounds from throat-voxes as their work was interrupted.

'Sorry…' the Dreadnought boomed in its true voice.

Deltrian bowed, reaper-like and sinuous. 'All is well, lord.'

'Fine,' Malcharion spoke into the vox again. 'Get on with it, Talos.'

'I had a vision, sir.'

'This is hardly remarkable to me.'

'This one was different. It is… wrong. Some of it, at least. It's not coming true. Right from the first moment I woke from it, everything within the images felt unlikely. It felt like a lie uncoiling inside my mind. Uzas of First Claw, killing Cyrion. And now, as the planet stands on the very precipice of being conquered, I wonder at the rest of the vision. Faroven has not died, as I dreamed he would.'

'Are you so certain these events must take place on Crythe?'

'I was,' Talos admitted. 'Now I am unsure they will take place at all. I look at so many of our brothers – even Cyrion and Uzas. I fear their taint has spread to me. Could my second sight be corrupted by exposure to the Ruinous Powers?'

'How many visions have you suffered? Are they as frequent as they were before my entombment?'

'More than before. They grow more frequent.'

'Hnnh. Maybe he will die on Crythe. Maybe he will die later. Maybe he will not die in the manner you have foreseen, and you worry over nothing. I don't recall you whining this much in the past.'

'Whining? Sir…'

'Even the primarch's visions were nebulous at times. Vague, he would say. Clouded. What right do you have to claim infallibility when even our gene-father's second sight was imperfect?'

'Wait. Wait.' Talos stared up the giant machine, his vision coloured killing-red. The image of Malcharion in life, clutching those three helms, stared back at him.

'Our father's dreams,' Talos whispered, 'were sometimes *wrong*?'

'The virtue of such dreams is sometimes in the symbolism.'

'This… cannot be true.'

'No? This is why you always bred enemies within our ranks, brother. A Legion is a hive of one million secrets. You, Soul Hunter, have always assumed you knew everything. I always liked that about you. Liked your confidence. Not everyone felt the same.'

'Did the gene-sire ever speak of me?'

'Only to tell me why you were named as you were. I laughed. I thought our father joked at my expense. It seemed so unlikely that anyone would disobey his final order.' Malcharion made the strange gear-changing growl again.

'Least of all you.'

XVII
SOUL HUNTER

'Because the name suits you.
One soul, my son. One hunt, in the name of revenge.
You will hunt one shining soul when all others turn their backs on
vengeance.'

– The Primarch Konrad Curze
Addressing Apothecary Talos of First Claw, Tenth Company

TALOS HAD CALLED to her from the darkness. He'd called the assassin's name, spoken in a whisper that emerged as a crackle of vox.

'M'Shen,' he hissed.

The assassin broke into a run. Talos followed.

The others would follow later. When the shock broke, when their tawdry and infantile ambitions overcame their grief. When they would look at the body of their slain father and weep not for his death, but for the fact his relics were taken from their greedy grasp.

Talos cared for none of this. The Imperial bitch had murdered his father, and she was going to die for it.

This was the age before *Aurum*. In his gauntlet he gripped a chainsword, gearing it into howling life as he pursued her. Although bareheaded, his vox-bead was in place. The shouts of his brothers transmitted with punishing clarity.

'Does he hunt her?'

'Brother, do not do this!'

'You defy the father's last wishes!'

Talos let them rant and rage. The hunter had no concern for anything beyond his prey. Bolts streaked past her as he fired and she dodged in blurs of dark lightning. Each bang was a storm's echo within the black halls of the Night Haunter's palace on Tsagualsa.

The assassin dared a laugh. And well she might. What was a lone Astartes to a trained agent of the Imperial Callidus Temple? Nothing. Less than nothing. She ducked and weaved and flipped over the bolts.

Outpaced with ease, Talos cursed as he slowed to a halt, and melted back into the shadows.

The hunt was not over.

M'SHEN LICKED HER lips to moisten them. The air of Tsagualsa was bitter and dry, an effect only magnified by the stilted air within this palace of the damned. Her fingers curled in the hair of her slain prey, the head of the Traitor Primarch clutched hard in her grip.

Drip. Drip. Drip.

She was painting the onyx floor with trickles of blood from the severed neck. The blood's scent was cloying and too rich, like powerful spices. This was the holy blood of the Emperor, soured into rancidity by corruption and evil. M'Shen resisted the urge to cast the grisly trophy away. Evidence. She needed evidence the deed was done.

It was strange. The primarch's genetic inhumanity was revealed once more even in death – the severed head had taken several minutes to start bleeding. Clotting agents within the blood were finally breaking down, releasing this dark trickle.

She could have simply taken the artefacts he wore, such as his simple crown circlet, the silver blade sheathed on his back, or the cloak of black feathers draped across his shoulders. But these relics, while valuable, could be stolen from the living as well as the dead. She needed overwhelming evidence to cast before her superiors. In the form of the dead god's head, the assassin had all she would require on that score.

The artefacts she'd taken were for her personal honour, not just the honour of her temple. *And oh, how they would praise her for this.*

M'Shen's pict-link back to her ship's data recorders, while scarcely reliable over such a distance, was gone now. She'd felt it die as she leapt at the Night Haunter and that, too, reeked of the most poetic corruption. The timing of such severance… Something about this place…

It made no sense. Her memory was as close to eidetic as the human mind allowed – yet still, she was lost. These black and bone-lined corridors, how they shifted and weaved. Sound carried strangely here. Sometimes it carried not at all.

The wall next to her head exploded in a shower of debris. She was already moving, already leaping to the side and falling back into her sprint with infinite grace. She was Callidus. She was the most murderous art rendered into human form.

On and on she ran. Constantly she passed Astartes in their outdated Mark III and newer Mark IV war-plate. At the sight of her, these warriors would freeze. Some trembled with the suppressed urge to draw weapons and meet her in combat. She felt their bloodthirst as an overwhelming presence in the air. A few, a rare few, shouted curses at her as she fled past. But not many. These were the stoic sons of a most moribund father.

And their gene-sire had died willingly. Still this most astonishing of developments assailed her thoughts. Fully half of the Callidus Temple, beloved instrument of the God-Emperor, hunted across the galaxy's Eastern Fringe for the lifeblood of Konrad Curze, Eighth primarch, father of the Night Lords Legion.

Here, on barren Tsagualsa, within this palatial fortress of onyx and obsidian, of ivory and bone and banners of flayed flesh she had found him.

Willingly, he surrendered his life.

She, M'Shen, was the death of a primarch. *Godslayer,* her mistresses would name her...

Tremendous weight smashed her to the ground. The primarch's head rolled from her clutch, her own face smashed against the tiled floor. Stimulants flooded her blood and she hurled the burden away. Within a heartbeat's span, the assassin was on her feet once more, looking back at the Astartes she'd thrown back against the wall.

Him. Again.

TALOS'S OWN BLOOD burned. His armour squirted fast spurts of searing chemicals into his body, through sockets in his spine, his neck, his chest and wrists. His chainblade shrieked in a series of enraged whines as it cut nothing but air. The assassin weaved aside from each blow, seeming barely to move, her body slipping into the minimal amount of movement necessary to dodge each swing.

The assassin's blue eyes, the blue of seas long boiled away on Terra, regarded him with fading amusement. She had nothing to say to him, and no reason to fear him, Astartes or otherwise. She was an Imperial assassin. She was the limit of human perf–

Talos's blade edge nicked her black weave armour, slashing a cut in the synskin over her bicep.

Eyes wide in alarm, she made a diving roll to the side, grabbed the trailing black hair of the primarch's head, and sprinted away faster than any Astartes could hope to follow.

Talos watched her go. The voices of his brothers were heated in his ear. Even his brothers within First Claw railed at him for this most disrespectful of disobediences.

'The Haunter *chose* this fate!' Vandred screamed.

'Talos, this was his final wish!' Cyrion implored him. 'She must escape back to Terra!'

Talos moved back into the shadows, a crooked smile on his face.

His vox-link screamed in a hundred tinny voices, others now joining the raging arguments.

The sons of Night Haunter had recovered their desperate ambitions quickly enough. Acerbus, Halasker, Sahaal and the others – the other captains, the other Chosen. Talos heard them whining and raging in his ears, and he found himself smiling at their furious and helpless disbelief.

'She has taken his signet ring,' one stormed.

'His crown!' another wailed like a lost child.

'Our father had not foreseen this,' one of them said. And then the ultimate hypocrisy – they demanded the entire Legion do now for greed what they had been cursing Talos for attempting in the name of vengeance.

'She must be slain for this!' they cried.

'She has transgressed against us all!'

The names of Legion relics stolen from their rightful inheritors was a litany Talos had no desire to listen to. He tuned out their voices, so suddenly full of righteous indignation.

How soon his brethren turned from faith and love in their gene-sire to grave doubts – the very same moment they realised the assassin had stolen weapons and relics they believed were theirs to inherit.

Such greed. Such pathetic, disgusting greed.

Talos despised them all in that moment. Never before had the sickening ambition of his corruptible brothers been shown so clearly.

And so was born the hatred that would never heal.

THE ASSASSIN ESCAPED the palace, and did so with apparent ease.

The Night Lords took their ships, ragtag gatherings of claws and companies, racing to their Thunderhawks to return to their vessels in orbit. The entire Night Lord fleet ringed the world of Tsagualsa, and they gave chase in unprecedented force.

Four vessels pulled ahead of the others. These were *Hunter's Premonition* of Third and 11th Companies; *Umbrea Insidior* of First Company; *The Silent Prince* of Fourth and Seventh Companies, and *Covenant of Blood*, of Tenth.

The assassin's ship, no matter how sleek, fast and exquisitely-wrought it was, stood no chance at all. As it powered away from the dark orb of Tsagualsa, the pursuing cruisers lanced in its wake, weapons roaring at their quarry's essential systems.

She fell from the warp, powerless and crippled, dead in space. Boarding pods spat from all four Astartes vessels, crashing home and locking fast in the metal flesh of the Imperial ship.

The hunters bit into their prey, each one desperate to be the first to taste blood, and with it, victory.

ON BOARD THE assassin's ship, Talos ran with the other hunters in his pack. Menials, mortals, servitors – all fell before the howling Night Lords as they flooded the decks from a hundred hull breaches.

It was to be a day forever imprinted in the annals of Legion history, as well as one held in the hearts of every Astartes present in that moment of denied vindication.

As the hunters found her – squads from First Company claiming that honour – a fresh anger broke out across the vox-network.

Talos stood in the charnel pit of the crew habitation quarters, surrounded by brothers from the Tenth and the ruined meat of so many mortal crew members. Blood painted the walls, the floor and the dark fronts of their armour plating. Not a soul would survive the culling of the murderer's ship.

At first, the reports had difficulty filtering through to the Astartes engaged in the hunt on board. Their blood was up, and the alerts were lost within the chaos of howling voices taking hold of the vox-channels.

Talos was one of the first to hear. He powered down his chainsword, tilting his head as he listened carefully.

How can this be?

'We are under attack,' he voxed to the others in proximity, his voice cold, calm, but edged with the taint of disbelief.

'We are under attack, *by the eldar.*'

IN THE CENTURIES to come, the warriors of the VIII Legion would argue over the exact nature of the xenos ambush. Riding from their unknowable pathways through the void, wraith-like eldar ships ghosted around the embattled Night Lords vessels, alien weapons bringing light to the blackness, cutting into yielding shields without mercy.

Some claimed the assault was to claim the relics of the primarch, just as the assassin had. Others argued that an alien race would have no need of such treasures, and it was either indecipherable xenos reasoning – or merely a night of ill-fortune conspired by fate – that brought the fleets into contact at such a moment.

Umbrea Insidior would be lost, and with it, the betrayer Sahaal. *The Silent Prince* would suffer devastating damage, but ultimately the xenos fleet would be annihilated.

Yet few of the Legion claimed any satisfaction in the hollow triumph won that night.

During the evacuation, eldar warriors materialised in the hallways of the assassin's ship, manifesting before the packs of enraged Night Lords to be cut down even before they were free of the shimmering smears that marked the aftermath of alien teleportation technology.

First Claw, along with the other squads on board, fought their way back to their boarding pods.

'Whatever they've come for,' Cyrion voxed as he cut the head from an eldar female even as she appeared, 'they want it badly.'

'Back to the ship!' Captain Malcharion was shouting over the disorderly fighting retreat. 'Back to the *Covenant*!'

The vox was no clearer now. Jubilant cries clashed with the calls for withdrawal and hateful curses levelled at the aliens. Somewhere in the verbal melee, Talos could hear the victorious shrieks of Captain Sahaal, and the fevered raging of First Company.

Something was wrong. He could hear it in their voices.

He slowed in his stride, falling behind the rest of his claw, his attention pouring into the myriad cries and conflicting reports coming over the vox. A pattern emerged soon enough.

Captain Sahaal had reclaimed one of the Night Haunter's relics... and immediately fled. He was taking *Umbrea Insidior* away from the fleet, breaking formation and trying to run from the eldar.

He has abandoned First Company. Talos swallowed. Had he heard that right? Had one of the Legion's most respected commanders left his own warriors to die at the hands of the eldar?

Talos stopped dead in his tracks, the corridor silent now that the rest of his squad had raced so far ahead.

Sahaal had fled with his treasure, running into the void. First Company were battling their way to their boarding pods, and would be stranded, forced to die fighting or rely on the charity of the other vessels to save them.

Talos cared little for most of this. The struggles of First Company were First Company's own trouble. The Legion was in retreat from this grotesque ambush, and Tenth Company would be fighting to save itself.

But M'Shen's death had still not been confirmed over the vox-network.

In his greed, Sahaal was fleeing with his trinket, all thoughts of vengeance forgotten... *and the assassin was still alive.*

Talos turned from his path of escape, and moved deeper into the ship.

THE POWER WAS out, leaving her in darkness, but she was safe at last.

As quickly as they'd come, the Astartes had fled.

Her ship still shuddered, but it seemed to her that the alien attackers, the filthy xenos creatures that named themselves eldar, had withdrawn with the Night Lords' retreat.

One of them had taken her hand with a swing of his blade. She could not fight off five of them at once, and the blow had severed her wrist in a clean slice. Her training made any pain from the wound utterly ignorable, but M'Shen bound her wrist with a tourniquet and a temporary seal of synthetic flesh nevertheless. The bleeding had been a danger, even if shock and pain had not.

She stood on the bloody ruin of her bridge, listening to the laboured breathing and shivers of the few crew members that yet drew breath.

None of them could see. The auxiliary power should have come online by now, resurrecting the lights. The continuing darkness was a bold enough statement that her ship was almost certainly damaged beyond easy repair.

M'Shen spun on her toes, her blade in her remaining hand. She could see nothing in the pure blackness, but she didn't need to. The thrum of live power armour filled her senses. The low growls of its servo-joints and false muscle fibres flexing told her all she needed to know. The Astartes's location, his posture, everything.

The assassin edged to the right, allowing herself a smile. Despite her exhaustion and blood loss, a lone Astartes would prove no threat. She–

TALOS CLOSED HIS hand around her throat.

He could sense she was duller, slower, and the beat of her heart was quicker than it had been in the palace. The assassin was weakened from her escape and the recent battle.

But she would kill him before his hearts had time to beat twice if he tried to hold her. Everything about this creature was engineered to end life, and with infinitely more skill and grace than the blunt efficiency of the Astartes. He was a warrior, but she was a murderer. He was trained for battle and war. She was bred only to kill.

The same second his hand gripped her throat, he was already acting.

Not to squeeze. Her armour of precious synskin would resist such trauma. He jerked her close, risking a headbutt to daze her. That was a mistake. The assassin leaned her head back like a recoiling serpent. Curse her, she was *fast*.

Talos felt her fisted hand coming up to unleash the lethality within her rings – each one a digital weapon of some unknown configuration. He wasted no time.

The Night Lord spat into her face, and hurled her away.

SHE HAD NOT screamed in many years.

It wasn't that pain was new to her, nor even a surprise, but this was no neat severance of limb from the body – this was the dissolving of her eyes in her skull, and never before had pain eclipsed her senses so completely. Even through the agony, she imagined the wretched Night Lord stumbling away in his cumbersome armour, amused at her momentary helplessness.

And she was right. In the darkness, Talos relished the sound of her scream. Even sweeter was the subtle, mellifluous hiss of acidic venom eating into the soft tissue of her beautiful blue eyes.

Panting now, seeing nothing but milky white sunfire, the assassin swallowed the pain, remembered her teachings, and used the agony as a focus. Over the vicious *tssssssshhhhh* of her melting eyes, she heard the humming rumbles of his armour.

He had to die. He had to die *now*.

She launched at him to make the need become reality.

* * *

TALOS FIRED AT the floor, bolt shells masking his movements as their rapid explosions overwhelmed the bridge chamber with noise. He cast a black-eyed glance at the assassin blindly fighting the air, her lashing kicks and blade sweeps utterly lethal – aimed at audible joints and weak points of his armour – but utterly useless. Talos was already across the bridge away from her, bolter still barking.

Deafened and disoriented, the assassin slowed her movements. Desperately poised, muscles taut, she seemed to be trying to filter the noise of his armour through the banging detonations.

He risked another shot to distract her, aiming squarely in her direction. She weaved a minimal amount, just as she had in the palace, and the bolt went wide.

Talos breathed out a curse as however she sought to sense him succeeded perfectly. The assassin turned to face him, and started running.

With his free hand, he slammed on his helm.

THE NIGHT LORD was a fool.

Every explosion ringing from the floor betrayed the shell's point of origin. It was complex, a matter of rigid concentration and training, and M'Shen was slowed by the pain she struggled to overcome. That was why triangulating his location took almost four entire seconds – an age to her preternatural senses.

Bolts started tearing directly at her, which confirmed her belief that the Astartes was a fool. Even rendered sightless, these she dodged with ease.

A new sound overrode the slicing whoosh of missing bolts. A sound she had only heard once before. His voice, speaking a single word.

'Preysight.'

HAD HER BLOWS landed, he would have died. He knew this with cold certainty.

Assassins, those from the Imperial-sanctioned temples, were already legends in the young Imperium. Her remaining hand would have thrust, blade-like and steel-hard, into the joints of his armour, crushing nerves and perhaps even breaking the enhanced bone of an Astartes warrior's skeleton. From there, his death would have taken mere moments. The pain he'd inflicted would be repaid tenfold.

None of her blows landed, because she made no attempt to strike him. As the blur of dull thermal movement came charging towards him, as every bolt he fired was dodged with ease, Talos filled his three lungs with the blood-rich air of her wrecked bridge.

As deep and echoing as the first thunderclap of a breaking storm, he roared his hatred at her.

* * *

WITHIN A CALLIDUS assassin, training and instinct met in honed, focused fusion. That fusion split within M'Shen as she lost the second of her senses. The depriving assault hit as hard and fast as the first. A moment of ear-splitting pain lanced through to the core of her mind, shaking her hearing, and all was suddenly silent.

She had no idea if the Night Lord was still screaming or had fallen quiet after detecting his triumph. Her senses were killed. She felt only the air shaking around her as her enemy moved again, and as bolts slashed past.

Blinded, deafened, clutching a shimmering blade that had taken the head of a fallen god, she twisted in her sprint and leapt at where she was certain the Astartes must be.

Her estimation was, as always, perfect.

TALOS HELD HER with the gentleness of a lover.

'My father told me of this night,' he whispered to her. 'And I never believed him. I never believed I would disobey him, until you came into our home and took him from us.'

M'Shen never heard his words. She would never hear anything again in her life, which was now measured in seconds. The assassin dropped her blade. As her gloved fingers uncurled almost against her will, she felt the heavy weapon thump against her foot.

Strengthless arms wouldn't move. Trembling fingers couldn't crook to fire digital weapons within the ornate rings. Painkillers choked her veins with no effect beyond an irritating tickle of sensation. Her stomach was aflame. It hurt even more than the hissing holes where her eyes had been. Some violation, some iron-hard presence pressed her in place, transfixing her torso.

She guessed correctly what it was. The Night Lord's chainsword. He had impaled her on his blade.

A dim, fading part of her mind tried to assess this damage, but the brutal and human edge to her consciousness overrode a life of combat narcotics and relentless training. She was dying. She would be dead within moments.

'Godslayer,' she said to him, never hearing her own words. 'That… is how I will… be remembered…'

Talos blinked stinging tears from his eyes. His thumb edged closer to the chainsword's activation rune.

Threat, threat, threat the warning runes flickered. Talos blink-clicked them away, clearing his red visor display of all but the assassin's masked face and her hollow, bleeding eye sockets.

'*Ave Dominus Nox*,' he whispered, and gunned the impaling chainsword into life.

* * *

HE DRIFTED FOR sixteen hours, alone in one of the boarding pods left by the ravaged survivors of First Company. In the absolute silence, he had only his grief and satisfaction to pass the time.

They did so admirably.

When his brothers found him, when the pod was brought aboard the *Covenant of Blood* as it returned to seek survivors and salvage, Talos was still sitting in one of the pod's thrones, his armour spotted with dried blood.

The pod's doors opened into ramps, and Talos looked out into the *Covenant*'s starboard launch bay.

First Claw stood watching him, their weapons raised.

'She's dead,' he told them, and rose to his feet, movements sluggish and weary.

His chainsword's teeth were clogged with dark, chewed meat and shards of bone. Before leaving her vessel, he had sawn her into nothing more than gobbets of biological matter, venting his final frustrations on her remains. In the darkness of the bridge, the surviving mortal crew members heard everything, with only their fearful imaginations to provide the imagery.

'Talos...' Captain Malcharion, the war-sage, approached slowly. 'Brother...'

Talos raised his head with equal slowness.

'She killed our father,' he said in a crackle of vox.

'I know, brother. We all know. Come, we must... deal with the aftermath.'

'The Haunter said I would do this,' Talos looked at the gore-caked blade. 'I did not believe him. Not until I felt the rage of her presence in our palace.'

'It is over,' said Malcharion. 'Come, Talos.'

'It will never be over.' Talos dropped the blade to the ground with a crash. 'But at least now I know why he named me as he did. *"One soul,"* he said. *"You will hunt one shining soul while all others turn their backs on vengeance".*'

'Brother, come...'

'If you touch me, Malcharion, I will kill you next. Leave me. I am going to my chambers. I need to... to think.' Talos left his weapons where they lay. Primus would gather them.

'As you wish,' the war-sage said, 'Soul Hunter.'

'Soul Hunter,' Talos chuckled in response, the sound laced with bitterness. 'I believe I could get used to that.'

XVIII
BROTHERHOOD

THE INTERLOCKING CAVERN network beneath the Omnissiah's Claw mountain range was home to miracles of immense scale and ingenuity. Here lay the living core of the Legio Maledictis, and the sacred heart of the Adeptus Mechanicus's operations on Crythe Prime.

A million humans, one million souls in varying states of augmentation, worked in these hallowed underground tunnels. The air was fever-hot with smoke, shimmering with heat blur, and rancid with the metallic reek of incense and industry.

Entire cave systems were given over to railroaded conveyor carriages, huge trains transporting resources, ammunition, servitors and machine parts from one colossal chamber to the other. The myriad chambers themselves reached hundreds of metres in height, each capable of housing a battle-ready Warlord-class Titan. The stone skin of this great lair was masked in machinework attached to the walls: consoles, sensor relays, gantries, elevators, storage loaders, promethium fuel tanks, and grand icons of the Mechanicus of Mars. Little remained of the original red stone that had once reached as far as – and indeed farther than – the mortal eye could see.

A city of factories and forges hidden beneath the armoured skin of the world's crust. A city founded to provide the Imperium of Man with invaluable god-machines to stride across distant battlefields in the crusades of a dying empire. A city that had prospered for almost two thousand years.

The plains before the mountain range had fallen to the Warmaster after the previous day's fighting. The Mechanicus's last-breath attempt to deter the siege of Seventeen-Seventeen's front gates had failed, and the evidence of that failure stretched from horizon to horizon. Troop bulk landers and Astartes Thunderhawks carried soldiers and warriors down from the void and from elsewhere on Crythe, massing on the plains in one unified horde. The bodies of slain skitarii and mortal fodder smothered the rest of the plain, punctuated by the occasional corpse of a downed Titan. The mortal dead bloated in the morning sun. The skitarii's flesh-parts were already starting to stink and discolour. The fallen Titans crawled with ants – the Warmaster's own tech-adepts recovering the slain god-machines for use on other worlds.

Crythe Prime was well-chosen by the Warmaster not only for its resources, but because the majority of its Titan Legion was engaged in battle elsewhere in the segmentum. Not only could resources be harvested from Seventeen-Seventeen if it fell, but the Imperium would be denied yet another bastion of strength in the future.

The great gates would not hold for long. Seventeen-Seventeen had grown too far beyond its original plans. The Avenue of Triumph leading into the main undercity now stood outside the protection of Site 017-017's invincible void shields. The main gate was naught but adamantium and Mechanicus ingenuity; despite its strength, it would fall to massed fire within hours. Wide enough to allow three Titans marching out abreast, it was also wide enough to allow the Warmaster's army within.

Under siege, threatened with destruction, the hidden city called upon its chosen sons. The few that remained answered this call. They marched through their home caverns, immense shoulders bristling with city-crushing weaponry, beneath banners of a hundred past glories. At their heels, a million adepts, servitors and skitarii warriors braced to repel the invaders.

The last sons of the Legio Maledictis had awoken, and Seventeen-Seventeen shook with their tread.

BLACKENED STOOD READY on the deck. It was a howling, dark-armoured vulture, with its engines whining as they gushed heat-shimmer into the air. It breathed readiness, and the Astartes felt inspired just seeing it.

First Claw marched in loose formation towards the lowered gang ramp, their armour as repaired as the handful of hours back on board the *Covenant* had allowed. Each suit of war-plate still bore a wealth of scars. Mercutian and Uzas, with no access to trained artificers, looked as though they had no right to walk away from the last battlefield. Pits, cracks, chips and cuts spoiled the surfaces of their ceramite plating.

Mercutian had complained of his armour's machine-spirit responding sluggishly. Small wonder, with the damage its skin had taken.

As he marched, he cycled through sight modes, swearing softly over the vox.

'My preysight is down.' The words came out hesitantly, and for good reason.

'Bad omen,' Uzas chuckled. 'Bad, bad omen.'

'I do not hold any faith in omens,' Adhemar said.

'Strange then,' Uzas replied, 'that you serve in a squad led by a prophet.'

'Uzas,' Talos said, turning to face him.

'What?'

Talos said nothing. He didn't move.

'What?' Uzas repeated. 'No lecture?'

Talos still said nothing, standing unmoving.

'His life signs are… insane,' Cyrion was watching his retinal displays. 'Oh, hell. Xarl!'

Talos half-turned, staggered, and fell on nerveless legs. Xarl caught him with a clash of battle armour.

'What ails him?' Mercutian asked.

'Seven eyes open without warning,' said Talos over the vox, 'and the sons of the Angel fly with vengeance in their hearts.'

'Isn't it obvious?' Cyrion said to Mercutian. 'Septimus! You are needed here.'

'The Angel's sons seek the blade of gold, and justice for their brothers with blackened souls…'

'Now, Septimus!' Cyrion yelled.

The Exalted turned its horned head to a mortal whose name he had never even tried to learn.

'Launch status,' he drawled.

The officer straightened his outdated uniform as he checked his console displays. 'Lord Malcharion's pod reads as already down, master. All squads already engaged or en route to the surface… except First Claw.'

The Exalted craned itself forward. Bone creaked and armour growled. 'What?'

'Confirming, master.' The officer affixed his vox-mic to his collar. 'This is the command deck. Report launch status, First Claw.'

The Exalted, ever a student of fear in the human form, watched in perverse fascination as the officer's face paled. The soft drumming of the mortal's heart thumped a touch harder and faster. Bad news, then. News the mortal feared to share.

'First Claw reports, master, that Lord Talos is incapacitated. He has suffered another… malady.'

'Order them to leave him and proceed to the surface at once.'

The officer relayed the order. As he listened, he managed to swallow on the third attempt.

'Master…'

'Speak.'

'First Claw has refused the order.'

'I see.' The Exalted's claws gripped the handrests of his exquisite throne. 'And on what grounds do they refuse to prosecute the enemy in this holy war?'

'Lord Cyrion said, master, that if you are so worried about the surface battle, you are free to borrow their Thunderhawk and take a look down there yourself.'

The fact the officer relayed all of this without more than a minor tremor in his voice impressed the Exalted considerably. He valued competence above all.

'Fine work… mortal. Inform First Claw their treachery has been noted.'

The officer saluted and did exactly that. The response, from the Astartes known as Lord Xarl, was immediate and obscene. The mortal decided not to relay that part back to the Exalted.

More voices buzzed in his ear. The Astartes of First Claw again.

'Lord?'

The Exalted turned, intrigued by the rising unease in the man's voice.

'Speak.'

'Lord Cyrion wishes a direct link to you. It's a most grave and urgent matter.'

'Open it.'

'Vandred,' Cyrion's voice echoed across the bridge. 'Recall the claws from the surface immediately.'

'And why would I do that, Brother Cyrion?'

'Because we do not have three weeks before the Blood Angels arrive.'

The Exalted tongued its lipless maw, feeling the veins under its cheeks ache in sharp pulses. 'Your belligerence grows tiresome, First Claw. I will listen to this and this alone. Link me to Talos's vox.'

'…breaching the hull. I kill him. He recognises my sword as he dies…'

The Exalted listened in silence for over a minute. When his next words came, they did so with savage reluctance.

'Open a channel to the *Vengeful Spirit*. I must speak with the Warmaster.'

MALCHARION TRUDGED THROUGH the cavernous chamber of the undermountain citadel. The siege had been grinding on for over an hour, and although Malcharion's forces from Tenth Company were charged with entering as part of the second wave, the reforming resistance in the early caverns was punishing the Chaos advance.

Flanking his hulking form, yet giving him respectful – and prudent – distance with which to fire his weapons, two Night Lord claws advanced, their bolters spitting into the disorganised ranks of the enemy.

The resurrected warrior knew them by name, knew their individual suits of armour even through the scars earned in the many battles each of them had survived and suffered without him.

Yet with the passion of battle-lust rendered cold in this immortal shell, he felt little connection to the brothers he once commanded as captain of the Tenth.

They fought because they still hated with a ferocity he no longer shared. They shrieked curses with a bitterness he no longer tasted.

Dark thoughts, these. Dark thoughts that threatened his focus.

The Dreadnought's armoured feet, splay-clawed and ponderous, crushed bodies beneath his weight. The double-barrelled cannon that served as his right arm boomed over and over, ripping vicious gaps in the skitarii's lines. On they came, drawn by the blasphemy of his existence, desiring nothing more than to end the unlife he suffered because of warped Mechanicum lore.

Perhaps a part of him was tempted to let them succeed. A small part. A part that remained silent and dead while battle raged. This was not joy – war had never been joyous for the war-sage – but the immersion allowed him to focus elsewhere, to concentrate upon the external. Such focus diminished his awareness of his true form, husk-like and cold within the sarcophagus.

A skitarii with four shrieking saw-blade limbs battered itself against the Dreadnought's front. Malcharion clutched it from the ground, squeezing it with the unbreakable strength of his power fist. Lightning flared into life as the dying tech-guard's blood spurted onto the electrified metal claw that crushed him. Malcharion fired his arm-mounted flamer unit, bathing the man in liquid flame, roasting the skitarii's flesh-parts even as the soldier was crunched into death. This organic wreckage he threw into the soldiers before him, lamenting their lobotomised indifference to such magnificent slaughter. Blood of the Ruinous Ones, what a foul waste of the Legion's talents this war was.

'Malcharion,' said a vox voice.

It was significant effort to tune into speaking within the vox-network instead of transmitting his voice to the speakers mounted within his armour. The battle raging in the caverns hardly helped.

'It is I.'

'It's Cyrion.'

His autocannon hammered shells into a towering skitarii – a champion or a captain, surely. The cyborged warrior fell into the teeming horde in pieces. The shouts of thousands of soldiers locked together rang around the arching cavern.

'You are supposed to be here, are you not? You woke me to kill everything for you?'

'Sir, you have to pull back from Seventeen-Seventeen. Lead the claws back to the Thunderhawks.'

Ghost-pain travelled through him in an acidic rush. Malcharion – his true form – screamed within the coffin of sustaining fluids. He felt the silken play of ooze across his ravaged face. Psychostigmata bruised his corpse's pale flesh.

The skitarii drilling into the Dreadnought's knee joint was pulped into a wet smear a moment later. Malcharion spun on his waist axis, power claw outstretched. Several other skitarii about to besiege his towering body flew back into their fellows, bones smashed to shards.

'We are within the cave city,' Malcharion boomed, his pain flooding his vox-voice. 'We cannot retreat. The day will be ours.'

Talos is being wracked by another vision. He says the Imperial relief fleet isn't weeks away. It's barely even hours away. The Blood Angels are coming.'

'What of Vandred?'

'He has apprised the Warmaster, but will not recall our forces. Likewise, the *Hunter's Premonition* has been ordered to keep its troops on the surface.'

Malcharion panned his power claw in an arc before him, unleashing streams of fire from the mounted flamer. Next to him, in orderly formation with bolters and blades striking, two squads of Tenth Company's Night Lords advanced in his shadow.

The Dreadnought halted. Slowly, he turned. Watching.

Noise erupted around him. Noises previously unheard over the snarling of his own joints and the rage of his weapons. Solid shells clanked and clinked from his armour. *Bizarre. Almost like rainfall.*

'The Black Legion and their mortal slaves are engaged alongside us. Are we to abandon them? The Soul Hunter's second sight is not without flaw.'

'Malcharion, my captain, what do you believe?'

The Dreadnought's power plant thrummed louder as Malcharion re-engaged the enemy, fist crushing, cannons firing. The speakers on his hull blared loud as he shouted in Nostraman.

'Night Lords! Fall back! Back to the ships!'

ABOARD THE COVENANT, the Exalted watched blurry pict feeds of the surface battle. The creature cycled through views – the helm picters of each squad leader and image-finders mounted on the hulls of Tenth Company's tanks. Orbital imagery was worthless with the battle now taking place in the opening chambers of the Omnissiah's Claw. It was left to this series of juddering, frenetic scenes out of necessity. It offended the Exalted's tactician sensibilities.

On its left stood Malek, on his right, Garadon.

'Do you see this?' The Exalted focused on the crimson view displayed by one Astartes's vision lenses.

'Yes, lord,' both Atramentar warriors said.

'Intriguing, is it not? Why would all of our squads be moving back through the Warmaster's forces? One has to wonder.'

'I can guess, lord,' Garadon said. His fist clutched the haft of his double-handed hammer tighter.

'Oh?' The Exalted allowed a rare smile to split its face. 'Indulge me, brother. Share your suspicions.'

Garadon growled before speaking, as if dredging up enough bitterness to put into the words. 'The prophet is making his move to usurp your leadership of the warband.'

Malek shook his bullish helm. 'Talos is incapacitated by his second sight. You are seeing conspiracies in guiltless corners, Garadon.'

'None of us are blind to your support of him,' Garadon replied. 'Your ardent defence of his every failure.'

'Brothers, brothers,' the Exalted no longer smiled. 'Peace. Watch. Listen. I suspect any moment now–'

'Incoming message, my prince,' the vox-officer called from his station.

'Delicious timing,' the Exalted breathed. 'Put it through.'

'This is Captain Halasker of the Third,' crackled the bridge speakers. All present knew the name. Halasker, Brother-Captain of Third Company, commander of the *Hunter's Premonition.*

'I am the Exalted, lord of the Tenth.'

'Hail, Vandred.'

'What do you wish, Halasker?'

'Why are your squads falling back to the landing site? Blood of the Father, the war-sage is ordering a retreat of all Eighth Legion forces. What the hell kind of game are you playing?'

'I did not order the withdrawal. Malcharion is acting according to his own maddened will. The Warmaster has demanded we continue the war's prosecution.'

'You cannot control your own forces?'

The Exalted breathed through its closed fangs. 'Not when the war-sage is on the surface, acting as if he ruled the Tenth.'

'And why are *you* not on the surface, Vandred?'

The edge of derision in Halasker's voice rankled more than anything the Exalted had endured in a long, long time... until the other captain's next words.

'Vandred, where is the prophet? Malcharion and your claws are voxing news of a new prophecy. I must speak with the Soul Hunter.'

'He is *incapacitated,*' the Exalted managed. Its teeth were clenched so forcefully that one cracked like porcelain. 'Our father's ailment has befallen him once more.'

'So it's true?'

'I did not sa–'

'Fall back!' Halasker cried to his squads over the vox. 'Fall back with the war-sage!'

The Exalted roared at the ceiling of the command deck, loud enough to send the mortal crew cowering.

HE OPENED HIS eyes. The sight of bright, proud armour faded from before him, replaced by the dark red of his visor display. Flickering, tiny runes streamed across his vision. His hearts slowed. He swallowed the coppery tang of blood in his mouth.

Targeting reticules locked on familiar aspects of his own chamber.

A quick glance at the digital chron reader in his lens display told him exactly how long he'd been lost to sense.

It could have been worse.

'Cyrion,' he voxed, and the door to his chambers opened the moment he spoke.

'Brother,' Cyrion said. He was still in full war-plate.

'Cy, the Throne's forces are coming. The Marines Errant, the Flesh Tearers. The Blood Angels, first of all. They are almost here.'

'You've been out three hours, Talos.'

'I know.'

'The Exalted has called a war council.' Cyrion moved away from the door, gesturing for him to follow. 'The Blood Angels are already here.'

XIX

FOR THE LEGION

THE WAR ROOM was being used for its intended purpose for the first time in decades.

Banks of monitors and consoles stood active, attended by servitors – many of whom were reprogrammed by Tech-Priest Deltrian following their capture on the asteroid chunk of Nostramo. A huge occulus screen showed the open link to a similar chamber on the *Hunter's Premonition*, though that room was far grander and larger than even this, the largest room on the *Covenant of Blood*. The battle-barge was built to carry three entire companies, whereas the strike cruiser housed only one.

A huge central table projected a distorted green hololithic display of Crythe and the dozens of ships surrounding it. In angry red blurs, a second fleet a short distance from the planet was depicted. They wavered in jagged, flickering detail.

The pict link to *Hunter's Premonition* showed Captain Halasker in his Terminator plate, unhelmed as he stood at the head of his own holo-projection table.

'They are holding off, then.'

The Exalted dragged its spiked bulk closer to the projected display, and gestured with a swollen, pale claw. 'Two battle-barges, three strike cruisers. This represents overwhelming force. Perhaps two-thirds of the entire Chapter.'

'We are aware of numbers. What we are not aware of is why they arrived so soon.' Malcharion stood opposite the Exalted, dwarfing the daemon-twisted former captain. The division in the room was obvious for all to see.

'The Warmaster lied to us,' Halasker insisted. 'He must have known.'

'Why would he lie and endanger his own forces on the surface?' the Exalted countered.

'Maybe so. But can that many seers truly be wrong?'

'Did not your own astropaths agree with the Warmaster's declaration?'

the Exalted asked. 'The wake of that many ships casts great waves through the sea of souls. Your astropaths confirmed the judgements of the Warmaster's own. The tide should not have broken upon us for another month.'

'The seers are mortal.' Halasker wouldn't concede the point. 'I placed no overt trust in them at all.'

Talos spoke from his place close to Malcharion. 'A larger fleet is still incoming. We are dealing with nuances in the immaterium – a dimension none of us understand. Can you, Captain Halasker, look into the warp and see which waves are natural tides in an unnatural realm? Can you, Captain Vandred, see whether the war-wake of one fleet is masked by the tidal wave caused by another? Everything we do is guesswork compounded by inexperienced estimation.'

The Exalted met Halasker's black eyes over the screen link. 'If the Blood Angels will remain at bay, they can be ignored while Crythe falls. We can recommit our forces and avoid the Warmaster's further displeasure.'

'You are free to commit the Tenth wherever you wish,' the other captain replied. 'I am done with this fool's errand. A fine concept in the simulation displays. A fine concept that has bled us dry when it came to the moments of bolter and blade.'

'The Warmaster has carelessly spent our blood,' Xarl snarled low. 'We owe him nothing.'

'I agree,' Talos said. 'We should disengage from the fleet as soon as all of our forces have been recovered from the surface.'

'Agreed,' said Halasker.

'Agreed.'

'I am enjoying this display of supreme naivety.' The Exalted's tongue bled as it licked its fangs. Eyes as black as dead stars turned upon Talos and Malcharion. 'But the Despoiler will not allow this. He has the strength to prevent us breaking away, and he will never forgive such a betrayal.'

'Enough, Vandred.' Halasker shook his head. 'Your loyalty to the Old War is commendable, but Abaddon is a fool. Yet again, he has committed too much, too hard, too far from support. He holds tenuous lordship over Legions that are greatly-enamoured of endless infighting. This is just one of many betrayals he will forgive because he will need allies again in the future.'

'Hear, hear,' the Dreadnought rumbled.

'The last of my forces will be on board the *Premonition* within the hour.'

'And how are we supposed to placate the Warmaster? I promise you, Halasker, he will fire upon us if we run.'

'Cripple his ships.'

All eyes turned to Talos.

'*What did you say?*' the Exalted asked, softer than he'd spoken in years.

'When we break from the fleet, we cripple the *Vengeful Spirit*, or any other vessel that challenges us.' Talos met the Exalted's stare.

'And leave them at the mercy of the Angels?'

'Do I look as though I will shed any tears over that?'

'Nor will I,' Halasker added. 'Abaddon is hardly short on ships. Even without us, he outnumbers the Blood Angels eleven to five.'

Chatter began to pick up around the room as the gathered Astartes discussed the imminent treachery.

'No,' the Exalted growled. 'This cannot, and will not be.'

'And why not?' Halasker narrowed his eyes.

'Almost all of the Warmaster's forces are engaged upon Crythe. If the Blood Angels strike – if they *board* the Black Legion's cruisers – the Warmaster will struggle to escape with any of his fleet intact. There might be as many as *six hundred* Blood Angels waiting on their ships on the other side of this world! They will sweep through any resistance on board the Black Legion's vessels.'

'Then he should have begun the recall of his men hours ago, as the prophet's vision suggested. Warnings were sent. You sent them yourself. Abaddon chose to leave them unheeded.'

'Malcharion,' Halasker addressed the Dreadnought now. 'Are the Tenth's full forces back on board the *Covenant*?'

'Yes, brother.'

'Then make preparations to leave. I still have fifteen squads on the surface, with armour support. They were deep in the caverns, and their fighting withdrawal is taking lamentably long. Vandred?'

'Yes, "brother"?'

'Even after all this time, you are still a worm,' Halasker finished. Then the screen went dead.

The Exalted looked at its shattered company, with no more than thirty Astartes remaining. They watched him from where they stood around the table. Their armour was pitted and cracked. Their bearing remained strong and tall despite this pointless war. How had it come to this? Betrayal after betrayal. The erosion of trust. The death of brotherhood.

'Incoming transmission,' a servitor intoned from a wall console.

The screen came alive again. This time, the face wasn't Halasker's, it was a dark helm with slanted eye lenses. The Astartes there inclined his head in greeting. Armour of black and gold shone in the flickering light of his own bridge.

'*Covenant of Blood*. The Warmaster demands to know why you have still not recommitted your troops.'

'Tell the Warmaster he will be losing this war without us, if he still aims to fight it. The Blood Angels have arrived, and more Imperial forces will be here soon.'

'Silence, Dead One. Exalted, hear me. You know who I was, and who I am now. As the Eyes of the Warmaster, I speak with the Despoiler's voice. Lord Abaddon cares nothing for the presence of the Sons of Sanguinius and their quaint fleet. He demands that the *Covenant* pull alongside the *Vengeful Spirit* in defensive formation.'

'No.'

'No? *No?* You will risk allowing them to board us?'

The Exalted shook its horned head. 'Ruven, you were once of the Tenth yourself. So you know we will not comply. We are not enslaved to the Warmaster's will. You know this as well as any other. Malcharion speaks the truth. Pull your own forces off Crythe before it's too late.'

'It is not that simple. We have committed much to the battle for Seventeen-Seventeen.'

'Leave the mortals. Let them die. Who cares if they do not live to be slaughtered on another world in a later war? Recover your Astartes and be ready to engage the Blood Angels. Perhaps if we move quickly, we can decimate them before other Chapters fall out of the warp in support.'

'We have *Titans* on that world. Thousands of Astartes. Hundreds of tanks. We are the Black Legion, not some shattered, impoverished horde weeping over its misfortunes and the memory of a martyred primarch.'

The Exalted tongued its broken teeth again, feeling his veins ache with the need to see this bastard's blood. Who was this wretch, this traitor, to speak of the Night Lords Legion in such a way...

'If you will not comply,' Ruven said, 'you will be fired upon for trying to flee.'

'The Throne's vengeance is here,' the Exalted spoke low. 'My prophet insists more will arrive within hours. We will not be selling our lives to preserve yours. We will not be repeating our warnings again.'

'Your prophet is unreliable. You have indicated as much yourself.'

The Exalted grunted a breathy sigh. 'That may be so. But he is my brother, and you are nothing more than a betrayer who fled to wear the black of Abaddon's many failures. I trust his words, as I trusted my father's.'

With a too-long claw, the Exalted dragged a finger across its throat in the demand for silence. The servitor at the vox console killed the link.

'Battle stations,' the Exalted said. 'Be ready to disengage from the fleet.'

THE MINUTES PASSED with agonising slowness. More signifier runes appeared on the hololithic display as the minutes became hours. Vessels belonging to the Marines Errant, and the cousin Chapters of the Blood Angels – the Flesh Tearers and the Angels Vermillion – pulled alongside their fellows.

The Exalted's expert eyes roamed over the formation, seeing the possibilities playing out within his mind. Loose. Their formation was loose, as if the captains had no experience with one another, or any desire to work together. This may indeed have been true, for all the Exalted knew. Either way, it was an opening.

They will come at us soon.

He knew that because, had he commanded the gathering fleet, it would have been what he'd do. Strike hard, ramming the point of the lance through the heart of the Warmaster's fleet. Such a gambit held grave risks and definite casualties. The Despoiler's ships bristled with immense firepower, and still outnumbered the loyalist vessels.

Strange, in truth. Not only had this approach been so masterfully masked, but the sense of opposition emerging between the two fleets was almost poetically startling. *The advantage we hold is in the external force we can bring to bear against them. The advantage they hold is in the internal threat they bring.* In a straight clash of vessels, the Throne's Astartes would be annihilated. But no void war was ever so clearly defined. When boarding actions came into consideration, the Warmaster's fleet would be lost.

Distances within void conflict are matters of thousands and thousands of kilometres. As the runes depicting the enemy fleet began to blink and move, the Exalted rose to its full height and addressed Malcharion – the only other Astartes still in the room.

'Alert the *Premonition*. We have forty minutes before they reach us.'

ORBITAL PICT IMAGERY was useful again with the ground forces in retreat. Talos watched on the bridge's occulus as the blurry forms of Astartes and rolling tank armour sheared back from their attack on the city beneath the mountains. Individuals were impossible to make out and the images were rendered even hazier by the shroud of pollution across the world's skies, but the stuttering, distorted picts still told their tale.

Talos saw the Black Legion falling back to their troopships spread across the conquered plain. Behind them in a routed wave came a teeming mass of humanity. Titans and tanks seemed like pockets of calm in the swarm.

'Will they be able to get more than a few hundred Astartes back into orbit before the Angels reach us?' he asked.

The Exalted watched the same picts. 'No. They will rely on the renegades that still have sizable forces on board their ships. The Purge, the Scourges of Quintus, the Violators... Here, look.' The Exalted gestured to other vessels in the fleet, their hololithic images flickering and sending streams of smaller craft between them.

'Thunderhawks,' Talos said.

'Exactly, my prophet. The Black Legion is begging its lesser allies for aid. Warriors from renegade Chapters are to be pressed into service, defending Abaddon's own ships.'

The Exalted shook its head as it sighed. 'Once more, our Warmaster has grievously overcommitted his forces onto a battlefield. At least he was wise enough to leave many of his allies in orbit in the event of disaster.'

Talos nodded to the creature on the throne. As much as it galled him to admit it, the Exalted was sinking into his element now. The myriad plays and ploys of void war lit up his eyes from within.

'If this is the spearhead of the Throne's force,' Talos said, 'I would hate to see the relief fleet arrive in full.'

'The odds still favour us.' The Exalted's gaze only left the pict screen to glance at a miniature hololithic tactical display generated from the armrest of his throne. 'Two battle-barges and six strike cruisers, with frigate support... We would survive, at crippling cost, should they be unable to board us.'

The Exalted summoned a naval rating to the side of his command throne. 'You. What's the status of the *Premonition*'s withdrawal?'

'The last report still has fifty Astartes and their transports on the surface, lord.'

'Get me a link to Captain Halasker.'

'Yes, my lord.'

'Halasker,' the Exalted said. 'What is taking your men so long?'

Pictureless, the vox-link crackled back. 'I have five squads fighting through to the landing site now. This is madness, Vandred. The Black Legion is shooting down our Thunderhawks.'

'I demand confirmation.'

'This is not the time to argue over picts! I have the sworn oaths of fifty men on the surface that they are embattled with the Black Legion, and that they have seen Abaddon's own forces tearing our gunships from the sky. They are led by some kind of warp-sorcerer... My men cannot kill him.'

'Ease your choler, brother. Be aware that no more than twenty minutes remain before we'll need to engage the Angels or break into the warp.'

'No. I will not leave half a company to die in the dust of a world Abaddon failed to take.'

'You are the commander of one of our Legion's last remaining battle-barges,' the Exalted's voice lowered to a dangerous snarl. 'If you are going to sell your lifeblood, do it in tearing down the Imperium, not a vainglorious last stand. I will recover your Astartes. I have Thunderhawks and transporters standing ready. We will rendezvous in the Great Eye as soon as we are able, where the dogs of the Throne will not follow.'

'Brave, Vandred. Very courageous. You think your little *Covenant* will survive where the *Premonition* would not?'

'Yes. It will.'

'Because it's a less tempting target, eh?'

'No. Not because of that.'

'I sense you have an idea, brother.'

'Halasker,' the Exalted's monstrous face lowered slightly, and its black eyes closed. 'Enough of this. Just run while you still can. Abaddon's mistake must not be allowed to kill us all. The *Premonition*, at the very least, must survive. Be ready to move the moment I give the word.'

'*Ave Dominus Nox*, Vandred. Glory to the Tenth. Die well, all of you.'

The Exalted took a rattling, sticky breath. 'We shall see.'

After the link was silent, it spoke again. 'Transmit the following message to the Warmaster's flagship: *"The Covenant of Blood is reengaging."* Then bring us alongside the *Vengeful Spirit*, as the Warmaster ordered.'

The vox-officer nodded, and did as he was told. The helmsman did the same. The vessel shuddered as its drive engines awoke.

'Vandred–' Talos began.

'All is not as it seems, my prophet.' He fixed Talos with a haunted, fierce look. The web-like veins splitting his cheeks curled as he smiled. 'Trust me.'

In the infinitely slow ballet of void movement, the *Covenant of Blood* drifted through the scattered fleet, coming alongside the Warmaster's flagship. A blue-black and bronze blade of a ship, it reached barely half the size of the *Vengeful Spirit*.

'Launch Thunderhawks,' the Exalted said, reclining once more in its command throne.

'Thunderhawks launching,' an officer called back.

'Report the moment they're clear of the fleet.'

It took less than a minute. 'Thunderhawks clear. All five are in the upper atmosphere.'

'Drift to the following heading.' The Exalted's claws hit keys embedded in his throne's console. 'Engines cold. That is imperative. *Drift*. Use attitude thrusters, and no greater duration than two seconds from each. Keep all thrust emissions untraceable by casual auspex sweeps.'

The *Covenant* obeyed. The Exalted watched the images displayed by the external picters, seeing the skin of the flagship edging closer to the hull of his own vessel. He was reminded briefly, as he always was in these dark and silent moments, of two sharks passing one another in the open ocean.

'Open a one-way channel to the *Premonition*. Do not allow a reply.'

'Done, lord.'

'Halasker, this is the Exalted. Run.'

Engines burned into angry life, propelling the *Hunter's Premonition* from its position in the invasion fleet. The Exalted watched the hololithic display and the sensor readings of his focused auspex scans, but spared no attention for the disengaging Night Lords battle-barge. His focus was on the rest of the fleet.

Several cruisers showed their weapons going live.

'Incoming message, lord.'

'From the *Vengeful Spirit*, I imagine,' the Exalted said.

'Yes, lord. They request we move, immediately, to a station at their starboard.'

'Oh, woe,' the Exalted grinned. 'Are we accidentally within their firing solution? My, however will they open fire on the *Premonition* before it breaks into the warp?'

Several of the bridge crew shared self-satisfied smiles.

'They've repeated the demand for immediate compliance,' the officer said.

'Inform the flagship we require confirmation of that order. Only a short while ago, we were ordered to this position. Now we are required to move? With the Blood Angels inbound?' The Exalted's smirk was as ugly and inhuman as the creature itself.

While the vox-officer sent the message, the Exalted watched the hololith again. Three other cruisers were powering up their lances to rip the *Premonition* apart for its betrayal. These, he disregarded. They would either be too slow to inflict more than minimal damage, or too late to do anything except watch the battle-barge escape.

Pride uncurled within his stomach, hot and welcome. Perhaps some nobility could be salvaged from this night after all.

'Orders confirmed,' the vox-officer called.

'Do as the flagship orders,' the creature nodded to the helm. 'They won't even be able to come about in time.'

As the *Covenant* shuddered in obedience, the Exalted opened a vox-link to every speaker on the ship.

'This is the Exalted. We are remaining within the fleet until the recovery of our brothers on the surface. We must buy our Thunderhawks time, during which we will endure assault from our former brethren, the Blood Angels. Seal all bulkheads. Atramentar, to the bridge. Claws, to your posts. All hands, to battle stations. Stand by to repel boarders.'

XX
THE ANGEL'S SONS

THE FLEETS MET only briefly.

'These battles are won and lost in the opening manoeuvres,' the Exalted said as it stared at the Astartes fleet bearing down upon them. 'If one side is in a strong enough position, the other – commanded by intelligent souls – would do better to retreat rather than be annihilated in a hopeless engagement.'

Garadon regarded the three-dimensional hololithic performance as a dull mystery. 'They will not back down, my prince.'

'No. They will not. Another opportunity lost. Helm, be ready to break orbit on my mark.'

'Break orbit?' Malek grunted. 'But lord–'

'We are not going away from Crythe, Malek. Quite the opposite.'

The Exalted closed its eyes, breathing deep and slow. It remained in this state for several moments. Finally, it spoke, without opening its jet eyes. 'The first lances will be firing… now.'

The Atramentar, all seven of them in their Terminator plate, watched as the hololithic display began to add weapons fire to its projection.

'The lead battle-barges, bearing the Blood Angels' insignia, will be hit by lance fire from the first of our perimeter ships… now.'

The Exalted opened its eyes, seeing its predictions confirmed. Officers and servitors at consoles started working frantically. 'We have a Blood Angels strike cruiser inbound, do we not?' the Exalted asked.

'Yes, lord!' called a rating.

'How predictable. Sometimes, we do not even need Talos to see the future for us. Our foes' grasp of tactical potential is so *coarse*.'

Garadon grunted acknowledgement, but said nothing.

'Fire lances,' the Exalted ordered, even as the weapons officer was drawing breath to announce the Blood Angels cruiser had just entered lance range.

'Firing lances, lord.'

The Exalted went back to its hololithic staring even as the ship started shuddering with the first impacts.

Shields holding. Six per cent drain.

'Shields holding!' an officer called. 'Seven per cent drain.'

Close enough.

'Weapon batteries, ready for my signal.'

'Weapon batteries, aye.'

Come on. Closer. Closer.

The bridge shivered again. The rune depicting the Blood Angels strike cruiser *Malevolence* bore down like a spear. That was the one. It would release boarders onto both the *Spirit* and the *Covenant*. They were well within scanning distance now. They would know how vulnerable the Warmaster's capital ships were. How empty the internal corridors stood without the Astartes to defend them.

The bridge lights dimmed, then failed for a handful of seconds. The fleets, as they crossed each other, exchanged a ferocious volley of fire. The smaller capital ships like the *Covenant* had void shields far below the punishment capacity of battleships like the *Vengeful Spirit*.

'Shields are down,' a rating called out on cue. The tremors shaking the ship intensified tenfold.

'My prince,' one of the weapons officers said. 'They're in weapon battery range.'

Wait. Wait…

'Lord, enemy cruiser *Malevolence* has fired boarding pods.'

The Exalted burbled a sound that might have once been a chuckle.

'All batteries fire.'

Two of the eight pod-runes flickered out of existence from the hololithic display. The others streamed home into their target ships. Four impacted into the *Covenant*.

The Exalted calmly demanded a vox-channel to the entire ship. A rating at the console nodded back.

'All claws, this is the Exalted. Between twenty and forty Blood Angels have breached us with assault pods. Hull impact locations are routed to squad leaders. Find the loyalists, my brothers. Kill them.'

The Exalted rose from its throne, dragging its armoured bulk to the dais railing. It stared into the occulus, at the greyish orb of Crythe below.

'Damage report.'

'Minor structural damage, primarily the starboard side.'

'Order the enginarium to vent plasma from the reactors. Bleed power directly into the void.'

'Sir?' his human bridge attendant stammered.

'Do as I command, mortal.'

'As you wish, lord.'

'Vox-officer.'

'Yes, my prince.'

'Transmit emergency crash landing signals to the *Vengeful Spirit*. Inform them we've taken glancing damage that has managed to wound our reactor. Tell them we are losing our orbit due to the pull of the planet's gravity, and our engines are locked at full power.'

As the confused vox-officer obeyed, the Exalted turned to face the row of helmsmen.

'Are we bleeding plasma? Self-scan the *Covenant*. Do we appear to be haemorrhaging from a reactor leakage?'

The helm officers bent over their consoles. 'Yes, lord,' one replied.

'Then dive,' the Exalted grinned.

'What?' Malek stepped forward. 'Lord, are you insane?'

'*Dive!*'

Like a sword falling from the sky, the *Covenant of Blood* tilted downward and fired its engines. Flame wreathed the shieldless strike cruiser as it tore through the pollution-clogged atmosphere.

SEPTIMUS BURNED BLACKENED'S engines, coming in tight and low over the plain. Behind him came another two Thunderhawks and two transporters, forming a loose 'V' formation.

'Be ready to break at the first sign of attack,' he warned over the vox.

'Compliance,' replied three servitors.

'Understood,' came a deeper voice. An Astartes. Septimus had no idea which one.

A trickle of sweat made its uncomfortable way down his back, seeming to pause at the bump of at each vertebra. It was one thing to know you'd eventually die in service to the VIII Legion. It was another thing to realise you were going to meet that fate imminently. Even if the Black Legion had stopped shooting down Night Lords gunships, what hope was there to get back into orbit and survive a docking operation in the middle of a void war?

Septimus swore under his breath and activated a general vox-channel.

'All Eighth Legion units, this is the Tenth Company Thunderhawk *Blackened*. Report your locations.'

The voices that came back to him were strained, angry, embattled. He throttled up, letting the engines shout harder, approaching the storm of disorder that engulfed the landing site of the Warmaster's forces.

'Look to the skies, Night Lords,' he said in fluent Nostraman. 'We are inbound.'

'Be swift,' one voice said. 'Most of us are down to killing them with our bare hands.'

The chorus of replies detailed exactly what needed to be recovered from the surface. A Land Raider, four Rhinos, a Vindicator and forty-one warriors.

Mere minutes later, Septimus kicked *Blackened* into hover, his altitude thrusters burning to keep the gunship aloft over the landing site. The landing platform erected by the 11th Company of the *Hunter's Premonition* was a bare bones setup – and Septimus was being generous calling it even that. The surviving tanks and men clustered around an engine-scorched patch of land, their weapons turned outwards into the ranks of the Black Legion's mortal slaves. The humans had seen the incoming gunships and sought to escape, charging the encircled Night Lords vehicles.

As the Astartes had said, several of the VIII Legion warriors were reduced to beating the mortals to death with their fists. Ammunition had not been landed and supplied to the front line in several hours. Even the guns of the tanks spat their deadly payloads only intermittently into the seething horde laying siege to their position.

'They've not got room to get the tanks into a loading position. Should we open fire on the crowd?' Septimus asked. 'My ammunition counters are practically voided.'

The gunship hovering fifty metres to his port bow immediately opened up with a vicious hail of heavy bolter fire, punching holes in the panicked mortal horde.

Foolish question to ask a Night Lord, really.

Septimus added his fire to the chaos below.

BROTHER-SERGEANT MELCHIAH MOVED with purpose.

In units of five, his men moved through the enemy ship.

The darkness was nothing to him. This, he pierced with the vision modes of his helm. The winding corridors offered no mystery to his senses. These, he navigated by memory, for one Astartes strike cruiser was the same as almost any other. Such was the wisdom contained with the Standard Template Construct patterns of all noble machines birthed by the Adeptus Mechanicus.

On he stalked, chainsword purring with rev-breaths, his plasma pistol raised before him. The blackness of the Traitors' vessel yielded before him, his vision stained emerald green by his helm's lenses, picking out details of walls, side corridors, and the heat smear of recent footsteps.

'Auspex,' he voxed to Hyralus.

'No movement,' Hyralus replied. 'Vague heat traces all around. A nexus of them in the chamber ahead.'

'Forward, in the name of the Emperor,' Melchiah said, moving on. He removed his helm, trusting to his own senses even in the pitch dark. He was Astartes. It was the way of things. Immediately, he felt more in tune with his surroundings, his senses no longer caged by the helm. Even with its enhancements, it was not always the perfect replacement for true perception.

Corruption was rife here. Even the air of the ship tasted foul. Too long in the warp, too long with the same recycled air. Warm and stale, it tingled against the steel studs implanted above Melchiah's eyebrow. Three of them, in recognition of his long service.

Upon the shoulders of each warrior, a ruby-red drop of blood the size of a mortal's fist was winged by marble angel pinions. It was a symbol that had endured for thousands of years, and one the Night Lords were sure to recognise. The Traitors' own symbol was the corrupt opposite – a fanged skull instead of a primarch's holy blood, and arching bat wings instead of the pure aileron of the murdered Angel, Sanguinius.

With the ancient hatreds hot in his heart, Melchiah entered the chamber, plasma pistol raised. The shuddering of the ship was growing savage. Curious, that it wasn't the jagged shaking of battle, but something much more regular. An atmospheric entry burn? Perhaps. But with little indication of why the Traitor Legion ship would be reacting this way, Melchiah put it out of his mind. He had a duty. He was oathed to this moment.

The chamber was large. Almost impressive. On board the *Malevolent*, this room was a chapel to the Emperor of Mankind. On the *Covenant*, it looked to be some kind of communal haven for slaves. Detritus decorated the floor. Tables stood abandoned and bare. Bedrolls lined one wall.

'Auspex?' he said. 'I see nothing.'

'And that's why you're dead,' Talos hissed as he dropped from the ceiling.

LIKE SPIDERS, THEY had lain in wait, clinging to the ceiling. With the Blood Angels in their midst, First Claw dropped the ten metres to the ground, their weapons spitting death at the loyalists below.

Talos hit first, *Aurum* deflecting a bolt from the Angels and lashing out to ram home in the chest of the helmless squad leader.

'*Aurum*!' the sergeant snarled. 'The blade!'

Talos's reply was a headbutt that crashed against his foe's reinforced skull, hammering the long-service studs through the bone and into the soft tissue of the brain beneath.

The two squads tore into each other, equal in all ways but for the fact First Claw had the advantage of surprise.

Talos powered the sword to the side, ripping through Melchiah's spinal column, lungs, one heart and his ceramite armour as if none of it existed. The blade's arc was as smooth as if Talos chopped air. As the Blood Angel staggered back, the Night Lord pounded a bolt into his neck, just a single shot. Melchiah had a single moment to claw at the wound before it exploded, removing his head in a shower of organic mess.

'For the Emperor!' one of the Angels cried. The darkness broke in the face of bolter flashes and clashing power weapons.

Talos leapt at the shouter, his golden sword cleaving through the warrior's bolter on the downswing. The Astartes met the blade's backslash with his own combat gladius.

'For the Emperor,' the Blood Angel said again, this time in a snarl.

'Your Emperor is dead,' Talos growled back. The moment came; the moment when the Angel's gaze flickered to the blade in the Night Lord's dark hands. Talos couldn't see his enemy's eyes, but he felt the minute movement of the Angel's muscles as his attention wavered. In that critical moment, Talos hurled the Blood Angel back against the wall. Three bolts to the head downed him for good, and Talos nodded his thanks to Cyrion.

Uzas, Mercutian, Xarl, Adhemar, Cyrion and Talos stood in the darkness, listening to the hiss of cooling bolter muzzles, watching the last Blood Angel in the doorway. He turned and ran, boots pounding down the corridor.

'I… wasn't expecting that,' Talos almost laughed. 'Uzas, do the honours.'

Uzas sprinted into the darkness, chainsword howling.

THE BLOOD ANGEL wasn't fleeing. Uzas knew that.

He hated to indulge the thought, even to himself, that the Angels were an admirable force – back in the Great Crusade, at least. These thinbloods left much to be desired. So far removed from the gene-seed of their primarch as to be almost mortal. But even so, the Angel wasn't fleeing. The only time an Astartes backed down from a battle was when he had an idea for how to fight it better elsewhere. The trick, Uzas had learned, was to kill the enemy before they got that chance.

He was on the Angel in under a minute, but the loyalist wasn't giving up easily. Without the element of surprise – and really, that was an inspired idea he grudgingly gave Talos credit for – the two of them were close-matched.

The Blood Angel pulled his gladius free from its ornate scabbard and lunged. Uzas parried the first thrust and dodged the second, third and fourth. *Kharnath's boiling blood*, the Angel was fast.

'I'm better than you,' the Angel mocked, backhanding the Night Lord with a fist that crashed hard against Uzas's helm. 'Will you call for your brothers, Traitor?'

Uzas gave ground, deflecting the gladius with his chainsword each time it sought his heart or throat. Teeth sprayed from his chainblade as the Angel hacked them away.

'I will eat your gene-seed,' Uzas grunted, 'after I claw it out of your throat with my bare hands.'

'You will die.' The Angel lashed out with a boot, thudding the Night Lord into the wall behind. 'And be forgotten.'

The Blood Angel's helm distorted with a tremendous *clang*, then exploded in a shower of red-painted shards.

Uzas breathed out slowly. The dead Blood Angel crashed to the ground in a metallic chorus of plate. Talos lowered his bolter and shook his head at his brother.

'You were taking too long,' he said, and moved back down the corridor.

THE *Covenant of Blood* was constructed in the shipyards of Mars in the age before Mankind's sundering. Since its birth in those fleet-raising forge-foundries, it had landed a total of zero times, and performed an equal number of atmospheric flights. As it burned through the atmosphere of Crythe and violently tore through the cloud cover, the Exalted's eyes remained closed, not seeing anything on the strategium command deck.

Its ship, the ship it knew better than the creature knew his own twisted body, was shaking itself apart. The painful shudders wracking the *Covenant* transmitted through to the Exalted's own spine in sympathetic torment.

But it vowed it would die before it failed in the promise to that preening glory-hound Halasker.

The bridge crew gripped their consoles or remained strapped into their own control thrones. The Atramentar Terminators were forced to their knees, even their enhanced muscle fibres unable to resist the gravity forces taking hold. They resembled worshippers before the Exalted's throne, which brought a sick little smile to the creature's face, even if only for a moment.

'Position,' it demanded of the helm. At the reply, the Exalted turned to the vox-officer. 'Hail our Thunderhawks. Inform them they have two minutes to be skyborne or they will have no mothership to return to.'

'We will be above Seventeen-Seventeen in ninety seconds, lord!'

'Slow my ship down, mortals. I care not how it's done, but make it happen. Give the Thunderhawks time to dock.'

THE SHAKING THREATENED the hunt.

Talos cursed as gravity reasserted its grip on them at another inconvenient moment, and his bolt went wide. Across the chamber, a second squad of Blood Angels stood their ground beside an unopened boarding pod. They crouched behind what little cover existed in the Blackmarket hall, returning fire at First Claw. Talos and his brothers used the corners of linking corridors as cover.

Neither side was getting anywhere.

'Brother, I have grim news,' Adhemar voxed. He crouched next to the prophet, twinning his fire with Talos's. 'That pod they're guarding?'

Talos unleashed another three bolts to no effect. 'I see it.' The hull was mangled and blackened where the red-metal pod had pierced the ship's skin. 'Hard to miss, Adhemar.'

'It's a Dreadnought pod.'

'What? How can you tell?'

'The size of the damn wound in our hull!'

Talos's retinal display outlined the measurements as he glanced around the corner. He resisted the powerful urge to sigh.

'You are right.'

'I'm always right.'

The ship juddered again, violently enough to throw two of the Blood Angels from their feet and onto the black decking. Uzas and Xarl similarly lost their footing, accompanied by Nostraman curses.

Like a steel bloom greeting the new season, the pod's cone-shaped front opened to the bay. The hulking form within began to grind forward, a tower of reddened metal and vox-roared challenges.

'I will end you, Traitors. I will end you *all.*'

The air between the squads roiled with barely-seen heat blurs, and the temperature readings on Talos's retinal displays shot up with sickening speed. The Dreadnought's massive multi-melta, capable of blistering tanks into sludge, was only just warming up.

'It's got a vaporiser cannon!' Mercutian voxed. 'We're dead.'

'Fine by me, I've had enough of your doom and gloom,' Cyrion answered.

Talos hunched behind his scarce cover, firing his bolter blindly around the corner and speaking into the vox.

'This is Talos of First Claw, requesting urgent reinforcements in the aft mortals' decks.'

The voice that answered was balm to his soul.

'Understood, my brother.'

XXI
FINAL UNITY

*'Many will claim to lead our Legion in the years after I am gone.
Many will claim that they – and they alone – are my appointed
successor.
I hate this Legion, Talos.
I destroyed its world to stem the flow of poison.
I will be vindicated soon, and the truest lesson of the Night Lords
will be taught.
Do you truly believe I care what happens to any of you after my
death?'*

– The Primarch Konrad Curze
Addressing Apothecary Talos of First Claw, Tenth Company

SEPTIMUS WRENCHED THE control sticks hard, begging for altitude. Crowded
around him were Astartes from 11th Company, each one a stranger to
him, each one now discovering the unwelcome fact that a blessed Legion
relic was being piloted by a mortal serf. He expected at any moment one
of them would demand the controls from him.

This didn't happen. He doubted it was because they were too exhausted
– in his experience, Astartes didn't tire as humans did – but they were
certainly worse for wear. Their dark, skulled plate was as shattered and
bloody as First Claw's had been.

Turbulence buffeted *Blackened* with an angry fist, and a sickening lurch
in his gut betrayed the loss of altitude even before his console instruments did. The serf threw levers and wrenched the sticks again. *Blackened*
climbed.

Behind them, a transporter exploded in mid-air. Its shell, and the hulks
of two Rhinos it was carrying, crashed to the ground in flames. Dozens
of mortal soldiers died beneath it.

'The Black Legion,' one of the Astartes said in a low, dangerous voice.
'They will bleed and scream for this. Each and every one of them.' The
promise met with general assent. Septimus swallowed; he couldn't have

273

cared less about vengeance in that moment. He just wanted the damn gunship to climb, climb, *climb*.

He had to break into orbit. He had to reach the *Covenant*.

And that's when he saw it.

'Throne of the God-Emperor,' he whispered for the first time since his capture.

The *Covenant of Blood* was on fire. It streaked across the sky like a burning meteorite, trailing flame and smoke in a thin plume. The heavens rang with thunder as it pounded through the sound barrier – not speeding up but slowing down.

'This is the Exalted,' the vox crackled live. 'Brothers of Seventh Company. We have come for you.'

THE VOX WAS alive with reports from the other claws. The Blood Angels, even with their numbers fewer than thirty, were spread throughout the ship and putting up ferocious resistance to the hunt that sought their lives.

Talos coughed blood. The bolts that had struck his chestplate and helm left his armour a broken ruin. Although his nerves were deadened to the worst of the pain by combat narcotics pulsing through his veins, he knew spitting blood onto the decking was a bad sign. His gene-enhanced healing was failing to heal whatever the hell was wrong with him.

He'd seen Adhemar die.

It was over in a moment.

A blur of motion as the former sergeant rushed the Dreadnought with his blade held high. The war machine had turned with unbelievable speed, whirring around on its waist axis, breathing invisible but searing heat from its multi-melta. Adhemar's armour baked and split within a heartbeat, the joints melted, the empty war-plate clattering to melt into sludge on the decking. Nothing biological remained.

Over in a moment.

All to save Mercutian and Uzas, who were wounded on the other side of the chamber. Talos had added his bolter fire to cover them, and taken hits from the Blood Angels for his trouble.

Were the Blood Angels suicidal? To fire a melta-weapon within a ship? It was a miracle the hull wasn't liquefied yet and every one of them torn out into the rushing air.

Talos gripped *Aurum*, feeling his strength waxing again. Good. Not lethal, perhaps. Something was wrong, but it could be dealt with later. The Blood Angels had to be slaughtered, skinned and crucified for their accursed presence on the *Covenant*.

At first he'd thought the deck shaking was merely more of the atmospheric turbulence. Shells still exploded around his fragile cover, and only when Malcharion strode past, his armoured bulk barely fitting within the linking corridors, did Talos realise what was happening. The Dreadnought stalked into the chamber, ignoring the small-arms fire from the Blood Angels.

Revitalised by the war-sage's presence, First Claw's survivors doubled their fire. Astartes armoured in red died. Mercutian and Cyrion went down as well, struck by bolts.

Talos felt his newly-recovered strength desert him. Back to the wall, he slid down to the decking, clutching his shattered breastplate. The Dreadnoughts regarded each other in a moment of almost hilarious calm.

'Kill it!' Talos screamed. *'Kill it now!'*

'I already have once,' Malcharion boomed.

The Blood Angels Dreadnought made the same gear-shifting grind of a sound Talos had heard from Malcharion. The Night Lord's eyes fell upon the sarcophagus mounted within the war-sage's new body. There stood the image of Malcharion in life, clutching the three helms. One of those belonged to…

The Blood Angel champion… Raguel the Sufferer.

'Even in death,' the Blood Angel growled, 'I will avenge myself,'

'You deserve the chance, Raguel.'

With power fists crackling, the two war machines did what they were resurrected to do.

The fight played out in two worlds, and until his dying night Talos was never sure which battle he truly witnessed. In the immediate, painful, shaking world of the shallowest senses, the two armoured behemoths tore at each other with rotating claws and bludgeoning fists. Ceramite ripped in those mauling hands, and shards of armour flew from the combatants like hail on some blizzard-touched deathworld.

Neither of the suspended corpses saw this, and neither felt it.

The walls were gold where these warriors duelled. Both men wore the proud armour of their Legion, and both men fought for Terra – one to defend it and die for the Imperium, one to conquer it and kill for the same reason.

Their blades spun and struck until both were broken. Then it came down to gauntleted fists and the strength to strangle.

Talos watched the Dreadnoughts tearing each other to scrap, and saw exactly what the dead men saw.

BLACKENED ROARED THROUGH the air, engines screaming as the racing Thunderhawk drew alongside the *Covenant*.

The others had already docked, bringing their precious cargo on board the strike cruiser as it tore across the sky. *Blackened* was the last.

Warning runes flashed across console displays as Septimus pushed the engines past all safe limits. The control sticks juddered in his fists, shaking almost in sync with the wailing sirens that screamed at him to cease what he was doing. The dark dart of the Thunderhawk banked closer to the racing shape of the *Covenant*, the turbulence intensified with *Blackened* on the edge of entering its mothership's slipstream.

It was starting to climb.

He could see it himself, even without the Astartes in the cockpit – warriors he didn't know – pointing it out in curses and complaints.

These, he did his best to ignore along with the warning runes blinking migraine-red everywhere.

But the *Covenant* was definitely climbing now, and even slowly, it made a near-impossible landing almost inconceivable. Its prow came up, cutting the polluted sky, in the beginning incline for orbital re-entry.

'Just a little more,' he mouthed the plea, wrenching the three thrust levers into the blank sockets past the red zones marked on the helm consoles. *Blackened* kicked, howling louder, and burst forward in pursuit of its carrier.

The thought occurred, as he climbed alongside the strike cruiser, banking ever closer to the open hangar bay, that there was a very good chance one – or all – of the Thunderhawk's engines would explode under this punishment.

Septimus pulled back, climbing parallel to the larger ship, boosting ahead of the open bay doors, ready to fall back and weave inside. The gunship veered gently, shaking hard, within thirty metres of the hangar bay.

They were going too fast to deploy the landing gear. The claws would be torn off the moment they cleared the hull. Septimus would need to lower them late, as soon as *Blackened* came into the bay, and pray they were down enough to take the ship's weight.

'Now or never,' he whispered, and banked hard right at more than full thrust. The Thunderhawk wrenched to the side, rolling directly at the hangar bay.

The next ten seconds lasted an age to Septimus – an eternity of insane shaking and the loudest noises he had ever heard.

The port booster exploded as the Thunderhawk veered home, amplifying the turbulence tenfold. Septimus had been ready for one or more of the engines to go, and compensated immediately. *Blackened* would have fallen short of its target, either smashing headlong into side of the *Covenant*, or glancing from the larger ship and then falling from the sky after sustaining severe damage in the impact. Septimus compensated by overloading the remaining boosters, destroying them all in one momentary burst of thrust that threw the gunship at the open bay.

He risked it, so close to the target, and deployed the landing gear. The hideous sound of wrenching metal told the fate of the front landing leg. The others held.

Darkness blanketed over the view windows as they hurtled at the

Covenant. Septimus had a split second to realise they were on course, but not *perfectly*, before they were in the bay itself with a blur of motion. Another almighty crash shook the Thunderhawk as the gunship's tail cleaved into the edge of the bay doors. *Blackened* bucked and lurched, twisted off its already chaotic course, and slammed into the floor with savage force.

The rear landing claws carved into the decking as the gunship's nose hammered down and ploughed a squealing, sparking furrow through the deck floor. After several dozen metres of skidding, the rear landing gear gave way, torn from their sockets and thudding the gunship's winged rear end to the decking with a thunderous crash.

With its engines dead and thrusters burned out, the only thing that brought the howling gunship to a final halt was its collision with the side wall of the hangar bay.

Septimus was jolted forward with this last indignity, but his restraint belts remained strong, keeping him in his throne.

Motionless at last, his heart pounding, Septimus let out the deepest breath he'd ever held.

'We're ... we're down,' he said, unsurprised at the tremor in his voice.

The Astartes squad unbuckled from their own thrones and left the cockpit without a word.

Even as the ruined engines continued the short process of terminally cycling down in an orchestra of mechanical whines, the Astartes on board were disembarking, summoned by the Exalted in defence of the *Covenant*. Throne-loyal Astartes were apparently on board.

Septimus was almost too tired to care as he stood slowly, trying to keep his balance on unsteady legs.

His neck ached. His back ached. His hands ached.

Everything ached. A pilot all his life, he'd not even believed such a docking was survivable. The Astartes left without a word of acknowledgement. He was also too tired to care.

Well. Almost.

Stumbling down the gang ramp, he blinked blurry stress-exhaustion from his eyes. *Blackened* creaked and hissed behind him as its strained hull settled into inactivity once more.

The gunship's tail was gone, torn off in the crash with the hull. The landing gear was a mangled memory. All across the Thunderhawk's proud, hunter's form, damage showed in stark, black burns and dark, twisted metal.

'I am never doing that again,' he said. Servitors approached, their simple programming taking several moments to calculate how to deal with the wreckage of what lay before them. Several looked at him curiously, wondering if he'd spoken a command.

'Get back to work,' Septimus said. He reached up to activate his vox-bead. 'Octavia?'

Her voice was weak. Wet with tears.

'You have to help me,' she said softly.

'Where are you?'

She told him, and Septimus broke into a pained run.

ON THE STRATEGIUM, the Exalted watched the mountain ranges below falling away. Its ship climbed, tearing into the sky like a spear. The bridge
crew cheered. The sound shook the Exalted, having never heard it before.

Within seconds, the blue palette of the occulus was replaced by black.

The black of the void. Blessedly, the *Covenant* ended its tormented
shaking. Artificial gravity resumed, and limbs became less heavy.

'Punch a hole through between these two ships,' the Exalted ordered.
It was already sat back in its throne, studying the reactivated hololithic
display. Keen senses raced to unravel the mysteries, the flight paths, the
destructions and deaths since he had last seen this image.

The shaking began again, and this time, damage reports flooded in.

'I do not care what damage is sustained.' The ship jolted hard under
another volley of lance strikes. 'Just get us into the warp.'

Arrow-straight and lethally fast, the *Covenant* ripped from Crythe
Prime's orbit, racing through the battling fleets.

'Navigator Etrigius,' the Exalted said. 'Answer me.'

'He's... he's dead,' said a female voice.

FIRST CLAW CAME to the downed machines.

The healthiest of the Astartes were limping. Uzas and Mercutian
dragged themselves by their hands.

The Blood Angel Dreadnought still twitched as it lay on its back. Its
claw opened and closed, grinding nothing but air. Talos nodded to the
sarcophagus, too pained to point.

'Cut that open.'

Xarl and Cyrion went to work with their chainswords, carving through
the coffin's surface, the tearing teeth offering no respect for the funerary
declarations and acid-etched glories depicted in Baalian glyphs. With
grunts of effort, the two warriors hauled the sarcophagus's lid away,
revealing the pilot within.

Their blades had ruptured the inner coffin. Clear amniotic fluid, blood-
pinked in patches, seeped from the pierced box in sloshing trickles.

Talos stepped on the downed Dreadnought's hull, looking down at the
limbless, augmented wreck of a human being.

'I am Talos of the Night Lords. Nod if you understand me.'

The slain hero nodded, skin tightening in doubtlessly painful spasms
as his life support interfeeds failed. Talos smiled at the sight.

'Know this, Blood Angel. Your final mission was a failure. Your brothers
are dead. We will wear their armour in battle against your False Emperor.

And know this also, champion of the Ninth Legion. Twice now, the sons of the Night Haunter have seen you slain. Greet the afterlife within the warp knowing you were too weak to triumph over us, even once.'

Talos locked eyes with the spasming remnant in its fluid-filled coffin. In a sure grip despite the weakness of his arm, Talos raised *Aurum*, the blade of another fallen Angel.

'Your bones will be made into trophies for our armour. We will feast upon your gene-seed. And whatever remains of this glorious walking tomb will be salvaged by our tech-priest to house a champion of our own Legion.'

He plunged the blade down. Its golden length stabbed through the casket, impaling the mutilated Imperial hero's open mouth.

'Die,' Talos finished, 'with the taste of your Chapter's eternal failure on your tongue.'

OCTAVIA WIPED THE blood from Etrigius's face.

The Navigator's eerie features seemed somehow childish in death, peaceful and innocent. She could almost believe he hadn't seen a lifetime of sights and secrets few mortals should be cursed to witness.

One of his rings had slipped from a too-long finger. She replaced it on his hand, not even sure why she bothered. It just felt right. Throne, she'd not even liked him. He was an insufferable and condescending ass.

Still. He'd not deserved this. No one did.

Octavia rested her hand over the bleeding puncture where his warp eye had been. A sniper... some kind of lightly-armoured Astartes youth... He'd stolen into the chamber and dropped Etrigius with a single shot. The Navigator died in the middle of complaining about the turbulence. Octavia had been too shocked to move, too stunned to reach for her autopistol, even when the Navigator's robed servitors deployed their claws and tore the Blood Angel youth limb from limb.

'He's dead,' she'd told the daemon-thing on the bridge when its voice blared over the vox. 'They killed him.'

The daemon-thing, the Exalted, had screamed. The ship shuddered as if in the grip of some huge, angry god.

Septimus's voice came to her again. Not over the vox this time. She looked up and saw him standing at the doorway.

'Octavia.'

'They killed him,' she said again, her teeth clenched. Throne, why was she crying? Why wouldn't the ship stop shaking... just for a moment...

'Octavia,' Septimus came to her, helping her to her feet. 'The *Covenant* is being destroyed. We are all dead, unless...'

'Unless... I guide us into the warp.'

'Yes.' He wiped flecks of blood from her face, his augmetic eye whirring as it focused. She heard it click once, very quietly.

'Did you just take my pict?'

'I may have,' he said. His smile answered for him, slow and mournful.

Octavia glanced at the bloodstained meditation couch, and did not look back at him. 'You should go. This is never pleasant to watch.'

He hesitated, reluctant to let her go even as the ship was being annihilated by Imperial guns. She pushed him away, not unkindly.

'You know,' she said, walking to the couch, 'I'll see you after. Maybe.'

'Maybe.'

She finally looked back, seeing him standing by the door. 'I have no idea what I'm doing. I can find the Astronomican, guide by the Emperor's light. But I have a feeling that would invite pursuit.'

'It would. Just... do your best.'

'I could kill you all, if I wanted to.' She grinned. 'You're heretics, you know.'

'I know.'

'You should go.'

He didn't know what else to say, so he left without saying anything at all. The door to Etrigius's – no, Octavia's chambers – sealed closed and locked tight.

'Navigator,' came a growl from the vox speakers around the room.

'Here,' she answered.

'I am the Exalted.'

'I know who you are.'

'Do you know the region of space, close to the galactic core, that houses a warp wound known as the Great Eye?'

Eurydice Mervallion, now called Octavia of the *Covenant*, took a deep breath.

'Link me to the helm,' she said, strength returning to her voice. 'I will commune with your pilots.'

IT WASN'T SO difficult, really.

The ship hated her. Oh, how it loathed her presence. She felt its soul recoil from her probing meditation, like a viper protecting its young.

I hate you, the *Covenant* hissed. Its presence thrashed in her mind, shrieking and hateful.

I hate you, it warned again, far from the docile and sedate soul of Kartan Syne's *Maiden of the Stars*.

You are not my Navigator, it spat.

'Yes,' she spoke to the chamber, empty except the corpse of her predecessor. 'I am.'

Octavia closed her human eyes, opened the third, and dragged the *Covenant of Blood* into the space between worlds.

* * *

'YOU FEEL THAT?' Xarl asked as the ship seemed to slip forward in a strangely smooth lurch that had no similarity to weapons fire.

Talos nodded. He'd felt the translation into the warp as well.

'We made it,' Cyrion grunted. 'Most of us.'

Malcharion was no longer moving at all. First Claw clustered around the ruined warrior, and Xarl's chainblade revved again.

'Should we?' he asked Talos. 'Deltrian might be able to save him, if he still lives within.'

'No. Let him sleep, as he wished. We already have an image of him that should stay with us down the ages.' The prophet's eyes didn't leave the triumphant engraving on the front of the sarcophagus for some time.

'It was grand to see him fight,' Uzas conceded, 'one last time.'

The others snorted or stared to hear such a thing from him.

'I swear, I saw the fight at the Palace of Terra again,' Cyrion said. 'Not these... war machines clubbing each other.'

Talos didn't reply.

'Deltrian,' he voxed to the Hall of Remembrance.

'Yes, One-Two-Ten. I am present, Talos.'

'Malcharion the War-Sage has fallen in battle.'

'Your voice indicates you grieve at this development. If condolences from others will ease your torment, I will offer them.'

'The sentiment is appreciated, but that is not all.'

'Your voice patterns now show a trace of amusement.'

'Send two teams of lifter servitors to the aft mortals' decks, to the area known as Blackmarket.'

'Processing. One team is enough to recover the holy relic of the entombed Malcharion. I require reasoning for your request of two lifter teams.'

'Because, honoured tech-priest,' Talos turned his gaze to the wreckage of Raguel the Sufferer in his priceless war machine shell, 'First Claw has a gift for you.'

With the link cut, Talos narrowed his eyes at the corpse of one dead Blood Angel. The warrior's breastplate remained intact despite grievous damage to his thigh, leg and shoulder armour. An Imperial eagle spread its wings proudly across the chestpiece, forged from platinum, gleaming gold in the dim light.

The prophet nodded weakly at the dead Blood Angel's beautiful armour.

'That is mine,' he said, and slid back down to the decking, too exhausted to move.

EPILOGUE
PORTENTS

IN THE BOWELS of the *Covenant of Blood*, a mother and father wept.

The human crew had not come through the battle unscathed. Some fell victim to the Blood Angel boarding teams, cut down as they fled from the righteous indignation of the Emperor's finest warriors. Others perished in the explosions that wracked the ship as it sustained severe damage from other Imperial cruisers. Still more died as gangs of mortals used the chaos of the orbital war as a cover to launch attacks on the rival gangs that shared the blackness with them.

One man clutched the body of his daughter, holding her light, lifeless form to his own scrawny chest. Blood still marked the girl's lips and face from where she had choked out her last wet breath, less than an hour before. Her eyes, dark from the eternal gloom, stared sightlessly at the crowd that came to gather.

She had no legs. These were lost to a Blood Angel chainblade as one of the Imperium's heroes had sought to exterminate his way through the heretic crew of the *Covenant*. His grinding blade had claimed the lives of many before he was finally slain by Astartes from one of the *Covenant*'s claws.

Her father cradled what remained of her, and cried out his sorrow.

The witnesses began to whisper, speaking in quiet tones of curses, of omens, of the blackest portents. On the girl's chest, a Legion medallion glinted in the dim light.

Her father held what remained of the ten-year-old girl, and yelled at the walls of the silent ship all around.

'This vessel is *cursed*! It is *damned*! *She has been taken from us!*'

More humans gathered in the darkness, their eyes wide and wet with tears, each of them sharing the same thoughts and fears as the mourning father.

* * *

TAISHA WAS NOT at peace, despite the harmony of the garden.

Beneath a dome that revealed the glory of the silent void, beneath the twinkling light of a million distant suns, Taisha came to the garden in search of answers. Her bare feet whispered over the cool soil, the grass soft on her toes. A robe of shimmering jade silk clung to her lithe figure, hanging off one shoulder to leave it bare. Hair the deep red of human blood, long enough to reach the small of her back, was tied up in a sharp topknot.

Her slanted eyes regarded a figure kneeling upon the grass. His own robes were the black of the unending space between the worlds. He spoke without looking up at her.

'Greetings, daughter of Khaine and Morai-Heg.'

Taisha inclined her head to the appropriate angle, politely acknowledging his superior rank and the honour he did her by speaking first. She did not kneel beside him. Such would be a breach of decorum. Instead she stayed several metres away, her fingers lightly stroking the wraithbone sword hilt at her waist. The curved blade's tip almost reached the ground, such was its length. The belt it hung from was all that kept her green robe closed.

'Greetings, noble farseer. Are you well?'

'I am well,' he said, still not looking up.

'Have I disturbed your meditations?'

'No, Taisha.' The kneeling male regarded the ground before him, where a spread of coin-sized rune stones lay among the dewy blades of grass. 'You have come for answers, yes?'

'I have, noble farseer.' She was not surprised he knew of her unease, or that she would be coming to him. 'My slumber is troubled.'

'You are not alone, Taisha.'

'So I have heard, noble farseer. Several of my sisters are likewise uneasy in their hours of rest.'

'Oh, but the turmoil reaches so much further.' Now he looked up at her, his ice-blue eyes like frozen crystals. 'War threatens the craftworld once more. A war that will see you shedding the blood of the mon-keigh, daughter of the Fate goddess.'

'We are Ulthwe.' She inclined her head again in respect. 'We know little else but war. But who comes, noble farseer? Which of the mon-keigh?'

The farseer scooped his runes from the grass of the garden, feeling them hot and portentous in his palm.

'The Hunter of Souls, Taisha. The one who will cross blades with the Void Stalker.'

THRONE OF LIES

THE *Covenant of Blood* tore through the warp, splitting the secret tides like a spear of stained cobalt and flawed gold. Its engines struggled, breathing white fire into the ever-shifting Sea of Souls. Pulsing like arrhythmic hearts, the thrusters laboured to propel the ship onwards. Its passage was a graceless dive, slipping through boiling waves of thrashing psychic energy.

Tormented fields of kinetic force shielded the craft from the warp's elemental rage, but the storm's force was merciless. Reaching out from the hurricane, the claws of vast creatures raked across the shields, each impact hammering the vessel farther from its course.

In a sealed chamber at the ship's prow, a lone figure knelt in silent repose. Her human eyes were closed, yet she was far from blind. Her secret eye, the eye she hid from the world beneath sweat-stained bandanas and uncomfortable helms, looked out into the void. The ship's hull was no barrier, and the crackling shields no obstacle. Her secret sight pierced them with effortless ease, and she stared into the storm beyond.

Like oil on water, the seas outside roiled in a sickening riot of colour. A beacon of light usually pierced the chaos – a lifeline of ephemeral radiance splitting the swirling murk. All she had to do was follow it.

There was no beacon this time. No radiant lifeline. The crackle of the shields buckling under pressure was all that illuminated the storm outside.

The tides rolled against the ship in jagged, unpredictable waves, too fast for human response. By the time she saw a flood of migraine-bright energy spilling towards her, the shields were already repelling it. They sparked with pained fire as they sent the assaulting wave back into the psychic filth from whence it came.

The *Covenant of Blood* trembled again, its engines giving a piteous whine as the tremor ran through the ship's steel bones. It couldn't take much more of this. The kneeling woman took a deep breath, and refocused.

Her lapse of attention had not gone unnoticed. The voice, when it came, was an insidious whisper breaching her heart, not her ears. Each word resonated, echo-faint, through her blood.

Centuries of conquering the void. Centuries of laying claim to the stars. The dance of hunter and hunted, predator and prey. You, Navigator, will be my end. The death of glory. The pain of failure.

The ship was threatening her again. She didn't take that as a good sign, and hissed a single word through clenched teeth.

'Silence.'

She swore that, somewhere on the edge of imagination, she sensed its laughter.

Above all else, she loathed the crude poetry of the ship's primal intelligence. The machine-spirit at the warship's core was a bestial, dominant consciousness. It had resisted its new Navigator for weeks now. She was beginning to fear she would never rise as its master.

The claws of the Neverborn tear at my hull-skin, promising to bleed my innards to the void, it whispered. *You are damnation. You are the bearer of blame. You will cast us into oblivion, Octavia.*

She bit back a reply, keeping her mouth as closed as her human eyes. Her third eye stared unblinking, seeing nothing but the storm raging outside.

No. No, there was something more now. Something else sailed the Sea of Souls, more suggestion and shadow than form and flesh. She pulsed a warning at once.

+Something beneath us, something vast. *Evade at once.*+

Octavia sent the command with all her strength, a desperate plea to the ship's pilots. At the speed of thought, she felt the response flash through the interface cables binding her to the throne of brass and bone. A dead voice, the tone of a lobotomised servitor at the ship's helm.

'Compliance.'

The *Covenant of Blood* shuddered now, its burning engines forcing it to climb through the psychic syrup of un-space. The predator, the vast presence beneath them, stirred in the aetheric fog. She felt it thrash, and saw a shadow the size of a sun ripple in the storm. It drew closer.

+It's chasing us.+

'Acknowledged,' the servitor replied.

+Go faster. Go much, *much* faster.+

'Compliance.'

The vast presence broke through the lashing waves of psychic mist, unaffected by their density. She was reminded, for an awful moment, of a vast shark pushing through the open ocean, dead-eyed and forever hungry.

+We have to break from the warp. We can't outrun this.+

This time, the answer was rich with emotion, none of it pleasant. It was deep, low, and tainted with inhuman resonance.

'How far are we from the Torias system?'

+Hours. Days. *I don't know*, my lord. But we're dead in minutes if we don't break from the warp.+

'Unacceptable,' growled the Exalted, master of the *Covenant of Blood*.

+Do you feel the way the *Covenant* is shaking? A psychic shadow made of black mist and hatred is reaching out to swallow us. I am the Navigator, my lord. I am dragging this ship from the Sea of Souls, no matter what you say.+

'Very well,' said the Exalted reluctantly. ' All stations, brace for re-entry to the void. And Octavia?'

+Yes, my lord?+

'You would do well to show me more respect when Talos is not aboard.'

She bared her teeth in a grin, feeling her heartbeat quicken at the threat.

+If you say so, Exalted One.+

THE HUNTRESS MOVED through the chamber, one of many in the cavernous palace, clad in a stolen crimson gown and someone else's skin. Her name, for the last two hours, had been Kalista Larhaven. This was even confirmed by the numeric identity code tattooed onto the flesh of her right wrist.

The true Kalista Larhaven, the original owner of both the name and the exquisite dress, was now folded with graceless, boneless ease into a thermo-ventilation shaft. There she lay, silent in death, an unknown martyr to a lost cause. She had her own hopes, dreams, joys and needs – all of which had ended in the shallow thrust of an envenomed blade. It had taken longer to hide the courtesan's body than it had to end her life.

The huntress passed a flock of acolyte clerics. They shuffled along the carpeted floor, chanting in heretical murmurs. The first of them bore an incense orb on a corroded chain, the bronze sphere seething with coils of thin, sugary mist. This priest greeted the courtesan by name, and the huntress smiled with the dead whore's lips.

'Do you go to attend upon the master?'

The huntress answered with wicked eyes and an indulgent smile.

'I wish you well, Kalista,' the priest replied. 'Go in peace.'

The huntress offered a graceful curtsey, subtly submissive, moving as one born to a life of giving pleasure. The true Kalista had moved this way. The huntress had watched it, gauged it, captured the essence of it – all in a handful of heartbeats.

As she walked away, she felt the eager eyes of the whispering priests following her movements. She exaggerated the swing of her hips, favouring them with a last glance over her bare shoulder. She read the hunger in their dark eyes, and much better, the idiotic conviction. Let them go about their business without knowing the truth: that the girl they desired was already dead, packed into a tube close to the thermal exchange processors elsewhere in the palace.

The heat would accelerate the process of decay, so the true Kalista would become a quick victim to the bacteria that always laid claim to a human body in the hours after it drew its last breath.

But the huntress was unconcerned. She would be gone by the time any discoveries were made; her duty done and her escape a source of infinite grief for the people of this worthless planet.

Before she had become Kalista Larhaven, the huntress had worn the skin of a nameless maidservant for almost an hour, using the shape to reach the lower levels and move through the slave tunnels. Before that, she had been a trader in the palace's vast courtyards, licensed to sell holy relics to pilgrims. And before that, a pilgrim herself, wearing the ragged clothes of a vagabond: a wandering beggar in search of spiritual enlightenment.

The huntress had been on the world of Torias Secondus for a single day, and a single night. Even as she drew close to completing her mission, she lamented the time spent so far. She was above this assignment. She knew it, her sisters knew it, and her superiors knew it. This was punishment – a punishment for the failures of the past.

Undeserved, perhaps. Yet duty was duty. She had to obey.

She moved on through the palace, passing chanting acolytes, scurrying clerks and raucous packs of intoxicated nobles. The halls were growing busy as noon approached, for with the coming of noon came the High Priest's long-awaited speech.

The woman who was not Kalista blended into the crowds, passing with smiles and feminine curtseys. Her irritation never showed on lips of rose-red, nor in eyes of ice-blue. The fact remained, though – this skin would not get her to the high priest's side at the right moment. Time was a vicious factor. If killing him was the only goal, he would be dead from a sniper's kiss already, long before taking to the podiums later today and addressing the people of the city.

But no. His death had to be choreographed along exact lines, played out like a performance for all to see.

The huntress sensed she was reaching the end of this skin's lifespan. Already, the chambers through which she moved were the domains of the chosen elite, with clothing becoming increasingly ostentatious and more expensive. The apparent courtesan graced her way through the carnival of colours, her stolen eyes flicking in predatory need.

Noblewoman to noblewoman, priestess to priestess, courtesan to courtesan.

None of them suited. None would allow her to finish what she had begun. She needed another skin. And soon.

* * *

THE DOOR TO the Navigator's chambers ground open on rough hydraulics. Nothing on this ship worked right. Octavia checked that her pistol was holstered at her hip, and left through the only portal leading out of her room. Her attendants, whom she despised as much as she loathed the ship itself, bustled around her, imploring her to return to her chambers.

She wanted to shoot them. She really, *really* wanted to shoot them. The most normal of them couldn't pass as a human even in poor lighting. It looked at her, smiling with too many teeth, clasping its hands together as if in prayer.

'Mistress,' it hissed. 'Return to chambers, mistress. For safety. For protection. Mistress must not be harmed. Mistress must not bleed.'

She shivered under its beseeching touch. Hands that possessed too many fingers stroked her clothes, and worse, her bare skin.

'Don't touch me,' she snapped.

'Forgive me, mistress. A thousand apologies, most sincere.'

'Get out of my way, please.'

'Please return, mistress,' it pleaded. 'Do not walk dark places of ship. Stay, for safety.'

She drew her pistol, sending the creatures scurrying back.

'Get out of my way. *Now.*'

'Someone comes, mistress. Another soul draws near.'

She stared into the blackened corridor outside her chamber, lit by weak illumination globes that did nothing to defeat the darkness. The figure emerging from the gloom wore a jacket of old leather, and carried two heavy pistols at his hips. A hacking blade – the kind of weapon one might find in the hands of a jungle world primitive – was strapped to his shin.

Half of his face glinted in the reflected light. Augmetic facial features, the most obvious of which was a red eye lens, were of expensive and rare craftsmanship. The human side of his face twisted in a crooked smile.

Octavia returned it.

'Septimus,' she said.

'Octavia. Forgive me for pointing out the obvious, but that was the roughest ride through the Sea of Souls I've ever had to suffer through.'

'The ship still hates me,' she scowled. 'Why are you here? Keeping me company?'

'Something like that. Let's go inside.'

She hesitated, but complied. Once they were back in her chamber, she ensured the door was locked. Anything to keep her annoying attendants away.

Octavia could, if one was being generous, be considered beautiful. But beauty needs light and warmth to bloom, and these were both denied to the young Navigator. Her skin was the unhealthy pale of unclean marble, marking her as a member of the crew aboard the lightless battleship, the *Covenant of Blood*. Her eyes were losing all colour as her pupils grew accustomed to remaining forever dilated. Her hair, once a tumbling fall of healthy dark locks, was a ragged mess held into false order by a ponytail.

She looked across to Septimus, who was absently picking his way through piles of discarded clothes and old food cartons.

'Look at this mess. You are a filthy creature.'

'Nice to see you, too. To what do I owe the pleasure?'

'You know why I'm here.' He paused. 'Talk of your attitude is beginning to spread. You're making the crew uneasy. They worry you're going to enrage the Legion because you can't follow orders.'

'So, let them worry.'

Septimus sighed. '*Asath Jirath Sor-sarassan.*'

'Speak Gothic, damn it. None of that whispery Nostraman, thank you. I know you were swearing. I'm not a fool.'

'If the crew worries, they might take matters into their own hands. They'd kill you without a second thought.'

'They need me. Everyone needs me. Without me, the ship has no Navigator.'

'Maybe,' said Septimus slowly. 'But no one wants tension with the Legion. Things are always on the edge, but when someone starts to breed difficulties? The crew has lynched troublemakers before. Dozens of times.'

'They wouldn't try that with me.'

He laughed bitterly. 'No? If they thought it would please the Legion, they'd hang you from a gantry in the engineering deck, or beat you to death and flush your body from an airlock. You need to tread with care. Talos is off the ship. When First Claw isn't on board, be cautious in how you deal with the Legion and the crew.'

'Don't give me this crap,' Octavia snapped. 'I was under more strain than you can even imagine. For Throne's sake, the Geller Field was dying. The ship was moments from falling apart.'

Septimus shook his head. 'Sometimes, you still forget where you are. Your talent spares you the worst treatment, but you're still a slave. Remember that. Delusions of equality will get you killed.'

'You're as bad as those things that try to keep me sealed in here. I've survived three weeks without Talos watching over me. A few more hours won't make any difference.'

She paused for a moment before changing the subject. 'Any word from the surface?'

'Nothing yet. As soon as they vox confirmation, I'll bring them back on board. It's close to noon in the capital city. The high priest will be speaking soon. Won't be long now.'

'I don't suppose you know what they're actually doing down there?'

Septimus shrugged.

'What they always do. They're hunting.'

AT THE HEART of Toriana, capital city of the world below, the masses waited for their leader. The plaza of the Primus Palace was flooded with an ocean of humanity - ninety thousand men, women and children. Each family had been carefully selected by the government's Departmento Culturum and marched to the gathering by armed enforcers.

Above the sea of cheering faces, an ornate balcony jutted from the palace's side. Ten figures stood in motionless silence, enduring the crowd's roars, with rifles clutched over armoured chestplates. Faceless black visors and carapace armour the colour of old blood marked these soldiers as the Red Sentinels, elite guard of the high priest himself. The back mounted power packs carried by each one hummed with suppressed tension, bonded to the ammunition sockets of their hellguns via thick, segmented cables.

The Sentinel leader kept up a constant stream of muttered words into the vox-network, checking on the position of his sniper teams situated on nearby rooftops. All was in readiness. Should trouble arise from the crowd, the Sentinels and the enforcers on the streets had enough firepower to paint the marble floors red and reduce the plaza to a charnel house.

The air itself thrummed as a Valkyrie gunship hovered overhead, its iron hull turned amber by the midday sun, and its cannons seeking targets in the windows of adjacent buildings. Satisfied, it moved away on growling engines, bathing the Red Sentinels below in a heated wind of thruster wash.

The Red Sentinel captain spoke a final order into the vox, and the massive double doors behind him opened. At the first sight of the robed figure walking onto the balcony, the crowd erupted in praising cheers.

High Priest Cyrus was the wrong side of middle age, and his fine encarmine robes looked painted onto his porcine form. Jowls shook as he raised fat hands to the sky.

'My people!' he proclaimed.

The high priest, once Imperial Governor of this world, licked his lips as he bathed in the cheers rising to meet him. His was a solemn duty: to herald in a world free of Imperial taxation and tithe. A world under his rule, aided by the council of cardinals, known collectively as the Benevolence.

'My people, hear my words!' he continued. 'We stand at the dawn of a new age of peace and prosperity! No more shall we hurl our faith and fortunes into the furnace of Imperial slavery. No more shall our world suffer alone, ignored by the Imperium of Man. No more shall we struggle

through famine and civil war, led into folly by self-serving ministers
appointed by distant Terra.'

Cyrus paused, waiting until the cheers died down before he continued.
'This is the age of the Benevolence! The new faith! The Benevolence
encircles us all, in hope and trust. Faith in one another! Faith in other
worlds that have thrown off the same shackles! Shoulder to shoulder, we
stand defiant against the oppression of the past!'

The crowd roared, as Cyrus had known it would. Already, they were
chanting his name as their saviour, their saint.

'Brothers and sisters, sons and daughters! We are free, united far from
the reach of the hated False Emperor! I... I...'

He never finished the sentence. The fat man staggered, gripping the
balcony's railing. The Red Sentinels moved as one, their rifles up and panning for threats. The cheering from the crowd was drowned in confusion.

The huntress smiled as she watched. The timing had been perfect; the
venom delivered the very moment this false prophet dared to decry the
God-Emperor. The crowd had seen it. The hololithic image feeds had
recorded it, so the whole planet had witnessed it. Now they knew the
price of blasphemy and secession.

The digital weapon concealed on her gauntlet was only good for a single
shot, one sliver-dart, rich with neurotoxin. The targeting laser was flashless,
and easily powerful enough to pierce the heretic's silk robes. She'd fired
it right into his spine, and none of the Red Sentinels were any the wiser.

The high priest tumbled forward and he pitched over the balcony's
edge. He didn't scream as he fell, for he was already dead.

The huntress smiled behind her faceless visor, moving with the other
Red Sentinels, feigning panic and anger to mirror theirs. She disliked the
bulky armour they wore, but the skin was a necessary one. The Sentinel
she'd killed to acquire it had put up a reasonable fight – for an unaugmented human, at least.

The huntress made a show of scanning for enemy targets on balconies
of adjacent buildings, relishing the panicked voices jabbering over the
vox. In a matter of minutes, she would be able to leave this wretched
gathering and make her way back through the city, in readiness to abandon this world forever.

She was already making her way to the double doors when the sun fell
dark, and heavy engines whined behind her. The huntress turned, her
eyes narrowed, her heart starting to beat faster.

Five shapes dropped from the sky. Armoured in massive suits of power
armour, they thudded down onto the balcony. Flame and smoke retched
from the thrust generators on their backs, and helms with painted skulls
for faces watched her with unerring focus. Not the other Red Sentinels.
Just her. These warriors had been waiting on the roof, knowing she would
make her move.

Each of the figures raised a bolter clutched in dark gauntlets.

'Assassin of the Callidus Temple,' intoned one, his voice a growl through his helmet's vox-caster. '*We have come for you.*'

There was no thought of fighting. The huntress turned and ran, preternatural agility blurring her form like quicksilver. Sentinel armour rained from her as she sprinted back through the palace, discarded as fast as she was able.

She heard them giving chase. The clanging thuds of ceramite boots on mosaic floors. The coughing bursts of jump-packs breathing fire, propelling the warriors down the halls faster than the huntress could run. Bystanders, innocent or otherwise, cried out as her pursuers cut down anyone in their way.

She heard the throaty crashing of bolters, and weaved across the detonating ground where shells hit home. She leapt as she ran, knowing they were targeting her legs, seeking to bring her down by an explosive shell to the back of the knee.

One shell impacted on the huntress's calf, but spun aside, deflected by her synthetic skin armour. Another exploded against the wall by her shoulder, sending chalky debris clattering over her face. Still, she ran.

When a shell finally struck home, it took her in the meat of the thigh. Despite years of pain resistance training and narcotic compounds introduced into her bloodstream to deaden her nerves, the agony was unrivalled. The huntress howled as she went down, her thigh reduced to nothing more than a ruin of hanging flesh and muscle stripped from the bloodstained, broken bone.

Spitting curses, she clawed herself forward, vicious even in futility. She had enough of a lead to drag herself to her feet, and round the next corner in an awkward, limping run.

Her flight to safety lasted mere seconds. As she rounded the corner, shoving her way through a milling crowd of servants, two immense, dark forms brought her to the ground. Her muscles stung with chemical enhancement, straining against the armoured warriors pinning her to the floor. She went to draw her blade from her thigh sheath, only to scream in frustrated rage when she realised the scabbard and blade had been torn from her body when the exploding shell struck her leg. She yelled fresh curses as her reaching forearm was smashed under the boot of another traitorous warrior.

She writhed under their oppressive strength, losing control in her anger, not even realising her face was flowing into the visages of a dozen women she'd killed in the last two days. From above, she heard the leader of the warriors speak while his men held her down.

'My name is Talos of the Night Lords Legion. And you are coming with me.'

* * *

THE HUNTRESS OPENED her eyes, feeling them ripe with stinging tears. The first thing to grace her senses was pain, jagged and unfamiliar in its intensity. Everything below her spine ached with sickening pulses in time to her heartbeat.

Immediately, training took over from disoriented instinct. She had to learn her whereabouts, then escape. Nothing else mattered. Her vision focused, resolving the blurred gloom into a semblance of clarity.

The chamber was intentionally dark, kept that way by low-burning wall globes. With no furnishings beyond the table she lay upon, it had all the charm of a prison cell. The huntress tried to rise, but her limbs wouldn't answer. She could barely even raise her head.

She became aware, at last, of rasping breath, with the teeth-aching rumble of active power armour.

'Do not try to rise.' The voice was the same rasping growl as before. 'Your legs have been amputated, as have your arms below the elbows. You are conscious only because of chemical pain-inhibitors flushed into your bloodstream.'

The armoured figure came into view, stalking to the edge of the table. Its face was a battered war helm, the visage painted bone white to resemble a human skull, and a rune from a filthy, forgotten language etched into its forehead. Across its breastplate, an Imperial eagle was ruined by ritual scarring, the holy aquila symbol no doubt profaned by the heretic warrior that wore it.

'You will not escape this chamber,' said the figure – Talos, she guessed. 'You will never return to your temple. There is no fate for you beyond the walls of this cell, and so I grant you a choice, assassin. Tell us what we wish to know, and earn yourself a quick death, or tell us after we have subjected you to several hours of excruciation.'

The huntress spoke through blood-flecked lips, her voice a ghost of its former strength.

'I will die before speaking secrets to a heretic.'

Even through the vox-crackle, the reply was tinged with amusement. 'Everyone says that.'

'Pain… pain is nothing to me,' said the huntress.

'Pain is nothing to you when what remains of your body is flooded with inhibitor narcotics,' replied Talos. 'The interface nodes implanted along your spinal cord will change your perception of pain soon enough.'

'I am Jezharra,' she said defiantly, 'daughter of the Callidus. You will get nothing from me, fallen one. Nothing but curses heaped upon your worthless life.'

Talos laughed.

'Stronger souls than yours have cracked in our claws, assassin. No one resists. Do not make me do this.'

'How did you know I would come?'

'I saw it,' he said. 'I am a prophet of the Eighth Legion. In moments of affliction, I can see along the path of a future yet to come.'

'Sorcery,' spat Jezharra. 'Black magic.'

'Perhaps. But it worked, did it not?'

'You think yourself cunning for arranging that ambush? For luring a daughter of the Callidus to this backwater world, and baiting the trap with a cult's high priest?'

'Cunning enough to have you here, at my mercy, with your arms and legs severed by my brothers' chainblades.'

'My death is meaningless,' Jezharra sighed. 'My life was lived in service to the Golden Throne, so do what you will. Agony will never twist me into a traitor.'

'Then you have chosen,' said Talos. 'These are your final moments of sanity, released from pain. Enjoy them while you can.'

'I am Jezharra, daughter of the Callidus. My mind is inviolate, my soul unbroken. I am Jezharra, daughter of the Callidus...'

The huntress grinned as she chanted the words. The warrior turned, addressing another presence in the room, a figure the bound assassin couldn't see.

'So be it. Excruciate her.'

JEZHARRA, THE HUNTRESS, resisted for seventeen days. It was by far the longest any human had lasted under the Legion's interrogation. When she broke at last, little remained of the woman she'd been, let alone the consummate killer.

She wheezed secrets from split lips, the words forming vapour in the chamber's freezing air. Once she had said all she needed to say, she lay slack in her restraints, trying to summon the strength to beg for death.

'The... Uriah System.'

'*Where* in the Uriah System?' asked Talos patiently.

'Uriah... is a dying star. Temple is... on the planet... farthest from it. Three. Uriah... Three.'

'What of the defences?' pressed Talos.

'Nothing in orbit. Nothing permanent. Local... local battlefleet patrols nearby.'

'And on the surface?'

'It... it is done,' breathed the dying huntress. 'Kill me...'

'What defences are on the surface of Uriah Three?' repeated Talos.

'Nothing... Just my sisters. Fifty... fifty daughters of Callidus. A lone fortress-temple... in the mountains.'

'Coordinates?'

'Please...'

'The coordinates, assassin,' insisted Talos. 'Then I will end this.'

'Twenty-six degrees... Eighteen... forty-four... point fifty-six. The heart of the tundra. Seventy degrees... Twenty-three, forty-nine point sixty-eight.'

'Is the temple shielded against orbital attack?'

'Yes,' she whispered.

'And the hololithic recording is there?'

'I... I saw it myself.'

'Very well,' said Talos.

The warrior drew a golden blade. Its craftsmanship was exquisite, forged in an age of inspiration long-forgotten by the Imperium. On a ship of ancient relics, this was by far the most revered. The Night Lord stepped closer to the husk on the Apothecarion table.

'Jezharra...'

The warrior let the assassin's name hang in the air. With his free hand, he disengaged the seals of his helm, pulling the death-mask off with a serpentine hiss of venting air pressure. The assassin's eyes were gone, taken from her in the interrogation, but she sensed what he had done in the way his voice changed.

'Thank you,' he said softly.

She spat at him before she died – one final act of defiance. In a way, it was hard not to admire her. But Talos's blade fell, embedding itself in the table as the assassin's head rolled free.

The warrior stood in the stinking chamber for an indeterminate number of heartbeats, before replacing his war helm. His vision drowned in the red wash of the eye lenses' tactical display. White runic text scrolled across his retinas. He blinked at the jagged symbol on the lens display – the Nostraman hieroglyph meaning brotherhood. A muted click signalled the opening of a vox-channel.

'This is Talos.'

'Speak, Soul Hunter,' growled the Exalted.

'The assassin has broken. Set course for the Uriah System. Her temple is on the world most distant from the sun. I have the coordinates.'

'We have been chasing this ghost for a very long time, Talos. The Legion has hurled itself at temple after temple after temple, across a hundred systems. You are certain the hololithic is there?'

Talos looked down, his targeting reticule locking onto the motionless, tortured body, then the severed head on the blood-slick floor.

'Summon the Legion, Exalted One. I'm certain it's there.'

SOME WORLDS, BY ill-fortune or intent, fall far from the countless billions of trade routes and pilgrimages that shape the Imperium of Man, linking untold numbers of stars in an astral cobweb. These worlds may be forgotten or ignored, but are never truly unknown. Every secret is laid bare somewhere, even if only a single reference in an abandoned archive in distant Terra's librariums.

Uriah was an unremarkable sun. It seemed notable only for the fact it scarcely burned bright enough to be called a star at all. The worlds turning around it in their measured, heavenly dance were all frost-locked spheres of eternal winter.

Above the third such world, a vessel fell into low orbit. It was a crenellated blade of darkened bronze and midnight blue, proudly displaying the skull insignia of the VIII Legion. It arrived alone, but did not remain that way for long.

Other vessels, warships all, tore holes in reality as they broke from the hell-space of the warp. Each bore the same insignia, each was armoured in the same colours – and each was an echo of a much finer age. The design of each warship was ancient, as if they'd burst from the Sea of Souls after travelling for millennia, rather than mere weeks.

Many of the warships were twisted, darkened, more brutish in aspect than their original architects had envisioned, but their lethal grandeur remained. As they came together, the fleet appeared to be something from ancestral memory, when humanity had reached out to rediscover the stars ten thousand years before.

Contact between the ships was hesitant. Greetings passed over crackling signals, many with tones of guarded reluctance. The Legion rarely gathered, and many of these captains were rivals. A hundred centuries of bloodshed, defeat, predation and pain made for short tempers and shorter alliances.

While warship commanders exchanged hails and veiled threats, the decks of every vessel came alive with preparation. Thousands upon thousands of Astartes warriors swore oaths of moment, machined armour into place and readied drop pods and Thunderhawk gunships, as well as grievously rare teleport platforms.

The Night Lords Legion was going to war.

Proximity alarms wailed only once, when a Navy patrol fleet ghosted within range of auspex sensors. A single Endeavour-class cruiser, its hull resplendent in Imperial gold, sought to come about and break into the warp, seeking the only realistic route of escape. Its lesser escorts remained behind, seeking to slow any pursuit. Despite the gesture's futility, every second the destroyers could buy for their retreating flagship was precious.

A single vessel broke from the Legion fleet formation, an agile strike cruiser bearing the name *Excoriator*. What followed was a massacre unworthy of record within any Hall of Remembrance. Stunted torpedoes crashed against *Excoriator*'s void shields, as effective as broken glass raining against steel. In reply, precise lance strikes cut into the iron meat of the three Imperial escorts, bursting their thin shields in a heartbeat and scoring the metal skin beneath. A second volley, mere moments after the first, carved them apart in dispassionate surgery.

Excoriator's shields briefly lit up again, kinetic pulses of light rippling across their surface as the cruiser glided through the debris.

With a shark's silent pursuit, the Legion battleship loomed close behind the fleeing cruiser. With game desperation, the Imperial vessel unleashed its meagre weapons, batteries of plasma and solid shot spilling into the void, clashing as they dissipated across *Excoriator*'s shields.

The Legion warship returned fire, its lance strikes rupturing the patrol vessel's shields with impunity. With the prey's shields down, the predator didn't leap upon its quarry with a hunger to destroy. *Excoriator*'s lances fell silent, and drew alongside the fleeing vessel. Instead of broadsides opening up and hammering the smaller ship into drifting scrap, the Legion warship disgorged boarding pods in an overwhelming wave. A dozen, spearing across space and digging into the vulnerable skin of the Imperial ship.

Excoriator didn't wait. Its engines, and the great warship veered in a lumbering arc, heading back to the fleet waiting in orbit. Aboard the Imperial ship, over a hundred Astartes of the Night Lords Legion went about the business of purging any crew too loyal or weak to be of use.

It took only three hours for the Endeavour-class patrol cruiser to pull into formation with the Legion ships, joining its might to theirs. It bore a new name, *The Faithless Song*, to go with its new allegiance.

The cold sun began to fade over the ice-rimed mountain range below the Legion's geostationary coordinates. Night was falling on the surface, and at last, with all in readiness, a voice carried over the fleet's communal vox-network. The words came in a dead language, spoken by no living soul outside the fractured brotherhood gathered here.

'*Acrius Toshallion. Jasith Raspatha vorvelliash kishall-kar.*'

Seated inside her sealed chamber at the prow of the *Covenant of Blood*, Octavia looked to Septimus.

'What did he say?'

'It doesn't translate easily,' Septimus replied.

'Humour me,' insisted Octavia. 'It's important. What did he say?'

'"Vengeance, as night falls. By dawn, none will ever recall the Legion's shame."'

'I don't understand,' said the Navigator, frowning. 'Why has the fleet gathered? What's so vital about one world out on the Rim?'

'If I knew, I'd tell you. I've never seen this many Legion ships in one place before. If I wasn't seeing it with my own eyes, I'd never believe it could happen.'

He moved to the bank of viewscreens adorning an entire wall. His gloved fingertip tapped ship after ship, each one a different class and size.

'These are supply ships. Promethium tankers, mostly. These look to be slave ships... Imperial Guard troop carriers, taken by the Night Lords over the years. These are Legion warships. There, the *Hunter's Premonition*.

That's the *Excoriator*, sister ship to the *Covenant of Blood*. This, here, is the *Serpent of the Black Sea*, one of the Legion's flagships from centuries ago. It was supposed to be lost in the Hades Veil. The Legion battleships alone could carry... ten, maybe twelve thousand Space Marines.'

'I didn't know they had that many warriors,' said Octavia, her voice tinged with worry.

'No records show how many there are. I doubt even the Exalted knows. These are just the ships close enough to answer the call, but even so, outside of the Warmaster's crusades, this is a gathering of rare significance.'

Septimus fell silent as he watched the warships shedding landing craft like a herd of beasts shaking off their fleas. Pods streaked planetward, trailing tails of flame, each one a meteor burning through the atmosphere. Following them in majestic, arcing dives, gunships and heavy landers swooped through the cloud cover, their hulls gleaming orange with the heat of atmospheric entry.

Octavia came over to him, staring into the viewscreens, unable to fixate upon a single image. It was all too much to take in.

'They're not sending any human craft down,' she noted. 'No slaves. No cultists.'

'It's fifty degrees below zero on the surface of Uriah Three. Even colder at night. Only legionaries can survive outside of shelter in those conditions.'

'How many of them are making planetfall?'

Septimus answered slowly. 'I believe... it looks like all of them.'

THE DROP POD threw up a torrent of snow and rock as it pounded into the earth. The edges of its dark hull glowed with fierce heat, its ceramite skin hissing and steaming in the air. Door seals spat free with mechanical clicks and vented steam, and like a flower in bloom, the ramps opened, lowered, and slammed into the melted slush around the pod's whining engines.

Talos was the first from the pod, his red-stained vision scanning the mountain pass ahead. His helm's auto-senses muted the roaring wind to a tolerable background level.

The ground trembled, an earthquake's echo, as more drop pods came down across the tundra. Already, the sky was darkened by landing craft and gunships fighting the vicious winds.

An identifier rune flashed white on the edge of Talos's retinal display. Mercutian's name glyph, though the vox gave all their voices a similar crackling cadence.

'We could do this alone. The five of us. But look up, brothers. The sky is black with Stormbirds and Thunderhawks. How many of the Legion muster with us? Nine thousand? Ten? We have no need of them to prosecute this war.'

Now Xarl's name-rune flashed, bold and urgent as the squad moved across the snow.

'He may be a miserable bastard, but he's right. This was our glory. We did the work. We sweated for weeks on that wretched world, living amongst that pathetic cult, waiting for the Callidus Temple to open their eyes and fall into our claws.'

Talos grunted his disagreement. Mercutian was morose at the best of times, and could always be trusted to see the darkest edge of any event. As for Xarl… he trusted no soul outside their own warband, and relatively few within it.

'This is not some personal glory to be etched onto our armour,' said Talos. 'This is the Legion's vindication. The others deserve to be here. Let them redden their claws alongside us.'

No name glyphs chimed in response. He was surprised the others were letting it slide so easily. Surprised, but grateful. Talos stalked on, his armoured boots crunching through the snow to crush the rocks beneath. Other squads fell into rough formation behind First Claw, but Talos and his brothers were allowed the honour of leading the advance.

The trek through the mountains would have killed a mortal in moments. Talos felt nothing, protected from even the void of space in his Mark V war-plate. Even so, to prevent his joints from freezing, his power pack's active hum had risen in pitch. The vox-network came alive with technical servitors reporting that the oil pipes and fuel tanks in the landed gunships were already icing up.

The temperature gauge on the edge of Talos's visor display remained unmercifully hostile. After only half an hour of trekking uphill, his power pack was humming with almost distracting intensity. He kept wiping frost from his faceplate when it threatened to form a crust.

The next warrior to speak was Cyrion. Despite the vox stealing all tone and humanity from his voice, his irritation bled through easily enough.

'I could have lived with annihilating this fortress from orbit. That would satisfy my honour, and spare us this tedious trudge.'

No one replied. Every one of them knew this mission required visual confirmation before it could be considered complete. Laying waste to the Callidus stronghold from orbit would achieve nothing.

'Don't everyone agree at once,' said Cyrion dryly.

Talos scowled behind his visor, but said nothing even as Cyrion continued.

'What if the Callidus bitch lied? What if we're marching half the Legion in neat formation through these mountain passes and a host of ambushes await? This is the most foolish advance in history.'

Now Talos replied, his own temper rising to the fore.

'Enough, Cyrion. Humans cannot survive outside shelter here. How will they ambush us? With thermal suits and hurled rocks from the cliff edges? If that were even a threat worth considering, orbital imagery would have caught it by now. This is a hidden temple. Defending it with a host of cannons upon the walls would require serious generation of power, and attract easy attention from orbital scanning.'

'I still do not like this march upland,' Cyrion grumbled.

'The march is symbolic, brother. The Legion commanders wished it, and so it shall be. Let the Callidus stare down from their fortress battlements, and bear witness to the doom that comes for them.'

Cyrion sighed. 'You have more faith in our leaders than I, Talos.'

Once more, the others fell silent. Above them, the looming fortress, hewn from the mountain rock, drew ever closer.

THE SIEGE OF Uriah 3 would enter the annals of the Night Lords Legion for its significance, if not its duration. The fortress rising from the side of the mountains was shielded against orbital bombardment, with multi-layered void fields offering dense resistance to any assault from the skies. As with many such defensive grids, the overlapping shields were considerably more vulnerable to attack from the ground.

Behind the marching warriors came entire battalions of Legion war machines: massive Land Raiders leading the way for the more compact Vindicator siege tanks, along with their Predator counterparts. Arrayed across ridges, nestled atop outcroppings and landed by Thunderhawk carriers along cliff edges, the Legion's armour battalions aimed cannons and turrets at the fortress's walls.

There was no heroic speech. No inspirational mantra. With a single word of order, the tanks opened fire as one, lighting the night with the brilliant flare of lascannon beams, and the incendiary bursts from demolisher turrets.

In the shadows cast by the flickering shield and the storm of assaulting fire, Talos watched the siege begin in earnest. Cyrion approached where he knelt on the lip of a cliff.

'How long do you think they can keep us out?' he asked.

Talos lowered his bolter, no longer looking through the gunsight. The fortress itself was blurred behind a mirage of wavering air – a haze that gave off no heat. The void shield distorted the view of what lay behind it, reducing the battlements to uneven silhouettes.

'With over five hundred tanks at the walls? This firepower would cripple an Imperator in a heartbeat. Blood of the Father, Cyrion... we've not gathered this much armour in one place since the Siege of Terra. The walls will fall, and we'll be inside before dawn.'

The prediction was true enough. The sky was not yet lightening when, four hours later, the void shield shimmered, fluttering like an ailing heartbeat, before disintegrating with a thunderclap of displaced air pressure. The Night Lords closest to the shield's edge were thrown from their feet, dozens of squads sent crashing across the icy landscape in the powerful rush of air, adding to the snowstorm's gale.

Without pause, without respite, the tanks turned their cannons upon the fortress's lower walls.

The first breach was torn exactly thirteen seconds later, a section of rock wall blasted inward under a demolisher shell. Squads broke into loping runs, moving around the still-firing tanks. They entered with the freezing wind, chainswords revving into life.

The defences were broken, and the slaughter could begin.

TALOS LED FIRST Claw through the catacombs, his boots crunching on the layer of ice already coating the stone. With the fortress breached, its innards were at the mercy of the blizzards tearing across the surface of Uriah 3. Many of the Imperial servants dwelling within the temple died from exposure within minutes of the walls coming down, and those that survived deeper within the complex soon fell victim to the grinding bite of Legion chainblades.

The Night Lords purged the fortress, chamber by chamber, level by level. In the combat arenas, where the Callidus agents were put through their rigorous training, banks of esoteric machinery lined the walls. Bolters made short work of the priceless bio-manipulation technology, explosive shells ripping apart the machines responsible for shaping generations of assassins.

First Claw moved through the catacombs, laying waste to the subterranean surgeries, their blades tearing medical equipment into ruin.

'These are the apothecarions where they implant muscle enhancers and the polymorphic compound that allow the Callidus to shapeshift,' said Talos. He reloaded his bolter, slamming a fresh magazine home and taking aim at an automated surgery table. 'Brothers. Leave nothing intact.'

Their bolters opened up with harsh chatters, detonating irreplaceable, priceless Imperial machines as the Night Lords left naught but scrap in their wake.

And yet, something was wrong. Cyrion voxed the others, lowering his bolter as they entered another underground apothecarion.

'As thrilling as this worthless vandalism is proving to be, I've been paying attention to the general channels. No squad has crossed paths with any assassins yet. Talos, brother, you were lied to. There are no Callidus here. It's an abandoned temple. This place is a tomb.'

Talos cursed, swinging his golden blade and splitting a surgical table in two. Both halves clattered to the tiled floor.

'She was *not* lying,' he said angrily. 'I have seen it in my visions. I heard the truth in her voice, after seventeen days of excruciation. The hololithic is *here.*'

The two warriors faced each other, edging closer to open argument. It was Cyrion that backed down, offering a salute, fist over his breastplate.

'As you say, brother.'

Talos cursed in Nostraman, a flowing sentence of bitter expletives leaving his lips and emerging harsh over the ragged vox- link. Just as he drew breath to order the squad onwards, the general channel sparked into life.

'Brothers, this is the Exalted. My honour guard has reached the thirtieth sub-level. It is a Hall of Archives. First Claw, come to me at once. Talos... You were right.'

TALOS ENTERED THE chamber, and confusion took hold before anything else. The librarium had clearly been swept clean long before the Legion had arrived in orbit, leaving empty bookshelves, blank display cases, and bare plinths.

Warriors from the Legion lined the walls – Night Lords from squads and warbands that First Claw didn't recognise. In the heart of the room stood the Exalted, its twisted bulk overshadowing the Astartes nearby. The daemon in its heart was forever reshaping the Exalted's outer flesh, and the Legion lord hadn't been human – or even Astartes – in many hundreds of years. A spined monstrosity of clawed hands and hulking armour breathed in a deep thunder rumble. It inclined its malformed head, grimacing through black fangs because it struggled to form any other facial expression through the mutations of its skull structure.

'Talos,' it said. 'The temple has been abandoned. The slaves left here were nothing more than custodians, remaining in the event of the Callidus's return.'

Talos stepped closer, his ceramite boots disturbing the dust of ages on the dark stone floor. Other footsteps tracked hither and thither across the ground. The tread of his Legion brothers. None were human. Humans had not walked these halls in years.

'I do not understand. You said I was right.'

The Exalted held out its claw, each bladed finger possessing too many joints. In the daemon creature's palm was a fist-sized sphere of discoloured bronze. A single lens peered from the sphere's side – a glaring eye of green glass.

A hololithic recorder.

'You *were* right. This remained, when all else was taken.'

'They wanted us to find it,' said Talos.

'It is not the original. Our hunt to destroy the original recording remains unfulfilled. But this... this is enough, for now. The Legion will thank you.'

Talos bit back his disgust at what the Exalted had become, taking the bronze sphere without comment. A simple twist of the top hemisphere caused a series of clicks from within, and the soft whirring of the lens brought itself into focus.

A grainy image beamed from the lens, monochrome green like watered-down jade. It showed...

'The Lord of the Night...' breathed Talos reverently.

It showed a hunched figure, its posture and musculature somewhere between human perfection and bestial corruption. The distortion stole too much clarity to make any true details, but the figure's face – his narrow eyes and fanged maw – smote the hearts of all bearing witness to it.

Primarch. Konrad Curze, the Night Haunter, Commander of the VIII Legion. Their father. The genetic forebear and biological template of every living Night Lord.

The flickering hololithic primarch rose from a throne stolen by distortion. He advanced in a silence that spoke of faulty recording, his movements jerky and interrupted by static interference.

None of that mattered. After centuries, the Lord of the Night's loyal sons were seeing him once again. Their father's ghost, here in this tomb of a temple.

If the Callidus had left the hololithic record to mock the Legion that would one day find it, they had severely misjudged the closure it offered, and the resurgence of purpose felt by every warrior present. Gauntlets clutched at bolters with inspired strength. Several warriors wept behind their skulled faceplates.

'Ave Dominus Nox.' They chanted the words in worshipful, thankful monotone. 'Ave Dominus Nox. Hail the Lord of the Night.'

The primarch's last moments of life unfolded before their eyes. The towering demigod laughed, still locked in eerie silence, and then leapt forward. A burst of visual static scratched the image into oblivion, only for it to reset and restart a moment later.

A wraith doomed to repeat its actions into eternity: the Night Lords primarch rose from his throne again, spoke words that went unheard, laughed without sound, and raced forward, only to vanish again.

'I remember seeing it in the flesh,' whispered the Exalted. 'I recall watching him rise from the throne, so many years ago, and obeying his order to watch as the assassin approached. I remember how he laughed before he leapt at her.'

Talos cancelled the archival playback, staring down at the metal orb in his hand. It had several settings, each one activated by turning the top hemisphere by a few degrees to the next frequency.

He lowered his hand, keeping the orb in his fist.

'We will ensure every Legion ship is granted a copy of the images contained here,' he said. 'Some things must be kept fresh in our memories. Come, brothers. We should return to orbit. There's nothing more for us to find here.'

THE DECK SHUDDERED beneath Talos's feet as the *Covenant of Blood* pulled out of orbit. He had stood with his brothers of First Claw on the command deck, as the Legion fleet bombarded the temple site from orbit.

The lances cut down into the planet below, a tectonic barrage that levelled the entire mountain range.

Then, one by one, the Night Lords warships broke away.

Alone in his meditation chamber, Talos regarded the hololithic recorder orb once more. He turned the device to its first setting, and watched his father laugh in the seconds before his death.

He watched this seven more times, before twisting the recorder to its next setting. Nothing happened. He tried the next, and received the same result.

Only the last setting contained another archive. A vox recording.

Talos recognised the voice immediately. It was the assassin who had slain his father in the age before the Long War. More than that, it was the woman he had disembowelled and torn apart himself, in pursuit of vengeance.

She spoke from the grave, ten thousand years dead, repeating the same words just as the primarch's spirit was caged into repeating the same actions.

This is M'Shen, daughter of the Callidus. I've found Commander Curze of the Night Lords Legion. I–

The recording broke into static.

This is M'Shen, daughter of the Callidus. I've found Commander Curze of the Night Lords Legion. I–

More static.

This is M'Shen, daughter of the Callidus. I've found Commander Curze of the Night Lords Legion. I–

Static.

BLOOD REAVER

PROLOGUE
A CRUCIFIED ANGEL

THE WARRIOR TURNED his helm over in his hands. Gauntleted fingertips stroked along the dents and scratches marring the midnight ceramite. The faceplate was painted white with an artisan's care, in stylised mimicry of a human skull. One scarlet eye lens was ruined, cobwebbed by cracks. The other stared, dispassionate in deactivation, reflecting the darkening sky above.

He told himself that this wasn't symbolic. His helm's ruination didn't reflect the damage done to his Legion. Even as he quenched the notion, he wondered from whence it came. The war had a proven and profane habit of fanning the embers of melancholy, but still. There were limits.

The warrior took a breath, seeing inhuman creatures dance and bleed behind his closed eyes. He'd been dreaming of the eldar lately, for months before setting foot on this desolate world. Thousands of them: spindly things with gaunt faces and hollow eyes, aboard a burning ship of black sails and false bone.

'Soul Hunter,' someone called. His brother's voice, making the name somewhere between a joke and a title of respect.

The warrior replaced his helm. One eye lens flickered live, bathing the vista in the killing-red of his targeting vision. The other showed angry grey static and the distracting after-images of visual input lag. It still echoed with a grainy and colourless view of the setting sun a few moments after he'd turned away from it.

'What?' the warrior asked.

'The Angel is breaking.'

The warrior smiled as he drew the gladius sheathed at his shin. Fading sunlight flashed off the blade's edge as the steel met cold air.

'Glorious.'

CRUCIFYING ONE OF the Imperial Astartes had been a delicious conceit, and served well as a means to an end. The warrior hung slack from his bonds, bathed in pain but surrendering no sound from his split lips. *The*

Emperor's 'Angels of Death', the warrior smiled. *Stoic to the last.*

With no iron spikes to hand, getting him up there required a degree of improvisation. Ultimately, the leader ordered his men to bind the Angel to the hull of their tank by impaling the prisoner's limbs with their gladii.

Blood still dripped to the decking in liquid percussion, but had long since ceased to trickle with rainwater eagerness. The Adeptus Astartes physiology, despite its gene-written immortality, only held so much blood.

Beneath the crucified captive, a helm rested in repose. The warrior dismissed another unwelcome tide of reflection at the sight of a helm so like his own but for the colours of allegiance and the bonds of a blood-line. With no real venom, he crushed it beneath his boot. How keen and insipid, the tendrils of melancholy lately.

The warrior looked up, baring features destroyed by mutilating knives. His armour was ceramite – halved with rich blue and pure white – pitted and cracked around the impaling short swords. His face, once so grim and proud, was a skinless display of bare veins and bloody, layered musculature. Even his eyelids had been cut away.

'Hail, brother,' the warrior greeted the captive. 'Do you know who we are?'

With the angel broken, a confession took no time at all. To speak the words, he came up close, the purred question rasping through his helm's vocabulator into the air between them. The warrior's faceplate was almost pressed to the Angel's flayed features – two skulls staring at one another as the sun went down.

'Where is Ganges?'

As his brothers prepared, the warrior watched the distant fortress burning on the horizon, paying heed to how it devoured the world around it. A sprawl of towers and landing platforms – its dark mass ate the land while its smoking breath choked the sky. And yet it offered so little of worth when laid bare to plundering hands. Why attack a world if the one node of resources was already drained dry? Piracy without profit was nothing more than begging.

Undignified. Oh, yes. And embarrassing.

The warrior stared at its distant battlements – a meagre stronghold on a lifeless world, claimed by a thin-blooded Chapter calling itself the Marines Errant. A raid for weapons, for supplies, for precious, precious ammunition... wasted. The Chapter's own crusades bled their reserves to nothing, leaving naught but scraps for the VIII Legion's grasping hands.

The fortress fell within a day, offering as little sport as plunder. Servitors and robed Mechanicum acolytes tore through the databanks in the nigh-abandoned stronghold, but discovered only what every warrior already knew: the raid was a waste of their diminishing ammunition reserves. The Marines Errant no longer stored their secondary armoury here.

'Things have changed since we last sailed these reaches of the void,' the Exalted growled to his command crew. The confession pained him, pained them all. 'We have hurled our last spears... to conquer a husk.'

Amidst the bitterness of desperation and disappointment, the embers of possibility still burned. One word cycled through the streams of data, over and over again. *Ganges.* Representing the ties in this sector of space between the Marines Errant and the Martian Mechanicus, a deep-void outpost was responsible for a significant supply of raw material for the Chapter's armoury. The Marines Errant, so proud in their armour of oceanic blue and marble white, maintained order within the subsector by vigilant destruction of human and alien pirates. In protecting Mechanicus interests, they earned the allegiance of Mars. In earning such unity, they garnered a share in the Mechanicus's significant munitions production. A circle of symbiosis, fuelled by mutual interest.

The warrior admired that.

What mattered most was this deep-space refinery's location, and that eluded all who sought to find it. Sealed behind unbreakable encryptions, the only answer that mattered remained known to none.

The few prisoners taken from the hollow monastery offered little in the way of information. Human attendants, lobotomised servitors, Chapter serfs... None knew where Ganges lay in the heavens. What few Imperial warriors had defended this worthless world died to their brothers' bolters and blades, embracing their deaths as honourable sacrifice rather than risk capture and desecration.

A single defender yet drew breath. The warrior dragged him onto the ash plains to be flayed under the setting sun.

Even now, the Errant still drew breath, though not for much longer. He had revealed all the VIII Legion needed to know.

Ganges. A raid there would reap much richer rewards.

In orbit, the Vectine system's sun was a vast orb of adrenal orange, a colour of deep fire and desperate strength. On the surface of the third world, it was a weeping eye, closed by the smog that blocked most of its brightness. The warrior watched it finally set behind the devastated stronghold.

A voice came to him, carried on the crackling waves of the vox network.

'Soul Hunter,' it said.

'Stop calling me that.'

'Sorry. Uzas is eating the Errant's gene-seed.'

'The Errant is dead? Already?'

'Not quite. But if you wish to execute him yourself, now is the time. Uzas is making a mess.'

The warrior shook his head, though there was no one to see it. He knew why his brother was asking: the Errant had been the one to break his helm, firing a bolter at close range during the assault and savaging the faceplate. Vengeance, even vengeance this petty, was tempting.

'We have all we need from him,' the warrior said. 'We should return to the ship soon.'

'As you say, brother.'

The warrior watched as the stars opened their eyes, scarcely piercing the dense cloud cover, little more than pinpricks of dull light. Ganges was out there, and with it, the chance to breathe easily again.

PART ONE

UNBOUND

I

ECHOES

THE SHIP WAS quiet as she walked its cobwebbing corridors.

Not quite a lack of sound, more a presence in itself that ghosted down the black iron hallways. Three days had passed since the *Covenant of Blood* last sailed under power. Now it coasted through space, its decks cold and its engines colder. *The hunt*, they called it, in their whispering tongue. This ethereal drift through the void, sailing in powerless silence closer to the target, seen and heard by none. *The hunt*.

Octavia called it *waiting*. Nothing was more tedious to a Navigator. The hull still creaked as abused steel settled, but the sounds of the crew were more muted than ever before. So few remained now.

One of her attendants trailed at her heels as she walked from her chamber. He was a scruffy, robed thing, more than half of his hunched form given over to crude bionics.

'Mistress,' he whispered over and over. 'Mistress, mistress. Yes. Mistress. I follow mistress.' He didn't seem able to lift his voice above a whisper.

Octavia was learning to ignore the annoying creatures. This one was one of the ugliest in the pack of augmented men and women that professed to serve her. It stood only as high as her shoulder, with its eyes sewn shut by thick, crude stitching. Whatever modifications were done to its body whirred, clicked, ticked and tocked as it loped along with a hunchback's gait. 'Mistress. Serve mistress. Protect mistress. Yes. All of these things.'

It regarded her with an eyeless face, looking up and seeing her through means she wasn't sure she wanted to understand. Bizarrely, he looked hopeful. He seemed to want praise for shuffling along by her side and occasionally bumping into walls.

'Shut up,' she told him, rather politely given the circumstances.

'Yes,' the hunched man agreed. 'Yes, mistress. Quiet for mistress. Yes. Silence now.'

Well, it'd been worth a try. 'Please go back to the chamber,' she said, and even smiled sweetly. 'I will return soon.'

315

'No, mistress. Must follow mistress.'

Her reply was an unladylike snort as their boots continued to clank along the hallway decking. Their images walked with them as they passed a hull section of reflective steel. Octavia couldn't resist a glance at herself, though she knew she wasn't going to like what she saw.

Ratty black hair, with its snarls only half tamed by a fraying ponytail. Pale skin, sunless and unhealthy. Her jaw line sported a faded bruise she couldn't recall earning, and her ragged clothes were smeared with oil and general deck-dirt, the rough fabric dyed the blue of a midnight sky back home on Terra. If her clothes had been tidier, they'd have formed a uniform: the attire of the ship's slave caste, loose and unwashed, hanging off her slender frame.

'Pretty as a picture,' she accused her scruffy reflection.

'Thank you, mistress.'

'Not you.'

The hunched fellow seemed to muse on this for a moment. 'Oh.'

A muffled weeping in the distance stole any further comment. Human emotion, helplessness without a shred of malice. A girl. The sound carried strangely down the hallway, resonating against the metal walls.

Octavia felt her skin prickling. She stared down the corridor, peering into the darkness that her hand-held lamp pack could only barely pierce. The beam of light lanced left and right, stabbing the gloom with weak illumination. Bare metal walls met her questing, until the light could reach no further down the long hallway.

'Not again,' she whispered, before calling out a hesitant greeting. No answer.

'Hello?' she tried again.

The girl's weeping stopped, fading away as Octavia's voice echoed.

'Hello, mistress.'

'Shut *up*, you.'

'Yes, mistress.'

She swallowed, and her throat clicked softly. There were no children on the ship. Not any more. Octavia reached for her hand vox, and almost thumbed the Send rune. But what was the point? Septimus wasn't on the ship. He'd been gone for almost two months now, leaving her alone.

Octavia clicked her fingers at her... servant? Attendant? Thing.

He turned blind eyes up to her. How he managed to stare adoringly when his eyes were sewn shut was quite beyond her.

'Come on,' she said.

'Yes, mistress.'

'You heard that, right? The girl?'

'No, mistress.'

She led him on, leaving her chamber far behind. As they walked, he picked at the dirty bandages wrapping his hands, but said nothing more.

Occasionally, a sound from deeper in the ship would carry through the hull's bones. The clanging of a machinist's tools or the clank of bootsteps several decks up. Occasionally, she heard muttered voices, sibilant in their murderer's tongue. She was struggling to learn even the basics of Nostraman since her capture. To listen to it, it sounded both seductive and mellifluous. To learn it was another matter. At its core, Nostraman was a nightmare of complex words and jumbled phrasing, scarcely related to Gothic at all. She suspected that despite Septimus's pleasant praise, she was mispronouncing everything, and she was fairly certain the vocabulary she'd mastered so far wasn't something even a particularly dim infant would be proud of.

They moved on through the gloom, nearing the passageway's end. In the darkness ahead, where the corridor branched into a junction, a figure dashed from one hallway to the next. It ran right across her path – too slight and small to be an adult, too tiny to be even a ruined thing like her attendant. A blur of blue clothing met her stare before the figure was gone. Octavia listened to its gentle, rapid footfalls running down the other corridor.

Again, she heard the childish weeping – the soft mewling of a child trying to keep her pain hidden.

'Hello?'

'*Ashilla sorsollun, ashilla uthullun,*' the little girl called back to her, as the sound of fleeing footsteps faded.

'I think I'm going back to my chamber,' Octavia said softly.

II

GANGES STATION

A SLIVER OF midnight drifted on dead engines, betraying nothing of its presence.

A world turned in the emptiness, its cloudless face one of grey stone and lifeless continents. Even an untrained eye needed only to glance at the rock to see its potential, not to nurture life, but to feed an industrious species with its precious ore.

The only evidence of human existence hung in orbit: a vast platform of gunmetal grey, its empty docking arms reaching into the void. Along the station's hull, stencilled in Imperial Gothic lettering, was the word GANGES.

The sliver of darkness drifted ever closer, as blind to astral scanners as it was to the naked eye. Within its blade-like body, a machine began to shriek.

MARUC CRASHED DOWN onto the couch, wanting nothing more than to stop moving. For a few moments, that was more than enough. He couldn't even be bothered to kick his boots off. Sixteen-hour shifts weren't the worst of his compulsory labour duties, but they were damn close. He drew in a breath that hurt his ribs, getting a lungful of his habitation pod's stuffy air. He smelled food cartons that needed throwing out days ago, and the ever-present suggestion of unwashed socks.

Home sweet home.

By the time the sigh finished leaving his lips, he was already thumbing at his closed eyes, trying to massage away some of the sting from staring at clanking conveyor belts all day. The earache, he couldn't do anything about. That had to stay.

With an exaggerated groan, he rolled to reach for the remote control palette where it lay in pieces on the floor. A few clicks later and he'd reattached the battery pack. He repeatedly speared the loose *ON* button with his fingertip, knowing it'd pick up on his intent at some point. For a wonder, it only took a few seconds this time. The screen mounted on the opposite wall flickered to life.

Well. Sort of.

It showed the kind of jagged distortion that spoke of something much worse than a mistuning. A technical fault, maybe. No picture, no sound, no nothing. Not that Ganges's endless cycle of Ecclesiarchial sermons, obituaries and technical safety broadcasts were exciting, but they beat seeing nothing but static.

He tapped the volume gauge. Silence became the dead-voiced whispery hiss of interference, even at full volume. Wonderful. No, really. Just great. Like he had the credits spare to call out the technical servitors again? Beautiful.

He let the remote fall from his oil-stained fingers, where it promptly ended up bisected on the floor, missing its battery pack again. He then said 'Balls to this' out loud to the empty habitation chamber, decided he was too tired to bother unfolding the couch into its bed position, and worked on sleeping off yet another pointless day in an increasingly pointless life.

Was he proud? No. But 'just' seven more years of this, and he'd have enough saved to drag himself off Ganges for good, catching a shuttle to somewhere else – somewhere with prospects slightly less grim. He'd have signed up for the Imperial Guard long ago if his eyes could see worth a damn. But they couldn't, so he hadn't.

Instead, he worked the construction belts here, sighing his way through a job deemed too menial to bother programming a servitor for.

Maruc drifted into sleep with these thoughts at the forefront of his aching head. It wasn't a restful sleep, but that didn't matter because it didn't last long anyway.

The screen started shrieking.

Maruc jerked back from the border of sleep with a series of curse words, grabbing at the remote and slapping the battery pack back into place. He dulled the volume while his free hand checked his ears to make sure they weren't bleeding.

They weren't. He was almost surprised.

A glance at the digital chron on his wall showed he'd been asleep, or almost there, for less than five minutes. Sound had evidently returned to the monitor, though it didn't sound like any distortion he'd heard before. This unit had given him a fair share of technical issues. His screen had crackled, buzzed, popped and hissed before. It had never shrieked.

Bleary-eyed, with a pounding headache, he raised the volume again. The sound grew louder, but no clearer. A tortured machine whine, pitched painfully high. A hundred human voices, formless and tuneless, rendered inhuman as they drowned in static. It was both, and neither.

The lights flickered above. Another power cut coming. Ganges was a run-down backwater at the best of times, stuck in orbit around a dead world at the arse end of nowhere. Last time the lights died, they'd been out for three day cycles before the tech crews had the illumination generators breathing again. Work hadn't ceased, of course. Not with the production schedules each sector had to meet. The entire western district of the station spent seventy hours working by torchlight. Dozens of menials had lost limbs or fingers in the machinery, and that week's obituaries ran as long as a saints' day prayer scroll.

Maruc hauled himself off the couch just as the lights went out. Fumbling in the dark brought him to the wall, and he opened the emergency supply cabinet containing his lamp pack, with a batch of standard-issue battery packs that would serve in every one of the hab-room's scarce and simple appliances. He was always lax in charging them, so which ones were still live remained a mystery for now. He stuffed all eight of the palm-sized discs into his overall pockets, operating under the shaky light of his hand-held torch, then crashed back onto the couch to await the inevitable personnel announcement that would demand they all 'Behave as normal', and that 'Illumination shall be restored at the earliest possible juncture'.

Throne. What a hole.

Two minutes went by, and became five. Five became ten. Every once in a while, Maruc would click on his lamp pack and aim the torch's beam at his wall chron, frowning at the passing of time.

At last, the chime sounded from the vox speaker mounted above the door. Instead of the automated message he'd been expecting, the stationwide vox system gave the same screaming whine as his screen, only twice as loud. His hands slammed to his ears, as if fingers and dirty palms could block over a hundred decibels of skull-aching shrieking. Maruc hammered the door release with his elbow, spilling out into the communal hallway on his knees. The sound followed him, crying from the deck speakers out there as well. Other doors slid open, but that only amplified the sound: the scream leapt from individual hab-rooms as other personnel staggered from their own chambers.

What the hell is going on?

He yelled the words, but never heard them leave his throat, nor did anyone nearby respond.

ARELLA HAD BEEN telling a story about her cat when everything went to hell. It hadn't been a particularly funny story, or an interesting one, but up on the overseer deck anything that passed the time was considered a welcome distraction. Their work shifts almost always consisted of twelve-hour stints spent watching scanner screens that showed nothing, reading crew reports that never looked any different from previous days, and discussing what they'd all do once they were transferred off this derelict munitions station, hopefully rotated back to actual fleet service.

Today, something had happened, and the crew on shift weren't exactly thrilled. Their chief officer, Arella Kor, was especially ardent in wishing things had just stayed quiet.

The weapons array was active, defensive turrets staring out into the void. The shields were live, layered spheres of invisible force protecting the station's hideous hull. Arella's eyes strayed to the timer on her console. Seven minutes and forty-one seconds had passed since the interference began. She was calling it 'interference' because that sounded a lot less worrying than 'the damn screaming'.

Currently, the damn scr– the interference was being broadcast through their internal vox-net, screeched onto every deck at an insane volume. They couldn't shut it down, and no one knew why.

'The lights have just died in Western-Two,' one of the others called out.

'Oh, shit... and Western-One. And Western-Three. And all of the Eastern sector. And–'

Fittingly, the lights died on the command deck at that same moment. Reserve generators cycled up, bathing them all in the headache red of emergency lighting.

'It's an external signal.' The officer at the console next to her tapped his screen – one of the few on the station that still seemed to be functioning. 'Whatever it is, it's coming from out there.'

Arella blew a lock of hair off her face. The command deck was always too hot, the air filtration had never worked right, and stress wasn't helping. 'Details?' She wiped her sweaty forehead on her sleeve.

The officer stabbed his screen with a fingertip again. 'A sourceless transmission, ten minutes ago. It's here, logged in the archive. When the signal was processed by our cogitators to be recorded and filed, it... spread. Like a disease, almost. It flooded specific station systems: the communications array, and the more primitive parts of the power grid.'

Arella sucked on her bottom lip, biting back the need to swear. 'Gravity?'

'Uncompromised.'

'Shields?'

'Still up.'

'Atmosphere. Life support. Weapons.'

'All still live. It's a simple, brutal, randomised blurt of scrap-code. It can't shut down anything complex. It's just communications, auspex and... it looks like the illumination network is offline. Only the most basic systems, but they're all filled with invasive code, impeding function.'

She looked back at her own scanner screen, at the same wash of corrupted feedback she'd been seeing for the last ten minutes. 'Scanners, lights and vox. We're blind, deaf and mute. And you *know* we'll get kicked in the teeth for this. The clankers will have demerits splashed all over our records. Just watch.' As if it would make any difference, she absently buttoned up her uniform jacket for the first time in countless shifts.

'You're not worried that this might be an attack?' the other officer asked.

Arella shook her head. 'Our weapons and shields still work. Nothing to worry about, except who the Mechanicus will hold accountable. And that'll be us. Pissing clankers and their profit margins.'

Only a few years ago, she'd have worried about all the people forced to work in the dark. Now her first fear was for herself: the Adeptus Mechanicus wouldn't take kindly to significant production delays, and this was going wrong in a hundred ways already. She might never get off Ganges at this rate.

The officer next to her, Sylus, scratched at his unshaven jawline. 'So we get jammed and fall off critical productivity. How is that our fault?'

Arella struggled to keep her patience. Sylus was new to the station, only two months into his tenure, and he hadn't mingled well. The bionics replacing his left cheek, temple and eye were ludicrously expensive – clearly he was a rich man playing at being a grunt. Maybe his wealthy father sent him here as some kind of punishment, or he was an Adeptus Mechanicus mole snooping for screw-ups. Whatever the truth, he was a stubborn bastard when he wanted to be.

She snorted. 'Who do you think the clankers will blame? "Pirates jammed us" isn't going to fly. Hell, why would anyone target a place like this? If whoever is out there could even get past our weapons, there's nothing here worth taking.'

Sylus was no longer listening. Arella rose from her seat, mouth hanging open, staring out the command deck window at a ship that shouldn't exist.

THE *Covenant of Blood* was born in an age when humanity did more than reach for the stars – mankind sought to conquer them. Great shipyards had ringed the planets of the Sol System, as the Emperor led the species back into the galaxy on a crusade to unite every world of worth within His aegis.

The vessels brought about in that era sailed the stars ten thousand years ago, before rediscovered Standard Template Constructs homogenised the technology of the entire human race. Innovation was not considered a sin. Deviation in the name of progress was visionary, not blasphemy. Like many of the warships born in those first fleets, the *Covenant*'s design was initially based on fragments of STC technology, but not limited to it. When it sailed under full power, it tore through space as a sleek hunter, owing as much to the contours of ancient Crusade-era warships as it did to the blocky structure of an Adeptus Astartes strike cruiser.

The Exalted's affection for its vessel went far beyond pride. It was a haven, the creature's sanctuary from a galaxy that desired its destruction, and the *Covenant* was the weapon it wielded in the Long War.

On its command throne, the creature licked its jaws, watching the image of Ganges Station expand in the occulus. They'd ghosted this close, undetected by the station's instruments or weapons batteries, but as they neared the invisible edge of the Ganges's void shields, they were close enough to be seen by the naked eye.

'Closer, closer,' the Exalted drawled to its bridge crew. 'Maintain the Shriek.'

ARELLA'S MONITOR STILL showed a confused storm of data; flickering after-images, information screeds and signals tracked that simply couldn't be there. One moment it registered fifty-three ships almost on top of each other. The next, nothing but empty space.

Outside the view window, the ship drifted closer. Armour plating – layers of black, bronze, cobalt and midnight – reflected the gaze of distant stars.

'It looks like an Errant strike cruiser,' she said. 'A big one.' She chewed on her bottom lip, unable to take her eyes from the ship drifting closer. 'The Marines Errant aren't due for resource collection until the end of the production cycle, nine and a half months from now.'

'It's not the Marines Errant,' Sylus replied. 'Not their colours, nor their symbol.'

'So who the hell are they?'

Sylus laughed, the sound soft and low. 'How am I supposed to know?'

Arella sat back down, breathing through her teeth. 'Why aren't we firing?' She felt the rise in her voice, perilously close to a whine. 'We have to fire.'

'At Imperial Space Marines?' One of the others looked appalled. 'Are you insane?'

'They're in our space with no clearance, are making no attempts to hail us, and are jamming all our sensors to worthlessness? Coming in on a docking drift with a Mechanicus outpost, full of resources to be shared with the Marines Errant Chapter? Yes, we should be defending ourselves.' She swore again. 'We have to fire, somehow.'

'With no target lock?' Sylus was resisting panic with much better grace. If anything, he looked almost bored, working his console and retuning dials with a safecracker's patience.

'Get Station Defence to fire their guns manually!'

Sylus scowled now, trying to listen to his earpiece. 'Internal vox is down. What do you want me to do, Arella? Shout down the corridor and hope the whole station hears? They're blind down there, anyway. Illumination is dead. How will they get to the turret platforms?'

She clenched her teeth, watching the warship drift closer. Almost three thousand people were on board Ganges, and they had the firepower to stave off an entire pirate fleet. Now, a single enemy ship was aiming for their heart, and the only people that knew couldn't say a damn thing to the people that could actually do something about it.

'Run out the guns,' she said.

'What?'

'Open the gun ports. We'll set the eastern weapon batteries to fire at the ship's rough coordinates. Program it as a live-fire drill. It'll work!'

'That's a good idea.' Sylus reached for his holstered side-arm, and without any hesitation at all, drew it and fired in a single smooth movement. The gunshot cracked in the small chamber, startlingly loud. Arella slumped from her chair into a boneless heap, with a hole drilled neatly through her forehead. Mushy wetness decorated the wall behind her. 'And it would've worked,' Sylus finished.

Of the three other officers on shift, two sat stunned, while the third reached for his own pistol. That one died first, sighing back in his chair as Sylus pumped three rounds into his chest. The other two both sought to run. Headshots ended their plans, spraying more skull fragments and dark paste around the control chamber.

'Messy work,' said Sylus.

He booted one of them out of the leather control throne and started working the console, tending to several of the station's primary systems in neat succession. The gun ports stayed sealed – a hundred turrets all denied the power they needed in order to activate. The launch bays and escape pod hives were locked, power completely siphoned away, trapping everyone on board the station. At last, the station's void shields collapsed, starved of nourishing energy and severed from their fallback generators. Alarms began to wail in the chamber, which he ended almost immediately. Irritating sound, that.

Sylus took a breath. He felt like lifting his boots up and resting them on the console, but – bizarrely – it seemed needlessly disrespectful. Instead, he rose to his feet, reloaded his pistol, and moved over to the vox console where he'd been sitting before.

A single blue light flickered. Incoming message. He clicked it live.

'Report.' The voice on the vox was between a gurgle and a growl.

'This is Septimus,' he replied. 'Ganges Station is yours, my lord.'

III

NIGHTFALL

Rats always survive.

Nothing to be proud of in that thought, yet it was shamefully apt. He'd lasted longer than most in this dim, crimson world of emergency lighting.

'Let's go,' Maruc whispered over his shoulder. With their lamp packs beaming thin slits of light ahead, the three men moved through the corridor. Each time a spear of torchlight brushed the wall, deck markers painted onto the hull proclaimed the passage as *E-31:F*. Maruc always did everything he could to keep off the station's main corridors. No part of Ganges was exactly safe since the killers had come, but Maruc had made it for a few day cycles longer than most by being cautious above all. He kept to the tertiary passages and maintenance ducts whenever possible.

He knew he stank from enduring seventy-nine hours of unwashed bodies crawling through the dark, and his eyes were aching pools, pained from the endless squinting. But he was alive. Like a rat, he'd survived, listening to the sounds of distant screaming, gunfire and laughter resonating through the iron bones of Ganges Station.

The worst thing was the cold. How could cold be so intense that it burned? Ice crystals painted diamonds across the metal walls around them. Their breath left their lips and noses in thin clouds, taking precious warmth with it. Maruc was no doctor, but he knew they'd not survive another night in this section of the station. The killers, whatever they were, had broken the heat exchangers in East Ganges. Maybe they wanted to flush the remaining crew out from hiding. It was possible. Or maybe they were bored with their hunt, and wished only to freeze the remaining crew to death wherever they'd gone to ground. Neither thought was exactly comforting.

'You hear that?' Maruc whispered.

Ahead of them, something metal rattled upon metal. He hissed the signal to halt, and three lamp packs peered down the hallway. Nothing. A bare corridor. The rattle carried on.

'It's a ventilation turbine,' Joroll whispered. 'Just a vent fan.' Maruc turned away from the other man's wide eyes and the airy press of his rancid breath.

'You sure?'

'It's just a vent fan. I think.' Joroll's voice was as shivery as his hands. 'I worked in those ducts. I know the sounds they make.'

Sure, Maruc thought, *but that was before you cracked.* Joroll was slipping faster than the rest of them. He'd already started to piss himself without realising. At least when Maruc did it, it was to keep warm. Another survival tactic. *Rats always survive,* he thought again with an ugly smile.

'Come on, then.'

They moved with exaggerated caution, not truly knowing what the killers could sense. Joroll had caught the best look at one, but wouldn't speak about it. Dath, bringing up the trio's rear, claimed to have seen more than Maruc, but it still wasn't much to go on – a huge figure with red eyes, screaming with a machine's voice. Dath had fled before seeing anything more, diving through a maintenance hatch and panting his way down the crawl-tunnels while his work crew were noisily torn apart behind him. One killer had been enough for fifteen people.

Maruc couldn't claim such a witness account himself. He suspected that was why he was still alive. He'd stuck to the smallest passages from when he'd first heard the reports of the killers coming aboard, leaving them only for necessities like raiding food stores or scavenging through stockrooms for battery packs.

Too cold for that now. Now they had to move, and pray other sections of the station still had heat.

For a time, he'd considered just giving up, just laying down in the confined crawlspace of a maintenance burrow and letting the ice take him. He'd probably never even decay after he died. At least, not until Adeptus Mechanicus salvage crews arrived to restart the heat exchangers... then no doubt he'd collapse and bubble away into a smear of rot along the steel.

At the next junction, Maruc waited a long time, doing his best to listen over the sound of his own heartbeat. He started to move down the left passage.

'I think we're okay,' he whispered.

Joroll shook his head. He wasn't moving. 'That's the wrong way.'

Maruc heard Dath sigh, but the other man said nothing. 'This is the way to the canteen,' Maruc said as softly and calmly as he could manage, 'and we need supplies. This isn't the time to argue, Jor.'

'That's not the way to the canteen. It's to the right.' Joroll pointed down the opposite corridor.

'That's towards the Eastern technical deck,' Maruc replied.

'No, it's not.' Joroll's voice was rising now, with a querulous edge. 'We should go this way.' The nearby ventilator fan continued its slow clicking.

'Let's just go,' Dath said to Maruc. 'Leave him.'

Joroll spoke before Maruc had to make the choice, for which the age-ing manufactorum worker was immensely grateful. 'No, no, I'll come. Don't leave me.'

'Keep your voice down,' Maruc said gently, having no idea if it would really make any difference. 'And keep your torches low.'

Maruc led them on. Another left. Another. A long corridor, then a right. He froze at the turn, reluctantly aiming his torch down the hallway at the double bulkhead entrance to the canteen.

'No...' his voice was soft, strengthless in a way even whispers weren't.

'What is it?' Joroll hissed.

Maruc narrowed his stinging eyes, letting the beam of light play around the sundered doorway. The bulkhead was off its joints, torn from the wall in a wrenched mess of abused metal.

'It's not good,' Maruc murmured. 'The killers have been here.'

'They've been everywhere,' said Dath. He almost sighed the words out.

Maruc stood shivering in the biting cold, his torch beam falling victim to the tremors of his hands. 'Let's go,' he whispered. '*Quietly.*'

As they drew near the broken doors, Joroll sniffed. 'I smell something.'

Maruc breathed in slowly. The air felt cold enough to scald his lungs with iceburn, but he didn't smell a damn thing beyond wet metal and his own stink. 'I don't. What is it?'

'Spices. Bad spices.'

Maruc turned away from the quivering look in Joroll's eyes. He was cracking now, no doubt about it.

Maruc was the first one to turn the corner. He crept to the edge of the torn doorway, looking around the large chamber in its wash of siren red lighting, unable to make any real detail out from the gloom. The tables, dozens of them, were overturned and thrown around, to be left wherever they landed. The walls were dark and pitted with gunfire's touch, and a horde of chairs were spilled across the floor – doubtless the remains of a worthless barricade. Bodies, lots of bodies, lay draped over the tables and stuck spread-eagled to the icy floor. Open eyes glinted with frost crystals, while smears of blood had become beautiful pools of ruby glass.

At least nothing was moving. Maruc lifted the torch and let the light shine in. The darkness parted before the torch, and the lamp pack revealed what the emergency lighting hadn't.

'Throne of the God-Emperor,' he whispered.

'What is it?'

Immediately, he lowered his torch beam. 'Stay here.' Maruc wasn't going to risk Joroll's patchwork sanity in there. 'Just stay here, I'll get what we need.'

He entered the canteen, boots crunching on the red glass puddles of frozen blood. His breath was white mist before his face, curling away in

the dim light as he moved. Giving the bodies a wide berth wasn't easy –
Maruc did all he could to avoid touching them, though he couldn't help
looking. What torchlight had shown in grim clarity was more obvious up
close: not a single corpse in this chamber had escaped desecration. He
stepped over a skinned woman with cringing care, and moved around a
heap of leathery strips, where her harvested flesh was frozen to the floor.
As he moved, her leering, skinless face of bared veins and blackening
muscle offered him a toothy smile.

Some of the bodies were little more than reddened skeletons, either
missing limbs or barely articulated at all, ice-dried and hard as they lay
across tables. The chill had done a lot to steal the smell, but Maruc could
tell now what Joroll was talking about. Bad spices, indeed.

He crept closer to the closed storage bulkhead, praying the wheel-lock
wouldn't squeal when he turned it. Maruc braced against the frostbitten
metal in his hands and twisted it. For once, fortune was on his side – it
gave with a sudden lurch and turned with well-oiled mercy. With a deep
breath, he hauled the bulkhead open, revealing the walk-in storage room
behind.

It looked unlooted. Shelves of dried ration packs in boxes, crates of
reconstituted meat product; every container stamped proud with the
aquila or the cog of Mars. Maruc was three steps in when he heard the
scream behind him.

He knew he could hide. He could shut the storage door and freeze to
death alone, or find a crawlspace and wait for whatever was happening to
be over. His only weapon was the lamp pack in his numb hand, after all.

Joroll screamed again, the sound disgustingly wet. Maruc was running
before he realised it, boots slapping on the cold floor.

A killer entered the canteen, dragging Joroll and Dath in its hands.
Throne, the thing was huge. Its black armour in the red gloom was a
smear of ink spilled into blood, and the vicious buzz rising from its
internal power generator was enough to make Maruc's teeth itch.

Joroll was dead weight in its hand, the dark fist wrapped around a
throat that shouldn't bend that far back. Dath was still kicking, still
screaming, dragged by a handful of hair in the killer's clutch.

Maruc threw the lamp pack from his sweaty grip. It clanged off the
killer's shoulder guard, spinning away from the icon of a winged skull
without leaving a dent.

It caused the killer to turn, and growl two words through its helm's
vox speakers.

'I see.'

With casual indifference, the killer hurled Joroll's corpse aside, dump-
ing it on a table alongside a skinless body. Dath thrashed in the monster's
grip, his heels kicking at the icy ground seeking purchase, his numb
hands clawing uselessly at the fist bunched in his long, greasy hair.

Maruc didn't run. He was sore to his bones from the cold and the cramped spaces, half-starved and exhausted from three nights without sleep. He was sick of living as a rat, with desperate fear the only emotion to break through the pains of hunger and the slow onset of frostbite. Too defeated to force a futile run, he stood in a chamber of skinned bodies and faced the killer. Would death be worse than living like this? Really?

'Why are you doing this?' he voiced the thought that had rattled around his head for days.

The killer didn't stop. An armoured hand, already coated in frost, thumped around Maruc's throat. The pressure was worse than the cold. He felt his spine creaking and crackling, felt his throat's sinews crushed together to feel like a bunch of grapes in his neck, choking off any breath. The killer lifted him with slow care, anger emanating from the skull painted across its faceplate.

'Is that a question?' The killer's head tilted, regarding him with its unblinking red eye lenses. 'Is that something you wish to know the answer to, or is your mind misfiring in a moment of panic?' The grip on his throat loosened enough to allow speech and a few gasps of precious breath. Each heave of Maruc's lungs drew stinking air into his body, cold enough to hurt.

'Why?' He forced the word through spit-wet teeth.

The killer growled its words from the skull-faced helm. 'I *made* this Imperium. I built it, night after night, with my sweat and my pride and a blade in my hands. I bought it with the blood in my brothers' veins, fighting at the Emperor's side, blinded by His light in the age before you entombed Him as a messiah. You live, mortal, only because of my work. Your existence is mine. Look at me. You know what I am. Look past what cannot be true, and see what holds your life in his hands.'

Maruc felt piss running down his leg, boiling hot against his skin. The Great Betrayer's fallen angels. Mythology. A legend. 'Just a legend,' he croaked as he dangled. 'Just a legend.' Breath from his denial steamed on the warrior's armour.

'We are not legends.' The killer's fist tightened again. 'We are the architects of your empire, banished from history's pages, betrayed by the husk you worship as it rots upon a throne of gold.'

Maruc's stinging eyes took in the silver aquila emblazoned across the killer's chestplate. The Imperial eagle, cracked and broken, worn by a heretic.

'You owe us your life, mortal, so I give you this choice. You will serve the Eighth Legion,' the killer promised, 'or you will die screaming.'

IV
ASUNDER

Taking the station had been as easy as any of them could've hoped. There was pride to be taken there, albeit not much. If a warrior could find glory in capturing a backwater manufactorum installation like this, then Talos wouldn't begrudge him for it. But as victories went, it rang hollow. A raid of necessity, not of vengeance. *A supply run*, the words taunted him, even as they dragged a smile across his lips. Not the kind of engagement that would be adorning the Legion's banners for centuries to come.

Still, he was pleased with Septimus. And glad to have him back aboard the ship – two months without an artificer had been an annoyance, to say the least.

Three nights ago, Talos had taken his first steps onto the station's decking. It was not a treasured memory. The boarding pod's doors flowering open, twisting the steel of the station's hull with that distinctive whine of protesting metal. Then, as always, emerging into a welcoming darkness. Visors pierced the black with programmed ease. Thermal blurs looked vaguely embryonic as they curled in upon themselves: humans on all fours; reaching blindly; cowering and weeping. Prey, crying around his ankles, resisting death by only the most pathetic and futile attempts.

Humanity was at its ugliest when desperate to survive. The indignities people did to themselves. The begging. The tears. The frantic gunfire that could never pierce ceramite.

The VIII Legion stalked through the station almost unopposed, stealing what little excitement there might've been. Talos spent several hours listening to the braying of other Claws over the vox. Several had run amok, butchering and relishing in their ability to inspire fear in the trapped humans. How they'd cried their joy to one another, during those long hours of maddened hunting.

'Those sounds,' Talos had said. 'The voices of our brothers. What we are hearing is the Legion's death rattle. Curious, how degeneration sounds so much like laughter.'

Xarl had grunted in reply. It might have been a chuckle. The others forbore comment as they moved down the lightless corridors.

Three nights had passed since then.

For those three nights, First Claw had done as the Exalted had ordered, overseeing the *Covenant*'s resupply. Promethium fuel was taken in barrels and vats. Raw, roiling plasma was leeched out of the station's generators. Ore of all kinds was taken in great loads to be turned into materiel in the *Covenant*'s artificer workshops. Useful members of the station's crew – of the few hundred that escaped the initial massacres – were dragged aboard the ship in chains. The vessel still remained docked, even now sucking what it needed through fuel lines and cargo loaders.

Six hours ago, Talos had been one of the last to drag slaves aboard, finding them hiding in a canteen that had clearly been a site for one of the Claws' butchery. According to the Exalted, the *Covenant of Blood* would remain docked another two weeks, leeching everything of worth from the processing plants and factory foundries.

All was as well as could be expected, until someone slipped the leash. The slaughter aboard Ganges was done, but some souls were never satisfied.

A lone warrior stalked the *Covenant*'s decks, blades in his hands, blood on his faceplate, and his thoughts poisoned by superstitions of a curse.

IT WAS A curse, to be a god's son.

Were these not the prophet's own whining words? *It was a curse to be a god's son*. Well, perhaps that was so. The hunter was willing to concede the point. Maybe it was a curse. But it was also a blessing.

In his quiet hours, when he was granted mercy for even a moment, the hunter believed that this was a truth the others too often forgot. Forever they looked to what they didn't have; what they no longer possessed; glories they would never achieve again. They saw only the lack, never the plenty, and stared into the future without drawing strength from the past. That was no way to live.

A familiar pressure grew behind his eyes, worming its way within his skull. He had lingered too long in the stillness of reflection, and a price would be paid in pain. Hungers had to be sated, and punishments were inflicted when they weren't.

The hunter moved on, his armoured boots echoing along the stone floor. The enemy fled before him, hearing the ticking thrum of active battle armour and the throaty rattle of an idling chainblade. The axe in his hands was a thing of fanged and functional beauty, its tooth-tracks oiled by sacred unguents as often as blood.

Blood. The word was a splash of acid across his cobwebbing thoughts. The unwanted scent of it, the unwelcome taste, the flowing of stinking scarlet from ruptured flesh. The hunter shivered, and looked to the gore lining his weapon's edge. Immediately, he regretted it – blood had dried in a crimson crust on the axe's chainsaw teeth. Pain flared again, as jagged as knives behind the eyes, and didn't fade this time. The blood was dry. He had waited too long between kills.

Screaming released the pressure, but his hearts were pounding now. The hunter broke into a run.

THE NEXT DEATH belonged to a soldier. He died with his hands smearing sweat-streaks over the hunter's eyes, while the ropey contents of his stomach spilled out in a wet mess down his legs.

The hunter cast the disembowelled human against the wall, breaking bones with barely a shove. With his gladius – a noble blade that had suffered a century's use as little more than a skinning knife – he severed the dying man's head. Blood painted his gauntlets as he held the harvest, turning it over in his hands, seeing the shape of the skull through the pale skin.

He imagined flaying it, first slicing pale peels of skin free, then carving ragged strips of veined meat from the bone itself. The eyes would be pulled from the sockets, and the innards flushed by acidic cleansing oils. He could picture it so clearly, for it was a ritual he'd performed many times before.

The pain started to recede.

In the returning calm, the hunter heard his brothers. There, the prophet's voice. Enraged, as always. There, the wretched one's laughter, grinding against the prophet's orders. The quiet one's questions were a muted percussion beneath all of this. And there, the dangerous one's snarls punctuated everything.

The hunter slowed as he tried to make out their words. They hunted as he hunted, that much he could make out from their distant buzzing. His name – they spoke it again and again. Confusion. Anger.

And yet they spoke of savage prey. Here? In the derelict hallways of this habitation tower? The only savagery was that which they brought themselves.

'Brothers?' he spoke into the vox.

'Where are you?' the prophet demanded. 'Uzas. Where. Are. You.'

'I...' He stopped. The skull lowered in a loosening hand, and the axe lowered alongside it. The walls leered with threatening duality, both stone and steel, both carved and forged. Impossible. Maddeningly impossible.

'Uzas.' That voice belonged to the snarling one. Xarl. 'I swear by my very soul, I will kill you for this.'

Threats. Always the threats. The hunter's lips peeled back from his teeth in a wet grin. The walls became stone once more, and the threatening voices of his brothers melted back into an ignorable buzz. Let them hunt as they wished, and catch up when they could.

Uzas broke into another run, mumbling demands to the god with a thousand names. No prayers left his lips, for no son of Curze would ever speak a word of worship. He commanded the divinities to bless his bloodshed, sparing no thought for whether they might refuse. They had never done so before, and they would not do so now.

MECHANICAL TEETH BIT into armour and flesh. Last cries left screaming mouths. Tears left silver trails down pale cheeks.

To the hunter, these things signified nothing more than the passing of time.

SOON ENOUGH, THE hunter stood within a chapel, licking his teeth, listening to the growl of his axe's engine echoing back off the stone. Broken bodies lay to his left and right, thickening the cool air with blood-stink. The surviving vermin were backed into a corner, raising weapons that couldn't harm him, pleading with words he would only ignore.

His thermal hunting vision cancelled, leaving him watching the prey through targeting locks and red eye lenses. The humans cringed back from him. None of them had even fired a shot.

'Lord...' one of them stammered.

The hunter hesitated. *Lord?* Begging, he was used to. The honorific, he was not.

This time the pain started at his temples, a pressing, knifing plunge to the centre of his skull. The hunter roared and raised his axe. As he moved closer, the humans cowered, embracing one another and weeping.

'A fine display,' the hunter drawled, 'of Imperial soldiering.'

He swung at them, and the axe-blade's grinding teeth met shining metal with a ringing crash.

Another figure stood before him – the whining prophet himself. Their weapons were locked, the blade of gold risen in defence of the cowering Imperials. His own brother was barring his bloodshed.

'Talos,' the hunter spoke the name through blood-wet lips. 'Blood. Blood for the Blood God. Do you see?'

'I am done with this.'

Each crash against his faceplate jerked his head and jarred his senses. His vision blurred over and over in quick succession, his neck snapping back hard enough to send him staggering. The corridor rang with the echo of metal on armour. Disoriented, the hunter snarled as he realised his brother had struck him in the face three times with the butt of his bolter. His mind was so slow. It was difficult to think through the pain. He sensed rather than felt his hands losing their grip on his weapons. The axe and the gladius fell to the ground.

As he regained his balance, he beheld the chapel, and... No. Wait. This was no chapel. It was a corridor. A corridor aboard the–

'Talos, I–'

The dull clang of steel on ceramite echoed again, and the hunter's head was wrenched to the side, the force pulling at his creaking backbone. Talos spun the blade of gold, while the hunter crashed down to the grilled decking onto his hands and knees.

'Brother?' Uzas managed the word through bleeding lips. It was spinal torment to raise his head, but there – behind an overturned table, the floor strewn with home-made trinkets and curios of scavenged metal – two ragged, filthy humans were recoiling from him. An ageing male and female, their faces streaked with grime. One wore a blindfold in the ever-present darkness. A *Covenant* tradition.

The hunter turned his head as his brother's footfalls drew closer. 'Talos. I didn't know I was on the ship. I needed...' He swallowed at the cold threat of judgment in his brother's emotionless eye lenses. 'I thought...'

The prophet aimed the point of his golden blade at the hunter's throat.

'Uzas, hear me well, even if only once in your wretched life. I will kill you the moment another word leaves your viperous lips.'

THE SMELL OF old blood and unwashed metal stained the air around them. Servitors hadn't been directed to clean this chamber in many months.

'He has gone too far.' Mercutian made no effort to hide the reprimand in his voice. 'When I stood with Seventh Claw, we didn't avoid gathering for fear of tearing out each others' throats.'

'Seventh Claw is dead,' Xarl grinned. 'So however they governed themselves, it didn't pay off in the end, did it?'

'With respect, brother, watch your mouth.' Mercutian's up-hiver accent was clipped and regal, while Xarl's swam in the gutter.

Xarl bared his teeth in what would, in a human, have been a smile. In his scarred legionary's features, it was a predator's challenge.

'Children, children,' Cyrion chuckled. 'Isn't it lovely when we gather like this?'

Talos let them argue. He watched from the side of the chamber, his eye lenses tracking every movement, his thoughts remaining his own. His brothers clashed with the banter and baiting so typical of warriors who struggled to keep each other's company away from the battlefield. Each of them wore their hybrid armour: repaired, repainted, re-engineered and resealed a thousand times since they were granted ownership of it so many years before. His own armour was an efficient mess of conflicting marks, formed of trophies taken from a century's worth of slain enemies.

Chained to the interrogation slab in the centre of the room, Uzas twitched again, a reflexive muscle spasm. The joints of his armour whirred with each tremor.

Sometimes, in rare moments of silence and introspection, the prophet wondered what their gene-sire would think of them now: broken,

corrupted, wearing stolen armour and bleeding through every battle
they couldn't flee from. He looked at each of his brothers in turn, a
targeting cross hair caressing their images in silent threat. The bleached
skulls and cracked helms of Blood Angels hung from their armour. Each
wore expressions that melded bitterness, dissatisfaction and directionless
anger. Like war hounds close to slipping the leash, they barked at one
another, and their fists forever strayed near holstered weapons.

His single footstep thudded an echo around the confines of the torture
chamber.

'Enough.'

They fell silent at last, but for Uzas, who was mumbling and drooling
again.

'Enough,' Talos repeated, gentler now. 'What do we do with him?'

'We kill him.' Xarl stroked a fingertip along his own jawline, where the
jagged scar from a Blood Angel gladius had refused to heal cleanly. 'We
break his back, slit his throat, and kick him out of the closest airlock.' He
pantomimed a slow, sad wave. 'Farewell, Uzas.'

Cyrion took a breath but said nothing. Mercutian shook his head, the
gesture one of lamentation, not disagreement.

'Xarl is right.' Mercutian gestured to the prone form of their brother
bound to the table. 'Uzas has fallen too far. With three nights to indulge
his bloodlust on the station, he had no excuse for losing control on
board the *Covenant*. Do we even know how many he killed?'

'Fourteen human crew, three servitors, and Tor Xal from Third Claw.'
As he spoke, Cyrion watched the prone form chained to the table. 'He
took five of their heads.'

'Tor Xal,' Xarl grunted. 'He was almost as bad as Uzas. His death is no
loss. Third Claw is little better. They're weak. We've all seen them in the
sparring circles. I could kill half of them alone.'

'Every death is a loss,' said Talos. 'Every death diminishes us. And the
Branded will want retribution.'

'Don't start that.' Xarl leaned back against the wall, rattling the meat-
hooks that hung there on corroded chains. 'No more lectures, thank you.
Look at the fool. He drools and twitches, after slaughtering twenty of the
crew on a deluded whim. Already, the serfs are whispering of rebellion.
Why is his life worth sparing?'

Mercutian turned black eyes to Talos. 'The Blood Angels cost us a lot of
crew. Even with the menials from Ganges, we must be careful in rationing
human life to a madman's chainblade. Xarl is right, brother. We should
cast the serpent aside.'

Talos said nothing, listening to each of them in turn.

Cyrion didn't meet any of their gazes. 'The Exalted has ordered him
destroyed, no matter what we decide here. If we're going against that
order, we need to have a damn fine reason.'

For a while, the brothers stood in silence, watching Uzas thrash against the chains that held him down. It was Cyrion who turned first, the servos in his neck purring smoothly as he regarded the door behind them.

'I hear something,' he said, reaching for his bolter. Talos was already sealing the collar locks on his helm.

And then, from the corridor beyond, came a vox-altered voice.

'First Claw... We have come for you.'

WITH TOR XAL dead, Dal Karus found himself shouldering an unexpected burden.

In better days, such potential promotion would have come with a ceremony and honour markings added to his armour. And in better days, it would have also been a promotion he actually desired, rather than one he fought for out of desperation. If he did not lead, then one of the others would. Such a catastrophe was to be avoided at all costs.

'I lead us now,' Garisath had said. He'd gestured with his chainsword, aiming the deactivated blade at Dal Karus's throat. 'I lead us.'

'No. You are unworthy.' The words were not Dal Karus's, despite how they echoed his thoughts.

Vejain had stepped forwards, his own weapons drawn, and started circling around Garisath. Before he realised what he was doing, Dal Karus found himself doing the same. The rest of the Branded retreated to the edges of the chamber, abstaining from the leadership challenge either from caution, prudence, or the simple knowledge that they could not best the three warriors that now advanced upon one another.

'Dal Karus?' Garisath's laughter crackled over the vox. Each of them had donned their helmets as soon as they'd learned of Tor Xal's demise. The action demanded retribution, and they would deal with it as soon as their new leader was affirmed. 'You cannot be serious.'

Dal Karus didn't answer. He drew his chainsword with one hand, leaving his pistol holstered, for these ritual challenges were made only with blades. Garisath hunched low, ready for either of the others to attack. Vejain, however, was edging aside, suddenly hesitant.

As with Garisath, Vejain hadn't expected Dal Karus to move into the heart of the chamber. He was more cautious, stepping away and casting red-lensed glances between his two opponents.

'Dal Karus,' Vejain turned the name into a bark of vox. 'Why do you step forward?'

In answer, Dal Karus inclined his head towards Garisath. 'You'd let him lead us? He must be challenged.'

Garisath's mouth grille emitted another grainy chuckle. The burn markings blackening his armour – those curving Nostraman runes branded deep into the ceramite – seemed to writhe in the gloom.

'I will take him,' Vejain grunted. His armour bore similar burns, depicting his own deeds in Nostraman glyphs. 'Will you then challenge me?'

Dal Karus exhaled slowly, letting the sound rasp from his helm's speaker grille. 'You won't win. He will kill you, Vejain. But I'll avenge you. I will cut him down when he's weakened.'

Garisath listened to this exchange with a smile behind his skullish faceplate. He couldn't resist gunning the trigger of his chainsword. It was all the bait Vejain needed.

'I will take him,' the warrior insisted, and charged forwards. The two Night Lords met in a circle of their brothers, chainswords snarling and revving as the blades scraped across layered armour the colour of Terran midnight.

Dal Karus looked away at the end, which came with both inevitability and infuriating speed. The blades were almost worthless against Legion war-plate, and both warriors fell into the practised, traitorous brutality of chopping at each other's armour joints. Vejain grunted as a fist cracked his head back, and the single second he bared his articulated throat armour was more than enough for Garisath to finish him. The chainblade crashed against the softer fibre-bundles encasing Vejain's neck and bit deep – deep enough to grind against bone. Shredded armour rained away. Blood slicked the machine-nerves that scattered across the chamber floor.

Vejain fell to his hands and knees with a clang of ceramite on steel, his life gushing away through a savaged throat. Garisath finished the decapitation with a second swing of his sword. The helm clattered to the decking. The head rolled free. Garisath stopped it with his boot, and crunched it underfoot.

He beckoned with his bloodied blade. 'Next?'

Dal Karus stepped forwards, feeling his blood sing with chemical stimulants – an aching song that spread from the pulse-point injection ports in his ancient armour. He had not raised his blade. Instead, he'd drawn his plasma pistol, which was met with disquieted mutterings. The magnetic coils ribbing the back of the weapon glowed with angry blue phosphorescence, painting a ghostly light over every Night Lord watching. The indrawn hiss of air through the muzzle's intake valves was a rattlesnake's blatant warning.

'Do you all see this?' Garisath put a sneer into his voice. 'Bear witness, all of you. Our brother defiles our laws.'

The pistol juddered in Dal Karus's grip now, the fusion weapon thrumming with the need to discharge its accrued power. 'I will serve no law that does not serve us in kind.' Dal Karus risked a glance to the others. Several of them nodded. Due to his lethality with a blade, Garisath was the leader Third Claw expected, not the one they unanimously desired. Dal Karus's gambit was founded upon it.

'You break tradition,' one of the others, Harugan, spoke into the silence. 'Lower the weapon, Dal Karus.'

'He breaks tradition only because he has the courage enough to do so,' Yan Sar replied, earning several vox-crackling murmurs.

'Garisath must not lead,' said another, and this too earned grunts of assent.

'I will lead!' Garisath snarled. 'It is my right!'

Dal Karus kept the weapon as steady as its shaking power cells would allow. The timing had to be perfect: the weapon needed to be at full charge, and he could not fire unprovoked. This must bear at least some pretence of a righteous execution, not a murder.

Acknowledgment runes chimed on his retinal display, as the members of Third Claw signalled their decision. Garisath must have seen the same, or else surrendered to his frustrations, for he gave a blurt of shrieking vox from his mouth grille and leapt forward. Dal Karus squeezed the trigger, and released the contained force of a newborn sun from the mouth of his pistol.

AFTERWARDS, WHEN SIGHT had returned to each of them, they stood motionless in their communal chamber. Each warrior's armour was dusted with a fine layer of ash: all that remained of Garisath after the blinding flash of plasma release.

'You made your point.' Harugan growled his disapproval, and even the smallest movement – a gesture towards Dal Karus's weapon – sent dust powdering off his armour plating. 'Nothing left to salvage now.'

Dal Karus answered by nodding down at Vejain. 'Some salvage exists. And we are not led by a madman. Take heart in that.'

The others came forwards now, treating Vejain's body with little more respect than they'd show to an enemy's corpse. The body would be dragged to the apothecarion, where its gene-seed organs would be extracted. The armour would be machined off into its component pieces and divided among Vejain's brothers.

'Now you lead,' said Yan Sar.

Dal Karus nodded, little pleased by the fact. 'I do. Will you challenge me? Will any of you challenge me?' He turned to his brothers. None answered immediately, and it was Yan Sar that replied again.

'We will not challenge you. But retribution beckons, and you must lead us to it. First Claw killed Tor Xal.'

'We have lost three souls this day. One to treachery, one to misfortune, one to necessity.' Dal Karus's own beaked faceplate was a Mark VI helm of avian design, painted a dull red to match the others of Third Claw. Snaking burn scars were branded deep into the composite metal. 'If we go against First Claw, we will lose more. And I have no wish to fight the prophet.'

He didn't add that one of the reasons he'd killed Garisath had been in the hope of avoiding the fight now threatening them. 'We are no longer of Halasker's companies. We are the Branded, Third Claw, of the Exalted's warband. We are Night Lords, born anew. A new beginning. Let us not baptise our genesis in the blood of our brothers.'

For a moment, he believed he'd swayed them. They shared glances and muttered words. But reality reasserted itself with crushing finality mere seconds later.

'Vengeance,' promised Yan Sar.

'Vengeance,' the others echoed.

'Then vengeance it is,' Dal Karus nodded, and led his brothers into the very battle he'd murdered Garisath to prevent.

Soon after the accord was reached, the remaining members of Third Claw stalked down the central spinal corridor of the prison deck, blades and bolters in gauntleted hands. What little light existed on the *Covenant of Blood* played across their armour, and shadows pooled in the black rune brands burned into the war-plate.

Voices ahead, from behind the closed bulkhead leading into a side chamber.

'Do we ambush them?' Yan Sar asked.

'No,' Harugan chuckled. 'They know we will not let Tor Xal go unavenged. They are already expecting us, I am sure of it.'

The Branded moved closer to the sealed door.

'First Claw,' Dal Karus called, taking pains to keep any reluctance from bleeding into his voice. 'We have come for you.'

Cyrion watched his auspex's monochrome display screen. The hand-held scanner clicked every few seconds, giving a wash of audible static.

'I count seven out there,' he said. 'Eight or nine, if they're bunched up.'

Talos moved to the doorway, uncoupling his bolter from the mag-lock plating on his thigh armour. The weapon was bulky, rendered ornate by bronzing, bearing two wide-mouth barrels. He still felt a stab of reluctance to carry it so openly. Its bulk didn't discomfort him, but its legacy did.

He called through the sealed door. 'We'll settle the blood debt with a duel. Xarl will fight for First Claw.'

In the chamber, Xarl gave a dirty laugh behind his faceplate. No answer came.

'I'll deal with this,' Talos said to First Claw. He blink-clicked icons on his retinal display, summoning up the runes for other squads in the vox array. The Branded, Third Claw, flashed active.

'Dal Karus?' he asked.

'Talos.' Dal Karus's voice was low over the occluded vox-channel. 'I am sorry for this.'

'How many of you are out there?'

'An interesting question, brother. Does it matter?'

Worth a try. Talos took a breath. 'We count seven of you.'

'Then let us settle on that. Seven still outnumbers four, prophet.'

'Five, if I free Uzas.'

'Seven still outnumbers five.'

'But one of my five is Xarl.'

Dal Karus grunted reluctant acknowledgement. 'That is indeed so.'

'How did you come to lead Third Claw?'

'I cheated,' said Dal Karus. With the words spoken as simple confession, he offered no justification, nor any excuse. Irritatingly, Talos found himself warming to the other warrior.

'This will bleed us both,' Talos said.

'I am not blind to that, prophet. And I did not spit on my allegiance to Halasker just to die on this crippled ship mere months later.' There was nothing of anger in Dal Karus's voice. 'I do not blame you for Uzas's... instability. I dealt with Tor Xal for long enough myself that I am all too familiar with the affliction of taint. But the blood debt must be paid, and the Branded will not settle for a duel of champions. My own actions may have annihilated any lingering worth in that tradition among us, but even before I acted, they were howling for revenge.'

'Then you shall have your blood-price,' the prophet said with a rueful smile, and severed the link.

Talos turned back to his brothers. Cyrion stood at ease, his weapon in his hands, only his slouched shoulder guards giving any indication of his reluctance to leave the chamber. Mercutian could have been carved from granite, so dark and motionless as he stood unbowed by the massive cannon in his fists. The heavy bolter's cavernous barrel thrust from a skull's open maw. Xarl clutched a two-handed chainblade in an easy grip, leaving his bolt weapons locked to his armour within quick reach.

'Let's get on with it,' he said, and even vox-corruption couldn't hide the smile in his voice.

Mercutian crouched, tending to his heavy bolter. The cannon was as unsubtle as Legion weaponry could be: wrapped in industrial chains and capable of vomiting a brutal rain of fire from its fat throat. 'Third Claw will use bolters over blades. If Tor Xal is dead, we won't have much to contend with once we stand within sword's reach. Getting into sword's reach will see us dead, though. They'll cut us to pieces with bolter fire.' He sounded as maudlin as ever.

Xarl barked a laugh and spoke in his gutter Nostraman. 'Smoke grenades as soon as the door opens. That buys us a couple of seconds before their preysight re-tunes. Then we'll bring blades to a gunfight.'

Silence reigned for a moment.

'Free me,' the last member of First Claw snarled.

Four helms turned to their brother, slanted red eyes judging without a trace of human emotion.

'Talos,' Uzas spat the name as he trembled, forcing his speech through clenched teeth. 'Talos. Brother. Free me. Let me stand in midnight clad.'

Something black trickled in a wet leak from his ear. The stink of Uzas's skin was cringingly ripe.

Talos spoke the words as he drew the relic sword from its sheath on his back.

'Release him.'

V

REVENGE

She found Septimus in Blackmarket, and saw him before he noticed her. Through the thin crowd, she watched him as he talked to the gathered serfs and crew. The scruffy fall of his hair almost covered the bionics on the left side of his face, where his temple and cheek had been rebuilt with subtle augmetics of composite metals, contoured to match his facial structure. It was a degree of surgical sophistication she'd rarely seen outside of the wealthiest theocratic covens and noble families of Terra's tallest spires. Even now, the other humans looked upon him with a varied clash of dislike, envy, trust and adoration. Few slaves aboard the *Covenant* wore their value to the Night Lords so openly.

With the communal market chamber less crowded than it had been before the Siege of Crythe, it was also less stifling and oppressive. Unfortunately, without the press of bodies, it was also colder – as cold as the rest of the ship. Her breath misted as she watched the crowd. The attendant hunched alongside her seemed content to mutter to himself.

'I thought we'd captured more... people,' she said to him. When he turned blind eyes up to her and didn't answer, she qualified her statement. 'The new slaves from Ganges. Where are they?'

'In chains, mistress. Chained in the hold. There they stay, until we leave dock.'

Octavia shuddered. This was her home now. She was an undeniable part of what went on here.

Across the chamber, Septimus was still speaking. She had no idea what he was saying. His Nostraman came in a whispering flow, and Octavia could make out maybe one word in ten. Instead of trying to follow the thread of what he was saying, she watched the faces of those he spoke to. Several were scowling or jostling their fellows, but most seemed placated by whatever he was telling them. She smothered a grin at his impassioned sincerity, the way he turned to people with a gentle gesture to make a point, the way he argued with his eyes as well as his words.

The smile died on her lips as she saw one of the faces in the crowd, darkened by weariness. It was a face in mourning, and coping by wearing a mask of grim anger. Rather than interrupt Septimus, Octavia moved through the crowd, apologising softly in Gothic as she made her way closer to the grief-stricken man. He noticed her as she neared, and she saw him swallow.

'*Asa fothala su'surushan,*' he said, dismissing her with a weak wave of his hand.

'*Vaya vey*... um... I...' she felt a blush rising to her cheeks as the words stuck in her mouth. '*Vaya vey ne'sha.*'

The people surrounding her were backing away now. She paid them no heed. Given what was hidden beneath the bandana around her forehead, she was used to being ostracised.

'I haven't seen you since... the battle,' she forced the words to her lips. 'I just wanted to say–'

'*Kishith val'veyalass, olmisay.*'

'But... *Vaya vey ne'sha,*' she repeated. 'I don't understand.' She said it in Gothic in case her halting Nostraman hadn't been clear enough.

'Of course you don't.' The man made the dismissive gesture again. His bloodshot eyes were ringed by the dark circles of a mounting sleep debt, and his voice cracked. 'I know what you wish to say, and I do not wish to hear. No words will bring back my daughter.' His Gothic was rusty from disuse, but emotion lent meaning to the words. '*Shrilla la lerril,*' he sneered at her with a whisper.

'*Vellith sar'darithas, volvallasha sor sul.*' The words came from Septimus, at the heart of the crowd. He pushed through the people to stand before the other man. Although the other slave was surely no older than forty, privation and sorrow had aged him far beyond his years – Septimus, as ragged as he was, was almost youthful in comparison. A brief flicker of greeting passed between Septimus and Octavia as their eyes met, but it was gone as soon as it showed. The artificer looked down at the hunched slave, anger in his human eye. 'Watch your tongue when I can hear the lies you speak,' he warned.

Octavia bristled at being defended when she still had no idea what had been said. She wasn't a bashful maid, needing to be protected to stave off a fainting attack. 'Septimus... I can deal with this. What did you say to me?' she asked the older man.

'I named you a whore that mates with dogs.'

Octavia shrugged, hoping her blush didn't show. 'I've been called worse.'

Septimus stood straighter. 'You are the heart of this unrest, Arkiah. I am not blind. Your daughter was avenged. As poor a fate as it was, that is all that can ever be.'

'She was avenged,' Arkiah answered in Gothic as well, 'but she was not protected.' In his hand, he clutched a Legion medallion. It caught the dim light with treacherous timing.

Septimus rested his hands on the pistols at his hips, hanging in battered leather holsters. 'We are slaves on a warship. I grieved with you at Talisha's loss, but we live dark lives in the darkest of places.' His accent was awkward, and he struggled to find the words. 'Often, we cannot even hope for vengeance, let alone safety. My master hunted her killer. The Blood Angel died a mongrel's death. I watched Lord Talos strangle the murderer, witnessing justice done with my own eyes.'

His own eyes. Octavia glanced automatically to see his human eye, dark and kind, next to the pale blue lens mounted in his chrome eye socket.

'*Tosha aurthilla vau veshi laliss,*' the other man gave a mirthless laugh. 'This vessel is cursed.' Murmurs of agreement started up. It was nothing new. Since the girl's death, talk of omens and misfortune were running rampant among the mortal crew. 'When the new slaves walk among us, we will tell them of the damnation in which they now dwell.'

Octavia couldn't understand Septimus's reply as he slipped back into Nostraman. She withdrew from the crowd, waiting for the gathering to finish, and at the edge of the huge chamber, she sat on an empty table. Her attendant trudged after her, as unbearably loyal as a stray dog she'd made the mistake of feeding.

'Hey,' she nudged him with her boot.

'Mistress?'

'Did you know the void-born?'

'Yes, mistress. The young girl. Only child ever born on the *Covenant.* Dead now, to the Angels of Blood.'

She lapsed back into silence for a while, watching Septimus arguing to quench all talk of rebellion. Strange, that on any given Imperial world, he would probably be a wealthy man with his skills in great demand. He could fly atmospheric and suborbital craft, he spoke several languages, he knew how to use and maintain weapons, and worked with an artisan's care and a mechanic's efficiency on reconstructive artificer duties. Yet here, he was just a slave. No future. No wealth. No children. Nothing.

No children.

A thought struck her, and she gave the little attendant another nudge.

'Please do not do that,' he grumbled.

'Sorry. I have a question.'

'Ask, mistress.'

'How is it that all these years, only one child was born on board?'

The attendant turned his blinded face up to her again. It reminded her of a dying flower trying to face the sun. 'The ship,' he said. 'The *Covenant* itself. It makes us sterile. Wombs wither and seed grows thin.' The little creature gave a childish shrug. 'The ship, the warp, this life. My eyes.' He touched a bandaged hand to his threaded eyes. 'This life changes everything. Poisons everything.'

Octavia chewed her bottom lip as she listened. Strictly speaking, she wasn't human in the most pedantic sense – the genetic coding in a Navigator's bloodline left her in an awkward evolutionary niche, close to being a sub-species of *Homo sapiens*. Her earliest years were filled with lessons and tutors hammering that very fact into her with stern lectures and complicated biological charts. Few Navigators ever bred easily, and children were an incredibly treasured commodity to a Navigator House – the coin with which to purchase a future. Had her life run its pre-planned course, she knew that after a century or two of service she'd be recalled to the family holdings on Terra and linked to another low-level scion from an equally minor house, expected to breed for the good of her father's financial empire. Her capture had rather done away with that idea, and it was one of the aspects of this greasy, dimly lit slavery she actually considered something of a perk.

Even so, her hand strayed to her stomach.

'What's your name?' she asked him.

The figure shrugged with a rustle of dirty rags. She wasn't sure if he'd never had a name, or simply forgotten it, but either way no answer was forthcoming. 'Well,' she forced a smile, 'would you like one?' He shrugged again, and this time, the gesture ended in a growl.

Octavia saw why. Septimus was approaching. Behind him, the crowd was dispersing, going back to their ramshackle market stalls or leaving the communal chamber in small groups.

'Hush, little hound,' the taller pilot smiled. His augmetic eye whirred as it focussed, the blue lens widening like a dilating pupil.

'It's fine,' Octavia patted the hunched man's shoulder. Beneath the ragged cloak, his arm felt cold and lumpy. Not human. Not completely.

'Yes, mistress,' the attendant said softly. The growling ceased, and there was the muffled *click-chuck* of a firearm chambering a round.

Septimus reached forward to brush a stray lock of Octavia's hair behind her ear. She almost tilted her cheek into his palm, warmed by the intimacy of the gesture.

'You look filthy,' he told her, as blunt and cheery as a little boy with good news. Octavia leaned away from his touch even as he was withdrawing his hand.

'Right,' she said. 'Well. Thank you for that observation.' *Idiot.*

'What?'

'Nothing.' As she said the word, her attendant started growling at Septimus again, obviously registering the annoyance in her voice. *Observant little fellow.* She considered giving him another pat on the shoulder. 'Still talking of rebellion?'

Septimus looked over at the diminishing crowds, masking a sigh. 'It is difficult to convince them the vessel is not cursed when we're being murdered by our own masters.' He hesitated, then turned back to her. 'I missed you.'

A nice try, but she wouldn't let herself warm to that. 'You were gone a long time,' she offered, keeping neutral.

'You sound displeased with me. Is it because I said you looked filthy?'

'No.' She barely resisted an irritated smile. *Idiot.* 'Did everything go well?'

Septimus knuckled his scruffy hair back from his face. 'Yes. Why are you angry with me? I don't understand.'

'No reason,' she smiled. *Because we've been docked for three days, and you haven't been to see me. Some friend you are.* 'I'm not angry.'

'You sound angry, mistress.'

'You're supposed to be on my side,' she told her attendant.

'Yes, mistress. Sorry, mistress.'

Octavia tried a change of tack. 'The murders. Was it Uzas?'

'It was, this time.' Septimus met her eyes again. 'First Claw have taken him to the prison deck.'

'He's captured. And there's an influx of new crew members. Maybe there'll be some stability now. Things can return to normal.'

Septimus gave his crooked smile. 'I keep trying to tell you: this *is* normal.'

'So you say,' she sniffed. 'What was the Shriek like? Inside the station, I mean.'

He grinned at the memory. 'It jammed the aura-scryers. Every auspex drowned in interference. Then it slaughtered all in-station and off-station vox, but there was more: it actually killed the lights all across Ganges. I have no idea if Deltrian and the Exalted planned it, or how it worked, but it was a surprise to me.'

'I'm glad you had fun.' She retied her ponytail and checked her bandana was tight. 'It was less amusing for us. The Shriek drinks power like you wouldn't believe. The engines dimmed to almost nothing, and the void shields were down the entire time. I had nothing to do but wait while we drifted for days. I hope we don't use it again.'

'You know they will. It worked, didn't it?' His grin faded when she didn't return it. 'What's wrong? What has happened?'

'*Ashilla sorsollun, ashilla uthullun,*' she said softly. 'What do those words mean?'

He raised an eyebrow. His artificial eye clicked as it tried to mimic the expression. 'It's a rhyme.'

'I know that.' She resisted the urge to sigh. He could be so slow, sometimes. 'What does it mean?'

'It doesn't translate directl–'

She held up a finger. 'If you say, "it doesn't translate directly", to me one more time, I will have my little friend here shoot you in the foot. Understood?'

'Understood, mistress.' Her attendant moved its hands beneath its overcloak.

'Well...' Septimus began with a scowl at the hunched slave. 'It doesn't rhyme in Gothic. That's what I meant. And both *sorsollun* and *uthullun* are words that mean "sunless", but with different... uh... emotions. It means, more or less, "I am blind, I am cold". Why do you ask? What's wrong?'

'Arkiah's daughter. The void-born.'

Septimus's hands, bound in fingerless gloves of scuffed leather, rested on his low-slung gun belt. He'd attended the girl's funeral only five months before, when her parents had let the shrouded corpse be released through the airlock with so many other slain human crew. 'What about her?'

Octavia met his eyes. 'I've been seeing her. I saw her while you were away on the station. And a week ago, I heard her. She called those words to me.'

THE DOOR DIDN'T open. It burst outwards in a storm of debris that filled the corridor with smoke. Emergency alarms sounded at once, sealing nearby bulkheads as the vessel's automated systems registered an enemy attack and the risk of hull breaches.

In the smoky mist, five towering silhouettes ghosted forwards, their slanted red eyes backlit and streaming with targeting data.

Bolter shells cracked and crashed against the walls around them, detonating with the crumpling pops of bursting grenades, showering the legionaries with fragments of iron and burning chunks of explosive shell. Third Claw had opened up the moment their preysight had adjusted to the smoke.

Talos emerged first from the mist, bolter rounds shredding the armour from his war-plate, ripping chunks of ceramite overlay from the cabled musculature. He closed the distance in the span of a heartbeat, swinging his sword in a carving arc. Retinal imagery displayed the grievous damage to his armour in aggressively bright runes, and was immediately joined by the flatline sound of a slain warrior's armour no longer transmitting life signs. – **Garius, Third Claw, Vital Signs Lost** – , his eye lenses warned. Such a shame.

'You've been fighting mortals for too long,' Talos spoke through the stinging bite of nerve nullifiers. His armour injected the fast-acting narcotics right into his heart, spine and bloodstream, but their effects were limited in the face of this horrendous fire. Bolters suffered against Legion armour – they were weapons far better at breaking flesh than ceramite – but despite his mockery, the massed assault was taking its toll.

He didn't even need to wrench his blade clear. The blow had cleaved

Garius's head clean from his shoulders. Talos gripped the bloody collar guard, ignoring his brother's life pissing out from the severed neck in red spurts all over his gauntlet. In death, Garius served as a shield of meat and armour. Detonating shells pounded into the headless corpse until Talos hurled it at the closest member of Third Claw.

Xarl was among them a moment later, his chainblade crashing against a brother's helm hard enough to send the warrior sprawling into the wall. Talos risked a momentary glance to see Xarl's war-plate as chewed up and broken as his own. Xarl was already leaping at another of the Branded, heedless of the damage he'd sustained.

Uzas, ever devoid of grace, had hurled himself at the closest of the enemy, and was doing his level best to punch his gladius through the other warrior's soft throat armour. All the while, he screamed a meaningless screed of syllables into the warrior's faceplate, giving voice to mindless hate. His armour wept fluid from a thousand cracks, but he rammed the short blade home with a howl. The Branded warrior jerked, polluting the vox with his gargling. Uzas laughed as he sawed ineffectively, his sword grating against the dying Night Lord's spine without severing it. A flatline chimed through everyone's helm receptors.

– Sarlath, Third Claw, Vital Signs Lost –

'Blades!' Dal Karus called to his surviving brothers.

Talos ran for him, the Blade of Angels swinging with a trail of crackling force streaming behind. Their swords crashed together, locking fast, neither one of them giving ground. Both warriors spoke through the breathy grunts of painful exertion. 'Foolish... to use... bolters...' Talos grinned behind his faceplate.

'It... was a risk... I admit,' Dal Karus grunted back. The grinding teeth of his chainsword clicked and ticked as they tried to whirr against the golden weapon it parried. Garius's blood spat and popped as it burned dry on Talos's energised blade.

– Vel Shan, Third Claw, Vital Signs Lost –

Talos couldn't see how the kill was made, but he heard Xarl give a roar over the whine of another flatline. He doubled his effort, leaning harder into the struggle, but his damaged armour was betraying his strength. As his muscles burned, his retinal display flickered twice. Power was flashing erratically through his armour systems, and it was all he could do to keep his blade locked to Dal Karus's. He felt the unwelcome drag of his arms growing heavier. A spray of sparks spat from a rent in his back-mounted power pack.

'You are weakening,' his enemy growled.

'And you... are outnumbered,' Talos grinned back.

Dal Karus broke the lock, disengaging savagely enough to send the prophet stumbling backwards. The chainsword skidded across Talos's sundered chestplate, scratching the defiled aquila emblazoned there.

With a curse at his overbalanced swing, Dal Karus did all he could to ignore the flatline chiming – a stream of tinnitus proclaiming the deaths of his brothers.

He moved back, sword up to guard against... against...

Against all of them. Against all of First Claw.

They stood as a pack, surrounded by the bodies of those they'd slain. In the clearing haze, Talos, Xarl, Uzas, Cyrion and Mercutian stood with bloodied blades in their fists. Their armour was shattered into ruin, and for the briefest moment of empathy, Dal Karus envisioned the amount of labour involved in repairing such punishment. Talos and Xarl stood shredded by gunfire, their armour plating ripped away and the under-layers blackened, punctured and burned. Their helms were dented to the point of malformation. Xarl was missing an eye lens, and both of Cyrion's were cracked beyond easy repair. Half of Uzas's features were visible through his broken faceplate. The leader of the Branded, the last soul to hold the title, locked eyes with the smirking, drooling fool.

'This is your fault,' Dal Karus said. 'Your madness has cost us every life taken this night.'

Uzas licked teeth made dark by bleeding gums. Dal Karus doubted the beast even understood his words.

'Let's finish this.' He set the teeth of his chainblade whirring again, chewing air. 'Do not dishonour Third Claw by making me wait for my death.'

Cyrion's laughter broke out, stripped raw by his vox-speakers. 'Dis-honour,' he wheezed the word through chuckles. 'A moment, please.' He disengaged the seals at his collar, removing his scarred helm and wiping his eyes on a deed-parchment he tore from his armour. '*Honour,* he says, as if it matters. These words from a warrior who was a murderer at thirteen, and a rapist two years later. *Now* he cares about honour. That's beautiful.'

Talos raised his bolter. The double-barrelled weapon was engraved with the deeds of a fallen warrior who'd achieved so much more than any of those in its new wielder's presence.

'Please,' Dal Karus sighed, 'do not execute me with Malcharion's weapon.'

'Remove your helm.' The prophet didn't move as he spoke. Sparks and lubricating oils still flicked and dripped from the wounds in his war-plate. 'You surrendered any right to choose your death the moment you forced this idiotic confrontation.'

Slowly, Dal Karus complied. Bareheaded, he faced First Claw. The deck smelled of blood's spicy scent, thinned by the chemical reek of bolter shell detonations. He offered a rueful smile, almost an apology.

'Why didn't you just kill Uzas?' he asked. 'It would have ended this before it began.'

'You are not foolish enough to truly believe that,' Talos spoke softly, 'and neither am I. This, as with all things in the Legion, is a wound torn open by revenge.'

'I wish to join First Claw.'

'Then you should not have come against us in midnight clad.' He kept his aim at Dal Karus's face. 'If you cannot dissuade your own squad from petty vengeance that costs loyal lives, what use are you to the remnants of the Legion?'

'You cannot control Uzas. Is there a difference? Are your lives worth so much more than ours?'

'Evidently they are,' Talos replied, 'because we are the ones with our guns to your face, Dal Karus.'

'Talos, I–'

Both barrels bellowed. Tiny gobbets of meat with wet fragments of skull clattered across the walls and against their armour. Headless, the body toppled, crashing against the corridor wall before sliding down, slumping in crooked, graceless repose.

They stood without speaking a word to one another for some time. Savaged armour sparked and made unwelcome joint-grinding sounds as they lingered in the slaughter they'd created.

At last, it was Talos who broke the stillness. He gestured at the bodies. 'Drag them. Septimus will strip their armour.'

'Two months.'

Talos laughed. 'Please do not joke with me, Septimus. I am not in the mood.'

The human slave scratched his cheek where the polished metal met pale skin, as he stared at the carnage strewn across his workshop. The seven corpses, with their armour suffering only minimal damage – they could be stripped and the meat flushed into the void within a day. But all five members of First Claw were barely able to stand with the damage done to their war-plate. Oil and lubricant ran in drying stains from cracked-open punctures. Dents needed to be beaten out, mangled ceramite had to be cut free and completely replaced, torn layers of composite metals needed to be resealed, repainted, reformed...

And the subdermal damage was even worse. False musculature made of fibre-bundle cables needed to be reworked, rethreaded and rebuilt. Joint servos and gears had to be replaced or repaired. Stimulant injectors needed sterilising and reconstructing. Interface ports had to be completely retuned, and all of that was before the most complicated repairs were undertaken: the sensory systems in each helm's retinal display.

'I'm not joking, master. Even using these parts as salvage, it will take more than a week for each suit of armour. Recoding their systems, rebuilding them to your bodies, retuning their interfaces to each of you... I cannot do it faster than that. I'm not sure anyone could.'

Cyrion stepped forward. A misfiring stabiliser in his left leg gave him a dragging limp, while his own features were cracked and bleeding.

'And if you worked on only mine and your master's?'

Septimus swallowed, careful to avoid Uzas's stare. 'Two weeks, Lord Cyrion. Perhaps three.'

'Mortal. Fix mine.' All eyes turned to Uzas. He snorted at them. 'What? I need my armour tended to, the same as each of you,' he said.

Talos disengaged his helm's seals with a snake's hiss of vented air pressure. Removing the mangled ceramite took three attempts, and the prophet's face was a bruised and bloody painting of varied wounds. One of his eyes was crusted closed by a foul-looking scab, and the other glared, clean and black, devoid of an iris like all of the Nostramo-born.

'Firstly, do not address my artificer – and our *pilot* – as if he were a hygiene slave. Show some respect.' He paused to wipe his bloody lips on the back of his gauntlet. 'Secondly, you bear the blame for putting us in these straits. Your urge to howl your way around the crew decks drinking the blood of mortals has removed us from being battle-ready for two months. Will you be the one to tell the Exalted he has lost two Claws in one night?'

Uzas licked his teeth. 'The Branded chose to face us. They should've walked away. Then they'd be alive.'

'It is always so simple for you.' Talos narrowed the one eye that still worked. He filtered his tone through a last attempt at patience, seeking to keep the strain of his wounds from reaching his lips. 'What madness infests your mind? What makes you incapable of understanding what you have cost us tonight?'

Uzas shrugged. The bloody handprint painted onto his faceplate was all the expression he showed to them. 'We won, didn't we? Nothing else matters.'

'Enough,' Cyrion shook his head, resting a cracked gauntlet on Talos's shoulder guard. 'It's like trying to teach a corpse to breathe. Give up, brother.'

Talos moved away from Cyrion's placating hand. 'There will come a night when the word *brother* is no longer enough to save you, Uzas.'

'Is that a prophecy, seer?' the other warrior grinned.

'Smile all you like, but remember these words. When that night comes, I will kill you myself.'

Each of them tensed as the door's chime sounded. 'Who comes?' Talos called. He had to blink to clear his blurring vision. The wounds he'd taken weren't healing with the alacrity he'd expected, and he had the grating sense that the damage beneath his armour was worse than he'd first thought.

A fist thumped against the door three times. 'Soul Hunter,' the voice on the other side crackled by way of greeting. Its tone was surprisingly rich with respect, despite being as harsh and dry as a vulture's caw. 'We must speak, Soul Hunter. So very much to speak of.'

'Lucoryphus,' Talos lowered his blade, 'of the Bleeding Eyes.'

VI

HONOUR THY FATHER

LUCORYPHUS ENTERED THE chamber in a bestial stalk, prowling on all fours. His feet, sheathed in ceramite boots, were warped into armoured claws: curling, multi-jointed and wickedly bladed, no different from a hawk's talons. Walking had been a bane to Lucoryphus for centuries – even this ungainly crawl was difficult – and the sloping thrusters mounted upon the warrior's back spoke of denied flight, a legionary caged by the confines of these corridors.

His eyes bled, and from this curse he took his name. Upon the white faceplate, twin scarlet tear-trails ran from the slanted eye lenses. Lucoryphus of the Bleeding Eyes, with his avian helm twisted into a daemon's visage mouthing a silent scream, watched with a predator's eyes. Machine-growls sounded in his cabled neck joints as the warrior's muscles tensed with unintentional tics. He regarded each of the gathered Night Lords in turn, the avian helm snapping left and right with an eye for prey.

He'd been like them once. Oh, yes. Just like them.

His armour bore little evidence of allegiance to his Legion or bloodline. Each of his warriors displayed their bond the same way: each bore the red tears of their leader reflected on their own faceplates. The Bleeding Eyes were a cult unto themselves first, and sons of the VIII Legion second. Talos wondered where the rest of them were at the moment. They represented fully half of the additional strength the Exalted's warband had taken on from recovering Halasker's companies on Crythe.

'The Exalted sends me to you.' Lucoryphus's voice made words from the sound of fingernails scratching down sandpaper. 'The Exalted is wrathful.'

'The Exalted is seldom ever anything else,' Talos pointed out.

'The Exalted,' Lucoryphus paused to hiss air in through his jagged mouth grille, 'is wrathful with First Claw.'

Cyrion snorted. 'That's not exactly a unique occurrence, either.'

Lucoryphus gave an irritated bark of noise, not far from a falcon's shriek, but flawed by vox corruption. 'Soul Hunter. The Exalted requests your presence. In the apothecarion.'

Talos placed his helm on the workshop table before Septimus. The mortal didn't disguise his sigh as he started turning it over in his hands.

'Soul Hunter,' Lucoryphus grated again. 'The Exalted requests your presence. *Now.*'

With his face marred by the wounds he'd suffered only an hour before, Talos stood motionless. He towered above the hunched Raptor, in armour devastated by his brothers' recent revenge. On his back, the golden blade stolen from the Blood Angels reflected what little light existed in the artificer's chamber. On his hip, clamped by magnetic seals, rested the massive double-barrelled bolter of an Eighth Legion hero.

By contrast, Lucoryphus of the Bleeding Eyes had come unarmed. A curious gesture from the Exalted.

'The Exalted requested,' Talos smiled, 'or demanded?'

Lucoryphus twitched with an involuntary muscle spasm. His avian head jerked, and the daemonic faceplate released a hissing breath. His left talon-hand snapped shut, the clawed fist trembling. When the fingers unlocked, they curled open on squealing metal joints.

'*Requested.*'

'First time for everything,' said Cyrion.

THE EXALTED LICKED its teeth.

It still wore its armour for the most part, though the ceramite plating had long since become part of its altered flesh. The apothecarion was expansive, but the Exalted's nature forced it into an uncomfortable hunch to avoid scraping its horned helm across the ceiling. All around it was silence – the silence of abandonment. This chamber hadn't seen any real use in many years. As the Exalted stroked a taloned finger across a surgical table, he reflected how the decades of neglect would soon be undone.

The creature moved over to the cryogenic vault. A wall of sealed glass cylinders, all racked and stored in perfect order, each etched in Nostraman with the names of the fallen. The Exalted growled low, a tormented breath, as its knife-like digits scratched squealing streaks down the metal vault racks. So many names. So very many.

It closed its eyes and listened, for a time, to the *Covenant*'s heartbeat. The Exalted breathed in unison with the distant rhythmic thrum of the fusion reactors, rumbling as the engines idled in dock. It listened to the whispers, the screams, the shouts and the blood-borne pulses of everyone on board. All of it echoed through the hull into the creature's mind – a constant sensory tide that took more and more effort to ignore as the years passed.

Rarely, it would hear laughter, almost always from the mortals as they endured their dim, dull existences within the ship's black bowels. The

Exalted was no longer sure how to react to the sound, nor what it could really signify. The *Covenant* was the creature's fortress, a monument to both its own pain and the pain it inflicted upon its grandfather's galaxy. Laughter was a sound that pulled at the Exalted, incapable of dredging any true memories, yet still whispering that, once, the creature would have understood such a sound. It would've made the sound itself, in the age when 'It' had been 'Him'.

Its lips peeled back from its shark's teeth in a grin it didn't feel. How times changed. And soon, they would change again.

Talos. Lucoryphus. The knowledge of their presence didn't come in simple recognition of their names. It was their thoughts drifting closer, bunched tight like fused writing and polluted by fragments of their personalities. Their approach came upon the Exalted like a whispering, unseen tide. The creature turned a moment before the apothecarion's doors opened on protesting gears.

Lucoryphus inclined his head. The Raptor stalked in on all fours, the sloping thrusters on its back shifting side to side in sympathy with the warrior's awkward gait. Talos didn't bother to salute. He didn't even acknowledge the Exalted with a nod. Instead, the prophet entered slowly, his armour a mauled palette of absolute ruination, and his face little better.

'What do you want?' he asked. One of his eyes was buried beneath strips of torn pale skin and weeping scabs. His head was laid open to the bone, and the flesh was scorched and angry. Damage from a bolter shell, and one that had almost killed him. Interesting.

Despite the prophet's typical undignified defiance, the Exalted felt a moment's gratitude that Talos had come in such a condition.

'You are wounded,' it pointed out, its voice a draconic murmur. 'I can hear your hearts labouring to beat. The blood-stink... the mushy, liquid concussion of overstrained organs... Talos, you are closer to death than you appear. And yet you come before me now. I appreciate your display of trust.'

'Third Claw is dead.' The prophet spoke as bluntly as always. 'First Claw is crippled. We need two months to recover.'

The Exalted inclined its tusked head in acknowledgement. It knew these things already, of course, but the fact the prophet reported it like an obedient soldier was enough to work with. For now.

'Who broke your face?'

'Dal Karus.'

'And how did Dal Karus die?'

Talos moved his hand from the great puncture wound in his side. The gauntlet came away coated in a sheen of blood. 'He died begging for mercy.'

Lucoryphus, hunched atop one of the surgical tables, emitted a shrieking snicker from his vocalisers. The Exalted grunted before speaking. 'Then we are stronger without him. Did you harvest Third Claw's gene-seed?'

The prophet wiped spittle from his lips. 'I had servitors store the bodies in the cryo-vaults. I will harvest them later, when we have a greater supply of preservative solution.'

The Exalted turned its gaze upon the mortuary vaults: a row of lockers built into the far wall.

'Very well.'

Talos didn't hide his wince as he took a breath. The pain of his wounds, the Exalted suspected, must border on excruciating. This, too, was interesting. Talos had not come out of obedience. Even grievously injured, he had come because of the location the Exalted had chosen. Curiosity could motivate even the most stubborn souls. There could be no other answer.

'I am tired of this existence, my prophet.' The creature let the words hang in the cold air between them. 'Aren't you?'

Talos seemed on edge, taken aback by the remark. 'Be specific,' he said through bleeding gums.

The Exalted stroked its claws down the sealed gene-seed pods again, leaving theatrical scratches on the precious containers. 'You and I, Talos. Each of us is a threat to the other's existence. Ah, ah. Do not even think to argue. I do not care whether you are as ambitionless as you claim, or if you dream of my death each time you allow yourself to sleep. You are a symbol, an icon, for the disenfranchised and the discontented. Your life is a blade at my throat.'

The prophet made his way to another operating table, idly inspecting the hanging steel arms that dangled slack from the ceiling-mounted surgical machinery. A rime of dust painted the table's surface grey. When he brushed the powder aside with his gauntlet, the surface beneath was stained brown by old blood.

'Doloron died here,' he said softly. 'Thirty-six years ago. I pulled his gene-seed myself.'

The Exalted watched as Talos indulged in memory. The creature could be patient, when the moment required it. Nothing would be gained by rushing now. When the prophet faced the Exalted once more, his good eye was narrowed.

'I know why you summoned me,' he said.

The Exalted inclined its head, grinning between its tusks. 'I suspect you do.'

'You want me to begin rebuilding our numbers.' Talos raised his left arm, holding it out for the Exalted's inspection. Something sparked in his elbow joint. 'I am no longer an Apothecary. I haven't carried the ritual tools for a long time. None of the fresh blood from Halasker's squads have endured the training, either.' Perversely warming to speaking of their dire straits, Talos gestured around the chamber. 'Look at this place. The ghosts of dead warriors locked in cold storage, and three dozen surgery tables gathering dust. The equipment is little more than scrap due to age, neglect and battle damage. Even Deltrian couldn't repair most of this.'

The Exalted licked its maw with a black tongue. 'What if I could replenish all that was lost? Would you then replenish our ranks?' The creature hesitated, and its deep voice drew in a breath somewhere between a growl and a snarl. 'We have no future if we remain divided. You must see it as clearly as I. Blood of the gods, Talos – don't you wish to be strong again? Don't you wish a return to the times when we could face our foes, to chase them down like prey, without endlessly fleeing before them?'

'We are above half-strength, but only barely.' Talos leaned on the surgical table. 'I've done a soul count myself. The Blood Angels butchered over a hundred of the crew, and almost thirty of our warriors. We are no better than before we inherited Halasker's men, but at least we are no worse.'

'No worse?' The Exalted tongued aside the stalactites of saliva that linked its teeth. '*No worse?* Do not turn a blind eye to your own sins, Talos. You have already slain seven of them this very night.'

Metal wrenched in protesting chorus with the harsh words. The Exalted's monstrous talon deformed the wall where the creature gripped too hard. With a grunt, it pulled its claw free. 'Halasker's warriors have been with us a matter of months, and already the infighting is savage enough to see bloodshed almost every night. We are dying, prophet. You, who can stare down the paths of the future, have no excuse to be so blind. Stare now, and tell me if you see us surviving another century.'

Talos didn't answer that. It didn't need an answer. 'You call me here, proposing a truce I don't understand to a conflict I'm not willingly fighting. I do not want to inherit Malcharion's mantle. I don't want to lead what remains of us. I am not your rival.'

Lucoryphus emitted another static-laden burst of noise – either a hissing laugh or a derisive snort. Talos didn't know the warrior well enough to tell. 'Soul Hunter carries the war-sage's weapon, yet claims not to be Malcharion's heir. Amusing.'

The prophet ignored the Raptor, focussing on the creature that had once been his commander. Before he spoke, he had to swallow a mouthful of blood that welled up from the back of his tongue.

'I do not understand, Vandred. What has changed to make you speak like this?'

'Ruven.' The name was spat as a curse as the Exalted turned its bulk, resting both of its warped claws against the vault wall. Hunched, growling, it stared at the genetic treasure within. 'At Crythe, when we fled before the wrath of the Blood Angels. That night poisons my thoughts even now. Ruven, that thrice-damned wretch, blithely dictating to us as if he were anything more than the Warmaster's peon. I will not be commanded by one who abandoned the Legion. I will not kneel before a traitor, nor heed the words of a weakling. I – *We* – are better than that.'

The Exalted turned again, its black eyes staring with the passionless, soulless intensity of a creature born in the ocean's silent depths. 'I wish to be proud once more. Proud of our war. Proud of my warriors. Proud to stand in midnight clad. We must rise again, greater than before, or be forgotten forever. I will fight that fate, brother. I want you to fight it with me.'

Talos looked over the decrepit machinery and the abandoned tables. The Exalted couldn't help but admire the warrior's restraint in swallowing the pain he must be feeling. Something, some restrained emotion, glinted behind the prophet's good eye.

'To repair the ship and restore our strength, we'll need to dock at Hell's Iris again.'

'We will,' the Exalted grunted.

Talos didn't reply to that. He let the silence speak for him.

The Exalted licked its blackened maw. 'Perhaps we won't see quite as much bloodshed this time.'

At that, Talos took a pained breath. 'I'll help you,' he said at last.

As the prophet walked from the room, the Exalted's cracked lips stretched back from its rows of stained teeth in something approximating a smile. Behind Talos, the door sealed with a grinding clunk.

'Of course you will,' the creature whispered wetly into the cold air.

THE DOOR CLOSED, leaving him alone in the sub-spinal corridor to reflect on the Exalted's words. Talos didn't labour under any delusion – the creature's offer of truce was founded in its own gain, and none of the Exalted's assurances would keep the prophet from watching his back at every opportunity. The *Covenant* wasn't safe. Not with the tensions boiling between Claws.

When he judged he'd come far enough, Talos slowed in his stride. Wiping his good eye free of blood was a constant irritant. The flayed half of his face was bitter with chill now, and the air stroked his skull with unpleasant fingers. Beneath it all, his pulse did little more than push pain around his body.

Remaining out here alone was unwise. Upon leaving the apothecarion, the first place he needed to reach was the slave holds. If the Exalted wished the warband to stand stronger than ever before, that required trained slaves, gunnery menials, artificers, manufacturers, and it required legionaries. This last need was the hardest to fulfil, but it could be done. Ganges Station had surrendered a bounty in flesh, as well as plunder.

The prophet turned into a side corridor, feeling his hearts clenching in his chest at the movement. They didn't beat, they hummed: buzzing as they overworked themselves. A fresh wave of nausea gripped him in an unwelcome and unfamiliar embrace. The genetic resculpting done to him as a youth had all but banished the capacity to feel dizzy in the human biological sense, but intense stimuli could still be disorienting. Evidently pain could, too.

Four steps. Four steps down the northward corridor, before he crashed against the wall. Blood tainted his tongue with a coppery sting, mixing with the caustic juices in his saliva glands. An exhalation became a purge as he vomited blood onto the decking. The puddle hissed and bubbled on the steel: just enough corrosive spit had washed into the blood for it to become acidic.

Something locked in his knee joint, almost definitely a cord of fibrous wirework too damaged to bend any more. The prophet pushed off from the wall and limped away from the still bubbling blood-vomit, moving alone through the ship's darkened tunnels. Each step brought fresh pain blooming beneath his skin. With a lurch, the world turned. Metal rang out against metal.

'Septimus,' he said to the darkness. For a time, he breathed in and out, working the ship's stale air through his body, feeling something hot and wet drip from his cracked skull. Shouting for a slave wasn't going to help him now. A curse upon Dal Karus's bones. For a vindictive moment, he imagined granting Dal Karus's helm to the slaves to use as a chamber pot. Tempting. Tempting. The prospect of such childish vengeance brought a guilty smile to his bleeding lips, even if the reality of such an act was too petty to really consider.

Forcing himself back to his feet took an age. Was he dying? He wasn't certain. He and Xarl had borne the brunt of Third Claw's bolter fire – their armour was devastated, and Talos was well aware how savage his wounds were if his blood wouldn't clot to seal the great rupture in his side. What remained of his face was a lesser concern, but if he didn't deal with that soon, he'd need extensive bionic implantation to repair the damage.

Another dozen steps sent his vision swimming. Blinking his eyes wasn't enough to clear them, and the telltale sting in pulse points was a stark indication that his armour had already flooded his system with synthetic adrenaline and chemical pain inhibitors to incautious levels.

The Exalted was right. His wounds were graver than he'd wished to reveal. Blood loss was starting to steal the sensation in his hands, and he felt leaden below his knees. The slave holds could wait an hour. Nerveless fingers felt for the secondary vox-link in his gorget.

'Cyrion,' he said into the link. 'Septimus.' How short, the scroll of names he could call to in perfect trust. 'Mercutian,' he breathed. And then, surprising himself, 'Xarl.'

'Prophet.' The reply came from behind. Talos turned, breathing heavily from the effort of staying on his feet. 'We must speak,' the newcomer said. It took a moment for the prophet to recognise the voice. His vision was getting no clearer.

'Not now.' He didn't reach for his weapons. As a threat it would be too obvious, and he wasn't sure he could grip them with any conviction anyway.

'Something wrong, brother?' Uzas delighted in tasting that last word. 'You look unwell.'

How to answer that? The constriction beneath his ribcage told of at least one lung collapsing. The fever had the sweaty, unclean edge of sepsis, a gift from the myriad bolter shell fragments punched into his body. Add the blood loss and severe biological trauma, coupled with his weakened state suffering an overdose on the automatically administered combat narcotics... The list went on. As for his left arm... that no longer moved at all. Perhaps it would need replacing. That thought was far from pleasant.

'I need to get to Cyrion,' he said.

'Cyrion is not here.' Uzas made a show of looking around the tunnel. 'Only you and I.' He stepped closer. 'Where were you going?'

'The slave holds. But they can wait.'

'So now you limp back to Cyrion.'

Talos spat a mouthful of corrosive, pinkish saliva. It ate into the decking with glee. 'No, now I stand here arguing with you. If you have something to say, make it quick. I have duties to perform.'

'I can smell your blood, Talos. It flows from your wounds like a prayer.'

'I have never prayed in my life. I'm not about to start now.'

'You're so literal. So blunt. So blind to anything outside your own pain.' The other warrior drew his blade – not the weighty chainaxe, but a silver gladius the length of his forearm. Like the rest of First Claw, he kept his weapon of last resort sheathed at his shin. 'So confident,' Uzas stroked the sword's edge, 'that you will always be obeyed.'

'I saved your life tonight. Twice.' Talos smiled through the blood sheeting his face. 'And you repay me by whining?'

Uzas still toyed with his gladius, turning it over in his gauntlets, examining the steel with false nonchalance. The bloodstained handprint was a painted smear across Uzas's faceplate. Once, on a single night long ago, it had been real blood. Talos remembered the moment a young woman had struggled in his brother's grip, her bloody fingers pushing with absolute futility against Uzas's helm. A city burned around them. She was writhing, struggling to avoid being disembowelled by the very blade now in his brother's hands.

After that night, Uzas ensured the image remained painted onto his faceplate. A reminder. A personal icon.

'I don't like how you look at me,' Uzas said. 'Like I am broken. Cracked by flaws.'

Talos leaned over, letting dark blood trickle between his teeth to drip onto the decking. 'Then change, brother.' The prophet straightened with a pained hiss, licking the taste of rich copper from his lips. 'I will not apologise for seeing what stands before me, Uzas.'

'You've never seen clearly.' The warrior's vox-voice was laden with static, flensing away any emotion. 'Always your way, Talos. Always the prophet's way.' He regarded his reflection in the gladius. 'Everything else is corrupt, or ruined, or wrong.'

The chemical taste of stimulants was acrid on the back of his tongue. Talos resisted the urge to reach for the Blood Angel blade strapped to his back. 'Is this going to be a lecture? I'm thrilled you've managed to piece more than four words together into a sentence, but could we discuss my perceptions when I'm not bleeding to death?'

'I could kill you now.' Uzas stepped closer still. He aimed the point of the blade at the defiled aquila sculpted over the prophet's chest, then let it rise to rest against Talos's throat. 'One cut, and you die.'

Blood trickled onto the blade, drip-drip-dripping from Talos's chin. It left the edges of his lips in trails like tears.

'Get to the point,' he said.

'You stare at me like I'm diseased. Like I'm cursed.' Uzas leaned closer, his painted faceplate glaring into his brother's eyes. 'You look upon the Legion the same way. If you hate your own bloodline, why remain part of it?'

Talos said nothing. The ghost of a smile played at the corner of his mouth.

'You are *wrong*,' Uzas hissed. The blade bit, the barest parting of skin against the metal's edge. With that gentle stroke of steel on skin, blood welled onto the silver. 'The Legion has always been this way. Your eyes have taken millennia to open, and you recoil from the truth. I honour the primarch. I walk in his shadow. I kill as he killed – *I kill because I can*, the way he could. I hear the cries of distant divinities, and I take power from them without offering worship. They were weapons in the Great Betrayal, and they remain weapons in the Long War. I honour my father, the way you never have. I am more his son than you've ever been.'

Talos stared into his brother's eye lenses, picturing the drooling visage behind the skulled faceplate. Slowly, he reached for the blade at his throat, lifting it away from his skin.

'Are you finished, Uzas?'

'I tried, Talos.' Uzas jerked the blade back, sheathing it in a smooth motion. 'I tried to salvage your pride by telling you honestly and clearly. Look at Xarl. Look at Lucoryphus. Look at the Exalted. Look at Halasker, or Dal Karus, or any son of the Eighth Legion. The blood on our hands is there because human fear tastes so very fine. Not through vengeance, or righteousness, or to ensure our father's name echoes through the ages.'

We are the Eighth Legion. We kill because we were born to kill. We slay because it is fuel for the soul. Nothing else remains to us. Accept that, and... and stand... with us.' Uzas finished with a wet, burbling growl, taking a step backwards to steady himself.

'What's wrong with you?'

'Too many words. Too much talk. The pain is back. Will you heed me?'

Talos shook his head. 'No. Not for a moment. You say our father accepted everything I hate. If that were true, whyſ did he consign our home world to flames? He burned a civilisation to ash, purely to stop the cancer spreading through his Legion. You're my brother, Uzas. I will never betray you. But you are wrong, and I will save you from this suffering if I can.'

'Don't need saving.' The other warrior turned his back, his tone ripe with disgust. 'Always so blind. I don't need to be saved. Tried to make you see, Talos. Remember. Remember tonight. I tried.'

Talos watched his brother's retreating back as Uzas moved into the shadows.

'I'll remember.'

VII

FLIGHT

FREEDOM.

A relative concept, Maruc reflected, *when I have no idea where I am*. But it was a start.

Time was fluid when nothing ever changed. At his best estimate, they'd kept him chained down here like a dog for six or seven days. With no way to know for sure, he founded the guess on the amount people slept, and how much they'd been forced to shit themselves.

His world was reduced to a blanket of darkness and the smell of human waste. Every so often in the numberless hours, dull light from lamp packs would spear around the grouped people as the ship's pale crew came in with salted strip-meat rations and tin mugs of brackish water. They spoke in a language Maruc had never heard before, hissing and *ash-ash-ash*-ing at each other. None of them ever addressed their captives. They came in, fed the prisoners, and left. Immersed in darkness again, the captives barely had enough chain between each of them to move more than a metre apart.

With the exaggerated stealth he'd used on Ganges, he slipped the iron ring off his chafed ankle. He was missing his boots, filthy and standing with his socks in a puddle of cold piss. *Still*, he thought again, *it's definitely a start*.

'What are you doing?' asked the man next to him.

'Leaving.' *What a question.* 'I'm getting out of here.'

'Help us. You can't just go, you have to help us.' He could hear heads turning in his direction, though none of them could see through the absolute blackness. More voices joined the plea.

'Help me.'

'Don't leave us here...'

'Who's free? Help us!'

He hissed at them to be quiet. The press of their stinking bodies was a clammy, meaty pressure all around. The slaves stood in the pitch darkness, shackled at the ankles, clad in whatever they'd been wearing when they'd been dragged from the decks of Ganges Station. Maruc had no idea how many of them were in this chamber with him, but it sounded like a few dozen. Their voices echoed off the walls. Whatever storage hold they'd been dumped in, it was big. The ship that had attacked Ganges was clearly not something to mess with, killers from myth or not.

I've decided not to die. It sounded foolish even to himself.

'I'm going for help,' he said, keeping his voice low. It was easy enough – dehydration roughened his throat, almost silencing him completely.

'Help?' Bodies jostled against him as someone way ahead moved position. 'I'm in Station Defence,' he called back in a harsh whisper. 'Everyone's dead on Ganges. How did you get free?'

'I worked my shackle loose.' He stepped away, blindly feeling through the press of bodies to where he hoped the door was. People cursed him and pushed back, as if offended by his freedom.

Relief flooded him when his outstretched hands grazed the cold metal wall. Maruc began to feel his way left, seeking the door with filthy fingertips. If he could open it, there was a chance that–

There. His questing hands met the door's ridged edge. Now, did it open by a pressure plate mounted on the wall, or a codepad?

Here. Here it is. Maruc brushed his fingertips along the raised keys, feeling a standard nine-button codepad. Each of the buttons was larger than he'd expected, and faintly indented by use.

Maruc held his breath, hoping to slow his clamouring heart. He keyed in six buttons at random.

The door slid open on ungreased tracks, groaning loud enough to wake the dead. Light from the other side spilled into Maruc's eyes.

'Uh... hello,' said a female voice.

'GET BACK,' SEPTIMUS warned. He had both pistols in his hands, aimed at the escaped slave's head. 'Another step. That's right.'

Octavia rolled her eyes. 'He's unarmed.'

Septimus didn't lower his bulky pistols. 'Shine the light inside. How many are free?' Octavia complied, panning the spear of light over the grim scene.

'Just him.'

'*Forfallian dal sur shissis lalil na sha dareel.*' Septimus's words were lost on her, but his face showed he was cursing. 'We must be cautious. Watch yourself.'

She glanced at him for a moment. *Watch yourself?* As if she needed to be told to be careful? *Idiot.*

'Of course,' she huffed. 'A real horde of danger here.'

'I protect mistress.' Her attendant, ever present at Octavia's side, had a grubby sawn-off shotgun clutched in his bandaged hands. His sealed eyes stared at the freed slave. She bit back the very real need to punch both of them for their overprotective swaggering.

'He's unarmed,' she repeated, gesturing at Maruc. 'He... *Sil vasha*... uh... *Sil vasha nuray.*'

Her attendant sniggered. Octavia shot him a look.

'That means, "He has no arms",' Septimus replied. He still hadn't lowered his guns. 'You. Slave. How did you get free?'

When the glare faded, Maruc found himself staring at three people. One was a hunchbacked little freak in a sackcloth cloak with his eyes sewn shut. Next to him, a tall girl with dark hair and the whitest skin he'd ever seen on a woman. And next to her, a scruffy fellow with bionics on his temple and cheekbone, with two pistols aimed right at Maruc's face.

'I worked my shackles loose,' he admitted. 'Look... Where are we? What are you doing to us?'

'My name is Septimus.' He still didn't lower the guns. 'I serve the Legiones Astartes aboard this ship.' His voice carried into the chamber. No one spoke. 'I'm here to find out each of your professions and areas of expertise, to determine your value to the Eighth Legion.'

Maruc swallowed. 'There is no Eighth Legion. I know my mythology.'

Septimus couldn't entirely fight down the smile. 'Talk like that will get you killed on this ship. What was your duty on Ganges?' As the guns came down, so did Maruc's hands. He was suddenly uncomfortably aware that he needed a shower like never before.

'Manufaction, mostly.'

'You worked in the refinery?'

'Construction. At the conveyance belts. Assembly line stuff.'

'And the machinery?'

'Some of it. When they broke down and needed a kick.'

Septimus hesitated. 'That was difficult work.'

'You're telling me.' A strange pride flowed through him at that moment. 'I know it was a grind. I was the one doing it.'

Septimus holstered his guns. 'After we have done this, you are coming with me.'

'I am?'

'You are.' Septimus coughed politely. 'You will also need to bathe.' He entered the chamber, and the others followed him. Octavia's attendant kept his shotgun gripped tight. The Navigator offered an awkward smile to Maruc.

'Don't try to run,' she said. 'Or he'll shoot you. This won't take long.'

One by one, Septimus gathered their former duties, noting them down on a data-slate. This was the third slave hold they'd visited. None of the prisoners had attacked him so far.

'Are they dosed with kalma?' she whispered at one point.

'What?'

'The pacifying narcotic. We use it on Terra, sometimes.' She sighed at his glance. 'Forget it. Are you slipping something into their water rations? Why don't they do something? Why not try to fight us?'

'Because what I'm offering them is no different from what they already did.' He hesitated and turned to her. 'As I remember, you didn't fight me, either.'

She gave him what would have been a coquettish smile, had it come from a noble-born scion of a Terran spire family, clad in her full finery. Instead, it looked a little sleazy and a little wicked. 'Well,' she toyed with her ponytail, 'you were much nicer to me than you were to these people.'

'Of course I was.' Septimus led the way out. Behind them both, Maruc and her attendant trailed along. The others had been instructed to wait until more crew came to take them to other parts of the ship, so they could clean themselves and begin their new duties.

'So *why* were you nicer to me?' she asked.

'Because you took me by surprise. I knew you were a Navigator, but I'd never seen one before.' His human eye glinted in the torchlight. 'I wasn't expecting you to be beautiful.'

She was glad the darkness hid her smile. When he tried, he could say just the right th–

'And because you were so valuable to the Legion,' he added. 'I had to be careful with you. The master ordered it.'

This time, the darkness hid her glare. *Idiot.*

'What's your name?' she asked Maruc.

'Maruc.'

A smile preceded her answer. It was the kind of look that made him suspect her father must've crumbled under glances like that. 'Don't get used to it,' she said. 'Our lord and master might have a different idea.'

'What's your name?' Maruc asked her.

'Octavia. I'm the eighth.'

Maruc nodded, gesturing at Septimus's back with a dirty finger. 'And he's Septimus, because he's the seventh?'

The taller man looked back over his shoulder. 'Exactly.'

'I do not have a name,' the hunched attendant provided helpfully. Stitched-shut eyes regarded him for a moment. 'But Septimus calls me Hound.'

Maruc already hated the creepy little thing. He forced an aching smile until the twisted fellow looked away, then he glanced at the girl again. 'Septimus and Octavia. The seventh and eighth,' he said. When she just nodded, he cleared his sore throat to ask. 'The seventh and eighth *what?*'

THE EXALTED SAT upon its throne at the heart of the strategium, brooding amongst its Atramentar. Garadon and Malek stood closest to their liege lord, both warriors casting hulking shadows in their tusked and horned

Terminator war-plate, with their weapons deactivated and sheathed.

Around the raised dais, the bridge crew worked under the harsh glare of spotlighting glaring down at each console. While most warships' command decks were bathed in illumination, the *Covenant of Blood* lingered in a welcome darkness broken only by pockets of light around the human crew.

The Exalted drew a breath, and listened for a voice it could no longer hear.

'What troubles you, lord?' This, from Garadon. The warrior shifted his stance, causing his war-plate's joints to sound in a clashing opera of grinding servos. Rather than answer, the Exalted ignored its bodyguard's concern, keeping its thoughts turned within. The mortal shell it wore – this swollen icon of daemonic strength – was its own, through and through. The creature had wormed its way within the legionary's form, hollowing it out and melting across its genetic coding in the most insidious and beautiful usurpation. The body that had once been Captain Vandred Anrathi of the VIII Legion was no more: now the Exalted reigned in this husk, proud of its theft and the comfortable malformation to suit its new owner.

But the mind, the memories – these were forever stained by the taste of another soul. To quest through the husk's thoughts was to bear distant witness to another being's memories, dredging them for meaning and lore. With each invasion, the Exalted's violating mental tendrils would meet the enraged – and helpless – presence curled foetal within the thoughts. Vandred's shade bunched itself tightly within his own brain, forever severed from the blood, bones and the flesh that he'd once commanded.

And now... silence. Silence for days, weeks.

Gone was the laughter that edged upon madness. Gone were the tormented cries promising vengeance each time the Exalted sifted through the psyche's accumulated knowledge and instinct.

The creature breathed through its open jaws, sending tendrils of thought back into its mind. Their questing reach spilled memories and emotions in a ransacking mess.

Life upon a world of eternal night.

The stars in the sky, bright enough to hurt the eyes on cloudless evenings.

The pride of watching an enemy ship burn up in orbit, trembling its way down to crash upon the world below.

The awe, the love, a devastating rush of emotion felt while staring at a primarch father that took no pride in any of his sons' accomplishments.

The same pale corpse of a father, broken by the lies he fed himself, inventing betrayals to sate his devouring madness.

These were fragments of what the husk's former owner had left behind:

shards of memory, scattered across the psyche in abandoned disorder.

The Exalted sifted through them, seeking anything that still lived. But... Nothing. Nothing existed within the bowels of this brain. Vandred, the scraps of him that had remained, were gone. Did this herald a new phase in the Exalted's evolution? Was it at last free of the clinging, sickening mortal soul that had resisted annihilation for so long?

Perhaps, perhaps.

It drew breath again, licking its maw clean of the acidic saliva. With a grunt, it summoned Malek closer and–

Vandred.

It was less a name, more a press of personality, a sudden aggressive burst of memory and emotion, boiling against the Exalted's brain. The creature laughed at the feeble assault, amused that the shadow of Vandred's soul would mount such an attack on the dominant consciousness after all this time. The silence hadn't been a symptom of the soul's destruction after all; Vandred had hidden, burrowing deeper within their twisted shared psyche, building his energy for this futile attempt at a coup.

Sleep, little fleshthing, the Exalted chuckled. *Back you go.*

The shrieks faded slowly, until they were swallowed once more, becoming the faintest background buzz at the very edge of the Exalted's inhuman perception.

Well. That had been an amusing distraction. The creature opened its eyes again, drawing breath into the husk to speak its decree to Malek.

A storm of light and sound awaited back in the external world: wailing sirens, rushing crew, shouting human voices. A laugh from within stroked at the Exalted's senses – the shadow of Vandred, revelling in his pathetic victory, distracting the daemon for a handful of moments.

The Exalted rose from its throne. Already, its inhuman mind stole answers from the barrage of sensory input. The sirens were low-threat proximity warnings. The ship was still docked. The auspex console chimed in urgent declaration, a tri-pulse that suggested either three inbound ships, or several smaller vessels bunched together. Given their location, it would be worthless haulier ships in service to the Adeptus Mechanicus; an Imperial Navy patrol blown far off-course by the winds of the warp; or, in all unfortunate probability, the arrival of a vanguard fleet in the colours of the Chapter Astartes sworn to defend this region of space.

'Disengage all umbilicals from the station.'

'Underway, my lord.' The mortal bridge attendant – *was it Dallow? Dathow?* Such insignificant details struggled to remain in the Exalted's mind – bent over his console, his former Imperial Navy uniform devoid of all allegiance markings. The man hadn't shaved in several days. His jawline was decorated with greying stubble.

Dallon, Vandred's voice ghosted through the creature's mind.

'All systems to full power. Bring us about immediately.'

'Aye, lord.'

The creature extended its senses, letting its hearing and sight bond with the *Covenant*'s far-reaching auspex sensors. There, burning in the deep void, the warm coals of enemy engine cores. The Exalted leaned into the sensation, wrapping its sightless vision around the approaching presences – a blind man counting the stones in his hand.

Three. Three smaller vessels. A frigate patrol.

The Exalted opened its eyes. 'Status report.'

'All systems, aye.' Dallon was still working his console as the Master of Auspex called out from his scanner table. 'Three ships inbound, my lord. Nova-class frigates.'

On the occulus screen, the view resolved into the form of three Adeptus Astartes vessels, cutting the night as they speared closer. Even at their speed, it would take over twenty minutes for them to reach weapon range. More than enough time to disengage and run.

Nova-class. Ship-killers. These carried weapons for void-duelling, rather than Imperial Space Marines for close-range boarding actions.

All faces turned to the Exalted – all except the servitors slaved to the ship's systems, who mumbled and drooled and cogitated, blind to anything outside their programming. The human crew watched expectantly, awaiting further orders.

It knew what they expected. It knew with sudden clarity that every human in the oval chamber expected the Exalted to order another retreat. To flee made perfect sense; the *Covenant* was still a shadow of its former might, limping from the scars earned during the brutality at Crythe.

The Exalted licked its maw with a black tongue. Three frigates. At optimal strength, the *Covenant* would drive through them like a spear, shattering all three with contemptuous ease. Perhaps, if the fates allowed it, the *Covenant* could still...

No.

The *Covenant* was close to complete ruin. Its ammunition loaders were empty, its plasma drives starved. They'd not used the Shriek on an amused whim – the Exalted ordered Deltrian to fashion it from necessity, along with the prophet's human slave serving on the station as a traitor on the inside. Attacking Ganges through conventional means had never been a viable possibility. Nor was surviving this fight, even against such insignificant prey.

Yet for a moment, the temptation was agonisingly strong. Could they win this? The Exalted let its consciousness dissipate through the vessel's iron bones. The plunder leeched from Ganges was still mostly in the ship's holds, not yet processed into usable compounds. All the raw material in the galaxy wouldn't help for a second.

Then the time for baring blades and showing fangs would come soon.

Now was the time to be ruled by reason, not rage. The Exalted clenched its teeth, forcing calm into its words.

'Come abeam of Ganges. All starboard broadsides to fire at will. If we cannot finish stripping our prize, then no one will.'

The ship shivered as it began to obey. The Exalted turned its horned head to its bridge attendant. 'Dallon. Ready for translation into the warp. Once Ganges is in pieces, we run.'

Again.

'As you command, lord.'

'Open a link to the Navigator,' the Exalted growled. 'Let us get this over with.'

SHE SPRINTED THROUGH the darkness, led by memory and the dull lance of illumination from her lamp pack. Her footsteps rang out down the metal corridors, echoing enough to become the panicked sound of a horde of fleeing people. Behind, she heard her attendant struggling to keep up.

'Mistress!' he called again. His wails were receding as she outpaced him.

She didn't slow down. The deck thrummed beneath her pounding feet. Power. Life. The *Covenant* was moving again, after days of sitting dead in dock.

'Get back to your chambers,' the Exalted's voice had drawled, irritation utterly unmasked. Even if the creature could threaten her, it didn't need to. She wanted this. She ached to sail again, and desire moved her limbs more than any devotion to duty.

She'd argued even as she obeyed. 'I thought the Marines Errant weren't due here for months.'

Before severing the link, the Exalted had grunted its disapproval. 'Evidently, destiny has a sense of humour.'

Octavia ran on.

Her quarters were nowhere near Blackmarket. Octavia scattered her attendants as she finally reached her chamber after almost ten minutes of running down stairs, along decking, and simply leaping down the smaller stairwells.

'Mistress, mistress, mistress,' they greeted her in an irritating chorus. Breathless and aching, she staggered past them, crashing down onto her interface throne. Responding to her presence, the wall of screens came to life before her. Picters and imagifiers mounted on the ship's hull opened their irises as one, staring out into the void from a hundred angles. As she caught her breath, she saw space, and space, and space – no different from the days before, as they'd sat here in the middle of nowhere, docked and half-crippled by damage. Only now, the stars moved. She smiled as she watched them starting their slow dance.

On a dozen screens, the stars meandered to the left. On a dozen others, they sailed right, or coasted down, or rose up. She leaned back into the throne of black iron and took a breath. The *Covenant* was coming about. Ganges hove into view, an ugly palace of black and grey. She felt the ship shiver as its weapons screamed. Despite herself, she smiled again. Throne, this ship was majestic when it chose to be.

Her attendants closed in around her, bandaged hands and dirty fingers holding interface cables and restraint straps.

'Piss off,' she told them, and snatched off her bandana. That sent them scattering.

I'm here, she said silently. *I'm back.*

From within her own mind, a presence that had lingered as a tiny, dense core of unrest began to unfold. It spread, great sheets of discordant emotion unwrapping to blanket her thoughts. It was a struggle to keep herself separate from the invader's passions.

You, the presence whispered. The recognition was laced with disgust, but it was a faint and distant thing.

Her heart was a thudding drum now. Not fear, she told herself. Anticipation. Anticipation, excitement, and... well, alright, fear. But the throne was all the interface she needed. Octavia refused the crude implantation of psy-feed cables, let alone needing restraints. Those were the crutches for the laziest Navigators, and while her bloodline might not be worth much in terms of breeding, she *felt* this ship well enough to reject the interface aids.

Not me. Us. Her inner voice tingled with savage joy.

Cold. Weary. Slow. The voice was the low rumble of something tectonic. *I awaken. But I am frozen by the void. I thirst and hunger.*

She wasn't sure what to say. It was strange to hear the ship address her with such tolerance, even if it was patience brought on by exhaustion.

It sensed her surprise through the resonant throne. *Soon, my heart will burn. Soon, we will dive through space and unspace. Soon, you will shriek and shed salt water. I remember, Navigator. I remember your fear of the endless dark, far from the Beacon of Pain.*

She refused to rise to its primitive baiting. The machine-spirit at the ship's heart was a vicious, tormented thing, and at best – at its absolute least unpleasant – it still loathed her. Much more often, it was a siege just to unify her thoughts with the vessel at all.

You are blind without me, she said. *When will you tire of this war between us?*

You are crippled without me, it countered. *When will you tire of believing you dominate our accord?*

She... she hadn't thought about it like that. Her hesitation must've flowed down the link, because she felt the ship's black heart beat faster, and another tremor ghosted through the *Covenant*'s bones. Runes flickered on several of her screens, all in Nostraman script. She knew enough to recognise an update of increased power capacity in the plasma generator. Septimus had taught her the Nostraman alphabet and pictographic signals pertaining to the ship's function. 'The essentials', he'd called it, as if she were a particularly dim child.

A coincidence, then? Just the engines building up energy, rather than her thoughts triggering the shipwide shiver?

I grow warm, the *Covenant* told her. *We hunt soon.*

No. We run.

Somehow, it sighed within her mind. At least, that was how her human awareness interpreted the breathless pulse of inhuman frustration that slid behind her eyes.

Still uneasy from the ship's accusation, she kept her thoughts back, holding them inside her skull, boxed away from the machine-spirit's reach. In silence, she watched Ganges burn, waiting for the order to guide the ship through a wound in reality.

THE WARP ENGINES came alive with a dragon's roar, echoing in two realms at once.

'Where?' Octavia spoke aloud, her voice a wet whisper.

'Make for the Maelstrom,' came the Exalted's reply, guttural over the vox. 'We cannot linger in Imperial space any longer.'

'I don't know how to reach it.'

Oh, but she did. Couldn't she feel it – a bloated, overripe migraine that hurt her head with each beat of her heart? Couldn't she sense it with the same ease as a blind woman feeling the sunrise on her face?

She didn't know the way there through the warp, that was true. She'd never sailed through a tempest to reach a hurricane's heart. But she could sense it, and she knew that was enough to reach it.

The Maelstrom. The *Covenant* heard her torment and responded itself. Waves of sickening familiarity washed over the Navigator as it felt the ship's primitive memory through the bond they shared. Her skin prickled and she needed to spit. The vessel's dull recollection became her own: a memory of the void boiling with cancerous ghosts, of tainted tides crashing against its hull. Whole worlds, entire suns, drowning in the Sea of Souls.

'I have never sailed into a warp rift,' she managed to say. If the Exalted replied, she never heard it.

But I have, the *Covenant* hissed.

She knew the tales, as every Navigator did. To plough into a warp rift was no different than swimming in acid. Each moment within its tides flayed ever more of a sailor's soul.

Legends and half-truths, the ship mocked her. *It is the warp, and it is the void. Calmer than the storm, louder than space.* And then, *Brace, Navigator.*

Octavia closed her human eyes and opened her truest one. Madness, in a million shades of black, swarmed towards her like a tide. Forever present in the darkness, a beam of abrasive light seared its way through the chaos, burning away the stuff of screaming souls and formless malice that rippled against its edges. A beacon in the black, the Golden Path, the Emperor's Light.

The Astronomican, she breathed in instinctive awe, and aimed the ship towards it. Solace, guidance, blessed light. Safety.

The *Covenant* rebelled, its hull straining against her, creaking and cracking under the strain.

No. Away from the Beacon of Pain. Into the tides of night.

The Navigator leaned back in her throne, licking sweat from her upper lip. The feeling taking hold reminded her of standing in the observatory atop her father's house-spire, feeling the unbelievable urge to leap from the balcony of the tallest tower. She'd felt it often as a child, that prickly sense of daring and doubt clashing inside her until the moment she leaned just a little too far. Her stomach would lurch and she'd come back to herself. She couldn't jump. She didn't want to – not really.

The ship roared in her mind as it rolled, the waters of hell crashing against its hull. Her ears hosted the unwelcome, ignorable sounds of human crew members shouting several decks above.

You will destroy us all, the ship spat into her brain. *Too weak, too weak.*

Octavia was faintly certain she'd puked on herself. It smelled like it. Claws stroked the ship's hull with the sound of squealing tyres, and the crashing of the warp's tides became the thudding beat of a mother's heart, overpoweringly loud to the child still slumbering in the womb.

She turned her head, watching the Astronomican darken and diminish. Was it rising away, out of her reach? Or was the ship falling from it, into th–

She suddenly tensed, blood like ice and muscles locked tighter than steel. They were free-falling through the warp. The Exalted's cry of desperate anger rang throughout every deck, carried over the vox.

Throne, she breathed the word, swearing with her heart and soul, barely cognisant of her lips speaking over the vox to the helmsmen on the command deck above. Her speech was automatic, as instinctive as breathing. The battle in her mind was what mattered.

Throne and shit and fu–

The ship righted. Not elegantly – she'd almost lost their way completely, and the vessel's recovery was anything but clean – but the ship pounded into a calmer stream with both relief and abandon. The *Covenant*'s hull gave a last horrendous spasm, rocked to its core as she stared the way she wished to go.

She felt the primal machine-spirit calming. The ship obeyed her course, as true and straight as a sword. Even if it loathed her, it flew far finer than the fat barge she'd suffered on under Kartan Syne. Where the *Maiden of the Stars* wallowed, the *Covenant of Blood* raced. Untouchable grace and wrath incarnate. No one in her bloodline, not in thirty-six generations, had guided such a vessel.

You are beautiful, she told the ship without meaning to.

And you are weak.

Octavia stared into the tides around the ship. Above, the Emperor's Light receded, while below, the faint outlines of great shapeless things thrashed in the infinite, turgid black. She sailed by instinct, blinder than she'd ever been before, guiding them all towards a distant eye in the storm.

PART TWO

HELL'S IRIS

VIII

THE CITY AT NIGHT

HE KNEW HE was one of the *slow* children.

That was the word his tutors used to describe the children that sat separate from the others, and he knew he belonged with them. In his class, four of the children were *slow* – already, he formed the word in his mind with the same delicate emphasis the adults around him used when they said it – and the four of them sat by the window, often completely ignoring the tutor's words, yet never suffering punishment for it.

The boy sat with them, the fourth and newest of the four, and stared out of the window with the others. Cars passed in the night, their front lamps dull to ease any strain on the eyes. The clouded sky was hidden by tower-tops, each spire decorated by great illuminated signs selling whatever it was that adults felt they needed.

The boy turned back to his tutor. For a while, he listened to her speaking about language, teaching the other children – the *not slow* children – words that were new to them. The boy didn't understand at all. Why were the words new to everyone? He'd read them in his mother's books a dozen times before.

The tutor hesitated as she noticed him looking. Usually she ignored him, forgetting he was there with casual, practised familiarity. The boy didn't look away from her. He wondered if she would try to teach him a new word.

As it happened, she did. She pointed to a word written across the flickering vid-screen and asked him if he knew its meaning.

The boy didn't answer. The boy only rarely answered his tutor. He suspected it was why the adults called him *slow*.

As the chime pulsed once, heralding the end of tuition for the night, all of the children rose from the seats. Most of them packed writing pads away. The *slow* ones put away scraps of paper with childish drawings. The boy had nothing to pack, for he'd done little but stare out the window all evening.

The walk home took over an hour, and was even slower in the rain. The boy walked past cars trapped in traffic queues, listening to the drivers scream at one other. Not far from where he walked, only a block or two away, he heard the popcorn crackle of gunfire. Two gangs fighting it out. He wondered which ones, and if many had died.

It wasn't a surprise when his friend caught up with him, but the boy had been hoping to be left alone tonight. He gave a smile to pretend he wasn't annoyed. His friend returned it.

His friend wasn't really his friend. They only called each other friends because their mothers were real friends, and the two families lived in hab-chambers next to each other.

'The tutor asked you a question tonight,' his friend said, as if the boy hadn't realised.

'I know.'

'But why didn't you answer? Didn't you know what to say?'

That was the problem. The boy never knew what to say, even when he knew the right answer.

'I don't understand why we go to tuition,' he said at last. Around them, the city lived and breathed as it always did. Tyres screeched in the next road. Shouted voices accused, demanded, pleaded with other shouting voices. Music pounded from inside nearby buildings.

'To learn,' his friend said. His mother had told the boy that his friend would grow up to 'break hearts one night'. The boy couldn't see it. To the boy, his friend always seemed confused, angry, or angry about being confused.

'Our tutor never says anything I didn't know before,' the boy shrugged. 'But why do we need to learn? That's what I don't understand.'

'Because... we do.' His friend looked confused, and that made the boy smile. 'When you even bother to speak, you ask some really stupid questions.'

The boy let it rest. His friend never understood this kind of thing.

About halfway home, well into the maze of alleys and back roads that the adults all called the Labyrinth, the boy stopped walking. He stared down a side alleyway, neither hiding nor making himself known. Just watching.

'What is it?' his friend asked. But the boy didn't need to answer. 'Oh,' his friend said a moment later. 'Come on, before they see us.'

The boy stayed where he was. Trash lined the alley's narrow walls. Amongst the refuse, a couple embraced. At least, the man embraced the woman. The woman's clothing was ruined, cut up and torn, and she remained limp on the dirty ground. Her head was turned to the boy. As the man moved on top of her, she watched both boys with black eyes.

'Come on...' his friend whispered, dragging him away. The boy said nothing for some time, but his friend made up for it, talking all the while.

'You're lucky we didn't get shot, staring like that. Didn't your mother teach you any manners? You can't just watch like that.'

'She was crying,' the boy said.

'You don't know that. You're just saying it.'

The boy looked at his friend. 'She was crying, Xarl.'

His friend shut up after that. They walked the rest of the Labyrinth in silence, and didn't say goodbye to each other when they finally reached their habitation spire.

The boy's mother was home early. He smelled noodles on the boil, and heard her voice humming in the hab-chamber's only other room: a small kitchen unit with a plastek screen door.

When she came into the main room, she rolled her sleeves down to her wrists. The gesture covered the tattoos along her arms, and the boy never commented on the way she always hid them like this. The coded symbols inked into her skin showed who owned her. The boy knew that at least, though he often wondered if perhaps they meant even more.

'Your tuition academy prelected me today,' she said. His mother nodded over to the prelector – it was blank now, but the boy could easily imagine his tutor's face on the flat, grainy wall screen.

'Because I'm slow?' the boy asked.

'Why do you assume that?'

'Because I did nothing wrong. I never do anything wrong. So it must be because I'm slow.'

His mother sat on the edge of the bed, her hands in her lap. Her hair was dark, wet from a recent wash. Usually, it was blonde – rare for the people of the city. 'Will you tell me what's wrong?' she asked.

The boy sat next to her, welcomed into her arms. 'I don't understand tuition,' he replied. 'We have to learn, but I don't understand why.'

'To better yourself,' she said. 'So you can live at City's Edge, and work somewhere... nicer than here.' She trailed off on the last words, idly scratching at the ownership tattoo on her forearm.

'That won't happen,' the boy said. He smiled for her benefit. She cradled him in response, the way she did on the nights after her owner hit her. On those nights, blood from her face dripped into his hair. Tonight, it was just her tears.

'Why not?' she asked.

'I'll join a gang, just like my father. Xarl will join a gang, just like his. And we'll both die on the streets, just like everyone else.' The boy seemed more thoughtful than melancholy. All the words that broke his mother's heart barely moved him at all. Facts were facts. 'It's not really any better at City's Edge, is it? Not *really*.'

She was crying now, just as the woman in the alley had cried. The same hollow look in her eyes, the same deadness.

'No,' she admitted in a whisper. 'It's no different there.'

'So why should I learn in tuition academy? Why do you waste money on all these books for me to read?'

She needed time before she could answer. The boy listened to her swallow, and felt her shaking.

'Mother?'

'There's something else you can do.' She was rocking him now, rocking him the way she had when he was even younger. 'If you stand out from the other children, if you're the best and the brightest and the cleverest, you'll never have to see this world again.'

The boy looked up at her. He wasn't certain he'd heard right, or that he liked the idea if he had.

'Leave the whole world? Who will...' He almost said *Who will take care of you*, but that would only make her cry again. 'Who will keep you company?'

'You never need to worry about me. I'll be fine. But please, *please* answer your tutor's questions. You have to show how clever you are. It's important.'

'But where would I go? What will I do?'

'Wherever you want to go, and whatever you want to do.' She gave him a smile now. 'Heroes can do whatever they want.'

'A hero?' The idea made him giggle. His laughter was balm to his mother's grief – he was old enough to notice it happen, but too young to know why such a simple thing could resonate within a parent's heart.

'Yes. If you pass the trials, you'll be taken by the Legion. You'll be a hero, a knight, sailing the stars.'

The boy looked at her for a long time. 'How old are you, mother?'

'Twenty-six revolutions.'

'Are you too old to take the trials?'

She kissed his forehead before she spoke. Suddenly she was smiling, and the tension in the small room evaporated. 'I can't take the trials. I'm a girl. And you won't be able to take them if you're just like your father was.'

'But the Legion takes boys from the gangs all the time.'

'It didn't always.' She lifted him away, and returned to stirring the noodles in the pan. 'Remember, it takes *some* boys from the gangs. But it's always looking for the best and brightest stars. Promise me you'll be one of those?'

'Yes, mother.'

'No more silence in tuition?'

'No, mother.'

'Good. How is your friend?'

'He's not really my friend, you know. He's always angry. And he wants to join a gang when he's older.'

His mother gave him another smile, though it was sadder, seeming like a wordless lie. 'Everyone gets into a gang, my little scholar. It's just one of those things. Everyone has a house, a gang, a job. Just remember, there's a difference between doing something because you have to, and doing it because you enjoy it.'

She placed their dinner onto the small table, her pale hands in little gloves to keep them from being burned on the tin bowls. Afterwards, she tossed the gloves on the bed, and smiled as he ate his first mouthful.

He looked up at her, seeing her face change in stuttering, flickering jerks. Her smile warped into a twisted sneer as her eyes tilted, pulled tighter, slanting with inhuman elegance towards her temples. Her wet hair rose as if charged by static, cresting into a stiffened plume of arterial red.

She screamed at him, a piercing shriek that shattered the windows, sending glass bursting out to rain down onto the street far below. The shrieking maiden reached for a curved blade on the nearby bed, and–

HE OPENED HIS eyes to the comforting darkness of his meditation chamber.

But the solace lasted no more than a moment. The alien witch had come through, following him back to the waking world. She said his name, her feminine voice breaking the black silence, her scent carried with her movements on the stale shipboard air.

The warrior reached for her throat, huge fist clutching the pale woman's neck as he rose to his feet and carried her with him. Her boots dangled and kicked in weak resistance, while her mouth worked without air to fuel her voice.

Talos released her. She fell a metre, crashing to the deck on boneless legs, falling to her hands and knees.

'Octavia.'

She coughed, spitting and catching her breath. 'No, really, who did you think it was?'

By the open doorway leading into his meditation chamber, one of the Navigator's attendants stood hunched and squirming, a scrap-metal shotgun in his trembling, bandaged hands.

'Need I remind you,' the Night Lord said, 'that it is a violation of *Covenant* law to aim that weapon at one of the Legion.'

'You hurt my mistress.' The man somehow stared with blinded eyes, his aim unwavering despite his obvious fear. 'You hurt her.'

Talos knelt down, offering his hand to help Octavia rise. She took it, but not before a moment's hesitation.

'I see you inspire great loyalty in your attendants. Etrigius never did.'

Octavia touched her throat, feeling the rawness there. 'It's fine, Hound. It's fine, don't worry.' The attendant lowered his gun, returning it beneath the ragged folds of his filthy cloak. The Navigator puffed a loose lock of hair from her face. 'What did I do to deserve that welcome? You said I could enter if the door was unlocked.'

'Nothing,' Talos returned to the slab of cold metal he used as a repose couch. 'Forgive me; I was troubled by something I saw in my dreams.'

'I knocked first,' she added.

'I am sure you did.' For a moment, he pressed his palms to his eyes, wiping away the after-images of the alien witch. The pain remained, undeniably worse than it had been in past years. His pulse thudded along the side of his head, the pain cobwebbing out from his temple. The injuries earned only a month before had done nothing but fuel the pain's growth. Now it hurt even to dream.

Slowly, he raised his head to look at her. 'You are not in your chambers. The ship is blessedly free from that horrendous shaking, as well. We cannot possibly have arrived already.'

Her reluctance to dwell on the topic was crystal clear. 'No,' she said, and left it at that.

'I see.' She required another rest, then. The Exalted would be less than thrilled. The three of them shared the silence, during which she flashed her lamp pack around the walls of his personal chamber. Nostraman writing, the flowing runes raggedly drawn, covered every surface. In some places, new prophecies overwrote older ones. Here was the prophet's mind, spilled onto the metal walls, scrawled in a dead language. Similar runic prophecy was carved over patches of his armour.

Talos seemed unconcerned with her scrutiny. 'You look unwell,' he said to her.

'Thank you very much.' She was well aware how sick she looked. Pasty skin and a sore back, with eyes so bloodshot and sore it hurt to blink. 'It isn't easy to fly a ship through psychic hell, you know.'

'I meant no offence.' He seemed more thoughtful than apologetic. 'The pleasantries go first, I think. The ability to make small talk. We lose that before anything else, when we leave our humanity behind.'

Octavia snorted, but she wouldn't be distracted. 'What was your nightmare about?'

Talos smiled at her, the same crooked smirk usually hidden by his helm. 'The eldar. Recently, it is nothing but the eldar.'

'Was it prophecy?' She rebound her ponytail, checking her bandana was still tight.

'I am no longer sure. The difference between prophecy and nightmare isn't always easy to perceive. This was a memory that became twisted and fouled towards the end. Neither a prophetic vision, nor a true dream.'

'You'd think you could tell the difference by now,' she said, not meeting his eyes.

He let her venom pass, knowing its source. She was afraid, rattled by his treatment of her upon awakening, and doing her best to mask the fear in condescending anger. Why humans let themselves become enslaved to such pettiness remained a mystery to him, but he could recognise it and acknowledge it, rendering it ignorable.

Encouraged by his tolerant silence, she said 'Sorry,' at last. Now their eyes met – hers the hazel of so many Terran-born, his the iris-less black of all Nostramo's sons. The gaze didn't last long. Octavia felt her skin crawl if she stared too long at any of the Night Lords' enhanced, proto-god features. Talos's face had healed well in the last month, but he was still a weapon before he was a man. The skull beneath his delicate features was reinforced and disgustingly heavy: a brick of bone, hard as steel. Surgical scars, white on white, almost concealed by his pale skin, ran down from both of his temples. A face that would've been handsome on a man was somehow profane when worn by one of these towering warriors. Eyes that might have been curious and kind were actually disquieting, always seething with something rancid and unconcealed.

Hatred, she suspected. The masters hated everything with unending ferocity, even one another.

He smiled at her scrutiny. That, at least, was still human. A crooked smile: once worn by a boy who knew much more than he wished to say. For a moment, he was something beyond this scarred statue of a hateful god.

'I assume there was a purpose to this visit,' he said, not quite a question.

'Maybe. What were you dreaming about... before the eldar came?'

'My home world. Before we returned to destroy it.' He'd slept in his armour, all but for his helm. Septimus had repaired it with Maruc's assistance, and Octavia had been present in the final moments, watching Talos re-breaking the aquila with a single ritual hammer blow.

'What was your family like?'

The warrior sheathed his golden blade in its scabbard, locking it to his back. The grip and winged crosspiece showed over his left shoulder, waiting to be drawn. He didn't look at her as he answered.

'My father was a murderer, as was his father before him, and his father before that. My mother was an indentured whore who grew old before her time. At fifty, she looked closer to seventy. I suspect she was diseased.'

'Sorry I asked,' she said with feeling.

Talos checked the magazine in his massive bolter, crunching it home with a neat slap. 'What do you want, Octavia?'

'Something Septimus told me once.'

He paused, turning to look down at her. She barely reached the base of his sternum. 'Continue.'

'He said you killed one of your servants, a long time ago.'

'Tertius. The warp took hold of him.' Talos frowned, almost offended. 'I killed him cleanly, and he suffered little. It was not a mindless murder, Octavia. I do not act without reason.'

She shook her head. 'I know. It's not that. But what happened? *"The warp has a million ways to poison the human heart".* She smiled, barely, at the ancient and melodramatic Navigator's quote. 'What happened to him?'

Talos locked his double-barrelled bolter to his armoured thigh plating. 'Tertius changed inside and out. He was always a curious soul. He liked to stand on the observation deck when we plied the warp's tides, staring out into the midst of madness. He looked into the abyss for long enough that it poured back into him. The signs were few at first – he would twitch and bleed from the nose – and I was younger then, I barely knew what to look for when it came to corruption. By the time I knew he was lost, he was a ravenous thing, crawling along the lower decks, hunting and eating the human crew.'

She shivered. Even the youngest Navigators knew the myriad degenerations that could take hold of humans in the warp, and despite her tedious career on *Maiden of the Stars,* Octavia had seen her fair share of taint in an unguarded crew. Nothing quite that bad, but still...

'And what happened to Secondus?' she asked.

'I have no desire to speak of the second. It is not something I recall with any pleasure, nor even any vindication when it was over.' He picked up his helm, turning it over in his hands. 'Just tell me what's wrong,' he said.

She narrowed her eyes. 'How do you know something's wrong?'

'Perhaps because I am not a complete fool.'

Octavia forced a smile. He could kill her; he *would* kill her, without a heartbeat's hesitation.

Now or never, she thought.

'I keep seeing the void-born.'

Talos breathed slowly, closing his eyes for several seconds. 'Go on.'

'I hear her weeping around corridor corners. I catch glimpses of her running down empty passages. It's her. I know it is. Hound hasn't seen her, though.'

Her attendant gave a bashful shrug, not enjoying the Night Lord's sudden scrutiny. Talos looked back to Octavia.

'So.' She tilted her head. 'Am I tainted?'

When he answered, it was with a tolerant sigh. 'You are nothing but trouble to me,' he said.

His words stoked the embers of her pride enough that she squared her shoulders, standing up straighter. 'I could say the same thing to you. My life has hardly been any easier since you captured me. And *you* hunted *me,* remember? Dragging me on board with your hand around my throat, like some prize pet.'

Talos laughed at that – his laughter was always the barest chuckle, little more than a soft exhalation through a crooked smile.

'I will never grow tired of your bladed Terran tongue.' The warrior took a breath. 'Guard yourself, Octavia. Despite your fears of your own weakness, the fault doesn't lie with you. This ship has spent an age within the warp. The corruption is not within you, but the *Covenant* itself. Taint rides in its bones, and we all breathe it in with the air supply. We are heretics. Such is our fate.'

'That... is hardly reassuring.'

He gave her a look then, almost achingly human. A raised eyebrow, a half-smile, a look that said: *Really, what did you expect from me?*

'The *Covenant* hates me,' she said. 'I know that. Its spirit recoils each time we touch. But it wouldn't haunt me like this, not on purpose. Its soul is too simple to consider such a thing.'

Talos nodded. 'Of course. But the *Covenant* is crewed by as many memories as living, breathing mortals. More have died on these decks than still work them. And the ship remembers every one of them. Think of all the blood soaked into the steel that surrounds us, and the hundreds of last breaths filtering through the ventilation cyclers. Forever recycled, breathed in and out of living lungs, over and over again. We walk within the *Covenant*'s memory, so we all see things at the edges of our vision from time to time.'

She shivered again. 'I hate this ship.'

'No,' he said, holding his helm once more. 'You don't.'

'It's nothing like I imagined, though. Guiding a Legiones Astartes warship – it's what every Navigator prays for. And the *Covenant* moves like something from a dream, twisting and turning like a serpent in oil. Nothing can compare to it. But everything here is so... sour.' Octavia's words trailed off. After a moment, she watched him closely, smelling the tang of acid on his breath.

'You are staring,' he pointed out.

'You were lucky not to lose your eye.'

'That is a curious choice of words. Half of my skull was replaced by layered metal bonding, and I am reliably informed by Cyrion that the left side of my face looks like I lost a fight with a crag cougar.'

He stroked gauntleted fingertips down the sides of his face, where the scars of surgery were slowly fading. Even his post-human biology struggled to erase the damage done. The scars on the left side of his face ran from his temple to the edge of his lips. 'These scars are not a mark of fine fortune, Octavia.'

'It's not that bad,' she said. Something in his manner put her at ease – a touch of almost fraternal familiarity in his measured tone and honest eyes. 'What's a crag cougar?'

'A beast of my home world. When next you see one of the Atramentar, look to their shoulder guards. The roaring lions on their pauldrons are what we called crag cougars on Nostramo. It was considered a mark of wealth for gang bosses to be able to leave the cities and hunt such creatures.'

'Mistress,' Hound interrupted. She turned at the break in her history lesson.

'What?'

Hound looked awkward. 'I killed a crag cat once.'

She tilted her head, but Talos answered before she could. 'Hill Folk?' His low voice resonated in the chamber.

Hound nodded his ruined head with its crown of scraggly grey hair. 'Yes, lord. And I killed a crag cat once. A small one. Then I ate it.'

'He probably did,' Talos conceded. 'The Hill Folk lived away from the cities, eking out an existence in the mountains.'

Octavia was still watching Hound. 'Just how old are you?'

'Older than you,' Hound confirmed, nodding again as if this answered everything. *Bizarre little thing,* she thought, turning back to Talos. 'How's the arm?'

The warrior had glanced down at his armoured left arm, closing the hand into a fist. On the surface, encased in armour, it looked no different to his right limb. A different story lay beneath the ceramite: a limb of dense metal bones and hydraulic joints. The subtle grind of false muscles and servos was still new enough to be novel. He still felt a faint amusement at the vibration of small gears in his wrist or the crunching clicks when the plasteel elbow joint moved too fast. For her benefit, he offered his hand, tapping his thumb to his fingertips over and over in quick succession. Even the most subtle movements made his growling armour thrum.

'Cyrion lost his arm at Crythe,' he said. 'I consider this an unfortunate thing to have in common with him.'

'How does it feel?'

'Like my own arm,' he shrugged, 'but less so.'

Despite herself, she felt a smile. 'I see.'

'I believe I will speak with Deltrian regarding the repairs,' he said. 'Do you wish to join me?'

'Not at all, thank you.'

'No,' Hound piped up, still lurking by the door. 'No, sir.'

Vox-speakers across the ship crackled to life. The Exalted's bass drawl rumbled through the corridors, *'Translation into the empyrean in thirty rotations. All crew to their stations.'*

Octavia looked up at the speaker mounted on the wall. 'A polite way of saying, "Octavia, get back to your room".'

Talos nodded. 'Return to your chamber, Navigator. Watch for the ghosts that walk these halls, but pay them no heed. How far are we from our destination?'

'A day from the Maelstrom's edge,' she said. 'Maybe two. There's one more thing.'

'Which is?'

'The void-born's father. Septimus told me not to trouble you with this, but I think you should know.'

Talos inclined his head for her to continue, but said nothing.

'Sometimes in Blackmarket, and elsewhere on the crew decks, he tells us all how the ship is damned, cursed to kill us all in the coming nights. Some of the older crew have been listening and agreeing for a while... You know how they were about the girl. But now the new crew, the Ganges crew, they're starting to listen. Arkiah blames you. The girl had your Legion medallion, and she still... you know.'

'Died.'

Octavia nodded.

'I told Septimus to deal with this,' the warrior intoned. 'But thank you for bringing it to my attention. I will end the situation myself.'

'Will you kill him?'

He wasn't deaf to the hesitation in her voice. 'Dead slaves are worthless,' he said. 'However, so are disobedient ones. I will kill him if he forces my hand, but I have no wish to end his life. He is an example of human resistance to corruption, for he was able to sire a child despite decades of life in the bowels of this ship. I am not an idiot, Octavia. He is as much an example as his daughter was. His murder would profit us little, and serve only to antagonise the mortal crew. They must be brought to obey through fear of the consequences, not crushed into obedience by hopeless depression. The former breeds motivated, willing workers who wish to survive. The latter breeds suicidal husks that care nothing for pleasing their masters.'

The air between them grew awkward, and Talos grunted an acknowledgement. 'Will that be all?'

'What awaits us in the Maelstrom? What is the Hell's Iris?'

Talos shook his head. 'You will see with your own eyes, if the ship manages to hold together for long enough to actually reach the docks there.'

'So it's a dock.'

'It's... Octavia. I am a warrior, not a scribe or a literist. I lack the words to do it justice. Yes, Hell's Iris is a dock.'

'You say that like it's a curse. "I am a warrior".' Octavia licked her dry lips before speaking. 'What did you want to do with your life?' she asked. 'I told you the truth: I'd always dreamed of guiding such a warship, and for better or worse, fate gave me what I wished for. But what about you? Do you mind if I ask?'

Talos laughed again, that same whispering chuckle, and tapped the defiled aquila emblazoned across his chest.

'I wanted to be a hero.' A moment later, he masked his scarred face behind his skulled helm. Red eye lenses stared at her, devoid of all emotion. 'And look how that worked out.'

IX
VOYAGE

REACTION WAS MIXED as one of the Legion masters strode into Blackmarket that night. Most stood stock still, freezing in place, variously wondering who had done something wrong, or if their own transgressions were about to be punished. Some fell to their knees in respect, or bowed their heads in greeting. Several fled at the first sight of the master's red eye lenses emerging from the blackness. Most of these – oil-stained workers from the engine decks – ran down the many corridors leading from the communal crew chamber.

Their escape went ignored. The warrior moved through the parting crowd to stand before a single man who tended a market table, selling scraps of white cloth and charms woven from female hair. Nearby, humans dimmed their lamp packs as a sign of respect in the presence of a Legion master.

'Arkiah,' the warrior growled. His vox-voice was a guttural snarl, a rasping coming through the vocabulator in the helm's mouth grille. The man flinched back, cowed by fear, kept straight only by his stubborn pride.

'Lord?'

The warrior reached for the gladius sheathed at his shin, his movements deliberate and slow. As he rose with the blade in his hand, eye lenses still locked to the mortal's sweating features, he growled another three words.

'Take this sword.'

Talos dropped the gladius onto the table with a clang, scattering trinkets off the edges. The blade was as long as the human's arm, its silver length turned amber in the dim lighting of the communal chamber.

'Take it. I am due to meet with the tech-adept, and that meeting goes delayed while I remain here. So take the sword, mortal. My patience is finite.'

With trembling fingers, the man did as he was ordered. 'Lord?' he asked again, his voice quavering now.

'The blade in your hands was forged on Mars in an age now believed to be myth by almost every soul in the Imperium. It has cut the heads from men, women, children, aliens and beasts. With these hands, I pushed it into the beating heart of a man who ruled an entire world.' The warrior reached to his belt, where an Adeptus Astartes helm hung on a short, thick chain against his hip. With a jerk, he wrenched the helm free, letting it thud onto the table where the sword had lain a moment before.

Red ceramite, marked by dents and scratches; green eye lenses, both cracked and lifeless. The helm stared at Arkiah in dead-eyed silence.

'This helm is all that remains of the warrior that murdered your daughter,' said Talos. 'I killed him myself, in the running battles that raged across the decks as we fled from Crythe. And when it was done, I severed his head from his shoulders with the very blade you now struggle to lift in your hands.'

The man made to lower the sword, to rest it back on the table. 'What do you wish of me, lord?'

'It is said you sow the seeds of discord among the mortal crew, that you preach this vessel is damned, and all who sail aboard her are destined to suffer the same fate as your daughter. Is that so?'

'The omens...'

'No.' Talos chuckled. 'If you wish to be alive at the end of this conversation, you will not speak of "omens". You will speak the truth, or you will never speak again. Do you preach of the *Covenant*'s damnation?'

Arkiah's breath misted in the cold air. 'Yes, my lord.'

The warrior nodded. 'Very well. That does not anger me. Slaves are not forbidden emotions and opinions, even misguided ones, as long as they obey their duties. What *are* your duties, Arkiah?'

The ageing man backed up a step. 'I... I am just a menial, lord. I do whatever is asked of me by the crew.'

Talos took a step closer. His active armour growled with teeth-itching resonance. 'And does the crew ask you to preach that every one of them is damned?'

'Please don't kill me, lord. Please.'

Talos stared down at the man. 'I did not come here to kill you, fool. I came to show you something, to teach you a lesson every one of us must learn if we are to remain sane in the lives we lead.'

Talos gestured to the helm as he continued. 'That warrior killed your daughter. His blade tore her in half, Arkiah. She would have taken several moments to die, and I promise you those moments were more painful than anything you can possibly imagine. Your wife also died in the raid, did she not? Slain by a Blood Angel blade? If she was with your daughter at the end, then this warrior likely butchered them both.'

Talos drew his own blade. A Blood Angel sword, as long as the human was tall, prised from the loose fingers of a slain hero. The polished and winged artefact was wrought of silver and gold: its craftsmanship unmistakable, its value uncountable. He slowly, gently, rested the golden blade on the ageing man's shoulder, the edge just shy of kissing the mortal's neck.

'Perhaps this was the last thing they both saw. A faceless warrior towering above them, blade ready to fall, to cut, to cleave them apart.'

Tears stood in the man's eyes now. When he blinked, they trailed down his cheeks in quicksilver rushes.

'Lord,' he said. One word, nothing more.

Talos read the question in the broken man's eyes. 'I have come to ease your doubts, Arkiah. I did what I could. I tore her murderer apart. I carry his memory with me, in the taste of his blood on my tongue as I ate his heart. Your daughter died, and you are entitled to your grief. But here, now, you have the murderer's remains. Use the sword. Break the helm. Take the vengeance you crave.'

At last he found his voice. 'I do not wish vengeance, lord.'

'No.' The Night Lord smiled behind the faceplate, pulling the healing muscles tight. Despite his words to Octavia, his face was a mask of constant aggravating pain now. He'd been considering stripping the skin from the left side of his skull, deadening the nerves, and replacing the scar tissue with bare augmetics. He still wasn't sure why he felt such reluctance to do so.

'If vengeance is hollow,' Talos continued, 'then you have simply not suffered enough. Revenge is all any of us can hope for, each time we must lick new wounds and wait for them to heal. Every soul on this ship, mortal and immortal alike, accepts that as truth. All except you. You, who insist you've been wronged more than any other. You, who dare to whisper dissent into the shadows, forgetting that your masters dwell within that same darkness. The shadows whisper to us, Arkiah. Remember, little human, treachery on this ship is punishable by being flayed alive.'

Talos was no longer speaking directly to him. The warrior turned, addressing the crowd that ringed them both, even as he aimed his words for Arkiah's ears.

'So answer me something: do you mumble your traitorous words because of selfish grief, as if you are the only one to have lost something precious, or is it because you truly think your fellows will rise up in rebellion against the Legion?'

'My daughter...'

The Night Lord was a blur of movement and a purr of servo-joints. One moment he faced the crowd, his back to Arkiah; the next, the weeping man was held aloft by a fistful of greying hair, boots hanging above the decking.

'Your daughter was one of hundreds to lose her life that night,' the Night Lord growled, 'on a ship that falls apart beneath our feet even now because of the damage it sustained. Do you want me to apologise for not protecting her? Or would that also change nothing? Would those words, even true, ring as hollow as worthless vengeance? Will they bring her back?'

Talos hurled the man aside, sending him crashing into a table that toppled under the impact. 'We lost dozens of warriors the same night you lost your daughter. Dozens of souls who'd stood on the very soil of Terra and watched the walls of the Emperor's palace tumble to the ground. Warriors who'd devoted eternity to fighting an unwinnable war in the name of vengeance. We lost hundreds of mortal crew. Every mortal on board lost someone or something precious that night, and they swallowed their grief, settling for the hope of revenge. But not you. *You* must tell everyone else that their losses mean nothing next to yours. *You* frantically whisper that everyone must piss themselves in fear at an unwritten future.'

Talos sheathed both blades and shook his head. 'I grieve for her loss, little father, for her life and what it represented in this wretched sanctuary we are all forced to suffer. I regret that all I could give her was the peace of vengeance. But let me be utterly clear, mortal. You live only because we allow it. You drew your first breath in an empire we built, and you serve us as we tear it down. Hate us. Despise us. We will never care, even as we shed blood to protect you when we must. Heed these words, human. Do not dare put your heart's losses above anyone else's. The warp always finds its way into fools. Poisonous thoughts are a beacon to the Neverborn.'

The crowd watched with rapt eyes. Talos turned, his eye lenses meeting the gaze of every serf in the chamber, one after the other.

'We sail through bleak tides, and I will lie to none of you about what awaits in our future. The *Covenant* bleeds, crying out for repair. We draw near to the dock at Hell's Iris, a place some of you will remember without affection. Once we are docked, remain locked in your quarters unless you are attending to essential duties. Every soul among you with access to a weapon, make sure you carry it with you at all times.'

One of the crowd, a new slave from the Ganges, stepped forward. 'What's happening?'

Talos turned to the man, looking down at his unshaven face. It was only then the Night Lord realised he'd been speaking Nostraman. Half the crew were new – they had no experience with the dead language.

'Trouble,' Talos spoke in Low Gothic, the Imperium's mongrel tongue. He was growing more comfortable with it since Octavia came on board. 'We are making for a haven of renegades in the heart of Imperial space, and will arrive at its borders within a handful of hours. There is a chance the ship will be boarded while we linger in dock. If that happens, defend the *Covenant* with your lives. The Eighth Legion are not generous masters, but we are saints compared to the depraved souls we must ally with. Remember that, should you find yourself tempted by thoughts of escape.'

Talos saved his last glance for Arkiah. 'Little father. If you defy the Legion with anything more than a selfish coward's whispered words in the future, I will carve the skin and muscle meat right from your bones. Your flayed skeleton will be crucified at the heart of this very chamber, hanging as a warning to all. Nod if you accept these terms.'

The ageing man nodded.

'A wise decision,' Talos replied, and stalked from the chamber. In the shadows of deeper corridors, he spoke four words into an open channel.

'First Claw, to me.'

HE SAT WITH his head cradled in shaking hands, gently rocking back and forth as he sat in the middle of a bare chamber, whispering the names of gods he hated.

One of his brothers called to him over the jagged soundwaves of the vox.

'I come,' Uzas replied, rising to his feet.

HE LOWERED THE immense blade, releasing the trigger to let the sword's teeth fall still. The engine in its hilt idled as the warrior listened to his brother's summons. Sweat bathed him beneath his armour, leaving his skin itching even as it soaked into the absorbent weave of his bodyglove.

'On my way,' Xarl voxed back.

THE QUILL SLOWED in its scratching path across the parchment, then finally stopped. The warrior looked to the skull-faced helm on his writing desk, watching him with its unblinking eyes. Reluctantly, he placed the quill back in its inkpot. A dusting of fine-grained sand trickled over the parchment to help the letters dry, before the warrior reached to activate the vox-mic in his collar.

'As you wish,' said Mercutian

HE WALKED THE ship's corridors, staring into the darkness through red-stained lenses and flickering white targeting cross hairs. A rune chimed on his retinal display, his brother's name-glyph pulsing for his attention. He blinked at it to reply.

'Something amiss?'

'We are gathering in the Hall of Remembrance,' Talos's voice came back.

'That sounds tedious. What might the occasion be?'

'I want a full report of the necessary repairs before we dock.'

'I was right,' Cyrion replied. 'That *is* tedious.'

'Just get there.' Talos severed the link.

* * *

THE HALL OF Remembrance echoed with the sound of divine industry. Servitors lifted and hauled, drilled and hammered; each one of them robed and hooded in black surplices, bearing the winged skull symbol of the Legion on their backs. Several had Nostraman glyphs tattooed on their foreheads – former serfs guilty of minor sins, sentenced to live out their lives as lobotomised, augmented drones.

Scores of menials and servitors laboured at tables and conveyor belts, constructing the explosive bolt shells used by the Legion's warriors, while others worked at wall-mounted consoles, deep-scrying parts of the ship and directing the repair teams. The entire hall resonated with the flood of chattering voices, clanging tools, and beaten metal.

Four great sarcophagi hung bound to one wall, wrapped in chains and supported by ceiling clamps. Only one remained within a protective stasis screen, its cracked surface halfway restored to perfection, though blurred by the field's blue mist.

The warband's Dreadnought coffins shivered as the ship gave another lurch, their chains rattling again. Each of the coffins' surfaces was immaculately wrought from precious metals, carvings lovingly etched into the armour. Such patient and diligent work was the responsibility of a master artisan, the craftsmanship a league apart from the simplistic repairs performed by most menials and slaves.

First Claw regarded one another around the chamber's central hololithic table. A three-dimensional image of the *Covenant of Blood* rotated before them all, its flickering, patchy contours flawed by stains of flashing red damage warnings. It pulsed in and out of existence in sympathy with the tremors shaking the ship.

'That doesn't look good,' Cyrion noted.

'It is not,' Lucoryphus rasped. 'Not good at all.' His presence had been an unwelcome surprise for First Claw upon entering. Talos knew without doubt that the Raptor had been sent by the Exalted to serve as the shipmaster's eyes.

'Tech-adept.' Talos turned to Deltrian. 'I need a complete listing of the repairs to be done, with the materials you'll need. I also need a time frame for how long the *Covenant* will be in dock undergoing overhaul.'

Talos stood with Deltrian, opposite Xarl and Lucoryphus. Little could be considered similar between the three warriors: Talos stood in his Legion war-plate, weapons sheathed, eyes calm, helm resting on the edge of the table. Lucoryphus kept his weeping mask in place – in truth, Talos had no idea if the other warrior could even remove it any more – and leaned forward with a graceless awkwardness, struggling to remain bipedal on his ceramite talons. Xarl was also bareheaded, the skull helm locked to his thigh. He stood impassive in his beaten armour, his scarred features a map of unpleasant memories, and his black eyes always moving between Talos and Lucoryphus. He wasn't subtle about it, wasn't even trying to be subtle – Xarl sensed the genesis of a rivalry between the two warriors, and watched with keen eyes.

Deltrian grinned because Deltrian always grinned. The chrome skeletal face beneath the black hood could form no other expression. As the tech-priest spoke, vein/wires and cable/muscles in his cheeks and neck tightened and flexed. His voice was an automaton's emotionless screed.

'The immaterium propulsion engines have been subjected to an inadvisable degree of damage in the last eight months–' here, Deltrian paused, turning his emerald eye lenses to Lucoryphus, '–but they function within permissible boundaries.'

The tech-adept's eyes hissed softly, moisturised by the coolant mist-sprays built into his tear ducts. Talos couldn't help but steal a glance. He kept his curiosity about Deltrian's personal reconstruction behind polite respect, but why even a tech-priest of the Martian Mechanicum would rebuild himself to resemble an augmetic image of a skinless human was a mystery. He suspected it was because of Deltrian's bond with the VIII Legion. This aspect, more given to inspiring fear in mortals, surely suited him better.

Or perhaps it was a matter of faith. Appearing as a synthetic version of the human skeleton, to show the many changes Deltrian had undergone in his quest for mechanical perfection, as well as evidence that he acknowledged his mortal beginnings.

Talos caught himself staring. With a guilty smile, he looked back at the hololithic.

Deltrian gestured with a chrome claw to red patches across the ship's hull. 'The flawed systems are located at these points. The hull sections in absolute need of complete reparation are located here, here, here, here and here. As for core systems, the Ninth Legion inflicted severe damage upon the actuality generators. Until this date, shipboard repairs have been sufficient to restore sustained empyrean flight. If we do not dock soon for an overhaul of the actuality generators, the immaterium engines will be throttled by failsafes, preventing their activation.'

'Meaning?' Xarl asked.

'Meaning the Geller field is damaged,' Talos answered. 'The warp engines won't work for much longer unless the shield generators are repaired.'

'Yes,' Deltrian confirmed. He appreciated the purity of precision in the warrior's words. He nodded to *Legiones Astartes One-Two-Ten; preferred appellation: Talos*. 'Precisely,' the tech-adept finished.

'Ninth... Blood Angels...' Lucoryphus rasped. 'No longer a Legion.'

'Acknowledged.' Deltrian tilted his head a moment. 'Recorded.'

Cyrion gestured to the hololithic. 'The Geller field is flawed?'

Deltrian's voxsponder unit built into his throat gave a blurt of machine-code. 'Terminally flawed. Temporary repairs will degrade with greater frequency. The longer we remain in the immaterium, the greater the potential of a breach-risk.'

'This is going to take weeks.' Talos shook his head as he watched the hololithic ship turn. 'Maybe even months.'

Deltrian gave another blurt of vocalised code in a static rush of numerals, as close as the adept ever came to cursing. 'The immaterium engine flaw is not the *Covenant's* principal concern. Observe.' His skeletal fingers keyed in a code on the table's keypad. The hololithic shivered before them, several other areas along the hull flickering red. When none of the warriors said anything, Deltrian emitted a tinny growl. 'I restate: *Observe.*'

'Yes, I see,' lied Cyrion. 'It all makes sense now. But explain it for Uzas.'

Talos silenced his brother with a glare. 'Humour us, tech-adept. What are we seeing here?'

For several seconds, Deltrian merely watched the warriors as if awaiting some kind of punchline. When nothing was forthcoming, the tech-adept pulled his black robe tighter, his silver facial features sinking deeper into the depths of his hood. Talos had never realised a mechanical skeleton could look exasperated while still grinning, but there it was.

'These are projected statistics equating to damage we will sustain in the remaining days of our journey, based on the turbulence of the immaterium so far.'

Talos smoothed his gauntleted fingertips over the scars streaking down from his temple, unaware of the unconscious habit in the making. 'That looks like enough to cripple the ship.'

'Almost,' Deltrian allowed. 'Our Navigator is untested and weak. She steers the ship through savage tides. She ploughs through warp-waves because she can sense no way around them. Visualise the damage her route is inflicting upon the *Covenant.*'

'So she's not a smooth sailor,' Xarl grunted. 'Get to the point, tech-adept.'

'In Nostraman vernacular, the Navigator is shaking the ship apart.' Deltrian cancelled the hololithic. 'I will state the situation in the simplest terms. Until this date, we have counted on ingenuity and the fictional concept of "fortune". These resources are no longer viable. Slave 3,101, preferred appellation: Octavia – will destroy this ship through incompetence if she fails to make peace with the machine-spirit and alter her techniques of navigation.'

The Raptor growled, drawing in breath through his speaker grille.

Deltrian raised a hand of chrome bones to forestall Lucoryphus's comment. 'No. Do not interrupt this vocalisation. There is more. We will reach the destination dock. I speak of eventualities and concerns for the future. She must learn to navigate with greater haste and proficiency, or she will continue wounding the *Covenant* each time she carries us into the immaterium.'

Talos said nothing.

'Furthermore,' Deltrian pressed on, 'our journey is hastening the erosion of several vital systems. Ventilation. Liquid waste recycling. The recharge generator pods supplying the port broadsides. The list is long and severe. Our vessel has sustained such a degree of damage in the last standard solar annum that less than thirty per cent of function is operating within reliable parameters. As my servitor crews move deeper through the ship's organs in reconstruction operations, they locate new flaws and bring them to my attention.'

Talos nodded, but remained silent.

'I lack expertise in reading unaugmented facial emotional signifiers.' Deltrian tilted his head. 'You seem to be experiencing an emotional reaction. Which is it?'

'He's annoyed with you.' Uzas licked his teeth. 'You're insulting his pet.'

'I do not understand,' Deltrian confessed. 'I speak only in realities.'

'Ignore him.' Talos gestured to Uzas. 'Tech-adept, I understand your concern, but we work with the tools we have.'

Lucoryphus, quiet for several minutes, broke his silence with a susurrating laugh. 'Is that so, Soul Hunter?'

Talos turned to the Raptor. 'You have something to say?'

'Did this warband not once have a warrior who could pilot vessels through the warp?' Lucoryphus twitched, hissing another laugh. 'Yes-yes. Oh, yes, it did.'

'Ruven is gone, leashed to the Warmaster's side, and we have no other sorcerers among us. No sorcerer is a match for a Navigator, brother. One possesses the lore to guide a vessel through the warp. The other was born to do nothing else.'

The Raptor snorted. 'Champion Halasker had sorcerers. Many Eighth Legion warbands treasure them.' Lucoryphus either gave a sharp nod or his neck twitched at the right moment. 'They speak of you, Soul Hunter. Talos of the Tenth, the warrior with the primarch's gift without ever staring into the warp's secrets. How many of our brothers only claim the father's foresight after mastering the secrets of the warp? But not you. No-no, not Talos of the Tenth.'

'Enough,' Talos narrowed his eyes. 'This is meaningless.'

'Not meaningless. Truth. You have been gone from the Great Eye too long, prophet. You are a wanted soul. Your talents should be shaped. Sorcery is as much a weapon of this war as the blade you stole and the bolter you inherited.'

Talos didn't answer. His skin crawled as his brothers in First Claw turned their eyes to him.

'Is this true?' Xarl asked. 'The Legion's warp-weavers want Talos?'

'Truth and true,' Lucoryphus rasped. His helm's bleeding eyes stared unwavering. 'Potential bleeds from the prophet like a black aura. Soul Hunter, did not Ruven seek to train you?'

'I refused.' Talos shrugged. 'If we could focus on the matter at hand...'

'I was there when he refused,' Cyrion smiled. 'And in my brother's defence, Ruven was – at the very best of times – a piss-drinking, snide little whoreson. I would have refused to loan him a weapon, let alone allow him to shape me into one.'

Lucoryphus crawled around the table on his metallic claws, the thrusters on his back swinging with his uneasy gait. For several steps, he rose to a bipedal stalk – standing as tall as his Legion brothers – but the movement clearly frustrated him. He dropped back down to all fours as he prowled by the chained sarcophagi, still idly musing in his serpent's voice.

'And what of you, First Claw? Xarl? Mercutian? Uzas? What are your thoughts on the prophet's reluctance? How do you see him now, in this new light?'

Xarl chuckled, offering no comment. Mercutian kept his stoic silence, his features betraying nothing.

'I think,' Uzas growled, 'you should watch your mouth. The prophet chose his path, same as all of us, same as every soul.' The warrior grunted in dismissal.

The others looked at him in undisguised surprise. Even Lucoryphus.

'*Enough,*' Talos snarled. 'Enough. Honoured tech-adept, please continue.'

Deltrian didn't miss a beat. '...and a discrepancy with the subsidiary feeds powering the forward lance array was acknowledged and recorded forty-six minutes and twelve seconds ago, Standard Terran Chronology. Fifteen seconds. Sixteen. Seventeen.'

Talos turned to the tech-adept. 'I think what you're trying to say is that we've been lucky so far, that the ship hasn't crumbled to pieces.'

Deltrian gave a faint machine-code hiss of disapproval. 'I would never vocalise the matter in those terms.'

'How long will this take to repair?' Xarl asked. 'All of it.'

Deltrian's hood turned to face the warrior. Emerald eye lenses and a silver smile glinted in the shadow. He had the exact calculations, but suspected the Night Lords would refuse to hear them anyway. 'With full crew workforce at eighty per cent efficiency: five-point-five months.' It almost pained him to be so imprecise, but their too-mortal intellects demanded compromise. 'Eighty per cent efficiency allows for mortal sickness, injury, death and incompetence in the repairs.'

'Five and a half months is a long time to be stranded in Hell's Iris,' Xarl scowled. 'What if we barter for the Blood Reaver's dock crews to aid us? We trade for materials and labour, rather than dealing with the labour ourselves.'

'Blood Reaver...' Talos was watching the hololithic, his voice distracted by the pain in his temples. 'A ridiculous title.'

Cyrion chuckled. 'A damning statement, from a warrior called "Soul Hunter".'

Talos covered his smile by scratching at his scarred cheek. 'Continue, tech-adept.'

'With the Hell's Iris work crews, the overhaul could be completed within a time frame of one month.'

'Forgive me for being the one to mention this, but we are not exactly beloved there,' Mercutian pointed out. 'There's every chance the Tyrant will refuse to let us dock, let alone lend us the services of his work crews. And we are not bearing a wealth of resources to barter with. We need everything we liberated from Ganges.'

'Just say "stole",' Xarl sneered at the other warrior. '*Liberated?* What does that even mean? You stinking City's Edgers, always dressing things up in pretty words.'

Mercutian returned the glare, anger in his eyes. 'Only Inner City gutter trash "steal". This is a war we're fighting, not robbing a store on a street corner for handfuls of copper coins.'

Xarl's nasty smile never faded. 'Stern talk from the rich man's son. Easy to use pretty words when you're up at the top of the tower, overseeing a crime syndicate where everyone else does all the dirty work. I used to shoot City's Edge juves when they came slumming in our sector. I loved every minute of it, too.'

Mercutian breathed through his teeth, not saying a word.

The pause lasted exactly 6.2113 seconds. Deltrian knew this, because his grasp of chronology was an exercise in numerical perfection. He ended the silence himself, offering a rare attempt at humour to pierce what he considered to be a tangential and bemusing confrontation.

'If we are not allowed to dock, to use Nostraman parlance, that would be very... unlucky.'

The word felt unclean and uncomfortable. He immediately wished he'd not vocalised it, and responded in two ways. The first was a human tic of sorts, a motion of pointless reassurance that felt intriguingly mortal to indulge: he pulled his robe tighter around his skeletal frame, as if cold.

He was not cold, of course. Deltrian had removed the capacity to register temperature against his epidermal surfaces, and only tracked such variances with detached measurements from thermal signifiers in his fingertips.

The second reaction, taking place in the very same split second, was to dump the word from his short-term memory with a calculated data-purge.

It worked, though. Talos smiled at the tech-adept's attempt at humour, and silenced the warriors with a soft, 'Brothers, enough, please. Even the tech-adept of the Machine-God looks awkward to witness yet another family argument.'

'As you wish,' Mercutian saluted, fist over his heart. Xarl feigned interest in the hololithic, his sneer remaining in place.

'Lucoryphus?' Talos asked.

'Soul Hunter.'

'Please do not call me that.'

The Raptor cackled. 'What do you want?'

'Inform the Exalted of the tech-priest's estimated time frames.'

'Very well,' the Raptor breathed, already turning to crawl from the room.

'I don't like him,' Cyrion thought aloud.

Talos ignored his brother's remark. 'Can you translate the details of the repairs to an encrypted data-slate? I will ensure everything proceeds apace once we reach dock.'

'Compliance.' Deltrian hesitated. 'But do you mean to imply that I will not be going ashore in Hell's Iris?'

'Do you want to?' Talos frowned. 'Forgive me, I hadn't considered it. First Claw will accompany you as an honour guard if you choose to leave the ship.'

'I offer you this expression of vocalised gratitude,' the tech-adept said. 'As an addendum to the exchange of vital linguistics, I apply a further question. Is your arm functioning to an acceptable degree?'

Talos nodded. 'It is. My thanks again, tech-adept.'

'I am proud of that work.' Deltrian grinned at him. But then, Deltrian always grinned.

MARUC LOOKED OVER to where Septimus was working. The lamplight was dim, doing no favours to Maruc's straining eyes, but he was slowly getting used to it over recent weeks.

'What's this?' He held up a metal object the size of his thumb.

Septimus glanced over to the older serf. Maruc's desk in the shared workchamber was a mess of drill bits, files and oiled cloths. A half-assembled bolt pistol was scattered over the surface. Septimus put down the creased schematics he'd been studying.

'A suspensor. It's for Lord Mercutian's heavy bolter.'

The ship gave another shiver.

'Was that–?'

'No.' Septimus turned from Maruc's worried gaze, silently hoping Octavia would head for calmer tides. 'Whatever you were going to ask, it wasn't that. Don't ask, just work.'

'Listen, Septimus...'

'I am listening.'

'This is a rough ride. Rougher than even the bulk transport rigs I've sailed on. What if something goes wrong?'

Septimus just stared at him. 'What do you plan to do? Run outside and bind the hull together with industrial adhesive? By all means, go ahead. There are a million monsters waiting to cut up your soul, and I'll have the unwelcome pleasure of training someone else.'

'How can you be so calm?' Maruc scratched his cheek, leaving a smear of oil on his skin.

'I am calm because there's nothing I can do about it.'

'I've heard stories about ships getting lost in the warp...'

Septimus went back to his reading, though one gloved hand rested on his holstered pistol. 'Trust me, the stories do not approach the truth. The reality is much worse than your Imperial fairy tales. And now is really not the time to dwell on it.'

The ship gave another shake, this one severe enough to throw them both from their seats. Yells from other decks echoed through the ship's hull in an eerie cacophony.

'Warp engines are dead again,' Maruc swore, touching his fingertips to a bleeding temple. He'd cracked his head on the table edge as he went down.

'*Sinthallia shar vor vall'velias,*' Septimus hissed as he picked himself up off the decking.

'What does that mean?'

The other serf brushed his gloved fingers through his hair, keeping it out of his face. 'It means, "That woman will be the death of us".'

OCTAVIA LEANED FORWARDS in her throne, knuckling her closed eyes. Sweat dripped from her forehead onto the decking, making the soft pitter-patter of gentle rainfall. She spat, tasting blood and choosing not to look. The eye in the middle of her forehead ached from staring too long, and itched from the sweat trickling at its edges.

With a sigh, she slouched back. At least the ship had ceased its trembling. If the last few times were anything to go by, she had between one and three hours' rest before the Exalted ordered her to pull the ship back into the warp. This last juddering fall from the Sea of Souls had been the worst by far. Octavia felt her lingering connection to the ship, and the distress of the crew bleeding through the vessel's steel bones. People were injured this time. She'd dropped out of the warp much too sharply, though she'd held on as long as she could, until she'd almost felt her blood starting to boil.

'Mistress?' she heard a voice ask.

She knew the voice, and felt how close it was. She knew if she opened her eyes, she'd see a dead girl staring back at her.

'You're not there,' she whispered.

The dead girl stroked her fingers along Octavia's knee. The Navigator's skin prickled, and she jerked back in her seat.

Opening her human eyes was exquisitely difficult. A moment of strangely pleasant reluctance preceded the closing of her third eye, and the thrashing uncolours faded to a more traditional nothingness. Her human eyes opened with some effort, gummy with tears.

Hound kneeled at the front of her throne, his bandaged hands on her knee.

'Mistress?' he almost whined.

Hound. It's just Hound. 'Water,' she managed to say.

'Already have water for mistress,' he replied. He reached beneath his tattered cloak, drawing forth a grubby-looking canteen. 'It is warm. For this, I am sorry.'

She forced a smile for the eyeless freak. 'It's fine, Hound. Thanks.' The first swallow was no different from drinking honeyed nectar. She could almost imagine the sweet, warm liquid rehydrating her sore muscles. Back on Terra, she drank imported wine from crystal glasses. Now she was pathetically grateful for lukewarm water, recycled from who knew what, offered by the hand of a heretic.

She was too tired to cry.

'Mistress?'

She handed him back the canteen. Her stomach sloshed with the warm water, but she didn't care. 'What is it?'

Hound wrung his wrapped hands, watching her with blind eyes. 'You are struggling to fly. I worry for you. You sweat and moan more than Etrigius ever did when he guided the ship into the secret tides.'

Octavia's smile was more sincere as she wiped her face with her bandana. 'He was probably a lot better at this than I am. And he'd had more practice. I'm used to sailing within the light, not through the darkness.'

Hound seemed to digest this. His withered, stitched eyes seemed to stare right at her. 'Will you be all right?' he asked.

She hesitated, and realised she wasn't too tired to cry at all. His concern touched her, tingling at the corners of her eyes. Of all the tainted souls on this ship, it was this abused, malformed little man that asked her the most obvious of questions – the one even Septimus avoided asking, out of his stupid, stubborn politeness.

'Yes,' she said, swallowing back the threat of tears. 'I'll be fi–'

The Exalted's decree cut across her words. 'All crew, remain on station. Reconfigure the immaterium drive for return to the warp.'

She sighed to herself, closing her eyes again.

X

THE FLAYER

THEY CALLED HIM the Flayer, for reasons he felt were obvious. It wasn't a name he cherished, nor was it one he reviled. It was – like so many other things in his existence – simply something that happened in his presence, a matter over which he could exercise no control.

He had unprepossessing eyes that usually failed to display any emotion beyond a distant disinterest, and a face so thin it bordered on gaunt. He worked in his armour, and laboured several times a day to cleanse and reconsecrate the layered ceramite. The scrub cloths always came away reddened by the blood that decorated his armour in random patterns, for his duty was not a clean one. His helm was white, though he rarely wore it on board the station.

'Flayer,' a weak voice pried at his attention. 'Don't let me die.'

Variel turned his cold eyes down to the warrior on the surgical table. The stink of his burned skin and baked blood was a pungent musk, while the warrior's armour of red ceramite and bronze trimmings was a cracked ruin. For several moments, the Flayer watched his brother's life leaking out from a hundred cracks.

'You are already dead,' Variel told him. 'Your body has just not accepted it yet.'

The warrior's attempt at a defiant cry emerged as a strangled choke. He managed to grip Variel's bulky narthecium gauntlet. Bloody fingers smeared filth over the buttons and scanner display.

'Please do not touch me.' Variel gently removed his arm from the dying warrior's grip. 'I do not like to be touched.'

'Flayer...'

'And please refrain from begging. It will avail you nothing.' Variel let his forearm hover over the warrior's cracked breastplate. The gore-grimed narthecium clicked as it cogitated. The scanner display chimed twice. 'You have suffered severe ruptures to one lung and both hearts. Sepsis has saturated your bloodstream with poison, straining your organs to the point of failure.'

'Flayer... Please... I wish only to serve our lord...'

Variel rested his fist by the warrior's sweating temple. 'I know you, Kallas Yurlon. Nothing will be lost when you expire.' Here, he paused, but not to smile. Variel was unable to recall the last time he smiled. Not in the last decade, certainly. 'Do you wish the Emperor's Peace?'

'How dare you mock me?' Kallas sought to rise. Blood ran from the cracks in his armour. 'I... will speak... with the Corpsemaster...'

'No,' Variel tensed his fist. 'Sleep.'

'I–'

A piston's *snick* sounded from the narthecium gauntlet, powering an adamantium drill-bore through the warrior's temple with a crack, lodging within the brain. Kallas Yurlon immediately sagged, lowered back to the surgical table in the Flayer's gentle arms.

'You will not speak to Lord Garreon at all. As I said, you are already dead.'

Variel opened his hand, lifting his fingertips from the pressure plate built into the palm of his gauntlet. The bloodied drill-spike retracted back into its housing along the Flayer's forearm, secure in its pod of sterilising fluid.

He keyed in a short command on his vambrace controls, triggering the deployment and activation of several more traditional tools: a las-scalpel, a motorised bone saw, and the silver claws of a thoracic vice.

Next, he began the task of burning, cutting, spreading bone and peeling back flesh. As always, he worked in absolute silence, reluctantly breathing in the smells of incinerated muscle and exposed organs. The first progenoid came free in a sticky withdrawal, clinging trails of sealant mucus forming gooey strings between the gene-seed and its gaping cavity.

Variel dropped the bleeding organ into a chemical preservative solution, before moving his narthecium's tools to the dead warrior's throat and repeating the extraction procedure. He worked quicker this time, his efficiency bordering on brutal. Through a vertical slit in the side of the neck, the Flayer inserted reinforced forceps from his vambrace kit. The cut flesh parted with a leathery rip, freeing more blood and exposing the viscera within Kallas's neck. The second progenoid node came loose from the sinew with greater ease, trailing a few snapped veins. Variel placed the organ in the same solution as the first and sealed both of them in a glass cylinder.

On a whim, he reactivated the laser scalpel that extended from his bracer. The post-mortem surgery was quickly completed, and Variel peeled away the harvested skin, leaving the corpse staring at the ceiling through a flayed face.

Slowly, his cold eyes as emotionless as ever, Variel looked up. With his duty done, the Flayer's focus diffused, spreading wide as he let his surroundings filter back into his senses. Around him, there was a carnival of noise: the shouts, the screams, the oaths and curses rising above the blood-stink.

Variel gestured to two medicae slaves, summoning them closer. The Star of the Pantheon had been crudely burned into the flesh of their faces, and they wore aprons streaked with bodily fluids. Their augmetic limbs allowed them to serve as corpse-bearers, dragging warriors in full war-plate.

'Take this husk to the incinerators,' he ordered them. As the Flayer watched the humans hauling the dead meat away, he slid the glass cylinder with its precious cargo into the storage pod sheathed to his thigh armour.

Lastly, he cleaned his narthecium with several bursts of disinfectant spray, before drawing breath to speak a single word.

'Next.'

THEY CAME FOR him several hours later, as he'd known they would. The only surprise was that he faced only two. It seemed Kallas Yurlon hadn't been as beloved by his brothers as Variel had suspected.

'Hello,' he greeted them. His voice echoed faintly in the corridor, but didn't carry far. They'd chosen their spot well, for here in one of the station's secondary thoroughfare spinals, few others would hear any screams or gunfire.

'Flayer,' the first one growled. 'We have come for Kallas.'

Variel still wore no helm. Nor did the two brother-warriors he faced, and their scarlet and black ceramite was a mirror to his own. He met their eyes in turn, taking heed of the ritual scarification blighting their faces. Both had mutilated their flesh with carvings of the Pantheon Star.

How very telling.

Variel spread his arms, the very image of benediction but for the lack of any warmth in his eyes. 'How may I be of service, brothers?'

The second warrior stepped forwards now, aiming a deactivated chainsword at the Apothecary's throat.

'You could've saved Kallas,' he snarled, his bloodshot eyes unblinking.

'No,' Variel lied, 'he was too far gone. I gave him the Emperor's Peace.'

'Deceiver,' the warrior laughed. 'Betrayer. Now you mock his shade with such words.'

'We have come for Kallas,' the first legionary growled again.

'Yes, I believe you mentioned that. I am not deaf.'

'His spirit besieges us, demanding vengeance in his name.'

'Indeed.' Variel moved slowly, not wishing to startle his brothers into attacking, and tapped the dry leathery memento on his shoulder guard. The skinned, stretched face of Kallas Yurlon stared eyelessly back at them. 'Here he is. He is most pleased to see you. See how he smiles?'

'You...'

If there was one thing Variel never understood about many of his brothers, it was their propensity – no, their *need* – to posture. Each of them seemed to consider himself the philosophical protagonist of his own saga. Their hatreds mattered more than anything else; their glories and the abuses against them had to be spoken of at every opportunity.

Baffling.

As his brother began to utter yet another threat, Variel went for his bolt pistol. Three shots cracked into the warrior's chest, detonating in a storm of debris, throwing the legionary back against the wall. Shrapnel cracked against the ceiling light, shattering it and plunging the narrow corridor into darkness. He was already running as the chainsword started up.

Variel blind-fired back in the seconds it took his gen-hanced eyes to adjust, explosions breeding light in flickering stutters as his second volley of shells struck home. He reloaded as he sprinted, slamming a fresh magazine home and weaving around three corners in quick succession. Around the last, he waited, drawing his carving knife.

'Flayer!' the second warrior screamed after him. The thunder of running boots came closer with each heartbeat. Variel's eyes focussed through the darkness, his weapons heavy in his hands.

His brother rounded the corner to be met with Variel's dagger punching into the soft armour at his collar. With an exaggerated gargle, the warrior's forward momentum sent him sprawling, tumbling to the decking in a heap of squealing ceramite and humming armour joints.

Variel stalked closer, his pistol aimed at his brother's head. His eyes widened at what he saw. The warrior fought his way to his knees, and was dragging the knife from his own throat with pained, voiceless breaths. How very tenacious.

'Your vocal chords are destroyed,' Variel said. 'Please stop trying to curse at me. It is embarrassing.'

The warrior tried to rise again. A brutal pistol-whipping put an end to that, breaking his skull with a wet crack. Variel rested his bolter's muzzle against the back of his fallen brother's neck.

'And blessedly, I am spared from hearing any ludicrous last words.'

Variel spat acid onto his brother's armour, where it began to eat into the clenched fist icon of the Red Corsairs.

'I assure you, that was unintentionally symbolic,' he told the doomed warrior, and pulled the trigger.

LORD GARREON WAS a warrior that – to use a Badabian expression – wore his wounds with a smile. In his case, the expression was far from literal: he smiled about as often as his favoured apprentice, yet he kept his visage with the corruption battle had placed upon it, rather than re-engineer himself with bionics. Garreon's face was a pale picture of tectonic ruination, the lacing scars serving only to make an ugly man uglier. The right side of his face pulled tight at his temple and cheek – the taut, dead muscles giving him a scarred, eternal sneer.

'Variel, my boy.' His voice was kind where his face was not: a grandfather's tone, belying the massacres ordered by the ageing warrior's thin lips.

Variel did not turn to the greeting. He remained as he was, staring through the observation dome at the smoky void and the world turning below. Wraiths, little more than formless mist, drifted past the glass, the spectral suggestion of faces and fingers finding no purchase as they ghosted by. Variel ignored them with ease. The pining of lost souls was of no interest to him at all.

'Hail, sire,' he replied.

'So formal?' Garreon approached, his own armour rattling with its profusion of vials, trinkets and talismans. Variel knew the sound well. Truly, the Apothecary Lord had embraced the Chapter's allegiance to the Pantheon.

'My mind wanders,' the younger warrior confessed.

'And where does it wander? To the globe turning beneath our feet?' Garreon paused to moisten his lips with a swipe of his quivering tongue. 'Or the two bodies in Subsidiary Spinal Eleven?'

Variel narrowed his eyes as he stared at the black world outside the glass. 'They were newbloods,' he said. 'Weak. Worthless.'

'You left them unharvested,' his mentor pointed out. 'Lord Huron would be less than pleased.'

'Nothing of value was lost,' Variel replied. He moved away from the edge of the observation platform, crossing to the other side. Here, the view was a deeper slice of the tempestuous, cloudy void and the metallic bulk of the station itself, reaching for kilometres in every direction. Variel watched the comings and goings of dozens of cruisers for several minutes, as well as the swimming dances of the parasitic lesser ships clinging close to each of them. The warships drifted in orbit around the station, or remained docked at its edges. The lights of the shuttle traffic painted the poisoned nebula with flickering stars racing hither and thither.

'Inspiring, is it not?' Garreon said at last. 'To think we once ruled one world. Now, we cradle a horde of systems in our tender grip. Billions of lives. Trillions. That is how power is measured, boy: in the souls one holds in his clutches, and the lives one can end with a word.'

Variel's grunt was patently noncommittal. 'I sense you bring news, master.'

'I do. And it is tied to your wastrel ways.' The edge of a lecture dwelled within those words, Variel knew. 'Our lord desires gene-seed. A great genetic harvest, to swell our ranks with fresh blood. He will commit to the siege soon – a battle two years in the making. He bids all of his fleshsmiths to be ready.'

Variel shook his head. 'I find it difficult to believe Lord Huron would truly commit to this undertaking. He would not spend the Corsairs so frivolously.' He gestured at the fleet of cruisers drifting around the station. Many bore the black and red armour of the Tyrant's Own, while others displayed the hues of allegiance to other disgraced Adeptus Astartes Chapters. By far the greatest number were Imperial Navy vessels, their hulls desecrated and branded with the Pantheon Star. 'Lord Huron's forces could break the back of any armada in the Holy Fleet,' Variel added, 'but this is not enough to lay siege to a fortress-monastery. We would be obliterated the moment we entered orbit. Imagine, master – all these beautiful ships becoming burning hulks, screaming down through the atmosphere.' Variel snorted without an iota of amusement. 'Such a graveyard they would make.'

'You are not a general, my boy. You are a bone-cutter, a flesh-crafter. When the lord desires your perception of his crusades, I am sure he will ask for it.' Garreon's sneer pulled tighter. 'But do not hold your breath in expectation for that day to ever come.'

Variel inclined his head, meeting his master's eyes at last. 'Forgive me. My humours are in flux today. What do you require of me, master?'

Garreon forgave his apprentice with a wave of dismissal, casting the topic from his mind. 'Lord Huron has not summoned us, but we will go to him before he does.'

Variel knew the purpose even before he asked. 'He suffers?'

'He always suffers.' Garreon licked his lips again. 'You know that as well as I. But come, let us ease it again for a time, if we are able.'

LUFGT HURON SAT in his ornate throne, armoured fists clutching at the armrests. The great Gothic chamber stood empty but for the Tyrant himself; all of his courtiers, attendants, bodyguards and beseechers sent away while his Apothecaries worked their trade. Variel had seen the expansive hall play host to hundreds of warriors at any given time, despite the fact that this deep-void station was far from the Tyrant's largest or most opulent bastion. Now, the vast chamber echoed with the sounds of Huron's ragged breathing and the tri-hum of the three renegades' war-plate.

'Garrlllmmmnnnuh...' the Tyrant drooled. 'Garrelllmmnuh.'

'Hush, Great One,' the Apothecary Lord replied, knuckle-deep in Huron's skull. 'I can correct the synapse relays,' he sighed. 'Again.'

Variel crouched by the side of the iron throne, his scalpel and microforceps picking at the Tyrant's throat. With each crackling breath, the reinforced hydraulics that mimicked Huron's neck muscles clicked and clanked. What little flesh remained was atrophied and almost nerveless, lumpy with scar tissue too degraded to bond with synthetic skin. The Tyrant had long ago endured injury to the very edge of destruction, and the mechanical repairs that kept him alive were crude, hideous, loud... but ultimately functional.

They were, however, temperamental.

Variel's memory, like most of the humans elevated into the ranks of the Adeptus Astartes, was as close to eidetic as mortality would allow. By his reckoning, this was the seventy-eighth instance he had been summoned to tend to his liege lord's augmetics, not including the initial surgeries performed with Garreon and two Techmarines in order to save the Tyrant's life.

Those first instances had been closer to engineering than surgery. A third of Huron's body was reduced to molten meat and burned bone, and in cutting away the ravaged flesh, a great deal more of his mortal frame had to be sacrificed to prepare attachment ports for extensive bionics. The right side of his body no longer existed beyond the clanking grind of Machine Cult ingenuity – all fibre-bundle muscles, piston joints and metal bones fused to the warrior's armour.

Variel had seen the bio-auspex readings at the time, just as he'd seen them each time since. The degree of pain registered within Huron's mind was far beyond the realms of human tolerance. Each time Lord Garreon or the Flayer burned out the synaptic relays, dulling their master's perception of his own agony, it would only be a matter of months before his enhanced physiology compensated for the damage, repairing the nerves enough to transmit pain again. Short of invasive lobotomising surgery that would risk what little brain tissue remained, there was nothing his healers could do to offer a permanent solution.

So he endured. He endured, and he suffered, and he channelled the torment into his piratical ambitions.

The Tyrant's throat and chest were bare now, his breastplate pulled away to reveal internal organs that bore closer resemblance to the filthy, oily innards of an engine than the organs of a human being. What was left of Huron's face – the grey, dead-fleshed parts that weren't given over to exposed bionics – twitched in response to unintentional tics as Garreon worked inside his lord's brain.

Huron hissed in a breath, recapturing some of the saliva trickling over his lips. 'Better,' he growled. 'Better, Garreon.'

Variel used a steel scalpel to peel back a layer of nerveless skin from where it was caught and mangled in the iron workings of the Tyrant's throat bionics. With patience and flesh-sealant, he reworked the flap of flesh, bonding it back in place. His eyes flicked upward, locking in place when he saw Huron's own gaze had dropped to meet his. The Tyrant's eyes blazed with the force of his ambition: each moment was lived in the path of pain, and every day saw him lording over an empire in the heart of madness.

'Variel.' The lord's voice was a bass rumble. 'I heard K-Kallas Yurlon died on your t-table today.' The spasms in his speech came with each probe of Garreon's scalpel.

'This is so, my lord.'

Huron bared his teeth in a savage smile. Variel stared back, seeing a warrior that should have died long ago – a creature held together as much by hate as by augmetic implantation. In any other living being, he'd have considered such a notion an idiotic attempt to forge a legend through hyperbole. But Lugft Huron, the Tyrant of Badab, known by the names Blackheart and the Blood Reaver, needed little assistance in turning his deeds into legend. The empire he ruled assured him of infamy; his conquests assured him of his place in history; and biologically speaking, the Flayer struggled to see how the Tyrant maintained a grip on life, let alone still displayed such prowess in battle.

The answer was as unpalatable as it was mythical: the Astral Claws only survived to become the Red Corsairs because Huron sold their souls to hidden masters within the warp. At the Chapter's darkest hour, he pledged them to the Unknown Pantheon, swearing them to an eternal crusade against the Imperium they'd once served.

After the Chapter's remnants fled here to the Maelstrom, mutation and instability began to settle into their gene-seed with corrosive rapidity. Variel had studied the changes, as had Lord Garreon and the other remaining Apothecaries. In mere centuries, many of the Red Corsairs were as victimised by genetic disorder as the Traitor Legions dwelling within the Eye of Terror for millennia.

Such a pact, Variel thought now. *Survival, at the price of corruption.*

'Kallas was close to taking the champion's mantle. You could have saved him, Variel.'

The Flayer didn't waste time asking how Huron knew the truth. 'Perhaps, my lord. I will not lie and say I liked him, but I did my duty. I weighed his life against the other work facing me. Keeping Kallas alive would have necessitated several hours of difficult surgery, ensuring the deaths of other warriors awaiting urgent treatment.'

The Tyrant shuddered as Garreon resealed his skull plating. 'I thank you, both of you. You've done well, as always.'

Both Apothecaries removed themselves from the dais as Huron rose to his feet. Ornate power armour thrummed and whirred, and the warrior breathed a satisfied sigh. The massive power claw serving as the Tyrant's right hand closed and opened, the talons curling in the cold air of the chamber. In the weapon's palm, Variel took note of the Pantheon Star carved into the crimson ceramite. It drew his eyes as it always did.

'I was informed, three hours ago, that we have uninvited guests in the northern reaches.' Distant light from the local sun reflected off the visible chrome portions of Huron's skull as he turned. 'A Legion ship. As tempting as it was to order one of our fleets to leave them as wreckage, I foresee a greater use for these visitors.'

Lord Garreon's sneer never wavered. Variel remained silent, wondering why the Tyrant chose to speak of such things before them both.

'It seems,' Huron bared teeth of solid metal, 'that they request sanctuary and succour. A long transcription of repairs and resupply accompanied their request to enter our space. They will reach us within two weeks, whereupon we shall discuss the price of our assistance.'

'You seem amused, my lord,' Variel said at last. 'But I am at a loss to see why.'

Huron chuckled, saliva stringing between his steel teeth. 'Because it is the *Covenant of Blood*. And if the Exalted and his prophet intend to leave Hell's Iris alive, let alone with their precious warship repaired, they have a great deal of bootlicking to do.'

XI
THE MAELSTROM

THE *Covenant of Blood* drifted through the roiling void, no longer buffeted by the tides of the true warp, yet still shivering in the weaker currents of...

Well. Of whatever this place was. Octavia wasn't sure. She reached up to check her bandana, as if to reassure herself it was still there, still blocking her secret sight.

As the daughter of a Navigator bloodline, she was hardly unfamiliar with the way the Sea of Souls spilled over into the material universe. Rifts in space were rare, but each was an ugly, dangerous scab – a tormenting hazard to stellar navigation, avoided by every Navigator with a desire to keep their sanity intact and their ship in one piece. It was the warp and natural space amalgamated in defiance of physical laws: a thinner breed of the former; a haunted, twisted reflection of the latter.

They'd already sailed past several worlds, through the heart of three systems. On one of the worlds, the oceans had boiled, visible even from orbit. Unnatural storms plagued the planet's face, raining piss, acid and blood onto the continents below.

Space itself was corrupted. She watched the bank of screens before her, seeing a thousand shades of violet and red pressing against the external lenses. The mess outside the hull clashed and swirled with the repellent properties of oil and water, always colliding, bonding without mixing. Her staring eyes interpreted the colourful dance as a liquid mist, thick enough to make the ship shudder, thin enough to show the stars beyond.

If she stared long enough, she could make out the suggestions of faces and fingers in the ooze, screaming, reaching, dissolving. Some seemed to taunt her with their maddening familiarity. She swore she saw Kartan Syne at one point – the last captain she'd served. And more than once, the rippling tides resolved into the face of her oldest brother, Lannic, dead these last six years after his trader vessel was warp-lost on the Eastern Fringe.

'Why do you watch, mistress?' one of her attendants asked. She glanced at the wretch, who was unhealthily tall and sexless in its overcloak, keeping its face behind stained bandages. Several others lurked close to the door, whispering amongst themselves. It was impossible not to smell their sweat, their stinking, bloodstained bandages, and the rancid oil-blood of their bionics.

'Because,' she said, 'it's like the warp, but... I can see it with my human eyes.' How to explain the difference to one not born to a Navigator bloodline? Impossible.

One of her attendants trudged closer. 'Mistress,' the hunched figure said.

'Hello, Hound. Could you get rid of the others?' She didn't say it was because of the smell – Hound didn't exactly come across as a floral garden himself, and she couldn't recall the last time she had a chance to bathe, either.

As Hound shooed the other attendants from her chamber, Octavia stared back at the screens. The ship was passing a cloudless planet that looked to be made of rusted iron. Whatever its true form, the Maelstrom had warped the world into a visage of grinding continental plates formed from scrap. Octavia stared at the great canyons carved into the planet's face, wondering what it would be like to walk on such a world.

'*Corshia sey,*' a female voice said behind her.

She was out of the throne in a heartbeat, spinning and drawing her pistol, aiming at–

'Now that's a curious welcome,' said Septimus. He rested his hands at his gun belt, thumbs hooked into the leather strap. 'Have I annoyed you in some unforeseen way?'

'How long have you been standing there?' Octavia narrowed her eyes. 'When did you come in?'

'Hound let me in a moment ago. He's outside with Maruc and the rest of your *nishallitha* coterie.'

Now that word she did know. *Nishallitha.* Poisonous.

Septimus came closer, and she let him pluck the gun from her hands. This close, he smelled of fresh sweat and the coppery oils he used to maintain First Claw's weapons. After placing her gun on the seat of her throne, he took her hands in his own, the beaten fingerless leather gloves wrapping her grubby, pale fingers.

'What's wrong?' he asked. 'Your hands are very cold.'

He was a head taller than her. She had to look up to meet his eyes, and the fall of his hair covered most of the chromed augmetics at his cheek and temple.

'This whole ship is cold,' she replied. It was difficult not to be aware of just how close he was now. She'd not been this close to another person in months – not since Talos had carried her from the prison facility. And that had been a cold salvation, relief permeating her more than any real comfort. This was human contact, the close warmth of a real person, not a towering fanatic in growling armour plating, or a hunched mutant with his eyes sewn shut.

'What is it?' he asked. The traces of blond stubble marked his jawline, where he'd not shaved in the last two days. Worry stained his features. She thought it again, despite herself: he'd be handsome, if he wasn't a heretic – if the darkness of this ship didn't run in his blood.

'I'm not used to being touched.' She tilted her head, little realising how imperious she suddenly looked. Her breeding as a noble scion of Terra wasn't as far behind her as she believed.

He released her hands, though not immediately. Slowly, his fingers unlocked from trapping hers, and the warmth he brought receded.

'Forgive me,' he said. 'Sometimes, I forget your unique upbringing.'

'That's one of the reasons I put up with you,' she smiled. 'What did you say when you came in?'

It broke the moment. Septimus narrowed his good eye, and the augmetic lens clicked and whirred as it struggled to mirror the movement. 'I didn't say anything. I entered and merely watched. You looked peaceful for once. I hesitated to disturb you.'

'*Corshia sey.*' She said it softly. 'What does it mean?'

'It means to beware,' said Septimus. 'Or, more literally, it is a slang threat from the Legion's home world. A warning given to those soon to die: "Breathe now". The implication is simple: breathe while you still can.'

'Yes, I got that.' She faked a smile. 'Charming culture.'

Septimus shrugged, his jacket rustling. 'Nostraman gutter threats. The lords speak them often. Did you hear it from one of the crew?'

'Stop worrying,' she shook her head, giving him her best, most convincingly irritated glare. 'And get your hands off your guns. I'm not a child, needing to be defended on the scholam playground every time you hear someone calling me a name.'

He looked away, suddenly awkward. 'I did not mean to imply anything.'

'It's fine,' she said, her tone suggesting quite the opposite. 'Just forget it.'

'As you wish.' He offered her a polite bow. 'I sense you wish to be alone, so I will comply.'

'*Wait.*'

He halted, and she cleared her throat. 'I mean, wait a moment. Did you want something? You don't come here much, any more.' She tried to keep the last comment casual, purging it of anything beyond neutrality.

She wasn't entirely successful. She saw it in the way he looked at her. 'The Exalted ordered your isolation,' he said. 'And I have been attending to my own duties. Maruc needed training. We had five suits of ceramite war-plate to restore, as well as First Claw's weapons.'

Octavia brushed his excuses away. 'So did you want something?'

He frowned. 'Forgive me, I am not sure I understand why you are so terse tonight. I wished to see you, nothing more.' He reached a hand into his jacket pocket, leaving it in there. After an awkward moment, he asked, 'How are you feeling?'

So it was going to be like that. Typical. The very last thing she needed. 'Can you just relax, please? For once? I'm not sure I can deal with your formal manners tonight, Septimus. I need a friend, not another handler. Choose which one you are, please, and stick to it.'

His jaw tightened, and she felt a guilty thrill of victory. She'd struck a mark there.

'It's not formality,' he replied. 'It's called respect.'

'Whatever it is, I prefer it when you leave it at the door.' She forced a smile, retying her ponytail. 'Have you looked out the window recently? Metaphorically speaking.'

'I try not to. You should probably do the same.' Instead of elaborating, he walked around her chamber, stepping over clothing and screwed up balls of paper from her many failed attempts to keep a journal. 'When was the last time you cleaned this chamber? Yet again, it appears you lost a fight with a storm in here.'

'It's not that bad.'

'By the standards of the slave holds, yes, it's quite the princess's palace.' He drew his hand from his pocket and tossed something to her. 'For you.'

Octavia caught it in both hands. A tiny bundle, no larger than her thumb, wrapped in blue cloth. The material looked ripped from a Legion slave uniform. She glanced at Septimus, but he was busy turning off her two dozen monitors, one by one. Slowly, she opened the ragged cloth.

A ring sat in the palm of her hand. A circle of light, creamy ivory, with elegant, miniscule Nostraman runes branded onto the surface.

'Oh,' she said, for want of anything better to say. She didn't know whether she should feel pleased, shocked or confused. All she knew for certain was that she felt all three.

'It's to thank you,' Septimus deactivated the last viewscreen, 'for Crythe. When you helped us run, rather than kill us all.'

'Oh,' she said again.

'I traded for it,' he said. 'In Blackmarket, of course.' He moved back over to her, standing by her throne. 'They're very rare. The material is difficult to cut into jewellery. Only those with access to machines are able to do it.'

She turned it over in her hands, unable to read the spidery Nostraman. 'What's it made from?'

'Bone. From a Blood Angel – one of the enemy warriors that died on board.'

Octavia looked up at him again. 'You bought me a gift made from the bones of an Imperial hero.' It wasn't a question, nor was it spoken with a smile.

He smiled, though. 'When you put it like that...'

'I don't want it.' She offered it back to him. 'You're unbelievable.' She shook her head as she met his eyes. 'You're also an idiot, and... and a heretic.'

He didn't take it back. He just walked away, nudging a pile of junk with the side of his boot. 'All of those accusations are true.'

Anger was getting the better of her now, but she let it flow, guiding her incautious words. 'Was this supposed to impress me?'

Septimus hesitated. 'Impress you? To what end?'

She glowered. 'You *know* to what end.'

His laughter annoyed her even more. 'You're serious,' he said, and laughed again.

'Get out.' She smiled thinly, 'Before I shoot you.'

He didn't leave. He came back over to her, taking her hand and slowly, carefully bringing her dirty knuckles to his lips. The kiss was as soft as the memory of a breeze.

'That is not how this works, Octavia. You are the most precious mortal commodity on this vessel, and a death sentence hangs over anyone that angers you, for you are the Legion's favoured prize. You are beautiful – the only beauty in this sunless world. But it has not crossed my mind to do anything more than watch you from afar. Why would I have ever considered it?'

He seemed genuinely amused, holding her by the hand as he spoke. 'I am not one to chase uncatchable prey. My normal duties are difficult enough.'

She still scowled up at him, resisting the need to lick her dry lips. His stare wasn't annoying, but she told herself it was.

'You should go,' she told him. Her voice caught on the words. Throne, he had the darkest eyes. Well... one, anyway. The lens was half-covered by his scruffy hair.

'Besides, I heard a tale,' he lowered his voice, 'that humans die from a Navigator's kiss.'

'That sounds like a legend to me,' she said, looking up at him. 'But you never know.' She tilted her head, her lips parting slightly. 'Navigators are dangerous creatures. Don't ever trust one.'

He trailed a thumb along her jawline, not saying anything. Octavia drew a breath, and–

–froze as the door opened on grinding tracks. After a split second, she stepped back from Septimus in an awkward hop, thumping her backside into her writing desk. Hound lumbered in, followed by Maruc. The older man looked like a beggar in his dishevelled slave uniform. He gave her a shy wave, sensing he was intruding.

'Mistress,' her attendant said. 'Mistress, forgive me.'

'It's fine.' She refused to look at Septimus. 'It's fine. What is it? What's wrong?'

'A guest, mistress. I could not refuse him entry.'

One of the Legion's warriors stalked into the room. His midnight armour caught what little light existed, its polished surface painted with bolts of lightning, akin to veins along the ceramite. His bare face was thin, unscarred, with emotive eyes despite their rich blackness. He was smiling, though only slightly.

'Lord Cyrion,' Septimus bowed.

'Septimus,' the warrior greeted him. 'We dock tonight. You are needed in the preparation chambers.' Cyrion gestured to Maruc, with a growl of armour joints. 'You too, Nonus. The thrills of hard labour await, my dear artificers.'

As the humans walked from the room, Cyrion looked over at the flushed Navigator. She seemed to be intrigued by a few scraps of paper on her desk, judiciously avoiding looking at anyone else.

'So,' he said to Octavia. 'How are you?'

HELL'S IRIS WELCOMED them two hours later with no shortage of posturing. Frigates declaring themselves as outriders for the Blood Reaver's fleet pulled into formation with the limping *Covenant*, escorting the larger cruiser closer to the station.

On the bridge, the Exalted sat enthroned, flanked by Garadon and Malek of the Atramentar in their hulking Terminator war-plate. The human crew worked around them, busy with the mathematical intricacies of guiding the massive warship into port.

'We made it,' the creature drawled.

Malek inclined his head in a purring growl of armour joints. His tusked helm swung to face his master. 'Now comes the hard part: staying alive until we leave.'

The Exalted grunted in acknowledgement as Hell's Iris grew larger on the occulus. It galled it to admire what it was seeing, but the Tyrant's resources were second only to the Despoiler's in scope and might. Hell's Iris triggered a very specific jealousy within the daemon's heart, for its past as much as what it represented now. The port was a nexus of secessionist activity, and it was far from the largest waypoint in the Tyrant's empire. The station itself had once been the Ramilies-class void fortress *Canaan's Eye*, positioned in deep space controlled by the Astral Claws Chapter. When indignity and betrayal swept through the region centuries before, during the Badab War, the fortress became one of many assets claimed by the rebels in their drive to secede from the Imperium. Imperial archives listed *Canaan's Eye* as destroyed by a battlefleet led by the Overlord-class cruiser *Aquiline*. What Terran records failed to state was the subsequent recapture and towing of the Ramilies hulk into the Maelstrom warp rift by the piratical renegades that rose in the wake of the Astral Claws' subjugation.

Centuries of raiding had only added to the rebuilt station. It sprawled in space around the dead, warp-corrupted world of Yrukhal, its metal halls home to tens of thousands of souls, serving as a port for hundreds of ships.

'My skin crawls to return here,' Malek admitted.

'Too many ships,' said Garadon. 'Even for Hell's Iris, this is too many.'

The Exalted nodded once, its eyes never leaving the occulus. Massive cruisers suckled at the station's fuel feeds, while smaller destroyers and frigates sailed at the outpost's perimeters.

A continent of steel, populated by carrion-feeders.

'Huron himself is here. Nothing else explains the presence of so many warships in his colours.'

Malek grunted. 'That will not make our dealings any easier.'

The Exalted ground its teeth together. 'Master of Auspex, sweep this fleet.'

'Aye, my lord,' a human officer called back.

The command deck doors rumbled open, admitting two more Legion warriors. Talos and Lucoryphus – the former striding in with his weapons sheathed, the latter crawling with all the monstrous grace of a gargoyle.

'Blood of the Legion,' Talos swore as he saw the occulus. 'What have we sailed into?'

'A sea of sharks,' Lucoryphus hissed. 'Very bad. Very, very bad.'

Belatedly, Talos made his salute to the Atramentar warriors on the Exalted's dais. Lucoryphus didn't bother. He prowled around the bridge, disconcerting the mortal crew by staring at them. His painted, crying faceplate watched with unblinking intensity.

'Greetings,' he leered at one officer. Even hunched on all fours, Lucoryphus was the height of the mortal man, and four times as bulky in his war-plate with its back-mounted thrusters.

'Hail, my lord,' the officer replied. He was a gunnery rating, clad in a faded Imperial Navy uniform stripped of insignia, his silvering hair thinning at the crown. Despite half a lifetime in the Legion's service – indeed, in the Exalted's presence – attracting the direct attention of a master was still something to make even the most jaded soul start sweating.

'I am Lucoryphus,' the Raptor cawed, 'of the Bleeding Eyes.'

'I... know who you are, my lord.'

The warrior crawled closer, its weeping eye lenses somehow alive with cold delight. The officer instinctively inched away.

'Do not run. That would be unwise. Bad things happen to humans who turn their backs on me.'

The officer swallowed. 'How may I serve you, lord?'

'You are not of the home world. Your eyes are not pure.'

'I was taken,' the officer cleared his throat, 'I was taken years ago, in a raid. I serve loyally, my lord.'

'You are not of the home world,' Lucoryphus hissed. 'Then you have never heard the hunting call of a Nostraman condor.' The Raptor's neck twitched, causing a growl of joint servos.

A second shadow, a taller one, fell over the mortal's face. He managed a salute, and the words, 'Lord Talos,' fell from his lips.

Lucoryphus turned on his claws. Talos stood behind him, his armour bedecked in skulls and Blood Angel helms.

'Soul Hunter?'

'Please do not call me that.' Talos gestured to the officer. 'This man's name is Antion. He has served us twenty-three standard years, in the destruction of exactly eighty-seven Imperial vessels, and more raids than I care to remember. Is that not true, Gunnery Officer Antion Kasel?'

The officer saluted again. 'It is true, my lord.'

Talos nodded, looking back down at Lucoryphus. 'We do not toy with the lives of those that serve us, Raptor.' His gauntlet rested on Malcharion's bolter mag-locked to his thigh. 'That would be counterproductive.'

'The mortal and I were merely having a conversation.' Lucoryphus's voice hinted at a smile behind the daemonic faceplate.

'The mortal has a duty to do. If we need to open fire, I would prefer all of our gunnery officers to be able to do so, rather than have them distracted in conversations with you.'

Lucoryphus gave a cackle and crawled away, armour joints snarling.

'Thank you, my lord,' the officer said quietly, saluting again.

Thank you. Those words again. Twice in one year. Talos almost smiled at the thought.

'Back to your duties, Kasel.' He moved away, returning to the Exalted's raised dais. A rune flickered on his retinal display – incoming message – the name-glyph signified Malek of the Atramentar. Talos blinked at the icon to activate it.

'Nicely done,' Malek voxed.

'Raptors,' replied Talos. 'Those things should be leashed.'

'And muzzled,' Malek agreed. 'Brother, a warning: the Exalted is uneasy. Huron is here, at Hell's Iris.'

'Understood.' Talos cancelled the link, standing on the steps leading up to the throne. Only the Atramentar and the Exalted itself were permitted to stand at the top of the dais.

'Auspex scan complete,' the Master of Vox called.

The Exalted's eyes were closed. It reached its senses beyond the heavy, cold hull, feeling the drifting warp-wind as the *Covenant* adjusted its course by guidance thrusters. The escorting frigates broke formation and pulled away, rejoining the patrolling fleet.

Something... the Exalted sensed it out there. *Something familiar...*

'Speak,' the creature demanded. Its black eyes flicked open. 'Ignore the names and classes of individual craft. Tell me only what matters.'

'My lord, the enemy fleet is–'

'They are not our enemy,' the Exalted snapped. '*Yet*. Continue.'

'The Corsair force is of considerable strength, but with unconventional fleet disposition. Many cruisers lack support craft, and several frigates and destroyers seem to lack any larger cohesion. This is a mustering of several flotillas, with at least nine marks of allegiance spread across various craft. They appear to be composed of renegade Adeptus Astartes Chapters and defected Imperial Navy vessels.'

'No,' the Exalted growled. 'There is something else at work, here.' The daemon stared into the occulus, its talons clicking at keys on the armrests of its throne, cycling through external views.

'There,' it barked, baring its teeth. 'That ship is no Red Corsair vessel, no matter what its colours claim.'

'It registers as the *Venomous Birthright*.'

The Exalted shook its horned, tusked head again. 'No. Probe deeper. Peel back the layers of auspex deception.'

'Focussed scanning, my lord.'

The Exalted narrowed its glinting eyes, unable to break its stare. The vessel was a weapon of crenellated, Gothic beauty, a sister to the *Covenant of Blood*, born of the same design and craftsmanship. Whereas the *Covenant*'s hull echoed from the earliest ages of the Great Crusade, before the full homogenisation wrought by the Standard Template Constructs of Mars, much of the Corsair fleet was wrought from the more codified principles of construction instituted on Mars in the last ten millennia.

The *Venomous Birthright* obeyed no such strictures. It could only have been born in the naively prosperous centuries of the Crusade itself, or in the bloody, hate-fuelled decade of the Horus Heresy. Whichever was true, it traced its roots to an era before the rest of this fleet had even been conceived.

'My lord?' The officer sounded uneasy.

'Speak.'

'The ship's transponder code has been altered. I read signs of encryption scarring in its identity broadcasts.'

'Break them. Now.'

'Aye, my lord.'

The Exalted closed its eyes again, reaching out with its hidden sense. With deceivingly gentle caresses, it ran ethereal feelers over the warship's hull, smoothing its psychic sense over the armoured contours. Yes, the vessel was old – ancient, even – so much older than these other craft. Its pedigree was a noble one, and it had sailed the stars since the Great Betrayal, ten thousand years before.

Greetings, void hunter, the Exalted whispered to the craft. *You are no weapon of the thin-blooded Corsairs. You are older, greater, and were once something so much more.*

Something within the ship, some cold-fire core of intelligence, responded with a predatory snarl. Its presence was goliath, its emotions too alien to contain within a human, or even daemonic, mind. Yet for all its immensity, it spared no more than a second's attention for the psychic intrusion.

Begone, its immense heart demanded, *little fleshthing*.

The second of connection was enough. The Exalted pulsed back into the body it wore, opening its eyes to see the bridge once more.

'My lord, the encryption was crude. I've managed to pierce it, and the vessel is–'

'I know what it is,' the Exalted growled. 'Or rather, what it was. Did you ascertain its former name?'

'Aye, my lord.'

'Speak it, for all to hear.'

'The original identity signifier reads as the *Echo of Damnation*.'

The Atramentar warriors tensed by the throne's sides, and Lucoryphus released a hissing stream of Nostraman invective. The Exalted gave a wet, grinding chuckle, feeling the name set Vandred's spirit writhing within.

'Yes,' it grunted. 'There, my brothers, is the reality of the carrion-feeders we are dealing with. The Corsairs, in their endless expansions, have claimed one of the Eighth Legion's warships. Look upon it, and tell me your thoughts.'

It was Talos who spoke. 'Some sins will not be allowed to stand.' He faced the Exalted, his words burning with conviction even through the crackling of his helm's vox-speakers.

'That's our ship.' The prophet clenched his teeth behind his faceplate. 'And we are not leaving until we take it back.'

EVEN IN DOCK, the Maelstrom's void-tides rippled against the *Covenant*, their gentle crashing formed from aetheric energies cooled in the icy nothingness of true space. The crew couldn't help but hear the polluted solar winds caressing the warship's hull, and despite all he'd seen and heard in the last ten years, it set Septimus's teeth on edge. He checked his pistols, thumbing the ammunition runes to check their power cells.

'Nonus,' he said.

Maruc clicked his tongue, not quite tutting. 'I'm not sure I'll be able to get used to that.'

'It's not that difficult, I assure you.' Septimus handed him one of the pistols. 'Have you ever fired one of these?'

The older man scratched at his unshaven jawline, which was well on its way to being buried beneath an itchy grey beard. 'Of course not.'

'Well, this is how you do it.' Septimus raised his pistol, mimed the activation, and dry-fired three times. 'It's not difficult. These were designed for use in the Imperial Guard, so they are far from complicated.'

'Hey.'

Septimus raised an eyebrow. 'Yes?'

'Don't you be mocking the Guard, son. They're heroes, one and all.'

Septimus smiled. 'Your perspective tends to change when your masters decorate their armour with Imperial Guard skulls for months after each encounter with them.'

'I wanted to be Guard, you know.'

Septimus let it drop. 'As I was saying, keep this weapon with you at all times. Hell's Iris is a particularly unpleasant port.'

Maruc – he still couldn't think of himself as 'Nonus' – blinked twice. 'We're going ashore?'

'Of course we are.' Septimus leashed his machete to his shin. 'We have a duty to do. This place is dangerous, but if we tread with care, no harm will come to us.'

'Is Octavia coming?'

Septimus gave him a look. 'She's a Navigator. The Legion can't risk her in a hellhole like this.'

'But it can risk you and me?'

The slave grinned. 'Can and will. Come, let's get this over with.'

First claw crossed the umbilical corridor into the station, to be met by a contingent of the Tyrant's warriors blocking the opposite bulkhead. Their ceramite war-plate, rendered in red, black and bronze, was a riotous contrast to the midnight and bone worn by the Night Lords.

'Nobody say anything foolish,' Talos warned First Claw over the vox.

'As if we ever would,' Cyrion replied.

Each of them openly carried their weapons drawn and ready, mirroring the posture of the Red Corsairs ahead.

'Halt,' the squad leader demanded. His horned helm regarded each of the Night Lords in turn. 'What brings you to Hell's Iris?'

Xarl snorted, resting his immense chainblade on his shoulder. 'I have a question of my own. Why do you thin-blooded little mongrels not kneel before warriors of the First Legions?'

Talos took a breath. 'You are an absolute gift to diplomacy, brother.'

Xarl just grunted in reply.

'Was that supposed to be humorous?' the Corsair leader asked.

Talos ignored the question. 'We need repairs. I am charged by my commander to speak with Lord Huron.'

The Corsairs exchanged glances. Most abstained from wearing their helms, leaving their scarred faces on hideous display. Talos marked the emblems of the Powers cut and branded into facial flesh. Such devotion. Such ardent, fevered devotion.

'I know your ship,' the Corsair leader said. 'I remember the *Covenant of*

Blood, and I remember you, "prophet". Your actions last time you walked these halls have earned you no friends.'

'If you know us, then further introductions are pointless,' said Talos. 'Now let us pass.'

'I am gatemaster for this dock,' the Corsair growled through his helm's vox-speakers. 'It would be wise for you to show a little respect.'

'And we,' Mercutian pointed out, 'were waging the Long War for several thousand years before you were born. Respect goes both ways, renegade.'

The Corsairs bristled, clutching their bolters tighter. 'Where was this vaunted respect last time you walked within our domain? I have warriors that still carry scars from the last time we met. What if I choose to send you back to the junker you arrived in?'

'That would be unwise. Lord Huron is expecting us.' Talos reached to unlock the seals at his collar, pulling his helm free with a hiss of vented air pressure. The corridor reeked of stale bodies and armour oils, with the faintest hint of something sulphurous beneath. He looked at the Corsairs, black eyes taking them in one by one.

'I appreciate the blow to your pride,' Talos said. 'We were less than courteous guests when we last came this way. But your master has already made his intentions clear by escorting us into dock. He wishes to see us. So if we could dispense with the posturing, nobody needs to die this time. We will go past you, or we will go through you.'

The Corsairs raised their weapons as one, bolter-stocks cracking back against shoulder guards. First Claw responded in kind, chainblades revving and pistols rising in unison. Talos held Malcharion's bolter in one hand, aiming both barrels at the Corsair leader's faceplate.

Cyrion chuckled over the vox. 'Another warm welcome.'

'Lower your weapons,' the Corsair commanded.

'Gatemaster...' Talos warned. 'It does not need to play out this way.'

'*Lower your weapons,*' he repeated.

'Talos,' another voice called in greeting. From behind the Corsair squad, another warrior wearing the armour of the fallen Chapter pushed through his brothers. The squad nodded in acknowledgement of the figure, though he paid them no heed in kind.

The Corsair stood between both squads, blocking the line of fire. Talos lowered his bolter at once. Xarl, Mercutian and Uzas did so with greater reluctance.

'Brother,' the Corsair said, and offered his hand to the prophet. Their armour clanked together as they gripped wrists for a moment, forming the traditional greeting between warriors since time immemorial.

'It is good to see you,' the prophet said. 'I'd hoped you would be here.'

The Corsair shook his head. 'I had hoped you wouldn't be. Your timing, Talos – as always – is venomous.' He turned to the warriors behind him. 'Stand down.'

They complied, saluting as they did so. The leader grunted a reluctant, 'As you wish, Flayer.'

'Come, all of you.' Variel's cold eyes drifted over First Claw. 'I will take you to Lord Huron.'

XII

PROPHET AND PRISONER

'YOU WILL COME with us to Vilamus.'

'I knew this was all going too well,' Cyrion voxed over a private channel. Talos ignored him.

'That is the price of my aid,' the seated figure added. 'When we lay siege to Vilamus, your forces will be in the vanguard.'

Lord Huron's throne room in Hell's Iris was hardly devoted to any suggestion of subtlety. The station's war room had been converted to a monarch's chamber, replete with a raised throne and rows of crusade banners hanging from the ceiling. Rows of bodyguards, supplicants and beseechers lined the walls: human, Renegade Astartes, and creatures lost in the mutable states of those in thrall to Chaos worship. The decking showed its stains with unwashed pride – blood, burns and greyish slime in equal measure – while the air bore the stink of something sulphurous, rising from the breath of the gathered warriors.

It all added to the pain-pulse buzzing inside the prophet's skull.

'Nothing,' Mercutian voxed quietly, 'bears the same stench as a Red Corsair haven.'

Talos had replaced his own helm upon entering the station. 'We have to agree to his wishes. Huron won't let us leave alive if we refuse.'

'His offer is suicide,' Cyrion pointed out. 'We're all aware of that.'

'We should confer with the Exalted,' replied Mercutian.

'Yes,' Xarl smiled behind his faceplate. 'I'm sure that will happen. Just agree, Talos. The smell of this place is seeping through my armour.'

'Well?' the enthroned figure asked.

Lord Huron's ravaged features stared with delighted interest. He was not a man with a mind to hide his emotions, and what remained of his human face was twisted into a leer that bled superiority. He knew he'd won even before these dregs of the VIII Legion came before him to beg, and he felt no qualms in showing the triumph across his brutalised visage. Yet, even in his monstrous exultation, little of pettiness showed. He almost seemed to share the joke with First Claw.

Talos rose from his knees. Behind him, First Claw did the same. Variel stood to the side, his face a careful mask of passionless boredom.

'It will be done, Lord Huron,' Talos said. 'We agree to your terms. When do we sail?'

Huron reclined in the osseous throne, the very image of an ancient, indecorous warlord. 'As soon as my work crews have resurrected your broken *Covenant of Blood*. A month, maybe less. You will provide the materials?'

Talos nodded. 'The Ganges raid was most fruitful, my lord.'

'Ah, but you fled from the Marines Errant. Not as fruitful as the venture might otherwise have been, eh?'

'No, lord.' The prophet watched the warlord, wishing it was easier to dislike Huron's disarming informality. A strange, reluctant charisma bled from the Corsair Lord's wounded carcass in a trickling aura.

'I watched the *Covenant* drift in, you know,' he said. 'How you let such a grand ship fall into ruin is, I suspect, something of a tale.'

'It is, sire,' Talos conceded. 'I would be glad to speak of it at a more opportune time.'

Huron blinked his dry eyes. Mirth enlivened them, and his shoulder guards rattled with the laughter he kept beneath his breath.

'Now seems the perfect time, Night Lord.' Around the chamber came the rumbling chuckles of legionary voices. 'Let us hear the story now.'

Talos swallowed, his mind racing beneath the pain. Huron's conversational noose was as simple and blunt as it was unavoidable. In a moment of foolish instinct, he almost glanced at Variel.

'My lord,' the prophet inclined his head, 'I believe you already know the vital aspects of our sufferance at Crythe. A more poetic voice than mine is required to do the tale any justice.'

Huron licked his corpse-lips. 'Indulge me. Speak to me of how you betrayed the Black Legion, and ran from the Blood Angels.'

More laughter from the armed audience.

'I curse the Exalted for sending us to do this,' Cyrion sighed.

'He's baiting us,' Xarl's voice was low, cold.

The prophet wasn't so sure. He bowed theatrically, feigning a role in the amusement at First Claw's expense. 'Forgive me, Lord Huron, I forgot how difficult it must be for you to receive pure information on the war waged by the First Legions. Those of us who once walked at the sides of primarchs tend to forget how distant and isolated the lesser Renegade Astartes must feel. I will tell you of Abaddon's preparations for the coming crusade and the Night Lords' place within it, of course. I only hope you will enlighten us as to whatever games you and your pirates have been playing, so far from the war's front lines.'

As Talos's words fell across the silent chamber, Uzas sniggered like a child over the vox.

'And you rebuke Xarl for his diplomacy?' Mercutian sounded aghast. 'You've killed us all, prophet.'

Talos said nothing. He merely watched the warlord upon the throne. Ranks of Red Corsairs stood at attention, waiting for the order to open fire. A stunted, inhuman creature skittered around their armoured boots, cackling to itself.

Huron, master of the Maelstrom and the largest pirate warfleet in the Eastern reaches of the galaxy, finally allowed his face to split into a smile. It took obvious effort to make the expression, the grin formed from twitching muscles and quivering, nerveless lips.

'I would have liked to walk upon Nostramo,' the Tyrant said at last. 'In my experience, its sons have an entertaining sense of humour.' Huron drummed his armoured talons on the armrests of his throne, releasing a mouthful of laughter closer to a gargle.

'I am glad to entertain you, lord, as always.' Talos was smiling himself. 'You are still a soul blinded by overconfidence, you know.'

'It is a curse,' the prophet agreed. The warlord gave another of his burbling, throaty chuckles – the sound of unspat bile trapped in wounded lungs. Thin pistons compressed with clicks, visible through the patchwork skin of the warlord's throat.

'And what if I'd not required you for this little task, legionary? Then what?'

'Then you'd have aided us from the goodness of your own heart, lord.'

'I can see why the Exalted loathes you.' The Corsair Lord grinned again. It bled the tension from the chamber in a rush of acidic breath. Huron rose, gesturing to the Night Lords with his oversized metal claw. At the movement, the creature loping around the chamber – a hairless, wretched little quadruped with skinny malformed limbs – scampered over to the warlord and climbed Huron's armour plating with its knobbly talons. The Corsair lord paid it no heed as it clutched onto his back-mounted power pack, gripping with its taloned hands. Swollen eyes glared at the Night Lords, and its awkward teeth clicked together with a stuttering rattle.

'What. The hell. Is *that?*' Cyrion breathed.

Talos whispered a reply. 'I'm not sure I want to know.'

'It looks like someone skinned the spawn of a monkey and a dog. I believe one of you should tell the Blood Reaver that he has an abomination crawling over his back.'

'I think he knows, Cy.'

Huron beckoned to them again, his claw squealing as its joints moved.

'Come, warriors of the First Legions. I have something of yours that you may wish to see.'

* * *

THE MYRIAD DECKS of Hell's Iris thronged with life, but the Tyrant's honour
guard had sequestered an entire level of the star-fortress for the Corsairs'
own use. Here, guarded by Huron's most capable warriors, the command
structure of the Red Corsairs made their plans to strike out against the
Imperium. And here, under the watchful eyes of the Chapter's elite, the
Tyrant liked to keep unwelcome guests incarcerated at his leisure.

As they walked through the quieter corridors, boots clanking on the
decking, Talos let his gaze drift over the profaned metal walls. Each bore
a manuscript's worth of blasphemous screeds and incantations, inked
and branded into the naked steel.

Huron's movements drew the prophet's eyes more than once. The
master of the Red Corsairs was a shattered creature, but his dragging
limp belied the suppressed power in every jerking movement. Seeing him
now, this close – close enough that the sickly flickering light glinted back
from his tarnished armour plating – it was no trouble at all to discern
why the former Tyrant of Badab remained alive. Some warriors were too
stubborn to die.

Had he been mortal, Talos suspected Huron's presence would be
enough to cow him into obeisance. Few other warleaders exuded such
an unpalatable aura of threat, born of a destroyed face, a pained smile,
and the growl of fibre-bundle cabling in his armour joints. But then, few
other warleaders commanded a secessionist empire, let alone an astral
kingdom of such immense size and might.

'Something in my face interests you, prophet?'

'Your wounds, my lord. Is there much pain?'

Huron bared his teeth to the curious question. Both warriors were the
painstaking product of extensive, archaic genetic manipulation and bio-
surgery, making pain a relative concept to post-human warriors with two
hearts, three lungs, and the habit of spitting acid.

'A great deal,' the Corsair lord said, leaving it at that.

Behind First Claw, the lumbering forms of Red Corsair Terminators
filled the corridor, plodding along in tank-like obstinance. The hairless
little mutant scrabbled around their heels. Cyrion kept casting looks
back at it.

'Before I give you this gift,' Huron's tongue moistened his cracked lips
again, 'tell me, Night Lord, why you risked that ludicrous jest with me
in the throne room.'

The answer came smoothly, relayed through his helm's vox-speakers.
'Your empire is a cancer webbing through the Imperium's heart, and it
is said you command as many warriors as any Legion lord except for
the Warmaster himself.' Talos turned to glance at Huron, the warlord's
broken features outlined by a target lock. 'I do not know if that is true,
Lord Huron, but I doubted such a man would be so petty or ungracious
as to vent his anger over a few spoken words.'

Huron's reply was no more than a flicker of amusement in his blood-shot eyes.

'Will we even want this gift?' Xarl voxed to the others.

'Not if it's what I think it is,' Cyrion's voice came back, a little distracted. 'That little thing is still following us. I may shoot it.'

'Ezhek jai grugull shivriek vagh skr,' Huron announced, bringing them all to a halt.

'I do not speak any of the Badab dialects,' Talos confessed.

Huron answered by gesturing at a sealed bulkhead door with his massive power claw. The curving talons had been painted the same red as his ceramite a long time ago, but battle had slowly disintegrated the weapon's appearance, leaving it scorched black from flame. The Tyrant inclined his head to the Night Lords, and the overhead illumination strips reflected their light back off the chrome portions of his bare skull.

'Here is what I wished you to see,' he said. 'Tormenting it has been both useful and entertaining, but I suspect you would take pleasure in seeing it, as well. Consider this viewing a token of gratitude for accepting my offer.'

The bulkhead began to rise, and Talos resisted the urge to draw his weapons.

'Keep your helms on,' the Tyrant warned.

HE COULDN'T TELL how long he'd waited: blind, alone, and feeling the unwanted sting of tears trailing down his face. The shackles were no punishment at all, despite how they gripped his wrists to bind him to the wall. Likewise, the onset of starvation was a pain to be overcome, something to be ignored along with the bite of desperate thirst that scratched like sand in his veins.

The collar leashing his throat – now that was punishment, but one born of a weaker breed. He couldn't see the runic scripture inscribed upon the cold metal, but it was impossible not to feel their emanations. *Pulse, pulse, pulse* in his neck, with the same, inevitable throbbing of an infected tooth. To be denied a voice and the power wrought by his every whispered word... it was humiliating, but that made it nothing more than another humiliation to be heaped upon so many other indignities.

No. He could, and would, withstand such things. He could even endure the other minds burrowing into his own, their careless, invisible probes thrashing aside his mental defences with all the ease of idiot children ripping through paper. It hurt to think; it hurt to remember; it hurt to do anything but force his mind to a meditative blankness.

Still. He could survive it, holding his psyche intact through shivering concentration.

But the light was another matter. He knew he'd screamed for a time, though he'd no perception of just how long. After the screaming, he'd rocked back and forth, head lowered to his bare chest, drooling acid through clenched teeth. The chlorine stink of dissolving metal had only added to his nausea, as his spit ate into the floor.

His strength deserted him at last. After weeks – months? – he now knelt with his arms wide, wrists bound to the wall behind, head loose on an aching neck, eyes dripping tears, unable to lubricate past the pain. The light splashed against his closed eyelids with corrosive intent, a press of misty white bright enough to drag tears from the eyes of a soul otherwise beyond sorrow.

Through this haze of pain and messy clouding of his thoughts, the prisoner heard the door to his cell opening once more. He took three slow breaths, as if they could expel the pain from his body, and breathed out the words he'd been waiting to say for the entirety of his bloodless crucifixion.

'When I am free,' he spat the words out with strings of saliva, 'I will kill every single one of you.'

One of his tormentors came closer. He heard it in the purr of armour joints, the soft grinding of machinery muscles.

'*Athrillay, vylas,*' his torturer whispered in a dead language, from a dead world. Yet his captors knew no such tongue.

The prisoner raised his head, staring blindly forward, and repeated the words back.

'Greetings,' he said, 'brother.'

Talos didn't want to imagine the prisoner's pain – his own retinal display struggled to dull the atrocious strength of the chamber's lights, and even behind his faceplate he felt the sting of tears at the aggravating brightness.

He curled his armoured fingers through the captive's unshaven, greasy hair, and yanked the prisoner's head back, baring the sweating throat. His words were a Nostraman hiss, pitched low to defeat unwanted ears.

'I swore to kill you when next we met.'

'I remember it.' Ruven smiled through the pain. 'Now is your chance, Talos.'

The prophet drew his gladius, pressing the blade's edge against the prisoner's cheek. 'Give me one reason not to peel the skin from your treacherous bones.'

Ruven choked out a laugh. As he shook his head, the sword rubbed against his flesh, slicing a shallow gash.

'I have no reasons to give you. Spare us both the pretence that I will beg for my life, and just do as you will.'

Talos withdrew the blade. For a moment, he did nothing but watch the drop of blood crawl its wet way down the steel. 'How did they catch you?'

Ruven swallowed. 'The Warmaster cast me aside. For my failures at Crythe.'

Talos couldn't help the crooked grin that took hold. 'And you fled *here?'*

'Of course. Where else? What other havens for our kind have such size and scope? Such potential? The Maelstrom was the only answer that made sense.' The prisoner's face twisted into a snarl. 'I did not know some of my erstwhile brothers had so harmed the Eighth Legion's reputation with the Corsairs.'

Talos was still watching the blood trickle down. 'We made few friends last time we were here,' he said. 'But that's not why Huron took you prisoner, is it? These might be your last words, brother. Lies have no place in a valediction.'

Ruven said nothing for a time. Then, in a sibilant whisper: 'Look at me.'

Talos did so. Streams of bio-data flickered across his visor. 'You are dehydrated to the point of tissue damage,' he noted.

The captive grunted. 'Is that so? You should be an Apothecary.'

'The truth, Ruven.'

'The "truth". Were it only so simple. Huron allowed me to remain at Hell's Iris if I traded away the secrets I'd spent decades prying from the warp. At first, I conceded. Then there was an... altercation.' Ruven's androgynous features split into a dry-gummed smile. 'Three Corsairs died summoning denizens of the warp many times more powerful than they could bind. Tragic, Talos. So very tragic. Evidently, the dabbling fools were considered promising candidates for Huron's Librarium.'

The prophet stared at the sorcerer for some time.

'You are still there, brother,' Ruven said. 'I hear you.'

'I am still here,' Talos agreed. 'I am trying to discern the truth from your lies.'

'I told you the truth. What purpose would lying serve? They have shackled me here for what feels like months, saturating my eyes with light. I cannot see. I cannot move. Abaddon cast me aside, stripping me of my role in his Black Legion. Why would I lie to you?'

'That is what I intend to find out,' Talos replied, and rose to his feet. 'Because I know you, Ruven. The truth is anathema to your tongue.'

'A TRAITOROUS PRIZE, is he not?' Lord Huron asked. 'I am almost done with him, for he is no longer worth any amusement, and I believe he holds little information back from my sorcerers now. They have peeled all the lore they need from his mind.'

'What were his crimes?' Talos glanced back at the kneeling form of his former brother bathed in the radiant light.

'He caused the death of three initiates, and refused to share his knowledge. He had to be... encouraged... to do so, by other means.' The Blood Reaver's cadaverous features peeled back into a smile. 'Rendering him helpless was a trial in itself. Collared as he is, he is no threat. He cannot whisper into the warp to call forth his powers. Binding his warpcraft was the very first precaution I took, immediately before blinding him.'

'Play this carefully,' Cyrion warned. 'This is a promise of our fate if we betray the Corsairs.'

'If?' Talos voxed back. 'They have the *Echo of Damnation*. I'm not leaving without it.'

'Very well. *When* we betray them.'

Talos clicked an acknowledgement pulse back over the vox in reply.

'Let him rot here,' the prophet said to the Corsair lord. 'What of his weapons and armour?'

Huron's split lips curled. 'I have his wargear. Consider it another gesture of goodwill that I offer it back to you.'

Ruven let out a moan that disintegrated as it left his slack jaws. Chains rattled as he tested his shackles for the first time in weeks.

'Do not leave me here...'

'Burn in the warp, traitor,' Xarl chuckled back.

'Thank you for the gift,' Talos said to Huron. 'It is always gratifying to see betrayers reap what they sow. Kill him if you wish. It matters nothing to us.'

'Talos,' Ruven whispered the name once – on the second effort, it became a scream. 'Talos.'

The prophet turned to the prisoner, his retinal display compensating for the insane glare once again. Ruven was staring at him now. Blood ran down his cheeks in twin tear-trails as the light burned out the sensitive tissue behind his eyes.

'I thought you said you wouldn't beg for your life,' Talos said.

The bulkhead slammed closed before Ruven could reply, sealing him inside the cell with his own screams.

XIII
REGENERATION

Septimus sipped the drink, forcing himself to go through the suddenly difficult ritual of actually swallowing. He considered it a fair bet the beverage was distilled from engine oil.

The bar, such as it was, was one of many on board Hell's Iris, no different from a hundred others of its filthy kind. Wretched men and women mixed in the gloom, drinking foulness as they laughed and argued and shouted in a dozen different tongues.

'Oh, Throne,' Maruc whispered.

Septimus scowled. 'Don't say that here if you wish to leave alive.'

The older man gestured to a lithe young woman across the room, moving from table to table. Her hair streamed down her naked back in a flawless fall of silken white, while an exaggerated femininity set her slender hips swinging with every step.

'Don't talk to it.' Septimus shook his head. For a moment, Maruc thought he saw a smile on the other serf's face.

It? Don't talk to it?

But she'd seen Maruc's interest. '*Friksh sarkarr,*' she purred as she approached, her dress of battered leather scraps whispering against her milky skin. Fingers the white of clean porcelain stroked his unshaven cheek. As if approving of something, she nodded to herself. '*Vrikaj ghu sneghrah?*' She had a child's voice: a girl on the edge of maidenhood.

'I... I don't...'

She shushed him with her fingertip, resting the pale digit on his dry lips. '*Vrikaj ghu sneghrah... sijakh...*'

'Septimus...' Maruc swallowed. Her eyes were wide, the rich green of forests he'd only seen in hololithics. Her fingertip tasted of some unknowable spicy musk.

Septimus cleared his throat. The maiden turned with a ghost's grace, moistening her lips with a forked tongue.

'*Trijakh mu sekh?*'

The slave drew back the edge of his jacket, revealing the holstered pistol at his hip. Slowly, pointedly, he shook his head, and gestured to another table.

The girl spat onto the floor by his boot, slinking away with her hips swinging.

'She's something else...' Maruc watched her moving away, leering at all the flesh on display.

'Skin-walker,' Septimus grimaced at the taste of his drink – he wasn't swallowing any more of the stuff, but it was grotesque enough even to pretend, when it lapped against his lips. 'That leather she's wearing, do you see how it is sewn together?'

'Yeah.'

'It isn't leather.'

Maruc watched the girl as she traced her fingernails gently across the back of a rough-looking man's neck. 'I don't think I can sit here much longer,' he said. 'That fat thing across the room has too many eyes. There's a beautiful girl with a snake's tongue, walking around wearing human skin. Everyone in here is armed to the teeth, and the sorry bastard under the next table looks like he died two days ago.'

'Be calm.' Septimus was watching him closely now. 'Be at ease. We are safe, as long as we don't attract attention to ourselves. If you give in to panic, we'll be dead before the first yell has finished leaving your lips.'

'I'll be fine.' Maruc calmed himself with a slug of his own drink. It spread a pleasant warmth through his gullet. 'This is good stuff.'

Septimus let his expression speak for him.

'What?' Maruc asked.

'For all we know, this is distilled rodent piss. Try not to drink too much of it.'

'Fine. Sure.' He made another subtle scan around the room. One of the other patrons seemed to be too small for his own skeleton: bones at every joint poked out from his flesh, even along the ridges of his spine and the stretched skin of his cheeks. 'Your lord was right, you know.'

'In what way?'

'About escaping when we docked. Being stranded here would be worse than staying on the *Covenant*. Throne...'

Septimus winced. 'Stop saying that.'

'Sorry. Look, have they even told you what the Legion agreed to?'

Septimus returned a shrug. 'First Claw pledged the Legion to a siege of some kind. They're calling it *Vilamus*.'

'A world? An enemy fleet? A hive city?'

'I've not had the chance to ask.'

Maruc's gaze drifted back to the beautiful girl. 'Are there many of those... people?'

Septimus nodded. 'The flaying of flesh is one of the more common traditions in many cults. Even the Legion does it, remember. Lord Uzas's ceremonial cloak was once the royal family of some insignificant back-water world the *Covenant* raided.'

'You mean the cloak once belonged to them?'

'No. *Was* them. It is not leather, either. But the skin-walkers are a common enough cult. Mutants, mostly. Avoid them at all costs.'

'I thought she wanted to–'

'She did.' Septimus's human eye glanced to the doorway, and he adjusted a silver ring on his finger. 'But she'd have skinned you afterwards. Come on.'

Maruc followed as Septimus led him to the door. The younger slave reached back to loosen his short ponytail, letting his scruffy hair fall to his chin, half-covering his subtle bionics.

'Keep your weapon ready,' he said. 'You never know when someone will take offence to us.'

'You still haven't said why we're here,' Maruc whispered.

'You're about to find out.'

OCTAVIA SIGHED – the kind of sigh where she felt she'd lost weight once it left her lips. As she breathed out, she exhaled months of tension, keeping her eyes closed as she tilted her head back.

The warm water rained against her face, tickling her eyelids, running in pleasant trickles along her lips and chin. She had nothing in the way of soap, but even that didn't dent her enthusiasm. She scrubbed at her body with a rough sponge, almost feeling the grime of neglectful months sloughing from her skin.

With the *Covenant* docked, taking on fresh water supplies, the refilled tanks took the strain off the depleted recycling processors.

She risked a glance down at her figure, though it took surprising courage to do so. While she was far from the emaciated wraith she'd expected to see, her skin was a pale palette, and the trails of blue veins showed faintly beneath her flesh. Still, she had to confess she felt unhealthier than she looked. Evidently the nutrient-rich gruel that served as ship-board fare was more nourishing than its sandpaper taste suggested.

With her nose wrinkled, she picked a little fluff, the same midnight blue of Legion slave clothing, from her navel. *Delightful.*

With a quiet laugh, she flicked it away.

'Mistress? Did you call?'

Octavia looked up with a start, covering herself with her hands. Octavia had at least a shadow of mundane human instinct within her, for she sought to ward her nakedness from a stranger's eyes. While one hand guarded her bare skin, the other flew to her forehead, palm covering everything beneath her hairline.

But it was there – a flicker of sight – the shadow of something either human or close to it, glimpsed through the turbulent vision offered by her genetic gift. She saw its stained, multi-hued soul as an imprint in the seething torment of the warp all around.

She'd looked at someone, stared right at them even if only for a heartbeat, with her truest eye.

Her attendant, standing at the communal ablution chamber's edge, made a throaty gagging sound. He reached up to his throat with trembling hands, choking on air he could no longer swallow. Darkness moved across the bandaged face: a wet, spreading darkness, broadcast from the attendant's black eyes and open mouth. The blood stained the dirty weave in moments, bathing the bandages in stinking red.

He collapsed against the wall behind, wracked by spasms, beating the back of his skull against the steel. Wrapped hands clawed at his head, pulling the bandages away to reveal a starkly human face, albeit one soured purple by asphyxiation. Bloody vomit emerged from the old man's lips in a reeking torrent, splashing across the chamber's wet floor.

He lay there, grunting, twitching, bleeding, as the warm water still rained upon her.

She swallowed, her human eyes still staring, as another of her attendants made his hunchbacked way inside. He spared her no glance, limping over to the dying elder, a beaten shotgun in his hands. He placed the sawn-off barrel in the older attendant's gaping, gushing mouth, and pulled the trigger. The chamber resonated with the gunshot's echo for several seconds. What remained of the old man – which was very little above the neck – fell still.

'It wasn't my fault.' Octavia breathed the words, caught between shock, anger, and shame.

'I know,' said Hound. He turned to his mistress, his blinded eyes fixed upon her. She still felt a strange reluctance to lower her hands. Either of them.

'I told you all to wait outside.'

'I know this, also.' Hound chambered another round with a sharp *click-chuck*. The spent shell tinkled across the dirty decking, rolling to a smoky rest against a wall. 'Telemach was in great pain. I entered only to end it. I will leave now, mistress.'

'I think I'm finished now...' She turned away from the headless body, and the ruination smearing the metal wall.

But she didn't leave with Hound. She stayed in the room with the dead body, her hands against the shower wall, head lowered into the jetting water. Her hair, almost long enough to reach her elbows now, was a black velvet drape hanging down.

She'd never killed with her eye before. The only time she'd ever tried had been a failure – at the moment of her capture so many months before, when Talos had dragged her into this new life with his hand around her throat. All the stories she'd heard over the years came flooding back to her in a bittersweet rush: sailors' legends that Kartan Syne's crew had whispered when they believed she couldn't hear them; the warning tales given to every scion of the Navis Nobilite in the years of their extensive tuition; the things she'd never learned from her teachers, but found herself believing after reading them in old family logbooks.

A Navigator cannot kill without consequence. So the stories said.

Blood of my blood, do not let your soul be stained by such a deed. Her father's words.

And a notation in an ancestral Mervallion journal, more damning than all else: *Every murdering glance is a beacon to the Neverborn, a light in their darkness.*

She didn't look over at the body. She didn't need to – its slumped repose was etched into her memory, scratched upon her senses with grotesque finality.

A tickle in her throat was all the weary warning she needed – a few seconds later, Octavia was on her knees, puking the day's gruel into the rusty drainage grate. Her tears mixed with the falling water, lost in the downpour, a secret to everyone but herself.

THE CORSAIRS' APOTHECARION saw a great deal of business. Many of the surgical tables held victims of the unending honour-duels and violent disagreements aboard Hell's Iris. Most were human, though plenty of others occupied their own mutational places on the charts of known natural species.

Deltrian moved through the chaos, his hooded features grinning at everything he saw. Talos walked behind him, as did Variel, the two warriors ostensibly acting as escorts. The tech-adept paused briefly to point at another ceiling-mounted auto-surgery unit, its mechandendrites hanging with the unpleasant curl of a dead spider's legs.

'We require one of these for stereotactic procedures, with the A, D and F socketed limbs.'

A dull-eyed servitor, wearing a robe similar to Deltrian's, trailed behind the other three. It drooled an acknowledgement, recording its master's wishes in an internal database.

Deltrian paused again, picking up a silver instrument. 'Tyndaller. Seven should suffice. A similar number of these occluders will be necessary.'

The servitor murmured another acknowledgement.

Variel tensed at the reaching hand of a Corsair grasping for his medicae vambrace. His thin features soured into a scowl.

'Do not touch me. Your wounds will be tended soon.' Variel disengaged himself smoothly, resisting the urge to sever the warrior's fingers as punishment. He rejoined Talos a moment later. 'Your facilities on the *Covenant* must be close to useless if you require so much from us.'

'You are not wrong. Battle and disuse have ruined almost all we have. In our last engagement, one of our squads was lost while flushing out a boarding party of Blood Angels from their refuge in the apothecarion chambers. You cannot imagine the damage the fools in red inflicted, let alone the dead Claw that failed to kill them.'

'A cryotome,' Deltrian interrupted. 'Interesting.'

Variel ignored him. 'The *Covenant* is a ruin, Talos, held together by luck. And you are starting to appear the same.'

Talos passed another table, stopping to slit the throat of the slave strapped there, killing him quicker than the death he was going to suffer by drowning in his own blood. The Night Lord licked the blood from his gladius, briefly lighting his senses with the flickering after-images of another mind's memories.

A chamber, messy, with the warmth of security; a trench, raining mud and shrapnel, clutching a sabre in his cold hands; the sickeningly mortal feelings of doubt, of fear, of weakness as all strength bled from his limbs... How did these people live and function, with such messy minds?

He supped a single taste, no more, and the insights were mist-thin, gripping his senses lightly before fading fast.

'My scars?' he asked Variel after sheathing his gladius again, and tracing a gloved fingertip along the faint scar tissue down the side of his face.

'Not your scars. The skin has regenerated and bonded well from whatever damage it sustained, and those markings will grow ever fainter. I am referring to the tracks of pain along your features less visible to untrained eyes.'

Variel held his gauntlet close to Talos's face, too astute to risk touching the other warrior. The fingers crescented, as if holding an orb over the Night Lord's temple. 'Here,' he said. 'Pain blooms from here, crackling beneath your skin in rhythm with your pulse, riding your veins like access tunnels to the rest of your skull.'

Talos shook his head, but not in disagreement. 'You are a better Apothecary than I ever was.'

'In some ways,' Variel withdrew his hand, 'almost certainly. As I remember it, you have little in the way of patience.'

Talos didn't argue the point. He watched Deltrian for a few moments, as the tech-priest peered down at a thrashing human, evidently intrigued by the analysis table upon which the wounded man lay.

'The head pain is getting worse, is it not?' Variel asked Talos.

'How could you possibly have guessed that?'

'Your left eye is irritated; the tear ducts are dilated by a measure of millimetres more than the other. The aqueous humour in the eye is also beginning to cloud with the suggestion of blood particles. As yet, these flaws remain hidden to mortal eyes, but the signs are there.'

'Servitors rebuilt my skull after a clash with Dal Karus and Third Claw.'

'A bolter shell?'

Talos nodded. 'Crashed into my helm. Sheared away a chunk of my head.' He made a chopping motion along his temple. 'For the first hour afterwards, I was able to get by with pain suppressors and adrenaline injectors. After that, I was oblivious for three nights while the medicae servitors worked their reconstruction.'

Variel's sneer came as close to a smile as he could manage. 'They did imperfect work, brother. But I appreciate circumstances were hardly in your favour.'

The Night Lord felt the petulant urge to shrug. 'I'm still alive,' he said.

'You are indeed. For now.'

Talos glared at the Apothecary. 'Go on...'

'The pain you are feeling is pressure on your brain, brought about from degenerating blood vessels, some of which are swollen, while others are likely to be on the edge of rupture. The braincase's new shape is also a contributing factor, and if the pressure continues to increase, it is likely you will haemorrhage blood from your optic cavity, which will occur after your eyeball is pushed out from its socket by the mounting strain. You will also likely sustain a degree of necrosis among the degrading blood vessels in your brain as well as in adjacent tissue, as you begin to suffer further cerebral vasospasms. However, I can rectify the servitors' flawed... tinkering... if you desire.'

Talos raised a black eyebrow, his face even paler than usual. 'I wouldn't trust one of my own squad to help me into my armour, and they all wear the winged skull of Nostramo. Why would I trust a warrior with Huron's claw on his shoulder to pry through my brain?'

Variel's amusement ended at his eyes. 'Because of Fryga, Talos. Because I still owe you.'

'Thank you for the offer. I will consider it.'

Variel keyed a command into his narthecium gauntlet. 'See that you do. If my estimate is correct, refusing means you will be dead by the end of the solar year.'

Talos's reply was broken off by Deltrian drifting back to them in a purr of smooth augmetics and a whisper of robes.

'I have collated the required data,' he declared in tinny pride.

Variel saluted, fist over his breastplate. 'I will take the data to my master. Lord Garreon is overseeing the resupply of your vessel.'

Talos caught himself thumbing his temple. With an irritated growl, he replaced his helm, clicking it into place and bathing his senses in the warm thrum of his armour's autosenses.

'I will escort you back to the *Covenant*, tech-adept. I must report to the Exalted myself.'

'Think on what I have said, brother,' Variel said.

Talos nodded, but didn't answer.

* * *

MARUC CAUGHT UP with Septimus, finding it harder to move through the crowded thoroughfare. He also couldn't quite keep revulsion from showing on his face; some of the creatures passing were brazen with their mutations. He almost collided with a spindly black-skinned woman, who cursed at him through a slack, rippling face like melting tallow. He muttered something loosely apologetic, and hurried on. The spicy stink of sweat mixed with the copper of spilled blood no matter where he turned his head. People – and 'people' – were shouting, growling, shoving and laughing in every direction.

Septimus reached out a hand to grip another walker's shoulder, halting the young woman in her stride. She turned, clutching an empty plastek bucket to her paunchy stomach.

'Jigrash kul kukh?' the serf asked her.

She shook her head.

' Low Gothic?' Septimus tried.

She shook her head again, her eyes wide at the expensive bionics just visible beneath the fall of his hair. She reached to touch them, to brush his hair aside, but he gently slapped her hand away.

'Operor vos agnosco?' he asked.

She narrowed her eyes and nodded, a quick bob of her head.

Wonderful, Septimus thought. Some backwater variant of High Gothic, a language he barely knew anyway.

Carefully, he led the woman, who looked to be wearing a plundered vestment of various discarded Imperial uniforms, to the edge of the wide hallway. It took him several minutes to explain what he needed. At the end of his halting explanation, she nodded again.

'Mihi inzizta,' she said, and gestured for him to follow.

'Finally,' Septimus said under his breath. Maruc followed again. As he peered at the woman's bucket, he realised it wasn't quite empty. Three fruits, like little brown apples, bumped about in the bottom.

'You wanted a fruit seller?' he asked Septimus, his expression showing what he was thinking – that the other serf was insane.

'Among other things, yes.' He kept his voice low in the crowd.

'Will you tell me why?'

Septimus cast a disparaging glance over his shoulder. 'Are you blind? She's pregnant.'

Maruc's mouth widened. 'No. You can't be serious.'

'How do you think the Legion makes new warriors?' hissed Septimus. 'Children. Untainted children.'

'Please tell me you're not going to–'

'I will leave you here, Maruc.' Septimus's tone froze. 'I swear to you, if you make this any harder than it has to be, I will leave you here.'

The three of them moved down an adjacent corridor, the woman leading them, still clutching her bucket. Less crowded here, but still too many witnesses. Septimus bided his time.

'What did you tell her?' Maruc asked at last.

'That I wished to purchase more fruit. She is taking us to another trader.' His voice thawed as he glanced at the older man again. 'We are not the only ones doing this. Across the station, serfs loyal to the Claws are playing the very same game. It's... It is just something that must be done.'

'Have you done this before?'

'No. And I plan to do it right, so it doesn't have to happen again soon.'

Maruc said nothing. They walked for another few minutes, before passing a smaller, darker side tunnel.

Septimus's eyes, human and the augmetic alike, washed slowly over the corridor entrance. Unless he was grossly off-course in this hideous labyrinth, this passage would lead back to the ship faster than returning down this particular thoroughfare.

'Be ready,' he whispered to Maruc, and tapped the woman on the shoulder again, the silver ring on his knuckle brushing the side of her neck. She stopped and turned.

'*Quis?*' She seemed confused. The crowd still sailed past, and she held her bucket protectively over her stomach.

Septimus kept his silence, watching for the droop in her eyelids. As soon as her eyes began to roll back, he caught her in a smooth motion, keeping her standing. To all observers – those few who paid any heed at all while going about their own dealings – it seemed he suddenly embraced her.

'Help me,' he ordered Maruc. 'We need to get her back to the ship before she comes to her senses.'

Maruc caught the bucket as it slipped from her slack fingers. They left it at the side of the corridor, as they carried her between them, the woman's arms around their shoulders. Her boots moved mechanically, her eyes rolling drunk in their sockets, as she accompanied her kidnappers to a new life in the slave holds of the *Covenant of Blood*.

OCTAVIA CLUTCHED HER jacket close as she left the communal ablution chamber. Several of the mortal crew waited in the corridor, kept out by her armed attendants, waiting their turn for the recharged cleansing racks. For obvious reasons, she had to bathe alone. Even though the crew knew the reasons, it seemed it only added to their dislike of her.

Most averted their eyes when Octavia came into the corridor. Several made superstitious motions to ward off evil, which she found bizarre, given where these people lived. Quietly, she asked two of her attendants to recover Telemach's body from the chamber and dispose of it however they wished.

Nostraman mutterings followed her as she walked away. In a solitary life, she'd never felt as lonely. At least on the *Maiden of the Stars* the crew hadn't hated her. Feared her, certainly, for fear in a Navigator's presence was a legacy of her bloodline as undeniable as the subspecies' third eye. But here, it was different. They loathed her. Even the ship despised her.

Hound loped along at her heels. For a while, they walked in silence. She didn't care where she was going.

'You smell very female now,' Hound said unhelpfully. She didn't ask what it meant. It probably meant nothing at all – just another of his blindingly obvious perceptions.

'I don't think I want to live like this any more,' she said over his head, staring at the walls as she walked.

'No choice, mistress. No other way to live.'

Throne, her eye ached. Beneath the bandana, an abrasive itch was steadily growing angrier. It took supreme effort not to claw at the skin around the closed eye, soothing the rawness with her fingernails.

Octavia walked on, taking lefts and rights at random. She was prepared to concede that she dwelled in self-pity, but she felt it was an indulgence she'd earned lately.

In the distance, she heard a faint shriek – it sounded female, though it cut off too quickly to be certain. Hammers, or something like them, crashed in dull industrial rhythm somewhere nearby, muted by the dense metal walls.

Her eye gave another dizzying throb. The pain was making her nauseous now.

'Hound?' She stopped walking.

'Yes, mistress.'

'Close your ey... Never mind.'

'Yes, mistress.' He paused in his hitched stride, looking around as Octavia removed her bandana. The skin of her forehead was sticky with sweat, the flesh almost burning to the touch. Blowing upwards did nothing but flutter a few wet locks of hair and make her feel foolish. It certainly didn't cool her down.

Sweat dripped onto her nose. She wiped it, catching sight of a dark smear on her fingers.

'Throne of the God-Emperor,' she swore, looking down at her hands. Hound shuddered at the curse.

'Mistress?'

'My eye,' she said, wiping her hands on her jacket. 'My eye is bleeding.' The hammering clanged louder as her words hovered in the air between them.

Touching her forehead made her wince, but she daubed the bandana over the sore flesh. Her eye wasn't bleeding, exactly. It was crying. The blood drops were its tears.

'Where are we?' she asked, her voice shaking as her breath misted before her face.

Hound sniffed. 'The apothecarion.'

'Why is it so cold?'

The hunched slave pulled his weathered shotgun from beneath his rags. 'I do not know, mistress. I, also, am cold.'

She retied the bandana while Hound aimed into the endless array of shadows.

Ahead of them both, the massive bulkhead leading into the apothecarion ground open on heavy gears. The hammering rang stronger, truer, coming from inside.

'Hound?' her voice was a whisper now.

'Yes, mistress?'

'Keep your voice down...'

'Sorry, mistress,' he whispered. His blunt-nosed shotgun tracked across the open door and the view beyond. Bare, silent surgical tables stood in the darkness.

'If you see the void-born in there, I want you to shoot her.'

'The void-born is dead, mistress.' He looked over his shoulder, mutilated face bunched in concern.

Octavia felt the blood running down her nose now, tickling her lips on its journey to drip from her chin. The bandana was no barrier, little more than a poor bandage. Soaked already, it did nothing to oppose the slow dripping.

She drew her own pistol as she neared the open door.

'Mistress.'

She glanced at Hound.

'I will go in first,' he stated. Without waiting for an answer, he moved inside, his hunch keeping him low, shotgun raised level with his unseeing eyes

She followed him in, sighting down her pistol.

The room was empty. Every surgery table was bare. The abandoned machinery made neither noise nor motion. Octavia blinked her human eyes to ward off the blood's stinging touch. It didn't help much.

Metal crashed against metal, almost deafeningly loud in the freezing chamber. She spun to face the far wall, aiming at ten sealed vault doors, each one the height and width of a human. One of them juddered in time to the hammering from behind. Whatever was within wanted to come out.

'Let's get the hell out of here,' she stammered.

Hound was less inclined to flee. 'Can it harm us, mistress?'

'It's just an echo,' she checked her pistol's ammunition counter. 'Just an echo. Like the girl. Just an echo. Echoes can't hurt anyone.'

Hound didn't have the chance to agree. The vault door burst outwards on squealing hinges. Something pale moved in the darkness inside.

'...not with Malcharion's bolter...' Its sepulchral voice, toneless yet sharp, cut the cold air. *'...wish to join First Claw...'*

Octavia backed away, eyes wide, murmuring for Hound to follow.

Another figure blocked the doorway. It stood tall, silhouetted against the gloom, red eye lenses tracking her movements with silent regard.

'Talos!' she breathed the name, relief flooding through her.

'No, Navigator.' The Night Lord stepped into the chamber, drawing his weapons. 'Not Talos.'

HE RETURNED, JUST as Variel had known he would. The Flayer acknowledged him with a nod, and deactivated the hololithic text he'd been studying.

Talos had not come alone. Cyrion, Xarl and Mercutian stood behind him, armoured, helmed and silent but for the chorus of growling armour.

'When I sleep,' the prophet seemed almost ashamed, 'I dream. My muscles react, but I do not wake. If I break the straps binding me to the table, my brothers will hold me down while you perform the surgery.'

'One is missing,' Variel noted.

'Uzas often chooses not to heed our summons,' Cyrion replied, 'unless war threatens.'

'Very well.' The Corsair Apothecary moved over to the lone table in his private chamber. 'Let us begin.'

XIV

LOYALTIES

His brothers' voices are dim, forgettable things, belonging to a world of sour smells, aching thoughts and sore muscles. Focussing on their words threatens to pull him from the dream, drawing him back to a freezing chamber where his body thrashes on a table, enslaved to its flawed biology.

The prophet releases his ties to that world, seeking sanctuary elsewhere. His brothers are gone when he...

...opened his eyes. Another shell crashed down nearby, shaking the grey battlements beneath his boots.

'Talos,' came the captain's voice. 'We move.'

'Harvesting,' he said through gritted teeth. His hands worked with mechanical familiarity, breaking, slicing, sawing, extracting. Something screamed overhead on failing engines. He risked a glance to see an Iron Warriors gunship whine above in a lethal spin, its thrusters aflame. The gene-seed cylinder snicked home into his gauntlet the very same moment the grey Thunderhawk ploughed into one of the hundred spires nearby. The battlements gave another horrendous shudder.

'Talos,' the captain's vox-voice crackled with urgency. 'Where are you?'

'It is finished.' He rose to his feet, retrieving his bolter and breaking into a run, leaving the body of a Legion brother sprawled on the stone.

'I'll go back for him,' one of his squad said over the channel.

'Be swift.' The captain was in grim humour, for obvious reasons.

The Apothecary's vision blurred as his helm struggled to filter out the sensory assault of another cannon barrage. Tower-top weapon batteries hurled their payloads into the sky, massive mouths thundering. Another wide spread of rampart stretched out ahead: where his brothers were making short work of the gun crews. The humans, ripped limb from limb, were hurled over the side of the battlements to fall hundreds of metres in grotesque imitation of hail.

A weight hit him from behind, powerful enough to send him crashing onto his hands and knees. For a moment, his retinal display flickered with meaningless static. Talos blinked once, thudding his forehead on the ground. Clarity returned immediately. He turned on the ground, bolter firing the moment it came level.

'Fists,' he voxed. 'Behind us.'

They ran, all formation broken, bolters clutched in golden hands. Despite their distance, another bolt shell cracked off his pauldron, sending shrapnel skittering across the battlements.

His attempted rise earned him a bolt shell to the chest, detonating against his chestplate and shattering the Legion symbol there. With a breathless grunt, he crashed back down.

'Stay down,' one of his brothers ordered. The name-rune flashed on his visor – his sergeant's name.

A dark gauntlet slammed into his armoured collar, gripping the ceramite. 'Keep firing,' the sergeant ordered. 'Cover us, or we're both dead.'

Talos reloaded, crunching the magazine home, and opened up again. His brother crouched behind him, firing with a pistol while dragging the Apothecary back.

The sergeant released him as they both took cover behind a section of loose rubble.

'Thank you, brother,' Talos said.

Sergeant Vandred reloaded his own pistol. 'It's nothing.'

'HOLD HIM STILL.'

There. His brothers' voices again, clearer than before.

'I am.' *Xarl. Irritated. The same grating disquiet that has always coloured his voice, present even in youth.*

The prophet feels his knuckles clacking against the table, a percussion born of twitching fingers. Sensation is returning, and with it, the pain. Breath rushes into his lungs, wickedly cold.

'Damn it.' *Variel's voice. A brother by oath, not by blood.* 'Is he aware, or fully somnolent? The readings state both.'

The prophet – no longer the Apothecary upon the battlements of Terra – mumbles saliva-drenched words.

'It's a vision.' *Cyrion. That was Cyrion.* 'It happens. Just deal with it.'

'It is affecting his slumber, and generating anomalous readings. Blood of the Pantheon, his catalepsean node may never function again after this – his body is trying to reject the implant.'

'His what?'

'I am not jesting. His physiology is in rebellion, rejecting any implantations linked to his brain. This must happen with every vision – his wounds are magnifying it. Whatever these dreams are, they are not a natural byproduct of the gene-seed.'

'You mean he's tainted? Warp-touched?'

'No. This is not mutation, but a matter of genetic development. In many initiates, the gene-seed doesn't take. You have all seen it, surely.'

'But his held. It did take.'

'It did, with tenacity, not grace. Look. Look at the bloodwork, and the signifiers here, and here. Look what his implants are doing to his human organs. His own gene-seed hates him. The chemicals and compounds that they released in adolescence to make him one of us still do not sit quietly in his blood. They try to change him even now, to develop him further. Like us, there is nothing he can develop into beyond the genhanced state. Yet his body still tries. The result is this... visionary state. Talos's body is too aggressive in processing your primarch's blood. His genetics are in constant flux.'

The prophet wonders, then, if this is what cursed his father. His gene-sire – his true father – the primarch, Lord Curze. Did the Emperor's machinations in genetic construction never settle within his father's bones? Did Curze's powers rise from a reaction to the Emperor's own blood in a lesser frame?

He tries to smile, but spit flies from his lips.

'Hold him.' Variel isn't angry, he is never angry, but he is certainly displeased. 'It is difficult enough with the convulsions, but we are risking severe brain damage now.'

'Please, Corsair, just do what you can.'

Mercutian. The rich man's son, heir to the City's Edge syndicate. So very polite. The prophet's smile registers across his face as a peeling rictus grin, formed not from humour, but the tight sneer of tensing musculature.

'He's suffering cardiac dysrhythmia. In both hearts. Talos. Talos?'

'He can't hear you. He can never hear anyone when these things take hold.'

'It is a wonder he survives these.' Variel stops speaking, and flashes of red pain jab into the prophet's head, flashing scarlet before his sightless eyes. 'I... need to... trigger his sus-an membrane, to stabilise the overworked core organs... Th...'

...HE WAS HOME.

He was home, and knowing it was a dream did nothing to diminish the rush of chill comfort. *A memory.* This had all happened before.

Not Nostramo, no. And not the *Covenant*. This was Tsagualsa, the refuge, their fortress on the fringe of space.

The doors to the Screaming Gallery stood open, Atramentar guardians barring passage to all but the primarch's chosen. They stood in defiant pride, not permitted to enter themselves, yet warding the doors against intrusion. The Legion's Terminator elite walked with heads high these nights; their refusal to serve the new First Captain was a festering wound that accorded them a subtle rise in prestige. With Sevatar dead and a Terran appointed to his role, the former First Captain's elite warriors splintered into hunting packs, binding themselves to company commanders they respected, rather than remain whole under a new master not of their home world.

One of the Terminators was Malek, his helm untusked, his red eye lenses bright with targeting acquisitions. Talos saluted the two Atramentar before making his way into the antechamber.

The walls, like so much of the Legion's fortress, were formed from black stone sculpted into forms of torment. Twist-backed humans arched and writhed motionlessly, captured at moments of supreme agony, their wide eyes and screaming mouths shaped by sadistic devotion.

Shaped. Not carved. Talos hesitated by the doors, his fingertips tracing over the open eyes of an infant girl reaching for the protective – worthless – embrace of an older man, perhaps her father. Who had she been, before the Legion raided her world? What had she done with her short life before she was dosed with paralytics and coated with rockrete? What dreams were quenched by her living entombment within the hardening walls of a primarch's inner sanctum?

Or did she know, on some panicked, animalistic strata of her dying mind, that in death she would be part of something more momentous than anything she'd achieved in life?

Within the stone, she would be long dead. The mask staring out at the world immortalised her in the naive perfection of youth. No tracks of time across her face; no scars from battles against an empire that no longer deserved to stand.

He withdrew his hand from her frozen face. The interior doors opened, bathing him in the warmth of the inner chamber.

The Screaming Gallery was in fine voice tonight – an opera of bass moans, piercing cries and the ululating chime of sobbing beneath the other sounds of sorrow.

Talos walked down the central pathway, boots thumping on the black stone, while the floor either side of the walkway rippled and tensed with the pliancy of human expression. Eyes, noses, teeth, and tongues poking from open mouths... The ground itself was a carpet of faces flesh-crafted together, kept alive by grotesque, baroque blood filters and organ simulator engines beneath the floor. As an Apothecary, Talos knew the machinery well: he was one of the few charged to maintain the foul ambience within the Screaming Gallery. Robed servitors mono-tasked for the duty sprayed gentle bursts of water vapour into the blinking eyes blanketing the floor, keeping them moist.

Several of the primarch's chosen were already gathered. Hellath, loyal beyond any other, preternaturally gifted with a blade, with the skull on his faceplate painted in streaky crimson; Sahaal, the Terran recently given First Captaincy – one of the few offworlders permitted here – the proud ice in his veins leaving him scorned by his brothers as often as heeded by them; Yash Kur, his fingers curling in twitch-spasms, breathing in a low rasp through his open mouth, the sound leaking from his helm's vocabulator; Tyridal, skulls rattling against his war-plate, as he dragged a whetstone along his gladius. His gauntlets were painted in sinners' red – a marker of the Legion's condemned: those warriors whose crimes against their own brothers meant they awaited execution at the primarch's own hands. A death sentence rode above Tyridal's head, to be exacted when Lord Curze decided his usefulness was at an end.

Malcharion stood to the side, arms crossed over his chest. No rank existed within the Screaming Gallery. Talos greeted his captain with nothing more than a quiet acknowledgement, inaudible over the wails rising from the floor.

When the primarch entered, it was with no flourish at all. Curze pushed open the double doors behind the Osseous Throne, his bare hands pale against the wrought iron. With no preamble, with no ritual greeting, the lord of the Legion took his throne.

'So few of us?' he asked. Thin lips revealed a shark's smile – the warlord's serrated teeth all filed to arrowhead points. 'Where is Jakr? And Fal Kata? Acerbus? Nadigrath?'

Malcharion cleared his throat. 'En route to the Anseladon Sector, lord.'

Curze turned his cadaverous visage to the Tenth Captain. The dark eyes were enlivened by a curdling brightness, suggesting some deep sickness within.

'Anseladon.' The primarch licked his corpse-lips. 'Why?'

'Because you ordered them there, my lord.'

Curze seemed to muse on this, his gaze slackening, seeing through the walls of his palace. All the while, the floor's wailing never ceased.

'Yes,' he said. 'Anseladon. The Ultramarine vanguard fleet.'

'Aye, lord.'

His hair had once been black, *Nostraman* black – the dark hair of those who grew without true light of the sun. Now its lustre was gone, and a frosting of grey patched close to his temples. The veins canalling below his white skin were bold enough to form a clear map of the subterranean biology at play beneath his face. Here was a fallen prince, gone to the grave, hollowed out by a hatred so strong he could not lie down and die.

'I have thirty-one fleets of varying force at work within my father's empire. I believe, at last, we have drawn enough of the Imperium's ire that Terra has no choice but to act against us. But they will not lay siege to Tsagualsa. I will not allow it. Instead, I will ensure my father's vengeance must assume a more elegant form.'

As he spoke, Curze fingered the old scars on his throat – those bitter gifts given by his brother, the Lion. 'And what will you do when I am gone, my sons? Scatter like vermin fleeing the rise of the sun? The Legion was born to teach a lesson, and that lesson will be taught. Look at you. Your lives already have such little purpose. When the blade finally falls, you will have nothing left at all.'

The chosen regarded each other with growing unease. Talos stepped forward. 'Father?'

The primarch chuckled, his laughter the sound of waves dragging over shale. 'The Hunter of One Soul. Speak.'

'The Legion wishes to know when you will lead us to war again.'

Curze sighed, a contemplative breath, leaning back in the ugly, shape-less throne of fused human bone. His battle armour, replete with its geography of scratches, dents and carvings, growled with idle power.

'The Legion asks this, does it?'

'Yes, father.'

'The Legion no longer needs my hand upon its shoulder, for it has already ripened. Soon, it will burst, spilling itself across the stars.' The primarch lowered his head slightly, fingernails scraping along the ivory armrests. 'For years, you have butchered to your hearts' content, all of you. As Nostramo collapsed back into anarchy, so has the Legion. That spread will only grow worse. It is the way of things. Human life taints everything it touches, if it spreads uncontrolled. Nostramo's sons are no exception. In truth, they are among the worst for such things. Disorder rides in their blood.'

Here, he smiled. 'But you know that, don't you, Soul Hunter? And you, war-sage? All of you, born of the sunless world? You watched your world burn because the flaws of its people infected the Night Lords. And how beautiful it was, to immolate that sphere of sin. How righteous it felt, to truly believe it would make a difference to a poisoned Legion.'

He snorted at the last. 'How very naive of me.'

The primarch cradled his head in his hands for several long seconds. As his sons watched, his shoulders rose and fell with slow, deliberate breathing.

'Lord?' several of them asked at once. Perhaps their concern caused his head to rise. With shaking hands, the primarch bound his long hair into a crested topknot, keeping the dark strands from his face.

'My thoughts are aflame this eve,' he confessed. Some of the sick gleam in his eyes faded as he reclined again, his intensity dimming. 'How fares the armada we sent to Anseladon?'

'They will arrive within the week, lord,' said Yash Kur.

'Excellent. An unpleasant surprise for Guilliman to deal with.' Curze gestured to two servitors standing behind his throne. Both were exten-sively modified beneath their robes, fitted with industrial lifter spades for forearms. Each one carried a weapon in its protective embrace: an over-sized gauntlet of scratched, abused ceramite, bearing slack metal talons as fingernails. Both augmented slaves approached in unison, raising their gear-driven arms with a reverent lack of haste. Like armourers of old, squires kneeling before a knight, they offered their service to their master.

Curze rose in kind, towering above every other living being in the chamber. The omnipresent wails became true screams.

'Sevatar,' the primarch intoned. 'Come forward.'

Hellath spoke up. 'Sevatar is dead, my prince.'

The warlord hesitated, his pale hands close to the gauntlets' waiting ceramite sleeves. 'What?'

'My prince.' Hellath bowed low. 'First Captain Sevatar is long dead.'

Curze thrust his hands into the gauntlets, linking them to his armour. The thrum of active war-plate grew louder, and the curving talons wavered as they powered up. The servitors backed away, blindly treading on several of the weeping faces, breaking noses and teeth under their heavy heels.

'Sevatar is dead?' the primarch snarled the words, his anger mounting. 'When? How?' Before Hellath could answer, the generators in Curze's gauntlets whined to life, dripping electrical ripples down the blades' edges.

'My prince...' Hellath tried again. 'He died in the war.'

Curze turned his head, as if seeking a sound none of his sons could hear. 'Yes. I remember it now.' The claws powered down, shedding their coating of artificial lightning. He stared around the Screaming Gallery, that unsubtle manifestation of his own inner conflict.

'Enough talk of the past. Muster what companies remain in local systems. We must prepare for–'

'...CONVULSIONS.'

'I need only to seal the skin. He metabolises even specially synthesised anaesthetic with irritating speed. Hold him.'

The prophet feels himself speaking, feels the words crawling past lips that aren't quite numb. But they have no meaning. He tries to tell his brothers of home, of Tsagualsa, of how it felt to stand in the darkening light of their fading father's last days.

'The...'

...WAR-SAGE PULLED HIS blade from the dying Blood Angel's throat, kicking the warrior's breastplate to send him crashing back into the chamber.

'Into the breach!' Captain Malcharion roared from his helm's vox-grille. '*Sons of the sunless world! Into the breach!*'

His shattered squads poured forwards, sinking another layer deeper into a palace the size of a continent. The chamber, a gallery of paintings and statuary, rained plasterwork from its ceiling onto the Night Lords below. Dust and grit clattered onto the Apothecary's shoulder guards.

Xarl fell into step alongside Talos as their bloodied boots crunched over marble and mosaic alike.

'Damn the Angels, eh? They're giving as good as they're getting.' Breathless from the fighting, his voice was harsher than ever. Meat clogged the idling teeth of his lengthened chainblade.

Talos could feel the weight of gene-seed vials in slot-racks attached to his armour. 'We're fighting to win. They're fighting to survive. They're giving it back much worse than we're giving it to them, brother. Trust me when I say that.'

'If you say so.' The other Night Lord stopped to crash his boot down on a mosaic relief of the Imperial aquila. Talos watched the symbol shatter, feeling his saliva glands tingle with the need to spit.

'Hold here!' the captain called back. 'Ready barricades, reinforce this chamber. Defensive positions!'

'Blood Angels!' yelled one of the warriors at the chamber's exit arch. The Night Lords toppled pillars and statues, using the priceless stonework as last-minute cover for the coming firefight.

'Apothecary,' one of the sergeants called. 'Talos, over here.'

'Duty calls.' Xarl was grinning behind his faceplate. Talos nodded, breaking cover to sprint over to where another of Malcharion's squads was taking shelter in the shadows of a fallen pillar.

'Sir,' he said to Sergeant Uzas of Fourth Claw.

Uzas was unhelmed, his keen eyes still watching for the Angels' arrival. The bolter clutched against his breastplate was exquisitely wrought – a gift commissioned from the Legion's armoury by Captain Malcharion, forged to commemorate Fourth Claw's victories in the Thramas Crusade.

'I've lost three warriors,' the sergeant confessed.

'Their bloodlines will live on,' he said, tensing his left hand into a fist, deploying a surgical spike from his narthecium gauntlet. 'I harvested each of them.'

'I know, brother, but watch yourself. Our enemies are not blind to the responsibility you carry on your arm, and they target you almost as much as they seek to bring down the war-sage.'

'For the Emperor!' came that inevitable cry from the chamber's mouth.

Talos rose with Fourth Claw, aiming above the pillar and opening fire at the Angels. Two of his shells detonated against the arch frame; the Blood Angels too canny to risk a frontal charge.

'I had rather hoped,' Uzas reloaded in a smooth motion, 'that bloodlust would drive them out into our gunfire.'

Talos dropped back behind the pillar. 'Their cover is better than ours. We have statues. They have walls.'

Another cluster of Night Lords scrambled into cover behind the immense pillar. Vandred and Xarl were among them.

'So much for squad cohesion,' grunted Talos.

'Oh, you noticed?' Vandred chuckled, and tapped his cracked helm. One eye lens sported a hairline fracture down its middle. 'My vox is down. Uzas?'

The other sergeant shook his head. 'Even Legion channels are corrupted. Thirty-First Company's channel is broadcasting nothing but shrieking. Whatever is happening to them, they're not enjoying it.'

'I thought it was just vox-breakage,' said Vandred. 'It's nice to know we're all suffering the same.'

One of the Night Lords nearby rose out of cover to send another volley at the Angels. A single bolt shell cracked into his helm, wrenching it from his head in a kicking burst of shrapnel. With a curse, he crouched again, wiping blood and acidic spit from his face.

'Do these bastards ever miss?'

Talos regarded the depleted Tenth Company spread across the chamber. 'Not often enough.'

The warrior, Hann Vel, blind-fired over the top of the fallen pillar. The bolter in his hand exploded before the third shot, taking the Night Lord's hand with it. Yet again the victim of Blood Angel marksmanship, Hann Vel bellowed with a drunkard's unfocussed fury, covering the burned stump with his remaining hand.

With bizarrely elegant elocution, Hann Vel shouted a curse. 'A plague on these red-clad sons of whores!'

That looks painful, Talos thought, and his crooked grin went unseen in his helm. Let the warp take Hann Vel, the warrior was a fool at the best of times.

'Captain,' Uzas was voxing. 'Captain, this is Uzas.'

The war-sage's reply grated back on the rasping tides of static. 'Yes?'

'Three squads to charge, the rest to rise in fire support?'

'My thoughts exactly – we're not breaking out of this vermin pit any other way. *First, Fourth and Ninth, make ready to charge.*'

'Lucky us.' Uzas smiled at the others. He drew his gladius, lifting his head to cry, 'For the Warmaster! Death to the False Emperor!'

The cheer was taken up by the others, warrior after warrior, squad after squad, screaming their hate at the Blood Angels.

With a curse through clenched teeth, Talos...

...SAW THE SCENE fading. That siege of sieges, the countless hours spent advancing chamber by bloody chamber through the Imperial Palace so long ago, drifted back into the recess of memory.

'How long do these episodes last?' Variel was asking.

'As long as they need to,' said Cyrion.

He...

...WATCHED IT MOVE, with its undulating, soft-spined flow. It was human only in the loosest sense: the way one might envisage humanity if the only lore available described the species in the vaguest terms. Two arms reached from its torso. Two legs propelled it forwards in a disgustingly fluid stagger. Each limb was a malformed thing of awkward joints and bones twisted beneath the veined skin.

Uzas's axe crashed against the creature, ripping smoking flesh and steaming fluid away in ragged gobbets. Mist armoured its white flesh – a sculpted haze clinging to its body, with its vaporous edges offering the sick suggestion of a legionary's armour.

The faint brume roiling in place of its head played the same misty trick, coalescing into the shape of a Night Lord's helm.

Around, behind, Talos saw the dark metal walls of the *Covenant*'s abandoned apothecarion. Octavia had her pistol braced in both hands, cracking off las-rounds as the creature slunk away from her. A repetitive booming announcement rose from her side, as the little attendant she favoured let loose with his shotgun.

Uzas gunned his chainaxe again.

Talos opened his eyes, to see that only Variel remained in the confines of the small chamber. The Apothecary worked alone, unarmoured now, greasing the component pieces of an array of dismantled pistols.

'Uzas,' the prophet said, though the word was broken by his own creaking voice. He swallowed, and tried the name again.

Variel's eyes were burdened and bloodshot by exhaustion. 'They know. Your brothers know. They heard your murmurings as you... dreamed.'

'How long ago?' The prophet rose on aching muscles. 'When did they go?'

The Corsair Apothecary scratched his cheek. 'I have spent four hours rebuilding your skull and brain with no fewer than thirteen separate tools, saving your sanity and your life in the process. But by all means, ignore that fact in favour of pointless overexcitement.'

'*Variel.*' He said nothing more. The look in his eyes said what his words did not.

The Flayer sighed. 'Nostramo bred ungrateful sons, didn't it? Very well. What do you wish to know?'

'Just tell me what happened.'

'It is a warp echo,' Uzas voiced from his helm's speakers. He derided the creature even as he stared at it. 'A phantom. A nothing.'

'I know what it is better than you.' She stood by the door, her laspistol raised. 'That's why I was running.'

The Night Lord seemed not to have heard her. 'And you are to blame for its presence here.' He turned from the vault, where a creature made of white skin and stinking mist was shivering its way from a morgue locker in bitter recreation of a stillbirth. Uzas's red eye lenses fixed upon Octavia. 'You did this.'

She wouldn't lower her pistol. 'I didn't mean to.'

The Night Lord turned back to the creature. On shaking limbs, it rose to its full height. The body had been dead for weeks, but refrigeration kept it untouched by the darkening stains of decay. It was naked, headless, grasping no weapon in its curling hands. But its identity was unmistakable.

'You are dead, Dal Karus,' Uzas sneered at the warp-thing.

'*...wish to join First Claw...*' Its voice was ice on the wind.

Uzas answered by squeezing the trigger on his chainblade's haft. The axe-teeth gave a throaty, revving whine, frustrated by a feast of thin air.

'*...not with Malcharion's bolter...*'

Octavia felt no shame at being immeasurably braver with a legionary – even this particular legionary – between her and the spiteful wraith. She fired three shots around Uzas's towering bulk, and, taking the cue, Hound fired with her. Spent shells rattled along the decking.

Dal Karus bled smoking, milky fluid from the gunshot wounds in his torso, but kept coming in the twisted, awkward stagger. The mist forming his helm stared at the three figures ahead, while his bare feet slapped on the cold floor with each lurch.

'No blood to offer. No skull to treasure.' The Night Lord's voice slurred, the words half-formed and wet. 'No blood. No skull. A waste. Such a waste.' The chainaxe howled louder. 'Die twice, Dal Karus. Die twice.'

Uzas charged, devoid of grace, fighting without finesse. He swung the axe wide, arcing down with heavy chops, while stabbing and carving with the gladius in his other hand. His thrashing would've been ludicrous had it not been performed by a warrior approaching three metres in height whose weapons tore the wraith apart. Steaming fluid splashed over nearby tables. Chunks of smoking flesh dissolved into sulphurous puddles, eagerly hissing as they devoured the decking.

The fight, such as it was, ended in a matter of moments.

'Hnnnh,' said Uzas in the aftermath. He dropped his weapons in disgust, letting them clatter to the floor. 'No blood. No skull. No gene-seed to taste. Just a husk of slime melting into the air.'

'Uzas?' Octavia called his name.

The Night Lord turned to face her. 'You do this. You summon the Neverborn to you. I know the stories. You killed with your mutant's eye. I know this. So the Neverborn come. Weak ones. Easy prey. Kill them before they grow strong. This time, this time. Navigator is lucky. This time, this time.'

'Thank you.' She had no idea if he could even hear her, or would care if he did. 'Thank you for killing it while it was... weak.'

The warrior left his weapons where they lay. 'The *Covenant* doesn't sail without you.' Uzas hesitated, looking back to the vaults. One locker stood open, its door wide and dark – a missing tooth among a multitude. 'The pain returns. Slay a piss-weak little daemon thing, and the pain returns. No blood. No skull. Nothing to offer, nothing to prove the deed was done. And the creature was too weak to matter. Not even a true daemon. A lost soul. A phantom. I said that first, didn't I? I killed your foolish little ghost. Others still chase you, don't they? Kill with your eye, and they grow stronger. Stories about Navigators. Heard many of them.'

She nodded, her skin crawling at his meandering speech. *He's no better than the warp-echo*, though she felt a flood of guilt for thinking it.

'Octavia. The Eighth.'

'Yes... lord.'

'Septimus. The Seventh. He refuses to repair my armour unless Talos commands it. The Seventh is like my brother. He watches me and sees a broken thing.'

She wasn't sure what to say.

'I am stronger now,' he said, and gave a hollow, quiet little laugh. 'But it hurts more. See the truth. Steal the power. A weapon. Not a faith. But it is hard to stay together when your thoughts fly apart.'

All three of them turned as the doors ground open again. Framed in the dim light, three Night Lords stood with raised weapons.

'Uzas,' Xarl fairly spat the name. 'What has happened here?'

The Night Lord gathered his dripping weapons. 'Nothing.'

'Answer us,' Mercutian warned. The heavy bolter in his hands – a weighty cannon of black iron – panned up and down the slouched figure at the centre of the chamber.

'Get out of my way,' Uzas grunted. 'I will go past you, or through you.'

Xarl's chuckle was sincere, crackling through his helm. 'You have quite an imagination, brother.'

'Let him go,' Cyrion moved aside. 'Octavia, are you well?'

The Navigator nodded, watching Uzas stalk from the chamber. 'I'm... Yes. I'm fine.'

She added the 'Lord' several moments too late, but at least she added it for once.

XV

DISQUIET

LUCORYPHUS OF THE Bleeding Eyes ran an oiled cloth between the teeth of his chainsword. Boredom didn't strike him often, for which he was grateful. On the rare occasions it took hold, he struggled to endure the sluggish state of mind that accompanied these prolonged periods of inactivity.

The *Covenant* functioned as any other Legion vessel in a neutral dock, which is to say it sucked up crew and supplies, stealing what it couldn't trade for, while vomiting out profit. And all to the dead melody clank-song of repairers' hammers ringing on the hull.

Vorasha, one of his best, stalked into the cargo hold the Bleeding Eyes had claimed for themselves. The Raptor moved on all fours, that same rapid crawl adopted by most of his kind, metal talons leaving indentations – or outright punctures – in the deck floor.

'Many weeks in dock, yes-yes.'

Lucoryphus exhaled through his vocabulator in reply. Vorasha's speech always grated against his nerves: the other Raptor barely formed words in full any more, conveying his meanings through a degenerate tongue of clicks and hisses. Statements were often punctuated by an almost infantile assurance. *Yes-yes*, he'd breathe, time and again. *Yes-yes*. If Vorasha wasn't so skilled, Lucoryphus would've cut him down long ago.

'Need to soar,' Vorasha stressed. 'Yes-yes.' The engine housings on his back coughed with denied flight, venting a slither of smoke. A charcoal reek of strangled thrust filled the air.

Lucoryphus prefaced his words with a bladed caw, signifying the ire behind his emotionless mask. 'Nothing to hunt. Be at ease, pack-brother.'

'Much to hunt,' Vorasha snickered. 'Could hunt Corsairs. Crack armour open. Drink the thin blood that runs from split veins.'

'Later.' Lucoryphus shook his head, a rare human gesture. 'The prophet agreed to serve the Blood Reaver. An alliance... for now. The betrayal comes later.' He went back to cleaning the teeth tracks of his gutting blade, though even this soured his mood. His bloodless sword needed no cleaning, and therein lay the problem.

The Raptor leader looked around the cargo hold, his neck cabling flexing with machinery purrs. Discarded weapons featured as much as furniture, while a cluster of robed Legion serfs spoke quietly amongst themselves in the far corner.

'Where are the Bleeding Eyes?'

'Some on station. Some on ship. Yes-yes. All waiting for Vilamus.'

Lucoryphus rattled out something like a laugh. *Ah, yes. Vilamus.*

TALOS AND MALEK stood on opposite sides of the table, unintentionally mirroring their positions on the debate.

'We have to sail with the Corsairs,' the prophet restated. 'I am not arguing against honouring our debt to Huron. But the *Covenant* is the equal to any two cruisers in their fleet. Once Huron's fleet is scattered at Vilamus, the *Covenant* will be able to hold off an assault for as long as we need. That is when we move against them. We withdraw quickly from Vilamus, while Huron's forces are still deployed. Then we take back the *Echo of Damnation*.'

'This is idiocy.' Malek turned his craggy features to the Exalted on its throne. 'My lord, you cannot be considering the prophet's plan.'

The creature gestured to them both with a magnanimous talon. 'Ah, but I like his plan. I share his passion for the blood we must shed, and I also refuse to see the *Echo of Damnation* commanded by any soul not born of Nostramo.'

'Lord, too much will be left to chance. The *Covenant* is likely to take massive damage even if we're successful. And what if we are boarded while the prophet's plan has left our decks empty?'

'Then the crew, and any of the Legion remaining on board, will die.' The daemon heaved its exoskeletal bulk out of the throne, armour joints creaking. 'Prophet.'

'Sir?'

'You are getting ahead of yourself in one regard. Before we retake the *Echo of Damnation*, we must aid Huron in taking Vilamus. How many men will we lose there? None, if luck dances to our tune. And what if fortune favours another song, as it always does? Every warrior we leave dead at Vilamus is a soul that cannot storm the *Echo* with you.'

Talos keyed a short code into the table's hololithic console. The cardinal projector generators blinked into life, beaming a lie before them. The shivering, rotating image of the Red Corsair strike cruiser, *Venomous Birthright*.

'Just give me the Bleeding Eyes,' he said. 'I will lead them in with First Claw. We will take the *Echo of Damnation* as we sail away from Vilamus.'

The daemon licked a black tongue along its maw. 'You ask for much.

My best squad, and my newly acquired Raptor cult. These resources are precious to me.'

'I will not fail the Legion,' Talos nodded to the hololithic. 'You were the one to come to me, Vandred. You wanted to reforge ourselves anew. Give me what I need, and I'll return with another warship.'

The Exalted looked long at the prophet. So rare, to see the light of conviction, of zeal, in the warrior's eyes.

'I trust you,' the daemon said. 'Brother. I will grant you the forces you need, and I will hold off the Blood Reaver's fleet while you enact your plan. I see only one true flaw with your thinking.'

'Name it, sir.'

'If you storm the ship and take it, its own Navigator may refuse to serve you. Worse, he will jump the ship back to Hell's Iris.'

'I will kill the *Birthright's* Navigator,' Talos admitted. 'The likelihood of betrayal already occurred to me.'

The daemon tilted its head. 'Then how do you plan to pull your new vessel into the warp?'

The prophet hesitated. *Ah,* the Exalted thought, *I am not going to like this.* 'Octavia,' the daemon said. 'You mean to take her with you.'

'Yes. I will take her in the assault. She will jump the ship once we've taken it.'

The Exalted growled in foul simulation of laughter. 'And the *Covenant?* Who will guide us through the warp while you race away, leaving us to face Huron's guns?'

Talos hesitated again. 'I... have an idea. It needs to be refined, but I believe I can make it work. I will only proceed with the plan if every piece of the puzzle falls into place. You have my word.'

'Very well. Then I grant you permission. But I need you to focus on the first of our problems. We need to live through our agreement with Huron before we can betray him.'

Malek took a breath, his greying stubble split by a scowl's trace. 'Vilamus.'

'Indeed,' the creature grunted. 'First, we must survive Vilamus.'

THE WEEKS PASSED, and her irritation grew. The Legion drilled and sparred, its warriors honing themselves for a battle no one cared to inform her about. None of First Claw came to see her in her chambers, not that she'd expected them to, but boredom was making her desperate.

Of the mortal crew, the only people she knew were Septimus, Maruc and Hound. The first of that list... Well, she had no desire to see him at the moment, anyway. The last time they'd met had been acutely uncomfortable. She was almost glad Cyrion had interrupted them, not that she was even sure what he'd interrupted.

The second name on the list was usually with Septimus, off-ship and engaged in some nefarious activity neither of them wanted to explain. That left her with Hound, who was – being fair to him – hardly the most cultured of conversationalists. Her royal blood might be watered down by the relative status of her lineage, but she was still a Terran noble, and had played hostess on several occasions to members of the Throne-world's ruling class.

Her attendant's main avenue of discussion was his own mistress. He seemed interested in little else, though he was good for helping her learn more Nostraman. The viperous tongue deviated from any possible Gothic roots more than any human language she'd encountered, but once she stopped seeking similarities, it became easier to begin afresh with a clearer outlook.

Still, boredom was always peering over her shoulder. Navigators were not born to sit idle.

Beyond Hound, all she had to distract herself were the endless repair updates, but even they'd dried to a trickle now the *Covenant* was ready to break dock.

Her door proximity sensor tolled again. Octavia caught herself halfway to reaching to check her bandana. Some habits shouldn't be developed, and that one was starting to stick. All too often she felt her hand twitch when Hound spoke to her, and she'd keep touching her covered eye with every loud noise echoing down from higher decks.

Hound stumbled his way around her messy chamber, tilting his face up to the viewscreen by the bulkhead.

'It is Septimus,' he said. 'He is alone.'

The Navigator made a point of studying her personal viewscreen, the one mounted on the armrest of her throne. Schematics, essays and jour-nal entries wiped across the screen as she cycled through the *Covenant's* datacore. The updated feed from Hell's Iris swelled the ship's onboard repository of knowledge with a great deal of recent lore about the local subsectors.

'Mistress?'

'I heard you.' Octavia frowned at the glowing screen, and typed *VILA-MUS* for the third time, refining the search.

'Shall I grant him entrance, mistress?'

She shook her head. 'No, thank you. Do you know what Vilamus is?'

'No, mistress.' Hound moved away from the door, resuming his place, sat with his back against the wall.

DATACORE MATCH blinked across her black screen in aggressively green script. She activated the entry, unlocking a stream of scrolling text and numbers.

'It would be useful,' she sighed, 'if I could read Badabian.'

Blurry orbital images accompanied the archive data. The Navigator breathed a little 'Huh' of surprise as the picts resolved to show a world no different from a thousand others – with one incredible exception. 'I don't see why we're... Oh. Oh, Throne of the God-Emperor... they can't mean to attack this.'

Octavia looked up at Hound, who was busy toying with the loose end of a wrist bandage.

'Hound,' she said. 'I think I know what Vilamus is.'

SEPTIMUS HEADED TO Blackmarket, determined not to let his mood get the better of him. Octavia was a fey creature even in her calmest moments. Trying to understand her was like trying to count the stars.

Several of the traders there greeted him with nods, a few with sneers, and many more with smiles. The massive chamber was a hub of activity, with new wares hawked as soon as they were smuggled on board from Hell's Iris. Several of the table stalls even had thuggish bodyguards on hand to defend presumably valuable merchandise. The serf raised his eyebrow as he passed a table laid out with what looked like plundered Imperial Guard weaponry – even a chainsword, scaled to fit a human hand. But that wasn't what drew his eye.

Septimus gestured to the stocky, long form of a lasrifle. Its body and stock looked to be formed of plain, dull metal. Scratches and burn marks along the rifle's length showed both signs of older wear and more recent desecration, likely the removal of all Imperial aquilas.

'*Vulusha?*' he asked the ageing merchant in the ragged Legion uniform. '*Vulusha sethrishan?*'

The man replied with a patently false laugh, naming a prince's ransom in trade items.

Septimus's smile was equally insincere. 'That's quite a price. It's a rifle, my friend. Not a wife.'

The trader picked up the chainsword, his knuckly fingers wrapping the hilt in an exaggerated grip that would see him disarmed in a heartbeat in an actual fight. With awkward chops, he cut the air a few times.

'I have more to trade than most of these others. How about this blade? Better than that chopping cleaver you keep strapped to your shin, isn't it? And look, it has perfect balance. See? This was once a hero's blade.'

'It's a chainsword, Melash. No chainsword has perfect balance. They're not balanced at all.'

'Why do you come to harass me, eh?'

'Because I want the rifle.'

Melash tongued a sore on his lip. 'Very well. But the gun was also the weapon of a hero. You know I would never lie to you.'

'Wrong again.' Septimus reached out to tap the Munitorum number code in faded stencilling along the rifle's stock. 'It looks like standard-issue Guard gear to me. What comes next, old man? Will you tell me you have a family to feed?'

The trader sighed. 'You wound me.'

'I'm sure I do.' Septimus moved aside as a small crowd of slaves moved past. Blackmarket had never looked busier. It was almost disorienting to be in the middle of so much life, like a real city night-market. Torches lit up dozens of unfamiliar faces. 'Just sell me the damn gun, Melash. What do you want in trade?'

The other man sucked his lower lip. 'Can you get me batteries? I need power cells, Septimus. Everyone is bringing lamp packs on board, but energy cells will be in short supply a few weeks after we set sail. And caffeine. Can you get me some powdered caffeine from the station?'

Septimus watched him closely. 'Now tell me what you really want, and stop avoiding it in case I refuse.'

The old man gave a more honest, but more awkward, smile. 'A labour trade?'

Septimus raised an eyebrow. His bionic eye clicked and purred as it sought to mirror the expression. 'Keep talking.'

Melash scratched at his bald pate. 'Some trouble with a gang on the lower decks. Hokroy's crew, a new pack from Ganges. A lot of the new blood, they haven't learned the laws, yet. They stole from me. Not much, but I didn't have much to begin with. Some coins, my pistol, some of my wife's jewellery... She's dead, dead in the Angel attack, but... I'd like it back, if you can arrange it.'

Septimus held out his hand. Melash spat into his own palm, and grasped the serf's hand in a shake.

'I meant *give me the rifle*, Melash.'

'Oh. Ah, I see.' The man wiped his hand along his uniform trousers. Septimus, wincing, did the same.

'Delightful,' he muttered. 'Did you get a strap when you stole the rifle?'

'A strap?'

'A strap, to carry it over your shoulder.'

'A strap, he says. I'm not an Imperial supply depot, boy.' The trader handed him the lasgun. 'It needs juice, by the way. I've not charged its power pack yet. Good hunting down there.'

Septimus moved back into the crowd, passing Arkiah's stall. The widower's table, once Blackmarket's hub, stood at the heart of the hurricane: a zone of stillness while chaos reigned all around.

He halted at the barren display. 'Where is Arkiah?' he asked a nearby woman.

'Septimus,' she greeted him with a shy smile. Despite being old enough to be his grandmother, she reached up to straighten her tangled grey hair. 'Have you not heard? Arkiah has left us.'

'Left?' He scanned the crowd for a moment. 'To live aboard the station? Or to dwell deeper within the ship?'

'He...' she hesitated once she saw the rifle in his gloved grip. 'He was killed a handful of nights after the Legion master came here to chastise him.'

'That was weeks ago. No one told me.'

Her shrug bordered on demure. 'You have been busy, Septimus. Chasing the Navigator and gathering for the Legion, I hear. Children and mothers... How many have you brought on board? When will they be released from the slave holds?'

He waved the questions aside. 'Tell me about Arkiah.'

The old woman made a face as the cold air graced one of her decaying teeth. 'When the Legion lord came, it made Arkiah a pariah in the nights that followed. People thought it bad luck to go near him, lest they risk earning the Legion's displeasure as he had. From there, it got worse – he started insisting he was seeing his daughter again, running through the corridors beyond Blackmarket. After that, he was always alone. We found his body a week later.'

She made no effort to hide her feelings from him, or the hurt in her eyes. Killings between the human crew were a fact of life on board the *Covenant*, frequent enough to put the crime figures in an Imperial hive to shame. Bodies showed up beaten and stabbed regularly enough for few mortals to bat an eyelid unless it was someone they knew. But then, everyone knew Arkiah, even if only because of his daughter.

'How did he die? What marks did you find on him?'

'He'd been gutted. We found him sat against a wall in one of the granary silos. Eyes open, mouth closed, one of his daughter's hair-trinkets in his hand. His insides were out, scattered over his lap and the floor nearby.'

Uzas. The thought rose unbidden, and Septimus fought to prevent it reaching his lips. The old woman didn't need to hear it, though. She saw it in his eyes.

'You know who did this.' She peered at him. 'Don't you? One of the Legion, perhaps. Maybe even your master.'

He faked nonchalance with an underplayed shrug. 'Talos would have skinned him and strung him up in Blackmarket, just as he'd promised. You should know that – he's done it before. If this was the Legion's doing, it was one of the others.'

Uzas.

It could be any of them, but the name stuck like a parasite as soon as it entered his mind. *Uzas.*

'I have to go.' He forced a smile. 'Thank you, Shalla.'

He DIDN'T CONSIDER himself a killer, though the gods on both sides of this war knew he was a murderer many times over. Duty called, and its calls often involved the fyceline-stinking thunder of gunfire in closed spaces, or the hacking crunch of a machete smacking into flesh. An unpleasant tingle crawled through the fingers of his right hand each time he recalled the grating nastiness of a machete blade sunk into flesh, only to be stopped by bone. He was just a man – it often took a second or third try to get through someone's arm, especially if they were waving it around, trying to claw at his face.

But he still didn't consider himself a killer. Not really.

In addition to clutching this denial around him, as if it offered some kind of protection, he took a faintly macabre pride in the fact he'd never enjoyed killing anyone. Not yet, at least. Most of the people who'd died at his hands in the last decade were fair game, one way or the other, because they'd simply been fighting for the enemy.

He could even salve his conscience when it came to the recent kidnappings, telling himself – and his victims – that life aboard the *Covenant* was immeasurably better than the Corsair hellhole he was abducting them from.

But this was different. Somehow, premeditation was the least of it. The entire endeavour, from agreement to commencement, set his skin crawling.

Octavia. Too long in her presence. Too many hours spent sitting with her, discussing life aboard the *Covenant*, being forced to examine and analyse his existence, instead of pushing ahead, outrunning the guilt, protected by familiar denial.

Once, not long ago, she'd asked him his name. 'Not "Septimus",' she'd laughed when he said it. 'What was your name before?'

He hadn't told her, because it no longer mattered. He was Septimus, the Seventh, and she was Octavia, the Eighth. Her former name hardly mattered, either: Eurydice Mervallion was dead. Did her family ties mean anything? Did her bloodline's wealth make any difference any more? And what of the fine manners she'd been taught as a scion of the Terran aristocracy?

The *Covenant* shaped them now. Septimus was a construct of these black corridors, a pale man who toiled for traitors, clutching two pistols, walking through the dark bowels of a blasphemous ship with a mind to commit murder. He was a pirate, a pilot, an artificer... and a heretic as truly as those he served.

It wasn't that the thoughts themselves were so sour; it was that he was thinking them at all. Damn that woman. Why was she doing this to him? Did she even know she was doing it? For weeks now, she'd refused to even see him. What the hell had he done wrong? She was the one whose questions dredged through silt best left untouched.

The door to First Claw's armoury parted before him on oiled hydraulics. He looked down at the lasrifle in his hands, checking it over one last time before giving it to its new owner.

'Maruc, I have something fo... Lord?'

Talos stood by his weapon rack, while Maruc worked with a hand-held broach, working the toothed tool along the side of the Night Lord's pauldron. Hardly a tall man, Maruc needed to stand on a stool in order to reach.

'Minor damage,' Talos said. Unhelmed, he turned his black eyes upon Septimus. 'I was sparring with Xarl. Where did you find a Kantrael-pattern Imperial Guard lasrifle?'

'Blackmarket. It's... a gift for Maruc.'

Talos tilted his head, something vulturine creeping across his gaze. 'How fares the harvest?'

'The slave holds are swelling again, my lord. Finding untainted children has been a challenge, though. Mutants abound on Hell's Iris.'

The Night Lord grunted in agreement. 'That is the truth. But what is wrong? You are uneasy. Do not waste time lying to me, I can see it etched on your face and inscribed within your voice.'

Septimus was long-used to his master's blunt, immediate honesty. Replying in kind was the only way to deal with Talos.

'Arkiah is dead. He was disembowelled and left in a grain chamber.'

The Night Lord didn't move. Maruc continued to work. 'The void-born's father?' Talos asked.

'Yes.'

'Who killed him?'

Septimus shook his head without any other answer.

'I see,' Talos said quietly. Silence resumed, but for the metallic rasp of Maruc's broach scraping at the armour's imperfections. Presumably, he had no idea what they were saying, for he didn't speak a word of Nostra-man. 'What else?'

Septimus placed the lasgun on Maruc's workbench. When he faced Talos again, it was with one eye narrowed, and his bionic eye dilated in sympathetic unity.

'How did you know there was more, lord?'

'A guess. Now speak.'

'I have to kill some people. Crew. No one important.'

Talos nodded, but his expression showed no sign of conceding to the point. 'Why do they need to die?'

'A trade agreement I made in Blackmarket. They're Ganges crew, and some of the newbloods are enjoying the lawless lower decks a little too much.'

'Tell me their names.'

'The gang leader is Hokroy. That's all I know.'

Talos still stared. 'And you assumed I would just allow you to do this? To wander the lower decks alone, murdering other members of the crew?'

'It... hadn't occurred to me that you would find fault with it, lord.'

'Ordinarily, I wouldn't.' The Night Lord grunted as he overlooked the repairs to his shoulder guard. 'Enough, thank you.' Maruc got down from the stool. 'It is not the crew's place to dispense justice, Septimus. It was not their place to kill Arkiah, nor yours to hunt down a pack of thieves. Times are changing, and we need to change with them. The new crew, those from Ganges, need to be faced with the consequences of lawlessness. The Exalted's choice to ignore the actions of mortals on board is no longer viable. We have too many new souls walking the hallways, and too many old souls used to living without consequence.'

Talos paused for a moment, striding over to where his helm lay on Septimus's work table. 'I believe it is time the Legion exercised more control over its subjects, reinstating the premise of iron law. Slaves cannot be given the keys to the kingdom. Anarchy is the result.' His smile was crooked, and more than a little bittersweet. 'Trust me, I have seen it before.'

'Nostramo?'

'Yes. Nostramo.' The warrior fastened his helm into place. Septimus listened to the snake-hiss of seals locking tight at the collar. 'I will deal with this, as I should have dealt with it weeks ago.'

'Lord, I–'

'No. You must do nothing. This is the Legion's work, Septimus, not yours. Now, ensure you are ready for the coming siege. We sail for Vilamus in mere days.'

The serf looked to his master. 'Is it true, what they say on the station?'

Talos snorted softly. 'That depends what they say on the station.'

'That Vilamus is an Adeptus Astartes fortress-monastery. That the Blood Reaver's entire fleet is laying siege to one of the best-defended worlds in the Imperium.'

Talos checked his weapons, before mag-locking them to his armour – the bolter to his thigh, the blade to his back.

'Yes,' he said. 'That is all true.'

'Are you not concerned about potential losses, lord?'

The legionary lifted a shoulder in the barest shrug. It sent skulls rattling against his armour, talking to one another in jawless clicks. 'No. All we have to do is stay alive, for the real battle will come after. That's when we'll bleed, Septimus. When we retake the *Echo of Damnation.*'

XVI

GAMBITS

THE MOOD IN Blackmarket was more subdued than usual, and it didn't take her long to see why. The reason – the seven skinless reasons – hung above everyone's heads, suspended from the ceiling on corroded chains.

Hound had stepped in some of the blood upon entering, which triggered a stream of muttered grumbling. 'The Legion is teaching a lesson to the crew,' he said, not bothering to clean his ragged boots.

The lesson was a wet one. Each of the seven bodies had dripped a great deal, if the stains on the decking were anything to go by. People were still tracking blood all over Blackmarket, and the smell, even for a heretics' ship, was something special. As Octavia watched, a tremor ran through the *Covenant*, more test-firing by the engine crews. The chained bodies swayed in their crucified moorings, and something long and stinking spilled from one's open stomach. It slapped onto the floor like a slimy cord of fat, glistening meat-rope.

Hound saw her staring, mistaking the disgust on her face for confusion. 'Intestines,' he said.

'Thank you, I guessed.'

'You shouldn't eat them.' He said these words with the sage wisdom of experience.

'I wasn't going to.'

'Good.'

Octavia turned her eyes back to the crowds. No one glanced her way for more than a moment. Before, she'd been a curiosity to some, and ignored by others. Now they all avoided her, from the oldest to the youngest, turning their heads from hers if she even looked their way.

She knew why, of course. The story had spread well over the weeks since she'd killed her attendant. Leaving her chamber already felt like a mistake, but sitting alone and hiding with her boredom wasn't an option any more. She'd go just as crazy in isolation as she would if she risked walking the ship's halls again.

One of the Legion strode through Blackmarket, helmed and armed. His loose gait suggested a routine patrol, though she'd never seen a legionary here before for anything other than specific business.

'Navigator,' the Night Lord greeted her, granting her a nod as he passed. Backswept wings, like those of a bat or a daemon from the pages of scripture, rose from his helm as a stylised crest.

She didn't recognise the warrior – he was from one of the other Claws – so she replied with a muted, 'Lord...' and left it at that.

The warrior left Blackmarket, heading deeper into the ship. 'That would also explain why everyone is behaving,' she mused.

The skinned bodies swung above in morbid echo of the Legion war banners on the bridge, drifting in the breeze of the air filtration system. A flayed hand hung not far from her face as she looked through the tin trinkets offered on one table. The trader quickly looked away after a giving a glassy smile.

Octavia walked on. When she reached Arkiah's table, she trailed her fingertips over the bare wooden surface, looking around for some explanation of his absence. No one would meet her eyes for long enough to ask. She checked her bandana, though she knew it was in place, and made a decision. Time to get out of here. One could find other places to walk; maybe the observation deck.

She turned and walked right into someone. Her face bounced off his chest, snapping her head back, and she thumped down onto the blood-slick deck with watering eyes and a sore backside.

'By shidding node,' she said, covering her mouth and nose. Blood dripped between her fingers.

'Forgive me.' Septimus offered his hand. 'I didn't expect to be headbutted.'

She took the offer, rising with his help. Hound offered her a scrap of cloth that looked as though he'd used it to wipe grime from parts of his body best left covered. She shook her head and used her sleeve instead. A bloody smear streaked over the dark material. Oh, if her father could see her now.

'Is it broken?' She wrinkled her nose.

'No.'

'It stings like it is.'

'As I said, forgive me. I've been looking for you. First Claw is gathering, and they ordered both of us present.'

That didn't sound good. 'Very well. After you.'

'You need me *to do what?*' Octavia asked. She didn't laugh. She wanted to, but she couldn't manage it.

First Claw gathered in their armoury, but they were not alone. Octavia had entered with Septimus and Hound, finding Maruc already present, which was no surprise. The tech-priest was another matter entirely. He seemed to be paying little heed to the Night Lords, occupying himself with drifting around their sanctum, an iron ghoul in whispering robes, examining curios and spare parts for their armour.

'I have never been granted access to a Legiones Astartes armoury chamber before,' he noted with tinny interest. 'Such intriguing disorder.' The tech-adept stood as tall as the warriors, though stick-thin by comparison. He arched over Maruc's desk, seemingly occupied by pushing a hand-held thermal counter across the wood, the way a child might nudge a dead pet to see if it still breathed.

'This is broken,' Deltrian observed to the rest of the room. When no one replied, he deployed digital micro-tools from his fingertips and began to repair it.

'You need me to do what?' Octavia asked again. Disbelief still coloured her voice, bleeding it dry of any respect. 'I don't understand.'

Talos spoke softly, calmly, as he always did when not wearing his helm. 'When the Siege of Vilamus is over, we intend to attack a Red Corsair vessel, one of their flagships, calling itself *Venemous Birthright*. You will be deploying with us in a boarding assault pod. Once we secure the ship, you will guide it into the warp with the *Covenant of Blood*, and we will make for the Great Eye in Segmentum Obscurus.'

Hound, like his namesake, made a growl at the back of his throat. Octavia could barely blink.

'How will the *Covenant* jump without me?'

'I will deal with that,' said Talos.

'And how will we take over an entire enemy warship?'

'I will deal with that, as well.'

She shook her head. 'I mean no disrespect, but... if it's a fair fight...'

Talos actually laughed. 'It will not be a fair fight. That's why we will win. The Eighth Legion has no passion for fighting fair.'

'We do tend to lose those,' Cyrion noted with a philosophical air.

'We'll handle the blood-work,' Xarl's voice was a vox growl, somehow still conveying his eternal eagerness. 'Don't you worry your fragile little skull about it.'

'But... how will you do it?' Octavia asked.

'Treachery.' Talos tilted his head. 'How else? The details are irrelevant. All you need to know is this: once we return from Vilamus, make sure you are armed and ready. You will join us in a boarding pod, and we will protect you as we move through the enemy decks. The *Birthright*'s Navigator has to die quickly, lest he jump the ship with us still on board. We will kill him, secure you in his place, and take control of the enemy bridge.'

Octavia's gaze drifted over to Deltrian. 'And... the honoured tech-adept?'

'He's coming with us,' Cyrion nodded.

The tech-priest turned in a graceful whirr of machine-joints. 'As requested, my servitors are re-tooled and poly-tasked for the planned eventualities.'

She glanced at Septimus, who gave her an awkward smile. 'I'm coming, too. So is Maruc.'

Maruc grunted. 'Punishment for my many sins.' He swallowed and shut up the moment Uzas turned towards him.

'I, also, am coming,' Hound announced. Silence greeted this proclamation. 'I am,' he insisted, and turned his blind eyes to Octavia. 'Mistress?'

'Fine,' Cyrion chuckled. 'Bring the little rat.'

'*Hound*,' Hound replied, almost sulkily. Now he had a name, he clung to it with tenacity.

'I know what Vilamus is,' she told them. 'And that's why I can't believe you're so confident about surviving it. A fortress-monastery? An Adeptus Astartes world?'

Cyrion turned to Talos. 'Why does she never say "Lord" when she addresses us? You used to train these mortals with a stricter hand, brother.'

Talos ignored him. 'None of us will die at Vilamus,' he said.

'You sound very sure... lord.'

The prophet nodded. 'I am sure. We are not taking part in the main siege. Huron will be tasking us with something else. If I'm correct, then for the first time since you've come aboard, we are going to fight a war our way.'

'And we tend not to lose those,' Cyrion added. For once, there wasn't a shadow of amusement in his voice.

VARIEL OPENED HIS eyes.

'Enter.'

The door raised on loud, unhappy tracks. The Apothecary loathed the times his Chapter based themselves at Hell's Iris. The station might be a military marvel, but it was filthy and run-down in a thousand offensive ways.

'Variel,' Talos greeted him, moving into the chamber.

Variel didn't rise from where he sat in the centre of the floor. The meditative control he'd held over his body loosened as awareness of the real world returned. His primary heart, slowed to a state of almost complete sedation, resumed its normal beat, and he felt the invasive warmth of his armour's interface spikes once more, buried in his body.

'I suspected you would be immersed in self-reflection,' Talos said through his mouth grille. 'But this can wait no longer.'

Variel motioned to the surgical table against one wall. 'Both of your post-surgery examinations have revealed no flaws in my work, or your healing processes.'

Talos shook his head. 'I did not come to speak of that.'

'Then what brings you here?'

'I came to speak with you, Variel, brother to brother. With neither my Legion overhearing, nor your Chapter.'

The Corsair narrowed his emotionless eyes. 'And yet you stand... what is your expression? In midnight clad? The winged skull of Nostramo stares at me from your armour, as surely as Huron's claw is clenched on my own war-plate.'

'Is. that an observation?' Talos smiled behind his skull mask, 'or a warning?'

Variel didn't answer. 'You do not even show me your face.'

'It is too bright in here.'

'Speak, then.'

'You are a brother to First Claw. Fryga forged that bond, and it has remained true for two decades. Before I can speak further, I have to know if you intend to honour the oath you took that night.'

Variel didn't blink much. Talos had noticed it before, and suspected the habit had an intensely disconcerting effect on humans. He wondered if the effect was something Variel had cultivated over time, or a natural proclivity that grew more obvious after gene-seed implantation.

'Fryga was almost thirty years ago for me. Only twenty for you, you say? Interesting. The warp has a wonderful sense of humour.'

'The oath, Variel,' said Talos.

'I never swore an oath on Fryga. I made a promise. There is a difference.'

Talos drew his sword, the weapon reflecting shards of the bright light back onto the austere walls.

'That is still one of the most exquisite blades I have ever seen,' Variel almost sighed.

'It saved your life,' the prophet said.

'And I saved yours mere weeks ago. One might say that we were even, and my promise has been kept. Tell me, are you still dreaming of the eldar?'

Talos nodded, but offered nothing more. 'Whether you saved my life or not, I need your help.'

Variel rose at last, moving over to the end section of his workstation – a sterile washbasin surrounded by racks of tools and fluids. With great care, he disengaged his gauntlets, stripping them off before slowly, slowly washing hands that were already perfectly clean.

'You want me to betray my Chapter, don't you?'

'No. I want you to betray them, steal from them, and abandon them.'

Variel blinked, slow, like a basking lizard. 'Abandon them. Interesting.'

'More than that. I want you to join First Claw. You should be with us, waging this war as part of the Eighth Legion.'

Variel dried his hands on a pristine towel-strip. 'Get to the point, brother. What are you planning?'

Talos produced an auspex from a belt pouch. The hand-held scanner had seen better days, scored by decades of use, but it functioned well enough when he activated it. A two-dimensional image resolved on the small screen, the subject of which Variel recognised immediately.

'The *Venomous Birthright*,' said the Apothecary. He looked up, attempting to meet the prophet's gaze for the first time. It worked, even through the other's eye lenses. 'I had wondered if you would ever detect its heritage, or even care if you did.'

'I care.' Talos deactivated the auspex. 'It's our ship, and after Vilamus, it will be in Eighth Legion hands again. But I need your help to take it back.'

On Variel's shoulder guard, the stretched face of Kallas Yurlon leered eyelessly in the Night Lord's direction. The Pantheon's Star still stood proudly on the leathery skin, black against the faded peach-pink of flayed flesh.

'And if I agreed... What would you need from me?' Variel asked.

'We cannot storm a cruiser full of Red Corsairs. I need the odds in our favour even before our boarding pods strike home.'

'Much of that crew is still Nostraman, you know.' Variel didn't look at Talos as he spoke. 'Survivors. Rejuvenated officers, valued for their expertise. Children of first generation exiles from your lost world. While the Night Lords are hardly a brotherhood of blessedly kind masters, I suspect many would prefer the cold embrace of Eighth Legion discipline to the lashes of Red Corsair slavedrivers.'

He snorted. 'Perhaps they will help you reclaim your ship. Not the Navigator, though. Ezmarellda is quite firmly one of Huron's creatures.'

Talos wouldn't be baited. 'I need your help, brother.'

The Apothecary closed his eyes for some time, leaning on his workstation, head lowered. Deep breaths carried through his war-plate, causing his shoulders to rise and fall with the hum of active armour.

He made a noise with his mouth, and shivered. Talos almost asked what was wrong, but Variel made the noise again, his shoulders shaking. When the Apothecary stepped away from the table, his eyes were bright, and his lips pliant in the dead-muscled parody of a smile. He kept making the noise, somewhere between a repetitive breathy grunt and a soft shout.

For the first time in decades, Variel the Flayer was laughing.

HE RAISED HIS head as the door opened again, though it took several attempts to speak.

'The weekly sip of water?' he sneered in Gothic.

The voice that answered was Nostraman. 'I see they still keep you here, leashed like a prized whore.'

Ruven gave a growl of guarded surprise. 'Come to mock me a second time, brother?'

Talos crouched by the captive in a purr of active armour. 'Not quite.

I have spoken of your fate with the Corsairs. They mean to execute you soon, for they can tear nothing more from your mind.'

Ruven breathed out slowly. 'I am not sure I can ever open my eyes again. My eyelids are no barrier to the light, and they feel fused shut.' He strained against the chains, but it was a weak, irritated gesture. 'Do not let them kill me, Talos. I would rather die by a Legion blade.'

'I owe you nothing.'

Ruven smiled, cracked lips peeling back from aching teeth. 'Aye, that's true enough. So why did you come?'

'I wanted to know something before you died, Ruven. What did you gain from that first betrayal? Why did you turn from the VIII Legion and wear the colours of Horus's sons?'

'We are all Horus's sons. We all carry his legacy with us.' Ruven couldn't help the edge of passion creeping into his tone. 'Abaddon is the Bane of the Imperium, brother. His is the name whispered by a trillion frightened souls. Have you heard the legends? The Imperium even believes him to be Horus's cloned son. And he bears that legend for a reason. The Imperium will fall. Perhaps not this century, and perhaps not the next. But it will fall, and Abaddon will be there, boot on the throat of the Emperor's bloodless corpse. Abaddon will be there the night the Astronomican dies, and the Imperium – at last – falls dark.'

'You still believe we can win this war?' Talos hesitated, for this was something he'd simply never expected. 'If Horus failed, what chance does his son have?'

'Every chance, for no matter what you or I might say, it's a destiny written in the stars themselves. How much larger are the forces in the Eye now, than those that first fled after the failed Siege of Terra? How many billions of men, how many countless thousands of ships, have rallied to the Warmaster's banner in ten millennia? Abaddon's might eclipses anything Horus ever commanded. You know that as well as I. If we could refrain from butchering one another for long enough, we'd already be pissing on the Imperium's bones.'

'Even the primarchs failed.' Talos wouldn't give ground. 'Terra burned, but rose again. They failed, brother.'

Ruven turned his face to the prophet, swallowing to ease the pain of speaking. 'That is why you remain blind to our destiny, Talos. You still idolise them. Why?'

'They were the best of us.' It was clear from the prophet's voice – Ruven knew he'd never even considered the question before.

'No. There speaks the voice of worship, and brother, you cannot afford to be so naive. The primarchs were humanity magnified – all of mankind's greatest attributes, balanced by its greatest flaws. For every triumph or flash of preternatural genius, there was a crushing defeat, or another step deeper on the descent into madness. And what are they now? Those that still exist are distant avatars, sworn to the gods they represent, ascended to devote their lives to the Great Game. Think of the Cyclops, staring into every possible eternity with his one poisoned eye, while a Legion of the walking dead does the bidding of his few surviving children. Think of Fulgrim, so enraptured by the glory of Chaos that he remains blind to his own Legion's shattering millennia ago. Think of our own father, who ended his life as a conflicted madman – dedicated one moment to teaching the Emperor some grand, idealistic lesson, and devoted the next moment to doing nothing but eating the heart of any slave within reach, while he sat in the Screaming Gallery, laughing and listening to the wails of the damned.'

'You are not answering my question, Ruven.'

He swallowed again. 'I am, Talos. I am. The Eighth Legion is a weak, unbalanced thing – a broken coalition devoted to its own sadistic pleasure. No greater goals beyond slaughter. No higher ambitions beyond surviving and slaughtering. That is no secret. I am no longer a Night Lord, but I am still Nostraman. Do you think I enjoyed kneeling before Abaddon? Do you think I relished that the Warmaster rose from another Legion, instead of my own? I loathed Abaddon, yet I respected him, for he will do what no other can. The gods have marked him, chosen him to remain in the material realm and do what the primarchs never could.'

Ruven took a shivering breath, visibly weakening as he finished. 'You asked why I joined the Despoiler, and the answer is in the fate of the primarchs. They were never intended to be the inheritors of this empire. Their fates were sealed with their births, let alone their ascensions. They are echoes, almost gone from the galaxy, engaged in the Great Game of Chaos far from mortal eyes. The empire belongs to us, for we are still here. We are the warriors that remained behind.'

Talos took several seconds to answer. 'You truly believe what you are saying. I can tell.'

Ruven gave a defeated laugh. 'Everyone believes it, Talos, because it is the truth. I left the Legion because I rejected the aimless butchery, and the naive, worthless hope of simply surviving this war. Survival wasn't enough for me. I wanted to win.'

The prisoner sagged in his chains. Instead of hanging slack, he fell forwards, crashing onto the cold deck. At first he couldn't move – the shock was too great, as was the pain of reawakening muscles abused in the fall.

'I... I am free,' he breathed.

'Yes, brother. You are free.' Talos helped the trembling sorcerer sit up. 'It will be several minutes before your legs are ready to be used again, but we must be quick. For now, here, drink this.'

Ruven reached out, his fingers curling around the offered cup. The tin was warm in his numb fingers. Sensation was returning to his extremities already.

'I understand none of this. What's happening?'

'I traded a supply of our gene-seed reserves to the Blood Reaver, in exchange for your life.' Talos let that sink in; the immense wealth of such an offer. 'And then I came to free you,' the prophet admitted, 'or slit your throat. Your fate depended on what you would say. And I agree with you in one respect, brother. I am also tired of just surviving this war. I want to start winning it.'

'I need my armour. And my weapons.'

'They are already in First Claw's armoury.'

Ruven gripped the iron collar around his throat. 'And this. This must be removed. I cannot summon my powers.'

'Septimus will remove it.'

The sorcerer chuckled. It sounded decidedly unhealthy. 'You are up to Septimus now? When I last walked the corridors of the *Covenant*, you were served by Quintus.'

'Quintus died. Can you stand, yet? I will support you, but time is short, and even through my helm, the light is beginning to pain me.'

'I will try. But I have to know, why did you free me? You are not a charitable soul, Talos. Not to your enemies. Give me the truth.'

The prophet hauled his former brother up, taking most of Ruven's weight. 'I need you to do something, in exchange for saving your life.'

'I will do it. Name it.'

'Very soon, the *Covenant* will have to fly without a Navigator.' The prophet's voice lowered and softened. 'We'll remove the collar, and restore your powers, for there is no one else who can do it, Ruven. I need you to jump the ship.'

ECHO OF DAMNATION

XVII

VILAMUS

Tareena thumbed her tired eyes, pushing hard enough to see colours. Once she was satisfied she'd numbed the itch into oblivion, she adjusted the vox-mic fastened to her ear and tapped it twice to assure herself that it was as useless as it'd been for the last few weeks.

Her auspex didn't so much chime lately as gargle, its rhythmic scanning note broken into an irregular stutter of audible static. The screen looked as clean as the scanner sounded, displaying a wash of distortion that meant nothing to anybody.

She knew the cause of the disruption. They all did. That didn't help in dealing with it, though. Tareena turned in her seat.

'Warden Primaris?' she called across the chamber.

Warden Primaris Mataska Shul came closer, bringing her austere silence with her. Tareena sensed a reprimand in the near future, for raising her voice.

'Yes, sister.' The old woman spoke with exaggerated care.

Tareena keyed in a retuning code, which changed absolutely nothing on her scanner display. 'Warden Primaris, forgive my interruption. I wished only to know if the augurs had refined their estimates on the duration of the interference.'

The Warden Primaris graced her with a thin-lipped smile. 'We are all troubled by the solar storm, sister. The Primaris Council meets with the Tenth Captain at the tolling of the bell for third reflection. Until then, trust in yourself, and your instruments, blinded as they may be for now.'

Tareena thanked her superior and returned to her console. The sun Vila, at the heart of the Vilamus system, was a temperamental benefactor, no doubt there. Tareena had only just entered her seventh year in the Wardens of Vilamus, and this was Vila's fifth outburst. None had lasted this long, though. Previous incidents of solar instability ended after a handful of days. This one was already into its third week, with no sign of abating.

She cycled through archived images of the bright, proud heart of fire in the system's centre. Several images, among the last recorded by the fortress-monastery's observation satellites before they lost connection to the surface, showed the sun spurting great arcs of misty plasma from its surface – far above typical solar flare activity.

Tareena's expertise training had been focussed on interstellar operation, for her placement in the fortress-monastery's command strategium. She knew what she was looking at, and though 'solar storm' was accurate enough, it wasn't the phenomenon's true title.

Coronal mass ejection. Natural, and not entirely uncommon among stars as aggressive as Vila. Still, it played sweet hell with the monastery's more sensitive electronics, and she'd rather not be caught on the surface of the planet without a reinforced radiation suit.

Not that there was anything out there, anyway. Vilamus itself, the fortress-monastery of the Marines Errant, was the only node of life upon the entire world. She was born here, she would die here, just as her parents had, and her children would.

'Sister Tareena,' said a voice farther down the main console. She turned, seeing Jekris looking her way. His hood was down, revealing a face worn by years of concern and a great deal of smiling. He was close to fifty now, and still unmated. She liked him, liked his fatherly face.

'Brother Jekris.' She kept her voice soft, aware of the Warden Primaris lurking nearby.

'Sister, I would ask you to aim a specific scrye-pulse to the east, at the following coordinates.'

She glanced at the coordinates he sent to her screen, but shook her head. 'My instruments fail me, brother. Do yours not do the same?'

'Please,' he said. 'Indulge me, if you would.'

She keyed in the digits, aiming a focussed auspex burst at the specified area of land. It took almost a minute, for the radar dishes on the fortress's battlements needed the time to turn and realign. She keyed in her personal code when the READY glyph flashed.

The imagery came back as a washed-over smear of meaningless junk. The charts came back with even less clarity.

'I see nothing through the storm,' she told him. 'I am sorry, brother.'

'Please, he said again, his gentle voice betraying a curious edge. 'Try again, if you would.'

She complied – it wasn't as if she had anything else to do anyway – and spent several moments looking at a returned spread of the same garbled results.

'I see nothing, brother.'

'Would you examine my results?'

She blinked. 'Of course.'

Jekris transmitted several images to her secondary monitor, which she cycled through in turn.

'Do you see it?' he asked.

She wasn't sure. In several of the images, there looked to be some kind of structure in the wastelands, but interference stole any chance of comprehending its scale, let alone if it was actually there. Little more than a thumb-sized smear marked the centre of several picts, almost lost in the turmoil of distortion.

'I don't think so,' she admitted. Tareena transferred them to her primary screen, coding in a demand for image recognition. No matches came up. 'It's a scanner ghost, brother. I'm certain of it.' She flicked a glance to the Warden Primaris, though. Such things had to be reported in times of auspex failure.

Jekris nodded, and summoned the elder with a raised hand.

Tareena focussed another scan at the location, tightening the auspex pulse to its smallest scope. The returning image was no clearer than anything else she'd performed in weeks, with no sign of the ghost image at all. As the senior scrye-mistress present, she initiated a purge of previous data from her scanner cache, and set up each element of her comprehensive scrying to run separately. Motion; thermal; bio-signs; everything. One by one, they came back negative, negative, negative.

All except the very last.

'I... have a reading,' she announced. 'Traces of iron detected, two hundred and sixty kilometres east of the fortress walls.'

'Mass readings?' The Warden Primaris was noticeably more alert all of sudden.

'No mass.' Tareena shook her head. 'The distortion won't allow specifics.'

'It is a drop pod,' said Jekris. 'Look at the shape.'

Tareena made a soft, 'Huh...' sound as she looked back at Jekris's images. *No. It couldn't be.*

'The Marines Errant have no forces in orbit,' she objected. 'Where would they have come from?'

'We have no idea what the Errants do or do not have in orbit, sister.' Jekris gave a shy smile, hesitant to disagree with her. 'For we cannot see what is up there.'

'It's likely one of our satellites. An observer, or a missile platform. With coronal mass ejection of this intensity, it's almost guaranteed that several of our satellites will malfunction, falling into degrading orbits.'

'So soon?

'Much depends on the satellites themselves, and the nature of the malfunction. But, yes, so soon.'

Jekris looked to the Warden Primaris, no longer trying to convince anyone but the elder.

'It's a drop pod, mistress. I am certain of it.'

Tareena stared at the imagery again, sucking her teeth. But, at last, she nodded. 'I cannot say, either way. It could be a satellite. It could be a drop pod.'

The Warden Primaris nodded. 'I will inform the Marines Errant at once. They will surely choose to investigate.'

THE RADIATION WAS brutal, so they sent Taras and Morthaud. Adeptus Astartes Scouts, despite their extensive modification, would still suffer out on the wastelands with the sunstorm raging through the system. That left the task to experienced Space Marines: Taras and Morthaud volunteered right away.

Both wore the heraldry of Eighth Company with pride, their squad designation emblazoned on their armour. Both wore their helms, split by halved paint schemes of white and blue. Both, as always, were arguing.

'This will be a false alarm,' Morthaud said. 'Mark my words, we are chasing a downed chunk of rock, or worse, an auspex ghost.' He delivered this proclamation from the Land Speeder's gunner seat, his hands gripping the heavy bolter's handles.

Taras, by contrast, worked the pilot's controls, easing the skimmer over the jagged landscape at full thrust. A cloudy plume of rock-dust streamed behind them, pushed into smoky shapes by the burning, howling engines.

They spoke over the vox, suit to suit, not afflicted by the stellar unrest taking place in the heavens. Their suits of armour were certainly miracles of machinery to the wider Imperium, but the relatively crude simplicity and limited sensor suites left war-plate immune to the kind of interference that slaughtered more sensitive and intricate systems.

'You'll see,' Morthaud finished his insistent little diatribe. The Speeder banked as it dodged around a smooth up-cropping of eroded stone, jostling both warriors in their seats. Taras didn't glance at his brother; his focus on the wastelands ripping past was absolute.

'Would that not be preferable to the alternative?'

Morthaud scoffed as he sighted through the cannon's targeting reticule. 'It would hardly be the first time we've had satellites degrade and strike the surface.'

'No,' said Taras. 'The other alternative.'

'Why would one of our ships–'

'I am not speaking of one of *our* ships. You know I am not. Cease being stubborn. The initiates may find it amusing, but I do not.'

Morthaud, like his brother, remained locked to his duty with unwavering resolution. Everywhere he looked, the heavy bolter's fat-mouthed muzzle followed. 'Now you speak in impossibilities.'

Taras said nothing for several moments. 'Chapter home worlds are not immune to attack,' he muttered.

'Perhaps. But we are far from the mindless xenos breeds that have attempted such things in the past. Come, brother, be serious. What is this bizarre melancholy?'

Taras veered sharply around a towering jut of rock, watching as the landscape grew harsher, cracking into ravines the deeper they travelled into the wastes. 'We have been garrisoned too long. That is all. I yearn to crusade once more.'

He seemed on the edge of saying more, but instead uttered a muted, 'Hold'. The Speeder's engines eased their prolonged roar, quieting to a throttled whine. The wastelands raced past at speed, instead of flashing by in an endless, colourless blur that almost defied perception.

'We're close now,' said Taras. 'Just over the next ridge.'

MORTHAUD RAN HIS gauntlet along the scarred heat-shielding, brushing away the sooty ash of atmospheric entry. It was undeniably a drop pod. And it was undeniably not one of theirs.

Before converging on the pod, they'd tried to raise Vilamus on the vox, with the expected result of such a futile gesture. Taras had led them in an extensive sweep of the local area, before they'd disembarked and made their way down into the canyon. Even without their squad, echoes of that unified loyalty showed in every movement – one would descend to a stable section of wall, while his brother covered him, aiming a bolter into the canyon below.

At the bottom, they split up, tracking separately while maintaining a steady stream of vox updates. The Marines Errant met again by the downed pod, once they were certain the area was secure.

'A single pod, in the midst of the storm.' Taras regarded the empty restraint thrones inside the open pod. 'And in this ravine... It is a wonder the scryers managed to track it at all.'

Morthaud hovered his hand-held auspex over the pod's scorched hull. 'The carbon-scoring is fresh. It's been down no longer than a week.'

'Look for marks of allegiance.' While his brother scanned, Taras kept his bolter up and ready, panning around for any signs of foes. 'Be swift. We must return to the fortress.'

Morthaud deactivated his scanner, brushing aside more of the cindery dust from the pod's armour plating. His efforts revealed a faded symbol: a horned skull, backed by splayed daemonic wings.

'Do you see anything?' Taras voxed.

'Aye.' Morthaud stared at the symbol, feeling his skin crawl. 'Traitors.'

FAILURE, THEY'D TOLD him, came with no shame. He was still useful. He still had a role to play in the Chapter's solemn duty. Indeed, failure came with its share of bittersweet triumph, for to even survive a failed trial was a feat relatively few managed to achieve, amongst the thousands that made the attempt. The rolls of the ignoble dead were long, their names listed as afterthoughts, for the sake of completion rather than remembrance.

Yet he was still human, and still at the mercy of his emotions. Each time he bowed before one of his masters, he would swallow the writhing twists of regret and jealousy. Always the same questions bubbled up from below: What if he'd tried harder? What if he'd managed to endure for a few more moments? Would he be the one now standing in blessed ceramite, while lowly humans bowed and scraped before him?

'*To serve is to know purity*': the words inscribed above each of the archways leading into the serf dormitories. He took great pride in his work, of course. All of the Wardens did. Their role was a vital one, and their diligence beyond question. From the lowliest programmer of servitors to the most respected of artificers, the Wardens treasured their irreplaceable position at the Chapter's heart.

This duality sat better in some hearts than others. He erred on the side of caution when discussing his regrets, though. Many of his robed brothers and sisters seemed to take nothing but joy in their duties, eager to serve the Chapter with no heed for what might have been.

Yeshic raised his hood against the ever-present chill permeating the great halls. His nightly duty stretched out before him – a long shift in the Meritoriam, writing the Chapter's deeds onto scrolls and purity seals for their suits of holy armour. Difficult work, for the scripture had to be exact and the writing perfectly formed. In some cases, the deeds were so extensive that the lettering on purity seal parchment was unreadable to the naked eye. Yeshic did good work, and he knew it. The Third Captain himself had once written him a commendation for his elegant poetry in expressing the officer's deeds. After taking the commendation to the Warden Primaris, he'd been honoured with a branding of the Chapter's holy sigil, the falling star, burned into the flesh of his forearm.

Upon entering Meritoriam Secondus, the lesser of the two chambers used for such work, he passed dozens of occupied desks, nodding in greeting at several of the other scribes. The wooden box under his arm contained his personal inks, which he placed at the edge of his table, pressing it into its waiting niche. With meticulous care, Yeshic prepared the inks, his quill pens, and the pots of sand used to help the lettering dry.

He was reaching for his first parchment when he heard the noise come from the antechamber.

'Did you hear that?' he asked Lissel, the young woman at the next table. She frowned at the interruption, her quill not resting in its scratching flow. Silence was rarely broken here. Lissel shook her head without looking up from her work.

There it was again. A muffled, minute clang, the report of metal against metal.

He looked over his shoulder, to the doorway leading into the antechamber.

'It's nothing,' Lissel murmured. 'Just Cadry, tidying the stores. He went in a few minutes before you arrived.'

Yeshic rose from his seat nevertheless, moving over to the closed door and keying the release code. As the portal opened on smooth hinges, nothing untoward met his questing gaze. Meritoriam Secondus had an immense storage chamber, with a shelf-forest of parchment racks, scroll tubes, ink vials and tools to mix pigments.

He stepped inside, closing the door so the others wouldn't be disturbed as he quietly called Cadry's name.

An irritating thrum in the air set his gums itching, though he couldn't fathom its source. A machine sound, without a doubt. Perhaps the grinder pestle was malfunctioning; not an unprecedented event, by any means. Yeshic moved deeper, heading through the rows of shelving. The feeling of static in his mouth grew stronger. The resonating hum grew louder in unison. It almost sounded like the growl of awakened ceramite, consecrated in the Emperor's name. But the Marines Errant never ventured into this wing of the fortress. Yeshic smiled at the very idea; an Errant would struggle to even fit through the doorway here.

'Cadry? Cad– Ah.' The elder sat hunched over the automated grinder, while the machine sat idle in its place on a workbench. The abrasive thrumming was everywhere now, more invasive than truly loud, strong enough to warm his eyes with subtle vibrations. He looked around for any sign of an Errant nearby, but saw nothing. All was in perfect order, bar Cadry's slack posture.

'Cadry? Are you well?' He touched the old man's shoulder. With a boneless slouch, Cadry fell face forwards onto the bench.

A heart attack, then. The poor old fool. Yeshic checked for a pulse at the elder's neck, and found nothing. His skin was still warm, though. The younger scribe muttered a prayer, stumbling over just what to say. Cadry had served with honour for seven decades. Many of the Wardens would attend his funerary rites, perhaps even one or two of the few Marines Errant remaining in Vilamus.

Yeshic turned the body to see the elder's face, intending to close the eyes before the funereal attendants arrived.

Blood painted the old man's chest. The eyes were gone. Hollow sockets wept and stared in their place, blackened by wounding, wet with fluid.

Yeshic turned, running only a single step before hitting the hand launching against his throat. Iron-skinned and shockingly cold, the grip clenched tight, leaving him capable of nothing but spraying wordless spit from flapping lips.

He looked up, following the arm that caught him. His attacker hung from the ceiling, armoured in ornate, ancient ceramite of a kind the serf had never seen. One of the Errant hands clutched the rim of a maintenance shaft, the other dragged the writhing serf up from the floor with no difficulty at all, no matter how the human thrashed.

Within three beats of Yeshic's heart, the Errant had hauled himself up into the maintenance conduit, dragging the serf with him.

Not an Errant not an Errant not an Errant.

'Do not pray...' the warrior whispered in a tinny crackle of vox, leering with red eye lenses, '...to your Emperor. Or you die even slower.'

Not an Errant... How... Who...

'Who–'

The warrior squeezed again, choking off his air. 'And do not ask foolish questions, or I will feed you your own eyes.'

The image of Cadry flashed back to him through his racing thoughts. The fat old man, blinded by mutilation, his eyes pulled from his head and placed upon his tongue. Maybe he'd even choked on them, before they went down...

'Thank you,' the warrior whispered. 'Your obedience has spared you the same last meal your friend enjoyed.'

The *not-an-Errant* drew a silver blade as he crouched, resting the tip beneath Yeshic's chin.

'Wait,' the serf wept. 'Please.'

The warrior exhaled something like a sigh, confessing three words to the whimpering human. 'I loathe begging.'

He thrust the blade upwards, burying it halfway to the hilt through tongue, palate, skull and brain. Yeshic convulsed, arms spasming against the duct's sides with quiet clangs.

At last, the Meritoriam scribe fell still. The warrior worked quickly, cracking the sternum with the pommel of his combat blade, and hacksawing through the ribcage with several chops. Once the ribs were broken, spread like open wings to reveal the harvest of organs beneath, the warrior kicked the corpse from the maintenance tunnel, letting it drop with a wet crack to the floor below. What had been inside the body began to leak out. That included the smell.

He regarded his rushed handiwork: the eyeless old man, the autopsied younger one; his ninth and tenth kills since arriving less than an hour before. What a fine discovery they would make for some oblivious menial.

The warrior paused only to clean his blade, sheathing it at his shin. The sirens chose that moment to begin.

Curious, Talos glanced back down at the gift he'd left, but the bodies were undisturbed. The sirens raged on. It sounded like the entire monastery was crying out in alarm, which, in a sense, was exactly the truth. Somewhere in this immense fortress, either his earlier handiwork – or that of his brothers – had been discovered.

XVIII
INFILTRATION

HURON'S PLAN HAD been easy to admire, as was the passion with which he'd presented it. Showing surprising humility and consideration to the one hundred warriors he was ordering to potential suicide, the Tyrant came on board the *Covenant of Blood* with a minimal honour guard to grant a personal address. On the *Covenant*'s bridge, flanked by two of his Terminator huscarls, the Corsair lord detailed his plan in full, highlighting the Night Lords' potential avenues of assault. He even conceded the point that, ultimately, the VIII Legion's arrival was a fortuitous event. Their warriors were much more suited to the first phase of the invasion, and although he entrusted the results to them, he knew their finest chances of achieving victory would be through their own methods.

Talos had watched all of this, gathered with First Claw in a loose pack around the hololithic table. The other Claws did the same. Only one Night Lord stood alone, his armour freshly repainted, diminished by his isolation yet standing proud. Ruven had no Claw, for each of them had refused him. The Exalted and its Atramentar reacted harshest of all, vocally promising to slay the betrayer if he was foolish enough to offend them even once.

Partway through the speech, the Blood Reaver summoned a hololithic projection of the Vilamus fortress-monastery. Even the rough, flickering image ignited something akin to envy in Talos's unwavering gaze. No fortress-monastery was the twin of any other, and Vilamus rose like an Ecclesiarchy cathedral, reinforced into a gothic bastion with staggered battlements, tiered ramparts, landing platforms and, on the highest levels, docks for warships drifting below low-orbit to be repaired at the Chapter's sanctuary.

'We could crash the *Covenant* into it,' Xarl mused, 'and it still wouldn't make a dent.' He carried his helm under his arm. For reasons Talos couldn't work out, since arriving at Hell's Iris, Xarl had taken to wearing his ceremonial helm. Its ornamentation was an echo of the Legion's emblem, with twin sleek, chiropteran wings rising in an elegant crest.

'Why are you wearing that?' Talos asked quietly, during the mission briefing.

Xarl looked at the helm in the crook of his arm, then scowled at the prophet. 'No harm in a little pride, brother.'

Talos let it go. Perhaps Xarl had a point.

Huron paused to clear bile from his throat. Gears clanked in his neck and chest as he swallowed. 'A fortress-monastery is a defensive bastion like no other. Each of you knows this, but even such strongholds have degrees of capability. Vilamus is no provincial castle on the Imperium's border. The hololithic simulations of even the entire Corsair armada attacking from orbit make for grim viewing. Even with our fleet, that battle would not earn any of us much glory, I assure you.'

Several of the gathered warriors chuckled.

'You are right to question why I am using you so harshly,' Huron allowed. 'And that is because if your Legion cannot complete the first steps of the invasion alone, then the siege itself has no hope of success. I am using you, but not as a master uses a slave. I am using you as a general wields a weapon.'

'What's in it for us?' one of the Bleeding Eyes called out. The question elicited a chorus of hissing chuckles from the others. Thirty of them in all, most crouched to accommodate their clawed feet, though several – the least-changed among them – stood tall.

Huron didn't smile. He inclined his head, as if acknowledging the question's wisdom. 'Some might say allowing your ship to enter my dock would be reward enough. But I am not selfish with the spoils of war. You know what I want from this assault. The Eighth Legion is free to plunder whatever it wishes, as long as the Marines Errant supply of gene-seed is left untouched. Take armour, relics, prisoners – I care for none of it. But if I find the gene vaults harvested, I will withdraw my amnesty. The *Covenant* will not simply be fired upon and chased from Corsair space as it was the last time you... stretched... my patience. It will be destroyed.'

The Exalted dragged its armoured bulk forwards, sending minute tremors through the deck. Massive claws came to rest on the table's surface, and tumourous black eyes half-lidded themselves, warding against even the anaemic light of the hololithic projectors.

'Every Claw will take part in the surface assault. The only warriors remaining on the ship will be the Atramentar.' The creature paused to drag air and spittle back through its teeth. 'I will deploy each Claw in drop pods.'

'And how do we breach the orbital defences?' Karsha, the leader of Second Claw, addressed his question to Huron rather than the Exalted. 'I assume you are not laying us all on the altar of fate in the hope a handful of us survive to do your bidding.'

Huron nodded again. 'I understand your scepticism, but this offensive has been years in the planning. Raider fleets have coordinated across the subsector for years, forcing the Marines Errant into increasingly wide patrol routes. For almost a decade, the Chapter has reached farther and farther from their fortress, its crusading fleets devoted to watching over vulnerable Imperial shipping routes. I have sacrificed more than my fair share of ships to engineer this opportunity, and committed more warriors to early graves than I care to admit. The fortress-monastery is defended by – at most – a single company's worth of Imperial Space Marines. Their fleet is gone, scattered across the subsector. All that remains are the orbital defence platforms, and though they are formidable, never in the Red Corsairs' history has such a prize been open for the taking.'

Huron's smile was every bit as predatory as any of the Night Lords. 'Do you believe I would be so careless as to simply hurl warriors at the world, ruining our one chance of a clean assault? No. What is your name, legionary?'

'Karsha.' The Night Lord didn't bother to salute. 'Karsha the Unsworn.'

'Karsha.' Huron gestured to the hololithic with his oversized power claw. The immense talons curled through a cluster of radar dishes mounted on one of the fortress's eastern walls. 'The sun, Vila, is being encouraged to bleed, haemorrhaging great flares into the void. Tides of solar wind and magnetic field disruption already flow through the Vilamus system. When the tides spill over the system's worlds, each will suffer geomagnetic storms, lighting the sky with aurorae at the planets' poles, and...'

Karsha growled in reluctant admiration. 'And slaying all vox and auspex on the surface.'

'And in orbit.' Huron corrected. 'Throughout the entire system, magnetic interference will butcher all scanning and transmission. The storm will leave our own assault practically blind, for we cannot rely on our own instruments when we commit to the siege. Infiltrating Vilamus will be no trial for any of you. The first phase should not test you at all. The second, however, will be when complications set in. We can discuss that later.'

Talos stepped forward. 'How will you trigger the sun to initiate a coronal mass ejection?' Though he aimed the question at Huron, his gaze drifted to Ruven at the crowd's edge. 'Such a thing cannot be artificially bred.'

Ruven didn't meet his eyes, but Huron did. 'Nothing is impossible, prophet. My warp-weavers are capable of more than you realise.' He spoke the words without boasting, merely stating a fact. 'It is a small thing, in truth, to reach into the heart of star and fire the arithmetic of fusion. My men know their task, and will die before failing me.'

'If you are able to blind the Marines Errant fortress-monastery,' Karsha affirmed, 'then we will not fail.' Grunts and murmurs of assent travelled through the ranks. Xarl was grinning; Mercutian muttered to himself; while Uzas stared off into the middle distance, his gaze slack and unfocussed. Cyrion met Talos's glance.

'Just as you said,' he agreed. 'We're fighting this one our way.'

The prophet nodded, but didn't reply.

The same night, the *Covenant of Blood* broke dock and entered the warp, making for the Vila system.

The drop pods fell nine days later.

As HE MOVED through the labyrinth of maintenance tunnels and ventilation shafts, he kept one thought primed in his mind: *as predators, they stood a chance; as prey, they'd not last a single night.*

First Claw's drop pod had come down to the east of the fortress, driving home in one ravine among a clawed landscape of many. Erosion and tectonics had enjoyed millennia to work their influence, giving the world's wastelands a scarred and hostile face. Once they'd climbed the canyon's wall, they'd headed west at a sustainable sprint, scattering across the empty plateaus after nothing more than a few irritated farewells.

With almost two hundred kilometres of lifeless, waterless barren landscape to cover, Talos had reached the walls of the fortress-monastery three nights after leaving the canyon. He used his gauntlets and boots to smash handholds in the fortress walls, and gained access through a wide-mouthed heat exchange venting tunnel. The flames were industrial – true fire, rather than the corrosive, clinging nightmare of a flame weapon's breath – and he walked through the thrashing orange heat with impunity, letting it scorch his armour and the skulls that hung from it.

Of his brothers' fates, he had no idea.

True stealth had never been a viable option for the assault's first phase. The battle armour of a Legiones Astartes warrior hardly allowed for one to become a consummate, untraceable assassin, not while it growled as loud as an idling engine, rendered him close to three metres in height, and bled a power signature detectable to even the crudest auspex readers. When the VIII Legion went to war, it wasn't under a veil of secrecy and the flawed hope of going unseen. Leave such cowardly hunts to the soulless bitch-creatures spawned by the Callidus Temple in their gestation vats.

He flicked a glance at his retinal chron. Two minutes had passed since the sirens began their tumultuous whine. The prophet consulted an archived hololith schematic on his left eye lens as he ran in a crouch through the maintenance tunnel. A large chamber waited ahead, almost certainly the hub of Chapter serf operations on this level. Killing everyone present but for a few screaming, fleeing survivors would surely attract some attention.

Not far now.

* * *

LUCORYPHUS CLAIMED NO great ties to being his gene-sire's favoured pet, nor did he care that other warriors lauded themselves as part of the primarch's inner circle. Like most of his brethren, his perspectives aligned along a different route in the generations since Curze's death. He was a Raptor, first and foremost, and a Bleeding Eye second. Thirdly, distantly, he was a Night Lord. He did not cast his Legion bond aside, but nor did he drape himself in icons of Nostramo's winged skull.

It was just a planet, after all. A sizeable minority of the Legion weren't even drawn from there. They were Terran, born on the Throneworld, descended directly from the bloodlines that begat the whole human race.

Vorasha was Earthborn, beneath the daemon-faced armour, the blood-weeping eyes, and the irritating cackles. This, too, meant nothing. Lucoryphus knew Vorasha thought as he did: Raptors first, Bleeding Eyes second, allegiance to the ancient Legions last. What was a birth world, anyway? Such details meant nothing. It maddened him to see others put so much stock in it; always, they looked to the past, refusing to face up to the glories of the present and conquests of the future.

The prophet was the worst of all. His grotesquely distorted perception of the primarch soured Lucoryphus's stomach. Curze killed because Curze wished to kill. His was a rotten soul. In death's vindication, he taught his idiotic lesson: that the evils of the species deserve to be destroyed.

The Raptor gave a grating cackle each time he thought of it. If the lesson was so vital, so pure, so necessary, why did Curze leave a Legion of murderers sailing the stars in his name? He died a broken thing, a husk of himself, with hatred the only emotion strong enough to pierce his own confusion. He died to teach a lesson to a father already slain; he died to show a truth that every soul in the empire already knew. That was not vindication, it was stupidity. Proud, blind, and deluded.

Primarchs. He wanted to spit at the thought of them. Useless, flawed creatures. Let the dead ones decay in poetic scripture throughout history's pages. Let those that survived dwell in the highest eyries of the immaterium, singing the ethereal praises of mad gods. He had a war to win, unshackled to failures from a time of legend.

The Exalted had asked much from him, and Lucoryphus willingly pledged a blood oath promising success. To be one of the Bleeding Eyes was a sacred bond; they were a populous brotherhood, spread across several sectors and allied to countless warbands. Lucoryphus prided his warriors' reputations among the best and brightest of the splintered cult. He led thirty of them, and many of those were insufferable wretches who'd claw his throat out if they believed they could take his place, but when blood called, they answered as a pack.

The labyrinth of maintenance tunnels hollowed through Vilamus had been built for teams of servitors to march through to fulfil their myriad repair functions. These, he crawled through with ease, a loping leopard's pace, claws hammering into the metal. He cared nothing for the noise he was making. Let the enemy come. Unlike the Claws, bound to the earth and forced to ascend slowly, every single one of the Bleeding Eyes had ascended to Vilamus's middle levels, riding the winds with their jetpacks before gaining entrance.

With the thrusters on his back, Lucoryphus was denied access to the smaller ventilation ducts, so his routes were limited. Caution was still a factor, as was his intended destination. A flickering schematic layout of the fortress overlaid his right eye, refocusing and turning as he rose through the monastery's levels. Frequently, the image would dissolve into a worthless wash of static, leaving the Raptor sneering irritated growls through his vox-caster speakers. They, at least, hadn't failed, but the coronal storm played havoc without regard for its victims' allegiances.

The sirens had been ringing for several minutes. Presumably, one of the Claws on the lower levels was beginning to enjoy themselves. Lucoryphus loped on, sloping facemask snarling left and right at the ornate gothic architecture. Even these access tunnels were wrought with an obscene amount of dedication and craftsmanship.

He ceased all movement. Dead still, he waited, muscles tensed. The only sound for several seconds was the beat of his primary heart and the ventilating rhythm of his breath. But there, at the edge of hearing...

He broke into a feral run, lamenting this undignified crawl and aching for the chance to soar. At the end of the tunnel awaited light, voices, and the sweat-stink of human flesh...

Prey.

Lucoryphus launched from the tunnel mouth, crashing through the thin iron grating with a condor's cry. They'd heard him coming – he'd made sure of it – and stood ready with their useless weapons clutched in steady hands. No fear in these ardent defenders, none at all, and why would there be? What had ever frightened them in the entire span of their threatless lives at the heart of this impregnable bastion? Fear was something they needed to be taught.

Las-fire scorched his armour with meaningless kisses, but the Raptor twisted as he fell, keeping his vulnerable armour joints protected. The ground shook with his landing, all four claws birthing cracks in the stone beneath his weight. In the span of two seconds, he'd taken another three las-round kicks against his pauldrons and tracked all four of the robed defenders, retinal targeting locks signalling the types of weapons in their grips, and giving dull-sensed representations of the humans' heart rates.

Lucoryphus took in their distance at the same moment all of these details flickered over his eyeballs. The humans were too far away for an efficient leap and an easy kill.

Irritating.

He turned to the wall, jumping as his engines fired – his posture betraying nothing of humanity, closer resembling the splay-limbed leap of a house lizard. He hit the wall with his hands and feet, sticking there for a moment in a parody of saurian inelegance. Then he was moving, muscles burning, joints growling. Claws and talons cracked into the stone as he climbed, his jerky reptile-scramble carrying him away from the enemy fire below. Once he'd clawed high enough, he kicked off from the ornate stonework, letting gravity and the weight of his armour bring him back down.

Better.

The Raptor plummeted, shrieking from his helm's vocalisers, outstretched claws still smeared with rock dust.

Though inexperienced, the serfs weren't devoid of training. Pride and devotion carried them, keeping their lasrifles firing, while lesser – or less-indoctrinated – souls might otherwise run. Lucoryphus was a great admirer of courage and the things it could achieve in those rare moments where fate and the human spirit met to create something unique. In most cases, bravery did little more than end lives several seconds quicker than cowardice. If the white-robed serfs had run, he'd have needed to give chase. Instead, they stood their ground and died for it. Quick deaths, but none of them painless.

Lucoryphus crouched down once the deed was done, returning to all fours. His weapons were still sheathed, but his claws ran red. With an impatient grunt, he shook his ankle, dislodging a gobbet of meat between his taloned toes. The corridor was an abattoir, decorated with scraps of cloth. When he listened closely, he heard sounds of approaching mortals; their tread too light to be anything more. Hunt-lust surged through him as he crouched in the gore, chilled by anticipation, his limbs trembling with unsated needs.

He said 'Preysight', though it left his helm's vocaliser just as it left his lips – a snarled, wet clicking from his throat. In his fury, the Raptor's Nostraman suffered similarly to Vorasha's. He felt saliva, thick and sticky, stringing between his tongue and the roof of his mouth.

Through his preysight, the wide corridor blurred into a world of tremulous greys. Even the bodies around him were bleached of detail, little more than vague shapes in the colourless nuance. Only when the enemy came around the corner did life and movement flicker through his eye lenses; jagged flashes of white against the dullness. Many of the VIII Legion rigged their helms to track by heat, or to home in on movement. Lucoryphus of the Bleeding Eyes preferred to do things his own way. He tracked by the visualisation of sound. The humanoid flickers painting over his eyes were formed from the percussion of footsteps and heartbeats, strengthened by voices and the crack of gunfire.

He met them with a shrieking charge of his own, drawing his weapons as his thrusters lifted him off the ground.

* * *

TALOS PICKED UP the severed head by its hair, ignoring the pissing trickle of its hewn neck. His blow hadn't been clean enough, and the stump wasn't cauterised by the power sword's chop – when the woman's head rolled from its perch, it was still free to bleed. Her body was an ungainly rug of tan flesh and twisted robes, sprawled across the floor.

He was no judge of these things – and the dead woman's slack-jawed, eye-rolled expression hardly made a judgement easier – but she seemed to have been attractive. Using the memento's hair, he tied it to one of the chains at his waist. The head thumped and bumped against the skulls already bound there. More blood seeped down the Night Lord's thigh and knee guard. He paid it no heed.

He rolled another body over with the edge of his boot. The young man's face gazed up at the ceiling, seeing through his murderer. Talos was turning away when his retinal display gave the tiniest flicker. Tilting his head, he looked back down at the dead man. A heartbeat?

A blood bubble burst at the corner of the serf's closed lips. Ah, so he still breathed. Not dead after all.

'You,' Talos told him, 'have earned yourself a place of honour.' He hauled the dying man across the room, dragging him by the ankle, their trail marked by a glossy arterial smear along the stone floor. Slaying these menials granted little joy, at least not to the prophet, beyond a short thrill of a successful hunt each time he cleansed another chamber or corridor of their lives. He was wondering again how his brothers were faring, when footfalls outside the chamber stole his attention.

Talos whirled, bolter up and aiming at the doorway. Uzas lowered his own weapons – the gladius and chainaxe were both burnished with slick red.

'Brother,' Uzas greeted him. 'Such hunting. Such prey. The blood-stink is almost enough to drown the senses.'

Talos lowered his own weapon, though not immediately.

'What do you plan to do with that?' Uzas gestured with his axe at the dying man.

'He was just about to help me make a blood condor.'

'Few still alive in this subdistrict...' Uzas was swaying slightly, though Talos doubted his brother was aware of it. 'No sense in making a blood condor. I killed many, Cyrion killed many. No one left alive to see it.'

Talos let the ankle drop. With a gentility born of inattention, he crushed the man's throat beneath his heel. All the while, he watched Uzas in the doorway. 'Where is Cyrion?'

Uzas didn't answer.

'Where is Cyrion?'

'Gone. Not here. I saw him before.'

'How long ago?'

'We killed together for a while. Then he left to go alone. He hates me.

I saw him strangling, and cutting, and eating the dead. Then he left to go alone.'

Talos snorted, the breathy, grunted challenge of a baited predator. 'I have something to ask you,' he said. 'Something important. I need you to focus on my words, brother.'

Uzas stopped swaying. His chainaxe stuttered at random intervals, as the Night Lord's finger twitched on the trigger. 'Ask.'

'The Void-born's father. The crew found him dead. These last weeks, I believed it was the deed of nameless members of the old crew. But it wasn't, was it?'

Uzas barked out something close to a cough. Whatever it was, it wasn't an answer.

'Why did you do it, Uzas?'

'Do what?'

Talos's voice showed nothing of anger, or even resignation. His tone was as neutral and plain as the dead rock remnants of their home world. 'I know you can hear me. I know you're in there.'

Uzas let the chainaxe whirr for several seconds. At last, he shook his head. 'Mortals die, sometimes. I am not always to blame.' He turned to look down the corridor. 'I go to hunt.' And he did, without another word.

The sirens still rang. Across the fortress-monastery now, the Claws were beginning to turn the lowest chambers into charnel houses, shrieking, roaring, doing everything they could to draw attention to themselves.

Talos stared at the empty doorway for several seconds, trying to decide if the conversation with Uzas was over.

With a murderer's grin, he decided it wasn't.

XARL DIDN'T SHARE his brothers' idiotic pleasure at being tasked with a duty so devoid of glory. To haunt the fortress's lower levels and butcher the indentured servants was one thing – someone had to be given that lamentable duty – but for First Claw to be ordered to do it was quite another.

He mused on this as he cleaned a meat clog from his chainsword's mechanics. This one was bad enough to jam the damn weapon, but given the harvest of life he'd reaped around him, it was to be expected. Seventeen Chapter serfs lay in pieces, spread over the corridor. Xarl couldn't grasp the mindset that allowed unaugmented humans to charge at him with nothing more than solid-shot pistols and knives, but that was ignorance he could easily live with. Evidently, those who could understand such things just ended up dead. Truly, not the most useful knowledge, then.

Distraction. The word itself was almost a curse. *The Claws will spread throughout the fortress-monastery*, the Exalted had ordained in its high and mighty drawl, *serving as distractions to allow the Bleeding Eyes to infiltrate the generatorum.*

And Talos just took it. He'd stood there, nodding his head, while the
Bleeding Eyes were tasked with taking the prize.

Xarl shook his head at the memory. 'I don't like this,' he said aloud.

Mercutian had forgone his heavy bolter in favour of a simple
chainsword. 'That can only be the fortieth time you've said so.'

The two had crossed paths before the alarms started ringing, both
chasing humans through the catacombs of this immense and loathsome
fortress. Mercutian admitted he'd tracked Xarl's rampage through the
hallways, hoping to link up with Talos.

Xarl's blade restarted, sprinkling blood from its wet teeth. 'You're usually the miserable one. It's not like you to be so sanguine.'

'I am far from sanguine, but anything is better than being on the
ship. And here, at least, we can hear the screams.' He seemed somehow
abashed by the confession. 'We've been out of battle for too long. I
needed this. I needed to know we were still fighting the war.'

Xarl's two-handed sword cycled down, idling at the ready. '*Fighting the
war.* You even sound like Talos now.'

Mercutian reacted to Xarl's tone in subtle, telling ways. His blade rose
slightly, and his helm lowered into a glare. 'And what of it?'

The other warrior chuckled. 'It's bad enough with him whining about
faded glories and the Legion's demise. If you commit to his delusions
about a noble past that never happened, I'll kill you myself in the name
of mercy.'

Xarl ventured down the corridor, beneath the skeletal arches of dark
basalt that rose to the ceiling. Mercutian followed, ill at ease. He considered, though only briefly, plunging his sword through the back of Xarl's
neck. Such treachery was beneath him, but the temptation was not. Xarl
was a vicious soul, despite the trust Talos placed in him. The prophet
considered him his most reliable brother, but Mercutian had always
believed Xarl reeked of betrayals yet to come.

The thought of murdering his brother triggered a grimmer one: how
many times had Xarl thought to do the same thing to him? He knew
he wouldn't like that answer. Some questions didn't need to be asked.

As they walked, the sirens continued their plaintive whine around
them, singing of excitement up in the higher levels.

Xarl's mood soured as he passed empty prayer chambers, bare of fur-
nishing and even barer of prey.

'Answer me something,' he demanded, apropos of nothing.

Mercutian kept turning to watch for any approaches from the rear. The
corridor, replete with its mutilated inhabitants, remained as silent as the
tomb they'd made of it.

'As you wish,' he said quietly.

'When was this grand and noble era that Talos describes? I was there, as
were you. I fought in the Thramas Crusade, beating myself bloody against

the Angels in Black. I was there when we pacified 66:12. I was there when Malcharion executed the king of that backwater pisshole, Ryle, and we broadcast his daughter's screams for three days and three nights, until his army threw down their arms. I remember nothing of glory. The glory came in the decades after Terra, when we finally slipped the Imperial leash. Our father was honest then – we crusaded because we were strong, and the enemy was weak. Their fear tasted fine, and the galaxy bled when we struck. So *when*, brother? When was this golden age?'

Mercutian looked back at the other Night Lord. 'It's perspective, Xarl. What's wrong with you? The venom in your voice borders on wrath.'

'*Talos*.' Xarl injected the word with acid. 'I wonder lately, just how far he can fall into his own ignorance. He wearies me. If he wishes to lie to himself, then he may do so, but I cannot take another lecture about a noble Legion that never existed.'

'I fail to understand why this anger surfaces now.' Mercutian stopped walking. Xarl turned, slowly, his voice brought low by ugly emotion.

'Because after this moronic siege, we will fight the battle that matters: the *Echo of Damnation*. And what happens then? Talos will begin his new duties. The Exalted wants to rebuild our forces. Who will control that gradual resurrection? Talos. Who will indoctrinate the newbloods after implanting them with gene-seed? Talos. Who will fill their minds with sour lies about how the Emperor demanded that we, the great and glorious Eighth Legion, became the Imperial weapon of fear that no other Legion dared to be? *Talos*.'

Xarl gave an uncharacteristic sigh. 'He will breed a generation of fools that share in his delusion. They will rise through our ranks, championing a cause that never existed, inheritors to a legacy that was never real.'

Mercutian said nothing. Xarl glanced at him. 'You feel as he does, don't you?'

'I was there as well, Xarl. We were the weapon humanity needed us to be. I cherish those memories, when entire worlds would surrender the moment they learned it was the Eighth Legion in orbit. Whether the Emperor demanded it of the primarch, we may never know. But we were that weapon, brother. I take pride in that.'

Xarl shook his head and carried on walking. 'I am surrounded by fools.'

XIX

MERCENARIES

THE EXALTED LEANED back in its throne, listening to the sounds of the strategium filtering through a veil of distracted thoughts. Around it, the sickening orchestra of human existence played out in its entirety: the grotesque, wet sound of moisture-laden respiration; the rustling hisses of clothing against flesh; the sibilant dryness of whispered words, spoken in the eternally misguided belief that the Legion masters couldn't hear.

Vandred had fallen blessedly silent again, and taken his lingering emotions with him. The Exalted only prayed it was a permanent oblivion this time, but held out little hope for such beneficence. The host body's former soul was likely folding back in on itself, hiding in the deepest recesses of their shared mind in the futile hope of making another attack.

Such desperation.

The Exalted let its gaze slide to the occulus, where a turbulent moon of methane oceans turned in the void. The moon was a shield, an aegis against the fortress-monastery's broken scanners somehow managing to detect them in orbit. Rather than linger in the upper atmosphere and risk discovery, the Exalted erred on the side of caution, withdrawing the *Covenant* to a safe distance after releasing the Legion's drop pods.

Musing in the calm before the storm, the daemon immersed itself within its own mind, seeking any memory-scent that might lead it to Vandred. When it discovered nothing, not even the ghost of a trace, it turned its amused senses back to the world below.

This was a far more difficult sending, requiring protracted, painful focus. The Exalted bared its fanged maw, acidic spittle drizzling from its gums.

Lucoryphus, it pulsed.

MARUC CLEANED THE rifle with practiced ease, vaguely listening to Septimus answering Octavia's endless questions.

As far as gifts went, the lasgun was a considerate one; the weapon of a

503

Guardsman, for someone who'd always wished to be in the Guard, but he wasn't sure exactly what Septimus expected him to do with it. His eyes were bad, and that was the beginning and end of the whole situation. He doubted he could hit anything past twenty metres or so, and he wasn't going to be earning any sharpshooter medals any time soon.

Hound sat close to Maruc, clutching a dirty shotgun in his lap, his hands wrapped in even dirtier bandages. The former station worker couldn't tell where Hound was 'looking' exactly, but if the angle of his face was anything to go by, the little blind man was watching Septimus and Octavia, brazenly doing what Maruc feigned disinterest in.

Meanwhile, Septimus and Octavia were doing what Septimus and Octavia always did best.

The seventh of Talos's slaves didn't look up from his work, tending to the engraved details on Lord Mercutian's heavy bolter. The file in his fingers made soft rasping sounds as it cleaned minor corrosion from the curving runes etched into the metal.

'Our Claws are nothing but distractions, moving upwards from the lowest levels.' Still, the file scratched. 'Vilamus has thousands of human defenders, but the Claws will go through them like sharks cutting the sea. The only concern is that the Marines Errant still have a skeleton garrison in place. Although they'll be unprepared for a strike at their home world's heart, they're still Imperial Space Marines, and they'll defend their monastery to the death. They have to be led away from the main objectives for this to work. That's where our Claws come in. They'll cleave through the monastery's population, drawing the Marines Errants' ire.'

Octavia, with nothing to do since they'd arrived in the Vila system, was lounging around Maruc and Septimus's workshop. She flicked a worthless Nostraman copper coin across the room. Hound shuffled after it to pick it up and return it to her.

This was a game she played fairly often. Hound didn't seem to mind.

'What about the ones who hiss and spit?' she asked. 'With the...' She curled her fingers into claws.

Septimus stopped to sip a cup of lukewarm water. 'You mean the Bleeding Eyes. The only thing that matters is shutting down the secondary generatorum. That's what the Bleeding Eyes have been ordered to do. Once they disable that, the orbital defence batteries will fall offline. Then we attack. The *Covenant*, and the rest of Huron's fleet, moves into the atmosphere. The siege can begin.'

'What if the Marines Errant attack the Bleeding Eyes, and not the Claws?'

'They won't.' He glanced up to read her expression, checking to see if she was merely trying to be difficult and contrary with this interrogation. For her part, she looked curious enough, but he couldn't be sure. 'They won't,' he continued, 'because the Claws will be attracting attention to themselves, while the Bleeding Eyes are sneaking in undetected. Have you seen the size of it on the hololithic? I've seen smaller hive cities. It's unlikely any of our warriors will see an Imperial Space Marine until the second phase of the siege. Even the distractions are likely unnecessary, but Talos is trying to be cautious. They need everyone to survive for what comes after.'

Octavia mused for a few moments. 'I almost feel guilty,' she admitted. 'If the ship was easier to fly, I'd not have wrecked it in the warp's tides, and we wouldn't need to take part in this madness.'

Septimus switched to a different scraper, scratching at another set of runes. 'The Claws don't care. The siege is meaningless, and they will do as little as possible while they're down there. Even in the siege, watch how the *Covenant* behaves. The Exalted will save almost all of the ship's ammunition for what comes after. Talos doesn't care about anything except retaking the *Echo of Damnation.*'

'But we've only just managed to build a crew large enough to run one ship. Why do they want two?'

'Why do they want anything?' Septimus shrugged, looking over at her. 'For skulls. For the fact they find it amusing to shed an enemy's blood. For the simple act of revenge, heedless of cost and consequence. I obey them, Octavia. I don't try to understand them.'

Octavia let the subject drop. Feints within feints, distractions within distractions... Nothing the VIII Legion did was ever simple. Well, except when they ran away.

She tossed the coin again, and dutifully, Hound stumbled over to get it. As he crouched by the door, wrapped hands struggling to scoop the coin from the floor, the bulkhead rattled open. Hound staggered back, trundling over to his mistress. The humans watched an immense figure filling the doorway, its helm panning left and right, examining them each in turn.

The legionary stepped into the chamber. His armour was almost devoid of ostentation, without a single skull or oath scroll bound to the ceramite. With every Night Lord bar the Atramentar deployed to the surface, Septimus knew who this had to be.

He didn't salute. He *wouldn't* salute.

The warrior regarded the four of them, silent but for his armour's voice, thrumming with each movement. In one hand he clutched a black staff, topped by the skull of a creature bearing a grotesque abundance of teeth.

'This chamber,' he growled in Gothic. 'It reeks of mating.'

Maruc's face screwed up in a crinkle of confusion. He wasn't sure he heard that right. Hound glanced blindly in the direction of Octavia and Septimus, which was the only cue the Night Lord needed.

'Ah. Not mating. Desire. The smell is your biological attraction to one another. Your scents are histologically compatible.' The Night Lord snorted, a beast snuffling an unpleasant scent from its senses. 'Another foul flaw of the human condition. When you do not stink of fear, you stink of lust.'

Octavia had narrowed her eyes at the beginning of his tirade. She had no idea who this was, but her value made her brave.

'I am not human,' she said, more cattily than she'd intended.

The warrior chuckled at that. 'A fact the slave staring at you with desire in his one remaining eye would do well to remember. *Homo sapiens* and *Homo navigo* were never meant to mix with any graceful genetic fusion. The balance of your pheromones is a curious one. I am surprised you do not repel one another.'

Septimus didn't hide the ice in his voice. 'What do you want, Ruven?'

'So you know me, then.' The legionary's slanted eye lenses fixed upon the artificer. 'You must be the seventh.'

'I am.'

'Then you should treat me with more respect, lest you share the same fate as the second.' Ruven chuckled again, a low baritone song. 'Have you ever seen a soul ripped from its housing of flesh? There is a moment, just a single, beautiful moment, when the body remains standing, every nerve transmitting a tide of electrical fire from the misfiring brain. The soul itself thrashes, still bound closely enough to its corpse that it shares the agony of a detonating nervous system, but unable to do anything beyond writhe in the aetheric currents.'

Ruven gave a contented sigh. 'Truthfully, I have rarely seen a more perfect embodiment of terror incarnate. I thanked the second for the gift of his death, for I learned a great deal about the warp, and my own powers, that night.'

'You killed Secundus.' Septimus blinked. '*You* killed him.'

The masked warrior performed a courtly bow. 'Guilty.'

'No.' Septimus swallowed, trying to force himself to think. 'Talos would have killed you.'

'He tried.' Ruven stalked around the armoury, examining the tools of Septimus's trade. He stopped when he reached Hound. 'And what are you, little wretch?' Ruven nudged the attendant with the side of his boot, knocking Hound from his seat. 'Navigator Etrigius took poor care of his slaves, didn't he?' He looked at Octavia. 'You have inherited the dregs, girl.'

Hound snarled up at him from the floor, but Ruven was already moving on. 'Septimus, you vastly overestimate your master's abilities – and his sense of prudence – if you believe Talos could ever kill me. After Secundus, he did try, and I commended his enthusiasm every time. Ultimately, while he never forgave me, he abandoned the tedious attempts at revenge. I believe he grew tired of failure.'

Octavia raised an eyebrow. Abandoning revenge? That didn't sound like Talos.

Septimus was less inclined to hold his tongue. 'You did this to my face,' he said. 'The prison world, in the Crythe system.'

Ruven peered down at the mortal, regarding the expensive, subtle augmetic work at his temple and eye socket.

'Ah, so you were the Thunderhawk pilot. What a well-trained rodent you are, boy.'

Septimus clenched his teeth, fisting his hands to fight the overwhelming urge to reach for his pistols. 'You sent those prisoners to kill us on Solace.'

Octavia's confidence was evaporating now. While Septimus had been left for dead on Solace, mutilated in the Thunderhawk's cockpit, the survivors had beaten her to the edge of consciousness and dragged her by her hair into the bowels of the prison complex.

'That was you? You sent them? Four hours,' she whispered. 'I was down there in the dark, with those... animals.. For. Four. Hours.'

Ruven shook his head, dismissing their melodramatic human nonsense. 'Enough of this whining. My armour requires maintenance.'

'I am not your artificer.' Septimus almost laughed.

'You tend First Claw's weapons and armour, do you not?'

'Yes, I do. And you are not one of First Claw.'

'I was once. I will be again.'

'Then you may order me to tend to your armour if First Claw ever accepts you again, and I will still refuse. Until then, get out.'

Ruven glanced at each of them in turn. 'What did you just say?'

'Get out.' Septimus rose to his feet. He didn't go for his guns, knowing such a gesture was worthless. The legionary could slaughter them all in a heartbeat if he chose. 'Get out of my master's armoury. This is the domain of First Claw and those in service to them.'

Ruven stood in impassive silence. This was something he'd simply not expected. Curiosity and amazement far outweighed any anger.

'Get out.' Octavia, unlike Septimus, had drawn her pistol. She aimed it up at the sorcerer's horned helm.

Hound followed suit, his grubby shotgun emerging from a split in his rags. 'Mistress says to go.'

Maruc was last, aiming his polished-iron lasrifle. 'The lady asked you to leave.'

Ruven still didn't move. 'Talos used to train his slaves to much higher standards,' he said.

Now Septimus drew his pistols, aiming both of them at the Night Lord's faceplate. Meaningless gesture or not, the slaves stood united.

'I told you to get out,' he repeated.

'You do not sincerely believe this display is actually threatening, do you?' Ruven took a step forward. Twin red dots wavered over his left eye lens, as Septimus thumbed the safeties off. The legionary shook his head.

'You live only because of your value to the Legion.'

'No,' Septimus glared, one of his eyes dark and human, the other glassy and artificial. 'We live because you are alone on this ship, and loathed by all who sail her. My master shares much with me. I know the Exalted seeks the smallest, meagre reason to execute you. I know First Claw would kill you before trusting you again. You have no rights over our lives. We live not because of our worth, but because you are worthless.'

Before Ruven could reply, Octavia reached her free hand to her bandana, hooking her fingers under the edge of the cloth.

'Get out.' The pistol trembled in her other fist. *'Get out.'*

Ruven inclined his head, conceding the point. 'This was most educational, slaves. I thank you for it.'

With that, he turned and stalked from the room. The bulkhead sealed behind him.

'Who the hell was that?' Maruc asked them.

'A bad soul,' Hound was scowling. His sewn eyes seemed puckered, squeezed tighter than usual. 'A very bad soul.'

Septimus holstered his guns. In three steps, he'd crossed the room, taking Octavia in his arms. Maruc looked away, a sudden feeling of awkwardness prickling his skin. It was the most he'd seen them touch, and he knew Septimus well enough to judge that it'd taken all of the artificer's courage to be so bold. He could point a gun at a demigod easily enough, but could barely muster the stones to offer a little comfort to someone he cared for.

She writhed out of his embrace almost immediately. 'Don't... touch me. Not right now.' Octavia shivered as she slipped from his arms, but her hands didn't stop shaking once she was free. 'Hound, let's go.' Her voice quavered on the simple command.

'Yes, mistress.'

Once the door sealed again, the two men were left alone. Maruc placed his rifle back on the workbench. 'Well, that was exciting.'

Septimus was still looking at the closed door. 'I'm going after her,' he said.

Maruc smiled for his friend's benefit, despite the way his heart still raced in the wake of the confrontation with the legionary.

'You picked the wrong time to grow a backbone. Let her be alone. What she said, about being taken by the prisoners on Solace – was that true?'

Septimus nodded.

'Then the last thing she wants at the moment is a man's arms around her,' Maruc pointed out.

Septimus crashed down onto his seat, leaning forwards, his arms on his knees and his head lowered. Ash-blond hair fell forwards, curtaining his pale features. His dark eye blinked, his blue lens clicked and whirred.

'I hate this ship.'

'That's just what she says.'

Septimus shook his head. 'It was so much easier before she joined the crew. Come when summoned, do the duty, know your value. I questioned nothing, because there was no one to answer to.' He took a breath, trying to frame his thoughts, but came up empty.

'How long has it been,' Maruc kept his voice gentle, 'since you judged yourself by human standards? Not as a slave without any choice, but as a man halfway through the only life he gets?'

Septimus raised his head, meeting Maruc's gaze. 'What do you mean?'

'Throne, it's cold on this ship. My bones ache.' He rubbed the back of his neck with oil-blackened hands. 'You know what I mean. Before Octavia, you did all of these things without ever needing to look at yourself. You did what you did because you had no choice, and you never judged any of your actions because there was no one else to see them. But now there's her, and there's me. And all of a sudden you feel like a heretic son of a bitch, don't you?'

Septimus said nothing.

'Well, *good*.' Maruc smiled, but it was merciful rather than mocking. 'You should feel like that, because that's what you are. You denied it to yourself for all those years, but now you've got other eyes watching you.'

Septimus was already buckling his machete to his shin in crude echo of First Claw's sheathed gladius blades.

'Going somewhere?' Maruc asked.

'I need some time to think. I'm going to check on my gunship.'

'*Your* gunship? *Your* gunship?'

Septimus adjusted his beaten jacket before heading to the door. 'You heard me.'

Cyrion reflected, as he occasionally did, on the attitudes of his brothers. After ascending another spiralling flight of stairs, he'd torn through several linked chambers, each with the austere chill and bare decoration of an Ecclesiarchy cathedral, and he was beginning to wonder just where the serfs on this level were hiding.

If this level was even used much at all.

Occasionally, he came across stragglers, but these were unarmed, terrified things, and he doubted killing them would draw much attention at all. Still, he cut most of them down, careful to let a handful flee, screaming, through the monastery.

Hopefully they'd bring the Marines Errant down here, so the Bleeding Eyes would finish their brutally simple missions, and the Claws could be done with the siege completely.

Cyrion was less enamoured of the plan than the rest of his brothers. He didn't care that the Bleeding Eyes had claimed the right to destroy the secondary generatorum – let them play whatever games they wished, and drape themselves in glory if they so chose. No, what stuck in Cyrion's craw was a much simpler, much less palatable notion.

He, like his brothers, didn't care about Vilamus.

The Imperium would no doubt consider this a great tragedy, and scribes were sure to waste oceans of ink in detailing the travesty of its loss. Lord Huron, likewise, would gain much from the siege, and this would be archived in history as one of his boldest, most daring raids.

The day the Marines Errant were doomed to a slow, ignoble demise. The night an Adeptus Astartes Chapter died.

And that was what troubled Cyrion. They were going to be instrumental in striking a vicious wound against the Imperium, yet neither he, nor any of his brothers, cared.

All eyes were on the true prize: the *Echo of Damnation*. Talos, Xarl, the Exalted, all of them – the battle they hungered for was going to be waged against fellow traitors. They would rather bleed their own allies than focus on injuring the Imperium.

The attitude was not a new one: Cyrion had ventured into the Eye of Terror on countless occasions, witnessing the brutal crusades waged by the remnants of the Legions against one another. Brother against brother, warband against warband – millions of souls shedding blood in the name of their chosen warlords.

He'd fought in those wars himself; against hordes of legionaries fighting for power, for faith, for conquest or for nothing beyond the pure release of rage, letting fury spill from them like corruption from a lanced boil. On more than one occasion, he'd opened fire on other Night Lords, gunning down brothers whose sin was no more than choosing to follow a different banner.

Their greatest enemy was their own inability to unite without unrivalled leadership. Few warriors possessed the strength and cunning to truly hold the disparate armies of the Eye together. Instead, loyalties were sworn at the lowest levels, and warbands formed from those who unified in the hope of surviving and raiding together. Betrayal was a way of life, for each and every soul in those armies was already a traitor once. What did one more treachery matter, when they'd already forsaken their oaths to mankind's empire?

Cyrion, for all his flaws, was no fool. He knew these fundamental truths, and he accepted them.

But he'd never seen it play out like this before. In the past, even at Crythe, inflicting harm upon the Imperium came before all else. It was the one goal guaranteed to force warbands to unite, even if only for a time.

Yet none of them cared about Vilamus. None of them cared about tearing this worthless, insignificant Chapter from the pages of history. Instead, they were ripping it from the galaxy's face with all the passion of wiping blood from their boots.

Was this how it began? Was this the path that ended with Uzas, snarling instead of speaking, blinded by his own hatred of everything that lived and breathed? Perhaps this was how all corruption began... in the quiet moments, facing the fact that avenging the sins of the past mattered more than any hope for the future?

Now there was a thought. What would they do, once the war was won? Cyrion grinned as he walked, enjoying the prospect of an unanswerable question.

He had to admit Vilamus was a bastion of the most majestic, bleak beauty, and such things appealed to him. In a way, it reminded him of Tsagualsa, stirring the faint embers of a long-fallow melancholy. Tsagualsa had been hauntingly beautiful – a bastion beyond words, raised by thousands of enslaved workers grinding their lives away into the dust of that barren world.

Cyrion replaced his helm, still tasting the blood of the last three serfs he'd slain. Flickering after-images danced behind his eyes, telling him nothing of any worth. Moments of great emotion in their lives... joy, terror, pain... All meaningless.

His bootsteps echoed as he left the chamber, moving back into the labyrinthine hallways and corridors that linked the subdistricts of this immense, baffling monastery. It would be glorious to be able to claim such a fortress as both haven and home, rather than the dank decks of the *Covenant*, or worse, the Legion's claimed worlds in the Eye – but its immensity was a weapon against invaders. His retinal map had failed a while ago, and he'd not studied enough sections to commit the entire thing to even an eidetic memory.

Stumbling around lost and butchering helpless Chapter servants was all very amusing, but it wasn't

A squad of liveried, armed Chapter serfs ran around the far end of the corridor, cracking lasrifle safeties off and taking firing positions. Cyrion heard the officer yelling orders. It was by far the most organised defence he'd witnessed yet. At last, Vilamus was reacting, its defenders hunting the intruders. He almost charged them, such was the call of instinct, despite the fact more and more of them were filling the corridor's far end. Their movements were a stampede of footsteps on stone.

In truth, he'd enjoyed the easy massacre so far, but things were about to become a measure more difficult.

Cyrion turned and broke into a run, leading his slow pursuers on a merry chase. Already, he heard them voxing for more of their kindred, calling for other squads to cut him off ahead.

Let them come. The more that arrived, the fewer would be left to defend the upper levels.

* * *

BREKASH VOCALISED HIS anger as a chittering hiss through his mouth grille. The nuances of language within that single sibilate were there for all to hear, but only his brothers in the Bleeding Eyes had any chance of understanding the meaning.

Lucoryphus understood all too well. He rounded on the other Raptor, his claws crackling in echo of his own irritation.

'Do not make me slay you,' he warned.

Brekash gestured to the whining generator, easily the size of a Land Raider battle tank. Another bark of un-language left his vocaliser.

'This is meaningless,' he insisted. 'How many of these have we destroyed? How many?'

Lucoryphus replied in kind with a condor's shriek, the cry of an apex predator foreshadowing his words. 'You are being moronic, and my patience bleeds dry. Destroy it, and let us move on.'

Brekash was one of the few warriors in the pack who preferred to stand on his altered foot-claws. He did so now, looking down at his crouching leader.

'You are leading us into folly. Where are the Marines Errant? They do not come to defend these places because these places have no worth.'

Lucoryphus's helm jerked in a brutal twitch of his neck. Several of the power cables and flexible pipes hanging from the back of his helmet thrashed as the Raptor spasmed, hanging loose like mechanical dreadlocks.

'We've seen no Marines Errant because this monastery is the *size of a hive city*, fool. Scarcely a hundred of them remain on the world. If the Imperial Ones have even had time to react in defence of their fortress, they are defending the lower levels against the Claws.' Lucoryphus punctuated his words with an aggressive growl.

Brekash wouldn't be cowed. 'Each of these we destroy makes no difference. Already, we've slain nine machines. Nothing has changed.'

Lucoryphus ordered two of the others to cease toying with the bodies of the dead serfs. 'Urith, Krail, destroy the generator.'

The Raptors obeyed, crossing the room in an arcing leap, carried by coughs of jetpack thrust. With nothing even approaching finesse, they laid into the juddering machine with their claws and fists, pounding dents into it and ripping hunks of steel away. Once they'd torn several openings to the generator's innards, the two Raptors let a handful of grenades clatter into the machine's core.

'Forty seconds, lord,' Krail hissed.

Lucoryphus nodded, but didn't leave. He turned back to Brekash. 'This fortress is a city, and we stand inside its guts, crawling north and south, up and down, poking at the organs. Think of a legionary's heart, brother.' The Raptor held out a claw as if carrying a human heart in his palm. 'It is a layered fruit, with chambers and pathways leading inside and out.

Cut one connection, and perhaps the body dies, perhaps the body lives. Cut many connections, and there is no doubt at all.'

Lucoryphus inclined his tendrilled helm towards the clanking generator. 'This is one of the heart-chambers of Vilamus. We have severed some of its bonds. We will sever more if we must. But the heart will fail, and the body will die.'

Brekash saluted, a clawed fist over his heart. 'I obey.'

The Raptor leader's bleeding lenses refocussed on his brother. 'Then we move.'

THE EXALTED'S SWOLLEN black eyes rolled to the occulus once again.

With the lashing return of an overstretched cord, the creature's senses snapped back into its own mind. Lucoryphus's perception took several sickening moments to fade – the disgusting feeling of too-human flesh; the repugnant sensation of staring with eyes forged in the material realm, blind to the minutiae of ethereal nuance.

'The Bleeding Eyes are on the edge of success,' the creature growled.

'Orders, my lord?' asked the deck officer.

The daemon leaned forwards in its throne, its armour growling, but not loud enough to mask the horrendous creak and crackle of inhuman sinew.

'Ahead two-thirds.'

'Aye, lord.'

The Exalted watched the occulus closely, before keying in several adjustments to the hololithic system display.

'Come abeam of the first orbital defence platform. Launch Thunderhawks to recover our drop pods before the Corsairs arrive.'

'As you wish, lord.'

'And ready the warp beacon. Summon Huron's fleet as soon as our Thunderhawks are on approach to dock.'

XX

THE FALL OF VILAMUS

CYRION WAS THE last to join them. He pounded into the room, bolter in hand, almost skidding to a halt on the litany-etched stone floor. Footsteps – a great many footsteps – clattered in the corridors some way behind him.

'I got lost,' he admitted.

Xarl and Talos moved with practised fluidity, their movements twinned as they took positions either side of the wide doorway Cyrion had just used as an entrance.

'It sounds as though you brought friends,' the prophet remarked. 'How many?'

Cyrion stood with Mercutian, both of them readying bolters. Uzas ignored his brothers, though his helmed head snapped around with a hunting dog's eagerness when he heard the approaching footsteps.

'Enough,' said Cyrion. 'Dozens. But they're only human. I haven't seen a single Marine Errant.' The warrior glanced around the chamber for the first time, seeing the immense circular hall cleared of all furniture – everything, every dead body, every pew seat and ornate table, had been dragged to the chamber's sides, leaving the middle bare. 'You've been busy,' Cyrion said. The others ignored his comment, which neither annoyed nor surprised him.

Talos slapped his crackling sword blade against the stonework to get Uzas's attention. It left a scorch mark.

'Bolter,' he said.

'What?'

'Use your bolter, brother. We're taking a defensive position in this chamber. Too many foes to charge.'

Uzas hesitated, perhaps not comprehending. He looked down at the axe and gladius in his hands.

'*Use your bolter*,' Xarl snapped. 'Look at us against this wall, freak. Does it look like we're charging?'

Uzas sheathed his weapons at last, and unlimbered his bolter. It caught the prophet's eye with the sting of memory; the same relic Malcharion had commissioned to honour Uzas's deeds in a brighter, better age.

'Uzas,' he said.

'Hnnh?'

Talos could hear the bootsteps drawing closer, along with the shouted, oath-rich encouragements of the squads' officers. 'Brother, I remember when you were given that weapon. Do you?'

Uzas clutched the bolter tighter. 'I... Yes.'

The prophet nodded. 'Use it well. Here they come.'

'I hear them,' came a human voice, frail and thin compared to the rumbling growls of the legionaries' speech.

Talos nodded to Xarl, and they moved around the corner as one. Bolters crashed in dark hands, shuddering as they spat shells down the corridor. Both warriors were back in cover before the first las-streaks slashed through the doorway in response.

'That one you hit in the face,' Xarl chuckled. 'Both bolts. His head turned into red mist. I can hear his men choking on it.'

Talos reloaded, catching the spent magazine and storing it away. 'Focus.'

The chains on his armour rattled against the ceramite, though he wasn't moving. Xarl flicked a glance at his own pauldron, where the chained skulls were knocking together as if in a breeze.

'About time,' Mercutian muttered.

First Claw averted their eyes from the centre of the room as the light first began to manifest. Sourceless wind rushed against their armour, a vortex in reverse, breathing cold air against the implacable ceramite. The faintest touch of ice rime formed on the edges of their armour, while the bloodstained clothing worn by the dead bodies spread around the chamber crumpled and flapped in the building gale.

'Such drama.' Cyrion bared his teeth behind his faceplate.

A sonic boom of violated air shattered several of the overturned tables, blasting their wreckage against the walls.

The light receded, crumbling back into the nothingness from whence it came.

Five figures stood in the chamber's heart: five figures in desecrated armour, strewn with talismans and engraved with bronze runes. Four of them eclipsed the fifth – their immense Terminator war-plate giving guttural snarls as they viewed their surroundings, tusked helms turning this way and that.

The fifth was bareheaded, dwarfed by the others in stature, yet emanating an amused, ugly charisma from the glint in his eyes to the confident smirk.

'You have done well,' grinned Lord Huron of the Red Corsairs.

* * *

VARIEL WALKED IN calm, impassive reflection, heading through countless corridors on his way to the observation deck. It was time to take stock, and drawing close to the time when a decision must be made. To that end, the Apothecary made his way to one of the few places he could be assured of some peace. He always felt his thoughts flowed clearest when staring out into the humbling reaches of space.

The first phase was complete, with the Night Lords evidently successful in shutting down one of the secondary power feeds within the walls of Vilamus. Huron had chosen his target well – with that subdistrict's generatorum offline, the fortress-monastery was vulnerable to an attack far more insidious than the relative barbarism of an orbital strike.

Rather than insist his oath-bound hirelings martyr themselves for his cause, Huron required them to do nothing more than deactivate the outlying shields preventing teleportation, and clear enough space in various chambers for several of his own squads to manifest directly within the fortress. Thus began the second phase, and if Huron's forces proceeded at the expected pace, they would still encounter insignificant resistance.

It was a plan not entirely without elegance, chosen because little else had any hope of success. Assaulting a fortress-monastery with anything other than esoteric cunning was doomed to failure. The fact this assault was deemed to be so decisive and without risk was, in the Flayer's mind, nothing short of miraculous. He could almost imagine Imperial archives referencing this defeat for centuries to come, citing the perils of leaving a Chapter's sanctuary so woefully unprotected.

With its initial defences rendered worthless, Vilamus now stood on the edge of true invasion.

Huron would drag his Terminators down to the surface through the arcane complexities of teleportation, manifesting at the preset coordinates cleared by the VIII Legion infiltrators. From there, each squad would seek to link up on the march to the primary power relay station deeper within the monastery's core. A Terminator advance, while ponderous, would break everything before it. With fifty of his chosen elite in the priceless suits of war-plate, reinforced by eight Claws from the *Covenant*, Variel doubted Huron would have anything to worry about.

The destruction of this inner sanctum would supposedly herald the endgame. For now, even with its orbital platforms blinded and powerless, and even with its protective shields dead, Vilamus remained an unapproachable bastion, capable of annihilating any ground forces that dared lay siege at its staggering walls. Any attempt to make a landing would be met with withering fire from the legion of turrets and missile silos lining the battlements.

Variel reached the observation deck, striding to one of the glass walls and gazing down at the barren rock of a world. From orbit, it seemed almost a stalemate. The raider fleet approaching the world couldn't drop warriors in support. Gunships and drop pods remained clutched in loading bays, filled with eager warriors unable to see battle.

Vilamus was visible to the naked eye even from this altitude, but it failed to inspire anything but contempt in the Flayer's thoughts. A vast spire of uninspiring red stone, soon to be cleansed of anything even remotely valuable.

The Tyrant's Terminator elite were at work down there, cutting their way to the primary energy relay sector, ready to starve Vilamus's last defences of the power they craved in order to fire.

Variel stared at the world in silence, severing himself from the vox-channels to avoid the pre-battle tedium of his brothers swearing oaths to powers they barely understood. He needed time to think, despite doing little else these last weeks.

At the cusp of the second phase's completion, Variel would need to act, one way or the other. With his best estimate, that gave him less than an hour to make a choice.

THE CREATURE GLARED at Talos as it clutched the Tyrant's shoulder guard. He was tempted to swat the ugly little thing with the flat of his blade, and wipe its alien stare clean off its beady-eyed face. Spindly, cursed in appearance with an excess of protruding bones at its ribs and ungainly joints, the xenos-wretch rode on the warlord's armour, occasionally twisting its features into a grimace.

Huron's focus was elsewhere. After greeting the warriors of the VIII Legion, he'd immediately set to advancing through the hallways, every tread crushing marble and onyx floor tiling beneath his boots, and testing the abused vox network in a bid to link up with his other squads. The Terminators flanked their lord, forming a ceramite shell as they marched, filling the breadth of even the widest corridors.

Behind them, First Claw walked in relative quiet, weapons lowered, each member's thoughts sealed within his own helm.

The few squads of uniformed Chapter serfs that didn't immediately flee died to the chattering crash of Terminator storm bolters. Several times, the horde stalked over ground thickly pasted with organic mush from shell-burst bodies. The Corsairs appeared no different, but First Claw was stained red to their shins.

Talos recognised the smell thickening the air, knowing the same spicy, sulphur-copper reek of ruptured human meat from every battlefield he could remember. Yet, most recently, it had been richest on the corrupted decks of Hell's Iris. The scent saturated even the metal hull of Huron's outpost, doubtless seeping in from the Maelstrom's poisoned winds. No wonder mutation ran rife.

'What *is* that thing?' Xarl voxed. In close proximity, communications worked, though in a scratchingly weak half-hearted way.

'I asked Variel once.' Talos couldn't stop staring at the little beast-thing. 'Huron calls it a *hamadrya*, apparently. It's a psychic creature, mind-bonded to the Tyrant.'

Xarl curled his lip. 'I want to slap it off his back and stamp on its leering face.'

'You and I both, brother.'

Huron brought the procession to a halt with a raised hand. 'Hold.' The Corsair's eyes, already bloodshot and narrowed by the pain of simply existing in his reconstructed state, twitched as he concentrated. The creature on his back drooled a viscous, silvery slime from its chittering maw. It bleached the paint from Huron's armour where it dripped.

'We are close now. And several of our kin-squads draw near. Come, brothers. The prize is almost ours, then this siege can truly begin.'

'Wait,' Uzas said. 'I hear something.'

TO SAY THEY arrived in orderly formation would be to do them an injustice, for the warriors' cohesion far exceeded anything seen in the Blood Reaver's attack force. In pristine ceramite of blue and white, matching the halved heraldries of ancient Terran knights, a single squad of warriors threw themselves into cover at the far end of the corridor. Their movements were utterly economical, ruthless in their soldierly precision, taking positions in total silence but for the growl of armour and the crack of bolter stocks against shoulder guards as each of them took aim.

Their leader was unhelmed, his stern features moulded into a mask of absolute resolve. Even over the distance, Talos knew that look, and could recall when he'd worn it himself. The defiance in the warrior's gaze made the prophet's skin crawl. Here was a man that believed in his cause. He felt no doubt, no hesitation, no temptation to wrack his mind in the futile second-guessing of sworn duty. His life was unclouded by broken oaths, and the legacy of mistrust and confusion that drifted in the wake of every betrayal.

Talos saw all of this in the time it took the warrior to raise his chainsword – a single second spent recognising the eyes of one who lived his life according to Talos's own long-abandoned convictions.

He heard Mercutian say, in rare Nostraman gutter-tongue, *'Oh, shit.'*

The prophet and his brothers moved in a unity of their own, despite no signal passing between any of them. Clutching weapons tightly to their chests, First Claw stepped into the hulking shadows of the Terminators.

'Kill them,' Huron sneered, already advancing in a halting, hitching stride. His Terminators followed, leaning forwards into onerous runs, keeping pace and enclosing their lord, shielding him with their armoured bodies. Their tread was enough to send an arrhythmic pulse through the ground.

Ahead of them, the brother-sergeant chopped the air with his howling chainblade, and the Marines Errant filled the corridor with a demolishing hail of bolter shells.

Detonating shells burst against the layered ceramite, shrapnel clattering against the walls in gritty hail. Even protected as they were in their armour, the Corsairs growled and cursed.

First Claw kept themselves in the Terminators' wake, shadowing their steps, letting the Corsair elite wade through the enemy fire. Xarl's snigger came over the vox, and Talos felt himself grinning.

'You're doing fine, brothers,' Cyrion mocked the Corsairs over the squad's secure vox-channel. The gore-scent was buried now, hidden beneath the chemical tang of bolter discharge and the powdery reek of fyceline dust.

'Fight,' one of the Terminators growled in a grey-voiced drone of vox. 'Fight, you spineless Nostraman bastards.' First Claw didn't answer, though their helms gave subtle clicks, betraying the laughter they shared in private. As the Corsair warrior reloaded his storm bolter, a shell cracked against his helm, shattering both tusks and earning a pained grunt.

The sound of so many bolts striking home was a rainstorm on a roof of corrugated iron. Over the din, Talos heard the Marines Errant sergeant give that ancient cry, 'For the Emperor!'

Ah, the whispery tendrils of nostalgia. The prophet smiled again, even as the warrior in front of him buckled and crashed to his knees, finally felled by massed bolter fire. Talos moved in the same moment, slipping into another Terminator's shadow, sharing the living, cursing cover with Mercutian.

'*Charge!*' Huron screamed the order in two voices, when the vocaliser built into his throat took over from his damaged vocal chords. His warriors powered forwards, lowering their bolters and hefting energised mauls.

'We should take these fools everywhere,' Cyrion suggested.

'Blood...' Uzas whispered over the vox. 'Blood for the Blood God.'

Xarl blind-fired around the bulk of the Terminator he was using as a shield. Talos and Mercutian joined in, and the prophet risked a glance around his reluctant protector's shoulder guard. He saw the Marines Errant falling back in supreme order, abandoning their dead, still pouring out half a squad's worth of fire.

Tenacious dogs, these Marines Errant.

Their sergeant was down, his legs stretched out slack and useless, while he used his own body to defend two of his men crouching behind him. The two warriors dragged him back as they fired over his shoulders, their gunfire adding to the meticulously clockwork *crack, crack, crack* of his pistol.

One of them struck Huron. They all heard the thudding kick of a bolt shell hitting home, and the crumpling burst of the reactive shell exploding against armour. The warlord staggered back between the members of First Claw. He had a single moment to curse the Night Lords for their apparent cowardice, and the fact he sensed the truth was written in a sneer across his features: he knew full well each of them was smiling behind their skulled helms.

The instant passed. Huron threw himself back into the relentless advance, raising his mechanical right arm as if to warn the Marines Errant away before they committed some grievous error. In the claw's palm, the spokes of an eight-bladed star led to a gaping, charred flamer nozzle, dripping colourless promethium fuel in its crudest, stinking raw form.

The Marines Errant broke ranks at last, only for their retreating forms to become statuesque silhouettes in the flooding wash of white fire. One of them unleashed a chemical torrent from his own flamer, dousing two of the Corsairs in corrosive splashes of liquid fire.

Girded in the technological marvels that comprised each suit of Tactical Dreadnought Armour, the Terminators shrugged their way through the flames.

But the Marines Errant burned. They roared as they died, fighting as they dissolved, lashing out with weapons fused to melting fists. With their armour joints liquefying, running under their ceramite plating as molten sludge, the last Marines Errant crashed to the ground.

The Corsairs kicked the burning husks aside, and marched on.

'We are close,' Huron growled between clenched steel teeth. 'So close.'

He turned to the VIII Legion warriors, to berate them for their pathetic show of timidity, to encourage them to push on and fight harder, so that they might all earn this great victory together. But when he turned, the hallway was empty but for the Marines Errant he'd killed. Flames still licked at exposed patches of skin. Bolters were reduced to pools of grey slag, halfpuddled on the stone.

The Night Lords were gone.

AN ASTRAL CONGREGATION came together in the skies above Vilamus. For some time, Variel was content to watch the gathering from the observation deck of the Corsair warship *Misery's Crown*, likening the drifting cruisers to sharks, assembling at the first scent of blood in the black water.

These were his brothers, and this mighty armada was the greatest embodiment of all they'd achieved together. Below them, powerless and unprotected, was their greatest prize yet.

The *Pride of Macragge* drifted past, another stolen ship, its repainted hull proudly bedecked in blasphemous symbols of brass. Variel spent several minutes watching it sail by, observing the Pantheon Stars carved into the warship's armour plating.

The deck vibrated beneath his feet as the *Crown* shivered in the planet's upper atmosphere, settling into a low orbit. He could make out the *Venomous Birthright* at the flotilla's edge, orbited almost parasitically by its support fleet. The lesser cruisers burned their engines hard to keep up with the warship as it coasted around the Red Corsair cruisers, unleashing its formidable weapon batteries on the deactivated orbital defences. It was hardly alone in this spiteful act of aggression; several vessels followed their own flight paths, reducing the missile platforms and defence satellites to wreck and ruin.

Debris flared briefly in the void as it crashed harmlessly against the *Birthright*'s shields, splashing gentle kaleidoscope ripples through the shimmering field of energy. Shoved by the momentum of their destruction, several of the large installations tumbled into the atmosphere in a slow motion that seemed almost graceful. Variel watched them burn and spin, dissolving in atmospheric fire as they fell to the planet below.

He turned, finding what he sought almost immediately. Midnight against the nothingness, the *Covenant of Blood* was a long-bladed spear at the armada's heart. The winged skull of Nostramo stared from its battlemented aftcastle, its eyeless gaze leering across the fleet to meet the Apothecary's stare.

Variel was still watching the VIII Legion warship when the drop sirens started their industrial caterwauling. He turned from the observation portal, affixed his helm in place, and tuned into the melee of clashing, crashing voices.

'This is Variel.'

'Flayer, this is Castellian.'

'Hail, Champion.'

'I have been trying to reach you, brother. Lord Huron has succeeded.' Bootsteps, clashes and clanks in the background. 'Where are you?'

'The... The gene-seed vaults are still exhibiting signs of terminal flux in the cryogenic process. We cannot receive and store plunder from the surface with them in this condition.'

'What do you mean, "still"? I don't understand.'

No, Variel thought. *Of course you don't.*

'I have recorded no fewer than thirteen specific notations in the last month, citing that our ship's vault is unacceptably temperamental.'

'Apothecary, I need a solution immediately. The Chapter is deploying as we speak. Vilamus's defences are broken, and we are needed on the surface.'

Variel let the silence run for ten long, long seconds. He could almost hear his captain squirming.

'Flayer?'

'I have destroyed the servitors responsible for the improper rites of maintenance, Champion. You have nothing to fear, the Tyrant will assign no blame to you.'

There was a pause. 'I... am grateful, Variel.'

'I need time, Castallian. We are one of the only vessels capable of transporting what we steal, and I have no desire to stand before Lord Huron with the confession that we allowed laxity to destroy a quarter of the genetic treasure harvested from the world below.'

Another pause. 'I am placing my trust and my life in your hands.'

'Not for the first time, brother. I will join you in the second wave. Good hunting.'

Variel waited for exactly one minute, counting the seconds in his head. Vox-channels scrambled as he tuned through several frequencies.

'This is the Flayer,' he said at last. 'Do you know that name?'

'My... my lord,' the voice replied. 'All know that name.'

'Very well. Secure an Arvus shuttle to be launched the moment the starboard docking bay is clear. I need transport to the *Venomous Birthright*.'

'As you command, Flayer.' Variel heard the officer speaking off-vox, making arrangements. The transfer of personnel from ship to ship during such an operation was hardly an anomaly, but it required some creative planning with the gunship fleet launching and the hangars so crowded by crew.

'Deck commander?' Variel interrupted the man's organising.

'Yes, sir?'

'I perform this duty for Lord Huron himself. If you fail me, you will be failing our master.'

'I will not fail, sir.'

Variel killed the link, and started walking.

'The Corsair fleet is moving into drop formation, my lord.'

The Exalted said nothing. It merely watched.

Malek of the Atramentar followed his master's gaze. 'Talos was right. The first phase was laughably easy.'

Garadon replied, the other Terminator clutching his massive warhammer in both hands, as if ready for a more immediate threat.

'Easy for us. I'm sure if he'd entrusted his Red Corsairs to infiltrate the fortress, they'd have wasted hours on uncoordinated killing sprees. Do you underestimate our Claws' finesse, brother?'

Malek just grunted for an answer.

The Exalted snarled its first order in some time, sending mortal bridge officers moving to obey. 'Launch Thunderhawks to retrieve the Claws.'

With a smile, or as close as the Exalted's twisted jaws ever came to one, it looked at its bodyguards. 'See what we have done here,' it murmured. The creature exhaled slowly, the sound a mimic of a dying man's last, difficult breath. 'See how we brought a storm to a weatherless world. Underbellies of dark-hulled warships form the clouds. The rain is the burning hail of a hundred drop pods.'

'It begins,' the creature said.

XXI
DEFIANCE

THEY CAME TO another four-way junction.

'I hate this place,' grumbled Mercutian.

'You hate everything,' Cyrion replied. He thudded a fist against the side of his head, trying to restart his failing retinal display. 'My hololith is still stuttering.'

Talos levelled his Blood Angel blade towards the eastern corridor. 'This way.'

The walls were shaking now. Huron had surely succeeded, stripping Vilamus of the power it needed to activate its last outer defences. The tremors in the air could only be the first wave of drop-ships coming down, and drop pods hammering through brittle stonework.

'Huron will be heading for the gene-vaults,' Mercutian voxed. 'That won't be a fast fight, but we're still not exactly blessed with an abundance of time.'

Talos vaulted a wall of bodies, no doubt left by an eager Corsair Terminator team on their march to the primary generatorum.

'He'll have to smash through a hundred Marines Errant,' the prophet said. 'They know why that scarred bastard is here now, and they'll be massing to stop him.'

First Claw was doing what they did best whenever a fair fight threatened to engulf them: they were running in the opposite direction. Talos led the pack in their headlong sprint.

'He'll divide his forces to split the remaining defenders. If the Marines Errant are in this subdistrict, the Red Corsairs will be bleeding for every step they take. Some enemies need to be divided before they can be conquered.'

Xarl laughed. 'When did you start paying attention to battle briefings?'

'When there was a chance I'd be caught up in something as foolish as this.'

A squad of serfs spilled into the hall from a side chamber ahead. Their tabards displayed the falling star of the Marines Errant, and by Talos's reckoning, you didn't need to be a prophet to see that was a bad omen.

Las-fire slashed past them, into them, leaving ugly charcoal marks on their armour. First Claw didn't even slow down – they blew through the troops like a winter wind, leaving tumbling bodies and severed limbs in their wake.

The Angel blade hissed and spat, its power field incinerating the smears of blood along its length. Each died in a flicker of smoky flame, evaporating to leave the weapon cleansed only seconds after it last took life.

Uzas stumbled, slowed, and broke ranks.

Talos cursed, looking over his shoulder. 'Leave the skulls,' he voxed.

'Skulls. Skulls for the Skull Throne. Blood for the–'

'Leave the damn skulls.'

Uzas complied, dragging himself away from the bodies and sprinting to catch up with his brothers. Perhaps the sense of urgency broke through his maddened perceptions, because Talos doubted his brother had obeyed out of a sudden ability to actually obey orders.

SEPTIMUS COULDN'T HELP it. He could never help it when he sat in this seat, always finding himself grinning like he had as a child – the boy who wanted to be a pilot.

Maruc checked his buckles in the co-pilot's throne. He was having a great deal less fun.

'You *can* fly this, right?'

Septimus spoke a smooth flow of Nostraman through his boyish smile.

'Is that a yes or a no?' Maruc buckled the last strap.

Septimus didn't answer. He reached a hand to his earpiece. *'Blackened,* primed for launch. Requesting clearance.'

The short-range vox snapped back a crackling reply.

Meanwhile, the gunship started to shake in sympathy with its own howling engines. Outside the reinforced window, the hangar was immersed in a concert of commotion, half-blanketed in rippling waves of heat exhaust. Maruc saw servitors staggering clear of the launch deck, loading trucks with empty claws retreating from the grounded flyers, and several Thunderhawks shivering with the whining build-up of their rear boosters. Each of the gunships seemed aggressively avian, unnecessarily so, with their sloping wings and leering noses. Each of them had a beast's wings painted on their hull armour, following the lines of their mechanical pinions. Septimus's craft, *Blackened,* had a crow's skeletal wingspan painted along the sloping metal, reaching to the wingtip gun turrets.

In all his life, despite working around finger-chopping, limb-mauling, eardrum-breaking industrial death traps, he'd never seen an angrier looking machine than a Thunderhawk gunship.

'I'm not in love with flying,' he admitted.

Septimus had one gloved hand on the flight stick, and the other on one of the many levers spread across the console.

'A strange thing for you to only mention now.'

The first gunship rose on a crest of polluted heat-shimmer. To Maruc's eyes, it was a graceless thing, a metal beast that wobbled in the air, its engines howling too loud.

Then came the sonic boom. A flare of white fire left him blinking; a bang that resonated like thunder in a cavern had him flinching; and the gunship tore forwards into the visible slit of space at the hangar's far end.

Not graceless at all, he thought. Throne, these things could move when they wanted.

'*Blackened*,' crackled the vox. 'Good hunting.'

Septimus grinned again.

THE BULKHEAD OPENED to reveal three robed serfs. The clenched claw icon of the Red Corsairs stood out in expensive gold-thread weave upon their chests. Their hoods were up, but their heads were lowered, bobbing in obsequious respect.

'Greetings, Flayer,' the first said. 'Welcome to the *Venomous Birthright*.'

Variel had forgone wearing his helm. Despite the innate intimidation it offered, he'd noticed over the years that humans reacted with greater discomfort to his bare face. He believed it was because of his eyes – eyes as light as polar ice often suggested some inhuman quality in mythological literature – but this was merely a guess. In truth, he'd never been bothered enough to ask.

'Do you know why I am here?' he asked them.

More obsequious bobbing of robed heads. 'I believe so, lord. The vox message was corrupted by the storm, but it pertained to the gene-vaults, did it not?'

'It did,' the Flayer nodded. 'And time is a commodity I cannot afford to waste,' he added.

'We will escort you to the gene-vaults.'

'Thank you,' Variel smiled. It was a gesture no warmer than his eyes, but it got the slaves moving. As they walked through the arched corridors, he noticed how much additional lighting the Tyrant's tech-adepts had installed since first claiming the *Echo of Damnation*. One of the most obvious aspects of its transformation into the *Venomous Birthright* was the profusion of lamp packs jury-rigged to the walls and ceilings, casting a harsher illumination than any VIII Legion warship crew would tolerate.

This would be one of the first things Talos would change, he was certain of it. Variel had visited Blackmarket once, out of idle curiosity. It was all too easy to imagine scavenger packs of those same Night Lord serfs stealing these lights for personal use, trading them, stealing power cells, or simply smashing them out of spite.

The hallways were wretchedly filthy, which was no surprise. Variel was long-used to the myriad corruptions that took hold in a poorly-maintained vessel. The Red Corsairs had owned the *Echo of Damnation* for six years now, and given her plenty of time to fester and grow foul.

After they'd been walking for several minutes, Variel calmly drew his bolt pistol and shot all three of his guides from behind. Their robes actually reduced the mess, keeping the exploded gore wrapped up, like wet gruel in a silk sack. He left what remained of the three slaves to twitch and bleed, their ruptured insides slowly soaking through their clothing.

A side door slid open, and a uniformed officer peered out. 'My lord?' Her eyes were wide in alarm.

'What is your rank?' he asked calmly.

'What happened, lord? Are you harmed?'

'What is your rank?' he asked again.

She lifted her gaze from the burst bodies, standing fully in the doorway now. He saw her insignia as she began to answer.

'Lieutenant Tertius, lor–'

Variel's bolt smacked into the woman's face, blasting the inside of her skull back into the room behind. Her headless body folded with curious tidiness, crumpling in a neat heap, blocking the automated door from sealing closed again. It bumped her thigh repeatedly as Variel walked past.

The bridge was a fair distance – and several decks – away, but reaching it would solve everything. What he needed was an officer of rank. These dregs simply wouldn't do.

No more than thirty seconds later, after ascending a crew ladder to the next level, he came face to face with an ageing man with his hood lowered. The elder's skin was jaundiced, and he reeked of the cancer that was devouring him from within.

But he had black eyes – all pupil, lacking an iris.

'My lord?' the man asked, edging away from the staring warrior.

'*Ajisha?*' said the Apothecary. '*Ajisha Nostramo?*'

RUVEN SENT THE attendants away with a curt dismissal. While he'd seen many degenerates in worse conditions during his years in service to the Warmaster, he'd always found Etrigius's servants to be particularly unwholesome things, and their service to the new Navigator had changed nothing of his opinion.

The chlorine reek of them offended his senses, the way it rose in a miasma from their antiseptic-soaked bandages, as if such trivial protections could ward against the changes of the warp.

'The mistress's chamber,' they whisper-hissed in some bizarre, sibilant choir. 'Not for intruders. Not for you.'

'Get out of my way or I will kill you all.' There. It couldn't be stated in plainer terms, could it? He levelled his staff for emphasis. The curved xenos skull leered down at them.

They still didn't move.

'Let him enter,' came the Navigator's voice over the wall-vox. Her words were punctuated by the door juddering open on ancient mechanisms dearly in need of oiling.

Ruven entered, shoving the slowest ones aside.

'Hello, Navigator,' he said. His amiability was so false it almost hurt the teeth to give it voice. 'I require the use of your chamber.'

Octavia was retying her dark hair into its usual ponytailed captivity. She didn't meet his eyes.

'It's all yours.'

Something growled in the corner of the room. Ruven turned to it, realising it was not a pile of discarded clothing, after all. A shotgun's barrel and a mutilated face peered out of the ragged heap.

'Please take your mutant with you,' Ruven chuckled.

'I will.'

Octavia left without another word. Hound followed obediently, his eyeless face turned to Ruven the whole time.

Once they were gone, the Night Lord circled her throne, taking note of the blanket covering the psychically-sensitive metal frame. Curious now, he lowered himself to press his cheek against the metal armrest. Cold, painfully cold for a human, but hardly fatal. He rose again, his disgust deepening.

This female was a lazy, weak-minded creature, and they would be better served without her. To slay her outright would only anger the prophet, but she could be replaced by other means. Ruven had never suffered in guiding vessels through the warp. Sorcery could achieve through strength of will that which a Navigator achieved by a twist of genetic fortune. He had no need to see into the warp, when he could simply carve a path through it.

The throne was too small for him, designed as it was for lesser beings. No matter. The walls were the reason he'd come. Nowhere else on the ship boasted such dense partitions to its surrounding chambers. A warship was not a quiet vessel, but a Navigator's chambers were as close to true silence as a soul could find.

Ruven sat on the floor, brushing aside more of the Navigator's mess. Scrunched parchment pages with unfinished log entries rolled across the decking.

He closed his eyes at last, and spoke murmured words from a nameless tongue. After only a few syllables, he tasted blood in his mouth. After several sentences, his hearts began to hurt. Witch-lightning coiled around his twitching fingers, maggoty crackles of the corposant stuff squirming over the ceramite.

The quicksilver pain running through his blood brought a smile to his serene features. Too many months had passed since he'd been free to work his wonders.

The ship's machine-spirit sensed his intrusion, reacting with a serpent's suspicion, coiling back into itself. Ruven ignored the artificial soul. He didn't need its compliance or its capitulation. He could drag this vessel through the Sea of Souls no matter what resided in the *Covenant*'s beating heart. Doubt's clinging fingers trailed over his skull, but he cast them aside with the same contempt he'd shown the Navigator. To doubt was to die. Mastery of the unseen world required focus above all else.

The ship gave a shudder. Instantly he was himself again, seeing nothing more than what his eyes showed before him.

And he was breathless, his respiration choppy, his hearts hammering. Perhaps he was weaker than he'd believed, after so long in chains. It was an unpleasant confession, even if only to himself.

Ruven gathered his concentration to make a second attempt, and stared at a burning chamber through another warrior's eyes.

THE MARINE ERRANT writhed in his grip, held off the ground by the massive clutching claw. Ceramite creaked, then cracked, split by lightning bolt fractures under the talon's pressure. With a grainy laugh, Huron hurled the warrior aside, paying no attention as the Errant slid down the stone wall. A bloody smear marked the dead soldier's trail. The inscription on his pauldron, etched in ornate High Gothic, read: *Taras*.

He had to admire them, though. Their predictability left them vulnerable, yet it also showed their dogged tenacity. With half of his Terminator assault marching to the gene-vaults, and half besieging the Chapter's Reclusiam, the depleted Vilamus garrison cut itself into two even smaller, weaker forces. The Reclusiam represented the Chapter's heart and soul; in the main chapel, where the Errants' loremasters had held court for centuries, the Chapter's relics were held in the trust of stasis fields. In the gene-vaults, a millennium's reserves of gene-seed was stored in cryogenically sealed vaults.

One target represented the Chapter's past, the other its future.

Conflicted sergeants led their squads to die at whichever shrine they chose to defend, while the fortress-monastery trembled with more Red Corsairs making planetfall every moment. In the wastelands outside the monastery, the Tyrant's warriors assailed the walls with an army of artillery, cracking breaches in the ancient stone for more Corsairs to spill inside.

Although the halls of Vilamus ran red, the fighting was most savage around the Corsair elite. Terminator kill-teams bulwarked themselves within their objective chambers and refused to give ground. Shrapnel grenades burst at their feet, going completely ignored. Any living being in the enemy's colours that crossed the flagstones ended its existence as a meaty stain on sacred floor, pulled apart by firepower capable of cracking tanks apart.

Huron swatted a kneeling serf aside with the flat of his axe, powdering the boy's ribs, sending him skidding away to die in a corner. The amusingly clockwork beat of his rebuilt hearts was a pleasant percussion to the chatter of mass-reactive shellfire.

Vilamus's Reclusiam had been an austere, orderly sanctuary, with its relics presented on marble plinths. He paused to examine a time-yellowed scroll suspended in an anti-gravitic aura. It listed the names of the First Company warriors who'd died in the Badab War, so many centuries ago.

Huron's teeth reflected the burning banners on the walls. With a care that bordered on reverence, he turned his palm to the preserved manuscript and discharged a gout of liquid flame. The papyrus dissolved, its edges drifting away on the smoky air.

Centuries' worth of gene-seed would soon be his. Let the Night Lords flee if they chose. They'd performed their mundane task with enough distinction that the Exalted could be forgiven for its past transgressions.

Someone screamed. Huron turned, axe in hand.

The heraldic armour of a Marine Errant was already aflame, and he raised a stolen relic above his head as he charged. Huron caught the hammer's haft with ludicrous ease, intercepting its killing fall.

'Stealing your own heroes' relics,' he sneered into the burning warrior's faceplate. 'You shame your Chapter.' Gears in Huron's knees droned as he levelled a kick into the warrior's stomach, sending him sprawling into a clanging heap on the sooty flagstones. 'Your brotherhood is about to die, and you profane it?'

The Errant tried to rise. Defiant to the last, reaching for Huron's shinguard with a dagger in his hands. The Tyrant caught a momentary glance of the warrior's breastplate, and the name *Morthaud* inscribed there upon the carved Imperial eagle.

'Enough.' Huron clutched the thunder hammer in his power claw, the way a man would hold a thin stick. Without activating either weapon, he pounded the maul into the back of the Errant's helm, relying on his own strength to do the deed. The sound of a tolling bell rang throughout the chamber.

Huron chuckled as he tossed the priceless weapon aside.

And Ruven opened his eyes.

VARIEL LET THE guards salute him.

'Flayer,' said the first.

'Welcome, lord,' added the second. He, too, had black eyes. 'We had received no word of your arrival.'

Variel answered as he always answered mortals greeting him: with the barest nod in their direction. Without further ado, he walked on to the strategium, entering through onto the rear concourse.

The Apothecary took a moment to process the scene. Over fifty human officers working at their various stations, much the same as any of Lord Huron's warships. The captain of the *Venomous Birthright*, who went by almost twenty irritatingly ostentatious titles, the shortest of which was 'Warleader Caleb the Chosen', was nowhere to be seen. His absence didn't trouble Variel at all. Quite the opposite, in fact – Caleb would surely be leading his company in the assault on Vilamus, as the Corsairs' battle companies joined up with the Tyrant's advance force.

He strode down the angled steps, descending to the main bridge. Mortals saluted as he went, to which he replied with the same customary nod as before. He took care to meet every face that looked his way, seeking pairs of black eyes among the human herd.

At least a third of the command crew possessed them. This was going to work. Variel approached the throne itself.

With the *Venomous Birthr*– the *Echo of Damnation* – hailing from an era when the legions commanded all of the Imperium's might, the throne was sized for a legionary. The human commander remained standing by its side, straightening as Variel drew near. His eyes were blue.

'Lord Flayer, it is an honour to have you aboard. Our vox is still crippled; we had no idea it was you on the shuttle...'

'I do not care. Where is your captain?'

'Warleader Caleb, Scourge of the–'

Variel raised a hand. 'I desire a new cloak. If you delay answering me each time to list the many titles your master has earned, I will make that garment out of your skin. That is a warning. Please heed it.'

The officer swallowed. 'Captain Caleb is overseeing the launch, my lord.'

'And what of his company?'

The officer broke attention to scratch at the cropped, greying hair by his temple. 'The Marauders are in the process of full deployment, my lord.'

'Why have they not deployed already?'

'I do not know, lord.'

Oh, but he did, and Variel saw the lie in his eyes. Caleb was a meticulous bastard, demanding no shortage of pomp and ceremony before every engagement. The Apothecary could easily imagine the battle company kneeling in reverence to the True Pantheon while their drop-ships were prepared and made ready around them, heedless of how their presence slowed the process.

When unleashed, the Marauders were one of Huron's most fearsome companies. It was why they'd been granted the *Echo of Damnation* as plunder – they'd been the ones to conquer it.

Their presence was going to be a problem.

Variel nodded. 'I understand, commander. I am here from the flagship because my message was too precious to entrust to a menial or the whims of flawed vox. Our situation is grave, commander. Show me the launch bays.'

'Grave, lord?'

'Show me the launch bays.'

The commander ordered a naval rating to bring a quad-split image of the four launch bays up onto the occulus. Two stood empty; two were still in extensive use. Variel saw docked Thunderhawks, cradled Land Raiders, and whole squads of Red Corsair warriors ready for embarkation.

'This will not do at all,' he murmured. Too many of his brothers remained on board. Far, far too many. Marauder Company wasn't even close to being fully deployed. It could take an hour or more. The Night Lords were preparing for a fight, but this would leave them grievously outnumbered.

'Lord?'

Variel turned to the man. Slowly.

'You know who I am,' Variel asked, 'do you not?'

'I... yes, my lord.'

'Listen well, commander. I am more than "the Flayer", more than the Corpsemaster's inheritor, and more than an honoured member of Lord Huron's inner circle. When I speak to you now, it is as a ranking member of the Chapter, here under the Tyrant's authority, empowered to exercise his will.'

The officer was getting nervous now. He nodded curtly.

'Then obey this order without question.' Variel fixed the man's gaze with his own. 'Seal both port launch bays at once, establishing bioweapon protocols for containment.'

The commander's confusion was apparent. It was apparent for just under three seconds, and ended when his face ceased to exist in a clap of detonative thunder.

Variel lowered his pistol, and looked at the closest living mortal officer. She looked right back at him. She had eyes for nothing else.

'You know who I am, do you not?'

The woman saluted, controlling herself admirably. 'Yes, lord.'

'Then obey this order without question: seal both port launch bays at once, establishing bioweapon protocols for containment.'

She moved to obey, shouldering one of the console officers aside. Her fingers began to hit keys, tip-tapping an override code across the small monitor.

'Lord, it requests a code for emergency command clearance.'

Variel dictated a long screed of a hundred and one alphanumeric characters from memory, ending with the words *Identity: Variel, Apothecary Secondus, Astral Claw Chapter.*

The officer paused at another obstacle. 'It requests a further unicode, lord.'

'Fryga.'

She entered the five letters, and sirens began to wail across the ship.

As HE RAN, his boots beat the worthless wasteland soil, unhindered by the thick dust at his ankles. The hovering gunship hurled a sandstorm against his armour, its engines giving an ululating whine as they kept it off the ground. The gritty wind abraded his war-plate's paintwork, leaving sliver-scratch slices of gunmetal grey showing through the blue.

First Claw had emerged from a blast-fissure blown in the fortress-monastery's outer wall, to be confronted with a battalion of Corsair battle tanks and cargo lifters massing on the desert. Landers and gunships still ferried warriors down from orbit, while drop pods hammered down in staccato thunderclaps, sending arid dust spraying up from their impact craters.

'Are they planning to stay here?' Cyrion voxed.

'They'll strip the fortress bare. With this many of them, it will not take long.' Talos turned away from the dust storm being dredged up by the landing gunship. Grit still clattered against his armour, but at least his eye lenses were clear now. 'Some of these transporters are already lifting siege tanks back into orbit.'

With the sigh of contented machinery settling, the gunship's landing claws crunched into the wasteland's skin.

Mercutian and Xarl were already running aboard.

'Lord,' Septimus's voice crackled from the cockpit. 'You're the last squad. The Exalted reports that all is ready for your return.'

Talos looked back at Vilamus. The fortress's towers reached too high to ascertain where they ended and the clouds began. By contrast, its lowest levels were practically aflame, thick smoke bleeding from the shell-cracks in the great walls.

A victory, but not *their* victory. This was a game played by another band of traitors, and it had tasted hollow from beginning to end.

Uzas remained with him.

'Are you ashamed?' he voxed.

Talos turned. 'What?'

Uzas gestured with his axe, aiming it at the fortress. 'Are you ashamed to be running from another fight, brother? You shouldn't be. This is meaningless. Our fight is about to begin.'

'Uzas?' Talos asked. 'Brother?'

'Hnnh?'

'You spoke with such clarity. It was... it was good to hear.'

Uzas nodded. 'Come. Prey waits in the heavens. Blood, skulls and souls.'

'And our ship.'

'Hnnh. And our ship.'

OCTAVIA WENT TO the one place she knew there'd be no one to talk to, while Hound waited outside.

She needed sleep. Just a few hours, maybe, before Talos returned and asked her to take part in the most dangerous and insane night of her life.

She'd never been in Septimus's room before. Given how he teased her for her mess, it wasn't as tidy as she'd expected. Mechanical innards and oiled cloths were spread over half the floor, as if he'd been summoned away in the middle of dissecting some unknown machine. A wide workbench stood against one wall, a low bunk against another. Several pairs of boots – one with its lost laces replaced by adhesive tape – were scattered in a tumble under the desk.

It smelled of him in the room, though – the rich, oaky incense of cleaning oils; the scent of a man's clean sweat while he worked; the spicy, almost antique smell of well-worn, well-loved leather.

Octavia turned one of his parchments over, into the light of the workbench lamp.

Her own face looked back at her.

Her own features, rendered in charcoal, sketched onto the paper. She wore her bandana, her face tilted slightly to the side, gazing off the page at something unseen. Above the corner of her lips was the little mole her maids had always insisted on calling a beauty mark.

She turned another sheet, revealing an unfinished vignette of her throne, with her blankets and a cushion heaped against one side. The third parchment was a self-portrait, rougher than the other sketches, with his augmetic left eye and temple undrawn. The fourth and fifth were both Octavia again; this time wearing a scowl in both images, her eyes narrowed and her lips between pursing and pouting. She wondered if she really looked like that when she was annoyed – it was a withering look, straight from the wealthy, spoiled halls of aristocratic Terra.

The next sheet showed a hand-drawn schematic of a legionary's gauntlet, and the next, a list of words in numbered order, all written in Nostraman. She could read enough to guess it pertained to the gauntlet diagram.

She turned the rest one by one, seeing herself several more times. By the end, she was blushing, no longer tired at all when Hound thumped on the door.

'Mistress, mistress... Wake up. The ship moves. It's time soon.'

CAPTAIN CALEB VALADAN looked up as the sirens began to wail. Hazard lights flashed yellow in their wall-mountings. The doors – *the accursed doors* – slammed closed with brutal finality, trapping over fifty of his men and their war machines in the hangar.

Corsairs rose from their knees, their oath-swearing rituals ending with an abruptness born of confusion.

'Commander,' Caleb voxed. He expected nothing but static, and his expectations were met. Curse the vox. Curse the solar storm. Curse the–

'*Initialising purge in: thirty seconds,*' announced the automated wall-speakers.

Every one of his warriors was standing now, their talismans and battle-trophies rattling against their armour. The hazard lights flashed brighter. He felt a sickening pull on his attention, and turned to face the shielded hangar bay opening.

The shield itself was a mellow screen of thin mist, clouding vision just enough to be noticeable. Beyond it, the void – the pinprick multitudes of distant suns, and a crescent slice of the thirsty, lifeless world below.

If this was a true purge...

'Sir?'

'Shut your mouth,' Caleb snapped. 'I'm thinking.'

'*Initialising purge in: twenty seconds.*'

'Into the gunships!' he ordered.

'Initialising purge in: *ten seconds.*'

Variel watched the occulus, his gaze flicking between both populated hangars.

'See? They are secure within the grounded gunships. All is well.'

Inwardly, he was cursing. It'd been too much to hope that this would work with such unbelievable ease, but trapping them like this was something, at least. He watched Caleb's armoured form sprint up a rising gang ramp, and silently wished him an intensely painful demise.

The picture was the same in both hangars. The Corsairs reacted with admirable haste, saving themselves. This would be a problem, but one that could be dealt with in the near future.

'*Initialising purge... Initialising purge...*'

The void shields covering the yawning hangar bays gave uncoordinated flutters, their radiance dimming. The primary hangar went first, its shield dissipating like engine exhaust in a gale, drifting out into the airless void. The second failed a moment later, repeating the same blown-smoke dissolution.

Variel watched the air roaring out in great flapping sheets of force, howling silently on the screen – an exhalation into space from lungs that could draw nothing back in. Crates rolled across the deck, spinning and leaping in their rush to fly into the void's gaping maw. Servitors, too brainless to realise the threat to their own lobotomised existences, went next. Dozens remained perfectly still as they flashed through the air, sucked out into space. Others still attempted to twist and turn as they flew, unable to understand why their limbs wouldn't respond. They mouthed error codes as they failed to attend their duties.

Racks of missiles, heavy bolter ammunition and unattached rocket pods spun and flew free in a near-constant stream. Variel winced as a hellstrike missile smashed into a wall on its way out.

The vehicles were next. The unsecured autoloaders and heavy lifter buggies crashed together and flipped end over end. A Land Raider in mid-loading slid back with punishing slowness, sparks spattering from its treads as they left grind-scars on the decking. When it fell from the hangar at last, it was with a jerking yank, as if some unseen hand finally claimed it as a prize.

In all, the vacuum took less than a minute to void both launch decks.

The three Thunderhawk gunships remained locked in their racks, filled with warriors Variel had hoped to see die. A similar scene appeared in the other hangar, but for the shuddering, squealing form of one gunship being dragged across the landing pad. Free of its rack, the vacuum had almost taken it before its pilot could fire the engines. Instead it lay scarred and wounded in the hangar's heart, all three landing claws severed by the strain.

Variel turned to the bridge commander.

'Illuminate the contamination warder beacons. We must ensure none of our sister ships attempt to lend aid until we have the situation under control.'

'Contamination warders alight, lord.' The occulus switched to a view of the warship's spine, where miserable, pulsing red lights flared along its vertebrae battlements. They put Variel in mind of boils, ready and ripe, in desperate need of suppuration.

'Bring the ship away from the fleet. High orbit.'

He waited, standing by the command throne, watching the sedate drift of stars.

'Should we re-pressurise the launch bays?'

'No. Our warriors are safe for now.'

'Lord, the Eighth Legion warship *Covenant of Blood* is shadowing us.'

The concourse doors opened before Variel could weave more deception into a plan quickly coming unravelled. A lone Red Corsair entered, his bolter in his hands, his helm crested by two curving horns of cracked ivory. With a measured tread, he descended to where Variel was standing.

'Flayer? Sir, what in the name of unholy piss is going on?'

Again, the Apothecary was denied the chance to answer. One of the console officers called back in a panic.

'Lord! The *Covenant* is launching boarding torpedoes.'

Now or never. Now or never. Now, or I die here.

'*Valmisai, shul'celadaan,*' he let his voice carry across the bridge. '*Flisha-tha sey shol voroshica.*'

The crew looked at one another. A few rested hands on holstered side-arms, but most looked confused.

His Red Corsair brother didn't move a muscle. 'And what does that mean?'

Variel drew and fired in a single movement, the shell pounding into the Corsair's throat armour and bursting inside his neck. There wasn't even a strangled cry. One moment two Corsairs stood speaking, and the next, one collapsed without a head.

Several seconds later, the spinning helm came back down and clattered onto the decking with the dull *clunnnggg* of ceramite on metal.

'It means the Eighth Legion is taking this ship back. We are about to receive guests, at which point, this ship must be made ready to make a brief warp jump. Anyone who opposes these actions should speak up now. I was not jesting when I said I needed a new cloak.'

XXII
ECHO OF DAMNATION

THE SHAKING SET Octavia's teeth knocking together. Being leashed into an oversized throne didn't help; she was clutching her restraint straps much tighter than they were returning the favour, and her hips thudded against the seat's sides as the turbulence rattled her around.

Maruc was next to her, his hands as white-knuckled as hers. He may have been yelling, but the noise stole any evidence of it.

'*Is it always like this?*' she cried out.

'*Yes,*' one of the legionaries voxed back. '*Always. Except Uzas is usually screaming about blood, and Xarl likes to howl.*'

'*Blood for the Blood God! Souls, skulls, souls, skulls...*'

'*See?*'

Octavia turned her juddering head to look over at Talos. He was sat calmly by comparison, his weapons locked to the pod's wall behind him. She wasn't even sure it had been him yelling back over his vox-speakers.

Xarl leaned back to give a full-throated howl. His helm's vox-speakers corrupted it, rendering it with a tinny edge, but that did nothing to diminish the volume. The four humans covered their ears – even Hound, who had not been able to say a word yet with the way the pod was shaking. His tiny voice had no hope of registering over the din.

'*Fifteen seconds,*' Talos yelled over to her.

'*Okay.*'

'*I always wanted my own ship,*' Cyrion leaned forward to shout. '*Talos, you can have the next one we steal.*'

She smiled even as she winced at the noise. Across the pod, she met Septimus's gaze. For the first time in a while, she found she couldn't hold it.

'*Five. Four. Three. Two. O–*'

THE IMPACT WAS like nothing she'd ever felt. For several heartstopping seconds, she genuinely thought she'd died. Surely, there was no way of

surviving the bone-jarring pound of slamming into a warship's hull at
such speed. The impact boom made the pod ride beforehand sound as
serene as her father's tower-top garden at midnight. It eclipsed thunder,
dwarfed even the rolling crashes of warp-waves hitting her hull... Even
with her ears covered, she was sure she'd be hearing that devastating
ocean-crash of sound for the rest of her short, deaf life.

She tried to say, 'I think I'm dead,' but couldn't hear her own voice.

Light streamed into the pod's far end. Artificial, pale and unhealthy
light, it rushed in and brought an unwelcome stink inside with it. She
coughed on the pungent stench of unwashed bodies, rusting metal, and
human beings shitting themselves for a moment's sick warmth in freezing corridors.

'Ugh,' one of the Night Lords snorted. 'It reeks like Hell's Iris in there.'

Talos tore his weapons from the wall, and left the pod without a word.
His brothers followed. His slaves had to jog to keep up. Octavia was the
last to leave, checking her pistol for what was surely the hundredth time.

'*Vishi tha?*' a voice asked from inside the pod.

She saw Septimus, Maruc, Hound and the giant forms of First Claw
ahead in the corridor. For a moment she couldn't follow, but nor could
she look round.

'*Vishi tha?*' the little girl asked again. It sounded as if she was sat in the
pod, waiting on one of the oversized thrones.

'You're dead.' Octavia squeezed the words through closed teeth. 'You're
dead and gone.'

'*I can still kill you,*' the girl said in sugar-sweet Gothic. Octavia turned,
pistol raised, aiming into an empty pod.

'Keep up,' Septimus called back to her. 'Come on.'

THUS FAR, IT had been a rather bloodless coup – barring a handful of
regrettable incidents – and Variel watched the occulus with something
approaching pride. The crew were nervous, unsure, excited, polluting the
air with sweat-scent and fear-breath, all of which Variel loathed inhaling.
He wore his helm just to keep the human stink from invading his lungs,
content to breathe his armour's stale air supply instead.

Why the Night Lords found such things intoxicating was beyond him.

The Red Corsair fleet remained in low orbit, its focus ostensibly on the
world beneath their hulls. With vox and auspex worthless, it was impossible to know if any other vessel had even witnessed the infinitesimal
boarding projectiles spearing through space to drive home in the *Echo*'s
hull.

The fleet's sheer scale was a disguise in itself. No armada this size could
allow its ships to drift near each other while they rode at orbital anchor,
and flotilla formation was a matter of calculating hundreds of kilometres between the biggest cruisers. The fleet's outrider vessels plied the

distances between the bulkier warships, ready to react to threats breaking from the warp farther out in the system.

He watched a destroyer squadron sail past, their sleek dagger-prows cutting between the *Covenant* and the *Echo*. The squadron's speed remained the same throughout; with fluid, arcing trajectories, they rode the void to another cluster of cruisers.

A routine patrol. All was well.

'Lord?' asked the female officer he'd unwittingly and unofficially promoted, purely by virtue of her proximity to him at the moment of a murder.

'Yes?'

'Captain Caleb is... active, sir.'

HE HADN'T WAITED long.

The purge was no accident, and no mere malfunction. Nothing had triggered the bioweapon alarms within the hangar, which ruled out any actual threat. The launch deck still lingered in vacuum, with the bay portal shieldless and left open to the void. Ice crystals glittered in a delicate rime across what little equipment remained in the hangar, painting the metal gunships with a patina of frost.

The gunships weren't fuelled yet. That ruled out the most obvious solution, even if their thrusters could be fired in cold vacuum.

Caleb Valadan possessed many virtues that made him an effective leader, but patience was most assuredly not one of them. Someone, somewhere, had tried to kill him on his own ship. And someone, somewhere, was going to pay for it very shortly.

He crossed the launch bay in a slow stride, his boots mag-locking with each step. Once he reached the immense doors leading back into the ship, he stroked his hand across the rimed steel, brushing aside the fast-forming ice dust.

These doors couldn't be cut, couldn't be cleaved. Depressurising the rest of the ship wasn't even a worry – the hangar doors were supremely thick, cored by dense metals, designed to resist anything that could endanger the vessel.

Beneath his helm, his brand-scars were itching again. The freshest one – imprinted for the sixth time in as many days to stave off his regenerative healing – was still raw enough to be painful. Balls of the Gods, what he wouldn't give to scratch it.

Caleb withdrew his hand, leaving crystals of glitter-frost drifting in the lack of air.

'Marauders,' he said over the short-range vox. 'If we can't cut our way in, we'll cut our way out.'

VARIEL TILTED HIS head. He'd not seen this coming, either.

The beetle forms of his distant brothers began their halting march across the weightless bay, boots keeping them tight to the deck. Caleb was at the lip, only metres from walking out onto the external hull.

Variel forced his teeth to unclench. This was not his role, and he was losing his temper. If he'd desired a position of command, he'd have betrayed his way to one long ago.

'Activate bay security fields,' he said.

Intolerable. Truly intolerable.

CALEB SPOKE SEVERAL languages, from Old Badabian to the trade-tongue of Hell's Iris, used as a communal lexicon by the station's native population. He swore now in every language he knew, which took some time. Then he turned to his men. Already, grey frost was lightening his blood-and-black ceramite. It sprinkled as powder from his joints as he moved.

'Squads Xalis and Dharvan – get over to the far side of the deck and load that Vindicator. We'll breach the external hull.'

'Sire...'

'Look around you, Xalis. Look around, drink in the beauty of this fine sight, and ask yourself if now is really the time to argue with me.'

THE IMAGE ON the occulus shook, but it was too distant from the bridge to feel any translated tremors.

A Vindicator siege tank's primary weapon mount was known among the Adeptus Astartes as a Demolisher Cannon. The weapon's most renowned use had been ten thousand years before, when the Traitor Legions used hordes of them at the feet of Titan god-machines to breach the walls of the Emperor's Palace.

Variel licked his teeth in distracted thought as the occulus image filled with drifting shards of twisted metal, chopping out of the smoke. He wondered how many of them had just died in that ill-advised escape plan, and suspected it was a great many.

'CLOSE YOUR EYES,' Talos warned.

Their pod had struck the ship's underbelly, not far from the prow, leaving them relatively close to their destination. She'd never really seen the Night Lords hunt before, never seen others' reactions to them. The crew members they did pass broke and fled at the first sight of the intruders. Whether they ran to hide or raise the alarm made no difference. First Claw let none of them live long enough to do either. Bolters banged and bucked in steady grips, implanting mass-reactive shells into the backs and legs of fleeing humans. Gladii and knives – a quick stab, a clean cut – finished off those who writhed on the ground.

Several of the people they passed were Nostraman. To a man, these fell to their knees before the warriors of the VIII Legion, speaking praises and blessings to see such a potent reminder of their annihilated home world.

The Night Lords moved quickly, efficiently, one of them always levelling a bolter to cover the others. Seeing them like this, it was almost hard to believe the truth of how they loathed each other.

She didn't hear them talk, just the clicking tells of vox-channel chatter. They weren't silent by any means, with their armour growling loud enough to wake the dead, but nor were they devoid of grace.

Septimus moved at her side, his pistols drawn. Maruc huffed and puffed, his lasgun tight against his heaving chest. Hound, shortest by far, struggled to keep up at all. His mutilated features were strained by the exertion. He used his shotgun as a walking stick, and yet again, she found herself wondering how old he was.

Throne, the ship stank. If they were supposed to live here after this, she prayed someone had plans to clean it. More than once they passed dead bodies stuck to the floor in stages of advanced decay. Rot hung in the air like it belonged.

Everything made of metal sported a wet tarnish of corrosion and grime.

The *Covenant* was cold, and it was dark, and it was often dank. But this matched sailors' tales of Archenemy ships. The *Venomous Birthright* was a Chaos ship, right through to its sickened core. She was already worried about bonding with the machine-spirit, and how abused the vessel's soul would be when she met it at the end of this journey.

'Close your eyes,' Talos warned.

HER NAME WAS Ezmarellda.

The fluid she bathed in was an ammoniac clash of nutrient-rich ooze long turned foetid, and half a decade's worth of her own urine. She was naked but for the scaling that hardened her flesh, and she was blind but for the fact she could stare into the Sea of Souls.

Her hovel was a dark chamber with the floor given over to a bowl depression, which she swam, drifted and walked through, as the mood took her. The edges of her rank pool were too high for her to reach, leaving her trapped in a pit of her own filth. She heard them enter, and her malformed face twitched this way and that. What should've been a mouth gummed ineffectively together, making wordless sounds whose meaning was lost to anyone but herself.

When Octavia saw her, she saw her own future laid bare. All Navigators suffered devolution as the centuries passed. She knew that. But this...

First Claw moved around the pool, and Ezmarellda tried to follow each of their movements by the tread of their armoured boots. She had no way of knowing that five bolters were aiming right at her.

Septimus covered his mouth, even though his eyes were closed. Maruc turned to throw up, though nothing he could've contributed to the pool would have made it any worse. Hound did nothing, either because he'd never been able to see, or because he was inured to such things. He stared at Octavia, as he always did.

Octavia had no reason to close her eyes. She was the only one bearing witness to this, and in a way, she was grateful. This was Navigator business. This was as *Navigator business* as things could possibly be.

'Can we use her?' Xarl asked in a crackle of vox. He'd not seen it, yet still his bolter tracked its every twitch.

Octavia didn't answer.

The Navigator turned at the sound of Xarl's voice. Ezmarellda waded through her liquid muck on clubbed limbs, drooling and smiling. She treaded water in the ripe, watery slime, and reached up with hands that had already begun a painful fusion into clawed flippers.

'Hello.' The Navigator's voice was creakingly infantile – a grandmother with her mind lost to dementia, speaking the way she had as a little girl. Saying a single word sent blood-pinked drool trickling down her chin, and she seemed eager to speak, to say more, apparently unaware of how difficult it was for her to form words.

Octavia touched the offered limb, her fingertips soft against its leathery flesh.

'Hello,' she said back. 'Did... Huron bring you here? To live?'

Ezmarellda turned in the water, her twisted spine making it difficult to remain in one position for long. As she moved, a bleached skull rolled up from below the water, bobbing on the scummy surface.

'This is my ship.' The Navigator licked at her melted lips with a flapping black tongue. *'This is my ship.'*

Octavia backed away.

'No,' she said. 'We really can't.'

Five bolters opened up in perfect unity.

THERE WAS NO way she'd get down in the water.

Octavia sat by the doorway, her back against a wall gone mouldy with eternal condensation.

'I can pilot us from here.'

Talos conceded to it easily, given the circumstances. 'I will leave Uzas and Xarl to watch over you.'

She nodded, but didn't thank him.

Maruc was still staring in horror at what floated face-down in the reddened ooze below. 'Throne of the God-Emperor,' he said for the fourth time.

'He wasn't a god,' Cyrion said with an edge of irritation in his tone. 'I know. I met him once.'

THE CHAMBER LOOKED worse with her eyes closed. She saw as Ezmarellda had seen, the layers of bloated, cancerous corruption clinging invisibly to everything around her. The Sea of Souls had lapped against this ship's hull in the past, but the taint hadn't yet taken true root. Its blight was brought by its crew, not nestled within the iron bones.

At first, the machine spirit flinched away from her, despite its power. She moaned as she reached to her wrist, screwing the connection valve implanted there and locking the interface cable tighter.

You are not my Navigator, it told her, just as the *Covenant* once had. Its voice was deeper, yet more guarded.

Yes, I am, she repeated the same words she'd pulsed to the other ship so many months before. *My name is Octavia. And I will treat you with more respect than any other Navigator you've sailed with.*

Suspicion. Disbelief. The suggestion of claws hidden in psychic sheaths. *Why?*

Because that is how my father raised me.

+Jump+ an intruding voice wavered through her thoughts. The sorcerer, Ruven, on the *Covenant*. +Octavia. Jump+

We have to sail, she told the *Echo*.

Show me the way.

+Now+

Now.

Now.

AT THE EDGE of the Red Corsair armada, two warships fired their engines with calculated precision. They both drifted forwards, gaining speed, their hulls parallel in form as well as formation.

Destroyer squadrons were already en route. Several other cruisers were coming about, their captains aiming to blockade the accelerating capital ships.

The void tore open before both ancient strike cruisers as their armoured prows punctured through from this realm into the next. With a swirl of colours reminiscent of migraines and madness, the twin wounds in reality burst open to swallow both vessels whole.

The inbound ships shivered as reality reasserted itself. On their bridges, captains cursed to find their weapons now locked on empty space.

THE *Covenant of Blood* tore back out of the warp soon after, manifesting several star systems away as its commander had intended.

Their warp-wake would take an age to track, mixing with the undercurrents already swirling around Vilamus from such a huge fleet arriving only hours before. The Exalted felt no cause for concern.

Freed of the coronal flares, the warship's systems came back to life with a rising swell of power and muted sighs of relief from the crew.

'Auspex, aye.'

'Vox, aye.'

But the Exalted was barely listening. The creature raised itself from its throne, and gazed out into the black.

'Where is the *Echo of Damnation?*'

XXIII
RESPITE

THE *Echo of Damnation* coasted to a drift, engine contrails streaming to misty points that vanished into the void.

Talos hadn't sat in the throne yet, and he wasn't certain he wanted to. Variel had been pleased to see him arrive on the command deck, insofar as Variel was ever pleased by anything.

'Tell me everything,' said Talos. 'We took the ship with no resistance at all. How did you manage it?'

'I attempted to jettison the Corsairs into space,' the Apothecary admitted. 'When that failed, I settled for imprisoning them.'

'Where?'

'The hangar bays. They sought to attempt an escape by loading and firing the main armament of a Vindicator siege tank.'

Talos cycled through live pict-feeds of the hangar bays. Two stood empty and powered down. The other two... Talos cast a slow look at the former Red Corsair.

'That explains the holes in the hull,' Cyrion said, looking around Talos's shoulder.

'I believe their short-range vox was active, for they attempted it in both bays at corresponding times. The results were very much as you'd imagine when a Demolisher cannon is fired at grievously short range.'

'It worked, though,' Mercutian pointed out.

'If you are referring to the twin hull-breaches, then yes, their mission was a resounding success. If you're referring to the fact the explosions and resulting blast-waves killed almost a quarter of them, then the results are somewhat less spectacular.'

Cyrion sucked air through his teeth. With his helm vocaliser on, it was a mechanical rattlesnake's hiss. 'You mean they went marching over the hull after they blew a hole in the landing bay?'

'Yes. Caleb led them out, no doubt seeking a judicious point of entry to cut their way back into the ship with power weapons.'

Talos chuckled, low and soft. 'Then they were on the external hull when we jumped.'

'Almost definitely. I watched it happening to several of them, who were in range of the external picters. It was an illuminating scene. To see armour, then flesh, then bone itself dissolve into the Sea of Souls. The speed with which they were flensed by the jagged tides of the warp was most humbling to witness. Most lost their holds on the hull the very same moment they were struck by the first waves. But I did get to study a few of them, watching them being utterly taken to pieces by tides of molten psychic energy.'

Even Cyrion winced.

'Blood of the Father, Variel.' Talos shook his helmed head. 'That is a cold way to kill.'

The Apothecary looked thoughtful. 'I was hoping you'd be impressed.'

'I am,' Talos confessed. 'I only wish I'd thought of it myself.' The prophet called over to the vox console, addressing the three officers there. 'Hail the *Covenant of Blood*.'

The lead officer lowered his hood, as if deciding the traditional scarlet robe of a Corsair serf was no longer appropriate given the vessel's new owners.

'Lord, the *Covenant of Blood* isn't in hail range.'

'Auspex,' Talos ordered. 'We cannot have arrived before them, the jump was too short.'

'Lord, the auspex is clean of ally and enemy alike. We're in the deep void.'

'Scan again. We were supposed to break from the warp in the Reghas system.'

The Master of Auspex consulted a data-slate. A moment later, he transmitted his findings directly to the hololithic projector table. The *Echo*'s signifier rune winked, gold and lonely, far from anything else of any import. Even the closest star was millions of kilometres away.

'We are approximately two hours' full sail from Reghas, lord.'

Every member of First Claw said the name in the same breath. '*Octavia*.'

SHE DISCONNECTED WITH a shiver, finding herself in the last place she wanted to be. The damp air moved through her lungs with the oily, cold feel of trapped mucus. Ezmarellda's body, as with her pool of fluids, enriched the air with the spicy stink of old disease.

Octavia wiped her eyes on her sleeves, still trembling a little from the *Echo*'s eagerness. Once she'd opened herself to the machine-spirit, it responded in kind, leaping forwards with a fierce will. It reminded her of a horse abused by its former master, as if the simple act of running free from its master would cleanse its body of whip scars. The *Echo* bolted forwards with the merest touch of her mind, clinging to that same desperation: as if by putting distance between itself and the Maelstrom, it could escape the indignities of its own recent past.

And like a spirited stallion, it had been a nightmare to control at first. It wanted to run, and it didn't care where. She'd managed to wrench its excitable kineticism vaguely in the right direction, but she suspected they were still a fair degree off-course.

Talos would likely be disappointed in her, but she couldn't bring herself to care just yet.

Octavia retied her bandana. Like the rest of her, like the rest of the chamber, it smelled somewhere between bad and awful.

'Mistress.'

Hound limped over to her, sitting heavily by her side. She could hear the ragged rhythm of the little man's heartbeat in his quavering breaths. In the marshy half-light of the fluid chamber, he looked even paler, even sicker, even older.

'I am tired,' he confessed, though she'd not asked. 'Running through the ship to keep up with you all. It made me tired.'

'Thank you for staying with me.'

'No need for thanks. Staying with you is what I always do.'

She rested her arm around his lumpy shoulders, leaned closer to him, and cried silently into his ragged cloak.

Awkwardly, he embraced her with his bandaged arms.

'I had a daughter once,' he admitted quietly. 'She sounded the same as you. Soft. Sad. Strong. Perhaps she looked the same as you, as well. I do not know. I have never really seen you.'

She sniffed. 'I've looked better, anyway.' After a pause, she smiled slightly. 'I have black hair. Did she?'

Hound's thin, chapped lips creased into a smile. 'She was Nostraman. All Nostramans have black hair.'

She drew breath to answer, but he hushed her with a quick *Shhh*.

'Mistress,' he said. 'Someone comes.'

The door opened to reveal Septimus. Beyond him, Xarl and Uzas still stood guard further down the corridor. She heard their helms clicking as they no doubt argued in private. Xarl seemed to be trying to make a point. Uzas seemed to be ignoring it.

'Apparently,' the other serf looked reluctant to speak, 'we missed our mark. Talos wants you to be ready to guide the ship again.'

Without a word, she reached for the connection cable. Until she fully bonded with the ship and had her own throne installed, it would have to do.

BREKASH OF THE Bleeding Eyes moved down the corridor, walking bipedal but pausing every few steps to sniff at the foul air. Like First Claw, the Bleeding Eyes had boarded and found little in the way of sport, and nothing in the way of resistance.

Brekash paused again, sniffing to his left.

Something scraped within the wall. Something with talons.

Brekash sent a questing blurt of noise from his mouth grille, not quite speech, not quite a screech.

A growl answered, muffled by the metalwork. Something trapped within the ship's iron skin? Vermin, perhaps.

Brekash wasn't sure what to do. He reached for his chainsword in a half-hearted, irritated way, but didn't key the activation rune. Another grunt preceded three dull thumps, as if knuckles knocked on the other side of the wall.

In reply, he scratched his clawed gauntlet down the side of the corridor as a warning to whatever mutated vermin dwelled back there.

'Lucoryphus,' he voxed. 'There is... a thing inside a wall, here.'

THE LEADER OF the Bleeding Eyes halted on his own patrol of the *Echo*'s filthy decks.

'Repeat,' he voxed.

Brekash's repetition came back garbled, and Lucoryphus let a mocking caw trickle over the vox. 'You leap at shadows, brother.'

Brekash gave a series of staccato, clipped shrieks – the most shameful sound Lucoryphus had ever heard a brother Raptor utter in his life, for it mimicked the distress cry of a Nostraman condor.

Then, with a porcelain crack of finality, the link went dead.

'Soul Hunter,' the Raptor leader voxed, 'something hunts us on this ship.'

THE WARRIOR WHO'D called himself Caleb Valadan – among a host of other titles earned in service to the Tyrant of Badab – had not died the glorious death he'd always foreseen for himself. There was no heaped pile of enemy dead to stand upon while he bled his last; no cheering voices as his honoured brothers saluted and praised the victorious dead.

He'd not even had a weapon in his hand when the last of his mortality fled, as if he'd been some toothless old man dying in a sickbed, rather than a champion of two centuries' worth of battle.

Caleb had known two things as he died. The first was pain. The second was fire.

He was unable to determine where one ended and the other began, or even if the two things held any distinction given what had happened. But he remembered them above all else.

The ship had entered the warp.

He'd seen it coming. They'd all seen it coming; the way the stars twisted in their astral sockets, and the way the ship itself groaned right through to its metal core. A few of his warriors had leapt from the ship's back – sailors abandoning a sinking ship – to die a freezing death in the endless void rather than be dragged into the Sea of Souls.

One moment he was boot-locked to the ship's hull, axe in hand, hewing into the sloped iron to hack his way back in. The next he was drowning, asphyxiating in liquid fire, suffocating even as it disintegrated him from the outside and incinerated him from within. He died a dozen deaths in a single heartbeat, and he felt every single one of them.

As had his brothers. When the molten sludge flowed over the ship, blanketing them all, he'd seen most of them lose their grips on the hull. Warriors he'd served with for decades, even centuries, spun away in the boiling madness of warp space, screaming as they dissolved. Several lingered by their burning bones in a shrieking, spectral form, before the raging tides ate at their very soul-stuff, immolating even that, before carrying the residue away to be diluted through the tumbling waves.

He refused to let go. The molten flood tore his axe from his grip, then his armour from his body, but he wouldn't relinquish his grip. It stripped his body from his bones, and his bones from his soul. Still, he held fast.

Then came the shadow, vast enough and dark enough to eclipse the howling witchlight of unspace.

Caleb had opened his eyes to the stars once more. True stars, the winking orbs of distant suns, flashing in the night, and the ship's hull beneath his boots.

Not dead. Not dead at all. Wreathed in Corsair ceramite, axe in his grip.

Alone, though. Utterly alone on the ship's skin, weapon in hand but a brother to none.

Caleb had cut, and cut, and cut, descending deeper into the ship with each fall of the energised axe blade.

He found his first prey within minutes, and when that shrieking, clawed warrior was dead, the Red Corsair hacked the Raptor's body into ceramite-coated chunks, and scooped the meat into his maw with trembling fingers.

Not enough. Not enough at all. He still hungered.

He could smell something, something sweet but indefinable, colouring the air of the ship's corridors. Caleb breathed slower, savouring the scent, almost able to taste it. Something touched by the warp, sickly-saccharine in its resistance to corruption, and with the rarest, sweetest blood in the human species. Every drop of sanguine life squeezed from its crushed heart would be divine nectar.

The Red Corsair loped forwards into a feral run.

XXIV

VANDRED

THE EXALTED STALKED the bridge, its many-knuckled claws clenching and releasing, forming gnarled fists one moment, and opening like ugly flowers in slow bloom the next.

The Atramentar – all seven that remained after Vraal's death at Crythe – had assembled on the strategium to attend their lord and master, for their lord and master was furious.

One of the Terminators hefted a two-handed maul, resting the massive hammerhead on his shoulder guard. The pauldron's sculpted face was the roaring visage of a Nostraman lion. Light reflecting from the hammer gave it eyes of staring gold.

'The prophet has not betrayed you, lord.'

'You cannot know that, Garadon.'

The Exalted still paced, albeit in a hunched, brutish stalk. Each of its footsteps sent a throb through the deck. The crew were growing uneasy, for the warlord scarcely left its throne unless something out of arm's reach needed berating or destroying.

'We cannot linger here indefinitely. They will track us... Hunt us down... Huron has warp-cunning magi who can part the Sea of Souls.'

Malek, Champion of the Atramentar, had occupied himself thus far by triggering his lightning claws every few minutes, repeatedly inspecting them. They'd scythe from their housings on the back of his power fists, only to snap-slide back after yet another brief examination.

'You also have a warp-cunning magus, lord.'

The Exalted spat acid onto the deck, dismissing the very idea. 'Ruven excels at three roles: that of a warlock, a traitor, and a waste of skin. If I have traded a genuine seer, a Navigator, and three dozen Bleeding Eye Raptors... in exchange for possessing *Ruven...*'

The Exalted spat again, and a crew member jumped out of the way of the lethal gobbet. '...then I will lose my temper,' the daemon finished. 'And those around me will lose their blood.'

'Auspex lock, my lord.'

The Exalted's wet-throated growl rippled around the bridge. 'At last, they return.'

'A second auspex lock, lord. And a third.'

Limbless servitors slaved to the scanner table began to murmur in binary cant, tracking the inbound vessels with the cogitators embedded in their skulls. The Exalted tuned into the babble breaking out across the strategium, already returning to its throne.

'Cobra-class destroyers,' called the Master of Auspex.

The daemon licked its maw, as if seeking forgotten morsels of food left between its teeth. The creature's tongue was long enough to lick the vitreous humours from its own eyes, which it occasionally did to clean them. Daemonic ascension had deprived the Exalted's face of eyelids. It did not miss them.

'Outriders?' asked Malek. 'Or the vanguard of something much more?'

'We will know after we destroy them.' Assurance flowed through the Exalted's tone again. *Void war. A void war they could win.* The salvage alone from breaking a tri-Cobra squadron, if the vessels could be kept reasonably intact, would be the haul of a solar year. 'All ahead full. Shields up, gun ports open, all lances online and weapon batteries live.'

A chorus of *Ayes* answered the creature's decrees. The *Covenant* itself leapt to obey, engines opening up hot, bright and wide, bellowing plumes of promethium thrust-fire into the silence of space.

The ship moved now as it once had, before the centuries of punishing crusades and patchwork repairs left her no more than a revenant with a majestic past. Between the Hell's Iris crews and the raw material from Ganges, the Exalted had done exactly what it set out to achieve: the years of neglect and shame were finally being cast aside in favour of reigniting an ancient aggression. They were hunters again. *Void hunters.*

The daemon's flesh-heart quickened behind the uncomfortable cage of its ribs. On the occulus, the three ships resolved into daggers of detail, their flanks, turrets and towers painted in the Tyrant's scarlet.

'Do not target their weapon arrays. I want those for the ripest salvage. When they launch torpedoes, take everything on the forward shields, only rolling and yawing to starboard if they buckle below one-third strength. Precision shield-breaking lance strikes as we dive towards the lead ship, then a one-quarter volley from the broadsides as we cut through their formation.'

A multitude of hungers, each unified only by how fierce they felt, gleamed in the daemon's black eyes.

'Lord, a new auspex lock. A cruiser, amalgamated class. And another, led by significant warp-wake... No, another three. It's another destroyer squadron – parasites to the cruiser.'

'They're a vanguard.' Malek cursed under his breath, but his tusked helm vocalised it as a buzzing sigh. 'We should run, lord. The *Covenant* has only just been reborn. To win a fight while sustaining crippling damage will be no victory at all.'

'You are beginning to sound like the prophet.' The Exalted leered at the occulus, paying Malek little heed. 'Six destroyers and a fat-bellied cruiser? We could run this gauntlet blind, and still come out unscathed. Still, I am not blind to the danger, here. After we destroy the first three ships, we will maintain a conservative distance until the scene is fully set. I have no wish to take an armada head-on.'

Several more auspex chimes rang out across the command deck.

'Lord...'

'Speak, fool.'

'Another nine ships have broken from the warp. Three of them are capital cruisers. We have a six-strong squadron of Iconoclast-class destroyers burning hot to flank us.'

The Exalted's nasty, feral sneer died on its face.

'All hands to battle stations. All Claws to defensive positions, standing by to repel boarders. Inform the "Navigator" that we will be needing his guidance very, very shortly.'

'Incoming torpedoes, lord.'

The Exalted licked corrosive saliva from its fanged teeth, and spoke the words it loathed more than any other.

'Brace for impact.'

SHE PUKED THIS time. It poured from her in wet, slapping chunks, spreading across the surface of the blood-tainted water.

'No more.' She breathed the words, unable to give them any truer voice. 'No more. Please, no more. Not until the ship is cleansed.'

Hound wiped her lips with the cleanest edge of his cloak. Over the vox-speakers, Talos's voice echoed around the befouled chamber.

'You did well, Navigator. Rest for now.'

'I DON'T BELIEVE what I'm seeing.'

Cyrion said the words in an awed whisper. Slowly, he removed his helm, needing to look upon the screen with unclouded eyes. 'I do not believe what I'm seeing.'

Talos didn't reply. The occulus focussed on a distant battle, following the twisting, wrenching, burning hulk at the heart of it all.

The *Covenant of Blood* tore through the centre of the enemy fleet, its shields flashing with oil-on-water iridescence. Wounds along its midnight hull spoke of previous shield ruptures, as fire-trails burned in ravine cracks along the ship's armour.

As they bore witness, the *Covenant* boosted even faster, pitching down at the last moment to glide beneath an enemy vessel of almost equal size. The bloated ship struggled in futility to come about in time, while the sleeker strike cruiser slipped underneath, rolling to present its starboard broadsides towards the enemy's underbelly. Every cannon on the *Covenant*'s side raged across the scarce distance between the two cruisers, massed plasma streams and clustered laser-fire raking the Corsair ship's keel.

'That's a kill,' Mercutian said softly. 'Watch, brothers. That's a kill.'

The *Covenant* didn't stay to observe. It thrust away, engines burning with unsustainable fury. In its wake, the Corsair cruiser rolled, cracked, and came apart along its underbelly. Detonations blazed along the length of the ship, as if it were a child's toy to be pulled apart at the seams. Within a handful of seconds it was a fireball, crumbling in on itself, towers toppling into its burning core. The shockwave of its exploding plasma core sent nearby smaller ships rocking, pushing them off course.

'Master of Auspex, how many enemy ships do we count?'

'Twelve, my lord. Wreckage shows four already destroyed.'

Talos stared at the *Covenant*, watching it burn.

'Accelerate to attack speed, and open a vox-channel to the *Covenant*.'

THE EXALTED PLAYED a dangerous game. It, the daemon itself, was no master of fleet warfare. It was a hunter, a predator, a killer without conscience or compare; but it was no void warrior.

To command a vessel in a void war was to immerse oneself in the absolute saturation of incoming information. Shouted numbers and binary codes were distances to and from other ships, pertaining to every vessel's projected pitch, roll and yaw, as well as the intricacies and vagaries of each object's estimated movements in three-dimensional space. The Exalted attuned itself to this state of ruthless focus by doing as it always had in the past: it reached back into the mind it now mastered, and peeled back the malingering human presence to reveal the core of relevant lore beneath.

Memories. Vandred's memories. While the understanding of these maddening astral dances was not something the Exalted possessed itself, it could flay its host's brain open with a thought and rifle through the Night Lord's psyche. Once inside, it took no more than a moment's concentration to wear the memories and drape itself in the comprehension as if these thoughts had always been the daemon's own.

Vandred possessed a wealth of such perceptions. In life, he'd been a void warrior without compare. It was what elevated him to the rank of Tenth Captain in the months following Malcharion's demise.

The Exalted plundered its host's mind with the same tenacity it plundered the Imperium's material wealth. No difference existed between the two acts. The strong took from the weak – it was the way of things.

But with Vandred's increasing withdrawal, the human's diminishing soul took his fading memories with him to the edge of oblivion.

The Exalted remained unconcerned at first. Vandred was a nuisance, but his consciousness could still be looted at will. It only became a trial when the human's remnant spark developed an irritating capacity for cunning. Vandred began to fall silent, instead of screaming uselessly, silently, at his former brethren for aid. He hid from the questing thought-tendrils the Exalted sent back into their shared brain. He buried his most valuable, useful memories, storing them away and defending them with vexing tenacity.

Even so, the Exalted tolerated it. It suspected enough of Vandred's imprint remained in the physical brain to allow shallow memory-stripping, even if the Night Lord's soul expired forever.

Their relationship of exploitive, hateful symbiosis had functioned – albeit with steady erosion – for over a century...

...until the moment sixteen Red Corsair warships shattered their way into realspace and locked weapons on the *Covenant of Blood*.

The Exalted watched the updating, evolving hololithic display, and while it could comprehend what it saw, it could infer little from its flickering runic displays, and could predict next to nothing. Without wearing Vandred's perceptions as a shroud over its own, the babbling behaviour of lesser species – the games of these flesh-things – made almost no sense at all.

Attack. Destroy. Plunder. The Exalted understood these terms. It grasped the basic precepts of void war. What it lacked was the comprehension of logistics; of strategy; of the masterful difference tactics, knowledge and prediction would make to any battle.

The warships came closer.

The Exalted reached back into its host's mind, and found nothing.

Mortal bridge crew began to request orders. The Exalted delayed them with irritated snarls, and ransacked the shared brain. Nothing. No memories at all. Vandred was still hiding, or gone completely.

It took several seconds in the material realm, and a great deal longer in the daemon's own time-loose psyche, but the Exalted closed its claw around Vandred's shrunken soul at last. The Night Lord put up little in the way of struggle, for erosion had weakened it unto extinction.

No matter. The Exalted peeled lore from its presence, layering its own essence with stolen understanding. This was a ritual between carcass and carrion-feeder that the two of them had played out many times before, even at Crythe, when the *Covenant*'s assault impressed even the Warmaster.

And as always, Vandred released his life's knowledge in weak spools for the Exalted to devour.

But it wasn't enough. The blinking runes made sense; the creature could guess the likeliest actions of the enemy vessels based on their bulk, armament and support craft; but it wasn't enough. To the Exalted's blossoming comprehension, every analysis it made of the situation led to the same result.

It was going to lose.

The Exalted was going to be destroyed here, cast back into the turmoil of the warp, forced to linger in the chaotic nothingness until another ideal host-husk made itself known.

The daemon clutched at the fading soul, leeching its life in a panicked suction for answers.

Vandred's embers resonated amusement. *The* Covenant *cannot stand against sixteen ships. To face the four cruisers alone would be mutually assured destruction. Their escorts tip the balance in the enemy's favour.*

Lies.

The Exalted could not, would not, die here.

What do you want from me, daemon? The Covenant *is a prince of ships, born in a greater age. But it is not invulnerable. You have spent lifetimes breaking it apart, piece by piece, only to lose it completely mere days after its resurrection.*

Panicked now, the Exalted ignored the demands of its bridge crew, ransacking random memories in the hope of finding something, anything to use as a weapon to save its own existence. For the first time in a century, the daemon had shown weakness. It had a brief, terrible second to sense the Night Lord's smile.

Vandred struck with the full force of everything he'd been hiding back. Memories of brotherhood, of wars waged under burning skies, of void duels won in the name of a Legion he would willingly die for. The full spectrum of human emotion and experience, from a child's barely remembered fears to the murderer's pride in the way blood trickles down pale flesh.

Memory after memory, perception after perception, spilled into the shared mind. And none of them belonged to the Exalted.

Vandred screamed. The cry began in his mind...

...and left his monstrous jaws in a roar.

The first thing to hit him was the way it felt to breathe. It hurt. His lungs burned. Sensation flooded over him as if he'd just been pushed from the womb into the bright, cold world. He roared again, and this time it ended as laughter.

The ship was shaking around him, already taking damage. The Corsairs were wily bastards; they knew how to strike, and it wouldn't be long before the *Covenant*'s warp engines were rendered worthless by enemy fire. If Vandred tried to run, he'd only hasten his death by offering a ripe target.

The other choice was the only choice. Stand. Fight.

'Gunnery Officer Jowun,' he growled through a lion's smile.

The man flinched as he was addressed. 'My lord?'

Vandred gestured to the hololithic, forcing himself not to be distracted by the clawed monstrosity that his right hand had become.

'We will begin with that Murder-class cruiser, Jowun. Ready the lances.'

THE COVENANT BURNED, and still it fought.

Its port broadsides were a black, smeared scar along its hull. Two of its primary booster vents were melted slag, causing fires throughout the enginarium deck and untold deaths among the most menial of the slave crew. Much of its battlement architecture and statuary simply didn't exist any more, torn from the ship's spine by massed enemy fire. Sections of the aftcastle had suffered a similar fate. Barely a square metre of armour plating had escaped charring, scoring, or outright ruination. Much of the vessel burned with ghostly, void-sucked flames, while water and air pissed and breathed into space from canyons carved in its hull – the former freezing to become streams of ice crystals; the latter dissipating, dying in the breathlessness of the deep void.

The destroyer *Lachesis* lost half of its superstructure in a reactor explosion, cut apart by the *Covenant's* forward lances. Half a minute later, the strike cruiser rammed its way through the frigate's spinning wreckage, pounding into the remaining hull section, batting it aside with its cracked prow as if merely swatting an insect.

Even limping, her legs broken and her skin aflame, the Night Lord warship clawed at the prey within her reach.

The cruiser *Labyrinthine*, now deprived of its last support ship, dived its ponderous way down onto the slowing *Covenant*. A volley of plasma cannon fire twinned with a knifing cut from its lances to rain devastation on the ship below. Too crippled to escape, the *Covenant* rolled with what little momentum remained, preparing for a final lance burst in spiteful retaliation.

The *Labyrinthine* fired again.

And missed.

Its entire payload splashed harmlessly across the rippling shields of another vessel – a warship twinned in size and lethal elegance to the dying *Covenant*. The intruder ship raced between the two cruisers, forcing them apart with proximity alarms wailing on both bridges.

After taking the kill-shot and letting it bleed across its shields, the newcomer lashed back with a withering hail of laser battery broadsides. The *Labyrinthine's* shields burst, and the ship rolled hard to starboard, desperate to avoid another barrage.

On the *Covenant's* bridge, a voice rang out over the hissing, spitting speakers.

'This is Talos of the Eighth Legion, warship *Echo of Damnation*.'

The reply crackled back on a wave of ravaged vox. 'Very amusing. But you should have stayed away from this battle, prophet. No sense in the Legion losing two ships this night.'

XARL AND UZAS listened to the newest slice of madness coming down the vox. The Bleeding Eyes, several of them at least, were filling the communication channel with the most annoying, piercing shrieks.

'What's your location?' Xarl was asking, and not for the first time. 'This is Xarl of First Claw; what's your location?'

The shrieking fell silent again. This had happened several times now, with each bout of eagle-crying rage preceded by talk of 'hunting those who would become hunters themselves' and 'stalking the prey with the broken soul'.

Xarl hated the Raptors.

'I hate those things,' he said. This, too, was not for the first time. 'I hate the way they talk, I hate the way they think and I hate the way they tell that tale about being first on the walls at the Emperor's Palace.'

Uzas didn't reply. He was trying to listen to the Raptors, as well.

'Their hunt is not going well,' he mused.

'Thank you for the translation, brother.' Xarl reached for his hand-held auspex, thumbing the activation rune. 'Wait here. I'll be back soon.'

Uzas tilted his head. 'Talos ordered us both to remain here.'

'*You* are lecturing *me* on appropriate reactions to orders?' Xarl made a show of looking around. 'Are you possessed, brother?'

Uzas didn't reply.

'I'll be back soon,' said Xarl. 'I want to join in the Bleeding Eyes' hunt for… whatever it is they're hunting. It sounds as if it's ripping them to pieces, and I like those odds.'

'I wish to hunt, as well.' Uzas grunted, sounding particularly petulant. 'You stay here. I will hunt with the shrieking idiots.'

Xarl shook his head. 'I think not.'

'Why?' Uzas asked. 'Why should I stay while you go?'

'Because even on my worst days, I'm the best with a blade. You, on the other hand, run around with an axe, screaming about gods while you butcher your own servants.'

Without waiting for a reply, Xarl strode off down the corridor, boots thudding on the deck.

VANDRED WAS ONE of the few still alive on the *Covenant*'s bridge. Flames coated the walls in a second skin, beginning to eat into the bodies of those who died doing their duty. He was half-blinded by the light of too many fires, and he could smell his ship's last breath in the acrid smoke.

Despite this body's raw strength, blood loss from several vicious gash wounds made it difficult to get back to his throne. The blood itself smelled foul, and dripped from his wounds in thick, adhesive clumps, barely liquid at all.

The remaining command deck crew were all servitors, their limited behavioural protocols keeping them bound to their duties no matter what external stimuli were at play. Two of them were burning, literally aflame as they stood at their stations: metal parts scorched, flesh blackening and bleeding. They keyed in commands to fire gun turrets that no longer existed.

Vandred hauled himself into the throne, and his wounds began to leak onto the black iron. The ship trembled again. Something burst in the occulus wall, venting pressurised steam.

'Talos.'

The prophet's voice came back choppy, but the fact it came back at all was close to a miracle.

'I hear you,' he said.

Vandred spat blood. It was difficult to speak with all these teeth. 'The *Covenant* is gone, brother. They're not even boarding us. They want us dead, and they'll get that wish very soon.'

Talos snarled. 'Run. We will cover your escape. The twin-jump will work this time, you have my word.'

'Why is there this maddening devotion to lose both ships? The *Covenant* can barely crawl, let alone run. Save the worthless heroics for when you have an audience to appreciate them, prophet. That night may yet come, but it is not tonight. *You* run. I will cover *your* escape.'

'As you command.'

'Come about to these coordinates. Stay out of the fight, keep the enemy at bay with lance strikes, and be ready to receive survivors. Do not engage. Do you understand?'

A pause. 'You will be remembered, Vandred.'

'I would rather not be.' He terminated the link with his bleeding claw, and switched to the shipwide vox, wondering just how many people remained alive to hear it.

'This is the captain. Seek succour aboard the *Echo of Damnation* at once. All hands, all hands...' He took a shivering breath.

'Abandon ship.'

XXV

LOSSES

THE FIRST CRAFT to spill from the *Covenant*'s burning form were the vulture silhouettes of the Legion's gunships. They shot out into the void, their engines streaming with comet-tails as they raced to put distance between themselves and their doomed vessel.

Talos watched them bank and turn, no evidence of formation in their selfish flight, as they each adjusted their course to aim for the sanctuary offered by the *Echo*.

'You have just inherited several Claws,' Mercutian pointed out.

Talos could tell the gunships apart by the pinions painted on their wings. He wondered if Ruven had managed to beg his way onto one of them.

Serf civilian craft came next, drifting from the launch bays, laden with supplies and refugees, their slow progress nothing like the racing dives of the Legion transports. The one exception was *Epsilon K-41 Sigma Sigma A:2*, Deltrian's armoured box of a ship, fattened by an expanded cargo hold and bristling with a ridiculous array of weapon turrets, as if it were a small mammal protecting itself with defensive spines. The *Epsilon* powered ahead of its contemporaries, fat-mouthed engines flaring. The automated turrets coating its structure like barnacles shot down any missile that came within range. Purely as a by-product of mechanical efficiency, the tech-adept saved more crew lives than any other evacuee.

All the while, the *Covenant* crawled on, its final volleys reaching out to strike home against the regrouping enemy fleet. The Red Corsair vessels returned long-range fire, setting more decks aflame, and several of the serf escapee shuttles had barely cleared the *Covenant*'s hull before they perished in the firestorm still tearing their mother ship apart.

Last came the escape pods – smallest and most numerous of all, and easily the most scattered. They spat into space, flitting on random trajectories, too small to attract notice but too slow to race for solace.

The *Echo of Damnation* ran as Vandred had ordered, withdrawing from the battle, absorbing these lost souls into its two functioning launch bays.

THE PROPHET MET many of the refugees on the primary port deck. His first concern was that he saw no sign of the Atramentar. His second concern wiped the first one away, stirring him from concern to outright anger.

Deltrian descended his vessel's gangramp at the head of a servitor parade: a hundred of the lobotomised slaves dragging his equipment with them. Cargo loaders on anti-gravitic runners carried the disassembled pieces of his largest relics, and the prophet was certain he saw a Dreadnought's arm on one of the transport pads. On another: a medical amniotic fluid cylinder, containing the drifting, sleeping form of the Titan princeps First Claw had offered Deltrian as a gift.

Several of the augmented servants had been fitted for industrial lifting work – these worked in small teams to bear the immense weight of mid-range machinery. Two packs of them carried ironclad coffins with eerie, dead-eyed reverence.

Talos watched the second team – and their burden – with narrowed eyes.

Before he could intercept the tech-adept, one of his brothers blocked his way.

'I survived, Talos!' Ruven was jubilant. 'What more evidence do we need of fate's hand at work? We shall both live to fight together again.'

'A moment, please.' Talos moved past, getting a second, better, glance at the burden being hefted by six of Deltrian's servitors.

'You traitorous bastard,' he whispered. Deltrian, far across the chamber, heard nothing. The tech-adept continued to inventory his salvage.

The prophet's vox crackled live, stealing his attention but lessening none of his anger. Xarl's name rune flashed.

'Xarl, you will not believe what Deltrian has done.'

'I doubt I'll care, either. This is much more important – brother, the Bleeding Eyes have found something down here. It's already killed eight of them.'

'What is it?'

'I barely saw it myself, but I think it's one of the Neverborn. And a damn ugly one, at that.'

LUCORYPHUS HUNTED WITH no regard for gravity. Denied flight in most of the confining corridors of shipboard pursuits, it made no difference to the Raptor whether he crawled along the ceiling, the walls or the floor. His jointed claws made all surfaces equally effortless.

As he clung to the roof of an empty serf refectory chamber, he tilted his head in aggressive, snapping movements, seeking any sign of motion below.

He could see nothing moving, and smell nothing bleeding. Neither of these things made sense. The wounded creature had fled into this chamber, and Lucoryphus had gathered packs of his Raptors to watch over each of the three exits. He'd entered alone, immediately rocketing up to the ceiling and sticking there.

'I see nothing,' he voxed. 'I hear nothing. I smell nothing.'

'Not possible,' Vorasha snapped back.

'It hides,' rasped Krail.

Lucoryphus crawled across the roof, clicking quietly to himself in contemplation, his weeping faceplate staring at the deck below.

CALEB WAS SLOWLY coming to terms with what his new form could do. The Pantheon had blessed his resurrected flesh with corporeal vitality, as they did for all of their servants, but with a twist of thought, a flash of concentration, the Corsair could reshape reality itself.

He knew a life of faith would be rewarded with great beneficence upon death, but this was no mere possession. He walked in the province of daemonhood now, mastering gifts no mortal should know.

The first thing he'd learned to do was to keep the flies quiet. They grumbled and droned in an ever-present cloud, hiving themselves within the cracked holes of his ceramite. The Night Lords had tracked him by the sound, until he'd learned to focus on it, rendering the insect host unheard with a flex of concentration.

They'd tracked him by smell, next. His veins bulged through his armour, as if the ceramite itself was a second layer of skin, and they writhed with his fluctuating heartbeats. The smell rose from this organic cabling beneath his skin, for his body couldn't contain the sulphurous reek of his own blood. One of the Raptors had managed to strike him, ripping strips of his neck away with a flailing talon, and the blood had bubbled in contact with the air, hissing and boiling away like evaporating acid.

Outside of his body, his blood simply burned away to nothingness, unable to exist unanchored to the material universe.

He'd blessed and thanked the Raptor, before strangling it with a smile. The lesson had been learned. Caleb was no longer a creature of this realm. His powers were unnatural for a mortal; they were entirely natural for a warp-spawned avatar of the Pantheon. He obeyed laws of a different reality now.

The next thing he'd learned had been the most useful. In seeking to hide from the gathering hunters, he'd rendered them blind to his presence. Unlike the other instinctive powers, this took his full focus, chanting the names of the Pantheon and deeds he would perform in their honour, if they'd bless him with the chance to reach his true prey.

And it seemed they had. Caleb drifted through the ship's walls, his boots soundless on the decking, until at last he felt his eyes, his finger-tips, his beating heart all *pulled* in one direction, tugged by secret strings.

He let his focus slip free, and manifested in a corridor deep in the ship's body. The corridor was darker than any other, because someone had recently shot out the overhead lighting strips.

He turned at a sound from behind, a sound he knew very well indeed.

THE CHAINAXE ROARED as its teeth ate air. Uzas shifted his grip, holding the weapon with both hands, ready to chop the creature in two the moment it dragged its filthy-looking carcass closer.

'Move,' it laughed at him. Flies had made a nest of its mouth.

'Protect the Navigator,' he said. Septimus and Maruc both fled behind the bulkhead, sealing it shut.

'Move,' the creature said again, walking towards him. He didn't comply. Instead, he gave the air an experimental hack, as if warming up his muscles.

Uzas expected a grand duel. Even with his consciousness torn, he sensed a battle he would remember with wrathful pride for the rest of his life. He didn't expect the creature to care so little for pointless violence that it would smash him aside with one blow and vanish, but that was exactly what happened.

The thing's claw took him in the chest, hurling him back into the wall hard enough to leave a two-metre long dent. Uzas had several seconds of consciousness, which he used to try and regain his feet. A broken skull, and the nausea it brought with it, denied him even that. A blow that could render a Legiones Astartes warrior out cold would be enough to kill a human, or put a hole in an armoured transport's hide. Uzas passed out – still furious – without even thinking to vox for aid.

THE HUMANS HEARD the dull clang of something heavy hitting the wall. Then came the smell, and yellow smoke sifting through the closed bulkhead.

Octavia stepped around the pool's edge, holding her pistol. The others were all armed, all ready, without knowing what they were ready for.

'Where do we shoot it?' Maruc asked.

Septimus didn't answer at first, and when he did, it was only to shrug. 'The head. I'm just guessing, though.'

'Uzas will stop it,' said Octavia. Even to her own mind, her voice held no sincerity. She sounded desperate to convince herself. She wanted to admit that she'd seen Uzas kill her warp-ghosts before, that she was sure he'd be able to kill this one as well, as long as it was still weak.

But that would mean admitting this was all her fault. She was the one drawing these restless dead upon them, and she was the one giving them strength every time she opened her third eye.

'The *Covenant* cursed me,' she said. It left her mouth as a strangled whisper. No one heard. They were all watching the smoke manifest into something loosely humanoid.

'I think that clang was Uzas trying and failing,' said Maruc, backing away. He raised his lasrifle.

THE COVENANT HAD the advantage of size, speed and power over each ship in the enemy fleet, but it was alone, encircled, and wounded unto death.

One of the destroyers made to break past, disengaging from the burning hulk to make a run for the *Echo of Damnation*. The *Covenant* dissuaded them all from such a course of action, protecting its sister ship by jettisoning its warp core. The destroyer veered away, as nimble as any vessel of that size could be, arcing away from the tumbling machinery.

It almost made it.

The *Covenant* fired the last of its defensive stern turrets, clipping the volatile engine core and setting it alight. The explosion lit up the void with purple-white flames, riding a spherical shockwave, catching two vessels in its anger. The first was the Cobra-class *Magnate*, which found itself bathed in nuclear fire, hurled off-course, and depleted of a third of its crew who died over the course of the next several minutes, fighting the flames threatening to take the whole ship to the grave.

The second vessel was the *Covenant* itself. Facing the enemy fleet, it found itself drawn further away from the *Echo*, but its limping pace was no match for the Red Corsair cruisers. They picked at it with long-range weapons, outrunning its feeble attempts to charge.

Lacking the speed to initiate a suicidal ram by traditional means, Vandred's only choice was to cheat.

The *Covenant*'s rear was fully immersed in the spreading detonation rising from its own purged and destroyed warp core. The shockwave smashed into the *Covenant*, breaking its rear half to pieces, powering the remaining hull wreckage forwards like a dying shark riding a wave crest.

The Red Corsair fleet turned, banked, opened fire – all to no avail. The *Covenant of Blood* speared right into the *Skies of Badab*, ramming the cruiser in the flank as it tried to turn away, and destroying both of them in an explosion that rocked the Corsair fleet to its heart, completely ruining their formation as every other ship sought to escape yet another critical core breach.

THE ONLY SOULS to hear Vandred's final words were the servitors still alive on the *Covenant*'s command deck, and it was uncertain if such wretches had souls at all.

As the occulus swelled with the image of the *Skies of Badab*, Vandred finally gave in to the urge that had plagued him every minute of every hour, every night of every year, for a century. All this time, he'd been fighting merely to exist. Now, he *let go*.

'I hope this hurts,' he said, and closed his eyes.

The body twitched. Its eyes opened again.

The Exalted's last words were a wordless scream devoid of anything except pain.

THE CREATURE TOOK shape. It was, roughly, one of the Red Corsairs.

All four of them opened fire, filling the pool chamber with the *crack-crack-crack* of las-weapons. Each bolt-beam slashed and scorched against the Corsair's armour, but did little beyond breeding a rain of burning flies from every wound.

Hound's weapon gave a throatier, angrier *boom, click-chuck* with each shot fired. Each shotgun shell scattered the flies for a moment, and hammered scattershot into the fleshy ceramite. The blood stank. Even over a lifetime spent on the *Covenant*, even above several hours spent in the same chamber as Ezmarellda's corpse, the creature's blood reeked like nothing else in life. Maruc vomited, firing blind as he did so.

The Red Corsair ran, untroubled by the slippery edges of the dank deck, and reached for the former station worker. Maruc screamed, inhaling flies as he was dragged from his feet with the creature's grip on his ankle. Hanging upside down, Maruc still fired through the flies, each shot stitching into the armour and doing nothing.

'Not you,' the Corsair told him. He slammed Maruc against the wall, breaking his head open, and tossed the ragdoll body into the sick fluid pool. 'Not him.'

Hound had to reload. His bandaged hands worked with surprising efficiency, slotting home shell after shell as he backed up, careful not to slip. Just as he cracked the shotgun straight and chambered a round, the Corsair leapt for him.

He didn't scream, or thrash, or soil himself as Maruc had done. He let the creature lift him, and once brought up to the monster's face, he fed it his shotgun barrel.

No defiant last words for Hound. No quip or courageous laugh. He clenched his teeth, stared with blind eyes, and pulled the trigger over. The first shot blasted the beast's fangs to powder and made mincemeat of its tongue. The second blew the contents of its maw out the back of its throat.

There was no third shot. The Corsair hammered its fist into Hound's chest with a wet, snapping *crunch*, and hurled the body aside with far greater malice than it had thrown Maruc. Hound missed the water completely, pitching clean over the pool and hitting the far wall with an ear-aching crack. He tumbled to the decking, boneless and still.

Septimus stood next to Octavia, their fire twinned and achieving next to nothing.

'Your eye...'

'Won't work,' she breathed.

'Then run.'

She stopped, almost trembling, a question in her eyes.

'*Run*,' he whispered again.

The Red Corsair sprinted for Septimus. He backed away, still firing, as Octavia reached the sealed bulkhead. It opened the moment her fingers touched it.

'Out of the way!' Uzas shoved her, pushing her down onto her backside. He hurled his axe.

HE COULD STILL feel pain.

Though the gunfire did little more than ache like scratches upon the skin, the little bastard's shotgun blasts left him reeling, muted by the wounds, and trembling with the lingering agony. It fuelled his anger, as was only righteous, but Blood of the Pantheon, it also *hurt*.

The axe cracked against his head with the same kind of kicking, slamming pain. He had a single second to grunt, before he realised the blade was still live. The teeth snagged in his skull right after impact, clicked once, twice... then started chewing.

The pain of his jaws and throat being blasted apart turned out to be nothing, after all, compared to the feeling of metal teeth eating inside his skull and shredding his brain into paste.

THE CREATURE ROARED, though no sound emerged from the remains of its face. Its head had a shattered eggshell look to it, while its throat was a bleeding mess of blood-gushes and abused meat. It turned from Septimus, feral and enraged, hunting the greatest threat – the causer of the greatest pain. To reach Uzas, it ran forwards, spilling into the pool of water, turning its charge into a thrashing wade.

Uzas was already firing his bolter. It crashed and bucked in his grip, spitting mass-reactive shells into the daemon's body. Each one popped inside its torso with no apparent effect. The soft, crumpling thuds of bolter shells bursting harmlessly were almost disheartening.

Xarl was at his brother's side, his two-handed chainblade ready. 'Give it up,' Xarl told him.

'It wants the Navigator.' Uzas reloaded, taking aim to fire again. His head snapped back as Xarl crashed an armoured elbow into his faceplate.

'*Give it up*,' the other Night Lord hissed again.

Uzas shook his head to clear it, glancing between Xarl and the nearing daemon. He scooped Octavia up by her throat, carrying her with neither grace nor kindness, and followed Xarl back into the corridor.

CALEB HAD NOTHING left except for his rage. He hauled himself from the pool, hurling himself through the door...

They were waiting for him. The things he'd hunted, gathered now into a great pack. They crouched on the deck, they gripped the walls, they clung to the ceiling – twenty sloping, iron daemon-masks, each one with two red eyes crying painted tears of silver and scarlet.

They chattered, and growled, and hissed and spat. In the midst of them, two Night Lords stood with bolters raised in one-handed pistol grips. One of them held his prize by the throat, heedless of her kicking and squirming.

Her blood smelled divine, but he couldn't focus on her. The pack tensed, moving in bestial unison. His anger drained, like pus from a lanced infection. It was as if the Pantheon abandoned him, sensing his worthlessness.

Caleb tried to summon it all back, to harness the anger again, to block out the pain and feed his muscles.

The bulkhead closed behind, sealing him in with the Raptors. The Red Corsair looked over his shoulder, seeing their armoured leader holding onto the ceiling, reaching down to shut the door with one claw.

'I am going to eat your eyes,' Lucoryphus promised him.

The Raptors dived as one.

SPEAKING WAS DIFFICULT, but she gave it her best.

'Hound?' She squeaked his name through a harsh throat. 'Hound, it's me.'

She rolled him over. He'd never been pretty, but there was even less left of him now. She caught at his trembling hand, squeezing it tight.

'Tired now, mistress.' His voice was as weak as hers. 'Thank you for my name.'

'You're welcome.' She had tears in her eyes. Tears, for a mutant heretic. Oh, if her father could see her now. 'Thank you for taking care of me.'

'It is dark in here. As dark as Nostramo.' He licked his bruised lips. 'Did it die? You are safe now?'

'Yes, Hound. It died, and I'm safe.'

He smiled, squeezed her hand with weak, dirty fingers. 'It is raining, mistress,' he chuckled softly.

Octavia wiped her tears from his scarred, wrinkled face, but he was already dead.

XXVI
AFTERMATH

UZAS TURNED TO face the opening door. He'd been standing in the centre of the cell, staring at the wall, thinking of blood's scent, the thin-oil feel of it on his face and fingers, and the stinging, addictive warmth of its bitter sweetness running over his gums and tongue. A god's name hid within that taste, within the touch, and within the scent. A god he loathed but praised, for the promise of power.

'I knew you would come,' he said to the figure in the doorway. 'After Vilamus. After what you said in the fortress. I knew you would come.'

His brother entered the small chamber – a spartan echo of Uzas's former bare cell back on the *Covenant*. Truly, it took little effort to recreate such a lack of comfort; all it lacked was the heap of skulls, bones and old scrolls forming a midden in the corner.

'I didn't kill him,' Uzas murmured. 'Does that matter?'

'It would matter if it was the truth.'

Uzas hunched his shoulders. Anger threaded through him at the accusation, but true rage, let alone wrath, was sluggish in his veins this night. He didn't rant and rave this time. He didn't have it in him; what use, to rebel against the inevitable?

'I did not kill Arkiah,' Uzas said, taking great care with each word. 'That is the last time I will tell you, Talos. Do whatever you wish.'

'Arkiah was the last in a long, long line, brother. Before him, there was Kzen and Grillath and Farik. Before them, there was Roveja. Before her, Jaena, Kerrin and Ulivan. You have butchered your way through the *Covenant*'s crew for more than a century, and you carry the blame for the deaths of Third Claw. I will not let you do that on the *Echo of Damnation*.'

Uzas actually chuckled. 'I am to blame for every murder that ever took place on the *Covenant*'s hallowed decks, am I?'

'All? No. But blood is on your hands from a great many of them. Do not deny it.'

571

He didn't deny it. Denial would neither serve him nor save him, anyway. 'My trial is done, then. Carry out the sentence.'

Uzas lowered his head, feeling both hearts beating harder. This... this was it. His skull would roll free. No more pain. Never, ever again.

But the prophet didn't reach for his weapons. The silence made Uzas raise his eyes in dull, slow surprise.

'You have been judged,' Talos said the words with a care equal to Uzas's denial, 'and you are bound by Legion law.'

Uzas stood impassive, saying nothing.

'The judgement is condemnation. You will stain your gauntlets with the red of a sinner's last oath, and when your lord demands your life, you will offer your throat to the edge of his blade.'

Uzas snorted, not far from a laugh. The tradition was rare even in the VIII Legion's glory days, and he doubted many warbands carried the practice with them down so many centuries. On Nostramo, members of gangs or families that betrayed their sworn oaths would sometimes be sentenced to delayed executions, so they might work off their sins in purgatorial duties before final justice was done. The home world's tradition of tattooing the condemned's hands bled into the Legion as a more obvious repainting of his gauntlets. To have hands stained sinners' red was to show the world that you lived on the sufferance of others, and that you could never be trusted again.

'Why not just execute me?'

'Because you have duties to fulfil for the Legion before you are allowed to die.'

Uzas mused on this, insofar as he ever mused on anything any more. 'The others wanted me dead, didn't they?'

'They did. But the others do not lead. I do. The judgement was mine to make.'

Uzas looked at his brother. After a time, he nodded. 'I hear and obey. I will stain my hands.'

Talos turned to leave. 'Meet me on the bridge in one hour. We have one last matter to deal with.'

'The Atramentar?'

'No. I think they went down with the *Covenant*.'

'That does not sound like the Atramentar,' Uzas pointed out.

Talos shrugged and left.

The door slid closed, and Uzas stood alone again. He looked down at his hands, seeing them for the last time in midnight clad. The sense of loss was real enough, cold enough, to make him shiver.

Then, with a moment of confusion, he glanced around and wondered where he was going to find red paint.

* * *

THE BACK OF her head thumped against the wall, hard enough to make her wince.

'Sorry,' Septimus whispered.

Octavia's eyes were watering despite all the blinking going on. 'Idiot,' she accused with a grin. 'Now put me down.'

'No.'

Their clothing whispered as it met. He kissed her, barely, the faintest brush of his lips on hers. He tasted of oil and sweat and sin. She smiled again.

'You taste like a heretic.'

'I am a heretic.' Septimus leaned closer. 'And so are you.'

'But you're not dead.' She tapped the corner of her mouth. 'That whole Navigator's Kiss thing was a myth, after all.'

He answered her smile with one of his own. 'Just keep your bandana on tonight. I don't want to die.'

The door chose that moment to open.

Talos stood in the arch, shaking his head. The towering warrior gave an irritated grunt.

'Stop that,' he said. 'Come to the bridge at once.'

She saw several of her attendants at his heels. Not Hound. The nameless ones. The ones she didn't like. She wilted in Septimus's arms, listening to his racing heartbeat with her head against his chest.

Closing her eyes was a mistake. Again, she saw Ezmarellda. Desire died within her, wholly and absolutely.

RUVEN WAS THE last to enter. He raised a hand in greeting to First Claw, who lurked in a loose crescent around the hololithic table.

A throne that mirrored the Exalted's seat of blackened bronze stood empty, as did the raised dais, once the province of the Atramentar. *That will change soon*, Ruven thought. *Talos may refuse that throne, but I will not.*

The thought was worth musing on; the prophet had never expressed any desire to lead, and First Claw would likely be honoured by promotion into the Atramentar themselves. They would be effective bodyguards for the time being, at least until the next generation of legionaries was raised from the fresh influx of infant slaves.

Ruven watched the strategium crew at work, taking note of the various uniforms on display. Most of the mortals were either in the insignia-stripped Naval uniforms of *Covenant* crew or the dark fatigues worn by the VIII Legion's serfs, but several dozen spread across various stations were clearly former Red Corsair slaves. Most of the latter wore the red robes of that fallen Chapter's servants.

The last time Ruven had walked the decks of a Night Lord vessel, the *Covenant*'s crew stank of misery – that heady compound of exhaustion, fear and doubt, forever in the air when mortals stood in proximity to the

Exalted. A nectar of sorts. Here, it was an undercurrent to the salty scent of tension. The sorcerer pitied them, so enslaved to their terrors. Such an existence would surely be intolerable.

He stood with First Claw at the hololithic table. Lucoryphus was present, crouched in his gargoyle's hunch on a nearby console. The two slaves, the seventh and eighth, were also present. He disregarded them without a greeting. They shouldn't even be here.

'Brothers. We have much to discuss. With a ship of our own, free of the Exalted's tedious paranoia, the galaxy is ours for the taking. Where do we sail?'

Talos seemed to be considering that very question, studying the transparent imagery of several nearby solar systems. Ruven used the moment to steal a glance at the others.

All of First Claw was looking at him. Mercutian, straight and proud; Xarl, leaning on his immense blade; Cyrion, arms crossed over his breastplate; Uzas, leaning forward, red-handed by Legion decree with his knuckles on the projector table; and Variel, their newblood, standing in midnight clad, his armour repainted and the Red Corsair clenched fist icon on his shoulder guard now shattered by hammer blows. The Apothecary still wore his narthecium vambrace, and was absently closing and opening his fist, triggering the impaling spike to release every few seconds. It *snicked* from its housing, retracting a moment later, before Variel's clenched fist deployed it again.

Even the slaves were watching him. The seventh, with his machine-eye and worthless weapons strapped to his frail, mortal shell. The eighth, pale and drawn, with her warp conduit hidden behind black cloth.

Ruven backed away from the table, but the prophet was already moving, a crescent of crepitating gold flashing out from his fists.

TALOS STOOD OVER the cleaved body, watching its hands still working, clawing at the decking.

'You...' Blood bubbled from Ruven's mouth, drowning the words. 'You...'

The prophet stepped closer. First Claw closed in with him, jackal-eyes glinting at the promise of carrion.

'You...' Ruven gargled again.

Talos rested his boot on Ruven's chestplate. The body ended there – everything from below the sternum had toppled the other way, leaving what was left to fall, crawl, and take almost a minute to die. Talos ignored the severed legs, only paying heed to the bisected less-than-half still capable of speech.

Blood ran in a forceful flow, pooling around the fallen halves, but gushing most fiercely from the cleaved torso with its straining, flapping arms. Discoloured innards spilled out with the sorcerer's thrashing, slick with blood still being uselessly regenerated in the dying body. A glimpse of bone led to the broken remnants of the ribcage, sheltering the dark, pulsing organs. Two of his three lungs had been halved by the single chop.

Talos kept his boot on Ruven's chest, preventing any more futile crawling. Xarl and Mercutian each placed a boot over Ruven's wrists, pinning him completely as his life flooded out onto the deck.

A crooked smile crept over the prophet's lips – his bitterly sincere, maliciously amused expression of subtle delight.

'Do you remember when you murdered Secondus?' he asked.

Ruven blinked, his shattered chest shaking as breath heaved through wounded lungs. Over the taste of his own blood, he supped the acrid iron of Talos's stolen sword, as the prophet rested the blade's razor tip against his lips.

'You sound just like he did,' Talos said. 'Gasping through dying lungs, panting like a beaten dog. And you look the same, eyes wide and flickering, dawning awareness of your coming death breaking through the pain and panic.'

He slid the blade's tip into the sorcerer's mouth. Blood gouted onto the silver metal. 'This is the fulfilment of a promise, "brother". You killed Secondus, you caused harm to sworn servants of the Eighth Legion, and you betrayed us once, just as you surely would again.'

He kept the sword in the sorcerer's mouth, feeling each flinch as Ruven split his lips and tongue on the blade's edges.

'Any last words?' Xarl grinned down at the fallen sorcerer.

Incredibly, he struggled. Ruven thrashed against his confines, against the inevitability of his own demise, but strength had fled, carried out by his spilling blood. Half-summoned warp-frost plastered his gauntleted fingers to the floor.

First Claw remained with their prey until it died, wheezing out its final breath, finally resting back onto the deck.

'Variel,' Talos said quietly.

The Apothecary stepped forwards. 'Yes, my lord.'

'Skin the body. I want his flayed bones to hang from chains, above the occulus.'

'As you wish, brother.'

'Octavia.'

She stopped chewing her bottom lip. 'Yes?'

'Return to your chambers and prepare to sail the Sea of Souls. I will do what I can to ensure you are not overexerted, but the journey will not be an easy one.'

She wiped sweaty palms on her trousers; her nose still wrinkled at the sight of Ruven's bisected body. Variel on his knees, cutting away armour and going to work with a flesh-saw, didn't exactly help.

'What's our destination?' she asked.

Talos called up an image on the central hololithic. Glittering stars cast a malignant glow down on upturned faces and faceplates.

'I want to return to the Eye, and make contact with some of the other Eighth Legion warbands. But for now, I do not care where we go. Anywhere but here, Octavia. Just get us there alive.'

She saluted for the first time in her life; fist over her heart, the way the Legion's warriors once saluted the Exalted.

'Quaint.' Talos's black eyes glinted in the reflected artificial starlight. 'To your station, Navigator.'

This time, she performed a Terran curtsey, as if she were back in the ballrooms of the distant Throneworld.

'Aye, my lord.'

Once she'd left the bridge, Talos turned to his brothers. 'I will return soon. If you need me, I will be with the tech-priest.'

'Wait, Talos,' Variel called, wrist-deep in the traitor's chest. 'What should I do with his gene-seed?'

'Destroy it.'

Variel squeezed, bursting the organ in his fist.

THE ECHO'S HALL of Reflection echoed, just as the *Covenant*'s Hall of Remembrance had echoed before it, with divine industry. Red Corsair plunder was dumped on the floor to be cleansed when Deltrian had time to attend to such insignificant details. Meanwhile, he observed his servitor army installing his precious Legion relics in places of pride.

The loss of every single artefact caused him a categorised host of digitally-interpreted approximations of negative emotion – what a human might call *regret* – but he was pleased with the modest horde of equipment he'd managed to salvage.

On an exceedingly positive note, the *Echo of Damnation* boasted an extremely well-appointed chamber for housing the treasures of his trade, and although rot had set in across the ship during its years in the Corsairs' clutches, nothing was ruined beyond the application of careful restoration and routine maintenance.

Deltrian passed a life support pod, stroking a steel finger down the glass. The way a man might tap to catch the attention of a pet fish, Deltrian's fingertip *tink-tink-tinked* on the glass as he admired one of the true gems in his collection. The Titan princeps, naked and hobbled, drifted unconscious in the amniotic ooze, curled almost foetal around the input/output cables implanted within his bowels and belly.

The sleeping man twitched at the second set of taps, as if he could actually hear the greeting. That was impossible, of course. Given the amount of narcotics flooding the princeps's bloodstream, he was locked in the deepest coils of a chemical coma. If he *had* been even remotely conscious, well, the pain would be indescribable, and almost certainly a detriment to sanity.

Deltrian watched the man twitch again. He made a note to monitor his unconscious ward closely in the coming nights, as they all acclimatised to their new sanctuary. The tech-adept moved on.

Lifter servitors were heaving one of the two saved sarcophagi into stasis racks. This one... This one caused Deltrian some degree of concern. *Legiones Astartes One-Two-Ten; preferred appellation: Talos* was in command now, and the existence of this particular sarcophagus directly contravened his emotive desires expressed at a past juncture.

Still, such an eventuality would be dealt with when the time arose. Deltrian considered the sarcophagus to be his finest work: a perfect representation of the warrior within. The Night Lord image engraved on the burnished platinum stood in a posture matching representations of heroic and mythic figures from at least sixteen other human cultures, with his limbs and armour sculpted to exacting standards. His helmed head was arched back to suggest some mythic roar of triumph aimed up at the heavens, while he clutched the helms of fallen warriors in each hand. His boot rested upon a third, signifying his absolute victory.

Yes, indeed. Deltrian was adamantly proud of his work with this particular unit, especially in the ferociously complex surgeries required to save the living remnant's life during the one and only time it had conceded to activation.

The tech-priest froze as the immense double doors opened on grinding hydraulics. In a curiously human gesture, he reached to pull his hood up around his features.

'Greetings, Talos,' he said, not turning around.

'Explain yourself.'

That made him turn. Not the anger in the prophet's voice, for there was none to be heard, but the gentility of the demand, that was most intriguing.

'I infer that you reference the continued existence of Sarcophagus Ten-Three. Correct?'

The prophet's black eyes flickered first, then his pale features turned to follow. He stared at the ornately rendered coffin for exactly six and a half seconds.

'Explain yourself,' he said again, colder now, his voice undergoing a significant reduction in vocalised temperance. Deltrian decided to frame this in the simplest terms.

'Your orders after the engagement at Crythe were countermanded by a higher authority.'

The prophet narrowed his eyes. 'The Exalted would never order such a thing. His relief at Malcharion's destruction was palpable. Satisfaction poured off him in waves, tech-adept. Trust me, I saw it myself when I informed him.'

Deltrian waited for an acceptable juncture in which to interject his own words. 'Incorrect assumption. The higher authority you are referencing is not the higher authority I inferred. The order to repair and sustain the life of the warrior within Sarcophagus Ten-Three did not originate with the Exalted. It was a command issued by Legiones Astartes *Distinctus-One-Ten/Previous-One*.'

Talos shook his head. 'Who?'

Deltrian hesitated. He didn't know the warrior's preferred appellation, for he'd never been told of it. 'The... Atramentar warrior, first of the Exalted's bodyguards, Tenth Company, previously of First Company.'

'Malek? *Malek* ordered it?'

Deltrian flinched back. 'The modulation of your voice indicates anger.'

'No. I am surprised, that is all.' Talos returned his gaze to the enshrined sarcophagus, already being attached to stasis feeds. 'Is he alive in there?'

Deltrian lowered his head and raised it, in the traditional human signifier for positive agreement.

'Did you just nod?' Talos asked.

'Affirmative.'

'It looked like a bow.'

'Negative.'

'So he's alive?'

Deltrian despaired, sometimes. Slowed by their organic flaws, these Night Lords were woefully difficult to deal with.

'Yes. This unit is ready for activation, and the warrior within is – as you say – alive.'

'Why wasn't I told of this? I walked the *Covenant*'s Hall of Remembrance many times. Why was his sarcophagus hidden?'

'The orders were to maintain silence. It was believed you would react violently to the knowledge if exposed to it.'

Talos shook his head again, though the tech-adept guessed it was an accompaniment to thought, rather than an indication of disagreement.

'Will you react with violence?' the tech-adept asked. 'This is sacred ground, already consecrated to the Machine-God, in honour of the oath between the Mechanicum and the Eighth Legion.'

The prophet's gaze lingered on the Dreadnought's sarcophagus.

'Do I look like a violent soul?' he asked.

Deltrian was unable to discern the exact ratio of sardonic humour to genuine inquiry contained in the Night Lord's question. With no comprehension of the question's nature, he couldn't formulate a customised answer. Lacking any other recourse, he answered honestly.

'Yes.'

Talos snorted, neither agreeing nor disagreeing. 'Awaken Malcharion if you are able,' he said. 'Then we will discuss what must be done.'

EPILOGUE
FATE

THE PROPHET SEES them die.

He sees them fall, one by one, until at last he stands alone, possessing nothing but a broken blade in his bleeding hands.

A warrior with no brothers.

A master with no slaves.

A soldier with no sword.

CYRION IS NOT the first to die, but his death is the worst to witness. The inhuman fire, burning dark with alien witchlight, eats at his motionless corpse.

An outstretched hand rests with its fingers blackened and curled, just shy of a fallen bolter.

XARL, THE STRONGEST of them, should be the last to die, not the first. Dismembered, reduced to hunks of armour-wrapped meat, his death is neither quick nor painless, and offers only a shadow of the glory he so craved.

It is not a death he would have welcomed, but his enemies – those few that still draw breath when the sun finally rises after the longest night of their lives – will remember him until their own eventual ends. That, at least, is a comfort he can take beyond the grave.

MERCUTIAN IS NOT the last, either. Miserable, loyal Mercutian, standing over his brothers' bodies, defending them against shrieking xenos bitch-creatures that take him to pieces with curved blades.

He fights past the point of death, fuelling his body with stubborn anger when organs and blood and air are no longer enough.

When he falls, it's with an apology on his lips.

VARIEL DIES WITH Cyrion.

The watcher feels a strange sorrow at that; Cyrion and Variel are not close, can barely stand to hear each others' voices. The same flames that embrace the former leap to embrace the latter, bringing death for one and pain for the other.

Variel dies unarmed, and he is the only one to do so.

UZAS IS THE last. Uzas, his soul etched with god-runes even if his armour is not.

He is the last to fall, his axe and gladius bathed red in stinking alien blood. Shadows dance in a closing circle around him, howling madness from inhuman throats. He meets them with cries of his own: first of rage, then of pain, and at last, of laughter.

THE NAVIGATOR COVERS both her secrets in black, but only one can be so easily hidden. As she runs through the night-time city streets, beneath starlight kinder to her pale skin than the Covenant's un-light could ever be, she looks over her shoulder for signs of pursuit.

For now, there are none.

The watcher feels her relief, even though this is a dream, and she cannot see him.

Breathless, hiding, she checks her secrets, ensuring both are safe. The bandana is still in place, sheathing her invaluable gift from those who would never understand. He watches as her shivering hands stray down her body, resting at her second secret.

Pale fingers stroke a swollen belly, barely concealed by her black jacket. The watcher knows that coat – it belongs to Septimus.

Voices shout for her, challenging and cursing in the same breath. A tall figure appears at the mouth of the alley. He is armoured lightly, for pursuit and the running gunfights of a street battle.

'Hold, heretic, in the name of the Holy Inquisition.'

Octavia runs again, cradling her rounded stomach as gunfire cracks at her heels.

THE PROPHET OPENED his eyes.

Around him, nothing more than a chamber – the cold comfort of his personal cell. The walls were already touched by Nostraman cuneiform, the flowing script written in some places, carved in others. The same etchings and scratchings were visible on the warrior's own armour, scrawled in mindless, prophectic decoration.

The dagger fell from his hand to clatter on the floor, leaving the final rune incomplete. He knew the sigil, and it wasn't one drawn from his birth-tongue.

A slanted eye stared back at him from the wall. It wept a single, unfinished tear.

An eldar rune, symbolising the grief of a goddess and the defiance of a species exiled to sail the stars.

Months of fever-dreaming suddenly made sense. He turned to a spiral carved into the steel wall, ringed by a crude circle ruined by its own elliptic sides.

Only it was not a spiral, and not a circle. It was a vortex that stared with one malignant eye, and a presence in orbit around it.

He traced his fingers along the orbiting oval. *What circles the Great Eye, trapped within its grip?*

'The *Song of Ulthanash*.' Talos broke the silence of the cold room, looking back at the weeping goddess.

'Craftworld Ulthwé.'

THE CORE

I

*"Look out at my father's Imperium.
Do not unroll a parchment map or analyse a hololithic starchart.
Merely raise your head to the night sky and open your eyes.*

*Stare into the blackness between worlds – that dark ocean, the silent sea.
Stare into the million eyes of firelight – each a sun to be subjugated in the Emperor's grip.*

*The age of the alien, the era of the inhuman, is over.
Mankind is in its ascendancy, and with ten thousand claws we will lay claim to the stars themselves.*

– Primarch Konrad Curze
Addressing the XIII Legion during the Great Crusade

IT KNEW ITSELF only as the Eldest.

More than its name, this was its place in creation. It was the oldest, the strongest, the fiercest, and it had tasted the most blood. Before it had become the Eldest, it had been one of the lesser breed. These weakling creatures were the Eldest's kin, though it remained distant from them now, seeking to quieten a hunger that could never fade with nothing to feed it.

The Eldest twitched in its repose, not quite asleep, not quite in hibernation, but a state of stillness that haunted between the two. Its thoughts were sluggish, a slow crawl of instinct and vague sensation behind its closed eyes. The consciousnesses of its kin whispered in the back of the Eldest's mind.

They spoke of weakness, of a lack of prey, and that made such whispers ignorable.

Nor was the Eldest a creature capable of dreaming. So instead of sleeping, instead of dreaming as a human would, it remained motionless in the deepest dark, ignoring the thought-pulses of its weakling kin, and allowed its somnolent thoughts to linger on the hateful hunger that pained it to its core.

Prey, its sluggish mind ached, burning with need.

Blood. Flesh. Hunger.

II

THE DEMIGODS MOVED through the darkness, and Septimus followed.

He was still unsure why the master had demanded he accompany them, but his duty was to obey, not to question. He'd buckled himself into his ragged atmosphere suit – a poor comparison to the demigods' all-enclosing Astartes war-plate – and he'd followed them down the gunship's ramp and into the blackness beyond.

'Why are you going with them?' a female voice had crackled over his suit's vox. To reply, Septimus had needed to switch channels manually, tuning a frequency dial built into the small suit control vambrace on his left arm. By the time he'd patched into the right channel, the female voice had repeated the question in a tone both more worried and more irritated.

'I said, why are you going with them?'

'I don't know,' the servant replied. He was already falling behind the Astartes, and was practically jogging to keep pace. For all the use it was, the luminator mounted on the side of his helm cast its weak lance of light wherever he looked. A beam of dull amber light speared ahead, cutting the darkness with illumination so thin and dim it was almost worthless.

The spotlight brushed over arched walls of unpolished metal, gantry floor decking, and – after only a few minutes – the first body.

The master and his brothers had already passed, but Septimus slowed in his stride, kneeling by the corpse.

'Keep up, slave,' one of them voxed back to him as they descended deeper into the dark tunnels. 'Ignore the bodies.'

Septimus allowed himself a last look at the body – human, male, frozen stiff in the heatless dark. He could have been dead a week, or a hundred years. All sense of decay was halted with the vessel powered down like this and open to the void.

A rime of frost coated everything like a crystalline second skin, from

585

the walls to the decking to the dead man's tortured face.

'Keep *up*, slave,' the voice called back again, snarling and low.

Septimus raised his gaze, and the weak beam trailed out into the darkness. He couldn't see the master, or the master's brothers. They'd moved too far ahead. What met his questing stare instead was altogether more gruesome, yet not entirely unexpected.

Three more corpses, each as frost-rimed and death-tensed as the first, and each one frozen tight to the metal floor of their corridor tomb. Septimus touched the closest ice-hardened wound with his gloved fingertips, making a face as he touched torn bones and red meat as unyielding as stone.

He felt the decking shiver under thudding footfalls. With the ship open to the void, the approaching demigod's steps were soundless, recognisable as heavy only because they sent tremors through the floor. Septimus raised his head again, and the lamp beam illuminated a suit of armour the troubled, turgid blue of flawed sapphire.

'Septimus,' the towering suit of armour voxed. In its dark fists was a heavy bolter of bulky, archaic design, much too large for a human to carry, adorned with bleached skulls hanging from chains of polished bronze. The cannon's muzzle had been forged into a wide-jawed skull, the barrel thrusting from the skeleton's screaming mouth.

Septimus knew the weapon well, for he was the one who maintained it, repaired it, and honoured the machine-spirit within. He rose to his feet.

'Forgive me, Lord Mercutian.'

The warrior's slanted eye lenses scanned him with unblinking scrutiny. 'Is something amiss?'

Mercutian's voice, even over the vox, had a quality most of the others lacked. Nestled among the inhuman depth and resonance was a hint of altered vowels, born of his accent. The refined edge to Mercutian's speech hinted at a youth of expensive education, and it coloured his Nostraman quite beautifully.

'No, lord. Nothing is amiss. Curiosity overtook me, that's all.'

The warrior inclined his head back down the corridor. 'Come, Septimus. Stay close. Does the additional weight trouble you?'

'No, lord.'

That was a lie, but not much of one. He carried a heavy ammunition canister over his shoulder, in addition to the oxygen tanks on his back. The canister was densely packed with folded belts of ammunition for the massive heavy bolter clutched in Mercutian's gauntlets. The warrior carried two similar containers himself, locked to his belt.

Another voice crackled over the vox – also speaking in Nostraman, but with a bladed end to each syllable. Septimus knew the hive ganger accent well enough. He'd learned to speak it himself, as a natural inflection when his master had taught him the language. Most of the demigods spoke in the same way.

'Hurry up, both of you,' the voice barked.

'We're coming, Xarl,' Mercutian replied.

The warrior led the way, immense gun lowered, boots thumping noise-lessly on the decking. He stepped over the dead bodies, paying them no heed.

Septimus moved around them, marking how each one had been dis-embowelled by sets of huge scythed claws he'd only ever seen before on hololithic biological displays.

As he followed Mercutian, the slave adjusted the tuning dial on his wrist.

'Genestealers,' he whispered into the private channel.

The woman on the other end was named Octavia, for she was the eighth, just as Septimus was the seventh.

'Be careful,' she said, and she meant it.

Septimus didn't reply at first. Octavia's tone showed she knew just how insane her own words were, given the existence they shared as pawns of the Night Lords.

'Have they told you why we're here? I'm not buying the salvage story.'

'Not a word,' she said. 'They've been silent with me since we left the Sea of Souls.'

'We used to salvage hulks all the time back on the *Covenant of Blood*, when we weren't engaging in acts of piracy or getting chopped to pieces by Imperial guns. But this feels different.'

'Different how?'

'Worse. For a start, this one is bigger.' Septimus checked his wrist chro-nometer again. He'd been on board the hulk for three hours now.

III

THREE HOURS BEFORE, a wicked blade of a vessel had translated in-system, leaving the warp's grip in a burst of plasma mist and engine fire.

The ship was the dark of a winter's midnight sky, its edges embossed in the kind of beaten, shining bronze that covered the armoured torsos of Terra's ancient heroes in those ignorant, impious generations before mankind had first reached out into the stars.

The ship was a thing of militaristic beauty – armoured ridges and gothic spinal architecture, presented in sleek viciousness. A barbed spear, all blackened-blue and golden bronze, surging through the void.

There were no active vessels nearby, Imperial, xenos or otherwise, but had any been present – and had they possessed the capacity to break the auspex encryption haze that the dark ship projected – they would have known the ship by the name it bore in the Horus Heresy ten thousand years before.

In that foulest of ages, this ship had hung in the skies above Holy Terra as the world's atmosphere burned. A million ships painted the void with flame as they raged at each other, while the planet below, the cradle of humanity, caught fire.

This ship had been there, and it had slain vessels loyal to the Golden Throne, casting them from orbit to tear through Terra's cloud cover and hammer into the Emperor's cities.

Its name was *Ashallius S'Veyval*, in a dead language, from a dead world. In Imperial Gothic, it translated loosely as *Echo of Damnation*.

THE *Echo of Damnation* had ghosted forward on low-burning engines, cutting space in silent repose. On its bridge, humans worked in unison with beings that hadn't been human in thousands of years.

In the centre of the ornate chamber, a figure sat on a throne of black iron and burnished bronze. The Astartes wore ancient armour, the pieces cannibalised from a dozen and more dead warriors over the years and repainted with great reverence. Jawless skulls hung on chains from his shoulder guards, rattling with each of the warrior's movements, and every shiver of the ship he commanded. The face he presented to the world was a skulled faceplate, with a single rune drawn from the same dead language branded into its forehead.

A hive of activity pulsed around the seated figure. Officers in outdated Imperial Naval uniforms bereft of insignia worked at various consoles, tables and cogitator screens. An ageing human at the broad helm console pushed a heavy steel lever into its locked position, and consulted the display screens before him, reading the scrolling runic text that spilled out in merciless reams. Such a flow of lore would be meaningless to inexpert eyes.

'Translation complete, my lord,' he called over his shoulder. 'All decks, all systems, all stable.'

The masked figure upon the throne inclined its head in a slow nod. It was still waiting for something.

A voice – female, young, but stained by exhaustion – spoke out across the bridge, emerging from speakers in the mouths of daemon-faced gargoyles sculpted into the metal walls.

'We made it,' the voiced breathed. 'We're here. As close as I could get.'

At last, the enthroned figure rose to its feet and spoke for the first time in several hours.

'Perfect,' its voice was deep, inhumanly low, yet possessed of a curiously soft edge. 'Octavia?'

'Yes?' the female voice asked again, breezing over the bridge. 'I... I need to rest, master.'

'Then rest, Navigator. You have done well.'

Several of the human bridge crew shared uncomfortable glances. This new commander was unlike the last. Acclimatisation was slow in coming, as most of them had served under the Exalted for many long years. None were used to hearing praise spoken in their presences, and it aroused suspicion before anything else.

From an alcove in the bridge chamber's western wall, the scrymaster called out his report. Although he was human, his voice was mechanical, with half of his face, throat and torso replaced by inexpensive, crude bionics. The augmetics that served in place of his human flesh had been earned for his actions in the death of the *Covenant of Blood*, five months before.

'Auspex is alive again, master,' he called.

'Illuminate me,' said the armoured commander. He was staring at the occulus, but the great screen at the front of the bridge chamber remained half-dead, blinded by ferocious interference. He seemed unconcerned; well-used to such static annoyance after a journey through the warp. The occulus always took a while to realign and revive.

Sometimes, he saw faces in the greyish storm of confused signals that blasted across the crackling viewscreen – faces of the fallen, the lost, the forgotten and the damned.

These always made him smile, even as they screamed at him in voices of tortured white noise.

The scrymaster spoke while staring down at his auspex displays, spread over four flickering screens, each one detailing a spread of numerical lore about the ship's surroundings.

'At three-quarters velocity, we're fifteen minutes and thirty-eight seconds from boarding pod range from intended target.'

The commander smiled behind his faceplate. *Blood of the father, Octavia, all praise to your skills for this.* To break from the Sea of Souls this close to a moving target… For such a young Navigator, she was skilled beyond all expectation, adapting to racing through the secret pathways of the empyrean with tenacity and instinct.

'Any contacts from nearby vessels?'

'None, master.'

All good so far. The commander nodded to the left side of the bridge, where the defensive stations were manned by ragged-uniformed officers and servitors capable of focusing on nothing else but their appointed duties.

'Maintain the Shriek,' he ordered.

'Yes, master,' one of the officers called. The man, an acolyte of the broken Mechanicum, possessed an additional pair of multi-jointed arms extending from his back-mounted power pack. These worked on a separate console beside the one he manipulated with his biological fingers.

'Plasma bleed is significant,' the acolyte intoned. 'The Shriek can be maintained for another two point one-five hours before aura-scrye inhibitors must be powered down.'

That would be long enough. The commander would cease the Shriek as soon as the region was absolutely secure. Until then, he was content to let the *Echo of Damnation* fill nearspace with a thousand frequencies of howling noise and wordless machine-screams. Any other vessels in range to trace the *Echo* on their scanners would find their auspex readers unable to detect definitive targets in the jamming field, and their vox channels conquered by the endless static-laden screams.

The Shriek had been Tech-priest Deltrian's most recent invention. Invisibility to Imperial scanning had its uses, but it also fed with greedy abandon on power that other areas of the ship needed to function. When the Shriek was live, the void shields were thin, and the prow lances were completely powered down.

'All remaining power to the engines,' the commander was still watching the distorted occulus. 'Bring us closer to the target.'

'Lord,' the scrymaster swallowed. 'The target is... it's vast.'

'It is a Mechanicus vessel. The fact it's huge is no surprise to me, nor should it be to you.'

'No, master. It reads as significantly larger than vessels of approximate design and specification.'

The Astartes aboard the *Echo of Damnation* were prepared for the eventuality that during its decades in the warp, their target would have meshed and malformed its way into a larger mass of lost vessels, as part of a serene, drifting space hulk.

Such was the fate of most warp-lost craft.

'Define "vast",' said the commander.

'Auspex reports indicate a mass in approximation of Jathis Secondus, master.'

There was a pause, during which the bridge fell almost silent. The loudest sound was the commander's breathing, which rasped in and out of his helm's vox-speaker. The crew were still unfamiliar with their new master, but they could all too easily recognise the harsh breathing of an Astartes on the edge of losing its temper.

'We have dropped from the warp,' the commander hissed through closed teeth, 'to seek a ship fused within a space hulk. And you are telling me the scryers indicate this hulk is *the size of a small moon?*'

'Yes, my lord,' the scrymaster cringed.

'Do not flinch when addressing me. I will not slay you for delivering irritating information.'

'Yes, master. Thank you, master.'

The commander's next reply was interrupted by the occulus, at last, resolving into focus. The static cleared, the distortion bled away.

The screen showed, with treacherous clarity, a distant mesh of conjoined, ruined spaceships, fused together as if by the will of some capricious, mad god.

And it was, as the commander had cursed, the size of a small moon.

One of the other Astartes by the commander's throne stepped forward, his own dark helm inclined towards the occulus.

'Blood of Horus... There must be two hundred ships in that.'

The commander nodded, unable to look away. It was the largest drifting hulk he'd ever seen. It was, he was almost certain, the largest any human or Astartes had ever seen.

'Scan that insane mess for the remnants of the Mechanicus exploratory vessel,' he growled. 'Hopefully it will be one of the ships merged at the outer layers. Acolyte, cease the Shriek. Helm, bring us in closer.'

A muted 'Compliance, master,' came from the primary helmsman.

'Make ready First Claw for boarding operations,' the commander said to the other Astartes.' As he re-seated himself on the metallic throne, he stared at the growing superstructure filling the occulus. Details, warped contours, mangled spires, were beginning to become visible.

'And inform Lucoryphus of the Bleeding Eyes that I wish to speak with him immediately.'

WHEN ITS CLAWS were not in use, they closed into awkward talons, curling in upon themselves and betraying a creature no longer suited to walking along the ground. Its movements had a jagged hesitance as it entered the chamber, punctuated by twitches in its limbs and flaw-born tics in its enhanced musculature. This spasming posture had nothing to do with cowardice, and everything to do with the fact that beast was caged - forced to act as one of its former brethren – forced to walk and speak.

Such things had been alien to the creature, if not completely anathema, for some time now. It walked on all fours, hunched over in a cautious stalk, hand-talons and foot-claws clanking on the deck. The cylindrical turbine engines on its back swayed with the creature's awkward gait.

The being's helmed face showed little evidence of the ties to its bloodline, now changed by war and the warp into something altogether more hateful. Gone were the runic markings and a painted skull over blessed ceramite. In place of traditional Legion signifiers, a sleek faceplate offered a howling daemon's visage to the world beyond, with a mouth grille set in a scream that had lasted since its god-father died.

The twisted face flicked to watch each of the other Astartes in turn, snapping left and right like a falcon choosing prey. The servos and fibre bundle cabling making up its armour's neck joints no longer purred with easy locomotion, they barked with each accusing twitch of its face.

'Why summon?' the creature demanded in a voice that wouldn't have been out of place creaking from the gnarled maw of a desert vulture. 'Why summon? Why?'

Talos rose from the command throne. First Claw moved as he moved, five other Astartes approaching the hunched creature, their weapons within easy reach.

'Lucoryphus,' Talos said, and inclined his head in respect before saluting, fist over both hearts, his gauntlet and forearm covering the ritually mutilated Imperial eagle emblazoned across his chest.

'Soul Hunter,' it snarled a chuckle from lungs that sounded much too dry. 'Speak, prophet. I listen.'

SOON AFTER, THE *Echo of Damnation* drifted in close, dwarfed by the immense hulk and utterly eclipsed in the shadow it cast from the light of a distant sun.

Two pods blasted from housings in the ship's belly, twisting like drills through the void until they pounded into the softer, twisted metal of the hulk's skin.

On the *Echo*'s bridge, two signals pulsed back to the communications array. The first was soft-voiced and coloured by vox crackle. The second was delivered in short, sharp hisses.

'This is Talos of First Claw. We're in.'

'Lucoryphus. Ninth Claw. Inside.'

IV

Ten hours in, and seven hours since he'd last spoken to Octavia.

Septimus knew better than to confess his hunger to the Astartes. They were above such things, and had no mind to be concerned with mortal needs. He had dehydrated ration tablets in his webbing, but they did little more than take the edge of his hunger. First Claw moved through the dark corridors with a relentlessness made sinister by their silence. An hour before, Septimus had risked stopping to take a piss against a bulkhead, and had needed to sprint to catch back up to them.

His return had been greeted with nothing more than a growl from one of the squad. Clad in ancient armour, a bloodied palm-print smeared across the faceplate, Uzas had snarled at the returning human.

As greetings went, by Uzas's standards it was almost cordial.

They'd travelled through fourteen vessels, though it was a nightmare to decide just where one finished and another started, or if they were moving through the aborted remnants of a malformed ship they'd already crossed in another section.

Most of the time was spent waiting for the servitors to cut – cutting through sealed bulkheads; cutting through warped walls of fuselage; cutting through mangled metal to reach a traversable area beyond.

The two servitors laboured with mindless diligence, their actions slaved to the signum control tablet held in Deltrian's skeletal hands. Drills, saws, laser cutters and plasma burners heated the air around the two bionic slaves as they carved their way through another blockage of twisted wall.

The tech-priest watched this through eyes of emerald, the gems sculpted into layered lenses and fixed into the sockets of his restructured face.

Deltrian had fashioned his own body to exacting standards. The schematics he had designed in the construction of his physique were, by the standards of human intellect, closer to art than engineering. Such was the effort necessary to survive the centuries alongside the Astartes, when one lacked the immortality allowed by their gene-forged physiology.

He knew he made the human uneasy. He was familiar with the effect his appearance had on unaugmented mortals. The equations in his mind that mimicked biological thought patterns reached no answer to rectify this adverse effect, and he was not certain it was – technically-speaking – an error to be corrected. Fear had its uses, when harvested from others. This was a lesson he had learned from his association with the Night Lords.

The tech-priest acknowledged the human now with an inclination of his head. The serf was one of the chosen, and deserved a modicum of respect due to his position as artificer for First Claw's armour and weapons.

'Septimus,' he said. The human started, while the servitors worked on.

'Honoured adept,' the slave nodded back. The corridor they occupied was low and claustrophobic. First Claw were busying themselves else-where, patrolling nearby chambers.

'Do you know why you are here, Septimus?'

SEPTIMUS DIDN'T HAVE an answer to that.

Deltrian was an ugly thing of darkened metal, fluid-filled wires and pol-ished chrome – a metallic skeleton complete with its circulatory system, and wreathed in an old robe of thick weave, the colour of blood at night.

It must've taken a perverse sense of humour to reforge your own body into something that looked like a bionic replica of some pre-Imperial Terran death god. Septimus didn't share the joke, if indeed it was one.

For the moment, Deltrian's eye lenses were deep green, likely cut from emeralds. This was by no means a permanent feature. Often, they were red, blue or transparent, showing the wire-works behind, linking to a brain that was at least partly still human.

'I do not know, honoured adept. The masters have not told me.'

'I believe I am able to make an approximate analysis,' Deltrian laughed, buzzing like a vox slipping from the right frequency.

There was a threat buried in that. Irritation made Septimus bold, but he kept his hands from resting on the two holstered laspistols at his hips. Deltrian may be favoured as an ally from the Mechanicus, but he was just as shackled in service to the VIII Legion as Septimus was.

'Feel free to enlighten me, honoured adept.'

'You are human,' the skinless creature turned its death's-head grin away to regard its servitors once more. 'Human, and unarmoured in enclos-ing ceramite. Your blood, your heartbeat, your sweat and breath – all of these biological details will be detected by the predatory xenos species aboard this hulk.'

'With all respect, Deltrian,' Septimus turned, looking back at the long corridor they'd walked down, 'you're deluded.'

'I see you and I hear you all too well, and my engineered stimulus array is comparable to the senses of the genestealer genus. My aural receptors register your breathing like a world's winds, and your beating heart like the primal drums of a primitive culture. If I sense this, Septimus – and I assure you that I do – then you should know that the many living beings sheltering on this derelict sense it as well.'

Septimus snorted. The idea of the Night Lords using him – one of their more valuable slaves – as bait, was...

'Contact,' voxed Talos.

In the distance, bolters began to bark.

THE ELDEST STIRRED from the cold, cold darkness of the nothingness that was as close to sleep as its species could know.

A faint pain echoed, faded but troubling, in the base of its curved skull. This weak pain soon spread with gentle insistence, beating through its blood vessels and twinning with the creature's pulse. The pain cobwebbed down the Eldest's spine and through its facial structure, emanating from its sluggish mind.

This was not the pain of a wound, of defeat, of a hunter denied. It did not eclipse the hunger-need, but it was even more unwelcome. Its taste and resonance were so very different, and the Eldest had not felt such a thing for... for some time.

Its kin were dying. The Eldest felt each puncturing hole, each ravaged limb, each bleeding socket, in this echoing ghost-pain.

In the darkness, it uncoiled its limbs. Joints clicked and cracked as they tensed and flexed once more.

Its killing claws shivered, opening and closing in the cool air. Digestive acid stung its tongue as its saliva ducts tingled back into life. The Eldest drew a shaking breath through rows of shark's teeth, and the cold air was a catalyst to its senses. Its featureless eyes opened, and thick ropes of drool slivered down its chin, dangling from its maw to fall in hissing spittle-droplets on the decking.

After dragging itself from the confines of its hiding place, the Eldest set out through the ship in search of the creatures killing its children.

It smelled blood in the air, heard the rhythm of a prey's heart, and scented salty sweat on soft skin. More than this, it sensed the buzzing hum of living sentience, the brain's fleshy electricity of emotion and thought.

Life.
Human.
Near.

The Eldest clicked to itself with bladed mouth-parts, and leaned forward into a hungry run, bolting through the black passageways with its claws hammering on the metal.

Kin, it sent silently, *I come.*

VI

Lucoryphus and his team were not slowed down by the presence of a human or a tech-priest. Nor did they rely on lobotomised servitors to breach obstructions. Instead, several of Lucorphus's raptors were armed with meltaguns, breathing out searing surges of gaseous heat intense enough to liquidate the metal it blasted.

As a pack, the Bleeding Eyes – still growing used to their new designation of Ninth Claw – moved at far greater speed through the amalgamation of twisted ships. Unlike Talos and First Claw, Lucoryphus and his brothers had no specific target. They scouted, they stalked, they sought whatever of worth they could find.

And so far, that had been nothing at all.

The boredom was made bitter by the fact that had they been heading deeper in search of the conjoined Mechanicus vessel at the hulk's core, Lucoryphus was sure the Bleeding Eyes would have been there by now, and on their way back out.

Vox was increasingly erratic as Ninth Claw pressed ahead of their brothers, and Lucoryphus was fast losing patience with First Claw's progress. The initial hesitations had come from their human slave holding them back. Then their tech-adept had forced them to lag behind while he – while *it* – had demanded to bleed information from various databanks and memory tablets in the ships First Claw was cutting through.

'Vaporiser weapons,' Lucoryphus's hissing voice carried over the vox, 'Melta-class weapons. No cutting. No cutting servitors. Much faster.'

Talos's reply was punctuated by the dull juddering of bolters. 'Noted. Be aware, we've encountered an insignificant genestealer threat. Minimal numbers, at least in this section. What is your location?'

Lucoryphus led his pack onward, through spacious corridors, each of the raptors hunched and loping beast-like on all fours. The construction of these passageways was utterly familiar.

'Astartes ship, Standard Template Construct. Not ours. Throne slaves.'

601

'Understood. Any xenos presence?'

'Some. Few. All dead now.' The cylindrical engine housings on his back idled in disuse, occasionally coughing black smoke from vent slits. 'Moving to enginarium. Vessel still has partial power. Some lights bright. Some doors open. Ship not ancient like others. This is close to hulk's edge.'

'Understood.' More bolter fire, and the dim sounds of other Astartes cursing as Talos replied, 'These things are stunted and weak. They seem almost decrepit.'

'Genestealer xenos present for many decades. No prey, no strength. Beasts grow old, grow frail. Still deadly.'

'It's no struggle, yet.' The chatter of bolters began to die down. 'Report status every ten minutes.'

'Yes, prophet. I obey.'

On four claws, the once-human stalked on, his slanted eye lenses following the contours of the walls.

The corridor at last opened up into a large room, blissful in its dark silence, populated by towering generators and a wall-mounted plasma chamber that still – against all expectations – emitted a faint orange glow from the volatile cocktail of liquids and gases roiling in the glass chamber's depths.

Without needing orders, the raptors spread across the engine deck, moving to consoles and gantries, taking up firing positions to cover the room's exits. Several of the pack let their thrusters whine into life, boosting their way up to the higher platforms.

With difficulty, Lucoryphus fought down the urge to soar with them. Even in the confines of the ship's interior, he ached to leave the trudging discomfort of the ground behind.

Indulging a little, he cycled his turbines live with an effort as simple and natural as drawing breath. The kick of thrust carried him across the enginarium, to land in a neat crouch before the main power console. Eight dead servitors lay scattered around the controls, reduced to figures of bone and bionics.

One of Lucoryphus's best, Vorasha, was already at the console, his curving finger-talons clicking at the controls.

'Plasma chamber depleted,' Vorasha's voice slithered from his helm's snarling speaker-grille. 'The power has bled from the chamber over decades, yes-yes.'

'Restore it,' the raptor leader emphasised the order with a short, sharp sound somewhere between a shriek and a whisper. 'Do this now.'

Vorasha's talons clicked on keys and worked levers. 'I am not able to do this. Most of the vessel is lifeless. Can send power from section to section, yes-yes. With ease. Open bulkheads too dense to burn through fast. Cannot restore all power to all sections.'

Lucoryphus's reply came in a keening, aggrieved tone. 'Many redundant sections. Kill power in them. Then we move.'

'It will be done,' said Vorasha, and began to divert what little power remained in the ship's blood vessels, forcing it into the sections that the Bleeding Eyes raptors had to cross. At his estimate, Vorasha was going to be able to save them almost an hour of burning through locked bulkhead doors on their way through the ship.

'What is this ship?' Lucoryphus asked, his faceplate turned to the ceiling, seeking any indication of allegiance or identity.

The answer came from one of the others. Zon La found a body no more than ten seconds after his leader had asked the question. Armoured in green, it lay on the raised gantry deck above the enginarium floor, cut into pieces by the violence of xenos claws, it displayed its brotherhood all too clearly in the bronze dragon emblem across its breastplate.

'Eighteenth Legion,' the raptor hissed, recoiling in disgust. Zon La's tongue ached with the sudden need to spit his corrosive saliva onto the skeletal corpse.

Vorasha, linked to the ship's faded power core, turned to Lucoryphus. 'Power killed in redundant decks. Ship name is *Protean*, yes-yes, Eighteenth Legion.'

Lucoryphus chuckled behind his faceplate. The red eye lenses stared out, with scarlet and silver tears painted in twin trails down his cheeks. It was a visage shared by all his bothers in the Bleeding Eyes. Each of them watched the world through helms with slanted eyes and cried tears of quicksilver and crimson.

'Salamanders. We killed so many in the Old War. Amazed any still draw breath.'

'Wait-wait,' Vorasha never really talked – he hissed and clicked in place of true speech, but the other raptors could make out the words from his broken language with ease. 'I sense others. I hear others nearby.'

Lucoryphus was as tense as his brothers, head tilted slightly as he listened with hearing preternatural by human standards.

He had heard it, too. Weapon fire.

'Salamanders,' Zon La rasped. 'Still alive on ship.'

Lucoryphus was already making his ungainly way to the double doors that led deeper into the ship's decks.

'Not for long. Nine of you, remain with Vorasha. Nine more, with me.'

XARL AND UZAS, both warriors of First Claw, sprayed the hallway with suppressive fire, bolters kicking in clenched fists. Uzas's field of fire was random, chewing down whichever alien beast drew his attention each particular second. Xarl was all controlled aggression, bolts punching home into the skulls of the closest aliens and crippling those that sought to rise again.

Both of them picked up the crackling declaration from Talos, and both were equally infuriated. The Bleeding Eyes, several hours deeper in the amalgamated hulk, had encountered loyalist Astartes.

Salamanders.

Too far away – far too far – for First Claw to reach them. Talos ordered his brothers to maintain the guardianship of Deltrian and purge the corridors of alien threats.

Xarl concentrated his anger into a killing urge, drawing his chainsword and tearing left and right, weaving wounds among the genestealers that reached the embattled warriors. Uzas, never one for subtlety or self-discipline, howled his bitterness through the uncaring hallways and tore into the aliens with his bolter, his chainblade, and even his bare hands.

'Lucoryphus, this is Talos.'

'No words now. Hunting.'

'Assess the enemy threat first. Do not engage without assured victory.'

'*Coward!*'

'We have the *Echo of Damnation* in the void nearby, fool. We can cripple their ship in space and deploy boarding bods at our leisure. Do not engage without assured victory. We do not have the strength here to face down Terminators.'

No reply came, except for the rabid charging of hand-claws and foot-talons on metal decking.

Talos exhaled slowly. It left his helm's vox-speakers as a daemonic rasp. This was not going to plan.

His standing orders for the strike cruiser had been to power down and activate the Shriek if any Imperial vessels came into the system. There was little chance the Salamanders' ship had detected and destroyed the *Echo*, but Talos was far from sanguine. Deltrian was taking too long, and Lucoryphus, as always, was an uncontrollable element.

'First Claw to *Echo of Damnation*.'

'...cr... s... aw...'

The vox was still worthless. They'd have to get back to the hulk's outer layers to restore contact.

'Deltrian,' Talos voxed, 'status report.'

VII

The eldest rounded a corner, clinging to the walls with claws that crunched purchase in the arched, ancient steel. It didn't slow down, not even for a fraction of a heartbeat. Burning saliva stung its jaws as it drooled down its chin.

Prey.

Two. Ahead.

The Eldest leaped over the bodies of fallen kin, moving its headlong dash to the ceiling as it tore forward, still not slowing in its stride. Claws ripped handholds in the corridor's roof with vicious speed. Bodily, it shoved its lesser kin aside, bashing through those tall enough to obstruct its passage. In better times, their links to the Eldest's own mind would have sent them scurrying aside respectfully, sensing their lord's approach.

'Reloading.' Mercutian dropped to one knee and ejected a spent ammunition belt from the massive heavy bolter.

At his side, Cyrion took aim with his own weapon, and the corridor echoed with the familiar *judda-judda-judda* of a bolter letting loose on full auto.

'Reload faster.'

'Keep shooting,' Mercutian snarled.

'It's on the damn ceiling...'

'*Keep shooting.*'

Beneath and around, the hard bodies of its kin were shattering and bursting under the prey's defences. The prey ahead – two of them – unleashed a sickening stream of burning anger that blasted the Eldest's kin apart.

The heated projectiles began to crash against the Eldest's skin.

It suddenly remembered what pain felt like.

* * *

MERCUTIAN BUCKLED THE ammo feed into place and lifted his heavy bolter again. It took three awful seconds to power up again, then its internal mechanisms clunked into life.

An instant's glance saw Cyrion's bolter fire laying waste to the weaker creatures, but the huge beast was shrieking its way through a volley of bolter fire, still sprinting across the ceiling, eating up the metres between them.

He didn't rise to his feet. Remaining where he was, he pulled the trigger handle and felt his armour's stabilisers kick in to compensate for the cannon's recoil.

The heavy bolter shook as it disgorged a stream of high-velocity explosive bolts, each one pounding chunks of chitinous meat from the creature's exoskeletal flesh.

As the twelfth bolt struck home, the beast fell from the ceiling, plunging into the seething mass of lesser creatures below. Mercutian lowered his aim, and let his cannon chew into them next.

THE ELDEST SMELLED its own blood, and this was somehow more shocking than the pain of its burst-open, bleeding wounds. The scent overpowered the wounds of its kin, eclipsing them in richness and potency.

The lord-creature drew in its damaged limbs, curling them close to its body. It had misjudged the prey. The prey was fierce. The prey could not be battled as equals, but must be stalked as meat to be hunted.

This was the Way. The Eldest's hunger had blinded it to the Way, but the pain of its mistake served as the most forceful of reminders.

Hunched and defeated but utterly devoid of shame, the Eldest tore its way back down the passageway, slaying its own kin in its need to retreat from the prey.

Minutes later, in the silent darkness again, it uncurled its wounded limbs, waiting for the blood to stop flowing.

A single thought-pulse screamed noiselessly through the decks above and below. More of its kin spread across the hive, weakened by hunger themselves, uncoiled and rose from their own states of near-slumber.

The Eldest moved away, seeking to come at the prey alone next time, and with greater patience.

MERCUTIAN LOWERED THE heavy bolter and sank back against the wall. Cyrion locked his bolter to his thigh, and drew a pistol and chainblade.

At last, the corridor was mercifully quiet. Occasionally, a dead alien would twitch.

'Talos, this is Cyrion.'

'Speak,' the prophet's voice crackled back over the vox.

'Area secure for now. Be warned, one of these genestealers is huge. Mercutian hit it dead-on with enough bolts to burst a daemon and it just howled and ran away. I swear by our father's name, it sounded like the bastard thing was laughing as it went. We're falling back to the irritating tech-priest now.'

'Understood. Deltrian insists this is the right ship. He has breached the starboard data storage pod. At last.'

'So it's a Titan-carrier?'

'It was. It looks like more of a xenos hive now. A nest of genestealers on the edge of starvation.'

'It would be pleasant to know we hadn't wasted a great deal of time in coming here.'

'That,' Talos laughed, 'would mean that something went right for once.' The link went silent.

A dead genestealer shivered no more than seven metres away from where Cyrion was standing. It was the creature at the head of the destroyed alien wave that had broken just shy of reaching the two Night Lords. Cyrion blew its head apart with a single shot from his bolt pistol.

Mercutian hauled himself to his feet with a grunt. 'I can see why the Throne sends Terminators into these places.'

THE ELDEST LOPED through the dark tunnels, its crouched run taking it along walls and ceilings without a thought. Deeper into the hive it ran, ever deeper, moving around the prey that reeked of strange metal and powdery fire. They were strong, and the Eldest was weaker than it had ever been before. It needed to feed on easier prey to regain its strength.

And there was other prey. The Eldest could still smell it, even over the reek of its own wounds.

The other prey-scent was salt-blooded and strong, and it was this meal that the Eldest sought with patient intent.

The armoured prey were defending it, though. They encircled it, blocking off passageways and lying in wait, ready to inflict more pain. The Eldest had to avoid them, clawing and crawling through the tightest spaces and ripping new tunnels in the hive's steel walls.

As it ran and tore and leaped and ripped, it could sense-hear more of its kin rising from their slumbers.

It came, at last, to an expansive section of the territory claimed by its kin, where few of its cousin creatures dwelled. The human prey was here, hiding in this immense chamber.

The Eldest unfolded its wounded limbs again. The blood no longer flowed. True regeneration might come in time. For now, a cessation of leakage and pain was enough.

In the darkness, the Eldest drooled and moved forward once more. Something primal and instinctive opened within its mind, and an unheard shriek tremored out through the ship.

Its kin must be summoned.

* * *

SEPTIMUS WATCHED THE servitors working in the chamber. Occasionally, his breath would mist the visor of his atmosphere suit, but when it cleared the scene was much the same: the bionic slaves were loading up with heavy cogitator memory pods and strapping them to their backs. Deltrian, the robed tech-adept, monitored their activity from beside the main console in a room full of stilled monitors and data processors.

Thousands of years before, this had been the heart of a Mechanicus warship, carrying Titans and enhanced soldiers across the stars. In this very room, tech-priests had worked their esoteric trade, storing the information of countless crusades, the gun camera footage of hundreds of battlefields, the countless vox transmissions from generations of Titan commanders and infantry officers, and most vital of all, the code-keys, voice imprints and encryption ciphers of the Titan Legion to whom this ship had once belonged.

All of it added up to what the skeletal tech-adept had come for: the chance to lay claim to a million secrets of the Cult Mechanicus. Such lore was worth any risk. Its potential uses were infinite in the Old War against the false Emperor and the dregs of the True Mechanicum that still lingered, gasping and ignorant, on the surface of Great Mars.

Yet it had been difficult to persuade the Night Lords of the necessity, of the possibilities on offer. They had been lured in with the temptation of potential scavenging. It was a crude compromise by the tech-priest's reasoning. Insofar as Deltrian was able to emulate human emotion anymore, he had a degree of regard for the warriors of the VIII Legion, but he mourned their lack of vision in regards to the lore he sought here.

Still, they were always reliably earnest in pursuit of piracy. He'd played to that predilection.

'Did you hear that?' Septimus asked, his breath audible over the vox. 'First Claw has engaged some kind of huge creature.'

Deltrian diverted an insignificant portion of his attention to replying. 'Corporaptor Primus.'

'What?'

The human's voice patterns indicated the confusion of misunderstanding, rather than not hearing correctly. Deltrian emitted an irritated spurt of static from his vocabulator – the closest he could come to a sigh.

'Corporaptor Primus. The patriarch of a genestealer brood. The alpha, apex predator.'

'How do you kill something like that?'

'We do not. If it finds us, we die. Now cease vocalisation. I am engaged in focused activity.'

Deltrian enjoyed another three minutes of relative silence, then the muffled clanking of distant footsteps, far too fast to be human, far too soft to be Astartes, echoed through the console as the adept worked. The distant tread vibrated the panels – the tremors imperceptible to a mortal, but registering on the sensitive pads of the tech-adept's metal fingers.

He spared a moment of his concentration to send a short burst of digital code to display written Gothic text across First Claw's visor displays:

```
GENESTEALER THREAT HAS BREACHED PERIMETER.
MY WORK IS AT A SENSITIVE STAGE.
```

WITH THIS TASK completed in less than the time it would take a human heart to beat, Deltrian continued working, entering numerical crack-keys to pierce the cogitator console's encoded information locks. He was close now, close to being able to bleed the console's memory banks, and loathed the fact a distraction would soon arrive.

VIII

THE BLEEDING EYES crouched in wait – gargoyles of ceramite with twisted faces rendered into silent howls. The tunnels here were wider, freer, with ceilings sporting secondary decking and mazes of overhead cables. It was on these decks, and among these dense cables serving the low-power ship as veins, that the Bleeding Eyes waited.

Beneath them, their prey had taken the bait. The green-armoured warrior in bulky Terminator plate stomped without a hint of grace, pounding his way through the corridors, firing at shadows and suggestions of foes with his underslung rotator cannon. Something was wrong, though. From their perches, the Night Lords listened to the Throne-loyal Astartes admonishing enemies that did not exist, evidently fighting a battle that had naught to do with the present. Burning holes streaked the walls where the cannon's stream of fire pitted the metal in long bursts of anger.

The Bleedings Eyes shared muted vox-chuckles and stared down at the deluded warrior. He was clearly afflicted by an amusing madness.

And yet... he *had* taken the bait. Shar Gan still led the Terminator on, appearing at junctions and corners, offering the flash of dark armour and screeching through his helm's vox-speakers. Whatever the Salamander believed he was seeing, he stiff gave relentless chase to Shar Gan, paying no heed to the Raptors crawling several metres above him, making their way on all fours across decking and power cables.

Only when Lucoryphus had deemed they'd come far enough, did they spring the trap.

'Seal the doors,' their leader hissed. Both bulkheads slammed closed, cutting the corridor off from the rest of the ship. At a distant control console elsewhere on the ship, Vorasha and the second team of Bleeding Eyes were laughing.

In the corridor below, the Terminator halted, retaining enough sense to realise it was trapped. The warrior looked up at last, as ten chainblades revved into snarling life.

Lucoryphus was closest, leading half the Bleeding Eyes, clinging the decking, the overhead cabling, even the walls and ceiling. The leader whispered into the vox, a moment before his Raptors pounced.

'Kill him.'

TALOS ENTERED THE data storage chamber. Gravity had been restored in this area of the Mechanicus ship, and with the recommencement of gravity came the reintroduction of an artificial atmosphere. The ship automatically sealed off the voided sections with bulkheads.

The restoration of air also brought a new aspect to this curious hunt. Sound had returned. It was unwelcome – the inner workings of the storage modules rattled and clanked like the engine of some struggling vehicle. Pistons hammered within the cogitators' innards. Talos had no desire to know why the archaic storage machinery required such moving parts, and the sound – in the six minutes since air had been restored by Deltrian's servitors – was growing steadily more irritating.

Variel had reached the chamber a few minutes before the prophet. As Talos entered, the newest member of First Claw nodded in greeting, but said nothing.

Variel's armour showed his newfound allegiance, but lacked much of the ornamentation worn by his brothers. On his pauldrons, instead of the VIII Legion's fanged skull flanked by daemon wings, Variel's insignia displayed a clawed fist rendered in black ceramite, broken by ritual hammering.

On Variel's left arm, his vambrace was a converted narthecium unit, containing liquid nitrogen storage pods, flesh drills, bone saws and surgical lasers. While his faceplate no longer bore the white paint of an Apothecary, he still carried the tools of his specialised craft. Instead of human skulls hanging from chains on his armour, Variel's war-plate was decorated in the sleek, elegant skulls of slain eldar. It was these differences, subtle but significant, that set him apart from the others of First Claw.

Both Talos and Variel clutched their bolters, barely watching Deltrian work, instead focusing their attentions around the spacious chamber and the rows of blank cogitator screens.

Septimus hadn't removed his helmet, even with breathable air restored. He walked closer to Talos, casting a sidelong glance at the busy tech-priest.

'Master,' he voxed to the towering Astartes.

Talos spared Septimus a momentary look. The slave's long hair, lank with sweat, was tied into a scruffy ponytail. The bionic portions of his face were glinting with reflection from the overhead lights – well-maintained and clean.

'Septimus. Be ready. The xenos are near.'

The Legion serf didn't ask how everyone but him seemed to know what was coming. He was long used to his all too human senses rendering him disadvantaged in the company of the warriors he still instinctively referred to as demigods.

'Master, why did you bring me here?'

Talos appeared to be watching a distant, shadowed wall.

'Master?'

'Why do you ask?' the warrior said, still paying little attention. 'You have never questioned your duty before.'

'I seek only to understand my place and role.'

Talos moved away, bolter at the ready. The Night Lord's mouth grille emitted a vox-distorted snarl. Septimus tensed, and didn't follow.

'I sense your fear. You are not here as bait. Remain sanguine. We will keep you alive.'

'Deltrian suggested otherwise.'

'We might be here for days, Septimus. If our armour needed repairing, I wanted you at hand to do your duty.'

Days...? Days?

'That long, master?'

There was a series of clicks as Talos changed to a limited vox channel, between himself and his slave. 'In respect for our honoured tech-adept, I will not say that Deltrian works slowly. I will alter the description, citing instead that he works meticulously. But you are not dense, Septimus. You know what he is like.'

Yes, but still... 'Master, could this really take days?'

'I sincerely hope not. It has already taken long enough. If the --'

'*Soul Hunter.*'

Talos swore softly, and in Nostraman the curse came out like gentle poetry. The voice coming over the vox was harsh, almost screeching. Lucoryphus's blood was up, and it filtered into his voice with astonishing clarity.

'Acknowledged, Lucoryphus.'

'Too many of them.'

'Confirm xenos sightings in–'

'Not the aliens! Bastard sons of Vulkan! Two full teams. They kill and kill. Nine Bleeding Eyes are dead. Nine to never rise again. Nine of twenty!'

'Be calm, brother.' Talos bit back the urge to rail at the Raptor leader for his accursed vainglory. Such idiocy had cost nine lives in a battle that could never have been won without patience and caution that the Bleeding Eyes utterly lacked.

Letting them slip the leash had been a mistake.

'I go now to Vorasha,' Lucoryphus hissed. 'We slaughter them all this time.'

'Enough. Will you fall back now? Will you wait until we regroup on the ship and strike from the void?'

'But the–'

'*Enough.* Fall back to your second team and abandon the *Protean.* Return to First Claw and we will make ready to leave. Let the Throne's slaves scurry around for their own salvage.'

'Understood.'

'Lucoryphus. Confirm your intentions.'

'Will fall back. Find Vorasha. Return to First Claw.'

'Good.' Talos terminated the vox-link, swallowing a mouthful of bitter, acidic saliva. Not for the first time, and not for the last, he reflected that he loathed the duties of command.

LUCORYPHUS CAST THE meltagun aside, letting it clatter to the deck. He wouldn't be needing it again. The thrusters on his back still streamed thin smoke from coolant vents, powering down after the sudden boost necessary to send him up into the ceiling in order to escape the chattering storm bolters of the Salamanders' elite warriors.

With the meltagun – a weapon stolen from the twitching corpse of Shar Gan – he had seared a whole in the ceiling and escaped onto the next deck.

He'd been hit himself. With a cracked breastplate, Lucoryphus could feel his armour's strength depleted, some vital power feeds cut by explosive bolter fire.

Bipedal walking was an awkward trial even when uninjured, so Lucoryphus crawled as he'd become accustomed, all four claws finding tight purchase on the gantry floor.

He moved with unnerving speed, though it hurt to do so.

'Vorasha...' his lips were wet with blood. The pain of his wounds was an irritant, but no more than that.

'Yes-yes,' the vox distortion was savage now. Lucorphus's war-plate was in worse shape than he'd first thought. His visor kept fuzzing with static at inconvenient moments.

'Orders are to return to First Claw.'

'I heard this,' Vorasha replied. 'I will obey.'

'Wait.'

'Wait?'

'More Salamanders than we first saw. Many more. Find xenos nests. Awaken aliens. Lead aliens to Salamanders. Both enemies fight, both enemies die. Vengeance for Bleeding Eyes.'

Vorasha's reply was a serpentine snigger, *Ss-ss-ss.*

'*Go now!*' Lucoryphus screeched. '*Lead xenos to Salamanders!*'

IX

With a moist *snick!* the membranes covering the Eldest's sensitive eyes peeled back. It looked down the long chamber, seeing telltale suggestions of flickering movement. The human-scent was stronger now. So much stronger.

The Eldest stalked forward, claws scraping on the metal floor. Two of the more dangerous prey-breed, those with the hammering weapons of punching fire, had entered the chamber. Though the Eldest's bestial intelligence did not count them capable of slaying the creature, it had learned its lesson well. This was not a hunt to make alone.

From its place of hiding in the shadows, The Eldest had been screaming in silence for some time. Its kin were coming, dozens upon dozens of them, coming through the tunnels and chambers nearby.

It would be enough to overwhelm even the most dangerous prey.

'I see it,' Talox voxed.

He stared into the darkness, looking away into the six hundred metres of shadowed chamber to the north. 'It emerged from the wall a moment ago.'

'I see it, too.' This, from Variel. He approached Talos and hefted his bolter, his thermal sight easily piercing the gloom. 'Blood of the Emperor, Mercutian wasn't lying.'

'A Broodlord,' the prophet murmured, watching the hideous alien – all chitinous limbs, clawed appendages and bulbous skull – creep closer. 'An immense one. Fire when it reaches optimal range. Avoid damage to the wall cogitators.'

'Compliance,' Variel said, and Talos could still hear the edge of reluctance in the newcomer's tone. His fall from grace and induction into the VIII Legion was still both fresh and bitter.

Talos raised his bolter, sighting through the targeter and drawing breath to summon the others. The vox chose that moment to erupt in sounds of gunfire and Nostraman curses. All of First Claw were engaged, flooded by waves of the weakened beasts.

The others evidently had their own problems.

On Talos's red-tinted visor, a proximity rune turned white. In the very same moment, Talos and Variel opened fire.

DELTRIAN'S FINGERS BLURRED as they tapped keys, pushed levers and adjusted dials. The locking code obscuring the information he desired was remarkably complex, and forced a degree of instrument adjustment even as his personally designed crack-keys did their work in the cogitator's programming. This was not an unexpected development, but it necessitated a division of attention that the tech-adept found galling. Added to the annoyance, the firefight fifty metres to his left was a raucous irritation, for bolters were hardly quiet weapons, and the Corporaptor Primus – a breed of xenos Deltrian had never witnessed firsthand – howled endlessly as it endured the process of being blown apart by explosive rounds.

The *crack-crack, crack-crack* of Septmus's laspistols joined the throaty chatter of boltgun fire, forming a curious percussion.

Almost... *Almost....*

Deltrian emitted a bleat of machine code from his vocabulator, the sound emerging as a tinny and flat pulse to anyone untrained in comprehending such a unique language. It was as close to a cheer as he had come in many years.

Sixteen separate memory tablets slid from the main cogitator's data sockets. Each one was the approximate size and shape of a human palm. Each contained a century of recorded lore, right back to the ship's founding decades.

And each was priceless – an artefact of unrivalled possibility.

'It is done,' the tech-adept said, and began to gather the data slates, apparently unaware that no one was paying him any heed at all.

He turned to the melee in time to see the alien beast, its body a mess of burst wounds and both ovoid eyes left as ragged, fluid-weeping craters, cleave Variel's leg at the knee with one of its few remaining limbs. A scythe of blackened bone, its bladed edge cracked and bleeding, chopped down in a lethal arc.

Ceramite armour shattered. The Astartes went down, his leg severed, and still he fired up at the horror drawing closer to slay him.

The death blow came from Talos. His armour a broken mess of claw-chopped metal plating, the prophet took another flailing limb strike to the side of the head in order to risk coming close enough to use his power sword. Lightning trembled along the golden blade as it sparked into life, even as the genestealer hive patriarch clashed a half-amputated sword-limb against the Night Lord's helm. White-painted shards of his faceplate tore free, scattering across the metal decking like hailstones.

Talos was close enough now. With half of his face laid bare and bleeding from the creature's last blow, he rammed the relic sword into the beast's spine, plunging it two-handed through exoskeletal armour, toughened subdermal muscle flesh, and finally into vulnerable meat and severable bone.

A twist, a wrench, a curse, and a pull. He sawed the sword left and right, foul-smelling and discoloured blood welling up from the widening wound.

The alien shrieked again, acidic ichor spraying from its damaged teeth to rain upon Variel's armour in hissing droplets. Talos gave his golden blade a final wrenching pull, and the beast's head came free.

The creature collapsed. It twitched once or twice, the savage wounds across its body leaking sour fluids as well as dark blood. The smell, Septimus would later tell other slaves back aboard the ship, was somewhere between a charnel house and a butcher's shop left open to the sun for a month.

Variel's armour was pockmarked gunmetal grey where the corrosive juices from the beast's maw scored away his war-plate's paint. His severed leg wasn't bleeding – the coagulants in Astartes blood were already working to seal the wound and scab it over. Any pain was dulled by his armour's narcotic injectors dispensing stimulants and pain suppressors into his bloodstream.

Yet he growled a curse as he dragged himself away from the stilled beast, and swore in a language only he understood. Deltrian analysed the linguistic pattern. It was most likely a dialect of Badab – a tongue from Variel's homeworld. The details were irrelevant.

Talos's suit of armour was almost entirely stripped of colour, the acids and burning blood having blistered the ceramite and scorched the dark paint away. He regarded the creature's steaming body, with half of his face visible due to the damage he'd taken to his helm.

The tech-adept saw the prophet scowl, and fire another bolter shell into the dead alien's severed head. What remained of the genestealer's skull vanished in an explosion of wet fragments that clacked off the walls, the floor, and Talos's own armour.

Septimus looked on, catching his breath. He knew repairing and repainting both of these ancient suits of battleplate was going to be a time-consuming process. He felt it was to his credit that he didn't say so here, and busied himself holstering his Guard-issue laspistols, before leaning against the wall.

Deltrian watched this scene for exactly four point two seconds.

'I said, "it is done"'. He couldn't keep the rising impatience from his tone. 'May we leave now?'

X

WHEN THE *Echo of Damnation* pulled away from the hulk, the Shriek fell silent as plasma contrails misted the void behind the ship. Engines running, breathing the mist into space, the *Echo* tore away from the vast amalgamation of forgotten ships.

On the command throne, his armour still a grey and cracked ruin, Talos watched to the occulus. It showed a slice of deep space – no more, no less.

'How long ago did they leave the system?' he asked. These were the first words he had uttered since returning and taking the throne. The answer came from one of the ageing human officers, still in his Imperial Navy uniform, albeit stripped of the Emperor's insignia.

'Just over two hours, my lord. The Salamander vessel was running dangerously hot. We think the Shriek unnerved them – they broke orbit and ran, rather than seek the signal's source.'

'They did not find the ship?'

'They barely even looked, my lord. They withdrew their boarding teams and fled.'

Talos shook his head. 'The sons of Vulkan are placid and slow, but they are Astartes and know no fear. Whatever sent them crawling from the system was a matter of grave import.'

'As you say, my lord. What are your orders?'

Talos snorted. 'Two hours is not an insurmountable head-start. Follow them. Make ready all Claws. Once we catch them, we will tear them from the warp and pick apart the bones of their ship.'

'Compliance, master.'

The prophet allowed his eyes to drift closed as the ship rumbled into activity around him.

He wanted to let his wrath fall upon Deltrian. More than that, and more difficult to admit, he wanted to *kill* Deltrian.

But given the results of the mission...

'Damn him,' the prophet breathed.

* * *

THE HALL OF reflection housed what few relics remained to the warriors of Talos's warband. In more glorious eras, such a chamber would have been a haven for prayer, for purification through meditation, and to witness the Legion's history through the weapons and armour once borne and worn by its heroes.

Now, it served as something not quite a workshop, and not quite a graveyard. Deltrian was lord of the chamber, and his will and word were law. Servitors worked at various stations, repairing pieces of armour, replacing the teeth-tracks of fouled chainswords, forging new bolter shells and creating the explosive innards.

And here, in ritually-preserved stasis fields, the ornate sarcophagi of fallen warriors were mounted on marble pedestals, awaiting the moment they would be mounted in the bodies of Dreadnoughts and sent to war once more. Several fluid-filled suspension tanks bubbled away, most empty – in need of flushing and scrubbing – and a few occupied by naked figures rendered indistinct by the milky, oxygen-rich amniotic fluids.

Deltrian had returned to his sanctum several minutes before, and was already inserted the data tablets into the sockets of his own cogitators, to drain the lore onto his own memory banks. The doors to the Hall of Reflection remained open. Deltrian allowed the data transfer to occur unwatched, and instead waited for the guests he was expecting.

At last, they arrived. Twelve warriors, in a ragged line. Each of the dozen Astartes showed signs of recent and grievous battle. Each of them had survived a harrowing six further hours on board the hulk, fending off genestealers and hunting the accursed creatures back to their nests.

The Salamanders had done an admirable job in their purging, but had still lost a total of six warriors on board the *Protean*, thanks to the efforts of Vorasha and the Bleeding Eyes diverting wave after wave of xenos beasts into their section of the ship.

Six souls lost, six warriors fallen. It did not seem many, on the surface of things. The Night Lords had lost fourteen – all of them from the Bleeding Eyes. Lucoryphus seemed untroubled.

'The weak fall, the strong rise,' he'd said as they boarded the *Echo of Damnation*. Deltrian observed that this was as close to philosophy as the degenerate warrior had ever come. The Bleeding Eyes leader had no reply to that.

Deltrian watched the twelve Astartes enter the Hall of Reflection now. Each pair carried a great weight between them: the broken bodies of armoured Salamander warriors. One of the butchered warriors was carved with both surgical precision and gleeful brutality, slain by the Bleeding Eyes and earning the ignoble honour of being the first to fall. The others showed a vicious spread of genestealer wounds: punctured breastplates, sundered limb guards, crushed helms.

But nothing, Deltrian mused, *that would be irreparable.*

The Night Lords arranged the bodies on the mosaic-inlaid floor. Six dead Salamanders. Six dead Salamanders in Terminator war-plate, complete with storm bolters, power weapons and a rare assault rotator cannon – practically unseen amongst the Traitor Legions, who were forced to wage war with scavenged equipment and ancient weaponry.

This haul, this sacred bounty in the blessed Machine-God's name, was worth infinitely more than the lives of fourteen Night Lords. Deltrian caressed the draconic emblem of the Salamanders Chapter, embossed in black stone on one dead warrior's pauldron. Such markings could be stripped, the armour itself modified and refashioned... the machine-spirits turned bitter and of more use to the VIII Legion.

Let the Night Lords spit and curse for now. He could see it in their black eyes; each one of them recognised the value of this haul, and each one hoped to be one of the elite few ordained to wear this holy armour once it was profaned and made ready.

Fourteen lives in exchange for the secrets of a Titan Legion and six suits of the most powerful armour created by mankind.

Deltrian always smiled, for that was how his skullish face was formed. Now, however, as he regarded his newfound riches, the expression was sincere.

VOID STALKER

'I have seen a time when the Imperium can no longer breathe.
When Man's empire chokes on its own corruption,
Poisoned by the filth and sin of five hundred deluded generations.

On that night, when madness becomes truth,
The Gate of Cadia will break open like an infected wound,
And the legions of the damned will spill into the kingdom they
created.

In this age at the end of all things,
Born of forbidden blood and fate's own foul humour,
Will rise the Prophet of the Eighth Legion.'

– 'The Crucible Premonition'

Recorded by an unknown VIII Legion sorcerer, M32

PROLOGUE
RAIN

THE PROPHET AND the murderess stood on the battlements of the dead citadel, weapons in their hands. Rain slashed in a miserable flood, thick enough to obscure vision, hissing against the stone even as it ran from the mouths of leering gargoyles, draining down the castle's sides. Above the rain, the only audible sounds came from the two figures: one human, standing in broken armour that thrummed with static crackles; the other an alien maiden in ancient and contoured war-plate, weathered by an eternity of scarring.

'This is where your Legion died, isn't it?' Her voice was modulated by the helm she wore, emerging from the death mask's open mouth with a curious sibilance that almost melted into the rain. 'We call this world *Shithr Vejruhk*. What is it in your serpent's tongue? *Tsagualsa*, yes? Answer me this, prophet. Why would you come back here?'

The prophet didn't answer. He spat acidic blood onto the dark stone floor, and drew in another ragged breath. The sword in his hands was a cleaved ruin, its shattered blade severed halfway along its length. He didn't know where his bolter was, and a smile crept across his split lips as he felt an instinctive tug of guilt. It was surely a sin to lose such a Legion relic.

'Talos.' The maiden smiled as she spoke, he could hear it in her voice. Her amusement was remarkable if only for the absence of mockery and malice. 'Do not be ashamed, human. Everyone dies.'

The prophet sank to one knee, blood leaking from the cracks in his armour. His attempt at speech left his lips as a grunt of pain. The only thing he could smell was the copper stench of his own injuries.

The maiden came closer, even daring to rest the scythe-bladed tip of her spear on the wounded warrior's shoulder guard.

'I speak only the truth, prophet. There's no shame in this moment. You have done well to even make it this far.'

Talos spat blood again, and hissed two words.

627

'*Valas Morovai.*'

The murderess tilted her head as she looked down at him. Her helm's crest of black and red hair was dreadlocked by the rain, plastered to her death mask. She looked like a woman sinking into water, shrieking silently as she drowned.

'Many of your bitter whisperings remain occluded to me,' she said. 'You speak... "First Claw", yes?' Her unnatural accent struggled with the words. 'They were your brothers? You call out to the dead, in the hopes they will yet save you?'

The blade fell from his grip, too heavy to hold any longer. He stared at it lying on the black stone, bathed in the downpour, silver and gold shining as clean as the day he'd stolen it.

Slowly, he lifted his head, facing his executioner. Rain showered the blood from his face, salty on his lips, stinging his eyes. He wondered if she was still smiling behind the mask.

On his knees, atop the battlements of his Legion's deserted fortress, the Night Lord started laughing.

Neither his laughter nor the storm above were loud enough to swallow the throaty sound of burning thrusters. A gunship – blue-hulled and blackly sinister – bellowed its way into view. As it rose above the battlements, rain sluiced from its avian hull in silver streams. Heavy bolter turrets aligned in a chorus of mechanical grinding, the sweetest music ever to grace the prophet's ears. Talos was still laughing as the Thunderhawk hovered in place, riding its own heat haze, with the dim lighting of the cockpit revealing two figures within.

The alien maiden was already moving. She became a black blur, dancing through the rain in a velvet sprint. Detonations clawed at her heels as the gunship opened fire, shredding the stone at her feet in a hurricane of explosive rounds.

One moment she fled across the parapets, the next she simply ceased to exist, vanishing into shadow.

Talos didn't rise to his feet, uncertain he'd manage it if he tried. He closed the only eye he had left. The other was a blind and bleeding orb of irritating pain, sending dull throbs back into his skull each time his two hearts beat. His bionic hand, shivering with joint glitches and flawed neural input damage, reached to activate the vox at his collar.

'I will listen to you, next time.'

Above the overbearing whine of downward thrusters, a voice buzzed over the gunship's external vox-speakers. Distortion stole all trace of tone and inflection.

'*If we don't disengage now, there won't be a next time.*'

'I told you to leave. I ordered it.'

'*Master,*' the external vox-speakers crackled back. '*I...*'

'Go, damn you.'

When he next glanced at the gunship, he could see the two figures more clearly. They sat side by side, in the pilots' thrones. 'You are formally discharged from my service.' He slurred the words as he voxed them, and started laughing again. 'For the second time.'

The gunship stayed aloft, engines giving out their horrendous whine, blasting hot air across the battlements.

The voice rasping over the vox was female this time. *'Talos.'*

'Run. Run far from here, and all the death this world offers. Flee to the last city, and catch the next vessel off-world. The Imperium is coming. They will be your salvation. But remember what I said. We are all slaves to fate. If Variel escapes this madness alive, he will come for the child one night, no matter where you run.'

'He might never find us.'

Talos's laughter finally faded, though he kept the smile. 'Pray that he doesn't.'

He drew in a knifing breath as he slumped with his back to the battlements, grunting at the stabs from his ruined lungs and shattered ribs. Grey drifted in from the edge of his vision, and he could no longer feel his fingers. One hand rested on his cracked breastplate, upon the ritually broken aquila, polished by the rain. The other rested on his fallen bolter, Malcharion's weapon, on its side from where he'd dropped it in the earlier battle. With numb hands, the prophet locked the double-barrelled bolter to his thigh, and took another slow pull of cold air into lungs that no longer wanted to breathe. His bleeding gums turned his teeth pink.

'I'm going after her.'

'Don't be a fool.'

Talos let the rain drench his upturned face. Strange, how a moment's mercy let them believe they could talk to him like that. He hauled himself to his feet, and started walking across the black stone battlements, a broken blade in hand.

'She killed my brothers,' he said. 'I'm going after her.'

PART ONE

THE CARRION WORLD

I
THE LONGEST DREAM

*'Because we are brothers. We've seen primarchs die to blade and fire,
and we've seen our actions set the galaxy aflame. We've betrayed
others and been betrayed in kind. We're bleeding for an uncertain
future, fighting a war for the lies our lords tell us. What do we have
left, if not blood's loyalty? I am here because you are here. Because
we are brothers.'*

– Jago Sevatarion, 'Sevatar', the Prince of Crows
As quoted in *The Tenebrous Path*, chapter VI. Unity

THE PROPHET'S EYES snapped open, bleaching his vision with the monochrome red of his tactical display. The familiarity was a comfort after the
madness of the dream. This was how he'd seen the world around him
for most of his life, and the dancing target locks following his gaze were
a welcome extension of natural sight.

Already, the nightmare fled before him, elusive and thread-thin, unrav-
elling as he sought to hold onto it. Rain on the battlements. An alien
swordswoman. A gunship, shooting up the black stone.

No. It was gone. Shadows remained, images and sensations, nothing
more.

That was happening more often, recently. The visions refused to stick
with any tenacity, whereas once they'd melded to his memory. It seemed
to be a side effect of their increasing frequency, though with no understanding of his gift's genesis and function, he had no way of knowing
the truth of the matter.

Talos rose from where he'd collapsed on the floor of his modest arming
chamber and stood in silence, tensing his muscles, bunching them and
rolling his neck, restoring circulation and checking the interface feeds of
his armour. The ceramite suit of layered war-plate – some of it ancient
and unique, some of it plundered much more recently – whirred and
growled in rhythm with his movements.

He moved slowly, carefully, feeling the quivering strain of muscles too long locked. Cramps played along his limbs, all except his augmetic arm, which responded sluggishly, its internal processors only now realigning with the impulses from his waking mind. The bionic limb was still the first section of his body to come back into full obedience, despite its halting sphere of motion. He used it, the iron hand gripping at the wall, to haul himself to his feet. Armour joints snarled at even these minor motions.

The pain was waiting for him back in the waking world. It crashed against him now, the same torture that always spiked through his blood like a toxin. He murmured breathless, defiant syllables behind his face-plate, uncaring how the words were vox-growled to the empty chamber.

The dream. Were they destined to be deceived, or destined to be the deceivers? Fate often played them the latter hand. The Exalted had said the words so many times: *Betray before you are betrayed.*

No matter how he reached for the dream, it dispersed ever further. The pain wasn't helping. It flooded back as if filling the hole in his memory. On several occasions in the past, the pain had been severe enough to leave him blind for entire nights. This eve was only just shy of the same torture.

He hesitated as he reached for his blade and bolter. They both rested as they should: racked against the wall and bound in place by strong leather straps. This, however, was rare. Talos was many things, but fastidiously tidy was not one of them. He couldn't recall the last time he'd returned to his room, replaced his weapons in perfect order, and promptly passed out comfortably in isolation. In fact, he couldn't ever recall it happening before. Not even once.

Someone had been in here. Septimus, perhaps, or his brothers when they'd dragged him from wherever he'd been when he fell prey to the vision.

Still, they'd never concern themselves with something as mundane as restoring his weapons to their racks. Septimus, then. That made sense. Uncommon behaviour, but it made sense. It was even laudable.

Talos pulled his weapons free before fastening them to his armour. The double-barrelled bolter mag-locked to his thigh, and the ornate golden blade sheathed at his back, ready to be drawn over his shoulder.

: COME TO THE BRIDGE

The words peeled across his visor display, spelled out in distinct Nostraman runes, clear white on the background red-tint like any other measure of tactical information or bio-data. He watched the cursor flicker at the end of the final word, blinking almost expectantly.

Quintus, the fifth of his slaves, had been rendered mute through battlefield injury. They'd communicated during the serf's years of service via hand signs or text uplink from a hand-held auspex to Talos's armour systems, and usually a fair degree of both at once. Quintus, much like

Septimus, was a good enough artificer that a little inconvenience was a small price to pay.

  : PROPHET
  : COME TO THE BRIDGE

Quintus, however, had never behaved so informally. He was also decades dead, slain by the Exalted in one of Vandred's many crazed outbursts.

Talos's retinal display responded to his desire, opening a vox-channel to First Claw.

'Brothers.'

They answered, but without anything resembling cohesion. Xarl's laughter machine-gunned across the vox-waves, followed by the others cursing and screaming oaths in equal measure. He could hear Mercutian's whisperingly polite swearing coming through clenched teeth, and the throaty chatter of bolters in their fusillade drumbeat.

The channel went dead. He tried several others: the strategium, Deltrian's Hall of Reflection, Septimus's armoury, Octavia's chamber, and even Lucoryphus of the Bleeding Eyes. All dead. All silent. The ship thrummed on, evidently active and running at speed.

He perversely relished these first pricklings of unease. It took a great deal to unnerve any of the Eighth Legion, and the ship's sudden emptiness was a pleasant mystery. He had the amusing feeling of being hunted, and it sent a smile creeping across his pale lips. This must be what his prey felt like, though he'd hardly lose control of his muscles and babble meaningless prayers to false gods the way humans usually did.

  : I AM WAITING

Talos drew his sword and left his chamber.

HE WAS FAR from shocked to find the bridge abandoned. It was no more than a minute's travel from his chamber on the deck below, but the *Echo of Damnation*'s central spinal thoroughfares were similarly empty when he'd passed through them.

The strategium was an expansive oval of gothic architecture, populated by leering gargoyles and sculpted grotesques clinging to the walls and ceiling. Here, a mutilated angel with eyes wrapped by barbed wire roared voicelessly at the central throne; there, a bat-winged daemon spread its pinions across the ceiling above the secondary gunnery platforms. The artistry involved in the *Echo*'s construction never failed to captivate him – for all the Eighth Legion's flaws as disciplined warriors, the Night Lords had managed to breed a few scholars and craftsmen with the same skill shown by the artisan-knights of the Emperor's Children and the Blood Angels. No matter their individual skills in craft, most VIII Legion vessels were decorated with blasphemous relish, depicting tortured divinities and captive daemons across the architecture.

A central throne rose above all else, its immense bulk aimed at the occulus viewscreen. Above the occulus, a legionary's broken skeleton was bound, crucified in place, hanging on chains.

In concentric circles around it were the banks of navigation, gunnery and operation stations. No robed heretic priests muttered their way between control tables. No uniformed crew relayed orders or adjusted settings. No branded servitors hardwired into their restraint thrones chattered and drawled their status reports in machine voices.

This was surely a dream, though it matched no vision he'd ever seen before. No other explanation fit.

'I am here,' Talos said aloud.

: YOU HAVE BEEN DREAMING MANY DREAMS
: NOW YOU ARE CLOSE TO WAKING ONCE MORE
: SIT BROTHER

He didn't smile. He rarely did, even when amused, though it was most definitely amusing to be told to take a seat in his own command throne. Talos complied, even if only to see what would happen.

: ALMOST CLOSE ENOUGH TO TOUCH

That prickled at the prophet's skin. He looked up at Ruven's crucified remains.

: YOU ARE NOT THE WARRIOR YOU SHOULD BE
: BUT YOU AND I MUST SPEAK
: IT MUST BE HERE AND IT MUST BE NOW
: THERE WILL NEVER BE ANOTHER CHANCE

Talos remained seated, the very picture of stoic patience. He refused to let his anger or doubts rise to the surface. Targeting reticules slid by without gaining a grip on Ruven's shattered skeleton.

: YOU MADE MY CORPSE INTO THE FINEST DECORATION
: THAT IS ALMOST AMUSING

Talos reclined in the throne the way he did on the true bridge.

'Can even death not render you silent?'

: YOUR OWN LIFE IS MEASURED IN MONTHS PROPHET

The skull, suspended on chains, leered with empty eye sockets. 'Is that so?' Talos asked it. 'And how do you come by this precious lore?'

: DO YOU PRETEND THIS MOMENT HAS NO SIGNIFICANCE
: DO YOU BELIEVE I CANNOT HEAR YOUR HEART BEATING FASTER

Talos stroked the hilt of the relic blade resting at his side. The restraint needed to resist demanding an explanation brought his headache to a crescendo.

'Get on with it,' he said, continuing his facade of bored indulgence. He had to collect his thoughts. At best, this was a trap. At worst, it was sorcery. More than likely, it was both.

That wasn't good.

: YOU REMEMBER NOTHING DO YOU
: YOU HAVE COME TO SEEK A PURE WAR
: A NOBLE WAR
: BUT YOU SHOULD NEVER HAVE RETURNED TO THE EAST-
ERN FRINGE
: OTHERS HAVE BEEN WAITING FOR YOUR RETURN WITH
REVENGE IN THEIR HEARTS

The prophet remained as he was, still stroking the blade's wingspread hilt. The Eastern Fringe. He couldn't think of anything that would ever drive him back there.

'I think you lie, husk.'

: WHY WOULD I LIE
: YOU RUN FROM THE EYE
: YOU RUN FROM THE ELDAR
: YOU RUN FROM DOOM AT THE HANDS OF ALIEN WITCHES
: WHERE BETTER TO FLEE THAN THE OTHER EDGE OF THE
GALAXY

Perhaps there was truth in that, but the prophet felt no urge to confess it. He remained silent.

: HOW LONG HAVE YOU WAGED THIS WAR TALOS

He shook his head, feeling the sudden need to swallow. 'A long time. The Heresy was the bloodiest decade. Then, the Raiding Years, when we called Tsagualsa home. Two centuries of bitter glory, before the Imperium came for us.'

: AND HOW LONG SINCE WE LEFT THE CARRION WORLD

'For the Imperium?' He narrowed his eyes at the question. 'Almost ten thousand ye–'

: NO
: HOW LONG FOR THE TRAITOR LEGIONS
: HOW LONG FOR YOU TALOS

He swallowed again, beginning to sense where this was leading. The warp stole all meaning from the material realm, even banishing all pretence of physics and temporal stability. The Great Heresy was days in the past for some of the Traitors within the Eye, and fifty thousand years gone for others. All of them, each and every soul to betray the Emperor in that golden age, could claim a different scale of time for the years since.

'A century since we left Tsagualsa.' Less than many, but more than some.

: A CENTURY FOR YOU
: A CENTURY FOR FIRST CLAW
: THAT MAKES YOU OVER THREE HUNDRED YEARS OLD PROPHET

Talos nodded, meeting the skull's hollow eyes. 'Close enough.'

: STILL SO YOUNG FOR A TRAITOR
: STILL NAIVE

    : BUT LONG ENOUGH THAT YOU SHOULD HAVE LEARNED CER-
TAIN LESSONS BY NOW
    : AND YET YOU HAVE NOT

The prophet stared up at the wreckage of crucified bone, and the letters superimposed over it. They flickered across his retinal display almost impatiently, as if awaiting an answer.

'If you find me lacking, revenant, then by all means enlighten me.'
    : WHY ARE YOU FIGHTING THIS WAR

The prophet snorted. 'For vengeance.'
    : REVENGE FOR WHAT

'To avenge the wrongs done to us.'
    : WHAT WRONGS DO YOU SPEAK OF

The legionary rose to his feet, feeling the skin crawling at the back of his neck. 'You *know* what wrongs. You *know* why the Eighth Legion fights.'
    : THE EIGHTH LEGION DOESN'T KNOW WHY IT FIGHTS
    : YOU CONCEIVE EXCUSES TO JUSTIFY A LIFETIME OF
WASTED HATE
    : THE LEGION FIGHTS ONLY BECAUSE IT IS AMUSING AND
PLEASURABLE TO DOMINATE WEAKER SOULS

'Unadulterated fantasy.' Talos laughed, though he'd never felt less like laughing. He considered shooting the chained skeleton down from its ungainly crucifixion, though it was doubtful whether the act of spite would achieve anything. 'We rebelled because we had to rebel. The Imperium's pacifism was destined to fail. Order can only be maintained through keeping its souls fearful of retribution. Control, through fear. *Peace* through fear. We were the weapon mankind needed. We still are.'
    : THE LEGION NEVER FOUGHT FOR THOSE IDEALS
    : YOUR DELUSION WAS NEVER EVEN POPULAR AMONG OUR
RANKS
    : BUT IT FADED WHEN THE TRUTH CAME
    : YOU CLING TO YOUR ILLUSIONS NOW BECAUSE HATE IS
ALL YOU HAVE LEFT

'Hate is all I need.' He drew the bolter now, aiming both barrels up at the corpse's shattered ribcage. 'My hatred runs pure. We *deserve* vengeance against the empire that abandoned us. We were *right* to punish those worlds for their sins, and threaten others with destruction if they ever broke our laws. Control. Through. Fear. The systems we pacified...'
    : THE SYSTEMS WE PACIFIED WERE BARELY HUMAN ANYMORE
    : WE MADE THE POPULATIONS INTO COWERING ANIMALS DIS-
POSSESSED OF FREE WILL
    : LIVING IN TERROR OF BREAKING THE LAW
    : LIKE THE WEEPING HERDS OF HUMANS LIVING IN THE
BOWELS OF OUR WARSHIPS NOW

'I stand by what I did.' The prophet was aware of his own maddening stance – he couldn't aim for much longer without making good on his threat to fire, but nor did he wish to strike in useless anger. 'I stand by what we all did.'

: MANY OF OUR BROTHERS NEVER CARED FOR ANY OF THOSE IDEALS

: THAT IS NO SECRET

: IT IS WHY CURZE DESTROYED NOSTRAMO

: TO STEM THE FLOW OF POISON INTO THE EIGHTH LEGION

: AND IT WAS WHY WE WERE PUNISHED BY THE IMPERIUM

'The lesson of the Legion.' Talos lowered the weapon. 'The primarch said those words many times.'

: WE BECAME THE VERY THING WE WARNED WHOLE WORLDS ABOUT

: WE WERE THE KILLERS AND THE MURDERERS WE TOLD THEM NEVER TO BE

: FREE TO SLAY AT WILL AND FREE FROM RETRIBUTION

There was a long pause. Talos felt the ship give a shudder, in sympathy to some external torment.

: THE BLOOD RAN COLD IN THAT AGE BEFORE THE GALAXY BURNED

: AND IT RAN IN RIVERS FROM THE VEINS OF THE GUILTY AND INNOCENT ALIKE

: BECAUSE WE WERE STRONG AND THEY WERE WEAK

'He hated us, I know that for certain. Curze loved us and hated us in equal measure.' Talos returned to his throne, his voice softened by contemplation. Ideas danced and died behind his black eyes, hidden beneath the monochrome red of his helm's eye lenses.

Much of it was true, and no mystery to the prophet. Curze had annihilated their home world in a melancholic decree, seeking to end the recruitment of rapists and murderers, but it was far too late by then. Much of the Legion was already given over to the very criminal scum he sought to purge from humanity. This was no secret. No revelation. Merely shameful truth.

But they'd still been right to fight. Pacification through overwhelming force, and ruling forever after by fear. It had worked, for a time. The resulting peace across dozens of systems had been a beautiful thing to behold. A population only dared rise in rebellion when the boot was lifted from their throat. In such cases, it was the fault of the oppressor for showing weakness, not the oppressed for rising up. To resist was human nature. The species couldn't be hated for it.

'Our way was not the way of the Imperium,' Talos quoted the ancient adage, 'but we were right. If the Legion had stayed pure...'

: BUT IT DID NOT

: THE LEGION WAS TAINTED BY SIN THE MOMENT THE FIRST

NOSTRAMAN-BORN WARRIOR SWORE HIS OATH OF SERVICE
  : AND WE DESERVED THE HATE OF OUR PRIMARCH
  : FOR WE WERE NOT THE WARRIORS HE WISHED US TO BE
Another pause. Another tremor quivered through the ship's bones.
'What's happening?'
  : REALITY IS SLIPPING THROUGH NOW
  : THE ECHO OF DAMNATION ARRIVES AT ITS DESTINATION
  : BUT YOU SHOULD NEVER HAVE COME BACK TO THE EAST-
ERN FRINGE
Talos looked up again. The corpse hadn't moved. 'You said that before.
I still don't recall ordering such a thing.'
  : YOU ORDERED IT IN SEARCH OF A PURE WAR TO ELEVATE
THE WARBAND
  : AND SEEK ANSWERS TO THE DOUBTS THAT PLAGUE YOU
  : BY WALKING UPON TSAGUALSA ONCE MORE
  : NOTHING I SAY NOW IS A REVELATION
  : I SPEAK ONLY THE SAME TRUTHS YOU ARE TOO PROUD
TO SPEAK ALOUD ·
  : YOU HAVE BEEN HOLLOW FOR A LONG TIME BROTHER
'Why am I seeing this?' He gestured around the chamber, at the body,
at himself. 'What... what is all this? A vision? A dream? A spell? The
tricks of my own mind, or something from the outside crawling into
my thoughts?'
  : ALL OF THOSE AND NONE OF THEM
  : PERHAPS THIS IS MERELY A MANIFESTATION OF YOUR
DOUBTS AND FEARS
  : IN THE WAKING WORLD YOU HAVE BEEN UNCONSCIOUS FOR
FIFTY-FIVE NIGHTS
  : YOU ARE CLOSE TO RISING
He was on his feet again, as the ship began to shake in prophetic ear-
nest. He heard the hull groaning with the sincerity of a gut-shot soldier.
Cracks began to lace their way across the occulus, sprinkling glass to the
decking. 'Fifty-five nights? That cannot be. How did this happen?'
  : YOU KNOW WHY
  : YOU HAVE ALWAYS KNOWN
  : SOME HUMAN CHILDREN ARE NOT MEANT TO CARRY GENE-
SEED
  : IT BREAKS THEM APART AT THE GENETIC LEVEL
  : SOME DIE FAST
  : SOME DIE SLOW
  : BUT AFTER THREE CENTURIES OF BIOLOGICAL FLUX YOUR
GENETIC INCOMPATIBILITIES ARE FINALLY CATCHING UP TO
YOU
'Lies.' Talos watched the ship coming apart around him. 'Lies and

madness are all you ever uttered in life, Ruven. The same holds true in death.'

  : VARIEL KNOWS THE TRUTH

  : CENTURIES OF INJURY

  : CENTURIES OF ENDURANCE AND PAIN

  : CENTURIES OF THE VISIONS BORN OF POISONOUS PRI-MARCH BLOOD

  : YOUR BODY CAN TAKE NO MORE PUNISHMENT

  : ENJOY WHAT TIME REMAINS TO YOU BROTHER

  : DUTY AWAITS IN THE WAKING WORLD AND YOU WILL RE-MEMBER PRECIOUS LITTLE OF OUR TALK

  : RISE TALOS

  : RISE AND SEE FOR YOURSELF

II
AWAKENING

LIGHT, MUTED AND bleached by the red of his visor display, filtered into his eyes.

The first thing he saw was the last thing he expected. His brothers. His crew. The strategium, with its two hundred souls engaged in their duties.

'I...' He tried to speak, but his voice was a dehydrated vox-rasp. Talos slumped in his throne, though a chain collar around his throat prevented him from falling too far forward. Voices babbled all around him, along with the growl of armour joints moving closer.

'I am not in my meditation chamber,' he said. He'd never woken from a vision anywhere else, let alone to rise and find himself on the warship's bridge. The prophet was struck by the image of his surroundings, wondering if he'd sat here in his armour the entire time, unconscious and screaming his delusional chants across the vox-network.

Chains rattled around his throat, wrists and ankles as he sought to rise. His brothers had bound him to the throne.

They had much to answer for.

Whispers of 'He returns' and 'He awakens' wove their way through the mortal crew. From his seat of honour on a raised dais at the heart of the bridge, Talos could see them pausing in their assigned duties, face after face turning to regard him. Their eyes were bright with surprise and reverence in equal measure. 'The prophet awakens,' kept leaving their pale lips.

This, he decided with a crawling feeling of spinal discomfort, was what being worshipped must feel like.

His brothers clustered around the throne, each of their faces masked behind their helms: Uzas, with his painted bloody handprint across the faceplate; Xarl, his helm crested by sweeping bat wings; Cyrion's eyes painted with streaking lightning bolt tears; Mercutian's helm topped by brutal, curving horns ringed with bronze.

Variel knelt before Talos, the Apothecary's bionic leg grinding and seizing, making the movement awkward. He alone wore no helm, his cold eyes fixed upon the prophet's own.

'A timely return,' he said. His curiously soft voice held no shade of amusement.

'We have arrived, Talos,' Cyrion qualified. There was a smile in *his* voice, at least.

'Fifty-five nights,' said Mercutian. 'We have never witnessed such a thing. What did you dream?'

'I remember almost none of it.' Talos looked past them all, at the world turning slowly within the elliptical frame of the occulus screen. 'I remember little of anything. Where are we?'

Variel turned his pale gaze upon the others. It was enough to get them to move back a little, no longer crowding the reawakened prophet. As he spoke, the Apothecary consulted his bulky narthecium gauntlet. Talos could hear the auspex scanner crackling with static and chiming with results.

'I administered supplemental narcotics and fluids to keep you in adequate health without activating your sus-an membrane these past two months. You are, however, going to be extremely weak for some days to come. The muscle wastage is minor, but significant enough for you to notice it.'

Talos tensed against the chains again, as if to make a point.

'Ah, yes,' said Variel. 'Of course.' He keyed in a code on his vambrace, deploying a circular cutting saw from his narthecium. The kiss of the saw along the chains was a high-pitched, irritating whine. One by one, the lengths of metallic binding fell free.

'Why was I restrained?'

'To prevent injury to yourself and others,' explained Variel.

'No.' Talos focused on his retinal display, activating a secure vox-link to his closest brothers. 'Why was I restrained here, on the bridge?'

The members of First Claw shared glances, their helms turning to face each other in some unknowable emotion.

'We took you to your chambers when you first succumbed,' said Cyrion. 'But...'

'But?'

'You broke out of the cell. You killed both of the brothers standing guard outside the door, and we lost you in the lower decks for almost a week.'

Talos tried to rise. Variel fixed him with the same glare he'd turned on the rest of First Claw, but the prophet ignored it. The Apothecary had been right, though. He felt as weak as a human. His muscles burned with cramps as blood trickled back into them.

'I do not understand,' Talos said at last.

'Neither did we,' replied Cyrion. 'You'd never acted in such a way while afflicted.'

Xarl took up the explanation. 'Guess who found you?'

The prophet shook his head, not knowing where to begin to make assumptions. 'Tell me.'

Uzas inclined his head. 'It was I.'

That would be a story in itself, Talos reckoned. He looked back at Cyrion. 'And then?'

'After several days, the crew and the other Claws began to grow uncomfortable. Morale, such as it is among we happy and loyal dregs, was suffering. Talk circulated that you'd died or were diseased. We brought you here to show the crew you were still among us, one way or the other.'

Talos snorted. 'Did it work?'

'See for yourself.' Cyrion gestured to the rapt, staring humans around the command deck. All eyes were upon him.

Talos swallowed the taste of something acrid. 'You made me into an icon. That treads close to heathenism.'

First Claw shared a low chuckle. Only Talos was unamused.

'Fifty-five days of silence,' Cyrion said, 'and all you have for us is displeasure?'

'Silence?' The prophet turned to look at each of them in turn. 'I never cried out? I never spoke my prophecies aloud?'

'Not this time,' Mercutian shook his head. 'Silence, from the moment you collapsed.'

'I do not even remember collapsing.' Talos moved past them, leaning on the rail ringing the central dais. He watched the grey world hanging in the void, surrounded by a dense asteroid field. 'Where are we?'

First Claw came to his side, forming up in a line of snarling joints and impassive, skullish facemasks.

'You don't recall your orders to us?' Xarl asked.

Talos tried not to let his impatience show. 'Just tell me where we are. That is a familiar sight, yet I struggle to believe we truly stand before it.'

'It is, and we do. We're on the Eastern Fringe,' said Xarl. 'Out of the Astronomican's light, and in orbit around the world you repeatedly demanded we travel to.'

Talos stared at it as it turned with indescribable slowness. He knew what world it was, even though he could remember nothing of these events his brothers insisted had happened. It took a great deal more effort than he'd expected to resist saying the words 'It cannot be'. Most unbelievable of all were the grey stains of cities scabbing over the dusty continents.

'It has changed,' he said. 'I don't understand how that can be true. The Imperium would never build here, yet I see cities. I see the stains of human civilisation scarring what should be worthless land.'

Cyrion nodded. 'We were just as surprised as you, brother.'

Talos let his gaze sweep across the rest of the bridge. 'To your stations, all of you.' The humans complied with salutes and murmurs of 'Yes, lord'.

It was Mercutian who broke the silence that followed. 'We are here, Talos. What should we do now?'

The prophet stared at a world that should have been long dead, purged of life ten thousand years before and abandoned by all who called it home. The Imperium of Man would never re-seed a cursed world, especially one beyond the holy rim of the Emperor's beacon of light. Reaching this world under standard propulsion would take months from even the closest border planet.

'Ready all Claws for planetfall.'

Cyrion cleared his throat. Talos turned at the surprisingly human gesture. 'You have missed much, brother. There is something that requires your attention before we become involved planetside. Something pertaining to Septimus and Octavia. We were unsure how to deal with it in your absence.'

'I am listening,' the prophet said. He wouldn't admit how his blood ran cold at the mention of those names.

'Go to her. See for yourself.'

See for yourself. The words echoed in his mind, clinging with an unnerving tenacity, feeling somewhere between prophecy and memory.

'Are you coming?' he asked his brothers.

Mercutian looked away. Xarl grunted a laugh.

'No,' Cyrion said. 'You should do this alone.'

HE REACHED HER chamber, appalled at the weakness in his own limbs. Fifty-five nights, almost two full months without the daily training rites, hadn't been kind to him. Octavia's servants lingered in the shadows around her door, hunchbacked royalty in the sunless alcoves.

'Lord,' they hissed through slits in their faces that were once lips. Their bloodstained bandages rustled as they shifted and lowered their weapons.

'Move aside,' Talos ordered them. They fled, as roaches flee a sudden light.

One of them stood its ground. For a moment, he thought it was Hound, Octavia's favoured attendant, but it was too slender. And Hound was months dead, slain in the ship's capture, scarcely twenty metres from this very spot.

'The mistress is weary,' the figure said. Its voice was somehow clenched, as though it strained through closed teeth. It was also a soft voice, too light to be male. She raised a bandaged hand, as if she could possibly bar the warrior's passage with a demand, let alone with her physical presence. The woman's cloth-wrapped face revealed nothing of her appearance, but her stature suggested she was less devolved – at least physically – than most of the others. Bulky glare-goggles covered her eyes, their black oval lenses amusingly insectile, giving the impression of mutation where none was immediately apparent. A thin red beam projected from the goggles' left edge, following the attendant's gaze. She'd welded a red dot laser sight to her facewear – for what reason, Talos couldn't begin to guess.

'Then she and I have much in common,' the prophet stated. 'Move.'

'She has no wish to be disturbed,' the strained voice insisted, growing even less friendly. The other attendants were beginning to return now.

'Your loyal defiance does your mistress credit, but we are now finished with this tedium.' Talos tilted his head down at the female. He had no wish to pointlessly slay her. 'Do you know who I am?'

'You are someone seeking to enter against my mistress's wishes.'

'That is true. It is also true that I am master of this vessel, and your mistress is my slave.'

The other attendants skulked back into the shadows, whispering the prophet's name. *Talos, Talos, Talos*... like the hissing of rock vipers.

'She is unwell,' the bandaged female said. Fear crept into her voice now.

'What is your name?' Talos asked her.

'Vularai,' she replied. The warrior smiled, barely, behind his faceplate. *Vularai* was the Nostraman word for *liar*.

'Amusing. I like you. Now move, before I begin to like you less.'

The attendant moved back, and Talos caught the glint of metal beneath the woman's ragged clothing.

'Is that a gladius?'

The figure froze. 'Lord?'

'Are you carrying a Legion gladius?'

She drew the blade at her hip. For a Night Lord, the traditional gladius was a short stabbing weapon the length of a warrior's forearm. In human hands, it became a sleek longsword. The swirling Nostraman runes etched into the dark iron were unmistakable.

'That,' said Talos, 'is a Legion weapon.'

'It was a gift, lord.'

'From whom?'

'From Lord Cyrion of First Claw. He said I needed a weapon.'

'Can you use it with any skill?'

The bandaged woman shrugged and said nothing.

'And if I'd merely shoved you aside and entered, Vularai? What would you have done then?'

He could hear the smile in her strained voice. 'I'd have cut out your heart, my lord.'

* * *

THE CHAMBER OF navigation offered a little more illumination than the rest of the ship's rooms and hallways, lit by the grainy, unhealthy half-light of almost thirty monitors linked to external pict-feeds. They cast their greyish glare across the rest of the wide chamber, bleaching the surface of the circular pool in the centre. The meaty reek of amniotic fluid was thick in the air.

She wasn't in the water. In the months since they'd taken the *Echo of Damnation*, even after half the ship had been scoured and purged clean with flame weapons, Octavia had vowed to only use the amniotic pool for warp flight, when she required her deepest connection to the ship's machine-spirit. Talos, having seen Ezmarellda, the chamber's previous prisoner, could understand all too well why the Navigator refused to spend too long in the nutrient-rich water.

Mixed in with the chemical stink of the thin ooze were the usual smells of Octavia's personal space: the tang of human sweat; the musty edge of her books and parchment scrolls; and the faint – not unpleasant – spice of the natural oil in her hair, even when recently washed.

And something else. Something close to the scent of a woman's monthly blood cycle, with the same rich piquancy. Close, but not quite.

Talos walked around the edge of the pool, approaching the throne facing the bank of monitors. Each screen showed a variant view of the ship's outer hull, and the cold void beyond. A few showed the grey face of the world they orbited, and its contrasting white rock moon.

'Octavia.'

She opened her eyes, looking up at him with the moment's bleariness that follows sleep but precedes comprehension. Her dark hair was bound in its usual ponytail, hanging from the back of the silk bandana.

'You're awake,' she said.

'As are you.'

'Yes,' she admitted, 'though I'd rather not be.' Her lips curved into a half-smile. 'What did you dream?'

'I can recall little of it.' The warrior gestured to the world on the screens before her. 'Do you know the name of this world?'

She nodded. 'Septimus told me. I don't know why you'd want to return here.'

Talos shook his head. 'Neither do I. My memory is in fragments from even before I succumbed to the vision.' He released his breath as a slow sigh. 'Home. Our second home, at least. After Nostramo, there was Tsagualsa, the carrion world.'

'It's been colonised. A small population, so it's a recent colonisation.'

'I know,' he said.

'So what will you do?'

'I don't know.'

Octavia shifted in her throne, still wrapped in her thin cloth blanket.

'This chamber is always cold.' She looked up at him, waiting for him to speak. When he said nothing, she filled the silence herself. 'It was difficult to sail here. The Astronomican doesn't shine this far from Terra, and the tides were blacker than black.'

'May I ask what it was like?'

The Navigator toyed with a stray lock of hair as she spoke. 'The warp is dark here. Utterly dark. The colours are all black. Can you imagine a thousand shades of black, each darker than the last?'

He shook his head. 'You are asking me to envisage a concept alien to the material universe.'

'It's cold,' she said, breaking eye contact. 'How can a colour be cold? In the blackness, I could feel the usual disgusting presences: the shrieking of souls against the hull, and the distant cancers, swimming alone in the deep.'

'Cancers?'

'It is the only way I can describe them. Great, nameless entities of poison and pain. Malignant intelligences.'

Talos nodded. 'The souls of false gods, perhaps.'

'Are they false if they're real?'

'I do not know,' he confessed.

She shivered. 'Where we've sailed before, even away from the Astronomican... those places were still dimly lit by the Emperor's beacon, no matter how far from it we sailed. You could see the shadows and shapes gliding through the tides. Daemons without form, swimming through liquid torment. Here, I can see nothing. It wasn't about finding my way through the storm, the way I've been trained. This was a matter of tumbling forward into blindness, seeking the calmest paths, where the shrieking winds were lessened, even if only for a moment.'

For a moment, he was struck by the similarity between her experiences and the sensation of falling into his own visions.

'We are here,' he said. 'You did well.'

'I felt something else, though. The faintest thing. These presences, warmer than the warp around them. Like eyes, watching me as I brought the ship closer.'

'Should we be concerned?'

Octavia shrugged. 'I don't know. It was one aspect of madness amongst a thousand others.'

'We've arrived. That is what matters.' Another silence threatened between them. This time, Talos broke it. 'We had a fortress here, long ago. A castle of black stone and twisting spires. The primarch dreamed of it one night, and set hundreds of thousands of slaves to making it. It took almost twenty years.'

He paused, and Octavia watched the passionless skull of his facemask, waiting for him to continue. Talos exhaled in a vox-growl.

'The inner sanctum was called the Screaming Gallery. Have any of the others ever spoken of this before?'

She shook her head. 'No, never.'

'The Screaming Gallery was a metaphor, of a kind. A god's torment, expressed in blood and pain. The primarch wanted to reshape the external world to match the sin within his mind. The walls were flesh – humans moulded and crafted into the architecture, formed as much from sorcery as from ingenuity. The floors were carpeted in living faces, preserved by feeder-servitors.'

He shook his head, the memory too strong to ever fade. 'The screaming, Octavia. You have never heard such a sound. They never stopped screaming. The people in the walls, crying and reaching out. The faces on the floor, weeping and shrieking.'

She forced a smile she didn't feel. 'That sounds like the warp.'

He glanced at her, and grunted acknowledgement. 'Forgive me. You know exactly what it sounds like.'

She nodded, but didn't say anything else.

'The foulest thing was the way you'd become immune to the wailing chorus. Those of us who attended the primarch in his last decades of madness spent much of our time in the Screaming Gallery. The sound of all that pain became tolerable. Soon after, you found yourself enjoying it. It was easier to think when surrounded by sin. The torment first became meaningless, but afterwards, it became music.'

The prophet fell silent for a moment. 'That was what he wanted, of course. He wanted us to understand the Legion's lesson, as he believed it to be.'

Octavia shuffled again as Talos knelt by her throne. 'I see no lesson in mindless brutality,' she said.

He unlocked his collar seals with a breath of air pressure, and removed his helm. She was struck, once again, by the thought that he'd have been handsome but for the cold eyes and the corpse-white skin. He was a statue, a scarred demigod of clean marble, dead-eyed, beautiful in his sterility, yet unlovely to look upon.

'It was not mindless brutality,' he said. 'That was the lesson. The primarch knew that law and order – the twin foundations of civilisation – are only maintained through fear of punishment. Man is not a peaceful animal. It is a creature of war and strife. To force the beasts into civilisation, one must remind them that excruciation awaits those who harm the herd. For a time, we believed the Emperor wanted this of us. He wanted us to be the Angels of Death. And for a time, we were.'

She blinked for the first time in almost a minute. In their many long discussions and reflections, he'd never spoken of this in such detail. 'Go on,' she pushed.

'Some say He betrayed us. Once our use was complete, He turned against us. Others claim that we'd merely taken our self-appointed role too far, and had to be put down like animals ourselves, for slipping our leashes.' He saw a question in her eyes and waved it away. 'None of that is important. What matters is how it began, and how it ended.'

'How did it begin?'

'The Legion had taken immense casualties in the Great Crusade, in service to the Emperor. Most of these were Terran. They came from Terra, from the Emperor's wars across humanity's birth planet. But all of our reinforcements came from our home world, Nostramo. Decades had passed since the primarch last walked upon the world's surface, and his lessons of law had long since died. The population slid back into lawless anarchy, with no fear of punishment from a distant Imperium. Do you understand how we were poisoning ourselves? We were repopulating the Legion with rapists and murderers, with children who were the blackest sinners before they'd even tasted adulthood. The primarch's lessons meant nothing to them, meant nothing to most of the Eighth Legion at the end. They were slayers, raised to become demigods, with the galaxy as their prize to plunder. In wrathful desperation, the primarch burned our home world. He destroyed it, breaking it apart from orbit with the firepower of the entire Legion fleet.'

Talos breathed, low and slow. 'It took hours, Octavia. All the while, we remained aboard our ships, listening to vox-calls from the surface, sending their screams and pleas up to us in the heavens. We never answered. Not even once. We stayed in space and watched our own cities burn. At the very end, we watched the planet heaving, breaking apart beneath the fleet's rage. Only then did we turn away. Nostramo disintegrated into the void. I have never seen anything like it again. I know, in my heart, I never will.'

A moment of foolishness almost made her reach a hand to touch his cheek. She knew better than to give in to that instinct. Still, the way he spoke, the look in his black eyes – he was a child, grown into a god's body without a man's comprehension of humanity. No wonder these creatures were so dangerous. Their stunted psyches worked on levels no human could quite comprehend: simplistic and passionate one moment, complex and inhuman the next.

'It didn't work,' he continued. 'The Legion was poisoned by then. You know that Xarl and I grew up together, murderers even as children. We joined the Legion late, when Nostramo's venom was already rich in the Legion's veins. And believe me when I say that where he and I grew up, among the street wars and the cheapness of human life, it was one of the more civilised regions of Nostramo's inner cities. Much of the planet was in the throes of devolution, lost to urban wastelands and scavenger armies. As the strongest candidates, they were usually the ones chosen for implantation and ascension to the Eighth. They were the ones to become legionaries.'

Talos finished with a smile that didn't reach his eyes. 'By then, it was too late. Primarch Curze was in the throes of degeneration himself. He hated himself, he hated his life, and he hated his Legion. All he craved was one last chance to be right, to show that he'd not wasted his entire existence. The rebellion against the Emperor – that war of myth that you call the Horus Heresy – was over. We'd turned against the Imperium that sought to punish us, and we'd lost. So we ran. We ran to Tsagualsa, a world outside the Imperium's borders, away from Terra's Beacon of Light that he claimed still stung his eyes.'

He gestured at the grey world. 'We ran here, and here is where it ended.'

Octavia's breath left her lips as mist. 'You fled a war you lost and constructed a castle of torture chambers. How noble of you, Talos. I still see no lesson in it.'

He nodded to that, conceding the point. 'You have to understand that by the end, the primarch was riddled through by madness. He cared nothing for the Long War, wanting nothing beyond bleeding the Imperium and vindicating his life's path. He knew he was going to die, Octavia. He wanted to be *right* when he died.'

'Septimus told me of this,' she said. 'But raiding the Imperium's edges for couple of centuries at the behest of a madman, and slaughtering entire worlds, is hardly a lesson of worthy ideals.'

Talos watched her with his soulless eyes unwavering. 'In that light, perhaps not. But humanity has to know fear, Navigator. Nothing else ensures compliance. By the very end, when the Screaming Gallery was the Legion's war room and council chamber alike, the primarch's degeneration had devoured him from within. He was rendered hollow by it. I still remember how regal he looked to us, how majestic our father was to our adoring eyes. But looking at him was like growing used to a disgusting smell. You could forget the foulness, just as you can ignore the scent, but when something reminds you of it, you perceive it with renewed strength. His soul had rotted away by the end, and on some nights you could see it in the flash of his dying eyes, or the bleak shine of his teeth. Some of my brothers asked if he were tainted by some outer power, but most of us no longer cared. What did it matter? The end result was the same.'

The lights chose that moment to flicker and fail. The warrior and the mutant remained in darkness for several heartbeats, illuminated only by the eye lenses of his armour and the grey glare from the screens.

'That's happening more and more lately,' she said. 'The *Covenant* hated me. The *Echo* seems to hate all of us.'

'An intriguing superstition,' he replied. The lights, dim as they were, came back on. Talos still didn't continue.

'And the assassination?' she prompted.

'The assassination came soon after, when his mad clarity was at its height. I have never seen a creature so placidly delighted by the thought of its own destruction. In death, he would be vindicated. Those who break the law must be dealt with in the most violent, lethal way, as an example to all who would consider betrayal. So he set us butchering across the galaxy, breaking every law against reason and rhyme, knowing the Emperor would prove the point all too well. The assassin came to slay Curze, the great Breaker of Imperial Law, and she did just that. I saw him die, vindicated, pleased for perhaps the first time in centuries.'

'That's grotesque,' she said. Her heart quickened at the thought he would take offence, but her fear was unfounded.

'Maybe so,' he nodded again. 'The universe has never seen a living being that loathed being alive as much as my father. His life was broken in seeking to prove how humanity could be controlled, and his death was a sacrifice to prove that the species was ultimately wretched.'

Talos withdrew a hololithic orb from his belt pouch, and thumbed the activation rune. A life-sized image of flickering blue light manifested before them both. A figure rose from an unseen throne, its hunched, feral posture still not entirely stealing the beauty of its muscled physique, or the savage nobility in its movements. The distortion robbed the image of clarity, but the figure's face – a wraith's visage of black eyes, gaunt cheekbones and filed fangs – was set in a vicious grin of sincere amusement.

The image died as Talos deactivated the orb. For a long time, neither of them said another word.

'Was there no one to lead you after his death?'

'The Legion broke down into companies and warbands, following individual lords. The primarch's presence was what inspired unity within us. Without him, the raiding parties sailed farther from Tsagualsa, staying away for longer periods. As the years passed, many stopped returning at all. Many captains and lords claimed they were the Night Haunter's heir, but each claim was refuted by the others. No one soul can bind a Traitor Legion together now. It is simply the way of things. As much as I loathe him, Abaddon's success is what sets him apart – and above – the rest of us. His is the name whispered across the Imperium. Abaddon. The Despoiler. The Chosen. *Abaddon*. Not Horus.'

Octavia shivered. She knew that name, she'd heard it whispered of in the halls of Terran power. Abaddon. The Great Enemy. The Death of the Imperium. Prophecies of his triumph in the final century of mankind were rampant among the psychically-gifted in thrall to the Emperor's throne.

'There was only one,' Talos said, 'who could have held the title without his brothers betraying him. At least, there was only one who would have survived his brothers' betrayals, but even he would have struggled to hold the Legion together. Too many ideologies. Too many conflicting desires and drives.'

'What was his name?'

'Sevatar,' the prophet said quietly. 'We called him the Prince of Crows. He was killed in the Heresy, long before our father.'

She hesitated before speaking. 'Mercutian has spoken of him.'

'Mercutian comes to speak with you?'

The Navigator grinned. Her teeth were whiter than any of the crew's, from so few years spent in the filth of slavery. 'You are not the only one with tales to tell, you know.'

'What does he speak of?'

'He's *your* brother. And one of the ones you don't spend your time trying to kill. You should be able to guess what he speaks of.'

The prophet's black eyes glinted with some repressed emotion. She couldn't tell if it was amusement or annoyance.

'I still do not know Mercutian well.'

'He speaks of the Heresy, mostly. He tells me stories about brothers that died in the Siege of the Emperor's Palace, or the Thramas Crusade against the Angels, and the centuries since. He likes to write about them, recording their deeds and deaths. Did you know that?'

Talos shook his head. He'd had no idea.

'What did he say about the Prince of Crows?' he asked.

'That Sevatar wasn't killed.'

The words brought the ghost of a smile to the prophet's lips. 'That is an entertaining fiction. Every Legion has its conspiracies and myths. The Eaters of Worlds claim that one of their captains is the chosen of a bloodthirsty god.'

Octavia didn't smile. 'When will you make planetfall?'

'My brothers wished for me to see you first.'

She raised an eyebrow, smiling as she clutched her blanket tighter. 'To give me a history lesson?'

'No. I do not know what they wished. They mentioned some problem, some flaw.'

'I don't know what they could mean. I'm tired, but the flight here was hellish. I think I earned a little sleep.'

'They said it concerned Septimus, as well.'

She shrugged again. 'I still can't guess. He hasn't been lax in his duties, and neither have I.'

Talos thought for a moment. 'Have you seen him often, recently?'

She looked away. Octavia might have been skilled at many things, but she was a poor deceiver. 'I do not see him much, these nights. When are you making planetfall?'

'Soon.'

'I've been thinking about what comes next.'

He regarded her with a curious expression; one she'd never seen before that wasn't quite puzzlement, nor was it exactly interest or suspicion. It seemed to be all three.

'What do you mean?' he asked.

'I thought we would make a run for the Eye of Terror.'

He chuckled. 'Do not call it that. Only mortal star-sailors, frightened of their own shadows, call it that. We simply call it the Eye, or the Wound, or… home. Are you so keen to drift into those polluted tides? Many Navigators lose their sanity, you know. It is one of the reasons so many of our vessels rely on sorcerers as guides in the Sea of Souls.'

'It is the last place in the galaxy I would like to go.' Octavia narrowed her eyes as she smiled. 'You're avoiding the question. Just like every other time I ask it.'

'We cannot return to the Eye,' Talos replied. 'I am not avoiding the question. You know why I am reluctant to sail there.'

She did know. At least, she could make a decent guess. 'The eldar dreams,' she said, not quite a question.

'Yes. The eldar dreams. Worse than before, now. I will not return there just to die.'

Octavia was quiet again for a time. 'I'm glad you're awake again.'

Talos didn't answer her. He didn't understand why he'd been sent here. For several seconds, he merely glanced around the chamber, listening to the ripple of the water, the thrumming pulse of the hull's rumble, and…

…and the two heartbeats.

One was Octavia's, a steady *thump, thump, thump* of wet thunder. The other was a muffled stutter, almost quick enough to be a buzz. Both came from within her body.

'I am a fool,' he said, rising to his feet in a snarl of armour joints.

'Talos?'

He drew in a breath, seeking to quell a surge of anger. His fingers were trembling, the micro-servos in his knuckles whirred as his hands clenched into fists. Had he not been so weary and his senses so dulled, he'd have heard the two heartbeats immediately.

'Talos?' she asked again. 'Talos?'

He walked from her chamber without a word.

III

HOMECOMING

As soon as the door opened, Septimus realised he was probably going to die.

He had half a second to draw breath before the hand was at his throat, and another half-second to croak out a denial. The gauntlet closed around his neck with enough strength to choke off any breath, let alone speech, and he struggled as he was lifted off the decking.

'I warned you,' the intruder said. Septimus tried to swallow, and gagged instead. In response, the Night Lord hurled him across the chamber. He hit hard, crashing against the wall and sinking to the floor in a heap of slack, shivering limbs. Blood marked the black iron where his head had struck.

'I warned you,' the warrior said again, filling the room with the sound of armour joints and bootsteps. 'Was I somehow not clear enough? Was my warning something to be ignored merely because I was unconscious for fifty-five nights?'

He hauled Septimus up by the hair, and threw him against the opposite wall. The slave went down again, this time without a sound. The warrior kept advancing, kept speaking, his voice twisted into machine-like impassivity by his helm's vocaliser grille. 'Did I perhaps fail to express my meaning in absolute terms? Is that it? Is that where this savage breakdown in communication has occurred?'

Septimus struggled to rise. For the first time in his life, he drew a weapon on his master. At least, he tried to. With a snort that might or might not have been a laugh, the towering warrior thudded a boot into his slave's side – not a battlefield kick, but rather the scuffing of refuse from underfoot. Still, the modest, messy chamber echoed with the twig-snaps of breaking ribs. Septimus swore through clenched teeth, reaching for the pistol he'd dropped.

'You son of a…' he began, but his master cut him off.

'Let us not compound disobedience with disrespect.' The Night Lord took two steps forward. The first crushed the laspistol into pieces, grinding them along the deck in a mangled spray of abused metal components. The second rested on Septimus's back, slamming him face-first onto the decking and knocking the wind from his lungs.

'Give me one reason not to kill you,' Talos snarled. 'And make it *incredibly* good.'

Breath sawed in and out of the human's lungs, through the heavy, jagged obstructions of broken ribs. He could taste blood at the back of his throat. Through all his years of captivity, all the years they'd forced him to serve and aid them in their heretical war, Septimus had never once begged for mercy.

He wasn't about to start now.

'*Tshiva keln,*' he grunted through the pain. Pinkish spit painted his lips as he fought to breathe.

It was a night for first occurrences. Septimus had never before drawn a pistol on his master, and Talos had never before had one of his slaves tell him to 'eat shit'.

The prophet hesitated. He felt his malign concentration suddenly broken by a short burst of bemused laughter. It echoed hollowly around the small chamber.

'Ask yourself this, Septimus: does it seem wise to annoy me even further?' He dragged the bleeding human up by the back of the neck, and threw him a third time against the sloping iron wall. When Septimus went down this time he didn't curse, or resist, or do much of anything at all.

'That's better.' Talos stalked closer, and knelt by his barely breathing slave. Septimus's facial augmetics were damaged, the eye lens split by an ugly crack. Spasms quivered through him, and it was clear from the angle of his left arm that it'd been wrenched from its shoulder socket. Blood bubbled from the man's swollen lips, but no words came forth. That last fact was probably for the best.

'I warned you.'

Septimus turned his head slowly, facing the voice. He either couldn't say anything, or intelligently chose not to. His master's boot pressed down on his back, a veritable weight of absolute threat. It would take no effort at all to stamp down and reduce the human's torso to a pulp of disordered meat and bone.

'She is the most precious thing on this ship. We cannot sail the Mad Sea with her health compromised. *I warned you.* You are fortunate I do not skin you and hang your bones from New Blackmarket's ceiling.'

Talos lifted his boot from the slave's back. Septimus hissed in a slow breath, rolling onto his side.

'Master...'

'Spare me any false apologies.' Talos shook his head, the skull-painted faceplate passionless in its red-lens gaze. 'I have broken between fourteen and seventeen of your bones, and your cranial bionics need mainte-nance. The focusing retinal lens also has a longitudinal crack. Consider that punishment enough.' He hesitated, looking down at the prone human on the deck. 'You are also fortunate I do not order surgery to eunuch you. On my soul, I swear these words are true, Septimus: if you touch her again, the merest brush of skin against skin, I will let Variel flay you. Then, while you are still alive as a skinless, weeping husk, I will pull you apart with my bare hands, and let you watch your own limbs being fed to the Bleeding Eyes.'

Talos didn't bother to draw weapons to heighten the threat. He merely stared down. 'I own you, Septimus. I have afforded you many freedoms in the past because of your usefulness, but I can always train other slaves. You are only human. Defy me again, and you will live just long enough to beg for death.'

With those words, he left in a thrum of whirring armour joints. In the sudden silence, Septimus dragged in a wracking breath and began to crawl across the deck of his chamber. Only one thing would have roused his master's ire like that. The very thing he and Octavia had feared had evidently come to pass, and the Night Lords had sensed the changes in her biology. The revelation wasn't quite drowned in the sea of pain from the beating he'd received.

Septimus spat out two of his back teeth, and the man who would soon be a father promptly lost consciousness.

TALOS GATHERED THE Claws in the war room around the long hololithic council table. Eighty-one warriors in total, each standing in midnight clad. Many were bloodied, or yet bore armour scars from the purgation duties still taking place in the bowels of the *Echo of Damnation*. Stealing the ship back from the Red Corsairs had only been the first step. Cleans-ing a warship of this size would take years, with flamer teams incinerating the worst touches of Chaos taint – where the hull was corroded with foulness, or worse, where the metal had mutated into living tissue.

The *Echo of Damnation*, much like the *Covenant of Blood* before it, was essentially a city in space, carrying a crew of over fifty thousand souls. She was, in all ways, a grander beast and a greater beauty than the Stand-ard Template Construct cruisers and barges of the Adeptus Astartes that patrolled the heavens of the modern Imperium. The *Echo* had first tasted the void in the Great Crusade ten thousand years before, when the war-riors of the Legiones Astartes claimed the finest vessels for themselves, and sailed their warships at the vanguard of expansionist fleets. A strike cruiser of yesteryear wasn't always equal to its Imperial counterpart, and the *Echo* showed how they often eclipsed their newer cousins in size and firepower.

Fifty thousand souls. Talos had never grown used to the number, even as they toiled for decades below his boots. His life was among the ever-diminishing elite, and their most favoured slaves.

On the rare occasions he descended into the ship's dank reaches, it was for the duty of purging any insidious taint that threatened the ship's optimal function, or for the more plebeian desire for murder. Most of the slave-caste workers dwelled in the deepest reaches and lowest bowel-decks of the immense warship, toiling their lives away in the darkness, working as engine crews and the other menial tasks suitable for human cattle. Hunting for skulls and screams among the mortal chattel was merely one of the traditional paths of training. It was undeniably the most pleasurable.

Talos regarded his brothers, the eighty-one warriors pulled together by fate into a fragile alliance, drawn from the remnants of the Night Lords' Tenth and Eleventh Companies. However he'd intended to begin the war council was discarded once he saw them all gathered. One thing was abundantly clear from their ragged ranks, with some squads reduced to two or three surviving members.

'We must restructure the Claws,' he said to them.

The warriors shared glances. Neck joints hummed as they turned to one another.

'The infighting ends here, brothers. First Claw will remain six-strong. The other Claws will reform as close to full strength as they are able.'

Xeverine, a warrior never without his ornate chainglaive, raised his voice to speak. 'And who leads these new Claws, Soul Hunter?'

'Honour duels,' answered Faroven, wearing a similar ceremonial helm to Xarl. The winged crest dipped as he nodded. 'We should commit to honour duels. The victors lead the seven new Claws.'

'Honour duels are for the weak and fearful,' said one of the scarred veterans nearby. 'Murder duels should settle an issue of leadership.'

'We do not have the numbers to bleed away in murder duels,' replied Carahd, leader of Faroven's Claw.

Arguments broke out among the gathered squads, each seeking to shout the others down.

'No one is reaching for a weapon yet,' Xarl said quietly, 'but give it time, and we'll be wading through a bloodbath.'

Talos nodded. This had gone on long enough.

'Brothers,' he said. He kept his voice coloured by nothing but patience. Sure enough, one by one they fell silent. Eighty helms regarded him, variously painted with skulls, Nostraman runes, crested with high wings, or darkened by battle damage. To First Claw's left, the five remaining Bleeding Eyes vox-buzzed and hissed amongst themselves, but Lucoryphus favoured the prophet with his full attention. The Raptor lord was even standing up, his foot-claws unsuited to the posture, watching Talos with his sloped daemon-mask.

'Brothers,' Talos said again. 'We have eleven squad leaders, with enough warriors to make seven full Claws. All who wish an honour duel to claim leadership are free to do so.'

'And murder duels?' asked Ulris.

'Murder duels will be fought against Xarl. Anyone who wishes to kill a brother for the honour of leading a Claw is free to challenge him. I will grant a full Claw to anyone that slays him.'

Grumbling simmered between several of the Claws.

'Yes,' said Talos, 'that is what I thought you would say. Now enough of this, we have gathered for a reason.'

'Why did you bring us back to Tsagualsa?' one of the warriors called out.

'Because I am such a sentimental soul.' Bitter, mirthless laughter broke out across the chamber in answer. 'For those of you that have not heard, the planetary sweeps have detected cities capable of housing a population of over twenty-five million, principally spread across six major cities.'

Talos gestured to a tech-adept, who stepped forward to the table. Deltrian, his skeletal form robed as always, deployed a plethora of micro-tools through the tips of his fingers. One of them, a neural interface trident-pin, clicked within the table console's manual socket. A sizeable hololithic image of the grey world appeared in the air above the table, fraught with eye-watering flickers.

'I am operating under the primary hypothesis that the world's past requires no explanation to the legionaries of the Eighth.'

'Get on with it,' muttered one of the Night Lords.

Such disrespect. It galled Deltrian to think of the ancient bonds of allegiance between the Martian Mechanicum and the Legiones Astartes, now degraded to this degree. All the oaths that had been sworn, and all the rituals of respect – reduced to ashes.

'Honoured adept,' said Talos. 'Please continue.'

Deltrian hesitated, fixing the prophet with his dilating eye lenses. Without realising he still possessed such a curiously human habit, Deltrian reached up to adjust his hood, and sank his metallic features deeper into shadow.

'I will vocalise the principal factors in the defence array. First, the–'

The Night Lords were already speaking over one another. Several shouted their objections.

'We cannot attack Tsagualsa,' said Carahd. 'We cannot set foot upon that world. It is cursed.' Murmurs of agreement grew in chorus.

Talos gave a short bark of a laugh, the sound shaped for mockery. 'Is this really the time for idiotic superstition?'

'It is cursed, Soul Hunter,' Carahd protested. 'All know it.' But the agreeing mutters were fainter this time.

Talos leaned his knuckles on the desk, watching the gathered warriors. 'I am willing to allow this world to rot, forgotten on the edge of space. But I am *not* willing to walk away when the world we called home for so many decades is infested with Imperial filth. *You* may run from this, Carahd. *You* may weep over a curse ten thousand years old, and long grown cold. *I* am taking First Claw down to the surface. *I* will show these intruders the unforgiving nature of the Eighth Legion. Twenty-five million souls, Carahd. Twenty-five million mouths to scream, and twenty-five million hearts to burst in our hands. You truly wish to remain in orbit while we bring this planet to its knees?'

Carahd smiled at that. 'Twenty-five million souls.' The prophet could already see the glint of avarice in the warrior's eyes.

'Is a world cursed simply because we left it in a moment of indignity? Or is the curse a beautifully convenient masquerade to conceal our shame at running from our second home world?'

Carahd didn't answer, but the answer was clear in his colourless eyes.

'I am pleased that we understand one another,' finished Talos. 'Now, Deltrian, please continue.'

Deltrian reactivated the hololithic image. It bred a ghostly gleam across the dark armour-plating of the gathered warriors. 'Tsagualsa is as lightly defended as most Imperial frontier worlds. We have no data on the frequency or size of Naval patrols in the subsector, but given the location, viable projections indicate minimal and irregular presence of the Imperial war machine. Three Chapters of the Adeptus Astartes are known to hold protectorates in approximate regions. Each of these claims descent from Thirteenth Legion gene stock. Each of these was also present in the year–'

Talos cleared his throat. 'The vital details, please, honoured adept.'

Deltrian repressed a blurt of irritated binary. 'The world is undefended from orbit, as is common among frontier worlds, with the exception of any Imperial void patrols that are willing to risk venturing this far from the Astronomican. Without the Emperor's warp beacon to guide their Navigators, destruction within the Sea of Souls is a significant threat. I struggle to process the reasons the Imperium would even establish a colony this far into the Eastern Fringe. The cities on the surface are likely to be self-sustaining society-states, almost certainly adapted to depend on global resources rather than the infrequent imports from the wider Imperium.'

'What of military movements upon the surface?' asked one of the warriors.

'Analysing,' Deltrian said. He turned his hand as though turning a key in a lock. The neural interface link clicked in the console, and the hololithic stuttered, several sections of the world now flashing red. 'We have monitored satellite vox-traffic for the last sixteen hours, since arrival. It was initially remarkable in that so little communication takes place at all. The world is almost silent, suggesting devolution and/or a primitive grasp of technology.'

'Easy prey,' another legionary grinned across the chamber.

Cease interrupting, Deltrian thought. 'Three point one per cent of planetary vox communication was military in nature – or could be interpreted as such, in matters of city-state security and law enforcement – suggesting two things: firstly, that this world maintains a minor – perhaps infinitesimal – garrison of conscripts for planetary defence. Secondly, it suggests that despite its reasonable population statistics by the standards of Apex Degree frontier worlds, it levies no regiments for service in the Imperial Guard.'

'Is that unusual?' asked Xarl.

Cyrion chuckled. 'What does he look like, an Imperial recruiter?'

Deltrian ignored the misguided attempt at wit. 'Twenty-five million souls could sustain an Imperial Guard Founding, but frontier worlds seem to be marked for other tithes. The remote location of Tsagualsa makes it increasingly unfavourable and unlikely for Guard recruitment. It should be noted that the planet's inhospitability renders it detrimental – almost hostile – to human life. Auspex readings indicate settlements capable of sustaining the stated numbers, but actual populations are likely to be lower.'

'How much lower?' another warrior asked.

'Conjecture is useless. We will see for ourselves soon enough. The world is undefended.'

'In short,' Talos said, 'this world is ours, brothers. We need only to reach out our claws and take it. We will divide before planetfall,' Talos explained. 'Each Claw will take a section of the city, to do with as they please.'

'Why?'

All eyes turned to Deltrian. 'You have something to say?' Talos asked him.

The tech-adept took a fraction of a second to frame his thoughts into a verbal formation and tone calculated to offer the least offence.

'I would ask, lord, why you seek to make planetfall here at all. What does this defenceless world offer us?'

Talos didn't look away. His black eyes drilled into the tech-adept's cowl, locking to the glimmering lenses therein.

'This is no different to any other raid, honoured adept. We are raiders. We raid. This is what we do, is it not?'

'Then I would form a further query. Why did we travel across a quarter of the galaxy to reach this location? I suspect I need not process the number of worlds in the Imperium and calculate the percentage that offer potential raid targets. So I would phrase my query thusly: Why did we come to Tsagualsa?'

The Night Lords fell silent again. They watched the prophet in wordless patience, for once.

'I want answers,' Talos said. 'I believe I will find them here.'

'Answers to what, Soul Hunter?' one of the warriors asked. He could see the question mirrored in many of their eyes.

'To why we are still fighting this war.'

As expected, his answer was met with laughter, with the answers 'To win it' and 'To survive' mixed in with the amusement. That suited Talos well enough. Let them believe it was a veteran's joke, shared with his kindred.

IT TOOK THREE hours for Xarl to speak the words Talos had been expecting.

'You shouldn't have said that.'

The arming chamber was a hive of industry, as Septimus and several servitors machined First Claw's war-plate onto their bodies.

Cyrion glanced at the human serf helping to drill his shin guard into its locking position.

'You look like death,' he pointed out. Septimus forced a smile, but said nothing. His face was a palette of bruised swelling.

'Talos,' Xarl said, 'you shouldn't have said that in the war council.'

Talos closed and opened his fist, testing the workings of his gauntlet. It purred in a muted orchestra of smooth servos.

'What, exactly, should I not have said?' he asked, though he already knew the answer.

Xarl shrugged his left shoulder as a servitor drilled the pauldron into place. 'No one respects a maudlin leader. You are too thoughtful, too introspective. They considered your words to be a jest, and that was a saving grace. But trust me, brother, none of the Claws would wish to descend onto that cursed world purely to satisfy your desire for soul-searching.'

Talos nodded, agreeing easily while checking his bolter. 'True. Their only reason for making planetfall is to spread terror through the population, is it not? There's no place for nuance or deeper emotion in such shallow, worthless psyches.'

First Claw looked at their leader in silence for several moments.

'What is wrong with you?' Xarl asked. 'What bitterness grips you these nights? You were speaking like this before you fell into the long dream, and have been twice as bad since awakening. You cannot keep shouting out against the Legion. We are what we are.'

The prophet locked his bolter to his thigh plating along the magnetic seal. 'I am tired of merely surviving this war. I want to win it. I want there to be meaning behind fighting it.'

'We are what we are, Talos.'

'Then we must be better. We must change and evolve, because this stasis is worthless.'

'You sound like Ruven before he left us.'

The prophet's lips curled in a snide sneer. 'I have carried this bitterness for a long time, Xarl. The only difference is that now I wish to speak of it. And I do not regret it. To speak of these flaws is like lancing a boil. I already feel the poison bleeding from me. It is no sin to wish to live a life that matters. We are supposed to be fighting a war and inflicting fear in the name of our father. We are sworn to bear his vengeance.'

Xarl didn't hide the confusion taking hold of his pale features. 'Are you insane? How many among the Legion truly paid heed to the rantings of a mad primarch spoken so long ago?'

'I am not saying the Legion has heeded those words,' Talos narrowed his eyes. 'I am saying that we *should* heed them. If we did, our lives would be worth more.'

'The Legion's lesson is taught. It was taught when he died. All that remains is to survive as best we can, and wait for the Imperium to fall.'

'And what happens when it falls? What then?'

Xarl looked at Talos for a moment. 'Who cares?'

'No. That is *not* enough. Not for me.' His muscles bunched as he clenched his teeth.

'Be calm, brother.'

Talos moved forward, immediately restrained by Mercutian and Cyrion, who struggled to hold him back.

'It is *not* enough, Xarl.'

'Talos…' Cyrion grunted, seeking to drag the prophet back with both arms.

Xarl watched with wide eyes, unsure whether to reach for his weapon. Talos still sought to throw his brothers free. Fire danced in his dark eyes.

'It is *not* enough. We stand in the dust at the end of centuries of useless sin and endless failure. The Legion was poisoned, and we sacrificed an entire world to cleanse it. We failed. We are the sons of the only primarch to hate his own Legion. There, again, we failed. We swore vengeance on the Imperium, yet we run from every battle where we don't possess overwhelming force over a crippled enemy. We fail, again and again and again. Have you ever fought a battle you'd struggle to win, with no hope of running away? Have any of us? Have you ever, since the Siege of Terra itself, drawn a weapon with the knowledge you might die?'

'Brother…' Xarl began, backing away as Talos took another step closer, despite Cyrion and Mercutian's best efforts.

'I will not see my life whored away without meaning. Do you hear me? Do you understand me, prince of cowards? I want vengeance against a galaxy that hates us. I want Imperial worlds to cower when we draw near. I want the weeping of this empire's souls to reach all the way to Holy Terra, and the sound of suffering will choke the corpse-god on his throne of gold.'

Variel had joined in, restraining Talos from getting any closer to Xarl. Only Uzas stood apart, watching with dead-eyed disinterest. The prophet thrashed in their grip, managing to kick Cyrion away.

'I will cast a shadow across this world. I will burn every man, woman and child so the smoke from the funeral pyres eclipses the sun. With the dust that remains, I will take the *Echo of Damnation* into the sacred skies above Terra, and rain the ashes of twenty million mortals down onto the Emperor's Palace. *Then* they will remember us. *Then* they will remember the Legion they once feared.'

Talos hammered his elbow into Mercutian's faceplate, knocking his brother back with a crack of ceramite. A fist into Variel's throat sent the Apothecary sprawling, until no one stood between Xarl and the prophet. Talos aimed *Aurum*'s golden blade at his squadmate's left eye.

'No more running. No more raiding to survive. When we see an Imperial world, we will no longer ask if it is worth attacking for plunder, we will ask how much harm its destruction would cause the Imperium. And when the Warmaster calls us for the Thirteenth Crusade, we will answer him. Night by night, we will bring this empire to its knees. I will cast aside what this Legion has become, and remake it into what it should be. Do I make myself clear?'

Xarl nodded, his eyes locked to the prophet's. 'I hear you, brother.'

Talos didn't lower the blade. He breathed in the stale, recycled air of the shipboard ventilation, tinged with the musk of weapon oils and Septimus's fear-sweat.

'What?' he asked the slave.

Septimus stood in his beaten jacket, his scruffy hair loose around his face, not quite hiding the damaged optic lens. He held his master's helm in his hands.

'You are bleeding from your ear, lord.'

Talos reached to check. Blood marked the fingers of his gauntlets. 'My skull is aflame,' he admitted. 'I have never felt my thoughts running clearer, but the trade in pain is extremely unpleasant.'

'Talos?' one of his brothers said. He wasn't sure which one. Through blurring vision, they all looked the same.

'It is nothing,' he told the faceless crowd.

'Talos?' a different voice called. He was struggling with the realisation that they couldn't understand what he was saying. His tongue had turned thick. Was he slurring his words?

The prophet stilled himself, taking a deep breath.

'I am fine,' he said.

Each of them looked at him with doubt in their eyes. Variel's cold gaze was keenest of all.

'We must speak in the apothecarion soon, Talos. There are tests to be run, and suspicions I hope are not confirmed.'

'As you wish,' he conceded. 'Once we return from Tsagualsa.'

IV
THE THREAT OF WINTER

THE CITY OF Sanctuary barely deserved the title, and it deserved its name even less. By far the largest of the settlements on the far-frontier world Darcharna, it was a mongrel cityscape formed from landed explorator ships, half-buried colonist cruisers, and simple prefabricated structures risen against the howling dust storms that blanketed the planet's face in place of real weather.

Walls of cheap rockcrete and corrugated iron ringed the city limits, patchworked by flakboard repairs and armour-plating pried from the beached spaceships.

The lord of this spit-and-bonding-tape settlement looked out at his domain from the relative quiet of his office. Once, the room had been the observation spire aboard the Ecclesiarchy pilgrim hauler *Currency of Solace*. Now it stood empty of the pews and viewing platforms, housing nothing beyond the archregent's personal effects. He called it his office, but it was his home, just as it had been the home of every single archregent for the last five generations, since the Day of Downfall.

The window-dome was thick enough to suppress the gritty winds into silence, no matter how they thrashed and raged at the settlement below. He watched the gale's shadow now, unable to see the howling winds but forever able to see their influence in the flapping of ragged flags and the crashing of armoured windows slamming closed.

Will we go dark, he wondered. *Will we go dark again? Is this the first storm of yet another Grey Winter?*

The archregent pressed his hand to the dense glass, as though he could feel the gale blowing through the bones of his junkyard city. He let his gaze drift upward, to the thin cloud cover and the stars beyond.

Darcharna – the *real* Darcharna – was still out there somewhere. Perhaps the Imperium had despatched another colonist fleet to replace the one that had been lost with all souls in the deepest depths of the warp, only to find itself vomited back into real space in the Eastern Fringe.

What little contact existed between this Darcharna, the Darcharna they called home, and the wider Imperium was limited, to say the least. It was also not a matter for the populace. Some things had to be kept secret.

The last had been several years before – another garbled vox message from a distant world, relaying the signal from deeper beyond. Throne only knew how it had reached them. The automated response to several centuries of pulsed calls for supplies and extraction was blunt to the point of crudity.

You are protected even in the darkness. Remember always, the Emperor knows all and sees all. Endure. Prosper.

The archregent breathed slowly as the memory curdled in his thoughts. Its meaning was clear enough: *Remain on your dead world. Live there as your fathers did. Die there as your fathers did. You are forgotten.*

During his rule, he'd personally spoken to only two souls off-world. The first was the magos captain of a deep-space explorator vessel, with no interest in any dialogue beyond cataloguing the world's usefulness and moving on. Finding little of worth meant the ship had left orbit after a handful of hours. The second soul was a lord among the sacred Adeptus Astartes, who had informed him this region of space came under the protectorate of his warriors, the Genesis Chapter. They sought a fleeing xenos fleet outside the Emperor's Light, and while the Imperial Space Marine lord had professed sympathy with the unwilling colonists of Darcharna, his warship was no place for, in his words, 'the tread of ten million mortal boots'.

The archregent had said he understood, of course. One did not argue with warriors of heroic mythology. No, indeed – especially not when they displayed such a thin veneer of patience.

'Do you have no astropaths?' the Space Marine lord had pressed. 'No psychic souls with the power to call out into the void?'

Oh, they did. Incidents of psychic occurrence were perhaps a little too common on Darcharna; a fact the archregent had considered wise to conceal from the Adeptus Astartes lord. Half of the psychically-aware men and women born to the colony cities suffered mutation or deviance beyond tolerable allowance. As for the other half, many were put down in peace when they showed signs of failing their training. What passed for an Astropathic Guild in Sanctuary was a collection of shamans and interpreters of dreams, forever whispering to ancestor-spirits only they could see, and insisting on worshipping the sun as a distant manifestation of the Emperor.

Those leaders who donned the mantles of Ecclesiarchs – the archregent and abettor among them – sympathised with the solar reverence on this darkest of worlds. Despite most of the cities' populations having access to the old archives, a huge number of them considered themselves among the faithful.

Even so, there were limits. At best, the Astropathic Cult was a den of deviancy waiting to happen, with little to no ability to actually communicate off-world. At worst, they were already heretics in dire need of purging, just as they'd been culled by former archregents in previous generations. How many times had they called out into the void never to receive an answer, never to even know if their cries were loud or strong enough to reach other minds?

The archregent stood at his window for some time, watching the stars decorating the sky. In his reverie, he didn't even hear the dull grind of the door opening on low power.

'Archregent?' came a tremulous voice.

He turned then, to be met by the thoughtful eyes and perpetual frown of Abettor Muvo. The younger man was slender to the point of ill health, and his bloodshot eyes and yellowing skin told of organs working poorly. In this regard, he was no different from any of the population in Sanctuary, or any of the other settlements across Darchana. Crude hydroponic plantations in the sunless bowels of beached void cruisers sustained the surviving descendants of the first colonists, but hardly enriched them. There was – the archregent had decided long ago – surely a difference between living and simply being alive.

'Hello, Muvo,' the ageing man smiled. It deepened the lines of his thin face. 'To what do I owe the pleasure of your company?'

'The storm-scryers have sent word from the east hills. I thought you'd want to know.'

'I thank you for your diligence. Am I to assume Grey Winter falls once more? It feels early this year.' But then, it felt earlier every year. One of the curses of getting old, he thought.

The abettor's scowl softened for a rare moment. 'Would you believe, we actually have an uplink?'

The archregent didn't bother to conceal his surprise. Vox and pict communication beyond Sanctuary's walls, and often within it, were so unreliable the technology bordered on being abandoned. He could count on one hand the number of times he'd spoken over a vox in the last two years, and even then, all three of those times had been within Sanctuary's city limits.

'I would like that very much,' he said. 'Visual?'

The abettor gave an abrupt grunt and said nothing.

'Ah,' the archregent nodded. 'I thought not.'

The two men moved to the archregent's battered desk, looking into the dead screen set in the wooden face. Several dials needed re-tuning before anything like a voice resolved itself.

RIVALL MEYD, THE son of Dannicen Meyd, was a technician in the same vein as his father. He carried the official rank of storm-scryer, which gave him no small pride, but travelling up into the hills and predicting weather patterns was only a small part of his duties. Most of the people walled up back in Sanctuary and the other encampments knew little of his work.

He was content with their ignorance. Using his heirloom meteorological auspex scanners was more glamorous to layfolk than the truth, which was that he spent most of his time bandaged and goggled against the grit of the dust plains, looking for things that didn't exist and wasting time on things that couldn't be repaired.

They needed metal. The people of Sanctuary needed metal almost as much as they needed food, but there was almost none to be found. Any veins of ore he found in his travels were hollow and worthless. Any scrap metal from damaged ships on the Day of Downfall had been vultured up by his predecessors decades ago.

The vox towers and storage bunkers were another matter, but enjoyed the same measure of failure. The first generation of colonists, fresh from the Day of Downfall, had clearly been optimistic and enterprising souls. They'd built relay networks of communication towers across the plains, binding each city by the dubious reassurance of vox contact. Bunkers had been established beneath the ground, to refuel and resupply travellers making the overland journey between cities and satellite settlements. Even from their first landing, it was little trouble to brew and refine promethium fuel for wheeled vehicles, though flyers and void-worthy vessels were grounded – thirsty for fuel and unable to sustain flight in the winds anyway.

Rivall stood at the cliff's edge, brushing dust from the lenses of his macrobinoculars and looking back at Sanctuary as a stain on the horizon. Most of the city stood empty now. The fleet had come to Darcharna with almost thirty million souls cramped in the confines of pilgrim carriers and repurposed troop ships serving as colonist vessels. Planetwide estimates now numbered them at fewer than a third of that, in the four hundred and seventieth year since the Day of Downfall.

'Meyd, get over here.'

'What is it?' He lowered the macrobinoculars and moved over the rocks back to his partner. Eruko was wrapped as he was, no skin showing against the abrading wind. His friend was crouched by the backpack vox-caster, working the dials.

'It's only the bloody archregent,' Eruko said. 'If you're not too busy staring at the horizon.'

Meyd crouched with him, straining to hear the voice.

'...fine work, storm-scryers,' it was saying between distortion crackles. '...Winter?'

Meyd was the one to answer. 'The scanners register a drop in temperature, as well as an increase in winds, over the last week. The first storms are coming, but Grey Winter is still a few weeks away, sire.'

'Repeat please,' the voice returned.

Meyd breathed in deep, and lowered the cloth strips wrapped around his face, baring his lips to the scratching wind. He repeated himself, word for word.

'Good news, gentlemen,' replied the archregent.

'So we're gentlemen now?' asked Eruko quietly. Meyd smiled back.

'Sire?' Meyd spoke into the speech-handle. 'Any word from Takis and Coruda?'

'Who? I am afraid I'm not familiar with their names.'

'The…' Meyd had to pause to cough glassy grit from his throat. 'The team responsible for the next eastern boundary. They went to scout last night's asteroid for iron.'

'Ah. Of course. No word yet,' the archregent replied. 'My apologies, gentlemen.' Rivall Meyd liked the old man's voice. He sounded kind, always patient, like he genuinely cared.

'I assume this contact is only possible because you managed to repair the erosion damage to East Pylon Twelve.'

Meyd smiled, despite the grit stinging his lips. 'It is, sire.' He didn't add that they'd needed to junk an old dune-runner buggy to get it done.

'A rare victory. You have my thanks and admiration, both of you. Come to my office when your rotation ends. I will offer you a glass of whatever passes for alcoholic finery in my admittedly limited cellar.'

Neither Meyd nor Eruko replied.

'Gentlemen?' the archregent's voice rang out. 'Ah, have we lost the link?'

Eruko hit the ground first, his cheek breaking against the stone. He said nothing. He did nothing, except bleed in silence. The blade through his heart had killed him instantly.

Meyd wasn't dead when he fell. He reached a bleeding hand to the vox-caster's emergency rune button, but lacked the strength to push it. Bloodstained fingertips smeared meaningless patterns over the button's plastek surface.

'Gentlemen?' asked the archregent again.

Meyd drew the last breath of his life, and used it to scream.

THE ARCHREGENT LOOKED at the abettor. The younger man toyed with the hem of his brown robe's sleeves.

'I would like you to tell me that was interference,' the archregent said.

The abettor sniffed. 'What else would it have been?'

'It sounded to me like someone was crying out, Muvo.'

The abettor attempted to force a smile. It wasn't entirely successful. With respect to the older man, his hearing wasn't what it once was. They both knew how often Muvo had to repeat himself for the archregent.

'I believe it was interference,' the abettor said again.

'Maybe so.' The archregent ran his hands through his thinning white hair, and took a breath. 'I would still feel more comfortable sending out a search team if those gentlemen have not restored contact within the hour. You heard the wind, Muvo. If they fell from those cliffs...'

'Then they're already dead, sire.'

'Or in need of help. But dead or alive, we are recovering them.' He felt curiously energised for a moment. The dust plains had taken too many of them over the years, and Eruko and Meyd were close enough to recover in a few days, if the dust storms were really going to stay away a while longer.

The vox-channel crackled live again, as though the channels were being tuned. The abettor gave a joyless smirk of triumph. The archregent smiled in response.

'Interference, indeed. You win this round,' the old man said, but his fingers froze before they touched the dial. The voice rasping from the speakers wasn't human. It was too low, too guttural, too cold.

'You should never have settled on this world. Our shame is our secret to keep. Tsagualsa will be clawed clean of life once more. Hide in your cities, mortals. Lock your doors, reach for your weapons, and wait until you hear us howl. Tonight, we come for you.'

V

A PURE WAR

DANNICEN MEYD HAD noted his fifty-eighth birthday a month before, and on Darcharna that made him practically ancient. The grit in his bones from a life on the dust plains meant that it ached to move and it ached to lie still, and these days he did a lot more of the latter than the former.

The plains gave a man a serious beating over the years. There were the skin abrasions to deal with, which came with their own infections soon after. Then you had black lung to worry about from the grit getting into your mouth and nose, eventually losing lung tissue to decay or infection, and spending most of your time coughing up bloody phlegm.

Sore eyes were a constant misery – always leaking, yet somehow always dry – and his vision was clouded over by years of particulates dulling his sight. He didn't hear so well, either. The Emperor only knew what decades of ashy grit had done to his ear canals, but when his blood was up and his heart beating fast, everything was muted and faint, like he was hearing things underwater.

His heart hurt worst of all. Now it rattled and raged at him every time he walked for more than a few minutes.

All in all, he was a man with every right to his complaints, yet he had very few. Dannicen Meyd wasn't a man given over to musing over misery. He'd tried to talk Rivall out of the plains life, though. That hadn't worked out so well. It went almost exactly the same as it'd gone when Dannicen's own father had tried to say the same words to him, way back in a life before all these aches and pains.

He was giving in to that often-replayed memory when the city's sirens started up their discordant wail.

'You're not serious,' he said aloud. Storms were starting damn early this year. Last he'd heard from Rivall, they were supposed to have a few weeks yet, maybe even a month.

Dannicen hauled himself from the couch that served as his bed, sucking air through his teeth as his knees crackled in chorus. Both joints came

673

awake with needling jabs beneath the bone. *Nasty, nasty. Getting old is a bitch, make no mistake.*

A shadow passed his window. He looked up just as fists started pounding on the flakboard plank that served as his door.

'Throne of the bloody Emperor,' he grunted as his knees gave another protest, but he was up and walking no matter what they had to say about it.

Romu Chayzek was on the other side of the door. Romu Chayzek was also armed. The battered Guard-issue lasrifle hadn't been new this side of the millennium's turning, but as Watchman for South-43 Street down to North/South Junction-55, he had the right to bear arms in his patrols.

'Going hunting for dust rabbits?' he almost laughed, gesturing to the gun. 'A little early to be shooting looters, kid.'

'The sirens,' Romu was panting. He'd obviously run here, down the muddy alley that served as a street for the prefabricated bunkerish buildings.

'Storms are early.' Dannicen leaned out of the door, but any view of the horizon was stolen by Sanctuary's broken-tooth skyline. Families were pouring from their homes, milling through the street in every direction.

Romu shook his head. 'Come on, you deaf old bastard. To the sub-shelters with you.'

'Not a chance.' The Meyd house had stood up to every Grey Winter so far, as had most of those in this section of the city. South Sector, 20 through 50, had the choicest picks of the troop landers way back at the Day of Downfall. All that armour did the deed when it came to keeping out the worst of the dust storms.

'Listen to me, it ain't the storms. The archregent's under attack.'

For a moment, Dannicen didn't know whether to laugh or go back to bed. '…he's what?'

'This ain't a joke. He could be dead already, or… I don't know what. Come on! Look at the sky, you son of a bitch.'

Dannicen had seen the panic in Romu's eyes before, on the faces of those he'd served with outside the walls. That animal fear of being lost on the plains, turned about and directionless as a dust blizzard bore down. Helplessness – sincere, absolute helplessness – painted across a man's face, turning it sick and ugly.

He looked to the west, towards the distant archregent's tower, where a faint orange gleam illuminated the evening sky behind the rows of awkward urban stalagmites serving as a cityscape horizon.

'Who?' he asked. 'Who would attack us? Who even knows we're here? Who even cares?'

Romu was already running, blending in with the crowd. Dannicen saw him reach a cloth-wrapped hand to help a young boy back to his feet, and shove him into the press of bodies.

Dannicen Meyd waited another moment, before he took his aching knees and arthritic hands back inside his house. When he emerged, he carried his own lasrifle – and this one worked just fine, thank you very much. He'd used it in his own days as a volunteer Watchman, shooting looters in the Grey Winters after his retirement from storm-scrying.

He kept to the edge of the crowd, walking west as they pressed east. If the archregent was under attack, to hell with running and hiding. Let it never be said that Dannicen Meyd didn't know how to do his bloody duty.

He looked down, just briefly, to check his lasgun. That was the moment he heard the dragon.

The crowd, every one of them, screamed and crouched, covering their heads as the beast roared overhead. They looked up with terrified eyes as the roar hurt their ears. Only Dannicen remained exactly as he was, his bloodshot eyes wide in awe.

The dragon was black against the grey sky, screaming above them on howling… engines. Not a dragon at all. A flyer. A gunship. But nothing had flown on Darcharna for centuries. The crowd was screaming now, thin parents carrying their even thinner children and hiding their eyes.

It banked above them, streaming fire from its thrusters as the wind rattled grit against its armour-plating. Its own momentum had it drifting as it hovered in the air, fighting the wind raging against the dark hull. Its leering prow seemed to watch the panicking people below before the gunship slowly veered away. Buildings shivered and cracked as its thrusters gave a thunderous boom, kicking the flyer across the sky and into the distance in the time it took Dannicen to blink.

He broke into a run, the pain in his joints all but forgotten. 'Let me through,' he said when he needed to, though the crowd parted and was fleeing in the opposite direction with little encouragement from him. The gunship had been more than enough.

He made it three streets before his knees gave up the fight. He leaned against a shack wall, cursing at the needles in his joints. His heart felt no better, racing to the point of strain, sending tendrils of tightness through his chest. Dannicen thumped a fist against his breastbone, as if anger would soothe the spreading fire.

More orange glows were showing stark against the clouds now. More of the city was burning.

He caught his breath, and forced his knees to obey him. They shivered but complied, and Dannicen stumbled forward on shaking legs. He made it another two streets before he had to stop and let his breathing catch up to him.

'Too old for this foolishness,' he coughed as he slumped against the wall of a grounded Arvus industrial shuttle now serving as a family home.

Legiones Astartes power armour makes a distinctive thrum: the loud, violent hum of immense energy waiting to be released. The armour joints, not coated in layers of ceramite, are still armoured against harm and filled with servos and fibre-bundle cabling in imitation of living muscles. They snarl and whine with even the most modest movement, from a tilt of the head to a clench of fist.

Dannicen Meyd didn't hear any of this, despite it taking place mere metres away from where he stood, struggling to catch his breath. His blood was up, and his ears deaf to all but the ragged drumbeat of his own heart.

He saw the street clearing of life as people fled. Many were looking back at him, their eyes and mouths wide in screams Dannicen couldn't quite hear. His teeth itched now, and his gums ached. There was a tremor in the softness of his eyes, as though an aggressive, subsonic sound pulsed nearby. Something he couldn't hear, but could feel like an unwanted caress.

He blinked, wiping away the sting of his watering eyes, and lifted his head at last. What he saw crouching on the roof of the shuttle was enough to tear the thin walls of his heart at last.

The figure wore ancient battle armour, contoured ceramite the colour of midnight. Lightning bolts marked the armour-plating in clawed streaks. Slanted red eyes stared down at him from their place in a skull-faced helm. Spikes and spines knifed up from the figure's bulky armour, glistening with moisture in the moonlight. Blood coated the thing, from its face to its heavy boots.

Three heads, their ripped necks still leaking, were tied to its shoulder guard by their own hair.

Dannicen was already on his knees, his burst heart losing all rhythm. Instead of blood, it pumped pain. Bizarrely, his hearing faded back into being.

'You are suffering heart failure,' the crouching figure told him in a deep, emotionless rumble. 'The constriction in your chest and throat. The breath that will not come. This would be more amusing if you feared me, but you do not, do you? How rare.'

Dannicen raised his lasrifle, even through the pain. The figure reached down to take it from his hands, as though stripping a toy from a child. Without looking, the warrior crushed the barrel in his fist, mangling it and casting it aside.

'Consider yourself fortunate.' The figure reached next to lift the ageing man by his grey hair. 'Your life ends in mere moments. You will never feel what it is like to be thrown into the skinning pits.'

Dannicen breathed out a strangled, wordless syllable. He was soiling himself, without feeling it, without realising, as he lost control of his body at the edge of death.

'This is our world,' Mercutian told the dying man. 'You should never have come here.'

TORA SEECH'S MOTHER worked in a hydroponics basement, her father taught sector children to read, write and pray. She hadn't seen either of them in several minutes, since they'd run into the street and told her to wait in the single room that served the family as a house.

Outside, she could hear everyone shouting and running. The city's sirens were wailing loud, but there'd been no storm warnings before this. Usually her parents gave her a few days to pack and get ready to head to the shelters before the sirens started up.

They wouldn't have left her here. They wouldn't have run away with everyone else and left her here alone.

The growl started from far away, and came closer each time her heart beat. It was a dog's growl, an angry dog fed up with being kicked. Then the footsteps followed it. Something blocked the pale light from her window, and she dragged her thin blanket higher. She hated the sheet, it had fleas that brought her out in itchy lumps, but it was too cold without it. Now she needed it to hide.

'I see you under there,' said a voice in the room. A low, snarling voice with a crackle, like a machine-spirit come to life. 'I see the heat of your little limbs. I hear the beat of your little heart. I taste your fear, and it is sweet indeed.'

GERRICK COLWEN SAW one of them when he went back for his pistol. At first he thought his street was empty. He was wrong.

His first clear glance was of a figure almost a metre taller than a normal man, wearing spiked armour drawn from the depths of mythology. A skinless, bleeding body hung over each shoulder, raining dark fluid onto the dark armour-plating. Three more cadavers trailed along behind in the dust, hooked to the walking warrior by bronze chains pushed into their spines. Each of them had been skinned in the same crude rush, the skin peeled and torn from their body in indelicate rips. Dusty soil coated them now like false skin, painting the exposed musculature dark with ash.

Gerrick raised his pistol, in the bravest moment of his life.

Variel turned to him, a bloody flesh-saw in one hand and an ornate bolt pistol in the other. A sourceless peal of thunder boomed between them.

Something hit Gerrick in the stomach with the force of a truck crash. He couldn't even shout, so fast did all air leave his lungs, nor did he have time to fall before the bolt in his belly detonated, taking him apart in a flash of light.

There was no pain. He saw the stars spinning, the buildings tumbling, and fell into blackness just as his legless torso struck the mud road. The life was gone from his eyes before his skull cracked open on the ground, spilling its contents into the dirt, leaving him long dead before Variel started skinning him.

AMAR MEDRIEN POUNDED his fists on the sealed door.

'Let us in!'

The shelter entrance for three streets of his subsector was in the basement of the Axle Grinder, a dive bar set on a tri-junction. He never drank there, and the only time he'd spent more than five minutes in the place was the Grey Winter four years before, when most of his district had endured three weeks underground during dust storms that ravaged their homes.

He stood outside the sealed bulkhead with a tide of others, locked out of their assigned emergency shelter.

'They locked it too early,' voices were saying, back and forth.

'It's not a storm.'

'Did you see the fires?'

'Why did they seal the doors?'

'Break them down.'

'The archregent is dead.'

Amar ran his fingers along the door's seams, knowing he wouldn't find any sign of weakness, but with nothing left to do in the press of bodies from behind. If they kept packing the basement – and the flood showed no sign of slowing – he'd be crushed against the old iron before long.

'They're not going to open it...'

'It's already full.'

He shook his head as he heard the last remark. How could it be full? The bunker had room for over four hundred people. Close to sixty were still out here with him. Someone's elbow dug into his side.

'Stop pushing!' someone else shouted. 'We can't get it open.'

Amar grunted as someone shoved him from behind. His face thumped against the cold iron, and he couldn't even get enough room to throw an elbow back to clear some space.

The tinny whine of the door release was the most beautiful song he'd ever heard. People around him cheered and wept, backing away at last. Sweating hands gripped at the door's seams, pulling it open on hinges in dire need of oiling.

'Merciful God-Emperor...' Amar whispered at the scene within. Bodies littered the bunker's floor, each one mutilated beyond recognition. Blood – a slow river of the thick, stinking fluid – gushed out across Amar's boots and over the ankles of those waiting behind him. Those who couldn't see what he saw were already shoving against those in the front rows, eager to get into their false solace.

Amar saw severed limbs cast in every direction; blood-spattered fingers gently curled as they dipped into the bloody pools across the floor. Body upon body upon body, many strewn where they had fallen, others heaped in piles. The walls were flecked with graceless sprays of red over the dark stone.

'Wait,' he said, so quiet that he couldn't even hear himself. The shoving from behind didn't cease. 'Wait...'

He stumbled with the pressure, staggering into the chamber. As soon as he crossed the threshold, he heard the roar of a chainblade revving up.

Streaked with blood, most notably a fresh palm-print on the faceplate of his helm, Uzas rose from his hiding place beneath a cairn of corpses.

'Blood for the Blood God.' He spoke through lips stringed by spit. 'Skulls for the Eighth Legion.'

THE ARCHREGENT LOOKED down at the fires, and wondered how metal ships could burn. He knew it wasn't the hull itself catching flame, but the flammable contents within the vessel's body. Still, it seemed strange to watch smoke and flame pouring from ruptures in the walls of his grounded ship. The wind couldn't steal all the smoke. Great plumes of it choked the air around the observation spire, severing his sight beyond the closest buildings.

'Do we know how much of the city is burning?' he asked the guard by his desk.

'What few reports we've had suggest most of the population is making it to their assigned shelters.'

'Good,' the archregent nodded. 'Very good.' *For whatever it's worth*, he thought. If their attackers had come to kill them, hiding in the subterranean shelters would achieve nothing beyond herding the people together like animals for the slaughter. Still, it reduced the chaos on the streets, and that made it progress of a kind.

'The lockdown list, sire,' another guard said. He wore the same bland uniform as the first, and carried a data slate in one gloved hand. The archregent glanced at it, noting the number of shelters reporting green light lockdowns.

'Very good,' he said again. 'If the raiders make demands, I want to be informed the moment the words have left their lips. Where is Abettor Muvo?'

Providence answered, as Muvo entered before any of the twelve guards could reply.

'Sire, the western granaries are burning.'

The archregent closed his eyes. He said nothing.

'Landers are coming down in the western districts, deploying servitors, mutants, machinery and... Throne only knows what else. They're excavating pits and hurling the bodies of our people into the holes.'

'Have we managed to send word to the other settlements?'

The abettor nodded. 'Respite and Sanctum both sent acknowledgements of warnings received.' He paused for a moment, his bloodshot eyes flicking to the scene beyond the glass dome walls. 'Neither of them will have any better chance at defending against this than we do.'

The archregent took a breath. 'What of our militia?'

'Some of them are gathering, others are heading into the shelters with their families. The Watchmen are organising shelter retreats. Should we call them off storm protocol?'

'Not yet. Spread word through the streets that all Watchmen and militia should gather at their assigned strongholds as soon as the shelters are locked down. We have to fight back, Muvo.'

He looked at his two guards, and cleared his throat. 'With that in mind, might I have a weapon, young man?'

The guard blinked. 'I... sire?'

'That pistol will do, thank you.'

'Do you know how to fire it, sire?'

The archregent forced a smile. 'I do indeed. Now then, Muvo, I need you to... Muvo?'

The abettor raised a shaking hand, pointing over the archregent's shoulder. Every man in the chamber turned, facing a huge vulture silhouette in the smoke. The dome was dense enough to drown out all sound, but the amber flare of the gunship's engines cast myriad reflections across the reinforced glass. They watched it rise higher, an avian wraith in the mist, until it hovered above the dome's ceiling. Fire washed down against the dome, spilling liquid-like over the surface, beautiful to behold from below.

The archregent saw the gunship's maw open, a ramp lowering into the air, and two figures fall from the sky. A flash of gold from one of their hands speared downward, splitting the dome with brutal cracks from the impaling point.

Both figures' boots struck the cracks as they fell, shattering the dome's ceiling in a storm of glass. Razor diamonds rained into the centre of the chamber, coupling with the breathy roar of the gunship's engines, no longer held silent by the transparent barrier.

The figures fell twenty metres before thudding down onto the deck with enough force to send tremors through the chamber. For a moment, they knelt in the dent they'd caused, crouched in their impact crater with their heads lowered. Glass hailstones broke almost musically against their armour.

Then they rose. One held an oversized chainsword, the other a golden blade. They moved in predatory unison, animalistic without intent, walking towards the desk. Each of their steps was a resonating thump of ceramite on iron.

Both of the archregent's guards opened fire. In the same moment, both armoured warriors threw their weapons. The first died as the golden sword speared him through the chest, dropping him to the floor in a twitching heap. The second went down as the chainsword smashed into his face and torso, the live teeth eating into his flesh. Streaks of warm meat and hot blood splashed across the abettor and archregent. Neither man had moved.

The archregent swallowed, watching the armoured figures approach. 'Why?' he asked. 'Why have you come here?'

'Wrong question,' Xarl smiled.

'And we owe you no answers,' said Talos.

The archregent raised the borrowed pistol and sighted down the barrel. The warriors kept walking. Next to him, Abettor Muvo was interlacing his fingers, seeking to quell their shaking.

'The Emperor protects,' the archregent said.

'If he did,' replied Talos, 'he would never have sent you to this world.'

Xarl hesitated. 'Brother,' he voxed, ignoring the old man with the gun. 'I am getting a signal from orbit. Something is wrong.'

Talos turned back to the other Night Lord. 'I hear it, also. Septimus, bring *Blackened* along the eastern edge of the spire. We must return to the void at once.'

'Compliance, master,' was the crackling reply. Within moments, the gunship was hovering by the dome's edge, gangramp lowering like an eagle's hooked maw.

'The Emperor protects,' the archregent whispered again, trembling now.

Talos turned his back on the mortal. 'It would seem that on rare occasions, he really does.'

Both Night Lords dragged their swords clear from the dead bodies as they ran, and drew bolters mid-sprint, opening fire on the reinforced glass. Their armoured forms crashed through the damaged barrier, taking them into the smoke and out of sight. The archregent watched their silhouettes vanish into the darkness of the gunship's innards, still unable to blink.

'The Emperor protects,' he said a third time, amazed that it was so very, tangibly true.

TALOS HELD HIS head in his hands. The pain was a rolling throb now, pushing at the back of his eyes. Around him, First Claw were readying their weapons, standing and holding to the handrails as the gunship climbed back into the sky.

'Is it a Navy vessel?' Cyrion was asking.

'They think it's an Adeptus Astartes cruiser,' Xarl held a hand to the side of his helm, as if it would aid his hearing. 'The vox reports are exciting, to say the least. The *Echo* is taking a beating.'

'We outgun any of their cruisers.' Mercutian was kneeling as he refitted his heavy bolter, not looking up at the others.

'We outgun them when they don't break into the system and knife us in the spine from a perfectly executed ambush,' Cyrion pointed out.

Talos drew breath to speak, but no words left his lips. He closed his eyes, feeling tears in his eyes and hoping it wasn't blood again. He knew it would be, but holding to hope prevented his temper from flashing free.

'The Sons of the Thirteenth Legion,' he said. 'Armour of scarlet and bronze.'

'What is he saying?'

'I...' Talos began, but the rest of the sentence fled from him. The sword hit the deck first. The prophet collapsed to his hands and knees a moment later. Behind his eyes, the darkness was returning in a tidal roar, hungry for his consciousness.

'Again?' Xarl sounded angry. 'What in hell's name is wrong with him?'

'I have my suspicions,' answered Variel, kneeling beside the prone warrior. 'We have to get him to the apothecarion.'

'We have to defend the damned ship when we reach it first,' Cyrion argued.

'I hear sirens,' Talos said, and fell forward once more into the yawning maw of nothingness.

VI
ASSAULT

He woke laughing because of Malcharion. The war-sage's deep, rumbling declaration from over a year before rattled through his aching head, when the Dreadnought had woken with the words *I heard bolter fire.*

He could hear bolter fire too. There it was, that unmistakable drumbeat – the heavy, juddering chatter of bolters opening up against one another. The distinctive thuds of fired shells and the echoing crash of them detonating against walls and armour set up a familiar cacophony.

The prophet dragged himself to his feet, smacking a hand to the side of his helm, forcing the retinal display to re-tune. He stared at his surroundings: the confined troop bay of his own Thunderhawk gunship.

'Fifty-three minutes, master,' said Septimus, relaying the exact duration of his unconsciousness. Talos turned to see his servant, clad in his usual ragged flight jacket, low-slung pistols at his hips.

'Tell me everything,' the warrior ordered. Septimus was already handing him his weapons, one after the other. The human needed both hands to lift each one.

'I know little. All Claws were recalled before a brief void battle began. We've been boarded by the enemy. I do not know if our shields are still down, but the enemy cruiser isn't firing with their own men on board. We came into the cortex hangar, under Lord Cyrion's orders. He wished to be close to the bridge for the defence.'

'Who boarded us?'

'Imperial Space Marines. I know nothing more. Did you not dream of them?'

'I do not remember what I dreamed. Just the pain. Stay here,' Talos ordered. 'My thanks for watching over me.'

'Always, lord.'

The prophet descended the gangramp, into the hangar. Mute servitors and skull drones watched him impassively, as if expectant he might offer them orders.

'Talos?' one of his brothers voxed.

'Was that Talos laughing?' came another voice.

'Fall back!' That was Lucoryphus. That was definitely Lucoryphus, he could tell from the bass-edged rasp. 'Fall back to the second concourse!'

'*Stand your ground!*' Cyrion? Yes... Cyrion. The vox made it hard to tell. '*Stand your ground, you carrion-eating bastards. You'll leave us without support.*'

From there, the vox-network degenerated back into a melee of conflicting voices.

'Is that Talos laughing?'

'This is Xan Kurus of Second Claw...'

'Where is that damned Apothecary?'

'This is Fourth Claw to First, we need Variel immediately.'

'Falling back from the tertiary spinal. Repeat, we've lost Spinal Tertius.'

'Who was laughing?'

'Talos? Is that you?'

The prophet heaved breath in through a throat that that felt atrophied from disuse. 'I am awake. First Claw, status report. All Claws, report in.'

He didn't receive an answer. The vox broke apart in a fresh gale of bolter fire.

Talos staggered from his small hangar, weapons loose in fists that still spasmed with residual pain. He followed the sounds of bolter fire, and made it no more than five hundred metres down the winding corridors before he found its closest source.

Indeed, he staggered on weak limbs right into the middle of a firefight, and promptly took a shell to the side of the head.

It LEFT HIM blind for a moment. The shell that cracked against the side of his helm was deflected by the angle, but hit with enough force to scramble the delicate electronics for an irritating cluster of seconds. Vision returned in a static-laden wash of red-tinted sight and flickering runic displays.

'Stay down,' warned a voice. Mercutian stood above him, hands shaking with the kickback from his bolter cannon. Bolt weaponry offered little in the way of muzzle flash, but the ignition from every self-propelled shell flickered a splash of amber across Mercutian's midnight armour.

'This is Mercutian of First Claw,' he voxed. 'The Bleeding Eyes have broken ranks. We are cut off in the primary concourse, strategium deck. Requesting immediate reinforcement.'

A voice crackled back, 'You are on your own, First Claw. Good hunting.'

Talos turned as Cyrion moved into view. His brother held a gore-wet gladius in one hand, and his bayoneted bolter in the other. Cyrion cracked off three shots, one-handed, barely aiming.

'Nice of you to wake up,' he commented with commendable calm, never once even glancing at Talos. Cyrion threw his gladius into the air, reloaded with smart precision, and caught the sword as it fell back into his grip. Several dozen metres down the corridor, the vague figures of their foes never moved from cover. The reason for their tactical concealment was Mercutian. Or, more accurately, Mercutian's booming heavy bolter.

'We're going to die here,' Mercutian grunted over the cacophony of his pounding weapon. He never stopped firing, the cannon kicking in bellowing three-round bursts, bathing himself in stark, amber flashes.

'Oh,' Cyrion agreed amiably, 'no doubt.'

'Those *kalshiel* Bleeding Eyes,' Mercutian swore as he dropped to one knee, reloading as fast as he could. Cyrion took up the screen of fire, bolter shells detonating down the length of the corridor.

'They'll charge any moment, Talos,' he warned. 'You could use that pretty bolter of yours, you know. There's no better time for it.'

Talos half-dragged himself into cover behind a wall arch. Both his blade and bolter were on the decking by his boots. These, he retrieved with a grunt at his unclear vision and the pain weaving its way down his spine. It took him two attempts to level his massive bolter, before he added its weight to the chorus of gunfire. Torrents of explosive shells barked down the yawning corridor. Thirty seconds passed in the stuttering melody of drumming gunfire.

'What happened?' he asked. 'Who boarded us? What Chapter?'

Cyrion laughed. 'You don't know? You dreamed this, didn't you? You said "armour of scarlet and bronze" before you lost consciousness.'

'I recall nothing,' Talos confessed.

'Reloading,' Mercutian called out. He dropped to one knee again, eyes still fixed on the tunnel, hands moving in dark blurs. A crunch, a click, and the heavy bolter sang its throaty song once more.

'What happened?' Talos repeated. 'Blood of the False Emperor, *someone* tell me what's happening.'

Cyrion's explanation broke off as Uzas crashed into the middle of the corridor. He dropped from the ceiling, falling from a crew ladder with his hands around the throat of a red-armoured Imperial Space Marine. Both warriors tumbled through the line of fire, causing the opposing squads to break off their attacks, even if only for a moment.

'Idiot,' Mercutian breathed, finger idling by his trigger.

The Imperial warrior threw a fist to Uzas's faceplate, snapping the Night Lord's head back with a bone-jarring echo. As their brother staggered, the rest of First Claw cut the Space Marine down with a blistering hail of bolter fire.

The Space Marine fell with a cry of his own. Unimpeded now, the enemy squad at the other end of the corridor advanced, bolters up and crashing with the same *thud, thud, thud* as First Claw's kicking guns. Shells exploded around Talos's cover, showering him with debris.

Uzas ran, and for once he maintained enough sense to run in the saner direction, back toward his brothers. Talos watched the warrior stagger as a shell took him high in the spine, and another clipped the back of his leg. Uzas smacked against the wall at Mercutian's side, rebounding from the steel in a hideous squealing crackle of abused ceramite. When he sank to the decking, his helmeted head crashed against the floor with the ringing finality of a funeral bell.

'Idiot,' Mercutian repeated, his heavy bolter rumbling. The enemy squad reached halfway along the corridor, leaving their dead and dying on the deck behind them. And still, they kept to the cover of the gothic-arched walls.

Talos's retinal display showed First Claw's vital signs still beating strong. With more trouble than he cared to confess, he moved to Uzas's side, dragging the twitching fool into cover. His brother's armour was scorched black, the shreds of flayed flesh serving as his cloak now burnt to cinders. Uzas had been drenched in flamer promethium more than once in the recent past. The chemical stink rose from his blackened battleplate in a miserable tang.

'Son of a...' Uzas mumbled, and fell into a coughing fit. His heaving chokes were sickly wet.

'Where's Variel?' Talos asked. 'Where's Xarl? I'll kill you myself if you don't start answering me.'

'Xarl and Variel are holding the rear tunnels.' Cyrion was reloading again. 'These wretches had already engaged the *Echo* in orbit before we docked. One way or another, the Imperium was waiting for us.'

Mercutian retreated a couple of steps as a lucky shell detonated against his shoulder guard, spraying all three of them with ceramite wreckage.

'Genesis Chapter,' he growled. 'Boarded us an hour ago. Scum-blooded cousins to the Ultramarines.'

'Perhaps we left the warp too close to Newfound before we drifted into the Tsagualsa system,' Cyrion admitted. 'I doubt it, though. More likely that they tracked us from warp beacons left by their Librarius division. Cunning fellows, these thin-bloods.'

'Very cunning,' Mercutian grumbled.

'You can blame your Navigator, of course,' Cyrion remarked. The wall by his head burst in a spread of sharp fragments. 'She should have sensed the beacons these tenacious dogs left in the warp.'

Talos slammed back into cover as he reloaded. 'She said she sensed something, but she had no idea what they were,' he said. 'We need to fall back. This corridor is lost.'

'We can't fall back from here, we're the only defenders on this arc. If they get onto the bridge, we'll lose the ship. The void shields are still down, as well. Deltrian is sweating oil and blood trying to repair the primary generator.'

'And we can't run,' Mercutian muttered. 'The Bleeding Eyes were hold-ing the southern walkways. The Imperials are closing on us from behind now, too.' Mercutian cursed and fell back another few steps. 'Oh, hell. *He* looks dangerous.'

The prophet left Uzas slouched and bleeding against the wall, mov-ing to his brothers and aiming down the corridor they were generously feeding with explosive fire. His vision had fully re-tuned at last, targeting locks flickering and zeroing in on individual enemies. He could make out the ornate chains and tabards draped across the foes' armour, and the emblems inscribed, worn with righteous pride. One warrior stood out above all, walking closer with inevitable purpose.

'Oh,' Talos said. What followed were several multi-syllabic curse words in Nostraman, with no literal Gothic translation. They were not fit for polite society, or even the less decadent tiers of impolite society.

Cyrion fired with his bolter at his cheek, laughing as he replied. 'At least we'll be killed by a hero.'

THE VOID SHIELDS weren't down. That wasn't the problem.

'Analysing,' the tech-adept said aloud. 'Analysing. Analysing.' He stared through ream upon ream of runic figures streaming through his mind. The link to the generator's cogitator was strong and fluid, but the amount of information was taking an unacceptable amount of time to filter.

The problem wasn't that the void shields were down. The problem was they had dropped for three minutes and nine seconds, and the ship had suffered an as yet unknown degree of infestation exactly forty-eight minutes and twelve seconds previously. In the battle with the enemy ship, those precious seconds of vulnerability had been enough for the enemy to board them in heavy numbers.

The thought of all those Imperial Space Marines tearing the *Echo* apart from within would have made Deltrian's skin crawl, had he any skin remaining.

The shields revived, but the generator itself was strained to the point of damaging itself. This led to a further problem: that unless he managed to bring the generator back to a semblance of stability, it might flicker-fail again if the enemy fleet fired another barrage. Perhaps it was unlikely they would, with scores of their own troops on board, but Deltrian hadn't achieved something close to immortality by relying on supposi-tion and assumption. He was a creature that didn't play the odds. He weighted them in his favour.

To extrapolate further, a second flicker-fail would potentially cost them the ship if the shields didn't revive quickly enough. Worse, it could lead to a complete failure, which would not only cost them their ship, but also their souls.

Deltrian had no intention of dying, especially not after investing so much time and meticulous care into resculpting so much of his biological frame into this artifice of mechanical perfection. Nor did he wish his immortal soul to spill out into the transmogrifying ether, to be pulled apart at the amused mercies of daemons and their mad gods.

That, as he was so fond of saying, would not be optimal.

'Analysing,' he said again.

And there it was. The bruise of flawed code, mixed in with the generator's scrambled cogitations, lost and found within a thousand thoughts per second. The damage was minimal, and focused around several of the external projector arrays on the starboard hull. They could be repaired, but not remotely. He'd need to send servitors, or go in person.

Deltrian didn't sigh. He registered his irritation with a non-linguistic blurt of machine-code, as if belching in binary. With an exaggerated patience he didn't possess, the tech-seer activated his epiglottal vox by simulating the act of swallowing.

'This is Deltrian.'

The vox-network replied with an overwhelming miasma of shouting and gunfire. Ah yes, the defence effort. Deltrian had quite forgotten. He disengaged from the terminal and re-tuned into his surroundings.

He considered the scene for a moment. The Void Generatorum was one of the largest chambers on the ship, with its walls layered in clanking power facilitators forged from bronze and sacred steel. All of these secondary nodes fed the central column, which itself was a black iron tower of throbbing plasma, with the churning liquid energy visible from the outside through the eyes and open mouths of gargoyles sculpted onto the pillar's sides.

Only now, as his focus returned to the external world, did he see the madness had ceased. The chamber around him, so recently alive with crashing gunfire and vox-altered screaming, was now beautifully silent.

The enemy boarders – or rather, the fleshy, broken things that had until so recently been the enemy boarders – lay in a ruptured carpet of blood-soaked ceramite across the chamber. Deltrian's olfaction sensors registered a severe level of vascular and excretory scents in the air, enough to make mortal digestive tracts rebel in protest. The smell of the slain was nothing to Deltrian, but he recorded the charnel house stench for the sake of completion in the reference notes he planned to compile later that evening.

His attackers hadn't come anywhere near him. That was because Deltrian, like many adepts of the Machine Cult, was first and foremost a believer in preparation to cover all contingencies, and secondly, a practitioner in the habit of overwhelming force. As soon as the void shields had failed for that split second, he knew the Night Lords would be scattered across the ship, defending every deck against the anomalous outbreak. So he took his safety into his own hands.

Admittedly, three-quarters of his servitors hadn't survived. He paced the chamber, taking stock of the variances in slaughter. Those still standing were slack-faced automatons, lobotomised past personality, their left arms amputated in favour of bulky heavy weaponry. Bionics covered at least half of their skin and replaced a great deal more of their internal functioning. Each one was a labour of faith, if not quite love, and required unswerving attention to detail.

He didn't thank them, nor offer congratulations on their victory. They'd never register it, either way. Still, to slay ten Imperial Space Marines was no mean feat, even at the cost of… (he counted in a heartbeat) …thirty-nine enhanced servitors and twelve gun-drones. A loss like that would inconvenience him for some time.

Deltrian paused a moment to regard the emblem on a dislocated shoulder guard. A white triangle, crossed by an inverted sigil. Their armour was a proud, defiant red.

'Recorded: Genesis Chapter. Thirteenth Legion genestock.' *How delightful. A reunion, of sorts.* He'd last encountered these warriors – or their genetic forefathers, at least – in the Tsagualsan Massacre.

'Phase One: complete,' he said aloud, as he pulsed the affirmation code to the surviving servitors' waiting minds. 'Commence Phase Two.'

The cyborgs fell into step, continuing the execution of their previously laid out order rotation. Half of the dozen remaining would move through the ship in a pack, carrying out seek-and-destroy subroutines. The other half would walk with Deltrian, back to the Hall of Reflection.

The ship quivered, hard enough for one of his servitors to miss its footing and emit an error message from its cybernetic jaw. Deltrian ignored it, tapping back into the vox.

'This is Deltrian to Talos of First Claw.'

Bolter fire answered, distant and crackly over the vox. 'He's dead.'

Deltrian hesitated. 'Confirm.'

'He's not dead,' came another voice. 'I heard him laughing. What do you want, tech-priest?'

'To whom am I speaking?' Deltrian asked, not bothering to inflect his voice with any aural signifiers of politeness.

'Carahd of Sixth Claw.' The warrior broke off, replaced for a moment by bolter chatter. 'We're holding the port landing platform.'

Deltrian's internal processors required a fraction of a heartbeat to recall Carahd's facial appearance, Legion record, and every modification made to his battle armour in the last three centuries.

'Yes,' he said, 'your situational update is fascinating. Where is Talos of First Claw?'

'First Claw is engaged on the primary concourse. What's wrong?'

'I have discovered and analysed the flaw in void shield function. I require the lord's order, and an escort, to–'

Carahd's vox-link deteriorated, breaking apart with the sound of furious screaming.

'Carahd? Carahd of Sixth Claw?'

Another voice took over. 'This is Faroven of Sixth Claw, we're falling back from the landing bays. Anyone still breathing in the sternward concourses, link up with us in New Blackmarket.'

'This is Deltrian, I require a Legion escort to–'

'For the love of all that is sacred, *shut up*, tech-priest. Sixth Claw falling back. Carahd and Iatus are down.'

Another voice crackled in reply. 'Faroven, this is Xan Kurus. Confirm Carahd is down.'

'I had visual confirmation. One of these aquila-bearers took his head off.'

Deltrian listened to the legionaries as they defended the ship. Perhaps their disrespect was excusable, given the circumstances.

Walking around the organic refuse that had once been loyal soldiers of the Golden Throne, and the mortuary of modified bodies that had been his own weaponised minions, Deltrian decided to take matters into his own hands yet again.

LUCORYPHUS OF THE Bleeding Eyes wasn't limited to the decking in the same way as his lesser kindred. He couldn't run though, not as he once might have done. His retreat was a surprisingly agile and unarguably feral race on all fours, his hands and foot-claws clanking on the deck grilles in bestial rhythm. He ran as an ape would, or a wolf, or – as he was – a warrior who'd not been fully human in many years, thanks first to Imperial genetic redesign, and later to the shifting tides of the warp.

Lucoryphus, perhaps more than most of his brothers, wanted to live. He refused to die for their cause, and refused to stand his ground in a hopeless battle, let alone one he was ill-suited to fight in the first place. Let the madness of futile last stands be something his brothers embraced. He lived his life, twisted as it was, by a code of abject rationality. Thus, as he fled, he felt nothing in the way of shame.

Responding to his feverish need for self-preservation (one couldn't call it fear, especially when it lay closer to anger), the thrusters on his back trailed thin, bleak coils of smoke. They were eager to breathe flame and howl loud, carrying him up into the sky. He was eager to give in to it. All he needed was somewhere to soar. Trapped on board the dying *Echo*, it wasn't a likely prospect.

Over the vox, First Claw were still berating the Bleeding Eyes for retreating.

'Let them whine,' Vorasha chuckled, his laughter a hissing '*Ss-ss-ss*'. Both of them were clinging to the ceiling as they fled. The other Bleeding Eyes, whittled down these last months to the most stubborn and brutal survivors, clawed their way across the walls and floor.

The ship shuddered again. Lucoryphus had to cling to the metal for a moment with his hands and foot-claws, to prevent being shaken free.

'No,' he hissed back. 'Wait.'

The Bleeding Eyes halted with inhuman union, each of them holding motionless, clinging to the walls around their leader: a pack meeting in three dimensions. Vorasha tilted his sloping helm, watching as a bird might. Each of them regarded their champion with the same tear-trails painted upon their daemonic iron faceplates.

'What? What is it?'

'You go.' Lucoryphus punctuated his order with an irritated shriek. 'Fall back to the second concourse. Reinforce Fourth Claw.'

Their muscles tensed as the instinct to obey ran through them. 'And you?' Vorasha hissed back. Lucoryphus gave a wordless cry, the call of a carrion crow, as he turned and moved back the way they'd come.

The Bleeding Eyes regarded each other as their leader tore back down the corridor, running along its ceiling. Instinct pulled at them: the pack hunted together, or not at all.

'Go,' Lucoryphus voxed back to them

Without sharing a word, they reluctantly obeyed.

FROM HIS BIRTH on an orderly, respected feudal world at the edges of Ultima Segmentum, the warrior had risen among the ranks of his Chapter through a liberal measure of discipline, focus, skill and peerless tactical acumen. None of his brothers had bested him in an honour duel for close to four decades. He'd been offered a company captaincy on three occasions – to assume the mantle of mastery over a hundred of the Emperor's chosen warriors – and had refused with humility and grace each time.

One shoulder guard was given over to the white stone majesty of the Crux Terminatus, the other bore the symbol of his Chapter carved in blue-veined marble and black iron.

To his brothers, he was simply Tolemion. In the archives of his Chapter, he was Tolemion Saralen, Champion of the Third Battle Company. To the enemies of Terra's Throne, he was vengeance incarnate clad in carnelian ceramite.

His armour was an ablative suit of composite metals, layered and reinforced through hundreds of hours of consummate craftsmanship. His helm, with its ornate faceguard and bronzed grille, was an imposing and crested relic from a bygone era, forged in the age of humanity's interstellar apex. One red gauntlet clutched a trembling thunder hammer, its power field charged to a teeth-aching whine. The other held a huge tower shield out ahead, the barrier's shape that of an aquila in profile, one golden wing spread to protect the bearer.

The order he growled to his kindred was a mere two words.

'Boarding blades.'

The warrior's remaining three brothers advanced alongside him, slinging their bolters and drawing pistols and short swords.

First Claw watched this implacable advance, pouring fire down the corridor, watching everything they had shatter harmlessly against the champion's tower shield.

Mercutian dumped his heavy bolter with a disgusted crash.

'I'm dry.' In mirror image of the closing Space Marines, he drew a bolt pistol and the gladius sheathed at his shin. 'I never thought I'd *want* to see Xarl,' he added.

Talos and Cyrion drew their blades a moment later. The prophet helped Uzas to his feet, expecting no word of thanks, and stunned when he actually received a grunt of acknowledgement.

In the moment before the squads came together, the Imperial shield-bearer growled through his amplifying vox-grille.

'I am the End of Heretics. I am the Bane of Traitors. I am Tolemion of the Genesis, Warden of the West Protectorate, Slayer of–'

First Claw didn't wait to be charged. They were already running forward.

'Death to the lackeys of the False Emperor!' Uzas cried. 'Blood for the Eighth Legion!'

VII

DEADLOCK

FIRST CLAW HAD one chance to survive the next few minutes, and they reached for it with everything they had left. The four of them hurled their weight forwards as one, shoulder-charging in a mass of midnight armour. Talos and Mercutian bore the responsibility of the vanguard, and both of them thudded their sloping, spiked shoulder guards against the half-aquila shield with a shared cry of wordless anger.

Tolemion braced against them, his boots chewing sparks from the decking as he was sent slowly skidding backwards. He had the shadow of a second to swing his hammer, pounding the maul into Mercutian's back-mounted power generator, discharging its gathered storm of force in a burst of energy and light.

Mercutian's backpack exploded, blasting debris in every direction. The hammer's concussive force threw him to the decking in a clatter of deactivated armour, to be trampled beneath the grinding feet of both squads. Talos saw Mercutian's life signs wipe blank from his retinal display, powered down before even registering a flatline.

Even as Mercutian was falling, Uzas took his place against the shield, sending the champion staggering backwards. Cyrion pounded into his brothers' backs, adding his strength and weight to the jury-rigged phalanx.

It turned the tide. First Claw and their majestic victim went down in a fighting tumble, cursing and spitting.

Cyrion was the first to rise, the first to face the Genesis Chapter's blades. His gladius punched into the abdomen of the closest Imperial Space Marine, eliciting an irritated, pained gurgle. The Space Marines hacked at his armour, their scoring blades leaving silver smears where they cleaved paint from the ceramite, and ceramite from the subdermal layers.

Uzas didn't even bother to rise. He cleaved with his chainaxe, severing one of the enemy at the knees. For his efforts, he was rewarded with another of the enemy warriors ramming a short sword into his back.

693

Talos, pinned atop Tolemion's shield, couldn't reach the champion through the aquila barricade. He caught an incoming sword from above with his augmetic hand, and yanked to pull the bearer off-balance. The Genesis warrior fell forward, his proud breastplate of beaten bronze meeting the rising gold of Talos's Blood Angel blade. A crunch. A squeal of metal on metal. The hiss of bubbling blood on charged iron.

The prophet rolled aside, kicking the dying Imperial's legs out from under him.

Two down. His senses thrumming in response to heightened synapses and reflexes, Talos scrambled up and launched at the last Genesis Space Marine in the same moment as Cyrion. Both Night Lords bore the warrior to the decking, slaking their blades' thirsts with each puncturing stab.

We are not soldiers. We are murderers first, last, and always.

Who wrote those words? Or spoke them? Was it Malcharion? Sevatar? Both were prone to those dramatic turns of phrase.

He was dizzy now. His vision watered as he dragged his sword from its scraping sheath in the Space Marine's collarbone. He'd never had to fight so soon after a prophetic dream. Tolemion rose on snarling armour joints, smashing Uzas aside with the edge of his shield. The legionary staggered back into his brothers, his helm mangled beyond recognition.

Mercutian lay unmoving at the champion's feet. The three Genesis warriors were down and just as dead. Talos, Uzas and Cyrion faced Tolemion, all of their bravado – in short supply even at the fight's beginning – now gone. Uzas and Talos were barely able to stand. In First Claw's infamous, not-quite-illustrious history, few battles had ever looked so one-sided.

'Come then,' the Space Marine intoned. They each heard the cold amusement in his voice, distorted as it was by the waspish buzz of vox-growl.

Despite the challenge, Tolemion didn't wait for them to charge, nor was he willing to risk them trying to flee. His crested helm dipped as he advanced, the hammer emitting its migraine whine as it made ready to fall.

Aurum, the Blade of Angels, caught the first blow. Gold scraped against gunmetal grey, with the prophet locked against the champion. Tolemion broke the deadlock with only the scarcest effort, levelling a second blow against the sword's crosspiece. The thundercrack was deflected enough to miss a direct strike, but pounded into the Night Lord's joined wrists. Talos lost hold of the blade, and Tolemion kicked the prophet against the arched wall, finishing him with a backhanded blow to the chest. The broken aquila on Talos's chestpiece burned black with scorch damage, while chasm-cracks ripped out in an unintentional star.

'Down you go, heretic.'

As Talos collapsed, joining Mercutian on the decking, Cyrion and Uzas descended as one. The former hurled himself onto the weighty shield, his gauntlets clawing at the edges. If he could tear it from Tolemion's grip, or even lower it enough, Uzas could deliver the death blow.

He realised his mistake as soon as he latched onto the ornate shield. Uzas, at his best, was sloppy beyond belief when it came to pack tactics. Desperation didn't focus him the way it did his brothers. And Tolemion was no fool; he recognised the threat as soon as it came near, and bashed Cyrion back against the wall the moment the Night Lord had a grip.

The pressure was somewhere close to falling beneath a Land Raider's treads. Cyrion voxed nothing beyond strangled breaths as he felt himself slowly crushed into the wall. Reaching around the shield's edge with his pistol allowed him to crack a shot into the champion's knee, which did nothing but scar the ceramite.

Tolemion used his backswing to finish the damage he'd already begun to inflict on Uzas. As the axe-wielder came in for a second strike, he met the thunder hammer face-on. It broke through his weak guard, pounding a half-second later into his breastplate. Lightning played across Uzas's armour in sick delight, even as the warrior toppled backward, dead-limbed, onto the decking next to his brothers.

With the others finished, Tolemion released Cyrion. The legionary staggered forward, weapons falling from numbed hands. A third and final shield bash rocked him back to his heels, sending him down to the deck in a weak heap.

'Your impurity sickens me.' The angry hum of Tolemion's armour was a rumbling percussion to the snarl of his words. He moved to stand over Cyrion, pressing a boot onto the Night Lord's chestplate. 'Was it worth it, to fall from the Emperor's grace? Do all of your viperous achievements validate your cancerous existence, now that your life comes to an end?'

Cyrion's laughter was broken by coughing, but it was laughter all the same. 'The Thirteenth Legion... always gave... the best battle sermons.'

Tolemion raised the hammer, his expression hidden by the dense metal facemask.

'Behind you,' Cyrion was still laughing.

Tolemion was no fool. Even an initiate wouldn't be deceived by such crude trickery. That fact, coupled with the noise of chatter from the boarding squads in constant communication over the vox, was why he was taken completely by surprise when Xarl came at him from behind.

Cyrion was the only one of First Claw to witness the duel that followed. What he saw stayed with him until the night he died.

They didn't engage at once. Xarl and Tolemion stared at each other for several moments, each taking in the trophies and honour markings displayed across their rival's suit of armour. Tolemion was a vision in Imperial accoutrement, with wax purity seals, honour scrolls and aquilas decorating his ornate war-plate. Xarl stood in filthy reflection, his armour adorned with skulls and Imperial Space Marine helms hanging from rusted chains, with swatches of flayed skin in place of parchment scrolls.

'I am Tolemion of the Genesis, Warden of the West Protectorate. I am the End of Heretics, the Bane of Traitors, and a loyal son of Lord Guilliman.'

'Oh,' Xarl chuckled through his voxsponder. 'You must be very proud.' He tossed something round and heavy onto the decking between them both. It rolled to knock gently against Tolemion's boot. A helm. A Genesis Space Marine's helm – the eye lenses put out, the faceplate smeared with blood.

'You'll scream just as he did,' Xarl said with a smile.

The Champion showed no reaction. He didn't even move. 'I knew that warrior,' he said with solemn care. 'He was Caleus, born of Newfound, and I know he died as he lived: with courage, honour, and knowing no fear.'

Xarl swept his chainsword across the scene, gesturing at the prone forms of First Claw. 'I know all of these warriors. They are First Claw, and I know they'll die as they lived: trying to run away.'

It was the laughter that did it. His mockery of the Genesis Champion's demeanour wasn't quite enough to incite the Imperial wretch to rage, but Xarl's laughter served as the coffin's final nail.

Tolemion advanced, shield high and hammer at the ready. 'Make peace with your black-hearted gods, heretic. Tonight, you will know the–'

Xarl gave a distinctly annoyed snort. 'I'd forgotten how much you heroes liked the sound of your own voices.' As Tolemion drew nearer, the Night Lord gripped his two-handed chainblade in a single gauntlet. In his other hand, Xarl caught the handle of Uzas's damaged chainaxe, as he kicked it up from the deck.

Both blades began to roar as their teeth chewed the air. He'd fought through seven Imperial Space Marines to get back here, and their blood flicked in a light spray from the whirring teeth of his chainsword. Beneath his armour, sweat bathed his skin in a greasy sheen, while amusement danced with the strain of pain and anger in his eyes. The sting of already suffered wounds knifed at him through the rents in his war-plate.

'Let's get this done,' he said, still smiling. 'I look forward to letting our slaves use your helm as a shitbucket.'

DELTRIAN DIDN'T NEED to breathe – that is, to respire in the conventional sense – but his remaining internal organics required an oxygenated system to function, and could only be slowed by necessity for so long. The augmetic equivalent of holding one's breath was to manipulate his inner chronometry, forcing it to operate at a fraction of optimal speed. It left him slower, near sluggish, but it meant he could operate in the void for up to three hours, by his closest prediction.

His robes drifted around him as he walked. Beneath his clawed feet, the ridged hull of the *Echo of Damnation* stretched out for kilometres both ahead and behind. To look in any other direction was to stare out into the far reaches of space, and the stars winking an infinity's distance away. The enemy vessel circled the *Echo of Damnation* with rapacious patience, casting shadows across the larger cruiser's hull as it eclipsed the distant sun. The ship was a battlemented void-cutter, a strike cruiser with the inscription *Diadem Mantle* along its prow. Almost against his will, he considered it a singularly beautiful name for a warship.

Deltrian took another step, making his cautious way across the outer hull, leading a phalanx of those in his service. Most wore environment suits and full rebreathers. Several were robed, as resistant to the void as Deltrian himself. The pack traversed brutalised sections of the ship's armoured skin, moving through craterous holes and across wrenched-steel terrain. A warship would endure an eternity of external damage with no concern, but a handful of unfortunate shots against certain sections, and havoc was the result.

'Your Reverence, please,' one of Deltrian's lesser adepts began over the vox. Lacking the human lexicon to continue in a formal complaint, the robed priest blurted a pulse of offended code over their communications link. Deltrian turned to face the other adept, his skullish face peering from beneath his red cowl with glittering eye lenses. While Deltrian's appearance was a calculated artifice to inspire discomfort in biologicals, his Mechanicum kindred could read the displeasure in the subtle kinetics of his facial movements, even down to the shutter-guarded glare of his focusing lenses.

The adept was already preparing to apologise when Deltrian spoke.

'Lacuna Absolutus, if you distract me with further objection, I will have you rendered down to your component pieces. Pulse me acknowledgement signifying your comprehension.'

Lacuna Absolutus transmitted a spurt of affirmative code.

'Good.' Deltrian returned his focus to his duty. 'Now is not the time to cite optimal operational specifics.'

It took the Mechanicum repair party exactly twelve minutes and two seconds to reach the first shield generation spire. The damage was immediately apparent: the pylon, reaching out six times as high as an unaugmented man, was a mangled tower of scrap iron in a crater of damage eaten into the metal meat of the hull.

'Analysing,' he said, devoting his sphere of attention to the damage he beheld. What required immediate maintenance? What was superficial hull-scoring, and could wait until dry dock?

'Sixteen composite metal girders to replace the focusing spire's damage.' Four servitors shambled to obey, their mag-locked boots sending minute tremors along the hull. Deltrian's eye lenses whirred as he sought to perceive through the outermost layers of the hull. He pressed his hand to the twisted metal, pulsing ultrasound into the damaged floor. 'The damage does not extend to any significant depth. Internal team, move ahead.'

'Compliance,' came the dead-voiced reply, from over a dozen metres beneath his feet.

'Your Reverence?' one of his adepts voxed.

Deltrian didn't turn. He was already walking into the crater, beginning the hike to the next spire.

'Vocalise, Lacuna Absolutus.'

'Have you determined the probability of the enemy craft detecting the attempted repairs on their narrow-band auspex sweeps?'

'Detecting us is irrelevant. The void shields are active. We are working to ensure they remain active. I had not realised the situation was beyond your cognition.'

'Your Reverence, the void shields are active *now*. If they fall again before we complete the repairs, the enemy will surely seek to interfere with our actions, will they not?'

Deltrian resisted the urge to emit an expletive. 'Be silent, Lacuna Absolutus.'

'Compliance, your Reverence.'

XARL CAUGHT ANOTHER hammer blow in the crossed blades. His own sword – the unimaginatively-named *Executioner* – was already reduced to ruin. In flashes of insight between blocking blows and swinging to kill, he sincerely doubted Septimus would be able to restore it to full working order.

If Septimus was even still alive. The ship was taking a hell of a beating, and the crew with it.

He'd miss this sword, no doubt there. Assuming he survived, of course. He trusted his skills in battle above any of First Claw (above any Night Lord except Malek of the Atramentar, if he was being perfectly honest), but duelling an Adeptus Astartes Company Champion was no laughing matter, especially not one this well armed and armoured.

Xarl knocked the thunder hammer aside with Uzas's damaged axe, lashing another fruitless strike against Tolemion's dense armour with his own blade. The chainsword, now almost toothless, skidded along the layered ceramite, leaving nothing but scratches. With so few teeth, it had almost no grip. No chain weapon could stand up to a protracted duel with a thunder hammer. Xarl cast it aside with a curse.

Three crashing strikes against Tolemion's shield drove the warrior back as far as Xarl needed. He repeated his kicking move, flipping Talos's stolen Blood Angel power sword off the deck and catching it in his spare hand. Clenching the grip was enough to activate it. The sword hissed and spat with lethal lightning dancing along its golden length, crackling as the energy discharged into the air.

Everything changed the moment he held the blade, for he had a weapon that could reliably parry the devastating maul. Xarl used both weapons to smash into the hammer's haft, knocking its descent aside. Conflicting power fields met with angry, snarling sparks. When Tolemion's shield came high, readying for a crushing bash, Xarl's axe hacked into the top rim. The Night Lord pulled the hooked axe, tearing the shield from the Space Marine's grip.

They backed away once more. Xarl kept both weapons live, one boot on the half-aquila of the fallen boarding shield. Tolemion gripped his hammer in both hands.

'You have done well, traitor, but this ends now.'

'I think I'm winning.' the Night Lord grinned behind his faceplate. 'What do you think?'

DELTRIAN REACHED THE third damaged generator pylon. This one, half a kilometre from the first, was a ruined stump of melted metal. Its severed nub scarcely poked from the ship's scorched armour-skin. The hull underfoot was a pitted, dissolved desert of abused steel, having suffered heavy damage in the last cannonade.

For the first time in several decades, Deltrian felt something akin to hopelessness. The emotion was simply too powerful, too sudden, to swallow back down in traditional Mechanicum repression of the mortal, the flawed, the organic.

'Lacuna Absolutus.'

'Your Reverence?'

'Take the last team ahead to the final damaged spire. I will deal with this one myself.'

Lacuna Absolutus stood next to his master, his own red hood drifting in the airless void. His face was a chrome-plated simulacrum of an ancient Terran death mask, expressionless, yet not without judgement. His voice issued forth from a coin-sized vocaliser tablet sutured into his throat.

'Understood. But how will you deal with this, your Reverence?'

Deltrian grinned, because he always grinned. His features left him no choice in the matter. 'You have your orders. Begone.'

A shiver wormed its way down his spine as he received information from his link to the ship.

'No,' he said aloud.

'Your Reverence?'

'No, no, no. The generator was stabilised.'

'*Void shields,*' came the voice across his uplink bond, '*failing.*'

VIII

TURNING THE TIDE

XARL HEAVED WITH the blade, each of his grunted breaths rasping blood flecks into the inside of his helm. The duel had lasted no longer than a handful of minutes, during which both warriors had melted into blurs of movement, each landing blows and smashing others aside with feverish desperation. All elegance had fled, coming down now to two warriors wishing nothing more than to kill the other.

It grieved him to realise it, but Xarl was already exhausted. Being hit with a tank-cracking thunder hammer was little different from being hit by a tank itself. His left arm was slack and useless, the pauldron broken along with the shoulder beneath it. Each breath was effort, rendered into needling torment from the way his destroyed breastplate had pierced his chest in several places.

'Just *die*,' he breathed, and heaved with the blade yet again. This time it came clear, ripping free of Tolemion's stomach with a spray of cleaved armour shards moistened by gore.

The Champion sagged, his armour reduced to similar wreckage, the cast-iron hammer now dragging against the decking.

'Heretic,' the Space Marine snarled. 'For your… impurity…'

Xarl's backhand ended the threatened chastisement, snapping the loyalist's helm to the side. 'I know, I know… You already said all that.'

The Night Lord staggered back himself, dropping the sword so his one good hand could claw at his collar locks. He had to disengage his helm's seals. He had to get the helmet off so he could see, and so he could breathe.

It came free with the *snap-hiss* of depressurising air. As soon as his eyes were clear of the blood-smeared lenses, Xarl raised Talos's blade again. The ship was shaking around them.

'Your shields are down.' Tolemion barked a harsh laugh. 'More of my brothers will be boarding.'

Xarl didn't reply. He charged forward with all the strength he could muster, muscles fuelled as much by anger as the adrenal sting of combat narcotics. Sword met hammer again and again, crashing and flashing as their opposing power fields protested each impact. Their blows were blurs as the wounded warriors spat and cursed, bleeding the last of their energy into the duel's final moments.

Tolemion gave no ground. Retreat was simply not within him. Xarl's blade cracked against his armour-plating, cutting cold and deep, each carve leeching precious portions of what little strength he had left. In return, his hammer was a slow, clumsy maul that rarely struck his opponent – but when it did, it echoed with vicious finality, throwing the Night Lord back against the wall.

Xarl jumped to his feet again, feeling split sections of his outer armour falling free. He shuddered to think how long these repairs were going to take First Claw's artificer, and stumbled, almost falling again as he stepped over Cyrion's body. The other Night Lord was trying to rise himself, to no avail.

'Xarl,' Cyrion growled through his helm. 'Help me up.'

'Stay down,' Xarl was panting. A single glance at his brother's prone form told him all he needed to know: Cyrion was too weak to do anything, anyway. 'I will be done in a moment,' he said.

Hammer and blade fell in the same moment, meeting midway between the bloody, swearing warriors. The flash was enough to leave a retinal bruise playing over Xarl's eyes, while his vision danced with flickering after-images.

He wasn't going to win this if it stayed a fair fight, and his options to cheat were getting thinner with each drop of blood that ran from his body. The bastard's armour was too thick, and one more hammerfall would keep him down long enough for Tolemion to finish the job.

The Genesis Space Marine drew breath for another chastisement. Xarl chose that moment to head-butt him.

A life of bloodshed and battle meant Xarl was no stranger to pain, but pounding his bare forehead against the riveted, dense helm of an Adeptus Astartes Company Champion immediately ranked as one of the most agonising moments of his existence. Tolemion's head snapped back, but Xarl wouldn't let him go. He leaned closer, around their waspishly buzzing weapons, and powered his head against the Space Marine's faceplate a second time. Then a third. The impacts made the corridor echo like a forge, and his nose gave way with a sickening snap on the fourth. On the fifth, something cracked in the front of his skull. Two more followed it. He was breaking his own face apart, and the feeling was both distantly indescribable, and painful beyond words.

Blood sheeted into his eyes. He could no longer see, but he could feel Tolemion's muscles loosening, and hear the gargling of a throat injury. He spat, then. A stringy gobbet of blood-diluted acidic saliva splashed against Tolemion's left eye lens, eating its hissing way into the flesh beneath.

An eighth head-butt was enough to send both of them reeling: Tolemion stumbling back against the wall, Xarl losing his balance and collapsing to his knees for several heartbeats. Talos's sword fell from his grip. Blinded, he felt along the floor for the fallen weapon.

He sensed the shadow rising above him, and heard the tense growl of wounded power armour. He knew the Genesis Space Marine was raising the hammer high, its distinctive thrum was unmistakable. Xarl's fingers closed around the hilt of Talos's energised sword. With a scream of effort, he rammed it upwards.

It bit, and bit deep. Xarl didn't hesitate – he started carving as soon as it sank in. His clumsy, brutal hacksawing tore through armour, flesh and bone with equal relish. Gore rained onto him, populated wormishly by the looping ropes of Tolemion's intestines. He felt them splash over his shoulders and circle his neck like oil-slick snakes. At any other time, he'd have been amused at the foul display.

Xarl yanked the sword free, hauling himself to his feet in a surge of renewed vitality. His next chop cleaved the champion's hammer-hand at the wrist, letting the weapon fall at last.

'I am taking your helm,' Xarl panted, 'as a trophy I think I earned it.'

Tolemion swayed on his feet, too strong and too stubborn to collapse. 'For... For the... Emp–'

Xarl took a step back, spun with all the strength he could muster, and powered the golden blade through his enemy's neck. It went through without slowing, as though it had nothing to chop but clean air. The head fell one way, the body another.

'To the abyss with your Emperor,' Xarl sighed.

DELTRIAN HAD NEVER worked faster, even with the relative limitations opposed by his slowed internal chronometry. He'd deployed his four auxiliary arms, activating them and letting them uncurl from their sockets in his resculpted back. These replicas of his skeletal main arms each gripped a blocky signum device, shaped as wire-encrusted rods. The adept couldn't trust his servitors to work with the speed and precision the moment required, and thus it fell to Deltrian to slave them to his more efficient output.

The four servitors responded in service to the merest movement of the signum controls in his hands, their every tic and breath controlled by his will. In a morbid ballet of lobotomised unity, the bionic slaves lifted girders into place, sealed them with fusing strips, and worked to rebuild the destroyed power pylon's external focusing spire.

Linking the spire's foundations to the flash-fried electronics being replaced in the hull itself was a much more difficult task. To that end,

Deltrian multisected his visual receptors, seeing with a fly's segmented vision through the eyes of the four servitors outside on the hull with him; through his own perspective as overseer at the crater's edge; and through the eyes of two of the servitors on board the ship, several metres below his feet. They were cramped into the crawlspace tunnels, their corpse-like flesh leaking its oily sweat as they laboured with fingertip micro-tools, re-bonding and rewiring the damage done.

Deltrian was a man (in the loosest sense) that usually enjoyed his work. Challenge motivated him, resulting in something akin to a pleasant emotive response as well as increased productivity. A fleshier creature would probably call it inspiration.

This, however, was an exercise in manipulation and haste far beyond preferred operational parameters. He'd fought wars with less effort than this.

The void shields had flicker-failed again, snapping out of existence for two minutes and forty-one seconds. During that time, as Deltrian multisected his attention between six servitors, he'd also looked out into the void and watched the distant red smear of the enemy ship in its far-ranged orbit of the wounded *Echo of Damnation*. Zooming his eye lenses had diverted even more of his precious attention span, but he had to know if the enemy cruiser was risking an attempt to deploy more warriors while the *Echo*'s shields were down.

The crew of the Genesis strike cruiser had surely been tempted to fire, but would never do so with so many of their loyal warriors on board. Instead, it launched another two boarding pods, surely now representing the warship's entire complement of Imperial Space Marines spent.

Deltrian had watched the pods diving closer, burning through the void. The *Echo*'s main broadside weapon batteries had no hope of shooting down such minute targets, but the servitor-manned defence turrets began spitting hard tracer fire into the void the moment the pods entered range. One had popped in silence, coming apart in the barrage, spilling its organic cargo into space. Deltrian hadn't seen the Imperial Space Marines and their pod's debris strike the hull with lethal inertia, but he'd allowed himself a brief imagining of the mess such an impact had likely made.

The second pod struck home in the ship's belly, far from the tech-adept's visual sphere. He pulsed a vox-screed detailing his estimated location for the pod's breaching, and hoped at least one of the Claws defending the ship would pay heed to it.

Seven minutes and thirty-seven seconds later, when the void shields were back up and his work on the reconstruction was nearing forty per cent complete, a shadow ghosted behind him. Deltrian reluctantly began to spare it a fraction of his attention, and was halfway turned when something with the force of a Titan's kick hammered into his side, detonating in a flash too fast for the human eye to follow. His ocular implants were technically capable of registering the spherical detonation as it dispersed at otherwise untrackable speeds, spreading its force into the void with no resistance to counter it. He didn't manage to track anything, however. The explosion against his ribcage blasted him from his grip on the hull, sending him skidding along the ship's outer skin.

As he tumbled away, several hands reaching out to latch onto the hull and arrest his fall, his cogitation processor did the following things: firstly, it catalogued an instant display of the damage his physical form had sustained; secondly, it felt all six of his servitors go mind-dead, defaulting to their slower, simpler behaviour; thirdly, it spared the runtime to pulse a warning to the other repair teams on the outside of the ship; and lastly, it allowed him a moment to wonder how in the infinite hells any of the Imperial Space Marines had survived their disintegrating pod, and managed to walk their way along the hull to shoot him in the back. That level of resilience was irritating when found in one's enemies.

All of this took less than a second. Deltrian's skidding, clawing slide ended three seconds after his cogitations, as he drifted out of reach from the hull, turning and spinning into the void. The stars twisted, unfocused, in his spiralling vision.

With no method of thrust or creating inertial force, he was almost certain to drift away until his death. This… this was not optimal.

Something caught his robe, jerking him in place. He turned in the weightless, airless nothingness, seeing the hand clutching the very edge of his cloak, and the warrior that the gauntlet belonged to.

The Night Lord regarded him through curving eye lenses. Tears, painted in red and silver streaks, ran down the daemonic faceplate.

'I heard you on the vox,' said Lucoryphus of the Bleeding Eyes.

'Praise be to the beneficence of the Machine-God,' Deltrian sent back over the communication link.

The Raptor pulled the adept back onto the hull, without bothering to be gentle about it.

'If you say so,' Lucoryphus rasped. 'Remain here. I will slit your ambusher's throat. Then get back to your repairs.'

The engines housed on his back cycled into silent life, their roars stolen by the airless void. With a burst of manoeuvring thrusters, the Night Lord kicked off from the ship's skin and boosted over to the damaged pylon.

Deltrian watched him depart, so overcome with relief he decided not to record the Raptor's disrespect for later archiving.

This time.

XARL DROPPED THE sword, and with almost insane patience, he moved to lean against the arched wall. He remained there for a timeless span, cataloguing his hurts, catching his breath. The blood leaking through his breastplate smelled too rich, too clean. Heartsblood, he knew. That wasn't good. If one of his hearts was sundered, he'd be laid up for weeks adapting to an augmetic replacement. He couldn't move one arm, and the other was numb from the elbow, the fingers starting to seize up. One knee was refusing to bend, and the pain in his chest was getting colder, spreading farther.

He grunted again, but couldn't move away from the wall just yet. *Another minute, perhaps.* Let his regenerative tissues catch up to the damage. That's all. That's all he needed.

Cyrion was the first to rise, pulling himself up by the opposite wall. His armour looked almost as ruined as Xarl's, and rather than help the others, he lifted the now-dead hammer in his hands.

'Its power cells are depleted to eighty per cent now. Perhaps it was hitting us harder than it hit you.'

Xarl didn't reply. He kept leaning against the wall.

'I've never seen a duel like that,' Cyrion added. He moved to where his brother stood.

'Get away from me. I need a moment to breathe.'

'As you wish.' Cyrion moved over to Talos, who still lay paralysed on the deck. A vial of chemical stimulant injected into the prophet's neck sent his muscles into spasm, and he rose, choking, a moment later.

'I have never been hit with a thunder hammer before. Variel will bore us all with details of what it does to a nervous system, but I never want to feel it again.'

'Be glad the blow was glancing.'

'It did not feel glancing,' Talos replied.

'If you're still alive, then it was glancing.'

One by one, First Claw rose to their feet.

'Xarl,' Talos said. 'I can't believe you killed him.'

The other warrior faced his brothers with an amused sneer. 'It was nothing.' He caught his helmet when Talos tossed it to him. For a moment, Xarl stroked his fingers along the winged crests – the ceremonial Legion decoration – looking down at the bitter visage he presented to the galaxy.

His eyes were clear of blood, but his skull was a shattered mash of bone and flesh. Even rolling his eyes in their sockets bred enough pain to drive him to his knees, but he wouldn't allow such weakness to show. Blinking was an agony so fierce he lacked the imagination to describe it even to himself. He didn't even want to know how much of his face was left. The others were looking at him with worry in their eyes, and that only made him angrier.

'Can you still fight?' Talos asked.

'I've felt better,' replied Xarl. 'But I can fight.'

'We need to move,' Mercutian said. He was the weakest of them all. Without power, his armour was almost useless, adding nothing to his strength or reflexes. The joints didn't whirr, and the backpack didn't hum. 'We need to link up with one of the other Claws if we're being boarded again.'

'Xarl,' Talos said again.

The warrior looked up. 'What?'

'Take the hammer. You earned it.'

Xarl lifted his helm back into place. It clicked once, sealing to his collar locks, and his voice left his vocaliser in its usual vox-altered snarl.

'Talos,' he said. 'My brother.'

'What is it?'

'I regret arguing with you before. It is no sin to wish for a life with meaning, or a way to win this war.'

'We will speak of this later, brother,' said Talos.

'Yes,' he replied. 'Later.'

Xarl took a single step closer. His head rolled forward in a slow nod, and his body followed in a boneless topple. He collapsed into the prophet's arms, utterly limp, his armour broadcasting the tuneless whine of a flatline signal.

IX
REPULSION

'I have broken a hundred oaths. Some by design, some by chance, some by misfortune. One of the few I still seek to honour is our pledge to the Mechanicum. No Legion can stand without the foundations provided by the exiles of Mars.'

– Konrad Curze, the Night Haunter,
Primarch of the VIII Legion

TALOS DRAGGED THE body onto the bridge. Xarl's armour growled along the decking, the ceramite grinding every step of the way.

'Leave him,' Mercutian said. He was bareheaded now, his powerless suit no longer tied into the vox. 'Talos, leave him. We have a battle to fight.'

The prophet hauled Xarl's body to the side of the chamber, leaving his brother lying by the western doors. When he rose, he took in the sight before him through impassive eyes. The bridge was deep in its usual bustle of noise and organised chaos, with officers and servitors calling back and forth, running between their stations. First Claw, what remained of them, moved to the eastern doors, checking their weapons as they walked. Humans scattered before them, all gestures of respect going ignored.

Only Talos lingered by the command throne. 'Why aren't we engaging the enemy ship?'

'You don't want it as plunder once we've beaten these dogs into their graves?' Cyrion voxed back.

Talos turned to the occulus, watching the scarlet strike cruiser drifting with excruciating patience. 'No,' he said, 'No, you should have known I would not.'

'But we can't board them with every squad engaged.'

'Are you insane? I don't want to board them,' the prophet said. 'I want them to burn.'

'They're half a system away, hanging back out of weapons range. They pulled away as soon as they released boarding pods.'

Talos looked at his brothers, then at the crew, as if they were deluded beyond comprehension. 'Then *chase them.*'

As the ship warmed up around them, Cyrion cleared his throat. 'You want to destroy that ship? Truly?'

The prophet shook his head, not in denial but confusion. 'Why is that so hard to understand?'

'Because it is hardly the province of pirates to annihilate any reward from their raids.' Cyrion looked at the distant ship. 'Think of the ammunition reserves on that cruiser. Think of the thousands of crew, the resources, the weapons we could take as plunder.'

'We have all we need on board the *Echo.* I do not want plunder. I want revenge.'

'But…' Cyrion trailed off as Talos watched him for a moment, his face without expression.

'No,' the prophet said. 'It burns. They die.'

The eastern doors opened on dense hydraulics. Variel limped in, his augmetic leg giving off sparks from its locked knee. Blood washed the flayed leathery flags of skin draped across his armour. The symbol of the Corsair's fist was a hammer-broken ruin on his shoulder guard, while the other pauldron showed the Legion's winged skull with bloodstained pride.

'Fifth Claw has purged the principal habitation decks,' he said. 'The Genesis warriors are bleeding us, but the tide is turning.'

Talos said nothing.

'Xarl?' Variel asked him.

'Dead.' Talos didn't glance at the body. He sat in the command throne, grunting at the pain of his wounds. Combat stimulants were holding off the worst of it, but he needed to get out of his armour soon. 'Take his gene-seed later.'

'I should harvest it at once,' Variel replied.

'*Later.* That is an order.' He looked over to his brothers, stood in a pack. 'The other Claws need Variel. Get to the Hall of Reflection and defend Deltrian at all costs. I will ensure all squads fall back to you once their killing is done.'

Cyrion stepped forward, as if to protest. 'What about you?'

Talos nodded to the occulus. 'I will join you, as soon as I finish this.'

THE RAPTOR WAITED at the crater's edge. Deltrian paid the warrior little heed, casting his attention back into the difficulties of multisecting vision. The replacement pylon was being capped by the conduction orb, while the deck crews worked to fuse the tower's electronics to the ship's main systems.

Despite the absence of nerves, and the resulting lack of pain, Deltrian's wound was a troubling one. He'd leaked precious haemo-lubricant oils in place of blood, and his minimal organic components were triggering internal alarms along his retinal displays. Worse, the straining organs were now putting increased pressure on his augmetic systems to keep him functional.

Time was more of a factor than ever. Thankfully, work was almost complete.

Blood crystals clattered gently against his deployed arms as he worked. The fate of Deltrian's ambusher had apparently been an unpleasant one. The body was gone, but crystalline evidence remained, frozen in the void.

He could hear Lucoryphus fighting again, hear it by the grunts and dull thumps over the vox, but the adept spared the Raptor no significant attention.

At that moment, the ship gave a colossal tremor beneath his feet. The stars began to turn in the night sky, and Deltrian lost several precious seconds watching the void dance before his eyes.

The ship was moving. An attack run, surely. He couldn't envisage a scenario where the Night Lords would run from a smaller vessel, especially not when it had arrived to guard the world they wished to take for themselves.

'This is Deltrian to the strategium. The shields will be secured within four minutes standard.'

'This is Talos,' came the crackling reply. 'The shields are already active.'

'I am aware of that. But they are unsecured, due to external pylon damage. They may yet fail again, and the probability rises to a near-certainty if kinetic force is a factor. Do not engage until the void generators are at a secure operational capacity. Four minutes. Acknowledge understanding of this critical proviso with an immediate response.'

'Understood, adept. Work fast.'

THE SHIP SHOOK around her. Octavia remained in her throne, watching the stars drift by on her wall of pict-feed monitors.

'They're running,' she said. 'The Genesis warship is trying to maintain distance.'

Septimus stood next to the throne, his wounds still bandaged, the bruises discolouring his face now at their ripest.

'Should you even be here?' Octavia asked, unwittingly sounding more like a Terran aristocrat than ever.

He ignored the question. 'I don't see how you can tell they're running,' he said, his throat tight and his voice scratchy. 'It's just a red speck in the blackness.'

She didn't lift her eyes from the screens. 'I can just tell.'

Several of her attendants bustled on the other side of the fluid pool, guarding the bulkhead door. One of them approached, the footsteps echoing around the humid chamber.

'Mistress.'

Octavia turned to glance at the bandaged, cloaked figure. 'What is it?'

'The door is sealed. Word from Fourth Claw promises this deck is safe from intrusion.'

'Thank you, Vularai.'

The figure bowed, and moved back to its brethren.

'You are treating them better,' Septimus pointed out. He knew she still missed Hound.

She smiled, patently forced, and looked back to the screens. 'We're catching up, but too slowly. The engines are taking too long to burn hotter. I can almost picture the enemy captain, watching us as we watch him, hoping his boarding teams will take our bridge before we reach his ship. And they might, for this chase will take hours. Maybe several days.'

'Octavia,' came a bass rumbling voice from the gargoyles carved into the chamber walls. Their wide maws were sculpted to hold vox-emitters.

She reached to the armrest of her throne and worked the cranking lever. It settled with a crunch.

'I'm here. How is the battle going?'

'Victory will have a high price. I need you to ready the ship for immediate warp entry.'

She blinked twice. 'I… what?'

'The void shields will be secured in two minutes. You will jump the ship shortly after. Understood?'

'But we're in orbit.'

'We are leaving orbit. You can see that.'

'But we're so close to the planet. And the enemy isn't even running to the system's warp beacons. They're not going into the Sea of Souls.'

'There is no time to debate this, Octavia. I am ordering you to engage the warp engines as soon as the void shields are secured.'

'I'll do it. But what's the destination?'

'Nowhere.' He sounded impatient now, which she found a rare change. 'Jump closer to the enemy. I want to… to shunt the ship through the empyrean, and ambush the enemy strike cruiser. I am not wasting days chasing these fools across the stars.'

She had to blink again. 'You're talking about ripping a hole in space to leap through the narrowest slice of the empyrean. The engines will barely be live before we'll need to kill power to them. It will be a jump of less than a second, and even then, we may overshoot by a long way.'

'I did not say I cared how it was done.'

'Talos, I'm not sure this *can* be done.'

'I did not ask that, either. I just want you to do it.'

'As you wish,' she said. Once she'd worked the lever back, cutting off her vox-link to the bridge, Octavia took a deep breath. 'This will be interesting.'

* * *

'CONSTRUCTION COMPLETE.'

Deltrian began to retract his augmetic arms, while the servitors fell back into a hear/obey pattern around him.

'Orders?' one of them voxed to him.

'Follow me.' Deltrian was already moving, his magnetic boots pounding along the hull in silent shivers. 'Lucoryphus?'

The Raptor waited at the crater's edge, three red helms in his clawed clutch. 'You are finished, at last? We must regain immediate access to the ship.'

Lucoryphus lifted from the decking on a gentle surge of thrust. Gone was the crawling, awkward creature – out here, freedom altered him into something much more lethal. Guidance thrusters breathed little jets of soundless pressure, keeping him suspended in place.

'Why?'

'Because Talos intends to jump the ship.'

'That is incorrect terminology.'

Lucoryphus merely snorted. 'It is still happening.'

'When?'

Deltrian didn't stop walking. He strode past the hovering Raptor, head down, eye lenses focused on the closest bulkhead set into the ship's skin. It was still over three hundred metres away.

'Must I truly answer that question with a detailed chain of events? He intends to engage the warp engines as soon as the void shields are secured. I have repaired the final pylon. Thus, they are secured. Thus, to clarify further, he intends to jump the ship now. Have you ever borne witness to a living organism left unprotected in the warp?'

Deltrian could hear something wet over the vox. He suspected it was the Raptor's smile.

'Oh yes, tech-priest. I most certainly have.'

The ship rumbled beneath the adept's boots, building strength and momentum the way a beast draws breath to roar.

Deltrian cycled through his epiglottal vox-triggers. 'Lacuna Absolutus?'

'Your Reverence?'

'Inform me of your location at once.'

A spurt of amused code fed back over the link. 'Do I detect trace amounts of concern in your query, Revered One?'

'An answer, if you please.'

'My team is between sixteen and twenty seconds' journey from our closest maintenance bulkhead, approximately six hundred metres roll-ward and prow-ward from your position. I believe the...' His words washed away in a flow of static.

'Lacuna Absolutus. Finish vocalisation.'

Static remained the only reply.

'Hold,' Deltrian ordered. The servitors obeyed. Lucoryphus did not, he was already at the next bulkhead, claws gripping the hull as he keyed in the access cipher.

'Lacuna Absolutus?' the adept tried again. The white noise continued unabated, until Deltrian applied audio filters to the vox-channel, scrambling through the chaos. It rendered one sound clearer than all else.

'Lucoryphus,' Deltrian said.

The Raptor hesitated, in the middle of hauling the circular bulkhead door wide open. 'What is it?'

'My subordinate, Lacuna Absolutus, has been engaged. I have deciphered the sound of servitor death across the vox-link.'

'So?' The Night Lord swung the door wide, peeling back the steel to expose the crawlspace within. Beneath their boots, the ship gave a premonitory shudder, its engines gaining power. 'Build another assistant, or whatever it is you do to engineer your slaves.'

'He is...' Deltrian trailed off, feeling the vibration through the ship's bones. They were less than a minute away from entry into the warp.

'He is already dead,' Lucoryphus reasoned. 'Get inside.'

'Your Reverence,' crackled Lacuna Absolutus's voice over the reconnection. '...Astartes...'

Logic and emotion warred within the ancient adept. He had several auxiliaries and subordinates, but few were as gifted as Lacuna Absolutus. Few also retained the same sense of personality and drive, which were aspects to be admired – at least when they blended with efficiency and ambition in that rare mesh of perfect fusion. More than the inconvenience involved in training a replacement, more than the vastly increased workload it would force him to endure – on a small, subtle and personal level it would also grieve Deltrian to lose his favoured aide.

The truth was an awkward one. Affection bred a cold, alien discomfort within his core. In an entity with more flesh to feel with, the sensation might be called a chill.

'I will not abandon him.'

Deltrian turned and made it seven steps before he heard Lucoryphus's disgusted sigh.

'Get inside.' The Raptor soared past him, thrusters trailing ghost-fire as he raced over the hull. 'I will deal with your lost friend.'

LUCORYPHUS OF THE Bleeding Eyes covered the distance in a matter of heartbeats. The hull flashed beneath him in a streaking blur the same colour as his armour, while his target stood out in the stark illumination of external siren lights.

A single red-armoured warrior guarded the maintenance hatch, clearly in the process of entering when he'd seen the adept's servitor pack approaching. Filthy Throne-worshippers. It was bad enough having them worming through the ship's bones, let alone having to endure them crawling over the *Echo*'s skin as well.

The hull veered beneath him with a slow, serene urgency. Enough of this. He would not be trapped outside when the *Echo* entered the warp. That was no way for a leader of the Bleeding Eyes cult to meet his end.

Lucoryphus turned in the void, angling his dive to bring him down atop the Genesis Space Marine. The warrior reared back, only in time to take both of the Raptor's clawed feet in the chest. Lucoryphus gripped with his hands, clutching at the Space Marine's helm while he kicked with his foot-talons, shredding the ceramite breastplate, the subdermal muscle cabling, and the soft flesh beneath. A vicious wrench broke the Space Marine's neck – Lucoryphus felt the muted, popping snaps of the vertebrae giving way even through the armour that separated him from his prey.

The Genesis warrior went slack, still standing straight with his boots mag-locked to the hull. Blood left his torn chest in a crystallised cascade.

Lucoryphus boosted up, twisting in space to land on the hull several metres back with his pistol drawn. A single bolt shell hammered into the Space Marine's breastplate, knocking the body from its magnetic perch, sending it tumbling into the nothingness.

Only then did Lucoryphus turn to find Lacuna Absolutus. The adept was cowering behind a ridged rise of hull armour, holding a laspistol. The safety settings were still showing as active along the weapon's side – not that such an insignificant weapon would enjoy much luck against an Imperial Space Marine even at the best of times.

'Have you never modified yourself for battle?' Lucoryphus asked, reaching for the adept's throat and hauling him out of hiding.

'Never.' The adept dangled in the warrior's grip. 'But after the events of this night, I plan to rectify that failing.'

'Just get inside,' the Raptor growled.

'TELL ME THAT worked,' Talos said to his crew.

While Octavia was heaving her guts up after the jump, purging the liquefied contents of her stomach, and while the warband's Claws were at last forming together to isolate and slay the final remnants of the enemy boarding parties, the *Echo of Damnation* trembled with the pressures of returning to real space. The warship burst back into reality, streaming the migraine-coloured unsmoke of the deep ether from its spinal battlements, after what was assuredly the shortest warp jump in Legion history.

The engines had flickered live for less than a single second, ripping a rift in the void at the vessel's prow. Even as the *Echo*'s entrance rip was sealing, another opened tens of thousands of kilometres away, disgorging the warship back into space.

No warp transit came without cost, but neither did the laws of logic apply when rushing through the hell behind the veil. A short flight was no guarantee of safety, and the ship's emergence mere heartbeats after entry still left it juddering, its Geller field made visible by the clinging pollutant mists.

The shaking bridge had the added rattling melody of chains clashing together as they dangled from the ceiling. The Night Lords occasionally used them to hang bodies – Ruven wasn't the only decoration.

'Speak to me,' Talos ordered.

'Systems realigning,' one of the bridge officers called back. 'Auspex live. I... It worked, lord. We're thirteen hundred kil–'

'Come about,' interrupted the prophet. 'I want that cruiser dead.'

'Coming about, sire,' called the Helmsmistress. The gravitic generators whined at the strain as the ship banked hard, and the occulus reactivated with a blast of static, resolving into a view of the distant red warship.

Talos spared a glance for the hololithic display, still scrambled and showing little of worth. They were too far ahead for any of their weapons to reach yet – still, it was an improvement over lagging so far behind. He had another idea, one that would work now.

'All power to the engines.'

'All power, aye.' The Master of Propulsion reached for his vox-caster, dialling the code for his subordinates on the enginarium control deck. 'All power to the engines,' the veteran officer said into the speech horn. 'We need every one of the reactors burning like a sun's core. Don't spare the slaves.'

Seven replies overlapped into one mess of agreement. Not all of the voices were human.

The *Echo of Damnation* kicked forward, tearing through space in pursuit of its prey.

Talos knew he wasn't a void warrior. He lacked the Exalted's patience, and he was a self-confessed creature of sensation – he waged war with a blade in his hand and blood on his face – the salty reek of an enemy's fear-sweat in his senses focused him, spurring him on. Void warfare required a measure of tolerance he'd never acquired. He knew it, and didn't berate himself for the deficiency. One couldn't be an expert at all things.

To that end, Talos spared no time after taking the *Echo*, almost immediately investing a great deal of trust in his mortal crew. Some of them were survivors from the *Covenant of Blood*, others were veterans of the Red Corsairs' fleet. When they spoke, he listened. When they advised, he considered their words. When he acted, it was with their counsel.

But patience had its limit. One brother had already died this day.

Another look at the resolving hololithic spoke of the shortening distance between the runes denoting both ships.

'We will catch them,' Talos said.

'They're running for the system's jump locus,' the Master of Auspex called out.

Talos turned to the hunchbacked former Corsair slave. The eight-bladed star blackened his face in a vicious burn marking.

'I do not believe they are. They are running to hide, not to flee.' He ordered the occulus to pan across the expanse of space, finally resting its gaze on a distant moon.

'There,' Talos said. 'They seek to purchase time, pulling further away from us to hide on the other side of that rock. They need only wait long enough for their boarding parties to take control of the ship, or for confirmation that the assault has failed. Then they can return or flee, whichever they deem necessary.'

The Master of Auspex was working his multi-jointed fingers along the clicking console keys. Each brass button clacked like some ancient typing machine.

'You may be correct, lord. Before the warp jump, such a manoeuvre would have bought them approximately seven hours.'

Talos felt his gaze drawn to Xarl again. He resisted it, knowing his brother would still be slouched against the wall. Nothing could be gained by staring at his corpse. 'And now?' he asked.

The robed officer scratched at the weeping sores that marked the edge of his lips. 'We will catch them in perhaps two hours.'

Better. Not good, but at least it was better. Still, a discomforting thought gnawed at him. Talos mused aloud, 'What if they realise their assault has failed beyond recovery?'

The robed man drew in a sticky breath. 'Then we will not catch them. The warp jump gave us a chance at an honest engagement. No more, lord. No less.'

Talos watched the ship running for respite, burning its engines hot as it made for the temporary sanctuary offered by the dead-rock planetoid. It didn't matter. His idea would work.

'Nostramo,' he whispered. Memory and imagination bred a fire in his dark eyes, though it was lost behind the skullish faceplate and slanted red eye lenses.

'Sire?'

The prophet took several moments to answer. 'Let them run. We are close enough now for the Shriek to work. Pursue, but let them reach orbit on the other side of that rock. Let them come close to it, believing they can buy a few more hours.'

'My lord?'

Talos gestured to the vox-mistress. 'Find Deltrian, if you please.'

The officer – heavily augmented, her remaining flesh pitted by acid scars – worked her console, and nodded a moment later. 'Ready, sire.'

'This is Talos to Deltrian. You have ten minutes to activate the Shriek. It is time we won this fight.'

When it came, the tech-adept's reply was overridden by Lucoryphus's husky drawl. 'We are in the starboard terminus arc. It will take us ten minutes to even reach the adept's chambers.'

'Then move swiftly.' Talos gestured for the Vox-mistress to terminate the link, and released a heavy breath. 'Master of Arms.'

The officer looked up from his console, his sleek and elegant uniform faded by time. 'My lord?'

'Ready cyclonic torpedoes,' the Night Lord ordered.

'Lord?' was the stunned reply.

'Ready cyclonic torpedoes,' he repeated in exactly the same tone.

'Lord, we only have five warheads.'

Talos swallowed, clenching his teeth and closing his eyes as if he could contain his anger by sealing the portals of his face.

'Ready cyclonic torpedoes.'

'Sire, I believe we should save them for–'

The human said nothing more. The front of his face came free with a sickly *crack*, the flesh and jagged bone crunching in the Night Lord's fist. Talos ignored the body as it toppled, spilling the insides of its halved skull onto the decking.

No one had even seen him move, such was the prophet's speed, clearing ten metres and vaulting a console table in the time it took a human heart to beat once.

'I am trying to be reasonable,' he said to the hundreds of watching crew members. His vox-voice carried across the chamber in a guttural, malign whisper. 'I am trying to end this battle so that we might all return to our insignificant lives, still wearing our skin around our souls. I am not, by nature, a choleric creature. I allow you to speak, to advise... but do not see my indulgence as weakness. When I order, you will obey. Please do not try my patience this night. You will regret it, as Armsmaster Sujev is so aptly demonstrating.'

The body at Talos's feet was still twitching, still leaking. The prophet handed his fistful of bloody facial wreckage to the nearest servitor.

'Dispose of this.'

The servitor watched him with dead-eyed devotion. 'How, my lord?' it asked in a monotone murmur.

'Eat it for all I care.'

The prophet stalked back to his throne, tracking through the organic filth running from Sujev's corpse. All the while, he resisted the need to cradle his aching head in his hands. Something inside his mind threatened to break out, shattering his skull with the strain.

The gene-seed is killing you. Some humans are not meant to survive implantation.

He looked up, where Ruven's remains hung on rusting chains.

'I killed you,' he told the bones.

'Sire?' asked a nearby officer. Talos looked over at the man. Mutation had ruined him, leaving one side of his body seized and muscle-locked, giving his face the perpetual leer of a stroke victim. He wiped his drooling, stretched lips on the back of his hand, frozen as it was into a half-claw.

Is this what we have fallen to? the prophet wondered.

'Nothing,' said Talos. 'All stations, ready for deployment of cyclonic torpedoes. When the Shriek is live and our torpedoes cannot be intercepted or tracked, destroy the moon.'

X
REVENGE

'Xarl is dead,' Mercutian said to the darkness. 'I can scarcely believe it. He was unkillable.'

Cyrion chuckled. 'Evidently not.'

The lights around them failed with a crack of overloading circuitry, and the ship groaned strangely beneath their boots. The air itself seemed to cling to them for a moment, pushing and pulling at their limbs.

'What was that sensation?' Variel asked. His shoulder-mounted lamp pack flared in response to the dimming lights, cutting a beam through the blackness. The slice of light panned across the empty iron tunnel ahead.

Even though their retinal displays filtered to compensate, the other Night Lords instinctively turned their eyes from the sharp glare.

'Deactivate that,' Cyrion said softly.

Variel obeyed, amused without possessing the grace to actually smile. 'Please answer my question,' he said. 'That sound, and the ship's shiver. What caused it?'

Cyrion led the remnants of First Claw through the tunnels, moving deeper into the ship. 'It was the inertial adjustment from releasing cyclonic warheads. Talos is doing something either very clever, or very, very foolish.'

'He is angry,' Mercutian added. His brothers, still wearing their helms, didn't pause to look back. They led the way, weapons in their fists. 'Talos will not take Xarl's death with any grace,' he continued. 'I could see it in the way he moved. He is wounded over this. Mark my words.'

Uzas breathed through his speaker-grille. 'Xarl is dead?'

The others ignored him, all but Mercutian. 'He died an hour ago, Uzas.'

'Oh. How?'

'You were there,' Mercutian said quietly.

'Oh.' The others could almost sense his attention sliding across the surface of the conversation, failing to hold.

Cyrion led the depleted Claw around another corner, descending the spiralling walkway to the next deck. Crew members scattered before them, like roaches fleeing a sudden light. Only a few of them, robed menials and beggars alike, remained to kneel and weep at the boots of their masters, pleading to be told what was happening.

Cyrion kicked one of them aside. First Claw made its way past the others. 'This ship is the size of a small city,' he said to his brethren. 'If the Genesis wretches go to ground, we may never dig them out. We've only just managed to cleanse the worst of the taint left over from the bastard Corsairs.'

'Did you hear what they found on deck thirty?' Mercutian asked.

Cyrion shook his head. 'Enlighten me.'

'The Bleeding Eyes reported it in a few nights before we arrived at Tsagualsa. They said the walls are alive down there. The metal has veins, a pulse, and sheds blood when cut.'

Cyrion turned his head to Variel, his disapproving sneer hidden behind the glaring helm. 'What did you tainted fools do to this ship before we stole it back?'

The Apothecary stomped on, his augmetic leg pistoning and hissing as its servos mimicked human joint structure as best they could.

'I have seen Night Lord vessels infinitely more corrupt than you seem to imply. I am hardly one of the faithful, Cyrion. I have never once spoken in reverence to the Powers That Be. The warp twists what it touches, I do not deny it. But do you pretend there were no poisoned decks on board your precious *Covenant of Blood*?'

'There were none.'

'Is that so? Or did you merely linger around the least-populated decks, where the touch of the Hidden Gods was lessened? Did you walk among the thousands of slaves toiling in the ship's engine-bowels? Was it all as pure and unchanged as you claim, despite all your decades in the Great Eye?'

Cyrion turned away, shaking his head, but Variel wouldn't let it lie. 'I loathe hypocrisy more than all else, Cyrion of Nostramo.'

'Be silent for a minute, and spare me your whining. I will never understand why Talos saved you on Fryga, nor will I understand why he allowed you to come with us when we left Hell's Iris.'

Variel said nothing. He was not a soul inclined to long arguments, nor did he feel a burning need to get the last word in a dispute. Such things mattered little.

As they descended to another deck, it was Mercutian who spoke, his voice accompanying their clanking tread. More slaves scattered before them – ragged and wretched things, all.

'He is with us because he is one of us,' Mercutian said.

'If you say so,' Cyrion replied.

'You think he isn't one of us, simply because sunlight doesn't hurt his eyes?'

Cyrion shook his head. 'I don't wish to argue, brother.'

'I am sincere when I say this,' Mercutian insisted. 'Talos believes it, too. To be Eighth Legion is to have a focus, a... dispassionate focus not shared by any of our kindred. You do not have to be born of the sunless world to be one of us. You merely need to understand fear. To take pleasure in inflicting it. To relish the salt-piss smell of it, emanating from mortal skin. You must think as we do. Variel does that.' He inclined his head to the Apothecary.

Cyrion cast a glance over his shoulder as they walked, his painted lightning tears splitting his helm's cheeks with what seemed like jagged relish. 'He is not Nostraman.'

Mercutian, never given to laughter, actually smiled. 'Almost half of the primarch's Chosen were Terran, Cyrion. Do you remember when First Captain Sevatar fell? Do you recall the Atramentar breaking up into scattered packs, because they refused to serve Sahaal? There is an example in this. Think on it.'

'I liked Sahaal,' said Uzas, from nowhere. 'I respected him.'

'As did I,' Mercutian allowed. 'I had no affection for him, but I respected him. And even when the Atramentar disbanded after Sevatar's death, we knew their resistance to Sahaal was born from something more than simple prejudice. Some of the First Company *were* Terran, the oldest warriors in the Legion. Even Malek was Terran. There was more to it than Sahaal's birth world. Being Terran, Nostraman, or born of any other world has never mattered to most of us. The gene-seed blackens our eyes the same, no matter the world of our birth. We divide because with the primarchs gone, that is every Legion's fate over time. We are warbands in a shared cause, with a shared legacy and ideology.'

'It is not so simple.' Cyrion wouldn't be moved. 'Variel's eyes are not black. He carries Corsair gene-seed in his throat and chest.'

Mercutian shook his head. 'I am surprised you cling to the ancient prejudice, brother. It will be as you wish, for I am done with this discussion.'

But Cyrion wasn't, not yet. He vaulted a guardrail, dropping the ten metres to the platform below. His brothers followed in a pack.

'Tell me something,' he said, his voice less edged now. 'Why did the First Company refuse to follow Sahaal?'

Mercutian drew in air between clenched teeth. 'I had little chance to speak with any of them. It didn't seem to be because of any flaw with Sahaal as Sevatar's replacement, and more due to the fact *no one* would ever live up to the true First Captain. No one *could* live up to him. The Atramentar would serve no other leader after Sevatar died. He'd made them into what they were, a brotherhood that couldn't be broken any other way. Just as the Legion would serve no single captain after the primarch died. It is not our way. I doubt we'd even follow the primarch now. It has been ten thousand years of change, of war, of chaos, of pain and survival.'

Uzas was trailing the inactive blade of his chainaxe across the iron wall, breeding a scraping shriek of metal on metal.

'Sevatar,' he said. 'Did Sevatar die?'

The others shared chuckles and snorts as First Claw's wounded remnants walked on, deeper into the darkness that filled their home.

TALOS WATCHED THE moon come apart. In times past, he might have marvelled at the power he commanded. Now he watched in silence, trying not to overlay the image of the disintegrating moon with the memory of Nostramo dying in the same way.

Rubicon-grade cyclonic torpedoes weren't enough to annihilate an entire world, but they ate into the small moon with voracity and speed.

'I want to hear the Shriek,' he said as he stared.

'Aye, lord.' The Vox-mistress tuned the bridge's speakers to project the aural aspect of Deltrian's jamming field. Sure enough, the sound matched its name. The air was filled with ululating cries of sonic resonance, hateful and somehow organic. Beneath the cries, beneath the screams of rage and vox-crackling torment, a lone man's voice fuelled it all.

The tech-adept had been exquisitely proud of designing the interference projector, and Talos was accordingly grateful for it. The Shriek made hunting so much easier, when enemy vessels were rendered auspex-blind, feeling their way through the cold void without scanners. The power drain was significant, though. The Shriek cloaked them in their prey's blindness, but suckled strength from every generator on the ship. They couldn't fire their energy weapons. They couldn't move at anything less than a half-speed crawl. They certainly couldn't raise void shields – the deflector screens operated on similar tuning to the Shriek itself, and siphoned power from the same sources.

Talos wondered what had happened on the enemy bridge, once the Shriek had caressed their systems. Secure in the cover of the moon's shadow, had the Chapter serfs panicked when they lost contact with their masters in the boarding parties? Perhaps, perhaps not, but no Adeptus Astartes vessel would be crewed by weaklings. Those officers and servants would be the pinnacle of unaugmented human possibility, trained in war academies reminiscent of those on the worlds of Ultramar.

The entire operation was flawlessly conducted according to their wretched Codex Astartes, from the precision first strike, through the meticulous and savage deck-by-deck fighting, to the cruiser's withdrawal to buy its warriors more time.

Victory would come by changing the nature of the game. Talos knew this, and never hesitated to cheat. Some cyclonic-grade weaponry ignited a planet's atmosphere when used in conjunction with other orbital bombardment. This moon had no atmosphere to speak of, and no population to burn, making such weapons useless even if the *Echo of Damnation* had possessed them.

Other cyclonics buried melta or plasma charges into a world's core, triggering fusion effects to either force cataclysmic tectonic activity, or birth a lesser sun at the heart of the world. Either way, no world would survive. Most died within minutes, taking their populations with them.

Rubicon-grade torpedoes were lesser examples of this latter breed. They were all Talos required. One would almost certainly be enough, but two would ensure the deed was done.

First, he had blinded the enemy by the Shriek. They had no way of tracking the torpedoes cutting towards them, and no way of sensing their impact on the moon until it was too late. Within minutes, the burrowing missiles had done their work. He'd seen no need to destroy the entire moon in a pinpointed spherical detonation at its core. To that end, the cyclonics had struck high in the northern hemisphere, drilling into the salt flats of the barren polar caps. Rather than detonate in the planetoid's core, they'd tunnelled through the moon's scalp, inspiring tectonic instability as they exploded in a series of timed chain reactions close to the world's far side, facing the enemy ship.

The moon came apart. Not neatly, by any means. A quarter of its surface shattered, bursting out into the void with such speed that the *Echo*'s own hololithic display lagged in displaying the changes taking place. No more than three minutes after the torpedoes struck the moon's surface, huge chunks of debris began to break free. Ravine-cracks cobwebbed across the satellite's surface, disgorging an atmosphere of dust into the moon's nearspace.

'Kill the Shriek,' Talos ordered. 'Raise shields, arm weapons. All ahead full.'

The *Echo* shivered as it came back to life, pushing though space with a shark's hunger. The strategium deck fell into its familiar organised chaos as officers and servitors attended to their battle duties. The rattle and clank of levers mixed with the murmur of voices and the clatter of fingers on clicking keys.

'Any sign of the Genesis cruiser?' Talos asked from his central throne. On the occulus, the scalped moon was a sorry looking ruin, already half-surrounded by its new asteroid field.

'I see them, sire.' The Master of Auspex drew in a wet breath through his rebreather mask. 'Rendering on the hololithic now.'

At first, Talos couldn't make out the vessel from the debris. The hololithic flickered with its usual unreliability, offering a scene with hundreds of targets. The moon's ruptured edge was a ragged curve at the image's side. Rocks of all shapes and sizes decorated the space above, along with a hazy mist representing particulate debris too small for focus on individual locks.

There they were. The telltale forked prow of an Adeptus Astartes warship, and the runic signifiers of its weapons firing into the void. Talos watched the hololithic ship as it manoeuvred, suddenly finding itself at the heart of an asteroid field, unloading its weapons on the surrounding rocks as it sought to cut its way free.

He was almost disappointed they'd not been destroyed in the initial burst, but at least he could witness it first-hand now.

'I cannot help but feel a moment of pride,' he said to the crew, 'You have done well, all of you.'

The drifting rocks tumbled through space, crashing into each other and shattering into yet more rubble. Talos watched the hololithic display as several large chunks collided with the flickering ship. The primitive imaging program displayed little of the immense damage such impacts must be inflicting.

'Bring us in for a visual confirmation.' Talos knew that would involve a wait of several hours to close the distance, and an idea took root to pass the time and tip the odds further against the Genesis warriors on board.

'Hail the enemy ship, and filter the feed so every vox outlet on the ship transmits the words we speak.'

Vox-mistress Auri did as she was told. The bridge had fallen quiet after the Shriek was deactivated. Now it rang again with the voices carrying from the enemy cruiser. Monotone servitor voices formed a background chorus to the crumpling thuds of rocks impacting on the hull, and a resonant voice speaking breathlessly.

'I am Captain Aeneas of the *Diadem Mantle*. I will not listen to your taunts, heretic, nor to your temptations.' An explosion cut the Space Marine's words off for a moment, punctuated by distant screams.

'This is Talos of the warship *Echo of Damnation*. I will speak no taunts, merely truths. Your assault has failed, as has your flight from our vengeance. We are watching you die on our auspex hololiths even as we speak. If you have any last words, speak them now for posterity. We will remember them. We are the Eighth Legion, and our memories are long.'

'Filthy, accursed traitors,' crackled the reply.

'He sounds angry,' a nearby officer joked. Talos silenced him with a wordless glare.

'Talos?' came the captain's voice again.

'Yes, Aeneas.'

'May you burn in whatever hell awaits the damned and the deceived.'

Talos nodded, though his counterpart had no hope of seeing the gesture. 'I am sure I will. But you will reach there before I do. Die now, captain. Burn and be mourned, for a wasted life.'

'I fear no sacrifice. The blood of martyrs is the seed of the Imperium. In Guilliman's name! Courage and hon–'

The link went dead. On the hololithic display the runic symboliser of the enemy warship blinked out of existence at the core of the brutal asteroid storm.

'The *Diadem Mantle*,' said the Vox-mistress, 'lost with all souls.'

'Bring us closer to the debris field, and annihilate whatever remains with a volley from our prow armaments.'

'Aye, lord.'

Talos rose from his throne, weary and aching. 'The entirety of our speech was broadcast across the ship?' he asked.

'Aye, lord.'

'Good. May it dishearten the Genesis bastards still alive, to hear their captain die and their warship burn.'

'Lord,' began the Master of Auspex. 'The use of torpedoes... That was a fine plan. It worked beautifully.'

Talos paid him scarce heed. 'As you say, Nallen.' He gestured to the closest officer. 'Kothis. You have the bridge.'

The named officer didn't salute. The masters paid no attention to such formalities. Still, he knew better than to sit in the lord's throne. Instead, he stood by it, taking control over those hunched below him.

Talos moved to the edge of the strategium, and lifted Xarl's corpse onto his shoulders.

'I am going to bury my brother. Summon me only if the need is dire.'

IT TOOK ALMOST an hour for First Claw to reach any of the other squads. Their journey through the *Echo*'s labyrinthine decks took them through chamber after chamber, tunnel after tunnel. At times they passed through crowds of idling slaves hiding in the dark, while other chambers were filled with the bustle of efficiency, as the Legion's servants went about their duties. Minor repair crews and teams of menial slaves were in the majority. Several they passed looked mauled from encounters with the Genesis Chapter, and Cyrion had the uncomfortable feeling that the final crew casualty lists would number in the thousands.

Mercutian was clearly thinking the same. 'They hit us even harder than the Blood Angels hit the *Covenant*.'

Cyrion nodded. Given the numbers of crew lost that night at Crythe, he'd not been keen to witness another boarding assault. Still, the *Echo* had the resources and manpower to compensate for such a grievous mauling; the *Covenant* hadn't.

As they walked, each of them grew aware of a moist, soft sound crackling over the vox. Uzas was licking his teeth again.

'Stop that,' Cyrion warned him.

Uzas either didn't hear or didn't care. His blood-palmed helm didn't even turn to regard the others.

'Uzas.' Cyrion resisted the urge to sigh. 'Brother, you are doing it again.'

'Hnh?'

Despite Mercutian's earlier lecture on prejudice, Cyrion didn't think of himself as a petty creature. However, the endless run of Uzas's tongue along his teeth was enough to make him grind his own.

'You are licking your teeth again.'

Variel cleared his throat with gentle politeness. 'Why does that cause you irritation?'

'The primarch did it. After he'd filed his teeth to points, he'd ceaselessly lick his teeth and lips while thinking, like some kind of animal. He'd often cut his tongue as he did it, and the blood would flow over his lips, driving us on edge with the scent.'

'Intriguing,' the Apothecary noted, 'that a primarch's blood should have such an effect. I have never envied you your existence in their shadows, but that sounds fascinating.'

The others said nothing, showing just how much they cared to discuss that particular subject again.

'I smell intestines,' Uzas grunted as they entered another chamber.

'I smell the Bleeding Eyes,' said Cyrion.

'Hail to First Claw,' cawed a voice from above.

They raised their bolters as one, aiming into the roof of the domed chamber. The room itself was a hollowed-out mess, signs of abandonment in every direction. A supply room or crew barracks, was Cyrion's guess. Four hunched figures squatted in the rafters, barely visible between the tendrilous forest of chains hanging from the ceiling.

Six Genesis warriors dangled, limp as broken marionettes, from hooks on the dirty chains. Their armour was torn open across each stomach – power cables split and layered ceramite shredded, pulled open by clawed hands. The flesh beneath was similarly mutilated, allowing their innards to rain in a slopping spill onto the decking below. Blood still dripped from three of them.

Against his instincts, Cyrion lowered his bolter. These wretches were barely his brothers, but they were murder in a fight, and the warband was fortunate to have them. The problem was keeping them in the fights they joined. *First in*, they always claimed, and that was true enough. The fact was also true that they were also *first out*.

'You have been busy,' he said. Despite the distance, he caught a glimpse of one of them without its helm on. Blood coated its hands and what little he could see of its face, as it fed upon the organs of the hanging warriors. A scalp of black veins and misaligned bone was immediately covered by the traditional sloping, daemon-shrieking helm.

'Throne of Lies,' he swore.

'What?' Mercutian asked, keeping his voice low.

'The warp beats in their blood more than I realised.'

The Raptors shared a series of clicks and growls, passing as discussion between the pack. One of them hissed at the Night Lords below, the sound breaking off into a rasping vox-cackle.

'This deck is clean, First Claw. We cleaned it of enemy heartbeats.' The Raptor's head jerked twice, on a twitching neck. 'You seek Lucoryphus?'

Cyrion shook his head. 'No. We are moving through to the Hall of Reflection. We seek Deltrian.'

'Then you seek Lucoryphus. He stands with the machine-speaker.'

'Very well. Our thanks to you.' Cyrion waved his brothers forward. First Claw walked around the hanging bodies, giving them a wide berth. The Bleeding Eyes never reacted well to others interfering with their kills, or with the feasts that followed.

As First Claw passed, one of the Raptors ignited the thrusters on its back, diving down from the ceiling with a thrust of smoky engine flare, sinking his claws into the exposed meat of a dead warrior's torso. First Claw paid no heed, and moved ahead without a word.

THE MAN WAS only a man in the loosest, most physiological sense. He had no comprehension that he'd ever possessed a name, nor was he truly sentient beyond an ability to express the same tortured emotion over and over again. His existence was divided into two planes of experience, which his strangled mind interpreted as Torpor and Scourging.

In moments of Torpor, which lasted for oceans of time between Scourges, he drifted in a milky haze of numbing sensation, doing nothing, seeing nothing, knowing nothing but an eternity of weightlessness and the taste of salty chemicals in his lungs and throat. The only thing that could be generously interpreted as thought was the faint, distant echo of anger. He didn't feel fury itself, but rather the memory of it: a recollection of once knowing rage, without knowing why.

When the Scourging came, it came in a storm of pain. The anger rose again, sparking through the veins of his head like misfiring power cables. He'd feel his jaws opening, his tongueless mouth silently screaming into the cold nothingness that cocooned him.

After a time, the pain would fade, and the false anger it brought would drift away with it.

It was happening now. The man once known as Princeps Arjuran of the Titan *Hunter in the Grey* breathed the cold liquid of his chemical womb, inhaling fluid and excreting filth as his ravaged body was at last allowed to rest.

Lucoryphus of the Bleeding Eyes stood before the glass tank containing the tortured man. He didn't like to stand upright, but some things bore closer investigation. The Raptor tapped a claw on the glass.

'Hello, little soul,' he rasped in a smiling whisper.

The body within the suspension tank had been hobbled, its legs ending below the knees and its hands amputated at the wrists. Lucoryphus watched the crippled figure writhing in the fluid, lost in whatever inner torments drifted through its drugged mind.

'Do not touch the glass,' Deltrian's toneless voice still conveyed his disapproval.

Lucoryphus jerked twice, his helmed head twitching on his neck. 'I will break nothing.'

'I did not ask you to break nothing. I asked you to refrain from touching the glass.'

The Raptor cawed a short whine and dropped back down to all fours. He watched the excruciation needles withdrawing from the prisoner's temples, and turned his attention to the tech-adept.

'This is how you make the Shriek?'

'It is.' Deltrian's chrome face was hidden in his hood, as he worked on powering down the pain engines feeding into the suspension tank. 'The prisoner was a gift from First Claw. They tore him from his throne in a Titan's mind-chamber.'

Lucoryphus hadn't heard the tale, but he could guess the details easily enough. In truth, the Shriek fascinated him. To render an enemy vessel's scanners inert and useless, to drown them in a voxed screed of tormented scrapcode... such technology was rare enough, but still possible in any one of a hundred ways with the right genius and the right materials. But to breed electronic interference from the pain of a single human soul, to filter organic agony through the ship's systems and use it to harm the enemy – that was poetry the Bleeding Eyes leader could sincerely appreciate.

He tapped the glass again, uttering a low snarl that wasn't quite a laugh.

'How much of your brain-flesh is still human?' he asked.

Deltrian paused, his multi-jointed fingers hovering over the console keys. 'That is a matter I have no desire or motivation to discuss. Why do you ask?'

Lucoryphus inclined his sloping daemon helm to the amniotic tank. 'Because of this. This is no cold, logical creation. This is the work of a mind that understands pain and fear.'

Deltrian hesitated again, unsure whether to process the Raptor's words as a compliment. It was always difficult to tell with the Bleeding Eyes. He was prevented from a need to answer, as the doors opened on grinding hydraulics. Four figures stood silhouetted by the red emergency lights beyond.

'Hail,' said Cyrion.

* * *

THE HALL OF Reflection was more museum than workshop, and within its walls Deltrian was monarch of all he surveyed. Cyrion watched him for a while, canting binary orders to his menials, directing their efforts to unknowable projects.

The Night Lord walked around the chamber, ignoring the bustle of robed adepts and mumbling servitors. His gaze fell upon the weapons being repaired, and the great Dreadnought sarcophagi chained to the walls, housing the Legion's revenants, forever awaiting reawakening.

The last of these armoured coffins depicted the triumphant image of Malcharion, rendered in burnished gold, as he'd been in life. He stood with the helms of two Imperial champions in his hands, crucified by the rays of a moonrise over Terra's most holy battlements.

'You,' Cyrion turned to a nearby adept.

The Mechanicus worker nodded his hooded head. 'My name is Lacuna Absolutus, sire.'

'Is work still proceeding on reawakening the war-sage?'

'The battle interrupted our rituals, sire.'

'Of course,' Cyrion said. 'Forgive me.' He crossed the chamber to where Deltrian stood. 'Talos ordered us here to protect you.'

Deltrian didn't look up from the console. His chrome fingers clicked and clacked at the keypad. 'I need no protection. Furthermore, reports from all Claws report the enemy resistance is ended.'

Cyrion had been listening to the same vox reports. That wasn't exactly what they'd said. 'It is not like you to be so imprecise, honoured adept.'

'Hostilities are almost at their conclusion, then.'

Cyrion was smiling now. 'You are annoyed, and trying not to let it show. Tell me why.'

Deltrian emitted an irritated blurt of code. 'Begone, warrior. Many demands press upon my time, and the array of my attention is limited.'

Cyrion laughed. 'Is this because your requests for assistance weren't answered? We were engaged in battle, honoured adept. If we'd had the time to walk on the ship's hull with you, I assure you we would have done as you asked.'

'My work was critical. The repairs had to be made. If we had committed to a void battle with the enemy cruiser–'

'But we did not,' Cyrion rejoined. 'Did we? Talos tore the moon apart instead. Beautiful overkill, that. The primarch would have laughed and laughed, loving every moment of it.'

Deltrian deactivated his vocabulator, preventing any response based on a moment of emotional temper. He merely nodded to indicate he'd heard the warrior's words, and continued his work.

It was Lucoryphus that answered, from his vigil by the torture tank. 'It does not matter. I answered his call.'

Cyrion and the rest of First Claw turned to the Raptor. 'Yes, after you fled with your rabid pack, leaving us to fight alone.'

'Enough whining.' The Raptor's head jerked on the servos in his neck. 'You survived, did you not?'

'No,' Cyrion replied. 'Not all of us.'

HE WORKED ALONE, with his brother's blood on his hands.

'Talos,' a voice carried over the vox. He ignored it, not even paying heed to whom it belonged.

The extraction of gene-seed wasn't a complicated process, but it required a degree of delicacy and efficiency made easier with the right tools. More than once in recent years, Talos had ruined gene-seed organs in the heat of battle, cutting them from a corpse with his gladius and pulling them free with his bare hands. Desperate times called for desperate measures.

This was different. He wasn't carving open one of his distant brothers under enemy fire.

'You were always a fool,' he told the dead body. 'I warned you it would see you dead one night.'

He worked in the stillness of his own meditation chamber, silent but for the humming of his armour joints and the wet-meat sounds of a blade going through flesh. His own narthecium was long gone, lost in a fight decades ago, yet he had no desire to allow Variel to do this.

Splitting the breastbone beneath the black carapace was the most difficult obstacle. The biological augmentations that rendered a legionary's bones stronger than a human's were also a bane to easy surgery. He briefly considered widening the wound close to Xarl's primary heart, but it would involve burrowing and pulling more meat free.

Talos hefted his gladius, testing the weight a few times. He brought the pommel orb down on Xarl's solar plexus once, twice, and a third time with a dull thud punctuating each impact. On the fourth, he pounded the pommel down with more strength, cracking the breastbone in a ragged split. Several more thumps widened the crack enough for Talos to curl his fingers around the ribcage, opening his brother's body like a creaking, cracking book. The smell of burned flesh and bare organs soon thickened the air in the small chamber. He reached a gloved hand into Xarl's chest cavity, pulling the first globular node free. It resisted at first, tightly bound to the nervous system; the heart of a mesh of veins and muscle meat.

He poured the handful of cold blood and stringy flesh into a medicae canister. In better times, there had been words to say and oaths to speak. None of them felt right now.

Talos clutched Xarl's limp head, turning it to the side. Moving the body caused a rattle of breath to leave the corpse's open mouth and exposed lungs. Despite his training, despite all the things he'd seen in his centuries of life, the sound caused his hands to freeze. Some instinctive responses were too human, too tightly bound to a warrior's core, to go ignored. Bodies breathing was one of them. He felt his blood run cold, just for that moment.

The progenoid organ in Xarl's throat was much easier to recover. Talos used the tip of his gladius to carve through the skin and sinewy muscle, making a wide wound in the dead flesh. He pulled out another handful of bloody tissue and vein-stringy meat, placing it in the canister with the first.

A twist, a seal, and the medicae canister locked tight. A green rune activated along its side.

For several slow breaths, Talos knelt next to his brother's body, saying nothing, thinking nothing. Xarl's mutilated remains scarcely resembled the warrior in life – he was a defeated, broken thing of ripped flesh and ruined ceramite. The traitorous thought entered his mind of scavenging his brother's armour, but Talos suppressed the vulture's urge. Not Xarl. And in truth, there was little remaining worth the effort of plunder.

'Talos,' the vox insisted. He still ignored it, though the voice pulled him from his dead-minded reverie.

'Brother,' he said to Xarl. 'A hero's burial awaits.'

Talos rose to his feet, moving to his weapon rack. An ancient flamer rested as it had for years, cleaned of all rust and corrosion, its unlit nozzle emerging from a brass daemon's wide maw. He'd never liked the weapon, scarcely even used it since first tearing it from the hands of a dead warrior of the Emperor's Children five decades before.

A click of his thumb activated the pilot light. It hissed in the chamber, an angry candle flame casting a sharp glare in the gloom. He slowly aimed the weapon at Xarl's body, breathing in the scent of his brother's ruptured flesh and the chemical tang of old promethium oil.

Xarl had been there when Talos first took a life: a shopkeeper slain by a boy in the lightless Nostramo night. He'd stood with him as the gang wars swept the cities, always cursing with gutter invective; always first to shoot and last to ask questions; always confident, never regretting a thing.

He was the weapon, Talos thought. Xarl had been First Claw's truest blade, and the controlled strength that formed their backbone in battle. He was the reason other Claws had always backed down from facing them. While Xarl lived, Talos had never feared First Claw losing a fight. They had never liked one another. Brotherhood asked for no friendship, only loyalty. They'd stood back to back as the galaxy burned – always brothers, never friends; traitors together unto the last.

But none of it seemed right to say. The flamer hissed on in the spreading silence.

'If there is a hell,' Talos said, 'you are walking there now.' He aimed the weapon again. 'I believe I will see you there soon, brother.'

He pulled the trigger. Chemical fire breathed out in a sudden roar, washing over the body in short bursts. Ceramite darkened. Joints melted. Flesh dissolved. He had a last sight of Xarl's blackening skull, the bones resting in a silent, eyeless laugh. Then it was lost in the smoke choking the air.

The fire quickly spread to the chamber's bedding and the scrolls on the walls. The spoiled-meat reek of burning human flesh turned the cloying air even fouler.

Talos washed the body in a final spread of liquid fire. He stowed the flamer over his shoulder, locked the medicae canister to his thigh, and reached for his weapons last of all. Talos took Xarl's helm with one hand and his own bolter with the other. Without looking backwards, he strode through the smoke and engaged the door release.

Thick, coiling smoke poured into the hallway beyond, and with it came the smell. Talos walked from the chamber, sealing the door behind him. The fires would die out soon enough, starved of oxygen and fuel in the chamber.

He'd not expected anyone to be waiting. The two humans stood quietly, their cupped hands shielding their mouths and noses from the thinning smoke.

Septimus and Octavia. The seventh and the eighth. Both tall, both dressed in dark Legion uniforms, both permitted, as so few slaves were, to carry weapons. The former stood with his damaged facial bionics clicking each time he blinked or moved his eyes. His long hair framed his face, and Talos – who had little gift for reading human expression beyond terror or anger – could make no sense of the emotion on Septimus's features. Octavia had her hair bound in its usual ponytail, her forehead covered by her bandana. She was getting thin now, and unhealthily pale. This life wasn't being kind to her, nor was her own biology, as her strength faded to be fed to the child growing inside her.

He recalled his order that the two humans remain apart, and his more recent demand that Septimus remain in the hangar. In this moment, neither seemed to matter.

'What do you want?' Talos asked them. 'There is nothing to salvage from Xarl's wargear, Septimus. Do not ask.'

'Variel ordered me to find you, lord. He requests your presence in the apothecarion as a matter of urgency.'

'And it took both of you to deliver this message?'

'No.' Octavia cleared her throat, lowering her hands. 'I heard about Xarl. I'm sorry. I think... by your standards, by the Legion's ideals, I mean... he was a good man.'

Talos's exhalation became a snort, which in turn became a chuckle.

'Yes,' he said. 'Xarl was a good man.'

Octavia shook her head at the warrior's sarcasm. 'You know what I mean. He and Uzas saved me once, just as you did.'

The prophet's chuckle became laughter. 'Of course. A good man. A heretic. A traitor. A murderer. A fool. My brother, the *good man*.'

Both humans stood in silence as, for the first time in many years, Talos laughed until his black eyes watered.

XI

FATE

CHAOS REIGNED IN the Primary Apothecarion. On the *Covenant of Blood*, the Legion's medicae sanctum had been more a morgue than a surgery, becoming a place of stillness and silence – a chamber of cold storage vaults, old bloodstains on the iron tables and memories hanging in the sterile air.

The opposite was true on the *Echo of Damnation*. Variel walked from table to table, through a sea of wounded humanity, his unhelmed face betraying no emotion. Human crew and legionaries alike cried out, reaching for him, filling the air with the reek of sweat, the heat of escaping life and the stink of chemical-rich blood.

Hundreds of tables lined the chamber in rows, almost all of them occupied. Mono-tasked lifter servitors hauled corpses from the slabs, dragging living wounded onto the tables in replacement. Drains in the floor suckled at the blood sloshing across the dirty tiles. Medicae servitors and crew members trained in surgery were sweating as they worked. Variel strode through it all, a gore-streaked conductor overseeing a wailing orchestra.

He paused by one gurney, glancing down at the tangled crewman's body laying there.

'You,' he said to a nearby medicae servitor. 'This one is dead. Remove his eyes and teeth for later use, before incinerating the remains.'

'Compliance,' murmured the bloodstained slave.

A hand gripped his vambrace. 'Variel…' The Night Lord on the next table swallowed blood before he spoke. His clutch tightened. 'Variel, graft the new legs onto the stumps and let's be done with it. Do not keep me here, when we have a world to conquer.'

'You need rather more than new legs,' Variel told him. 'Now remove your hand.'

The warrior gripped tighter. 'I have to be on Tsagualsa. Don't keep me here.'

The Apothecary looked down at the wounded legionary. The warrior's

737

face was half-lost in a wash of blood and burned tissue, baring the skull beneath. One of his arms ended at the bicep, and both legs were fleshy stalks leaking fluid from the ravaged ceramite where his knees had once been. The Genesis Chapter had almost killed this one, no doubt about it.

'Remove your hand,' Variel said again. 'We have discussed this, Murilash. I do not like to be touched.'

The grip only grew tighter. 'Listen to me...'

Variel clenched the warrior's hand with his own, prying the fingers back and holding tight. Without a word, he deployed the laser cutters and bone saw from his narthecium gauntlet. The saw bit down.

The warrior cried out.

'What did you just learn?' Variel asked.

'You wretched bastard!'

Variel tossed the severed hand to another servitor. 'Incinerate this. Ready a bionic left hand with the rest of his planned augmentations.'

'Compliance.'

In the corner of the apothecarion, where they leaned against the wall watching the organised chaos, Cyrion chuckled and voxed to Mercutian.

'You were right,' he said. 'Variel really is one of us.'

'I would have cut out Murilash's heart,' Mercutian replied. 'I've always loathed him.' The two warriors lapsed into silence for a time.

'Deltrian reported they're back to working on reawakening Malcharion.'

Mercutian's reply was to sigh. Through the vox, it was a breathy crackle. 'What?' Cyrion asked.

'He will not thank us for awakening him a second time. I would give much to know why Malek of the Atramentar spared the war-sage's existence.'

'I would give much to know where in the infinite hells the Atramentar are. Do you believe they went down with the *Covenant*?'

Mercutian shook his head. 'Not for a moment.'

'Nor I,' Cyrion agreed. 'They didn't evacuate with the mortals, nor in a Legion gunship. They never reached the *Echo of Damnation*. Which leaves only one choice – they boarded an enemy vessel. They teleported onto a Corsair ship.'

'Perhaps,' Mercutian allowed. His tone walked the border between thoughtful and doubting. 'They would never be able to take a Corsair ship alone.'

'Are you truly this naive?' Cyrion grinned behind a faceplate that wept painted lightning. 'Look how the Blood Reaver treats his Terminator elite. They're his Chosen. I'm not suggesting the Atramentar mounted an assault on the Corsairs, fool. They betrayed us to them. They *joined* them.'

Mercutian snorted. 'Never.'

'No? How many warriors have cast aside the bonds of the First Legions? How many find them irrelevant as the years become decades, and the decades twist into centuries? How many are legionaries only in name, after finding a more satisfying, more purposeful path instead of eternally whining over a final vengeance never taken? Every one of us has his own path to walk. Power is a greater temptation for some than ancient, lofty ideals. Some things matter more than old bonds.'

'Not to me,' Mercutian said at last.

'Not to most of us. I am merely saying–'

'I know what you are saying. I am saying I have no wish to speak of this.'

'Very well. But there is a tale behind the Atramentar's disappearance, brother. One we may never know.'

'Someone knows.'

'That they do. And I would enjoy excruciating the truth from them.'

Mercutian didn't reply, and Cyrion allowed the discussion to wane into an awkward lull. Uzas, standing a few metres away from them, was looking down at his red-painted gauntlets.

'What's wrong with you now?' Cyrion asked.

'My hands are red,' said Uzas. 'Sinners have red hands. The Primarch's Law.' Uzas lifted his head, turning his bruised and bloody face to Cyrion. 'What did I do wrong? Why are my hands painted in sinners' scarlet?'

Mercutian and Cyrion shared a glance. Another moment of rare clarity from their degenerating brother caught them by surprise.

'You killed many of the *Covenant*'s crew, brother,' Mercutian told him. 'Months ago. One of them was the father of the void-born girl.'

'That wasn't me,' Uzas had bitten his tongue, and blood flowed over his lips, slowly raining down his white chin. 'I didn't kill him.'

'As you say, brother,' Mercutian replied.

'Where is Talos? Does Talos know I did not do this?'

'Peace, Uzas,' Cyrion rested a hand on the other warrior's shoulder guard. 'Peace. Do not let yourself grow aggravated.'

'Where's Talos?' Uzas asked again, slurring now.

'He will be here soon,' said Mercutian. 'The Flayer has summoned him.'

Uzas half-lidded his black eyes, drooling saliva and blood in equal measure. 'Who?'

'Talos. You just… You just asked where he was.'

Uzas stood slack-jawed. Blood bubbled at the corner of his thin lips. Even without Legion modification, even had he been left alone as a human boy and never swollen into this broken, avataric living weapon stitched back together after hundreds of battlefields, Uzas would have been a singularly unwholesome and unattractive creature. Everything in the years since only made him fouler to look upon.

'Uzas?' Mercutian pressed.

'Hnnh?'

'Nothing, brother.' He shared another glance with Cyrion. 'It is nothing.'

The three warriors remained silent as the minutes passed on. Again and again, the northern doors opened on grinding tracks. More packs of crew members were arriving each minute, dragging and carrying their wounded.

'It is surprising to see so many mortals flocking here,' Mercutian mused.

With medicae stations on many decks, the crew knew that the Primary Apothecarion was the Flayer's haunt, and few would willingly put themselves beneath his cold gaze and the pressing cuts of his blades.

'They know their own expendability,' Cyrion nodded. 'Only desperation drives them here.'

Talos entered with the latest batch. The prophet ignored the humans around his boots, crossing straight to Variel. Septimus and Octavia trailed him in. The former immediately moved to one of the tables, working to assist the medicae attendant there.

'Septimus,' the surgeon grunted in greeting. 'Start stitching the stomach wound.'

Octavia watched him working, knowing better than to try and offer her help. The mortal crew flinched back from her at all times, no matter her intentions. The curse of the third eye, even when it was hidden beneath her grimy bandana. They all knew what she was, what she did for their lords and masters. None of them wanted to look her way, let alone touch her. So she followed Talos, hanging back what she judged a respectful distance.

Talos walked to Variel, the damage to his armour showing starkly in the apothecarion's harsher light.

'Where is Xarl's corpse?' the Apothecary asked.

Talos handed him the sealed cryo-canister. 'That is all you need,' he said.

Variel took it, his fingers subtly twitching. He disliked others doing inexpert work when he could have performed it to perfection. 'Very well.'

'Is that all?' Talos looked over to Cyrion, Uzas and Mercutian, ready to join them.

'No. We are long overdue a discussion, prophet.'

'We have a world to bring to its knees,' Talos reminded him.

Variel's eyes – ice-blue to the Nostraman's inky black – still flitted around the chamber, drinking in the details. It was the one way Talos thought Variel still differed from the Nostraman-born Night Lords. Whether by genetic legacy or simple habit, a great many VIII Legion warriors would stare in autistic silence, gazing at those they were speaking to. Variel's attention was altogether more fractured.

'We also have half of our warriors dead or dying,' the Apothecary pointed out, 'along with hundreds of mortal crew. There is gene-seed to harvest, and augmetic grafting to perform.'

Talos fingered his temples. 'Then do what needs to be done. I will take the others down to the surface.'

Variel said nothing for a moment, absorbing the words. 'Why?' he said at last. Around him, men and women were still weeping, moaning, screaming. It put Talos in mind of the primarch's Screaming Gallery, with all the shivering hands reaching out from the walls in fruitful torment. He felt like smiling, really smiling, without knowing why.

'Why what?' asked Talos.

'Why attack Tsagualsa? Why attack it in the first place? Why rush down there to finish the deed now? You have been less than forthcoming with answers on the matter.'

The blue veins beneath Talos's cheeks twisted like lightning, following the contours of his scowl. 'To let the hounds slip the leash and torture as they desire. To let the Eighth Legion be itself. And above all, for the symbolism. This was our world, and we left it barren of life. It should remain that way.'

Variel breathed slowly, his eyes settling on Talos for a long, rare moment. 'The populace of Tsagualsa, such as it is, are now cowering in their storm shelters, fearful of the nameless wrath that attacked their capital city. They know it will return, and yes – I suspect you are correct – once the Legion slips its leash and toys with the lives of those souls on the surface, every warrior will be energised by the infliction of fear and the wanton slaughter to inevitably follow. But that is not a good enough answer. You are dreaming without recalling what you see. You are acting on visions you scarcely remember, and barely understand.'

Talos remembered the first moment of awakening once more, finding himself chained in the command throne, with the occulus showing Tsagualsa's grey face from the silent safety of orbit.

'Where are we?' he'd said.

First Claw had walked to his side, forming up in a line of snarling joints and impassive, skullish facemasks.

'You don't recall your orders to us?' Xarl had asked.

'Just tell me where we are,' he'd demanded.

'The Eastern Fringe,' Xarl had answered. 'Out of the Astronomican's light, and in orbit around the world you repeatedly demanded we travel to.'

Variel broke through the prophet's reverie with a murmur of displeasure. 'You have not been the same since we took the *Echo of Damnation*. Are you aware of this?'

They could have been alone, discussing such things in the stillness of a meditation chamber rather than the abattoir of the Primary Apothecarion.

'I do not know,' Talos confessed. 'My memory is a jagged thing of plateaux and shadows, ripe one moment, hollow the next. I am no longer sure I even see the future. What little I remember is tangled, like fate's skeins matted together. It is no longer prophecy, at least not as I understand it.'

If any of this surprised Variel, he didn't let it show. 'You told me months ago why you wished to travel here, brother. You told me you'd dreamed of human life on Tsagualsa's face once more, and that you wished to see it with your own eyes.'

Talos moved aside as two members of Third Claw dragged a slain brother onto a table.

'Soul Hunter,' one of them greeted him. Talos gave him a withering look, and led Variel away from them both.

'I recall no such dream,' he told the Apothecary.

'It was months ago. You have been slipping for a long time, but the rate of degeneration is accelerating. Focus on this fact, Talos: you wanted to sail back into these skies. Now we are here. Now those same humans you dreamed of crawl into the earth, weak and weaponless, wailing that we have returned. And even as you fulfil your desire, you are still hollow, still void of memory. You are breaking apart, Talos. Fracturing, if you will. *Why* are we here, brother? Focus. Think. Tell me. *Why?*'

'I do not remember.'

Variel's reply was to strike him. The blow came from nowhere, the back of the Apothecary's gauntlet smashing backhanded into the side of Talos's face.

'I did not ask you to remember. I asked you to use your gods-damned mind, Talos. *Think*. If you cannot recall, then work out the answer from what you know of yourself. You brought us here. Why? What benefit is there? How does it serve us?'

The prophet spat acidic saliva onto the floor. When he turned back to Variel, a viperous smile played across his pale, bloody lips. He didn't strike back. He did nothing but smile with bleeding gums.

'Thank you,' he said as the moment passed. 'Your point is taken.'

Variel nodded. 'I had hoped it would be.' He met the prophet's dark eyes. 'I apologise for striking you.'

'I deserved it.'

'You did. However, I still apologise.'

'I said it is fine, brother. No apology is necessary.'

Variel nodded again. 'If that is the case, would you ask the others to cease aiming their weapons at me?'

Talos looked around the chamber. Both members of Third Claw had their bolters raised. First Claw was a mirror of the image, their own guns lifted and aimed. Even several Night Lords on tables awaiting surgery were holding their pistols level and ready to fire.

'Ivalastisha,' said Talos. 'Peace.'

The warriors lowered their weapons at once, in slow unison.

Variel gestured to one of the side chambers. 'Come. There are tests on your blood that I must–'

'The tests can wait, Variel.'

Variel's cold eyes flickered with something, some unknowable emotion never given the grace to flash in full across his features.

'I believe you are dying.' He lowered his voice. 'I have saved you before. Let me analyse you now, and we will see if I can save you a second time.'

'A trifle melodramatic,' Talos replied, though his blood ran cold, feeling like a flush of nerve-killing combat narcotics.

'Your body is rejecting the modifications wrought by the gene-seed. As you age, as you take wound after wound, your regenerative processes are breaking down. You can no longer heal the damage Curze's blood is doing to your body. Some humans are simply unsuitable for gene-seed implantation. You are one of them.'

Talos said nothing for a moment. Ruven's dream-words replayed through his mind, in savage chorus with Variel's. The prophet's marble visage turned to the rest of the chamber.

'This is conjecture,' he said.

'It is,' Variel admitted. 'I have had little experience in dealing with the physiology of first-generation Legiones Astartes. But I was able to sustain my Lord Blackheart's life for centuries, through a mix of ingenuity, ancient science, and working with fools who practised powerful blood magic. I know my art, Talos. You are dying. Your body no longer functions as it should.'

Talos followed him as he spoke. In the side chamber, the Apothecary gestured to an excruciation table replete with chains. The room's ceiling was given over to a multi-limbed arachnid machine, with various scanners, cutters and probes at the end of each jointed iron limb.

'There is no need to lie down at first. The more detailed tests will come after these preliminaries, but I wish only to draw blood from the veins in your throat for now. Then we will scan your skull. Only then will we proceed deeper.'

Talos acquiesced in silence.

ANOTHER ONE DIED beneath Septimus's hands. He swore in Nostraman.

The surgeon he was working with wiped bloody hands across his own face, as if it would clean away the stains already there rather than add to them.

'Next,' the man said to the closest servitors. They dragged a writhing woman in a filthy crew uniform onto the table. She'd lost a leg to a bolter round, but the tourniquet at her thigh had spared her a cold, shivering death from blood loss. Septimus winced at the biological ruin left of her leg below the knee. Her eyes were wide, the pupils narrow. She hissed air in and out through clenched teeth.

'Who are you?' he asked gently, in the same moment the medicae said 'Name and role.'

'Marlonah,' she said to Septimus. 'Starboard tertiary munitions deck.

I'm a loader.' She squeezed her eyes closed for a moment. 'Don't servitor me. Please.'

'He won't,' Septimus told her.

'Thank you. Are you Septimus?'

He nodded.

'Heard about you,' she said, and lapsed back onto the table, covering her eyes against the bright glare of the lights above.

The medicae wiped his face again, clearly weighing the effort and value of the diminishing cheap augmetic supplies he had at his disposal. Only officers could count on their chances of a bionic organ or limb, but she was hardly underdeck scum.

'She can't do her duty with one leg,' Septimus said, sensing this game was already lost.

'Another could perform a loader's duties just as easily,' the medicae replied. 'Menials are hardly difficult to replace.'

'Primaris,' Marlonah said, the words hissed through the pain. Sweat bathed her in feverish droplets. 'Primaris qualified. Not… not just a hauler. Cart driver, too. Cannon loader.'

The surgeon tightened the tourniquet, eliciting a fresh grunt. 'If I find out you're lying to me,' he told her, 'I will inform the Legion.'

'Not lying. Primaris qualified. I swear.' Her voice was growing weaker now, and her eyes unfocused.

'Record her for omega-grade augmentation after the crisis is over,' the medicae said to his attendant servitor. 'Stabilise her, and pitch the stump until then.'

Marlonah was unconscious now. Septimus suspected that applying hot pitch to her raw stump to prevent any future bleeding would rouse her, though. He released a pent-up breath, cursing the Genesis Chapter for their fanatical assault. Throne in flames, they'd given the ship a beating.

The medicae moved away, seeking another patient on another table, in this endless supply of them. As Septimus followed, his glance fell on Octavia across the room. She stood at the heart of carnage's aftermath, her pale skin ungraced by the blood marking the dead and dying around her.

He watched her retying her ponytail, seeing the hesitance in her fingers as she walked from table to table, careful not to touch anyone. She only paused by the unconscious ones, resting her fingers on their skin, saying a few words of comfort or checking their pulses.

In the middle of this stinking den of dying heretics, Septimus smiled.

VARIEL TAPPED THE display monitor, overlaying the hololithic charts.

'Do you see the correlation?'

Talos stared at the distorted hololithic of conflicting charts and hundreds of rows of runic symbols signifying numbers.

He had to shake his head. 'No, I do not.'

'It is difficult to believe you were once an Apothecary,' Variel told him, in a rare moment of pique.

Talos gestured to the overlaid readings. 'I can see the flaws and failings in the body's kinetics. I can see the impairment and the unwarranted spikes in cortical activity.' How easy it was, to speak of his own degeneration so impartially. The idea almost made him bare his teeth in a smile that would have done Uzas proud. 'I am not saying I cannot understand what I am seeing, Variel. I am saying I do not see what you find so unique in it.'

Variel hesitated, trying a new tack. 'Do you at least recognise the spikes in limbic activity, and see the other signs listed as potentially terminal?'

'I recognise the possibility,' Talos allowed. 'It is hardly conclusive. This suggests I will be in pain for the rest of my life, not that my life will be cut short.'

Variel's exhalation trod perilously close to a sigh. 'That will do. But look here.'

Talos watched the looping results flicker and restart, again and again. The rune-numbers cycled, the charts flowed in some hololithic dance, devoid of all rhythm.

'I see it,' he said at last. 'My progenoid glands are... I do not know how to describe it. They are too active. It seems they are still absorbing and processing genetic markers.' He touched the side of his neck, recalling the removal of Xarl's gene-seed only hours before.

Variel nodded, allowing himself the smallest of smiles. 'Mature progenoids will always react with a subsistent level of activity – a base level of processing genetic matter, collating a biological record of the experiences and traumas of the warrior they serve.'

'I know how progenoids function, brother.'

Variel raised a hand to placate the prophet. 'That is my point. Yours have always been overactive, as we already knew. Much too efficient. They rendered your physiology unstable and were, perhaps, the cause of your prophetic vision. Now, however, they are in rebellion. Previously, they were still trying to *improve* you, from human to one of the Legiones Astartes. But that development was a dead end. You could improve no more. You were already one of us. Their overefficiency has now passed a critical juncture. In many cases, the implanted organs would wither and die within the body. Yours are too strong. They are affecting the host, rather than withering themselves.'

'As I said: pain while I still draw breath, but it is not terminal.'

Variel conceded the point with a flash of thought in his pale eyes. 'Perhaps. Either way, removal of the progenoids is no longer an option. It would make no difference, for your organs are already–'

Talos interrupted with an irritated wave of his hand, as if giving the order to fire. 'Enough. I can read the accursed hololithic. Come, Variel. Deal with the wounded, and let us retake Tsagualsa.'

The Flayer exhaled slowly. The dim illumination of the side chamber painted the skinned faces across his pauldrons in a greasy, pallid light.

'What is it?' asked Talos.

'Were you to die, and a suitable host be found for your gene-seed organs, there is a chance the new host would carry the same curse as you – but with the ability to control it. Your gene-seed is uncorrupted, but unsuited to you. In a better host, with true symbiosis, they would be...'

'Be what?' His dark eyes flickered with thought now, possibilities playing out in their depths.

Variel was staring at the charts. 'Powerful. Imagine your prophetic gift without the false visions that increase as time passes, or the headaches that drive you to your knees, or the unconsciousness that lasts weeks or months. Imagine it without the broken memory, or the other debilitating symptoms that plague you. When you die, brother, you will leave a powerful legacy for the future.'

'The future,' Talos said, his black eyes unfocusing. He almost smiled. 'Of course.'

Variel turned back from the hololithic. 'What is it?'

'That is why we are here.' Talos tongued his split lip, tasting his own blood – a lesser reflection of Uzas and the dead primarch. 'I know what I want from this world.'

'I am pleased to hear it. I had hoped this discussion would have that effect on you. Am I to assume you have changed your perspective, or are you still content to allow the Legion to slip its leash and slaughter everyone on the world below?'

'No. The pure war is not enough. This is Tsagualsa, Variel. The carrion world... now with life tenaciously clinging to its scabbed surface. We can claw more than some tawdry, bloodthirsty satisfaction from this.'

The Apothecary disengaged the hand scanner, letting it power down. 'Then what, Talos?'

The prophet stared past Variel, stared past the chamber's walls, looking at something only he could see.

'We can reforge the Legion. We can lay down an example for our brothers to follow. We can cast aside the hatred between warbands, with these painful first steps. Do you see, Variel?'

He turned at last, his black eyes shining. 'We can make it glorious, this time. We can begin again.'

The Apothecary wheeled several of his full-body scanners into place. Buttons and dials on his narthecium gauntlet activated the jointed arms reaching down from the ceiling. Chemicals sloshed in glass vials.

'Lie down,' he said.

Talos complied, still staring with unfocused eyes. 'Will I lose consciousness?'

'Without a doubt,' Variel replied. 'Tell me, is Tsagualsa the right place to begin such a reforging?'

'I believe so. As an example, as a… symbol. Have any of the others told you what happened when we left this world?'

'I have heard of the Tsagualsan Retaliation, yes.'

Talos was seeing past him again, staring now into memory rather than the paths of possibility.

'That makes it seem so placid. No, Variel, it was much worse than that. With the primarch gone, we'd been decaying for years – scattering to the stars, guarding our own supplies from the claws of our brothers as much as from the preying hands of our enemies. But at the end of it all, when the grey sky caught fire with the contrails of ten thousand drop pods, that was the day a Legion died.'

Variel felt his skin crawling. He loathed being near any expression of emotion, even the bitterness of old memory. But curiosity forced his tongue.

'Who came for you?' he asked. 'What size was the force to dare attack an entire Legion?'

'It was the Ultramarines.' Talos lowered his head, surrendering to the memory now

'A thousand warriors?' The Apothecary's eyes widened. 'That's all?'

'You think in such small terms,' Talos chuckled. 'The Ultramarines. Their sons. Their brothers. Their cousins. The entire Legion, reborn after the Heresy, wearing hundreds of icons proclaiming their new allegiances. They called themselves the Primogenitors. I believe their descendants still do.'

'You mean the Ultramarines' kindred Chapters?' Variel could almost picture it now. 'How many of them?'

'All of them, Variel,' Talos said softly, seeing the sky once again on that distant day. 'All of them.'

PART TWO

THE LAST DAY

XII
THE PRIMOGENITORS' RAGE

He knew he was dreaming.

It didn't help. It didn't make anything less real. The smells were no weaker, the pain was no fainter.

'Get to the ships,' *he said aloud. He could sense Variel moving around the chamber, though he could see nothing outside the pictures his mind was painting. The tests being run on his blood, on his brain, on his heart... none of it meant anything, for he felt nothing at all.*

'Get to the ships,'

'Peace, Talos,' *came Variel's voice, from a great distance.* 'Peace.'

He couldn't remember a time of peace. There had never been peace in the purgatory of Tsagualsa.

His first memory of the last day was the sunrise.

They came for vengeance as the weak sun rose.

Tsagualsa's star was a cold heart at the system's core – a source of anaemic, thin light that scarcely brightened the lone world in its care. Its pale radiance spread across the planet's lifeless surface, at last painting bleak illumination across the battlements of a black stone fortress. On the plains, a dust storm was brewing. It would crash over the fortress within the hour.

Before Mercutian, before Variel, before Uzas – there was Sar Zell, Ruven, Xarl and Cyrion.

Sar Zell was the one to come running. His boots pounded across the battlements as the heavens caught fire.

'They're here,' he voxed to Talos. 'They've come at last.'

In a moment of divine atmospheric poetry, it started to rain from an amber sky.

In the years following the primarch's death, more and more warbands cut loose from Tsagualsa's skies and took their raiding deeper into the

Imperium. Many were already carving out havens in the Great Eye with the other Legions, spending as much time waging war against former kin as against the minions of the False Emperor.

A battlefleet of staggering size rested above the grey world's barren face, each warship marked by the winged skull of the VIII Legion. Here was a fleet that could devastate entire solar systems. It had done so before, many times.

Across the Tsagualsan System, rifts in reality tore open in the silence of the void. They bled foul, daemonic matter into the clean silence of real space, while shuddering battleships strained their way back into the material universe. As with almost all warp flight, there was little cohesion, no alignment of arrival vectors and formations maintained through the rage of empyrean flight. Instead, one by one, the invaders burst from the warp and powered towards the grey world.

At first, they matched the Night Lords' numbers. Soon, they overshadowed them. As the battle began, by the time the skies of Tsagualsa started to burn, they eclipsed the VIII Legion fleet completely. More warships arrived with each passing minute, vomited from the warp and streaming trails of poisonous mist.

They needed no formation. They needed no strategic assault plan. That many ships needed nothing else to win a war. The Primogenitor Chapters, the XIII Legion in all but name, had come to end the cancer of heresy once and for all.

Captains and commanders filled the vox-net with recriminations; with orders no one else was following; with tactics few souls were willing to hear.

Talos remained on the battlements, listening to the thousands of screaming voices. Always in the past, the screams were those of their prey. Now the cries were torn from the mouths of brothers, brothers that had survived the Heresy and the two centuries of warfare since.

One order was damning in its repetition. He heard it over and over again, screamed and cried and yelled. *Get to the ships. Get to the ships. Get to the ships.*

'We have to defend the fortress,' Talos voxed back to his commander.

The Exalted's voice was a bass drawl, rasping and wet over the scrambled vox. 'You do not see the madness taking place up here, prophet. The Thirteenth Legion will crucify us if we remain.'

'Vandred, we cannot abandon all of the fortress's resources...'

'There is no time for this, Talos. Dozens of our warships are already running. We are more than outnumbered; we are at risk of being overwhelmed. Get back to the ship.'

The prophet activated his narthecium gauntlet, tracking First Claw's armour runic signifiers. Xarl and Cyrion were close, perhaps in one of the armouries nearby. Sar Zell waited only a few metres away, listening in to the vox-chatter. Ruven was deeper in the fortress, doing the gods only knew what.

'Vandred,' said Talos. 'We are already seeing drop pods coming down. The sky is aflame with engine wash.'

'Of course it is. They outnumber our ships five to one. We can barely keep them from orbital bombardment, do you think we have any chance of preventing them making planetfall?'

Talos watched the pods raining down, trailing fire from the sky.

'This is Talos to all Tenth Company Claws.' His voice was merely one of many, strangled in the miasma of conflicting vox traffic. 'All Claws, get to the gunships. We have to reach the *Covenant*.'

'As you command, Soul Hunter,' replied several squad leaders.

Soul Hunter, he thought, with a cringing sneer. The name given by his father, for the killing of a single soul – avenging his primarch's murder. Talos earnestly hoped that the ludicrously theatrical title would fade out of use in the years to come.

THE FORTRESS WAS not without defences. Even as enemy gunships shrieked over the battlements, even as drop pods plunged through the scorching atmosphere and impacted in the ash wastes, along the walls, and in the courtyards – the fortress itself resisted the assault.

Anti-air turrets spat hard shells into the sky, hurling Thunderhawks to the ground in flames. Servitor-manned weapons platforms aimed at the landers coming down on the ash wastes, launching missiles and eye-aching streams of laser fire at the vehicles grinding their way overland towards the high walls.

Talos ran across the battlements, Sar Zell a step behind. As they passed turret platforms, their helm's audio sensors parsed down the crashing chatter of autocannon fire, as well as the strangely monotone shouts of gun-slaved servitors mumbling their aiming vectors aloud. The black stone beneath the legionaries' boots shook with the rage of the fortress's response.

'The gunship is in the western quadrant, secondary hangar,' Sar Zell voxed. 'That's if it's not stolen by another company before we reach it.'

'I–'

The explosion from nowhere hurled them from their feet. Talos stumbled forward, smashing headfirst into the rampart wall. Sar Zell tumbled across the stone, slipping over the battlement's edge.

Chunks of servitor and weapon battery rained down, clattering off Talos's armour as he hauled himself back to his feet. Above them, the enemy gunship – its hull painted in royal blue and clean, Imperial white – angled away as its rocket pods reloaded. A thunderclap of thrust sent it streaking through the sky again, seeking more turret platforms to destroy.

'Sar Zell,' he voxed, blinking to clear his senses. His retinal display re-tuned to pierce the smoke, but a more tellingly mundane disorientation clouded his eyes for a moment.

The only reply he received over the vox was a grunt of effort. Talos saw the hands gripping the battlement's lip. He offered his own, as his brother hung there two hundred metres above the desert below. The weight of the immense lascannon chained across Sar Zell's back pre-vented the warrior from pulling himself up with ease.

'My thanks,' Sar Zell voxed back, as his boots thudded on the cold stone again. 'That would have been a singularly ignoble way to die.'

'Perhaps you should leave the cannon,' Talos said.

'Perhaps you should stop speaking madness.'

The prophet nodded. Hard to argue with that.

THEY MET XARL and Cyrion in the armoury level of the closest spire. The walls shook around them as the tiers of autocannons rattled and banged, filling the air with noise. Gunships whined overhead, several ending in the piteous wails of engines spiralling down to the ground.

Xarl wore his wing-crested ceremonial helm, in the midst of looting the armoury. A crate of replacement chainsword teeth-tracks was weighed against one hip.

'I can't find any melta charges,' he told Cyrion, without looking away from his plundering.

Cyrion nodded to Talos and Sar Zell. 'Tell me you have a plan.' The chamber gave a horrendous shudder in time to the tectonic thunder of battlements giving way nearby. 'And tell me it doesn't involve fighting our way across half of the fortress to get to *Dirge*. These Imperial dogs are inside the walls. We won't survive a long journey.'

Talos drew his chainsword. 'In that case, I think it best if I remain silent. Where is Ruven?'

Xarl finally turned from his looting. 'Who cares?'

Get to the ships. The vox-chatter was a repetitive storm of voices all say-ing the same thing. *Get to the ships. Get to the ships.*

'With the Legion scattered, the fortress will fall,' said Sar Zell. 'We were fools not to remain united.'

Talos shook his head. 'The fortress was always going to fall one night. Unity was never an option with the primarch gone. We are fools, but only for still being here when so many of our brothers have already taken to the stars.'

THEY MET RESISTANCE three levels down, as their boots hammered across the black stone floor of a primary thoroughfare corridor. Dead slaves lined the walls, some wearing the Legion's blue uniform, others in the rags that made up their only remaining possessions. Each of the bodies lay in burst repose, broken apart by bolter shells. Blood lined the walls in an uneven layer of greasy, stinking paint.

Talos held up a fist and opened his fingers, making the hand signal to spread out. As his armour's kinetic systems recognised the gesture, corresponding runes flashed on First Claw's retinal displays, relaying the order.

'The invaders decorate the same way we do,' Cyrion noted, eyeing the bodies as the squad moved apart.

'Focus,' Xarl grunted in reply. Cyrion lowered his bolter and withdrew his auspex. It crackled as it tuned into their surroundings.

'Contact,' he announced. 'Dead ahead, and moving back this way. They've either got scanners, or they heard us coming.'

Talos checked his bolter as he crouched by a gore-streaked wall. 'Sar Zell,' he said.

Without a word, the warrior braced against the weight of his lascannon and lifted it to aim down the corridor.

'Are we shooting this out?' Xarl asked.

'No.' The prophet listened to the approaching bootsteps. 'Charge after the initial burst.'

Talos felt his teeth itching, alongside the telltale ache in his tongue and gums as the lascannon drew in power. The consistent thrum made the hair on the back of his neck rise, despite the sanctity of his armoured suit.

Their foes were disciplined veterans, too canny to fall prey to easy traps. They fanned out at the corridor's junction, taking cover where the hallway joined a large chamber beyond.

Both squads immediately started the crashing exchange of bolter fire. Chunks of stone flew through the dusty smoke of shell impacts.

'They're bringing up a heavy bolter,' Cyrion voxed, his autosenses filtering through the smoke. 'He's moved behind the left wall.'

'Sar Zell,' Talos said again.

The lascannon drew in one final exhalation of energy before roaring down the corridor with a discordant *freem* of unrestrained blue-white power. The blade-beam of crisp, sun-bright force burned through one of the stone walls, disintegrating a hole clean through the torso of the warrior taking refuge behind it.

'They're not bringing up a heavy bolter anymore,' Cyrion noted.

'Until someone else picks it up,' Talos replied. 'Another volley, then charge.'

The lascannon shuddered in Sar Zell's hands, rattling and steaming with the expulsion of force. Another of the distant enemies clattered down in a heap of ceramite-clad limbs.

First Claw drew their blades and started running.

* * *

No more than three minutes later, they almost ran headlong into another enemy squad. Another Claw was pinned down at the far end of a sparring chamber, returning a decreasing level of fire as the Imperial Space Marines gunned them down.

Talos dropped into a crouch, leaning by the wall and raising his bolter. Where Guilliman's sons worked and fought with absolute efficiency, First Claw moved with the shadowed, ragged remnants of discipline. Talos gave no order to fire this time. He didn't need to. Their bolters opened up with throaty barks, utterly without unity, picking their targets with impunity. Of the seven remaining, three went down under the fresh hail of fire.

The four Imperial Space Marines turned to face this new assault, half the squad moving to divide their fire with inhuman precision. Their armour was a clashing mix of grey and green, their shoulder guards marked by eagles of silver.

Sar Zell leaned around the corner long enough to unleash a single shot, blasting a tank-killing stream of laser through the groin and thighs of the squad's grey-helmed sergeant, annihilating him below the waist.

Three left.

'I remember these bastards.' Sar Zell lowered his cannon, brushing away stone debris from its power tubing. Pressurised air, scalding enough to melt skin, vented in a hissing cloud from the weapon's bulky generator.

Talos remembered them, as well. The Silver Eagles and the Aurora Chapter had beaten elements of the VIII Legion back from a series of targeted void raids only a handful of years before.

'We need to do this quickly,' Xarl voxed, holstering his empty pistol and revving his chainblade. 'Who's with me?'

Sar Zell shook his head. 'A moment.'

He braced again, lifting the cannon and leaning around the corner while First Claw gave covering fire. The lascannon bucked in his fists, thumping back with violent recoil as it screamed out a beam of savage light. The torrent cleaved through one of the last Imperial warriors, disintegrating his head, shoulders and chest.

Two left.

'Ready,' he said, lowering the overheating cannon. Stress vanes along the weapon's side were protesting now. The barrel would need replacing soon.

First Claw charged forward as one, chainswords grinding down against ceramite and pistols kicking at lethal range. Xarl and Talos took the kills, the former decapitating his enemy, the latter tearing his foe's helmet off and feeding him the muzzle of a bolt pistol.

The sergeant, bisected by lascannon fire, still lived. He dragged his way across the floor, nothing more than a legless torso.

Cyrion and Xarl circled him, looking down and sneering.

'No time for games,' Talos warned them.

'But...'

Talos's pistol banged once. The shell blasted the sergeant's head and helm to shrapnel, clattering against their boots and knee-guards.

'I said *no time for games.*'

First Claw moved across the chamber, through the wreckage of sparring equipment, to the squad they'd saved. Only one remained. He was crouched by the bodies of his brothers looting them for weapons, ammunition and trinkets.

'Sergeant,' Talos greeted him.

The legionary sucked in air through his teeth, lifting a chainaxe from a warrior's lifeless fingers. He cast his broken bolter aside, and stole another from a second corpse.

'Sergeant,' Talos said again. 'Time is short.'

'Not a sergeant, anymore.' The Night Lord rested a boot on the back of a slain warrior. With the axe, he severed the corpse's head, and dragged the helmet free. 'I lost a duel to Zal Haran.'

He placed the helmet on his head and sealed the seams at his collar. 'Now I have Zal Haran's helm, and he is carrion. A poetic cycle.' The warrior looked at them for a long moment, while the fortress shook to its foundations around them. 'First Claw,' he said. 'Soul Hunter.'

'Uzas,' Talos said to him. 'We have to go.'

'Hnh,' he grunted, uncaring of the saliva stringing down from the edge of his lips. 'Very well.'

XIII

LEGACY OF THE VIII LEGION

AND STILL HE dreamed.

He thought not of the blood analysis taking place, nor of the drills opening his skull to the cold air and the press of curious blades.

He thought only of the time before, when the enemy had come to Tsagualsa ten thousand years ago, bringing punishment for so many sins.

AFTER AN HOUR had passed since the sky first caught fire, Talos had to admit the fatigue was getting to him. The vox was alive with brutal reports of walls falling to enemy artillery; of tanks spilling into the fortress through holes blown in the barricades; of drop pods crashing through the parapets to disgorge hundreds of enemy squads into the castle's outer districts.

He'd lost all contact with the fleet above, beyond the choppiest, most nonsensical eruptions of curses and screams. He was no longer even sure the *Covenant* was in orbit.

First Claw had quickly abandoned their headlong flight through the fortress, moving to take subsidiary corridors, ventilation shafts, slave tunnels and maintenance crawlways in order to avoid the enemy flooding through their haven.

The vox, what little of it still made any sense, spoke of a bleak picture. Casualties were more than high; the Legion forces still on the ground were being devastated. Squads of enemy Space Marines were fighting with an efficiency that had no place on such a vast scale. Legion Claws were shouting of enemy soldiers linking up with their brethren with vicious frequency, forming overwhelming numbers as they stormed through the primary chambers, forcing the defenders into an ever-heightening state of disorder and retreat. Every Night Lord counter-attack was met with waves of reinforcements, as the Imperials fell back in organised withdrawals, sinking to fall-back points already being reinforced by their freshly landed brethren.

The squad halted in a maintenance duct, so confined that they had to crouch, and for some stretches, move on all fours. Cyrion's auspex wavered in and out of readable resolution.

'We're lost,' Xarl mumbled. 'Accursed servitor tunnels. We should've stayed on the concourses.'

'And be dead like the others?' Sar Zell asked from the rear. He was dragging his lascannon behind him, as careful as he could be with the relic weapon. 'I will take sanity over madness, thank you. I want to live to fight another day, in a war we can win.'

'This is like fighting a virus,' Talos breathed over the vox. 'Like fighting a terminal infection. They're everywhere. They know how best to counter us as soon as we do something. They studied us before committing to this attack. This was all planned to the last detail.'

'Who were the first ones we killed?' asked Sar Zell.

'Before the Silver Eagles? The ones in armour the same green as Rodara's sky were the Aurora Chapter. We fought them at Spansreach. I do not know many of the others,' Talos confessed. 'The vox is alive with names I've never heard. The Novamarines. The Black Consuls. The Genesis Chapter. Titles of the Chapters whose protectorates we've been raiding and punishing for decades. This was what our father felt, before he died. Our sins have come home to roost, just as his did.'

'It doesn't matter,' Xarl interrupted. 'They're all Ultramarines. They bled in the Great War. They'll bleed now.'

'He has a point,' said Sar Zell. 'Better the Thirteenth than the gods-damned Blood Angels, with all their screaming kith and kin.'

'Is *now* truly the time for this argument?' Talos asked quietly. The others fell silent.

'This way,' said Cyrion. 'The hangar isn't far.'

First Claw emerged into relative quiet. The cacophony of thudding bolters and roaring engines hadn't faded completely, but at least here the halls were free of shrieking slaves and the bootsteps and gunshots of conflicting squads.

'We missed the battle here,' Talos voxed to his brethren. Bodies already littered the floor – some in VIII Legion ceramite, others in the colours of the Primogenitor Chapters. 'Praetors of Orpheus,' he said. 'I recognise their colours.'

It wasn't hard to make out the scene's details. The invaders had breached the fortress at countless points nearby, rather than risk running directly against the hangar's immense defence batteries. From their intrusion points, they'd focused their aggression inwards, splitting their landing forces between penetrating deeper into the bastion and slaughtering all who fled for the safety of the hangar on this level.

The prophet narrowed his eyes, imagining the same scene playing out on every level, through all of the hangars around the fortress, imagining the breaches in every wall.

'They will have left a rearguard,' he warned. 'They are too precise to forget such a thing.'

'No life signs,' Cyrion replied.

'Even so.'

Talos was the one to defile the stillness, kicking out a ventilator grille and dropping to the deck below. Despite the negative scans, he panned his bolter across the scene.

'Nothing,' he said. 'No one. This place is a tomb.'

Cyrion's voice was coloured by a smile over the vox, 'Cowardice has never been so rewarding.'

'We are not safe yet,' said the prophet.

THE HANGAR STRETCHED out before them. Despite being one of the fortress's more modest launch platforms, the western quadrant's secondary hangar bay still housed over two dozen gunships and storage shuttles. At capacity, the workforce would number over two hundred souls; servitors and slaves alike engaged in the duties of maintenance, refuelling, rearming and repair.

Talos breathed out slowly, and swore under his breath. The ground was littered with the remains of the slain. Half of the gunships and shuttles were wrecked by sustained weapons fire. Several were now little more than smoking hulls, while others had had their landing gear carved out from under them, now resting crashed down onto the deck.

'There's no need for a rearguard when they were this thorough,' said Sar Zell. 'Come on.'

The gunship *Dirge* nestled at the far end of the hangar, still held ten metres above the ground in its docking clamps. Speckles of tracer fire dotted the gunship's armour-plating, but the principal damage wasn't to the flyer itself.

'Oh no,' Sar Zell complained. 'No, no, no.' The others stood in silence, watching for a moment.

'Focus,' Talos ordered them. 'Stay alert.'

First Claw, still accompanied by Uzas, fanned out through the hangar, their bolters up. Talos remained with Sar Zell, and gestured to the gunship. 'We need to get off this world, brother.'

'We're not leaving in that,' Sar Zell replied. The Thunderhawk had escaped most of the harm inflicted upon the rest of the bay, but the sabotage was still complete. The docking clamps gripping the gunship were shattered; the fact they still held the Thunderhawk aloft was a miracle in itself.

'We can destroy the docking clamps,' Talos said. '*Dirge* will survive a ten metre fall.'

Sar Zell nodded, though it was vague and almost devoid of actual agreement. 'The rotating platforms along the deck are inactive. The control chamber is ruined.' He gestured to a raised deck overseeing the hangar's operation below. More bodies lay across the consoles – many of them scorched husks of charred meat – and every machine in sight was gouged by blades or darkened by flamer wash.

'We can take off with the positioning carousels,' Talos breathed slowly.

Sar Zell turned his gesturing arm to take in the wreckage lying across the hangar floor, many of the hulks reaching halfway to the ceiling.

'And what do you want to do with all of this detritus? Blast it aside with rocket volleys at suicidal range? I can't fly a gunship through this. We need the hangar systems operational to clear the way. Without them, it will take days.'

Talos held his tongue as he scanned across the husks and wounded gunships. 'There. That one. That will fly.'

Sar Zell's gaze lingered on the burned husk for several seconds, his keen eyes flickering over the condition of the hull. The Thunderhawk stood close to the hangar bay doors, ruthlessly stitched by heavy-calibre fire that had clearly and cleanly punched through its layered armour-plating. Its midnight paint was left charcoal grey-black, the crow-like hull entirely seared by flamer weapons. Even the reinforced windows had melted, leaving the cockpit unprotected. Smoke breathed from the shattered window, evidence of earlier internal grenade detonations.

'It might,' Sar Zell said at last. 'It will mean taking off through the dust storm, and the smoke rising from the burning fortress. The engines may suffocate in the ash.'

'Better than dying here,' the prophet replied. 'Get to work.'

Weighed down by his lascannon, Sar Zell made his way across the hangar and went to find out if the gunship would fly, one way or the other.

THE HANGAR'S FUNEREAL serenity lasted a handful of minutes before it was breached by Imperial soldiers in white livery.

Sar Zell was already in the pilot's throne, relieved by the sound of the engines cycling up to readiness. The gunship had taken a beating, but it would fly.

Admittedly, he knew they'd be without heat-shielding when they went through the atmosphere (solvable, by sealing themselves outside of the cockpit, behind the bulkhead, leaving the gunship's machine-spirit to take over), and in vacuum once they reached the void (no real threat, if their armour was sealed), but first things first, at least the Thunderhawk would take off.

'More Praetors,' Sar Zell voxed.

The rest of First Claw came running. Five of the enemy left the odds close to even, and both squads took cover among the endless opportunities within the wreckage. Talos crouched with Cyrion, checking his ammunition reserves.

'We are cursed,' he said. 'No one alive should have our luck.'

'No?' Cyrion blind-fired over the debris they were hiding behind. 'If anyone deserves to die for their crimes, brother, it's *us.*'

Talos lifted his bolter to add his fire to Cyrion's. In the same moment, all firepower from the enemy ceased.

Talos and Cyrion exchanged glances. Both of them slowly looked above their barricade, letting their bolters lead the way.

All five of the Praetors had left the safety of their cover. All five stood in the open, their limbs locked tight, shuddering as spasms wracked their bodies. As First Claw watched, two of them dropped their weapons. Their unburdened fingers trembled and curled, all control lost.

A figure stepped into view behind them. Horns curled in an elegant rise from his skull-faced helm, and his T-shaped visor looked upon the scene in expressionless silence. In one armoured fist, the figure held an ancient bolter; in the other, a staff of mercury-threaded black iron, topped by a cluster of human skulls.

The Praetors' shaking helms clicked with flawed vox signals, as they tried to vocalise their torment. Smoke hissed from their melting armour joints, and their epileptic quivers redoubled. As holes appeared in their armour-plating, the screams finally broke free from the molten decay.

One by one, they collapsed to the hangar decking, liquidised organic filth spilling in slow gushes from each armoured suit.

The figure lowered its staff, and walked calmly towards First Claw.

'You weren't thinking of leaving without me, were you?' asked Ruven. His voice lacked even the shadow of emotion.

'No,' Talos lied. 'Not for a moment.'

WIND ROARED IN through the sundered cockpit window. Uzas's cloak of flayed skin flapped in the rushing gale, and the skulls hanging on Xarl's armour-chains rattled in bony chorus. Sar Zell sat in the pilot's throne with the comfortable lean of a soul born to be there.

From the air, the fortress was a stain across the landscape – a castle in the first throes of becoming devastation incarnate. Smoke poured from its broken battlements, with rows of defence batteries aflame and the outer levels ravaged. Scars across the stone showed the impact craters of drop pods, while a haze of whining, roaring gunships and Land Speeders swarmed through the burning skies in an insectile cloud.

First Claw's stolen gunship juddered as it climbed, its intake valves breathing in smoke and its engines exhaling raw fire. It took no more than a few heartbeats to boost up into the pall of smoke now hanging over the fortress. Tracer fire chattered past them from below, knocking on the hull as it scratched home.

'We're fine,' Sar Zell voxed over their shared link.

'It did not sound fine,' Talos ventured, from his own shaking restraint throne.

'We're in the smoke. We're fine now, at least until the ash slays the engines.'

Talos pointed ahead of their ascent. 'What is that?' the prophet asked. A bright blur, fierce as a second sun, blossomed in the black smoke-clouds above them. Veins of fiery light spread in every direction from its white-hot core.

'It's a–' Sar Zell never finished the sentence. He wrenched the control columns, banking the gunship so sharply that every bolt and plate within its construction heaved in torment.

The second sun flashed past them with a carnodon's roar, still streaming atmospheric fire on its insane descent.

Talos released a breath he'd not realised he'd been holding. The drop pod plummeted from sight.

'That was close,' Sar Zell admitted.

'Brother…' Talos gestured the same moment the proximity alarms caught up and started their tuneless pulse. 'Something else.'

'I see it, I see it.'

Whatever it was, it strafed alongside them – a mirror image in ascension – streaming the same fire from its engines. For a moment, the avian shadow broke through the plumes of smoke, just long enough to reveal the markings along its hull, visible even through the char damage.

'Ultramarines Thunderhawk,' Talos warned.

'I said I *see it*.'

'Then shoot it down.'

'With what? Curses and prayers? Did you have time to load the turrets before we left, and simply chose not to tell me?'

Talos's skulled helm snapped around to face the pilot. 'Will you shut your mouth and just get us into the void?'

'The engines are choking with ash. I told you this would happen. We're not going to clear orbit.'

'*Try*.'

In the same moment, more tracer fire zipped across their prow, tinnily hammering into the gunship's nose. Half of the control console went dark.

'Hold on,' Sar Zell muttered, an ocean of bizarre calm.

The Thunderhawk banked in a hard roll, driving them all against their restraint thrones. The shaking – already brutal – magnified tenfold. Something burst outside on the hull with a rattle of metal.

'Primary engines are dead,' said Sar Zell.

'The worst… pilot in… all of… Tenth Company…' Cyrion managed to vox through the crushing gravitational forces.

Talos watched the smoke cloud twisting in all directions, feeling the gunship lurch beneath him again. A second detonation was a muffled *crump* on the edge of hearing.

'Secondary engines are dead,' intoned Sar Zell.

There was no single serene moment where the Thunderhawk hovered at the apex of its flight before gently beginning a plummet. They rolled and shuddered in a powerless freefall, listening to the piteous machine-scream of the ash-choked engines. Each of them was shouting over the vox to be heard, even their audio-receptors unable to filter out the storm of noise.

'*We're dead in the air,*' Sar Zell called, still hauling on the levers to drag some stability back from their death-dive.

'*Jump packs,*' Talos shouted over the chaos.

First Claw locked their boots to the deck and rose from their restraint thrones. Step by halting step, they made their way to the crew bay, magnetic bootsteps thumping. Loose debris crashed against their armour-plating. Xarl's crate of replacement chain-teeth shattered on Ruven's helm, eliciting a muttered curse over the vox.

Talos was the first to reach the racked jump packs. He locked the harness over his shoulder guards, secured the seals to his armour, and readied to thud his armoured fist into the bay door release.

'*We're going to die today,*' Cyrion voxed, sounding more amused than anything else.

Talos hit the ramp release, and stared out into the roaring wind, choking smoke, and the horizon spinning beyond sanity.

'*I have an idea,*' the prophet replied with a shout. '*But we'll need to be careful. Follow me.*'

'*The ash will choke our jump pack engines,*' Sar Zell called out. '*We'll have a minute, maybe two. Make it count.*'

Talos didn't reply. He unlocked his boots from the deck and started running, leaping out into the burning sky.

XIV
COVENANT OF BLOOD

FIRST CLAW HAD gathered.

'When will he awaken?' one of them asked. 'The humans below are still in their shelters, but we should act soon.'

'He will be awake within the hour. He is close to the surface now.'

'His eyes are open.'

'They have been for hours, yet he cannot see us. His mind is unresponsive to most external stimuli. He may be able to hear us. The analysis on that matter is inconclusive.'

'You said he was going to die. He said he was going to live, but suffer pain. Which one of you is right?'

'I believe he was correct. His physiology is in flux, and it may not be terminal. But the pain will destroy him over time, one way or another. And his prophetic gift is no longer reliable. There is no distinguishable brain pattern between his natural nightmares and his visions now. Whatever biological miracle, whatever mix of genetic coding bestowed the gift upon him is beginning to fade from his blood.'

Talos smiled without smiling. He would weep no tears if he lost his foresight. Perhaps freedom would even be worth the price of pain.

'We've sensed it for a while now, Flayer. He was wrong about Faroven on Crythe. Since then, he's been wrong more and more often. He was wrong about Uzas killing me in the shadow of a Titan. He was wrong about all of us dying at the hands of the eldar. Xarl's already dead.'

For a time, the dreamer heard no more voices. The silence seemed important somehow; bloated with tension.

'His gene-seed still manipulates his body more aggressively than it should. It also ingurgitates more of his genetic memory and biological distinctiveness.'

'...ingurgitates?'

'Absorbs. Soaks up, if you will. His progenoid glands are receptors for the unique flaws in his genetic code. In another host, those flaws may not be flaws at all. They might make a legionary of vicious, vicious quality.'

'I do not like that look in your eyes, Variel.'

'You like nothing about me, Cyrion. Your thoughts on the matter are meaningless to me.'

Once more, a pregnant silence reigned.

'The Legion has always said that Tsagualsa is cursed. I feel it in my blood. We will die here.'

'Now you sound like Mercutian. No jokes, Nostraman? No toothed smile to hide your own sins and instability from your brothers?'

'Watch your tongue.'

'You do not intimidate me, Cyrion. Perhaps this world is indeed cursed, but a curse can bring clarity. Before he fell into this slumber, Talos spoke of knowing what to do with the world beneath us. We will linger only long enough to achieve our goals. '

'I hope that you are right. He is no longer mumbling or screaming in his sleep.'

'That was prophecy. This is a memory, not a vision. What was, not what will be. He dreams of the past, and the part he played within it.'

THE ULTRAMARINES THUNDERHAWK shuddered on its hover jets, drifting over the fortress's battlements in lethal serenity. Its rocket pods were empty, its squads deployed, and it hovered on-station, sweeping its bow across the fortress's defence platforms, raking them with merciless fire from its heavy bolters. Every thirty seconds, the gunship's spinal turbolaser discharged a beam of force, annihilating another of the weapons platforms in a bolt of blue light.

Brother Tyrus of the Demes Collegiate saw through flickering pictscreens as the gunship moved in another hulking drift. With his gauntlets on the control levers, he forced the heavy bolters to chew through one of the last remaining servitor weapons teams still alive on the castle's parapets.

'Kill confirmed,' he voxed to the pilot. 'Sabre defence platform, two servitor crew.'

Brother Gedean of the Arteus Collegiate didn't turn from the view through the gunship's blastshield. 'Ammunition reserves?' he voxed back.

'Remain on-station for another six strafing runs,' said Tyrus. 'Advise rearmament thereafter.'

'Understood,' the pilot replied.

There was a distinctive, undeniable bang of metal on metal from above. The pilot, co-pilot, gunner and navigator – each of them Ultramarines drawn from separate training collegiates throughout the worlds of distant Ultramar – all looked up in the same moment.

A second thud sounded from above. Then another, and another.

Brother Constantinus, enthroned in the navigator's seat, drew his bolt pistol. 'Something is–' he began, though he was interrupted by two more thuds on the ceiling above. The thuds made their way down the side of the hull in a feral, hurried drumbeat.

Constantinus and Remar, the co-pilot, disengaged their throne-locks at once, moving from the flight deck and descending via crew ladder into the loading bay.

As soon as they entered, they were greeted by the sight of the external bulkhead being wrenched from its hinges with a tearing whine of abused metal. The crash and boom of the siege poured in with the air outside, and the enemy came in with it.

'Emergency boarding protocol,' Brother Remar voxed to Gedean in the cockpit above. The Thunderhawk immediately started to climb, boosting high on angry engines. Remar and Constantinus kept their backs to the crew ladder, raising their weapons.

The first thing to enter was a broken chainaxe, the adamantine teeth snarled into ruin by chewing through the bulkhead hinges. It crashed onto the deck, tossed inside with casual abandon. The second thing to enter was a warrior of the VIII Legion, his skull-faced helm leering through the smoke as he slid into the bay with almost serpentine desperation. The huge jump pack turbines on his back made his entrance through the bulkhead altogether less graceful.

Constantinus and Remar opened up with their pistols, taking the warrior down even as he twisted to present his reinforced shoulder guard to protect his head. Before the first boarder had even hit the floor, others were spilling in through the hole. They came armed, their own bolters lashing back with a greater storm of fire.

Both Ultramarines went down – Remar dead, his armour and flesh pulped against the crew ladder behind; Constantinus haemorrhaging from terminal wounds to his chest, throat and stomach.

'Move, move,' Xarl voxed. He led Uzas and Ruven up the crew ladder. Cyrion hesitated, turning back to where Talos remained crouched by their last brother. Blood and broken armour lay in a smear across the floor where Sar Zell had fallen.

'He's dead,' the prophet said. He didn't deploy his reductor to begin harvesting Sar Zell's gene-seed, nor did he make any move to follow the others up the ladder to the cockpit. He remained where he was, Sar Zell's broken helmet in his hands. Blood streaked what was left of the warrior's face.

Cyrion could hear the shouts and blade-grinds from above. He almost resented Talos for making him miss it.

'Leave him,' he said. 'Xarl can fly the gunship.'

'I know.' Talos hauled the body to the side of the bay, leashing it with binding straps. Cyrion helped, albeit belatedly. The gunship juddered as it climbed higher.

'He was a fool to go in first,' Cyrion continued. 'We should have sent Uzas in after he carved the door open. Then–'

Three bolt shells hammered into Cyrion's side, blasting armour wreckage against the bay walls with ringing resonance. The warrior staggered back with a pained cry across the vox, and crashed against the bulkhead's edges before falling from the gunship.

The dying Brother Constantinus still held the empty bolt pistol in a trembling hand. He clicked the trigger three more times, aiming at the remaining Night Lord. In reply, Talos rammed his chainsword through the Ultramarine's spine, letting the teeth chew through everything they could find to bite. For what it was worth, Constantinus died in bitter, angry silence, never once howling in pain.

'Cyrion,' he voxed as he tore his sword free. 'Cyrion?'

'I can't... He hit my jump pack,' was the hissed reply.

Talos ran to the sundered bulkhead, gripped the edges, and hurled himself out into the sky again.

Xarl's voice crackled in his helmet mic. 'Did you just–'

'Yes.' Talos's retinal display flickered as he fell, the runes cycling as they recorded his dropping altitude. Responding to his fevered attention, his target lock pinpointed the tiny figure of Cyrion, detailing a host of life sign bio-data in Nostraman runic script. Talos ignored it, and fired the turbines on his back. He just wasn't falling then, but powering towards the ground. The fortress, faint behind a gauzy veil of smoke, lurched closer as the thrusters kicked harder. He ignored the Land Speeders and gunships raging over the battlements.

Nearer now, he could see Cyrion's jump pack flaring with sparks and false thrust. A Thunderhawk in the green of the Aurora Chapter heaved past, unconcerned with such small targets as it strafed the battlements.

And still, Cyrion tumbled through the smoke. The ground surged up to meet them. Too fast, far too fast.

'I thank you...' Cyrion grunted, '...for making the attempt.'

'Brace,' Talos warned, and his straining engines gave another coughing burst of thrust, propelling him downward. Three seconds later, they collided in mid-air, ceramite screeching as they crashed together.

Their contact was utterly devoid of grace. Talos smashed into his brother, his gauntleted fingers scrabbling for purchase, at last clutching Cyrion by the shoulder guard. The other Night Lord reached up, and their hands slammed closed, gripping one another's wrists.

Talos focused on shifting his thrust, forcing the jump pack's antigravitic suspensors to prime along with the adjusted turbines. It made little difference. The two of them tumbled through the sky together, slowed by Talos's jump engines. The thruster pack – despite the archaic design better designed for sustained flight – was already straining from its journeys through the ash storm and clouds of smoke. Talos had the briefest moment of selfish panic: he could let go and save himself dying in a smear across the Tsagualsan dust plains. None of the others would know.

'Drop me,' Cyrion voxed, his lightning-streaked helm facing up to his brother.

'Shut up,' Talos voxed back.

'This will kill us both.'

'Shut up, Cy.'

'Talos...'

They plunged into another column of smoke, the runic numbers on the prophet's retinal altitude chiming red. In the same moment, Cyrion released his grip. Talos clutched harder, cursing in breathless anger.

'Drop me,' Cyrion said again.

'Lose... the... jump pack...'

Cyrion restored his grip with a curse that mirrored his brother's a moment before. With his free hand, he disengaged the seals that bound the boosters to his backpack. As the turbines fell free, the lessened weight pulled them from their freefall.

Slowly, much too slowly, they began to rise.

'We're going to be shot to pieces,' Cyrion voxed, 'even if your engines don't fail in the ash.'

The prophet struggled to keep them steady as they ascended, his gaze ticking back and forth between the burning sky above and the thrust gauge at the edge of his vision. Gunships and Land Speeders slashed past, some zipping by hundreds of metres away, others roaring by much closer. Wake turbulence threw the brothers around, buffeting them in the air as an armoured Land Speeder sliced past, almost close enough to touch.

'They're coming back,' Cyrion voxed.

Talos spared a glance over his shoulder. Cyrion was right; the Speeder banked into a skyborne swerve, racing to come about on an attack run.

'No one deserves our luck,' Talos said, for the second time in less than an hour. He fired at the swooping craft despite its distance, the bolter shells going wide in the wind. It bore down on them, turbines howling, the underslung multi-barrelled assault cannon already spinning, winding up to fire.

Tracer fire slashed from above in a flaming hail. The Speeder jinked, evading the first streams of the sudden barrage, but the falling firepower shattered through the craft's hull with explosive force.

Trailing fire, the Speeder's wreckage hurtled past the defenceless Night Lords, screaming on its way to the ash plains below.

An Ultramarines Thunderhawk darkened the sky before them, its bulky, active engines causing the air itself to throb. Slowly, the forward gangramp started to lower, a vulture's beak opening to shriek.

'Are you finished?' voxed Xarl. 'Can we get the hell out of here now?'

* * *

ONCE THEY CLEARED the ash cloud, the true scale of the invasion force became agonisingly apparent. Talos leaned forward in the co-pilot's throne, watching the sky twist from clouds of fire to become a heaven of stars and steel. Next to him, Xarl gave a soft curse.

The void above Tsagualsa was wretched with enemy vessels, cruisers and barges of standardised classes, deadlocked in the sky with the Legion's remaining fleet. The Imperial Space Marine fleet dwarfed the Night Lords' in numbers and scope, but the Legion's primary warships eclipsed the loyalists' vessels in size by vast degrees. Smaller cruisers ringed the Legion battleships, trading fire against rippling, iridescent void shields.

'The Codex Astartes in action,' Ruven smirked. 'Surrendering their largest and finest warships to the newborn Imperial Navy. I pray that today the Thirteenth learn a lesson in whoring away their most potent firepower to lesser men.'

Talos didn't take his eyes from the fleet engagement filling the heavens. 'The Codex Astartes was responsible for our fortress falling in the most brutally efficient assault I have seen since the Siege of Terra,' he said quietly. 'I would watch your tongue until you're certain we will survive this, brother. The Navy will be blockading the system's outer reaches, one way or another.'

'As you say,' Ruven conceded with an unpleasant smile in his voice. 'Find the *Covenant*, Xarl.'

Xarl was already watching the gunship's primitive hololithic auspex display. Hundreds of runes conflicted across its surface.

'I think it's gone. The Exalted must have run.'

'A fact that will surprise none of us,' Cyrion remarked from the navigator's seat. The bodies of the dead Ultramarines pilot and gunner lay at his feet, where Xarl, Uzas and Ruven had dumped them. Uzas watched the others, saying nothing, his finger occasionally squeezing the trigger of his chainaxe, causing the teeth to chew air.

'That is Sar Zell's axe,' Talos said.

'Sar Zell is dead,' Uzas replied. 'Now it is my axe.'

Talos turned back to the scene beyond the cockpit windshield. Xarl abandoned any false hope of keeping his distance from the battle, taking the gunship through the drifting hulks and doing his best to veer around any storms of battery fire.

'This is First Claw, Tenth Company, to any Legion ships taking survivors.'

A dozen immediately voices crackled back, all asking after Talos. Some were concerned for his safety; the others earnestly appealing that he lie dead in the fortress below.

'Oh,' Ruven chuckled without any amusement, 'to be one of the Night Haunter's Chosen.'

'You could have hunted down our father's killer,' Talos rounded on him. 'I am weary of your whining, sorcerer. Do not hate me because I was the one to avenge the primarch's murder.'

'Vengeance against the primarch's own wishes,' Ruven snorted.

'But it was still *vengeance*. That was enough for me. Why do you still hiss and spit over it?'

'So you gain renown and infamy in equal measure, purely for disobeying our father's last wish. How wonderful for you. Never before has a lack of discipline granted such glory.'

'You...' Talos trailed off, tired of the old argument. 'You speak like a child, deprived of its mother's milk. No more whining, Ruven.'

The sorcerer didn't reply. His creeping amusement was as palpable in the small cockpit as condensation on the walls.

Talos didn't answer the vox. He knew that outside Tenth Company, he was hardly regarded with any real universal admiration – he guessed the same number of his brothers wanted him dead as those that admired him – but avenging the primarch's murder had earned him savage notoriety. He suspected their disregard was more from their own shame at not hunting down the Night Haunter's killer. It was certainly the case with Ruven.

Xarl was the one to reply. 'Yes, yes, the Legion's good luck charm is still breathing. I need a list of ships in a position to take survivors.'

Almost thirty transponder codes bled across the relay monitor in the course of the next sixty seconds.

'That's the *Covenant*'s code,' Talos tapped the monitor. 'They're still here...'

They stared out into the orbital view, seeing the immense bulks of battleships gliding past each other. Ahead, above, and in every direction besides, the two fleets were meeting in the eerily silent, sedate fury of a void war.

'...somewhere,' Talos finished, a little lamely.

Xarl switched from atmospheric thrust to orbital burn, kicking the gunship forward. Something deep in the Thunderhawk's bowels gave an unpleasant rumble.

'This is why Sar Zell flies,' Cyrion pointed out.

'I am not piloting for the Claw in the future,' Xarl replied. 'You think you can leave me behind on raids while you have all the fun? We'll train a slave to do this. Quintus, maybe.'

'Perhaps,' Talos allowed.

Small enough to escape notice, the gunship powered on. The stellar ballet of orbital battle played out before them. There, the massive, dark hull of the *Hunter's Premonition* rolled in agonisingly slow motion, its void shields splashing with bruised colour; and there, two Primogenitor strike cruisers shuddering away from the crippled *Loyalty's Lament*, their incidental fire blasting wreckage out of their paths as they escaped the larger ship before it could detonate.

Wings of VIII Legion fighters, piloted by servitors and Naval slaves, swarmed the Primogenitor cruisers, miniscule weapons sparking against the warships' shields. Carriers and battleships alike, resplendent in midnight clad, bore the brunt of enemy fire in return. Ships that had seen service for centuries ceased to exist with the passing of each moment, collapsing in on themselves before their wreckage flew apart on concentric rings of force, born of destabilised power cores. Others fell silent and cold, ruined to the point of drifting hulks, the fires that would lick at their hulls unable to survive in the airless void.

Xarl banked close to the hull of the *Premonition*, racing across its superstructure, weaving through the spinal battlements. A cacophony of light burst on all sides as the warship fired its backbone armaments at the lesser ships above. Xarl cursed at the brightness, flying with clenched teeth.

'I can't do this,' he said.

'We die if you don't,' replied Talos.

Xarl's agreement was a noncommittal grunt.

'Break left,' Cyrion called, staring at the hololithic display. 'You're heading towards the–'

'I see it, I see it.'

'Left, Xarl,' urged Talos. 'Left now...'

'Do you fools want to fly this thing? Shut your mouths.'

Even Uzas was on his feet now, staring out of the windshield. 'I think we should–'

'I think you should *shut up.*'

The gunship boosted faster, breaking away from the *Premonition*'s spinal ramparts, cutting towards two huge cruisers drifting closer together. To port, the Night Lords' warship *Third Eclipse*; to starboard, the Aurora Chapter battle-barge *In Pale Reverence*. Both vessels exchanged withering hails of fire as they readied to pass by.

The Thunderhawk bolted between them, its engines screaming and shaking the cockpit.

'There...' Xarl breathed, facing ahead again.

And there it was. The great ship burned, rolling in space, ringed by lesser cruisers that lashed their fire against its unprotected hull. Its spinal structures and broadside batteries spat back, forcing the invaders to drift away and regroup for another attack run. Along its midnight hull, the Nostraman script read, in immense letters of beaten bronze, *Covenant of Blood*.

'This is Talos to the *Covenant*.'

'You still live,' drawled the Exalted. 'This is a day of so many surprises.'

'We are in a Thirteenth Legion Thunderhawk, approaching the prow. Do not shoot us down.'

The warrior on the other end of the vox gargled something like a laugh. 'I will see what I can do.'

'Vandred is getting worse,' Uzas mused aloud in a dead voice. 'He doesn't blink now. I noticed that.' And then, apropos of nothing and in the same lifeless tone: 'Talos. When you jumped to save Cyrion, Ruven told us not to come back for you.'

'I'm sure he did.' The prophet almost smiled.

TALOS OPENED HIS eyes. The apothecarion's lights glared down, forcing him to turn his head and shield his sight.

'Am I going to die, then?' he asked.

Variel shook his head. 'Not today.'

'How long was I gone?'

'Exactly two hours and nine minutes. Not long at all.'

The prophet rose, wincing at pains in his joints. 'Then I have a world to make an example of. Are we finished here?'

'For now, brother.'

'Come. We are going back to Tsagualsa, you and I. I have something to show you.'

A SONG IN THE DARK

XV
BEACON IN THE NIGHT

THE PEOPLE REMAINED as they were, lingering in their underground storm shelters. The few that stayed above ground crouched in hiding or set up street-end barricades, ready to defend their territory with iron bars, tools, pylon spears and limited numbers of small arms. They were the first to die when the Night Lords returned. Their bodies were the first cast into the skinning pits.

Servitor excavation teams pulled up entire sections of streets, digging ever-expanding holes to pile the skinless dead. Floating servo-skulls and the Night Lords' own helm-feeds recorded the carnage, archiving it for later use.

The archregent never left his desk. Dawn, as weak as it was on this world, was only an hour away. With the attackers returned, he intended to get some answers, one way or another. If today would see him die, he wouldn't go in ignorance.

Abettor Muvo hurried into the chamber, his shaking hands clutching printed reports as his robe swished across the sooty floor. No servants remained above ground to sweep the debris away.

'The militia is practically gone,' he said. 'The vox is... There's no reason to listen to it any more. It's just screaming, sire.'

The archregent nodded. 'Stay with me, Muvo. All will be well.'

'How can you say that?'

'A bad habit,' the older man confessed. 'All will not be well, but we can face it with dignity nevertheless. I believe I hear gunfire on the decks below.'

Muvo crossed to the desk. 'I... I hear it, too. Where are your guards?'

The archregent took his seat, steepling his fingers. 'I sent them to the closest shelter hours ago, though they did seem likely to remain out of some admirably foolish desire to do their duty. Perhaps that is them deeper in the ship, selling their lives to delay this meeting by a handful of seconds. I hope it's not them, though. That would be quite a waste.'

The abettor gave him a sideways glance. 'If you say so, lord.'

'Stand straight, Muvo. We are about to have guests.'

FIRST CLAW WALKED into the chamber, their armour still decorated in the blood of the tower's defenders. Talos led them in, immediately dropping a red helm onto the archregent's desk. It sent cracks through the wood.

'This desk is an heirloom,' the old man stated with admirable calm. The archregent's hands didn't even tremble as he leaned back in his chair. Talos liked him immediately – not that it would affect the Legion's actions one iota. 'I take it,' the statesman continued, 'that this is the helmet of an Imperial Space Marine belonging to the Genesis Chapter?'

'You presume correctly,' came the warrior's voice, in a snarl of brutal vox. 'Your defenders came to interfere with our plans for this world. It was the last mistake they ever made.'

The warrior turned away, walking around the observation dome, staring out over the city stretching in every direction. He finally looked back at the archregent, the skull helm staring without remorse, but curiously, without the hot-blooded shadow of malice – it was a cold, hollow visage, betraying nothing of the thoughts of the creature wearing it.

The archregent sat straighter and cleared his throat. 'I am Jirus Urumal, Archregent of Darcharna.'

Talos tilted his head. 'Darcharna,' he said without inflection.

'The world had no Imperial designation. *Darcharna* was the name of the first ship from our fleet to land h–'

'This world is called Tsagualsa. You, old man, are archregent of a lie. Tsagualsa had a king once. His throne stands empty at the heart of a forgotten fortress, and he needs no regent.'

The prophet looked back across the city, listening to the music within both mortals' heartbeats. Both were accelerating now, the wet drum tempo increasing in speed, and the salty tang of fear-sweat was beginning to reach his senses. Humanity always smelled its sourest when afraid.

'I will tell you why the Imperium has never come for you,' Talos said at length. 'It is the same reason this world bore no name in Imperial record. Tsagualsa once sheltered a Legion of arch-heretics, in the years after a war now lost to legend. The Imperium wishes only to forget about this world, and all those who walked upon it.

He turned back to the archregent. 'That includes you, Jirus. You are tainted by association.'

The archregent looked at each of them in turn – the skull trophies and ornate weapons; their red eye lenses and thrumming battle armour powered by the bulky backpack generators.

'And what is your name?' he asked, amazed that his voice didn't strangle in the tightness of his throat.

'Talos,' the towering warrior's vox-voice growled. 'My name is Talos of the Eighth Legion, master of the warship *Echo of Damnation.*'

'And what do you hope to accomplish here, Talos?'

'I will bring the Imperium to this world. I will drag them back to the world they so ardently wish to forget.'

'We have been awaiting Imperial rescue for four centuries. They don't hear us.'

The Night Lord shook his head, making the servos in his damaged armour buzz. 'Of course they hear you. They merely choose not to answer.'

'We are too far from the Astronomican for them to risk travel.'

'Enough excuses. I have told you why they abandoned you here.' Talos breathed slowly, weighing his next words with care. 'They will answer this time. I will make sure of that. Do you have an Astropathic Consortium in this husk of a society?'

'A… guild? Yes, of course.'

'And other psychically gifted souls?'

'Only those within the guild.'

'You cannot lie to me. When you lie, your body betrays you in a thousand subtle signals. Each of those signs is a clarion call to me. What are you seeking to hide?'

'There is mutation, at times, among the psychic. The guild deals with them.'

'Very well. Bring this guild to me. Now.'

The archregent made no attempt to move. 'Will you let us live?' the old man asked.

'That depends. How many draw breath upon this world?'

'Our last census collated ten million, across seven settlements. Life is unkind to us here.'

'Life is unkind everywhere. The galaxy has no love for any of us. I will let some of you live, to eke out an existence in the ruins while you wait for the Imperium. If none survived, there would be no one to speak of what they saw. Perhaps one in every thousand will live to greet the Imperium's arrival. It is not necessary, but it will be amusingly dramatic.'

'How… How can you speak of such dest–'

Talos cleared his throat. Through his helm's vocaliser, it sounded like a tank changing gears.

'I am bored of this conversation, archregent. Comply with my wishes, and you may still be one of those who survives the night.'

The old man rose to his feet. 'No.'

'It is a fine thing, to see a man with a backbone. I admire that. I respect it. But dubious courage has no place here, now, in this moment. I shall show you why.'

Cyrion stepped forward, his hand closing with a fistful of the abettor's lank hair. The man cried out as his boots left the floor.

'Please…' the man stammered. Cyrion drew his gladius, drawing it in a workmanlike carve along the abettor's belly. Blood gushed in a torrent, while looping innards threatened to spill out, held inside the body by nothing more than the man's own fingers. His pleading immediately warped into worthless screaming.

'This,' the prophet said to the archregent, 'is happening right now, across the stain of wreckage you call a city. This is what we are doing to your people.'

Cyrion, still holding the abettor aloft by his greasy hair, shook the man in his grip. More screaming, now punctuated by the wet slops of reeking intestinal meat slapping onto the decking.

'Do you see?' Talos's eyes never left the archregent. 'You fled to the shelters, trapping yourselves with nowhere to run. Now we will find all of you, and my brothers and I will do as we always do with those who flee like verminous prey.'

He reached for the man in Cyrion's grip, taking the convulsing, still-living figure in an iron hold around the throat. Without ceremony, he dumped the bleeding body on the archregent's desk.

'Comply with me, and one in a thousand of your people will avoid this fate. You will be one of them. Defy me, and not only will I no longer spare any of the others, you yourself will die now. My brothers and I will skin you, while you still live. We are masters of prolonging the experience, so the prey only dies in the hours after the surgery is performed. Once, a woman lived for six nights, wailing throughout the hours of crippling agony, only dying at last from infection in her filthy cell.'

'Your finest work,' Cyrion mused aloud.

The old man swallowed, trembling now. 'Your threats mean nothing to me.'

The Night Lord pressed his gauntleted fingers to the archregent's face, cold ceramite fingertips following the contours of the weathered skin and fragile bone beneath.

'No? The human body does wondrous things when its mind feels fear. It becomes an avatar of the pressure within a single paradox: to fight, or to flee. Your breath sours from the chemicals at work in your system. The clenching of internal musculature affects digestion, reflexes, and the ability to concentrate on anything but the threat. Meanwhile, the heart's wet rhythm becomes a war drum, beating blood for your muscles to use in order to escape harm. Your sweat smells different, muskier, like an animal trembling in terror, hopelessly marking its territory one last time. The edges of your eyes quiver, answering hidden signals from the brain, caught between wanting to stare to see the source of your fear, or to seal shut, hiding your vision from having to see what threatens you.'

Talos clutched the back of the archregent's head, his skulled faceplate centimetres from the old man's face.

'I can sense all of that on you. I see it in every twitch of your soft, soft skin. I smell it peeling off your body in a thick stink. Do not lie to me, human. My threats mean *everything* to you.'

'What...' The archregent had to swallow again. 'What do you want?'

'I have already told you what I want. Bring me your astropaths.'

As THEY WAITED, the archregent watched his city die.

The enemy lord, the one naming himself Talos, stood by the edge of the observation dome, in constant communication with his brethren across Sanctuary. His voice was a low, feral murmur, updating squads on each others' positions and mapping their progress. Every few minutes he would fall silent for a time, and simply watch the fires spread.

One of the other warriors, the one with the bulky heavy bolter slung on his back, activated a handheld hololithic emitter. He altered the scene it displayed each time Talos ordered him to focus upon the pict-feeds from a different squad.

Abettor Muvo had fallen silent. The archregent had closed his friend's eyes, choking on the smell rising from the split corpse.

'You get used to it,' one of the warriors had said with a black laugh.

The archregent watched the hololithic feed, seeing Sanctuary's death playing out clearly enough despite the visual distortion. The armoured warriors projected before him, silent in their hololithic incarnation, tore through shelter bulkheads and ripped through the huddled masses within. He watched them drag men, women and children by the hair out into the street, to be skinned and carried away by servitors, or crucified on the side of buildings, to mark that the closest shelter had been raided and cleaned out of all life. He saw the bodies hauled into the skinning pits; great mounds of flayed corpses stacked higher and higher – monuments of raw flesh in honour of nothing more than suffering and pain.

'Why?' he whispered, without realising he'd spoken aloud.

Talos didn't turn from watching the city burn. 'Some of us do it because we enjoy it. Some of us do it simply because we can. Some of us do it because this is our empire, and you do not deserve to live within it, enslaved to a lie.'

The slaughter didn't cease when the sun rose. Some primitive, foolish part of the archregent's hindbrain had hoped against hope that these creatures would vanish with the coming of the light.

'Do you have communication with the other cities?' Talos asked.

The archregent gave a weak nod. 'But it is infrequent at best. The astropaths sometimes manage to communicate with other guild members in the other cities. But even that is rare enough.'

'It is rare because they have no focus. I will deal with that. We have Mechanicum adepts among our crew – they will make planetfall and attend to your flawed equipment. We will then broadcast these images to the other cities, as a sign of what comes for them.'

The archregent's mouth was dry. 'You will give them time to organise resistance?' There was no hiding the hope in his voice.

'Nothing on this world is capable of resisting us,' answered Talos. 'They are free to prepare however they wish.'

'What is the Mechanicum?'

'You would know it by their slave-name: the *Adeptus Mechanicus*.' Talos fairly spat the cult's Imperial title. 'Cy?'

Cyrion walked over, his eyes never leaving the burning city. He hungered to be down there – they all did – and it showed in the movement of every muscle.

'You are enjoying this,' he said, seeing no need to make it a question.

Talos's nod was subtle enough to almost go unseen. 'It reminds me of the days before the Great Betrayal.'

And that was true enough. In that age, in the farthest, shadowed reaches of the Emperor's Light, the VIII Legion had slaughtered whole cities to 'inspire' the other settlements across a given world into obedience of Imperial Law. 'Peace through justice,' Talos said. 'And justice through fear of punishment.'

'Aye. It reminds me of the same. But most of our brothers down there are doing it for the thrill of the hunt, and the pleasure of slaughtering terrified mortals. Remember that, before you graft a false layer of high ideals over what we do here.'

'I am no longer so deluded,' Talos admitted. 'I know what we are. But they do not need to share my ideals for my plan to work.'

'*Will* this work?' Cyrion asked. 'We are on the wrong side of the Imperium's border. They may never know what we do here.'

'They will know,' said Talos. 'Trust me, they will hear this, and come running.'

'Then my advice is this: we should not be here when they arrive. We are down to four Claws, brother. After this, we have to return to the Eye, and link up with whatever Legion forces we can ally with there.'

Talos nodded again, but said nothing.

'Are you even listening to me?' Cyrion asked.

'Just get me the astropaths.'

THEY NUMBERED ONE hundred and thirty-eight in total. The astropaths marched in as a disorderly pack, dressed in the same ragged clothing so typical of Sanctuary's citizens and the detritus caste of humanity found on frontier worlds across the Imperium's edges.

Yuris of the newly-organised Second Claw led them in. Blood marked his armour in dry splotches.

'There was a struggle,' he admitted. 'We tore our way into their guild shelter, and seven of them died. The rest of them came without a fight.'

'A ragged conclave,' Talos noted, walking around the prisoners. An equal mix of men and women; most of them were filthy. Several were children. Most interesting of all, none of them were blind.

'They still have their eyes,' Yuris said, noting Talos's stare. 'Will they still be of use to us if they've not been soul-bound to the False Emperor's Throne?'

'I believe so. They are not a true choir, and enslavement to the Golden Throne has not refined their power. In truth, they are barely worthy of the name *astropaths*. These are closer to telepaths, dabblers, witches and wyrds. But I can still make their powers work as we require.'

'We will return to the city,' Yuris said.

'As you will. My thanks, brother.'

'Good fortune, Talos. *Ave dominus nox.*'

Second Claw left the chamber in a loose pack, no more organised than the prisoners they'd brought in.

Talos faced the wretches, his targeting reticule flicking from face to face.

'Who leads you?' he asked. One woman stepped forward, her ragged robe seeming no different to any of the others.

'I do.'

'My name is Talos of the Eighth Legion.'

Confusion momentarily shone through the dullness of her eyes. 'What is the Eighth Legion?'

Talos's black eyes burned. He inclined his head, as if she had somehow proved a point.

'I am in no frame of mind to provide a lesson in history and myth,' he said, 'so let us simply say that I am one of the original architects of the Imperium. I hold to its founding ideal: that the species must know peace through obedience. I aim to bring the Imperium back into these skies. A lesson was once learned on this world. I find an amusing poetry in using this world to teach a lesson in return.'

'What lesson?' she asked. Unlike many of the others, she showed little overt fear. On the cusp of middle-age, she was likely at the height of her powers, not yet bled dry by them. Perhaps that was why she led them all. Talos didn't care, either way.

'Seal the doors,' he voxed to First Claw. Uzas, Cyrion, Mercutian and Variel moved to guard the chamber's two exits, their weapons clutched in loose fists.

'Do you know of the warp?' he asked the leader.

'We have stories, and the city's archives.'

'Allow me to guess. To you, the warp is the afterlife, a sunless underworld where those disloyal to the Emperor are punished for their faithless ways.'

'This is what we believe. All the archives state–'

'I do not care how you have misinterpreted your records. You are the strongest of your guild, are you not?'

'I am.'

'Good.'

Her head burst in a rupture of blood and bone. Talos lowered his bolter.

'Close your eyes,' he said. 'All of you.'

They didn't obey. The children drew close to their parents, and panicked murmurs broke out, as did intermittent weeping. The guild mistress's body hit the decking with a bony clang.

'Close your eyes,' Talos repeated. 'Commune with your power in whatever way works best. Reach out now, and feel for the soul of your dead leader. All who can hear her spirit still shrieking in the air around us, step forward.'

Three of them stepped forward, their eyes uncertain, their limbs quivering.

'Only three?' Talos asked. 'How very disappointing. I would hate to have to start shooting again.'

Another dozen stepped forward. Another handful followed.

'That is better. Tell me when she falls silent.'

He waited in silence, watching the faces of those who claimed to hear their dead mistress. One woman in particular winced and cringed as if suffering tics. When all others claimed to hear her no longer, she only relaxed a full minute afterwards.

'Now she is gone,' she said, scratching her thin, lank hair. 'Thank the Throne.'

Talos drew his gladius, tossing it and catching it three times. As it smacked into his palm on the last catch, he turned and hurled it across the chamber. One of the men who'd stepped forward sank to the deck, gasping soundlessly, his eyes wide and his mouth working like a fish deprived of air. The sword impaling through his chest made a gentle, tinny sound as it tapped on the deck with each spasm.

At last, he lay still.

'He was lying,' Talos told the rest. 'I saw it in his eyes. He could not hear her, and I do not like being lied to.'

The air around the crowded guilders was charged now, alive with overlapping tiers of ripe tension.

'The warp is nothing so mundane. Beneath what we see of the universe is a layer we do not. Through this unseen Sea of Souls, an infinity of daemons swim. They are, even now, digesting the spirits of your murdered kin. The warp is not sentient, neither is it malicious. It simply *is*, and it responds to human emotion. Most of all, it responds to suffering, to fear, to hatred, for in such moments humanity is at its strongest and most honest. Suffering colours the warp, and the suffering of psychic souls is like a beacon. Your Emperor uses that suffering as fuel for his Golden Throne, to project the Astronomican.'

Talos could see few of them followed his words. Ignorance stunted their intellects, and fear blinded them to the nuance of his explanation. This, too, he found grimly amusing, as his red eye lenses drifted from face to face.

'I will use your suffering to breed a beacon of my own. The slaughter and torture of this city's people is merely the beginning. You can already feel the pain and death pressing against your minds. I know you can. Do not resist it. Let it saturate you. Listen to the screaming of souls as they dissolve from this realm into the next. Let their torment ripen within you. Carry it with you as an honour, for together you will become an instrument no different from your beloved, distant Emperor. You, like he, will become beacons in the endless night, bred from agony.

'To do that, I will break each one of you. Slowly, so very slowly, so that madness breeds within the pain. I will take you up into our warship, and over the course of the coming weeks, I will have you crippled, flayed, excoriated and excruciated. I will consign your ruined, pained forms – kept alive by our expert grace – to prison-laboratories where your only company will be the skinned carcasses of your children, your parents, and the corpses of others from your dead world.

'With the pain I give you, with your prolonged agonies, I will choke the warp at the Imperium's edge. Fleets will come to investigate, fearing nearby worlds may succumb to daemonic intrusion. Mankind's empire will ignore Tsagualsa no longer, and will learn an old lesson. It is not enough to force criminals and sinners into exile. You must make an example of them, and crush them utterly. Leniency, mercy, trust – these are weaknesses that the Imperium must pay for. The Imperium should have destroyed us here when it had the chance. Let them learn that once more.

'Your lives are over, but in death you will achieve something almost divine. You have prayed for so long to leave this world. Be pleased, for I am granting you that wish.'

As he fell silent, he watched the dawn of horrified disbelief on their faces. They could scarcely imagine what he was saying, but no matter. They'd understand soon enough.

'Don't do this,' came a voice from behind.

Talos turned to face the archregent. 'No? Why should I not?'

'It... I...' the old man trailed off.

'Strange.' Talos shook his head. 'Your kind never has an answer to that question.'

XVI
SCREAMING

Septimus made his way through the dark corridors without any obvious effort. His pistols were holstered at his thighs, and his repaired facial bionics no longer clicked each time he blinked, smiled, or spoke. He could see clearly enough with his augmetic eye piercing the gloom, and a photo-contact lens over the iris of the other – yet another perk of being one of the more valuable slaves on board.

His hands ached though, right to the knuckles. Nine hours of armour maintenance would do that. In the three weeks since Talos had returned from Tsagualsa, he'd managed to repair most of the damage to First Claw's armour. A treasure trove of salvage and spare parts from the Genesis Space Marines and slain Night Lords left the artificer spoiled for choice. Trading with artificers who served the other Claws had never been easier, nor as fruitful.

An hour ago, Iruk, one of Second Claw's slaves, had spat something brown between his blackening teeth while they'd traded for torso cabling.

'The warband's dying, Septimus. You feel that? That's the wind of change, boy.'

Septimus had tried to avoid the conversation, but Iruk wouldn't be swayed. Second Claw's arming chamber was on the same deck as First Claw's, and just as chaotic with all the junked armour and weapon parts lying everywhere.

'They're still following Talos,' Septimus said at last, looking for a way out of the discussion.

Iruk had spat again. 'Your master makes them crazy. You should hear Lord Yuris and the others speak about him. Lord Talos is... They know he's not a leader, but they follow him. They know he's losing his mind, but they listen to every word he speaks. They say the same things about him and the primarch: broken, flawed, but... inspiring. Makes them think of a better time.'

'My thanks for the trading,' said Septimus. 'I have work to do.'

'Oh, I'm sure you do.'

He didn't like the amused glint in Iruk's eye. 'You have something to say?'

'Nothing that needs speaking out loud.'

'Then I'll leave you to your work,' Septimus said. 'I'm sure you have as much to do as I have.'

'I do indeed,' Iruk replied. 'But my "work" doesn't involve stroking that three-eyed witch's pale arse.'

Septimus made eye contact for the first time in several minutes. The kit bag full of spare parts slung over his shoulder suddenly felt heavier – as weighty as a weapon.

'She isn't a witch.'

'You want to be careful,' Iruk smiled, showing several missing teeth among the darkened ones remaining. 'Navigator spit is supposed to be poisonous, they say. Must be a lie though, eh? You're still breathing.'

He turned from Second Claw's crew, moving away and hitting the door release.

'Don't take it so hard, boy. She's lovely to look at, for a mutant. Has your master allowed you to start sniffing around her heels again?'

He genuinely considered braining Iruk with the sack and drawing his pistols to shoot the older man on the floor. Worse, it felt like the easiest, most satisfying answer to the man's idiotic barbs.

With teeth clenched, he walked from the chamber, wondering at what point in his life murdering someone became the easiest solution to a moment's discomfort.

'I've been with the Legion too long,' he'd said to the darkness.

An hour later, with servitors left to deal with the final work on Lord Mercutian's chestplate, Septimus was drawing close to what Octavia unsmilingly called her 'suite' of chambers. He could hear screaming from some directionless distance. The *Echo of Damnation* was named well: its halls and decks rang with faint screams, generated from mortal mouths elsewhere on the ship and carried wherever the *Echo*'s steel bones and cold air willed.

He shivered at the sound, still not used to its infrequent rise from nowhere. He had no desire to be illuminated on whatever the Legion was doing to those astropaths, or what they were inflicting on the countless other people brought up from the cities.

Rats, or things like them that he felt no need to examine closer, scampered off ahead of him through the darkness, skittering into side passages and maintenance ducts.

'You again,' said a voice ahead, by the main bulkhead leading into Octavia's chambers.

'Vularai,' Septimus greeted her. 'Herac, Lylaras,' he greeted the other two figures. All three were wrapped in filthy bandaging, clutching weapons. Vularai held her Legion gladius resting on one cloaked shoulder.

'Not supposed to come anymore,' the shortest of the figures hissed.

'And yet, Herac, here I am. Move aside.'

OCTAVIA SLEPT IN her throne, curled up in the huge seat and blanketed against the chill. She awoke at the sound of bootsteps approaching, instinctively reaching to check her bandana hadn't slipped.

It had. She adjusted it quickly.

'You shouldn't be here,' she said to her visitor.

Septimus didn't answer at once. He looked at her, seeing the bandana over her third eye; seeing her reclining in a throne made for its mistress to use in sailing the Sea of Souls. Her clothes were filthy, her pale skin unwashed, and she'd aged a year for every month she'd been on board the *Echo* and the *Covenant* before it. The dark rings of sleep debt decorated her eyes, and her hair – once a cascade of black silk – was bound back in a straggly and frayed rat's tail.

But she smiled, and she was beautiful.

'We have to get off this ship,' Septimus said to her.

Octavia took too long to laugh. It betrayed more surprise than amusement. 'We... what?'

He'd not meant to say it out loud. He'd scarcely even realised he was thinking it.

'My hands ache,' he said. 'They ache every night. All I ever hear is gunfire and screaming, and orders spat at me by inhuman voices.'

She leaned on her throne's armrest. 'You lived with it before I joined the crew.'

'I have something to live for, now.' He met her eyes. 'I have something to lose.'

'How rare.' She didn't seem overly impressed, but he could see the hidden light in her eyes. 'Even in your atrocious accent, those words bordered on being romantic. Did our master give you another head wound, for you to speak so strangely?'

Septimus didn't look away as he usually would. 'Listen to me. Talos is driven by something I cannot comprehend. He is arranging... something. Some grand performance. Some great point to prove.'

'Like his father,' Octavia pointed out.

'Exactly. And look what happened to the primarch. His tale ended in death through sacrifice.'

Octavia rose to her feet, casting the blanket aside. She was still not showing, though Septimus had too little experience to know if her belly should be beginning to round yet or not. She seemed unconcerned, either way. He felt a brief, guilty flush of thanks that she was strong enough for the both of them, sometimes.

'You think he is leading us towards some kind of last stand?' Octavia asked. 'That seems unlikely.'

'Not intentionally. But he has no desire to lead these warriors, and nor does he wish to return to the Eye of Terror.'

'You're just guessing.'

'Perhaps I am. It doesn't matter, either way. Tell me you want our child born on this ship, into this life. Tell me you want him taken by the Legion and shaped into one of them, or to grow in the darkness of these decks, starved of sunlight his whole life. No. Octavia, we have to get off the *Echo of Damnation.*'

'I am a Navigator,' she replied, though there was no longer any amusement in her eyes. 'I was born to sail the stars. Sunlight is overrated.'

'Why is this a joke to you?'

The wrong words. He knew it as soon as he'd spoken them. Her gaze flashed as her smile became glass.

'It is not a joke to me. I merely resent your patronising assumption.' In all her time there, she'd never sounded quite so like the aristocrat she'd once been. 'I am not so weak that I need *saving*, Septimus.'

'That is not what I meant.' But that was the problem. He wasn't sure what he meant. He'd not even meant to speak the thought aloud.

'If I wished to leave the ship,' she said, lowering her voice, 'how could we do it?'

'There are ways,' said Septimus. 'We'd think of something.'

'That's very vague.' She watched him as he moved around her chamber, absently tidying away old food ration containers and data-slates her attendants had brought her as entertainment. Octavia witnessed the bizarre domestic ritual with her arms crossed beneath her breasts.

'You are still filthy,' he said, distracted.

'So you say. What are you thinking?'

Septimus stopped for a moment. 'What if Talos knows more than he's telling his brothers? What if he's seen how this all ends, and works now to his own plan? Perhaps he knows we'll all die here.'

'Even one of the Legion wouldn't be that treacherous.'

He shook his head, watching her with those mismatched eyes. 'Sometimes, I swear you forget just where you are.'

She wasn't blind to the change within him tonight. Gone was his cautious, endearing tenderness, as if fearful she would either break at a touch or kill him with an accidental glance. Gone was his vulnerability. In place of his patient virtues, frustration left him raw and curiously bare before her.

'Has he spoken to you recently?' Septimus asked her. 'Is there anything different in his words?'

She moved over to her bank of monitors, reaching for several tools in a nearby crate. 'He's always spoken like someone expecting to die sooner rather than later,' she ventured. 'Everything from his mouth is like some painful confession. I've always seen it in him – he never became what he wanted to be, and instead hates what he's become. The others… deal with it better. First Claw and the others – they enjoy this life. But he has nothing but hatred, and even that is growing hollow.'

Septimus sat next to her throne, closing his human eye in thought. His augmetic eye sealed closed in response, like a picter lens whirling shut. Screams filled the silence: distant but resonant, anonymous but so very human. He was no stranger to the sounds on an VIII Legion vessel, but too much had changed now. He couldn't tune it all out the way he'd done for years before. Now, no matter what he did, no matter where he worked, he could still hear the pain in those crying voices.

'Those poor bastards being skinned alive – do they deserve it?'

'Of course they don't,' she replied. 'Why would you even ask such a stupid question?'

'Because it was the kind of question I'd stopped asking years ago.' He turned to look at Octavia, holding her gaze for several long moments. 'This is your fault,' he told her. 'Maruc understood, but I tried to ignore him. You did this to me. You came here, and made me human again. The guilt, the fear, the desire to live and feel and…' He trailed off. 'You brought it all back. I should hate you for this.'

'You are welcome to do so,' she said as she worked on rewiring one of her external viewfinder monitors. Octavia was hardly in love with the work, but the little tasks of maintenance helped pass the time. 'But you'll be hating me because I returned something valuable to you.'

Septimus gave a noncommittal grunt.

'Do not huff and sigh at Terran aristocracy,' she said. 'That's childish.'

'Then stop… I don't know the words in Gothic. *Yrosia se naur tay helshival*,' he said in Nostraman. 'Smiling to mock me.'

'You mean "teasing". And I'm not teasing you. Just say what you want to say.'

'We need to get off this ship,' he said again, watching her as she worked, sat there with a wire-stripping tool between her teeth.

Octavia spat it out, using it with one dirty hand. 'Maybe we do. That doesn't mean we'll be able to do it. The ship can't go anywhere without me. We'll hardly get very far before they realise we're gone.'

'I'll think of something.' Septimus moved over to her, embracing her from behind. 'I love you,' he said, speaking into her hair.

'*Vel jaesha lai*,' she replied.

AN HOUR LATER, she was making her way through the *Echo*'s tunnels at the head of her attendants, loosely clustered behind her in a ragged pack. The screams were omnipresent now, echoing through the air and travelling through the walls with the same insistence as a natural wind.

The excruciation chambers were several decks down, and hardly a short walk. In terms of territory on board the warship, she knew they were deeper in more dangerous sectors, where the crew weren't as valuable, and life was accordingly cheaper.

'We come with mistress,' one of her attendants had said.

'We'll all come,' Vularai amended, resting her hand on the prized Legion sword she wore at her hip.

'Whatever you wish,' Octavia had said, though she was secretly glad of their devotion.

A pack of equally ragged deck-dwellers fled before her group – the third to run rather than remain. Several had watched her pass, hissing in Gothic, Nostraman, and languages she couldn't even guess let alone comprehend. One pack had challenged her advance, demanding their tradable possessions.

'My name is Octavia,' she'd told the grimy leader with the laspistol.

'That means exactly nothing to me, girl.'

'It means I'm the ship's Navigator.' She'd forced a smile.

'That means as much to me as your name does.'

Octavia had taken a breath, glancing at Vularai. Most of humanity, in all its huddled, unenlightened masses, might be essentially blind to the existence of Navigators, but she had no desire to explain her heritage – or worse, demonstrate it – here.

That's when he made his mistake. The pistol held loosely in his hand was a concern, but hardly a threat. When he waved it in her direction, however, her attendants stiffened. Their whispers overlapped into a serpentine layer of 'Mistress, mistress, mistress…'

The gang leader didn't conceal his unease as well as he'd hoped. He was outnumbered, and as he learned from the solid-slug shotguns being pulled from filthy robes, he was outgunned as well. The iron bars and chains carried by most of his kindred suddenly seemed less impressive.

'You're not deck vermin,' he said. 'I see that now, all right? I didn't know.'

'Now you do,' Vularai rested the oversized gladius on her shoulder, where its edge caught what little light existed.

'Just leave,' Octavia told him. Her hand strayed to her stomach without conscious thought. 'There's already enough death on this ship.'

Although her attendants moved on in peace, their blood was up now. They didn't bother hiding their weapons as they walked on, deeper into the ship.

No one challenged them again.

SHE FOUND TALOS in one of the excruciation chambers, just as she'd expected.

Before entering, she'd placed her hand on the sealed door, ready to go in.

'Stop looking at me like that,' she chided Vularai. 'Navigators keep a hundred secrets, Vularai. Whatever waits behind these doors is nothing compared to the secrets kept in the sublevels of the Navis Nobilite's spires.'

'As you say, mistress.'

The door opened on grinding hydraulics. She saw Talos for less than a second, and then she saw nothing at all. The smell that struck her was strong enough to have an obscene physicality – it quite literally hammered against her the moment the bulkhead rolled open. Her eyes squeezed closed, stinging like salt in an open wound. The reek seeped into the soft tissue of her eyes, choked her throat, cramped her lungs, and lashed at her skin with a disgusting, damp warmth. Even her sworn curse was a mistake, for the moment the air hit her tongue, the stench became a taste as well.

Octavia collapsed to her hands and knees, throwing up onto the deck. She had to get out of the room, but her eyes wouldn't open, and she couldn't catch her breath between her spasming lungs and rebelling stomach.

Talos watched this spectacle from his place by the surgery table. His attention remained rapt as she vomited a second time.

'I am given to understand,' he said, 'that it is common for females in your... condition... to regurgitate as part of the natural process.'

'It's not that,' she breathed, before her guts clenched again, forcing her to heave out another tide of thin, sour gruel.

'I have almost no experience with such things,' he admitted. 'We studied little of the human condition in regards to gestation of children.'

'*It's not that,*' she wheezed. Inhuman fool, he had no idea. Several of her attendants were similarly struck down, gagging and choking on what they could see and smell.

She crawled from the chamber, half-dragged by Vularai and one other. Only when they had her outside did she manage to rise to her feet, catching her breath as her eyes watered.

'Seal the door...' she panted.

'Mistress?' one of her attendants asked, confused. 'I thought you wished to come here?'

'*Close the door!*' she hissed, feeling her stomach heave again. Three of the other attendants still hadn't recovered either, but they'd made it out of the room.

Vularai was the one to obey. The bulkhead leading into the excruciation chamber rumbled closed. Despite the mask of bandages, she was gagging and choking herself, barely able to speak.

'Those people on the tables,' she said. 'How are they still alive?'

Octavia spat the last of the bile from her lips, and reached back to retie her ponytail.

'Someone get me a rebreather. I'm going back in.'

* * *

'WE HAVE TO talk,' she said to him.

The body on the surgery table moaned, too breathless and ruined to scream anymore. So little of it remained that Octavia could no longer determine its gender.

Talos looked over at her. The blades in his hands were wet and red. Four bodies, skinned and dripping, hung from dirty chains around the central table. He saw her eyes flicker to the hanging bodies, and explained their presence in a voice of inhuman calm.

'They are still alive. Their pain bleeds into this one's mind.' The Night Lord stroked the bloody knife along the prisoner's flayed face. 'It ripens now, swollen with agony. They no longer beg for death with their throats, tongues and lungs... but I can hear their whispers stroking inside my skull. Not long now. We are so very close to the end. What did you want to speak of, Navigator?'

Octavia took a breath through the rebreather mask over her mouth and nose. 'I want the truth from you.'

Talos watched her again, while the bodies drip, drip, dripped.

'I have never lied to you, Octavia.'

'I'll never understand how you can make a credible attempt at sounding virtuous while standing in an abattoir, Talos.' She wiped her eyes; the sick heat bleeding from the ruptured bodies was making them water.

'I am what I am,' he replied. 'You are distracting me, so I would ask you to make this quick.'

'And the manners of a nobleman,' she said softly, trying not to look at the butchery hanging on display. Blood trickled into a gutter grille beneath the table. She didn't want to guess where it led. She suspected something, somewhere down there on a lower deck, was feeding.

'Octavia...' he warned.

'I need to know something,' she said. 'I need to know the truth about all of this.'

'I have told you the truth, including what I expect from you.'

'No. You got it into your head that we had to come here. Now there's this... carnage. You know more than you're telling us. You know if the Imperium comes to answer these atrocities, it will come in force.'

He nodded. 'That seems likely.'

'And we may not escape.'

'That also seems likely.'

Octavia's rebreather clicked at the zenith of each slow breath. 'You are doing what he did, aren't you? Your primarch died to prove a point.'

'I do not plan to die here, Terran.'

'No? You don't *plan* to die here? Your plans aren't worth a damn, Talos. They never are.'

'The raid on Ganges Station seemed to go well enough,' he pointed out. 'And we sent the Salamanders running at Vykon Point.'

His amusement only fuelled her temper. 'You're supposed to be our leader. You command thousands of souls, not just your handful of warriors.'

He growled a laugh. 'Throne in flames, do you truly think I care about every single creature that draws breath on this ship? Are you mad, girl? I am a legionary of the Eighth. Nothing more, nothing less.'

'You could have killed Septimus.'

'And I will, if he defies me again. The moment his usefulness is outweighed by his defiance, he dies skinless and eyeless on this very table.'

'You're lying. You're evil, heart and soul, but you're not the monster you pretend to be.'

'And you are trying my patience, Terran. Get out of my presence before I lose the last vestiges of my tolerance for your irritating ethical theatrics.'

But she was going nowhere. Octavia took another calming breath, trying to control her stubborn anger.

'Talos, you are going to kill all of us unless you're careful. What if the Imperium's answer isn't some ship of salvation to carry the survivors away to tell some awful story, but a vast Navy battlefleet? It'll likely be both. We're as good as dead if they find us nearby.' She gestured to the quivering wretch on the table. 'You want to poison the warp with their pain and annihilate any hope of safe flight through the Sea of Souls, but it will be as much of a struggle for me. I cannot guide us through broken tides.'

Talos said nothing for several seconds. 'I know,' he finally replied.

'And yet you're going through with this?'

'This is one of the precious few times since the Great Betrayal that my brothers and I have felt like the sons of our father again. No longer raiding, no longer merely surviving – we are once more doing what we were born to do. It is worth the risk.'

'Half of them are just killing for the sake of it.'

'True. That, also, is the Eighth Legion way. Nostramo was not a wholesome birthworld.'

'You're not listening to me.'

'I listen, but you speak in ignorance. You do not understand us, Octavia. We are not what you think we are, because you have always misunderstood us. You judge us by human morality, as if we have ever been chained to those ideals. Life means something different to the Eighth Legion.'

She closed her eyes for a long moment. 'I hate this ship. I hate this life. I hate you.'

'Those are the most intelligent words you have ever said to me.'

'We're going to die here,' she said at last. Her hands bunched into helpless fists.

'Everyone dies, Octavia. Death is nothing compared to vindication.'

XVII

GAMBITS

CYRION WAS ALONE, now that his latest victim lay dead.

He sat with his back to the wall, breathing through spit-wet teeth. The gladius in his hand clattered to the stained decking. Shivers still rippled through him; pleasant aftershocks as the man's death played out again in his mind. Real fear. Real terror. Not the dull haze of pain that was all that remained among the astropaths and their other victims. This had been a vital, strong man with no desire to die. Cyrion had cherished the look in his eyes as the gladius hacked and carved. He'd been scared to the bitter end: a dirty, unwarranted death, replete with begging, deep in the ship's lower decks.

The Night Lord had needed it – water to a parched man after all the clinical infliction of pain on their captives. The crew member's final moments, as his weak fingers scratched uselessly at Cyrion's faceplate, were the final, perfect touch. Such delicious futility. He tasted that desperate fear, its actual tactile sweetness, like nectar on the tongue.

A groan escaped his lips through the tingling rush of chemicals flooding his brain and blood. It was good to be a god's son, even one with a curse. Even when the gods themselves watched a little too closely.

Someone, somewhere, was saying his name. Cyrion ignored it. He had no mind to return to the higher decks and go back to the surgical carving that needed to be done. That could wait. The flood was beginning to fade now, and with it, the tremor in his fingers.

A strange name, that. *The flood.* He couldn't recall when he'd first come to know his gift by that name, but it fit well enough. Latent psychic strength wasn't miraculously rare in the VIII Legion – or any of the Legions beyond – but his remained a source of quiet pride. Cyrion had never been born psychic, or else his touch of the sixth sense was weak enough to go unnoticed by the extensive tests upon Legion indoctrination. It had simply happened over time, during the years they'd spent in the Eye of Terror. His awareness had blossomed, like a flower opening in the light of the sun.

799

The wordless whispers began at the edge of his hearing, night after night. Soon enough he could make sense from the hissed phrases, stealing a word here or a sentence there. Each of them shared a single strain of familiarity: they were all fearful utterances, unspoken but still audible, pulsing from those he killed.

In the beginning, he'd merely found it amusing. To hear the fearful final words of those he butchered.

'I do not see why you find this so funny,' Talos had rebuked him. 'The Eye is influencing you.'

'There are those who bear worse curses than I,' Cyrion pointed out. Talos had let it rest, never mentioning it again. Xarl hadn't acted with the same restraint. The stronger the gift became, the less inclined Cyrion was to hide it, and the filthier Xarl found his presence. *Corruption*, Xarl had called it. He'd never trusted psykers, no matter the benevolence of the powers they claimed.

'Cyrion.'

His name brought him back to the present, back to the stink of oily metal walls and newly dead bodies.

'What is it?' he voxed back.

'It's Malcharion,' came the response. 'He… he has awakened.'

'Is this a hilarious jest?' Cyrion hauled himself to his feet with a grunt. 'Deltrian swore there was no progress.'

'Just get up here. Talos warned you about hunting in the ship's bowels when we have work to do.'

'You're as bad as he is, sometimes. Has the war-sage spoken?'

'Not exactly.' Mercutian broke off the contact.

Cyrion started walking, leaving the bodies behind. No one would miss the lower-deck trash that lay in bloody pieces behind him. Hunting in the *Echo*'s deep levels was a forgivable sin, unlike Uzas's occasional mad slayings through Blackmarket and the officer decks, butchering the most valuable members of the crew.

'Hello,' said a soft, quiet voice from nearby. Too low to be human, but unrecognisable in the vox distortion.

He looked up. There, in the chamber's iron rafters, one of the Bleeding Eyes crouched with a gargoyle's patience. Cyrion felt his skin crawl; a rare sensation indeed.

'Lucoryphus.'

'Cyrion,' came the reply. 'I have been thinking.'

'And evidently following me.'

The Raptor nodded his sloping helm. 'Aye. That also. Tell me, little Lord of Smiles, why do you come down here so often to sniff out the excretion-reek of fear?'

'These are our hunting grounds,' Cyrion replied. 'Talos spends long enough down here, himself.'

'Maybe so.' The Raptor's head jerked once, either a flaw in his armour's systems or the result of warp-flawed genetics. 'But he kills for release, for pleasure, for the surge of adrenaline stinging in his veins. He was born a killer, therefore he kills. You hunt to sate another appetite. An appetite that has bloomed within you, not one you were born with. I find that interesting. Oh, yes.'

'You may think whatever you choose.'

The angled, almond-shaped eye lenses showed Cyrion's reflection in miniature. 'We have watched you, Cyrion. The Bleeding Eyes see everything. We know your secrets. Yes we do.'

'I have no secrets to keep, brother.'

'No?' Lucoryphus's laugh was somewhere between a chuckle and a caw. 'A lie doesn't become truth simply because you give it voice.'

Cyrion said nothing. He briefly considered reaching for his bolter. His fingers must've twitched, for Lucoryphus laughed again.

'Try it, Cyrion. Just try.'

'Make your point,' the warrior said.

Lucoryphus leered. 'Why must there be a point to a conversation between kindred? Do you assume every soul is as treacherous as you are? The Bleeding Eyes follow Talos because of that oldest axiom: he breeds trouble wherever he walks. The primarch paid attention to him, and that is an interest still fascinating all these centuries later. He has a destiny, one way or another. I wish to witness that destiny. You, however, have the potential to become a nuisance. How long have you fed on human fear?'

Cyrion breathed slowly before answering, suppressing the tempting flood of chemical stimulants from intravenous feeds in his wrists and spine.

'A long time. Decades. I have never kept track.'

'A very weak breed of psychic vampirism.' The Raptor exhaled a thin breath of steam from his vocabulator grille. 'I am not one to question the gifts of the warp.'

'Then why question me at all?'

He realised his mistake as soon as the question left his lips. Delaying had cost him the edge of opportunity. From the corridor he'd come down, another of the Bleeding Eyes crawled on all fours, blocking the doorway.

'Cyrion,' it said, seeming to struggle with speech. 'Yes-yes.'

'Vorasha,' he replied. It was no surprise when another three Raptors crawled out of the tunnel ahead, their sloping daemon-masks watching him with unblinking scrutiny.

'We question you,' Lucoryphus rasped, 'because while I would never speak out against the warp's changes, I have much less patience for treachery so close to the prophet. Stability is vital now. He is planning something secret, something he has chosen not to share. We all sense it, like... like a static charge in the air. We walk now in the pressure of a storm yet-to-be.'

'We trust him,' said one of the other Raptors.

'We do not trust you,' finished a third.

Lucoryphus's voice was ripened by a smile. 'Stability, Cyrion. Remember that word. Now run along and witness the war-sage's flawed resurrection. And remember this talk. The Bleeding Eyes see all.'

The Raptors scattered back into the tunnels, worming their way deeper into the ship.

'That isn't good,' Cyrion said to himself in the silent darkness.

HE WAS THE last to arrive, entering the Hall of Reflection almost thirty minutes after the initial summons. The chamber's usual industry was halted in surreal immobility. None of the servitors went about their business, while dozens of low-tier Mechanicum adepts looked on in relative silence. If they communicated with each other, it was via means that the legionaries couldn't discern.

Cyrion walked to First Claw, who stood by the circular bulkhead entrance to one of the antechambers. The barrier itself was rolled open, revealing the stasis chamber within. Cyrion felt something at the edge of his hearing, like the threat of thunder on the horizon. He cycled through his helm's audio receptor modes, picking up the same almost-audible infrasound murmur no matter the frequency.

'Do you hear that?' he asked Talos.

The prophet stood with Mercutian and Uzas, saying nothing. Variel and Deltrian conferred in hushed voices by the adept's central control tables.

'What's wrong?' Cyrion asked.

Talos turned his skulled faceplate to him. 'We are still not certain.'

'But Malcharion is awake?'

Talos led him into the stasis chamber. Their boots sent resonant echoes clanging off the iron walls. Malcharion's sarcophagus remained on its marble plinth, chained in place, supported by hundreds of copper filament wires, power cables and life support tubes. The sarcophagus displayed Malcharion's triumphant death in exquisite detail: gold, adamantine and bronze worked into a vision of a Night Lord victorious, head tilted back to roar at a starry sky. In one hand, the tail-crested helm of a White Scar khan; in the other, the helmet of an Imperial Fist champion. Last of all, his boot rested on the proud helm of a Blood Angels lord-captain, grinding it into the Terran dirt.

'The stasis field is down,' Cyrion pointed out.

'It is,' Talos nodded, crossing to one of the secondary consoles ringing the central plinth. His fingers tapped against several plastek keys. As soon as the final key clicked, the chamber burst with a flood of agonised screaming. The cries were organic, human, but with a tinny edge and an undertone of buzzing crackle.

Cyrion winced, it was that loud. His helm took a couple of seconds to filter the sound to tolerable levels. He didn't need to ask the screams' origin.

'What have we done to him?' he asked. The screaming died as Talos killed the power feed from the sarcophagus to the external speakers.

'That is what Variel and Deltrian are working on. It seems likely that Malcharion's wounds at Crythe have left his mind shattered beyond recovery. There is no telling what he would do if we connected him to a Dreadnought chassis. For all we know, he would turn on all of us.'

Cyrion thought over his next words with exceptional care. 'Brother...'

Talos turned to him. 'Speak.'

'I have supported you, haven't I? You wear the mantle of our commander, but it doesn't quite fit.'

The prophet nodded. 'I have no desire to lead anything. I'm hardly keeping it a secret. Can you not see me doing all I can to restore our true captain?'

'I know, brother. You are the living embodiment of someone in the wrong place at the wrong time. But you are coping. The raid on Tsagualsa was a fine touch, as was sending the Salamanders running at Vykon Point. I don't care what you're planning – the others are either content to trust your judgement, or lose themselves in indulgence in the meantime. But this...'

'I know,' Talos said. 'Trust me, I know.'

'He's a Legion hero. You will live and die by how you treat him, Talos.'

'I am not blind to that.' The prophet ran his hand across the graven image on the surface of the sarcophagus. 'I told them to let him die after Crythe. He'd earned the respite of oblivion. But Malek – a curse upon him, wherever he is – countermanded my order. And when Deltrian smuggled the coffin aboard, it changed everything. He hadn't died, after all. Perhaps I was wrong to believe him too melancholy to survive in this shell, since he'd fought for life when he could so easily have died. We could have used his guidance, Cyrion. He should have stood with us again.'

Cyrion gripped his brother's shoulder guard. 'Tread with care, Talos. We stand on the edge of everything coming unravelled.' He looked at the sarcophagus himself for several long moments. 'What did the Flayer and the tech-adept suggest?'

'Both of them believe he is ruined beyond recovery. They also both concur that he could still be formidable – if unreliable – in battle. Variel suggested controlling Malcharion with pain injectors and focused excruciators.' Talos shook his head. 'Like an animal, collared by unkind masters and trained by beatings.'

Cyrion expected no less from either of those two. 'And what will you do?'

Talos hesitated. 'What would you do, in my place?'

'Truly? I'd flush the organic remains into the void without any of the Legion knowing, and install one of the grievously wounded warriors in his place. Spread the word that Malcharion died during the rituals of resurrection. Then there would be no one to blame.'

The prophet turned to face him. 'How noble of you.'

'Look at the armour we wear. Witness the cloak of flayed flesh worn by Uzas, the skulls hanging from our belts, the skinned faces draped over Variel's pauldrons. There is nothing of nobility in us. Necessity is all we know.'

Talos watched him for what seemed an age. 'Is there a reason for this sudden proselytising?'

Cyrion thought of Lucoryphus, and the Bleeding Eyes' words. 'Just my caring nature,' he smiled. 'So what will you do?'

'I have ordered Variel and Deltrian to see if they can calm him down with synapse suppressors and chemicals. There may be a way to reach him yet.'

'And if that fails?'

'I will deal with that possibility when it becomes an unarguable truth. For now, it is time we played our hand. Octavia's time has come.'

'The Navigator? Is she ready for this?' *Whatever 'this' is*, he added silently.

'Her readiness is immaterial,' said Talos, 'for she has no choice.'

THE *Echo of Damnation* rode the tides, powered by plasma fusion, driven by the sentient heart at the ship's core, and guided by the third eye of a woman born of humanity's ancestral home world.

Talos stood by her throne, his own eyes closed, listening to the sounds of the screaming sea. Souls crashed against the hull, mixed in with the very life-flesh of daemons, shaking the warship and rippling over them in an endless, howling tide. He listened, for the first time in decades he truly listened, and heard once more the music of his father's throne room.

A breathy sigh hissed from his parted lips. Gone was the doubt. Gone were the concerns of how best to lead the few warriors that remained to him, and how he should spend the lives of his slaves. Why hadn't he done this before? Why had he never noticed the similarity in sound until Octavia pointed it out? He knew all the tales that warned of listening too close to the warp's song, but they all went blissfully ignored.

The Navigator was sweating, staring into a thousand shades of black. One moment the darkness screamed at her, expressing its pain through souls bursting against the hull. The next, it called to her; nameless things beckoning with the same claws that raked along the ship's metal skin.

The tides writhed with the same coiling chaos found within a nest of serpents. Flashes of sick light winked between the overlapping warp-stuff, either the distant Astronomican or the deceptions of daemons – it didn't matter to Octavia. She aimed the ship for every pulse of light that flickered ahead, crashing through the void-tides with the power and weight behind one of the species' oldest warships. The cold waves of unreality burst apart at their prow, and trembled in their wake, forming shapes no human eyes could ever perceive.

The *Echo* itself remained in the back of her consciousness. Unlike the sullen, contrary soul of the *Covenant*, the *Echo of Damnation* had a great, eager heart. Terra had no sharks, but she knew of them from the Throneworld's archives. Predators within the ancient seas, forever needing to move forward lest they die. That was the *Echo* in a single, simple concept. It desired nothing more than to run with all its strength, breaking through the barriers of the warp and leaving the material realm behind.

You have listened too long and too hard to the warp's call, she chided the ship as sweat ran down her temples.

Burn, burn, burn, it pulsed back. *More strength to engines. More fire in core.*

She felt the ship racing harder in response. Her own instinctive impulses flashed through the neural-sensitive cables plugged into her temples and wrists, curbing the sudden leap in thrust. The *Echo*'s primal excitement snapped back, entering her body through the same ports, sending her into a delicious shiver.

Calm, she pulsed. *Calm.*

The ship's reply was another effort to increase thrust. Octavia could almost see the slave crews in the cavernous chambers of the engine decks, sweating and shouting and dying to feed the generators at the pace demanded of them. For a moment, she thought she could feel them all the way the *Echo* felt them: as a hive of flea-like, insignificant sentience, itching within her bones.

The Navigator pulled back from the mesh of sensation, rejecting the ship's primitive emotions and settling firmer within herself. The cold kiss of her chamber's air supply touched her sweating skin, causing another involuntary shudder. She felt as though she'd been holding her breath under boiling water.

'Starboard,' she whispered into the vox-orb drifting before her face. Its tiny suspensors kept it afloat – a half-skull rendered into a portable vocabulator – and transmitted her words to the crew and servitors on the command deck above. 'Starboard, three degrees, pressurised thrust to compensate for warp density. Axial stabilisers are…'

On and on she mumbled, staring into the darkness, sharing control of the warship with the vessel's crew and its own angry heart.

Outside, the pantheon of ethereal inhumanity raged against the ship's

Geller field. The tide itself recoiled, burned and bleeding, each time it broke against the diving vessel. Octavia scarcely spared a thought for the deep, cold intelligences hiding in the endless void. It took all her concentration to focus on the narrow path she was ramming through the Sea of Souls. She could endure the screaming, for she was born to see through the unseeable – the warp held few secrets or surprises for her. But the *Echo's* eager joy threatened her focus like nothing else ever had; even the *Covenant's* mulish resistance had been easier to overcome. That required force. This required temperance. It required a lie told to herself: that she didn't share the same savage joy, that she didn't feel the same need to burn the engines unto self-destruction, running faster and diving deeper than any soul – artificial or otherwise – had ever done before.

The *Echo's* dark delight filtered back through the neural feeds, spicing her blood with excitement's charge. Octavia pulled back from the bond, forcing her breathing to slow as her body reacted to the symbiotic pleasure in the most primal of ways.

Slower, she breathed, sending the word back to the ship's core even as she spoke it aloud. *Geller stability is wavering.*

You are wavering, the *Echo's* dull sentience pulsed back. *A slave to reason.*

The ship gave another shiver in sympathy to her own. This one was tighter, born of tensed muscles and clenched teeth. It spoke of control and focus, as Octavia's will blanketed the ship's machine-spirit.

I am your Navigator, she whisper-hissed the silent words. *And I guide you.*

The *Echo of Damnation* never communicated with actual language; its pulses of emotion and urges formed words only as Octavia's human mind fought to find meaning in them. Its surrender now never even manifested as false utterances, though. She merely felt it cower back from her surge of willpower, taking its inflicted emotions with it.

Better, she smiled through the tears of sweat. *Better.*

Close now, Navigator, it sent back.

I know.

'Beacons,' she mumbled aloud. 'Beacons in the night. The blade of light. The Emperor's Will given shape. A trillion screaming souls. Every man and woman and child ever given to the Golden Throne's soul engines, since the dawn of the One Empire. I see them. I hear them. I see the sound. I hear the light.'

Whispering voices slithered into her ears. Deck by deck, the word was being passed, so pathetically slow in its reliance on mortal speech. Octavia had no need to stare at hololithic star maps. She cared nothing for the rattle and clang of deep-void auspex readers.

'All stop,' she whispered through lips bright with spit. 'All stop.'

The hand on her shoulder could have come a minute, an hour, or a year later. She wasn't sure.

'Octavia,' said the low, low voice.

She closed her secret eye, and opened her human ones. Vitreous humour gummed them, leaving them sore as she forced them open. She felt the soft caress of her bandana being draped over her forehead.

'Water,' she demanded, her voice a horse rasp. Her attendants muttered nearby, but the hands bringing the dirty canteen to her lips were armoured in midnight blue. Even the tiniest knuckle-joints gave soft growls.

She swallowed, caught her breath, and swallowed more. With trembling hands, she wiped the cooling sweat from her face, then pulled the intravenous feeds from her arms. The cables in her temples and throat could remain there, for now.

'How long?' she asked at last.

'Sixteen nights,' said Talos. 'We are where we need to be.'

Octavia closed her eyes as she sank back into the throne. She was asleep before Vularai covered her shivering form with a blanket.

'She must eat,' the attendant pointed out. 'Over two weeks... The baby...'

'Do whatever you wish,' Talos said to the bandaged mortal. 'That is none of my concern. Wake her in six hours and bring her to the excruciation chambers. All will be ready by then.'

SHE WORE HER rebreather again, listening to the sound of her own respiration turned low and throaty. The mask over her nose and mouth stole all sense of taste and scent, leaving only the stale musk of her own breath, tinged with a chlorine edge that stung the back of her tongue.

Talos stood behind her, ostensibly to oversee the moment. She wondered if he'd really remained in order to prevent her from running.

Six hours' sleep wasn't enough, not even nearly enough. Octavia felt her weariness as a physical sickness, leaving her weak and slow, as if her blood beat around her body at a muted rate.

'Do it,' Talos ordered her.

She didn't – at least, not immediately. She walked among the chained bodies, between the slabs on which they lay, weaving through the medicae servitors mono-tasked with keeping the carcasses alive just a little while longer.

The husks laid out on each table scarcely resembled humans in any real sense. One was a mess of musculature and stripped veins, twitching its final moments away on the surgery table. The flayed ones were little better; neither were those now deprived of their tongues, lips, hands and noses. Ruination was complete on each and every one of them – desecration had never seen such variety. She was walking through a living monument to fear and pain: this was the Legion's imagination given form.

Octavia looked back at Talos, glad he still wore his helm. If she'd seen any pride in his naked eyes in that moment, she would have never been able to tolerate his presence again.

'The Screaming Gallery,' she said, above the muffled moans and beep of pulse trackers. 'Was it like this?'

The Night Lord nodded. 'Very much so. Now do it,' he said again.

Octavia took a stale breath, moved to the closest table, and removed her bandana.

'I will end it for you,' she whispered to the organic wreckage that had once been a man.

It turned its eyes towards her with the last of its strength, lifted its wet gaze to the Navigator's third eye, and looked into absolute oblivion.

XVIII

A SONG IN THE NIGHT

THE WORLD ARTARION III.

In the Tower of the Emperor Eternal, Godwyne Trismejion watched the astropath writhing against the restraining straps. This was nothing unusual. It was his job to watch over his wards when they dreamed, monitoring them as they sent their somnolent messages to receptive minds on other worlds. He found it amusing – in his own dullish, slow-witted sort of way – that in an empire of a million worlds, the most reliable way to carry a message to another world was to take it there yourself.

Even so, his wards had their roles to play. Astropathic contact saw a great deal of use on Artarion III, as might be expected of any world so heavily populated by guild trade interests.

The astropath started to bleed from the nose. This, too, was within tolerable parameters. Godwyne clicked a steel switch and spoke into his console's vox-input.

'Vital signs for Unon fluctuating within… tolerable…' he trailed off, his eyes locked to the spiking polylithic printout. The readings spiked harsher with each passing second.

'Sudden heart failure, and…' Godwyne looked back to the astropath, seeing the onset of real convulsions now. 'Heart failure and… Throne of the God-Emperor.'

Something wet and red burst against the viewscreen window. He couldn't see through the mess to be sure, but when a purification team entered six minutes later, they would learn it was Astropath Unon's heart and brain, burst by unprecedented external psychic pressure.

By that time, Godwyne was on the edge of panic as he worked at his console, his hands full of vague printed images from the minds of his astropathic wards, and his head full of the wailing sirens as more and more of them died.

'What are they hearing?' he screamed at the chaotic spill of frantic information. 'What are they seeing?'

The Tower of the Emperor Eternal, as a precious and expensive psychic node – warded and strengthened against daemonic intrusion – absorbed all the death and pain taking place within its walls. It didn't distil it or filter it; it merely fused the sudden fears and mortal agonies with the hideous incoming transmission, and beamed the foul whole back into the void.

The notes of the song sailed on through the night, now with a new chorus.

Each world hearing the song would add another chorus in turn.

THE WORLD VOL-HEYN.

On the agricultural world's northernmost archipelago, an Administratum overseer blinked at the spots of blood dropping onto his manuscript. He blinked and looked up, where his advisor – Sor Merem, local provost of the Adeptus Astra Telepathica – was twitching and curling into himself.

The overseer recoiled at the man's fit, activating his hand-vox. 'Inform the medicae division that the Telepathica provost has fallen victim to some kind of seizure.' He almost laughed, seeing the man collapse and smack his head on the table edge on the way down. Bloody drool spurted from his lips.

'What madness is this?' the overseer half-laughed, biting back his unease.

Shouting reached his ears from elsewhere in the building. Other astropaths? Their guardians and keepers? The poor fools 'gifted' with the sacred speech were never stable, never healthy – each one rendered blind and feeble by their soulbinding to the Golden Throne. Shouting in the halls was commonplace as they sent and received their many messages each night. Each one would burn out in under a decade. The overseer didn't relish the fact – it was simply the way of things.

The provost was thudding the back of his head on the stone floor now, beating himself bloody and biting his tongue. The overseer didn't understand. The provost was newly appointed only the previous season. He had many years of use before burning out.

'Merem?' the overseer asked the twitching body. Froth at the man's lips was the only answer. His eyes were wide, terrified by something only he could see.

'Overseer Kalkus,' his hand-vox crackled.

'Speak,' the overseer said. 'I demand to know what's happening.'

'Overseer... the–'

'The what? Who is this?'

Something screamed down the vox connection. It didn't sound human. The overseer would find exactly how true that was in a handful of minutes, when it reached his door.

* * *

On New Plateau, it came to be known as the Night of the Mad Song, as tens of thousands of hive residents dreamed the same torturous dreams.

On Jyre, the central fortress of the Adeptus Astra Telepathica was destroyed in a riot from within, that spread onto the streets and lasted three weeks before the planetary defence forces quelled the uprising.

On Garanel IV, almost all off-world business within Capital City was brought to its knees by an outbreak of an unnamed contagion in the astropathic guild's sector of the city.

The song carried on into the night.

The world Orvalas.

The world itself was largely worthless. Its ore deposits had long since been carved bare, leaving great, dry canyon-scars across the planet's tectonic visage. What few humans remained maintained an astropathic relay station in high orbit. Their sworn duty was as simple as it was vital: to interpret the dreams, images, nightmares and voices of the warp reaching them from other worlds, and relay them onward down the 001.2.57718 Astra Telepathica Duct.

Sixteen minutes after its contingent of psychically-gifted souls received the mortis-cry from several worlds elsewhere along the Duct, the astropathic relay station at Orvalas went dark. No trace of its further existence was ever noted in Imperial record. All five hundred and forty souls aboard were entered into the Adeptus Astra Telepathica's Chronicles of the Lost, at their headquarter bastion on the world Heras, Corosia Subsector, in Ultima Segmentum.

The final astropathic transmissions from Orvalas reached thirty-four other worlds, strengthening the bleak song past its already potent voice.

It took four hours.

One by one, she killed them with her secret sight. Each of them looked into her hidden eye, and though she never knew what they saw, she knew what would happen. The first howled and reached for her with handless arms, banging its amputated wrists against her face as it died. A single glance at her third eye was all it took. No more lethal weapon existed in all of humanity's long and bloody history. Any sailor of the stars knew that to look into a Navigator's warp eye was to know death. No tales existed of what the doomed ones ever saw in those depths. No one had ever lived to tell of it.

Octavia had her own guesses, though. Her tutors had hinted of their own research, and of archival evidence noted by previous scholars. Her bloodline's priceless mutation allowed her immunity to the warp's taint, but for one without Navigator blood, the third eye was a death sentence. Each of these poor, excruciated remnants looked through the window into Chaos Incarnate. Their minds opened to the horror beyond the veil, and their mortal forms ruptured, unable to contain it.

Some of them simply expired, their spirits at last drifting from the tortured husks that contained them. Others twitched against their restraints, possessing a vitality they'd lacked at any other time, writhing as they died from agonising organ failure. Several of them burst in front of her, drenching her with stinking viscera. Jagged shards of bone cut and bruised her with each disgusting detonation, and the air soon turned thick with the reek. She had blood on her tongue and shit on her face by the time she'd killed the seventh.

By the twelfth, she was drooling herself, trembling, bleeding from her third eye. By the fifteenth, she could barely stand. By the eighteenth, she could no longer recall who she was.

She passed out as she murdered the nineteenth.

Talos didn't let her fall. He gripped the back of her head in his gauntleted hand, forcing her unconscious visage into the faces of those doomed to die. He held her secret eye open with the tip of one finger, slaying wherever he aimed her limp body.

By the end, she was barely breathing. Her attendants rushed to her, but the Night Lord warned them back with a glare.

'I will take her back to her chamber.' He opened his vox-link with a moment's concentration. A rune flashed live on his retinal display. 'Variel, attend to the Navigator in her chambers. She is wounded from her efforts.'

'As you wish,' crackled back the Flayer's reply. 'First Claw awaits you on the bridge, Talos. Will you finally tell us what you've been doing in there for the last four hours?'

'Yes,' Talos replied. 'Yes, I will.'

FIRST CLAW GATHERED around the command throne. The hololithic table's anaemic blue light flickered against their armour as they watched a growing cross-section of the galaxy, increasingly expansive in scope. First, it showed a single system; then several nearby; soon, it was displaying a wide swathe of Ultima Segmentum, with auspex corrosion leaving the picture hazy and indistinct in many places.

'Here.' Talos gestured with the point of his golden sword. The Blade of Angels gently carved through the misty hololithic, in a loose arc that covered hundreds upon hundreds of stars and the worlds enslaved to them.

'What am I looking at?' Cyrion asked.

Talos removed his helm, resting it on the table edge. His black eyes never left the shimmering three-dimensional display.

'A galactic ballet,' he said with a crooked smile. 'More specifically, you are looking at the Zero-Zero-One point Two point Five-Seven-Seven-One-Eight Astra Telepathica Duct.'

'Oh,' Cyrion nodded, none the wiser. 'Of course. How foolish of me.'

Talos pointed to world after world in turn. 'Each Astra Telepathica Duct is as unique as a fingerprint. One might be created by artifice and intent: several worlds being colonised in alignment near stable warp transit routes, allowing the psychic dreamers on each planet to speak across the untold distance. Others are born of chance and happenstance, boosted by the warp itself, or by a simple twist of fate that allows a number of disparate worlds the chance to call to each other across the solar winds.

'The Imperium has hundreds of these ducts,' Talos was smiling now. They grow, they fade, they rise and degrade, always in flux. With few other ways to make astropathy even an iota more reliable, there is little other choice. And still, it is an art of casting runestones and heeding whispers from nowhere. Utilising a duct is no stroke of genius. But this one... What we did here, brothers...'

Mercutian leaned forward, shaking his head. 'Blood of the False Emperor,' he swore. 'Talos, *this* was your plan?'

The prophet gave a sadist's smile.

Cyrion watched the arc of stars and worlds for a few more moments before looking at his brothers.

'Wait.' Realisation sank in, running through his blood as an unwelcome chill. 'Wait. You've just sent over a hundred astropathic mortis-cries through an established psychic duct?'

'I have indeed.'

Mercutian's voice had the edge of panic. 'You killed them with... with a Navigator. That's what you were doing in there, wasn't it?'

'It was.'

'This is bigger than us, Talos,' Mercutian said. 'So much bigger than us. I admire you for the ambitious spear thrust at the crag cat's heart, but if this works, the retaliation will wipe us from the face of history.'

Talos's expression never changed.

'Will you stop smiling?' Cyrion asked him. 'I'm not used to it. You're making my skin crawl.'

'What do you anticipate will happen?' asked Mercutian. 'At the very least, this will isolate several worlds for decades. At worst, it will devastate them.'

Talos nodded again. 'I know.'

'Then speak,' Mercutian pressed. 'Stop grinning and *speak*. Our lives could be measured in hours.'

The prophet sheathed his sword again. 'The idea came to me when Deltrian first constructed the Shriek. His craft was to turn fear and pain into a source of power. It made fear into a weapon once more. Terror became a means to an end, rather than the end itself.' Talos met their eyes, lowering all pretence of grandeur. 'I needed that. I needed to focus on a life worth living.'

Cyrion nodded. Mercutian watched in silence. Uzas stared into the

shimmering hololithic; whether or not he heard the prophet's words
was anyone's guess.

Cyrion turned slightly, realising the entire command deck had fallen
silent. Talos was no longer addressing First Claw. He was speaking to the
hundreds of mortals and servitors on the bridge, most of whom were
now watching the prophet to the exclusion of all else. He'd never seen
this side of his brother before. Here was a glimpse of what might yet be
– a warrior ready to assume the mantle of leadership; a warlord ready to
live up to his vision of what the VIII Legion once was, and could be again.

And it was working. Cyrion could see it in their eyes. Talos's mix of
hesitant confidence and vulnerable fanaticism had them enraptured.

'Tsagualsa,' Talos said, his voice softer now. 'Our refuge, and second
home. To find it crawling with vermin left a bitter trail on my tongue.
But why punish them? Why destroy these weak, lost colonists? Their sin
was nothing more than drifting through the warp to a world that offered
cold welcome. That was no crime, except perhaps one of misfortune. And
yet, there they were. Millions of them. Lost. Alone. *Prey*, scratching in
the dirt. How poetic, to find them here, of all places. Rather than punish
them for punishment's sake, we could use them. What better weapon
to wield against the Imperium than the souls of its own lost children?'

Talos gestured to the sweep of worlds and suns in the hololithic display. 'Humans die every night. They die in their millions, in their billions,
feeding the warp with emotion at the moment of death. Astropaths are
no different, except by virtue of degrees. An astropath dies, and a psychic
soul cries out that much louder upon final death. The warp boils around
those souls, when they are unleashed from their mortal shells.'

The hololithic image turned, refocusing on several worlds not far from
the warship's current location. Population and defence data, almost certainly outdated, spilled out in static-blurred lines.

'Purely by excruciating the astropaths, we could have created a song of
screams, loud enough to be heard and felt by psychic souls on several
nearby worlds. But it wouldn't be enough. The butchery of astropaths is
hardly a rarity. How many Legion warbands have done the same over
the millennia? I couldn't even begin to guess. Raiders have used the ploy
since time out of mind, as a means to cover their tracks. What better way
to mask your escape than to stir the cauldron of the warp, thickening the
primordial ooze to slow any pursuers? Even with the risk of daemonic
contagion, it often works well enough to be worth the risk.'

Talos walked around the chamber, addressing the mortal crew, meeting their eyes in turn. 'All this power and pain at our fingertips. Weapons
that can level cities. A warship capable of breaking entire fleet blockades.
But that means nothing in the Long War. We can leave scars on steel,
but so can any ragged pirate vessel with a battery of macro-cannons. We
are the Eighth Legion. We wound flesh, steel and souls alike. We scar

memories. We scar minds. Our actions must mean something, or we deserve to be forgotten, left to rot amongst ancient mythology.'

Talos took a breath, his voice growing soft again. 'So I gave voice to the song. The song means something: a truer weapon than any laser battery or bombardment cannon. But how best to twist this silent song into a blade that might bleed the Imperium?'

Cyrion watched the crew's faces. Several of them seemed keen to answer, while others waited with eyes lit by interest. Throne in flames, it was really working. He'd never have believed it possible.

Uzas was the one to answer. He looked up, as if he'd been paying attention all along. 'Sing it louder,' he said.

Talos's lips curled into the same sick smile as before. He looked to several of the crew, as if sharing some jest with them.

'*Sing it louder*,' he smiled. 'We turned our singers into a screaming chorus. Weeks and weeks of pain and fear, condensed into the purity of absolute agony. Then add the torture of others to their own torment. The butchery of thousands of humans is nothing – a drop in the warp's ocean. But the astropaths drank it in. They had no choice but to hear, and see, and feel what was taking place. When the psykers finally died, they expired as husks bloated by genocidal suffering, blinded by the ghosts of the dead all around them. We fed them agony and fear, night after night. They screamed it out as psychic pain. They screamed it out upon the moment of death, right here, into the astropathic duct. World after world is hearing it, even now. The astropaths on those worlds magnify it with their own miseries, adding verses and choruses to the song, sharing it with the other worlds in line.'

Talos paused, the smile finally fading. His eyes slid from all others, now reflecting the bluish gleam of the hololithic.

'All of this was possible because of one final gamble. One last way to make the song louder than we could ever have imagined.'

'The Navigator,' Mercutian breathed. He could scarce give the idea countenance.

Talos nodded. 'Octavia.'

SHE AWOKE TO find she wasn't alone.

One of the Night Lords stood nearby, consulting an auspex reader mounted on his bulky vambrace.

'Flayer,' she said. Her own voice horrified her, to hear it so scratchy and weak. Her hands went to her stomach on instinct.

'Your progeny still lives,' Variel said distractedly. 'Though by all rights, he should not.'

Octavia swallowed the lump in her throat. 'He? It's a boy?'

'Yes.' Variel didn't look up from his scanner, still making adjustments and turning dials. 'Was I unclear? The child is in possession of all attributes and biological distinctions implicit in the term *he*. Thus it is, as you say, a male.'

He looked up at her at last. 'You have a long list of biorhythmic anomalies and physiological deficiencies that need addressing in the coming weeks if you are to regain full health. Your attendants have been briefed in full of the sustenance you require, and the chemicals you are to ingest.' He paused for a moment, watching her with his pale blue eyes never blinking once. 'Am I speaking too quickly?'

'No.' She swallowed again. Truth told, her head was swimming and she was relatively sure she'd be throwing up in the next couple of minutes.

'You do not seem to be following me,' Variel said.

'Just get on with it, you son of a bitch,' she snapped.

He ignored the insult. 'You are also risking dehydration, Kings' Disease, rachitis, and an acute scorbutus flaw. Your attendants are aware of how to treat the symptoms and prevent further development. I have left the relevant medicinal narcotics with them.'

'And the baby?'

Variel blinked. 'What of it?'

'Is it... healthy? What will all of these treatments do to him?'

'What does that matter?' Variel blinked a second time. 'My mandate is to ensure your continuance in serving as the ship's Navigator. I have no interest in the misbegotten fruit of your womb.'

'Then why haven't you... ended it?'

'Because if it survives gestation and infancy, it will eventually undergo implantation to serve in the Legion. I had thought that was obvious, Octavia.'

The Apothecary checked his narthecium readings one more time, and made his way to the chamber door, boots thudding as he went.

'He won't be one of the Legion,' she said to his back, feeling her tongue tingle with a rush of saliva. 'You'll never have him.'

'Oh?' Variel turned enough to look over his shoulder. 'You seem very certain.'

He walked from the room, scattering her attendants before him. Octavia stared at the bulkhead as it whined closed in his wake. Once he was gone, she threw up a thin trickle of sticky bile, and blacked out again, slumped in her throne. That was how Septimus found her, almost half an hour later.

By the time he entered, Vularai and the other attendants had connected the nutrient feeds to the implanted sockets on Octavia's limbs.

'Move aside,' he told them as they barred his way.

'Mistress is resting.'

'I said, move aside.'

Several of them started to reach for their scavenged pistols and the shotguns concealed beneath dirty robes. Septimus drew both of his pistols in a smooth movement, aiming them at two separate hunched attendants.

'Let's not do this,' he said to them.

Before he even knew Vularai was there, he felt the keen edge of her blade at the back of his neck.

'She needs her rest,' the attendant hissed. Septimus had never paid heed to just how snake-like her voice really was. He wouldn't have been surprised to learn her tongue was forked beneath all that bandaging. 'And you are not supposed to be here.'

'And yet here I am, and I am not leaving.'

'Septimus,' came Octavia's weak voice.

All of them turned at the whispered word. 'You woke her,' accused Vularai.

He didn't bother answering. Septimus shrugged her off, and moved to sit by Octavia's throne.

She was pale – as pale as if she'd been born to this life – and she was almost cadaverously thin, but for the swell of her stomach. Blood scabbed her forehead and nose, where it had dried after running down from beneath her bandana. He wasn't sure why, but one of her eyes wasn't opening, and she licked cracked, split lips before speaking.

It must have shown on his face.

'I look that awful, do I?' she asked.

'You... have looked better.'

Her fingertips managed a weak brush along his unshaven cheek, before she sagged back into her throne. 'I'm sure I have.'

'I heard what they did to you. What they made you do.'

She closed her eyes and nodded. When she spoke, only one side of her mouth moved. 'It was quite clever, really.'

'Clever?' he asked, his teeth clenching. '*Clever?*'

'To use a Navigator,' she sighed. 'The secret sight. To rip their souls from their bodies... with the purest, strongest... connection to the warp...' She laughed without breath, doing little more than shivering. 'My precious eye. I saw them dying. I saw them torn loose. Souls cast into the warp. Like mist. Pulled apart by the wind.'

He stroked her hair back from her sweating face. Her skin was ice. 'Enough,' he said. 'It's over.'

'My father told me there was no worse way to die. Nothing more painful. Nothing more damning. A hundred souls, driven mad by fear and torture, killed by looking into the warp itself.' She gave another quivering, breathless laugh. 'I can't even imagine how many people are hearing those mortis-cries now. I can't picture how many are dying.'

'Octavia,' he said, resting his hand on her stomach. 'Rest. Recover your strength. We're getting off this ship.'

'They'll find us.'

Septimus kissed her wet temple. 'They are welcome to try.'

XIX
FALSE PROPHECY

TALOS REFLECTED ALONE, sat in the silence of First Claw's arming chamber. After the activity of recent weeks, he craved the calm.

The *Echo of Damnation* remained in its sedate drift, waiting for its Navigator to recover before they risked the flight back to the Great Eye. Even a short flight was likely to kill Octavia in her current condition, let alone a journey lasting months or years, sailing across most of the galaxy.

Talos was all too cognisant of the fact she'd never sailed into a true warp storm. The Eye was an unwelcoming haven, even for experienced sorcerers. An untested Navigator, especially an exhausted one, was a liability he had no wish to test until he had no other choice.

He still saw the eldar when he closed his eyes. Their lithe figures danced in flickering after-images, shadows against shadows – black and silent one moment, silver and screaming the next.

The eldar. He no longer needed to be asleep to see them. That, too, was a problem. Was Tsagualsa to blame? If that was the case, breathing the carrion world's air had done the opposite of what he'd hoped. Despite gifting him with the inspiration he'd desired, had it also accelerated his degeneration like some cure for cancer that did nothing but fuel the tumours' black spread?

He'd argued with Variel in the apothecarion all those weeks ago, but the truth had a cold core. He needed no auspex reading or biorhythmic scan to tell him he was falling apart. The dreams were evidence enough. They'd been growing worse since Crythe – more crippling, less reliable – but even that had been manageable. For a time, at least.

No. The eldar dreams were different, because they were more than mere dreams. He no longer needed to be asleep to feel them. The howls and blades of mad aliens were becoming as real as the walls around him, as true as the voices of his brothers.

What plagued him most was the question of why he still saw them at all. Since Hell's Iris, when the dreams had first come, he'd been unashamed in his reluctance to return to the Eye. Now, though, the prophecy seemed void. Xarl couldn't die twice. He'd never been so relieved to be wrong.

It wasn't easy to decide how much to tell the others. Too much, and they'd never follow him. Too little, and they'd yank at their chains, resisting his guidance.

'Talos,' said a shadow at the edge of his vision. Instinct forced him to glance left. Nothing. No figure. No sound. As he exhaled, he heard the clash of a blade against ceramite, as faint and misty as a memory. It could have been coming from somewhere nearby on board the ship; it could have been in his mind.

His brothers' objections coiled amongst the eldar-thoughts. The other legionaries wanted to run right away, heedless of killing the Navigator in the process. Lucoryphus had advocated pushing Octavia as far as they could, then simply trusting the warp's currents to lead them home once she was dead. Voices from among the other Claws raised similar desires. Even if the warp carried them elsewhere, the risk was better than remaining here for the certainty of Imperial vengeance.

He'd calmed them down, forcing himself not to show disgust. They sounded craven, either without realising or simply without caring. Imperial revenge would take a great many months to arrive, at best. Warp flight close to the afflicted worlds would be ruined for a long while yet. Then subsector command nodes would have to realise a pattern in the planets affected, which would take months – even years – leaving them here, untouched, with impunity. Even after the pattern was recognised, the Imperium's own disparate worlds would take an unknowable age to seek the song's origin in the telepathic duct.

No, there was nothing to fear just yet. Not from the Imperium, anyway.

'Talos,' another voice whispered. Something black and slender flitted across his vision. He glanced its way to see it vanish.

'Talos,' the air whispered again.

He lowered his head, breathing slowly, perversely enjoying the pulsating throb of veins in his skull. The pain was a reminder that he was awake. A small blessing, but one he was thankful for.

'Talos.' There was a click, followed by a soft metallic whine as a laspistol charged.

With his head still in his hands, he felt the threat of a smile tease the corner of his lips. So it was finally happening. He'd been expecting this for so long now: the seventh slave had changed since the eighth came aboard, and this was a confrontation he'd been anticipating with very little relish.

'Septimus,' he sighed. 'A poor choice of moment to make your move.'

'Look at me, heretic.' The voice wasn't his slave's. Slowly, he lifted his head.

'Oh,' Talos said. 'Greetings, archregent. However did you find yourself here?'

He watched the old man with an almost distracted air. The liver-spotted hands shivered as they held the stolen pistol. Blood flushed the old man's cheeks; blood that in a true warrior would have flooded to the muscles, ready for battle. Here was an old fool thinking with his head, not fighting with his heart. Talos doubted he would even shoot.

'As a point of interest,' the prophet said, 'from the angle of the weapon, you are aiming too low.'

The Archregent of Darcharna, still clad in his filthy robes of state, lifted the pistol higher.

'Better,' Talos allowed. 'However, even if you were to shoot me at this range, it is still unlikely to kill me. Humanity breeds its demigods from hardy stock, you know.'

The old man kept his silence. He seemed caught between the urge to cry, to pull the trigger, or to flee the room.

'I would be intrigued to learn how you are here,' Talos added. 'You should be on Tsagualsa with the others we spared. Did one of the other Claws bring you up here to serve as a slave?'

Still no answer.

'Your silence is vexing, old one, and this conversation grows increasingly one-sided. I would also like to know how you managed to survive several weeks on board without meeting an unpleasant demise in the *Echo's* halls.'

'One of... of the others...'

'Yes. One of the other Claws brought you aboard as a toy. I had guessed. Now what brings you to this ill-advised assassination, so painfully destined to fail?'

For a moment, just a moment, the old man's face pulled taut, lengthening into something inhumanly elegant that regarded him with soulless and slanted eyes. Talos swallowed. The eldar visage vanished, leaving only the old man.

The archregent didn't reply.

'Did you intend to speak, or did you simply come here in order to aim that useless weapon at me?'

Talos rose to his feet. The gun followed him up, shaking more noticeably now. Without any sign of haste or impatience, Talos took the pistol from the old man's hands. He crunched it in his fist, and dropped the wreckage to the decking.

'I am too tired to kill you, old man. Please just go.'

'Thousands of people,' the archregent whispered through spit-wet lips. 'Thousands and thousands... You...'

'Yes,' Talos nodded. 'I am a terrible creature likely to burn in the eternal fire of your beloved Emperor's judgement. You cannot imagine how many times I have heard similar threats, always whispered by the downtrodden, the powerless, and the desperate. They change nothing, neither the words nor the people that weep them. Is there anything else?'

'All those people…'

'Yes. All those people. They are dead, and you have been broken by what you saw. That is no excuse to whine at me, human.'

Talos picked the old man up by the throat and hurled him into the corridor beyond. He heard the twiggish snap of brittle bones breaking, but couldn't bring himself to care. *Irritating old fool.*

'Talos,' said a voice within the room. His eyes flicked left and right, revealing nothing. He wasn't surprised.

As he lowered himself down again, hanging his aching head, he heard the dream-sounds of rainfall and female laughter drifting back once again.

No, the thought came unbidden, cold and rancid with sudden truth. *The Imperium will not come to answer this atrocity. Someone else will.*

'This is Talos,' he voxed. 'How long has the Navigator been at rest?'

A servitor's voice replied after a seven-second delay. 'Thirty-two hours, fift–'

'That's long enough. Ready the ship to leave the system.'

The next voice was Cyrion's, still on the bridge where Talos had left him in command.

'Brother, even Variel said we shouldn't risk pushing her for a week or more.'

Talos heard a howl behind Cyrion's voice – strangely feral and feminine all at once. It was too clear to be vox corruption, but couldn't possibly be real.

Yet the howl unlocked another memory, granting it like an unwanted gift. *Rainfall.* Talos closed his eyes to focus. *A murderess in the rain. Somewhere… Beneath a storm…*

No, no, no. It was starting to make a sick sense now. He'd avoided taking them to the Eye, unwilling to face the eldar of Ulthwé, refusing to bow to the fate that his brothers would die at their hands. When Xarl had fallen at Tsagualsa, he'd dared to believe the prophecy broken. Surely, once broken, it could be ignored as another false dream.

Surely, his own thoughts mocked him. *Surely we're safe now.*

'Ready the ship to sail the warp,' Talos ordered. 'We need to leave immediately.'

'It will take hours just to prepare the–'

Talos ignored whatever Cyrion was saying. He was already out of First Claw's arming chamber, vaulting the slumped body of the archregent and running through the twisting corridors, sprinting towards the prow.

No, no, no…

'I do not care about the preparations,' he voxed. 'We'll sail blind if we have to.'

'Are you insane?' Cyrion spat back. 'What are you thinking?'

Just a little more time, his racing mind begged. *We have to get away from here.*

He was halfway to Octavia's chambers when the sirens began their careening wail.

'All hands,' came Cyrion's voice over the shipwide address system. 'All hands to battle stations. Eldar warships inbound.'

AN IMPERIAL CRUISER doesn't merely slip back into reality from passage through the warp; it breaks back into the material universe from a wound in the void, trailing the smoky tides of madness still clinging to its hull. Their passage through the Sea of Souls was a storm of colour, sound, and screaming devilry.

Cyrion had to admit, for all the violence and trauma of such travel, it was at least familiar.

The eldar warships played their own games with the warp. They showed no contrails of clinging ethereal energy, nor did they herald their arrival by vicious detonations in the fabric of space and time. One moment he saw stars. The next, eldar vessels shimmered into being, shadows ghosting out of other shadows, gliding towards the drifting *Echo of Damnation.*

Cyrion knew next to nothing about the metaphysics of eldar void travel, nor was he of a mind to care. He'd heard, at some point, the word 'webway' spoken of in regards to their eerie interstellar wanderings, but the concept meant nothing to him. Meeting the eldar in the past had rarely ended well, and he loathed them even more than he loathed most of his brothers, which made it a very rich hatred indeed. They repulsed him, and it was not a discomfort that he cherished, even perversely.

He saw the warships coming on the occulus, as if space itself had breathed them into being, and he acted on instinct. Being Cyrion, the first thing he did was to swear, loudly and with feeling. The second thing he did was to order the crew to battle stations. The third thing he did was to swear again; a long river of curses that might've made even the primarch blink.

They came on in grand, sweeping arcs, never sailing straight. Each one was forever banking and weaving through the void in dramatic arcs that would have been impressive – as well as impossible – for an Imperial vessel. As he watched the eldar warships dancing with such foul grace, he felt a raw, stale taste on the tongue. Even his acidic saliva glands instinctively reacted to his disgust, for mankind's technology, even flavoured by the taint of Chaos, could never emulate that alien swooping. It was difficult to reconcile what his senses were seeing with what was physically possible in the depths of space.

'You there,' he said to one of the crew. 'Yes, you. Ready the ship for a warp run.'

'Under way, lord. We heard Lord Talos's orders.'

'Good,' said Cyrion, already ignoring the man. 'Activate void shields, run out the guns... All the usual furore, if you please.'

He sat in the command throne – Talos's throne, if he was being perfectly honest – and watched the occulus with a wary eye.

'Should we engage, lord?' one of the uniformed crew asked.

'Tempting. We outsize them both by a measure of magnitudes. But they're likely outriders – hold back for now, focus on getting ready to break into the warp when the Navigator decides to grace us with her attention.'

On the occulus, a distant image resolved behind the first two. This one was much larger, sporting great angled wings of bone and shimmering scales. The glassy serpent-skin sails flashed as they reflected the sun, and the warship gathered speed.

'Another eldar warship entering long range scanning,' the scrymaster called out. 'Capital class.'

'So I see. And we don't outsize that one quite so convincingly,' Cyrion admitted. 'How long until they reach us?'

The hunchbacked Master of Auspex shook his burn-scarred head. 'Difficult to say, lord. A projection based on conventional thrust would be almost thirty minutes. If they keep dancing through the void like this, it could be five, it could be twenty.'

Cyrion reclined, putting his boots up on the throne's armrest. 'Well then, my dear and loyal crew. We have a short while to enjoy each other's company before we die. Isn't that *delightful*?'

TALOS CAME THROUGH the bulkhead in a blur of blue ceramite and a roar of armour joints. Octavia's attendants scattered before him, bolting with all the haste of rats fleeing a hunting cat. Even Vularai flinched back, unsurprised that her query of 'My lord?' went unanswered.

Octavia was already coming around, awoken by the emergency sirens. She jumped in her seat as Talos thudded to a halt, boots hammering into the deck hard enough to shake her throne.

She looked almost dizzy with exhaustion. Despite sleeping for hours on end and having her nutrient feeds tailored to her specific needs, the ordeal of the murders he'd forced her to commit mere days ago still played out in dark patches across her features, as did the long flight to reach this point at the Imperium's edge. Weary circles noosed her eyes, and her clammy skin looked greasy in the chamber's dull light.

She looked up at Talos, the sway of her head on sore neck muscles betraying the migraine going on behind her face.

'Eldar?' she asked, confused. 'Did I hear that correctly?'

'Jump the ship,' he demanded. 'Do it now.'

'I... What?'

'Listen to me,' he growled. 'The eldar are here. They sensed the psychic scream we made – or worse, their witches predicted it beforehand, and they had a fleet lying in wait. More will come, Octavia. Jump the ship now, or we all die.'

She swallowed, reaching for the first of her throne-union link cables. Weakness left her hands shaking, but her voice was firm and clear.

'Where? Where should we go? The Eye?'

'Anywhere but *here* or *there*, Octavia. You have a whole galaxy. Just find us somewhere to hide.'

PART FOUR

VOID STALKER

XX

FLIGHT

THE WARSHIP RAN, again and again and again.

Two days after its initial flight, it sailed back into the true void only to find a blockade of eldar cruisers hanging silently in space, lying in wait. The *Echo of Damnation* came about in a wrenching arc, diving as it rolled, and thrust its way back beyond the physical universe and into the relative safety of the warp.

Three days later, it dropped from its interstellar journeying to drift closer to the world Vanahym, only to find five eldar cruisers already orbiting the world. The alien ships angled their reflective sails as the Night Lord vessel came closer, cutting out of orbit to intercept the VIII Legion warship.

Again, the *Echo* ran.

The third time it left the warp, it didn't slow down for the eldar blockade. The *Echo of Damnation* surged through the cold tides of real space, broadsides singing into the dark, railing at the alien vessels as it screamed between them. The eldar ships banked and turned with impossible grace, even those with their solar sails shattered by VIII Legion weapons batteries. The *Echo* outran a fight it couldn't win, concentrating all of its retaliatory fire on holding the xenos warships at bay long enough for a return to the warp.

The fourth, the fifth, the sixth – each successive emergence met with greater resistance, the farther they flew from their point of origin.

'They're herding us,' Cyrion said after the eighth re-entry and subsequent flight.

Talos had simply nodded. 'I know.'

'We're not going to reach the Great Eye, brother. They won't let us. You know that, don't you?'

'I know.'

A week passed. Two weeks. Three.

On its fourteenth exit from the warp, the *Echo of Damnation* broke the peace of a silent sky. It tore its way back into the material realm, riding a storm of violet lightning and carnelian smoke. This time, there was no rupturing re-entry to the depths of clean space; no pause to gather their bearings and scan for enemies.

This time, the *Echo* ripped into reality and kept running, engines flaring hot. The warship powered its way through the psychotic hues of the Praxis Nebula, diving ever deeper into the immense gaseous cloud. Talos let the engines rage on, powering the ship ahead at hull-rattling speed.

'No eldar,' Cyrion observed.

'No eldar yet,' Talos replied. 'All ahead full. Bury the ship in the nebula, as deep as she'll go.'

The scrymaster called out as his servitors began to chatter. 'Lord Talos, the–'

'The scanner interference,' Talos calmly interrupted, 'is why we're here. I am aware of it, scrymaster.'

First Claw gathered around the central throne, maintaining vigil with their leader. One by one, the other surviving Night Lords walked onto the command deck, their eyes lifted to the occulus, watching in silent unity.

THE HOURS PASSED.

Talos occasionally let his gaze leave the stars to glance again at the tactical hololithic. Like the viewscreen, the hololithic projection showed stars, a world turning in the void, and nothing else.

'How long?' he asked.

'Four hours,' said Cyrion. He walked by the prow weapons console, looking over the shoulders of the seven uniformed officers stationed there. 'Four hours and thirty-seven minutes.'

'The longest yet,' Talos observed.

'By far.'

The prophet leaned forward in the ornate command throne. The golden Blood Angels blade rested against one of the throne's arms, the prophet's bolter rested on the other. A great high seat of fire-blackened bronze, the throne itself loomed above the rest of the command deck from its central dais.

Talos had always known the Exalted relished being in such a position, lifted above his brethren on the *Covenant of Blood*. The prophet didn't share the sentiment. If anything, he felt detached from his kindred, and the thought wasn't a comfortable one.

'I believe we're clear,' Cyrion ventured.

'Don't say that,' replied Talos. 'Don't even *think* it.'

Cyrion listened to the sounds of the command deck, which had a melody all its own: the grind of levers, the mumble of servitors, the thump of boots. A soothing sound.

'You should rest,' he said to Talos. 'When did you last sleep?'

'I still haven't slept.'

'You're joking.'

Talos turned to Cyrion, his white face drawn, his dark eyes dulled by sleeplessness. 'Do I look as though I'm joking?'

'No, you look as though you died and forgot to stop moving. It's been three weeks now. You're being foolish, Talos. Go. Rest.'

The prophet turned back to the occulus. 'Not yet. Not until we've escaped.'

'And if I summon the Flayer to give you a lecture?'

'Variel has already lectured me on the matter.' Talos gave a rueful sigh. 'He had charts and everything. In meticulous detail, he noted the strain I was putting on my mind, citing the catalepsean node's operational limit of keeping a legionary awake for two weeks.'

'A physiology lecture. I sometimes think he forgets you were once an Apothecary.'

Talos didn't answer. He kept watching the stars on the occulus.

Three weeks, the prophet thought. He'd not slept since the endless chase began, when the eldar ghosted out of the void mere hours after he'd murdered the astropaths. How many times had they ripped their way in and out of the warp since then? How many times had they emerged back into real space, only to find yet another eldar squadron waiting for them?

Three weeks.

'We can't keep running, Cyrion. Octavia will die. We'll be stranded.'

Cyrion looked up at Ruven's crucified bones, hanging in state. 'I almost regret the fact you killed the sorcerer. His powers would be a boon now.'

Talos turned weary eyes to his brother. Something akin to amusement gleamed in those black depths.

'Perhaps so,' Talos allowed. 'But then we'd have to suffer through his endless conversation.'

'A fine point,' Cyrion replied. As soon as he finished the words, sirens started to cry out in ululating unity across the deck.

'They've found us,' Talos leaned back in the throne, his voice an exhausted whisper. 'They've found us *again*. Octavia, this is the bridge.'

Her voice sounded as weary as Talos looked. 'I'm here,' she said over the chamber's vox-speakers.

'So are the eldar,' said Talos. 'Ready the ship to run again.'

'I can't keep this up,' she said. 'I can't. I'm sorry, I can't.'

'They'll be on us in twenty minutes at the most. Get us out of here.'

'I *can't.*'

'You've been saying that for over a week.'

'Talos, please, listen to what I'm saying. This will kill me. One more jump. Two more. It doesn't matter. You're killing me.'

He rose from the command throne, walking to the dais rail and leaning down, watching the organised chaos of the bridge below. The hololithic table flickered with ghostly threats sailing closer: six eldar warships, their wing-sails lost in the mist of distortion.

'Octavia,' he said, softening his voice. 'They can't chase us forever. I need a little more from you. Please.'

It took several seconds, but the ship itself gave the answer. Shaking gripped the deck as the warp drive began to amass the energy required to break through one reality into another.

'Do you remember,' her voice echoed across the command deck, 'when I first took control of the *Covenant*?' There was a curious duality in her tone as she bonded with the ship's machine-spirit, an unwholesome unity that made Talos's skin crawl.

'I remember,' he voxed back. 'You said you could kill us all, for we were heretics.'

'I was angrier then. And scared.' He heard her take a breath. 'All hands, brace for entry into the Sea of Souls.'

'Thank you, Octavia.'

'You shouldn't thank slaves,' she replied, her twinned voice resonating around the chamber. 'They'll get delusions of equality. And besides, this hasn't worked yet. Save your thanks for when we're sure we'll survive. Are we running or hiding this time?'

'Neither,' said Talos.

Every eye on the bridge turned towards him. The Legion warriors still on the command deck watched keenest of all.

'We're not running,' Talos voxed to Octavia, well aware that everyone was watching him, 'and we're not hiding. We're making a stand.'

Talos relayed the coordinates through the keypad on the arm of his throne. 'Take us back there.'

'Throne,' Octavia swore, making half the bridge crew wince at the Imperial expletive. 'Are you sure?'

'We don't have the fuel to keep dancing to their song, and we can't break their blockade. If we're being herded like prey, then I'll at least choose where we'll fight back.'

Cyrion came to the throne's side again. 'And if they're waiting for us there?'

Talos looked at his brother for a long moment. 'What do you want me to say, Cyrion? We'll do what we always do: we'll kill them until they kill us.'

WITH THE SHIP in the warp, Talos walked to meet with the one soul he had every reason – yet no desire – to see once again. Sword in hand, he headed down the winding corridors, his thoughts dark and his options even darker. He was going to do something he should've done a long time ago.

The immense doors leading into the Hall of Reflection rumbled open as he stood before them. Menial adepts turned to regard his entrance, while servitors went about their business.

'Soul Hunter,' said one of the robed Mechanicum priests in respectful greeting.

'My name is Talos,' the prophet replied, walking past the man. 'Please use it.'

He felt a hand grip his shoulder guard, and turned to face the one who dared touch him. Such a breach of decorum was most unlike any of the adepts.

'Talos,' said Deltrian, inclining the staring skull that served as his face. 'Your presence, while not a violation of any behavioural code, is unexpected. Our last interaction ended with the agreement you would be summoned if there was any change in the subject.'

The subject, thought Talos. *Very quaint.*

'I am aware of our agreement, Deltrian.'

The robed, chrome cadaver lifted his hand from the warrior's pauldron. 'Yet you come here armed, a blade drawn in this holy place. In processing your demeanour, only one outcome holds any significant probability.'

'And that would be?'

'You have come to destroy the sarcophagus, and slay Malcharion within it.'

'Good guess.' Talos turned away, heading into the annexed chamber where the war-sage's ornate coffin was being held.

'Wait.'

Talos halted, but not because Deltrian ordered it. His shock froze him in his tracks, the blade still held in a loose fist. He took in the sight before him: the ornate sarcophagus linked and chained into place, mounted on the ceramite shell of an armoured Dreadnought. The blue aura of weak, focused stasis fields still played around the war machine's limbs – locking them into immobility.

'Why have you done this?' Talos didn't look away. 'I gave no orders to prepare him as a Dreadnought.'

Deltrian hesitated before speaking. 'The later rituals of resurrection require the subject's installation within the holy shell.'

Talos wasn't sure what to say. He wanted to object, but knew nothing was likely to move Deltrian to see any kind of sense. His surprise doubled when he saw another figure was already in the chamber. He sat with his back to the wall, idly squeezing the trigger of a chainaxe, listening to the blades whine.

'Brother,' the other Night Lord greeted him.

'Uzas. What brings you here?'

Uzas shrugged. 'I come here often, to watch him. He should come back to us. We need him, but he doesn't want to be needed.'

Talos breathed, low and slow, before addressing Deltrian. 'Activate the vox-speakers.'

'Lord, I–'

'Activate the vox-speakers or I will kill you.'

'As you command.' Deltrian walked on his stick-thin legs, clicking his way over to the primary control console. Several levers cranked with unhealthy grinding sounds.

The chamber filled with screaming. Breathless, animalistic, exhausted screaming. Somehow, it sounded like an old man – that degree of ancient, weary weakness.

Talos closed his eyes for a moment, though his helm stared ahead, as remorseless as ever.

'No more,' he whispered. 'I am ending this.'

'The subject is biologically stable,' Deltrian vocalised louder, to speak over the screaming. 'He has also been rendered into a state of mental stability, as well.'

'You think this sounds like mental stability?' The prophet still hadn't turned around. 'Can't you hear the screaming?'

'I can hear it,' Uzas interrupted. 'Bitter, bitter music.'

'I am indeed aware of the vocalised pain response,' Deltrian said. 'I believe it indicates–'

'No.' Talos shook his head. 'No. Don't try that with me, Deltrian. I *know* there's something human inside you. This isn't a "vocalised pain response". It's screaming, and you know it. Lucoryphus was right about you: no mind could conceive of the Shriek and be as truly detached as you claim. You understand fear and pain. I know you do. You are one of us, whether you wear ceramite or not.'

'The "screaming" then,' Deltrian allowed. For the first time, there was a nuance of tone in his voice: an iota of displeasure. 'We have brought him to a state of mental stability,' he continued, 'relatively speaking.'

'And if you deactivated the stasis locks on the machine-body?'

Deltrian had to pause again. 'It is likely that the subject would kill us all.'

'Stop saying *the subject*. This is Malcharion, a hero of our Legion.'

'A hero you mean to murder.'

Talos rounded on the tech-priest, the blade flaring to electric life in his hand. 'He has already died twice. A fool's hope allowed me to let you play your games with his corpse, but he is not coming back to us. I see that now. It is wrong to even try, for it goes against his final wish. You are no longer allowed to toy with his remains when it keeps him locked in some eternal, dead-minded agony. He deserves better than this.'

Deltrian hesitated again, processing through potential responses, seeking one to appease the ship's master in this uncomfortably mortal outburst. During the short pauses, the screaming continued unabated.

'The subject – that is to say, Malcharion – can still serve the Legion. With applied excruciation and the correct pain control, he would be a devastating presence on the battlefield.'

'I've already refused that path.' Talos still hadn't deactivated his sword. 'I will not tolerate abuse of his body, and in his madness he'd be just as likely to shoot our own forces.'

'But I can–'

'*Enough.* Throne in flames, this is why Vandred lost his mind. The infighting. The bickering. The Claws killing one another with knives in the dark. I may not have desired this idiotic pedestal my brothers have placed me upon, but I am here now, Deltrian. The *Echo of Damnation* is *my* ship. We may be running, we may be doomed, but I will not die without a fight, and I will not meet my end condoning this disgusting indignity. Do you understand me?'

Deltrian didn't, of course. This all sounded so very mortal to his audio receptors. Any actions based on emotion or mortal chemical processes were to be purged and ignored.

'Yes,' he said.

Talos laughed, little more than a bitter bark of amusement against the backdrop of the Dreadnought's screams. 'You're an awful liar. I doubt you even recall what it means to have any regard or trust in another soul.'

He turned his back on the priest, hauling himself up the sarcophagus, climbing it one-handed. The power sword crackled with a buzzing drone as it came close to brushing the stasis fields.

Talos stared at the image of Malcharion wrought in precious metals – his lord, his true lord before the years of Vandred's reign – resplendent in that ancient moment of ultimate glory.

'How different all of this might've been,' Talos said, 'had you lived.'

'Do not do this,' Deltrian vocalised his final objection. 'This course of action violates the tenets of my circle's oath to the Eighth Legion.'

Talos ignored him. 'Forgive me, captain,' he said to the graven image as he raised his blade.

'Wait.'

Talos turned, but only from surprise at who'd spoken. He remained as he was, halfway up the Dreadnought's armoured body, ready to sever the power feeds linking the life support machinery to the sarcophagus.

'Wait,' Uzas said again. The other Night Lord still hadn't risen to his feet. He tapped the blade of his axe on the decking, *tap-tap… tap-tap… tap-tap.* 'I hear something. A pattern. A pattern in the chaos.'

Talos turned to Deltrian. 'What does he mean?'

The tech-adept was so confused by the exchange that he almost shrugged. Assuming a less-human behaviour instead, he emitted a spurt of negative code.

'Clarification required. You are querying me as to the meaning of your own brother's words, in the expectation I can provide some insight?'

'I take your point,' said Talos. He dropped from the sarcophagus, boots thudding onto the deck. 'Uzas. Speak to me.'

Uzas still tapped the axe in a soft, clanging rhythm. 'Beneath the screams. Listen, Talos. Listen to the pattern.'

Talos glanced at Deltrian. 'Adept, can you not scan for what he might be speaking of? I hear only the screams.'

'I have sixteen slave processes running continual diagnostics.'

Uzas looked up at last. The bloody palm-print over his faceplate caught the chamber's dull light. 'The pattern is still there, Talos.'

'*What* pattern?'

'The… the pattern,' Uzas said. 'Malcharion lives.'

Talos turned back to the sarcophagus. 'Honoured adept, would you do me the service of explaining exactly what constitutes your order's ritual of resurrection?'

'That lore is forbidden.'

'Of course. Then maintain the secrets, simply… be vague.'

'That lore is forbidden.'

The prophet almost laughed. 'This is like drawing blood from a stone. Work with me, Deltrian. I need to know what you are doing to my captain in there.'

'A combination of synaptic enhancement pulses, electrical life support feeds, chemical stimulants and invasive physiological stabilisers.'

'A long time since you played Apothecary.' Uzas's grin was obvious from his tone. 'Shall I run and find the Flayer?'

Talos almost smiled despite himself, at hearing his lost brother making a jest. 'That sounds close to several of the methods we use in excruciation, Deltrian.'

'This is so. The subj– Malcharion has always been a troubling project. Awakening him requires an unusual degree of effort and focus.'

'But he's awake now,' Talos said. 'He's *awake*. Why maintain the ritual?'

Deltrian emitted an irritated blurt from his throat vocaliser.

'What in the warp's many hells was that?' Talos asked.

'A declaration of impatience,' the adept answered.

'How very mortal of you.'

Deltrian made the sound again, louder this time. 'With respect, you are speaking in ignorance. The rituals of resurrection do not cease purely because the subject is physically awakened. His mind is not cognisant of his surroundings. We have awakened his physical remnants, allowing him to bond with the holy war machine. But his mind is still lost. The ritual proceeds in order to refuel and restore his anima.'

'His… what?'

'His sense of self-awareness and capacity to reason in response to stimuli. His conscious sentience, as the manifestation of his living spirit.'

'His soul, you mean. His mind.'

'As you say. We have brought forth his brain and body, but not his mind and soul. There is a difference.'

Talos breathed in stale, recycled air through his teeth. 'I had a dog once. Xarl used to poke it with sticks.'

Deltrian froze. Although his eye lenses remained focused and unmoving, his internal processors raced for some kind of comprehension to find purchase with the current conversation.

'Dog,' he said aloud. 'Quadrupedal mammal. Family Canidae, Genus Canis, Order Carnivora.'

Talos was watching the sarcophagus again, listening to the screams. 'Yes, Deltrian. A dog. This was before Nostramo burned, before Xarl and I joined the Legion. We were children on the streets most nights, little knowing of the lawless madness taking hold of the world outside our city. We thought we lived at the heart of the gang warfare. That delusion came to be almost amusing, in time.'

Talos's tone never changed as he continued. 'The dog was a stray. I fed her, and she followed me forever afterwards. A mean bitch, never shy to show her teeth. Xarl would poke her with sticks when she slept. He found it hilarious to have the dog waking up, barking and snapping her jaws. He kept poking her once, even when she was up and barking at him. After a few minutes of his teasing, she went for his throat. He got his arm up in time, but she savaged his hand and forearm.'

'What happened to the dog?' Uzas asked, surprising Talos with the curiosity in his voice.

'Xarl killed her. He broke her head open with a tyre iron the next morning, while she was asleep.'

'She didn't wake up barking that time,' Uzas observed, in the same strange, soft tone.

Deltrian hesitated before replying. 'The relevance of this adjacent conversational pathway eludes me.'

Talos inclined his head to the sarcophagus. 'I am saying he's already awake, Deltrian. What have you done since he awoke? You told me he needed to be stabilised, but the fact remains: he's awake now. What have you been doing?'

'The rituals of resurrection. As stated: synaptic enhancement pulses, electrical life support feeds, chemical stimulants and invasive physiological stabilisers.'

'So you've filtered maddening chemicals and electrical stimulants through the body of a warrior wounded unto death, who has already demonstrated his symbiosis with the sarcophagus doesn't follow standard patterns.'

'But...'

'He's awake now, and in his madness, he's trying to go for your face. You've poked him with sticks, Deltrian.'

Deltrian mused on that. 'Processing,' he said. 'Processing.'

Talos was still listening to the screaming. 'Process faster. My captain's screams aren't music to me, Deltrian.'

'At no juncture has the subject registered within acceptable levels of higher cognitive function. If he had, then the rituals of resurrection would immediately be terminated.'

'But you said, Malcharion's reawakenings never followed conventional patterns.'

'I…' Deltrian, for the first time in centuries, began to doubt his findings. 'I… Processing.'

'You process that,' said Talos, walking away. 'Sometimes, Deltrian, it pays to share your secrets with those you can trust. And it isn't always a curse to think like a mortal.'

'A potential flaw occurs,' Deltrian vocalised, still watching the reams of calculations playing out on his retinas. 'Your supposition breaks the established and most holy ritual for a guess based primarily on emotion. Should your assumption prove incorrect, the damage to the subject physiology may be irreparable.'

'Does it seem as if I care?' Lightning danced down the golden blade as Talos drew near the central control console. He glanced across it, at the army of dials, scanning screens, thermal gauges, levers and switches. This was what pumped poison and pain into the body of his captain.

'Shut this down,' he said.

'Negative. I cannot allow such an event to come to pass, based on something as flawed as mortal supposition and a metaphor centred on the interrupted sleep of a quadruped mammal. Talos. Talos, do you hear me? Deactivate your sword, my lord, please.'

Talos raised the blade, and Uzas started laughing.

'*NO.*' Deltrian vocalised a piercing, weaponised burst of sound that would deafen any mortal and render them incapacitated. Talos's helm left him immune to such theatrics. He'd used the same scream himself as a weapon too many times to fall for it now. '*TALOS, NO.*'

The blade fell, and the repellent union of the power field and the console's delicate machinery bred an explosion that hurled debris across the chamber.

TALOS ROSE TO his feet in the silent aftermath, and his first thought was a bizarre one: Uzas was no longer gunning the chainaxe's trigger. Through the thin smoke, he saw his brother standing by the wall, and Deltrian halfway across the chamber floor.

The stasis fields were still active, imprisoning the Dreadnought's limbs, generating a hum severe enough to make the prophet's teeth itch. But the screaming had ceased – the sterile chamber felt somehow charged by its absence, akin to the richness of ozone in the air after a storm.

Talos watched the towering war machine, waiting, listening – his senses keen for any change at all.

'Talos,' Uzas called.

'Brother?'

'What was your dog's name?'

Keza, he thought. 'Be silent, Uzas,' he said.

'Hnnh,' the other Night Lord replied.

The Dreadnought didn't move. It didn't speak a word. It stood in silence, finally, *finally* dead.

'You killed Malcharion,' Uzas said as he walked closer. 'That was always your intent. All those things you said... You wanted to help him die, no matter what else you said.'

Victory had a foully hollow taste. Talos swallowed it back before speaking. 'If he lived, so be it. If he died, then the torture would end and we'd have complied with his final wish. But either way, I was ending it.'

Deltrian circled the ruined control console, his auxiliary arms deployed and picking up chunks of smoking debris.

'No,' he was saying. 'Unacceptable. Simply unacceptable. No, no, no.'

Talos couldn't keep from smiling an awkward, bitter smile. 'It's done.' The relief was palpable.

'Talos,' said a voice, avatarically guttural, loud enough to make the deck rumble.

In the same moment, the chamber's doors opened on grinding hydraulics. Cyrion entered, tossing a skull into the air and catching it each time it fell. Clearly it was one of the skulls from his armour, the chain broken and rattling at his hip.

He stopped, took in the scene – Talos and Uzas standing together, staring at the Dreadnought; Deltrian standing with all arms deployed, staring in the same way as the legionaries.

'Talos,' repeated the booming, vox-altered voice. 'I can't move.'

Cyrion laughed as he heard the voice. 'Captain Malcharion is awake again? Wasn't that worthy of a shipwide message?'

'Cyrion...' Talos managed to whisper. 'Cyrion, wait...'

'Cyrion,' the Dreadnought intoned. 'You're still alive. Wonders will never cease.'

'It's a fine thing to see you again, captain.' Cyrion walked over to the Dreadnought's chassis, looking up at the sarcophagus chained into its armoured housing. He caught the skull one more time.

'So,' he said to the immense war machine. 'Where should I begin? Here's a list of what's taken place while you slumbered...'

XXI
DEAD WEIGHT

THE LAST WARRIORS of the Tenth and Eleventh Companies had gathered in the *Echo of Damnation*'s war room. For seven hours, none of them moved, all remaining around the prophet and the war-sage. Occasionally, one of the warriors from the other Claws would speak up, adding their recollections to those spoken by Talos.

At last, Talos released a long, slow breath. 'And then you awoke,' he said.

The Dreadnought made a grinding sound deep within its innards, akin to a tank slipping gears. Talos wondered if that was the equivalent of a grunt, or a curse, or simply clearing your throat when there was no longer a throat to speak of.

'You did well.'

Talos almost flinched at the sudden proclamation. 'I see,' he said, purely from a need to say something, anything at all.

'You seem surprised. Did you expect my anger?'

Talos was acutely aware of the others watching him. 'I had expected to kill you at best, or awaken you at worst. Your anger – either way – hadn't occurred to me.'

Malcharion was the only thing in the room standing truly motionless. Though the others remained in place, they'd shift their posture from time to time, or tilt their heads, or share quiet words between Claw-kin. Malcharion was monumental in his stillness, never breathing, never moving at all.

'I should kill that accursed tech-priest,' he growled.

Across the chamber, Cyrion chuckled. Convincing Malcharion not to annihilate Deltrian for the traumatic and agonising resurrection had taken the two brothers some time. Deltrian, for his part, had been mortified – albeit in his subtle and unemotional way – at the failure of his resurrection rituals.

'But the eldar…' Talos wasn't sure how to finish the sentence.

841

'With no officers, you've managed to keep us alive this long, Talos. Reclaiming the Echo was a fine gesture, as well. The eldar's trap is meaningless. The only way to avoid it would have been to continue existing on the fringes, accomplishing nothing, making no difference to the galaxy. How many worlds will have fallen dark from your psychic scream?'

He shook his head, unsure of the specifics. 'Dozens. Perhaps a hundred. There is no way to know without accessing Imperial archives once the dust has settled on every afflicted world. Even then, we may never know.'

'That is more than Vandred ever did, even if it wasn't done on the field of battle. Do not be ashamed for fighting with your mind instead of your claws, for a change. The Imperium knows *something* happened out here. You've sown the seeds of a subsector legend. The night a hundred worlds fell dark. Some will be silent for months. Some will be lost to warp storms for years. Some will never be heard from again – the Imperium will no doubt arrive to find them reaved clean of life by the daemons loosed upon them. I confess, Talos, you are colder than I ever imagined, to dream up such a fate.'

Talos fought to turn the subject away from himself. 'You say the Imperium will know something happened here, but the eldar already know. For them to have reacted as fast as they did, their witches must have peered into the future and seen something in the tides of alien prophecy.'

The Dreadnought moved for the first time, turning on its waist axis to look over the gathered Night Lords.

'And this troubles you?'

Several heads nodded, while other warriors replied with 'Yes, captain.'

'I see what you are all thinking now.'

The Night Lords looked back at their captain, incarnated in his hulking shell, a towering monument to a life lived in devoted service.

'You do not wish to die. The eldar herd us into a final fight, and you fear the call of the grave. You think only of escape, of living to fight another day, of preserving your lives at the cost of all else.'

Lucoryphus hissed before speaking. 'You make us sound craven.'

Malcharion turned to the Raptor, his armoured joints grinding. 'You have changed, Luc.'

'Time changes all things, Mal.' The Raptor's head jerked to the side, with a whine of servos. 'We were the first on the walls at the Siege of Terra. We were the blades of the Eleventh before we were the Bleeding Eyes. And we are no cravens, Captain of the Tenth.'

'You have forgotten the lesson of the Legion. Death is nothing compared to vindication.'

The Raptor gave a harsh croak, his equivalent of a laugh. 'Death is still an ending I would rather avoid. Let us teach the lesson and live to teach it again another day.'

The Dreadnought gave a rumbling growl in response. 'The lesson wasn't learned if you have to teach it twice. Now stop whining. We'll face these aliens down before we worry about dying at the day's end.'

'It's good to have you back, captain,' said Cyrion.

'Then stop sniggering like an infant,' the Dreadnought replied. 'Talos. What is your plan? It had better be grand, brother. I have no desire to die a third time in anything less than glory.'

Several of the gathered legionaries shared a grim chuckle.

'That was no joke,' Malcharion growled.

'We didn't take it as one, captain,' said Mercutian.

The prophet activated the tactical hololithic. A dense spread of asteroids filled the space above the projection table, densest in the void above a shattered sphere. At the heart of the cluster, a pulsing rune showed the *Echo of Damnation*.

'We're safe for now, within the Tsagualsan asteroid field.'

Malcharion made the gear-grinding sound again. 'Why is the asteroid field so dense in this region? Even allowing for drift patterns, this is different to what I remember.'

Lucoryphus gestured to the hololithic. 'Talos shattered half of the moon.'

'Well.' Cyrion cleared his throat. 'Perhaps a fifth of it.'

'You have been busy, Soul Hunter.'

'How many times must I drag you back from the grave and tell you to stop calling me that?' Talos keyed in another set of coordinates. The hololithic shrank, zooming out to show Tsagualsa itself, and a host of other flickering runes ringing the world and its wounded moon.

'The enemy fleet is gathering beyond the field's perimeters. They're holding off from coming in after us, and are refraining from attacking the several thousand souls we left alive on the planet itself. For now, they seem content to wait, but this is it. The noose has tightened. Each time we sought to run forward, they forced us back. They know we have no choice but to fight. Our backs are to the wall.'

He looked around the war room, meeting the eyes of his last living brothers. The warriors of Tenth and Eleventh Companies, now grouped into four final Claws.

'You have a plan,' Malcharion rumbled. It wasn't a question this time.

Talos nodded. 'They've tightened the noose to force us into a fight, true enough. They have the firepower to annihilate the *Echo of Damnation*, without a shadow of a doubt. More of their vessels are arriving every hour. But we can still surprise them. They're expecting us to cut out of our hiding place and make a last stand in the void. I have a better idea.'

'Tsagualsa,' one of the other Night Lords said. 'You can't be serious, brother. We stand a better chance in the void.'

'No.' Talos refocused the hololithic. 'We don't. And this is why.' The flickering image resolved to show a spread of Tsagualsa's polar region, and the jagged remnants of a structure that had once rivalled the sky with its towers. Several of the gathered legionaries shared quiet words, or shook their heads in disbelief.

'Our fortress scarcely stands,' Talos said. 'Ten thousand years haven't been kind to the spires and battlements. But beneath the remains...'

'The catacombs,' Malcharion growled.

'Exactly so, captain. Auspex scans show the catacombs are largely unchanged. They still reach for kilometres in every direction, with entire sections of the labyrinth immune to orbital bombardment. A fight on *our* terms. If the eldar want us, they're welcome to come down into the dark. We'll hunt them as they hunt us.'

'How long can we last down there?' Lucoryphus asked, his vox-voice crackling.

'Hours. Days. Everything depends on the force they deploy to chase us. Assuming they land an army and flood into the tunnels, we'll still bleed them more savagely than we could in a fair fight. Hours and days are both longer than lasting a handful of minutes. I know which one I'll choose.'

The warriors were leaning forward now, hands resting on weapons. The atmosphere had turned, all reluctance filtering away. Talos continued, addressing the Claws.

'The *Echo of Damnation* is unlikely to survive even the brief run to the planet's atmosphere. Once we break from the densest region of the asteroid field, the eldar will be on us like a second skin. Everyone who intends to survive must be ready to evacuate the ship.'

'And the crew? How many souls aboard?'

'We're not certain. Thirty thousand, at least.'

'We cannot evacuate that many, nor can we afford essential crew members leaving their stations. What will you tell them?'

'Nothing,' replied Talos. 'They'll burn with the *Echo*. I'll remain on the bridge until the last moments, so the command crew doesn't realise the Legion is abandoning them to die.'

'Cold.'

'Necessity. There's more. This is our final stand, and we damn ourselves if we hold anything back. First Claw will remain with me, to arrange our final surprise for the eldar. The rest of you will make planetfall via drop pods and Thunderhawks as soon as you can. Lose yourself beneath Tsagualsa's surface, and be ready for what follows. Remember, even if we survive this, the Imperium is coming. They will find the survivors we left in Sanctuary, and spread the story of our deeds. The eldar care nothing for the populace. They're here for our blood.'

Fal Torm of the newly-gathered Second Claw gave a wicked chuckle.

'Suddenly you're talking of survival. What are the odds of us actually surviving this, brother?'

Talos's only reply was a singularly unpleasant smile.

HOURS LATER, THE prophet and the Flayer walked together through Variel's personal apothecarion. The facilities here were more specific in scope, with far fewer attendant slaves and servitors to get underfoot.

'Do you realise,' Variel asked, 'how much work you are asking me to simply cast aside?'

Cast aside, thought Talos. *And Malcharion calls me cold.*

'That's why I've come to you,' he said. As he spoke, he ran his hand along the mechanical arm of a surgical machine, imagining it in motion, in sacred use. 'Show me your work.'

Variel led Talos to the holding chambers at the apothecarion's rear. Both warriors looked in, where the Flayer's charges huddled in their bare cells, chained to the walls by collars around their throats.

'They look cold,' Talos noted.

'They probably are. I keep them in aseptic containment.' Variel gestured at the first of the children. The boy was no older than nine, yet his flesh showed the ragged pink scars of recent invasive surgery along his chest, back and throat.

'How many do you have?'

Variel didn't need to consult his narthecium for exact figures. 'Sixty-one between the ages of eight and fifteen, adapting well to the various stages of implantation. A further one hundred and nine of harvestable age, yet not ripe for implantation. Over two hundred have died so far.'

Talos knew those kinds of figures well enough. 'Those are very good survival rates.'

'I know that.' Variel almost sounded piqued. 'I am skilled at what I do.'

'That's why I need you to keep doing it.'

Variel entered one of the cells, where one of the children lay on his front, unmoving. The Flayer turned the boy over with the edge of his armoured boot. Dead eyes stared back up.

'Two hundred and thirteen,' he said, and gestured for a servitor to drag the infant's body away. 'Incinerate this,' he ordered.

'Compliance.'

Talos paid no heed to the servitor as it went about its funereal work. 'Brother, listen to me for a moment.'

'I am listening.' Variel didn't stop keying in notes on his vambrace, recording yet more details.

'You cannot stand with us on Tsagualsa.'

That made him stop. Variel's eyes – ice-blue to Talos's black – lifted in a slow, sterile stare.

'You tell a hilarious jest,' the Flayer said, utterly without warmth.

'No jest, Variel. You are holding the key to a significant piece of the Legion's future. I am sending you away before the battle. Deltrian's ship is capable of warp flight. You'll be going with him, as will your equipment and your work.'

'No.'

'This is not a debate, brother.'

'*No.*' Variel tore the flayed skin from his pauldron, revealing the winged skull beneath. The symbol of the VIII Legion stared back at Talos with hollow eye sockets. 'I wear the winged skull of Nostramo, the same as you. I will fight and die with you, on that worthless little world.'

'You owe me nothing, Variel. Not anymore.'

For once, Variel looked close to stunned. 'Owe you? *Owe you?* Is that how you see our brotherhood? A series of favours to be repaid? I *owe you* nothing. I will stand with you because we are both Eighth Legion. Brothers, Talos. Brothers unto death.'

'Not this time.'

'You cannot–'

'I can do whatever I wish. Captain Malcharion agrees with me. There is no room on Deltrian's vessel for more than ten additional warriors, and even that is better devoted to relics that must be returned to the Legion. You and your work must be preserved above all.'

Variel took a breath. 'Have you ever realised how often you interrupt those you are speaking with? It is almost as irritating a habit as Uzas constantly licking his teeth.'

'I'll bear that in mind,' Talos replied. 'I'll work on this alarming character flaw in the many years of life I have left. Now, will you be ready? If I give you twelve hours and as many servitors as you need, can you ensure your equipment is loaded aboard Deltrian's ship?'

Variel bared his teeth in an uncharacteristic angry smile. 'It will be done.'

'I've not seen you lose your temper since Fryga.'

'Fryga was an exceptional circumstance. As is this.' Variel pressed his fingertips to massage his closed eyes. 'You are asking much of me.'

'Don't I always? And I need you to do something else, Variel.'

The Apothecary met the prophet's eyes again, sensing something disquieting in the other Night Lord's tone. 'Ask.'

'Once you're gone, I want you to find Malek of the Atramentar.'

Variel raised a thin eyebrow. 'I am never returning to the Maelstrom, Talos. Huron will have my head.'

'I don't believe Malek will have remained there, nor do I believe the Atramentar would willingly join with the Blood Reaver. If they boarded a Corsair vessel, it was for another reason. I don't know what that reason was, but I trust him despite what happened. Find him if you can, and tell him his plan worked. Malcharion lived. The war-sage resumed command, leading the Tenth again in its final nights.'

'Is that all?'

'No. Give him my thanks.'

'I will do all of that, if you wish. But Deltrian's ship will not get far without needing to refuel. It is too small for long-range flight. We both know this.'

'It doesn't have to get far. Not at first. It just needs to get away from here.'

Variel gave a grunt of displeasure. 'The eldar may chase us.'

'Yes. They may. Any other complaints? You're wasting what little time I can give you.'

'What of Octavia? How will we sail the Sea of Souls without a Navigator?'

'You won't,' Talos replied. 'That's why she's going with you.'

HE COULD HAVE guessed her reaction would be somewhat less polite than Variel's. Had he bothered to predict such a thing, he'd have been quite correct.

'I think,' she said, 'I'm sick and tired of doing what you tell me.'

Talos wasn't looking directly at her. He walked around her throne, casting his gaze across the fluid pool, remembering the chamber's previous occupant. She'd died in filth, broken apart by the bolters of First Claw. Despite a memory that bordered on eidetic, Talos found he couldn't recall the creature's name now. *How rare.*

'Are you listening to me?' Octavia asked. The tone of her voice, so exquisitely courtly, drew his attention back.

'Yes.'

'Good.' She sat in her throne, one hand cradling her swelling stomach. Her near-emaciation made the pregnancy all the more prominent.

'What are the chances that Deltrian's ship will even make it to safety?'

Talos saw no sense in lying to her. He looked at her long and hard, letting the seconds pass by to the rhythm of her heartbeat. 'Your chance of survival is almost amusingly small. But a chance, nevertheless.'

'And Septimus?'

'He is our pilot and my slave.'

'He's the father of–'

Talos held up a hand in warning. 'Be careful, Octavia. Do not mistake me for a being able to be moved by emotional pleas. I have skinned children before their parents' eyes, you know.'

Octavia clenched her teeth. 'So he's staying.' She wasn't sure why she said it, but it came out in a spill, nevertheless. 'He'll follow me, somehow. You can't keep him here. I know him better than you do.'

'I have not yet decided his fate,' Talos replied.

'And what about you? What's your "fate"?'

'Do not speak to me in that tone of voice. This is not the Imperial Court of Terra, little highness. I am not impressed or awed by a haughty tone, so save your breath.'

'Sorry,' she said. 'I'm... just angry.'

'Understandable.'

'So what will you do? You're just going to let them kill you?'

'Of course not. You saw what happened when we tried to run, how we battered our prow against blockade after blockade. They won't let us run to the Great Eye. The noose started to close around us the moment I let out the psychic scream. We make our stand here, Octavia. If we leave it any longer, we'll lose our last chance to choose where this war will be fought.'

'You're not answering my question.'

'We're going to die.' Talos gestured to her bank of wall monitors, each one showing a different angle outside the ship – each one an eye staring upon the millions of rocks drifting in the void. 'How can I be clearer? How can it be more obvious? Outside this asteroid field, alien warships wait for us to make our move. We're dead, Octavia. That's all there is to it. Now ensure you are ready to leave the ship. Take whatever you wish, it matters nothing to me. You have eleven hours before I never want to see you again.'

He turned and left, shoving aside two of her attendants that didn't scatter quickly enough. She watched him walk away, tasting freedom on her tongue for the first time since she was captured, and unsure whether the taste was as pleasant as she remembered.

THE DOOR OPENED with smooth traction, revealing his master in the entrance arch.

Septimus looked up, Uzas's helm still in his hands. He'd been making the final repairs to the left eye lens socket.

'Lord?' he said.

Talos walked in, filling the humble chamber with a chorus of snarling joints and the ever-present hum of live armour.

'Octavia leaves the ship in eleven hours,' the Night Lord said. 'Your unborn child goes with her.'

Septimus nodded. His eyes never left his master's faceplate. 'With respect, lord, I had already guessed.'

Talos walked around the room, casting his attention here and there, never lingering for long on one thing. He took in the half-repaired pistols on the desk; the sketches of schematics; the charcoal drawings of his lover Octavia; and the clothing left in messy heaps. Above all, the small space bled a sense of life, of personality, of being the sanctum of one specific living soul.

A human's room, Talos thought, reflecting on the empty lifelessness of his own personal chambers – chambers resembling the quarters of any other legionary, except for the prophecies scrawled on the iron walls. *How different they are to us, to leave their imprint so sternly on the places they live.*

He turned back to Septimus, the man that had served him for almost a decade now.

'We must speak, you and I.'

'As you wish, master.' Septimus put the helm down.

'No. For the next few minutes, we will forget the roles of those who serve and those who are served. For now, I am neither *master*, nor *lord*. I am Talos.' The warrior removed his helm, looking down with his pale features calm.

Septimus felt the mad urge to reach for a weapon, unnerved by this strange familiarity.

'Why do I feel like this is some frightening prelude to slitting my throat?' he asked.

The prophet's smile never reached his dark eyes.

OCTAVIA AND DELTRIAN weren't getting along, which was a surprise to neither of them. She thought he was unbearably impatient for such an augmented creature, and he thought she smelled unpleasantly of the biological chemicals and organic fluids involved in mammalian reproduction. Their relationship had started with those first impressions, and gone downhill from there. It was a relief for both of them when she went to her quarters for her final preparations before flight.

She strapped herself into the uncomfortable throne in the belly of Deltrian's squat insectoid ship. Her 'chamber', such as it was, offered a single picter-screen and barely enough room to stretch her legs.

'Has anyone ever sat here and tested this equipment?' she asked as a servitor slid a slender neural spike into the modest and elegantly-crafted socket at her temple. '*Ouch*. Careful with that.'

'Compliance,' murmured the cyborg, staring with dead eyes. It was all the answer she received, which didn't surprise her, either.

'You push until it clicks,' she told the lobotomised slave. 'Not until it comes out my other bloody ear.'

The servitor drooled a little. 'Compliance.'

'Throne, just go away.'

'Compliance,' it said for a third time, and did exactly that. She heard it bumping into something in the corridor outside, while the ship shook on the deck with final armament loading. Octavia's box of a room had no porthole windows, so she cycled through the external picter feeds. Image after image of the *Echo*'s main hangar deck flickered across the screen. Thunderhawks were being loaded with full payloads, and drop pods were winched into position. Octavia watched with emotionless eyes, not sure what to feel. Was this home? Would she miss all of it? Where would they even go, if they managed to get away?

'Oh,' she whispered, watching the screen. 'Oh, shit.'

She paused the scrolling feed, keying in a code to tilt one of the image-finders on the ship's hull. Loader buggies and crew transports ferried back and forth; a lifter Sentinel, stolen from some long-past raid, clanked its way past, steel feet thumping on the deck.

Septimus, with a beaten leather bag over one shoulder, was speaking with Deltrian by the main gangramp. His long hair covered his facial augmetics, and he wore a subtly armoured bodysuit beneath his heavy jacket. A machete was sheathed at his right shin, and both pistols hung low at his hips.

She had no idea what he was saying. The external viewfinders didn't offer sound. She watched him slap Deltrian on the shoulder, which the stick-thin cadaver of chrome didn't seem to appreciate, if his recoil was anything to go by.

Septimus made his way up the gangramp, and vanished from view. The screen showed Deltrian return to directing his loader servitors, and the endless flow of machinery being brought aboard.

She heard the knock at her bulkhead door almost immediately after.

'Tell me you've got your bandana on,' she heard him call through the metal.

She smiled, reaching a hand to check, just in case. 'You're safe.'

The door opened, and he dumped his gear the moment he'd closed it behind him. 'I was dismissed from service,' he said. 'Just like you.'

'Who'll fly *Blackened* down to the surface?'

'No one. There are only enough squads for three gunships. *Blackened* has been loaded into this ship's conveyance claws already. Talos has bequeathed it to Variel, full of his apothecarion equipment and relics from the Hall of Reflection. It's to be returned to the Legion in the Eye, if we ever make it that far.'

Her smiled faded, the sun going behind the horizon. 'We're not going to make it that far. You know that, don't you?'

He shrugged, evidently sanguine. 'We'll see.'

WORD HAD SURELY spread throughout the ship of the upcoming battle, but the *Echo* was a city in space, with all the various multitudes such scope implied. On the highest crew decks, the battle to come was a matter of focus – the officers and ratings knew their parts to play, and went about their duties with all the professionalism of those aboard an Imperial Navy warship.

On the lower decks, as one ventured deeper into the ship's innards, the battle was either a matter of prayer, ignorance, or helpless muttering. The thousands who fed the ship with their blood and sweat, toiling in the reactor chambers and the weapon battery platforms, had no wider under-standing of the situation beyond the fact a battle would soon be fought.

Talos went alone to the primary hangar deck. Tenth Company's surviving warriors were already on board their drop pods, while their Thunderhawks were loaded with wargear to be ferried down to them on the surface. Servitors stood in idle silence here and there, waiting for the next order that would engage their limited response arrays.

The prophet crossed the quiet landing bay, to where Deltrian was descending down his ship's gangramp.

'All is in readiness,' Deltrian vocalised.

Talos regarded the adept with unblinking red eye lenses. 'Swear to me you'll do as I say. Those three sarcophagi are priceless. Malcharion will stand with us, but the other three tomb-pods have to reach the Legion. They are relics beyond price. They cannot die here with us.'

'All is in readiness,' Deltrian said a second time.

'The gene-seed matters most of all,' Talos pressed him. 'The gene-seed supplies in storage must reach the Eye, at all costs. Swear to me.'

'All is in readiness,' Deltrian repeated. He had scant regard for the swearing of oaths. In his view, promises were something sworn by biologicals seeking to use hope in place of calculated likelihood. In short: an agreement made on flawed parameters.

'Swear to me, Deltrian.'

The tech-priest made an error sound, vocalising it in a low burr. 'Very well. In an effort to end this vocalisation exchange, I give my oath that the plan will be followed to precise parameters, to the best of my ability and capacity to oversee the efforts of others.'

'That'll do.'

Deltrian wasn't quite finished. 'Estimates suggest we will remain in the asteroid field for several hours after your departure before we know for certain if every xenos vessel is giving chase. Auspex unreliability is a factor. Drift jamming is a factor. Alien interference is a factor. The logistics of–'

'There are many factors,' Talos interrupted. 'I understand. Hide as long as you need to, and run when you can.'

'As you will it, so shall it be.'

The tech-priest turned, then hesitated. Talos wasn't moving away.

'Do you linger here in the desire that I will wish you luck?' Deltrian tilted his leering skull of a face. 'You must be aware that the very idea of fortune is anathema to me. Existence is arbitrary, Talos.'

The Night Lord held out his hand. Deltrian's eye lenses focused on the offered gauntlet for a moment, soft whirrings in his facial structure giving away the fact his eyes were refocusing.

'Intriguing,' he said. 'Processing.'

A moment later, he gripped the legionary's wrist. Talos gripped the adept's, returning the VIII Legion's traditional warrior handshake.

'It's been a privilege, honoured adept.'

Deltrian searched for the appropriate response. He was an outsider, but the ancient formal words, traditionally spoken between warriors of the VIII Legion on the eve of hopeless battles, came to him with an alacrity he found surprising.

'Die as you lived, Son of the Eighth Legion. In midnight clad.'

The two broke apart. Deltrian, as dead to patience as he was to subtlety, immediately turned and walked up the gangramp, heading into the ship.

Talos hesitated, seeing Septimus at the top of the ramp. The slave raised his gloved hand in farewell.

Talos snorted at the gesture. *Humans. The things emotion forces them to do.*

He acknowledged his former slave with a nod, and left the hangar without a word.

XXII
GAUNTLET

THE ECHO POWERED through the asteroid field with no concern for ammunition reserves or void shield charges. The smaller rocks crashed aside, repelled by the ship's crackling shields as the cruiser rammed the asteroids out of the way. The larger rocks died in invisible detonations, as the warship's guns pounded them into rubble.

It didn't turn to avoid any impacts. It didn't slow down, or manoeuvre, or deploy drones to break up any debris in its path. The *Echo of Damnation* was done hiding. It tore its way from its volatile sanctuary, every cannon along its sides and spine swinging forward, ready to cry out in anger for the final time.

On the bridge, Talos watched from his throne. The command crew, mortals all, were almost silent in their focused devotion. Servitors relayed printed reports, several of them emitting slow rolls of inked parchment from augmetic jaws. The prophet's eyes never left the occulus. Beyond the twisting rocks, past even those that weren't yet bursting apart under the *Echo*'s weapons fire, the alien fleet lay in wait. He saw them moving through the void in a tidal drift, disgustingly harmonious, their glittering solar sails tilted to catch the distant sun's weak light.

'Report,' Talos said.

The responses came from every section of the command deck. Calls of 'aye' and 'ready' hailed back in an orderly verse. To coin Deltrian's phrase, all was in readiness. There was nothing he could do now beyond wait.

'Alien fleet moving to intercept. They're positioned in the clearest paths through the rest of the asteroid field.'

He could see that well enough. The smaller vessels, shaped of contoured bone, remained around their motherships – lesser fish feeding from sharks – but the bigger cruisers moved with a speed no less impressive. They came about in fluid arcs, sails banking, running to head off the *Echo of Damnation* as soon as it left the densest sector of the asteroid field.

He didn't like how they moved; not only because of the grotesque agility far beyond human capability, but because outrunning and out-gunning this fleet was already impossible, and they were making it look like outmanoeuvring them was an equal fiction.

'Forty-five seconds, lord.'

Talos leaned back in the throne. He knew full well there was a chance he'd never get off this deck alive. The run to the planet was looking to be the hardest part; slaughtering these skeletal alien wretches in the Tsa-gualsan catacombs would be a delightful treat by comparison, and one that almost made his mouth water.

'Thirty seconds.'

'All targets marked and locked,' called out the weapons overseer. 'We'll need a full minute of uninterrupted bearing to unleash the entire first volley.'

'You'll have it, Armsmaster,' Talos replied. 'How many targets will that hit?'

'If the aliens behave as eldar fleets usually do, rather than running alongside us for a broadside exchange... Fifteen targets, my lord.'

Talos felt his lips twitch behind his faceplate, not quite a smile. *Fifteen targets in one volley.* Blood of Horus, he'd miss this ship. She'd been a beautiful twin sister to the *Covenant*, and it would be churlish to begrudge the armament improvements performed by the Corsairs in the centuries they'd claimed her.

'Twenty seconds.'

'Give me shipwide vox address.'

'Done, lord.'

Talos drew a breath, knowing his words were being heard by thousands upon thousands of slaves, mutants, heretics and serfs across the ship's myriad decks.

'This is the captain,' he said. 'I am Talos, of the bloodline of the Eighth Primarch, and a son of the sunless world. A storm like no other bears down upon us, ready to break against the ship's skin. Survival rides on your blood and sweat, no matter the deck you toil upon. Every life counts in the minutes to come. All hands, all souls, brace for battle.'

'Five seconds, lord.'

'Start the Shriek.'

'Aye, lord.'

'First volley as planned, then fire at will.'

'Aye, lord.'

'Lord, we're clear of the Talosian Density. Enemy fleet is moving to eng–'

'*Open fire.*'

The *Echo of Damnation* ran with all its heart, streaming plasma flame in contrails almost beautiful in their devastating heat.

The wider asteroid field's presence was one of the many unwelcoming aspects that made Tsagualsa such a secure haven for so many years after the Heresy. It was significantly less of a hazard to navigation than the denser debris around the shattered moon, but the eldar ships still ghosted and looped around any loose rock rather than risk impact.

The *Echo of Damnation* took no such care. It ploughed ahead, relying on its void shields and forward weapons array to ram aside any impending threats.

Their initial dives were somewhat less graceful than their previous void dancing, for their prey was playing a different game. The *Echo* obeyed no conventional logic, never once turning for better angles with its weapon batteries, making no adjustments to its flight vectors. The warship wasn't where the alien vessels expected it to be, nor was it going where they'd prepared for it to go. By simply carving its way through the asteroid field, the *Echo* was sacrificing an insane amount of ammunition and shield power, knifing directly towards the world ahead.

The eldar ships ready to engage, laying in wait throughout the clearer routes in the debris field, now found themselves far away from the path of their fleeing prey.

'Is it working?' Talos asked. He could see it working – it was obvious in the way several alien vessels were coming about at speed to adjust their attack runs – but he wanted to hear it, nevertheless.

The officers stared down at their consoles, none more keenly than those stationed at the auspex hololithic projectors.

'The eldar fleet is struggling to come about to our trajectory. Several cruisers are already failing their intercept courses.'

'It's working.' Talos remained in the throne, resisting the desire to pace the deck. The ship shook with the firing of the guns, and the hammering shivers of rocks pounding against the void shields. 'We're outrunning almost half of them.'

The alien ships were elongated, contoured things – all smooth bone and shining wing-sails. He suspected the distant sun made the eldar warships sluggish, starved of the heat they needed on their solar sails, but he hardly had a wealth of experience in the function of alien vessels. With the eldar, everything always felt like guesswork.

'Xenos vanguard ships entering maximum weapons range.'

Talos thought of his brothers in their drop pods, and the gunships warmed and waiting in the landing bays. On the occulus, the coin-sized grey sphere of Tsagualsa grew by the second. Proximity alarms wailed at each and every asteroid that went spinning aside from the inexorable advance, and servitors slaved to their stations chattered at the threat of incoming warheads.

For no reason he could adequately explain, Talos felt a smile creeping across his face. A crooked, sincere smirk of inappropriate amusement.

'Lord,' called out one of the auspex officers. 'Alien torpedoes are resistant to our interference.'

'Even to the Shriek?' He knew it was calibrated to Imperial technology, but even so, he'd been hoping it would make a difference.

'Several have lost their bearings, others are ploughing into the debris field. But more than three-quarters are still on target.'

'Time to impact?'

'The first will be upon us in less than twenty seconds.'

'That's good enough. All hands, brace for impact.'

Soon enough, the hull's rattling became shaking, and the shaking in turn became violent convulsions. Talos felt the creeping of some new and unwelcome unease worming its way up his backbone; how many times had he been aboard a warship in a void battle? A difficult question. One might as well ask how many breaths he'd drawn over the centuries. But this was different. This time, he was the one guiding the ship's path. He couldn't just leave it in Vandred's hands and focus on his own lesser conflicts.

Malcharion should be here. Talos quashed the treacherous thought, true as it might be.

'Shields holding,' a servitor chattered nearby. 'Two-thirds strength.'

Talos watched the grey world growing as the *Echo of Damnation* cried out around him.

'Come on,' he whispered. 'Come on.'

THE VIII LEGION warship hammered her way onward, ramming through the asteroids lying in her path.

The eldar captains were hardly novices in void warfare, nor could any of their craftworld home on the edge of the Great Eye ever be truly surprised by the tactics of an Archenemy warship. Solar sails aligned across the fleet as the alien cruisers swam through their haunting, beautiful attack runs, filling the rocky void with flashing streams of pulsar fire.

Individually, each pulsar beam was as thin as string against the background of infinite black, but they streaked across the void in a cobweb of shining force, raining and lashing against the *Echo*'s suffering void shields.

The *Echo of Damnation* rolled as it ran, offering its broadsides and spinal batteries to the enemy. Return fire burst from the Eighth Legion cruiser – corruption bursting from suppurated wounds – as the warship lashed back with its own guns. Such was their grace, several of the eldar vessels seemed to shimmer out of existence, vanishing from the path of incoming fire. Others took the onslaught, letting it starburst across their shields, secure in the knowledge that the *Echo*'s flight forced it to devote the majority of its armament to clearing a way through the rocks.

The first alien ship to fall was a minor escort ship bearing a name no human could accurately pronounce. Certainly, none of those present on the *Echo of Damnation* cared to try, yet they cheered and laughed when it broke apart before their eyes, ruined by a barrage of plasma and hard-shell fire from the spinal batteries.

A lucky shot, and Talos knew it. Nevertheless, his skin prickled at the sight.

The second xenos vessel died as much from the random tides of fate as from Night Lord malice. With no time to turn, the *Echo of Damnation* poured all of its forward fire into a huge asteroid ahead. Its lances carved into the frozen stone, splitting the rock along fault lines in time for the ship's shielded prow to ram straight into the surface. As the asteroid broke apart, scattering from the crackling and protesting shields, spinning rocks tumbled in all directions. The eldar fleet, for all their arcing agility, were hampered by the oppressing rocks all around. Even as they scattered to fly aside, several of them took incidental damage from the spreading rubble.

Talos gave a crooked smile as one of the heaviest chunks crashed into the slender form of a swooping enemy warship. The debris shattered a solar sail into nothing more than beautiful diamond glass, before grinding into the vessel's body of supernatural bone. The ship twisted, suffering and straining, before diving directly into another asteroid ahead.

'Even if we die here,' the Night Lord chuckled, 'that was worth seeing.'

'Three minutes until we pass Tsagualsa, lord.'

'Good.' The smile died on his lips as he remembered the betrayal to come. Given the ship's trajectory and the overwhelming force against them, many of these poor souls had surely already guessed the only way this could possibly end.

'Should we ready the ship for warp flight?' asked one of the closest officers. Talos heard it in the man's voice; the officer had surrendered his hope, and sought to hide his unrest. The prophet admired him for that. Cowardice had no place on this bridge.

'No,' Talos replied. 'Do you genuinely believe we will make it to safety?' The ship shuddered around them, forcing several mortal crew members to cling to railings and consoles. 'Even with this successful run, do you believe we'll evade them for much longer?'

'No, lord. Of course not.'

'A wise answer,' Talos told him. 'Focus on your duties, Lieutenant Rawlen. Don't worry what will come after.'

Septimus and Deltrian stood in the modest, cramped chamber that the tech-adept announced, with no trace of pride or shame either way, as *Epsilon K-41 Sigma Sigma A:2*'s bridge.

He'd also demanded Septimus leave the deck, to which the human had replied in Nostraman, with something dubiously biological about Deltrian's mother.

'I'm a pilot,' he added. 'I'm going to help fly this thing.'

'Your augmetic aspects, while impressive, are far too limited for you to interface with the machine-spirit of my vessel.'

He gestured to the rocks quivering on the unreliable hololithic. 'You trust servitors and a machine-spirit to fly out of *this?*'

Deltrian made an affirmative sound. 'More than any human. What... what a strange query.'

Septimus had relented, but remained on the bridge by the pilot-servitor's throne.

The slave and the adept, along with the two-dozen servitors and robed crew, were watching the hololithic projection that served as tactical map and occulus alike. Unlike the *Echo*'s holo-imagery, Deltrian's was watery and flickered at intervals that pained Septimus's human eye. Looking through his bionic took away the ache, and helped resolve some of the flickering interference. Only then did he realise it was a projection designed to be viewed by augmetic eyes.

The ship itself was a rounded, bloated beetle of a vessel, bristling with defensive turrets, with almost three-quarters of its length given up to the drive engines and warp generators. Bulkheads sealed those areas of the ship off from the habitable areas, and Septimus had seen several of the adepts wearing rebreather masks while entering and leaving the engine decks.

The entire vessel was cramped to the point of madness. To make room for the vessel's armour, weapons systems and propulsion, every tunnel was a narrow walkway, and every chamber was a squat box featuring the essential systems and enough room for a single operator. The command deck was the most spacious area of the whole ship, and even that offered no room to move if eight people were present at once.

Septimus watched the ship's identifier rune pulsing on the hololithic, attached to an asteroid as it hid from the aliens' scanners. Far across the field of malformed rocks, the rune signifying the *Echo* was a speck among a nest of angry signals.

'The *Echo* is almost there,' he said. 'They're going to make it.'

Septimus turned his head at a familiar sound. Variel walked in, his armour joints humming with every movement.

'Tell me what's happening,' he demanded, as calm as ever.

'It doesn't look like they know we're here,' Septimus let his eyes drift back to the hololithic.

'Tell me about the *Echo*, idiotic mortal.'

Septimus had the grace to force a smile, abashed at the obviousness of his mistake. 'They're going to make it, Lord Variel.'

The Apothecary showed no emotion at the use of the honorific, just as he never showed any emotion the many times Septimus had or hadn't used it before. Such things were less than meaningless to him.

'Am I to assume we will be departing soon?'

Deltrian nodded, doing his best to simulate the human movement on a neck not designed to flex in such subtle ways. Something locked at the top of his spine, and he had to take a moment to will the vertebrae coupling to loosen.

'Affirmative,' he vocalised.

Variel moved to where Septimus stood, watching the hololithic himself. 'What is that?' he gestured to another runic signifier.

'That…' Septimus reached down to the servitor pilot's console, and adjusted the hololithic display with a few tapped keys. '…is the Genesis Chapter's strike cruiser we destroyed months ago.'

Variel didn't smile, which was no surprise to Septimus. His pale blue eyes blinked once as he regarded the hololithic image of the broken cruiser, its hull left open to the void. He reached down to magnify the image, taking in the absolute devastation where the warship lay dead at the heart of the Talosian Density, among the thickest cluster of asteroids above the broken moon.

'That was a particularly satisfying kill,' the Night Lord noted.

'Aye, lord.'

Variel glanced at him with those disquieting eyes. After almost ten years in service to the VIII Legion, Septimus would have gambled on nothing being able to unnerve him anymore. Variel's eyes seemed to be a rare exception.

'What is wrong with you?' the Apothecary asked. 'Your heart rate is elevated. You reek of some moronic, emotional excitement.'

Septimus inclined his head to the hololithic. 'It's difficult to watch them fight without us. Serving the Legion is all I've done for most of my adult life. Without that… I'm not even sure I know who I am.'

'Yes, yes. Fascinating.' He turned to Deltrian. 'Tech-priest. A question, to alleviate my boredom. I want to listen to the eldar's communications. Can you leech their signal?'

'Of course.' Deltrian deployed two of his secondary limbs, letting them arch over his shoulders to work on a separate console. 'I have no capacity to translate eldar linguistic vocalisations.'

That caught Variel's attention. 'Truly? Curious. I'd thought you'd be more enlightened than that.'

'An adept of the Mechanicum has more pressing matters to attend to than the mumblings of wretched xenos-kind.'

'No need to become irritated,' Variel offered a momentary smile, as false as it was brief. 'I speak several eldar dialects. Just leech the signal, if you are able.'

Deltrian paused before pulling the last lever. 'Explain your mastery of the alien tongue.'

'There is nothing to explain, honoured adept. I dislike ignorance.

When the chance to learn something arises, I take it.' He looked over at the robed figure. 'Do you believe the Red Corsairs only battled the corrupt Imperium? We fought the eldar countless times. Captives were not unknown, either. You have one chance at guessing who extracted information from them through excruciation.'

'I see.' Deltrian accepted the answer with another attempt to simulate a nod. His spinal column, made of various precious metals reinforced by tiny plates of ceramite, clicked and whirred with the movement. As he engaged the lever, the bridge was flooded by sibilant alien whispers, distorted by vox crackle.

Variel spoke a word of thanks, and returned his attention to the hololithic. Septimus stood with him, his attention alternating between the unfolding battle and Variel's pale face.

'Stop looking at me,' Variel said after a minute had passed. 'It is getting annoying.'

'What are the eldar saying?' Septimus asked.

Variel listened for another half-minute, not seeming to pay overmuch attention. 'They speak of manoeuvres in three dimensions, comparing warship movements to ghosts and beasts of the sea. It is all very poetic, in a bland, worthless and alien way. No casualty reports yet. No sound of any eldar captains shrieking as their souls are cast adrift.'

It was suddenly clear to Septimus what Variel was really listening for. First Claw had been right; Variel really was one of the VIII Legion, no matter the origins of his gene-seed.

'I...' the Apothecary started, then fell silent. The eldar voices whispered on in the background.

Septimus drew breath to ask, 'What are they–'

Variel silenced him with a glare, his pale eyes narrowed in suspicious concentration. The slave crossed his arms over his chest, waiting and hoping for an explanation, but hardly expecting one.

'Wait,' Variel finally breathed, closing his eyes to better focus on the alien tongue. 'Something is wrong.'

XXIII
A FATE DENIED

OCTAVIA WAS DOING something she'd not dared in a long while. She was using her gift for pleasure, not for duty or necessity.

The Sea of Souls was not a source of easy indulgence, and her childhood was littered with a thousand tales told of Navigators who looked too long, too deep, into the warp's tides. They never saw anything the same afterwards. One of the Mervallion family's own scions – her cousin Tralen Premar Mervallion – was locked beneath the family spire in an isolation tank where he could do himself no more harm. The last time she'd seen him, he'd been floating in the murky fluids of an amniotic pool, leashed by restraint straps, now the proud and laughing owner of a ragged hole in the middle of his forehead where his third eye had been. She shivered at the memory, seeing the bubbles spilling up from his laughing mouth. He always laughed now. She'd hoped whatever fuelled his manic amusement offered some kind of solace, but she wasn't naive enough to believe it.

She didn't like to think of Tralen. Navigators were said to die from the removal of their warp eyes. It seemed there were some few, rare exceptions to that vile rule.

It had taken long enough to calm her nerves before risking her needless viewing, but with her human eyes closed and her bandana pulled free, the rest took no time at all. In truth, it was almost frighteningly easy – a similar sensation to falling from halfway up a difficult climb – but she knew she had the strength to pull herself back.

Octavia, once Eurydice of House Mervallion, might not have been born to a bloodline blessed as strong Navigators, but experience aboard the temperamental, wilful vessels of the VIII Legion had honed what skills she possessed. She couldn't help but wonder, as she gazed into the infinite black tides, how she would perform on the aptitude judgement arrays back on Holy Terra now. Had she grown stronger, or was it merely a matter of familiarity and confidence?

She'd never know. The odds of her ever setting foot on the Throne-world again were millions to one. That thought didn't seem as bleak as it once had. She wasn't sure why.

Curiosity forced her hand now, though. A less selfish, more perverse curiosity than dwelling on her own fate. *Seeing* into the Sea of Souls was as simple as opening her third eye. She didn't need to be in the warp, though she knew some Navigators did. Few of them could compare the use of their gift with absolute common ground. Her father could only see into the warp with all three of his eyes open. She'd never known why; they all had their personal habits.

When she *saw*, she merely stared with her secret sight, watching the shadowy ebb and flow of the half-formed nothingness, shapeless yet tidal, formless yet serpentine. Shamans and witches from the primitive ages of Old Earth would consider it no different than a ritual allowing them to look into the layers of their mythical Hell.

But when she *searched*, she couldn't help but hold her breath each time, until her hammering heart and aching lungs forced her to breathe again. She was aware, on some logical level, that she was projecting her sight through the unholy tides, perhaps even casting a fragment of consciousness into the ether – but Octavia cared little for the metaphysics at play. All that mattered was what she could find with her second sight.

In the madness of the eldar blockades, they'd run again and again, flowing through the tides along the path of least resistance. Talos's psychic scream left the warp raw and abused, its veins swollen and its rivers in turmoil. She'd guided the ship as best she could, riding the winds rather than fighting too hard and risk the *Echo* breaking apart. All the while, she'd been caught between two states, seeing the sundered warp and feeling her hand resting on her swelling stomach.

Now, free from the pressure of navigating the warp, she was free to stare into it. Octavia stared harder, her sight reaching deeper, past the hundred shades of black outside the Astronomican's light, seeking any source of light between the conflicting clouds.

For the first time, she started to see what Talos had done. The colliding waves of daemonic matter bled before her eyes, riven by savage wounds and leaking into one another. She watched them splitting and reforming, meshing and dividing, birthing screaming faces and dissolving them just as quickly. Hands reached out from the thrashing tide, melting and burning even as they gripped the outstretched claws of other nearby souls.

Octavia steadied herself, staring deeper. The wounded warp – *no*, she realised, *not wounded…. energised* – stretched on and on, the bleeding rivers meeting to become a bleeding ocean. How many worlds were choking in this invisible storm? How much terror would this spread?

She could hear her name in the crashing waves. A whisper, a scream, a plaintive cry…

Octavia pulled back. Her eye closed. Her eyes opened.

For a moment, fascination at what Talos had spread through dozens of solar systems gripped her more than the fear of having to fly through it. The warp was always in eternal flux, and in the hours after the scream first sounded, it had boiled with rejuvenation. Now, however, she was preparing to guide an unfamiliar ship into unsailable seas.

The Navigator replaced her bandana, retied her ponytail, and stretched in the uncomfortable throne, trying to ease the pressure on her backbone. She gave an idle thought for her attendants stationed outside the door, no doubt cramped in the narrow corridor. She missed Hound with a dull ferocity, and that in itself was painful to admit. More than that – *and how I hate to confess this, even to myself* – she wished Septimus was with her. He was incapable of ever saying the right thing, but even so. His self-conscious smile; the edge of amusement in his occasional glances; the way he slouched into his throne no matter how dire the threat seemed…

What a stupid, stupid place to fall in love, she thought. *If that's what it even is.*

As Octavia shuffled in her seat, her eyes widened in sudden shock. As if afraid to touch her own flesh, she rested a hesitant hand on her stomach, where for the first time she felt the new life moving within her.

When the shields died, Talos never moved in his throne. The crew – those standing, at least – were thrown from their feet in the sudden resurgence in violent shaking that gripped the ship. Two legless servitors fell from their installation sockets, mouths opening and closing as their useless hands worked at the floor, mimicking motions on consoles they could no longer reach.

'Shields down, lord…' called out one of the officers.

No, really? Talos thought.

'Understood,' he replied through gritted teeth.

'Orders, sire?'

The prophet had watched the grey world grow until it became a swollen orb taking up the occulus with its dreary, pockmarked visage.

Close now. So very close.

'Damage report,' he ordered.

As if the ship's heaving wasn't report enough. As if he needed some other confirmation that they were being cut apart in record time by alien pulsar fire. This many eldar ships, with that much firepower… the *Covenant of Blood* had never had to withstand that much damage in its distinguished career. The *Echo of Damnation* was enduring it for the first, and the last, time.

The officer, Rawlen, couldn't tear his wide eyes from the console screen. 'There's… Lord, there's too much to…'

'Are we in drop pod range for a surface assault?'

'I...'

Talos vaulted the railing and landed with a crashing thud next to the officer. He turned to the screen himself, calculating the scrolling runes into some semblance of sense. With a snarl, he turned to the vox-mistress.

'Deploy the Legion,' he growled over the chaos taking hold around them.

The woman, uniformed and branded in service to the Red Corsairs, started hitting key commands on her desk. 'Legion deploying, lord.'

'Vox-links,' he demanded. 'Vox-links now.'

'Vox, aye.'

The voices of his brothers rasped their way across the shaking bridge, half-lost in the storm of noise and fire.

'This is Talos to all Legion forces,' he shouted. 'Soul count. Report affirmative deployments.'

One by one, they called back to him. He heard the exultant yells of his brothers in their drop pods as they reported back: 'Second Claw away,' 'Fourth Claw deployed,' and 'Third Claw launched.' The occulus re-tuned to show several Thunderhawk gunships blasting from the hangars for the final time, engines flaring white hot as they raced out into the stars.

Malcharion's bass rumble heralded the war-sage's departure.

'I'll see you on the carrion world, Soul Hunter.'

Three more confirmations followed, each with the same machine-growl voices. The occulus flashed back to show a scene from some mythical hell, fiery tides washing over the viewscreen like liquid flame.

'We're in the atmosphere,' yelled one of the officers. 'Orders?'

'Does it matter?' another screamed back.

'Pull the ship up!' one of the helmsmen shouted to the others.

Even Talos had to clutch at a railing as the *Echo* gave a horrendous kick, lurching into an uncontrolled dive. He didn't want to imagine how little of the ship was still in one piece – not after running that insane gauntlet.

The western bridge doors opened on grumbling hydraulics, showing Cyrion silhouetted by fire in the doorway.

'Are you mad?' he voxed. 'Hurry the hell up.'

Now or never, thought Talos. He sprinted up the dais to his command throne, needing to hold the armrest to stay on his feet. The melting view on the occulus showed thin clouds, then stars, then the ground, all in an endless, random cycle.

With his free hand, he pulled his sword from its place locked at the throne's side, and sheathed it on his back.

'You should be in the drop pod,' he voxed back to Cyrion.

'I wish I was,' his brother replied. 'The ship's backside just fell off.'

'You're joking.'

'No engines. No joke. We're in freefall.' Cyrion was gripping the door frame, as human crew flooded around him, trying to flee the bridge. 'Come *on*,' he urged.

Talos ran to him, keeping his balance despite the humans falling underfoot and the deck seeming to disregard all pretence of physics.

Their swords didn't stay sheathed for long. As they forced their way through corridors turned thick with the press of panicked human bodies, both blades fell and carved, hewing a way through the living forest. Blood joined the sweat-stink and fear-scent, aching in Talos's senses. Through the screams, he was dimly aware that he was butchering his own crew, but what did it matter? They'd be dead in moments, anyway.

Cyrion was breathing heavily, kicking out at the humans to break legs and backs as often as he lashed out with his gladius.

'We're going to die,' he breathed over the vox, 'and it's your fault for waiting so long.'

Talos cleaved his sword through a mortal's body, splitting the human from neck to pelvis and shouldering through the falling pieces.

'You didn't have to come back just to whine at me.'

'I didn't have to, no,' Cyrion allowed. 'But no one should die without being reminded of their mistakes.'

'*Where in the infinite hells are you?*' came Mercutian's voice over the vox.

Talos disembowelled one of the fleeing crew from behind, hurling the biological wreckage aside. He was sweating beneath his armour, already feeling the strain of the endless chopping through the panicked humans blocking the tunnels. A horde of them, hundreds – and soon to be thousands – were fleeing for the escape pods. Exhaustion wasn't a factor; he could carve all day and all night without rest. The problem was purely one of time.

'Launch the drop pod,' Talos voxed. 'Mercutian, Uzas, get down to Tsagualsa.'

'*Are you insane?*' Mercutian's strained reply came back.

'We're closer to the command deck's escape pods. Just go.'

Cyrion pulled his gladius from the spine of a uniformed deck officer, his own breath starting to come through ragged. 'If there are any escape pods left after these vermin have run away, that is.'

'*Ave dominus nox, Talos. We'll see you in the catacombs.*'

Talos heard the massive grind of the drop pod's clamps disengaging, and Uzas's joyful howling. Their descent through the atmosphere carried them out of vox range in a matter of heartbeats, silencing Mercutian's curses and Uzas's laughter in the same second.

Talos and Cyrion butchered their way onward.

THE WHISPERING CONTINUED. A chorus of soft voices exchanged words and laughter, each of them like silken mist on the ears, even through the hiss of vox distortion.

Variel had been listening to it for almost half an hour, his casual interest becoming keen attention, quickly evolving into rapt focus. Septimus watched the Apothecary more often than he watched the hololithic now. Variel's colourless lips never stopped moving, softly mouthing the alien words as he translated them in his mind.

'What are–' Septimus tried again, only to be silenced by a raised fist. Variel made ready to backhand him if he spoke again.

'Deltrian,' the Apothecary said after several heartbeats had passed.

'Flayer,' acknowledged the adept.

'The game has changed. Get me within vox reach of Tsagualsa's surface.'

Deltrian's eye lenses rotated and refocused in their sockets. 'I request a reason for a course of action in utter opposition to our orders and planned processes.'

Variel was still distracted, listening to the breathy purring of eldar language. Septimus thought it sounded like a song of sorts, sung by those who hoped no one hears their voices. It was beautiful, yet it still made his skin crawl.

'The game has changed,' Variel repeated. 'How could we have known? We couldn't. We could never have guessed this.' He turned around the humble command deck, his ice-blue eyes looking through everything, alighting on nothing.

Deltrian was unfazed by Variel's distant murmurs. 'I restate my request, altering the terms to make it a demand. Provide adequate reasoning, or cease your vocalisation of orders you have no authority to give.'

Variel finally fixed his gaze on something – specifically, Deltrian, in his red robes of office, with his chrome skull face half-hidden in the folds of his hood.

'The eldar,' said Variel. 'They whisper of their own prophecies, of the Eighth Legion bleeding them without mercy in the decades that follow. Do you understand? They are not here because of Talos's psychic scream. They have never once spoken of it. They speak of nothing but our foolishness and their need to sever the strands of an unwanted future from the skeins of fate.'

Deltrian made an error-abort sound, in his equivalent of a dismissive grunt. 'Enough,' the adept said. 'Alien witchery is irrelevant. Xenos superstition is irrelevant. Our orders are all that remains relevant.'

Variel's eyes were distant again. He was listening to the aliens' sibilant voices sing in their whispery tongue.

'No.' He blinked, staring at the adept once more. 'You do not understand. They seek to prevent some future... some event yet to come, where Talos leads the Eighth Legion in a crusade against their dying species. They chant of it, like children offering prayers in the hope of a god taking pity upon them. Do you hear me? Are you listening to the words I speak?'

Septimus backed away as Variel walked to stare down at the seated adept. He'd never seen Variel's blood up like this.

'They fight to prevent a future that frightens them,' he said through clenched teeth. 'One they cannot allow to come to pass. These ships... This is a vast risk for them. A colossal gamble. They've backed us into a corner, using ships crewed by spirits, saving their precious alien lives for the final blow. *That* is how much they need Talos dead.'

Deltrian repeated the negative sound. 'Purely supposition based on xenos whisperings.'

'And if they're right? The Prophet of the Eighth Legion will rise at the end of the Dark Millennium and bleed the Ulthwéan eldar far beyond what their dwindling population can sustain. Are you so blind and deaf to everything outside your work that you can't hear my words? Listen to me, you heathen warlock: in these futures they've seen, he brings the Legion itself against them. These alien dogs believe he *unites* the Eighth Legion.'

LOADER PRIMARIS MARLONAH secured herself in the restraint throne, shaking hands fumbling with the buckles. *Click*, went the first lock. *Click*, went the second. She didn't know it, but she was mumbling and swearing to herself as she worked.

Dumb luck had found her on the primary crew decks rather than at her station when the battle took a turn for the worst. She'd been on her way back to the starboard tertiary munitions deck, after an emergency discharge from the apothecarion in the wake of another malfunction in her augmetic leg.

The limb itself was still a bit of a bitch. She doubted she'd ever get used to it, no matter what the sawbones said.

The sirens screamed before she'd even managed to hobble halfway back to her duty shift. These weren't the rapid pulses of a call to battle stations, or the long caterwauling of pre-warp flight readiness. She'd never heard this siren before, but she knew what it was the moment it started screaming.

Evacuation.

Panic flooded the decks, with crew running in every direction. She'd been close enough that even her limping run kept her ahead of the pack, but the corridors leading to the pod bays were choked by the many dozens of souls that had been even faster, even closer, or even luckier.

When her time had come, she was a trembling, sweating wreck that fairly spilled into the last throne inside the pod. Outside the pod's closing doors, people were shouting and beating on the walls. Some were trampling each other. Others were stabbing and shooting, desperate to get to the pods before the ship's remains made one brutal bitch of a crater in the grey landscape.

Even through her relief as the last buckled *click*, she felt the ache of sympathy for those still trapped outside, hunting for pods. She couldn't look away from their faces and fists, pressed to the dense glass.

As she watched, mouthing the word 'sorry' to each pair of eyes she met, the clamouring faces were swept aside in a blur of cold blue and wet red. Blood smeared across the viewing glass, while shadows danced beyond, just out of sight.

'What the...' one of the other crew members stammered from his seat in the opposite restraint throne.

The door shuddered in a way no amount of beating fists and yelled curses had managed to inflict. The second time was worse: it shook to its reinforced hinges.

It came away the third time, letting in a burst of sickeningly hot air, and revealing a scene from a carcass pit.

Two of the masters stood outside, ankle-deep in the dead, their blades dripping with blood. One of them hunched down to enter the confines of the pod. No thrones remained untaken, and even if they had been free, none of the Legion could fit their bulky armoured forms into a human restraint throne.

There was no debate, no hesitation. The Night Lord rammed his golden sword through the chest of the closest human, ending any resistance, and dragged the spasming body from its seat. The harnesses snapped as the legionary pulled with one, hard tug, before hurling the body outside into the corridor to lie amongst the slain.

The second legionary entered, his armour joints snarling as he mimicked the first murder. The second man to die shamed himself by weeping and begging before he was cut apart. Two of the restraint thrones followed, torn from their moorings and hurled out into the corridor. The towering figures meant to empty the pod in order to create the room they needed to stand within it.

Marlonah was scrambling to unlock her restraints when the third man was killed and thrown outside.

'I'll get out!' she was yelling. 'I'll get out, *I'll get out* – I swear I will.'

She looked up as the hunched shadow fell across her, blocking out the dim red illumination from the central emergency light.

'I know you,' the master growled in his vox-voice. 'Septimus argued with one of the human surgeons to grant you that leg.'

'Yes... Yes...' She thought she was agreeing. In truth, she had no idea whether she was even speaking aloud.

The Night Lord reached to slam the reinforced door closed, leaving the bloodbath on the other side.

'Go,' he growled to his brother.

The other warrior, who was forced to stand stooped in the same half-crouch, reached to the central column and pulled the release levers – one, *crunch*; two, *crunch*; three, *crunch*.

The pod lurched in its cradle, and the whine of its propulsion systems became a forlorn roar.

When the escape pod fell, Marlonah felt the floor drop out from under her in the same moment that her stomach tried to find a new home in her throat. She wasn't sure if she was screaming or laughing as they rattled their way down to safety, but in actuality, she was doing both.

DELTRIAN HAD TO admit, he was struggling to make a decision. Talos had demanded a set process of actions from him, but the Apothecary (while grotesquely emotional) made a persuasive case.

And yet it still came down to practicalities and probability. Deltrian knew this better than anyone.

'To process the odds of this vessel surviving a direct engagement with the enemy fleet requires a calculation few biological minds would be able to comprehend. Suffice to say, in terms you will understand, the odds are not in our favour.'

Had he been able to smile sincerely rather than as a natural by-product of a metallic skull for a face, Deltrian would probably have grinned in that moment. He was extremely proud of his mastery of understatement.

Variel wasn't moved, nor was he amused. 'Focus the cogs and gears that rattle behind your eyes,' he said. 'If the eldar are so fearful of this prophecy coming to pass, then it means there's a chance Talos *does* survive the war down there. And *we* are that chance. My brother has a destiny beyond a miserable death in the dust of this worthless world, and I mean to give him the chance to seize it.'

Deltrian's emotionless facade didn't even alter. 'Talos's final orders are all that remain relevant,' he stated. 'This vessel is now the gene-seed repository for over one hundred slain legionaries of the Eighth. This genetic material must reach the Great Eye. That is my oath to Talos. My sworn promise.' Those last words made him acutely uncomfortable.

'You run, then. I will not.' Variel turned back to Septimus. 'You. The Seventh.'

'Lord?'

'Ready your gunship. Get me down to Tsagualsa.'

XXIV
CATACOMBS

TEN THOUSAND YEARS ago, the fortress stood defiant as one of the last great bastions of Legiones Astartes invincibility in the material universe. The coming of the Primogenitors made a lie of that claim. The centuries since had been no kinder. Jagged, eroded battlements thrust up from the lifeless earth, broken by ancient explosives and the bite of a million dust storms.

Little remained of the fortress's great walls beyond hills of rubble, half-swallowed by the grey soil. Where the battlements still existed, they were toothless and tumbledown things, devoid of grandeur, brought low to the ground with the passing of the years.

Talos stood in the grey ruins, watching the *Echo of Damnation* die. Grit in the wind crackled against his armour as he stood in the open, surrounded by defanged, fallen walls. The warship made an agonisingly slow dive towards the horizon, shedding wreckage as it burned, trailing a thick plume of smoke.

'How many were still on the ship?' asked a female voice at his side. Talos didn't glance down at her; he'd forgotten Marlonah was still there. The fact she'd even considered the question was the starkest difference between them both in that moment.

'I don't know,' he said. The truth was that he didn't care. His masters had made him into a weapon. He felt no guilt at the loss of his humanity, even when it caught him by surprise in times like these.

The *Echo of Damnation* went down behind the southern mountains. Talos saw the flash of its reactor flare going critical, lighting the sky like a second sunset for a single, painful heartbeat.

'One,' he counted. 'Two. Three. Four. Five.'

A roll of thunder broke above them, fainter than the voice of a true storm, but all the sweeter for it.

'The *Echo*'s final cry,' Cyrion said from behind.

Talos nodded. 'Come. The eldar will be on us soon.'

The two warriors walked past their downed escape pod, through the uneven remnants of the landscape left by the erosion. Marlonah kept pace as best she could, watching them hunting through the broken buildings and ruined walls, seeking an uncollapsed tunnel that would lead deeper into the labyrinth.

After several minutes, they came across an empty Legion drop pod, its paint seared off during descent, and its doors open in full bloom. It had shattered through a weak roof in what had once been a large domed chamber. Little else but two walls and a span of arcing ceiling remained, like the filthy ruins discovered by xenoarchaeologists on long-dead worlds. What was left of their grand fortress looked like nothing more than the remains of a dead civilisation, unearthed millennia after a great extinction.

Marlonah heard the clicking of the two warriors conversing over their helm voxes.

'Can I come with you?' she mustered the courage to ask.

'That is unwise,' Cyrion told her. 'If you wish to live, your best chance at survival is making the three-week journey south, towards the city we allowed to survive. If the scream was loud enough, the Imperium will come one night, and save those souls.'

She didn't know what any of that meant. All she knew was that there was no way she'd survive walking for three weeks with no food and no water, let alone make it through the dust storms.

'Cy,' said the other Night Lord. 'Does it matter if she follows us?'

'Fine then.'

'Descend into the catacombs if you wish, human,' said Talos. 'Just remember that our own lives are measured in mere hours. Death will come quicker than in the desert of dust, and we cannot afford to linger with you. We have a battle to fight.'

Marlonah tested her aching knee. The bionic was throbbing where it joined to her leg.

'I can't stay up here. Will there be places to hide?'

'Of course,' Talos replied. 'But you'll be blind. There's no light where we're going.'

Septimus listened to the engines whining into life. Nowhere else was as comfortable for him as the very seat he now occupied – the pilot's throne of the Thunderhawk gunship *Blackened*.

Variel sat in the co-pilot's throne, still unhelmed, staring off into the middle distance. Once in a while, he'd absently reach to run a thumb along his pale lips, lost in thought.

'Septimus,' he said, as the engines cycled live.

'Lord?'

'What are the chances of us reaching Tsagualsa undetected?'

The serf couldn't even begin to guess. 'I... know nothing about the eldar, lord, or their scanning technology.'

Variel was clearly still distracted. '*Blackened* is small, and the void is close to infinite in scope and span. Play to those advantages. Stay close to the asteroids.'

Septimus checked the bay doors ahead. Beyond the gunship and several stacks of what Deltrian insisted was essential equipment, there was precious little room in *Epsilon K-41 Sigma Sigma A:2*'s only landing bay. Even the Thunderhawk was loaded with vital supplies and relic machinery from the Hall of Reflection, denying any room for extra crew. Deltrian was less than thrilled to see it departing.

There'd been no time to speak with Octavia. A short vox message to her private chamber was all he'd been able to arrange, and he'd barely known what to say, anyway. How best to tell her he was probably going to die down there, after all? What would reassure her that Deltrian would protect her once they reached the Great Eye?

In the end, he'd mumbled in his usual awkward tone, in a mixed mess of Gothic and Nostraman. He tried to tell her he loved her, but even in that inspiration deserted him. It was hardly an elegant declaration of emotion.

She'd not replied. He still didn't even know if she'd received the message at all. Perhaps that was for the best.

Septimus triggered the launch cycle, closing the forward gangramp. It shut beneath the cockpit with a mechanical slam.

'We're sealed and ready,' he said.

Variel still seemed to be paying little attention. 'Go.'

Septimus gripped the control levers, feeling his skin prickle as the engines shouted harder in sympathy. With a deep breath, he guided the gunship out from the confined hangar bay, and back out into the void.

'Have you considered the fact you might be wrong?' he asked the Flayer. 'Wrong about Talos surviving, I mean.'

The Apothecary nodded. 'It has crossed my mind, slave. That possibility is something else that interests me.'

TIME PASSED IN darkness, but not silence.

Talos viewed the subterranean world through a red veil, his eye lenses piercing the lightless corridors without strain. Tactical data in tiny white runes scrolled in an endless stream down the edges of his vision. He paid no heed to any of it, beyond the healthy signals of his brothers' life signs.

Tsagualsa had never been home. Not in truth. Returning to walk its forgotten halls bred a certain uneasy melancholy, but nothing of sorrow, or of rage.

The human serf hadn't remained with them for long. They'd outpaced her limping stride in a matter of minutes, ghosting through the corridors as they tracked their brethren's vox-signals. For a time, Talos had heard her shouting and weeping in the dark, far behind them. He saw Cyrion shiver, surely a physical reaction to her fear, and felt the acid tang of corrosive saliva on his tongue. He didn't like to be reminded of his brother's corruption, even as subtle and unobtrusive as it was.

'She'd have been better off on the plains,' Cyrion voxed.

Talos didn't reply. He led the way through the tunnels, listening to the vox-net alive with so many voices. His brothers in the other Claws were laughing, making ready, swearing oaths to bleed the eldar dry before they finally fell themselves.

He smiled behind his faceplate, amused by all he heard. The remnants of Tenth and Eleventh Companies were on the edge of death, cornered like vermin, yet he'd never heard them sound so alive.

Malcharion reported that he was alone, walking through the tunnels closest to the surface. When the Claws protested and argued they should fight alongside him, he'd cursed them for fools and severed his vox-link.

They found Mercutian and Uzas before the first hour fully passed. The former embraced Talos, wrist-to-wrist in greeting. The latter stood in mute inattention, breathing heavily over the vox. They could all hear Uzas licking his teeth.

'The other Claws are getting ready to make their stands in similar chambers.' Mercutian gestured to the northern and southern doorways – open now that the doors themselves had long since rotted away to memory. Talos took his brother's point: the two entrances would make the chamber relatively easy to defend compared to many others of comparable size, while still giving them room to move. He followed Mercutian's second gesture, indicating a crawlspace high in the western wall that had once been an access point to the maintenance ducts. 'When they fall back, they'll move through the service tunnels.'

'Will we fit?' Cyrion was checking his bolter with meticulous care. 'They were built for servitors. When we left this place, half the ducts were too small for us.'

'I've scouted the closest ones,' said Mercutian. 'There are several dead ends where we can't make it through, but there are always alternate routes. Our only other choice is to dig through the countless collapsed tunnels.'

Talos took in the whole chamber. It had once belonged to another company, used as a training hall. Nothing remained of the room's former decoration. When viewed through the red wash of his eye lenses, Talos saw nothing but bleak, bare stone. The rest of the catacombs looked no different. The entire labyrinth was the same naked, hollow ruin.

'Our ammunition?'

Mercutian nodded again. 'Already done. The servitors who came down in the other pods landed close to the Claws. As for gunships, it's less obvious which ones made it down. Our mules are down here, and safe. I'll take you to them – they're idling in a chamber half a kilometre to the west. With so many tunnels collapsed between here and there, it's quicker to take the maintenance ducts.'

'They made it, then,' Cyrion said. 'A slice of precious luck, at last.'

'Many didn't,' Talos amended, 'if the vox is anything to go by. But we've smuggled enough ammunition down here to give the eldar a thousand new funeral songs.'

'Is our primary cargo intact?' Cyrion asked.

For once, it was Uzas who answered. 'Oh, yes. I'm looking forward to that part.'

As First Claw made their way in ragged, hunched formation, clattering their way down the service ducts, Talos heard the first report of battle over the vox.

'This is Third Claw,' came the voice, still coloured by laughter. 'Brothers, the aliens have found us.'

SEPTIMUS HUNTED FOR the right touch. Speed was of the essence, but he had to fly close to every asteroid – hugging them, staying in their shadows wherever possible, before sprinting to the next closest. Beyond that, which was easily enough to worry about already, he was careful not to push the engines too hard in case the eldar vessels now stationed in high orbit above the fortress had the capacity to detect their presence via heat signature.

They'd only been flying for ten minutes when Variel closed his eyes, shaking his head in gentle disbelief.

'We have been boarded,' the Flayer said softly, to no one in particular. Bootsteps from behind forced Septimus to crane his neck to look over his shoulder. The gunship slowed in response to his wavering attention.

Three of Octavia's attendants stood by the doorway leading into the confined cockpit. He recognised Vularai at once; the others were most likely Herac and Folly, though their ragged cloaks and bandaged hands meant they could be almost anyone.

Septimus looked back at the windshield, bringing the gunship in a slow bank around another small rock. Smaller dust particles ceaselessly rattled against the hull.

'You stowed aboard before we left?' he asked.

'Yes,' said one of the males.

'Did she send you?' Septimus asked.

'We obey the mistress,' replied the one who was probably Herac. In fairness, they all sounded similar, too. Voices didn't always make it any easier to tell them apart.

Variel's unwholesome blue eyes fixed on Vularai. The attendant was wrapped in a thick cloak, and though she wore her glare-goggles, the bandaging around her face and arms was loose and hanging in places, revealing pale skin beneath.

'That deception would fool a disinterested Mechanicum menial,' Variel said, 'but it is almost tragically comical to attempt the same with me.'

Vularai started to unwrap her bandaging, freeing her hands. Septimus risked another glance over his shoulder.

'*Fly.*' Variel's eyes were enough of a threat. 'Focus on your duty.'

Vularai let the wrappings fall at last, and cast aside the heavy cloak. She reached up to her face, removed the glare-goggles and checked her bandana was in place.

'You're not leaving me alone on that piece of crap ship, with that mechanical abomination,' said Octavia. 'I'm coming with you.'

DELTRIAN MADE HIS way to Octavia's chamber in the vessel's bulbous belly, seeking to contain any traces of irritation from manifesting in his movements or vocalisations.

When he'd given the order to his servitor-pilots to make their way through the asteroid field, all had been well.

When he'd calculated the best prospective location to risk entering the warp without attracting attention from eldar raiders *or* risking a hull breach from accidental collision during acceleration and reality dispersion, all had still been well.

When he'd ordered the warp engines to begin opening the tear in the fabric of the material void, all had still been well.

When he'd ordered Octavia to ready herself, and received no reply of confirmation... he encountered the first flaw in an otherwise perfect process.

Repeated attempts to contact her elicited the same response.

Unacceptable.

Truly, utterly unacceptable.

He'd ordered the vessel back into hiding, and started to make his way down to her chamber himself.

A handful of her attendants scampered aside from his hurried advance down the corridor. That in itself would have been curious to anyone that knew the Navigator well, but Deltrian was not such a soul.

His thin fingers overrode the lock on her bulkhead, and he stepped into the cramped chamber, standing before the cabled throne.

'You,' he said, preparing to initiate a long and accusatory tirade, centred on themes of obedience and duty, with subsidiary aspects of self-preservation to appeal to her biological fear of corporeal demise.

Vularai sat back in Octavia's throne with her boots up on the armrest. Without her bandaging, she was a wretched thing – anaemic flesh showed the veins underneath, swollen and black like cobwebs beneath the thinnest skin. Her eyes were watery, half-blinded by cataracts, and ringed by dark circles.

For several seconds, Deltrian catalogued a list of visual mutations in the woman he was seeing before him. Her warp-changes seemed subtle by some standards, but the overall effect was a fascinating one: beneath her thin flesh, it was possible to see the shadow of bones, veins, muscle clusters and even the beating silhouette of her heart, moving in disharmony with her swelling, contracting lungs.

'You are not Octavia,' he vocalised.

Vularai grinned, showing scabby gums populated by cheap iron teeth. 'What gave it away?'

Talos was last to enter the chamber. The prophet panned his gaze around the empty hall again, alighting at last on the only other living souls. Fifteen servitors stood in slack-jawed repose, too dead of mind to be considered truly patient. Almost all of them had their arms replaced by lifter claws or machine tools.

First Claw moved over to the stowage crates the lobotomised slaves had hauled down into the depths.

Talos was the first to pull something forth. He held a massive cannon in his gauntlets – a lengthy, multi-barrelled weapon rarely used by the VIII Legion.

With a glance at the closest servitors, he dumped the cannon back in its crate. It rested atop a ceramite breastplate, densely armoured and proudly displaying its aquila shattered with ritual care.

'We don't have long,' he said. 'Let's get this started.'

XXV
SHADOWS

THEY GHOSTED DOWN the corridor, blacker than the shadows that shielded them. His eyes weren't what they once were – relying on movement as much as shape – but he watched them draw nearer, moving in a haunting, sinuous unity he could only call alien. *Alien.* While the term was accurate, even as the creatures bore down on him, he felt the term lacked a certain poetry.

He knew little about this xenos breed. They burst the same as any human under the grinding hail of autocannon fire, which was reassuring but hardly a surprise. Watching them shatter and crumble in wet showers told him very little he didn't already know.

Had he been able, he'd crouch over one of their corpses, peeling the broken armour back, and learn all he needed in a feast of flesh. With the taste of blood on his lips, his enhanced physiology would infuse him with instinctive knowledge about the fallen prey. In an existence he still barely understood, the pleasure of tasting fallen foes' lost lives was one of the things he missed most of all.

Eldar. He admired them for their disciplined silence even as he found their bending grace repulsive. One of them, evidently unprotected by its fragile interlocking plates, burst across the left wall in a wet slap of gore and clattering armour.

He couldn't kill them all with the sluggish cannon that served as his arm. Several of the aliens ducked and weaved beneath his arc of fire, conjuring chainblades into their thin-fingered hands.

The Night Lord laughed. At least, he tried to. He gagged on the pipes and wires impaling his mouth and throat, while the sound emerged as a gear-shifting grind.

With no hope of outrunning them, he still needed to step back to brace himself. The feeling of them chopping and carving at his vulnerable joints was an unusual one – without pain, without *skin*, the sensation became an almost amusing dull scrape. He couldn't make out individual

879

figures when they were this close, but the corridor lightning-bolted with
sparks from the blades chewing into his connective joints.

'Enough of that,' he grunted, and lashed down with his other fist.
The servos and cable-muscles of his new body lent strength and speed
beyond anything he'd known in life. The fist hammered into the stone
floor, shaking the entire corridor and breeding a rain of dust from the
ceiling. The alien wretch caught beneath his downswing was a pulped
ruin, smeared across the ground.

Malcharion turned on his waist axis, lashing out again, crushing with
his fist even as it spewed liquid fire from its mounted flamer. The aliens
weaved back, but not fast enough. Two died beneath his pounding fist;
one wailed as it dissolved in the torrent of corrosive fire.

The Dreadnought breathed in deep, inhaling the scent of the now
empty corridor. Instead of cold air filling his lungs with the scent of
murder, he felt the oxygen-rich fluid of his coffin bubbling with his
breath, and smelled nothing at all beyond the chemical stink-taste of
his tepid confines.

When he shivered, it translated as his metal body juddering, reloading his autocannon with a *clunk* and a *click*. When he sighed, it left his
sarcophagus as a machine's snarl.

Temptation almost made him open the vox-net again, but the fawning
regard of those he'd once commanded was an irritant he had no desire
to deal with. Instead, he hunted alone, stealing what pleasure he could
from how things had changed.

Malcharion moved around the slender corpses, his waddling stalk
shaking the tunnel with each tread. Without hope of stealth, he had to
play a different game.

'Eldar...' he growled. 'I come for you.'

LUCORYPHUS CROUCHED ATOP the ruined battlements, watching the sky. He
could hear his brothers eating the eldar behind him, but hadn't partaken
himself. He'd eaten their flesh before, and felt no compulsion to repeat
the experience. Their blood was thin and sour, and their skin lacked any
of the salty richness found in a mouthful of human meat.

The leader of the Bleeding Eyes wasn't sure where the eldar were
appearing from. Despite maintaining a vigil of the sky and refusing to
descend into the catacombs, he'd seen no sign of alien landing craft. Yet
they kept appearing, here and there, moving from behind broken walls
or manifesting atop fallen spires.

The fortress ruins spread for kilometres in every direction. He knew
his Raptors couldn't cover all that ground alone, though he drove them
hard, making the attempt. What confused him most of all was that the
aliens didn't seem to be appearing in the numbers he'd been expecting.
They had enough ships in the void above to land an army. Instead, he

was witnessing small fire teams and scout parties descending into the labyrinth, and butchering those few that remained on the surface.

The thrusters on his back gave a sympathetic whine in response to his musing.

'Ghost ships,' he said.

Only one of the Bleeding Eyes bothered to look up from their meal. 'You speak?' Vorasha hissed.

Lucoryphus gestured upward with a deactivated lightning claw. 'Ghost ships. Vessels of bone and soul in the void. No crew but the ghosts of dead eldar.'

'Ulthwé,' Vorasha said, as if that was agreement enough.

'Silent ships, piloted by bones, captained by memories. An unbreakable armada in the heavens, but on the ground?' His head jerked with a muscle tic. 'They are not so strong. Not so numerous. Now we know why they owned the heavens, but fear the earth.'

The Raptor breathed slowly, inhaling the planet's unhealthy air through his mouth grille. Mist rose with each exhalation.

'I see something,' he said.

'More eldar?' asked one of the pack.

'A shadow within another shadow. There,' he pointed to the overhang of a rotted stone building. 'And there. And there. Many somethings, it seems.'

When the challenge came, it was given in a tongue Lucoryphus couldn't understand, shouted from a throat he ached to slit. The eldar warrior knelt atop a wall two hundred metres away, a crescent blade in one hand, and great eagle wings arcing up from his shoulder blades.

As soon as the cry carried across the air, another four winged figures revealed themselves, each one crouched atop a broken tower or ruined wall.

'Bleeding Eyes,' Lucoryphus whispered to his kin. 'At last, some prey worth hunting.'

UZAS AND MERCUTIAN were first. With none of the Mechanicum's blessings or prayers, it took significantly less time for them to get ready. While they waited, Talos and Cyrion stood watch in the northern and southern tunnels, listening to the sounds of battle carrying over the vox.

'Armour primed,' Mercutian voxed to Talos. 'Uzas is ready, too.'

'That took almost half an hour,' Cyrion noted. 'Still not a rapid process, even without the Machine Cult's ramblings.'

'It's fast enough,' Talos replied. 'Mercutian, Uzas, cover us.'

Talos waited until a low, industrial grinding sound echoed down the tunnel. The fall of each bootstep was a roll of thunder.

'Your turn,' came Uzas's vox-altered growl. The new helm was a muzzled and tusked visage, sporting eye lenses of ruby red and a painted daemon skull. The armour itself emitted a constant, guttural hum, and was wide enough to fill half the corridor on its own.

'How does it feel?' Talos asked his brother.

Uzas stood straighter, against the war-plate's natural hunch, and the power generators hummed louder. In one hand, he held a new-model storm bolter, the aquila markings defiled by scratches or melted away completely. His other arm ended in a power fist, the thick fingers crunching closed in reverse bloom.

On one shoulder, the broken draconic symbol of the Salamanders Chapter was buried beneath a bronze icon of the VIII Legion, hammered into place by thick steel rivets.

'It feels powerful,' said Uzas. 'Now hurry. I wish to hunt.'

SHE ANSWERED HIM, shriek for shriek and blade for blade. The Bleeding Eyes took to the air on howling thrusters, filling the sky with filthy exhaust fumes in their pursuit of their prey. The eldar, armoured in contoured war-plate of innocent blue, replied to the hateful shrieking with war-calls of their own – each one a piercing, dismissive cry.

The fight was an ugly one; Lucoryphus knew how it would play out the moment they first clashed. The eldar ran and the Raptors gave chase. Most of the alien sky-maidens were armed with slender, tapered laser rifles, spitting out coruscating stabs of energy. They needed distance to use them, while the Raptors filled the sky with the clatter of short-range bolt pistols and the desperate whine of slashing chainblades eating air and going hungry.

The first to fall from the sky was his brother Tzek. Lucoryphus heard the death rattle over the vox – a choking gargle from bloody lungs and a ruptured throat – followed by the spiralling whine of engines failing to fire. The Raptor twisted in the air, keeping his own foe back by lashing out with his clawed feet, just in time to see Tzek's body crash into the uneven ground.

The sight caused his tongue to ache, filling his mouth with hissing ichor. Tzek had been with him down the many years of twisted time, since the first night of the Last Siege. To see such a noble soul broken by alien filth made him angry enough to spit.

The eldar leaned back, hawkish wings vibrating with a melodic chime as she flipped in the air, swooping as true and elegantly as a bird of prey. The gobbet of corrosive slime missed her completely.

Lucoryphus followed her, engines roaring and breathing smoke in opposition to her musical glide. Each cut from his claws sliced nothing more than air, as the alien bitch danced back, diving and arcing aside, seeming to soar on thermals.

The Raptor released the frustrated scream he could no longer contain. Either the wind stole much of its potency, or her sloping, crested helm inured her to burst eardrums, for she ignored it completely.

She soared higher, spinning through the sky, her blade trailing electric fire. Lucoryphus of the Bleeding Eyes chased her, his fanged maw screaming as loudly as his protesting engines.

Her grace counted only when she danced through the air; in a straight and honest chase, he had her dead. They both realised it in the same moment. Lucoryphus caught her from behind, carving through her wings with his lightning-kissed claws. They cleaved through the alien-forged material, crippling her in mid-flight.

With another war cry, she twisted in the air, bringing her sword to bear even as she started to fall. The Raptor parried her blade, letting it rasp against his charged talons. His free hand gripped her throat, keeping her aloft and in his arms for a precious second more.

'Goodnight, my sweet,' he breathed into her faceplate. Lucoryphus released her, letting her tumble from the sky in mirror of Tzek's ignoble demise.

His laugh died as soon as it began. She'd not fallen more than three seconds before one of her kin caught her at the end of a swooping dive, angling down to bear her to the ground.

'I think not,' the Raptor hissed, leaning forward into a dive of his own. He could hear them over the wind, shouting to one another in their babbling tongue. He had to bank sharply to avoid her pistol spitting its jagged light back up at him, but with the eldar's erstwhile saviour encumbered, they had no chance of outrunning the Raptor's second assault. Lucoryphus hit them both like a bolt from above, latching his claws into both torsos and tearing the two figures apart.

He screamed at the effort it took, his rapturous shriek echoing across the sky. The wingless maiden went one way, falling and spinning down through the air to crash in a mangled heap, smeared over the ground. The male fell in similar reflection, blood raining from the wounds in his breastplate. His wings quivered, seeking a final flight, but the drying blood on Lucoryphus's claws told the last of that particular tale. The Raptor sneered as the eldar struck the earth, flopping over the rocks as he came to pieces in the tumbling impact.

He was still smiling when he turned in time to see Vorasha die next. His brother fell back from a mid-air grapple, his body raining meat and shards of armour-plating as it plummeted. The eldar who'd shot Vorasha at point-blank range turned in the air, bringing his rifle up to aim at Lucoryphus.

The Raptor leader tilted forward and boosted closer, another shriek leaving his scarred lips.

TALOS LED FIRST Claw through the corridors in a new kind of hunt. With no need to heed any caution, the four Terminators thudded their way onward in a loose phalanx, unfamiliar weapons aimed at the ready.

'This will take some getting used to,' Cyrion voxed. He was still bemused at the aquila showing on the edge of his retinal display. In Deltrian's many modifications and reconfigurings, he'd evidently not managed to scrub that detail from the armour's internal systems.

Talos was distracted by the vox-net; the reports of Second and Third Claws engaging the enemy higher up in the catacombs, and the Bleeding Eyes' savage curses as they fought on the surface. He tried not to wonder what Malcharion was doing – the captain had decided to die alone, and he couldn't find flaw with that desire. First Claw would have to split up soon enough. Once unified resistance became impossible against greater numbers, it would come down to murder in the dark, and every soul for himself.

He'd never worn Tactical Dreadnought war-plate before, and the sensation was a surprising one. His battle armour was as familiar as his own skin, and as comfortable as clothing once wearer and suit bonded over time. Terminator plate was a different beast from tusked helm to spiked boots; every muscle in his body felt revitalised, stinging with strength. He'd expected to feel sluggish, but the range of motion and speed of movement was little different from the times he'd trained out of his armour. The only disconcerting aspect was the forward-leaning hunch, leaving him always on the edge of breaking into a run.

Talos had tried running. It resulted in a quicker, more forceful tread that was somewhere between a stagger and a sprint. Compensatory servos and stabilisers wouldn't allow him to pitch forward and fall, though the shift in the centre of his balance still felt unusual after so many centuries crusading in his modified Mark V plate.

One of his hands was an armoured glove the size of a legionary's torso – the power fist active and rippling with a passive force field. The other clutched a heavy rotary cannon, his finger resting on the curved trigger. They didn't have much ammunition for the assault cannon. When First Claw scavenged the suits from the Salamanders, they soon learned the Imperials had used most of their reserves. He carried his double-barrelled bolter locked to his thigh, ready to draw it the moment he dumped the empty cannon.

Mercutian reached with his oversized power fist, tapping at the ornate tusks Deltrian had grafted to the muzzle of his bullish helm.

'I once saw Malek of the Atramentar head-butt someone with his tusks,' he said. 'I'd like to try that.'

Talos held up a fist for silence – or as close as they could come to silence while in suits of armour rumbling like the idling engines of four battle tanks.

A hail of razor-edged discs sliced out from the corridor ahead, followed by the advancing forms of eldar warriors. They hesitated in their tracks when they saw what was stalking towards them. Several of them scattered, while others fell back, still firing. Talos heard the shuriken projectiles clattering against his armour, with the same tinkling sound of glass shards breaking on the floor.

In reply, he squeezed his trigger, filling the tunnel with the distinctive flashing roar of an Imperial assault cannon. Suspensors in his elbow, wrist and the gun's grip counterbalanced any recoil, letting him aim without distraction, but his retinal feed had to dim to compensate for the brightness of the muzzle flash.

First Claw stood in disbelief ten seconds later. Talos tilted the cannon to get a better look at its steaming, reddening barrels.

'Now *that's* a cannon,' said Cyrion, as the four of them waded through the organic mess left in the corridor. 'Can I use it for a while?'

MARLONAH WASN'T SURE what she was hearing anymore. Sometimes the stone hallways echoed with what sounded like distant gunfire, other times it seemed like nothing more than the wind, weaving through the dark at her side.

She had a lamp pack – no crew member on an VIII Legion vessel would walk a ship's halls without one – and she knew the power cell would be good for another few hours at least. What she didn't know was what to do, or where to go.

Does is make a difference? What does it matter if I die down here or on the plains?

She still had her stub gun, for what it was worth – a primitive little slug-thrower compared to a Legiones Astartes bolter, make no mistake. It'd be fine for shooting herself in the head before she died of thirst, but it wasn't much use if she walked into a battle. Slaves weren't permitted weapons on the *Echo of Damnation*, but the thriving black market trading going on in every level of life took care of that. The Legion never enforced such a law anyway, for they feared no uprising. She suspected they enjoyed a little spice to the challenge when they hunted crew members for sport, as well.

Marlonah wasn't sure how long she'd been alone before the thumping started. She made her way through the deserted catacombs, sending her torch beam ahead, letting it cut the blackness as best it could. All sense of direction had long since abandoned her. Sound echoed strangely down here, to the point she wasn't even sure whether she was heading towards the thumping or avoiding it completely. It never seemed to fade or grow any stronger.

She never saw what knocked the lamp pack from her grip. A breath of air passed by the back of her neck, and a rough impact against her hand sent the torch clattering to the ground. For a split second, its spinning beam sent insane shadows against the walls: the silhouettes of witch-thin figures with elongated, inhuman helms.

Marlonah went for her gun before the torch had fallen still. That, too, left her hand with what felt like a kick to her fist.

The second time she felt the breath, it was against her face. The voice emerging from the darkness was as unwelcomingly soft as velvet on bleeding skin.

'Where is the Prophet of the Eighth Legion?'

She aimed her fist at the voice in the blackness, but her punch met nothing but air. A second, third and fourth swiped through the same nothingness. She could hear the subtle movement and breathing of something dodging her in the dark, betrayed by the smooth scrape of armour plates sliding with every weave.

A hand bolted around her throat, collaring her with thin fingers sheathed in cold iron. She managed a single blow against the unmoving arm, before she was slammed back against the wall. Her boots scrabbled against the stone, unable to reach the ground. Her rough augmetic leg made clicking, whirring sounds as it struggled to find the floor.

'Where is the Prophet of the Eighth Legion?'

'I've lived my whole life in the dark,' she told the unseen voice. 'Do you think *this* scares me?'

The collar of fingers tightened enough to cut off her breath. She wasn't sure if the thumping was getting louder, or if she was being deceived by her own rising heartbeat.

'Filthy, blind, poisonous, cancerous mon-keigh animal. Where is the Prophet of the Eighth Legion? Thousands of souls remain at stake while he draws breath.'

Marlonah thrashed in the stronger grip, beating her fists against the armoured arm.

'Stubborn creature. Know this, human: the silent storm approaches. The Void Stalker comes.'

The clutch at her throat vanished as fast as it appeared, dropping her to the ground. The first thing she thought, as she heaved the stale air back into her body, was that her heartbeat hadn't lied. The thumping was all around her now, the thudding crunch of steel on stone. It sent trembles through the ground beneath her, and the wall against her back.

Marlonah scrabbled for her lamp wand, chopping its thin blade of illumination around the chamber. She saw stone, and stone, and stone, and... something immense, and dark, and leering down at her with rumbling joints.

'What are you doing down here?'

HE CAME IN too hard, at a bad angle, and tumbled across the dusty ground. It took a moment to haul himself back up to all-fours, and another two attempts to stand straight. His metallic foot-claws splayed to compensate, digging into the soft dust.

The pain was… quite something. He tasted blood with each breath, and the ache of his muscles put him in firm mind of the three nights he'd been racked by Lord Jiruvius of the Emperor's Children.

That hadn't been a pleasant war. Losing it had felt even worse.

Lucoryphus hadn't landed far from the last eldar. He walked over to her prone form, noting the trail of bloody fluid leaking from several of his armour joints. His war-plate was an interesting display of battle cartography, marked by laser burns and punctures from the aliens' short bone-daggers.

The Raptor rolled the sky-maiden's corpse with his foot-claw. Her slanted eyes, as lifeless as sapphires and much the same colour, stared up into the grey heavens. On her chest was a smooth red jewel, named by her kindred as a soulstone. Lucoryphus tore it from the armour and swallowed it whole. He hoped her immortal spirit would enjoy its fate to dwell forever within his bowels.

'Soul Hunter,' he voxed at last.

The prophet's voice was flawed by distance distortion and gunfire crackles. 'I hear you, Lucoryphus.'

'The Bleeding Eyes are dead. I am the last.'

He heard Talos give a grunt of effort. 'It grieves me to hear that, brother. Will you join us down here?'

The Raptor looked to the fallen walls, the remnants of once-great battlements. Storm clouds were gathering above them – an anomaly on this weatherless world.

'Not yet. Something comes, Talos. Watch yourselves.'

XXVI
STORM

THE RAIN STARTED the very moment her boots touched the Tsagualsan soil.

Lucoryphus watched her from his tenuous perch, crouched on what remained of a long stretch of battlement wall. Five eldar soulstones sat cold in his guts. When he closed his eyes, even just to blink, he was certain he could hear five voices screaming in a lamenting dirge.

How curious, he thought, as she manifested. She stepped from a heat shimmer in the air itself, falling a dozen feet to land on her toes, with arms outspread. Her armour consisted of silver plating, shaped like slender musculature over a black bodysuit that shimmered like fish scales. In one hand was a staff – scimitar-bladed at both ends and wet with slow ripples of liquid lightning. In her other fist, she clutched a throwing star the size of a battle shield, ending in three hooked dagger blades. The fire that danced along the alien steel was black, forged through a craft Lucoryphus wasn't certain he wished to know.

Her face was shielded by a silver death mask, sculpted in the cold-eyed image of a screaming goddess. A high, long crest of black hair flowed down her shoulders and back, somehow immune to the wind sending dust-wraiths haunting through the ruins.

Everything about her radiated wrongness, even to a creature as warp-touched as he. For several seconds, the heat haze remained around her, as if she were at risk of being rejected by reality.

This is no eldar maiden, the Raptor knew. *Perhaps she was, once. Now... she is something much more.*

Lucoryphus's claws tightened on the stone as the eldar war-goddess flew across the ground in a blurred sprint, her feet barely gracing the earth. One moment she was a silver blur in the ruins; the next she was gone, either vanished into thin air or descended underground – Lucoryphus wasn't certain.

'Talos.' He opened the vox-link again. 'I have seen what hunts us.'

* * *

SECOND CLAW HAD survived for over three hours in a series of running gunfights, repelling wave after wave of alien attackers. The only lights to flash down the tunnels and illuminate the chambers came from the staccato flicker of weapons fire, or the rare clash of opposing energy fields when a power sword met another of its kind.

Yuris was limping from the blade wound to his thigh. He knew his brothers would leave him behind soon. It wasn't a matter of needing to talk them into abandoning him, nor did it come down to something as noble as self-sacrifice. They'd leave him behind because he was getting slower, and getting weaker. His life had become a liability to theirs.

The Night Lord caught his breath with his back to a wall. He locked his bolter to his thigh for a moment, reloading it with a crunching smack, and only a single hand.

'My last,' he voxed to the other two survivors. 'I'm out of ammunition.'

'We'll fall back to the reserve crates,' replied Fal Torm. The truth was implicit in the other warrior's words: they would fall back to the ammunition reserves, but they'd almost certainly leave him behind. If Yuris's death bought them a few more seconds, then all the better.

'You're hurt worse than you're admitting,' said Xan Kurus. The backswept wings on Xan Kurus's helm had been shattered off hours before, broken away by an alien blade. 'I can smell your lifeblood, and hear the strain in your hearts.'

Yuris couldn't catch his breath. It was difficult to inhale, forcing air into a throat that felt too tight.

Is this what dying feels like?

'I'm still standing,' he voxed back. 'Come. Let's move.'

The three survivors of Second Claw retreated further into the dark, breaking into a ragged run. Mere hours before, Yuris had led nine other souls. Now he was the high and mighty lord over two warriors, both of whom were preparing to abandon him the moment the opportunity presented itself.

As with humans, all eldar were not created equal. Yuris had learned that at great cost. The ones with weak projectile rifles and thin armour of black plate and mesh weave – they died like weak children and shot with all the skill expected of any hive-born member drawn from humanity's urban dregs. But the others... The shrieking witches and the sword-killers...

Six warriors dead in three hours. The alien maidens would dissolve out of the dark, weaving past any gunfire, and lock blades with the Night Lords in a storm of blows. Whether they killed or not didn't seem to change their behaviour; as soon as the first blade clashes were done, they'd break away and flee back through the tunnels.

The howling was the worst part of every charge – they'd scream a dirge long and loud enough to wake the forgotten dead of this accursed world.

Each howl knifed a sliver of ice right into the back of his head, doing something to his brain, slowing his reactions enough to leave him straining to parry every blow.

Ah, but Second Claw hadn't gone down easy. They were the hunters, after all. Yuris had slit three of the maidens' pale throats himself, grappling them from behind and ending them with a quick, sawing caress of his gladius.

Back and forth it went: charge, defend, hunt, slice, retreat…

Yuris stumbled in his run, his hand resting on the wall for balance. He'd run ahead of his brothers, but that soon became limping alongside them, and at last, limping and lagging behind.

'Goodbye, Yuris,' Xan Kurus voxed from up ahead. Fal Torm didn't even stop – he carried on at a dead sprint.

'Wait,' Yuris said to Xan Kurus. 'Wait, brother.'

'Why?' Xan Kurus was already running again. 'Die well.'

Yuris listened to his kindred's bootsteps growing fainter. His stumbling run devolved into a simple stagger, and he crashed against the wall, sliding down to his knees.

I don't want to die on Tsagualsa. The thought rose, sourceless and unbidden. Was Tsagualsa truly a worse place to die than any other?

Yes, he thought. *The carrion world is cursed. We should never have returned here.*

The ancient superstition brought a painful smile to his bloody lips. And what did it matter? He'd served, hadn't he? He'd served loyally down the centuries, and ripped pleasure from a galaxy that had never been able to deny him. *Until now…*

Yuris tried to grin again, but blood spilled from his mangled lips in a black gush.

No matter. No matter. It was a fine thing, to be alive and to be strong.

His helm tipped forward as that strength finally faded, seeping out with his blood.

'Yuris,' the vox crackled.

Begone, Fal Torm. Run ahead, if you wish. Let me die alone and in peace, bastards.

'Yuris,' the voice repeated.

He opened his eyes without realising they'd been closed. Red-tinted vision returned, showing his cracked breastplate and the stump where his left hand had been less than an hour before.

What? he asked, and had to make a second attempt to speak it out loud. 'What?' he voxed.

His retinal display feeds were white blurs of scrolling gibberish. Blinking twice brought them back into resolution.

Xan Kurus's life signals registered as a flatline. As did Fal Torm's.

That cannot be. Yuris forced himself to his feet, biting back a groan at the agony of his broken knee and missing hand. His armour's damage prevented it from flooding pain inhibitors into his bloodstream, only compounding his torment.

He found his last two brothers in the hallways ahead, and shook with suppressed laughter. Both bodies were sprawled across the stone floor, their ruination exacting and complete. Xan Kurus and Fal Torm were both cleaved in half at the waist, their bodies separated from their legs. Blood decorated the floor in patternless blotching.

Neither of them had a head. Their helms were free of their severed necks, released to roll against the wall once the corpses fell.

Yuris couldn't bite back the laughter. Despite abandoning him, they'd died before him, anyway. Even through the pain, the notion appealed to his sense of poetic justice.

The blade that killed Yuris struck first in the back, driving through his lower spine and bursting from the layered armour over his belly. Foul, glistening ropes of offal followed it out, as his insides tumbled in a sick heap at his boots.

Yuris managed to remain standing for another couple of heartbeats before the blade struck again. He saw it this time; a blur of spinning silver and burning black, slashing through the air quicker than a blink. It cleaved into his ripped stomach and tore out from his lower back, and this time Yuris fell to the ground with a cry and a crash.

For one grotesque moment, he found himself on his back, reaching with his one remaining hand to drag himself back over to his legs.

Then she was above him. The creature Lucoryphus had warned them about. His racing, firing, dying mind screamed at him to act. He had to vox the others. He had to warn them she was already down here.

But that didn't happen. He said nothing. He warned no one. Yuris opened his mouth, only to choke a hot flood of bile and blood down his neck.

The silent witch-queen lifted the spear cradled in her other hand, and lifted it high above. She said a single word in crude Gothic, her accent spicing it almost beyond recognition.

'Sleep.'

For Yuris, blessed blackness dawned at last, with the fall of an alien blade.

THE FIRST HOWLS had caught him unprepared. He wouldn't make that mistake again.

When First Claw linked up with Faroven's Third Claw, both squads readied to hold an expansive network of chambers for as long as they could, replete with annex rooms, fall back tunnels and defensible junctions.

'Have you seen Malcharion?' was Faroven's first question.

'He still hunts alone,' Talos had replied.

The screaming maidens came in the wake of those words. After fighting the weakling warriors of the last few hours, the shrieking assault had been an unpleasant change in pace and tactics. Still, it had at least stopped Cyrion from pining to use the assault cannon.

The first howls had caught them unprepared. Before the blade-witches attacked, they shrieked their mournful cries, using the song itself as a weapon. Immunity to fear meant nothing in that song's shadow – Talos felt his blood run cold, felt his muscles slowing, felt sweat break out at his temples, as his body reacted the way any terrified mortal's flesh might.

The sensation had been... incredible, almost intoxicating in its unnatural force. Like nothing he'd ever felt in all the long decades of his life. No soul enhanced by gene-seed could feel terror, yet even though the creeping doubt never touched his mind, the physical sensation of feeling fear still forced a laugh from his throat. To think *this* was a pale reflection of what he inflicted on those he killed? To sense it first-hand?

How educational, he'd thought, grinning his crooked grin. The amusement was admittedly dampened by the deadness in his limbs, and short-lived enough to burn away in his anger a moment later.

But the aliens were among them by then. They cut and cleaved and carved with their mirrored blades, savaging the ranks of the last two Night Lord Claws left standing. They danced as they killed, as though performing some inhuman dance to music only they could hear. Each of their helms was sculpted into a shouting death mask, open mouths projecting the psychically amplified shriek.

A lovely trick, he thought, hating himself for admiring anything an alien breed could create.

As the prophet deflected a descending sword with the back of his armoured glove, he fancied – in his fever – he could sense the song's edges himself. The crash of blades on ceramite was the rapid clash of soft drums; the grunts and cries of his dying brothers became the rhythm beneath it.

'Be silent,' he snarled, backhanding the alien wretch with his power fist. Her shrieking ended along with her life: with a wet crack against the stone wall behind.

The eldar were gone as quickly as they'd come, fleeing back into the tunnels.

'They're not howling now,' Cyrion had laughed.

Talos hadn't laughed. Three of Third Claw lay dead, cut to pieces by the banshees' blades. Only one of the eldar had fallen; the one he'd smashed aside with his fist.

Talos walked his careful, crunching way across the chamber. As he drew near, he saw her fingers twitch.

'She still lives,' Faroven warned.

'So I see.'

Talos pressed his boot down on her hand, the gears grinding in his knees. It took no effort at all – the Terminator suit made it no harder than drawing breath – to crush her hand into a bloody smear of paste.

That woke her up, and she woke up screaming. He dragged the helm from her head, and the psychic cry died, leaving an almost-human moan in its place.

Talos rested the assault cannon on her chest.

'I know you,' she said in awkward Gothic, as though the words tasted foul. Her slanted eyes narrowed, showing the lush green of long-lost forests. 'I am Taisha, Daughter of Morai-Heg, and I know you, Soul Hunter.'

'Whatever your alien witchery has told you,' his voice was a vox-altered snarl, 'is meaningless. For you lie at death's edge, and I am the one to kick you over it.'

Trapped with her arm ruined beneath his boot, she still managed to smile through agony's breathless panting.

'You will cross blades with the Void Stalker,' she grinned with bloody gums. 'And you will die on this world.'

'And who is the Void Stalker?'

Her answer was to lash out with a kick. He'd tortured eldar countless times before – they never broke under excruciation, and never whispered a word they didn't wish to speak.

Talos lifted his boot and walked away.

'End her,' he voxed, not caring who did the deed.

Lucoryphus wasn't ashamed of the feast. Just as the VIII Legion scavenged wargear from the slain, so too did the Bleeding Eyes scavenge flesh.

He knew if Talos or any of the others saw him pulling apart his brothers' bodies to devour the meat within, they'd be unlikely to see it in such generous terms, but with events unfolding as they were, that hardly seemed to matter.

And it wasn't as if Vorasha and the others needed their flesh anymore. Lucoryphus was careful, between mouthfuls, to save their gene-seed. No ceremonial extraction for a fallen Raptor, and no emotional butchery at a brother's hands. Lucoryphus pulled the fleshy nodes out with handfuls of meat around them, and stored them in a cryo-canister at his thigh.

Then went right back to devouring the dead in the rain.

He looked up every now and again, his bare face tingling in the unfamiliar feel of wind as he scanned for signs of eldar arrival. What scraps of chatter he caught from the vox sounded as though the subterranean hunts were no longer of interest. They were all as good as dead.

He wasn't even sure why he was taking the Bleeding Eyes' gene-seed. Some traditions were tenacious, even in the face of death.

When he heard the gunship's engine, his instinctive reaction was to tense, claws activating as he turned to face the growing sound. Without his helm's vision cycles, his sight suffered at a distance. He needed movement to follow, motion to track, else he was close to blind past a hundred paces.

Lucoryphus was reaching for his helm when the gunship reached him, hovering overhead, breathing engine wash downward and blasting dust across the ruins. He watched without expression as the gangramp opened, and felt no pulse of surprise at the figure that dropped from the sky.

The Night Lord landed with a smooth thud, and voxed back up to the gunship. 'I am down. Land on the battlements over there. Stay away from any eldar ground forces. If you are engaged from the air, run. That is all I desire from you. Understood.'

The gunship banked without the pilot replying, thrusters flaring as it obeyed.

'Lucoryphus of the Bleeding Eyes,' said Variel.

'Variel the Flayer.'

'I have never seen you with your helmet off.'

Lucoryphus replaced his helm, fixing the daemon's visage back over his face.

'You look like a drowned corpse,' Variel noted.

'I know what I look like. Why are you here?'

Variel let his gaze drift around the ruins. 'A fool's hope. Where is Talos?'

Lucoryphus gestured with his claw, the blades angled down. 'Beneath.'

'I cannot reach him on the vox.'

'Contact breaks down. They're deep under, and fighting.'

'Where is the closest entrance to the catacombs?'

Lucoryphus gestured again. The Apothecary started walking, his own dense bionic leg making a *thunk, thunk, thunk* on the dusty soil. Pistons hissed in his cybernetic knee.

Lucoryphus followed, dropping to all fours in a graceful prowl that never failed to impress Variel for its unexpected elegance.

'How did you get past the blockade?' the Raptor asked.

'There is no blockade. Two-dozen vessels wait in high orbit, with little sign of landing craft. We didn't even detect a sensor sweep. It took hours to reach this far, but twenty vessels cannot keep an entire world in their eyes. You may as well ask a blind man to count each rock that makes up a mountain.'

Lucoryphus said nothing as they passed Vorasha's mutilated, half-eaten body. Variel wasn't so silent.

'In a time now considered myth, cannibalism was considered good for the body and soul.' He looked at the Raptor for a moment. 'If we survive this, I would like a sample of your blood.'

'Not a prayer.'

Variel nodded, expecting that answer. 'You are aware, Lucoryphus, that such degrees of *livor mortis* and bacterial decomposition on your face and throat would simply not manifest on a living being? Your biology is in a stage of autolysis. Your cells are eating themselves. Does the feasting on fraternal flesh regenerate the process?'

Lucoryphus didn't reply. Variel continued nevertheless. 'How then do you live? Are you dead, yet still alive? Or has the warp played a greater game with you?'

'I no longer know what I am. I haven't known for centuries. Now tell me why you're here.'

Above the forgotten fortress, the storm finally showed its strength. Lightning lit up the grey sky, while heavier rain lashed down on their armour. Variel's flayed shoulder guard, the skinned face of a brother he'd slain long ago, seemed to be weeping.

'TALOS.'

He didn't reply. Teeth clenched, he kept the cannon's trigger pulled tight, streaming out tracer fire to illuminate the dark tunnel. The numeric runes on his retinal display depleted away, shrinking by the second, even as the cannon's spinning barrels began to glow a brighter red with the pressure of overheating.

'Talos,' the voice crackled again. 'Don't move too far ahead.'

The assault cannon eased off with a descending whine. He bit back a harsh reply, knowing it would make no difference. Cyrion was right; still, the frustration remained. The hunt had changed once more. When the eldar stopped coming to them, they'd taken the fight to the eldar.

Talos stalked to a stop, letting the stabilisers and servos in his leg armour settle once more. The cannon hissed in the cold air, while dead aliens lay strewn at his feet.

Cyrion and Mercutian stomped closer, filling the tunnel with their whirring joints and pounding footsteps. Both of their storm bolters showed defiled Imperial aquilas. Both weapons also had smoking barrels.

'I'm almost out of ammunition,' voxed Mercutian. 'It's time to get back into our battle armour and split up. The butchery was enjoyable, but they're avoiding us as a pack.'

Talos nodded. 'I'll miss the armament.'

'As will I,' Mercutian replied. 'And I've lost count how many of these wretches we've killed. I lost count at seventy, at the last intersection. This group makes...' Mercutian panned his storm bolter across the destroyed, bloody bodies. 'Ninety-four.'

'These are nothing more than dregs.' Cyrion turned his tusked helm towards Mercutian. 'But the shrieking maidens? I've not managed to hit one, yet.'

'Nor I,' said Talos. 'Not since the first one. The weaker ones die like vermin. The howling ones are a breed apart.'

Uzas came last of all, his armour washed by blood. Instead of tusks, his helm sported a brutal, curved horn from the bridge of the faceplate's nose.

'They are warrior-priestesses of their war god's daughter.' First Claw turned to look at him, none of them saying a word for a moment. 'What?' Uzas grunted. 'I have excruciated eldar captives in the past, just as you have.'

'Whatever they are, we should get back to Third Claw.'

'*Talos.*'

The prophet hesitated. No name rune flashed on his retinal display. 'Variel?'

'Brother, I am in the ruins above with Lucoryphus. We must speak.'

'No. Please let this be a foul jest. I ordered you away for a reason, fool.'

Talos listened to his brother's explanation, as hurried and fragmented as it was. He took several long moments to reply.

'Back to Third Claw,' he ordered the others. 'Variel, do not descend into the ruins. The tunnels are infested with eldar.'

'Are you returning to the surface?'

Talos wasn't even sure of that himself. 'Just stay hidden.'

THE HOWLING MAIDENS returned as soon as First Claw rejoined Faroven and the Third. Faroven was down to four warriors; their slain brethren were left in the corridors, while the remnants of the Claw moved as a unified pack.

This time, the Night Lords were ready. Pursuing their prey through the corridors for the last couple of hours had fed their hearts in a way forming defensive lines never could.

The aliens spilled through the VIII Legion's ranks, blades blurring and hair-crests flowing. Talos caught a growled 'We're outnumbered,' from one of his brothers, but the press of limbs and blades made the details hopeless.

The two maidens before him both screamed at once, raising their blades. He felt the same ice crawl through his muscles, dragging him back, slowing him down.

Two... can play... that game...

The Night Lord released a scream of his own – a roar from three lungs and an enhanced respiratory system, heightened tenfold by the vox-speakers in his snarling helm. The surviving Night Lords heard the cry and took it up a heartbeat later.

He'd used his cry to shatter windows and deafen crowds of humans to soften them up for the kill; now he used it in opposition to those who sought to turn his own weapon against him.

Three of the maidens' swords shattered outright. Several of the alien warriors lost eye lenses to splitting cracks as the harmonious, savage scream reached its apex. In the same moment the Night Lords' cry hit its crescendo, the eldar's howl died a sudden death.

Talos killed the first of the warriors before him with a fist around her head, crushing the skull and bones of her shoulders before hurling her away. The second died while still staggering back from the shout, cut to pieces by the final hail from his assault cannon. He dropped the empty weapon and reached for his relic bolter, drawing in breath to scream a second time.

With the tide turned, with the maidens stumbling back and succumbing to the butchery they'd inflicted on the legionaries, a new sound invaded the warriors' senses.

Uzas hammered his fist into one of the alien's stomachs, breaking her breastbone and spine in the same blow. As she fell against him on strengthless legs, he lowered his head and rammed his helm-horn through her torso.

'Do you hear that?' the others were voxing.

'Footsteps.'

'Those aren't footsteps. They're too fast.'

He couldn't hear a thing beyond the beating of his hearts, and the blood rain streaming down his helm and shoulders. It took two heaves to shove the twitching body off his horn. His neck gave a stiff crackle as he stood up straight again.

Then he heard it. And Talos was right. It was footsteps.

'I know what that is,' he said. The steps had the rhythm of a racing heartbeat, soft against the stone yet still echoing down the hallways, loud as the winds of the warp.

Talos stood above two slain maidens, blood dripping from his curled fingers. The only sound was the footsteps, now all the screeching had fallen still.

'What is it?' he asked.

'A storm in flesh, with a rain of blades. She Who Stalks the Void.' Uzas ran his tongue across his teeth, tasting the acid on his gums. 'The Storm of Silence.'

XXVII
VOID STALKER

SHE CAME FROM the darkness, just as her sisters had done. Varthon was the first to see her, and shouted a warning to the others. The cry died in his throat as soon as it started, ended by the spear blade punched through his breastplate, bursting both of his hearts in a single blow. A full metre of the black spear thrust out from his spine for a single moment, until the weapon slid back from his flesh with vicious patience.

She watched each of them as she let the body fall, while a flatline tune played out in every Night Lord's helm.

Every figure moved at once. The legionaries lifted their bolters and opened fire, each of them unleashing a torrent of explosive shells and none of them coming close to striking her.

Flatline wails rang in Talos's ears as he fired at the dancing, flickering figure. Centuries of training and battle aligned with the targeting processors in his Terminator plate and retinal display, guiding his aim as much as instinct. The storm bolter bucked and banged in his grip, spitting shells in a tide that only relented when he had to reload.

He backed away, crunching another magazine home. All of them were reloading out of sync, all sense of unity and covering fire gone in a moment. Talos saw, in one blurry scan of the chamber, how their bolter fire had savaged every single wall without once hitting their prey.

Jekrish White-Eyes died next, his head cleaved clean from his shoulders. As the body started to topple, Talos lifted his fist to block his brother's spinning helm from hitting him. It clanged aside, dropping to the floor. He was already firing at the black blur, aiming in the places instinct and his targeting reticule said she'd be. More stonework died in detonation craters and splintering chips.

She didn't even slow down to kill. The spear reaped right through Gol Tatha's waist, severing him from his legs. In the same second, Faroven died halfway across the chamber, a three-bladed throwing star forged of alien iron and black fire cracking his head down the middle. Both bodies fell, twinning their thuds as they struck stone.

Mercutian cried out, his bulky suit of armour arching its back as he cursed. Talos caught a flicker of movement in his visor display as the spear lanced back out from his brother's back. Mercutian staggered forward, only prevented from falling by the artificial ironclad muscles in his armour's joints. His storm bolter boomed once more, before spilling from his grip.

When the throwing blade hit Uzas, it crashed against his horned helm, sending ceramite chunks clattering off the walls. He didn't stagger as Mercutian had; he tumbled one step and dropped to his hands and knees, heavy enough to send tremors through the floor. Talos saw blood drip to the dark stone ground, pooling between Uzas's shaking hands.

'Talos…' crackled the vox.

'Not now.'

'Brother,' said Variel, 'when are you returning to the surf–'

'*Not now!*'

He followed the blur with his storm bolter, just as it danced behind Korosa, the last soul standing in Third Claw. Korosa turned, as fast as a genhanced human body was capable of moving, lashing out with his howling chainsword. In the single second it took Talos to draw aim, Korosa was lurching backwards, blood gouting from his severed arm. He made it two steps before the spear's backswing disembowelled him, spilling a wet slop of innards down the front of his war-plate.

Talos fired over Korosa's shoulder. The single *crack* and the throaty burst that followed were the sweetest sounds he'd ever heard. He saw the blur resolve into a female figure, as tall as any of them in their Terminator ceramite, falling back with her head snapped to the side.

Mercutian was struggling to reach for his dropped bolter and Uzas was still down, but Cyrion aligned his aim the same moment Talos fired again. A silver crescent arc blurred before her, detonating shell after shell before they could touch her. It took the prophet's eyes a couple of precious seconds to adjust to the speed, before he realised she was blocking their incoming fire with the blade of her spear.

She couldn't shatter them all. A withering spit of shells crashed against her black-and-bone armour, sending her reeling again.

Talos broke off to reload. Cyrion did the same, a second later. Both of them froze with their bolters empty, staring at the damaged wall where she'd been a moment before.

Korosa crashed to the ground, breaking the sudden silence.

For a long moment, Cyrion turned in place, unwilling to believe she was gone. Other, less intrusive sounds filtered back into being: Mercutian's choking breaths, Uzas's pained grunts, and the hiss of cooling bolter muzzles.

'I can't see her,' Cyrion voxed over their squad link. 'And I'm out of ammunition.'

'As am I.' Talos resisted the need to check on Uzas and Mercutian, never taking his eyes from the walls as he turned, back-to-back with Cyrion.

'She's still here,' said Cyrion. 'She must be.'

'No.' Talos gestured with his power fist. A trail of blood spatters led from the chamber, back into the tunnels. 'She's running.'

Cyrion threw his empty storm bolter away, discarding it without care. 'We should be doing the same.'

THE SERVITORS AWAITED them, still silent in their dead-minded reverie. Talos was first into the chamber, gesturing for the augmented slaves to attend him.

'Get me out of this armour.'

'Compliance,' uttered twelve voices at once.

'And me,' said Mercutian. Unhelmed now, he spat blood onto the floor. It started dissolving the stone at once.

'Compliance,' said the rest of the servitors.

'Make it quick,' Cyrion voxed, taking guard with Uzas at the entrance archway. Mercutian threw him his storm bolter as the servitors closed around. Cyrion checked the ammunition feed on his retinal display, and readied the weapon. Despite his wound, Uzas stood straight and speechless; the only sound registering from him was the tidal flow of his slow breathing. His helmet was a cracked ruin, baring most of his bloodstained face beneath. Unfocused eyes stared into the tunnel, as did the twin barrels of his storm bolter.

'I'll miss this armour,' Cyrion said. 'Uzas and Mercutian are only still alive because of this war-plate. That spear went through battle armour like a knife through flesh.'

Mercutian muttered a reluctant agreement. He was struggling to stand, and each movement brought a fresh muscle cramp, with another pulse of pain slithering up his spine.

'I'm not going to make it much further,' he said, needing to spit the blood from his mouth again.

The servitors' machine-tools went to work – drilling; unscrewing; prising plates clear. Talos felt himself breathing easier with each layer that came free. 'None of us are,' he said. 'We didn't come down here to win.'

Uzas chuckled at that, but said nothing more.

'Brother?' Talos voxed. 'Uzas?'

The other Night Lord turned his broken helm, bloody features looking back at Talos. 'What is it?'

The Terminator shoulder guards were machined free, coming loose with a series of crunches and clicks, and carried away by the servitors.

Talos met Uzas's eyes, black to black, sensing something had changed in his brother's face but unable to decide what.

'Are you well?'

'Aye, brother.' Uzas turned back to his guard duty. 'Never better.'

'You sound well. You sound very... clear.'

'I imagine I do.' Uzas's armour gave a slow growl as he glanced at Cyrion. 'I feel clearer.'

The servitors were removing Mercutian's power fist when his legs gave way. He stumbled, needing to lean against the wall to remain standing. Blood was running from the corner of his mouth.

'Leave me behind when you go,' he said. 'My spine's aflame, and it's spreading to my legs. I can't run like this.'

Cyrion was the one to answer. 'He's right, anyway. It's time to split up, Talos. She'll go through us like a cold wind if we hunt her as a pack.'

Uzas gave another guttural chuckle. 'You just want to hide.'

'Enough of your perspective, drooling one.'

Mercutian bit back a growl. 'Enough talk of splitting up. Leave me, and get the prophet back to the surface. Variel's come for a reason, fools. Talos can't die here.'

'Shut up, all of you.' Talos breathed deep as the helm was lifted clear. 'Uzas, Cyrion, be silent and watch the tunnels.'

MALCHARION'S HUNT WAS slower, but no less purposeful. He made his way through the tunnels, backtracking when he encountered a collapsed passageway or a hall too narrow and low for him to traverse.

'This was once a laborium. The Legion's Techmarines worked here. Not all of them, of course. But many.'

Marlonah limped alongside the colossal war machine. Her torchlight flickered and died yet again, and this time, smacking it against her thigh didn't bring it back to life. For several seconds she stood in the darkness, listening to the dusty ghosts of the forgotten fortress.

'Our Techmarines and trained serfs constructed servitors in a ceaseless horde. Captives. Failed aspirants. Humans harvested from a hundred worlds, brought here to serve. Can you imagine that? Can you picture the production lines filling this bare hall?'

'I... I can't see anything, lord.'

'Oh.'

Light returned with a crack. A lance of illumination burned from the Dreadnought's shoulder.

'Is that better?'

'Yes, lord.'

'Stop using that word. I am no one's lord.'

Marlonah swallowed, looking around where the beam of light pointed. 'As you wish, lord.'

Malcharion made his slow, grinding way across the large chamber. 'It is all so different now. This is no longer my home, and it is no longer my war. One last hunt, though. For all of the pain, it was worth it to hunt one last time.'

'Yes, lord. If you say so, lord.'

The Dreadnought whirred on its waist axis, coming about to a new direction and stomping that way when its legs realigned. Sparks briefly lit up the tarnished armour-plating. Their last few run-ins with the masked aliens had left their mark on the war machine's iron body. Still, he'd slaughtered them all before they could come anywhere near her.

'Are you alive, lord? I mean... You speak of death and resurrection. What are you?'

The Dreadnought made an awkward gear-grinding sound. 'I was Captain Malcharion of Tenth Company, called war-sage by my primarch, who found my long treatises on warfare to be pointless, but amusing. He lectured me more than once, you know. Told me to serve with the Thirteenth, where my wit would be more welcome.'

She nodded slowly, seeing her breath mist in the air. 'What's a primarch?'

Malcharion made the same gear-shifting noise again. 'Just a myth,' the vox-speakers boomed. 'Forget I spoke.'

For a time, they stood in silence. Malcharion tuned back into the vox, listening in contemplative quiet to the words of Variel, Talos, Lucoryphus and the last surviving members of his company. The arrival of the Flayer was a surprise, as was the presence of the gunship he brought. Beyond that, they all seemed to be dying just as they'd desired: falling only after reaving countless enemy lives, watering the stones of their ancient castle with the blood of their foes one last time.

Perhaps it wasn't glorious, but it was right. They weren't the Imperial Fists, to stand in gold beneath the burning sun and scream the names of their heroes to the uncaring sky. This was how the VIII Legion fought, and how all sons of the sunless world should finally die – screaming their anger, alone, down in the dark.

He thought for a moment of the lie he'd told the human by his side; the lie that he relished this last hunt. He was perversely thankful for the chance to witness his former brethren meet their ends as true sons of the VIII, but he cared nothing for shedding the cursed blood of these foolish xenos heathens. What grudge did he bear against them? None. None at all. Killing them was only a pleasure to teach them the ways of the VIII, and the flaws of their inhuman arrogance.

He considered it unlikely they could kill him with their scattered, weakling war parties. Perhaps twenty or thirty of them with better blades might be able to overwhelm him, but even then...

No.

He'd meet his end in this cold tomb, already interred within his coffin, finally falling into silence when the Dreadnought shell ran out of power. It could be ten years. It could be ten thousand. He had no way of knowing.

Malcharion shut off the vox, and once more considered the human by his side. What was her name again? Had he even asked? Did it matter?

'Do you want to die down here, human?'

She hugged herself against the cold. 'I don't want to die at all.'

'I am not a god, to forge miracles from nothingness. Everything dies.'

'Yes, lord.' Again, the silence. 'I hear more whispers,' she confessed. 'The aliens are coming again.'

The immense cannon on the Dreadnought's right arm lifted and made the clanking reloading sounds that were already becoming so familiar to her. The whispers were already growing stronger. She could almost feel the warmth of breath stroking the back of her neck.

'My chronicle already ends in glory. Captain Malcharion, reborn in unbreakable iron, slaying Raguel the Suffer of the Ninth Legion for the second time, before at last passing into eternal slumber. That is a fine legend, is it not?'

Even without understanding the meaning of the words, she felt their significance. 'Yes, lord.'

'Who would ruin their legend with one last, untold tale? Who would cast aside the slaughter of an Imperial hero in favour of saving a single human from death in the infinite dark?'

Malcharion never gave her time to answer. His weapons rose even as he pivoted, and filled the chamber with echoing, deafening gunfire.

FIRST CLAW STOOD ready, surrounded by inactive servitors and priceless, precious suits of Terminator war-plate that would never see sunlight again.

Talos sheathed his gladius along his shin, locked his empty bolter to his thigh, and drew the Blade of Angels. His skull-painted faceplate – marked with the forehead rune depicting the title he so often hated – regarded his brothers in turn.

Mercutian's breathing came in ragged growls, sounding wet over the vox, but he stood straight enough to hold his heavy bolter. He regarded the others through a dispassionate helm, crested by twin curved horns.

Uzas wore his palm-printed helmet of ancient design, his chainaxe in one hand, his gladius in the other. His cloak of skinned flesh was draped over one shoulder in grim, regal contrast to the skulls hanging from his armour.

Cyrion readied his chainsword and his bolter, the lightning bolt markings of his faceplate looking like jagged tear trails.

'Let's end this,' he said. 'I was bored of being alive, anyway.'

Talos smiled, though he'd never felt less amused. Uzas said nothing at all. Mercutian nodded, his words coming after a grunt.

'We'll get you to the surface, brother. Then when Variel's had his chatter, we'll get back to skinning that alien harpy.'

'Simple plans are often the best,' Cyrion noted.

Talos led them from the chamber, leaving their abandoned relics and mindless slaves to waste away in the dark.

XXVIII
A TRUTH NEVER TOLD

AFTER AN HOUR, it became a hindrance. After two, a problem. In the third hour, they were barely moving at all.

'Just leave me,' Mercutian said, supported on Talos's shoulder. He was dragging them back, slowing them down. Talos knew it. Cyrion and Uzas knew it, and Mercutian knew it better than any of them.

'Leave me,' he kept saying.

'Leave the cannon,' Talos replied. 'It isn't helping.'

Mercutian clutched the heavy bolter tighter. 'Just leave me. I'll cut down any of the xenos wretches that come here to find me. If they're behind us, I'll buy you some time.'

Cyrion walked alongside Talos and the limping warrior. Over a private link, he took a deep breath. 'We should leave him, brother.'

Talos didn't even glance Cyrion's way. 'You should be silent.'

'We're going to die, Talos. That's why we're here. Mercutian is already dying, and the head wound Uzas is wearing doesn't look like it's left him all in one piece, either. His skull is bare to the bone, and we left one of his eyes back in the chamber where Third Claw died.'

Talos didn't argue. 'Uzas is worrying me as much as Mercutian. He seems... cold, distant.'

'To say the least. Come, what does it matter if Variel overhead a whisper of alien witchery? We're dead men. If we don't die here, we'll die in orbit.'

Talos didn't answer at once. 'The gunship slipped in. It can slip out. You heard what Variel said about the wraithships. The game has changed.'

'And you believe him? You think you're destined to live on, and unite the Legion?'

'I don't know what I believe.'

'Very well. If you're not supposed to die here, what visions of the future have you seen beyond tonight?'

'None.'

'There's your answer. You die here. We all do. Don't let our last hunt fail because we had to limp and flee like wounded dogs. We should find her while she's wounded, not let her come to us in another ambush. It's not our way.'

Talos shook his head as he adjusted Mercutian's weight on his shoulder. 'Enough, Cy. I'm not leaving him. And I have to get to Variel.'

'Your trust in the Flayer is your own flaw to fight. Don't drag our lives into it. If you're really turning your back on our last hunt, then Mercutian is *still* right. You want to reach the surface, and he's slowing us down.'

Talos narrowed his eyes as he walked. 'Sometimes, Cy, you make it easy to see why Xarl hated you.'

'Is that so?' Cyrion snorted. 'Don't hide behind his ghost as if he'd smile and nod and cheer you on for the sentiment. Xarl would be the first to leave him behind. You know that as well as I. It would be one of the few things he and I ever agreed on.'

Talos had no answer to that.

'Brothers,' Uzas said, with serene calm. 'I hear her. She comes, sprinting through the black.'

First Claw redoubled their efforts. Cyrion took Mercutian's other side, helping the wounded warrior limp onward.

'Talos,' Mercutian grunted.

'Shut up. Just move.'

'*Talos,*' he snapped. 'It's time. Throne in flames, Soul Hunter. It's time. Leave me. *Run.*'

SHE CAME FROM the darkness again, eldritch blades in bone-armoured fists. The throwing star burned black with warp-tempered fire; the spear hissed like fresh iron in a forge trough, spitting-hot to the touch.

One figure stood in the hallway before her. She smelled the chemical reek of its weapon oils and the dirty blood leaking from its wounds. She'd marked this one. She knew the scent of his life.

A lone mon-keigh from their unclean warrior caste, abandoned by his kindred to bleed out the last of his life alone. How little these creatures knew of loyalty or nobility.

As she drew near, she saw him strain to lift his weapon, and heard a single word in one of the human species' filthy tongues.

'*Juthai'lah,*' said the dying soul of the warrior caste.

MERCUTIAN DRAGGED IN cold air through his mouth grille. The target locks on his retinal display struggled to align on the advancing witch-queen, as though reality itself resisted her presence.

He blinked to clear his vision, braced back against the weight of his heavy bolter, and lifted the muzzle to aim down the hallway.

She walked closer, and still he couldn't lock onto her. To the hells with augmented targeting then. Back to simple purity.

Mercutian breathed the word aloud into the corridor, uncaring whether she knew its meaning or not.

'Preysight.'

His bolter kicked in his fists a second later, hammering in anger and filling the narrow tunnel with explosive shells.

THE SURVIVORS RAN.

Their boots pounded onto the stone as they sprinted, never once looking back. Genetically enhanced muscles bunched and moved within the fibre-bundle cabling that augmented their strength, while three lungs and two hearts worked to capacity inside their heaving chests.

Talos vaulted a pile of rocks, his boots crashing down on the other side and never missing a stride. His eye lenses flickered runic sigils between eighty-four and eighty-seven kilometres per hour. Those figures sank lower each time he was forced to slide and skid around a corner, or leap up and kick off from an adjacent wall at a junction in order to maintain a semblance of speed.

They'd been running for a full seven minutes before Talos cursed under his breath. At the edge of his retinal display, the three remaining life signs became two, and a flatline whined its way across the vox.

MERCUTIAN TREMBLED AS he died in her grip. Even through his fading vision, he noted the damage done to her helm and breastplate – the armour was cracked, letting some of her stinkingly ripe alien blood trickle through. He'd only managed to graze her a handful of times with over forty shells from his heavy bolter, but the detonations left her charred and wounded, even if he'd failed to cripple her as he'd hoped.

'Sleep,' she caressed him with her voice, somehow mocking despite its gentleness.

Mercutian gripped the spear that impaled his chest, and *pulled*. He slid half a metre closer to her, feeling the horrendous, squealing scrape of the metal pole grating against his destroyed ribcage and burned flesh.

'Sleep,' she said again, laughing this time. A full-throated and melodious laugh, that only ground Mercutian's teeth together even harder. He gripped again, and pulled a second time. He barely moved – strength was fleeing him, along with his blood.

She whipped the spear back, and the pain of the withdrawal was worse by far than the *crack* of it going in. With nothing to support him, he crumpled to the ground on dead legs, his armour crash reverberating through the tunnel.

For a moment, he lay foetal, trying to suck in air that wouldn't come. He was drowning without being underwater, his vision already greying at the edges.

She walked past him. The sight of her boots swishing past were a catalyst, shocking him back to his weakening senses. In his preysight, she was little more than a thermal blur, but training allowed him to make out the details he needed.

With a roar of effort and pain mixed into one screamed song, Mercutian moved as fast as he ever had in his life, and faster than he ever would again. The gladius in his hand rammed through the back of the maiden's leg, bursting through the front of her shin, and sticking fast. She cried out in kind, spinning to ram her spear down through his chest a second time.

Mercutian grinned up at her as his last breath left him. He spent it speaking a final sentence, meeting the witch-queen's eyes.

'*Now* try running...'

LUCORYPHUS LANDED IN a haze of spreading dust. Variel ignored it, breathing the recycled air within his sealed suit as he stood in the rain.

'I see them,' the Raptor said. 'They surfaced to the west, on the battlements.'

Variel immediately started to run. He heard Lucoryphus laughing, and the Raptor's engines cycling back up to power. The Apothecary had a handful of seconds before Lucoryphus struck him from behind, grabbing his shoulder guards, and lifted him off the ground.

Variel – who had no love for flying, but even less affection for any of the Bleeding Eyes – clung on in undignified silence as the ruins passed below.

HIS FIRST SIGHTING of Variel wasn't actually when the Apothecary was dropped rather crudely onto the battlements from above. It was when his eye lens display acknowledged his Badabian brother's proximity, and linked a third vital sign feed to join Uzas and Cyrion's. Xarl's name rune, along with Mercutian's, were silent and faded by comparison.

Lucoryphus touched down with considerably more grace, his claws gripping the ramparts of the crooked, leaning battlement wall.

Talos approached the Apothecary as Variel was picking himself up. 'I want answers, Variel, and I want them now.'

'My explanation may take some time. I can call the gunship.'

'Septimus and Octavia are truly here? On this world?'

'That, also, will take time to explain.'

'We are short of many things, brother: ammunition, hope, warriors. You can add time to that list. Where's *Blackened*?'

'The battlements, to the north. Perhaps four minutes' flight.'

Talos re-tuned his vox to the familiar channel he never thought he'd contact again. 'Septimus.'

'Lord? It's good to hear your voi–'

'Get the gunship in the air, and fly over the central ruins. We are proceeding there now. Don't land until we call you in – it's too dangerous for you to remain on the ground any longer than you have to. Do you understand me?'

'Aye, lord.'

'And if by chance you catch an eldar maiden in armour of bone in your gunsights, I would appreciate you shooting her into red mist.'

'Uh… as you say, lord.'

Talos severed the link, and looked back to the others. 'Scatter into the ruins until the gunship comes in. Don't let her find you. Now move. Variel, you're with me. Start explaining.'

CYRION SPRINTED THROUGH the rain. Erosion had left this stretch of ruined battlements a mere seven metres above the ground, which Cyrion cleared in a casual drop down to ground level. His boots crunched on the rocky earth, and he broke back into his run.

Taking cover in the ruins of the gigantic fortress was hardly difficult; even on the surface, weathering had left an abandoned city of rubble and tilted walls on the grey plains. He ran for several minutes, stopping at last when he reached a slope of rubble that had once served as a barracks wall, next to the battlements.

The Night Lord started to climb, his gauntlets punching and clawing handholds in the stone where it was too smooth to grip in the rain.

'Cyrion,' said a voice. Not over the vox. Over the rain. It was that near.

Cyrion looked up. Uzas crouched at the top of the wide wall, looking down at him. The painted palm-print was smeared over his ancient faceplate, untouched by the cold rainfall.

'Brother,' Cyrion replied. A pregnant pause reached between them. Cyrion hauled himself the rest of the way up. Uzas rose to his feet, and backed away. His chainaxe and gladius were still in his fists.

'Let us speak,' Uzas said. The storm heaved harder, lightning splitting the sky above them both.

'Talos told us to split up.'

Uzas never turned his red eye lenses away. 'Talos. Yes, let us speak of Talos.' His voice had never sounded so clear – at least not in the centuries since the Great Heresy. Cyrion couldn't help but wonder just what the head wound had done.

'What of Talos?' he asked.

Uzas gunned the trigger of the chainaxe for a moment. Raindrops sprayed from the whirring teeth.

'Talos has lost his patience with me many times in the decades since we fled Tsagualsa. Yet he has always treated me fairly. Always defended me. Always remembered that I am his brother, and that he is mine.'

Cyrion rested his hand on his sheathed chainsword. 'Aye. He has.'

Uzas tilted his head. 'But you have not.'

Cyrion forced a laugh. It sounded as insincere as it was.

'Cyrion, Cyrion, Cyrion. I have been thinking, as I look down at these red hands of mine. I bear the sinner's red hands because of my many, many rampages through the mortal crew of the *Covenant*. The void-born's father was the last, wasn't it? That foolish, fearful old man, who would sweat and weep and cringe every time we walked near.'

Uzas took a step closer to Cyrion. 'How did his fear taste, Cyrion? How did it taste when you killed him? Was it still tingling on your tongue when you stood by and let the others blame me?'

Cyrion drew both blades as Uzas took another step closer. 'Lucoryphus told you, then.'

'Lucoryphus told me nothing. I have been playing the past through my mind these last hours, and the conclusion was simple enough. No one else would have found the old fool a tempting target. None of the others would have been able to taste his cowardice the way you could. And any of them would simply confess to Talos what they'd done. But not you, *oh no*. Not the perfect Cyrion.'

Cyrion glanced behind. He was close to the wall's edge now, and the long drop down to the rubble that came with it.

'Uzas...'

'I've been so blind, haven't I? Answer me this, Cyrion. How many times did you slay to sup on the crew's fear, and stand by while I was blamed? As I pull through the broken memories, I can recall my true hunts, and too many instances of losing control. But nothing like the amount I've been blamed for.'

'Don't seek to blame me for t–'

'*Answer me!*' Uzas pulled his helm clear, hurling it aside and facing Cyrion barefaced. His scarred, stitched, broken-angel features were contorted by hate. Blood still painted one side of his head, and one eye socket stared hollow, still not quite wedged shut by the wound. 'How many of your sins have damned me?'

Cyrion smiled at his brother's slipping control. 'Over the centuries? Dozens. Hundreds. Take your pick, madman. What do a few more souls matter in the harvest you've reaped alone?'

'It matters because I am punished for your sins!' Spit sprayed from Uzas's lips as he screamed. 'The others despised me! How much of that blame can be laid at your feet?'

'The others are dead, Uzas.' Cyrion kept his voice calm, cold. 'What they believed no longer means anything. You damned yourself in their eyes by forever screaming about your Blood God each time you drew a blade in battle.'

'I. Never. Worshipped. Anything.' Uzas aimed the chainaxe at his brother's head. 'You never understood it. The Legion raises icons to the Powers when it suits them. Whatever the cost, wars must be won. I am no different. *No different!*'

'If you say so, Uzas.'

'Do you know how many times my thoughts have cleared, only to be confronted by a brother enraged at me for slaying some vital member of the crew?' Uzas spat over the side, his face even more hideous now the rain had washed away the blood. His skull showed where the left half of his head had suffered the skin being ripped away. 'I killed dozens, yet bore the blame for hundreds!' He raised the weapons in his fists, displaying his red gauntlets. 'These are your marks of shame, Cyrion. I wear them because you are too weak to do so yourself.'

The rage bled from him as abruptly as it had risen. 'I... I will tell Talos. And you will confess what you've done. He must know the depths of your... appetite. The things it has forced you to do.'

'If you say so,' Cyrion repeated, 'brother.'

'Forgive my anger. The wrath is difficult to bite back, some nights. I know the feel of the warp's caress, as surely as you do. I feel for you, my brother. I truly do. We are more alike than either of us has ever admitted.'

Uzas sighed and closed his eyes. A smile – the first sincere smile in centuries – spread across his broken face.

Cyrion moved the moment Uzas's eyes closed. He lashed out with both blades at once, aiming for the pale flesh of Uzas's throat. The other Night Lord flinched, barely blocking with his own weapons, and hit back with a kick that rang against his brother's breastplate like a tolling temple bell. Cyrion staggered, boots loose on the edge, and plummeted from view without a sound.

Uzas howled, a full-throated cry to the unquiet sky, his clarity shattered and his vision bathed red. The heaven's thunder melted into his throbbing heartbeat, and the rain in his eyes stung like his own acid-spit. He took a running leap, chainaxe snarling, and threw himself after his treacherous brother.

HE HEARD THE howl, but saw no source.

Lightning forked the sky again, a pulse of daylight's brightness bathing the ruins for a single second. For a moment, the toppled walls and spires resembled a dead city, and the legs of Titans.

Talos stopped running. He slowed to a halt, looking around with narrowed eyes, ignoring the pointless data streaming across his eye lenses.

'No,' he said, to no one but himself. 'I've seen this before.'

The lightning flashed again, drenching the ruins in short-lived light. Again, in the fragmentary sight, he saw Titans formed from the tilting walls, and tanks revealed as lifeless stone when the blinding brightness faded.

He leaned against –

Flash!

– the hull of a Land Raider –

– the stone wall of a fallen building, and looks for signs of his brothers. He sees Cyrion, half-buried in a mound of rubble, almost a thousand metres away by the testimony of scrolling retinal tactical data.

He watches another struggling figure emerging from the wreckage, and his visor locks onto Uzas, approaching Cyrion's prone form from behind.

And, at last, he knows where he's seen this.

It was never at Crythe. I read my own vision wrong. Uzas… He kills him here. He kills Cyrion here.

He broke into a run, the golden sword's power field flaring to life.

CYRION WINCED AT the pain in his thigh, feeling fairly certain his leg was broken by the twenty-metre fall. His helm's display was a haze of static, stealing any chance of checking his bio-readings, but having lost an arm in battle and feeling a haunting sense of familiarity in the sensation now, he felt he could make a fair guess.

He tried to claw his way free of the rubble. He had to get away from–

'Cyrionnnnn.' The low growl lingered on the final syllable, lost in drooling confusion. He heard Uzas scrabbling across the rocks behind, and thrashed in the rubble's grip, pulling himself half-clear. He could hear footsteps, heavy and swift, but couldn't twist to see.

The shadow above him lengthened across the rocks, as Uzas raised the axe. Cyrion was still reaching for his fallen sword when the blade descended.

UZAS STIFFENED, THE chainaxe falling from loose fingers to clatter onto the rubble. He looked down, no longer seeing Cyrion trapped beneath him, his eyes drawn to nothing but the golden sword extending through his chest.

I know that sword, he thought, and started laughing. But no breath meant no laughter, and he did nothing more than wheeze through bloody lips. The golden blade was already cleansed of his blood, washed clean by the rain. Even so, the cold droplets aggravated the shimmering energy field, breeding a buzzing aura around the steel, spiced with sparks.

He sighed, almost in relief, as the sword slid back out. Surprisingly, he felt nothing in the way of pain, though the pressure in his chest was mounting to the point he feared his hearts would rupture.

He turned to face his murderer. Talos stood in the rain, red eye lenses offering nothing of mercy.

Talos, he tried to say. *My brother.*

'You…' The prophet readied the blade again, clutching it in two hands. 'I trusted you. I argued again and again and again for your life to be spared. I swore to the others you were still inside there somewhere. Still a shred of nobility, waiting to be reborn. Still a fragment of worth, deserving of hope.'

Talos. He tried to say again. *Thank you.*

'You are the foulest, basest, most treacherous creature ever to the wear the winged skull of Nostramo. Ruven was a prince by comparison. At least he was in control of himself.'

Talos... Uzas's vision swam. He blinked, and upon opening his eyes, he found he was looking up at his brother towering over him. Had he fallen to his knees? *I... I...*

'Wait...' Uzas managed to say. He was appalled and amused in equal measure by the weakling's whisper his voice had become. 'Talos.'

The prophet kicked him in the chest, sending him toppling onto his back. His head cracked on the jagged rocks, but he didn't feel any pain beyond the press of cold stone.

No more words would come. Every breath sent black blood, deliciously warm, spilling over his chin.

He saw Talos rise above him, the golden sword spitting sparks in the storm. 'I should have killed you years ago.'

Uzas grinned, just as Mercutian had grinned, at the moment of death. *You probably should have, brother.*

He saw Talos turn and move away, out of sight. Variel replaced him, the Apothecary's icy eyes staring down with polite disinterest. Drills and saws deployed from his narthecium gauntlet.

'His gene-seed?' Variel asked.

Talos voice carried back from nearby. 'If you harvest it from him, I will kill you, too.'

Variel rose to his feet with one last dispassionate look, and moved away as well. The last words Uzas heard were those spoken by Cyrion, grunting as he was pulled from the rubble.

'He came at me from behind, screaming his endless devotions to the Blood God. My thanks, Talos.'

XXIX
ENDINGS

THE GUNSHIP CAME in low across the battlements, thrusters roaring as it hovered. Heat-shimmer turned the air as murky as water beneath the flaring jump jets. Steam rose from their armour, all traces of rainfall evaporating away.

Cyrion was limping, but able to stand unaided. Variel and Lucoryphus remained unharmed, but Talos hadn't spoken since he'd butchered his brother. He was a silent presence in the group's core, meeting no one's eyes as they climbed the ramparts, and avoiding eye contact afterwards.

Cyrion moved back and looked up to the sky beyond the gunship's scissoring searchlights, letting the rain wash across his painted faceplate.

'Have you noticed that it always rains here when we lose a war? The gods have a curious sense of humour.'

None of the others said a word in reply. Talos spoke, but it was only to Septimus.

'Bring her down. Be ready for immediate dust-off.'

'Yes, lord.'

The gunship kissed Tsagualsa's lifeless soil. Slowly, too slowly, the gangramp started to descend.

'This world is a tomb,' Talos said softly. 'For the Legion, and the hundreds of eldar that died down there tonight.'

'Then let's leave,' Cyrion hardly sounded impressed, 'and die in orbit, in defiance of the Flayer's moronic superstition.'

'All Claws, all souls of the Eighth Legion, this is Talos. Answer me if you still breathe.'

Silence replied, thick and cold, over the vox. True to his words, he felt as though he was shouting across a graveyard.

Even Malcharion is dead. The thought made him shiver.

'Variel,' he said, as the ramp lowered fully. 'It isn't me.'

The Apothecary hesitated. 'I do not understand.'

For a moment, Talos just watched his own retinal display. Xarl.

Mercutian. Uzas. All faded. All silent. All gone.

'It isn't me. I doubt any prophet will rise to unite the Eighth Legion, but if one does, it will not be me. I couldn't unite a single Claw.'

'Well,' Cyrion interrupted, 'we were a difficult group at the finest of times.'

'I mean it, Variel. It isn't me. It was never me. Look at me, brother. Tell me you believe *I* could unite tens of thousands of murderers, rapists, traitors, thieves and assassins. I don't think like them. I don't even want to be one of them, anymore. They damn themselves. That was always the Legion's flaw. We damned ourselves.'

'Your loyalty to your brothers does you credit, but you are speaking while affected by mourning.'

'No.' Talos shook his head, taking a step back. 'I'm speaking the truth. One of the many, many writings that remain with us from the era after the Heresy speaks of this "prophet". We call it the Crucible Premonition, though it was never shared past a few captains. And whether it's a destined fate or not, I am not that prophet.'

Variel nodded. Talos read the look in his brother's pale eyes, and smiled. 'You've considered the alternative,' he said, and it wasn't a question. 'I can tell.'

'The concept has remained with me since I ran the tests on your physiology.' Variel inclined his head to the gunship. 'A child that grows with your gene-seed implanted within its body will have all the makings of a powerful seer.'

'You're guessing.'

'I am. But it's a good guess.'

Cyrion cursed at them from the ramp. 'Can we leave, if we're going at all?' Lucoryphus crawled up the ramp, but Talos and Variel remained as they were.

'My father said something to me, in the hours before he died. Words for my ears alone; words I've never shared before tonight. He said: *"Many will claim to lead our Legion in the years after I am gone. Many will claim that they – and they alone – are my appointed successor. I hate this Legion, Talos. I destroyed its world to stem the flow of poison. I will be vindicated soon, and the truest lesson of the Night Lords will be taught. Do you truly believe I care what happens to any of you after my death?"'*

The Apothecary stood motionless, as Talos took a breath. 'Sometimes, I almost know how he felt, Variel. The war drags on for an eternity, and victory comes at an agonising pace. Meanwhile, we endure betrayals. We hide, we run and flee, we raid and ambush and skin and flay and kill, we loot our own dead, we drink the blood of our enemies, and suffer the endless tide of fratricide. I killed my own mother without knowing her face. I have killed nineteen of my own brothers in the last century alone, almost always in idiotic battles for possession of this sword, or over matters of bruised pride. I have no wish to unite the Legion. I *hate* the Legion. Not for what it is, but for what it made me become.'

Variel still said nothing. Rather than seeming lost for words, he simply seemed to lack any desire to speak at all.

'There's one thing I want,' said Talos. 'I want that alien witch's head. I want to plant it on her spear at the heart of these ruins.' Talos turned away from the gunship, walking away. 'And I mean to have it. Stay in the air, Variel. Land once it's over. Whether I live or die this night, you are welcome to my gene-seed come the dawn.'

Cyrion left the ramp, following Talos. 'I'm coming with you.'

Lucoryphus's head jerked with a muscle tic in his neck. He briefly rose to his clawed feet, and stalked after the others. 'I will join you. One more dead eldar will bring the Bleeding Eyes to two score. I like the sound of that number.'

Variel stood by the gunship, fighting the urge to follow. 'Talos,' he said.

The prophet looked over his shoulder in time to see blood burst from Variel's body. The Apothecary shouted – the first time Talos had ever heard an utterance of such volume from the Flayer's lips – and reached his hands to his bloody mouth, as if he could stem the flow of lifeblood gushing from his lips.

The black spear pulled out, staggering him as it withdrew from his back and cleaved through both of his legs on the backswing. The bionic leg gave crackling sparks of protest as its sundered systems tried to restore balance. His human leg bled, and bled, and bled.

The three Night Lords were already running, weapons alive in their fists.

'*Get in the air,*' Talos yelled into the vox. 'Consider it your final order.'

The gunship immediately rose, unsteady on its whining thrusters.

'You dismissed me back on board the *Echo*, Talos. I don't have to follow your orders, do I? Come with us.'

'*Don't die with us, Septimus. Run. Anywhere but here.*'

Talos was the first to reach the eldar maiden, as she was releasing the first notes of her paralysing shriek. He charged with a raised sword, telegraphing his intent to give a two-handed cleave. At the last second, as her spear came around to offer a perfect parry, he launched up and thundered a kick to the front of her facemask. Her head snapped back, the howl ended as her helm cracked, and she caught herself in a graceful handspring to avoid falling to the floor.

Talos landed hard and rolled back to his feet, the golden blade coming up again. He grinned at the sight of her deathmask split down the middle by a brutal faultline crack.

'You have no idea how satisfying that was,' he told her.

'*You,*' she said in mangled Gothic. Her helm's vocaliser grille was damaged, deforming her speech. '*Hunter of Souls.*'

He met her again, blade on blade, their power weapons resisting one another like opposing magnetic fields.

'I'm so tired of that name,' Talos breathed. He head-butted her, shattering the mask a second time. He saw her eye – her alien eye, slanted and unlovely – through the crack.

Cyrion and Lucoryphus came at her from opposite sides. The former had his chainblade parried by the three-knived throwing blade in her other hand; the latter missed with both lightning claws as the maiden danced out of the warriors' triangle, flipping and leaping aside.

She stumbled as she landed, the first sign of gracelessness in her movements, and they all heard the rasping hiss of pain. Blood sheeted her left leg from the shin down. Whatever had wounded her had done a beautiful job of hobbling her. Wounded, she was barely faster than them.

Lucoryphus wasn't part of First Claw, and lacked the unity of purpose that showed so clearly in the other two brothers. He leapt ahead of them with a roar that wouldn't have shamed a Nostraman lion, clawed fingers curled and aiming for her heart.

The spear met him in the chest, annihilating his breastplate and casting him to the ground. Even as the maiden rammed her spear one-handed through the prone Raptor's stomach, she was hurling her throwing star.

Cyrion's enhanced reactions were honed from centuries of battle, and years of training even before that. In his lifetime, he'd blocked solid-slug bullets on his vambrace, and weaved to avoid laser fire without feeling its heat. His reflexes, like all of the warriors within the Legiones Astartes, were so far beyond human that they bordered on supernatural. He was already moving to dodge aside before the blade left her fingers.

It wasn't enough. Not even close. The spinning knives took him in the chest, crunching deep as they bit, and black fire burst across his armour.

The witch-queen held her hand to recall the throwing star. As it flashed through the air, Talos broke it in half with a swing of his power blade. The maiden tried to wrench her spear back out of Lucoryphus's belly, but the Raptor gripped the haft in his metal claws, keeping it lodged inside his body and the stone ramparts beneath.

The prophet was on her a heartbeat later. She weaved aside from the first swing, and the second, and the third, leaping back and dodging each ponderous carve. Despite moving faster than the human eye could follow, his heavy swings wouldn't land.

On another flip, her wounded leg gave out again. Talos swept her leg out from under her as she staggered to recover her balance, and at last *Aurum* struck home. The golden sword cleaved through her right arm, severing the limb close to the elbow.

She shrieked, then – an unamplified shriek of pain and frustration that sounded almost mortal. Dirty alien blood hissed and crackled as it burned away on the blade.

Her reply was a firm-fingered chop to the soft armour at his throat, crunching the cables there and thudding into his larynx hard enough to kill a human outright. It was enough to make him fall back, raising his blade defensively, struggling to catch his breath.

Talos felt his head snap to the right from a blow he never saw coming, and had a brief glimpse of Lucoryphus on his back, like some kind of iron-skinned helpless testudeen reptile, turned over on its shell.

The sword flew from his grip, kicked from his hand by a bloodstained boot. Another kick smashed into the scarred aquila on his chestplate, hurling him backward, barely keeping his balance. The combat narcotics flooding his muscles did nothing; he couldn't block her, he couldn't dodge her – he could scarcely even see her.

'Preysi–'

His own sword interrupted him as it crashed against his helm. Pain flared white-hot, cobwebbing out from his temple in the same moment his arc of vision halved. Before he could even process the notion he'd been blinded in one eye, the blade hammered home again. It slid into his chest with a loving lack of haste, stealing all breath, all energy, all thought, beyond one truth.

She killed me with my own sword.

He laughed without a sound, spraying flecks of blood into his helm. When she dragged the blade free, he first thought she'd cast it aside; instead, she broke it across her knee.

The pain burrowing through his chest finally embraced his spine, clinging with fervour. That's when he fell – but only to his knees. Somehow, that was worse.

'So falls the Hunter of Souls,' she said, pulling her helm off to stare down with slanted, milky grey eyes. She'd have been beautiful, had she not been so disgustingly inhuman. One of her ears twitched in the rain, as sensing a sound only she could hear.

He rose to his feet again, removed his own helmet, and looked out at another vision finally coming true.

The details were close. Not perfect, but so very close. His fevered mind had coloured places with ancient memory, making the fortress appear still standing in desolate glory, rather than the tumbled ruin he saw now.

But the rest was so clear, he had to smile. Talos took a step closer to her, and stooped despite the flare of agony in his chest, reaching to pick up the broken blade.

'In my dreams,' he breathed, 'you still had your helm on.'

She nodded – a slow and grave acknowledgement. 'In the dreams of Ulthwé's seers, they saw the same. Fate is fluid, Hunter of Souls. Some futures cannot be allowed to pass. There shall be no Prophet of the Eighth Legion. There shall be no Night of Blood, when the Tears of Isha are drunk by your thirsting brethren. You die here. All is well.'

He held a hand to his ruptured chest, feeling the aching beat of at least one heart. His breathing was tight, but his redundant organs had come to life, sustaining him past mortal death.

The maiden walked to pull her spear from Lucoryphus's chest. The Raptor made no movement beyond a limp twitch.

As she moved back to him, her black spear in her remaining hand, dream and reality melted together, becoming one at long last.

XXX
LESSONS

THE PROPHET AND the murderess stood on the battlements of the dead citadel, weapons in their hands. Rain slashed in a miserable flood, thick enough to obscure vision, draining down the wall's sides. Above the rain, the only audible sounds came from the two figures: one human, standing in broken armour that thrummed with static crackles; the other an alien maiden in ancient and contoured war-plate, weathered by an eternity of scarring.

'This is where your Legion died, is it not? We call this world *Shithr Vejruhk*. What is it in your serpent's tongue? *Tsagualsa*, yes? Answer me this, prophet. Why would you come back here?'

Talos didn't answer. He spat acidic blood onto the dark stone floor, and drew in another ragged breath. The sword in his hands was a cleaved ruin, its shattered blade severed halfway along its length. He didn't know where his bolter was, and a smile crept across his split lips as he felt an instinctive tug of guilt.

Malcharion would not be proud, he thought.

'Talos.' The maiden smiled as she spoke. Her amusement was remarkable if only for the absence of mockery and malice. 'Do not be ashamed, human. Everyone dies.'

He couldn't stand. Even pride has limits over what it can force from a body. The prophet sank to one knee, blood leaking from the cracks in his armour. His attempt at speech left his lips as a grunt of pain. The only thing he could smell was the copper stench of his own injuries. Battle stimulants ran thick in his blood.

The maiden came closer, even daring to rest the scythe-bladed tip of her spear on his shoulder guard.

'I speak only the truth, prophet. There's no shame in this moment. You have done well to even make it this far.'

Talos spat blood again, and hissed two words.

'*Valas Morovai.*'

The murderess tilted her head as she looked down at him. Her long, ember-red hair was dreadlocked by the rain, plastered to her pale features. She looked like a woman sinking into water, serene as a saint while she drowned.

'Many of your bitter whisperings remain occluded to me,' she said. 'You speak... "First Claw", yes?' Her unnatural accent struggled with the words. 'They were your brothers? You call out to the dead, in the hopes they will yet save you?'

The blade fell from his grip, too heavy to hold any longer. He stared at it lying on the black stone, bathed in the downpour, silver and gold shining as clean as the day he'd stolen it.

Slowly, he lifted his head, facing his executioner. Rain showered the blood from his face, salty on his lips, stinging his eyes. He didn't need to wonder if she was still smiling. He saw it on her face, and loathed the kindliness of the gesture. Was it sympathy? Truly?

On his knees, atop the fallen battlements of his Legion's deserted fortress, the Night Lord started laughing.

Neither his laughter nor the storm above were loud enough to swallow the heavy sound of burning thrusters. A gunship – blue-hulled and blackly sinister – bellowed its way into view. As it rose above the battlements, rain sluiced from its avian hull in silver streams. Heavy bolter turrets aligned in a chorus of mechanical grinding, the sweetest music ever to grace the prophet's ears. Talos was still laughing as the Thunderhawk hovered in place, riding its own heat haze, with the dim lighting of the cockpit revealing two figures within.

'I saw this,' he told her. 'Didn't you?'

The alien maiden was already moving. She became a black blur, dancing through the rain in a velvet sprint. Detonations clawed at her heels as the gunship opened fire, shredding the stone at her feet in a hurricane of explosive rounds.

One moment she fled across the parapets, the next she simply ceased to exist, vanishing into shadow.

Talos didn't rise to his feet, uncertain he'd manage it if he tried. He closed the only eye he had left. The other was a blind and bleeding orb of irritating pain, sending dull throbs back into his skull each time his two hearts beat. His bionic hand, shivering with joint glitches and flawed neural input damage, reached to activate the vox at his collar.

'I will listen to you, next time.'

Above the overbearing whine of downward thrusters, a voice buzzed over the gunship's external vox-speakers. Distortion stole all trace of tone and inflection.

'If we don't disengage now, there won't be a next time.'

'I told you to leave. I ordered it.'

'Master,' the external vox-speakers crackled back. *'I...'*

'Go, damn you.' When he next glanced at the gunship, he could see the two figures more clearly. They sat side by side, in the pilots' thrones. 'You are formally discharged from my service.' He slurred the words as he voxed them, and started laughing again. 'For the second time.'

The gunship stayed aloft, engines giving out their strained whine, blasting hot air across the battlements.

The voice rasping over the vox was female this time. *'Talos.'*

'Run. Run far from here, and all the death this world offers. Flee to the last city, and catch the next vessel off-world. The Imperium is coming. They will be your salvation. But remember what I said. We are all slaves to fate. If Variel escapes this madness alive, he will come for the child one night, no matter where you run.'

'He might never find us.'

Talos's laughter finally faded, though he kept the smile. 'Pray that he doesn't.'

He drew in a knifing breath as he slumped with his back to the battlements, grunting at the stabs from his ruined lungs and shattered ribs. Grey drifted in from the edge of his vision, and he could no longer feel his fingers. One hand rested on his cracked breastplate, upon the ritually-broken aquila, polished by the rain. The other rested on his fallen bolter, Malcharion's weapon, on its side from where he'd dropped it in the earlier battle. With numb hands, the prophet locked the double-barrelled bolter to his thigh, and took another slow pull of cold air into lungs that no longer wanted to breathe. His bleeding gums turned his teeth pink.

'I'm going after her.'

'Don't be a fool.'

Talos let the rain drench his upturned face. Strange, how a moment's mercy let them believe they could talk to him like that. He hauled himself to his feet, and started walking across the weathered, sunken battlements, a broken blade in hand.

'She killed my brothers,' he said. 'I'm going after her.'

HE MOVED FIRST to where Cyrion lay. The throwing star had left almost nothing of his chest, its black fire eating much of the bone and meat of his sternum and the organs beneath. He removed Cyrion's helm with a careful touch brought on as much by his own wounds as respect for the dead.

Talos blinked when Cyrion's hand gripped his wrist. His brother's black eyes rolled in their sockets, seeing nothing, trailing raindrop tears in mimicry of the lightning bolts on his faceplate.

'Uzas,' Cyrion said. One lung quivered in the exposed crater of his chest. One heart still gave a weak pound.

'It's Talos. Uzas is dead.'

'Uzas,' Cyrion said again. 'I hate you. Always hated you. But I'm sorry.'

'Brother.' Talos moved his hand before Cyrion's eyes, with no reaction. The blindness was complete.

'Talos?'

He took Cyrion's hand, gripping his arm wrist-to-wrist. 'I'm here, Cy.'

'Good. Good. Didn't want to die alone.' He sank back against the stone, relaxing in his hunched lean. 'Don't take my gene-seed.' He reached up a hand to touch his own eyes. 'I… I think I'm blind. It's the wrong kind of dark here.' Cyrion wiped a trickle of spit from his lips. 'You won't take my gene-seed, will you?'

'No.'

'Don't let Variel take it, either. Don't let him touch me.'

'I won't.'

'Good. Those words you said. About the war. I liked them. Don't pass my gene-seed on. I'm… done with the war… as well.'

'I hear you.'

Cyrion had to swallow three times before he could speak again. 'Feel like I'm drowning in spit.'

He wasn't – it was blood. Talos said nothing about it, either way. 'Septimus and Octavia got away.'

'That's good. That's good.' Cyrion drooled blood through a loose smile, his body starting to twitch with the onset of convulsions.

Talos held him still as he shivered, saying nothing. Cyrion filled the silence, as he always did.

'I'm dying,' he said. 'Everyone else is dead. The slaves escaped. So…' he breathed out slowly, '…how are you?'

Talos waited for the last breath to leave his brother's lips before gently closing Cyrion's eyes.

He took three things from the body – no more, no less.

LUCORYPHUS WAS A motionless husk. Talos gave the corpse a wide berth, making his way to Variel.

The Apothecary was far from dead. The prophet caught up with him as he crawled, straining and legless, across the stone. Becoming crippled from the knees down hadn't improved his demeanour at all.

'Don't touch me,' he said to Talos, who promptly ignored him. The prophet dragged him to the ramparts, a little more shielded from the rain.

Several compartments of Variel's narthecium were open, their contents dispensed, mostly into the Apothecary's bloodstream.

'I won't die,' he told Talos. 'I have staunched the flow of blood, eliminated the risk of sepsis and other infections, applied synthetic skin and armour sealant, while also–'

'Shut up, Variel.'

'Forgive me. The stimulants in my system are volatile and strong by virtue of their emergency requirements. I am not used to–'

'Shut up, Variel.' Talos clasped his brother's arm, wrist-to-wrist. 'I'm going after her.'

'Please do not endanger your gene-seed.'

'In truth, you'll be fortunate if it survives intact.'

'That grieves me.'

'And if you ever escape this cursed world, leave Cyrion's gene-seed untouched. Let him rest in peace.'

Variel tilted his head in the rainfall. 'As you wish. Where is the gunship? Will it be returning?'

'Goodbye, Variel. You'll do the Eighth Legion proud. I do not need to be a prophet to know that.' He gestured to Variel's belt, at the pouches, the bandolier and ammunition straps. 'I will take those, if you do not mind.'

Variel allowed it. 'How will I leave Tsagualsa if the gunship does not return me to Deltrian's vessel?'

'I have a feeling some of the Legion will come one night, to see what happened here for themselves.'

'A guess?' Variel started tapping keys on his vambrace.

'A good guess,' Talos replied. 'Goodbye, brother.'

'Die well, Talos. Thank you for Fryga.'

The prophet nodded, and left his last living brother in the rain.

SHE CAME FOR him when she could no longer hear the cold iron huntercraft in the air, when distance had at last swallowed its engine-roar. She moved from the shadows, sprinting down the battlements, her spear held loosely, with perfect balance, in her remaining hand.

Silken hair streamed back in a sword-dancer's tail, kept out of her eyes as she ran. Ulthwé's banshee shrine had needed her, and to Ulthwé's banshee shrine she'd come. The division between the craftworld's seers was an unfortunate one, as was the separation of forces that followed.

Few of the other Path shrines would walk with her, no matter their respect for the armour she wore and the blades she bore. They would not leave Ulthwé so undefended, and thus, the armada had been a thin and hollow enterprise, populated by wraiths, with few able to risk setting foot on the unholy world.

Losses this eve had still been grievous. Ulthwé could ill afford to lose so many to the blades of blasphemers, but the Hunter of Souls was fated to fall, before he could become the Bane of Isha at the dawning of the Rhana Dandra.

So it was written. So shall it be.

In all the years since her most recent Becoming, few events had shown the portents aligning as fiercely those speaking of this very night. The very rightness of her actions, and the gravity of her cause, leant speed and strength to her aching limbs.

This time, he was hunting her, in his own slow, limping way. The blade in his hands rang with ancient resonance, the crude metals used in its forging dating back to the Humans' Hubris, when their arrogance burst open the Gate of Sha'eil like a great eye in the heavens. She did not fear it. She feared nothing. Even her damaged accoutrements would manifest whole once more, when the fates aligned.

She ran faster, the rain cold on her skin, the blade high in her hand.

TALOS OFFERED NO resistance.

The black spear cleaved through him, finishing the work his own sword had started in her hands. He didn't smile, or curse, or whisper any last testament. She kept him at arm's length, the impaling spear forcing him back.

As the sword dropped from his grip, Talos opened his other hand. The grenade in his fist activated the moment his fingers slipped from the thumb-plate. It exploded, triggering the three grenades he'd taken from Cyrion, the two he'd taken from Variel, and the power generator on his back.

With the exception of the fire that incinerated half of an alien immortal's physical form, Talos Valcoran of Nostramo died much the same way he'd been born: with black eyes open, staring at the world around, and silence on his lips.

MARLONAH LIMPED INTO the rainstorm, closing her eyes and letting the cool water rinse her body of hours of sweat. She felt like weeping. Running her hands through her soaking hair was a pleasure she couldn't put into words.

The Dreadnought preceded her, but took no similar joy. The war machine dragged one leg, scraping sparks with every step and leaving a mangled engraved path along the ground. Its armour-plating was blackened in places, melted to sludge and hardened again in others, or riddled with silver shuriken discs like misaligned fish scales. His joints no longer whirred with confident, heavy grinding – they crackled and sparked and clanked, as gears and servos slipped across each other's loose teeth, finding only occasional purchase.

The construct walked onward, out onto the battlements, both its arms lowered and loose. Dozens of cables linking the sarcophagus to the main body were severed, either venting vapour, leaking fluid, or simply dried up completely.

She didn't know how many of them Malcharion had killed during their journey and ascent. They'd come at him with chainswords, with knives, with pistols, with rifles, with laser weapons and projectile-throwers and claws and spears, and even rocks and curses. He showed the impact of every single one of them on his ruined adamantite hull.

'I heard a gunship...' the Dreadnought growled. 'I... I will contact it. Talos's human slaves. They will come back for you. Then. Then I sleep.'

On the battlements ahead of them, she saw the devastated body of a legionary slumped against one wall, his armour burned black and every joint melted and fused. Smoke rose from the corpse, tangling with the downpour.

Closer to where they walked, one of the alien maidens still moaned and crawled across the stone. She only had one arm, the other lost to savage burn wounds, and one leg that ended below her thigh. The other was nowhere to be seen. All hair was seared from her body, as was most of her flesh. She writhed and groaned and bled, shivering and twitching in the rain.

'Jain Zar,' she whisper-croaked, struggling to speak with a scorched tongue. 'Jain Zar.'

Impossibly, the only unharmed part of her body was her left eye, which watched Marlonah with sour, sentient malice.

'Jain Zar,' the dying alien rasped again.

Malcharion crushed the living wreckage under his armoured foot, smearing it across the battlements. He lifted a protesting arm on whining joints, to gesture to the legionary's corpse.

'I... have to finish everything... for that boy.'

EPILOGUE PRIMUS
NAMES

THE SLAVES HUDDLED together in the darkness, the male cradling the female. It wouldn't be long now. Their confines shivered as the shuttle rose, labouring on its way back into the atmosphere.

The evacuation began five days before, when the Navy's first envoy made planetfall. A hundred other refugees sat in the near-dark, speaking in quiet voices, several weeping with relief, others with fear. The people of Darcharna had never left their world. Even those taught to cherish the distant Imperium as their saviour were bound to be frightened now they were finally in the empire's less than tender care.

The slaves had spent two long months in the Last City. Two months of lying to blend in with the other survivors; two months of hiding her third eye; two months of hoping Variel wouldn't appear in the doorway of their scavenged shack. She dreamed of that confrontation all too often, picturing his red eye lenses, hearing the snarl of armour joints. She always woke the moment his gloves of cold ceramite stroked across her belly.

But he never came.

In quiet moments, she still recalled Talos's words: 'If Variel escapes this madness alive, he will come for the child one night, no matter where you run.'

But where was he? Had he fled Tsagualsa with Deltrian after all? She didn't dare believe they were safe from Variel's knives, but she was beginning to hope.

Octavia's hands rested on her stomach. The baby would be with them soon – a month or two at most. She wondered if he'd be born in the void, like that poor girl on board the *Covenant*, or if she'd first breathe the air of whatever world they'd call home once they'd lied their way through Imperial processing.

He'd agreed to act as a manual worker from one of the smaller southern cities. She was going to claim descent from the planet's original Navigators, from the colony fleet four hundred years before. It still amused her,

in her calmer moments, to think that with Navigator biology, her story
was technically the more likely one. She doubted she'd have any difficulty
with whatever dubious authority finally processed the survivors of Darcharna. As a Navigator – precious as she was – they'd be likely to send her
to a stronghold of the Navis Nobilite in a nearby sector, but pilgrims and
refugees were one of the Imperium's many lifebloods. Losing themselves
among the teeming billions would be no trouble.

They'd be fine, she knew, as long as the Inquisition didn't get involved.

Octavia nodded to Marlonah across the cargo hold. She nodded back,
returning a nervous smile. It'd been good to have her around these last
months, and she shared Octavia's amusement that all three of them only
still lived because the Legion had – at various points – saved their lives.
Such bizarre behaviour from soul-sworn murderers. Even after a year and
more in their company, she'd never understood any of them.

Well. Perhaps Talos.

For the first time in longer than she cared to remember, she let let her
thoughts drift to the future.

'I just had a thought,' she said, in a strange voice.

Septimus kissed her sweaty forehead. 'What is it?'

'What's your name?' she asked.

'What do you mean?'

'You *know* what I mean. Your real name, before you were the seventh.'

'Oh.' Septimus smiled, and though she had no hope of seeing it in the
dark, she heard the grin in his whisper. 'Coreth. My name was Coreth.'

Eurydice – once Octavia – tasted the word, then turned to taste his lips.
'Coreth,' she said, her mouth against his. 'Pleased to meet you.'

EPILOGUE SECUNDUS
THE MONTHS OF MADNESS

[EXCERPT BEGINS]
...from the rogue trader vessel *Quietude*, that the eldar of Segmentum Obscura name that specific date 'the Night of Sacred Sorrow', with no record of...
[EXCERPT ENDS]

[EXCERPT BEGINS]
...personally report contact lost with subsector guild interests on thirty-seven worlds, nine of which still remain dark. We await the reports of scout vessels and Imperial Navy forces in the area, but...
[EXCERPT ENDS]

[EXCERPT BEGINS]
...don't trade there, anymore. Rumours of warp storm geneses, and temperamental tides. It's not worth the money in repairs. The *Iago*'s Navigator went blind...
[EXCERPT ENDS]

[EXCERPT BEGINS]
...without confirmation of this 'sizeable Archenemy fleet' on the Eastern Fringes, it is a fool's crusade to petition for...
[EXCERPT ENDS]

[EXCERPT BEGINS]
...Golar, the second world of the system of the same name, simply no longer exists in any habitable capacity. The population of the capital city was recorded in the last referenced census as four million. Extensive planetary tectonic activity left the city...
[EXCERPT ENDS]

[EXCERPT BEGINS]

...which is why, if you will heed the archival data, you will see fluctuations in the quality of astropathic contact, alongside severe...

[EXCERPT ENDS]

[EXCERPT BEGINS]

...is meaningless. Tell the Mechanicus representative that we've scryed the region *twice* now, at a cost in fuel and crew lives I struggle to tally without a cogitator...

[EXCERPT ENDS]

[EXCERPT BEGINS]

...in the region of one of the dead worlds, but no recognised Imperial tongue...

[EXCERPT ENDS]

[EXCERPT BEGINS]

...Viris colratha dath sethicara tesh dasovallian. Solruthis veh za jass...

[EXCERPT ENDS]

EPILOGUE TERTIUS
PROPHET OF THE VIII LEGION

1

THE PROPHET LOOKED up as the bulkhead opened on squealing hinges. He wasn't surprised to see who stood there.

'Apothecary,' he said without a smile. 'Greetings.'

The Apothecary avoided all eye contact. 'It is time,' he said.

The prophet rose to his feet, hearing the healthy grind of his armour joints. 'I presume the others are already waiting?'

The Apothecary nodded. 'They will join us on the way. You are ready?'

'Of course.'

'Then let us go. The council is already in session.'

As they walked the winding, twisting hallways at the heart of the *Sun's Scourge*, screams and moans sounded in the distance, on the many decks below. The prophet let his gauntleted hand brush along the ornate steel walls.

'I will claim a ship like this one night,' he said.

'Is that a prophecy,' the Apothecary replied, 'or a hope?'

'A hope,' the prophet confessed. 'But it seems likely, if all goes well tonight.'

The two of them continued walking, their armoured boots thudding on the decking. Soon enough, they were joined by a third figure. This one wore the same midnight-blue ceramite, though its helm was a sloping, snarling daemon mask. Twin tear trails graced its face, painted in scarlet and silver. The figure crawl-walked on all fours, hunched over and loping along behind them like a loyal hound.

'Variel,' the newcomer said in a burst of crackling vox. 'And hail to you, prophet.'

Variel said nothing, though the prophet inclined his head in greeting. 'Lucoryphus,' he said. 'Have you spoken to the other Bleeding Eyes?'

935

'Yes. Over three hundred of the cult have attended the gathering. I spoke with several Bleeding Eye leaders among the other warbands. A dozen other cults are also in evidence. All is well. A gathering of the rarest significance, I believe.'

'True enough.'

They walked on, heading deeper. Variel occasionally checked the readings from his narthecium gauntlet, adjusting dials seemingly on a whim. The prophet didn't bother to ask what was occupying the Apothecary's mind. Variel's thoughts were forever his own; he was not a man that enjoyed sharing counsel.

The three figures soon joined another two; both of these stood in hulking suits of Terminator war-plate, their tusked, horned helms lowering in respectful greeting. The Legion's winged skull stood proud on their curving shoulder guards.

'Malek,' said the prophet. 'Garadon. It is good to see you again.'

'It's nothing,' Garadon said. An immense war maul was slung over one shoulder.

'We would be nowhere else,' Malek added. His massive gauntlets carried the scythe-like claws retracted in armoured housings.

'Not meeting with the other Atramentar?' asked the Raptor, now crawling above them, hanging on the ceiling.

'That can come after this,' Malek replied. 'The survivors of the old First Company have precious little to say to one another, these nights. Meetings always degenerate into duels over their warlords' respective strengths.'

'The cults are the same. As are the Legions themselves.' Lucoryphus seemed amused by the idea. 'Your decades in the Maelstrom were ill spent if you believed anything would change.'

'The Maelstrom,' Garadon chuckled. 'An entertaining guess. How little you know, screecher.' Malek simply snorted, not quite an argument, and left it at that.

Malek and Garadon fell in alongside the prophet, flanking him as they marched three abreast down the labyrinth of corridors. Variel allowed himself to drift behind. The prophet's entrance should be alongside two of the Legion's most respected Atramentar warriors. He had no wish to debate the point.

They came, at last, to the council chamber at the very heart of the ship. The sound of raised voices and cursing could be heard even through the sealed bulkhead.

'Do they scream or laugh?' Lucoryphus rasped.

'Both,' said Malek, hauling the door open.

The group stalked into the chamber, joining one of the largest gatherings of VIII Legion commanders in ten thousand years.

* * *

2

FOR ALMOST THREE hours, the prophet simply listened in silence. His attention drifted from figure to figure around the central table, drinking in the details of their armour, their terror markings, their warpaint and the stories scratched across ceramite in burn marks, scars and dents.

The Legion's gathered lords and sorcerers were as divided as ever. Many called out for allegiance, no matter how temporary, to Abaddon's rising Crusade. This would be the Thirteenth, and the first with a goal to truly wound the Imperium's fortress world of Cadia beyond recovery. Others called out for patience and discretion, letting the Black Legion bear the brunt of the initial assaults while the Night Lords devoted themselves to raids away from the front lines.

Still more would hear none of it, refusing to join the Black Crusade, no matter the prize or threat of retribution. They were souls who'd abandoned the Long War, living only for themselves and the glory they could claw from existence as raiders.

The prophet didn't judge any of them, no matter their choices – courageous or craven, wise or wasteful, all of them were his brothers, for better or worse.

Talk turned to individual assaults. What fleets could strike where. What slivers of tactical intention the Despoiler had revealed so far. How best to capitalise on it for success against the Imperium, or as a means of betraying the Black Legion and cannibalising false allies in the name of spoils.

When the prophet finally spoke, it was a single word.

'No.'

3

THE NIGHT LORDS didn't fall silent immediately. Several arguments raged too hot, too loud, for an immediate quiet to descend. Instead, those nearest the prophet turned to him with cautious eyes. The lords and their honour guards – some of warriors, some of Terminators, some of Raptors – watched with sudden and cold interest, as the unknown lord spoke at last. Thus far, he'd not even named himself, yet many of those present recognised the warriors at his side.

'What did you say?' asked the nearby lord whose tirade the prophet had interrupted.

The prophet stepped forward, taking a place at the table. 'I said "No". You asserted that you will stand triumphant at the coming battle in the Alsir Divide. You will not. You will die aboard your command ship, mutilated and screaming in rage. Your final thoughts will be to wonder where your legs and right arm have gone.'

The lord hissed something low and vile through his helm's vocaliser. 'You threaten me?'

'No, Zar Tavik. I do not. But I have seen your death. I have no reason to lie.'

The named lord barked a laugh. 'No reason? Perhaps by keeping me away, you hope to secure the victory there for yourself.'

The prophet lowered his helm, conceding the point. 'I am unwilling to argue. Where you die means nothing to me.'

Silence was spreading around the table now, as infectious as a foul scent. One of the other commanders, a Raptor in silvered war-plate, turned his daemon mask to the prophet.

'And how do I die, seer?'

The prophet didn't even turn to look at the Raptor. 'You die here, Captain Kalex. This very night. Your final thoughts are of disbelief.'

There was a moment's hesitation. Kalex's claws closed around the hilts of his sheathed chainswords.

'And how could you possibly know such th–'

The Raptor crashed back from the table, blood spattering those nearest him. Malek of the Atramentar lowered a double-barrelled bolter, smoke coiling from its brazen mouths.

'As I said,' the prophet smiled.

Lords nearby were edging away from him now; some in caution, others readying weapons. Kalex was one of the few to lack an honour guard. No warriors pulled iron in a bid to avenge him. Instead, a tense silence flooded the chamber, rippling out from the prophet and his brothers.

'Many of us will fall in the coming Crusade, whether we swear allegiance or abstain entirely.'

'Seize the moment…' Lucoryphus's voice came over the vox.

The prophet pointed to lord after lord, each in turn.

'Darjyr, you will be betrayed by the Word Bearers at Corsh Point, when they leave you to face the Imperial blockade alone. Yem Kereel, you will fall in the last charge at the Greson Breach, against the Subjugators. You will be succeeded by your lieutenant, Skallika, who will be killed three nights later, when his Land Raider is toppled by a Titan and overrun by Guard platoons. Toriel the White Handed, the Legion will consider you lost to the warp when you leave here, swearing never to fight under what you call Abaddon's "slave mark". The truth is close. You are attacked by one of your own Claw leaders while under way in the warp, and as you lose your hold on your ship's path, the Sea of Souls floods into your warship.'

On and on, the prophet spoke, until a full third of the gathered warriors had been named as doomed to die in the coming Black Crusade, or while they abandoned it.

'This war will cost us. We will pay in blood and souls, night after night. But the price will be victory. The Imperium's defences will be broken, and we will never need to sneak and fight our way from the Eye again.

The empire's throat shall be forevermore bared to our blades. That is what Abaddon offers us.'

'He's offered us the same thing before,' one of the lords called.

'No,' Lucoryphus hissed. 'He hasn't. The other Crusades were merely *crusades*. The Despoiler left the Eye to achieve whatever Black Legion madness he wished to achieve. This one is different. It will be a war. We will break Cadia, and forever after be free to raid the Imperium at will.'

The prophet nodded to the Raptor's words. 'Some of us have remained Legion brothers down the centuries. Others have splintered from the Legion in all but name, while still others among us have cast aside the colours entirely. I see several warbands now wearing the colours and honours of their own factions, for they've been strong enough to rise from the old ranks and claim mastery over their own paths. Yet we are all bonded by the fact that this Crusade, this Thirteenth Uprising, will be the war we've waited for. The more of our blood we add to the tides, the greater our triumph.'

'But so many deaths…' Another lord nearly spat the words. 'The price is high, if you even speak the truth.'

'I see these deaths in thick, spiteful dreams each time I close my eyes,' the prophet said. 'I dream of nothing else. I see the death of every single warrior bearing Eighth Legion blood in his veins. Just as our primarch knew he was destined to fall – just as our sorcerers suffer visions of their own deaths, and the demises of those near them. But my soul sight goes… further. Your worlds of birth mean nothing. If we are connected by gene-seed, then I have watched your last breaths. If you have Eighth Legion blood beating through your veins, then I have seen you die. Most are vague, indistinct endings, ripe for change with a twist of fate. A few may be ironclad, the same in a hundred visions, and all that remains is for you to sell your lives dearly. But most are not. Fate is not etched in stone, brothers.'

Silence reigned now, almost majestic in its oppressive totality. Variel and Lucoryphus stepped closer, alongside Malek and Garadon, as the prophet drew breath to speak again.

'Do you know what one of the greatest threats to victory will be in Abaddon's Final War?' he asked the gathered warleaders.

'Each other,' several of them joked at once. The prophet waited for the laughter to die down.

'For once, no. The Imperium will claim an ally of desperate strength, and one we cannot afford to leave at our backs. What ancient detritus is caught within the Great Eye's eternal grip? What haven of alien filth still holds out against the forces of the Enlightened Legions?'

'Ulthwé,' said one lord.

'The Black Eldar,' said another. Disgruntled murmurs started up, just as the prophet knew they would. The VIII Legion – like all of the Eye's forces – had lost their fair share of warriors and warships over the millennia due to the interference of the accursed Ulthwé eldar.

The prophet nodded again. 'Craftworld Ulthwé. They came for Tenth Company once, decades ago. They chased the Tenth across the stars, feverish in their need to end a single life before prophecy could become truth. They failed in that quest, though they never knew it. Their witches and warlocks scryed a future they could not allow to come to pass: a future where the Prophet of the Eighth Legion rallied his kindred to bring fear and flame upon their precious craftworld in an unrelenting storm. These creatures, with their species so close to extinction, fear damnation more than anything else. *That* is where the Eighth Legion will strike first. *That* is where we will devote our initial assault, raining bloodshed and terror onto the eldar, drenching their dying craftworld in the tears of the slain.'

'And why should we?' called Lord Hemek of the Nightwing. 'Why should we spill eldar blood, when we have hordes of Imperial Guard to slake our thirsts?'

'Revenge,' argued another. 'For vengeance.'

'I need no vengeance against the eldar,' said Hemek. His Legion-crested helm was resplendent with its wings of black-veined cobalt. 'We all carry our own grudges, and mine have nothing to do with Ulthwé.'

The prophet let the arguments rage for a few minutes.

'This is getting out of hand,' Variel privately voxed.

'Let me handle it,' the prophet replied. He raised his hand for silence. Peace was a while coming, but the others eventually fell silent.

'I have seen you die,' he said. 'All of you. All of your warriors. These fates may be promised by destiny, but destiny can always be denied. The eldar cannot be allowed to join this war with their forces untouched. None of you can imagine how many of us will die. These are losses I would spare the Eighth Legion from suffering, if you will heed my words.'

'My sorcerers speak of the same ill omens,' one of the other lords announced. 'Their warpsight afflictions are hardly as reliable as Talos's visions once were, but they have served me well in the past.'

Several voices rose in agreement. Clearly, it was a sentiment many shared within the councils of their own warbands.

'And you are?' the prophet asked politely.

'Kar Zoruul, of what was once Fortieth Company. On the guidance of my sorcerers, I was already planning to assault the eldar, as were several of our brother warbands.'

Hemek wasn't convinced. 'So you come to bring us a warning of the eldar?'

All or nothing, thought the prophet.

'The eldar are a threat to be considered now,' he said, 'but they are not the true reason I came here. What matters is what comes after. Some of you have already met Abaddon, while others will meet with him in the coming months, as his Crusade gathers potency. To survive, to break the Imperium's back and enter the Emperor's final nights, we must join this war, no matter our reservations. The future holds great things for us, my brothers. The Last Age of the Emperor is drawing to a close, as the Dark Millennium ends. This is it, my lords. With the Legions and their forces no longer contained in the Eye, we stand on the edge of final victory.'

More silence, for several moments. The prophet smiled behind his faceplate; it was enough to get them thinking. This wasn't a war he expected to win in a single night. Slowly, slowly, he'd win them to his side, offering counsel and aiding them in avoiding the bitter fates awaiting them.

'There was talk,' Toriel the White Handed said softly, 'that Talos survived the carrion world. It was said Malek and Garadon returned to stand by him, and here we see both of those honoured Atramentar among us. How much of this is true, Variel?'

The Apothecary didn't answer. He merely turned to the prophet.

'Does it matter?' Lord Darjyr snorted. 'Why should we believe this thin-blooded wretch? I scent the changes in you, young one. Your gene-seed is old, but it has scarcely ripened within you. You are an infant, standing in the shadows of gods.'

'You do not have to believe what I say.' The prophet smiled behind his faceplate. 'It makes no difference to me, or to my kindred.'

'You are not Talos, then? This isn't some trick?'

'No,' the prophet replied. 'I am not Talos, and this is no trick.'

'Tell us your name,' demanded one of the others, one of those not named to die in the coming months.

The prophet leaned on the central table, red eye lenses panning across them all. His armour was a scavenged mesh of conflicting marks, each ceramite plate showing carved Nostraman runes. His breastplate bore the image of an aquila, its spread wings ritually broken by hammer blows. Over one shoulder was a sweep of pale age-browned flesh, flayed into a cloak with thick black stitches. Skulls and Imperial Space Marine helms hung on bronze chains from his belt and pauldrons, while two weapons were sheathed at his hips: the first was a double-barrelled bolter, inscribed with ancient writings and depicting the name *Malcharion*; the second was a relic blade stolen from the Blood Angels Chapter a forgotten number of centuries ago. Its once-golden length was discoloured silver, evidence of a recent reforging.

The prophet's helm was a studded, brutal affair with a skull-painted faceplate, and sweeping ceremonial Legion wings rising up in an elegant crest. The skull's eyes wept black lightning bolts, as if the bone itself was cracked. In the centre of its forehead, a single Nostraman rune gleamed black against the bone white.

He removed the helmet slowly, making no sudden moves, and regarded them all with a youthful, unscarred face. Dark eyes glinted in the chamber's low light, drifting from warrior to warrior.

'My name is Decimus,' the Night Lord replied. 'The Prophet of the Eighth Legion.'

ABOUT THE AUTHOR

Aaron Dembski-Bowden is the author of the New York Times bestselling novel *The First Heretic* for the Horus Heresy series. He has also written *Betrayer* and *Aurelian* for that series. His work in the Warhammer 40,000 universe includes *Armageddon*, *The Emperor's Gift* and the acclaimed *Night Lords* trilogy. He lives and works in Ireland, hiding from the world in the middle of nowhere.